MAR 25

THE TANYUIN ACADEMY

THE COMPLETE SERIES

BOOKS 1-3

CARLY STEVENS

Omnibus copyright © 2024 by Carly Stevens

All rights reserved.

No part of this book may be reproduced in any form or by any electronic or mechanical means, including information storage and retrieval systems, without written permission from the author, except for the use of brief quotations in a book review.

For information about permission to reproduce selections from this book, write to carly@carly-stevens.com

https://www.carly-stevens.com

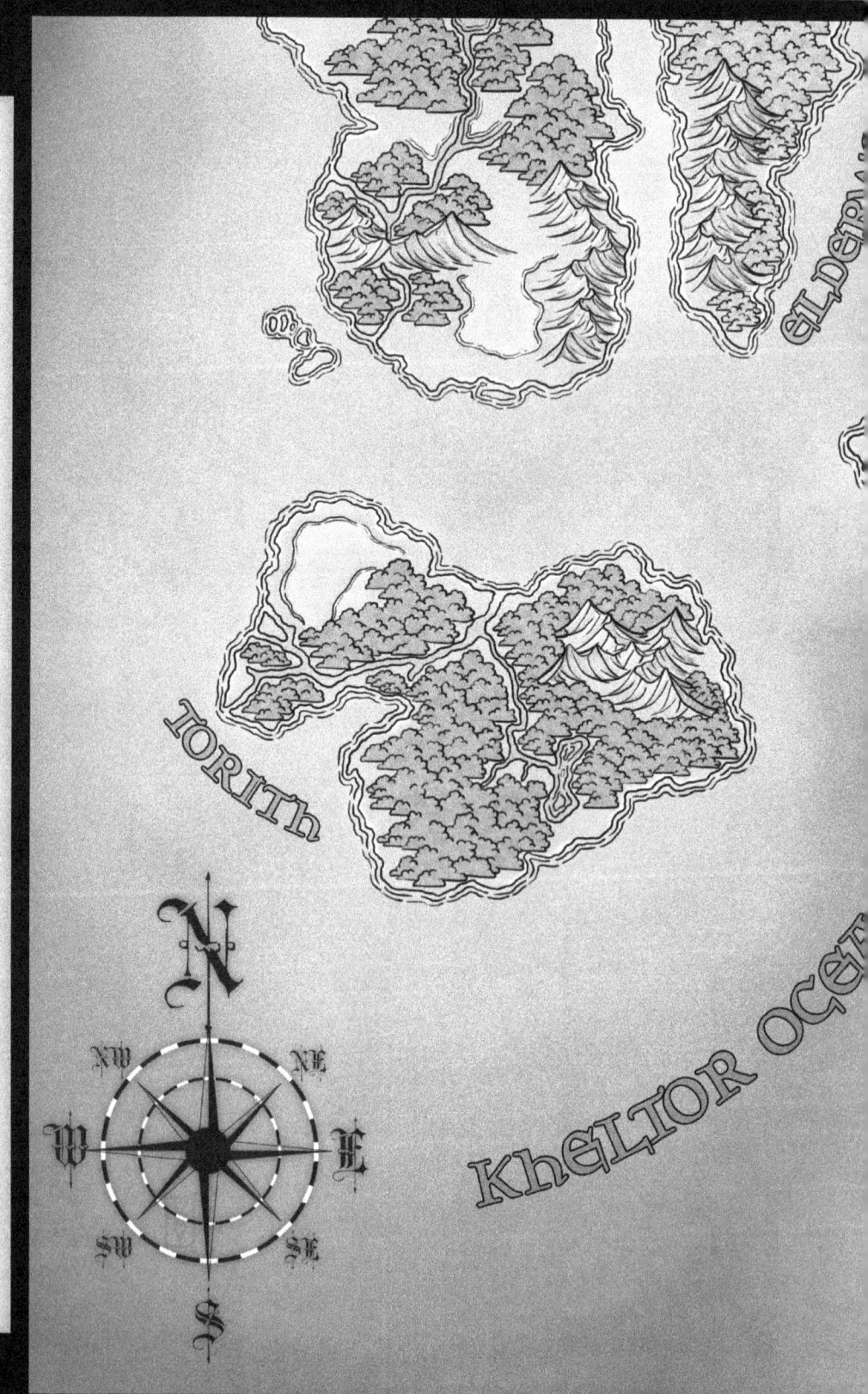

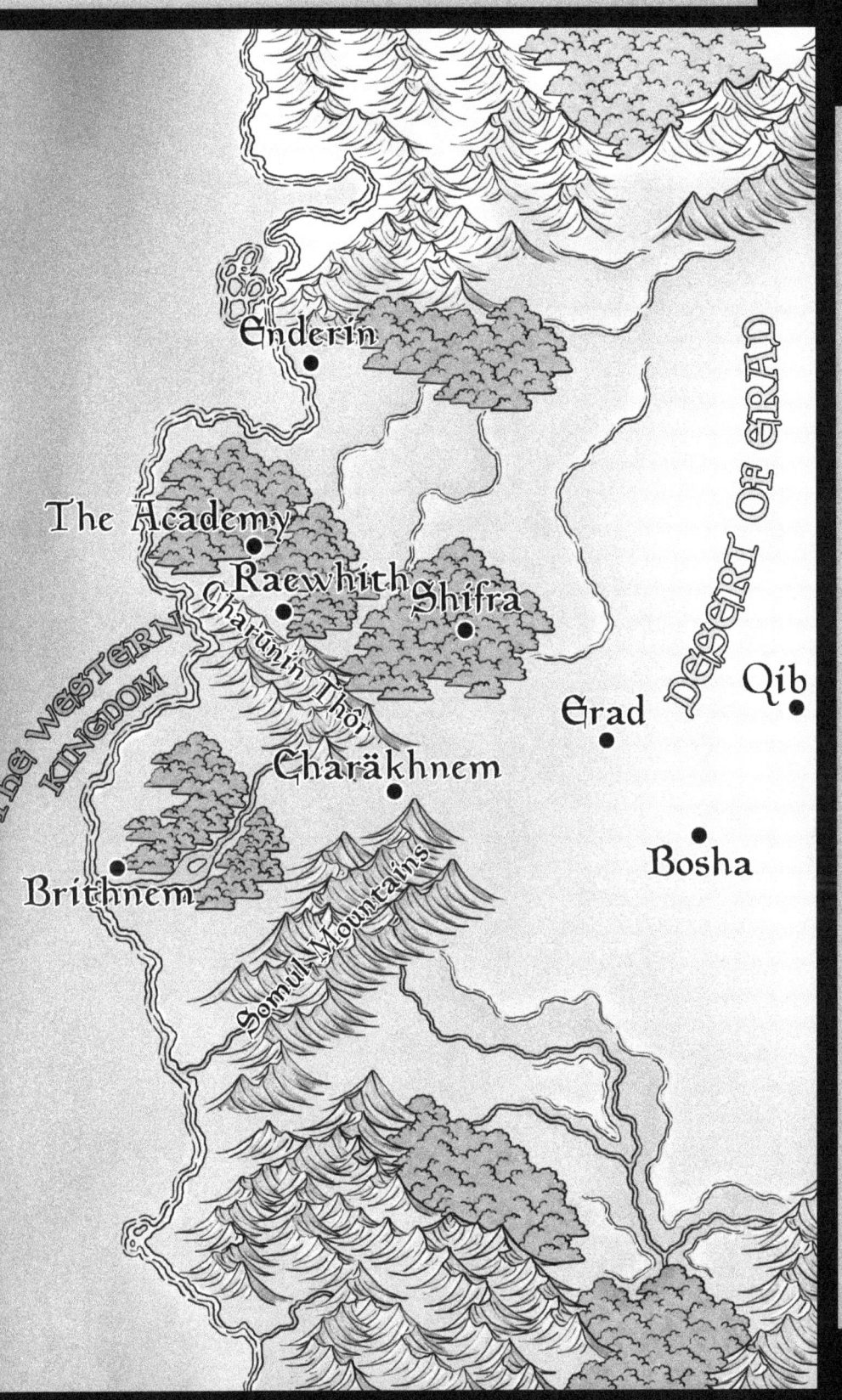

FIRIAN RISING

BOOK 1 OF THE TANYUIN ACADEMY SERIES

PART I

LEARNER (AGE 11)

1

FIRIAN

Firian inched forward on his elbows to see over the ridge. Rocks cut into his arms, but he barely noticed the pain. When he reached the edge, he crouched down in the moon-shadow of a large tree to his right. Scanning the dark valley carefully, he saw what he had been hunting: a mountain-ghost. It glimmered faintly under the shadow of another tree. Then it drifted on across an open field, unaware of his presence.

His stomach flipped. The ghost was huge and tall, with fierce fire in its eyes. Firian squared his shoulders. Maybe others would be afraid. Not him.

He moved his eyes a fraction to the left, expecting to find his friend Caedmon lying flat on the tough grasses beside him. But no one was there.

Wait, where was he?

Firian spun his head around, only to see Caedmon standing sullenly a little way down the hill.

"What are you doing?" Firian whispered.

"I don't feel like doing this," he said in his normal speaking voice.

"But right over there," he hissed, "I found the—"

Caedmon idly picked up a rock and chucked it at the tree where Firian was hiding. The rock pinged above him as he ducked. Chunks of bark pattered on his head.

He turned back to the ghost. To his horror he found that it had discovered their position and was rushing toward them, faster than any man could run. The edges of its shimmering cloak now burned with a bright light.

"Idiot!" he screamed as he jumped up and ran back down the hill, dragging Caedmon along with him.

They couldn't outrun it this way. They'd be killed.

"Firian! Firian, stop! I don't want to play this game anymore. Let me go!" Caedmon wrenched Firian's hand off his arm and jogged to a halt.

The night and the mountains melted away, transforming into the bright, stark dirt that hurt Firian's eyes. Low brown buildings sprang up here and there, the nearest one facing the clearing where a group of children played. He was back at the trade schools of Raewhith.

"I don't feel like playing this anymore. I don't feel like doing anything," he repeated.

"Are you sick?" asked Firian. After all, Caedmon hadn't come to school the day before.

Looking irritated and tired, he scrunched his forehead down. "Maybe. I don't know."

"Is that why you weren't here yesterday?"

Caedmon shot him a black look and stalked away to be by himself.

It was just a question.

Firian was alone again, and fighting a mountain-ghost wasn't as fun by himself. He imagined other adventures all the time at home. Here at least, he could play with other people. Sure, sometimes he got hurt when he imagined battles, but it was still more fun than trade school. He just couldn't let his father see his scars.

One of his teachers, Mr. Harlenn, stepped out of the small school building. "Come on," he cried, clapping his hands. "Break is over. It's time for lesson."

With many groans and derogatory remarks, all the children followed him inside. Firian only realized that he had forgotten to eat lunch after he had been swept inside. Somewhere out in the little dirt clearing there was some bread and cheese and even a cookie that his mother had made. Now ants were probably eating it and he wouldn't be allowed to have anything else until later that night. If only he'd stowed the cookie away in his pocket.

Sighing, he slid down to his section of the long, pockmarked bench. The rough-hewn bench had never been comfortable, but he suspected that that was all part of Mr. Harlenn's plan to get them to pay attention.

His teacher walked slowly up the aisle between benches, inspecting the boys. His eyes rested a little longer on Firian than on the rest. Firian didn't look back, and instead reached under the seat and took out his lead piece and something to write on. Some drawings were left from the last time he'd sat in that class, so he scratched them out before anyone could see. The teachers thought he had an unhealthy imagination, but he thought it was much more enjoyable than the real world of overbearing teachers.

"We're going to continue talking about multiplication today," Mr. Harlenn said.

This information would probably be important when Firian made glass like his father, but now it was unbearably boring. After all, he was only eleven and his apprenticeship was a year away.

"If you sell seven items for three tokens each, how many tokens have you earned?"

Mr. Harlenn called on another student for the answer, so Firian focused instead on the globes. Once he had seen his teacher blowing through a long tube with a glowing glob of glass on the end. Slowly, the glob expanded like a soap bubble until it looked like an eggplant. Before that, he had thought glass was always solid, like a sort of rock that his father cut into windows. But it could change and morph into all kinds of shapes. Sometimes he felt like asking if he could try shaping the fiery glass in a new way. But no one would let him do that. The globes were for the palace of Brithnem, the capital of the Western Kingdom. Raewhith, on the very outskirts of the Kingdom, separated from Brithnem by mountains, still had to do their part to support the huge nation.

Next to him, Ewin was drawing squares, triangles, swirls, eyes. Firian leaned over to him. "Do you know where Caedmon was yesterday?" he breathed.

"He was being tested," came the quiet reply.

"Why?"

"To see if he was good enough to be a Tanyu, stupid."

"A *Tanyu*?"

Ewin nodded slightly. "Before he left, he made it sound like he was a Tanyu already. Everyone wanted to slug him by the end of the day." A smug smile flashed across his mouth. "He didn't make it. He won't even talk about it."

"I know *that*," said Firian. "You stay if you're accepted."

"Aw, he deserved it, after talking that way yesterday."

"Have you ever been tested, Ewin?"

"No."

Caedmon hit him on the back of the head. "Yes, you have, you liar!"

Ewin turned very red.

"Sorry," Firian said.

"Shut up," Ewin replied.

"Ewin!" Mr. Harlenn said next. "If you've earned twenty-one tokens, how many coins does that equal? And how many coins will you need to earn to create the same amount of stock?"

Firian bit his lip and looked down. The first question was easy, but the second was ridiculous. Did Mr. Harlenn ever say how much the items cost to make in the first place? He didn't think so.

There was a short pause. "I think Firian should answer that question, sir," Ewin said.

"Why is that?"

"Because he was making me talk in your class, Mr. Harlenn."

"Is that so, Firian?"

"He thinks it is, sir," he replied, tight-lipped. He clamped his jaw tight and looked down. The room felt hot, and he twirled the lead piece in his fingers.

The teacher peered down at him. "Well. Same question."

"Two coins, one token, sir." He took a breath and felt anger choke him. He knew he should stop there, but he couldn't. "You never said how much the items cost to make so there's no way I can answer the second part. Make your questions clearer next time, sir. Most of the time you don't even teach us the answer before you ask. You just assume we weren't listening to anything you were saying, sir."

A few boys giggled under their breath at his boldness.

Mr. Harlenn set his mouth in a hard line and lifted an eyebrow. His eyes became flecks of black stone and his rigid body was framed starkly against the wall of globes. "I believe that you want to leave this room as much as we want you to," he said coldly, pointing toward the door. "You may go now."

Everyone watched Firian as he deliberately set his things back under the bench and left, closing the door behind him.

The air was colder and less musty outside. With calculated breathing, he marched to the nearest tree and punched it as hard as he could. The bark scraped the skin off his knuckles but the pain helped to soothe his rage.

It wasn't fair. He'd told the truth. But his teachers never wanted the truth.

He looked around. He couldn't go home early again. So he found his lunch in a little grove of trees. The bread was a little dirty but ants weren't swarming it. Even the cookie was still there. He stuffed it in his mouth whole. A few crumbs spilled from his open mouth as he chewed. His mother would have been angry with him for eating his sweets first, but he didn't care.

Gripping the rest of his lunch, he took everything past his trade school and across the dirt road. Several shops where real tradesmen worked lined the street. He kept his face aimed straight ahead toward his sister's school, but he still felt the eyes of Rhys, the town's rope and basket maker, following him. Sometimes he told on him, the sneak.

Finally out of sight of the road, he found a stump where he could eat the rest of his food in peace.

Several hours later, boys and girls started pouring out of the school buildings, most of them eager to be gone. Firian stopped sucking his stinging knuckles and perked his ears for the sound of his sister's voice. He stood up, dusting off the seat of his pants, and ran to entrance of the girls' school.

There she was, saying goodbye to a few friends. Brett was always surrounded by friends. He didn't like them. Brett had been his best friend for a long time when they were younger, but now she was almost thirteen and had other friends.

He ran up to her, ignoring the other girls. "Come on, Brett. Time to go home," he said as he began to lead her away.

"You're out early," she replied, pacing after him. She waved backward to a girl with short black hair, and then jogged up to match his fierce pace.

"I walked fast," he said, irritated that she would mention it.

Her soft blue eyes filled with concern. He had her full attention now. "Is something wrong, Firian?"

"No. I'm fine."

"Did you get out early again?"

How does she always know? "It's not your business what I do," said Firian sullenly.

Pursing her lips, Brett tossed her long glossy hair back over her shoulder. "That's the third time this month. Mother and Father won't be happy about that."

"They won't learn about it."

A strain passed over her fine features and Firian knew she was torn between siding with her him or their parents.

"I'll let you have all the rest of the cookies if you won't say anything about this one time," he said.

"Well... all right," she conceded, breaking into a smile. "But if you do it again, you'll be in trouble. What do you do to get the teachers so mad all the time?"

He shrugged. "I don't know. They just don't like me."

"Sometimes I think that Miss Dasa doesn't like me, but she never throws me out of her class."

Brett didn't understand. Firian shook his head, wishing he could get angry with her, but... he loved her too much. Just like everybody else.

"You just don't understand," he told her. "I don't like trade school and they don't like me there either. I wish I could be twelve now and get away from all those people." But then he would have to be Father's apprentice for six years before he'd be considered a man and could start his own shop. He squinted down at the road. *Awful choices.*

"I'm sorry, Firian," she said, and she meant it.

Cresting the top of the hill, a horse and rider clomped toward them, pulling a cart behind. Firian grabbed Brett's hand and dragged her to the side of the road. Her face twisted in an amused grimace, but she went with him anyway. Firian put himself between her and the rider as it passed.

From the top of that hill, they could see their little cottage. It sat back from the road, but part of the roof peeked out from the trees. Small, with a wooden roof and a wooden door, it was just like all the others in the little town of Raewhith. Behind it was a small garden where they grew vegetables and herbs.

Firian bustled inside and kicked off his dusty shoes.

Mother set down the rag she had been running over the furniture and gave them both a wan smile. She wasn't an emotional woman, didn't hug them as his friends' mothers did. Instead, she stayed careful and still. She glanced at Brett and then at Firian a moment. Seeming preoccupied, she picked up the cloth again. A hint of pink colored her gray cheeks. "You better start dinner, Brett. Your father will be home soon."

Brett dashed through to the second room, toward the food pantry and the stove. Firian tromped after her. She busied herself with the food and he headed toward the small pile of firewood in the corner. It wasn't very cold, but Father always liked to have a fire going.

He stacked the wood in one arm, a piece at a time. Clonk, clonk. How much could he carry? One time he had carried seven pieces at once. Maybe he could do better. The load grew until it reached eye level. His muscles strained and he finally had to use the other arm to stop all the wood from dropping.

He spun around, just able to see over the top log. The knife Brett was holding stopped in midair above a handful of spring onions. Her eyes widened, exasperated, but a smile spread across her face as she turned to chopping again.

The door creaked open. Father was home.

Firian only hesitated a moment before hefting his load of firewood into the front room. He chanced a look at Father. His tough, thin frame looked bent like a spring. He rarely smiled, but today his lips were pursed. A bad sign.

Mother smiled politely and looked around the room a little as if to present it to him. Father followed her eyes and apparently found everything in his house satisfactory.

"How was your day at the shop, dear?" Mother asked, moving some of her ashy hair away from her face.

At the fireplace, Firian tried to set down his load quietly, but the freshly cut wood went tumbling, crashing out of his arms. He cringed and caught his breath. Not daring to look up, he started putting the pieces gently into the fireplace, his stomach in knots.

"Not very good," Father said with gritted teeth. More of his materials must have been stolen by thieves from Archer's Point again. Coke for the furnace, molds, cooling windowpanes.... He knew his family couldn't afford to lose any more. And whenever there was trouble at the shop, they felt it at home.

Firian braced himself.

"Hello, Father!" Brett's voice.

"Hello, darling." Father's voice softened just a little as he greeted his favorite child. Sweet Brett never contradicted him. Ever since Firian could remember, Father had never acted like he hated her.

With Brett in the room, Firian could stand up and turn around.

Father's tired gaze strayed over to him.

"Yanon," Mother said quietly, "I have—"

"What is that, Firian?"

Father was looking at Firian's scabbed knuckles. One of them was bleeding again. Firian put his hands behind his back, but it was too late.

"How have you hurt yourself? Come here. Let me see," Father said, coming forward and gesturing with a finger.

Firian's pounding heart hurt against his ribcage. Having no other choice, he presented his hands to his father.

Mother sucked in a startled gasp. "Oh, Yanon, I'm sorry! How could I have missed...?"

Father hummed, like the low growl of an animal. "How did this happen, Firian?"

Firian's blood was pumping. "I..." – he felt the attention of all his family – "I fell," he said.

"And only scraped your hands?" Father raised a dark eyebrow. "You didn't get in a fight again, did you? You didn't hurt anyone?"

He always seemed to get into fights with his schoolmates. And he would win, which got him into more trouble. That wasn't the case this time, but how could he tell them that he had punched a tree? It sounded stupid now. Besides, then they would find out why he was so angry and he couldn't let that happen.

"Brett, darling? Do *you* know why he is hurt?" Father asked, turning to her.

All the cookies, Brett. Firian put as much meaning in his look as he could muster without drawing attention to himself. It was a large sacrifice for him for her silence. He knew she could easily assume why he had bloody knuckles.

"Brett?"

Seeing the indecision on his sister's face, Mother turned back to Firian, her face drawn with disappointment. "You didn't get dismissed from school again, did you?"

"Did you?" pressed his father.

Firian hesitated.

Striking him hard across the face, Father snapped, "Answer me, Firian. Did you?"

"Yes, I did, sir," he mumbled.

Both his parents rolled their eyes in disbelief. "Firian!" Even Brett seemed amazed that he confessed.

He planned on taking at least a few cookies now.

Father seized one of his injured hands, and tossed it away in disgust. "What did you do?"

"I answered a question correctly, sir."

"Firian! No one asked you to leave for answering a question correctly. I've had enough of this. What did you do to your hands?"

"I hit something, sir."

"What did you hit?"

"A... tree."

"A tree?"

"I was angry, sir."

Father huffed out a disgusted breath. "Firian, quit talking back or I'll pull you out of the school!"

"I would like that, sir," Firian murmured.

"That's *enough*!" Father roared, grabbing him roughly and dragging him across the room. His fingers dug deep into his thin shoulder. "No dinner tonight!"

He hurled Firian away in exasperation. When Firian glanced back over his shoulder, he saw Mother backing away from Father as he stalked toward their room.

"How did I get such a scut for a son?" he growled, disappearing into the room.

"Firian, go to your room," Mother said quietly, picking up the rag and starting to clean once again.

2

FIRIAN

"Firian! Come down here!"

Firian jolted awake. Wiping the drool from his face, he ran out of his room.

He found his parents eating at the table with Brett. The room smelled like cabbage and cumin, which set his mouth watering. Mother gestured for him to sit down. Could he have dinner after all? That never happened once he was sent to his room. He glanced at Father, who regarded him with an undefinable emotion.

What's going on?

"Something came for you today," he said, edging a piece of paper across the table with a finger. His mouth pinched in what might have been a smile as he looked up from his meal.

Firian eyed them all as he took the note.

To Firian Kess, *son of Yanon and Lithia Kess.*

Firian shall come to the watchtower in Raewhith tomorrow afternoon. From there, he will be taken to the Tanyuin Academy to be tested for Ability. The presence of both Yanon and Lithia shall be required as well.

Sias Jairon
Tanyuin Head

Firian clutched the paper until it crumpled. Tested for the Academy. With his greatest dream in front of him, he felt suddenly terrified. This chance could be taken away as easily as it was given. His face went hot, then clammy. He looked up, barely breathing.

His family was all smiling—Brett biggest of all. She knew what this meant to him.

"You are going to be tested to become a Tanyu, Firian. Do you know what that means?" asked Father, matter-of-fact.

He nodded. It was everyone's dream to live the exciting life of a Tanyuin warrior, someone who mattered. It was the highest honor that anyone could get, so it was no wonder that the boys who were not chosen—like Caedmon—were somber and moody when they had to face their friends.

Tanyu. The word tasted like adrenaline. *Is it... possible?*

"We'll take you," Father said, "but don't get your hopes up. The Tanyu are warriors. Disciplined. Respected. They don't take boys like you."

Mother had tears in her eyes, happy despite his Father's negativity. She rarely showed this much emotion. At least she believed a little in his chances.

"If" – Father scoffed the word – "they let you in, you'd have to leave everything." He took a thoughtful bite of cabbage. Firian guessed he was weighing the merits of that idea. Father would lose a worker but also rid himself of a burden. Having a son in the Tanyuin Academy would also be a reason to be proud of Firian, maybe for the first time.

Father looked at Brett and Mother, giving them leave to speak.

"Oh, Firian!" Brett cried. "It's wonderful. You could do what you've always wanted—fighting for us and flying and everyone, everyone in the Kingdom would love you..."

"Now Brett, darling, flying is only a rumor," said Mother. "But this is amazing! Not everyone gets asked to come! They must think you're very special."

Firian nodded. "We're going tomorrow, sir?"

"Of course," Father answered. "Remember, not everyone gets chosen. But for some reason you got an invitation, so do everything you can to get in."

Brett sniffed and kept clearing her throat. "It's wonderful. I'm so happy for you, Firian," she said, a slight break in her voice. She wiped her shadowed eyes. "I hope they choose you."

"We all do," said Mother, holding Father's hand on the table.

Firian could have said a thousand things as he walked to the watchtower with his parents, but he kept quiet, glancing occasionally at Father.

Had the watchtower always been so far?

No one knew anything about the Tanyuin arts, really, even though the others in trade school pretended to know sometimes. He grew up hearing vague stories of battles, flying, and other worlds he could reach only by closing his eyes. Sometimes he imagined that he was in a world like that, but those were just his games.

He closed his eyes to calm down. *A Tanyu!* The possibility was real!

Now he just needed to be brilliant enough, strong enough, *and* have the Talent. He had no idea how they would figure out those things, since he wasn't sure exactly what the Talent was, but it didn't matter. He would die if he had to go back to his schoolmates dejected like Caedmon.

He *would* pass, no matter what he had to do.

They turned a corner and the tall stone outpost slid slowly into view through the trees. Firian sucked in a breath.

The building grew as they approached, getting taller and taller. *You?* it laughed. *But you're that little boy who's failing trade school. How can you hope to become a Tanyu if you can't even do that?*

Firian stuck out his chest as they came to the guard-flanked double doors. The walls seemed to loom not straight upward but over him as he passed through.

Even your parents like your sister better than they like you.

At that, his eyes stung, but only for a moment. He couldn't have the Tanyu see him cry. After all, he was far too old to be crying over silly little things. He closed his eyes and imagined that he was already a Tanyu, the very best. He saw himself walking through the same corridor, except now it was filled with people, all giving him respect. *They* thought he was worth something. He smiled in his vision and nodded to the people right and left of him as they stopped going about their business to bow and touch their foreheads in admiration.

Then one older man looked up. Straight into his eyes. "Firian?" he asked, an amazed smile forming on his lips.

Firian's eyes shot open and the vision fled. *What was that?* His imagination never talked back to him before. He had to calm down. He was far too nervous.

"Watch where you're going," said his father softly. The hard-edged sound of a voice connected to blood and flesh made him aware that he had strayed toward the left-hand wall.

"Yes, sir," he replied, correcting his error.

A tall man in a long black coat stepped soundlessly out of the stairwell right in front of them. Mother jumped, her hand fluttering to her chest.

"Firian?" the man asked.

His deep voice resonated and the very word seemed to make Firian the best and most significant person in the room. The man's features were severe, but his manner held something like kindness behind it. His eyes and skin were very dark, like a polished stone, both soft and hard. He wore a close-fitted black shirt and looser pants tucked into black boots. When he shifted his weight, Firian saw a sheathed knife on his belt. Even without the weapon, power seemed to flow around this deadly man.

A Tanyu. Firian would have smiled if he hadn't been so nervous. All he managed was a nod.

Without another word, the man headed back up the narrow winding stairs, his boots barely making a sound. Firian followed, his parents trailing behind him. Up and up he climbed until they reached a room off to one side of a landing.

In the small room sat two black chairs and a desk with no one behind it. *Wouldn't it be fun to sit there...* Wordlessly, the Tanyu strode to his seat behind the desk. He seemed more comfortable standing than sitting, but he still felt dangerous, sitting poised and ready to strike at the desk.

"Sit," the man said to his parents, flicking his wrist carelessly toward the other chairs.

The man gave Firian courage simply by being in the same room. *He* was not afraid of his parents.

Father flexed his hand open and closed. No one ever told him what to do. Still, his parents obeyed and sat. A smile flickered over Firian's face.

The Tanyu's gaze shifted to him, and he remembered that this man had come for *him*. Would the man see through him? Judge him instantly?

"Firian," he confirmed again.

He swallowed. "Yes, sir."

The man stared at him a moment before turning to his parents. "We don't know how long the Test will take," he said, "and we do not know what effects it may produce in your son, nor the outcome."

The blood drained from Firian's head and hands. He swallowed, his throat suddenly dry.

"You must understand—many are chosen for testing, but very few actually succeed in advancing."

Father's lips pursed knowingly.

"I hope you have not planted false hopes in this boy. More than likely he will be sent home tonight or tomorrow. A messenger will bring him home when he is finished, or, if he passes, he will stay at the Academy. If he advances, you may not ask about him or try to contact him. Your failure to comply may have dangerous results."

Firian shuddered. He realized he was holding his breath.

"Do you agree to these terms?"

His mother's eyes shifted to his father nervously and even his father seemed surprised by the intensity of the terms. He shot a hard glance at Firian, and nodded.

"Yes or no?" the man asked sharply.

"Yes," they replied, somewhat taken aback.

"Very well," said the Tanyu. "Come with me." He stood quickly and walked out of the room, not looking back to see if Firian followed.

"Goodbye, Firian," his mother said, suddenly animated now that he was leaving. She reached for his scabbed hand and pulled him in for a hug. It was paper-light, as though she would break or anger him. Firian mostly felt impatience rather than love or sadness. When she pulled away, the flyaways around her face gave her the breathless look of someone returning from a fast wagon ride. Sadness and pride flickered like light and shadow in her eyes. The end result was confusion, as though she couldn't fully comprehend what was happening.

Father stood and looked down at him, his light blue eyes narrowing. "Make sure you pass, son." He put a strong hand on his mother's arm to lead them out.

"Say goodbye to Brett for me," he replied. Then he swiftly walked out of the room. His parents would not miss him. Brett would miss him though.

Once out the door, he couldn't see the man. How could he fail already? Then —there!—he caught a ripple of black out of the corner of his eye and rushed after it down a hall on his right.

Never breaking his stride, the Tanyu looked back at him for a moment. "Quicker than most," he said.

He couldn't tell whether that was good or bad. The inflection offered no clue.

Questions boiled in his mind, but he kept silent as they walked, walked,

walked down the hallway, upstairs, down a different set of stairs—seeming to get no place at all.

"Will your parents leave soon, boy?"

He jerked his head up. "Yes, sir. They've probably already left." An oddly desolate feeling swept over him at the thought.

"Down the street by now?"

"Probably, sir."

"Good. Precautions, you know."

He didn't know, but he didn't ask. They took a sharp turn around a corner, down another winding staircase, and then out a side door into the open air. He hadn't realized how stuffy it had been inside. He savored the breath of freshness in his lungs. It made him want to take off running.

They kept walking deeper into Esmeroth, the pine forest that surrounded Raewhith. The Tanyu led, swift and silent, and Firian followed.

Tree shadows began to lengthen. How much longer would it take to get there? If he asked, that might show weakness, and every move he made was important now. So he said nothing.

The little winding paths through the thick woods finally took them to a stream. The Tanyu halted and refilled a flask that had lain inside his coat. At a motion from the warrior, Firian drank some of the water out of cupped hands, not knowing how long it would be before he would get another drink. He had to keep up his strength for as long as possible. Still the man said nothing, but he seemed to be thinking hard about something.

Firian's burning adrenaline began to cool inside him. He needed that adrenaline—it would help him focus. Maybe all of this was just part of the test. Could he keep up, keep going, not complain, do... something right?

The shadows deepened into pools of darkness and the sky grew dim. They only stopped once the trees turned black. The Tanyu didn't make any sort of camp. "Only one night," he explained, as he stretched himself out on the ground to sleep.

As Firian lay down at a respectful distance, rocks and sticks dug into his back. He twitched and rolled over. This side was a little more comfortable. Underneath him, something squirmed.

He shot to his feet, electrified with disgust, and stamped the place where he'd been lying. In a frenzy, he crushed the pine needles and dirt until he was sure nothing could have survived.

A single laugh made him remember the Tanyu, who had seen it all. Firian's insides chilled with embarrassment and fear, but he thought he saw a slight smile on his dark face. At least he wasn't angry. "Get some sleep," the man said.

WHEN FIRIAN WOKE up the next morning, nothing looked familiar. The stream wasn't there, and the pine trees looked taller. He shook himself and looked around, and still had no idea how he had gotten to this part of the forest. The sensation was like dizziness. "Where are we?" he asked the dark man, who had crouched down to get something out of his pack. His long black coat draped over the ground around his feet.

The man smiled grimly and tossed him some food, a piece of dried meat and a plum. Firian took and ate it gratefully as they began to walk again, but he still felt uneasy.

They walked through the fir trees for a very long time—into the afternoon.

Firian had started to wiggle his toes to stop his feet from aching when he caught a glimpse of a huge stone structure jutting out ahead of them. It filled the spaces between the pines; battlements rose dimly into the air.

The tree line stopped abruptly and the two of them came to a clearing. In front of them stood what looked like a castle, a barracks, a fortress without banners. *The Academy.* Even the building seemed proud. It had none of the airy quality of castles in pictures. This was rooted to the earth like a mountain. The walls, made of solid dark stone, looked as though they had been carved with a giant's knife, sheer sides and massive rounded battlements. For such an enormous building, there weren't many windows. Firian was glad they had come to it in daylight.

They hiked around the left side, which must have been the main entrance. The Tanyu tugged the iron handle, and the massive double doors swung open silently toward them.

The dark man gave Firian a knowing look as they entered. Firian could never tell anyone where the Academy really was, not his family, not his school friends... He gazed reverently at the worn wooden doors. Who else had touched them?

His mouth fell open as he looked inside. Men and women in black—many of them in their teens—walked around a massive indoor courtyard with a fountain in the middle. The high ceiling drew his eyes upward. A chandelier hung from an inverted dome high above, and a railed-in second story looked down at the open area. Most of the Tanyu in the courtyard walked with purpose, like his guide, but there didn't seem to be a rule about where they were going. A couple girls sat on the lip of the fountain, talking. Overall, the atmosphere was hushed and business-like, as though they had better things to do than socialize.

Many of the Tanyu noticed Firian. It was no more than a piercing glance, but even that was something. They almost all looked severe, focused, but not aggressive—Firian knew the difference. Their eyes burned with so much awareness that he was sure they would remember him. He was only eleven and now Tanyuin warriors knew his face. He would make sure they knew more of it. One day he would be famous, even among them, maybe even feared. He stood taller and tried to walk stealthily like one of them. The dark man led him down a hallway off to the side.

"In here," said the man, leading him through the last door at the end. The space was large with one long table in the middle of the room. Eight Tanyu sat around it. All of them looked at him intently. His throat closed tight.

The man closed the door behind him.

"Master Jairon," he said, acknowledging the man at the head of the table.

Firian paled at the name. *The Tanyuin Head.*

Master Jairon looked a little familiar. He had short graying hair, now with an iron circle over it like some kind of crown. His face was more good-natured than the man who'd brought him, but, unlike his guide, there was not kindness beneath the surface, but someone precise and dangerous. "Thank you, Master Makai," he said. "So this is Firian."

"Yes, sir," he replied. His voice sounded loud and high and empty.

"Firian," Master Jairon said again, lowering his head confidentially as if trying to spark his memory.

Then Firian remembered. "You're the man who—!" For fear of looking foolish, he allowed the statement to drift away. Better to be silent than ruin his chances.

"Who what, Firian?"

Hesitantly, he answered. "You were the man in my... imagination."

The leader laughed and the others peered around at each other in muted astonishment. "Very good, boy! You're right. I saw you there as well."

"What do you mean?"

"Come, come!" he cried, not answering the question. "Sit down if you like."

All of chairs had armrests, a small luxury for someone who grew up poor. He chose the most comfortable-looking one close to the door and sat down. His guide sat opposite him.

Master Jairon leaned back in his chair.

"It is an honor to get so far," said a woman, who looked too young to have her short, wavy, white-gray hair.

"Quite an honor."

Firian nodded wisely, laying his arms on the rests. He noticed as he looked around that the others all wore dark rings each with a pinpoint red stone.

There was a pause.

The dark man, Master Makai, spoke. "Do you know how many people have come into this room thinking they would succeed?" he asked in his low voice. "Nine hundred and sixty-one in the last five years alone. You make nine hundred and sixty-two. And do you know how many stayed? Hmm? Ninety-five—ten of them were eleven years old at the time." He relaxed in his seat. "This age is beginning to lose the Talent, Firian. Years ago, there were many who were gifted enough to become warriors in the Tanyuin arts. Now there is a surprising lack."

Firian listened attentively. He'd known his chances were slim; the odds didn't deter him.

Master Jairon continued the explanation. "The Khelê founded the Tanyuin Academy when they were still new."

Firian knew about strange-looking Khelê—no two alike, and they usually had tattoos as well. They visited Raewhith sometimes. The white-haired woman was probably one of them.

He continued. "We were a branch of the Exmorei. You've heard of the Exmorei? They were the Khelê elite. Religious at first. Then over time they broke into factions. The Tanyu were the stronger branch, appointed for defense."

That sounded a little familiar. Exmorei... *Wasn't that a secret organization?*

"The Tanyu are the only ones who test those who wish to join, who *require* Talent. The Amir care only for the Sacred Scroll, for study. They are still loyal only to the Western Kingdom, but we have broken free of those constraints and help anyone in need of our great strength. The Tanyuin Academy is the greatest lasting organization of the Exmorei in the world."

There was a pause.

"Are you beginning to see what you're trying to do, boy?" the dark man asked. "Only the best have even been allowed to see this building, much less be tested. People know who we are, but no one knows what we do for them. *You* don't even know what we do."

Firian's stomach felt sour and he swallowed roughly. Master Jairon watched him closely. His face and neck felt hot.

The dark man continued, relentless. "Only the best. Only the best, Firian, get to know the secrets of the Tanyu. Every person who passes inspection must be deadly focused, extremely gifted, and willing to pledge their loyalty to the order. We are... almost like our own race. Not anyone can join us. Very few do—the chosen, you see. The best are usually trained for at least thirteen years. Are you able and willing to practice intensely, every day, until you are twenty-four years old?"

Twenty-four? That seemed very far away. But it still would be better than facing everyone at trade school again. At the end of those thirteen years, he would be a Tanyuin warrior. Yes, he could wait if he had to.

His guide watched him intently. Firian's hands shook and he could hardly breathe, but he managed to keep his face still. A deep silence covered the room and he suddenly wondered if he was supposed to answer the question.

"You must realize that you'll probably prove worthless like all the rest," said a large blond man to his left before he could give his answer. "Can you live with that?"

Firian was about to say *I already do,* but someone else spoke first. "Tests have broken people's minds before, boy."

"So what chance do you think you have?" finished Master Makai.

No face seemed especially friendly toward him, not even the leader, so he found no comfort there. There was no Brett to look at him with sympathy. All the warriors waited for him to speak. He felt horribly unqualified to say anything, but he knew he had to. All the warriors were now silent, waiting for him to speak.

"I think I should take the test before I decide that," Firian replied stoutly, dry-mouthed.

Master Jairon laughed. "And spirit too!" he cried suddenly. "Take him away!"

Immediately, the guide got up from his seat and jerked his head for Firian to follow. Again he was out the door following the man, bewildered. He could barely feel his legs as he hurried off.

Had they dismissed him without even testing him? His heart thumped fast and heavy in his chest. Before, he had learned to deal with failure, but not this time. This was his one chance to get away, to get out and become something great. If they denied him his only chance for freedom without even testing him...

It was not a long walk this time. They came out into the hall, then up a large, curved set of stairs that led to the second-story hallway he had seen from the courtyard. Doors lined the left side and a short railing closed them in on the right. Below, students still meandered around the indoor stone courtyard.

Misty tears started to fill his eyes before he remembered to stand up tall.

They stopped. The man produced a key and unlocked one of the rooms. Inside the very small chamber was a bunk on the left, a dresser on the right, and a window. Firian turned to the guide. "What is this?"

"This is your room. Congratulations. You passed the test."

3

KIRIA

This was the night to try again.

A small painting crashed off the wall. "*Shhhh!*" Kiria hissed. It was probably Atty's fault; he was clumsier than his brother Jori even though he was two years older.

The three of them crouched low, hurrying through the wide corridors. Living in Brithnem's palace, Mon Párinath, had its advantages. They didn't need to see the grand sculptures and potted trees to know which way to turn next. Since Kiria lived on the opposite side from the Calthwaite brothers, in the royal wings that fanned back into the gardens toward the sea, they had met in the front section of the palace. In her excitement, Kiria had jogged the entire way from her chamber near her mother, the Second Keeper, all the way to the Main, where important official meetings took place during the day.

All they could see was darkness but they knew that they were approaching the huge doors. No one stood guard, as they had last week after reports that people were sneaking into the grand hall—running around, creating disturbances. Atty reached up and cracked the carved door open enough to admit the three of them.

Not so much as a lantern shone around the Main tonight.

"Jori? Did you bring a match?" Kiria whispered.

"Of course I did," he replied, and a bright light struck up and underlit his face. He went over to the nearest round lantern hanging from the wall. He wasn't tall enough to light the wick inside and the match burned close to his fingers. "Atty! Take it!" he said, reaching up.

"Here. Strike me another one," said his brother.

Jori shook out the first one and there was a moment of blackness before he fumbled and lit a second. Gingerly, Atty took the match and lit the lantern. It was still too dark to see most of the room, so he lit one more.

Now they could dimly see the entire space. Banners, light blue and deep purple, hung like clouds from the ceiling, each one marked with a laird flower, the symbol of peace. Where the wall met the high ceilings, verses from the Sacred Scroll had been etched into the stone. Kiria's mother said the words were there to remind them of their devotion to God. Three large carved thrones, one for each monarch, stood side by side on a raised platform in front of them.

Smooth stone tiles, the pattern broken by a large circular mosaic in the center, stretched across to a crowd of chairs. Set in the floor, the mosaic depicted Shane and Mari Calthwaite at the center and their four children in four quadrants around them. Three of the children began the lines of Keepers, but the fourth son died and was called the Father of the Lost Line. Kiria's favorite had always been her ancestor Maril, the only woman. She was depicted in blue and white, holding a knife and a sprig of lavender.

She knew that Atty and Jori preferred their own Line, the Third, which still carried the Calthwaite name. Only the Second Line, passed on from daughter to daughter, kept Maril's married name: Arioc. Calthwaite for the men, Arioc for the women.

Statues of four war heroes, including Shane and Mari, towered twelve feet high in their respective corners. In the light of the flickering lanterns, the figures appeared to smile and wink at the intruders.

Kiria ran over to the raised chairs and sat in the middle one, where her mother usually sat. Her feet barely touched the floor. "What do you think?" she asked grandly as she laid her arms on the armrests.

"Wait!" Atty cried as he jumped up and sat on her left. They both gazed imperiously down at Jori, who stood alone in the middle of the floor.

"That's not fair," he said.

"Well, *you* can't be Keeper!" said Atty. As the second-born, Jori wasn't in line for any of the three thrones.

"You wouldn't like it anyway," said Kiria, looking out over the group of smaller chairs facing them. *That's where the advisors sit. And there is the place for the Keepers' families...* "This is weird."

Atty nodded solemnly.

Jori huffed and strode over to the place where the First Keeper, Cúron, sat. "I'll sit *here*," he said.

"You can't sit there." Atty leaned over to see around Kiria. "Even if I died or something and you had to be a Keeper, you'd sit in *this* seat."

"I'll sit where I like."

Kiria kicked at the floor with her feet. "*Kader* will sit there before you do, Jori," she told him. Kader was Cúron's two-year-old son, the heir to the first throne, just as she and Atty were heirs to the second and third.

Jori rested his chin on his fist and sighed. "It doesn't matter. Keepers do boring things anyway. People say they do exciting stuff, but Dad does boring things all the time. Lucky you, *Atael*."

"It's not that boring," Atty said. "Dad's been all the way out to the Pillars of Awel before. And he went to visit the Tanyuin Academy once, remember?"

"Oh yeah." A dreamy look stole over Jori's face. "I want to go to the Academy."

Kiria wasn't so sure she'd want to visit. Her mother said that the Tanyu protected the Kingdom, but they acted as though they were out for themselves, like a tiny kingdom of their own. Remembering the strong, stern men that came to the palace maybe once a year unsettled her. They didn't seem very nice. They looked like they were ready to hurt everybody who disagreed with them. Even though they were a little… terrifying, she liked watching them. It was like watching the large desert cats she had seen in the royal zoo when she visited the large neighboring kingdom of Charäkhnem a few years before.

Once, Jori dared her to stick her foot out and see if she could make a Tanyu trip. She tried it but he only adjusted his pace to step over her. He hadn't even glanced down.

"Why does every boy want to go to the Academy?" she asked. "We have the Amiran Academy right here."

They both looked shocked. "Are you serious?" Jori asked, sounding scandalized.

"Tanyu," said Atty. "They're amazing."

"They're really mean," she said.

"No, they're not!" Jori cried, leaping to his feet. "It's just that they can do all kinds of things that normal people can't. They're the best warriors in the world…"

Kiria stood up too. "I know people who don't like Tanyu—"

"They're jealous," said Atty, as though he was explaining something extremely simple. "They wish they were Tanyu too."

"Yeah," Jori agreed. "But they're stuck doing boring stuff and memorizing all of the Sacred Scroll."

"That's important for the Kingdom," Kiria protested, but they would hear none of it.

"Girls just don't understand," said Jori, knowing that that would bait her.

"What do you mean we don't understand?" she cried. "There are girls at the Academy!"

"How do you know?"

"Our advisor's sister goes there! And I heard she's better than a lot of the boys."

"Mm hm," said Jori. "Sure she is." He grinned evilly at her.

She narrowed her eyes. "Be quiet!" she hissed, leaping at him to cover his mouth. Jori stumbled backward.

Atty jumped up from the throne, offering to pin Jori's arms to his sides so Kiria could close his mouth. Jori couldn't beat both of them together. The scuffle afterward left all three of them on the floor, laughing.

Then they went back to exploring the huge forbidden room with the thrill of knowing that as long as they weren't too loud, they could stay up until their servants awoke at daybreak and no one would know.

KIRIA SMIRKED as she watched Atty, Jori, and their father through the window. The boys struggled to keep their whole bodies from drooping. Even from here, their eyes looked saggy with sleep as they trudged alongside their father and a handful of servants. They always missed their father when he traveled, so it surprised her that they had forgotten about their early morning hunting trip.

Their father Aylmor, the tallest man in the group, sported a trimmed brown beard and dark brown traveling cloak pinned with the royal insignia. He stopped on the path for a moment and turned to Atty, who—now that she noticed—carried nothing but the bow and quiver slung over his back. His father bent down kindly and handed him one of the rabbits he carried. Jori already held two by the feet, and stood a little straighter.

They wound their way up the path, past the curved walls of the Amiran Academy. She imagined her tutor was studying in one of the rooms, as usual. Everyone in the domed Amiran Academy acted much friendlier than they did in the Tanyuin one. At least the Amir weren't all about fighting.

Two servants opened the palace doors for the Third Keeper's family, where she stood waiting.

"Welcome back!" said a booming voice behind her.

Kiria whirled around to see Cúron, the oldest of the three Keepers, looking particularly regal in long purple and blue robes. *What's the special occasion?*

He spread his arms. "A successful trip, Aylmor?"

Kiria glanced at Atty. The boys' father nodded, slinging his bow off his shoulder and handing it to the nearest servant. "Yes, we all managed to make a few kills."

"I'm glad your boys are growing up so well. I'll let the kitchen know to prepare rabbit tonight." He cast a smile at the boys, but as he turned back to their father, his tone turned businesslike. "Aylmor, the ambassador from Charäkhnem has just arrived. He is still settling in, but you had better get ready."

The Charäkhni ambassador? That sounded important. "Should I tell my mother?" Kiria asked, ready to run down the hall.

Cúron smiled down at her. "If she wants to come, she certainly may."

Kiria knit her brows. Something about his tone didn't sit right with her. Shouldn't her mother be at the meeting? She ruled the Western Kingdom just as much as he did. Why did he make it sound as though she didn't need to come?

"I'll tell her," Kiria said, running off down the wide hallway.

Her parents' room was all the way at the end of the huge palace wing. Not stopping to catch her breath, she knocked on the door, ignoring the two guards.

Her father answered the door, looking concerned. He and Aylmor had become friends in the army and they shared the same style of clipped beard, not like Cúron's longer gray one. He had the intense eyes of a general, deep-set and focused, even though he didn't campaign very often any more. He looked at eye level first, and then down at her. "Kiria, what's wrong?"

"Where's Mother?"

"Right here," came a softer voice from inside the room. "Is everything all right?"

"The ambassador from Charäkhnem has just arrived!" Kiria cried, projecting her voice past her father, hoping her mother would hear.

"Not so loud, honey," Father said. "Sometimes these things are secrets."

"She should be at the meeting."

Firian Rising

Finally, Mother came to the door. "Hello, Kiria," she said kindly, soothingly.

Her mother's dress was all wrong for an official meeting. It was an everyday dress, Brithnem blue but made of rougher material. She ought to be wearing something flowing and gauzy, maybe with jewels... And where was her crown? "You should get ready to see the ambassador," Kiria said, and then realized that she had forgotten to greet either of her parents. "Hello."

"I'm sure Aylmor can handle that meeting," she replied, perfectly calm. "Is he back from his hunting trip?"

"But Cúron will be there, too," Kiria insisted.

"He likes to know what's going on."

"You should know, too."

"Kiria," Mom said, tampering down her enthusiasm with a word, "having three Keepers wouldn't work if we didn't trust each other. I trust the two of them. I'm sure they'll tell me if they come to an important agreement."

Kiria pursed her lips.

"You have to trust me. It'll be fine." Her mother smiled.

She tried, but she couldn't smile back.

4

FIRIAN

HE HAD PASSED THE TEST.

With a satisfied sigh Firian sat down on the edge of the lower bunk. No one was there to take the top one, but he decided that if anyone did come, he would rather have the bottom. He had more privacy down there and could get in and out without disturbing anyone.

He had passed the test and didn't even know how he had done it.

His mouth broke open in a smile and he jumped up, screaming. "Ha, *ha!*" he screamed, not caring who heard. "I'm free! I passed! *Ha!*" He fell back on the bed laughing and panting. He was going to be a Tanyu. A Tanyuin warrior. He took on the expression a fully trained Tanyu would have—utmost seriousness, of course—and attacked his pillow expertly.

The door opened.

"I'm sure it's not the pillow's fault," said a man Firian hadn't seen before.

He stopped beating it and stood.

"This is your room," said the new man to someone Firian couldn't see. Then from behind him came a boy who looked about his age, except that he was smaller and looked weaker. His strength wasn't in his muscles but in the energy gleaming bright from his large black eyes. His hair spiked wildly. The boy's eyebrows twitched down when he saw Firian standing there, but his curiosity gave way to a grin.

"I'll send for your things," the man said, closing them into the room.

A second of silence, then, "I'm Bard. Who are you?"

"Firian."

"How long have you been here?"

"I just got here. I passed the test," he added proudly.

"I did too... barely," said Bard, craning his head to look around the room. "Where are you from?"

"Raewhith." Bard's skin was a little darker than his and his features were smaller. And he spoke with a lilting accent. He certainly had never seen eyes like his back home.

"I'm from Enderin. You're lucky to have the Academy so close to your house."

Firian had no idea that people came from so far away. It had just never crossed his mind. Enderin was as far north as the capital city Brithnem was south. The Academy wanted the best, after all, and that meant from anywhere in the world, even Enderin. Tanyu weren't just connected to the Western Kingdom, but had all the world's best.

"So which bed is mine?" Bard asked.

"The top one. What do you mean you barely passed the test? They said I passed but they didn't even test me."

Bard was already trying to scramble up to his bunk. "They didn't even test you? They just let you in without all that mind stuff?"

"Mind stuff? I guess. They said the 'tests can break your mind,' but then they just took me here and said I passed."

"Weird."

"I thought the test was maybe seeing how I would react when they said I probably wouldn't get in, but that doesn't make any sense. What'd they do to you?"

Dragging himself noisily to the top, Bard reached his bed and sat down on the edge with his feet dangling. "They told me to close my eyes and think of different things. They said I wasn't thinking hard enough. Then they told me to stop thinking."

The Tanyu hadn't made Firian do any of those things. It didn't make sense. "Stop thinking? What do you mean? How do you do that?"

"Think of nothing. That part was easy."

Firian had never tried to think of nothing. His vivid imagination would always take over and sometimes he would have visions even in the daytime. *Nothing... nothing...* It wasn't black and it wasn't white. It was clear and there was nothing on the other side. It covered him and he ceased to exist...

"Firian!"

"Hmm. What'd you say?" The fuzz of nothing cleared and he saw Bard staring at him from his perch.

"You're not paying attention."

"Yes, I was."

"What did I just say?"

"You're not paying attention."

Bard swatted at him but Firian ducked and grabbed a dangling leg. Shrieking, Bard held onto the mattress as Firian tried to pull him off. The mattress lifted and bent upward as Firian dragged him from the bed, laughing and screaming. Bard fell sprawling on top of him.

"We're Tanyu!" Bard yelled, springing up again. He kicked Firian in the side as he attempted to get up again. "We're Tanyu!"

Firian thought his face would split with happiness.

IT TOOK Firian far too long to find Mr. Belik's room. He hated that he was late for his first lesson. When he finally found the right place, he knocked. Silence. He knocked again, harder this time.

"Not so loud, boy!" cried a voice. Firian's fist froze in the air, mid-knock. "Just come in."

He cracked open the door. The room was dim and tiny. A man—the only person in the room—sat in one of two chairs. Large and imposing, he looked too big for the room, as if he were caged. A hint of softness gleamed behind his intense eyes, but Firian knew better than to appeal to it. No man had ever shown him unearned kindness. So he would earn it.

Mr. Belik glanced at a piece of paper he held in his lap. "You are Firian Kess," he said deliberately, peering over his glasses as he waved for him to sit.

"Yes, I am," Firian said, sitting in the other chair.

"Very good. I hear you have some ability."

"I hope so, sir."

"You will call me Master Belik if you call me anything at all."

"Yes, s— I will." He hoped his habit of respect would die easily. He suspected it would.

"It says here you're eleven years old."

"Yes, I am."

"Why do you talk like that?"

"Like what, si... Master Belik?"

"Like *that*."

"My father, sir." He clamped his teeth shut when the word escaped.

Belik smiled grimly and looked at the paper again. "Do you know what we do here, Firian?"

He had an idea, but figured that it would be better not to answer.

"We *fight* here, boy. We don't curtsy. So cut out the nice stuff. Your dad won't be here to tell you to shut up from now on. Now *I* tell you when to shut up. Got that?"

Firian nodded, pleased.

Belik dropped his paper on the floor beside him. "Close your eyes," he commanded.

Firian shut them tight.

"Pretend you are in your old house, in your old room..."

Firian instantly pictured the old board house nestled uncomfortably in the trees as if it wanted to shy away from the road. Then he stood in his little room, with the low bed pressed against the far wall, under the window. Grayish-yellow plaster above the paneling emphasized the dusty light coming in. Maybe that was one of the reasons his parents never thought it was clean enough, even if everything was put away...

"Now you are in the outpost with your parents..."

He saw it all again, as if he were reliving it.

"Now you're back in your room."

He was.

"Now in the outpost."

He was.

Belik's voice took a less commanding tone. "Your father is tall and thin, with short brown hair and a mustache, your mother is a hand shorter, with medium-length brown hair and blue eyes, just like yours, and there is a window above the bed in your room."

Firian opened his eyes. "How did you know that?" he whispered. Could everyone in this place read his mind? In his sudden fear, he instinctively thought of the worst thing he knew, then flushed hot as Belik laughed.

"I could see almost everything," said Belik. "Do you know how?"

"No."

"You have an imagination. I have an imagination. I just have to imagine that I see what you're imagining, see?"

Firian thought about it for a moment. "Not really, Master Belik."

"Close your eyes again. You'll see what I mean."

His lids lowered.

"Now, clear your thoughts and our minds can meet halfway in the Unreal."

He tried to empty his mind and figure out what the Master was thinking at the same time. It wasn't easy, but slowly he saw the trade school and his teachers there moving around and telling him to pay more attention.

"Explain," Belik demanded.

"What?" His eyes popped open, his stomach churning uncomfortably.

"What did you see?"

"My... trade school teachers."

Belik leaned forward with a sardonic look on his face. "Why would I think about them?"

"Maybe to show me the differences between you and them?"

"I don't even know your trade school teachers. I was thinking of something completely different." He paused. "When did you arrive here?" He asked the question as though he already knew the answer.

"Just yesterday."

"Ah," he said, nodding. "And they just let you in?"

Firian's throat constricted.

Belik narrowed his eyes. "The Head was there for your test, wasn't he? He doesn't bother with new recruits unless he has a reason. He went because he knew you had the Talent before you arrived. That's why you passed. So come on," he said, clapping his dry hands together, "try again. What am I picturing? It's just a picture so it won't be hard for you."

Again in darkness, Firian's heart pounded. Nothing came to him. He still had no idea what Belik was thinking. How could they all expect him to read minds on the first day? It wasn't as if he'd been practicing. He hadn't known it was possible until now.

Then something Bard had said came back to him. *Nothing. Think of nothing.*

Nothing... nothing...

Then... something! Just one image, unmoving, unwavering, came slowly into view in the clear mirror. It was a person, a woman that he'd never seen before. The image was so detailed that she could have been standing in front of him.

"What does she look like?" Belik's voice echoed.

"She has dark skin and big eyes," he answered, without opening his eyes, "some kind of ring in her nose, and short, reddish-brown hair and… she's wearing a green dress."

"Shoes?"

"Shoes are yellow."

"There you have it!" Belik shouted so loudly it made Firian jump. "Look at me."

He looked up and the image lingered a little before his mind before flickering out completely.

Belik seemed pleased. "That's Chetana."

"Who's she?"

"That doesn't matter. Do you understand now? Do you understand?" His large, rough hands twitched with anticipation.

Firian swallowed. For a moment, he'd really done it. "I think so."

"Could you do it again?"

Firian nodded vigorously and beamed with pride.

"Well then, do it. Now!"

For hours, they practiced techniques for meeting in the Unreal until Firian was sure it must be well past lunchtime.

Before Belik let him go, he told Firian the rest of his class schedule, which all sounded more interesting than anything he had learned at trade school.

After a quick meal, Strategy was next.

It took a moment for Firian's eyes to adjust to the darkness. Six students sat on chairs and a Master sat facing them, her hair slicked back in a braid and her eyes calmly closed. Firian silently moved toward the one empty seat.

No one shifted or made a noise. They almost seemed asleep. He wouldn't mind a class like that at all… But they couldn't be sleeping.

An energy buzzed under the surface of the room. All the students were sharing one thought. He dove in, drenching himself in nothing as he had done over and over with Master Belik.

A bright moving picture materialized. Two men, one dressed in red and the other in white, stood in a square, black room with gleaming sides. Their slick, colored images reflected in the floor.

"Success depends on creativity, on calmness in whatever situation," he heard a woman's voice say. "None of the battlegrounds should be so simple, but your lesson begins here. There are two men, endless possibilities. Most of the battles you will be engaged in—if you make it—will be between you and one other person. So we begin Strategy here."

Long, thin swords appeared in the hands of each man. "In the Unreal, you have everything, and nothing. Thought is your only restraint. Any weapon you can devise, any way you want to move, is possible if you have mastery. Mastery is key. Strength of mind."

The men ran at each other, blades raised, whirling their swords expertly at each other, and clashed. The weapons gleamed deep white in the sheen of the floor.

"This is one method," said the female voice, as the fight continued before Firian's mind. "But this is too simple. If your opponent has any skill at all, you must use more advanced tactics."

All of a sudden, the red and white men left the ground and slid on a film of air like ice, gaining height as they fought harder. Someone gasped—a sound heard from underwater. Soon the two were flying through the air, rotating in every direction as though no one way could pull them down.

"Typical," the voice said. "Most warriors are advanced enough to fly. The next step is to change weapons, like this."

The red man's sword dissolved into smoke and a spear appeared in its place. The white man kept his sword, but gained a knife. The fight moved faster, faster. Firian gaped as he watched. If the fight got too close, could it hurt him? He flexed, steeling himself, and focused on the complicated moves. Tonight, he would try to remember every last step in detail.

Then everything went blank.

"That's enough for today. Remember all that for tomorrow."

Firian opened his eyes and peered cautiously around. The room seemed brighter now.

During the rest of the lesson, the Master (he hadn't caught her name) spoke and drew diagrams of strategies that worked or didn't work and why. Her long, thick braid swung with each measured movement. The Unreal fight was much easier to remember than the diagrams.

When the class ended, Firian followed everyone out the door.

One day down...

He found his way back to his upstairs room, hoping he could find more food.

No one was there, not even Bard. But on the lower bunk was a small, bulging knapsack. He worked open the leather strap at the top and found his winter boots from home. The Tanyu must have sent for his belongings immediately for them to arrive so quickly. Not even a day had passed since he arrived.

He pulled out the items one by one and laid them on the bed. A note or gesture of good-bye from his parents was not among the items he received. He didn't really expect one. But there was a scrap of paper from Brett. *Congratulations,* it said. *I knew you could do it! Now you'll be a warrior—a Tanyu—one of the bravest and smartest people in the world! I love you. I won't forget you.*

He wouldn't forget Brett either. Based on what Master Makai had said at the watchtower, it was unlikely that his family could come often. And she is the only one who would want to.

With a sewing needle, he tacked the paper to the wooden bedpost beside the bottom bunk pillow.

He put away all his other clothes and belongings quickly. Since he didn't own very much, he noticed that a couple items of clothing were missing, but he wasn't going to ask about them. Maybe the Academy would provide him with clothes.

When he was finished, he threw himself down on the bunk and began to pick at the bedpost, tossing the flakes away with his fingernail.

The door swung heavily on its hinges and Bard stepped in, looking very small, followed by a stream of yellow-white light. He shut the door behind him and opened a dresser drawer, bringing out two oranges and a small loaf of brown bread. Though he looked tired, he smiled. "Hungry?"

"Yeah!" Firian hopped off the bed.

"A last gift from my parents," he said, handing him an orange and breaking off a hunk of bread.

Firian didn't feel like responding to that, so he peeled the orange instead. Mist spritzed from the peel as he ripped it off.

After a while, Bard finally said, "Is there anything else planned for today?"

"I don't think so," Firian replied with his mouth full of orange slices.

"Then I'm going to bed," said Bard. At that, he undressed and climbed up into his bunk.

Firian didn't feel tired, so he just sat at the edge of his mattress, chewing thoughtfully, reviewing all that he had learned in his mind. He reviewed his lessons in the dark. He didn't intend to take thirteen years to learn how to fight. Already, the Tanyuin Head himself had let him in, and he'd gotten a Master's approval on the first day. Once he believed he could remember every detail of Belik's teaching and the Strategy lessons, he blew out the light and lay down.

The only light in the room came from the moon and stars peering in the small window. Bard softly started to cry. The sound was painful and left Firian at a loss. He angled up on his elbow, wanting to comfort Bard but not having the slightest idea where to begin. Bard probably just missed home—something Firian couldn't fully understand. Maybe it was better to give him his privacy.

He settled himself back down. Drowsiness overtook him and he fell slowly asleep to the sound of Bard sniffing and quietly choking on sobs.

5

KIRIA

"Kiria."

Her daydream vanished—something about leading a battle or dancing with a prince. Blinking in the sunlight streaming in from the window, she looked up at her tutor, Daelon. He smiled at her, crinkling his deep eyes. Though Daelon wore the same high-collared long robe of dark blue-gray that all other Amir wore, he wasn't intimidating like some of the others. "Where have you been?" he asked.

"Right here."

The study rooms in the Amiran Academy were traditionally small, and held only a copy of the Scroll or some other guide for meditation. Royalty and other noble families sent their children there for their whole education. Right now, the room only contained the two of them and a large map spread over a table.

Daelon sighed. "I'm trying my best to keep your attention, my Kepress."

She smiled defiantly at him. "Just say it again. I'll remember this time."

She obediently turned to the map. Only the right-hand side was well filled out. The left side consisted mostly of the Kheltor Ocean, which she would be able to see if she could leave this lesson and go outside. Inlaid silver marked her city of Brithnem, the capital of the Western Kingdom, on the coast directly between two slanting mountain ranges.

Running his finger across the huge distance from the southern mountain range to the area just north of the second range, Daelon said, "The Western Kingdom stretches from the Somul Mountains in the south to Esmeroth Forest in the north."

A barely perceptible line of silver marked the country's boundaries. She followed the line with her eyes. It enclosed almost the whole space between the mountain ranges and beyond, like tea spilling from a cup. One day, she would help to rule that whole area. She could hardly suppress a grin at the thought.

"Now, my Kepress," he continued, "without looking, tell me what kingdom lies directly east of ours."

She met his eyes, aware of her peripheral vision as she tried to remember. *Of course.* Her parents talked about this kingdom all the time. "Charäkhnem!" she cried. The kingdom of Charäkhnem held the pass where the mountains met.

Daelon looked as though he would ask another question, but he glanced at the sun first. "Speaking of Charäkhnem, we don't have much longer. You're supposed to meet the prince later."

"Oh!" That was good. If Mother wouldn't meet with the ambassador, at least she could meet with the prince. She wasn't a grown-up, but even an eleven-year-old could make a good impression, and maybe get some information that would be helpful to the other Keepers.

He opened the door for her and they both went out into the bright palace gardens. Gravel crunched beneath their feet as they strolled back to the castle.

"Okay, is there anything else I have to learn?" she said quickly.

Amused, Daelon shook his head, looking older than his twenty years. Memorizing the Sacred Scroll must make people look old. Amir always had lines around their eyes.

"History was going to be the last subject of the day," he said, gesturing to a corner of the palace as they strolled by—the corner with the ugliest stones near the foundation. Blackened and chipped, they looked much older than the rest of the castle. The adults seemed to love the old stones, though, and never let her say anything against them.

"Like the War of the Kingdom Rebels?" she asked, proud that she knew what that was.

"Right. Who fought in that war?"

"The Kingdom Dwellers and the founders!"

"Don't forget..." he prompted, lowering his head as he looked at her.

"The Khelê." She felt a little bad leaving that out. Daelon was Khelê himself.

She had mostly descended from Kingdom Dwellers, so she had a more traditional look. Even now, their people were generally tall, strong, light-skinned, dark-haired, with defined lines and grayish eyes, beautiful with the kind of beauty her mother had—refined without losing a rugged edge. Kiria was probably going to be shorter than a true Kingdom woman, and her hair was a lighter brown.

The Khelê, on the other hand, varied from person to person. Skin color, hair color, even last name—none of it passed from generation to generation. At first, Kingdom Dwellers had considered them cursed, but now the Khelê wore their uniqueness as a badge of honor.

"Right," Daelon said. "The founders were the ones that burned the palace."

Kiria had heard all this before. "I know that," she said. "Can we do the Scroll game?"

Daelon could never resist that, and she knew it. "If you want to." His eyes sparkled even as he shook his head. "*And for as long as I live—*"

"*—I will set my God before me,*" she finished.

"Very good. '*The gifts of God are irrevocable—*'"

"'—what the Perfect One gives is given.' Now let me do one!" She cleared her throat, ready to chant the way Daelon had chanted the Scroll to her when she was younger. "'*God supports the just man's cause—*'"

He laughed.

Daelon hardly ever laughed, so she smiled at the sound. Too bad they weren't brother and sister. He would make a good brother.

"'*—and dawns upon him light in darkness,*'" he said in the same cadence. A smile stretched across his face. "It's about time to meet the prince."

"Okay!" She started to run back to the palace. "Wait." She stopped and spun around. "What's his name?"

"Prince Amrit of Charäkhnem," he said slowly.

She nodded seriously and mimicked his tone. "I will meet Prince Amrit of Charäkhnem."

"Yeah, you will," said a voice behind her. She jumped and turned around. Jori. "He's waiting for you, I think." He shrugged. "Atty wanted me to look for you. He's already there."

The three of them hurried back to the palace.

"They're in the meeting room next to the Main," Jori explained as they hustled down the wide corridor.

In minutes, they made it to the right place. Kiria stopped and caught her breath—dignified Keepers were never out of breath—and a large guard let her into the room. Jori and Daelon stayed outside in the hall.

The space wasn't very large, about as big and dark as the formal dining room, where her parents sometimes had meetings over dinner. This room had a table too and the walls were covered in wood paneling and tapestries.

Atty stood awkwardly by the big table. A look of relief crossed his face when she entered. Two Charäkhni guards in pointed helmets and embroidered uniforms stood in the corner of the room. Swords hung at their sides. Kiria glanced sideways at the door she had just come through and was happy to find Brithnem guards at the ready too. At the center of the room was a gangly boy, maybe eleven or twelve, with toughened desert skin and light red hair, wearing a formal outfit much too big on him. He looked lost.

"Prince Amrit?" Kiria began, addressing him.

"Yes," he replied in a thick accent. He touched the middle of his chest. "Prince Amrit."

"I'm Kiria Arioc, the Kepress of Brithnem," she said. She loved the way her title sounded. Technically, she was the Kepress of the whole Western Kingdom, but Brithnem was a prettier word.

"And I'm Atael Calthwaite," said Atty, stepping forward. "I'm—I'm a Kepron."

Amrit bowed a little from the waist, first to Atty, then to Kiria.

"I'm glad you have come to the palace," Kiria said, speaking slowly. Hopefully it wasn't too slowly.

"Yes." Amrit narrowed his eyes. "You are a leader?" he asked.

She knit her brows. "Yes, I'm the heir to the Second Line," she said. Atty nodded in confirmation.

"Oh."

Oh? What's that supposed to mean?

"Shall we sit?" she asked, gesturing to the table. It sounded like something her mother would say, and she wasn't sure what else to do.

She and the two boys sat around the table, the awkwardness getting thicker.

Finally, Amrit spoke to Atty, who kept looking nervously down at his hands. "My ambassador is here to talk about an alliance." It was clear that he had memorized just enough words in their language to get that sentence out.

Kiria nodded, prompting him to go on.

But Amrit's pained look meant he had already run out of words to say. He seemed caught between speaking and not speaking. He called one of his guards over and spoke to him rapidly over his shoulder in Charäkhni. The guard whispered back.

The chair dug into Kiria's back. *Will he ever get to the point?*

Amrit centered himself again, ready to perform another sentence.

He turned his eyes to her. "I don't think we should make an alliance."

She didn't know what she had expected, but it wasn't that. "What? Why not?" she burst out. An alliance was a good thing, wasn't it?

He made an unreadable face.

She continued. "I think our countries would make great allies." It was probably true. Daelon was always telling her about how allies helped in times of war. Just think of the War of the Kingdom Rebels. They couldn't have won without allies. Right now, there were no wars, but it was never bad to have more friends in other countries, just in case.

Amrit shook his head. This skinny boy was getting on her nerves.

Atty finally joined the conversation. "Yeah," he agreed. "It would be good to have peace with each other." A slight slur crept into his voice, as it did whenever he felt overwhelmed.

The door behind them opened. Relieved to have someone else take the pressure off her, Kiria twisted to see who it was. Her mother.

"Hello," she said, "I'm Merian Arioc, Second Keeper."

Amrit stood in a gesture of respect, and bowed to her. At least he got that right.

"Thank you for meeting with my daughter and Kepron Atael," she continued. "But I must pull them away. I hope you have a pleasant stay, Prince Amrit."

Kiria and Atty got up and followed her mother out of the room.

"We were trying to make an alliance," Kiria whispered. Surely her mother would see how helpful that was.

Her mother smiled, almost amused. "Aylmor and Cúron have already negotiated that."

Kiria deflated. It was a little silly, in retrospect, to think that she would have that much power to make political decisions.

"Amrit was being rude," she said.

Mom laughed humorlessly. "His father suggested that he marry you to firm up the alliance. I thought it was well known that Second Keepers can't be married off like that..."

Amrit's disgusted face made more sense now. But why should he be disgusted?

He would be lucky to marry Kiria. Well, she didn't want him either. He was a gross boy.

"They should have known," said Atty, chiming in.

"Yes," Mom replied, turning to him. "They should have. Still, the Keepers have managed to make the ambassador come around." She sighed, a tired sound.

"As long as I don't have to marry Amrit!" said Kiria, not caring if he heard.

6

FIRIAN

Knock, knock, knock!

"You're late for class! Report to Master Jovan immediately!"

Bard rolled over and nearly fell off the bed. Firian saw his arm flail into view above him.

How did I sleep late? Frantic, Firian grabbed yesterday's clothes from the floor and pulled them on. Running into the hall, he left Bard standing there, still muttering and blinking the sleep out of his eyes.

He ran past the other rooms, down the stairs, and out again into the common area. He didn't see any trace of the person who had knocked on his door. Still groggy, he approached the nearest Tanyu, a tall older girl. "Excuse me," he said. If he hadn't been so desperate, he would never have spoken to her like this. She turned and looked at him. "Excuse me, I'm looking for Master Jovan."

Almost imperceptibly, her eyes widened. "Down that hall." She pointed. "It's the third room on the left."

He rushed off, frantic, without a thank you, almost barreling into two more students. The hallway was longer than he expected. There it was—third door on the left! He burst in.

Twenty people stopped and stared at him.

He froze. Facing the door, Master Jovan stood in front of the class, an angry look on his face. His tanned skin looked tough like leather. The black shirt he wore showed off the gigantic muscles on his arms. The smooth stone room he commanded looked just like Master Belik's, except much bigger. This one had a window and no chairs. Across the large room, arranged in rows, students around his age stood at attention. It certainly looked like more than ten students. *Did Master Jairon lie about that number?* Every one of them wore a long-sleeved black shirt and black pants tucked into short black boots. Firian looked down at his dirty green and brown outfit.

"Who are you?" Jovan demanded.

"Fi... Firian Kess."

"Get in line, Firian Kess! Don't stand there like you're stupid. We have no time to wait for gory students who are late." The curse word knifed through him. Jovan's voice became dangerously low. "Meet me after."

Firian's face felt on fire as he scrambled into an empty spot in one of the rows with the others. He held his hands behind his back to keep them from trembling. One boy sniggered at him.

"Do you have something to add, Shiro?" the Master barked, turning on the boy who had laughed.

"No, Master Jovan."

The door behind them flung open and Bard ran in. His eyes widened and he stopped.

"And here's another," Jovan said.

Bard swallowed visibly. Unable to face him, Firian looked away.

"And who are you?"

He hesitated for several seconds. "Bardhon Tanery."

"Come here, Tanery."

Firian raised his eyes to Master Jovan, who pointed to the floor beside him. His fierce gaze burned as he looked at Bard. Instinctively, Firian flexed, ready to take a blow. This man was so much bigger than Father. Whatever he did to Bard was bound to hurt.

Firian heard stumbling footsteps as Bard appeared beside the Master. Bard's dark eyes rounded, huge with fear. At the first sound of the Master's voice, Bard flinched.

"There are many ways to kill a man," Jovan cried, so the class could hear.

The blood seeped from Bard's face until it was ashen. Firian stopped breathing.

"But we don't want to kill someone unless it's necessary. More often it's a better idea to injure in order to get information, or distract to get away. There are many ways to do those as well." He turned back to Bard, whose breathing rasped in and out, shallow and rushed. "One easy thing to do" – he raised his leg before Bard could move away, and stamped hard on his foot, scraping his boot down across the bridge – "is to step on the person's foot like that."

Bard screamed and his anguish-lined face glistened with tears that didn't fall.

"Don't merely crush the toes, but stomp higher up. Some people can still run with crushed toes. This will slow them for a while."

Firian tasted blood and realized he had bit his tongue.

"You will all practice that later, but now we're working on the basics—go line up, Tanery—so get in position," said the Master.

Limping, Bard slid into line, avoiding everyone's eyes. His ragged breathing betrayed that he was crying.

All the other students spread their legs a little and put their hands behind their backs. Firian followed their example and so did Bard, wincing.

Meet me after... He had heard those words many times from his trade school teachers, but they were harmless. Master Jovan could kill him if he wanted to.

During the rest of class, the Master showed them all basic strength techniques: three different kinds of push-ups, deliberate postures flexing the abdomen or the legs, crouching jumps... Jovan corrected every weak repetition or wrong angle, and mocked anyone who struggled to keep up. By the end, Firian's muscles quivered, completely strained. Bard had trouble matching the pace but he managed. Finally, Jovan announced a short break for breakfast. The children scattered quickly, eager to escape his watchful eyes.

Everyone left but Firian and the Master. The room felt huge and empty.

"Kess!" Jovan cried suddenly. The name reverberated around the room.

"Yes, sir!" he answered, forcing himself to look the Master in the eyes. "Yes, Master Jovan?"

He laughed loudly and began to walk out through a back door that Firian hadn't seen until then. "With me, Kess," he said, disappearing through the opening.

The door led to a dark, stone hallway covered in dust. Obviously, people didn't use it often. A door rimmed with yellow light blocked the other end of the corridor. With one hand, Jovan opened it and blinding light burst in.

After they walked outside, the Master closed the door behind them. Huge weathered pines grew close together all around the Academy. The wall behind him rose tall and impassible, made completely with rough stones fitted together without mortar. No way to escape.

"Run."

Firian looked up. Master Jovan cocked his head to the left. "Around the building. Now. Run. As fast as you can. Go!"

Firian took off sprinting. Dread faded away the farther he went. He ran like a hunted thing, but his muscles already ached from the workout during class. He didn't know how far he'd gotten before he slowed to a jog. Around the building, Jovan had said. All the way around. So he stumbled forward as fast as he could, keeping close to the wall.

Finally, he rounded the corner to see Master Jovan waiting there for him. Firian stopped, panting.

"Very good," Jovan said. "But you were too slow. Do it again."

Again?

He peered back, completely stoic. "Faster. Go."

Firian had no choice but to follow orders. *Warrior... warrior...* It was all for the sake of becoming a Tanyu. He had to do anything they said or they could send him home. So he ran even faster than he had before, though it used up all of his remaining strength. His legs burned, his breathing rushed against raw, dry lungs. *Keep going... keep going... keep going...*

He ran now to send a message to the other Tanyuin warriors. Grown and strong, he wore all black, running. He ran for the safety of the other Tanyu still trapped in that battle. Slowly the enemy troops were advancing to the real location of the Academy. They all knew where it was. So Firian ran to take his message to... Master Jovan.

He snapped from his thoughts and realized that he could hardly breathe. He slowed, and his muscles recoiled. He twisted in pain, but had no breath to scream.

Bent almost double, he began to go again. He never should have stopped. *Faster... faster... faster than the last time...* He began to feel lightheaded and the tendons in his legs tightened more with every step. *Faster...* His side began to ache. *Faster.* He could see Master Jovan now, leaning with his back against the wall, watching him.

"Faster!" Jovan yelled when he saw him stumbling toward him. "It's taken you just as long as last time! How will this teach you to get to class on time if you don't HURRY?"

Firian tried to straighten and run again.

"Faster!"

He ran faster, and though his nostrils were flared like a running horse, he couldn't breathe at all. Only a few more steps. The Master grew closer. Closer.

Firian collapsed at his feet and vomited.

Master Jovan looked unconcerned. "You'll get to class on time tomorrow?" he asked.

Firian nodded miserably.

"Good," he said, going back inside. "That's enough for today."

The door clicked into place and Firian still lay there, panting like a dog. Stabbing pain seared his legs and his side.

Once he had gathered enough breath, he stood up painfully, wiped his mouth, and went back inside. He had missed breakfast.

PART II

DEFENDER (AGE 15)

7

FIRIAN

Master Jovan laughed. "Run!" he yelled.

Determined to beat his record, Firian finished his second lap around the Academy. Although he had moved on to weapons training and more advanced techniques, Jovan still insisted on ending every session with the same laps around the building that had ended his initial lesson. Now, the new muscle Firian had gained over the past four years made him look bigger and more impressive than he had when he had first arrived.

He jogged to a halt. Master Jovan crossed his large arms as he looked down at Firian. "Well," he said slowly, "you're getting better."

Those were some of the first words of encouragement he had ever heard Jovan say. Firian nodded as he caught his breath.

"That means you can do better tomorrow," he said, disappearing again through the door back into the Academy. Firian followed at a respectful distance, smiling.

You're getting better.

Jovan's leaving always signaled the end of the lesson, so Firian was free to go back to his room.

Bard wasn't there. Probably in class.

Firian slipped into the Unreal, felt its power sizzle under his skin. How could he practice today? He was improving physically, but would his skill be enough to pass the hall test later today? Their hall master Erron tested the guys on his hall every year or so. Even though Erron, at eighteen, was a Defender, not a Master, he was in charge of making sure they were all keeping up with their training. At least, that's how the Masters had explained this to Firian the first time. Almost everyone treated these tests less like an exam than a competition. Firian had always been a standout among people his age, but today he wanted to show up Erron. And today he could do it. He felt powerful, ready.

He stood in a shapeless space, idly switching out weapons in his hands. Bow, knife, sword. He could only do so much by himself, but he could practice the latest technique Belik had taught him. Become something else—maybe something from a nightmare. He shrank and grew, feeling the wind rush by as he changed. What would be frightening? A ghost, the kind he used to imagine as a kid? That sounded like a challenge, so he let the thought of it consume him. Ghosts were partially transparent—at least the ones in his imagination. He wasn't sure whether or not they really existed. If the stories were true, they stood a head taller than a tall man, so he grew. Flowing robes. Flashing eyes. That felt right, but he couldn't be absolutely sure he was doing it right unless somebody checked for him.

As though on cue, he heard the faint sound of a door opening. Bard was back.

Firian swam up through the layers of his imagination and broke the surface of reality again. The room smelled like sweat.

"Hey, Fir!" said Bard, closing the door behind him.

"Bard, look at this," he called, his voice deeper now. It hadn't cracked in over a year. He sat on the edge of his bed and shut his eyes.

Bard hesitated. "I'm kind of tired."

"Come on!"

His friend gave a barely audible sigh. "Just don't practice attack moves on me, okay?"

Firian nodded impatiently.

Nothingness gave way to a meadow. Bard materialized a few feet away, looking around apprehensively. "What do you want me to see?" he asked.

Firian didn't answer, but called for the energy to become the ghost he had imagined.

Bard's large eyes got even bigger. "Gore, Firian!" he swore. "What are you trying to do?"

Firian subsided into himself again.

Suddenly sheepish, Bard took a deep breath. "Sorry," he said, apologizing for the language. "Are you going to use that during the hall test?"

"I was thinking about it." It depended on the rules Erron set up. Sometimes there were restrictions so that the boys could prove their skills without actually hurting each other. Other years, it was a free-for-all. Hopefully today he could do whatever he wanted.

It was almost time.

The two of them opened their eyes and headed out the door. More students than usual crowded the hallway. Tiev, Shiro, and Rian walked past in the same direction, with Erron leading the way to the room at the hall bend. Across the courtyard, in the girls' hallway, another group headed to their test. Rhea, a girl from the little town of King's Heights, glanced over at him as she went down the staircase leading to the main level, her long blonde hair waving on the air. He rubbed his lips together and shook his head. Today, he couldn't be distracted.

Erron held the door open for all of them to enter. It was another typical Academy classroom—bare of decoration, only a couple of chairs in a stone room.

The boys filed in, filling almost the entire space. Erron was the last to come in and silently stand behind one of the two chairs facing each other.

The door creaked open again, and Firian spun around to see Master Belik limping into the room. *Why is he here?* He had never come to any of the other tests.

Bard smacked Firian's arm and nodded toward Belik.

Students made way for the Master, pressing out of the way. Despite the limp, he commanded respect. Once, with a sarcastic yet meaningful look, he'd told Firian, "Whatever hurts makes you work harder."

Belik's face remained impassive as he claimed a spot against the wall. Erron raised his eyebrows at him to give him the floor, but Belik held up a hand. He didn't want to speak. He was here to observe.

Erron continued with the test protocol. "Shiro and Firian!" he said.

Firian nodded confidently. Shiro came from the same desert city as Tiev, so they both had dusty tan skin, black hair, and thin green-brown eyes. They were both about as tall as Firian, but more compact. The two of them roomed together, but Tiev, though a better friend, was the bigger threat, both in person and in the Unreal. Shiro, by comparison, should be much easier to beat.

The chairs were so close Firian had to spread his knees so they didn't knock against Shiro's.

"No shots to the head or heart. Hall master's choice." Erron wasn't one to waste words.

The three of them—Firian, Shiro, and Erron—closed their eyes and waited for a moment in darkness. Master's choice meant that Erron would control the environment. Firian and Shiro could only control themselves.

Blue. Blue and black and white. The colors came into focus, surging, waving. Firian's body heaved upward with the color and he realized. They were in the ocean. That was new.

Erron floated above the sea like a deity, watching from a distance. Firian and his opponent floated in the water. He had never seen the ocean, so he took in as many details as he could—the wet, heaving waves, cold on the surface, the salt in his mouth, the depths below, the sky reflecting hard like glass.

A wave raised them both up as high as the Academy walls. Shiro, rising mechanically instead of organically, was struggling to find the reality in the situation. Without that belief, he couldn't hope to win. Firian brought his hands out of the water and slicked back his hair, feeling the cool sea splash his face.

Time to go. If he couldn't attack Shiro's face, the only part of his body peeking up over the water, he would have to go below. So he sank down, heavy as a stone.

Blackout. Water pressed in heavy on him. Shiro had to be roughly in that direction...

A current forced him deeper. Had he turned around? The sunlight filtered dim above him. His limbs burned. He couldn't breathe. He flailed convulsively, lungs on fire.

Where are you? You're in the room. You're fine.

He still couldn't make himself breathe. But if he didn't, he would pass out. Out of options, he gasped. No water entered his lungs. He could still feel it on his face, but none in his body. Panting, he smiled. This was exactly as it was supposed to be—believe without believing.

There was Shiro, shooting silver darts from his feet as they dangled under the surface. They passed harmlessly through Firian as he approached.

Now he could have a bit of fun. He'd heard of sea creatures, some menacing and horrible. Thank goodness he had a good imagination as a kid. He didn't need to have seen something to visualize it.

A huge, gaping mouth, full of teeth. Bigger. He could make himself even bigger. He wouldn't need to worry about realistic gills and all that if he could just scare Shiro back to reality, like a person falling to wake up from a nightmare. Firian's rubbery skin stretched over his enormous body, tiny eyes squinting at his prey, gigantic mouth ready to open at the right moment. Looking around at the blackened deep, even Firian shuddered at the idea of a creature like him controlling the water.

Closer, closer... Shiro's body and legs looked frail now. The surface of the water turned red, ablaze with fire. Shiro's trap couldn't hurt him, he was sure. The knowledge buzzed in his mind like a strong drink from the pub.

He swam closer, Shiro getting larger. Soon... closer... now!

With a roar of air and water, five rows of teeth burst high above the surface, water streaming down the head and long throat. Below him, Shiro screamed like a lost soul and disappeared.

It took Firian a shaky moment to get back into his own skin.

When he opened his eyes, Shiro was glaring at him, beet red. He hurled a curse at him and left, passing Belik on the way out.

Bard, Erron, and the others looked at him aghast. Hardly anybody won so decisively.

"Wow, nice job!" said Bard, as though he couldn't keep the words in.

Firian smiled as Belik silently left the room.

THE NEXT DAY during their lesson, Master Belik opened his eyes and squinted. Then he hummed, a noncommittal sound.

Firian treated it as positive. Stiff from sitting too long in the chair, he nodded, ready for the next scenario. The Unreal was always better than reality. There, he could feel like he was flying or standing or rolling or running...

"How did you do?" Belik asked, staring intensely as though Firian's response was crucial.

Firian's hands fidgeted.

"How did you do today?"

"What do you mean?" Firian asked, cracking his knuckles.

"I mean, you did as well as any other student," he said slowly. "But you, Firian, are not any other student. Your work today has been mediocre. Have you even seen half of the things I've shown you?"

Firian began to shrug and thought better of it.

"No," Belik answered. "Where's your focus? If you can't work with everything you have, then leave!" His tone grated, worn out. Belik was a hard man, but his edges were crumbling today.

"There are all kinds of things..."

"Anything more important than this?" he snapped.

"I'm sorry. I'll work harder."

"Yes, you *will* work harder. Why do you think we let you into this Academy? Because we liked your smile? No" – emotion lifted him a little from his chair – "the moment you walked into my room, you swore to me you'd work as hard you needed to become the best!"

Firian's throat constricted enough to force his breathing. Adrenaline snaked like lightning through his body, and he gripped the armrests until his knuckles lost their blood. "Of course! Let's do it again."

"Not until you stop being so gory distracted!" Belik roared suddenly.

Firian's chest rose and fell with hurried breaths. He fought to keep his wide eyes from rolling.

Master Belik slowly raised an eyebrow high above his glasses. Besides that, the lines on his face seemed immovable. "It's a *very* good thing you're as Talented as you are, and that I like you. People *die* in war, and you're dicking around like none of it matters. You're not finished yet."

"But we're not in a war now," Firian found himself saying.

"That you know of." Belik's eye twitched evasively, and he resettled his glasses on his nose with a finger. The Academy loved their secrets.

Maybe they have too many.

Firian bit the inside of his lip hard. Belik saw the fight with Shiro. Why was he giving him such a hard time? "I am Talented, though," he muttered, unable to hold back the words.

"So am I," Belik replied. He laughed humorlessly through his nose. "I was in line for the Headship, once. And look where I am now." He exhaled a deep breath, his anger deflating. "Trust me. I understand." His tone had completely changed into something almost fatherly. "I could go to the Second Level of the Unreal before I was twenty years old. No one goes to the Second Level."

Firian's eyes widened. He'd tried to get to the Second Level before but almost suffocated. It was the Unreal within the Unreal. It took a dangerous amount of belief to establish the first layer, the one they could all reach, in such a way that it was a stepping stone to a level further down.

Belik continued. "That's how Anewa got Lost, the idiot. But anybody who can..." His gaze shifted to the floor, as close to vulnerability as Firian had ever seen. "Those skills earn you high positions. Strategic positions."

"What position did you have?"

Belik blinked, becoming aware of the room again. His mouth hardened. "It doesn't matter now, does it?" He drew himself up in the chair, his dark ring digging into his finger as he gripped the armrests. "I should have given everything. Everything. And so should you."

Firian cleared his throat. "Show me that last one, Master Belik. I'm focusing now." He closed his eyes. Only darkness and nothingness appeared behind his lids. Seconds passed, but he refused to open them until something happened.

Slowly, he was in a strange gray-white room with many half-guessed suspended platforms above and below him. Maybe fifteen feet overhead, Master Belik appeared, standing on one of them. This wasn't what the last scenario had been, but at least he was out from under Belik's penetrating glare, so he jumped up and Belik jumped down until they met in the middle.

"The object of this exercise," the Master began, "is to... Come with me." Walking away, he said nothing more, so Firian followed him up and up onto new platforms only distinguishable by a darker gray outline of shadow. Up and up.

Climb up. Above him, the room soared neverendingly upward into a haze. Firian jumped to catch the next ledge. Up and up. Most of the landings came to about his waist and he would pull himself onto them, accepting Belik's unstated rule that whenever *he* acted like there was gravity, Firian acted the same way. No flying. No floating. No growing or shrinking. He was just himself. Something exceptionally human in Belik's movements let him know when the rule was in play. The only difference from real-life movement was that Belik's leg never hurt in the Unreal, as it did from a war injury that kept him cooped in the Academy.

Finally, on a large platform that took up half the space in the room, the Master halted.

Turning slow eyes upon him, Belik looked Firian quickly up and down as he hoisted himself up to stand. "Why are you out of breath?" he asked. "Where have you gone?"

Firian hadn't even thought about it. None of his muscles were really tired at all. He slowed his breathing to a normal pace. "Nowhere."

"Are you sure?"

Doubt—just one unreasonable moment—entered Firian's mind as he looked down into the formless depths, then back at his teacher... who rushed at him with a knife! Firian didn't have time to think before he was stabbed and hurled powerfully backward into nothing.

Fly! Just fly, you idiot! He jolted to a halt again in mid-air and settled lightly onto a platform. Jerking his head up, he saw Belik standing there, disapproving.

"Open your eyes," Belik's mind said impatiently.

They opened.

"What was that?" Belik cried. "You know better than to believe in the Unreal! I could have killed you. You could have been Lost."

Belief was reality. If he had believed he died, then he would be dead. "I didn't believe in it, Master Belik," Firian said, fighting the urge to dab his fingers to his chest to check for blood. He glanced down.

"But you doubted, Firian, you doubted!" He motioned to the thin line of blood welling up near Firian's collarbone. "We have lost many good soldiers because they doubted for an instant. It's a good thing I've at least taught you enough to stop yourself from falling."

Rage coursed through him, but he held his tongue. He'd done enough damage for one day.

"Firian, at your level, you need to know this. We can't afford to lose even one soldier to their own stupidity!"

Firian lowered his head. *How dare...*

No. Master Belik was a full Tanyu. Firian calmed himself.

"Do you want to end up useless like Anewa?"

Belik referenced Anewa almost every week, so Firian was sick of hearing about him. He had been Lost a year before Firian entered the Academy. He was the best, they said—so good that his Talent undid him. He went into the Unreal one day and never returned. Belik, being in Retrieval, had tried to rescue him, but failed. The other Tanyu waited months for him to come back to his right mind, but in the end, it became too costly to take care of his unconscious body and they were forced to kill him.

"No Unreal for five days!" pronounced Belik. "Starting tomorrow, I'll post Sentries to make sure."

No Unreal? None? The one time he had experienced Sentries was terrible. Master Asoka had appointed a Sentry over the entire strategy class so she could teach them what it felt like: a painful buzz, a net preventing entry to the Unreal. "As you would have it, Master Belik," he said, each rehearsed word tasting sour.

"You have to want it." The lines around Belik's eyes deepened slightly before his face became a mask harder than before. Even a tiny misgiving—a little doubt—was good to see. Maybe he would regret his decision. Firian's lips almost twisted into a bitter smile at the thought.

"That's all. Leave. Now! Mistakes like that can't happen again."

Firian closed the door behind him without a word. He went to the courtyard and sat on the edge of the fountain, but he knew that his lesson wasn't supposed to be over for a long time, so instead he went to his room and dozed. *That* would prevent him from slipping into the Unreal, because this certainly seemed like a good time to go there.

8

FIRIAN

Firian hadn't gone home in four years.

He practiced so much that thin white scars laced his torso from the times he had practiced too hard, been too focused in the Unreal. So how dare Belik tell him that he was distracted?

"Stop! Fir, what are you doing?" cried Bard.

Firian jumped back from the doorway to their room. "What?" he snapped.

Bard presented the broom in his hand. "Erron told me to sweep and you wrecked everything."

"Why do you have to clean?" he asked, amused now, stepping over the scattered pile of dust.

"Because we've hardly cleaned anything since we came."

Firian laughed. "If we don't mind, why should Erron care?"

Bard swept out Firian's footprints with gusto. "It's his job to tell us what to do," he grumbled.

Firian jumped onto his bed and sat cross-legged to avoid touching the floor. "It seems that way." He thought for a minute. "Bard?"

"Yeah?"

"How many times have you gone back to see your parents?"

He had just come back from his latest trip a few days ago, when he had returned earlier than Firian had expected. He picked at the wood on the top of the broomstick. "This was the third time."

"I've never gone home."

Bard squinted. "Haven't you?"

"No."

Bard leaned on the broom, his look puzzled as though he were trying to remember a time when Firian had left. "Why not?"

"They never said I could."

"It's been four years, and they haven't given you leave yet?"

"No." Firian reclined against the hard wall. "I think everybody's been able to leave but me. Even Rian's been able to go, and his parents hate him. And you. You live pretty far away."

"I don't know," said Bard. "I can't think of any reason they would keep you here. It's been a long time."

Firian scratched the back of his neck and searched for his family in his mind, but he couldn't find them. He had forgotten. None of them had the Talent. Not even Brett.

"Do you want to see them? You don't really talk about them at all."

Firian wouldn't mind if Brett visited, but he thought better of mentioning it and leaned back again, dull anger stirring in his gut. "No. I don't want to see them. I was just wondering why they would keep me locked up like some prisoner without the chance to go."

Bard leaned harder on the broom and almost lost his balance. Falling silent, he began sweeping again and didn't pry.

"They should let you go," said Bard finally. "You learn everything faster than anybody else, practically. You deserve to have a day or two to yourself."

Firian laughed, half from resentment and half from amusement. "Yeah, they should. I should just leave without permission…"

"They'd have your head," said Bard.

They both knew that he wouldn't leave the Academy's grounds unauthorized. It would jeopardize everything he'd worked for. Students had been dismissed for that, even though it had been a mistake. Everyone suspected the worst for anyone kicked out, but no one talked about it. In any case, the consequences were more than he was willing to risk.

Firian had known that he belonged to the Tanyu from the moment he passed the test. Until now, he hadn't minded. The organization could do what they liked, could push him, could work him to the bone. Loyalty until death was part of the Tanyuin code, and he was proud to be a part of it. Honestly, he was excited to become the one to whom others pledged their loyalty. And they would one day.

The Tanyu could train him until he almost dropped dead, but Firian wouldn't stand to be manipulated. If there was a reason that he wasn't given leave, he wanted to know it.

"I could ask Erron why I'm still here," said Firian. Masters seemed to tell hall masters extra information about their group.

"He'll make you do chores," replied Bard, finishing his cleaning. "He'll probably ask me to do something else too, if we aren't careful." He shook out the broom in the hallway, and then hastily closed the door. "I wish I could burn that thing," he said, staring contemptuously at the brush.

Making himself more comfortable, Firian laughed. "I would like to watch that, just because you'd dance around like a giddy girl."

"Erron never asks you to sweep," Bard muttered.

"That's because I'm stuck here forever."

"Then go find out why."

Firian slapped him on the shoulder and slipped out of the room. Erron had earned everyone's respect. Students only became hall masters if they had done exceptionally well every year at the Academy and were at least seventeen years old. Because of Erron's reputation as a ruthless fighter in the Unreal, many boys on the hall feared him but not Firian.

The hall felt claustrophobic now, narrow and unchanging. The thought of having another free day in Tánuil didn't cheer him much. He knew almost everyone there and had done everything there was to do. He didn't even *have* to see his family. If he could even visit someplace else, like Brithnem—that was supposed to be a great city—or if he could go with Bard to see *his* family....

He knocked curtly on Erron's door.

"Yes? Who is it?"

"Firian."

"Is it important?" Erron didn't open up much and kept mostly to himself. Only his imagination was savage, apparently.

"...yes."

"Very important?"

"Yes."

"Come in. I don't feel like talking to anyone for very long."

Firian hurried in.

"Close the door, Kess," said Erron, seated in a chair with his name carved in both armrests. He'd threatened death to anyone who attempted to steal it from him. No one had, but the thought had crossed every boy's mind more than once. "What is it?"

"Why haven't I been allowed to leave the Academy?" Firian asked. Small talk was a waste of time.

Erron arched an eyebrow. "What do you mean?"

Firian looked into Erron's large eyes. All his features were large, especially his nose. "I mean I've been here for four years and have never been given leave to go."

"You've never been into Tánuil," he said dryly, blanking his eyes. With one large finger, he tapped the dark band of his Defender ring inlaid with a light blue stone against the armrest.

"You know what I mean."

"You want to see your family?"

Firian shrugged, avoiding the question. "That doesn't matter. I've never been allowed to leave the grounds since I've gotten here. Everyone else has been given permission to visit their homes at least once in the last four years. I never have."

"Why does that bother you?"

"Erron. Can you tell me or not? That's why I came. I want to know. *Do* you know?"

"I have no idea," he said. "You should ask someone else."

Firian pursed his lips. Belik would know, but they weren't on the best terms right now. "Okay." He headed back out of the room, leaving Erron to himself.

The question grew in Firian's mind. He paused, gnawing his lip. *Is there anyone else I can ask?*

No. Belik was the only one guaranteed to have the answer. The food he had eaten earlier that day sat heavy in his stomach as he contemplated going back to the Master's room.

Why haven't I been allowed to leave? It was a fair question. And he was afraid of nothing. At least, that's what he told himself. Sticking out his chest and huffing out a breath, he turned on his heel and headed back toward Belik's room. Hopefully he wasn't teaching or doing Retrieval right now.

Firian stepped lightly down the stairs and through the fountain courtyard to the hallway where Belik's room was. After only a second's worth of hesitation, he knocked on the door.

"Firian," came Belik's voice. A flat, knowing acknowledgment, almost as though he expected him.

Firian opened the door and leaned in. Master Belik was alone.

"Master Belik," he said, "I... have a question."

Belik's face was impassive. He didn't respond, but instead waited for Firian to continue.

Firian's face flushed hot with sudden embarrassment. "I was just thinking, why haven't I ever been allowed to leave?" He didn't mean that he wanted to really leave the Academy, so he rushed on. "I mean, other people have been able to visit their families, but I've never been given permission."

Master Belik dropped his eyes and he opened his mouth to take a breath. Apart from Master Jovan, Belik was the strongest person Firian had ever met. He was always in control. Something about his uncharacteristic hesitation made sickness slowly start to rise in Firian's belly. He waited while the Master looked around for words. *What could be so hard to explain?*

"We should have told you sooner," he began in a low voice. Careful, almost tender. Compared to earlier that day, the tone sounded like a different person, a kinder person.

Forcing breath in and out became a difficult task.

Belik sighed and raised his eyes to meet Firian's. "Firian, two years ago your family was killed in a fire."

Firian's face went cold and his hands started shaking. "No. I want the truth," he said faintly. *Why haven't you let me go? That's impossible.*

The sympathy in Belik's look deepened. Regret, too. "I'm sorry. We should have told you. You had a visit coming up when we got the news, and then we thought it was better that you stay here. Focus on your training."

Firian's tongue stuck to the roof of his mouth and he found no other words to say but an automatic "goodbye." His mind registered nothing but pain and confusion. Fighting for breath, he vaguely headed in the direction of his room. No one else was in the hallway and the courtyard beneath the railing grew darker, lost in shadows.

Brett...

At the thought of her name, her face, she was with him. She smiled sweetly. She looked so different now that she was seventeen.

"Down that hallway is Master Belik's room," Firian said, pointing over the railing.

"Who's he?" Brett asked.

"He's my personal trainer."

"Your personal trainer!" Impressed, her eyes lit up.

He took a long look at the face he hadn't seen in years. Her glossy hair had grown even longer; she was still as tall as he was, and her features were still delicate and innocent, but more mature somehow. "I'm glad you came to visit me, Brett."

"Me too," she said.

Suddenly, he bumped into Bard and realized that he had taken her to see his room. "Brett, this is Bard. Bardhon Tanery." He smiled as he related the full name. "He's my roommate."

Brett shook his limp hand politely, but Bard looked confused. "You have a beautiful sister," Bard said, but it seemed forced, as though he spoke against his will. His lips barely moved when he said it. Then he said "Firian" and it sounded clear, but far away... and somehow more real than his compliment to Brett.

Firian thought about answering the call, but decided against it. "This is where I've been living for the past four years. I've missed you."

"I've missed you too." She looked around the room. "This place is a mess," she teased.

Bard gave Firian a meaningful look.

"I know," said Firian.

"What?" said Bard, squinting like a deaf man.

"You don't mind living here?" she asked, looking around.

Firian shrugged with one shoulder. "I... I think I like it here. I like it here a lot. But it's hard. Not like Mother and Father, but... it's like it means something."

"Firian, what are you talking about?" said the small, muffled voice of Bard. Firian ignored him.

Brett kissed Firian on the cheek. "I wouldn't have the courage to do this," she said in a low voice. "It would be too hard to move away from everything and have personal trainers and... what else do you do?"

"I'm not supposed to tell you any of this but we run and do things like that for some of the day but most of the practice has to do with the Talent—the mind Talent we have," he said. *Or has she heard of that already?*

Bard gave him an admonishing look. Or maybe he was scared. Firian had forgotten he wasn't supposed to say so much to someone from outside the Academy.

Brett carefully changed the subject to something that she understood a little better. Firian didn't begrudge her for not understanding him. He was almost glad that she didn't. That way he could have something that even Brett couldn't touch, that he could know and she wouldn't. She was smart, he knew that, but she couldn't understand how hard he had worked to become what he was. "You've grown since I saw you last," she said.

"You too," he replied.

She felt his arms. "You're a lot stronger than that scrawny boy I remember," she said, smiling.

"I wasn't scrawny. I was strong then too," he said in his defense, but he was proud anyway.

"Fir!" He heard the far-off voice calling him again. "Firian!" The voice grew more insistent.

Then Brett let go of his hand and left the room. "I have to go, Firian," she said. "I love you and I'll tell Father and Mother you're doing well. I'll visit again as soon as I can. Goodbye!" And she was gone.

"Firian!"

"What?" he cried. Then it was as if the room settled into itself and he suddenly knew none of it had been real. The Sentries just hadn't been posted yet to bar him from the Unreal. Brett had never come.

"What's wrong, Firian?" asked Bard, who stood before him, tense, like he was ready to fight or run.

Heat flooded his face as he realized what a fool he must have looked just now. And that Brett never would come. "What was I saying?" he mumbled as he closed the door.

"You sounded like you were talking to someone," Bard said apprehensively. "Are you sure you're all right?"

"I'm fine!" he said, taking off his clothes and getting in bed.

Brett's note, yellow and stained, still curled away from the wooden bunk post. He had pinned and repinned it until it was barely legible. He rolled over and scrubbed his eyes so fiercely they hurt.

9

KIRIA

Kiria lay on her bed, crying. The closed curtains let in no light, so no one could see her, so she couldn't see herself. She had told her two serving girls to watch the door and not to let anyone in the room. She hardly ever cried. In fact, her parents always said that she kept her head about her and would make a great Keeper of Brithnem someday. They were proud that she was the heir to continue the Second Line.

But none of that was a comfort right now.

Someone had said she was ugly. And the worst part was that he meant it.

She squeezed her hands into fists.

Stupid boy! I've never liked people from Charäkhnem anyway. Ever since Prince Amrit had visited the first time four years ago, she knew she didn't like him. Her face burned with how much she hated that skinny, mean prince.

If only Jori could punch him, but she was never going to tell him what happened because... because what if... what if he *agreed*?

She felt the blood drain from her face and suddenly felt cold. Everybody knew her as brave, and usually she was. She didn't mind standing up to the occasional person who told her that it was stupid to have her mother as a Keeper since she was a woman. She would even stand up to Cúron, the oldest and most experienced Keeper of the three, if she didn't agree with him.

But was she brave enough to face this truth? What if she *was* ugly?

She squeezed her eyes shut. It was a desolating thought. The heir to the Arioc throne was supposed to be beautiful, like in the stories. Like the statue of Mari in the Main—strong and beautiful.

Violently, she jerked back the curtains around her bed and ran to the looking glass. She didn't really look at herself much. Action had always excited her more than looks. Her serving girls picked out her outfit in the morning and combed her hair when it got ratty. She'd always assumed that when she got older, she would be beautiful. She hadn't thought much about it, but now that she *was* older, already fifteen... she needed to know.

There she was.

Her dry and ash-colored hair hung limply around her face. The freckles on her nose weren't cute; they looked like a mistake. Pudge puffed around her light brown eyes and her mouth was small and thin. Her ears stuck out too much. She was short and had no figure at all. On anyone else it would have been average—she wouldn't have thought twice about it—but on herself it was unacceptable.

Ugly.

She stood in pain for a moment, staring at the creature in the glass. She had never thought that there was something wrong with her—maybe even thought that she was a little bit pretty. The girl that looked back at her wasn't pretty.

"She's sort of ugly, isn't she? I expected her to look different. Weren't the other Keepers beautiful...?"

His halting words hit her over and over again in different ways, in different places, like torture. *Stupid boy.* Her nose turned red as she started to cry again. She wouldn't bear to look at herself anymore. Gritting her teeth hard, she felt stuck in her own body. It couldn't ever change. She would look the same, just older, when she grew up. No one would look at her and think that she was beautiful. Men wouldn't want to marry her and Brithnem wouldn't be proud to have her lead them.

All because of something she couldn't control.

A wild, desperate idea came to her. What if she *could* change? She had heard of things like that happening in stories.

She closed her eyes and thought hard about it, picturing long glistening hair, perfect skin, a figure. She thought for a long time, until her eyelids tingled from being shut so tightly. The tingling in her eyelids spread over her whole body as she kept wishing.

Then she opened her eyes and looked into the glass.

And nearly choked.

After she finished coughing, she cautiously looked up again, afraid of what she might see. It was true! She had changed! She was the most beautiful girl she had ever seen.

It was hard to pinpoint the changes. Everything she had seen a moment ago remained, except now it was all perfect. She was *breathtaking.*

Looking at that gorgeous face, foreign but familiar, she couldn't breathe. How was this possible? She didn't have time to think it through before the beauty faded into her average reflection.

What... what did I do? What was that?

Gingerly, she touched her face. After she convinced herself that she wasn't crazy, she tore out of the room with her maids jogging after her.

"I need to see my parents," she told the guards when she was outside her parents' room, panting from the run. "Let me in."

She didn't have to convince them.

Another fit of sobs rose up in her throat as she crossed the thick maroon carpet to the window where her parents sat talking.

Alarmed, her mother jumped up and rushed over to her daughter. "Kiria!" she said, taking her into her arms. "What's the matter?"

"I..." She realized that she didn't know how to begin, so she just cried until she didn't have any tears left.

By the time she looked up, both of her parents were looking down at her, extremely concerned.

"You have to tell us what happened, Kiria," said her father. Sternness and fear shone in his eyes. "Did something happen to you?"

"Well..." She took a deep breath, suddenly not wanting to tell them her story since she knew by now they were expecting something much worse. Once they found out what she was really crying about, it would seem so small. "I... I was looking at myself in the glass and..." – she felt her mother's arms relax around her – "and I don't know what happened. I *changed*. Does that happen?" she finished in a small voice. In the arms of her mother, she felt like a child.

"What do you mean, you 'changed?'" her mother asked her.

"I was... I turned... beautiful..."

"Beautiful?"

"I was the prettiest girl I'd ever seen," she whispered, feeling stupid for saying it, but it was true.

"Kiria!" her mother cried, excited. "You have an Ability!" She grabbed her shoulders gently and held her at arm's length.

Through her tears, Kiria saw her mother smile. "Ability?"

"The gift," her mother said.

In her shock, Kiria had forgotten all about them. They were so rare. Of course she knew about Abilities.

Her mother still continued. "Abilities show us our original state before men started worshiping other gods. Some people are given Original Knowledge, which allows them to know something without having heard it or seen it for themselves, and others were given Original Harmony, that deals with nature. Those people can walk out into a storm and none of the elements hurt them. My sister had that one. Other people can speak the Original Language. Tanyu have the Original Talent, allowing them access to imagination and the Unreal. And the last Ability is Original Beauty. Those people can make themselves appear like they were originally intended to look, before the world fell. Is that what happened to you?"

"I guess so." *Original Beauty*. It was real. She could *become* beautiful. Her mind flashed to Tanis, the new guard in training.

"You have Beauty! What a gift!" her mother cried, delighted. "But Kiria, listen to me." She became much more serious. "Now that you've found out your Ability, guard it. Abilities are dangerous gifts. Don't show your Beauty to anyone yet."

Kiria's mouth fell open. Just as joy began to well inside her, her mother had to dampen it.

"She's right," her father added. "Beauty is one of the most dangerous gifts. You need to be careful."

Kiria screwed her brows together. This seemed to be getting out of hand. Surely it couldn't be that dangerous to look one way instead of another.

"Yes," her mother continued, "never change unless you have a reason."

"But... why can't I?" Kiria asked, feeling as though the biggest discovery of her life was going to be swept out of sight in a drawer somewhere.

Her mother smiled more weakly now. "For now, only show your Beauty to those you can absolutely trust. We'll discuss a time when you can reveal yourself to the people."

"Why?" Kiria thought of the look on Prince Amrit's face if she walked up to him in all her beauty. He would choke on his horrible words.

"Beauty is powerful," her father answered. It wasn't a good enough answer to her question.

Her mother stepped in again. "You need to learn how to deal with this gift before you reveal it to other people," she said. "Many will treat you differently when you're Beautiful. Some of the attention can be good, but" – her eyes flashed to Father – "some can also be harmful. There are many benefits to staying just as you are."

"Why would I—"

"You don't have to make a decision right now, but you'll eventually have to choose which appearance to use when you're a leader. Once you decide, you'll have to remain consistent."

Seeing the look on her face, her father added, "We're only thinking of you."

She didn't have to think about it. She would use her Beauty all the time as Keeper. She would have so much more confidence. There was no point in staying ugly.

"Of course," her mother agreed. "What you have is a more perfect beauty than this world knows right now, so guard it for now."

Kiria nodded. She would be careful, but she would change as often as she could get away with it. Scenarios whirled in her head. She wanted to change again right now. "Can I show Jori and Atty?" *And Tanis.*

For one maddening second, her parents hesitated. It seemed her father was about to protest when her mother said, "I think they've proven themselves. Yes. You may."

Kiria didn't need more encouragement. "Thank you!" she said, and rushed out of the room.

For a terrifying second, Kiria felt nothing. Could she only change once? Had it been her imagination after all? Her forehead furrowed with intensity as she tightly shut her eyes.

Finally, a tingle. She kept her eyes closed for a while, just in case. Shivers ran over her body, crackling like her leg did when it fell asleep.

She popped her eyes open and checked her hand, holding it close to her face. There was something elegant about it. *Perfect.*

Staying mostly hidden behind the palace wall, she peered across the open green field, beaten yellow in the center, to where a crowd of guards, warriors, and trainees gathered. She would be careful not to let all of them see her, and then she'd go to Atty and Jori. For now, Tanis' training session was almost finished.

A month ago, she had seen him accompany her mother's guards. He had been dressed in full uniform, though he was still in training. His long blond hair falling to his square jawline revealed him to be a Khelê. Every Kingdom Dweller had darker hair than that. She didn't know how old he was—seventeen? She just knew that he had made her stomach drop when she looked at him. At first she thought she might be sick, but then thoughts of him intruded in her mind all day. The smallest thing reminded her of him. It had been this way for weeks.

This is stupid. She was a Kepress, and was going to be a great leader. She didn't have time to go running after boys. Jori and Atty would laugh. Well, Jori would laugh. They both knew that Atty fell hard for almost every kitchen maid. As far as she knew, not many looked back at *him* either.

She peeked around the corner. Back by the well where the trainees crowded around, strong arms pulled a helmet off a blond head, the long strands settling down separately. Her heart suddenly beat in her throat.

Maybe it wasn't stupid. Maybe he would think of *her* all day.

Tanis shot back a cup of water and broke free from the others as he headed back to the gate leading out of the palace grounds. Toward where she hid waiting for him. Kiria watched him, suddenly clammy. What to say? Every option she played out sounded idiotic. She was better than this—more elegant, brave, intelligent...

"Oh, hello!" His tone revealed that she had caught him off guard.

She looked up from her shoes to his blue eyes. He was very close. No, it was a normal distance, but closer than she had ever been to him. How had he come up so quickly? Her heart pounded.

"Hello."

His eyes rounded as he stared at her. He closed his mouth and cleared his throat. "Did you come to watch the practice?" He shifted the metal helmet under his arm, where it reflected the sun into her eyes.

"Mm hm." She nodded and swallowed. "Yes, you all are doing very well out there."

He gave a lopsided smile. "Thank you." When he lowered his head to meet her gaze, her arms felt a little weaker. "You are?"

"Oh yes. I'm Kiria. Arioc. The Kepress."

When she spoke her name, his roving eyes widened even further. He blinked a couple times. Bowing a little from the waist, he said, "My name is Tanis, at your service. You... look very nice today. Is it okay to say that?"

For a split second, she thought this was a joke. Had someone told him to say that? Everything was happening too perfectly. "Yeah, yes," she corrected. *You look good too. That uniform...*

"Are you going to come see us again tomorrow?" he asked.

Her face flushed hot with surprise. *He wants to see me again!*

She recovered her dignity as quickly as she could. "I'll try. I'll see what I can do. You have a good evening, Tanis." A pleasant churning in her stomach made her smile as she walked away.

10

FIRIAN

The more Firian's arms shook, the more the water in the buckets rippled. He tried to tighten his core, his chest, anything to take the pressure off his arms as he held them straight out.

Master Jovan watched impassively.

Firian huffed out a breath, fighting the urge to glare at him. At least this was physical pain, not mental pain. This was only the second day without the Unreal and he felt parched, like a man dying of thirst. He could do anything there, in that semi-actual imaginary space. Here, he was too weak.

He rolled his shoulders and adjusted his grip on the wooden handle. *Mind over body.* Like falling down a slide, his mind descended to the comfort of the Unreal. He could endure so much more that way.

Red pain exploded behind his eyes. Yelling, he vaguely heard water slosh out of the buckets as they tumbled to the ground. Sentries. His brain ached from the aftershock.

"Firian!" Jovan cried, scooping up the bucket handles. The sun glinted on his bald head as he bent down. "You did better last time."

Alarmed by the warmth of embarrassment creeping up his neck, Firian muttered, "I'll do better next time, Master Jovan." His eyes felt prickly, so he rotated his shoulders, twisting at the waist away from Jovan's gaze.

"Yes, you will. That's all for today."

"As you would have it." Firian practically ran back inside before he finished the phrase. He hurried down the stone corridor out into the courtyard, dodging the fountain on the way to the stairs. Movement helped him stay out of his thoughts.

A swish of brown hair caught his peripheral vision and a hard lump lodged in his throat. When he swallowed over and over, it didn't budge. *Mind over body.* He always had somewhere to go when he was in pain, but not now. For the past two days, he'd felt the dull buzz of Sentries, like madness, press against his skull. If he tried to pass the barrier, to reach the Unreal, pain would incapacitate him as it did in front of Jovan. And that hadn't been the only time. Desperate to find relief, he'd hurled himself against the barrier at first. Almost missed his strategy class.

He wasn't as rash as he had been, but he also hadn't resigned himself to three more days of this torture. Those Sentries were experts. They had been Tanyu who deserved the terrible punishment of focusing on nothing, creating a painful, disembodied barrier to the Unreal. At least, that's what the stories said. The threat of becoming a Sentry cowed even strong Tanyu. It was a horrific fate, even worse than a Master ordering a Sentry to temporarily block the Unreal.

Firian had been punished before, but not like this. He felt cut off from air.

He flung the door open to his room to find Bard and their friend Tiev Gelir sitting on the ground around an Indisfate board. Tiev raised his knee to avoid the door, tipping over a Falcon. The tiny click of the wooden figure falling echoed in the little room. Firian let out a breath. Had Bard said anything about company?

"Hey, Fir!" Bard waved for Firian to take a seat, so he lowered himself cross-legged beside the board. It was an even game.

"You can play after Tawn and me," Tiev said, squinting his green eyes as he contemplated his next move. Everyone had started calling Bard that after someone had made fun of his accent—"tawn-yoo." Now, whenever he said the word, somebody laughed. Firian still called him by his name, but he was one of the last.

Firian had better things to do than watch two people play a game, but he didn't have the energy to leave.

Tiev moved the Man, a larger piece than the others on the board. "Ha!" he said under his breath. A smile crept onto his face.

Firian sucked the inside of his lip. It was a good move. Hopefully Bard could counteract it.

He glanced back at Tiev. Tiev often acted as though he were much older than Firian, even though the age difference was only a year. Besides that, his hair was always perfect. Every guy on the floor envied it.

Firian drew his aching arm across his chest, holding it at the elbow to stretch it, while watching Bard worry over his pieces.

Never looking away from the game, Bard absently pulled a slice from a partially-peeled orange and put it in his mouth. His brows creased together in concentration. Normally, he'd be smiling. Coming to a conclusion, he nodded to himself and moved the Viper two spaces.

Tiev pursed his mouth. Apparently, that isn't what he wanted. Firian's mouth curled up in a sardonic smile. *Good for you, Bard!*

"What's that big, ugly piece?" Firian asked, pointing to the Man looming over the other wooden game pieces.

A grin flashed over Bard's features. "It's not ugly. It's just a figure I got when I was home. It's Corso!"

"They sell Tanyu figures there?" Firian grabbed it off the board. Tiev's fingers twitched to stop him but he reconsidered.

He held the figure up to his face and spun it in his fingers. Corso wore a long

Academy jacket and held two knives crossed in front of him. His bearded face looked grim and determined, with deep eyes and long hair. After the rebel loss at Carradoc, the real Corso had risen up and fought in ways that no one up to that time had been able to. His name was a rallying cry for anyone fighting for the liberation of Brithnem in the War of the Kingdom Rebels.

"He was always my favorite," Bard said.

Tiev stuck his neck out to look more closely at the figure. "My mom would tell stories about him when I was a kid." The contented haze of memory crossed his features.

Firian flexed his jaw. He'd heard the stories too, from schoolmates. Disjointed stories. Sometimes Corso could lead a fleet of a thousand ships, sometimes he could fly across the plain from the Charúnin Thôr to the capital, sometimes he just carved a bloody swath in the war, so fearsome that none could touch him. Firian's favorite story was about the time he got captured and taken to the arena to be killed, but then he made a knife from the meat bone they gave him and killed four guards. He escaped and freed all the animals and prisoners, who helped him storm the palace in one of the decisive battles of the war.

Tanyu had changed since then. Firian wished they fought physically more often, but that wasn't the way anymore. Since the Tanyu had hidden the Academy, they hadn't kept large standing armies. They relied on mental warfare and individual missions now.

"I'd pretend to be him sometimes," Bard continued. "Well, I wanted to, but Jac always took that one. But then I got to be a Tanyu. Weird, huh?"

Firian couldn't help but agree. Everything he heard about Bard's older brother actually reminded him of himself, much more suited to the Academy than Bard was.

"So, were you Fern or Zhelan?" Tiev laughed. Love interest or villain?

"No!" Bard cried. And then, more quietly, "Neither, not most of the time."

Firian snickered at the image, but Bard didn't laugh with them.

Tiev took the figure of Corso and put it back on the board, lazily moving another piece.

After watching Tiev's move, Bard shot a glance at Firian. They both saw it. He could use Soldier's Pass to win in the next move. Almost imperceptibly, Firian nodded. *Do it.* This time, Bard was quick. His fingers flashed over the game and he sat back satisfied.

It took Tiev a moment to realize Bard had won. His smile faded. "Okay," he said, taking in the loss.

Bard angled up to stand. "Better luck next time, yeah?" he said, popping up his eyebrows.

"Yeah." Tiev wasn't happy. He stood up in a motion so smooth it made Firian jealous. "That was good. I'll see you later," he said, waving a cursory hand at both of them.

"Yeah, all right." Bard gave a little nod, squatting back down to clean up the pieces. The measured way he did it confirmed that something was bothering him. One at a time. Firian grabbed the pair of Vipers to help. After an agitated breath, Bard stole a glance at him. "Did you hear that Enderin was attacked?"

Firian's pieces froze in midair on their way to the bag. That would explain why Bard returned early from his last trip home.

Bard cast his eyes back down to the board. "I don't... I just hope..." He cleared his throat. "I don't think anything's happened to them," he murmured, chewing his lip. Bard came from a family so big that it had taken a year before Firian could keep them all straight. "Do you think—"

"No!" Firian cried. "Of course not."

Silence followed. Game pieces clattered into the bag.

"But what if—"

"That didn't happen."

"How do you know?" Bard asked, his voice louder now. "Why do you think they took me away so soon? Why couldn't I have stayed unless it was dangerous?"

"They're all fine."

Bard clenched his fist around the figure of Corso. "Jac was going into the army anyway."

"Look, you don't even know if anything bad's happened." Firian's chest tightened. *Maybe they wouldn't tell him. They didn't tell me.* His secret built like fire inside him until he burned with it. His heart pounded heavily and the ache in his arms spread over the rest of his body.

Bard's forehead scrunched downward in concern. He always read him better than other people could.

Firian settled his shoulders. It might have been a shrug. "You know why—" He tried again. "You know why *I* haven't left the Academy?"

"Why?"

Why am I even talking about this? "Because..." He blew out a long breath to steady himself. "Because my whole family was killed in a fire." He twitched his head as though hair had fallen in his face.

Shock and sympathy filled Bard's eyes. "Oh, Fir... I'm so sorry!" He sat back from his crouch to the floor, ready to listen.

Firian stood up and waved a dismissive hand, like someone shooing a fly. His mouth felt dry. "Yeah. Well." He wasn't going to talk about his feelings. But Bard would find out about his family eventually—it might as well be now. It had to be now, when the secret burned him like acid. His roommate was the safest person to tell. And he had to tell someone.

Bard's tears glistened on his lower lid.

Tanyu never cried. *Tanyu never cried.*

But suddenly, Brett's death, the punishment, it all caught in his throat. Blood rushed to his face and a sob broke from him. He tried to stop but it was all he could do to suck air into his hot lungs. Gasping for breath, he crouched on the floor, howling, all snot and tears. People in the hall could hear, but he couldn't stop himself. He wept until he felt he was going to be sick.

Hiccupping to silence, he subsided to a profound calm. Thoroughly ashamed of himself, he sat up. Fifteen-year-olds—Tanyu!—never cried, no matter what.

Bard, with red, puffy eyes, handed him a towel. He leaned his fist on his mouth. "It's okay," he said softly. He meant the crying, not the death. Firian knew that. Death—Brett's death—would never be okay.

Numbly, Firian took the towel and rubbed it over his wet face. He took a breath in through the nose, deep in the lungs, and out through his mouth. He had no more words.

Bard seemed to understand. And Firian knew that Bard would never tell anyone about this.

Together they sat in silence until the light in the room started to fade to orange.

11

KIRIA

Late the next afternoon, suitably beautiful, Kiria invited Tanis to walk with her through the grounds. She told Candrae and Vayci, her two serving girls, that they could stay behind. He had eased off his armor—*oh my goodness!*—and accepted her invitation.

She didn't know why she was so excited when he agreed to walk with her. Could he even say no to a Kepress? She doubted it. Be that as it may, he was here now, walking close beside her along the pathways behind the palace, and she felt the thrill of it down her spine. The training grounds were out of the way, so they had a little while to walk before they even reached the Amiran Academy. It felt like they were alone.

"Don't you have servants or something? Do they always let you take walks like this by yourself?" he asked, a glimmer in his eye.

He knows I shouldn't be out here. But she was a Kepress; he couldn't get her in trouble.

Probably.

"I do this sometimes," she said. Technically, she wasn't supposed to, but she managed to get out now and then. She was always careful. "I like to come out and look at the ocean or the new flowers."

The newest was some kind of lavender lily that she liked very much. It almost looked like the laird flower on the flag. Patches of them lined the far end of the field where they were walking.

"You know, you should have a guard with you," he said.

"I know, but..."

"I can be your guard." He ran a hand through his long hair.

Her heart skipped. This was silly. Now that she had his attention, what was she supposed to do with it? She probably looked like a fish, wide-eyed and gaping.

His touch sent a shock through her hand. He eased his fingers through hers and held her hand close. Breathing was complicated. She managed to smile encouragingly at him. At least, that's how she hoped he would take it.

The dome of the Amiran Academy was getting closer. *I have to go back.* The thought hit her hard and it was worse because she should have thought of it sooner. Showing her Ability to one person didn't seem so bad—judging from how the night was going, it wasn't bad at all—but waltzing back into the palace grounds where hundreds of Amir lived and worked wasn't smart.

"I'm surprised I never noticed you before," Tanis said, squeezing her hand, which was getting sweaty.

"It's okay," Kiria said. She wouldn't have noticed herself either. "You know why I look this way now?" She lowered her voice, even though no one else was around. "I have an Ability. It's Original Beauty." Anyone with eyes could already tell, but she felt a thrill as she told him.

He chuckled, half to himself. "No wonder," he said. "Did you just find out?"

He seemed eager to learn more, but they were getting too close to the palace. *Why can't I just stay beautiful?* "Yes, let me show you," she said, although it didn't seem right to ruin the moment. "I *have* to change because not everyone knows yet. And you can't tell anyone!"

"Okay, okay, if you're sure." He let go of her hand and stepped back, as though she would burst into flame.

She didn't want to close her eyes with his stunning blue ones looking back at her. Who wanted to look *worse* in front of someone so gorgeous? But it had to be done.

Before opening her eyes again, she heaved a sigh. "So there you go!" she said, trying to sound more lighthearted than she felt.

He looked over her whole body, clearly masking disappointment. "Yeah, I'm happy you got your Ability," he said. "You can switch back, right?"

"Of course." She nodded.

A crooked smile crossed his features. "So I can't tell anybody?"

"No! No, no. I have some matters to discuss before officially revealing it." Why was her tone so formal all the sudden? "But I'm glad I showed you." She gave him a little smile.

He nodded, his glance darting toward the far gate.

"I think I might come by tomorrow to watch the training again." She fought for a second to catch his eye. "I'll be beautiful again. It's just that here... so close to the palace..."

"Do you want to walk again?"

The question stung. *Don't you?* she wanted to ask. She had shown him far more than was wise, just so he would be impressed and like her. She'd abandoned some of her good sense just to know what it felt like to be wanted. And now he acted as though he wasn't attracted to her at all.

She shoved down her hurt feelings. Maybe he didn't mean anything by it. "Let's do it."

Spurred by the churning in her stomach, she grabbed Tanis' hand and led him out of sight of the Amiran Academy, into a grove of shady trees. She closed her eyes again and a moment later was beautiful.

Tanis broke into a grin. "Okay, I'll be waiting," he said. Before he left, he kissed her softly on the cheek.

"So I don't have an Ability," said Jori over the noise of people, stretching out in his chair in a leisurely way. "Everything I do is an Ability."

Atael smacked him on the chest, making him double over in his chair. "He's just jealous," he told Kiria.

Jori huffed with scorn as Kiria smiled. "Keep your voices down," she said. "I don't think everyone is supposed to hear us talking about it."

About a hundred brilliantly dressed people meandered around the circular stone courtyard behind the palace. Among them were two of the Keepers, Cúron and Merian. They couldn't stay long because they had called an emergency session in the Main. Torith had attacked Enderin, the main city in the northern region of Phlaxtin, and they had to decide how much help to send their ally to the north. The island of Torith was mostly peaceful, her mother had explained to her that morning, but years ago an enormous coalition of pirates set up their base on the eastern side and ran it as their own country. These mercenaries raided and terrorized both the big island north of Torith and now the continent. They had to be stopped.

The straightness of her mother's back was the only hint of her stress. Cúron didn't betray any at all. Aylmor, Atty and Jori's father, was away on business near the base of the Charúnin Thôr mountains, where the range met the ocean directly north of Brithnem.

The grounds looked amazing from here—winding paths, rolling lawns, the forest, the hedges. A few chairs and benches strategically littered the flagstone but most of the people chose to stand and talk. The two huge wings of the castle flanked them on either side, soaring up past the trees. Long, shimmering blue flags waved limply in the breeze along the peak of the roof.

Every few months or so the Keepers would host a gathering like this one, inviting merchants and wealthy businessmen, fishermen and maids. It was a way to maintain morale among the people. If someone were lucky enough to be noticed and chosen for one of these exclusive parties, that person could brag about it for years. Kiria and the Calthwaites didn't find the atmosphere quite so intoxicating (with the possible exception of Jori, whom Kiria suspected of sneaking a glass of ale or two while she and Atty had been talking).

"Why not?" Jori asked loudly.

Atty leaned over to his brother from the opposite side. "You're an ass," he muttered.

"I haven't shown the people yet," Kiria whispered. "I will, but don't go telling everyone ahead of time."

Kiria put a finger to her lips as little Kader, who was six now, climbed into one of the shady seats next to them, pretending to be grown-up and interested in their conversation. He tugged at his buttoned, embroidered vest.

Jori watched Kader, who wiggled with boredom after only a moment of silence. "I think it's dumb that Atty gets to be Keeper."

She shushed him. Jori was so fun when he wasn't in one of his moods. Why did he have to be in a mood today? "Stop acting stupid. You know it has to be this way," she said. Younger siblings never inherited the throne. "Besides, that won't be for a while." Their parents were both relatively young. Younger than Cúron, anyway.

Launching himself off the seat, Kader ran off, weaving between the legs of the adults. He was too young to sit still for long. In moments his nurse caught up with him and brought him inside.

Atty nodded thoughtfully, looking away from them.

"See, Atty doesn't even want it," Jori goaded him.

"Shut up, *Jori*," he said sharply, looking at them again, slightly embarrassed. "Of course I do."

To be honest, Kiria was a little nervous for Atty. He didn't do very well in his studies, and Jori had always been more charismatic. Whenever becoming a Keeper came up, Atty would lift his head and say he wanted to be just like his father. Those might even be little hairs on his chin.

"Of course he does," she affirmed. "We'll do it together." She didn't know much more than he did about running a country, but they would help each other.

"My idea's more fun," Jori said, eyeing a plate of smoked fish as it went by. Part of her believed him.

Guards milled around the many party guests. Since the guest selection was all but random, they posted extra guards to make sure that the Keepers and their families were safe. Kiria found herself scanning the faces beneath the helmets. Was that a trainee she had seen earlier? *Are all the trainees here?*

Sitting made her antsy, so she stood up. "Do you want to get some food?" The parties might be boring, but the food always tasted amazing. Ten or twelve extra cooks were brought in just to help prepare the food for these events, nearly doubling the number of kitchen servants.

The boys had already leapt to their feet. "That looks good," said Jori, going for the tray of fish.

"Kepron Atael! And Kepress Kiria!" someone cried delightedly. A large woman came into view, mouth gaping, eyes popping. Her dress wasn't quite as fine as most of the others. Her eyes were a little glazed over too. "To think...! Just to think I'm meeting the future Keepers of Brithnem! I am honored!"

"Oh." Atty looked lost.

"How nice," Kiria said, trying to recover from Atty's fumble. "It's lovely to meet you." She offered her hand to the woman politely as her eyes strayed once again toward the guards. There he was, across the garden! "You must excuse me."

Somehow she extricated herself from the enthusiastic woman and wedged her way through the crowd to get to Tanis. They couldn't talk for long—he was on duty—but she had to say hello.

When she reached where he was, she pretended to be nonchalant. Her parents were at this party, and the Calthwaite boys might notice. "Hello," she whispered. Her dress restricted her breathing more than she remembered.

His helmet shone in the sunshine, like his hair and his eyes. His lips pursed in an expression of utmost seriousness. He kept his hand on the hilt of his sword where it hung by his side. He nodded to her. "My Kepress."

The words sounded so good coming from him. "I think you're doing a good job," she said. "This is good practice for the real thing."

He flashed her a quick smile. "So... you still haven't told anybody yet?"

She wilted a little, burying her hands in the folds of her skirt. "No. But I will, though."

"It's okay. You'll tell them soon."

She got just a little closer to him. "It's our secret," she whispered. Her breath fogged the shoulder of his armor.

"You're still coming tomorrow, right?"

She flushed, pleased. "Yes, I'll be there." The Keepers and their advisors would be in meetings all day tomorrow because of the attack, but she wasn't required to go to the Main with them yet, not until she was eighteen.

Beauty is not for the beautiful. The line from the Sacred Scroll popped into her head. Hadn't Daelon said something like that? Or was it her mother?

Her Ability wasn't just for her, but for others.

She could be beautiful just for him.

Together they sat against the wall that enclosed the palace grounds. The setting sun shone in their faces as it set over the Kheltor Ocean, bleaching Tanis' hair white gold. Kiria wanted to reach up and touch the strands as they curled at his shoulder. She wouldn't have to reach far. They sat very close.

"Where does your family come from?" she asked.

"My family are all farmers," Tanis said, leaning his head back lazily. "We live on the outer edge, growing crops." The outer edge was far to walk every day. Even on a horse, it usually took at least an hour to get to the palace from the outer edge, just outside the city wall. Kiria had only been there two or three times. The land gave farmers more room for their crops. They were still officially part of Brithnem, though they were separated.

He turned to look at her. "But I'm glad I got in this program. Farming isn't very fun."

"Why not?"

Tanis shrugged and picked one blade of grass. Two.

"Do you come all that way every day?" she asked, smoothing her light blue dress.

"It's worth it." He smiled with gleaming teeth, lolling his head in her direction.

Her stomach clenched, and she edged her fingers closer to his. "Really?" she asked, pretending this was normal. She half-smiled back.

"Yes. I got to meet you." His hand closed the gap between them and rested on top of hers.

She sighed happily and looked ahead. The green field in front of them sloped gently down to the gardens, the dome of the Amiran Academy, the towering palace. It all glittered in the sunlight. Even the breeze playing with their hair and the fabric of their clothes felt warm and magical.

He was already looking at her, taking her in, when she looked back at him. "You look pretty tonight."

The words were music. "Yeah, what else do you like about me?" she teased.

He laughed. "What do you like about *me?*"

"You first."

He looked up, his forehead creasing in thought for a little while. "You're smart," he began, "and sweet... and sneaky!" He drew his legs in and crossed them, a deep breath rising in his chest that almost seemed like relief.

She couldn't stop the smile lifting at the sides of her mouth. "And you" – she crossed her legs and faced him – "are... cute" – she blushed – "and strong and nice." The somewhat uncomfortable yet warm thrill she felt with him intoxicated her. She was slowly getting used to the fluttery feeling.

He squeezed her hand reassuringly and brushed his blond hair out of his face with the other. "I wish other people could see what I see," he said.

It took her a moment to understand his meaning. "You mean... the Ability?"

"Yeah."

She smiled, lowering her head. "But you would still like me without it. Right?"

"Of course, yeah," he said, taking her other hand. "Of course I would. But you have to show other people sometime."

"Maybe I won't," she said, just to be contrary.

"Yes, you will. You wouldn't want to be ugly forever when you could be so beautiful." He reached up to touch her cheek.

She recoiled. The words hit her like a battering ram. "Ugly?"

"That's not what I meant."

"That's what you said." She pulled her hands away.

"But that's not what I meant," he protested.

"If I didn't look like this" – her breath hitched – "I'd still be... smart."

"Of course you would," he said, reaching for her hands again, a hint of exasperation in his face.

She shook her head, her eyes getting hotter. She had to leave before he saw her cry. "No, you wouldn't like me." A tear trailed down her face as she stood up.

"Wait," he said, standing too. His brow furrowed, that golden hair tumbling in his face. "I didn't mean what I said."

She set her jaw. After backing away a few steps, she closed her eyes and changed back to her usual self. "Yes, you did," she said and ran back to the palace.

PART III

MASTER (AGE 18)

12

KIRIA

Kiria and Jori went out of the palace to escape their guards, though guilt threaded through Kiria as she did so. Her guards had to be getting worried with all the time she spent sneaking off. Maybe it was unfair to them, but she wanted to be alone with somebody who wouldn't expect anything from her and wouldn't talk about anything serious. Jori was her best bet. And she wouldn't be gone long.

He ambled along beside her down the gravel paths of the garden, hands in his pockets. Far away, the splash of waves floated up from the coast. The air smelled like water. She lost herself in the smell, the touch of the cool air on her face. As she breathed in, her shoulders began to loosen. Here there were no responsibilities, no decisions about whether to lead with her Beauty or not, no people to treat her differently depending on what she chose. No one to disappoint.

The weight of one day becoming Keeper pressed more heavily every day. In just a few days she would turn eighteen and be expected to attend every session, begin her formal apprenticeship, as it were. She couldn't even live up to her Beauty. It presented her as far better than she was inside. How would she live up to a kingdom full of expectations? Her chest tightened again.

Jori's unbuttoned embroidered vest flapped as he turned toward her. "Kiria, you need a snack? A drink? You look sad."

Wonderful. Already her plan wasn't working. "You know you shouldn't drink," she said. They were seventeen, old enough to drink, but Jori tended to overindulge.

He waggled his head, noncommittal. "Sometimes that makes it more fun."

Smiling, she smacked him lightly on the arm. "You say such ridiculous things!"

"Right, though?" he said, raising both eyebrows until they almost reached the wavy dark hair falling over his forehead. "You know I'm right."

She smirked.

"Come on, I'll get you something," he said. "Nothing a drink can't fix."

"No! No… It's okay. I'm fine." But his offer had managed to cheer her up.

He shrugged. "Suit yourself. Just trying to help a friend in need," he said, winking at her.

She looked up at the churning gray sky. "Do you want to head inside?" She pulled her cloak tighter around her. It staved off the cold and covered her body like a shapeless blanket, which fit her mood.

"Sure," he said, following her gaze. "I like rain, though."

"Jori! They'll know we snuck outside. Besides, I'm sure someone will miss us if we're out much longer."

"They probably already do. Don't you like being missed? And anyway, if we're found out here, their relief will make up for everything."

"I'm glad you're not the oldest," she said, laughing. "You'd make the worst Keeper I've ever seen."

"Ah, well," he said, smiling. "Do you still want to go inside?"

Muffled thunder rumbled around them. "Yes. We can't have somebody worried. Mother will kill me if she found me out here with nobody but you."

"Afraid of what she'd say?" His gray eyes teased her.

"I don't have any protection and we're at war." None of the frontiers were close to the palace—the real conflict took place far away—but it was still better to be safe.

"I can't protect you?" he said, cocking an eyebrow.

"You know what I mean. Not really." He attempted to steer her away from the palace. "You can be so difficult," she added, steering them back.

"Thank goodness!" he said. "Imagine how boring life would be if I was easy to be around."

She laughed in spite of herself. "You're absurd."

"I know. Might as well be."

A large drop of water landed on her face. "Come on! It's starting to rain," she said, breaking into a jog as they neared the castle.

"I told you I like rain," he said again, refusing to follow at her speed.

"Jori!"

Once inside, she tried to shake the water off her clothes, but it had soaked in. "I really shouldn't do that so often. Candrae and Vayci will be so worried."

"Oh well," he replied, popping his shoulders up and down to resettle his wet coat. "I think Sen and Wyat actually like it when I'm gone. It gives them a chance to do what they want for once." Those were his servants, the sons of Ataël's tutor.

"Stop getting water on me," she said, shooing the drops away with her hand.

He shook his head like a dog in answer and droplets went flying everywhere from the tips of his dark brown hair. "What do you mean 'so often'? We don't run around like we used to as kids." He smiled impishly. "Have you been sneaking off?"

There was that word again. The one Tanis had used when she was fifteen, and then again a couple weeks ago when she finally found someone else and thought she would try again. This time, it'd been a soldier. Anton seemed different. But in the end, he didn't care about her either. She was a political stepping stone, a beautiful face, and nothing more. She had only managed to be alone with him once before he was sent to the field. They hadn't so much as kissed before she realized the kind of person he was.

Was she really that sneaky? Apparently not, since Jori had caught on. She lowered her voice to a whisper. "No." But her heartbeat betrayed her lie, and she tried never to lie. "Okay, yes, just a little."

"Oh, tell me!"

"Shh! It doesn't matter."

"A *boy*, then," he said, coming closer to hear. "Have you finally had a crush? Atty will be so sad."

The truth balled up like pain inside her.

When she didn't protest his comment about Atty, he looked fractionally more concerned. "Who wouldn't like a Kepress?" he asked in an uncharacteristically soothing way.

"It doesn't matter," she repeated, not looking at him. "I have bigger things to worry about..." *Like learning to lead the nation, like the war, like choosing whether or not to show the whole country my Ability...*

"Let's not worry about them," he said, and then fell easily back into his usual laid-back attitude. "That's what I try to do at all costs. Worrying doesn't help anybody. Sen and Wyat will make sure I eat." Those poor serving boys. Jori always had been a handful.

"Nobody needs to tell you that," she said.

"There you go. I'll live another day. It's a whole lot easier when you let things go." He sailed a hand off into the imaginary distance.

I'll live another day. Maybe she had been carrying too much on her shoulders. She wasn't a Keeper yet.

She shot a glance down the hallway back to her room where her serving girls and guards were probably wondering where she had gone. "Okay," she said. "How about that drink?"

THE NEXT DAY, accompanied by her longsuffering maids, Kiria walked up to the door and knocked. The guards ignored her. The door swung open heavily and Jori looked out. "Oh, it's you," he said, opening it wider to let them enter.

As usual, Candrae remained at the door and Sen, Jori's servant, came inside with Vayci. One servant inside, one servant outside.

Jori grinned and sank indolently into a chair. "What brings you here? I was just about to get some food."

Too many thoughts hounded her, and she had to talk to somebody. Maybe Jori was a bad idea. He took nothing seriously. "Don't let me keep you," she said.

He smiled knowingly at her. "Well, if you didn't come for anything specific, can I get you something?" He rose from his chair and went over to a small cabinet in the wall. "They don't allow me to keep much in here," he said, "but I have a little bread and wine, if you want some."

She breathed out a short laugh. "You don't have to act like I'm a stranger," she said, coming over and taking a sugared slice of dried orange from the cabinet. She smiled, popping the candy into her mouth.

He pulled the wine and two glasses out of the cabinet and closed it with his elbow. After setting them down on a small table by his seat, he pulled an upholstered chair over so it was across from his own and gestured for her to sit down. "I guess you're right," he said, sinking down again, "it's almost brunch anyway. No use spoiling our appetites."

"None at all." She swallowed the candy and sat down. "Pass me a glass."

"Certainly, my lady," he said, pouring them both some from the bottle.

She reached over as he passed her the glass half full of dark wine. "Thanks, Jori."

"Hard day?" He looked at her over the rim of the glass as he drank.

"Not really."

"Then what's the matter?"

"Oh..." She shrugged. "I think I've decided to reveal my Ability to the public soon, but I don't feel ready." For a split second, she had considered leading as she had always looked, but that option was silly compared to the other. The people expected greatness in their leaders, and Beauty would help them see that. Even if she already felt a little resentful because of it.

"You seem ready to me," he replied, mouth full of bread.

"You're such a liar, Jori! I think I'll be ready when I have to be but... it... I wish I were more ready now. I used to look forward to being a Keeper." Her own words surprised her.

"I'm sure you'll do fine. You don't have to be a Keeper now. I know I'd much rather lie around here doing nothing and be *almost* famous while I do it." He threw back his head and finished his wine in a gulp.

"Sounds good," she said honestly. The people of Brithnem couldn't judge her for taking time for herself, could they? "I could never picture you in the Main anyway."

"I have been there, you know," he said seriously, nodding his head.

"Really?" she teased.

"Yes, my father's made me go a few times," he said. "And I roamed around it as a kid. You might remember. So I do know how it tends to function, though most people wouldn't think it."

When they were all kids—Kiria and Atty and Jori—the Main had seemed so immense and dark, a hall of kings and princesses, solemn judgments and dances. These illusions were only partly true, she learned as she grew up. "I'll wager Kader goes in there too when no one is watching," she said.

"How old is he now?"

"Just turned nine, and he already likes to go to meetings and order people around."

Jori barked out a humorless laugh. "Now *he's* one I would bet on to be a good Keeper."

"The First Line, what can you expect?"

"That doesn't mean anything." He scoffed. "Oldest child... Just because his last name's Calthwaite doesn't mean he has to be boring and responsible."

She raised her eyebrows. "You're not, anyway."

"Those Ariocs, though," he said wistfully, gazing at the ceiling.

She leaned over and hit him on the shoulder. "I can have fun," she said.

He hummed thoughtfully, clearly cooking up a test of her words. Something glinted in his eye as he looked at her. "There's music in the front lawn tonight," he said. "It's for the people, but we can still go." His gaze drifted lazily to the ceiling again.

Tonight. She squinted, trying to look impish, despite the reality that more obligations crowded her schedule. Being irresponsible sounded so freeing.

"I have a lesson with Daelon," she finally said.

"And you said you could have fun." Jori stood up, cracked his neck, and smoothed his collar. Then he offered her his arm.

She took it and they swept out of the room together, their servants trailing behind. Despite running off to escape her maids now and then, she did what she was supposed to: she attended sessions in the Main (even boring ones) and she tried to pay attention during lessons. Ever since she could remember, she had always looked forward to being a Keeper... until lately. The idea of the people judging her for her looks or decisions gave her directionless anger. Her pace slowed.

"So, music?" he prompted.

"I'll decide later," she said. Skipping a lesson was a bigger step than she had taken. It was a crossroad, and she wasn't sure she was prepared for it.

They turned the corner into the huge hallway that led from the Third Keeper's wing to the front of the palace. Guards and portraits and potted trees rushed by on either side of them as they walked.

"You know how much I love later," Jori said in an undertone as he gave a guard a familiar nod. "But now is always better."

Like a closing door, the moment she would succeed her mother as Keeper threatened her, ready to shut off any possibility of relaxation and cheer. She almost felt the weight of that responsibility already. Would it be so bad to find out what a little rebellion felt like first?

She shook off the stress like a physical thing and turned to Jori.

"Let's do it," she said.

13

FIRIAN

The Academy didn't heat many fires. Some students from wealthy families wore fur-lined coats they had picked up on a visit home. Firian could have worn his Academy-issued black coat, but the cold made him feel more alive. It kept his senses sharp and muscles tense. He was almost glad he didn't have a comfortable overcoat.

It had been a little over three years since he'd heard about his family's death, so the thought didn't bother him like it used to. Well, it still bothered him, but it didn't sting anymore. The pain had dulled.

Now he had other things to worry about. He bit down hard as he passed the hall master's room, swearing to himself. What was Tiev doing that the Masters liked so much? He couldn't figure it out. Tiev seemed only a little better than average, and yet here he was—the hall master. He didn't deserve that level of respect, especially not when Firian did everything he could to earn more.

Firian reached the courtyard and jogged to his first class. Impatiently, he sat down across from Master Belik, ready to go. Belik sat in uncomfortable silence for a few moments. It was long enough for Firian to realize his muscles still ached from the night before when he stayed up late doing training exercises. The last pose he had held for two hundred breaths left his side burning. The extra work he had done early that morning hadn't helped the soreness. He bit the inside of his lip as the Master peered at him over his glasses with a familiar, scrutinizing gaze. Why couldn't the Master see all his work, his progress? At this point, he should know that Firian wasn't a child anymore. He needed to be promoted to Defender. If he could jump or swim or fight to get that blue-stoned ring, he would already have it.

"Firian," he said, "something's bothering you. What is it?"

"Master Belik..." He hesitated. "How do I get better?"

A half-smile cracked the older man's features. "Better at what?"

"Faster. Smarter. Better at fighting. Better at the Unreal!" Firian burst out. Each word deflated the pressure that had built up in his chest.

"What do you think I'm teaching you?"

"No. You are—but... How do I get better faster?"

The Master raised an eyebrow.

"I'll do anything."

Belik's eyes became suddenly intense. "Anything?" he asked in a low voice.

Firian nodded, but the way he repeated the word brimmed with hidden motives, secret knowledge, as though he'd have to give his soul.

Belik fell back into his normal mode. "The faster you want to learn, the more you have to be willing to endure. Pain forces us to be better." He laid a hand, perhaps unconsciously, on his bad leg. "Test yourself. But be careful. Remember, the better you are, the more danger you're in of believing yourself to be dead or injured." His eyes flickered to the white scars on Firian's hands.

"I've been training myself, working out all the time..."

Belik snorted. "What do we do here, Firian?"

Taken aback, he answered, "Train for war—defense."

"And how do we do that?"

"...Mental warfare."

Belik's eyes shone. "*Mental* warfare. There you go. You have to get tougher in your mind."

"But—"

"But you're good for your age?" Belik snapped. "No one becomes the best by being good at something. You become the best by sacrificing everything else." He stared into Firian's face. "Are you ready to do that?"

"Yes," Firian answered, no hesitation.

"Then show me."

Tánuil was covered in icy, glittering snow. Huge icicles dangled off the houses like liquid diamonds. A fresh layer of snow dusted over even new footprints.

Belik's words still echoed in Firian's ears. *You become the best by sacrificing everything else.* This town day could not have come at a worse time. The Academy required students to take time off periodically, to renew their energy and focus for the coming days. Firian usually looked forward to a little time off, but he wanted to practice today. To push himself.

He wanted to bleed.

It was so cold that Bard's nose and ears looked frozen and red, and he kept shivering as they walked together to the Old Pub. Firian welcomed the slicing wind as it cut across them, but he kept seeing Bard shoot him concerned looks. If he'd had an extra coat, he was sure Bard would have offered it to him. As it was, even the black Academy coat he had on didn't seem to help.

The sign above the low door simply read OLD PUB: Kiegan, proprietor. Firian had learned early on that Kiegan wasn't really the proprietor. It was just a tradition to leave his name there. The Old Pub was one of the only remaining buildings left from the original settlement of Tánuil. In World Events, he'd learned that Kiegan had been a friend of the legendary General Brishen, one of the heroes of the War of the Kingdom Rebels. He, along with Shane and Mari Calthwaite, whose descendants were the Keepers of Brithnem, had stopped here on the road to Carradoc. So the sign stayed as it was.

The two of them hurried inside. Even though there were only a few people, the small room seemed crowded. The air was muggy and thick with a chilling draft. A few rough-hewn chairs were strewn about the room, all taken, and there were stools lining the chunky wooden counter. All the surfaces in Kiegan's old house had worn thin and dull from use.

Bard rubbed his running nose and puffed out a breath that formed ice clouds in the air.

Firian jostled his way to the counter. "Two ciders!" he shouted over the noise to the real proprietor, Hyrum, a haggard-looking man with thin hair and dark, rough skin like unsoftened leather.

Firian turned to Bard and held out his palm for a token.

Moments later they managed to find two empty seats in a corner where most people didn't like to sit. The draft, the tight space, and the grimy windows didn't make it appealing. Good thing the hot cider came right away. It would warm him up and not dull his brain.

Bard sipped his with relish. "You know, those are made in Enderin," he said, tipping his chin toward a carved sconce on the wall. The dark, sealed wood had been carved with a branching tree.

Firian did know. Bard never lost an opportunity to point out Endrian work.

"There's a place by the tanner's that does carvings like that. I wonder if Samson's dad carved that one..."

"I doubt it." Firian ran his finger over the mug handle. "I'm sure that's been on the wall since the Calthwaites."

"Maybe you're right. And how would they get it here?" He popped his eyebrows up. There was hardly any trading in or out of Tánuil, and the border patrollers dealt with what little got through. Bard huffed a laugh through his nose. "It *is* from Enderin, though. Yeah, it wouldn't be Samson. His family hasn't traveled since his daughter died anyway." He paused as the memory hit him. "She was little." When he looked up, his face lightened and he waved. "Tiev!"

A jolt ran through Firian's body. Too late to stop Bard from calling him over. Seeing Tiev's smug face, his perfect hair, made the drink in his stomach sour.

Tiev, bundled in his coat, wove his way through the crowd and stood across from Firian. His desert complexion looked strangely pale in the cold. He shook the wetness from his hair and a drop landed in Firian's cider.

Firian ground his teeth, rounding his shoulders around the mug.

"Hey, Tiev," Bard said, grinning. "I didn't know you had a town day too."

"Just a few hours." He had to speak loudly so they could hear him over the cacophony of voices. He didn't need to bother. "Why'd you choose this spot?"

Why'd you choose to come over?

"Last place open," Bard said.

Tiev cast his narrow eyes to the grimy window. "Everyone's getting an ale."

"Or a cider," said Bard, as a shiver racked him again.

Tiev nodded. "I have an ale coming." He flattened his hand on the scored little table, showing off his dark blue Defender ring. He preened like a village girl in that thing.

Firian let out a breath through his nose. So he wasn't just planning to harass them for a moment, but to stay for a while. Perfect.

Even Bard eyed the ring with something like awe. "It's good. It's so cold today!"

"I hope it comes fast. I have a lot to do. Could use the warmth before I go."

Bard nodded, but Firian picked his teeth with his tongue.

They sat for a few moments in tense silence.

"You know," said Bard, "now that you mention it, I need to finish packing actually. Get a couple things before I go home." He quickly gulped the rest of the steaming cider.

Firian cast him a look. Bard stood and wrapped his jacket close.

"I'm going to go, Fir. You coming?"

Firian glanced at his mug. "I'll finish my drink first. Go ahead."

Bard nodded. "I'll see you later, Tiev?"

Of course you'll see him later—he's our hall master. He didn't understand why Bard was so nice to him. Tiev deserved none of it.

With Bard gone, Tiev turned to Firian. "So, I hope you haven't been sneaking out at night." His tone was light, but he smiled and twisted the dark Defender ring on his finger as he waited for an answer. They had snuck out together plenty of times when he was a Learner, but this had an air of threat to it—not friendly at all.

"What?" Firian snapped, casting him a black look.

Tiev's lips twisted in another smile.

He likes this power over me.

He leaned forward to speak again, but Hyrum interrupted with a mug of ale plunked between them. Tiev pulled it toward him. "I don't want to kick you off my floor, you know," he said. "I have always wondered how one becomes a Sentry, though."

Only truly disgraced Tanyu ever became Sentries. They all knew that. It was an inhuman punishment—no creativity, no freedom, only intense focus on the boundaries they needed to build. Yes, Sentries were essential in times of war so that no one could harm a sleeping Tanyu through his or her dreams. But it was the worst fate one of them could suffer.

How dare he threaten me?

Firian's face felt hot despite the cold and his next words exploded from him. "Just because you have a gory ring doesn't mean you're any better than I am!"

Tiev's eyes dilated and his mouth twitched downward.

Good. Firian tried to hide his deep breath.

"Actually, it does," Tiev said, stopping to smirk, "and I was thinking about setting up a proficiency test. A few of the Masters suggested it."

Here was his chance to prove himself to Belik. He wouldn't just pass the test. He'd crush Tiev, and prove that if anybody deserved to be a Defender, he did. "I'd be ready right now." He paused, then said in a low voice, "I could kill you in the Unreal if I wanted to."

"I'll give you one thing," said Tiev, fighting to keep his voice steady. "You're brave to speak to a Defender that way. I've spoken personally to the Tanyuin Head. I could get you kicked out of the Academy."

Firian took in Tiev's perfect hair, thin eyes, heavy coat, Defender ring... But his hands had only one scar. Firian stretched his jaw and peered into Tiev's face. "Try."

14

KIRIA

Two weeks later, the day came.

Kiria smoothed her long dress again and touched her hair. The tailor had brought a large looking glass down at her request, so she could check herself one last time as she waited in the side hallway that opened into the Main. She wore a floor-length dress of deep red, with gold tracery that flowed like water down the neckline and bodice, twisting around the waist in royal symbols, and down to the end of the short train. The skirt was full but simple, not too gathered or fluffed.

Looking herself up and down, she straightened her shoulders, stood tall. Every movement she made didn't seem to fit the radiant image before her. She made her form less perfect when she wasn't graceful or elegant, when her expression wasn't serene or joyful. The look on her face was just too human. Her Beauty was too beautiful to fit into.

She cleared her throat. Regardless of how she felt, the people of the Western Kingdom wanted their leaders to be the best, and this was part of what she had to offer. Over the past couple days, her feelings had alternated between excitement—who didn't want to look ravishingly beautiful?—and crippling insecurity. With Beauty she felt naked, as though there were nothing left to reveal. The surprise was ruined. Kiria Arioc was a hollow thing.

Only her serving girls stood with her, but she could hear crowds of happy voices seeping through the thick door to the Main. The wild thought crossed her mind that she could still go back to being plain. Almost no one had seen her like this yet. She could hide in the comfort of invisibility. *No, this is for the people, not for me... at least, not completely for me.* Besides, this late birthday party existed to reveal her to the world. She felt sick.

"Vayci," she whispered, leaning toward her serving girl's dark head. Vayci was as tall as she was now. "Find Jori and Atty for me and bring them here."

Vayci obliged and, minutes later, she slipped back through the door with the two brothers, both dapper in their leather vests and embroidered jackets. Kiria tried to peek through the momentary crack in the door, but it didn't reveal much but warm yellow light. Once the door closed, she shot out questions like demands. "What's it like out there? Are there many people yet?"

Instead of answering, Jori's eyes widened. "Look at you," he said. Atty didn't speak, but held the hilt of his ceremonial sword uncomfortably.

Kiria's face washed hot. Even around the Calthwaite boys, she didn't usually reveal her Ability like this. And it was a particularly nice dress. "Thank you," she said shortly. "I haven't been announced yet. I have to know what's going on." Nervously, she rearranged the gold bracelets on her wrists and checked her dangling gold earrings.

"The room's filling up," Jori said idly. "Lots of people here to see you in all your glory."

"The Keepers aren't here yet," Atty added. "But a couple ambassadors came, I think."

Jori shrugged. "The most interesting thing out there is the food."

"Food!" she cried. Remembering that it existed gave her great comfort. "Would you get me something?" She laid a hand on her churning stomach.

"Get her something," Atty said.

After hesitating a moment, Jori squeezed himself out the door. Chatter and glasses tinkling amplified through the crack in the door. The sound muted again when it shut behind him.

Atty swallowed visibly. "You shouldn't be nervous," he said.

Awkward silence followed. The girls stood at attention, but she didn't have anything for them to do.

Happily, Jori soon emerged with a glazed tart in one hand and wine in the other. Kiria snatched the tart from him and stuffed it all in her mouth at once. It did nothing to ease her stomach but it took her mind off her nerves for a moment. "Mmm," she hummed, rubbing her fingers together to get rid of the crumbs. "Thank you."

Lively string music began in the next room. One of her favorite songs. She closed her eyes and breathed once.

"Ready?" Atty asked.

Jori leaned toward her, smiling. "Ready as she'll ever be, right?"

She felt too sick to answer.

The music suddenly stopped and a voice announced something. At first, she thought Amir Chetana was announcing her and she felt bile rising in her throat before realizing that the voice had named Cúron and her mother. Aylmor couldn't come because he was somewhere near the Charúnin Thôr mountains once again for a political meeting.

"We've got to get back," Atty said apologetically.

"That's okay," she managed.

The Calthwaites both cast encouraging looks her way as they went out.

Alone with her girls again, she turned feverishly to Candrae, intending to ask her to fix her hair. Was it perfect? Of course it was. There was no use asking. She was beautiful.

It was only seconds now. *Good. Less waiting. ...When will they play that music?* She centered herself toward the door. It would open inward to present her. She just needed to stand and be beautiful, walk in, sit down, wait a moment, wander, talk amiably, dance, eat, and leave. That was it—

The door opened, washing her with light. "...Kepress, Lady Kiria—" was all she heard. Her name resounded in her head like a bell. Nine musicians played music off to the left against the wall but all other human sounds hushed. All the partitions had been removed, making the room huge. It was awash with bright flowing fabric and perfumes. Normal sessions in the Main only took up about a quarter of the space. She'd forgotten how big the room could become, with its vaulted ceiling. Everything was heady and alive, done up perfectly.

Slowly, she walked into the room. Loud gasps echoed through the room as scores of faces watched her. Before she even reached her seat at the foot of the Keepers' dais, whispers filled the space. Amir, soldiers, citizens, servants, noble families all leaned confidentially to talk low in each other's ears. Bold men tried to catch her gaze, their intentions clear. Other people, with flushed faces and misty eyes, watched her silently. The shock and reverence and excitement were all for her. Surreal.

By the time she smoothly made her way past the Keepers to her seat facing them below, she felt exhausted. After bowing to them respectfully, she sat down. An odd mixture of blue-hot pride and crippling embarrassment alternated in her body. If only she could hide and observe everyone's reactions.

She closed her eyes a moment. Maybe things would come into focus again. Her limbs felt heavy and her eyes tired as she sat there, wilting, relaxing. The initial shock was over. Short, painful, but it was over. The ball, however, was not. The players started up a lively dancing tune and she sensed exhaled breath and movement as the people began to talk and choose partners again.

"Kiria?"

She snapped out of her daze. Jori, dressed to the nines, offered her his arm. A few grumpy-looking men stood just behind him as though they'd just been pushed to the side. "Would you consent to dance with me?" he asked.

"'Would I consent?'" she repeated, rising and linking her arm around the soft fabric of his dress coat. "What way is that to ask someone?"

"*You're* the Kepress, especially now," he pointed out. "*I'm* just someone's brother." He squinted and whirled her onto the best spot on the floor, in front of the musicians, as he'd done last week when they had disguised themselves and snuck into the city for a party. "Almost famous."

"Notorious," she said, smiling. Talking to someone relieved some pressure, but she still felt everyone's eyes following her every move.

The tip of her shoe caught the dance floor and she stumbled forward a little. A hundred eyes widened. Jori laughed, stepping away from a man who let go of his dance partner to offer Kiria a hand, and simplified the dance. "Thank you," she said under her breath.

He smiled disarmingly and stumbled forward too. "Didn't know you could even trip looking like that."

"I'm still the same," she said. An ambassador's daughter sneered with her friend on the edge of the dance floor. Kiria lowered her eyes. The gold encircling her wrists glowed against her skin.

She looked up again at Jori, who raised his eyebrows disbelievingly.

"I am," she insisted.

He spun her again before replying. "You might be the same, but now you'll have to look out for yourself. Just look at you!"

She automatically scanned the curved walls where the guards held their positions. "Jori, if you say anything like that again…"

"It was an attempt at a compliment."

The music began to shift. In the pause between pieces, Kiria heard her name whispered by about eight voices around the room. She caught the eye of a middle-aged man who was dancing near her. He promptly turned back to his wife, pretending never to have seen her.

Maybe revealing her Beauty was a mistake. Everything she did seemed wrong, wooden and false when so many people were watching her. She tried to ignore them. "'You'll have to look out for yourself…'" she mimicked. "Poor excuse for a compliment. Should I be afraid of you too?"

"Oh yes," he said, escorting her off the dance floor and back to her seat. "I will have you for my wife now, because I saw you once in a nice dress." He leaned confidentially toward her. "If you need rescuing from someone who *actually* thinks that, let me know. Wink at me or something. I'll probably come help you. If I don't, then know that I'm laughing, right over there." He pointed to the table with sparkling wine and headed toward it.

She shook her head, glad that somebody could take her mind off her nerves and remind her that the world would not end tonight.

"These people have never seen anyone as beautiful as you," her father said behind her. She hadn't even heard her parents approach. They stood behind her in full Brithnem finery—all light blue, dark purple, and silver. The thought struck her that she should have worn those colors instead. After all, wasn't she supposed to serve the people of the Western Kingdom? Instead she chose the colors she thought would show off her Beauty. She swallowed down her embarrassment, her inadequacy, so no one would see.

"How are you doing, dear?" her mother asked.

"Very well, thank you," she replied, aware once again of all the eyes on her. Her folded hands gave away her nervousness, didn't they? *How does Mother hold her hands as she sits?*

Her mother smiled at a few of the dignitaries who hovered near them. "Jorrim was the first to ask you to dance," she observed.

"Of course he was. I don't know who else I'd want to dance with first. I get the feeling they don't even believe it's me."

"I'm sure they know it's you, Kiria," said her father. "Shall we dance the next, since everyone else is too afraid to ask you?" Her father rarely danced.

She smiled and accepted his offer. Plenty of others waited on the fringes for their chance, but she'd rather dance with her father.

Years ago, generals and soldiers all danced before campaigns, a last taste of joy before months of darkness and pain. But those days were over. Even the war with the Torithians felt far removed. Lately, she hadn't even thought about it.

"You're doing well, I think," her father said quietly. Even as he took her hand in the formal dancing position, his eyes darted around the room. Ever the military man, concerned with security. His thick eyebrows twitched down a couple of times as he saw something he didn't like.

"I'm doing better now," she said honestly.

He gave a half-smile. "Ready to lead a kingdom."

She swallowed. *Not quite.* But his eyes softened at the edges when he looked at her, so he thought she could do it. A well of thankfulness bubbled up. "When the time comes," she said.

"You'll make the Arioc name proud." Although others had talked down to her over the years, her father never had. Now, he saw her as strong and capable. That confidence radiated from him. Her father had never feared women in power. After all, he had married her mother and taken her name, a unique situation in a country where people either took their husband's last names or didn't have surnames altogether.

Their dance was short but meaningful. As the last note sang out, the room erupted in clapping, though she couldn't have been very graceful.

Her mother's wild face caught her attention. "Rhet!" Her hushed tone was urgent as she called them over.

They hurried to her.

Daelon stood next to her, his face pale. Kiria's stomach clenched. Something was wrong.

Her mother stood on the dais step and bent over to speak in an undertone. "Kiria, do you know where Atael and Jorrim are?"

Daelon touched her mother respectfully on the shoulder and cast a look across the room. "There they are, my Keeper." Without waiting longer, he rushed over to them—at least, that's as quickly as Kiria had ever seen him go.

"Rhet, I need to talk to you." In a flash, her mother had ushered her father away from her.

Cold with fear, she practically jogged to catch up with Daelon. If she reached him in time, she could overhear his news.

Atty and Jori were both talking casually to one of the guests, a military strategist named Petra. Kiria had always found her more approachable than most of the other high-ranking soldiers. "Excuse me, madam," Daelon cut in, "but I must speak with Kepron Atael immediately."

She'd never seen him look so serious. Often he was stern, but never this upset. He fairly dragged Atty off, with Jori in tow. A few people began to notice the disturbance.

"Excuse me," Kiria said, moving away from someone who had come up to talk to her. *This dress...* Why had she ever liked it? She couldn't move fast enough.

People, maybe well-meaning, blocked her path, as she watched the three of them disappear through the carved doors.

She spun around to catch her parents. Maybe she could get them to tell her what they knew. But she knew her mother's body language well. She wasn't ready to talk.

The only thing to do was to follow Daelon and the Calthwaites out into the hall.

As soon as she slid between the huge wooden doors, shutting out the sounds of the ball, she spotted Daelon walking briskly down the hall away from her, his feet clipping the floor.

"Daelon!" she cried, a loud, empty sound.

He turned around. Even at that distance, his face looked strained and pale. "What is it, my Kepress?" he asked.

"Where are Att... Atael and Jorrim?" Only their formal names seemed to fit the moment.

"Unavailable."

"What do you mean?" They were always available. Jori made himself so available that they had spent the last six months having fun, going to parties, and escaping the responsibilities of the palace far more often than they should have. "Is everything all right?"

He didn't respond but stood awhile, considering. His eyes softened. "Why don't you go back to the party?" he finally said.

Her breathing tightened. "What happened?" *Not something terrible. Please.*

After pausing for a few moments in indecision, he strode toward her.

"Would you like to sit down, Kepress?" he said, motioning to the built-in bench against the wall.

She needed no argument; her legs felt shaky with apprehension. It had to be something serious to rattle Daelon this way.

He sat down next to her and ran his hands over his face that normally looked so young. "This will be announced very soon," he began solemnly, "so don't tell anyone. Not a soul."

She nodded, frowning.

"There has been... an accident."

"Who?" she cut in, but even as she said the word, she knew.

"Keeper Aylmor has been killed," he said very softly. Atty and Jori's father.

"Oh no! What happened?" she cried, swallowing against the rock in her throat.

"The report said that he was thrown from his horse. There was no pain." He cleared his throat. "Remember that you can't tell anyone."

"I won't. You know me." She let out an unsteady breath. Too many thoughts assaulted her at once. She had to go comfort them, but she was too shaken from the news. Better if she composed herself first. *Third Keeper gone.* "Then there's no... Wait! Atty's not ready to lead the country!" Her voice broke a little.

"He is a bit inexperienced," the Amir agreed. "But we will probably have the coronation ceremony before the new moon."

"Coronation..." It was too much to take in all at once.

"Unfortunately, I have to go tell the other advisors the news. It just arrived by messenger." He got up to leave.

"Okay."

Aylmor had been such a staple in her life. It never occurred to her that this would actually happen. Of course Atty would one day become the Keeper of Brithnem, but that was *one day*, not *now*. Not in the face of tragedy. But then, tragedy always preceded the crowning of a new monarch. One had to fall for the next to rise. Too suddenly, her friend was one of the most important leaders in the world.

She sat alone on the bench, shoulders heavy, and felt her Beauty seeping back to normalcy.

15

FIRIAN

With Bard gone to visit his family in Enderin, a visit that was sure to be brief, considering the conflict there, Firian had the room to himself. He could invite a girl over, but he wasn't in the mood. It had been too long since he had been alone with his thoughts. He dropped to the floor and started doing pushups. After all the practice, his muscles barely felt the strain.

"Isn't your Defender giving tests now?" The deep voice belonged to Master Makai, the man who had brought him to the Academy all those years ago.

Firian's joints suddenly felt wooden and cold. He sat up on his knees. "What?" he snapped, before adding an apologetic "...Master."

"I was told that Defender Tiev is giving his first tests now," Makai replied, seemingly unaffected by Firian's tone. "He should have told *you*, at least, Kess." Apparently, the whole Academy knew about the competition that had grown between the two of them lately.

"He's testing now?"

"Yes, now. Better hurry."

Firian fought the urge to run. At least Tiev wouldn't get the pleasure of seeing him rush to be on time to his little meeting, panting in the doorway like somebody begging to be forgiven for his tardiness. As far as he was concerned, Tiev could wait for him forever, except that he'd miss the chance to outdo him and prove his superiority.

Eventually he arrived at the meeting room for his floor, the one Erron had used for his tests. Each hall had one on the far end: a larger, open room used for gatherings, announcements, and testing. It looked like everybody else had already arrived. Boys overflowed out of the room, all craning their necks over the rest of the crowd, trying to see. Firian raised an eyebrow. What could they want to see? From the outside, testing normally looked like two people sitting and facing each other with their eyes closed—nothing great to look at. His curiosity took over.

Obviously, something out of the ordinary was happening. Discreetly, he glanced over the other people's heads to the two chairs in the middle of the room.

"Out of the way!" Master Belik roared as he arrived. He looked haggard with suppressed excitement. Firian and the others automatically clamored to the side, creating a path for him.

The break in the sea of people allowed Firian to see what was happening. Tiev sat in one seat, with a look of perfect concentration on his face, and Rian sat in the other, sweating and twitching as though somebody were hitting him repeatedly.

"*Move!*" cried the Master again, though no one was in his way. "Tiev!"

Tiev snapped open his eyes and Rian slumped off his chair to the floor. He lay there, limp. The crowd at the door closed again, but Firian could just make out Tiev's face. The blood drained out of it as he glanced first at the unconscious form of Rian, then at Master Belik.

Belik toed Rian with his shoe, then sighed. "Gelir," he said to Tiev in a low voice. "This isn't a war." He jerked his head toward Rian. "He's alive, but if I find that you've 'tested' others like you tested him…"

"I didn't—"

"Shut up! And don't use all your Talent at once."

There was a very awkward silence while everyone waited for the Master to leave, but he didn't. Tiev seemed unsure whether to call up the next person, especially with Rian still lying by the chair.

"Well?" Belik prompted.

"Kess!" Tiev blurted. "Firian Kess!"

Firian felt numb. What just happened? Was Tiev *that* good?

Firian muscled his way through the crowd and sat calmly in the seat, making sure his feet didn't touch the prostrate form of Rian, which nobody had bothered to move. He pursed his mouth as he looked straight into Tiev's eyes. *You don't need to hold back on me.*

Tiev cleared his throat quietly. "Ready?" he whispered.

The crowd went very quiet. Firian lifted a corner of his mouth. "As long as you are."

"Hall master's choice."

They both closed their eyes. Firian let himself sink into nothingness.

There were no doors in the spotless paneled room. The walls shot upward and upward until they vanished, yielding to a thin prick of light hardly visible above. Circular windows formed an endless pattern, curling upward along the walls, allowing some sunlight to enter.

Firian stood at one end of the room, intense and calculating, with his legs slightly spread apart and his hands behind his back. Tiev stood in the same position opposite him.

"Do you see it?" Tiev asked customarily.

"Of course. Your choice," Firian added with a shrug, clenching his teeth in his mouth. He breathed the musty air, loving the possibilities sparking in his mind like flint.

A little smirk spread over Tiev's face.

To think that I was ever friends with this sniveling…

He calmed himself down. It was just a test, even if it was being administered by someone his own age.

"Can we start?" Firian asked, bringing his hands slowly to his sides.

"Sure." Two identical knives appeared in Tiev's hands and he twirled them expertly.

Please.

It was easy to look intimidating in the Unreal, but it was just that—Unreal.

Hard leather formed under Firian's palms. Whips in hand, he ran at Tiev, who started running along the circumference of the room. With superhuman speed, Firian ran in front of him.

Enough on the ground. He rose up so he was above the Defender. It took a moment for Tiev to realize where Firian was, and then he flew to meet him.

Setting his teeth, Firian mussed Tiev's perfect hair hard as he rose up beside him. Tiev's only answer was to jab his knives at him, but Firian flew out of the way.

This is all you have? It was almost laughable. Or it would be, if it weren't so insulting.

Master Asoka had told them once to be like water in the Unreal—liquid, solid, or gas. It didn't matter which, as long as it fit the situation. Every time Tiev knifed him, he pretended to be water and just let it go through him. Here he was immortal.

Bending his thought entirely on Tiev, he imagined no knives, no weapons of any kind in his opponent's hand. The endeavor was successful: Tiev's knives dissolved. In his instant of opportunity, his whips dissolved into blue smoke, leaving his hand in a tight fist. *What next?* Stars. Throwing stars. Shooting up in the air, he felt the cold bite of metal in his closed hand. Throwing feverishly, two stars at a time, he saw them sink deep into the paneling, always where Tiev had been a moment before. Then... a hit! Tiev recoiled in pain. Wild joy rose up in Firian, and he was almost ashamed of it.

He had won!

The rest of the stars melted into the air like smoke.

But just as the real world started to enter his mind and he could feel the open air of the meeting room, he felt himself being dragged back.

What?

That had never happened before. Tiev stood in the middle of the room again, and Firian got in the starting position to fight, still confused.

A blazing light began to pulse brighter and brighter around Tiev, spinning into him. *What?* he thought again. *This can't be real.*

After a few seconds, Firian had to look away. Watching Tiev was like looking straight at the noon sun, especially in that dim room. Whatever was happening made Firian nauseated. Something was wrong.

Firian's Academy coat whipped in front of his body as a gale swept past him from behind. He squinted forward again through his wildly blowing hair, trying to adjust his eyes enough to look. All the light and all the wind were sucked into Tiev with an energy that Firian had never witnessed before—like the energy of two or three Masters at once.

His mouth went thick and dry.

Here was power.

All the energy penned up in Tiev exploded out with fierce brightness and swept Firian off his feet. He hit his head hard against the wall as he fell, skidding.

"Time's up," said a faint voice, probably from the real world.

Painfully, he opened his eyes. So did Tiev. Once his eyes adjusted to the dark room—when did it become so dark?—Tiev said one word. "Difficult?"

Firian felt cold sweat dry on the backs of his hands. "Not at all," he lied, still shaken.

It seemed quiet without Bard moving around and talking in his sleep. Firian lay in bed with his hands behind his head, staring at the plywood of the bunk above him. The testing a few days ago was still bothering him. In fact, it was almost all he thought about. Where had the power come from? It couldn't have been Tiev. It *couldn't*.

Everyone else, however, thought that it had been. The story had spread over the whole Academy with amazing speed. People asked Rian about his experience in almost every class. He'd recovered quickly after Firian's test was over and since then everyone had been curious about what had really happened to him. At first, he'd seemed a little resentful to bring up the subject but, after he got more attention than ever before, he started relating the incident to everyone who would listen. Predictably, his stories had gotten wilder and wilder with each telling. No one understood fully what had happened and Firian refused to give any details about his own experience, though he was asked almost as often as Rian.

Meanwhile, people treated Tiev like a prodigy or a god. People feared him, spoke about him in whispers, and argued about the significance of his Talent. Even the Masters were beginning to treat him almost like an equal. Firian's stomach felt sick and frozen whenever he thought of the possibility of Tiev being promoted to Master. Many people talked about the chance it would happen. Others followed Tiev as though he alone held the secret to being the perfect Tanyu. In the minds of almost everyone at the Academy, Tiev was in a class by himself and that caused many to revere him.

Firian pursed his lips together in the darkness. He knew he worked harder than any other student his age, including Tiev, whatever everyone else may think. As it was, he only slept four hours a night. It didn't really matter to him that he had to practice his skills in the dark cold of early morning much of the time. He'd always liked the cold season better anyway. It made him feel more alive.

He took a deep breath and sat up at the edge of his bunk. Closing his eyes, he concentrated hard on visualizing different objects, on visualizing himself as towering, as tiny, as air, as fire itself... *Fire! Is that how he did it?*

"Stop losing focus," he muttered to himself.

He was fire—all flame, but not consumed. Consum*ing*. That was it.

Powerful bright light. Burning. Power.

He lay down again as he became fire in his mind. It was abstract, but not much different than the lessons he'd been given on becoming like water, able to shift.

They were both just natural elements. He would probably learn this stuff as a Defender anyway, or even later on that year.

The flames danced before him. Changing. Shifting. Burning. Flickering...

Firian was alone in a dark room. He felt cold and could only see about two feet ahead of him. Walking cautiously ahead, he found a blank wall, so he turned. After maybe five minutes, he found another wall, identical to the one he just left. Weaving his way around the new wall, he found more. These walls obviously formed some sort of maze. Without knowing why, he felt strongly that the answer to all of his problems waited in the middle and he needed to find it. He broke into a run toward what he knew instinctively was the center of the maze. It grew colder every minute. His clothes did nothing to fight off the icy chill that now bit on every side. Soon, the cold surpassed ordinary winter cold and starting gnawing inside him. He felt as though he were freezing to death. His fingers felt too fat to bend and his face was a mass of pain. *Need to finish* ... All of his answers were waiting.

He ran harder. The walls rose up closer together. Everywhere he went, there they were. Desperation set in. He was close to panic.

A cold wind blew past him. The fear that shook him wasn't enough to make him stop. He trudged ahead and a weak glow emerged from where the wind had blown. Now he could see more than one wall at a time. The center was close. His limbs moved as though he were wading through syrup.

He turned a corner. There it was.

A little wood fire burned sickly pale in the center of the maze and a huddle of people crouched around it. Firian could have cried with joy. He wasn't going to freeze and die in that meaningless maze. He must have laughed or gasped with relief because everyone around the fire turned to look at him.

Suddenly ashamed, he felt naked beneath their stares. None of the people said a word. After a moment or two, he almost wanted to sneak back into the maze to avoid them. The worst thing was that they *knew* him. Firian's breathing became thin and shallow.

"Stop looking at me," he breathed, turning away.

When he finally had the courage to look back, he saw the features of those who stared at him.

"Father?" he whispered. "Bard? Master Jovan?" He scanned a whole line of familiar faces until he lighted on one. His throat caught. "Brett."

Forgetting his fear, he threw himself around his sister's neck and broke down crying. She felt stiff in his arms, but his joy couldn't be stifled by a little thing like that. "Brett. I thought...." He shook his head into her shoulder.

When he pulled away from her, she said his name with such an odd expression that some of his apprehension returned. "What's wrong?" he asked.

"Get away from her," said his father's voice.

A creepy feeling crawled in his stomach at his tone of voice. It was as if he'd walked into a congregation of the dead. "I didn't..." he began to protest. "I just... It was cold."

A joyless laugh. "Worthless," someone muttered.

Firian bristled. "I'm a Tanyu," he said.

"He's not worth it," Master Belik broke in. "We let him in out of pity."

Master Jovan nodded his assent.

His mother didn't say anything, but he felt her sad eyes boring into him. She seemed on the verge of despairing tears and somehow all of it was his fault. Bitter disappointment etched deep into her lined features. He couldn't help her.

"Stop it," he said quietly, shaking.

"We knew you'd never amount to anything," his father said.

"Stop!" Firian said, with more force.

"What? Because *you* want us to? Just shut up," said Tiev cruelly. "No one cares what you say. Do us a favor and kill yourself so we don't have to worry about you anymore."

Firian's throat had closed so tightly he could barely breathe.

"Get away from me," Brett said softly at his side. "I can't stand it anymore."

Tears rimmed his eyes. Even Brett.

"You'll always be worthless, Firian," said someone, or it could have been all of them.

"*Stop!*" he yelled as loudly as he could.

The word echoed around the little room as Firian jolted awake. Pale rays of first light eked through the heavy curtains of his room. His chest rose and fell with heaving breaths. It took a moment for everything to spiral into silence again.

Time for more practice.

16

KIRIA

Candrae, the little serving girl, put another pearl-tipped pin into Kiria's hair. Kiria tapped her foot distractedly, screwing up her nose as she looked as herself in the glass, her head framed by Candrae's voluminous blonde hair. Hopefully her Beauty wouldn't distract anyone from the gravity of the ceremony.

"How much time do we have?" she asked.

"About twenty minutes, my Kepress."

"Right. Okay." She didn't know why she was so nervous. This was the time for Atty to be nervous, not her. But this proved that one day it would be her turn. Just because she'd never seen a coronation before didn't mean they never happened. She would be a Keeper of Brithnem too, just like Atty. "We have to get in place," she said, standing to her feet. She wasn't tall, but Candrae still had to reach up in order to keep the pin from falling out when she moved. "Vayci! Are you almost ready?" she called.

Frantically, her other serving girl emerged from the adjoining room, still holding one shoe in her hand. The servants' dresses weren't nearly as nice as hers, but they were still beautiful in a way: plain, in rich colors, with a thin decorative belt around the waist. Vayci had even tied Candrae's hair in knots before they went to bed the night before so that it would curl in the morning, and Candrae had helped Vayci with the swirling designs on her head. Kiria's silky blue dress reached down to the floor. It was almost impossible to walk because of the length, let alone the elaborate shoes she wore with it.

"We have to get to the Main," Kiria said.

Vayci nodded and put her shoe on awkwardly before standing up.

Seeing them both in their nice things watching and waiting for her made her suddenly proud of them. Usually she didn't think about them at all, but they were brought up to serve her and were doing it so well. They never complained or hesitated. It was people like these two girls that made the whole Western Kingdom work properly. "You both look lovely," she told them, smiling.

They blushed and ran to open the door for her. She swept through it and into the common area, where her parents were waiting with all six of their attendants —guards, ladies-in-waiting, and her Amiran advisor Chetana. She'd never seen her mother look so amazingly beautiful. Merian, her mother, had always had natural beauty—an outdoor kind that was best left untampered-with—but today she wore a green dress with diamond studs and diamonds in her ears. Even her father was transformed. He wore several rings that he usually kept stowed away, and he wore his best vest, with gold thread throughout it and a dark blue coat. Normally they didn't go out in all this finery, but this was a special occasion: part Aylmor's funeral, part Atael's coronation celebration.

"Are you ready, Kiria?" her mother asked.

She sucked in a breath and nodded.

Her mother took her father's arm and promenaded with him down into the wide hall that led down to the Main. Kiria had trouble keeping up because of her tall shoes, but somehow all eleven of them managed to make the long walk to the Main without making fools of themselves. Well, of course her mother and father wouldn't make fools of themselves, but she was glad that she hadn't.

A low murmur of voices came from inside the room and low lights flickered through the crack in the door. Four guards stood outside the room. They all instantly recognized them and moved aside.

The First Keeper, Aylmor's relatives, the Amir, nobles, and servants all crowded into the large room, standing mainly toward the edges of the room where dark purple fabric covered the multi-paned windows. Except for the dim lighting and serious occasion, it seemed nothing like a funeral. Everyone looked stunning, sipping cold drinks and talking in huddles. The chairs had been taken away, at least for the moment, as they did for parties.

Kiria saw almost everyone bow their heads respectfully as her family entered. Keepers didn't require any elaborate form of deference, as long as some kind of deference existed.

Kiria scanned the room for Jori. He was leaning against the opposite wall, looking sullen until someone came up to talk to him. His grin came easily until the person walked away again. He kept picking at the sleeves of his maroon tunic and glancing uneasily around the room. She almost went over to stand by him before remembering that she couldn't leave her family during the ceremony. So she tried to get his attention instead, looking intently at his face in order to catch his eye, waving discreetly. He refused to notice any of it.

Atty, on the other hand, was nowhere to be seen. But that was no surprise.

Nearby, to her family's right, stood Cúron with Kader and his wife, Varinna. Cúron's particularly splendid robe matched Kiria's dress, all light blue, one of the official colors of Brithnem. It complimented his short gray beard and hair that fell to his collar. Varinna looked like a queen in purple, with her hair done up in twists like a crown.

Her mother and father made quiet, polite conversation with Cúron and his family for several minutes. Having two Keeper families speak to each other made

Jori look even more separate and dejected. He had no one left but Atty. Again, Kiria wished she could go over to him.

Daelon appeared and stood beside her. He winked and she knew it was just to make her feel better. Winking was inappropriate at a gathering like this, but not so much that people would comment.

Soon Cúron walked up onto the dais where the Keepers' chairs were and stood there alone, facing the crowd. Everyone quieted and turned to the front of the room. "Keepers, Amir, and people of Brithnem," he began in a loud voice, "we have come here today to honor the Third Line of Keepers. The descendants of Caedmon, the son of Shane and Mari Calthwaite, have served this country well through all its trials and successes. Today we witness the future and remember the past." He acknowledged his Amiran advisor standing just below him to the left. "Parohim."

Parohim strode up the steps. He was tall and thin, rather gray, and he wore the traditional coat with a high neck. Without any preamble, he began a recitation from the Sacred Scroll.

"*Forever shall you worship God. In whatever you do, worship Him.*

For not only the race of Khelê shall be called the Chosen Ones, but you also, as their descendants, may partake of their glory. In days of wickedness you were ignorant and evil, but now a great good is restored to you and God speaks among you once more. Be wise, therefore, and follow no other words but those of God. If you do not chase after other gods and invent them for yourself, He shall remain present among His people. Then you shall all be as the Khelê, seeing God's goodness in the ways that He chooses you for Himself.

Forever shall you worship God. In whatever you do, worship Him."

Kiria mouthed the familiar passage as the advisor proclaimed it. All her life, she'd seen those words written along the walls of the Main, reminding the Keepers of their duty to God. They spoke of the time when the race of the Kingdom Dwellers had decided to follow a false god, giving it the name of the only God. To draw their attention rightfully back to himself, God had sent them children who looked nothing like them. The people misunderstood and thought they had been cursed. In the panic that followed, a leader (the Kingdom's first king) rose up and declared that they should kill all the strange-looking children. They even created ceremonies for these killings, and did it all in the name of God, who in his wisdom engineered ways for many of the innocent children to escape. Those people grew up and formed an army that attacked the Kingdom, which was built in the very spot that Brithnem was now, and were called the Khelê—God's chosen people. At the time, only a few Kingdom Dwellers saw the justice in what the Khelê were doing. Among them were Shane and Mari Calthwaite, who converted and were the first to willingly ally themselves with the Khelê. They were heroes, and their children began the three royal Lines of Brithnem.

Parohim stepped down from the platform. "Aylmor Calthwaite fulfilled his duty to God and to the Western Kingdom and now the Holy One has taken him, leaving his son, Atael Calthwaite, to serve in his stead."

Then there was a dead silence. A rasping breath came from somewhere, loud in the quiet. Cúron walked off the dais and back to his family, his feet hitting the floor softly.

The heavy door at the side creaked open, the same one she had stood behind, waiting to reveal her Beauty. No servant had opened it, but a figure in rags appeared, standing out in stark contrast to the overwhelming finery around him. His hair was uncombed and his feet had no shoes. He didn't raise his eyes to meet the dozens of pairs transfixed on him. His dress was worse than a servant's.

The figure wove through the crowd and approached Cúron. A large circle formed around the two of them as the man in rags dropped to his knees and pulled out a wet strip of cloth from his belt and ran it over the ruler's feet. Once he had finished, Cúron said, "Thank you." The man nodded.

Then he moved on to one of Jori's servants, named Sen, and proceeded to do the exact same thing. "Thus will I serve my country; thus will I serve my God," said the man, lifting his head.

It was Atael. Kiria had never seen him look so ragged and drawn.

"Bring a robe for his back," said Cúron.

"Bring shoes for his feet," said Merian.

A pause.

"Bring a crown for his head," said Jori finally, "that he may represent our Third Line." He shifted slightly to stand upright. Kiria understood that the next of kin was supposed to say this line; normally that would be his mother, but Ladima had died when they were very young.

At Jori's words, the Third Line's Amiran advisor and Atael's two servants left the room.

Kiria leaned over to her mother. "Isn't he supposed to wash your feet?" she breathed. It seemed odd that Cúron was the only Keeper who was part of the ceremony.

Merian held up a hand. *Impatient? Irritated?* Hopefully that meant she would give an explanation later.

In moments the servants returned with the robe and shoes, and the Amir with the crown.

"Approach the throne, servant of Brithnem," said Atty's advisor, Reynard. Atty obeyed him and stood in front of his throne. His advisor followed him onto the platform. A servant came up quickly and put a thick robe around his shoulders while another bent down to strap shoes to his feet. Once the two servants stepped down, Cúron and Merian of the First and Second Lines took their seats at the front. They had never looked so splendid as far as she remembered, but she couldn't look away from Atty long. He set his face very seriously as he stood there in a poor man's tunic and a Keeper's robe. It all struck her as a game—they were all playacting, speaking in turn when their parts came. If not for the look on Atty's face she may really have believed that this was all an elaborate joke. But this was no joke. This was how someone became a Keeper. A wave of nausea hit her suddenly. One day this would be her ceremony.

"What do you swear?" asked the Amir holding the crown.

Kiria mouthed the words with him, words she had learned since childhood. "I swear to serve my country, the Western Kingdom, and its capital, Brithnem, to the best of my ability, to guide her through war and peace, freedom and judgment, with wisdom and integrity, for as long as I live." He said the words softly and clearly, with almost no lisp. The words shifted something inside Kiria. She felt breathless and small and yet completely, finally, secure. These were the words she'd forgotten. These were the words that meant everything.

The Amir turned to the other seated Keepers. "Do you accept Atael Calthwaite as the heir to this Line and consequently to this throne?" he asked.

"I do," Cúron and her mother stated.

"And do you, people of Brithnem?" he addressed the crowd.

"We do," came the murmur of dozens of voices.

The Amir turned back to Atty. "Please be seated, my Kepron." Atty sat in the throne they had played on as children.

Reynard took a deep breath, probably for effect. "We now call you Atael Calthwaite, Third Keeper of Brithnem." And he slowly placed the crown on Atty's mussed hair. It fell into place there like a door sealed shut.

The Amir came off the platform and bowed before the new Keeper. One by one the people began to fall on one knee before him, starting with the servants, then the guests, the Amir, and finally the Keepers' families including Kiria. Then applause erupted as he stood, a Keeper of Brithnem.

Once the clapping had died down, his two servants came up to him and escorted him from the room. Everyone else followed. Kiria came to her feet as her family rose and ushered her out.

Kiria tried to see Atty, her friend, but he was soon lost in the crowd. She had expected the ceremony to be longer. It really was nothing more than a formality, establishing something that was true to begin with.

Heirs to the throne of Brithnem served the country with their lives.

Lately she had forgotten. She'd let simple insecurity shake her resolve. No more. Let people say what they wanted about her looks, her youth, her femininity, her inexperience. She felt something harden within her. *I swear to serve my country, the Western Kingdom, and its capital, Brithnem, to the best of my ability, to guide her through war and peace...*

17

FIRIAN

Bard snorted in his sleep. "Where's the... lace?" he muttered. "I lost... tuft of lace...." He rolled over. "Really? I thought... brush had it... Maybe..."

Town day... Knuckling his eyes, Firian rolled off the bed and started getting dressed. Despite Bard's being gone for a few days, he was still used to these lively one-sided conversations.

"Stop... jumping," Bard murmured under his breath.

"I'm not," Firian whispered, absently scratching the back of his neck. The whole room still smelled of the cinnamon that Bard's mother had packed with his clothes. It was pretty, like a woman's perfume, which Firian liked on girls but not in their little space, where it felt stifling.

"Lace..."

Dressed and ready, Firian stood and smacked Bard on the arm. "Get up!" he said loudly. "It's a town day."

"S'early..." Bard slurred with his back to him.

"I'm going now," he said.

Bard sniffed as he rolled over and peered at Firian with puffy eyes. "Fine," he sighed and cleared his throat. "I'll come. Give us a minute."

"Still can't find that tuft of lace, can you?" he said.

"What?" Bard grunted. "What are you talking about?"

"Just a moment ago—in your sleep."

He groaned. "Don't tell anyone."

Grinning, Firian said, "Why would I want to do that?"

Bard threw his pillow at him and collapsed again from the effort.

Leaving the sounds of discontented muttering behind him, Firian headed toward the washroom at the end of the hall.

The door swished over a thin film of water as he entered. Tiev, Shiro, and their lanky friend Braden were the only ones there. Tiev hardly traveled alone these days. All his newfound friends followed him wherever he went. Firian ignored them and went to the nearest sink to splash his face with the cold water. It was fiercely refreshing. He slicked the wetness off with his hands and flicked it at the sink, eyeing Tiev, who eyed him back.

"You're up early," Firian told him, giving in to the temptation to poke at the bear.

"So are you."

"You're not practicing on a town day, are you?" Firian continued idly.

"What's that to you?" Tiev asked, scooping up some water in his hand and splashing it on the back of his neck.

"Just, if you were..." He shrugged.

"What?"

"You don't feel like you *need* to practice this early on an off day, do you?" Firian was satisfied when Tiev bit his lip in agitation. Apparently he'd hit a nerve.

Shiro and Braden tried not to look interested in what was happening between the two of them, but they weren't doing a very good job.

"I'm not!" Tiev exclaimed.

"Hm. Lately you've just seemed... more motivated than usual."

Tiev straightened. "I'm not afraid of you, Firian," he said angrily. "Remember the test day."

When Firian set his mouth a little tighter in response, Shiro sniggered. Firian shot him a black look. Why had he started this row in the first place? "Right! I remember. Good job attacking Learners during a test."

"At least I *could*," Tiev replied coolly.

"You had no idea what you were doing." It had to be true. Firian smiled a little.

Shiro and Braden stopped pretending to wash up. Tiev colored slightly and narrowed his eyes. "I knew exactly what I was doing." He set his jaw forward.

"That would explain the terrified look on your face."

Tiev stepped forward violently. "Shut up, Firian! If you want to be nearly killed again today—"

"What time?" Firian shouted, his voice echoing off the damp walls. He was startled by the vehemence of his own voice. His hands had become fists at his sides.

A glint of apprehension flashed in Tiev's eyes for a moment. Firian fought back a smirk of triumph. Then Tiev said, "Why not now?"

Of course he would suggest that. No Masters to judge. "Afraid someone will see?" Firian taunted.

Tiev waved a cursory hand at his two friends watching them. "Everybody *saw* the last time!"

"Fine!" Firian walked over to the tubs lining the side of the room and sat on the edge of one. Close enough to a chair. He turned to the two onlookers. "Watch. When he starts twitching and begging to be let out, just leave him there. I'm sure he's *Talented* enough to save himself. And I'll make sure I don't kill him. He just needs a lesson after all—"

One side of his face exploded in pain. He couldn't see. Reeling, he stood to his feet. "You gory—"

Tiev glared at him, shaking out the pain in his hand. Blinded with rage, Firian jumped on him, swinging both fists at his face. They scrabbled frantically over the wet floor, punching, kicking, grabbing. Firian vaguely heard Shiro and Braden, and then others, crying, "Fight! Fight!" His fury didn't allow him to think of anything but hurting Tiev. He'd gotten the position that Firian rightly deserved; he'd mocked him for the last time.

Finally he got on top of Tiev enough to sit on his chest and pin down his arms with his knees. With Tiev helpless to defend himself, Firian punched at his head. Even when his fists hurt, he kept going.

Breathing heavily, he realized that Tiev wasn't fighting back anymore, but had gone slack. Slowly, Firian stood to his feet. Blood trickled a red trail from Tiev's nose into the water pooling on the floor.

Firian sniffed. His nose was bleeding too. He ran the back of his hand across his face. He hardly knew what to think, looking down at Tiev's still body. It didn't register.

He was suddenly aware of a small crowd of boys all crammed into the little washroom. Some grudgingly exchanged coins and others bent down, trying to revive Tiev, splashing water on his face and lifting him awkwardly off the ground. He groaned and twitched a finger.

Numb, unsure of what to do, Firian just left the washroom with people talking in his wake.

As he walked back down the hall, he realized that his clothes were soaked and sticking to him. He took a deep breath. *Served him right... He started it. Somebody needed to show him to mind his own gory business.* Bitter satisfaction thrilled through him. He was better after all—as long as the Masters didn't find out. Maybe they wouldn't care, but Tiev was their special little boy now. They'd probably all go running to help him as soon as they found out.

"Why are you all wet?" Bard asked, walking toward him in the hallway. When he got closer, he squinted at his face and stained hands. "What were you *doing*?"

"Oh. Tiev..." he answered vaguely.

Bard's eyes popped. "*Really?* Firian!"

A corner of his mouth lifted to see Bard so concerned. Tiev would live. "See him. He's still in there," he said, jabbing his thumb at the washroom, which was so crowded by now that boys overflowed out the door. Firian shrugged.

Bard didn't reply. He just looked at Firian, stunned. Red-faced with concern, he moved stiffly toward the washroom, as if he were being drawn there against his will.

From the sounds of people yelling, it seemed that Tiev was conscious again. Somebody was trying to get him back to his room.

By the time Firian returned to his own room, freezing cold and dripping, he decided that the sooner he got into town, the better. He threw on some dry clothes and got the water out of his hair by sopping it with some of Bard's clothes.

He was a Defender, said a voice in his head. It sounded a lot like Bard.

Damn idiot too.

The Masters will find out, Firian.

They... they would want us to sort it out ourselves.

Careful or they'll throw you out...
Firian shook himself.

He felt cold again and grabbed his jacket. He wouldn't be thrown out. Of course not. The Academy needed as many people as they could get since the Talent was so rare now. A stupid thing like this wouldn't get someone thrown out...

Hyrum's large hand drummed once on the counter with black-rimmed nails. He made no move to get the ales they had just ordered. "Master Jovan needs to talk to you," he said, his eyes darting between Firian and Bard, gauging their reactions.

Firian blinked. "When?" Was he so predictable that Jovan could give Hyrum the message and know it would get to him?

"Right now."

Bard looked at him, worry radiating from him. Firian didn't look back, but ran both his hands distractedly through his hair. "Did he say why?"

Hyrum shook his head, not sorry that he had no more to offer. Sometimes people of Tánuil liked to see Tanyu squirm.

Without another word, Firian turned away back to the Academy. He had the distinct feeling that he was in trouble.

He broke into a run until he reached the doors of the Academy. Jovan would probably be in his classroom about now. He never took town days. Other Masters rarely did, but Firian realized that he had never seen Jovan in Tánuil at all.

Upon reaching the Master's door, he tried to remember whether or not the he was teaching a class.

"Come in," Jovan's deep voice said from inside.

Firian hadn't even knocked.

He opened the door and saw the large room empty save for two people: Master Jovan and Tiev, who was sporting a black eye, bruised chin, and several cuts. It looked as though he'd washed up as well as he could though—his hair was perfect again. Tiev glared at him through red eyes as he came in.

Master Jovan let them both stand there in excruciating silence while he merely looked at them with his hands behind his back. His hard-set face made it impossible to tell what he was thinking. The quiet crackled.

"So, I hear," began Master Jovan, in a deadly subdued voice, "that you two have been fighting. Is that correct?"

They both nodded, trying not to look at each other.

"Speak when I ask you a question!" he barked, taking his hands from behind his back.

"Yes, Master Jovan," they said in unison.

"Normally this would not be a problem," he continued. "It happens. Just let it be. *But*—this case is different. Kess" - he started involuntarily at the sound of his name – "are you aware that Tiev is a Defender?"

"Yes, Master Jovan."

"And that you are merely a Learner."

He gritted his teeth. It was just as he thought. The Masters were stepping in to help their favorite boy. He forced down shame and disappointment, stood up a little straighter, and said, "I was aware, Master Jovan."

"Gelir," he said, addressing Tiev, as he addressed everyone, by last name, "were you also aware of this distinction?"

Firian was glad to see that he seemed nervous too. "Yes, Master Jovan."

"Then what the gore were you thinking?"

It struck Firian how even a big room like this seemed too small for Jovan. He and his presence took up the whole room and left Firian feeling stifled.

When neither of his victims answered, the Master said, "Apparently you both need to learn something about the distinction of rank. You want to be equal. Very well. Kess, you move in with Tiev for a week and see how that suits you."

Tiev's mouth fell open. Then his jaw worked furiously but he wisely held his tongue.

Firian went numb. Live with Tiev for a week? That would be torture.

He tried to rationalize. *He'll be taking different classes and I'm out all the time too. We won't even have to see each other more than a minute or two a day...*

It didn't help much.

"Don't stand there gaping like idiots," said Jovan. "Move your things. Now."

18

KIRIA

Kiria's serving girls watched her pace outside the doors of the Main. They'd given up on following her from one end of the hall to the other. Sometimes she would stop, listening, but she could hear nothing through the impenetrable doors. It seemed childish to press her ear against the door with the guards watching. She could tell her pacing irritated them enough.

"My Kepress," said one guard, finally. Guards almost never began conversations with Keepers or their families, so it proved just how exasperated he was. "May I ask what it is you'd like to know?"

"Nothing," she said quickly. The session should be out soon anyway and she knew very well that the guards couldn't tell her what they discussed in there, or how Atty was doing in his first session. If she had arrived on time, she wouldn't have been in this position. No one short of a Keeper could come into the middle of a session in the Main—not even a Kepress who had been required to attend.

Tight-lipped, the guard looked straight ahead as she continued to pace, sit, stand, listen, pace again....

When the latch finally clicked and the small crowd streamed out of the Main, everyone was relieved. Uniforms, armor, robes... "Atty!" she called out when she saw him, then realized how informal that sounded. "Atael." But his real name sounded strange on her tongue—too formal.

Completely surrounded by people, he didn't hear her. She cocked her jaw in frustration. Then she saw a tall regal figure.

"Mother!" she called.

Her mother did hear her and came over, breaking away from the crowd. "What is it, Kiria?" she asked, looking serious and drawn.

"How was Atty?" Kiria whispered.

"He handled it very well. His advisor spoke more than he did, but that's normal for the first time. Everyone has to adjust after such a big change. But he's young. He'll be all right. He seems to have a rather good grasp on politics. Now I have to discuss some things with Cúron."

"But..." She still had questions, but her mother had already rejoined the crowd flowing out of the hall. Despondently, she watched the rest of the people go by. Who else could she ask?

Short, curly hair bobbed above the crowd as Chetana, her mother's Amiran advisor, walked by just a few feet away. She would know. She attended all the sessions, and she was Daelon's mother, even though they didn't look alike. Kiria could never tell who was related in Khelê families.

Kiria ran up to her, but stopped short. Chetana, not the most approachable person, was exceptionally tall, dark-skinned, and carried herself with a rigid military bearing. Kiria only came up to her graceful neck, so Chetana's far-away, Amiran gaze usually skimmed the top of her head and soared past her to more important matters.

"Amir Chetana?" she began.

She looked down at her. "Yes, my Kepress?" Her face was stoic—no... upset, though not at her.

"How did Atael do on his first day?"

Chetana's hardened face thawed into a smile, punctuated by her lace septum ring. "He's new," she replied. "He's..." Her voice drifted off, unsure.

"Tell me, please." As a Kepress, she didn't need to add "please" but it never hurt to be polite.

More people came out of the Main, but the wide hallway didn't become any louder. Everyone's brows furrowed or eyes widened, deep in thought.

"What's wrong?" Kiria insisted.

"Nothing is wrong." Seeing that she wouldn't accept that answer and go away, Chetana lowered her voice and continued. "The Torithians attacked our outpost, so our allies think we should send more troops. Many more."

Poor Atty didn't have an easy first day. "Do you think we should?" Kiria asked.

"Cúron elected to send soldiers, but your mother thought we should wait and see."

She didn't answer the question. "What about Atty?"

"He didn't say very much," she replied. "But I think he agrees with Cúron."

"Do they need us?" It felt like a naïve question, and Kiria hated feeling stupid.

"I've already said enough," said Chetana, firmly but kindly.

The air felt stuffy and close. Now Atty had to choose whether to risk the war or risk more Kingdom lives. If only she had gone to the session herself to support him. Heaven only knew how much help a new Keeper needed to lead well. At least she had Chetana and Daelon to help prepare her.

Kiria's first chance to speak with Atty face to face since the coronation came when he fell ill.

One of the two guards outside his door drew his shoulders back before looking straight ahead. "Keeper Atael is sick and will not take any visitors, My Kepress."

"He'll let me in," she insisted. "Ask him."

The guards looked at each other and came to a wordless agreement. One of the guards went into the room while the other stared as she tried to see through the crack in the door. She looked back at him and she assured him, "He'll let me in."

When the guard came out of the room, his expression hadn't changed. "My Kepress is allowed to enter for a short time," he announced, a flicker of disappointment dashing over his face.

She raised an eyebrow at the guards as she passed them and entered. To her irritation, two more guards already stood inside by the door. She should have guessed. That was the system arranged for her mother on most days, but Atty had always been different, just like her—famous, learning, waiting.

Atty lay in his huge four-poster bed, looking specter pale, his face framed by stringy hair. His Keeper room seemed to swallow him, it was so big.

"Atty! How are you?" she asked, rushing up to him.

He smiled faintly. "Look at me," he said, gesturing down at the covers. His black Keeper tattoo reaching out from beneath his sleeve seemed to sit on top of the white skin on his hand. Kiria's stomach dropped. It was exactly like Aylmor's. "But I'm doing all right."

"I haven't seen you in ages!"

"I know. I've been busy. I've seen you in the Main, though." He nodded slightly in encouragement.

She tilted her head from shoulder to shoulder. "I'm trying to be responsible. It gets a little boring after a while though."

He blew a laugh. "Try going to every session." He settled his big shoulders on the pillow.

"Good point." Atty disliked politics more than she did. Her trick was to focus on the parts she cared about, where she felt she could make a difference when she was older. She sat down next to him and leaned over. "I brought you something," she said quietly, taking a few small sweets out of her cloak pocket and stuffing them under the cover. "I figured they wouldn't let you have these since you're sick."

Without hesitation, he made his face blank as if nothing had happened. A holdover from their younger days.

"So how is it being a Keeper?" she asked in a normal tone.

"Busy," he answered, and coughed.

"You've been Keeper for a couple months, though. What's it like?"

He paused, thinking. "To tell the truth, it's hard. For one thing, people never leave you alone." He indicated the guards with his eyes.

"But you had that before. Is there anything that really changes?"

"People expect you to be perfect, to *be* the Third Line..." He paused and looked down at the covers. "I don't know how Father did it. He always—" He stopped to clear his throat. "He always seemed to know what he was doing. But you can't make a mistake. That's the hardest thing." His voice sounded thick as it started to slur.

Perfect. That was comforting. She sighed and a wisp of mousy hair floated up.

"You'll do great, though," he said, catching her worry. That sent him coughing for a while, deep coughs from his lungs.

"Are you sure you're all right?" Kiria asked, now worried for a different reason.

He nodded, unable to catch his breath. A guard approached him with a glass of water, and then he bent down to tell him something in his ear. Atty nodded again.

The door opened and Jori appeared, wearing tall gray boots and an embroidered purple jacket, almost as though he were going to a party. He probably was.

Catching the fact that Atty couldn't speak at the moment, Jori turned to Kiria. "So how does he look? Any better?"

"He's all right," Kiria replied confidently.

"Made a big announcement yesterday, didn't you?" Jori said to Atty. Kiria couldn't read his tone. Jori rarely talked politics, so maybe it was a personal announcement.

Atty's breathing finally calmed. "Yes."

Before he could continue, Jori burst out, "He suggested that Amir get a vote in the Main."

If Kiria had been drinking water, she would have spit it out. "What? A *vote*?" She turned to Atty.

"Just half a vote," he said. "Cúron suggested it, and I think it's a good idea."

"They already advise us, and they do it exceptionally well," Kiria said. "If the Amir get a vote, others will want one too."

Part of her regretted saying the words the moment she spoke them. It wasn't that she didn't trust Daelon or Chetana, but she knew that giving them all a vote would start a chain reaction of consequences that Atty couldn't anticipate. If the Amir got a vote, then the military, the noble families, maybe even the Tanyu would want one too. The bond between the Western Kingdom and the Tanyu wasn't as strong as it had once been, but she would be surprised if they didn't claim their old alliance to gain more power in the Kingdom. In name, they were still the last line of defense, the elite fighters Keepers could summon in times of crisis. But the Tanyu were warriors—practically mercenaries for hire—and the Amir religious scholars and advisors.

She and Atty had been trained from birth to know and foster the people groups, treaties, alliances, geography, economy, and culture of Brithnem. Not every well-meaning person could lead a country. She even doubted her own ability at times.

The Kingdom's system of three monarchs had worked for a long time. Why did he want to change it? Why did *Cúron* want to change it? The idea didn't sit well with her at all.

"Your mother shot him down," said Jori carelessly, sitting on the opposite side of the bed. His eyes wandered to the lump under the covers by Atty's left elbow.

"But we're still debating it," said Atty. "I think it's a good idea." He almost looked ashamed.

Kiria held her tongue. She'd already given him her reaction.

Jori pulled one of the sweets out from under the blanket and popped it in his mouth. Atty set his drawn lips flat in annoyance but didn't correct him.

"Oooh!" Jori shivered pleasurably, chewing the sweet. "Just imagine what the Tanyu will think when they find out."

19

FIRIAN

Bard slid onto the bench next to Firian in the community dining room. "What did they do to you?" he asked. "Why weren't you in the room last night?"

"I have to stay in Tiev's room until the end of the week," Firian muttered, not looking up from his food. Last night was awful. Neither of them had breached the icy silence. People were constantly knocking and coming in and going out, asking for things, playing a game of Indisfate... Even Rian came and knocked his drink over Firian's blanket on the floor, obviously in a ploy to get on Tiev's good side. The result was a clammy, miserable night and he didn't want to talk about it.

"Because of the fight?" Bard continued, ripping a small loaf of bread and shoving a bite in his mouth.

Firian nodded.

Bard swallowed. "Have you heard anything more about Enderin?" he asked anxiously, leaning in a little so he wouldn't be heard. The war wasn't going well.

"No. They'll probably say something about it in World Events tomorrow."

Bard sighed and went back to eating.

Kaori, a Charäkhni boy from their hall sitting on the bench behind Firian, leaned backward to speak to him. "So, you and Tiev got in a scrape yesterday," he said.

Firian didn't respond. Whenever Kaori spoke, it seemed like he was talking too much.

"I heard you knocked him cold."

"Yeah, I did."

Kaori laughed. "What made you do it?"

"Nothing."

"Well, obviously it was some—"

"Nothing! Shut up and eat," said Firian, grouchier than ever.

"You're acting like they called *katah* on you," Kaori muttered.

"Ha ha," he replied tonelessly.

Katah was considered a Tanyuin death sentence. It was a focused connection forged between two people. Tanyu, usually women, trained in the art of *katah* learned how to focus unrelentingly on their target, seducing him into believing that their lives were linked, that they *needed* each other. Eventually, the victim, often a high-ranking general or strategist, couldn't tell the difference between imagination and reality when the Tanyu was there because he wanted her to be real, to be present. At that point, the Master could kill the target easily in the Unreal. Belief became reality.

"Wish I'd've been there."

"I'll bet."

"Nice eye, by the way."

"Sure." Firian hunkered over his food again and wouldn't look back at him.

Just then, Master Belik came to stand beside the table. Firian looked up, confused. Belik never ate lunch at that time, especially not with Learners. He felt Bard shrink at his side.

"Firian," the Master said curtly, "our classes are canceled for the next three days."

His eye throbbed and his heart pounded heavily. "Why?" He couldn't help himself.

"They will resume the day after that. I have business."

He opened his mouth to protest, but revised his response. "As you would have it, Master Belik."

"In four days, then." And Belik turned and left with many curious eyes trailing after him.

Bard waited until the Master was gone before he spoke. "What was *that* about?" he said.

Firian shrugged. "Maybe he has Retrieval work."

"Then why would he come all this way to tell you about it?"

Firian had been wondering the same thing.

"Maybe somebody really important got Lost!" put in Kaori, who had heard the whole thing.

"Like the Head," said Rian, who sat next to Kaori at the other table. Kaori's eyes rounded.

Bard gave a very incredulous look. "That's... no."

"Of course not," said Firian. Though that wouldn't be so bad. The Head had made many bad decisions since he'd been here. When Firian had first arrived, Master Jairon had seemed friendly, almost like a grandfather, but now that he had spent more time talking to other Tanyu and people in the village, very few actually liked his leadership.

But this whole conversation was ridiculous. Belik could be gone for a number of reasons. He probably couldn't get someone to send the message for him so he came himself. It was a little weird, but not reason enough to suppose that the Tanyuin Head had gotten Lost in the Unreal. That news would get out no matter how much everybody tried to keep it secret. "It's probably somebody unimportant," he said. "He does this kind of thing sometimes."

But despite Firian's logic, the rest of lunch was taken up with radical hypotheses about Belik's appearance.

Tap, tap, tap.

Firian looked up from visualizing the scenarios for Strategy homework. Tiev wasn't in the room at the moment, which was the whole reason for Firian's choosing to use the space. He sighed. It was probably one of Tiev's friends or stupid admirers at the door, as usual. He lay back down on his stomach on the floor mat.

Tap, tap, tap. Tap, tap.

"Who is it?" he snapped. Maybe refusing entry outright was a better tactic with this person than simply ignoring him.

"...Just delivering something," replied a rather high-pitched voice.

"For who?"

"Defender Tiev Gelir." The boy spoke as though he were reading the name.

"Leave it at the door," Firian instructed.

"Well... as you would have it, Defender," he said hastily. There was a dull thud and the sound of retreating footsteps. Firian waited until the sound faded completely before opening the door and pulling the small package inside. Wrapped simply in brown paper, it had good weight to it. *Who's delivering something to Tiev? Defenders don't just get packages out of nowhere...* He shook it but it felt solid. Then he noticed a few words drawn on the corner of the paper:

To Defender Tiev Gelir.

It was a pleasure meeting you today. I hear your future is bright. Perhaps this will make it brighter.

Amir Murali

– Keep the gift a secret.

Firian's mind spun. *An Amir in the Academy? Sending Tiev a gift?* The situation seemed absurd, but slowly, it started to make sense. It gave Belik a reason to cancel classes, and if anyone were to receive a secret gift from the Amir it might be Tiev, the Academy's precious prodigy boy.

He glanced up at the light leaking through the curtains. Tiev probably wasn't due back for several minutes.

Leaping to his feet, he put the package under his arm and left the room, practically jogging back to his own.

From the top bed, Bard jerked around to see who it was. "Firian?"

Firian closed the door behind him. "Come here," he said, holding out the package.

Bard jumped lightly onto the ground to see it. "What is it?"

"Something for Tiev" – he lowered his voice – "from an Amir."

Bard's mouth grew slack. "Tiev knows an *Amir*?" he hissed.

Firian shrugged. "Looks that way. I think there's one in the Academy."

"That's why Belik...!"

Firian nodded.

Wide-eyed, Bard let out a breath, trying to process everything. "Have you seen him?"

"No, but there's a note…" He pointed to the scrawled writing. Bard turned his head sideways to read it. A few moments later, he looked up.

"Wicked," he pronounced.

"Mmm hm." Firian began tearing at the paper.

"Wait, Fir! You're opening it?"

"Of course. You thought I just wanted you to read the nice note before giving it back?"

"…No."

"Tiev doesn't even know about this. He wasn't there when it was delivered." He ripped the last of the paper off. In his hands sat a rather large book with a plain tan cover. His heart sank. *That's it?*

Bard stared at it in awe. "What does it say?" he whispered.

"I don't know." He flipped it open to the first page. There was no title. He flipped through more pages until he reached the end. Pages of small, neat writing followed elaborately illustrated letters. This book was carefully, even reverently, done. "Of course!" he said. "What gift would an Amir give? This is a copy of the Sacred Scroll! They love this thing."

"Can I see it?"

He handed it over.

Bard turned the book over in his hands, opened to a random page and read a sentence with his eyes. "That's amazing," he said. "I'll bet only the Head has one of these."

"Probably." Firian took the book back. These words held even more importance than the Tanyuin Academy to some people. And he didn't even know what they said. There was no debate in his mind. He was keeping it. Tiev would never know it was gone.

At the thought of Tiev, he cursed to himself. Gathering the book in his arms, he pulled open his dresser drawer and shoved it inside, under his clothes. "I've got to go," he told Bard on his way out.

He could sense a protest, and he didn't want to hear it.

Stalking back down the hall, he prayed that Tiev wasn't there already. He couldn't handle the arrogant questions he was sure to get. If he could just fall asleep—or at least pretend to sleep—first, then sharing the same space would be a bit more bearable.

He edged his fingers around the door as he creaked it open. Success! Tiev wasn't back yet. He stripped off his shirt and crawled into his bed on the floor.

Seconds later, the door opened again. They had just missed each other. Not bad timing. Firian kept his eyes shut. Brief shuffling meant that Tiev was getting in bed too, and wouldn't bother him. Even better.

Tap. Tap, tap, tap, tap.

"Go away, Rian! I'm sleeping!" Tiev called out.

The knocking abruptly stopped.

Tiev sighed and gave a stretching yawn. *Here it comes.*

"An Amir came to visit today," he whispered.

Firian didn't respond.

"Have you ever met one?"

Silence.

Tiev soldiered on. "Master Belik took me to meet him in the Head's office."

He must know that using Belik's name would rattle him. Those should have been Firian's rewards. He fought to keep his breathing even.

"This is all confidential, so they'll have your head if you tell anyone. Thought you might be interested."

Firian breathed through gritted teeth.

He could almost hear the smile in Tiev's next words. "G'night."

Firian lay for an hour with his mind spinning before he opened his eyes in the darkness. Tiev was snoring softly on his bed. He should've expected him to crow about his meeting, but the gallingly innocent way he'd said it reached the end of Firian's patience.

He *couldn't* stay another night.

Getting up softly, he left the room and went down to his own. He always woke up earlier than Tiev, so he wouldn't be missed. As long as no one saw him coming of his usual room, no one would know the difference.

He slipped inside. Not tired, he lit a candle. Orange-gray shadows leapt up on the wall, waving and flickering. Bard slept so hard that the light wouldn't wake him.

Firian bit the inside of his lip. Being angry with Tiev would do nothing but hurt him, unless he decided to turn it into motivation.

It was never too late for a little mental training.

Yanking out the dresser drawer, he rifled around for the book under his clothes. There it was. He cleared a space on the floor littered with clothes and wrappers and in the dim lamplight began to read. *Not like an Amir*, he assured himself. He still knew that defense was more important than the words of this book, but memorizing sections of the Sacred Scroll would give him more elite knowledge. When *he* met an Amir, he would know how they think, what advice they would give before they gave it, and God knew what else. He would strip their power with their own words. And if he found that it wasn't useful, he would just stop reading.

I hear your future is bright. Perhaps this will make it brighter.

He mouthed the words soundlessly as his eyes scanned the page. Sitting cross-legged on the floor, with the sounds of Bard murmuring above him, he shoved back the dark hair falling in front of his face. Concentrating hard on the words, he tried to memorize as fast as he read. The words slipped through like water, but he caught some of them. The burning of his focus, sheer force of will, would imprint the words in his mind.

The book began by speaking mainly of God and what He did among His people, called the Khelê, the main people group that the Tanyu had been set up to protect. Firian had learned about all that in World Events. Many of his classmates were Khelê. The Talent ran more strongly through that bloodline.

When their race began, they were a completely mish-mashed band of people who had survived a racial purging in Brithnem. They built a fortress named

Carradoc in Shifra, a swamp that wasn't far from Tánuil, and that was where they took the name "Khelê." Master Ardal, who taught World Events, said that meant "the divine human race" in an older language.

Apparently, the people of the Kingdom were tyrannical, controlling the lives of its people. The Khelê claimed that God had called *them* His chosen, instead of the Kingdom Dwellers, and launched a minority campaign against the Kingdom. After a bloody war, they managed to kill the evil king.

Somewhere around that time, the Exmorei was founded to defend the people and study the Sacred Scroll, which had been revealed to the Khelê only a year or two before. Later the Exmorei split into the Tanyu, who believed that defending the people was most important, and the Amir, who only studied the Scroll.

The Tanyuin mission had changed since those times, but their divine appointment and elite status as defenders had not. How could Amir not see that the Scroll was dead, history? Time had moved beyond it. But even the Keepers of the Western Kingdom were still guided by its principles.

What Tanyu has this advantage? Firian reminded himself, shifting on the floor as he hunched over the book. *The Head might have a copy, but he would be the only one.*

An image of himself sitting in *that* chair rose before him, almost spiritual. It glowed inside him. In the semi-darkness, he smiled. He would memorize the whole damn book if he had to. Anything that gave him an edge above Tiev, who now seemed smaller—the first step in a staircase to the top of the Academy.

A week spent in Tiev's room convinced Firian firmly of one thing.

They had prodded each other in their minds, of course. There, Tiev was still maddeningly cocky. Carefully, Firian observed his methods, how he practiced, what he did to be so powerful. His thought processes—at least as many as Firian could observe without getting caught—were only a little above average.

Unless there was a deep seed of unlimited Talent that he just couldn't see, there was nothing special about Tiev at all.

"Firian, stop!" Tiev snapped, glaring at him across a blank mindfield. The setting dissolved. "Go back to your own damn business!"

Firian clenched his teeth to stop a knee-jerk reply. Instead, he paraphrased the Scroll: "'*Strength is not just for the strong.*' I was hoping to learn something." He gave him a half-smile. He couldn't help it.

Tiev shook his head. "You do it again and I'll hurt you."

"Oh, okay. In *that* case...." He raised an eyebrow. They both knew Tiev couldn't make good on his threat. But Firian let him rant. It seemed to give him a fleeting sense of power.

The problem was, he *did* have power. *Why? Why did the Masters promote him and not me?*

The question bubbled up in his gut as he walked to his lesson, but he had to be careful. He didn't want his prison sentence doubled.

In Belik's little room, Firian faced the Master as they ran through drills. Firian ploughed through them with the force of a sprinter.

"Good," said Belik. "Again."

They went back to a scenario Firian had learned about in Strategy the day before. *"What if your opponent changes the location? Can you reorient yourself fast enough to believe and not believe?"* That was one of Master Asoka's favorite phrases: "believe and not believe."

Belik changed the background at a dizzying pace. Different countries, settings, sizes. One place was even upside down.

Firian continued to attack. For this drill, he couldn't change his weapon, but had to focus on what he could do given the new environment. All he had was a sword. Firian flew, reappeared, sank through the floor, ran forward, sword flashing...

"Enough," Belik said calmly. They both opened their eyes. Belik's face was impassive. *Does nothing impress him?* "That's good."

"I don't want to be good!" Firian cried, surprising himself.

Belik's eyes widened, curious. "Then what do you want?" he asked.

"I want to be the best."

Belik smiled with closed lips, a private smile. He wiped his glasses on his trousers and put them back on.

Surely he could see well enough into Firian's mind to know the question burning there. Tiev's face wouldn't leave him. "How long do you think it will take before I am promoted to Defender?" he asked.

"A couple of years. If you're lucky, two."

"Tiev got promoted when he was my age."

"You are not Tiev," the Master said decidedly, raising both eyebrows. "You know how to get better. Double your efforts if you're concerned."

Firian smiled. Belik didn't say that Tiev was better, and he would have if it were true.

"What?" Belik said, looking intently at him.

"Nothing."

"Is something funny?"

"No, Master Belik." He deadened his eyes and let his face fall back into a stoic position. He took a deep breath. "Nothing's funny."

Belik crossed his arms. "So you've finally figured it out, have you?"

Firian's heart leapt. He wasn't imagining it!

"Gore," Belik muttered, almost to himself. "I was wondering how long it would take." His eyes shot up to meet Firian's. "You were getting lazy." His stony face cracked into a smile. Behind the glasses, his eyes shone brightly. "And look how hard you practice now."

Firian didn't dare respond. They'd promoted Tiev to get *him* to work harder?

"Tiev's an idiot," Belik breathed.

"Then how...?" The question half-escaped him before he could stop it. *What about the burst of energy during the hall test?*

Belik tapped his own chest with a blunt finger. "Now that you know how to work hard, I can tell you. More people should have figured it out, but even...

others... took the promotion seriously." He laughed once, sarcastic. Running his tongue over his bottom lip distractedly, he said, "Tiev never should have met the Amir. Or the Head. It all got out of hand. At least you finally got there."

Relief, confusion, anger, and pride all swirled through Firian's body. His emotions culminated in a single word. "Why?"

The Master weighed his answer, leaning back in his chair. "You've got something," he said. He opened his mouth again, reconsidered, closed it. "Don't waste it."

20

FIRIAN

Does a man want influence? Does a man want power? Greatness is found in service and majesty in love. Remember a heritage of evil but a future of hope. This is the history that can be for every man. Therefore, do not exalt yourself above another. Rather, lift up your brother to see what you too have been given.

Firian had to read the passage four times to commit it to memory. It was getting late, so he jumped to his feet from where he had been lying on the floor and found a flint among the clutter on the dresser. He lit two candles and lay back down, flipping lazily to the second page of the Scroll. It was blank, but he had sealed a note on it with wax. The seal was already starting to chip off in soft, jagged edges. He waited until the wax from one of the candles was hot and clear enough to drip over it.

Congratulations. I knew you could do it! Now you'll be a warrior—a Tanyu—one of the bravest and smartest people in the world! I love you. I won't forget you. He didn't know why he had kept it. He wasn't sentimental like Bard. It just reminded him of who he was and who he could have been—nothing. He had fulfilled the vision that he'd set out for himself when he arrived. With Tiev and others trying to convince him otherwise, the note convinced him that his younger self would approve of his present one.

After pouring the hot wax over the sides of the note and blowing on it until it hardened, he closed the book and shoved it back in the drawer.

Without a knock, the door slammed open. Master Jovan stood huge in the doorway. Firian leapt up and stood straight.

"Come with me, Kess."

Heart pounding, Firian followed him as he strode quickly down the hall toward the stairs. They passed Bard coming back to the room. He stood almost flat against the wall as he saw them coming. His face creased anxiously and he looked to Firian for an explanation, but he didn't have one to give.

Heavily, Master Jovan descended the steps. Instead of turning left to the courtyard, he turned right, toward the wooden double doors leading out to Tánuil. Jovan opened the front door with one massive hand and led him outside.

An early evening wind cut dryly through the trees. It made Firian glad he had brought a shirt and shoes. The sky was still light blue in the west, but it quickly drained dark without the sun. They passed carts, shopkeepers heading home for the night, and wives lighting lanterns outside their doors.

Images flipped before Firian's mind. *Scroll... practice... class... I did visit Maya...* Nothing merited punishment, since he hadn't been caught visiting anyone or reading the Scroll, if that was an offense.

Jovan turned onto the path that led to the unused house that Firian passed sometimes when he met girls secretly. The stifling silence and unnatural combination of two parts of his life almost stole Firian's breath.

Firian followed Jovan inside the house. Embers from a large fireplace glowed brightly, but there was still barely enough smoky orange light to see by. A rough-hewn table with a bottle on it and two chairs sat off to one side. One of the chairs had a footstool. On the floor was a wooden box with parchment in it. A polished bronze ewer hung on the wall along with three swords of different makes and sizes; a bright stuffed bird and an urn made of blue stone glittered in the firelight. Through an open door on the left, Firian saw a cot sitting on the hardwood floor and an immense shield inlaid with gold and pearls leaned in a corner. There were no windows.

"Close the door," the Master growled.

Firian obeyed.

"Sit."

He sat. Jovan did not.

"I see you think you have Talent. Others think the same. Do you have more Talent than Defender Tiev?" The Master fixed him with a glare, forcing up his scarred forehead to open his eyes wider.

Back to this, are we? Still, it was a loaded question. Anything he said would probably get him in trouble, so why not say the truth? "Yes, Master Jovan."

Jovan didn't move for a moment, then he hummed deeply and walked toward the room with the cot. Instead of going inside, he reached in around the corner and pulled out an amber drinking glass. He picked up the bottle on the table by Firian and poured its dark contents into the glass. "Then have something to drink," he said, offering it to Firian.

Firian took the cup. Jovan hadn't poured himself any. Still, he knew better than to ask what it was.

"Drink!" Jovan ordered.

Firian had no choice. It tasted like ale. It could even have been from the Old Pub. Jovan stood looming silent before him, so Firian just drank obediently and waited.

Firian Rising

FIRIAN WOKE up in chilly darkness. Small rocks dug into his back and arms as he rolled over. Squinting into the dark, he made out black trunks rising around him. Pine needles rasped, but otherwise there was no sound. His head felt heavy and his thoughts ran sluggish. Had he fallen asleep there? *Did I get drunk or something?* He didn't often have alcohol, preferring a clear mind, and he only remembered having one drink in front of Master Jovan...

Master Jovan! He must have put him here. But why? *I said I was better than Tiev.*

Shivers ran up and down the skin of Firian's back. He wasn't kicked out of the Academy, was he? Bard's voice rang in his head—all the warnings, all the ways to get kicked out, all the things he shouldn't have done.

Fighting with Tiev wouldn't be enough to merit...

No. There was only a small number of Tanyu in the world and he was one of the rising champions—or at least he was good enough to fight in a war if they needed him. And they'd already given him a punishment for that fight. Unless they'd learned about his Scroll, he couldn't imagine anything he'd done since to get kicked out. His heart thumped dangerously and he ran his hands over his arms to warm them.

Then he felt something attached to his left forearm with rough string. Yanking it off, he found it was a small, folded piece of parchment. He unfolded it and held it an inch before his face, but it only looked gray. Something was written on it. He bared his teeth. The darkness maddened him, crushed him.

He had to see.

Looking up, the moonless stars were too dim. He'd have to make a fire. He remembered putting a piece of flint in his pocket earlier that day. He felt in his pockets for what he had. Nothing. Master Jovan must have taken everything out. He swallowed on a dry mouth and blindly began to dig a shallow pit with his fingernails to put dry brush into.

Within ten minutes he'd built a little fire. Instinctively, he kept it low in case someone unwanted should find him. He grabbed the parchment and held it near the flame.

Come back after two weeks. Train until then.

His relief made him realize how hard he'd been breathing. Even his hands had been shaking.

It's only training. He wasn't kicked out.

This must be a physical survival test. He blew out a breath. A wilderness test showed that the Masters acknowledged his ability to the point of considering him for a physical mission.

Between his panic and the aftereffects of the drug, sleep pressed down heavily on him. So he ran his fingers through his hair to get the dirt off, burned the note, covered the fire, and went back to sleep until the sun rose.

IT WAS Firian's third night in the wilderness. He lay on his back by a smokeless fire. Deep heat seeped over his right side but his left was dark and blue and cold.

Since no bears or tree cats had appeared for the last two nights, he wasn't as concerned about them as he had been. After all, he'd had no idea where he was at first. Peering up through the black web of pine needles, he saw dotted blue and white stars. He blinked his cold eyes. The fire died down slowly to glowing black and gold embers.

This wasn't so bad, even without much food. Physical training with Jovan was harder. In fact, the time alone allowed him to exercise both his mind and his body as much as he liked. Sinking into nothing, he leisurely searched around in his mind. Before reaching far, he felt the faint buzz of Sentries.

His eyes snapped open. That was odd. The Sentries weren't guarding him, but they were blocking someone's access to the Unreal close by. Slowly, he sat up and squinted into the space between the gray trunks. He couldn't see far. Feeling again in his mind, he hit something.

He tensed. Something was very close.

A rattle of dead pine needles and he was on his feet. He had no weapons. He took a steady breath. Should he build up the fire so he could see or would that alert the person to his presence? *Safer to let it be.* He peered harder into the darkness, slowly making his way away from the spot.

Someone wrapped a thick, hairy arm around his neck from behind. Without a thought, Firian jerked his elbow up into the man's nose. The man cried in surprise and yanked his arm back. Firian pivoted to see a stolid, husky man with thinning hair that looked black in the dimness. Blood from his nose ran down his hands as he bent over in pain. The bone hadn't gone all the way into his brain.

Firian's legs suddenly buckled. Another man had kicked him hard in the back of the knees with a boot. He crumpled in pain. Regaining himself, Firian grabbed savagely at the man's legs to bring him down but he couldn't reach, so he jumped back up again, ignoring the jabbing pain in his legs.

Five more large men jumped within the reach of the ember-light. Three gripped knives in their right hands. Firian struck out madly, rolled, broke a man's finger to kick the knife away. He hurled himself toward the knife. Hitting the ground, he grabbed a rock to toss behind him in a man's face. *Where's the gory knife?* He felt madly in the darkness, fingers scrabbling over loose dirt.

But then they were all on top of him, smothering. He couldn't breathe, struggled to move, mouth open, too hot, gasping, no air...

He tried blindly to pry himself out from underneath them all but they held him down harder the more he struggled. His flattened, ragged lungs burned, sucking at air that wouldn't come.

Now? he pleaded. *But I'm not a Master... not respected... I was never...*

"TANYU!" a man yelled from close above him, grating into his ear. Firian was lying on his back with his hands bound underneath him. Piercing pain cut into his wrists.

He pried his eyelids open but couldn't see anything beyond the slightly darker figures of the men standing above him. Breathing shallow, he felt something slide sideways down his face. Spit.

"Walk!" One of them dug his boot into Firian's side.

They already knew he was awake. If he resisted, they'd beat him, and neither would get what they wanted. He couldn't fight this many from his back, so he trundled up onto his feet. From behind him, a man grabbed the end of the rope tying his wrists. Firian writhed his hands, trying to ease the pain of the sharp cords. Pebbles and dirt fell out of the deep grooves in his skin. It was useless.

Mind over body. The mind makes what is and is not. Firian only used his physical senses enough to see where to step. The rest of his powers retreated into the Unreal. His attackers, who didn't speak, even among themselves, had set up a rudimentary Sentry on his mind, but he broke it without a second thought. They must have known it, but still they didn't say anything or retaliate.

He threw himself into the Unreal until the sound of a horse pulled him out.

He came to himself among five large horses. Three of the men mounted silently. He clenched his swollen hands as his captor led him to one of the horses. They were going to drag him.

Almost automatically, he flung himself backward onto the ground, biting back a yell as he landed on his hands. The man holding the rope flew on top of him. Firian put up his knee and caught him in the gut. His captor wheezed forcefully and rolled to the side, still clutching the end of the line.

The three who had already mounted jumped off again and attacked. From his back, Firian kicked the shortest man in the jaw. His teeth cracked together as he stumbled backward. A horse screamed and reared.

Someone pulled Firian's hair from the roots and yanked his head back. With a metallic ring a blade lay across Firian's straining neck. "Be still or die."

Firian's knees fell to the ground.

"Now stand."

He stood slowly.

Four panting men glowered around him. One of them couldn't resist slicing his arm lightly with a dagger.

Firian gritted his teeth in a closed mouth. The motion moved a tendon in his neck against the dagger.

"Tanyu can run, can't they? We'll see. Otherwise you'll be going backward."

The man holding his slack rope walked deliberately to one of the horses and tied him tightly to the baggage on the saddle. Once he found the knot strong enough, he came back to Firian with a savage light in his eyes.

Firian's muscles went taut. The dagger nicked his skin as his neck muscles contracted. If he only knew why they wanted him, he'd know how soon they intended to kill him. The man's stare left little room for doubt that they ultimately did intend to kill him.

Firian heard another scrape of metal on metal. *Is it now?* He struggled to think of a counterattack.

"Stop! Don't touch him!" a man cried to his left.

"I said not yet," hissed the man with the rope.

A knife was sheathed.

Not yet.

"Where's the Academy?"

Firian only sat up to preserve whatever dignity he had left.

Blood streamed from his nose and his head pounded, crashing in his ears. His shins and knees were ripped and swollen from the run and now his feet were asleep because of how tightly they had bound his ankles once they finally stopped riding. Rocks pierced his back when he spun to the ground, unable to keep upright for a moment. One shoulder was dislocated and his entire body ached from bruises.

He swallowed and tasted blood like copper.

A man he'd heard called Den brought out a bowl of water and held it in the light of a single candle, just out of his reach. Firian stared disdainfully, too tired to do anything else.

"I'm not thirsty." Even the lie felt thick, but satisfying enough to keep his spirit up for another moment. At least they wouldn't have the victory of seeing him beg.

"Where's the Academy? We already know the area, and all we need is you to confirm it. You aren't helping anyone by keeping the secret. There is no secret. You're only making a gory fool of yourself."

Firian had no reason to tell them where it was. The Academy was his life, all that he had worked for. Everything and everyone he cared about was there. If he betrayed it, he might as well kill himself. So he just shut his eyes again and began to sink into the comfort of the Unreal, but even that didn't block out all of the pain. There was too much of it. But it helped.

Someone struck him.

"Where is the Academy?"

He had to choose some dying words, some battle cry to sum up his life. Urgency pressured him even in the Unreal, where he was suspended in darkness like an ocean.

The Academy will never be taken. I choose death.

I will tell you nothing, because I'm Firian Kess, the Tanyu.

A man screamed, a hideous sound.

Firian's swollen eyes sprang open. The room—or... cave?—was too dark to see much of what was happening, but he could make out that all the men who had gathered around him had scrambled to their feet, facing the blackness. One lay face down on the ground. Then another.

"Come with me," whispered someone behind him, who grabbed Firian's wrists and sliced the twine off them and off his ankles. The voice seemed familiar.

Firian leapt to his feet and immediately collapsed. After a second of red darkness, he climbed to his feet again.

"You can walk," said his helper in the darkness. "Follow me."

He could hardly see the moving figure in front of him, but he stumbled and followed. He didn't care if it was a trap.

After they had gone some distance, out of the cave and into the forest, the man guiding him began to talk to him, steadily asking simple questions.

"What's your name?"

Firian didn't answer. He wasn't in an answering mood.

"I'm here to help you. What forest is this?"

"Esmeroth."

"Who are the three Keepers of Brithnem?"

"Cúron, Merian, and Atael."

"What's your name?"

"Firian Kess, a Tanyu of the Academy," he said. He knew it was a fit of dying eloquence, but he didn't care. He'd earned those words.

"How did you get here?"

Firian told him a very simple version of the story, and then ran out of breath and couldn't speak for another five minutes.

When did I lose my shoes? The sky was gray and the air was cool with dawn. The green tree moss stood out in sharp relief against the trunks. It was almost peaceful.

The man led him to a large horse. Firian didn't have much experience with riding horses, but happily he didn't have to know what he was doing. His guide helped him up behind him and galloped away.

Scenery passed hazily by him—gray pillars of trees and whirring stones and grasses. *Wish I could ride by myself,* he thought. But it didn't seem to matter very much after a few minutes. He wouldn't have had the strength even if he had been given his own horse.

Other riders rode up alongside them. Since they didn't attack, Firian assumed they were friendly.

Slowly, slowly, everything went black.

A VOICE SPOKE. Firian felt as though he were under a great depth of water, hearing someone above the surface. "Fir? Firian?"

His whole body ached, destroying any will to move or respond.

"Firian?" He finally recognized Bard's voice, full of bottled panic.

His breath became hot as something obscured his mouth. A hand? Dimly, he realized that Bard was checking to see if he was still alive. Firian moved his head just a little. That should confirm his test.

A few seconds later, the light touch of a blanket fell across him. It fell on bare skin in unexpected places. His clothes must have torn.

"Do you want me to stay with you?" Bard asked, the words getting louder as Firian's consciousness surged toward the surface.

He wished it wouldn't. With consciousness came pain. "Yes." Only the hiss of the final letter whistled between his teeth. When he tried to open his eyes, he found that one was swollen shut. He could only see the bottom of the bunk above him. Easing his eye closed, he prayed for sleep. Bard would leave soon, maybe get a doctor.

A creaking door. Many muted footsteps. The sense of new nearness.

"He'll be fine." A cursory statement to Bard. The voice sounded like Belik's.

Someone, neither Belik nor Bard, moved the blanket away and lifted Firian's heavy arm. Some kind of rough fabric had been tied around his bicep. A stabbing pain screamed through his shoulder as his arm was raised higher. Firian twisted convulsively away. The strong hands placed his arm back down on the mattress.

"Any broken bones?" Belik again.

"Not from what I can see. His shoulder is dislocated. Bruises. Lacerations." He felt expert hands probing along his other arm, his abdomen, his legs. Firian gasped as the man found all the deep bruises. "No broken bones. He should remain in bed for at least three days, and I doubt he'll be ready for any kind of physical training for twelve to fourteen days after that."

Firian hated being useless, but he had no energy to protest. He knew his body wouldn't let him stand, much less train.

"Good. Thank you, doctor," Belik said.

"I'll come back today to dress the wounds."

"What happened to him?" Bard asked quietly. Firian had almost forgotten he was there.

"Just be glad it didn't happen to you," said Belik.

Even hazy, blind, and in pain, Firian knew vaguely that he hadn't answered the question.

More footsteps, now retreating. The feather's-weight of the blanket draped over him again, and he fell asleep almost instantly.

21

KIRIA

After Daelon's lesson, Kiria went up to the second floor of the Amiran Academy, to the holy place. More often over the past few weeks, she had come to say prayers. A Keeper's main duty was to God, after all. The Amir advised them so they didn't forget his words. Atty's coronation reminded her of the privilege and responsibility of being a Keeper. She hadn't missed a session since Atty's first.

She rounded the last corner of the claustrophobic stone staircase and stepped into the upper room. Smaller religious ceremonies occurred there. Once a year, on Dedication Day, all the Keepers and their families fasted all day and came into this space at nightfall. She remembered that, as a child, she was struck by the somber mood in the palace that day as they considered the seriousness of straying from God's will. But the night was about mercy, rebirth, rededication. The celebration took place on the day Mon Párinath was completed, the palace built on the ruins of the first. A new piece of music was written each year for the occasion and Brithnem's most talented musicians performed it in that upper room.

Normally, the Amir preserved an attitude of silence there, and could come and go as they pleased. Young Amiran students often sat there for hours, memorizing the Sacred Scroll, chanting it to themselves under their breath. On certain days, anyone from Brithnem was welcome to come and pray.

She gazed up at the vaulted ceiling, painted blue, a darker blue than the color on the flag. Strips of gold outlined the architectural segments of the dome. It almost looked like a diagram of the night sky.

As soon as she got back to the palace, she would study her lesson. Rather than dry information, the lessons now seemed like a way to whet her mind like a knife. The more she learned, the more she could rule with wisdom and justice, and fulfill the oath she would make in the Main one day. The Scroll, the laws, they were like advisors or friends that would prevent her from making mistakes.

Finally, she had found her purpose. When she was a little girl, she had wanted to be Keeper. Now, she knew what it would take, and she welcomed the challenge.

Sneaking away with Jori had lost its luster. Now it left her feeling hollow and guilty. But it was hard to explain to him that she didn't want to shirk her responsibilities. Still, he seemed to understand why she didn't spend as much time with him.

She murmured a prayer and stood in reverent silence for a moment before turning to leave. The holy place was so peaceful. Why didn't she spend more time there?

Everyone could only reach the second floor by one of two tiny spiral staircases accessible only from outside. The first floor was reserved for Amiran study cells and bedchambers. There was no access to the holy place from inside either of those. She went down the staircase and breathed in the fresh air.

Peace seemed to follow her into the light outside. At this moment, her Beauty seemed more integrated into who she was. It was always better when it began inside.

She passed several servants and Amir, all of whom turned to watch her, as she wandered dreamily toward the ocean. It churned and crashed a rhythm in the far distance. From the edge of the palace grounds, she had the best view of the bay.

She squinted. That was odd. There were more ships moored than usual. She looked them over carefully, but she didn't recognize many of them. They didn't look like they came from Brithnem or Phlaxtin or any of the other nations that sometimes traded with them.

Whose ships are those?

A muted shout filtered up from the port. Another. Her heart beat faster. The note of urgency in those shouts sent a shock through her fingers.

She needed to find someone. At best, there was a disturbance at the harbor. At worst...

She broke into a run back toward the castle. "There's an attack!" she shouted. "Attack at the harbor!"

Something slammed into her shoulder. She pitched backward, pivoting as she fell. The ground rose up and crashed into her chest, her cheek.

Confused, she looked up and saw a thick arrow sticking out of her. She felt sick. She couldn't breathe, and then her breath came too fast. Her hands started shaking, but she still couldn't scream. Pain started forcing gorge up her throat.

She saw the next one coming. It arched toward the sun and rushed at her, whistling in the air, getting bigger and bigger. She kicked back to avoid it, but it pierced the meat of her thigh, pinning her to the ground at an odd angle.

Her vision narrowed to a blackening circle. Warm liquid from her shoulder flowed across her neck onto the ground.

Above her, eyes appeared, red-rimmed and frantic. Daelon's face.

"Kiria! My God!" He knelt next to her and started tearing her skirt. She dimly wondered what he was doing. He tore the dress all the way up to her hip and she felt his hands on the upper part of her leg. His touch had never made her uncomfortable before, but she cringed now. Something tightened over her upper thigh. Fabric. A tourniquet.

Her voice came back in a sobbing scream.

Daelon took her hand. "You're going to be all right," he said. "You'll be all right. Hold on. Kiria, hold on. They're coming."

And he began to pray.

22

FIRIAN

Firian could see his breath in clouds as he stretched out his legs and leaned back in his chair in World Events class. His injuries had healed, although he still had scars on his shins. He'd passed the "training" and, apparently pleased with his loyalty, the Masters gave him even more work to do. Now he rode horses regularly. He and Bard had been trying to figure out what his mission would be, but the scenarios felt limitless.

Pretending to suppress a quick yawn, he shut his eyes and briefly found Maya in the Unreal to wink at her. She smiled at him from across the room. A little warmth filled his core. He sat forward and refocused on the lesson.

"This morning," said Master Ardal, "the Kepress Kiria Arioc was brutally attacked by a band of Torithians who managed to get onto the grounds of the palace, Mon Párinath. The details are still unclear, but our sources say she'll probably live. Some say that a Tanyu ought to have been there to keep her safe, but it has been many years since Tanyu were stationed in Brithnem." His straight nose wrinkled. "The Keepers prefer the help of the Amir, who clearly were not able to help her, although she was reportedly near their living quarters at the time. Many of the threats on the Keepers have been directed at her and the heir to the First Line specifically. The Torithians apparently view them as the weakest links in the lines of succession. This event, of course, seriously affects our relations with the Western Kingdom."

Interesting. I wonder what Brithnem's move will be now.

As he tried to catch the Master's eye to see if his mission would be related to this attack, his mind whirled with possibilities. Perhaps they'd send more troops to the battlefront? Get more aggressive? Suggest that Tanyu fight in their war? Firian would do all three, if he were a Keeper of the Western Kingdom, one of the only titles more prestigious than a Tanyu. He would make them pay for harming her.

Weren't the Tanyu supposed to protect Brithnem? Yet they hadn't gotten involved in their war against the Torithians. Maybe he didn't know the Kepress, but he knew Bard, and wished he could protect his homeland from those pirates.

And why did the Torithians target Kiria Arioc specifically? It made better strategic sense to get rid of Ataei, who was new and had no battle experience or heir.

But Master Ardal simply shifted to the next bit of news and the rest of the class gave no hint that they'd get to see war action any time soon.

Belik's class was next. After saying goodbye to Maya in one of the side hallways, he headed to the familiar blank room, clapping his hands against his legs to warm them.

Belik's door was open when he arrived and the Master was standing. With something like nervous energy, he shifted his weight when he saw Firian.

"We did it," he said in a husky voice.

Something in his tone made Firian stop short. "What?"

"I got you a mission."

The words echoed around his head, seductive. He turned them over and looked at all sides. Firian's hands nearly shook with excitement and his heart pounded thickly. *A mission.* Belik look on with pride as he puzzled out his meaning. "What is the mission? Master Belik?" He hastily added the proper title he too often left off. He knew he was ready for a mission, but he'd thought Belik wouldn't allow him to go until he could reach the Second Level of the Unreal or something equally impossible.

Belik's eyes sparkled. "The Kepress was attacked this morning. Torithians."

Firian nodded, almost afraid to break the silence.

"The Keepers called for someone to keep her safe, so we're sending you to Brithnem."

A confusing mix of exhilaration and disappointment filled him. He wanted to fight, to go into the enemy's territory and save someone, or kill someone. He hadn't thought about following a princess around. But her life *was* in danger. And it was a great honor. Master Jovan had been a bodyguard to the King of Charäkhnem for several years. At least the danger suggested some action, didn't it?

"So—a bodyguard?"

"Firian," Belik said, lowering his chin and his voice in warning, "I had to convince the Head to choose you. This task puts you in a prime position, if you do it right."

"When do I leave?"

"Tomorrow," he said simply. "We need time to get supplies together. Master Gerand will go too."

The *katah* teacher? "Do I need her?" Firian asked. A chaperone was an affront to his independence.

"The Master'll speak to the Keepers when you get there, as I understand," he explained, then raised an eyebrow. "Of course you need her. Don't doubt a Master, especially me. If you do, you're not fit for this."

"As you would have it, Master Belik."

The Master nodded and then cast him a softer glance. "You want a drink tonight, Defender?"

"Yes," Firian answered, too abruptly.

Defender. He couldn't help but smile. It was about damn time. Masters couldn't look down on him from such a height and Tiev couldn't look down on him at all.

"I'll see you then. Go to your room and prepare for the journey."

All his trials up to that point had been deliberate to get him here, to be an emissary for the Academy, recognized as one of the best up and coming Tanyuin warriors. He wanted to shout with joy, but instead calmly bowed his head and left the room.

Later that night Master Belik and Firian went to the Old Pub. The Master immediately demanded two large dark ales of Hyrum, the proprietor, and sat down at a little table in the corner. As the Master cleaned his glasses between fingers of his black shirt, Firian thought the place looked a little too cramped and grimy to house Belik. For all their stealth, Tanyu had an enormous presence.

"I knew you'd be good for a mission once you shut up and practiced," Belik said, breaking the silence. A smile laced his words but not his stoic mouth. "Maybe even good for more."

"Thank you, Master Belik," said Firian. Not every Defender had drinks with Masters, so he knew to be as respectful as possible.

The ale appeared and they each took a mug. Belik didn't offer any more conversation (or explanation of "more") but only sat drinking thoughtfully. His small, dark eyes seemed to recede into him.

Since Firian didn't know what to say, he remained quiet as well. At least this drink was more enjoyable than Master Jovan's had been.

Belik flicked two rough fingers at Hyrum without turning his eyes. The proprietor, who had been rubbing down the tables with a greasy rag, returned behind the counter to fetch the order.

Belik spoke again. "We'll tell you what to do when you're there," he said. "I'll be watching your progress. Hopefully they'll let you out of sight of the palace." He spat the last words with surprising vitriol. Some old grievance. "They know we can get the job done, but they don't trust Tanyu like they used to." He finished his tankard in one long swig. Hyrum clanked the next two ales down on the table.

"As you would have it," Firian replied. Now wasn't the time for all his questions, so he'd have to be selective. Perhaps he should cast a broad net. "Is there anything else I should know?" he asked, unsure of how much others in the pub should hear but wanting to get as much information as he could.

"No," Belik said. He took another long sip, then his eyes slowly turned outward again and he looked Firian meaningfully in the face. "You deserve this mission, Firian, after how you... handled things," he said, continuing to look at him, as though he expected a reply.

Master Belik had not mentioned Firian's three tortuous nights before except to commend him vaguely once or twice. Pride swelled in him. "Thank you," he said. He flexed his feet up and down under the table.

Without mental training to talk about, they ran out of topics and spent most of the night in silence. Firian drank three mugs and Belik drank five. Neither even began to slur. Firian couldn't afford to have his head ache on the first morning of his mission.

Afterward, Master Belik led him to the blacksmith's where they picked up a long knife and a belt with a sheath. Firian wrapped it around himself and tested out the blade. Learners couldn't carry more than a small boot knife, so Firian had never had anything larger, though Jovan had taught him the skills.

They walked back together along the dark road to the Academy looming in the distance like a black cliff of rock. At the walkway to the main doors, Belik stopped and turned to him. In the darkness, he looked like a living shadow. Firian stood at attention.

After a pause, he said, "Remember to do anything we tell you."

The Master had turned to him so deliberately, he had expected something more profound. This was common sense. "Of course, Master Belik."

Lightening his grim manner slightly, Belik added, "I hear the girl is beautiful."

Firian imagined rather than saw his knowing glance. Belik was no fool and knew Firian better than most people. He knew that Firian had been sneaking off with girls for years. Firian grunted noncommittally in reply.

"Enjoy yourself," Belik continued, "but don't get caught up. Always focus on the mission. We already have your supplies. Be ready to leave with the sun." With that, Belik left Firian to return to the Academy alone. The Master turned off the road to his house. It was odd to see him going into a house.

As Firian walked back through the Academy, with its huge stone pillars and staircases, high-roofed ceiling and fountain, his thoughts refused to settle but seemed to fly around in fragments that made it difficult to believe that his time had actually come. Only last night, he had known nothing of his mission, and now he knew what he had been working toward all this time.

But now he knew. His mission, although shrunken now that it was finite, held great importance. It also held the potential for more. Firian hadn't been working in the dark, solitary hours of the morning and night for years just to protect a princess. No, this was a mere stepping stone, but a crucial one.

If they had only given him more than one day to prepare, he could have told Tiev... Maybe his sudden disappearance would work just as well.

He topped the stairs and walked down to his room. Bard was asleep when he entered, already snuffling to himself with one arm slung over the edge of the bed. He would tell him about it in the morning. Now that he had the mission he had waited for, the room looked more comfortable than it had in a long time.

23

KIRIA

She heard someone say, "No one can see the Kepress."

"Who is it?" Kiria asked. After staying in her room for a week, alone except for the doctor and visits from her parents, she was anxious to see someone else. She was too weak to be very good company, but hours without human voices grated on her. It felt as though no one else existed. The silence gave her too much time to focus on the pain.

The guard didn't seem to have heard her. "Who is it?" she asked again.

"Amir Daelon," he replied.

Images flooded over her against her will. Searing pain and the look of panic in his face. She was struggling in her own blood with the thick arrow standing upright in her shoulder, he was ripping her dress, applying a tourniquet, and praying... She remembered hearing him pray before she lost consciousness.

She hadn't spoken to him since. "Please let him in."

"My orders do not permit me."

"Whose orders?"

He ignored her.

"The Keepers?" she snapped. Never had she felt so helpless. Just as she was beginning to feel she could be a strong leader, she was cut down and everyone started treating her like a helpless child. Rage and disappointment filled her. "May I at least see him? Can you open the door?"

To this, the guard reluctantly consented. The heavy door swung open to reveal Daelon, immaculate in his high-necked robe. He bowed his head. "My Kepress," he began. "You seem much improved." His eyes, darkened with bags, rested on the sling holding her shoulder in place.

"Of course, especially since the last time you saw me," she said, shifting. Burning pain flashed along her left arm. Her voice sounded loud and dry after such a long silence.

"Has the Second Keeper informed you that we have sent for a Tanyuin bodyguard?" he said, very formally.

"She has," she said. She wished they could just use one of the palace guards instead, since the Tanyu were such a touchy subject with both Daelon and his mother Chetana. There was some bitterness there, bad blood. She didn't want to stir up any old wounds.

He released a breath. "My Kepress, when I found you..."

"Don't," she cut him off. "Let's not talk about it."

He looked at the ground. In the slit of his eyes, she saw tears. If he hadn't come just at that moment... Without warning, tears welled up in her eyes too, hot and stinging. They shared a thick silence.

"It's too quiet here," she said. "I'd like you to come and talk to me sometimes."

"It's true that only one voice is wearisome," he said with a small smile. She recognized the line from the Scroll. "I'd be glad to keep you company. I could resume our lessons." The thought seemed to cheer him up.

She nodded, but the attack had dampened her enthusiasm.

As she'd lain in bed the past few days, there were times when she felt ready to hobble into the Main and become a Keeper that very minute. She'd proven her mettle, her survivor spirit. But, other times, anxiety choked her mind, sending it spiraling into darkness and fear. She couldn't know the right decision to make. Even as a Keeper, she wouldn't wield real power. Cúron would take care of everything, and the Amir too—thanks to Atty. Every halting step she took would please some and anger others. She could never be sure that she was making the right choice. The very thought made her feel trapped...

And then she would breathe.

"The Second Keeper, Merian Arioc," one of the door guards announced, as her mother appeared at the open door. And she wasn't alone. Chetana was with her, striding purposefully by her side up to Kiria's bed. It always amazed Kiria that Chetana and Daelon were related. She was martial; he was academic. She was dark-skinned; he was much lighter. They both were smart and composed, proud of the Amir and the Khelê, but that was the extent of the similarity Kiria could see.

Her mother swept to the side of the bed and knelt down. "Kiria, how are you feeling this morning?"

"A little better."

Her mother took her right hand and kissed it. "I'm so glad! Our troops killed or chased off the last Torithians this morning. They won't come to our harbor anymore." She smiled as though that were the end of it, the soothing end of a fairy tale.

Standing by her son, Chetana chimed in. "But there is still a threat to you."

Daelon looked at his mother in surprise.

Another threat? The idea made Kiria feel sick. She moved her injured leg a fractional amount, trying it out. The burning pain made her grit her teeth.

Her mother chastised the Amir with a look, as though the pain had been her fault, but Chetana didn't flinch. Even a Keeper couldn't intimidate her. "Our sources say that there might be someone inside the palace, so we've doubled your guards."

"Yes," her mother said quickly. "We have six guards outside your room now, so you're perfectly safe. And I already told you that we've called for a personal bodyguard, who will be here in less than two weeks."

"But why are they targeting me?" It seemed odd that the Torithians weren't threatening everyone in the palace.

Her mother cast her eyes to the far end of the room, clearly uncomfortable. "They haven't said, but it must have to do with your Beauty. I don't see any other reason."

Chetana nodded her agreement. She had a military background, so she would probably understand their rationale. "It would end the Second Line, the female line, and they would have your legendary Beauty to do with as they wanted. It's a first step." She said the words with perfect composure.

Her throat tightened. "Do they think I'm weak?" It felt strange having everyone croon over her, guarding her, reassuring her, looking at her. The last thing Kiria wanted was pity, so she sat up, trying not to flinch with the pain. She'd bring up her thoughts about the Tanyu now, even with the Amir here. It wasn't appealing to have someone else fussing over her. "I'm not sure I want a bodyguard. We can use guards from the palace, can't we? Until the threat is dealt with?"

"She has a point," said Chetana. "We have excellent guards here. Even I have some experience—"

"The Tanyu are the best warriors in the world," her mother explained, looking only at her, as though Kiria hadn't heard it before. "And we need all the guards here at the palace for the war, now that it has come to our shores..." She looked abstracted for a moment. "A Tanyu can protect you single-handedly as you move to a safe location."

"Wait, I'm leaving the palace?" Kiria cried.

"It's only temporary," said her mother. "I don't want you to leave either, but it's the best choice for now. As soon as we eliminate the threat, you'll come home." She smiled weakly.

"My Keeper," Chetana prompted. Her face was like thunder, restrained and angry. "Do we know which Tanyu is coming to take away your daughter?" The question was pointed.

Her mother clearly didn't appreciate her advisor's tone, but she didn't correct her. "Yes, I know the name."

Daelon paled as he waited. His demeanor made him seem many years younger. Why should he be so anxious?

Her mother's hesitation showed that she knew the names wouldn't be well received. Kiria's stomach twisted. Chetana and her mother were rarely at such odds.

"They are Defender Kess and... Master Gerand."

"Gerand! You know you can't trust my sister!" Chetana burst out. But Daelon loosened his shoulders, clearly relieved.

"Chetana!" her mother snapped, rising to her feet, suddenly a Keeper. "The Tanyu won't let anything happen to my daughter. They have sworn to protect us. I know that the Amir and Tanyu have a rocky history, but you have to put your prejudice aside."

Their history had been more than rocky if Daelon's lessons were right. He lived by a code of scrupulous honesty, so Kiria had no reason to doubt him. The two groups worked together at times, but individuals within both organizations perpetuated an ever-growing feud. She'd even heard rumors of a militant Amiran group whose main target were Tanyu, although that was hard to picture. The opposite was much easier to conceive. Maybe that was just a rumor.

Chetana drew herself up. "It isn't—"

"I know your feelings about Master Gerand. She will not be the one taking Kiria alone. *Defender Kess* will be her bodyguard, and I assume you have nothing against him!"

Chetana's eyes flashed, but she said nothing.

Her mother turned back to Kiria. "All we want is to keep you safe," she said. "And we're doing that the best way we know how."

Kiria nodded. If she had doubts before, Chetana's reaction made them worse. But it was true—Tanyu really were supposed to be the best—so she would have to trust her mother and the others who made the decision to send for them. Honestly, she was curious to meet Defender Kess, the man who could stir up such radically different reactions.

24

FIRIAN

The journey to Brithnem passed silently and uneventfully. They stayed off the main roads and bypassed towns whenever possible. Twice Master Gerand sent Firian into a village to buy food and supplies, but otherwise they fled from the sight of people like fugitives. The fewer people recognized them, the better. They could blend in if they wanted to, hide in a crowd, as long as no one knew their faces. That was a helpful ability to have on a mission like this.

The mountains harbored no ghosts; the road hid no robbers. Yet they set up a watch rotation at night regardless.

Now, almost three weeks later, they had to be getting close to Brithnem.

He pictured the map he had studied right before he left. They must be riding through the forest called Á Quihilmar—an old name that meant "Of Gray." Several passages in the Scroll referenced it. Bored, he tried to remember some of them, but they wouldn't come. The monotony of this trip was getting to him. Still, he knew that this forest meant they were getting close.

His horse nickered and tossed his head. The trees thinned. Firian caught a whiff of salt on the air and sat up straighter.

The trees ended and he saw, far away, the falling sun glinting on the surface of the sea. It shone like metal, blazing where it melded with the sky. Black against the shining ocean, thick turrets rose high above the small buildings clustering around it, spreading out evenly beyond the wall around the city. Raewhith could fit inside the city walls many times. And this was the city that had called for him.

Gerand rode up next to him and nodded toward Brithnem. For a glorious second, he had forgotten about her, and the gesture irritated him. Firian put up with Gerand's arrogance all the way over the mountains and he didn't want to have it interrupt this moment now. He turned away from her and looked back at the city.

They rode through stretches of farmland before they reached the wall. It soared above them, ancient, but without the primal power of the Academy. This wall had seen war, but it was still light, almost graceful. Firian was surprised no one had conquered it.

They trotted up to what looked like the main gate, since it was the biggest and had the most elaborate metal designs. Six men stood guard. Two of them came forward as they approached.

"State your business with Brithnem," one said.

Gerand answered, "We are Tanyu of the Academy. My name is Master Gerand, and this is Defender Firian Kess. Your Keepers summoned us to come to Mon Párinath as soon as possible on a matter of security."

One of the four guards remaining at the gate whispered to his neighbor.

"Very well," said the first guard. "We've been expecting you."

Four men hauled open the great gate for them. Firian kicked his horse with his heel, and she lumbered forward. The cobblestone road leading up to the wall continued into the city. The simple stone houses lining the roads reminded him of Tánuil. In the distance, the palace rose, majestic.

A man in a blue-gray robe came down the street toward them. "Welcome to Brithnem," he said loudly. "I am Amir Parohim, advisor to the First Keeper." *An Amir.* He looked about the same as Firian had pictured. His long, high-collared robes wouldn't allow him to run; his face was pale, creased with study, not with work; his hands were the same, long and pale, without callouses. His slicked-back hair reminded him of boys in Tánuil when they courted a girl for the first time.

Parohim turned to Master Gerand. "You must be Amir Chetana's sister." His face was not as carefree as his voice.

Gerand's sister is an Amir? The revelation made Firian uncomfortable, though he couldn't pinpoint why.

"I am," she said shortly. "Shall we go to the palace?"

Parohim ignored her, turning instead to Firian. "Is this your first time in Brithnem, Defender Kess?"

"Yes, it is," Firian said.

"Then let's walk to Mon Párinath together," said the Amir, gesturing to a woman who stood nearby. They all dismounted and she led the horses to a stable attached to the city wall. "They'll be well taken care of," Parohim said, leading them along one of the streets to the right.

The city was alive with people talking, trading, walking, washing, and even singing. All of them looked so strange to him. For years, Firian had recognized almost everyone around him. Now he saw no familiar face. It encouraged him to think that if he didn't recognize them, they wouldn't recognize him. Still, wasn't this supposed to be a secret mission? Did everyone in Brithnem need to see them? Firian knew they were conspicuous in Academy black. Parohim led them down the middle of the road, exposed to everyone's view, forcing them to move around carts.

One came up the road toward them, and Firian shuffled to the side to avoid it. Suddenly he felt young again, and bile churned in his stomach. He wasn't that pathetic little boy anymore, cringing at the sound of his father's voice. This wasn't

Raewhith. It was one of the most powerful nations in the world, and its leaders wanted him, Firian, to protect their princess.

He looked back at the palace, visible from everywhere, and threw back his shoulders. He clenched and unclenched his hands as he walked.

About twenty minutes later, they reached what seemed to be a great arena. Gold leaf sparkled in patches on the crumbling stone. Large flags, light blue and dark purple rimmed with silver with a flower in the center, flapped on the walls. Parohim led them in through a dark corridor.

"Why are you taking us here?" Master Gerand demanded.

"I want to show you some of the glories of Brithnem," he said.

They came out into a large open oval, with benches rising up in tiers around the sides. In the center rose a crowd of statues in a tight circle facing outward.

In a reverent voice, Parohim explained who they were. There were Shane and Mari Calthwaite and their four children, ancestors of the current Keepers. There was General Brishen, the Khelê war hero who led Shane and Mari and a small band to fight for God's people against the evil king who created the Kingdom.

Firian listened impatiently. He already knew some of the quotations that Parohim recited from the Scroll. Master Gerand tapped her foot as the Amir continued to explain. She probably had never read the entire Scroll, much less memorized portions of it.

A while later Parohim lifted his dry face to the sky. "I'm afraid it's getting late," he said without a hint of apology. "We ought to go to the palace now."

Through many twisting streets he led them until Firian approached Master Gerand and expressed his doubts with a look. She shook her head dismissively. Parohim was no threat. The long tour through the city still made him uneasy. Too many people had seen them.

The air grew thicker with the mist and flavor of the sea. Then, finally, the palace. It had three huge wings: one in front, and two thrust back into the grounds. Flags waved from turrets that rose victoriously above the city. Over the doors and windows, relief sculptures depicted historical scenes or flower patterns or lines from the Scroll. Firian saw no immediate evidence of a threat.

Parohim led them along the wall until they were well to the side of the palace, rather than the front, and let them in by a small door made of dark wood and intricately worked iron that led to the gardens.

"You will stay in the Amiran quarters," Parohim explained, gesturing toward it. The round, domed building was attractive in the extensive gardens, almost like a huge ornament. It had little of the Academy's ancient, forbidding mass. This was a place to study in peace, a place to stay in times of war, a quiet place. Pillars created a colonnade. All the way along the outside rim of the building hung burning lamps.

Round, white lanterns. Firian squinted at them. They were blown glass. He had completely forgotten about his class, his early vocation, and those glass balls that Raewhith always sent to Brithnem. Seeing them here was surreal. He closed his open mouth.

Although the sun was setting, darkness hadn't crept in yet. The ghost-lanterns staved off the dark.

Firian Rising

Servants conducted Firian to his room while Master Gerand discussed details with Brithnem's officials. Firian's room had thick carpet and was much bigger than the room he shared with Bard at the Academy. On the wall hung an old tapestry of a ship called the *Paladin* approaching land. He looked for a picture of the Second Line, but there was none. He'd just have to wait to meet the Kepress in person. Across from the tapestry was a small window. The way the warm yellow light streamed in made him feel much younger. Light had come through his window the same way in Raewhith. Academy light seemed different—purposeful, not so flippant with its wasted beauty.

Firian hadn't expected to recognize so many things here. It was almost like going home, and he wasn't sure he liked the familiarity.

He looked down at the cloth wrapped around his arm, staunching the cut he'd accidentally given himself while practicing the Unreal on the road. *Believe and not believe.* That was the life he wanted, power and respect. The cloth looked very similar to the one he'd worn years ago. Black was the standard Academy color, but a scrap of black around the wrist meant mourning.

He shouldn't be thinking like this. He wasn't sentimental. And he shouldn't be, especially now.

Unable to stay still, he checked that everything was in his bag. Nothing lost. Surely he could walk around outside without someone stopping him. The palace and its Amiran Academy were walled in, and he was a Tanyu.

He slipped out and walked along the colonnade. Dusk had washed the rounded walls in dark gray. Far away, he heard the cries of birds and the splash of waves. Busy servants maintenanced the gardens, snipping and watering.

Just in front of him an Amir emerged from his room. They quickly sized each other up, recognizing the outfits instantly. Every Amir seemed to wear the same bluish-gray cloak with the stiff collar reaching around their neck. This one was younger than Parohim, but his exact age was hard to pin down. They were the same height, but Firian could take him down easily if he needed to.

"Hello," Firian said, forcing a smile. It was always better to give a good first impression.

"Are you the Tanyu that the Keepers requested?" The Amir closed the door behind him.

The words sounded good coming out of the man's mouth. "I am. My name's Firian Kess."

"I'm the Kepress's tutor, Daelon."

One name. Must be Khelê.

"What brings you outside?" Daelon asked. His gaze showed marked distrust.

"Just some fresh air."

"I thought you would be eager to settle in after a long day of traveling."

"I don't get tired easily."

There was an awkward pause.

Firian had never been alone with an Amir. As much as he disagreed with them, this was an opportunity. And this man was the Kepress's personal tutor. "So, what is the Kepress learning now? Maybe I can encourage her in her lessons." *When she's away.* The unspoken words hung frostily in the air.

"That's private information," said Daelon.

"The Scroll? I assume that's part of it."

The Amir's eyes narrowed as though Firian had insulted someone close to him. "Of course it is. The Scroll teaches us all wisdom."

"I only asked because I have great respect for the Scroll." It wasn't hard to guess how to get on an Amir's good side.

Daelon sucked his teeth. "I haven't met many Tanyu with that view. Have you read it?"

"I have. It's very interesting." Seeing Daelon's skepticism, he added, "We have a few copies at the Academy."

Daelon's face began to thaw. He lifted his chin and his eyes softened with amusement, but his voice became an instructor's. *"For as long as I speak, I will speak the praise of God. For as long as I hear—"* He stopped and waited. It was a famous passage, a test.

"—I will heed God's wisdom," Firian finished. "I think that's it." *Heed* sounded fancy. The word was something like that, at least.

"It is, it is!" Daelon said with the sparkling joy of a teacher. An encouraging smile lit up his face. "The Kepress will be glad to know you've read it."

It was always about the Scroll. But it could only do so much; otherwise, why would they have called for people who could actually take care of her? "Good," he replied. "How is she feeling?"

"She's doing much better now. The doctor says she's well enough to travel." A shadow darkened his face again at the thought.

Is he interested in her, or is he just concerned?

Firian smiled. "That's good. I look forward to meeting her. Is there a specific time...?"

"No. No," Daelon said. "I was just about to announce your arrival to her now. Will you be the only bodyguard? I know you came with some others." He laid slight stress on the last two words, enough to tell Firian that he knew more than he said.

"I am the only one." Gerand was welcome to leave immediately, as far as he was concerned. Even being reminded of her sent him into a glowering mood. As though he needed to be babysat... But he wanted to meet the princess, so he arranged his face to look neutral. "Would it be too much to ask to meet her now?"

This way he could be rid of Master Gerand looking over his shoulder. Besides, he was curious about how beautiful she really was. The tales were legendary.

Daelon looked over his face again, searching for something, maybe an ulterior motive. Firian gazed back innocently. Daelon turned away and walked toward the palace. "Come with me," he said. "I'll ask her if she wants to meet you."

25

KIRIA

There was a session going on in the Main, but Kiria wasn't there. Her shoulder and anxiety were acting up, so she asked to be excused.

She was waiting for Jori, whom she had seen more often in the last couple weeks than she had for months before that. She could use some of his levity right now.

The sling was almost a novelty at first, but now it annoyed her. She wondered how people without maids dressed themselves if they were injured. As she sat in front of the mirror, she tried shifting her arm but she couldn't find a comfortable position.

The door opened. "Hello, darling," Jori said lightly, coming in. "I thought you'd be in here." A guard closed the door after him.

"I'm always in here," she said, looking at herself as Candrae did her hair. Her Beauty was comforting. When she was upset, she experimented with new fashions. In fact, that was the only time she tried them.

He eyed her new hairstyle appreciatively. "You know, you're late for the Main."

She groaned with guilt. "Don't even say that. I know. I'll go back soon. I just..."

"Here." He saved her from having to explain her feelings by settling a glass in front of her. "Let's forget about the Main."

Part of the reason he always redirected the conversation was his jealousy for Atty's position. He never said it outright, but she knew. His eyes crinkled and his jaw flexed when Atty brought up the important decisions Keepers got to make. But Atty also envied Jori's easy charm. No one had everything.

"All right," she said, picking up the glass with her good hand. He poured something into it. She took a burning sip.

He poured some for himself and downed half of it in one gulp.

"You're going to hurt yourself," she laughed, loosening the pins Candrae was trying to hold in place. "That's all right, Candrae," she said, dismissing her.

Jori pulled up a chair and clinked his glass against hers. After taking a pointedly smaller sip, he said, "Speaking of, how's the arm?"

"I think I can take the sling off soon. Thank goodness!" She couldn't play her instruments with it on, and baths were painful as she struggled to hold her arm in one position.

"Ah!" he exclaimed, topping off with more. "That's my girl! Always moving forward. It'll be a shame to take care of yourself again." His eyes twinkled.

She knew trying to make him talk seriously about the attack would be useless. Jori didn't want to think about it in those terms. To him, everything was all right. So she gave a little hum and retreated to her drink.

"Are you planning to go to an event this evening?" he asked, eyeing her nice outfit and half-done hair.

"No. I was just trying something out."

"Shame no one gets to see."

She smiled. When he complimented her Beauty, it felt different. He had always had a breezy way of complimenting her, no matter what she looked like, so it didn't feel fake like some of the others. "You're seeing," she said, and held out her glass for more.

A knock on the door made her jump. Daelon came in. His gaze swept over the two of them with their drinks and his face became unreadable. For some reason, Kiria felt a little ashamed. "My Kepress, I'm sorry to interrupt, but your bodyguard would like to meet you," he said. She was about to dismiss the idea when he added, "He's waiting just outside."

She twisted her mouth to the side. She was in no mood to meet a grim Tanyu that would remind her of the danger she lived in. But she nodded. She had to meet him sometime. "Just give me a moment, Daelon."

He nodded once and went back out the door.

Jori should have known to excuse himself, but he didn't. He was curious.

Kiria set down her glass. "Turn around," she told him. For some reason, she hated using her Ability in front of anyone but her serving girls. It exposed her, like changing clothes.

Her mother, Chetana, and guards had told her not to reveal her Ability to the Tanyu. It was a kind of compromise her mother made to settle their worries. Besides, they said her plain face would act as a sort of disguise when they left the palace—better for avoiding attention.

A tingling sensation and she was plain again. "Okay," she announced so Jori would know it was safe to turn around, and Daelon would know he could bring in the bodyguard.

After a soft snick of the lock, Daelon entered with the Tanyu—a handsome young man about her own age, lean but muscular. He strode in confidently, right beside Daelon, not behind. In her experience, Tanyu never liked to be second. He wore a long-sleeve black shirt and dark pants tucked into dirty boots. He hadn't cleaned up before meeting her, so he must have just arrived. His dark hair and eyebrows contrasted strikingly with his light skin. Like every Tanyu she'd met, his moves were calculated and powerful.

She had expected someone older, who would hover around her invisibly, detached from everything but his duty. This man looked right into her eyes, almost as though he were trying to communicate with her, but she couldn't read his face. She suddenly felt ugly and it bothered her. Her sling must make her look so helpless, and she hated to be helpless.

"My Kepress, this is Firian Kess, the bodyguard that the Keepers ordered."

She'd heard that name before. Daelon had taught it to her. *Firian, just like Mari's nephew in the story.*

Daelon turned to the Tanyu, who bristled at the introduction. She wondered why. "Defender Kess, this is Kiria Arioc, heir to the Second Line, Kepress of Brithnem and the Western Kingdom." He gave her title much more weight than his, slowing down the words as though he wanted to impress their importance on the Tanyu.

Firian made a small bow from the waist. Some of his disheveled hair fell into his face. He looked up at her and smiled a little as he bowed. She couldn't remember ever having seen a Tanyu smile.

She set her jaw hard. Firian was already trying to get on her good side, but it suddenly irritated her and she didn't know why. "Pleased to meet you," she said, sensing Jori's excitement as he stood beside her.

"You as well, Kepress," Firian replied. The words were just formal enough, but skirted the edge of casual.

Kiria had known Daelon long enough to know that he was annoyed, although his face betrayed nothing. He always wanted people to show her the utmost respect. "Defender Kess will accompany you when you leave in a couple days. I'm sure he'll do his work admirably." His eyes flashed to the floor as he paused. "We don't want to keep you," he said, beginning to back toward the door.

"Why don't you stay a little?" Jori chimed in. The words were obviously aimed at the Tanyu, not Daelon.

Firian glanced back at the Amir, a question.

Daelon paused. "Only if the Kepress agrees."

Kiria had never cared for Tanyu—they were so hardened and proud—but Jori seemed so happy with his huge smile that she didn't contradict him. He had never been able to spend time with a Tanyu, only admire them from afar. "Of course he can join us for a while," she said. "You can come pick him up in an hour."

Jori was already pulling up another chair, almost giddy with excitement. "Come, come!" he said, presenting the seat with a theatrical gesture.

"You don't have to stay if you don't want to," Kiria said quietly.

"No, I'll stay." Firian came forward easily and sat down with them as Daelon excused himself from the room. She trusted Daelon in most things, but he did have a bias against the Tanyu. To be honest, maybe she did too.

"Firian Kess?" Jori said, settling into the chair closest to hers. "Fresh from the Academy. I think you're the youngest Tanyu I've ever seen."

Firian's deep-set eyes sparkled a little at the compliment. "Do you see many here?" he asked.

"An ambassador comes once a year, but that's about it. Do you care for a drink?" Jori plucked the bottle and two glasses from where they had been sitting. He didn't have a third glass, so how he thought he could offer, Kiria didn't know.

She and Jori could share drinks together in her room, laugh and pass the time, but it felt strange to have Firian with them. They didn't know him. All in all, she didn't feel like herself, dressed up, hair half done, arm in a sling, drinking in her room with Jori and a stranger. She was better than that. Though she sometimes wanted to forget, she was the heir to a throne of Brithnem. Shouldn't he meet her in a formal capacity first? They were skipping steps. She would (she realized) be alone with Firian at some point, but to spend such relaxed time with him now didn't feel right.

She stepped in, addressing Firian. "This is Jorrim Calthwaite," she said, knowing the last name would register with him.

"Jori. Third Keeper's brother," her friend clarified, handing her the half-empty glass she had set down earlier.

Firian nodded. He didn't seem awed by either of their ranks.

Jori offered to pass Firian the bottle. Thankfully, he gestured that he didn't want any.

"So I've wondered," Jori said, twisting around to put the bottle back on the vanity counter, "what do you do all the way out there at the Academy?"

"I can't say." One side of his mouth lifted in a smile.

"That's what they all say." Jori took a drink. "But I'm sure you can tell us something. Do they hang you up by your ankles, or pit you against each other in boxing matches? We only hear little pieces, and I've always wanted to know."

He was teasing, but Kiria colored. "I'm sure they don't do either of those things," she said.

"Just know that we can offer the greatest security," Firian said, setting his hands on his knees. They were calloused with many light scars. She wondered how he got them.

"Well, I hope so," said Jori. "That's why you're here. We can't let this happen again." He lifted his chin at Kiria's sling. "You have to take care of our girl." He smiled at Firian, but his eyes were serious.

She sighed through her nose, running her finger along the base of the glass. "It *won't* happen again," she said. Even without a bodyguard, she could be more careful, and be just fine. She shifted in her seat. "I'm not afraid of the Torithians, and I don't want to be away for very long."

"Then I'll just make sure you're safe, and we'll return to the palace as soon as possible," Firian said.

"Good, because everything I know is here, and it feels terrible to be taken away just because I'm being targeted!" The words gushed out of her. To her, the bodyguard embodied her unfamiliar situation. It wasn't that she disliked him, but his presence put her in a testy mood. "Honestly, I wish you didn't need to be here. But we'll get through it."

Firian leaned forward on his elbows. "We will," he said earnestly, although the last reminder had been for herself.

She was a little taken aback by the intensity with which he looked at her.

"I wish I could go with you." Jori ran his fingers through his hair, practically pulling at the roots. He wasn't kidding.

"I'm sure you do," Kiria said, suddenly laughing. "I doubt it'll be very fun, though." She turned to Firian. "Do you know where we're going?"

"The Keepers are discussing that now," he said, a shadow falling over his face. "They'll tell us both in the morning."

26

FIRIAN

Firian returned to his room that night deep in thought. So far, many parts of the mission had been disappointing, but spending time with the princess and the Third Keeper's brother was a welcome break from Gerand's company. The princess wasn't as beautiful as everyone said. Frankly, her reputation of extreme beauty was a little baffling. He saw servants better looking than she was. But she was powerful, so it didn't matter.

Her friend Jori, more than anyone else so far, seemed to respect Tanyu. And he didn't respect very much. It was odd that more people didn't seem impressed. Of course, he had mostly met Amir and they tended not to like the Academy.

He had barely entered his room when he heard a knock. Without waiting for an answer, Master Gerand entered, the lines on her face deeper than when he had seen her last. "Here you are," she said, as though she had found a little boy. "The Keepers have asked to meet you. Come with me." She turned without seeing if he followed.

His fists turned numb with anger. At least no one else had been there to see how she treated him.

He had no choice but to chase after her. No matter how he felt, he couldn't be late to meet the Keepers of Brithnem.

Cúron, Merian, and Aylmor. He had memorized their names in school. He knew that Aylmor's son, Atael, was the Third Keeper now, but the sing-song voice in Firian's head still said the father's name. And Kiria would become the Second someday.

Gerand and Firian rushed through the gardens through one of the palace's back entrances. Daelon had taken him through a different entrance before. This one opened into an enormous hallway, all but abandoned except for a few guards who seemed to expect them. At least, Firian hoped so. *No wonder the Torithians chose to attack near the palace.* Deep rugs stretched over the spacious floor, and tall potted trees and portraits lined the walls. The palace was a glassmaker's dream—so many intricate panes forming patterns on the windows.

Gerand led them both to the left, where wooden doors as tall as two stories rose to the ceiling. Intricate carvings covered the entire face of them, probably depicting historical scenes, though none of them registered in Firian's memory.

The Master halted in front of the four guards that stood at attention beside the huge doors. "Master Gerand and Defender Kess," she said in a clear voice. "The Keepers are expecting us."

The soldiers recognized the names and cracked the door open enough to admit them. The space inside was round, with four large statues staggered across the circumference—three men and one woman. The vaulted roof went higher than the Academy's. Three thrones stood in the middle of a floor mosaic on a little raised platform. Before the thrones stood a small knot of people.

A guard conducted the two of them to the group in the center. Firian saw Cúron immediately. He had to be the bearded one wearing sweeping blue robes with long gray hair and flashing blue eyes. His every movement was royal.

If it had not been for the understated crowns on the two others, he wouldn't have been able to pick them out. Merian, Kiria's mother, was taller than her daughter, and frankly more beautiful, but she had little of the commanding presence Firian expected from a leader. Her expression, though strained in concern, settled into a look of calm distraction. Atael looked even more out of place. He resembled his brother, but his features were less refined, clumsier. He had a redder complexion and bigger bones, although he wasn't taller. He gave the impression that his clothes had been misbuttoned.

Besides the Keepers, there were several others—guards and Amir, by the look of it. He only recognized Parohim. Judging by the look of hatred on Gerand's face, she recognized someone else in the group too.

Cúron moved toward them with the expansive gesture of a benefactor. "We're so glad you've arrived!" he said. "Master Gerand and Defender Kess, welcome." He cast a tiny look at a dark-skinned woman standing by Merian.

The guard beside Firian introduced the three Keepers but said nothing of the others.

Merian stepped forward, covertly looking Firian up and down. "We're glad you could come for this temporary measure," she said. "We have agreed that you and my daughter Kiria will go to Carradoc until we have assessed the danger here at the palace."

The fortress of Carradoc featured in many parts of the Scroll. Firian should have guessed that's where they would send him. "I'm honored to be able to protect her," he said, bowing. Now was not the time to give these leaders any doubts about him.

The tall, dark woman pursed her lips, obviously unhappy. The more Firian looked at her, the more he got the impression he'd seen her before.

Cúron addressed the woman. "Only Defender Kess will go with the Kepress, and soon the danger will have passed."

The woman's face, severe and proud, punctuated with a septum ring, remained impassive. She kept casting distrustful looks at Gerand. Even though the two looked very different, this had to be Gerand's sister.

The Master turned to Firian, maybe to get away from the woman's gaze. "You will leave tomorrow and as soon as the threat is eliminated, their Watchman will inform you."

Firian had never had the chance to hear from a Watchman, so that would be interesting. He wondered if it was just an Amir with the Talent. *Probably.*

"Have you met Kiria?" Atael finally said something.

Before he could answer, Merian replied, "No, not yet. Could someone conduct us to a place where we could all meet?"

The dark-skinned woman spoke up. "I don't think Master Gerand needs to meet the Kepress," she said pointedly. Her whole manner reminded Firian of a Tanyu, but she wore the high-collared robes of an Amir. "Defender Kess will meet her by himself."

Firian felt the heat of Gerand's anger like a physical presence.

"I'll have someone introduce them tomorrow morning," Merian said, playing the peacemaker. "And now, I'm sure you're tired from your journey and would like to go back to your rooms." She nodded at a guard.

"Yes," Cúron said, booming, final. "We thank you for coming. The Defender will meet the Kepress tomorrow and they'll begin their journey to Carradoc." The guard took the hint and ushered Gerand and Firian out of the room.

27

KIRIA

THAT NIGHT, Kiria shuffled around her room with Candrae and Vayci, quietly packing. She set an extra pair of shoes by the pack lying open on her bed. Would she need more than two pairs? That might be too much.

She bit her lip. She had no idea how long she would be gone, and the whole situation put her stomach in knots. Hopefully she would arrive in Carradoc—that part excited her, at least—and then turn around to come home. *Strange that they chose a safe place so far away...* Surely it wouldn't take long to find the mole inside the castle.

She pointed at a pair of beige pants. "Bring those over," she told Vayci. Those would be good for traveling. She probably shouldn't bring any of her nice dresses. Even the thought made her blush. No wonder she wasn't ready to lead. Who would think to bring royal dresses on such a long clandestine trip? She might as well not hide her Beauty.

Yes, she would bring mostly pants. That would help her to ride horses more easily and walk over rough terrain. Her Tanyuin bodyguard had more experience, but she was determined to keep up even with her healing leg.

Her bedroom door opened and the guard announced her mother and father. Kiria turned to say hello and felt an unexpected lump in her throat. She tried to swallow it down but it wouldn't budge. Her mother's eyes softened when she saw her standing in front of the half-packed bag.

"Kiria," she began, but Kiria was already in her arms with tears stinging her eyes. Her father reached over and stroked her hair. *Why am I crying?* she thought. *I'm stronger than this.* Kiria knuckled her eyes with her good hand and stood up straight.

Her mother patted her arm. "I just met your bodyguard," she said. "Chetana's sister was there too. I'm not sure why she came after the first negotiation." Her eyebrows furrowed. "Only Defender Kess will be going with you in the morning."

She caught Kiria's eye. "I'll do everything I can to make sure you come home as soon as possible."

"We'll miss you while you're gone," her father added. Something in his tone suggested more than he said.

She furrowed her eyebrows. "I'll miss you too," she said. Even though she'd been spending less time with them lately, the idea of going so far away made her sad. She and mother didn't always agree, but her parents both loved her. She wished there was something she could do to make them proud.

"Oh!" her mother cried and wrapped her up again in a hug. Kiria's face only came to the beading on her neckline, now pressed against her cheek.

"Remember not to show your Ability to the young man," her father said.

She couldn't forget even if she wanted to. "I'll remember."

"And stay safe," said her mother, rubbing her back gently. "The girls will help you pack and then you'll be all ready to go in the morning." Her mother had a habit of saying obvious things like that, but now, with the windows dark and a journey with a stranger ahead of her, Kiria didn't mind. Her parents' love filled her like a warm cup of tea.

"Make sure you get that threat," Kiria said, separating from her mother. "And don't let Cúron do all the work." She couldn't help adding that last part.

"Oh, Kiria, of course I won't," her mother said like someone who'd ripped off an old scab.

"It's too bad," her father said. "I know you've wanted to see Carradoc. It's a beautiful place." Because he was a general, he had been there a couple of times. "But I'm afraid we'll have to bring you back before you reach it."

Amused, Kiria nodded, torn between wanting to see the fortress and hoping he was right.

"We'll let you get back to your packing," he said, putting his hand on her mother's shoulder.

She reached up to hold it as she looked down at Kiria one last time. "It won't be long," she said. "And the bodyguard seems like he'll do a good job."

Her father gave a look that said he'd better. "Let's go," he said gently.

"Good night, Kiria!" said her mother as they both went out.

"Good night," she called after them. "Ah!" She turned to her serving girls. "I'll be so glad when this is over."

Candrae gave a ghost of a smile. Both of her girls had always served her nearly in silence as all the servants did, waiting to be asked before interjecting an opinion. Kiria liked to hear what they thought, but they respected her position too much to speak first.

"What do you think would go with these pants?" she asked, coming back to mull over her outfits.

Vayci raised her head to speak when another knock sounded at the door.

Kiria made an exasperated sound as the door opened again. "Oh, it's you!"

"That's a way to say hello," Atty said as he came in hesitantly. He looked thin and pale compared to the last time she had seen him. His brown hair curled around his bronze crown. "I just came to say goodbye."

"I'm sorry to be leaving you like this," she said. Even though they didn't spend the same time together that they did as children, she knew he valued her support, especially now that he was a Keeper.

He waved the apology away. "It's not your choice. I know you would stay if you could. I wish you could stay." His eyes strayed to the bed. "Getting ready?"

Another obvious question. "Yes. Just about there."

Knock knock knock. *Again?* One of her guards cracked the door open and announced Jorrim Calthwaite and Firian Kess.

She would never finish packing. "Let them in." Maybe Jori wanted to say goodbye again, too.

The two of them sauntered in, Jori looking proud to be with a Tanyu. He stopped when he saw Atty. "Oh, I didn't know you'd be here," he said. "All saying goodbye, I guess?"

Atty nodded.

"Well, that's not why I'm here," Jori went on, turning deliberately to Kiria. "Since it's your last night here, I thought we'd have a bit of fun. Since you're here, Atty, you can join."

Atty's mouth lifted in an offended smile.

"You've met Firian?" Jori asked off-handedly.

"We've met," Atty said.

Firian nodded in agreement.

"So, what do you have in mind? I do have to get ready..." Kiria said. It did sound better to have fun with her friends than continue worrying about tomorrow.

"Oh, it won't take long." Jori walked forward. "We're going to sneak into the Main."

Atty made a face. "We have guards posted all the time now. Should we really sneak around the palace, especially considering...?" He gestured to Kiria.

"I could do it," she said.

"I don't think it's a great idea," Atty said.

"Then if we can't get into the Main, we could go somewhere else." Jori jabbed a thumb toward Firian. "He can keep us safe. No worries." He flashed a smile.

It did sound fun, a throwback to their younger days, before the war had any effect on them. "As long as we aren't gone too long." She ducked to catch Atty's line of sight. "You should come with us. It'll be fun!"

"We won't be caught." Atty said it like a warning.

"No," Jori said lightly. "We have a Tanyu."

Firian hadn't spoken yet. Maybe he disapproved of sneaking around. It wasn't exactly the best idea for someone whose life was in jeopardy. "You'll come with us, right?" she asked him.

"Sure. You can do anything you want," he replied.

"That's it then!" Jori rubbed his hands together. "Serving quarters? Kitchen? Garden?"

"Not the garden," Kiria said. Too many memories.

"Kitchen," said Atty.

Jori smiled at his brother. "Midnight snack? I like it."

It really did feel like old times. Minus the bodyguard, of course, but he was starting to do a better job of being invisible.

"Do we have to wait?" Kiria asked. In the past, they had waited until all the adults went to bed. Based on the traffic her room had seen this evening, none of them had turned in for the night.

"What if we didn't?" Jori said. "Make it more exciting."

"Unless we're caught," said Atty.

"Doesn't being a Keeper have any perks? I'm sure you can go to the kitchen and eat whenever you want. Don't be boring."

Kiria looked at Firian. "Do you think you can get us around the guards even if everyone isn't sleeping?"

His deep eyes regarded her seriously, and the question felt childish. Still, this could be a good test of his skills, and she hoped he had a sense of fun sometimes. It would make traveling with him easier.

"Of course I can," Firian said.

"See, there!" Jori raised his hands as though that settled the matter. "We'll go where we want, grab a snack, and be right back." He winked at the serving girls. Candrae blushed.

Atty set his mouth in a line, tired of his brother's antics.

The humor of the situation struck her. What a miss-matched group! A Keeper, his brother, an heir, and a bodyguard they had all just met, sneaking around Mon Párinath like a troop of children. She couldn't stifle a laugh.

"See there," said Jori, setting a hand on her good shoulder. "This is just what you needed. Everyone's been far too serious." He clapped his hands. "Everyone ready to go?"

Kiria and Atty nodded. Firian didn't respond, but he had the Tanyuin quality of looking ready at all times. He ran his thumb over his jawline.

Jori led the way, although Kiria thought Firian should go first. She wanted to know what he was made of. Did he walk cat-like, aware of everything, invisible when he wanted to go unnoticed? She wouldn't be surprised, based on what she'd seen of him, but this was a good test.

They passed the guards outside her door, who let them all pass without comment. If Kiria had been alone, they probably would have stopped her, but here she was with a Keeper and a Tanyu. Jori nodded jovially at them.

Firian bent down to speak quietly to Jori. "It looks like we won't have a problem. Who is it you want to avoid?"

Jori shushed him. "It's all in fun," he said.

Firian remained alert, but clearly didn't appreciate the response.

It was true. They could go almost anywhere they wanted if they were all together. Eating from the kitchens was bad form, but not forbidden. They could even go up to the Watchman Tower if they wanted to, although no one was supposed to disturb the person meditating up there.

They walked along the edges of the hallway, making sure to step on the rugs to dampen any sound. Kiria saw the Tanyu's shoulders relax. Maybe he was disappointed in the lack of danger. He had seemed more excited back in her room.

The main kitchen was in the front section of the palace. The four of them

Firian Rising

slipped through the archway that led downstairs. Kiria's mouth started watering at the smell of baking bread. A snack was a good idea. Jori's plans weren't always the best—she had to vet them, even before the coronation when they would sneak into the city together—but she appreciated this one.

At the bottom of the stairs, the kitchen felt humid and warm. It was like easing into a bath. A few staff stopped bustling around the room and looked at them, wide-eyed.

"My Keeper," said one, addressing Atty since he had the highest title. They all dipped a little bow. "How may we serve you?"

Jori gave Kiria an almost imperceptible little wink before he stepped forward. "We smelled your cooking and couldn't resist coming down," he said, moving toward a young female baker.

"Thank you," she replied, her eyes widening.

"I've always wanted to know how you make such wonderful things. Could you show us the ovens, the mixers...?" He started to walk with her to the far end of the kitchens.

Kiria realized what he was doing. She nudged Firian, who bent down to hear her. "Take some things for us while they're distracted," she breathed into his ear.

She hoped he heard her because he didn't respond. He only stood up straight when she finished giving instructions.

"Oh yes," she chimed in, walking forward. "I want to see too."

Atty still didn't see what was so exciting about the ovens, so Kiria leaned toward him. "He'll pick up some food," she whispered. "They won't mind."

Atty mouthed "okay" and they all went back for a little tour. The kitchen staff seemed perplexed by their visit, but they were clearly proud of their work. Kiria actually learned a few things.

A few minutes later, they said goodbye, thanked everyone, and left. Kiria felt a little bad about tricking them. It was a small thing, and she knew the staff wouldn't mind—they might not even be surprised, with Jori in the group—but she still felt a pang of guilt.

When they reached the top of the steps, Firian strode away, forcing everyone else to catch up. He went straight through the garden doors and took a sharp right, hugging the exterior wall of the palace so closely that they had to squeeze past hedges. Kiria fought to keep her arm in the right position as she shuffled sideways behind the plants. They scratched her good arm lightly and she wondered if spiders lived in those bushes. She couldn't see the webs very well because the sun was going down. There was enough light to see, but not much. *Where is he going?* It seemed odd that Firian was suddenly taking control. Jori nearly skipped with excitement.

Suddenly, Firian halted beside a large window far from any door. He reached above his head, shoulders straining, and pulled himself up to see through the window. Apparently the view satisfied him, because he let himself fall lightly back to the ground. Businesslike, he began pulling things out of his pockets—bread, sweets, oranges. Kiria held out her hand to take something. She had no idea there were so many places to hide things. His shirt was form-fitting. How had he gotten anything in there?

Even Atty looked excited now as he held snacks and waited to see what Firian would do.

Again, the Tanyu reached up to the window ledge, but this time he pulled himself all the way up so he could stand on the narrow, rocky strip. He arched backward enough to survey the whole window. Then he leaned against it and started feeling each panel, reaching blindly with his fingers. Kiria heard a lower one scrape. Firian smiled and crouched down, gently pushing that panel in with both hands. It gave. Her breath caught, but he caught the top edge of it before it fell. He turned the glass panel sideways and eased it through the hole, hanging on to hand it down to Atty, who took it and set it down against the castle wall.

"Make sure you put that back," Kiria said, fascinated.

Atty agreed. "Yeah, you can't leave it open."

Firian didn't answer. He just jumped through the opening, landed on the ground, and then leaned out again. He extended his hand. They were all going through the window.

Kiria made a face. She should have expected this from the moment Firian stopped at that odd place along the wall, but she had been so curious about what he was going to do that she didn't realize it meant her climbing through a window with a sling.

"The Kepress first," Firian said, stretching his hand toward her. "Help her up," he told the others.

They all handed their food to Jori. Atty laced his big fingers together to make a step. She took a deep breath and put her foot on his hands. The window wasn't very high, just enough to be inconvenient.

The thought crossed her mind that she should have worn pants today too. Dresses made it harder to climb. She reached up and took his hand. Atty lifted her foot and Firian pulled her up, squeezing her hand, so that she could rest her good elbow on the ledge.

"I'm going to lift you," Firian said, letting go of her hand, reaching down, and holding her just below her ribcage. She opened her mouth to protest, but then she realized it was the only way she could do this. Stones from the palace wall scraped her skin as he dragged her up and through the opening. She swung her legs over and landed beside him in the darkened room. He let go of her and stuck his head out to check on Jori and Atty. Her waist was probably bruised, he had held her so tightly.

Firian handed food backward to her. She had to cradle it in her arm to hold it all.

Atty appeared next, crawling through the missing pane, then Jori. Even the softest sound echoed. Kiria spun around to look. They were in the Main.

"Just like old times," Jori said, a little out of breath.

Firian smirked. "You should post a guard out there," he said.

28

FIRIAN

Firian forgot to put the windowpane back in after the four of them left the Main the night before. Hopefully that would teach them to put a guard outside. At least the Kepress and her friends seemed impressed by what he could do. That was the main thing. And he'd had a surprisingly fun time outsmarting the soldiers.

They left in the gray of the morning. Fog from the ocean blanketed the city in ghostly white. Cloudy shapes of buildings and, far off, the dark smudge of the city wall made Brithnem magical. He'd never seen a city look so beautiful.

As they walked silently through the mist, the cool, wet fog on his skin energized him. He finally felt alive.

Master Gerand was gone. It was just him and the princess now. His mission had truly begun. If any threat came, he was the only line of defense. No backup, no teacher, no supervisor.

Kiria rode silently by his side. He carried both of their packs since her arm still rested in a sling. Her face was hard to read, uncomplaining but unhappy. Maybe determined was the best way to describe it.

Frankly, she had disappointed him at first. On the long journey to Brithnem, he had lain awake at night picturing his mission as dangerous and even glamorous: combating enemies with a beautiful girl at his side, who was either his or his to be won. The reality of the mission so far paled in comparison. She wasn't hideously ugly by any means, just a bit plain. But the reports of her great beauty had been bald lies, all of them. Maybe they were designed to tempt him into accepting the mission. But that was impossible. Who in their right mind would refuse an opportunity like this? Even if she had been too ugly to show her face, he still would have come.

But his original daydreams aside, last night had shown him that the attack hadn't made her timid at least. She'd kept up with the rest of them and even seemed more confident than the Keeper Atael. He appreciated that. And the men at the palace certainly seemed to care about her. Maybe it was just her position as their Kepress, but there could be something more that inspired their loyalty. He would watch for it.

She looked up at the sky, squinting so hard that her whole face looked comically angry. "How long will it take us to get there?" she asked.

"It depends on how quickly we go," he said. "It should be less than two weeks."

She pushed the hair out of her face. "I'd like to go as quickly as possible."

"We have to take care of your leg." He had already noticed her wincing when she thought he wasn't looking.

"I've always wanted to see Carradoc, and I'm sure they'll catch the threat soon."

Firian secretly hoped they wouldn't. If they caught the threat inside the palace, the Watchman would call for him and his mission would be over. He had to be useful first. "When can you take off the sling?" he asked, returning to the topic of her injuries.

"Just a few days." A smile flashed across her face. "I can't wait."

He grunted. In her place, he would feel the same way.

She pointed to the left. Through the mist, he could just make out a large, empty plaza with a statue in the middle—maybe a fountain. "That's one of my favorite places in Brithnem. I've only been there a couple times, but it's beautiful. Daelon showed me. It's a statue of my great-grandmother and the other Keepers. They look so amazing!" She strained to see better through the fog, sitting higher on her saddle.

"Maybe they'll make a statue of you," Firian said.

Her forehead wrinkled in thought. "Maybe," she conceded. It seemed she wanted to say more, but she fell quiet.

The horses' hooves clopped in the silence.

THEIR FIRST REST stop was an old Exmorei outpost. Tanyu had commandeered it after the order split into two groups: Tanyu and Amir. Made of rough, dark stones, the outpost looked a bit like a little Academy, about the size of his house in Raewhith. There were four rooms, the largest in front, kitchen beyond, and two smaller rooms across from each other on the side, where they would sleep. Beyond it grew a garden overgrown with mint and stunted strawberry plants. Enough to eat for dinner.

Firian set up the horses outside, scanning the forest for the best entry points. Even with the slitted windows, the outpost presented some problems. Master Gerand might have been wrong when she suggested this place. A skilled attacker could come through the thatched roof, and a boot could break the lock on the front door.

The fog had burned off long since, but the deep shadows kept him from seeing very far. He squinted into the forest. Some of the trees had leaves instead of needles and he heard running water nearby. Nothing else seemed to move.

Easy enough. Firian slapped his horse and went inside, where it smelled moldy. Kiria was already busy preparing the cot in one of the smaller rooms.

"I thought we'd be camping," she said as he walked in.

"Not tonight."

"So we will later." It was a question.

Of course. "We'll have to," he said.

She quirked her mouth. Was she excited or disappointed? "I've never camped before."

"It's not so bad." He smiled.

"It actually sounds kind of fun," she said, smoothing out her bedroll with her good hand.

He just nodded. She really wasn't as plain as he had first thought. His first impression—that she was far less beautiful than the reports had said—had been premature, maybe. In his surprise he hadn't noticed that she had a decent figure and bright, intelligent eyes.

"Do you need anything?" he asked. Maids always helped her, Amir taught her, Keepers probably scheduled her days. Living rough would be good for her, but it couldn't hurt to get on her good side.

"Where will you be?" she asked after a pause.

"Front room." He could observe everything that went on from there. "I have some food when you're ready."

She nodded and turned back to her cot. He had no idea what else she wanted to set up. It all looked finished to him. Maybe she expected art to appear on the walls. But she looked busy, so he left and rolled out a blanket on the wooden floor of the main room.

Soon she emerged for the food he'd mentioned. She strolled up to him, but there was a fragility to her ease, as though she were covering up her real worry. "Hello," she said, looking around for a place to sit. There wasn't one. "What did you bring?"

He gestured to the floor. "There's a garden out back," he said.

She didn't understand.

"We'll eat food from there." He sat down cross-legged on the floor.

She eased herself down. It hadn't occurred to him that sitting this way might hurt her. "I think I got sunburned," she said, settling into a more comfortable position. She pressed the tip of her finger to her skin. When she lifted it up, her skin flashed white and then red.

"That's going to happen." He didn't notice burns anymore, if he still got them. He spent enough time outside to tan. Tentatively, she poked her arm again. It was just a sunburn, nothing to be upset about. "I'll get something for it in the morning," he said.

"Thank you."

He was used to getting up early anyway. Hopefully, she wouldn't sleep too long after the long day's ride. Maybe she was used to sleeping in every day. *What is a princess's schedule?* All the awkward dead space in their conversations started to grate on him. He had forgotten to be charming, too focused on the intoxication of freedom. Now that they were out of the palace, and away from Master Gerand, he should get to know her, and get her to know him as well.

In several short years, she would be a Keeper, one of the most powerful leaders in the world. And here she was at his disposal. Just the two of them, alone. He scooted closer to her.

"It doesn't look too bad," he said, touching her arm.

She flinched at his touch and her eyes hardened. "Do we still need to pick food from the garden?" she asked, matter-of-fact.

Annoyed, he bit the inside of his lip. "I have some of it here," he said, stretching backward to gather what he had collected when he was outside with the horses. He'd laid it by the kitchen area. They would supplement the strawberries and mint with bread they'd brought from the palace. It would go bad in another day anyway.

He would have to try another tactic. "Have you ever been this far from Brithnem before?" he asked, rubbing the dirt off the strawberries before handing them to her one by one.

"A couple times, yes." She spoke in a more business-like tone, taking the strawberries, but still inspecting each one. "I've been to Charäkhnem, and I took a boat to Phlaxtin once."

"What was Charäkhnem like?" There weren't many Charäkhni at the Academy. Kaori and Tesni, a girl with hair and skin the color of sand, were the only ones he knew for sure. Tiev and Shiro lived farther east.

"I mostly remember the zoo, and that the trip was kind of awful. You have to go over the Salt Fields. There's not much to see for miles and miles, but the city itself is very interesting." She balanced the strawberries carefully on her knee, not looking at him.

"The zoo?" he asked.

"Yes, Shear Ganesha has a whole collection of animals that he keeps on the palace grounds. I loved them when I was little. I used to draw them all the time." She bit into one small strawberry. Her face announced it was sour. Princesses were so delicate. "Where have you been?" she asked.

He paused. He hadn't been anywhere. "I've been training at the Academy since I was very young," he said. "That kind of focus doesn't allow for much traveling."

She eyed him. "So is this your first time away?"

"To Brithnem, yes." Hopefully she wouldn't see through him to the truth. Was it so bad that he had never traveled?

"I'm glad you got to see it," she said. "The Tanyu who come never seem to appreciate it. They're always so stern and stoic, but the city is beautiful. They should be impressed." She got the same look in her face that she had gazing toward the statue of the Keepers they had passed on their way out.

"You love the city," he murmured, passing her another strawberry. "That's good, since you'll be in charge someday."

"Not in charge," she said, and then checked herself as though she had said too much.

"What do you mean?" he asked, edging closer. How could the Keeper of Brithnem not be in charge? He had learned their names since childhood as some of the most powerful people in the world. Even Raewhith skirted the Western Kingdom's huge domain.

The air buzzed with a secret.

She edged away. "Nothing. It doesn't matter. Yes, I'll be the Keeper someday," she said. She chewed another strawberry. This time she didn't make a face.

"What do you mean?" he insisted. "Who's in charge if it isn't you?"

"Of course I'll be in charge, and that's not your concern, Defender Kess," she said, separating them with the name, as though a Tanyu were beneath her.

"You can call me Firian."

She hummed in acknowledgement and focused on her dinner. He broke a small loaf of bread in half and handed her a piece. It wouldn't be long before he would break down her walls. The princess had her secrets on the surface, not buried deep like so many Tanyu. Warriors were hard to crack; Kiria wouldn't be. Yesterday, in the Main, he had seen her blush. And it wasn't for Jori or Atael or Daelon. It was for him.

29

KIRIA

KIRIA WOKE to the sound of irregular thumping in the other room. Her heart pounded fast and she tried to sit up. An attacker wouldn't be making so much noise, would he?

Groaning, she realized how sore her neck and back felt. It had only been one day, and already she missed her bed. Yesterday had felt like an adventure, leaving early, alone with a stranger. It helped that the Tanyu was handsome, but that also made her a little nervous for some reason. That feeling had begun to wear off by the end of the day, but then he had touched her. It was innocent enough, but he should have asked first. Part of his job was to make her feel comfortable. He, clearly, felt comfortable around her despite her title, but she wasn't sure about him.

Firian wasn't one for conversation, so she had to find some way to stay positive and energetic today. She wouldn't be away long, but even a short stint away from the palace wore on her.

The thumping continued. *What is that sound?* She eased herself up, careful with her bad arm. Rubbing the sleep out of her eyes, she came out of her room.

Firian had already packed his bedroll and set it by the door, ready to go. He stretched out in the middle of the room, shirtless, doing some kind of exercise. Balancing on the balls of his feet, he pushed off with his hands, landed, and eased his straightened body down again. It didn't look like he was exerting himself very much, although the muscles in his shoulders and back moved and strained with each motion.

When he saw her, he jumped to his feet. She realized she had been staring.

He dusted off his hands, clapping them together. "Did I wake you up?" he asked. He didn't seem very concerned.

She shrugged, looking away. The sunlight already shone through the windows, so it was probably time they left anyway.

"I didn't realize I would wake you up." He went to the door and fished out something from his pack. It was a plant. He held it out to her. "Here. I found it this morning. You can put it on your sunburn."

She had forgotten about the sunburn. Why didn't he put on a shirt? She glanced down at her arms. They weren't nearly as red today as they had been last night. "Thank you," she said as she took it from him. "I'll get ready to go." Quickly, she turned around and headed back to her room.

When she closed the door, she stared at the plant in her hand. How was she supposed to put this on her sunburn? The leaves looked too small to cover it. She might look foolish trying to get out any sap or juice. She patted her skin with it experimentally a few times. The leaves were cool, but that was all the relief the plant seemed to offer. With a fingernail, she pealed back the skin of one of the leaves, hoping to find answers. The pulp looked wet underneath, so she pressed the opened leaf to her arm instead. It left a slimy gel that actually was very soothing.

She covered the whole sunburn with the stuff and turned to the task of getting dressed to go. With Candrae and Vayci, this step was easy. They always dressed her in the morning. She had been especially grateful for them since the attack.

It took her a long time to get on her travel gear, tenderly avoiding the fresh scar on her leg and keeping her left elbow at an angle. But she refused to ask for help. Finally, she finished and came out.

Firian, now with his black shirt on, had more strawberries for her. She set her pack by his at the door and ate her breakfast standing.

"Are you going to work out every morning?" she asked between bites. "We're already riding a long way." She flexed her foot and the movement sent an ache all the way up her thigh.

He smiled. An image of Tanis flashed before her mind, self-assured, entitled, and part of her was disgusted. "I can be quieter," he said.

For some reason, she felt annoyed. "I just don't see why you need to do it at all."

"I want to protect you. And I want to be the best. I've always practiced this way."

"Aren't you already the best? Why would they send anyone else to be my bodyguard?" It struck her again how young he was. Every other Tanyu she had seen looked at least ten years older than Firian. Did they think she would be more comfortable with someone her own age? Or did the Tanyu not respect Brithnem as much as she thought?

"I am the best," he said simply.

"But you're so young."

He popped a strawberry into his mouth. "Yes, I am."

She decided to drop the conversation. His arrogance irritated her. "So, are we leaving?" she asked.

"I'll saddle the horses," he replied, heading out the door.

She took off her sling two days later and stretched her elbow thoughtfully, feeling for discomfort. The wounds on her shoulder and leg still felt tender, but now she could function. She packed the sling away, grateful to be rid of it.

As the day dragged on, again mostly in silence—that seemed to be Firian's natural state—her shoulder ached more and more. Maybe taking off her sling was a bad idea.

She watched the slow rocking of the horses as they picked their way over the rocks of the foothills. Dark clouds came in. She looked up and one huge raindrop fell on her face, narrowly missing her eye. She blinked the water out.

"It's starting to rain," she said. "Should we find a place to stay?"

Firian didn't respond right away. It was just the early afternoon, much earlier than they had stopped any other day. But today her arm ached, she was tired, and the sky looked ready for a downpour. She wouldn't mind settling in early.

"If that's what you would like," Firian said, slowing his horse to speak to her more easily.

"It is. Do you know of a place close by?" she said, pulling her hood over her head as the raindrops began to fall more steadily.

"I'm sure I can find something."

She pursed her lips. Firian was handy in situations like this, but even he didn't know where they could go. Getting caught in the rain at the palace was one thing; she could always go inside. Here, the elements could dominate them. She kicked her horse lightly to hurry.

Cold wind whipped through the trees, over the rocks, and across her shivering body. She held her hood together with one hand and rode with the other. The blackened sky let out a faint thunder roar.

"Do you see anything?" she asked above the sound of the wind.

"There's probably something up here," he said, pointing vaguely over a shallow ridge. The land dipped down to cliffs rising on the right.

Water began pouring down in torrents, blowing in their eyes. In seconds, she was drenched. The poor horse, soaked through, had to clop through puddles. There wasn't so much as a cabin over the ridge.

Kiria lowered her head as they kept on, the lightning getting closer. Piercing pain in her shoulder made her let go of the coat's hood. She couldn't hold on anymore. Compared to the discomfort she felt hanging on to the hood, letting her arm rest was a relief, even though rain poured freely over her head. The horse steamed as it trod through thickening mud.

Firian seemed relatively unaffected. He rode high, didn't put up his hood, and kept swinging his head to look for a place to stay. His black figure got dimmer in the darkness.

What would her mother think of this? Was this any way to keep her safe? Thunder boomed. The reminder that she could be struck by lightning at any moment made her flinch. A few weeks ago, she wouldn't have been as afraid, but now she felt like a target, so high up on that horse with the lightning igniting the sky.

As time wore on, she started to accept the misery. The rain mixed with her running nose. Every few minutes, she slicked wet strands of mousy hair from her face so she could see. When was Firian going to stop?

Then he pointed ahead, sure of himself. Kiria's heart leapt. *Finally, finally!* She urged her horse to go faster, bobbing in the saddle. It couldn't pick up the pace, but at least there was a roof ahead.

Ahead of them, through darkening trees whose leaves spilled steady streams of water, was a shack. It hardly deserved a better name, but at that moment, she didn't care. It was tucked into a thick part of the forest, maybe a trapper's cabin. As soon as she got close enough, she heaved her way off the horse, hopping awkwardly on her bad leg. Firian ran up splashing and took the reins from her. She handed them over and ran inside, head ducked down.

She reached the doorway panting. The dry cabin was tiny but so much warmer and safer than outside. She never thought she'd be so thankful to see one drafty little room. Cold water drained from her sleeves into her hands. A puddle already pooled on the floor beneath her.

Leaning her head back out the doorway, she squeezed out her hair. Even though she was cold, she should probably take off her coat too and wring it out before she made the whole place sopping wet. She unbuttoned the front, but the wet cloth stuck to her as she tried to peel the coat off her arms.

Firian rushed in behind her with the bags and strode right into the room, his heavy black coat leaving a thick film of water leaking across the little floor.

"What are you doing?" she snapped. She hadn't meant for her tone to be so sharp.

"What?" He spun around and glared at her.

"You're getting the floor wet!"

He raised his dark eyebrows in surprise. "I hadn't noticed." And he hadn't cared either, judging from his expression.

"We're going to sleep here, right?" she asked pointedly, still struggling with her sleeve.

Firian came over and pulled her arm through. Stabbing pain shot down from her shoulder and she gasped.

Firian stepped back. "Did I do something wrong?" Barely restrained irritation showed through his voice. His eyes flashed darkly and rivulets of water ran from his hair into his face.

"My shoulder," she explained, easing carefully out of the other sleeve. "I just took the sling off today."

A tense silence filled the little space.

"I found us some shelter. You should be glad," he said, turning away from her. "We'll stay here tonight." With that, he knelt down by the packs and fished inside.

Her chest twisted angrily. She felt the retort bubbling up inside her before it came out. "Why are you so arrogant?"

He stood up more calmly than she would have expected, a flint from his pack in one hand. Taking a calculated breath, he faced her. "And why are you so entitled?"

"I'm not entitled!" she cried, shocked that he insulted her. "I just—"

"I don't control the weather. I found a place to stay, and you're complaining that I get the floor wet." His low tone almost scared her. His lip almost imperceptibly started to curl.

"It's better to keep it dry if we can," she said. She still believed that was the best way. Let him try to intimidate her. She had stood up to greater powers than he.

Her heart beat hard as he gave her a pointed look. The rain roared outside. He turned away and began to light the two torches hung just inside the door. Once they were lit, he reached past her and closed the door.

An odd relief flooded her heart as she took one side of the room and he took the other. At least they had rest now.

Deep, flickering shadows coiled over the walls. Monstrous shadows followed them whenever they moved. They reminded her that she wasn't outside in the rain, so she almost welcomed them as friends. *I'm not entitled. Right?* She shoved her hand inside her pack to feel for drier clothes. Something at the bottom didn't feel soaked. It might even be dry. *I don't expect Keeper treatment. I've been keeping up despite my injuries, and I've been traveling without using my Ability or bringing my serving girls or guards. We've barely eaten anything. And I've been in pain. How dare he accuse me of being entitled?* She started steaming again, and glared at him out of the corner of her eye. This was the first time she'd done anything like this. She hadn't trained as a warrior for years, and she was still doing pretty well. His expectations were too high.

He shook off his long coat and peeled off the shirt underneath. She turned back to her pack. He needed to learn how to act in front of a Kepress, but maybe now wasn't the time to tell him. She busied herself digging out the dry clothes at the bottom of her bag. A pair of brown pants and a shirt came out as she tugged. Her nightgown was sopping. If she didn't pull them out of the bag and lay them out, they would just stay that way, so she took out almost everything and started to lay the clothes flat. She hung a shirt on each sconce.

"You really don't like rain, do you?"

She looked back at Firian, still shirtless, who watched her with amusement in his eyes. A few of the small, white scars that laced his hands covered his strong chest.

"Put on a shirt," she said, not answering his ridiculous question. "And turn around, please. Or you can go outside. I want to dry off before I go to sleep."

"It's too early to sleep," he said, facing the wall.

She hurriedly changed into the dry clothes, watching him the entire time. When she was done, she said, "I really don't think I'm entitled. I've been doing a good job so far."

Firian turned around. "All my clothes are wet," he explained carelessly. "I'm not putting them on."

He wasn't going to obey her? "I'm a Kepress," she began.

"I know." His tone shifted from harsh to mischievous. "Do I make you uncomfortable?" He knew exactly how good looking he was.

Heat rushed to her cheeks. And he didn't make her that uncomfortable. Why did her face have to make him think otherwise? "No," she snapped. "But when I ask you to do something…"

"I have to obey you?" He wasn't taking her seriously.

"Yes," she said coldly. She was used to people underestimating her or her mother, but it was always done in subtle ways. She could work around that, rise above it. She'd practiced for years. But this blatant disrespect was something new. A chill replaced the heat in her face. "Yes, you do. *We* hired *you*."

"To do what you couldn't do for yourself. Tanyu *earn* their respect."

"We should never have hired you!" she cried. "Our own guards could have done this. Chetana was right." Firian had seemed different at first, when he spent time with them in the Main, but he was just as egotistical as every other Tanyu she'd met. So self-assured that even Keepers didn't deserve their full attention.

His face reddened. "Wait until somebody attacks. You'll see why they called for me."

The rage of their argument subsided into the sound of the rain.

She realized she was out of breath.

His voice rose just above a whisper. "I've practiced every day for seven years. You won't question me." He was so sure that she shivered, almost afraid.

She narrowed her eyes. Defending her position meant more than defending herself. Leaders of Brithnem deserved esteem, no matter who sat on the thrones. She suddenly wished she weren't alone. "I will if you need to be questioned." She drew herself up to her full height, still not higher than his chin. "Firian," she said, leaving out his title, "whatever you think about me, I still outrank you. And you've sworn to protect me, so you'll do that without question." She set her mouth in a hard line. Her heart beat heavily in her chest.

He licked his lips, considering how to respond. After a while, he nodded, ending the discussion. But he still didn't reach for a new shirt as he laid out his bedroll as far against the opposite wall as it could go.

Kiria watched as Firian moved a Bird across the board.

"So that's... Overbridge?"

He smiled, his stoic face creasing. "Yes."

This was the second straight day of the downpour. It didn't make sense to try to travel in this weather, so they were stuck in the little trapper's cabin. At least, that's what Kiria had decided to call it. They both had woken up feeling frosty toward each other, but that got so boring after a while that she finally broke the silence. Indisfate had come up and he spoke as though he needed to explain what that was. So she got the brilliant idea to have him teach her. It was a matter of an hour to gather enough matching stones, leaves, and other small items to imitate an Indisfate board.

Kiria kept back her smile, pretending to struggle with her next move. She picked up a Falcon, hesitated, put it down. Taking the Man two spaces forward would throw Firian off.

His smile faded as he realized what she had done. "You learn quickly," he said, a hint of uncertainty in his tone. His eyebrows beetled. Clearly, he wasn't used to being beaten.

She burst out laughing. "I've known how to play for ages," she said. "I just wanted you to teach me."

He raised one eyebrow. "Why?"

"So I could see that look on your face. It was worth it." Her giggles subsided. Maybe all this was childish, but how else were they supposed to pass the time? "Did you grow up knowing how to play?"

He paused, looking suddenly thoughtful. "No. I learned after I got to the Academy."

She drew up her knees and hugged them to her chest. "How long have you been at the Academy? You're the youngest Tanyu I've ever seen. What are you? Eighteen?"

He tilted his head down and looked straight into her eyes. For a second, she felt uncomfortable. "I got in when I was eleven," he finally said.

"That's really young."

"Yeah." A touch of a smile passed his lips.

"What did they teach you when you first got there? Indisfate? I knew people who really wanted to get in, so they would want to know." It was all for the best that Jori and Atty didn't get invited.

"You can't tell anyone." He touched her to punctuate his point. The room felt warmer than it had though the fire was dying.

She nodded at him. She wouldn't tell.

"Everyone who gets in needs to have the Ability and strength for it," he began.

"Okay," she prompted.

"They teach you how to use the Ability to go... into the Unreal."

"That sounds fake."

He pursed his lips, indignant. "It isn't."

A crackling silence passed between them. She was only kidding. Why did he have to take everything so seriously?

He started again. "They show you how to control your Ability, how to strategize, how to kill if you need to."

"When you were eleven?" She looked down, thinking. "When I was eleven, they were teaching me geography and music and the Scroll. Killing only came up in history, not in real life. Until the Torithians attacked, of course." When she looked up, he was studying her. "So... what's the Unreal?" That actually did sound vaguely familiar. Maybe Chetana or Daelon had brought it up at some point.

"Close your eyes," he said.

"What?" She wouldn't close her eyes alone with him. He wasn't a guard. He was serious and deadly and cocksure. And they were sitting so close.

"Do it." He demonstrated, keeping his own eyes closed.

Hesitantly, she did it. "Okay."

"Now," he said soothingly, "clear your mind."

Every attempt brought up more thoughts—her mother, tomorrow's food, the new bandage she needed, where they were going—*where are we going?*

"Are you doing it?"

"I'm not sure. Where are we going next?"

"Focus."

"No, I should know where we're going." She opened her eyes. His were still closed.

"If you try this, I'll tell you," he said.

She chewed the inside of her lip for a few seconds, and then closed her eyes again. Still, thoughts bombarded her—what else was north? The mountains, Enderin, Shifra—the difficult passage in her music. Blood. Her arm had been sliced. Firian's intense eyes.

"How do I clear my mind?" she asked.

"Nothing."

"Excuse me?"

"Think of nothing."

"I can't do that."

At least she knew they were going to Shifra. The picture had always looked lovely. Green swampland with guardian trees rising from the shallow water and overshadowing the paths. Wooden walkways still crisscrossed the marsh on the way to the fortress of Carradoc. But the part that sounded so beautiful in the old stories were the lanterns. The round lanterns at the palace were meant to echo them, but the originals shone many different colors. A celebration of color, casting festival light glowing over the walkways as she walked serenely over them. Fireflies rose over the water, twinkling. The smell of the trees filled the humid air with musk. Old yet fresh. A fish splashed gently in the water as she walked by.

And almost ran into Firian. His wide eyes were glowing.

She opened her eyes. Firian was looking straight in her face, as he had done in her imagination. His breathing was excited and an enthralled smile played on the edges of his mouth. "You have the Talent!" he said.

"What?"

"You have the Talent," he repeated. "Has no one told you?"

"No..."

"Did you see me?" He grinned, happier than she had ever seen him.

She nodded. "Yes. What does that mean?"

"Could you see me clearly?"

"Pretty clear."

"How did nobody know about this?" he said, almost to himself.

She bent down to catch his eyeline. "Hey, what does this mean?"

"You can go in the Unreal. I can see you there."

She scrunched her eyebrows together. She wasn't sure she wanted him to be able to see her in her imagination. "Are you saying you can read my thoughts?" she asked, a little disgusted.

"Not exactly." He stood up, clearly still processing the new information. "I'm going to tend to the horses," he said.

"Wait! You'll explain later?" she said, standing up and dusting herself off. *What a time to go out to the horses!*

"I'll explain later." He pulled on his coat and went outside into the rain.

30

FIRIAN

Firian cast his mind back into the little cabin as he stood by the horses, the soft rain falling less torrentially than before. Kiria would appreciate that the weather was clearing up. They might be able to get in a few miles before the end of the day.

He patted his horse's flank absently. His mind hit a slight buzz, but nothing constant. It was no wonder he hadn't noticed it.

She had the Talent.

As he stood in the rain, he smiled. The Academy would love this information. But he had only left Gerand a few days ago—he had no desire to get more instructions. For now, he would keep this to himself, a juicy secret. The Academy already had plenty of those. He just had to decide what he would do with it. Would it be stupid to train her? She had power, but she wasn't part of the Academy. *What would Bard say?* He would probably say they should all be friends, and that Firian should contact the Academy for permission first. He wasn't doing that.

Kiria in the Unreal. Even though it had only been a couple days, he did already miss being surrounded by people with the Talent. Until today, she had bored him a little. Her power enticed him, but her company offered very little. With extra possibilities, the trip wouldn't feel as mundane. Besides, he could be a good teacher.

The horses had banded together under a clump of trees. They looked uncomfortable, but they weren't in need of anything. He couldn't stall any longer.

He creaked open the door to the cabin and went inside. Kiria was cleaning up the game of Indisfate, carefully storing the pieces for another day.

"So, if I have the Talent," she said without introduction, "then I can do everything you can do?"

"I suppose so," he replied. What exactly did she think he could do?

"Why couldn't you teach me?"

He looked up into her earnest eyes. The firelight from the torches glowed on her face. Even though she wasn't very pretty, there was something that was alive about her. It gave her some beauty where she had none. And Brithnem and the Academy were supposed to be allies, after all. "Of course I could teach you," he said.

She smiled, full teeth. "Good. It'll give me something to do." After a moment, her mouth twitched again in a private smile as she said, "Jori will be so jealous. Atty too. They've always wondered what you do there in the Tanyuin Academy. They're royal, so they didn't have a chance to try out for it. They had to stay in Brithnem," she explained.

"But you'll get to find out," Firian said.

Kiria looked at Firian warmly, as though they were co-conspirators. Apparently she didn't mind his arrogance so much now. This felt more like it did back at the palace. Part of her loved adventure, and he would feed that side.

"Let's start," she said. "As long as you can be civil. I don't have to do anything I don't want to."

He sucked his teeth and reminded himself that this was a princess. If he indulged her, good things might happen. He'd had to do that with other girls he'd been with. It was worth it in the short term. "Okay," he said. "Sit down." There were no chairs, so they sat across from each other as they had while they played the game. "Close your eyes," he told her. That was the way that Belik always started his lessons. "The way it works—" He paused. It felt illegal to teach the inner workings of the Academy to an outsider. "Swear you won't tell anyone what I'm teaching you," he said abruptly.

Her eyes popped open, one eyebrow lifted. "Sure," she said, looking amused at how serious he was.

"Swear."

She twisted her lips to the side, but consented. "I swear."

"Good. Now close your eyes. Now think of nothing."

"I still have no idea what you mean by that," she said.

"Just don't think—no color, an empty space..." he chanted, hoping this was worthwhile after all. In his mind, he pictured Bard as vividly as he could: small, tan skin, black eyes, wild black hair, concerned expression, quick smile... "Tell me when you see something," he said.

The quiet stretched for such a long time that he wondered if she would ever see it. Maybe this whole thing was a waste of time.

Finally, "There's a person," she said slowly.

A chill ran through him. She did have it. "Good. Describe him for me," he said.

"He's... he's... wait, he's getting clearer. I don't think I know him. He looks like he sees something but it worries him. Short black hair. He's wearing all black, too. Is he a Tanyu?" she said.

The success was so heady it surprised him. "That's right," he said. "That's... someone I know from the Academy."

"He looks nice," she stated, as though that defied expectation.

He ignored her comment. "That's the basic idea behind using the Talent.

That's what starts everything. That way you can see what I see. Later, we can both visualize into the same place. Does that make sense?"

"I didn't realize it was so simple."

"All right, now you picture something and I'll tell you what it is. It works both ways. Make sure I've never seen it before," he added.

Instantly, he could see a domed room made of sandstone, the edges segmented into cages. Only pieces of it appeared at one time. He had to swing around to catch the details, which came into focus piecemeal. A bird squawked loudly from somewhere. Behind one set of bars, a cat-like creature about knee-high with a long nose and dusty stripes bared its teeth at him. *The zoo in Charäkhnem.*

"Ambitious for a first try!" he said. "It's the zoo. There's a cat and a bird."

The vision disappeared, so he assumed she had opened her eyes again. He quickly tried to sense any other minds that might be near their cabin but all was quiet. He couldn't let his guard down completely for this.

Back in the real world, he looked back at her and smiled. Belik's excitement over Firian's victories made more sense now. It was easier to see why he hungered for Firian's success, through any means possible. Looking at Kiria, he knew how Belik felt.

Kiria smiled back, glowing with pride. "That's what I was picturing!" she said.

"I know, I know." Automatically, he reached out to touch her, but pulled his hand back. "You'll get better at picturing different things, and seeing what I see."

"That's amazing..." She looked off to the side, musing. "But how does any of that help you be a warrior?"

"Watch this. Picture it again."

He dove back into the zoo scene, focusing specifically on the desert cat. Its slender tail balanced behind it as it walked forward to the bars. Triangular ears perked toward him. He filled in detail: velvety texture, glint of wetness in the black eyes, small paws slicked wet by licking. Reaching his hand into the cage, he caught the creature's attention. It regarded him warily before striking with sharp teeth that sank into his finger. He hissed and drew his hand back.

Swimming back to reality's surface, he held his hand out to Kiria. Blood dripped from the finger. "All it takes is belief."

She creased her forehead in surprise, staring at the blood.

He smirked at her concern. "There are lots of different ways to hurt somebody," he said. Maybe that's where he should draw the line with her. She didn't need to know how to fight. "But there's no time to go over all of those today. The rain is letting up, so we should pack up to leave soon."

"That was a short lesson," she said, catching onto his evasiveness. She didn't move from her position on the floor.

"Have to leave you wanting more," he replied, getting to his feet. Bending over her, he gave her another smile, hoping that would be enough. Honestly, he wanted more too. He wanted to see how her mind worked. And there would be time for that, he reminded himself.

They only got a couple hours of riding in that day. The paths were mucky with sludge and the rocks were too slick for the horses to get over easily. They were getting close to the most treacherous part of the journey, going through the mountains. Firian remembered the passes that he had taken to get to Brithnem, and didn't look forward to traversing them with someone unused to travel.

Kiria skipped out of the little shack, glad to be free. Almost immediately she said something about the ground smelling like artichokes. No one he knew talked like that, but he supposed she was right.

The next stop was a cave carved into the mountainside, as close as they could get without actually beginning to go over. Night fell as they went inside with the horses. The cave was big enough to house all four of them. Sounds echoed loudly, but Firian knew that the cave didn't go very far back. No enemies could attack from inside. It was a dry, strategic position where they could even build a fire without fear. Firian went to work on that immediately, gathering kindling from just outside the mouth of the cave. The larger sticks were still wet from the rain, but some smaller pieces of leaves and brush had dried.

Kiria dismounted and patted her horse gently on the face, happy for it. She whispered something to it. Probably its name. He had never considered names for the horses.

As he brought the brush back inside, Kiria laid out her bedroll. Even a few hours of riding had tired her out, apparently. Firian didn't mind. If she slept, it gave him more time to think. Their argument the day before still strained their conversations. The two of them would get along until something small turned the ankle of the discussion and brought it falling on its face. The simplest things offended her, but when she wasn't acting like a princess, she was all right. At least she tried to keep up with him and didn't complain very much.

He watched her out of the corner of his eye as he bent over the small pile of kindling, coaxing sparks out of the flint with his knife. She sat cross-legged on the bedroll, eating some rations. At times, her gaze flickered back at him.

He didn't want to give her another lesson today. He'd just stand watch over the cave most of the night, considering what to do. Little sleep didn't bother him at all.

Another few moments and she lay down to sleep, curled up, facing away from him. The trip must have exhausted her, because her breathing became deep and steady before he needed to add larger twigs to his little fire.

There wasn't much to see from the wide mouth of the cave. Even the rising moon was blocked by the mountain behind them. A blackened mass of trees was the only scenery. He turned back to Kiria's sleeping form, peaceful and innocently sensual there. Her shoulder sloped down to her waist and back up to her hip. At that moment, peace and restlessness wrestled in his chest. He missed the comfort and certainty of the Academy but he wanted to be here, the princess's sole protector. Despite her insults, she must trust him.

He worked his jaw. What was she dreaming about? He'd never gone into anyone's dreams before—well, once, for an assignment. But even Bard's colorful dreams had never interested him. He figured that if they sent him to war and he had to intimidate someone as part of a fear campaign, it wouldn't be that difficult.

People's subconscious intersected with the Unreal in dreams, so even people who didn't have the Talent could potentially be vulnerable.

The temptation of the Unreal pulled at his brain like a caught thread. Maybe it wouldn't be interesting. But it would be something.

He nudged his mind in her direction. Right away he saw a section of Mon Párinath. Deeply carved double doors of dark wood stood at the end of a hall lined with exotic potted trees and a mosaic floor. Two young women stood talking by the large doors. One had a parchment clutched in her hand but she faded in an instant. The other drew his gaze and kept it prisoner.

She was the most beautiful woman he had ever seen. Her hair fell long and full on her smoothly glowing skin. The floor-length blue dress fit her perfectly, its golden edges almost necessary to adorn her strong curves. Power spoke in her features—large, focused eyes, graceful hands, a mouth that could speak truth. Truth so piercing and final that it could shatter him.

Pleasure ran through him at the thought. Who was this goddess? To hold her would surpass any petty relationship he'd had. All of them looked as hollow as eggshells now.

Oddly, the gorgeous woman moved in a familiar way, although he would remember meeting anyone who looked like that. She was beautiful in a way that women never were, or maybe never had been. Her form made him ache, but even her *soul* was beautiful. He realized he was breathing fast as he watched her talk with that other girl.

The beauty turned toward him before vanishing. A stab of recognition shot through him. As he opened his eyes, he felt winded.

Kiria? Kiria can look like that? The vision seemed like too much to imagine casually. Did women imagine themselves as devastatingly brilliant in their dreams? His chest still constricted painfully at the memory. He had never wanted anything so much, except his position at the Academy, and at this moment, even that seemed on par.

He stared fiercely at Kiria's back. It couldn't be. He'd seen a vision, just a tantalizing vision. But he couldn't go back to seeing her the same way. If that divinely attractive woman in any way reflected Kiria, he would dig that part out of her. She would share it with him.

The night passed slowly. Firian hardly slept, even when the fire burned out. He'd always liked the cold, so he intentionally felt the breeze flow over him. Cold had the power to harden, to break. Heat tended to weaken.

He flexed his hands in the darkness, open and closed. He couldn't get the vision out of his mind. Maya waited for him back at the Academy—or at least she would come back to him when he returned—but she, despite her figure and her fierceness, didn't shine out like the negative image of Kiria burned into his brain.

A couple times he almost woke her, but he resisted, proud of his resolve.

As the morning sun leaked into the bare cave, she rolled onto her back. His heart gave a hard beat. She threw her arm over her eyes like Bard used to do and groaned.

"It's time to get moving," he said, surprising himself. He rarely spoke first in the morning. But now that he had her attention, he continued. "We have to get over the mountains today if we can." He almost leapt to his feet. Despite not sleeping, he didn't feel tired at all.

She brought her eyebrows together skeptically as she peeked above her arm. "We're going over the mountains in one day?" she asked, her voice husky with sleep.

"If we can," he repeated, cleaning up the fire and getting rid of its traces. He moved quickly, rushing from that to the horses, where he began to heave the saddles onto their backs.

Resigned, she grabbed her knees and sat up.

He carefully watched her stand and slowly repack her bag. Compared to the stunning woman, she moved heavily, clumsily. Her hair wasn't as thick or rich. It hung limply around her face. She wasn't ugly, but she was another eggshell person. He had to have imagined it. There was no way Kiria could have been the woman in the vision.

As soon as the horses were saddled, he jogged over and grabbed her pack.

"Thank you," she murmured, yawning. "You seem like you're in a good mood."

He tilted his head back and forth.

"I can't believe I slept so well. Did you watch all night? Did anybody come?" She looked at him with trust in her eyes.

Maybe a glimpse of the beautiful woman shone there, like sunlight on a flipped coin. Enough to give him hope. "Nobody came. There aren't many people around here," he said.

"I'm glad we're going through the mountains, then," she replied, passing him on the way to her horse. She worked her fingers through the knots in her hair. Her face showed that she wasn't used to wearing the same clothes multiple days in a row. Now she knew better than to mention it, though.

He handed her some dried fruit for breakfast. Their store had gotten a little slimy in the rain, but they couldn't be picky. Soon enough—nine days or so—they would be in Carradoc and get new food. He fished through the pack for his helping and realized their rations wouldn't last that long, not with two people. Only lone hunters and meager tribes lived in the mountains themselves. If they cut straight north instead of northeast, they could shave off a day and restock their food supplies in Raewhith.

The thought stopped him short. He hadn't seen Raewhith since he was a boy. On the bright side, no one there would recognize him as a grown man. He swallowed. *Not even my family.* They were all gone.

Now was not the time to feel sentimental. They had to go to Raewhith to replenish their food, and then they would cut east to Shifra from there. They wouldn't lose more than two days. The leaders at Brithnem seemed a little jumpy, so he would let them know about the change of plan when they got closer.

"Have you heard anything from the Watchman?" Kiria asked, nibbling on the fruit and struggling not to let disgust show on her face.

"Not yet." In fact, he'd almost completely forgotten about him. Besides a cursory check at sunrise and sunset, per their agreement, he didn't waste a thought on him. And he didn't check in last night.

How could he say what he'd seen in her dream? He looked for a way to bring it up and nothing sounded right. "Kiria, you did a good job yesterday," he said finally. Using names usually brought good results. "I'm amazed you haven't used the Talent before."

She smiled at the compliment. Her horse stamped the ground beside her. "I didn't even know I had it. It's crazy that I can do that. I thought everybody imagined things," she said, running her hand over the saddle. "You should give me another lesson today. The last one was terrible."

"What? Terrible?" *What does she mean by that?*

"It was too short."

"Oh." He leaned just a little closer, trying to hide his smirk. "You want *more* of my lessons?"

"Not like that," she said, waving him away. "It's just interesting. I want to know more about what you do."

"The Amir never told you?" he asked because they both knew the answer.

"No," she said pointedly, finishing her tiny portion and getting up on her horse.

He felt the conversation fizzle to a stop. That wasn't good. He had to know—was she or was she not the gorgeous girl in her vision? He stalled. "You know, I heard... before I came down to Brithnem... that you were very beautiful," he said, hating that he sounded unsure.

She looked at him sideways, as though reading his thoughts, almost accusingly. Even without answering, she confirmed it. A pleasurable chill ran through his body. "We decided that I wouldn't use my Ability on this trip," she said. "It would just draw attention, so it's better that I stay this way."

He fought to keep the excitement out of his voice. "But you have the Ability to change?"

"Yes." She raised the end of the word in a question and note of caution. "But I'm not going to. Why are you suddenly so interested?"

Watching her dreams sounded creepy, so he couldn't tell her the real story. "I just thought I should know. That information is important. If I'm going to keep track of you, I need to know all the ways you can look." As the words came out, he realized how stupid they sounded.

"Really?" She raised her eyebrows and looked like she knew exactly what he really wanted. "It doesn't just happen on its own."

The memory of her Beauty burned inside him like rage. He mounted his horse to see her at eye level. "I think you should show me. The whole Kingdom has seen you that way."

"I don't want to," she said quietly but firmly.

"I'm not going to do anything to you," he said, moving his horse parallel to hers.

Still she shook her head.

The absurdity of it all hit him then. "Why do you hide these things about yourself? You're beautiful and you don't show it. You're the heir to a kingdom and you act like you have no power. You have the Talent and didn't even know. It's ridiculous! You've been given everything, and you act like it's nothing!" He realized he was standing high on the stirrups, his stomach knotted in frustration.

She blinked fast but didn't recoil.

"I came from nothing and I worked. Harder than anybody else. I practice—I still practice!" He swept his arm over where she had slept. "I've given up sleep and comfort to be here. You sit there like a princess, expecting everything. What have you done to earn this? And why do you act like you have nothing?" The silence surged in like noise after his words. He exhaled the breath he'd been holding tight in his chest.

Kiria flushed bright red and her eyes glistened, but she didn't bite back, as though she feared the words that would come out. Something fierce lay coiled behind her expression.

His throat constricted uncomfortably. He had told the truth, but he'd ruined his chances with her. Certainly today, maybe for a very long time. What was he thinking?

She opened her mouth to speak, tasting the words beforehand. "You will not speak to me until I speak to you," she said, each word deliberate and distinct. She held up a hand as though he were about to protest. "No. You will do your job, and that is all. One day you will regret speaking to me as you just have. You have no right. I forgave you the first time, but this proves that you think yourself above an heir of Brithnem, and I will not tolerate that." With a finger, she gestured that they should begin riding.

Firian's mouth tasted like bile, but every word he had said to this girl was true. He bit his tongue until it bled, almost unaware of the pain, or thankful for it. The horses clearly felt the tension and tossed their heads uneasily, taking more than once to get over obstacles. The frustration cooled his bones, running like iron through his veins.

He had no words to speak. That should please her.

31

KIRIA

Gray light, just enough to see by, streamed into the outpost. Kiria grated her eyes open. The tension between her and Firian these past two days had made her jumpy and anxious. Every noise sounded like an enemy. All news was bad news. Anger radiated like heat off Firian even as he rode.

Alone with her thoughts, she listened as Firian's words hurdled down familiar tracks in her mind. He never should have said those things. The memory made her so angry she could cry. Tanyu would see that as weakness, though, so she swallowed tears down into bitterness. *You act like you have nothing.* He'd spat the words, so angry that she was given everything *he* wanted. That she wanted the same things, but she got them without working as hard. His arrogance made more sense now, but she couldn't excuse it.

The small, round outpost had two floors, so she had taken the second and he the first. Quiet thuds rose up from the first floor. He was practicing again, doing some kind of exercise.

She closed her eyes. If not for hunger, she doubted she would ever go downstairs. If only Jori or her mother could be here. Firian didn't scare her as much as he should, she realized. He could hurt her easily if he wanted to. If he did, though, the Keepers would kill him. She had absolutely no doubt.

Why do you act like you have no power?

She chewed her lip. That line had grown on her mind. Easing herself up, she looked around the little circular room. Wooden floors, stone walls, two embrasures in place of windows. And a staircase leading down. Firian was arrogant and wrong about a lot of things, but something about that line hit her strangely. Maybe it was true. What had she done with all her power? As a child, she anticipated being the Keeper, but she lost that fire when she grew up. It had all happened so slowly. Before Atty's coronation, she had done everything she could to forget she was an heir at all. There would always be time... and then there wasn't.

She winced as she stood up on her bad leg. Her back ached in a dozen places and a crick twinged in her neck. Traveling wasn't very fun, but she would be tougher at the end of it. And she was starting to realize that that's what she wanted. A Keeper shouldn't be soft. She should be able to battle injustice, weather storms, mete out wisdom, rise as a symbol of hope for a nation, never to be crushed.

From now on, if Firian was awake, so was she.

She stood up and stretched. Her bouts of anxiety wouldn't keep her from becoming the Keeper she dreamed of being. During these in-between hours she could practice visualizing things in the Unreal, exercise like Firian did, quote the Scroll to keep it fresh in her mind, or start thinking seriously about what she wanted to change about Brithnem when she was its leader. Darkness provided plenty of opportunity.

But it was still early, and her limbs felt tired. If she went downstairs, she couldn't sit and relax, not with Firian watching.

It's good for me. This is good for me, she told herself. Hopefully that was true.

Slowly, she packed her bedroll and slung it over her shoulder as she headed down the stairs. Firian sat on the ground doing sit-ups, covered in a light sheen of sweat. Small scars shone white on the ridges of his abs.

When she came in, he didn't stop. They just gave each other a piercing look. Firian's eyes flashed with suspicion but not anger. His dark eyebrows came together and his concentration redoubled. Maybe the icy attitude had thawed a little on both sides overnight.

She slumped her pack by the door next to his. Automatically, she checked her hands. Still plain.

A little self-conscious, she sat on the floor and began to stretch her bad leg. Her movement was so much easier than his, but it was all she could manage at this hour. She leaned down and reached for her outstretched foot. Ignoring Firian, she closed her eyes. Dark sleep surged near her like the tide. That wasn't going to work. She needed something else to keep her awake. Under her breath, she murmured a passage of the Sacred Scroll that Daelon had made her memorize years ago. It was a long passage, so that should keep her focused for a while. Her lips formed the words as she felt the stretch burn up her calf to her thigh. *Careful.* The last thing she wanted was to reopen that scab-covered wound. She switched to the other leg, wrapping her hand around that foot. This actually felt good. Maybe waking up so early wouldn't be terrible.

A small shuffle meant that Firian was on his feet. She opened her eyes and saw him nibble on one of their rations. He had been taking less. Probably thought she didn't notice.

He looked down at her and held up the piece of hardtack in a question. She shrugged and nodded. He had to reach past her to get a new piece out of his bag. He smelled like musk and pine.

After he handed her the food, she said, "We don't need to leave right away."

He raised his eyebrows. She had broken the endless silence.

"I just figured that as long as you were awake, I should be up." The first bite of hardtack dried out her mouth. She kept chewing, trying to moisten the crumbs, but she had no saliva. "Are we getting close to Shifra?" she asked, clearing her throat.

Firian searched her face. "Five more days. We'll need to stop for food."

"Where?"

"Raewhith. It's a little town just north." He pointed vaguely without looking.

She hadn't heard of it. It must not be big enough to merit a place on the palace maps. Still, speaking to him without antagonism was a relief. Neither apologized, but they had moved on. "I thought we might run out," she said, swallowing the dry crumbs.

He grunted. "The rain took out half the supply."

She pursed her lips. *Shouldn't he have known to plan better?* He reached past her again to get his black shirt and stretch it over his head.

She sat, considering him. "I was thinking," she said, "shouldn't I know more about defending myself? Maybe you could show me a couple things."

She flushed, suddenly angry with herself. Firian made her uncomfortable. Did she really want him teaching her self-defense? If only she could ask someone else, but they were alone, and the Torithians still targeted her. What if Firian couldn't manage on his own? She had to know *something*. Daelon's image flashed through her mind, knowledgeable and gentle. Not the sort to teach her anything but disembodied warfare tactics. And her mother never prioritized safety as highly as she should.

"I know the emergency procedures in the palace if something goes wrong," she added quickly, "but that mostly involves hiding in safe rooms. I didn't know what to do when…" Her voice and gaze drifted off to her wounds. She hadn't meant to bring those up.

"You know I can take care of you," Firian said in typical fashion, offering his hand to pull her up.

Kiria almost rolled her eyes. She got up by herself. "Don't be like that. You know what I mean. I would feel better knowing that I could do something if anything… were to happen again. Honestly, I'm a little surprised something didn't happen earlier." The more she'd thought about it—and the attack had consumed her thoughts these past couple days—the more surprising it seemed.

"What do you mean?"

She lowered her voice, as though others stood in the next room with their ears cocked. "It wouldn't be hard to besiege the city if they came in with enough troops."

Firian blinked once, his only sign of surprise.

"Tell them when the sun comes up," she said. The Watchman would relay all her updates to the Keepers. They might all know that a siege posed a great threat, but then, if they did, no one had told her.

"Sure," said Firian, glancing at the gray light rimming the door. Dawn would come soon. The cold breath of air ushering through the room announced it. "And I can show you a couple moves." He took another bite of his dry breakfast.

She waited. He didn't move. "Why don't you show me now?" she asked, pleased that he could see she didn't mean to sit around as he served her. He hadn't done a great job of that anyway.

He shoved the rest of the hardtack in his mouth and wiped the crumbs off his hands. She smirked as he kept chewing the dry biscuit.

"Main thing is mindset," he managed through the crumbs. Irritation showed through his face, but his full mouth just made it funny. She held back a laugh. He swallowed half of what filled his mouth and tried again. "The main thing is mindset. Always be aware. Always look people in the eye."

She nodded. "Okay."

"Now, if someone comes up to attack you, there are a lot of options." He held up a hand to number his points. "You can run, get away. You can hide. You can fight back."

"How do I fight back?" Not a lot she could do against a flying arrow, but maybe she could take out an attacker close by.

"There are many ways to kill a man—"

"I don't want to kill him."

A smile played on the corners of his mouth. "What if you have to?"

"I just want to hurt him."

"You might have to kill him."

"Just show me how to stop someone."

He actually smiled at that. She squinted at him. It didn't look like a bitter smile. Was he mocking her? "Okay. I'll show you how to stop someone," he said. "There are many ways to *stop* a person. You want to focus on a couple areas, if you can. Everyone has weak points, so exploit those." He paused fractionally, maybe remembering her angry speech. "The eyes, the throat, the groin. Use anything you can to strike those. Just one should make anyone stop."

"I just punch him in the throat?" It sounded too easy.

"Or scratch his eyes. Knee him in the balls. Whatever you can," he said almost lazily.

"What if they have a knife?" A thousand scenarios floated up in her mind. What if her arms were pinned to her sides? What if two people came at her at once?

"The sun's rising," he said, turning away.

"Wait! Pretend to attack me." She needed to get at least some sense of what he was saying.

He shook his head. "Pretend to attack you? You don't want me to do that." He didn't say it out of fear. It was as though he knew that, if he did, she would get angry again. And their relationship was just starting to be bearable again.

"Here, just be careful," she said, spreading her feet to brace herself.

Before she could get out of the way, his hands shot forward and grabbed her wrists. He twisted her arms behind her back and turned her around, pinning her against the wall with his body. She felt his breath by her ear. "What would you do?" he asked.

Her insides squirmed. With a heave, she pushed back against him and he let her go. She rounded on him. "I'd... kick you where it hurts!" she said fiercely. He was right. She was fuming, and smelled faintly like pine.

"That's what you should do," he said, crossing his arms, smiling, "but I thought you wouldn't hurt me. For a real attacker, just act. Don't think. You have too much sympathy."

"At least I have some."

He paused, his smile fading. "I need to check in with the Watchman," he said, turning away briefly.

The door outside beckoned. She would rather be with the horses than with Firian right now. But she needed not to put herself in any danger, for her family's sake and for Brithnem's. Her sense of helplessness returned. Back in the palace, she could be independent, but this journey locked her in a cage, tethered to someone she didn't even like.

Happily, Firian's silent update didn't take long. The way he returned showed her that the Torithian threat still lurked in the palace and that they still had to continue. "Ready?" she asked, impatient.

"Let's go."

Outside, the horses were already saddled. Kiria didn't relish the idea of waking up even earlier, but she would if it meant matching Firian's dedication. *Eyes, throat, groin.* She could remember that. Maybe tonight she would suggest playing Indisfate instead of a lesson. She could beat him at that. Teach him not to be so cocky.

"Today," Firian announced as Kiria swept Indisfate pieces into her pack, "we'll see if you can imagine an environment that we can both be in. This can be a little difficult at first, because you have to hold the place together enough for the other to move around in it. Understand?"

She picked the hay out of the handful of rocks and pinecones that served as game pieces. Beating him at the game had put Kiria in a better mood, and he seemed glad to move on to something he knew better. "Do you want it to be any place in particular?" she asked.

"Someplace familiar is all right," he replied. "Later you can create new places, so you don't have to use memories, but it's easier if you can remember something. Just plant something unfamiliar in it—an object or a different color—so you can remind yourself it isn't real."

She nodded, trying to come up with a place. Coming up with anything besides the palace proved difficult. She missed it. Grime covered the abandoned barn where they sat, but the space was warm. She couldn't wait to return to her clean bed. But at least she had beaten Firian at something.

She could picture the arena. Statues and rows of seats rose above her. Gold burned brightly in the sunlight. She stood on hard-packed sand in the shade of the magnificent figures. The smell of the dusty barn filled her nose, and straw ends poked into her legs as she sat cross-legged on the ground. *No, it smells like hot sand and a breeze. The sun hurts my eyes.* It took a few minutes for the shelter to fade away completely and for the arena to take hard-edged shape. Once the setting stabilized, she looked around for Firian. Turning around, she found herself face to face with him.

She jumped and the image wavered. Elements vanished.

"Get it back," he said patiently and leaned back against the statue of Shane Calthwaite. He watched her, smiling slightly as she struggled to restore the image.

The arena materialized around her, complete again. "There."

"Very good," he said. "Now talk to me. You have to get used to interacting in this space. It has to be second nature."

The statue wobbled. She forced it back. "What should I talk about?"

"It doesn't matter. Just look at me and talk."

She eyed him, clear-cut in the arena. He aggravated her, but being friendly and showing some goodwill might go a long way. "Where are you from?"

He chewed his lip before answering. Always so secretive. "Raewhith," he said.

His answer sent the soaring risers to dust. "The town where we're headed?" A few seconds later the background returned.

He nodded, scratching the back of his neck.

"Is that why we're going there?" she asked.

"No. No, we just need supplies. I wasn't lying about that."

"Is your family still there?" Firian acted so independent that it was almost hard to picture him with a family.

At her question, his thoughts became so loud that her vision darkened again, oppressed by an almost audible buzzing. "No," he said.

"Where are they now?"

He picked at the foot of the statue with his fingernail. "They're dead." His voice was small, matter-of-fact, but he didn't meet her eye.

She gasped. "I'm so sorry! I didn't know... What happened?"

"There was a fire." The two of them now stood in darkness with only the statues rising behind them. Firian's gaze flickered up to her. "Get it back," he said again, waiting.

She struggled to put the arena together again. *Why did I choose something so complicated?* The last seats, the blue of the sky, the expanse of sand, all settled into place. Firian waited for her, lost in thought. She saw Atty in his eyes. "I'm sure they'd be proud of you," she said gently.

He scoffed. An honest reaction, unedited.

"No, really," she said. There was no sense in bringing up his shortcomings now. Surely his family would be impressed by his accomplishments. "You come from a little town and now you're a Tanyu. That's impressive. Look what you taught me." She cast her eyes around the arena she loved so well.

He tipped his mouth, weighing her words.

"You could do so much good with what you have! I'm sure they'd be happy with that."

"They were never happy with me." He whispered the words almost to himself as though he couldn't hold them in. After they escaped, his face darkened.

Something twisted in her gut. Firian was usually all callous bravado, trying to cultivate a sense of mystery. But here was the truth, the pain that lay beneath. She didn't know what to say. "Well, look where you are now," she tried.

He looked up from the sand at his feet and gazed at her steadily, seriously, as though trying to find meaning in her face. He read her features like a scroll, scrutinizing them for signs of deception. His brow furrowed in concentration. To speak now would mean breaking his trust in this moment of vulnerability, but she felt uncomfortable. Maybe he wouldn't find the meaning he wanted.

His gaze dropped. A sarcastic smile spread over his face. "It's true. They never expected this."

"Did you?"

"What?"

"Did you expect this?"

He considered for a moment. "Yes, I did. I knew I could make it happen." There wasn't as much arrogance in this statement as she was used to. He just stated the truth as he saw it. Coming back to the present, he shook himself and changed the subject. "You keep talking about doing good. What will you do when you're the Keeper? Keep looking at me."

That's right—we're still practicing. "I used to think a lot about it," she confessed. "Anybody who's going to be put in that kind of position should think about it very seriously, I think. I would... Well, I've thought about making more copies of the Scroll so they wouldn't be confined to the Amiran Academy. I'm trying to work out how to improve our defenses and our alliances." She tried to gauge Firian's reaction so far. He took it all stoically. She continued, remembering some of the notes she had years ago, along with ideas she'd had just before the attack. "Some of the roads are very bad, so I'd fix those. Relations between Kingdom and Khelê are strained in some places, so I'd do my best to make peace between those groups. And there ought to be more beautiful statues and paintings because it's good to remember heroes and appreciate what we have. People will protect something they love. Those are some of my ideas." They sounded too simple when she stated them in a row like that, but many nights of thought had brought her to those conclusions. It had been a while since anyone had asked.

"That's not a bad beginning," Firian said thoughtfully.

"Beginning?" she asked. "What would *you* do?"

He just smiled.

Her own laugh surprised her. To feel comfortable enough to laugh was a relief. It made her burst out laughing harder. "What do you mean that it's not a bad beginning?" she said.

"You think too small," he said, clearly glad that they weren't talking about his past anymore. This topic made him stand taller, look bigger. She got the sense that he was flexing his arms. "You only live one time. You get *one* shot. Is that what you're going to do with it? Or do you have the courage to do what isn't safe?"

She fell through his words into a vision of herself, beautiful and admired, victoriously bringing peace, well-being, and the knowledge of God to every person in Brithnem, now celebrated as the center of all culture and learning, and as the home of the world's best warriors. Wise and well loved, her life was filled with romance and adventure. She, alone, overturned expectations by bringing wars to an end. Strong in mind and body, she made bold decisions, saving her people and enlightening the other Keepers.

The vision was vague but powerful, like strong perfume. Uneasy, she shook it off.

He looked expectantly at her.

"You didn't answer my question," she said.

"You're right. I didn't," he agreed. "Your plans aren't bad, but I prefer action to words. Maybe I'll show you someday."

She rolled her eyes. "Stop trying to be mysterious."

"I'm being honest," he replied. It seemed like he used honesty, rather than being an honest person. A moment ago, she had seen through the veneer, but it was back.

"Still, I'd like to know what you'd do," she said. "You won't ever control the Kingdom, so it's best to tell me now so I can be impressed." She quirked her mouth in a smile. "If your ideas are good enough, maybe I'll do something about them." She stood tall, squaring her shoulders. "It's a rare opportunity."

"I prefer the surprise," he said, mouth lifting in a smirk.

"Well, you're not going—"

A soft scuffling noise bled through the Unreal. Firian's image popped like a bubble as he went back to reality. Kiria froze, her breath hitched in sudden terror. *They found me.* The arena disappeared completely until all she saw was the back of her eyelids. She focused all her energy on hearing until the barn seemed loud in the silence. The hair that had fallen in front of her ears rubbed together like dry straw, a tree creaked outside, a breeze hissed through the barn slats, bringing the pattering of blown hay with it. Firian's quick, gentle footsteps echoed. She curled further into herself, braced for what would come.

Firian laughed.

Her eyes sprang open. She didn't hear that sound often. Firian stood in the middle of the shadowy barn and pointed to the corner. A brown cat arched its back to slink through a gap below the boards. Its soft tail darted out behind it.

She exhaled. *Only a cat.* After a few more heavy breaths of relief, she grinned and put her hand over her face. She peered at Firian through her spread fingers. "It's a good thing you were here," she said.

He popped his dark eyebrows up in mock agreement. "That cat would have gotten you otherwise."

32

FIRIAN

Firian's muscles strained as he pushed himself up. Power flowed through his arms, his back, his shoulders pinching together. Riding horses only worked out a couple muscles and left him feeling sore but not strong. The morning routine he'd had back at the Academy made him feel more like himself.

In the middle of the barn floor, Kiria rolled over and sat up, woozy from sleep. She leaned over her knees in an easy motion that reminded him of the grace he'd seen in her glorious dream. Though he might want to, he couldn't forget the burning beauty he'd witnessed. If he forced her to show him, though, he would only gain an enemy. The greater challenge was winning her trust and inspiring her to become beautiful of her own free will. And he never shied away from the greater challenge.

Eyes half-mast, Kiria struggled to sit cross-legged. She worked both hands through her long hair and muttered something to herself. Maybe she was praying. She did that sometimes.

He eased himself up slowly, precisely, to his feet.

"Good morning," she murmured.

Half his mouth lifted. "Morning," he said. She was like Bard, in love with sleep, and yet she woke up early every morning since she had committed to keeping pace with him. And her training in the Unreal was going well, as far as he could tell. At least she progressed fairly quickly. Her ideas were naïve, but she had a streak of independent thought. All her criticism at the beginning left a bad taste in his mouth, but he could learn a lot about Brithnem from her. Sometimes she surprised him with her knowledge of large-scale warfare. She didn't talk about it often, but there was an ease that made him want to lean in close. His training had been almost exclusively on individual tactics—the work of a person, not an army. But what kind of warrior was he if he didn't understand as much as she did about clashing nations?

Her head hung low, weighed down with sleep. Tangles of mousy brown hair fell into her lap. Her lips continued to move in some kind of plea or recitation. He got out a water skin and sat across from her. When he thrust it into her hands, she started and looked up, straining to see through the dimness. Blinking, she took a drink.

"Lessons this morning?" he asked.

She looked at the ground, thinking. "Just don't..." she began, but her thought trailed off.

He knew what she was thinking. As much as she liked his lessons in the Unreal, she'd gotten angry when he showed her basic self-defense, as though he should have gone easy on her. That's not how self-defense worked. Enemies wouldn't match their strength to hers. It was best for her to learn that right away. And besides, he liked the feel of her body against his. Maybe she did too.

Yes, he would prefer to teach physical than mental self-defense today. Yesterday, he had revealed too much about himself. Hardly anyone knew those things. Frankly, though, she was a good person to tell. His confession made her soften toward him, yet she didn't patronize him.

"I don't think there's enough time," she said in a husky voice, looking at the dusty light beginning to stream in. It was still ghostly gray, but she was right. He had to check in with the Watchman soon.

"Later," he said, leaving her to her water and prayers.

Maybe the Watchman would be ready now. A little early, but they were a priority, so the Watchman's mind definitely turned their way. He cast his mind south toward Brithnem. Only silence, stretching like a sea into darkness. There wasn't much to report—and he wasn't going to tell them about her Talent—so would it be terrible to miss a day?

He waited in silence. Hazily, he felt the light grow around him. Kiria's whispering made the quiet almost religious, or at least meditative. Deep in his lungs, air dragged in and out. Blood beat in his ears. Still no Watchman. Firian had practiced patience all his life, but he had none when another was supposed to come and didn't arrive on time. His mind began to buzz with suppressed fury, growing low like a mold. He wouldn't wait forever.

A flash of thought dawned so brightly that he squinted before remembering they were in the Unreal. There was no light.

He stood face to face with Brithnem's Watchman, whose wizened face, rubbed to a smoothness of deep wrinkles, now contorted with urgency. Firian was usually the first to speak, but now wasn't the time. Something was wrong. The Watchman's usually impassive eyes glinted with the whites. "Defender Kess, is My Kepress with you?" he said quickly.

"Yes," Firian said, his own eyes widening. He reached out into the Unreal, like feeling blindly with one hand, to check for dangers around the barn. Nothing.

"I have terrible news," the Watchman said. "General Rhet has been killed. Do *not* bring the Kepress back to the palace. Take her to the safety of Carradoc as planned. A full-scale search for the Torithians will continue until they are caught and executed."

Firian's face went cold. His heart beat thickly in his chest. "Yes," he said stupidly.

"You must tell the Kepress."

He licked his lips. "I will." What else could he say?

The Watchman nodded once and vanished to complete other business.

Firian let the real world in slowly, seeping back into his consciousness like blood.

It's just an assignment. Just an assignment. Just tell her.

Thankful that his back was to her, he let his eyes dart around the room. *Just say the words.* He tried to form his tongue around them, but they puffed like cotton in his mouth.

He steadied his breathing and turned around. Kiria was on her feet, watching him with suspicion. His back must have shown his tension. Stalling, he grabbed his shirt and put it on. She always wanted him to cover up. At this moment, she didn't know about her father. Her fragile peace was about to break.

"What is it?" she asked, her voice nervous.

His guts squirmed. He had to do it now. And he was usually so good at hiding things. Why couldn't he have bought himself some time, been kind to her for a while? Maybe this was better—just getting it out. This news would have soured every hour he held it inside.

He cleared his throat. Kiria turned pale, realizing how serious he was. "The Watchman" – he swallowed, out of breath – "he just said that... um, General Rhet has... been killed..."

"What?" Her face was bloodless.

He tried to say the words again, but they wouldn't come. So he only nodded.

Her body twitched, convulsing in small ways as though she was about to be sick. Shaking her head once, she tried to speak, confusion pooling in her eyes.

He nodded again, answering her unsaid protest. It was true.

With a pitched groan, her knees buckled. He almost caught her before she collapsed to the floor. Kneeling with her, he tried to set her down but she lay across his knees, as though unable to sit up. She shook violently in his arms. The first sob came in a burst, almost a scream. The sound twisted through his gut, painfully recognizable.

More violent sobs chased the first, as though the noise had admitted the truth that he was dead, had sealed his fate. Words tried to form, almost screamed out, but they died in a chaos of pain. Her hands moved in confusion, up to her mouth, down in a question. His left knee grew warm and wet with her tears. He heaved her up to a more comfortable position with her face in his shoulder.

The light grew around them as she bared her teeth, shuddering with grief. Finally, she pulled herself up to sit. "What happened?" she stammered, her chest rising and falling raggedly, convulsively.

"Torithians," he replied quietly.

A fresh gush of sobbing made her cling to him, grabbing his shoulders so hard her nails dug into his skin. She pressed her face into one shoulder as weeping rocked her again. She moved as though trapped in her own body. Unsure of what else to do, he held her close to his chest, swallowing against the rock in his throat.

Tears and snot smeared the shoulder of his black shirt, and he felt her hot breath as her crying began to subside from the screams of shock to the weeping of grief.

He shifted her just enough to reach for the dagger he kept by his side. Bending his leg toward himself, he reached for his ankle and sawed off the cuff of his black pants. Sheathing the knife, he drew the fabric around one of Kiria's wrists and tied it there.

She looked at it, uncomprehending at first. She stretched her fingers and balled them back into a fist, watching the tendons in her wrist shift against the mourning bracelet. He drew her back in. She didn't protest and held him like a ledge to keep her from falling.

THEY COULDN'T TRAVEL FAR that day. Kiria was too distraught. Firian offered her his share of the food, knowing that their rations wouldn't stretch the extra day, but she refused. No appetite.

He went to check on the horses, who would be getting a long rest today. They both chomped contentedly at the grasses around the barn.

Possibilities. Belik's words from a recent lesson came to him. *Possibilities are currency. Always think of more. Death is just the end of one possibility. For better or worse, you won't see that person anymore. Without possibilities, our lives would snuff in the present moment, all the air sucked out. But there are always more.*

As soon as he walked back in, he sensed the energy in the barn had shifted. "We have to go back to Brithnem," she said sternly. The sun was high and her eyes burned red.

"We can't—"

"We *have to*. They'll target my mother next. I can't believe I was so selfish!" Tears sprang again to her eyes as she looked up at the roof. "We have to leave now."

He shook his head. "We can't leave now."

"But—"

"The Watchman told me to keep you safe. So that's what I'm doing."

"Take me back!" She demanded with the voice of a queen, eyes flashing.

"No."

She stomped toward him with fists balling at her sides, the ragged scrap of black fabric still tied around one wrist.

"I can't," he said calmly, refusing to take a step back as she charged at him. "Just think. You couldn't do any good there. If you're right, then you're just making yourself an easy target, too. Remember, your mother hired me to look out for you. She doesn't want you to come home."

Her words barely made it out. "But she's alone." Her determined steps wavered to a shuffling stop. Her gaze dropped to his feet.

"I'm sure she's surrounded by guards now," he said, trying to catch her eyeline, but she shrugged off his comment as though it meant nothing. "She's safe."

"I need to be there for her," she insisted. Their only course of action was obvious, but she kept letting her pain speak for her.

"Think about the Kingdom," he said. If she was so worried about being selfish, then this would catch her attention. "What would they do if they lost the Second Line?"

She swallowed visibly. "I can't let that happen," she said so quietly that it barely went beyond moving her lips.

"See? There."

"Chetana is with her, and Daelon," she said to herself. "And she knows I would come if I could..."

He nodded solemnly in agreement. After a moment, he asked, "Do you think you can ride today?"

She tucked her hair behind her ear, still avoiding his gaze. "That might be good. I'll go crazy if I stay here."

He felt the same way. The shadows in the drafty barn replayed the past few hours in a relentless loop. He preferred to remain stoic, not rocked by memories.

A buzz. He snapped his head around to look behind him. Someone was very close. He dove into the Unreal, grateful that Kiria had turned away. *More news? No, it's coming from the wrong direction.*

Dark, spiky hair on a slight frame, dressed all in Academy black. He knew it as clearly as the smell of cinnamon. Bard. Firian let out a sigh of relief, but his insides clenched again with the uncertainty of why he had come. "Bard! What are you doing here?"

Bard grinned wide, a smile that split his face. "Hey, Fir!" he said. Neither one of them bothered with a background. Just the two of them floating in space.

"Wait, what are you doing here?" Firian repeated, though his stomach relaxed at Bard's happy expression.

"Just seeing how you're doing." Bard's black eyes darted down, then up. He was hiding something.

"Checking on me?" Firian asked, almost moved. The death of Kiria's father had weakened him. He pushed out his chest.

"Yeah. Well, I have to. It's for an assignment. Master Gerand got back yesterday so she's teaching *katah* again. We're supposed to practice—"

"You're declaring *katah* on me?" Firian grimaced, torn between feeling disgusted and amused. It was still a mystery why the Masters had added *katah* to Bard's schedule. He was a guy, and the word "sex" made him blush. Usually, women learned the craft and seduced opposing generals and tacticians. That's how *katah* worked.

"No, no," Bard said quickly. "It's not that. And *katah* isn't what you think." He turned his pleading gaze to Firian's face. "I need somebody to focus on, Fir. You're the only one I could think of."

Firian huffed a laugh through his nose.

"Please, Fir? You know how Master Gerand is."

He raised an eyebrow and tipped his head to the side. He really did know. Two weeks of traveling with that woman was more than enough.

"Are you coming back soon too?" Bard asked, barely masking the hope in his voice.

"I don't think so."

"Are you still with the Kepress?"

Leave it to Bard to use her accurate title the first time. "Yes, she's here."

"What's she like?" Bard had a question beneath this one: *Are you behaving yourself around her?*

It would be fun to pretend that he had struck Kiria with a wild passion for him the moment they met, but he couldn't lie. Not when the Masters might find out somehow. Kiria was too important an asset for him to mess with right now. Besides, if *she* found out, she'd hate him after all she had been through today, and she didn't need any more pain.

"She's..." Firian struggled for a word. "She's not bad. She's tougher than I thought."

Judging from Bard's expression, he hadn't expected that answer. "I wish I could meet her," he said. "It isn't the same here without you around. It feels like we're moving. The Head keeps ordering us to clear out rooms. It's weird."

Firian knit his brows. "That's strange."

"Yeah," said Bard, encouraged by Firian's interest. "But I'm sure it's much more interesting where you are. Have you seen any Torithians yet?"

"No." Firian shook his head. "I don't think we'll see any. I'm going to stock up on food and then we'll head to a safe location." The Torithians' easy window was rapidly closing. Which reminded him. "We're actually leaving now," he said.

"Okay," Bard replied, with the awkwardness of expecting the other to leave first. That meant he would keep watching him, per Master Gerand's orders. With enough focus, the kind required for *katah,* any Tanyu could sense another person's mind and even watch their thoughts to some extent, even when they weren't consciously in the Unreal together. Firian had never practiced the discipline. Did Gerand want to learn about his mission through Bard? Firian had a feeling she did. The look Bard gave him confirmed his suspicion. His friend shrugged apologetically.

Curse her.

Firian regarded Bard for a few seconds. "S'okay," he finally said.

Bard looked relieved, a little smile forming in his eyes and around his mouth.

Let Gerand look. She would find nothing to criticize.

33

FIRIAN

Now that they were over the mountains, Firian recognized this part of the woods. He had always had a pretty good idea of where they were, but now he knew every path and tree. The nearness of Raewhith settled like a weight in his chest. All at once, his situation felt surreal. He was returning to the town where he grew up, now as a Tanyuin bodyguard for the Kepress of Brithnem. He glanced at her riding beside him. She had struggled with the reality of her father's death the past few days, but their lessons in the Unreal had helped. She was coming along nicely, able to keep a strong image steady and talk to him at the same time. They stuck with safe, non-emotional subjects: her interest in music, Jori's antics, her love for fruit tarts. Even though she trusted him more now, she never brought up her Ability, and they hadn't spoken of the general.

A few low buildings peeped through the trees. Their memory smelled like dust or a familiar meal. He lifted his head to see around the little brown shops. Did he recognize anyone? Should he hide if he did?

Why am I so nervous?

They emerged by the edge of a bustling street lined with shops. Memories piled thickly over him. To the left, just out of sight was the trade school where he had gone as a boy. To the right was the road to his house where he had grown up.

Jovan's voice came to mind. *Even when you're in the Unreal, remember where you are. Never lose your balance in the moment.* Firian fought to stay aware of the present when the past and even the Unreal washed over him like a strong current. He rotated his shoulders and cracked his neck, just to feel them.

Next to the blacksmith's was the stable. He had learned the order of the shops as he had learned his numbers: *the tailor, the fruit seller, the cooper, the blacksmith, the stable... one, two, three, four, five...* Despite his unease, their order felt correct, like puzzle pieces fitting together. Exactly as they should be.

They dismounted and led their horses to the stable. After a brief exchange with the boy on duty, the two of them set out on foot, weaving through the little crowd buying and selling.

He kept his head down and his eyes up as they edged past other shoppers. Schoolchildren peeked through the alleys between shops to watch them as they passed. Raewhith didn't get very many visitors.

"Plums! Nice juicy plums!" cried the man at the fruit stand, holding up a purple plum in three fingers, as others would hold up a prized possession. "Plums! Only one token each!" Kiria, hurrying beside him in her plain brown dress, shot him a glance, concern glinting in her eyes. He tilted his head forward to urge her to walk on, looking into her eyes. *There's nothing to get nervous about.* Fruit wouldn't last long, although Shifra wasn't far, maybe four days.

He knew an inn stood down the road on the outskirts, past the spot where his house had been. As a kid, he'd had almost no chance to go there, but he heard that travelers came to get rest, food, and drink. He wouldn't say no to any of those.

A large wagon rumbled toward them and he grabbed Kiria's arm. She looked surprised as he brought her out of its path.

Pain twisted in his chest. *I'm sorry, Brett.* He wasn't sure why he felt sorry. Maybe because he hadn't been there when she died. He couldn't save her. At least he could save Kiria.

The weight of memory kept him silent as they traced his steps from the school, up the hard-packed dirt road up the hill. Sunlight reflected the road to white as the knot of people thinned, leaving the way clear for the two of them.

"You grew up here?" Kiria said in an undertone.

"Yes," he said, feeling the absurdity of it. His world had been so small. "I was going to be a glassmaker." The word tasted like ashes, and he spat on the side of the road. A few more steps and he would see the burned house. His chest tightened.

She replied but he didn't hear what she said. The house they'd rebuilt over his old one looked remarkably similar. It was a little smaller but that was the only difference. Maybe he had expected to see smoke still rising out of its charred remains. Briefly, he realized that his former neighbors would be the most likely people in town to identify him, and that his plan was not very safe. Of course, it probably didn't matter if they knew his name. He was a Tanyu now, far beyond that worthless eleven-year-old in skill and importance. And no one would recognize Kiria this far north, especially without her Beauty.

"Are you ignoring me?" Kiria asked as they crossed the street.

The new house's chimney leaned a little to the right too. Firian dropped his voice low. "No, I'm not. It's just… Just go along with me here." He knocked on the door, hardly aware of what he was doing.

Moments later, the door opened. Blood drained his face cold.

It was his mother.

"Hello. Who are you?" she asked, eyeing them. She wiped her hands on an apron worn to translucency. Her wispy hair now streaked gray. She had tied it in a knot behind her head but flyaways crowned her face. Her thin lips had wrinkles and her eyes were milky.

Firian closed his mouth. "I'm...." Indecision paralyzed him. "Is Mr. Kess at home?"

"No."

A baby started crying inside the house. *What does that mean?* The mystery seemed impenetrable, like a note in a song that didn't match the rest. It was just there.

"Can we come in?" Firian asked breathlessly.

His mother's gaze grew suspicious as she stared at him. "You look so much like someone I know," she finally said.

"I..."

Brett appeared at the door, holding the baby on her hip. Firian's breath caught. She was so beautiful, fully a woman now, but her face showed the same sweet spirit that defended him as a child. The baby reached for the end of Brett's long, glossy braid. Her face had filled out, and she wore a stained dress. But he saw himself in her eyes. At the sight of Firian, her mouth dropped open and her eyes rounded. "Mother," she breathed.

His mother's eyes narrowed. "Firian?" said his mother. She blinked away wetness.

"Can we come in?" he asked, with renewed urgency. He didn't want anyone else overhearing their conversation or getting a good look at them.

"Of course!" Brett said.

His mother opened the door wider. "Firian, come in, come in!"

Nothing had changed in the main room. Besides a few additions that looked like they belonged to Brett and the baby, everything was exactly as it had been, just distorted. He was bigger now, so the room was smaller. The little fireplace on the wall to the right, the table in the center of the room, the kitchen through the doorway on the left, the door to the garden straight ahead...

"Firian," said Brett, disbelieving. She handed the baby to their mother. "You've come back!"

He had no idea what to say, so he nodded and sat down. The house hadn't changed at all. It hadn't burned down. Everyone was still alive. There never had been a fire.

"Can I have a drink?" he asked. His mother went to get water from the kitchen. That was not what he had had in mind.

"It is you." A question bled through Brett's tone. She stared down at him, looking over his eyes, his hair, his clothes.

He was afraid to speak, afraid she would disappear if he broke the spell, so he just nodded again, almost holding his breath.

"Firian!" His name came out as a sob. She threw herself toward him, but checked herself. It had been so long, and he was a Tanyu. Could she touch him?

Sniffing back a tear, he stood and welcomed her into his arms. She squeezed him tight, as though he would run away if she didn't hold him down. It was surreal, surreal. His tightly closed eyes pressed out tears he couldn't stop. "We didn't know where you were," Brett said into his chest.

"I'm okay," he said. "I'm okay."

He remembered himself and let her go, and Brett's face glowed with happiness.

Their mother returned with two cups of water. Firian really was very thirsty. Looking around at the familiar room, he felt oddly disconnected from it. He was disconnected from them too. It was as though they were ghosts or figures intruding upon the Unreal. Something tightened in his chest. As he gulped down his water, he seethed. Why had the Academy told him they were dead? How could they have caused him so much pain?

"You have a baby," Firian said to Brett, feeling oddly empty. Everything felt like too much.

She laughed and said, "Yes, this is Sabir." She didn't seem old enough to have a baby. She had been so much younger when he saw her last. Seeing an opening, Brett introduced herself to Kiria, who had stood silently by the door during their reunion. "I'm Firian's sister, Brett," she prompted.

"Lovely to meet you," Kiria said, offering no more information. She hid her surprise well. He was almost impressed.

"This is my wife, Maya," he said when he had finished his water. Kiria didn't deny it. The truth could be damning, so he was glad she saw the sense in his story.

"Oh my goodness! It's wonderful to meet you," said his mother, who kept a respectful distance despite looking like she would like nothing better than to embrace her new daughter-in-law. Brett ran forward warmly and hugged Kiria with her free arm as though they were sisters.

The baby kept crying, fraying his nerves and trivializing this meeting that, for him, was monumental.

Brett caught him looking at the baby. She looked at him with eyes bright with concern. She was always the first to notice that something was wrong.

"Where's your husband?" Firian asked curtly before she could fuss over him. "Why isn't he here?"

"Gaius is fighting in the Torithian War. We expect him to come back in about three months to recuperate before returning to the front. I'm living here until then." Brett shifted the baby, the only sign that the arrangement made her uncomfortable.

Back with Father. The idea horrified him.

"How long will you be staying?" she asked.

"I'm not staying," he said, more forcefully than he intended. "In fact, we're leaving now." He took Kiria's hand. "We have to reach the Farmer's Inn."

"You can't leave now! Firian, it's been so long!" his mother cried.

Brett looked stern. "You've only just gotten here. I'm sure Father will let you borrow a horse and cart when he gets home so you can reach the inn in time if you really have to go."

"No, we have to leave now. Academy business." That should silence them.

His mother sniffed. Her eyes glazed over with bright tears. "Firian...." She had never shown this much desire to spend time with him. Maybe she regretted those years when she ignored him and thought he wouldn't amount to anything. He stood up straighter, his shoulders back. She had been wrong about him. He had amounted to something, but that didn't mean that he wanted to give in to her tears now. He almost wished he could, but that would have to be under different circumstances. At that moment he felt a little repulsed.

"We'll see each other again," he said dismissively. "Goodbye!"

"Nice to meet you all," Kiria added as they swept out the door.

Walking very quickly, he led them away from the part of town he recognized. In the new silence, he breathed deep into his chest. The baby's crying had finally stopped.

His head spun. *What just happened? Why didn't I know before?* Heavy in the stomach sat the certainty that the Academy had lied. Raewhith hadn't reported a fire. The Academy, for some gory, godforsaken reason, had pretended they were dead. Red rage filled his body. Even Kiria's presence irritated him, reminded him of his loyalty. Had Belik known about this? He'd lied to him before.

"Are you all right?" Kiria asked, breaking through his thoughts.

Firian shook his head as if he could send his doubts flying like cobwebs. "I'm fine."

"You're not fine," she said in an undertone. Her concerned look made him wonder if he had fallen into the Unreal for a moment as they walked. Shock could send a person there, make him abstracted. It was a dangerous place, to be in the Unreal without knowing it.

"Here's the inn," he muttered. They went inside the two-story wooden building that he hadn't been allowed to visit as a child. Of course, he had snuck up the hill to come here and listen to travelers' stories a few times.

The clunk of his shoes on the wooden boards echoed back those memories. Hooks for coats lined the walls just inside the door, leading through the empty entryway to the innkeeper's counter. A staircase led up to the rooms on the left and a small room crowded with round tables opened on the right. Even vacant, the entire place felt cramped, claustrophobic.

He edged his way to one of the wooden tables. Kiria followed, her expression both concerned and accusatory.

Moments later, a barman thunked two mugs of ale in front of them. Firian drank his gratefully.

"What happened back there?" Kiria asked.

He didn't answer, taking refuge in his ale.

Her eyebrows came together and she leaned her elbows on the table. She tried to meet his eyes, but he didn't take the bait. He wasn't in the mood to explain himself. "Why did you lie to me?" she said in a low voice so the barman and one grizzly-looking guest couldn't hear.

"I didn't lie to you."

Her light brown eyes flashed, even as they filled with tears. "You told me your family was dead."

"I thought they were!"

"Don't play with me," she said dangerously. Her face was red with the grief that welled just below the surface.

"I'm not. I didn't know they'd be here."

"Then why did you think...?"

Firian set his jaw in a hard line. "They told me," he muttered, taking another swig.

She slid her elbows off the table in disbelief. "Why would they do that?"

He was done answering questions. Everything still felt hollow. The memory of an hour before ambushed him unexpectedly, obtruding, making his stomach drop.

This time she accepted his silence and didn't push him for more answers. Instead, she changed the subject. "Are we staying here for the night?"

"Sure," he said, glad to move on from emotional subjects.

"We can get food here," she continued, now business-like. A much safer attitude. "And I need a bath. I've never gone this long without one."

His mouth quirked up in a half-smile. He wasn't sure why. "I'll make sure they draw one for you." He could probably use one too. Slicking his face and hair with stream water wasn't enough.

"And then off to... our destination," she said, almost letting the word slip. Even here, they couldn't say the place aloud.

He nodded once.

She said something else but he wasn't listening. Muffled scraping reverberated by the front door of the inn, but no one came inside. "Shut up," he whispered.

She scrunched her face in disgusted disbelief. "Firian, if you—"

He scraped back his chair just as the door burst open and six men piled into the tiny space. They brandished weapons as they barreled toward the princess, their bald heads glistening with sweat. Their thick necks strained forward. Light from the oil lamps glinted yellow on the knives and axe blades.

Ale sloshed everywhere as Firian yanked Kiria to her feet. "Here!" he yelled, pulling her in front of him. Picking up a chair that blocked their way to the back room, he hurled it at the Torithians. With no room to maneuver out of the way, they ducked and leaned to avoid it but it still struck one hard in the head.

Kiria almost collided with the barman, who emerged from the narrow kitchen doorway to see what was going on. She sidestepped. Firian punched the man hard in the face and then flung him around by the front of his shirt to shield them from the fighters, who shouted to each other to kill him, to cut them off, to follow them.

"Go!" he screamed at Kiria, cursing loudly to himself because he hadn't seen this coming. A few men struggled to get around the tables while the others ran back out the front door. If they didn't have men posted at the other exits, he could escape these idiots.

Kiria ran into the kitchen. Firian heaved the barman's unconscious body at the two men still hurdling toward them through the dining room, and ran to follow her. He couldn't leave her alone. The kitchen steamed with stuffy, hot air. He scanned the room. On the right, a large fire burned in an oven. Over the flames was a spit but no meat on it. Beside the fireplace someone had stacked piles of wood and a bellows. On the other side of the room, shelves held stacks of plates and mugs. Below them was a large, covered barrel of ale with a ladle sticking out.

In the back wall was a door. A way out. Firian grabbed the enormous ladle as he ran. It wasn't at all balanced like a sword, but it felt heavy enough to withstand one. And he always had the knives—large one on his belt, small one in his boot.

Ahead of him, Kiria stopped at the back door. Firian flung the door open. His eyes adjusted to the bright sunlight just in time to see one of the Torithians swing his sword. His shadow filled the doorway.

Kiria screamed and covered her face.

Firian swung the ladle full-force at the man's head. Using the man's hesitation, Firian pulled him closer and slammed the door on his sword hand. Kiria gasped as the bones in his arm crunched and the man screamed in pain. The sword fell to the ground.

Firian scrambled to pick it up. Sword in one hand, ladle in the other. The door bounced back open and the brawny man, snarling like an animal in his rage, threw himself at Firian. His huge body caught Firian by surprise and he stumbled backward, slamming into the shelves. Pottery crashed around him. Gigantic hands, worn like leather, crushed Firian's windpipe. A jagged purple vein traced up the Torithian's large nose. *Broken.* The man's face, like a mask of rage, streamed red, sticky blood onto Firian's neck and chest.

A jolt and more pottery shards told him that Kiria had smashed something on the man's head, but his thick skull didn't register the pain.

Bursts of dark stars clouded Firian's eyes and he gurgled in his fight for breath. His muscles recoiled from lack of air, stiffening, the veins standing out on his skin.

He had a sword. He was an idiot! He'd practiced for moments like this. Rolling the force of his body with his arm, he thrust the sword into the man's back. Firian felt the man go rigid with shock, and he heaved the man to the floor. The Torithian fell on his back, stunned. Firian stabbed him in the neck. The quick well of blood told him he was dead.

Kiria's hands covered her mouth, her eyes grown wide. The swift crunch of gravel told him that more were coming. Two other men ran up, clenching weapons in their fists. Maybe they had been guarding the other doors. Firian took one deep breath. *Many ways to kill a man...*

"Give us the Kepress!" one barked.

"To you?" Firian bared his teeth. It could have been a grin. "No."

Provoking them worked. They swung at him but he was ready this time. He'd practiced this with Jovan a hundred times. The moment's pause allowed him to calm his mind a little, to notice where they were coming instead of striking blindly or by instinct. They both came head-on, making them easier to see.

With the ladle, he reached toward the first man and twisted the sword out of his grip with the spoon end. Using the momentum, he struck under the man's chin with his elbow, cracking his teeth together. The man couldn't see with his head tilted up by the blow. Any sword swing would be blind.

Safe in his shadow for a split second, Firian ducked in time to avoid the second swinging sword. Unwilling to hurt his partner, the second man pulled back just shy of Firian. Grabbing his chance, Firian swung at the second man's sword arm but missed, cutting a huge gash in his calf. For a second, it looked like the man would strike again, but the shock gave way to pain and he dropped to his knees, puffing moans of pain. Firian finished him quickly.

"No! Let me go!" The scream was Kiria's.

Firian spun around. The two men from the inn had made it through the kitchen to the outside. The tallest one grabbed Kiria, pinning her hands to her sides. She tried stomping on his instep but it didn't work. The other man shielded him from attack as they hauled her away. *No!*

A movement in his peripheral vision. Firian jumped away from the first man whose jaw he'd elbowed but fiery pain sliced and burned along his back. He screamed and stabbed the man in the gut before running to get Kiria. Nausea rose up, slicking sweat on his cold face, but he forced it down.

He threw the ladle at the two men retreating around the building into the woods. It hit one in the back, but didn't seem to hurt. One man stopped to face him, knowing he had to be dealt with before they could have Kiria.

One at a time. I can do one at a time. Firian paused a little farther away than he had the last time, his back still stinging. The muscular, ax-wielding Torithian weighed more than he did. He'd have to rely on speed and surprise. *To the calm mind, everything is a servant.* Anything could be a weapon.

Of course, weapons could be weapons too.

Quick as a swallow, he took the small knife from his boot. *Disadvantage—no hands free. Advantage—two weapons.*

This Torithian wasn't a fool like some of the others. He took his time while his partner got farther away.

Firian's heart beat harder in his chest, impatient. Finally, he threw the small knife, just as he had practiced digging into the flesh of trees. The man doubled over and the knife flew harmlessly over his head.

This was Firian's chance! A moment's window. Firian started forward, but the man rose with dust in his hand, acrid and stinging in Firian's face. As the man hurled toward him, Firian forced his eyes open and stupidly held his sword straight out in front of him with both hands. His lesson with Kiria came back to him just as the man got close. He parried the axe and brought his knee up hard between the man's legs.

Taking the risk, Firian sprinted past the man paralyzed with pain. He could finish him later if he had to. Right now, he had one job. He needed to get Kiria.

It didn't take him long to catch up. The tall man moved slowly. Kiria writhed and dragged her heels in the dirt as he manhandled her forward.

She and the Torithian saw him coming at the same time. Firian's mind whirled. How to get her away from him unscathed?

Kiria opened her mouth, maybe to yell for him, but shut it again. She twisted violently and started shouting, forcing the man to pay attention to her.

He could go for the Torithian's head. That way he wouldn't touch Kiria at all. The man was a giant, much taller than she was.

But he'd seen Firian coming. He could use her as a shield.

Firian hesitated. Then Kiria began to glimmer. Even the Torithian noticed. She glowed like a mirage. In seconds, the goddess he had seen in her dream stood in the arms of the tall fighter.

Firian's heart stopped.

Then he realized what she'd done. She had changed to give him an opening. The enemy's eyes burned as he looked at her, forgetting about Firian. Firian lunged at the man, cutting his head almost completely off. His sword only stopped at the spine. His limp body collapsed to the ground, almost taking her with him.

For a blazing second, Firian looked at Kiria. Her glistening hair dripped with the man's blood. He could barely breathe as he looked into her wide golden eyes. A hint of pale fear shone through her radiant skin.

A heavy breath reminded him of where he was. Behind them came the last fighter, enraged. Firian grabbed Kiria's hand. Her soft skin tingled against him. He yanked the sword free of the man's neck and bolted into the woods.

34

KIRIA

"Go, go!" Firian's voice grated.

Kiria's legs started to burn, the initial adrenaline wearing off. But she forced them to keep moving, one in front of the other, jumping over fallen branches, climbing up large rocks, forward and forward, her breath coming out ragged and her scars aching.

She paused for a second when the realization hit her that Firian wasn't wearing the packs. They had left all their supplies at the inn.

He touched her back to make her keep moving. She knew he could run faster, but he kept her in front. She twisted her head around to see whether any of the Torithians still followed. The air blew her tears cold. She hadn't realized she was crying.

No one seemed to be after them. When she looked at Firian, he seemed to think the same thing. They jogged to a stop and silently crept to a thick grove of young pine trees. He motioned for her to go inside. Prickly needles scraped her arms and legs and chest, but she didn't care. She took the opportunity for a moment's focus, enough to make herself plain again. With that change, she felt smaller, deflated, harder to see, which was a relief. Being beautiful was horrible when it came with danger. At least her plan had worked. She shut her eyes tight, shaking.

If it hadn't...

Firian came in after her. They stood chest to chest, with no space to move. Kiria strained her ears for any sound of the Torithians. Nothing. But every time they had surprised her. She kept listening until she felt that she had gone almost deaf. No sound except for a falling pine cone and their own breathing.

She arched backward to give herself enough space to rub the tears off her face with the back of her shaking hand. For a while they stayed like that, just listening.

Finally, Firian held up his free hand to indicate that she should stay while he looked out. His last two fingers bloomed black and yellow and red, the middle knuckles swollen.

She tried not to breathe as he edged past her, threading through the spindly trees into the open woods.

He wasn't gone long. He returned to her line of sight and beckoned her out of the grove. "Let's go," he said, so quietly he might have mouthed the words.

She hurried out, ready to follow him. He gave no hint of where they were going for several long minutes. Aching bruises grew along her arms and waist where that monster had touched her. The breeze revealed something wet on her forehead. She gingerly touched it with one finger. Blood.

Glancing at Firian's sword, covered in gore, she suddenly felt sick. Saliva pooled in her mouth and she had to stop walking. Her body wouldn't go any further. Her stomach churned up bile. She couldn't get air in her lungs. Her quick breaths did no good. The air wouldn't stay in. Her fingers numbed and her limbs shook. Firian got farther away, striding with sure steps, gripping his sword. Streaks of blood painted both his hands.

"Wait, wait," she said breathlessly, hoping he could hear.

He did.

She sank to her knees, completely overwhelmed.

He jogged to reach her. "Are you hurt?" he whispered urgently.

"I don't think so," she managed through the thin air.

"We just have to get over that hill," he said, pointing ahead. "Can you make it?"

The distance seemed impossible. She started crying, overcome by helplessness.

"Up, up," he said, lifting her to her feet.

She knew that they had no time for this, but the ground wavered in darkness. When she stumbled, he caught her, but he grunted when he did. "You're hurt," she said, coming back to the present. She stood, her strength returning in small waves.

Denying it, he shook his head. His dark hair was wild. "Take a deep breath," he said.

It took her a few tries, but she managed to do it.

"Just over that hill," he repeated. He linked his free arm in hers and they went as quickly and quietly as they could.

From the top of the hill she could see another village in a valley far away. She couldn't make it all that way.

"We have no horses," she murmured.

Firian looked grim. "No," he agreed.

They couldn't go back to get them. Not now that the Torithians expected them to do that.

Tears threatened again. It was too much.

Uncharacteristically tender, Firian touched her arm and said, "Here. We can stay here for the night. I'll keep watch." He still held the bloody sword in his fist.

She nodded. At least one Torithian from that group was still alive and looking for them, and there could be more. Firian had killed two in front of her. That left —what? four?—that she wasn't sure about. Had he killed them all? He must have at least incapacitated them. How had he done that all on his own? She had tried to help, but didn't have the right training. She'd done all she could think of, and it wasn't enough. Despite all his flaws, she was deeply grateful for Firian in that moment.

"Thank you," she said.

He turned around, maybe to scan for a sheltered spot. A ragged tear in his black shirt ran from his right shoulder blade down to his waist, wet with dark blood.

She gasped. If that wound ran deep, he wouldn't last the night. "You're hurt. You're bleeding!"

"I'm okay."

"Shut up!" she said. "You're not okay. Your back..."

He reached back and grimaced before his hand reached the wound. "It's not too bad," he said.

"How are you still standing?" she asked. "Sit down."

He actually did as she said, going to a hollow just out of easy view and sitting on a large rock. She understood that's where they would stay the night. Despite her nausea, she came over to him. The least she could do was make sure he was all right.

A tiny stream ran into the hollow, pooling at the bottom, hardly enough to scoop up for drinking. She untied the sash from around her waist, hating the bruises there, and dipped the end of it in the cold water. Though she was no doctor, she knew it was important to clean cuts. The sash would be long enough to bind it too.

Firian didn't need her to explain what she was doing. He set down the sword only as long as it took to pull the shirt carefully over his head. His sharp breath betrayed how much that motion hurt.

A bloody gash ran down the length of his muscular back. She fought back sickness as she looked at it. Blood covered his whole right side.

"I'm going to clean you off," she said, hovering the damp sash over his cut.

He gave a single nod of acknowledgment, bracing himself.

His skin flinched only slightly at her touch as she sopped up the flowing blood, working mechanically from the top to the bottom. The end of the sash kept getting saturated. When it did, she wrung it out in the water and started again. By the time she finished, the little stream ran pink. "I don't think it's very deep," she said, watching the blood flow out of the cut again. The gash stretched along his entire back, but at the bottom it was little more than a scratch that looked nastier than it was.

He didn't respond, his head tilted, dazed, toward the sword in his hand. He ran his finger along the crossguard.

"Here, help me bind this up," she said, pressing one end of the sash to his back and handing him the rest to wrap around the front.

He lifted his arms and passed the fabric back around to her. They passed the sash back and forth, crisscrossing his chest and back until they ran out of fabric. She tightened the end and tucked it in, hoping it would stay. The deepest part of the injury was protected now, anyway.

Heavy silence fell.

Firian fingered the hole in his shirt. The needle and thread were in the lost pack.

Kiria felt numb, remembering the attack as though it had just been a nightmare. She never thought her life would look like this.

If her mother could see her now... dirty and plain, dripping with the blood of her enemies, alone with an armed Tanyu, with no food and no place to sleep. It was good that her mother couldn't see her. She didn't need more heartache.

But at least Kiria was alive. She looked at the back of Firian's head, now eye-level, and felt a rush of warmth. All his bravado didn't matter as much anymore.

Kiria woke up screaming. Blank terror covered her body like a physical force. Her heart pounded, heavy and painful.

A hand closed over her mouth. Feverish and wild, she looked around in the dark for her attacker.

"Shh, shh!" someone said. His breath felt hot in her ear. "It's all right."

She rolled her eyes to see him. It was just Firian. She stopped screaming against his hand, so he took it away, letting her breathe. Her heart didn't slow down. Any moment now, something horrible would emerge from the darkness.

Anger mixed with her fear. This was the third night she couldn't sleep because of nightmares. Exhausted and afraid, she sat up beside Firian. Forest mold dropped softly from her back. Maybe if she acted as though she felt normal, the reality would follow.

Today they were supposed to reach Shifra. Hopefully she would feel safer in the fortress of Carradoc than she did here in the forest. Firian had chosen a spot overhung with boulders since the trees thinned out here and they needed some kind of cover. She hated the rocks suddenly, longing for someplace with a locked door and a hot bath.

She chewed her fingernail, and Firian passed her a water skin they had gotten in Imlin, the town they had seen from the hollow. The last two times this had happened, she asked for water. Now she didn't need to ask.

She sucked in a deep breath to steady herself. "Have you seen anything?" she whispered, carefully taking a drink.

"No. I think we're safe tonight," he said. They sat close enough that their hips touched. The rewrapped sash puffed a little under his blue shirt, the darkest one he could find in town. It had cost the last tokens Firian had had in his pockets.

She needed a distraction. Briefly, her mind flitted to the pen and paper he'd gotten for her along with the food and water. She had started writing down all her ideas for ruling the Kingdom, protecting it from the Torithians and improving the lives of its citizens. But keeping her mind focused on something serious felt beyond her reach. In the morning she could begin again.

She closed her eyes, trying to reach the Unreal, something new to occupy her mind. Firian always met her there. Since the attack, they had practiced multiple times a day. Though it started as more of a distraction, she could tell she was getting better at entering their shared mental space and maneuvering in it. And the more she did it, the more she liked it.

She chose an easy place, a safe place. Her room in Mon Párinath. It fitted together, piece by piece. Each piece of furniture, carpet, and item soothed her, like old friends.

Firian appeared beside her. "Practicing again?" he said, his blue eyes smiling.

She nodded solemnly, taking in the therapeutic view. "I still don't see how any of this could be used for attack," she said. Her eyes swept over the familiar objects. How could even a trained warrior hurt her here? She could go back to reality at will.

He closed the space between them until she could feel his body heat. After a silent pause that made her gut twist a little, he said, "You can do anything here."

She flushed and cast him a look. What did he mean?

"You can bend the rules of reality." Casually, he began to levitate. She backed up, eyes wide. He would have to show her how to do that. "Your ability to fight and come up with new strategies is much better here." His mouth lifted with pride, but he hesitated as though he shouldn't explain any more. But then he continued. "During war, every sunup and sundown, people with the Talent meet to fight, pitting their best against our best. That means less bloodshed, usually, and a quicker end to war. Tanyuin minds tend to be good at strategy, so most generals and tacticians have some Talent. That gives us easy access to the top people. They often come willingly and, if not, there are other ways to get to them. Belief allows you to kill and be killed. The more you believe in the Unreal, the better you are at attacking and the more vulnerable you are at the same time."

"Do Torithian generals have it?" The mention of generals made her uncomfortable. *Is that what happened to Father?*

Firian floated down, landing lightly on the deep carpet. The fibers moved against his feet, a detail she hadn't added. "I'm not sure. We're not officially involved in your war."

She knit her brows together, knowing exactly what to write that morning. "Why not?" It was a real question, but also a challenge.

"I don't know. We should be," he said, deep anger coloring his features as he looked down at the patterned rug, but only for a moment. "If I were in charge, I would end this war. We could do it." He looked back at her. "You're not bad at strategy either."

It took her a moment to realize what he was talking about. "It was all I could think of," she muttered.

"I thought it was brilliant," he said, looking at her in a way that made her uncomfortable. His eyes burned with desire, flattering, attractive. She didn't want to like it as much as she did.

He hadn't brought it up before this. Her stomach coiled with the thought that he had seen her beautiful. Someone dangerous and powerful seeing her so exposed. No, not exposed, though it still felt like it sometimes. She looked back at him, trying not to acknowledge the invitation in his eyes. Though she felt drawn to him, his wild unpredictability stopped her from considering him as a partner. But, if she was honest, part of her was also glad he'd seen her that way.

Furtively, she checked her hands—still plain. "It was necessary." She cleared her throat. "So, is that it? Is that what you practice at the Academy?"

He shrugged one shoulder. "There are more ways to get to people. Everybody's mind touches the Unreal when they sleep."

"Is that what keeps happening to me?" she asked quietly, crossing her arms across her body. "Can they hurt me in my nightmares?"

A chill ran through her when he didn't answer right away. "No," he said slowly. "I would sense it."

"But people *can* be killed in their dreams?"

His eyes flashed regret. "Yes, but you're safe with me."

Those words would have rung boastful a few days ago, but they both felt the weight of their truth now. The memory of Firian standing guard that first night after the attack filled her face with heat. They looked at each other, suddenly serious with anticipation. Her heart started beating hard again, but not with the same kind of fear. He stepped forward, closer...

Her eyes shot open. After the lighted room, everything looked even darker, even though the sky had lightened from black to dark blue. The cool night air washed over her. "You should let the Watchman know we're safe," she said.

35

FIRIAN

So close.

Firian didn't want to check in with the Watchman. The man might tell him that they had eliminated the threat in the palace, and that the two of them could come back. Firian just needed a little more time.

Just now he had almost managed to kiss her, but she startled like a wild rabbit. What was she afraid of? He looked back at her in the space beneath the rocks, but she sat, eyes down, braiding her hair over her shoulder. The moment had passed. And yet she was tempted. He saw it in her eyes.

His mind spun with questions and the image of her terrified face, transformed into painful brilliance, came to him again. If he came back with a successful mission *and* the love of the Kepress, he could have two worlds at his disposal. Or could he? The Academy told him his family was dead, and ever since the moment he saw them alive, other lies cropped up in his memory like symptoms of a disease. The torture before the mission. Tiev's promotion.

Too early to call the Watchman, Firian looked northwest. Through those woods rose the Academy. Rage and confusion welled in his chest any time he thought about it, but he had to say something.

Reaching in his mind, he searched for Belik. It didn't take long.

When he saw the Master, Firian's arguments seemed smaller, as though he had imagined them. Belik was just the same. He couldn't have started the lie about his family.

"Master Belik."

"Firian!" The Master resettled his glasses on his nose, raising his eyebrows just a little to reveal his surprise.

They stood in a blank space. No need for ceremony.

"I heard about the attack," Belik said. "I'm glad you were able to protect the princess—"

"Kepress." It felt good to correct him.

Belik pursed his lips ironically, apparently starting to sense Firian's mood. "But I thought you could avoid being seen at all."

Firian gritted his teeth to stop himself from saying anything rash. He took a couple steadying breaths so he could match Belik's stoicism. Normally that wasn't a challenge. "I saw my family," he said, clear and matter-of-fact, watching Belik's expression. Except for a blink, it didn't change.

"Did you?" The question was careful, almost a statement.

Firian tensed. He felt strength run through his arms and back. "Yes. The Academy told me they were dead."

Belik considered. "With good reason," he said slowly. "You didn't like them and you didn't need the distraction."

A wave of dizziness flowed through him. He snarled. "How could—"

"Consider this." Calmly, Belik raised a weathered hand.

Firian's fingers gripped into a fist.

"I saw you and I saw myself." Though his voice was as steady as ever, Belik's face revealed the honesty of his words. He never spoke about his past, of which Firian had only learned bits and pieces. Was he going to now? Curiosity dulled the sharp edge of Firian's rage, and his hands relaxed just a little.

"I was like you," Belik continued. "I was good. Everybody knew it." He held up a finger. "But then I got distracted. I thought it didn't matter, thought I was better than that. I could do what I wanted." His mouth twitched. "But then it all went to hell," he said, pounding his bad leg in frustration and emphasis. "So now you know. I did what I thought was best for you."

Firian didn't say a word. Resentment mixed with pride and anger. No one had supported him and aggravated him more than Belik. No response felt right.

"Don't hold this against me or you'll put yourself and the princess in danger," Belik said. "I need you focused. I recommended you for this mission. Don't let me down."

Firian swallowed on a dry throat. He couldn't take this anymore. Without more than a curt nod, he left back to reality.

"I RECOGNIZE THIS!" Kiria said, her eyes shining as she moved closer to Firian. Their feet rasped against the stiff yellow grass of the animal track leading toward a dense, wet forest. Just ahead, huge trees hung with long, knotted, gray moss stood like gnarled old men. Water glinted through the dark trees, as though the forest stood in a marsh or lake. "It looks like the painting of Shifra we have up in the Palace." She cast Firian a smile, all her sorrows forgotten.

He wasn't surprised at her reaction. Shifra played a central role in the stories from the Scroll she'd heard thousands of times. Outcasts built Carradoc, the secret Khelê fortress, during the War of the Kingdom Rebels. In the days of the first Kingdom, its evil king killed any person he found different and therefore defective. According to the Scroll, God protected some of those persecuted people and named them his chosen race, the Khelê, "divine people." The ones who escaped from the Kingdom fled to Carradoc where they built an army to overthrow the king. Around the same time, the Scroll itself was written there. Shane and Mari Calthwaite, the non-Khelê founders of the three lines that now ruled the Kingdom, trained there.

Firian watched Kiria from the corner of his eye, a smile playing on the edges of his mouth. She practically skipped with excitement. Turning back to him, she swept her hair behind her ear. Had he ever been that innocent? Though she had power he wanted, she was pretty and pure like water. And he had set it boiling.

"*Out of Shifra will spring my chosen race,*" he said slowly, "*out of the fortress Carradoc, and those who once were abandoned will be found again, a united people. Their God will be their strength and never will they—*"

"*—vanish from the earth.*" Kiria jumped ahead and faced him, hands on hips. "That's really close," she said. Almost like a child in her excitement, she twirled around again and headed to the murky forest. Cheerfulness made her talkative. "I wonder if they still have the lanterns. I've always thought they were so beautiful. I didn't know if I'd make it to Shifra. They don't include it on the coronation tour because it's so far away."

"I'm glad you want to see it," he said. Apart from its history, the bedraggled forest wouldn't impress many people. The girl in front of him was more impressive. Her passion reminded him of the intoxicating secret she held just beneath the surface.

"I've wanted to for ages." She shook her head. "Daelon will be so jealous when I tell him about this. His family fought in the war, and he loves telling that story."

"What about the other Keepers?" Kiria didn't talk about them very much.

"My mother doesn't like traveling," she said, "but I'll tell her about it anyway. Atty'll be interested, I think." She turned back to look at him. "The Third Line is usually the one that travels, but he hasn't really done that. Cúron's probably already been here."

She tossed out the last sentence with a little resentment. *Interesting.*

As the ground started to squish beneath their feet, he could see why attacking Carradoc had been so difficult. Soon they waded through boggy grass that swallowed their shoes whole with each step. Even Kiria, despite her excitement, became momentarily disgruntled, her face scrunching.

"Here it is!" she said, louder than she should have. A rickety wooden walkway stretched like a long water snake through the swamp trees. He gave her a hand as she hoisted herself onto it. His foot splashed as he stepped up beside her.

"It's Shifra!" She clasped her hands in amazement. One sleeve fell down enough to reveal the black cloth around her wrist.

Firian blew a laugh through his nose. Her joy transfigured the gloomy swamp, elevating it by association. She hadn't been this happy their entire journey. The initial threat, her father's death, Torithians attacking in Raewhith... She hadn't had much reason to be.

The boards groaned and creaked as the two travelers walked single file along the narrow path. Great mossy trees blocked out the sun, but there were no lanterns yet.

Kiria slowed and turned to look at him. "Do you think we can reach Carradoc before nightfall?"

The pathway wound so much that Firian wasn't sure. According to the maps he'd studied, they could make it in a straight line, but this old trail twisted and doubled back constantly. No one was following them—that much was clear.

At the fortress, people waited for Kiria. Maybe they waited to congratulate him, too, for getting her there safely. He wanted to hear those words, but he wanted another night with Kiria to himself. She felt generous now, happy.

"I don't think so," he replied. "We'll find a place where the path widens out and we'll stay there. We'll find the fortress tomorrow morning."

She nodded, and then something caught her eye. "Lanterns!" she cried, pointing.

In the distance, a red light glimmered. He bowed his head to encourage her toward it. She scampered off. Just before the light, the path grew wider and sturdier, so more than two people could walk abreast. Even armed men didn't need to fear falling through a rotten board on this part of the walkway.

On either side, hanging from iron rods, glowed round lanterns of all colors. Unlike the ones hanging around the Amiran Academy in Brithnem, these weren't made of glass but dyed and woven fabric. Glass didn't belong here.

As they paced down the walkway, Kiria stopped now and then to lightly touch one of the spheres. Her hands, not used to hard labor, felt so soft. Their memory occupied Firian for a while.

Carradoc could appear any time now. They were clearly going the right way, and the path twisted less than before, heading straight for the fortress. At the next landing, Firian shouldered off the small pack they'd gotten to replace the old one.

"But we're almost there," Kiria said, backtracking to him.

He flashed her a smile. "It's farther than it looks. We'll get there in the morning." He stretched his arms behind his back, squeezing his shoulder blades together. His cut still stung. At the Academy, he wouldn't mention it. "Can you check my back?" he said. "I think it might need to be wrapped again."

"I'm sure it's fine. Are you sure we can't get there today?" She twisted a piece of her hair around her finger.

He grimaced as he pulled his blue shirt over his head. Strange to see any color but black. "Please?" he said, starting to unwrap the sash. It smelled musty, like everything else. He couldn't be certain, but he thought he saw her eyes widen. A good sign.

"You seem to be all right." She paused a moment, but he kept unraveling. With a sigh, she said, "I'll check."

He wrapped the sweaty fabric, now completely undone, around one hand and set it down in a pile. Then he turned around like an obedient child with his back to her.

Her warm breath breezed over his skin as she scrutinized the wound. "It's healing nicely," she said after a moment. "I don't think you need the sash anymore if you don't want it." She stepped back with a rattling creak.

When he turned around, she'd already started rummaging through her pack. Probably looking for pen and paper. Since they had picked it up in Imlin, she scribbled constantly. "New ideas for the Kingdom. I don't want to forget," she'd told him.

"Having an idea?" he asked, crouching beside her after throwing his shirt back on.

"I always have ideas," she replied absently, drawing out a pen from the bottom of the bag. "Why, do you want to add something?" Next came the notebook, which had cost more than he had in his pocket at the time, but he doubted she would want to know that.

"Can I?" He sat down.

She hugged the notebook to her chest, suddenly shy. "If I like your idea, I'll write it down."

"I feel like we've done this before."

"But not with this," she said, waving the pen in the air.

"End the war," he said playfully, nudging her. "Then your problems will be gone."

"Never mind. Your time's up." She turned her eyes in mock seriousness to the page.

"You know," he said, "if you weren't so frustrating, you'd be pretty wonderful."

She looked up at him, bright red.

He'd tried that line before, but this time it felt different. He said the word as he never had before, finally starting to realize what it meant. No other girl knew as much about him as Kiria did. She saw his family and helped him kill a man. Everything he had worked for led to this. Kiria, the beautiful Kepress of Brithnem, was the height of his ambition.

But it didn't feel that way now. At this moment, she meant more. He wanted to know her thoughts, to spend time with her, to touch her. Other girls had been a balm, a pastime, but Kiria offered substance.

Her brown eyes searched his as though she were trying to read his thoughts. Concern lined her small features, all bathed in orange light.

His gut squirmed. He was never uncomfortable like this. Hating his own weakness, he forced himself to meet her eyes, thoughtful in a heart-shaped face. If she hadn't been the Kepress, and hadn't possessed any of her Abilities, he'd still want to look in that face. And that power over him that she didn't know she wielded made his mouth go dry.

The silence weighed heavy. A fish splashed.

She didn't run like last time, but he held his body still as though any movement would spook her.

"You're wonderful too," she said thickly, barely above a whisper.

His heart thumped hard at the words. Slowly, he moved her hair from her shoulder, brushing his fingers against the hollow of her neck. Her pulse pounded under his fingertips. She leaned closer as he stroked her arm all the way down to her hand, hot and soft in his. He brought his face to her small one, breathing against her mouth.

A scuffle on the walkway made him look. A sturdy, red-haired woman bustled from light to light, refilling the oil. She carried a small vat that banged against her wide hip each time she stepped.

Damn. Firian exhaled in frustration just before she saw them.

Kiria sucked in a breath and pulled away. At the sight of the woman, she hopped to her feet.

"Who's there?" called the woman warily, holding a tiny spoon in one fist. Oil dripped from it onto her heavily tattooed hand.

"It's..." Kiria started, sounding a little hoarse. She cast a quick look at him as he stood and confirmed this woman was no threat with a nod. "It's... the two you were expecting."

The woman walked closer for a better look, her short steps echoing. He hated the sound and wished he could toss her into the swamp. "So it is!" she cried, giving a tight-lipped smile. "Come with me, eh?"

Firian picked up the pack and followed Kiria's eager feet. So they were close to the fortress after all.

36

KIRIA

Kiria knelt at the grave, distracted as her kneecap hit the cobblestones. Shane Calthwaite and his son Sandor (father of the Lost Line) had fought and died here. The first time Daelon told her the story, she cried. The Khelê had tucked the memorial in a corner of the enormous open courtyard of Carradoc, carving the names deep into the stone wall. Small offerings littered the ground beneath the gravestone: tokens, herbs, candles.

She touched her forehead in respect, feeling the eyes of the Khelê scrutinizing her. The question in their gazes told it all. They wondered about her Ability. After her eighteenth birthday, when she'd been publicly introduced, everyone in the Kingdom knew that she possessed overwhelming Beauty. They were waiting.

Firian just stood next to her, looking out, acting the bodyguard. She caught his eye and beckoned for him to show his respects. He hesitated before quickly bowing to one knee before the memorial.

Wishing she could have a quiet moment alone with her thoughts, she cast one more look at the grave she had longed for years to see. Slowly, she stood and faced the small crowd gathered behind her. The fortress still functioned as a military barracks and training ground, but now parts of it seemed to function more like a small city. Civilian Khelê like the stout red-haired woman formed the majority of the group wanting to see the Kepress.

Her hands tingled. If wouldn't take much to change, to impress them all, to set Firian on fire... She closed her hands gently into fists. Should she? She stood for a moment in indecision as she looked at the people of Carradoc, trying to ignore her peripheral vision.

She should be enough, even without her Beauty.

But she had made this choice. The Kingdom mattered more than her personal comfort, and right now these kind people offering her refuge were looking for their Kepress. So she transformed.

Several gasped and brought their hands to their mouths. One woman began to cry quietly, overcome by the sight. Some stepped forward, some back. A few crossed their arms, defensive, self-comforting. In one way or another, every person was moved. Firian tensed beside her. She felt his hungry stare move over her body. Her breathing grew shallow.

The tension she felt built within her. The people still waited.

"Thank you for welcoming us to this place," she said. Her voice sounded small and she was shorter than almost everyone around her. Usually Cúron did this sort of thing. Kiria just greeted guests.

She glanced at Firian. He looked back before scanning the crowd again.

What am I afraid of? This is nothing.

"It's been my dream," she continued, "to visit the fortress of Carradoc since I was a little girl. My tutor at the Amiran Academy loves to tell stories of his Khelê ancestors fighting alongside the founders." She smiled and gestured to the grave. "I pray we live up to their bravery, whether we are Keepers or tradesmen, Amir or Tanyu. But now, it's getting late, so I thank you all."

Hopefully that would be enough. It was risky to mention Amir and Tanyu together, since supporters tended to favor one heavily over the other. But her little speech didn't sound too bad. The miss-matched group of soldiers and civilians nodded and shifted, still wide-eyed.

Humid darkness filled the large courtyard like water and made the bright torches hazy. Warm firelight glowed on the faces. The lazy clunk of slow wagon wheels over cobblestones magnified in the waiting stillness. After all the day's excitement, Kiria's eyes burned for sleep.

Firian touched her waist. She spun to face him. He looked meaningfully at Matthan, the man charged with showing them around, who had approached the side of the empty semi-circle where she stood by the grave. The after-image of Firian's fingers felt warm.

"You must have had a long day of travel, my Kepress," said Matthan. "Let me show you to your room."

"Yes, thank you."

Matthan led them away from the crowd though a passage as wide as a street. Maybe it was a road. Like other soldiers in the complex, Matthan wore complete metal armor up to the neck. He had light green eyes, tanned skin, and a light beard that covered some of the tattooed symbols on his face. Kiria hadn't decided on a design for her royal tattoo, but she wanted it on her back and arms, not her face.

Firian followed behind. Since their moment on the platform, they hadn't spoken. The more time passed, the more she doubted her decision to respond to him. As Matthan led them to their secure quarters, she felt his eyes on her. He wanted to figure her out, to open her up, to protect her. For all his maddening qualities, she'd be lying if she said that part of her didn't want to yield to him. Just a small part. But it was selfish to want Firian's arms around her. Nothing could come of it. He had saved her, taught her, comforted her, become a friend. But he lacked respect, and his wild ambition could bring down the Kingdom.

It wasn't that he was a Tanyu that prevented her from being with him, despite some of the prejudices in Brithnem. Tanyuin skills fascinated her. It was that he was Firian. To give into desire would show nothing but weakness. She couldn't be with him, and she shouldn't lead him to think so.

"Here we are!" Matthan opened a wooden door set into the stone. It opened onto a chamber big enough for the two of them. "This is our finest room. I'll send an additional guard to watch the door and someone will come in the morning to draw you a bath before breakfast."

A bath. Her chest ached with gratitude. "Thank you very much," she said, going inside.

Dark red blankets covered a large bed. *Is that a down pillow?* The sight brought a lump to her throat. After weeks in the wilderness, she'd almost forgotten how wonderful it was to sleep in a comfortable bed. A large blue rug covered most of the stone floor, and even amenities like a mirror and sink stood in corners, ready for use.

She sighed deeply, the beauty and comfort of the place soothing her soul. The room wasn't nearly as grand as hers in the palace, but she felt more thankful for it. Before this journey, she hadn't considered how much luxury she had. Now she did, and promised herself to be more grateful.

She fell on the bed and hugged the soft pillow. A sharp twist in her gut reminded her of the night terrors. Hopefully tonight she could sleep in peace.

Firian didn't seem tired. Did he ever sleep? She had woken up with him in the morning, but she couldn't match his stamina to stay up late at night.

"No lesson tonight," she murmured, closing her eyes.

As the door latched closed, memory fell thick between them. She opened one eye to see where he was. He didn't expect to pick up where they left off, did he?

He leaned over her to grab the other pillow. He dropped it on the floor. "Sure?" he asked.

"I need some rest." Then, after a moment, "Maybe tomorrow."

The snick of a lock woke her. When the door opened silently on its hinges, the contrasting moonlight revealed the outline of a man in armor. The guard. It must be. What was he doing here at this hour?

She rolled her head luxuriously to the side and squinted into the thick darkness. The man didn't bring a light. Her gut twisted.

The bed sank down as Firian sat on the edge, half leaning over her. She felt his tense heat through the blankets. He put one strong hand on her leg. His other hand must have strayed to his knife, because of the slight, leathern sound of metal against the sheath.

Her breath caught in a tight ball under her ribcage. If this really were their guard, why did no one use a light? And why didn't Firian trust him? Carradoc was supposed to be safe.

Firian's voice made her jump. "State your business." The weight on her leg disappeared. He'd stood up to face the intruder.

Alone in the bed, she realized how paper-thin her nightgown was. The blankets were a welcome barrier, but not enough. Her unshod feet went cold.

"The girl—" His words strangled away into a gasp, a chokehold. Electricity jolted through her veins. She tucked her legs in and sat up.

"Firian! Master Firian! I'm—let go!—I'm..." He coughed, able to breathe a little better. "I'm Tanyu."

"What are you doing here?" Firian growled.

"Tanyu are everywhere."

"You're not from the Academy."

"Not for a long time. I'm supposed to deliver a message."

The shuffle of feet. Firian had let him go. He was a Defender, not a Master, wasn't he?

"Who sent you?"

"Master Belik."

The hum in the air stilled. Kiria's heart beat hollow in her chest. The name didn't sound familiar, at least not in a way she could place, but something had shifted for Firian.

"What does he say?" Firian whispered through his teeth.

"Strike a light," said the other.

She hated the command but couldn't stand the darkness any longer herself. She lit the candle on the side table. Huge, bloated shadows twisted over the walls. She drew the blankets up higher. At the foot of the bed stood Firian with a knife in his hand, stiff-shouldered. He didn't spare a look for her when the light flared up. All his energy focused on the man before him. Dark eyebrows lowered over his glaring eyes. He practically vibrated with intensity.

The other man didn't cower under the attention, even though Firian had shown how effectively he could attack. His long blond hair had been tied back at the nape of his neck. He had to be ten years older than the two of them. His torso, longer than average, sat on strong, thick legs. The sharp panes of his face looked severe in profile.

"What does he say?" Firian repeated, fractionally drawing out each word.

The blond man flicked a look at Kiria and adjusted his clothes. "The Amir have been given a vote in the Main."

It passed. How could it pass?

Her eyes widened, glad at least that the conversation now veered into something she knew. Except, it didn't make sense that this Tanyu from Carradoc would know about it.

"So your situation has changed." He glanced at Firian's knife. Apparently satisfied that he wouldn't aim it at his throat, he looked again at her, turning his head completely. His rugged face looked sharp from this angle too. Something about the glint in his eye made her insides squirm. It was predatory, like an animal gloating over prey.

Firian stepped between them with his back to her.

"The Tanyu sent their request and they were denied the same vote." The blond man's voice dripped with languid confidence now. He, at least, thought his danger had passed.

Watching Firian's back, she wasn't so sure.

Pieces started clicking into place in her mind. *Atty, what have you done?*

Amir and Tanyu had never seen eye to eye. If the Amir could vote in the most powerful kingdom on the continent, the Tanyu would expect the same treatment. Why hadn't she warned Atty when she had the chance?

The man continued. "So, you're not her bodyguard anymore. You'll keep her as a hostage until we finish negotiations."

A shock ran through Kiria's veins. All of the air sucked out of the room. Was she in the Unreal? Was this a dream? She drew one bare foot over the other. The clammy cold of the toes dragged over the bridge of her foot confirmed the reality of where she was.

The knife loosened in Firian's grip and he drew it back in, twisting it in his fist. He didn't reply.

"Don't kill her or hurt her. We're still in talks. But you can have some fun."

Her mouth went dry.

"Get out of here tonight. We'll know where you are."

"How?" The first word Firian had spoken in too long. Would he really choose the corrupt Tanyu over her?

The man's cheek creased in a smile she could see around the side of Firian's neck. "That was the whole message." The man leaned over to leer at her.

Hot fury roared through her body. No one looked at a Kepress like that. If Firian wouldn't defend her, then she would do it herself.

Surprising herself, she stood. The sensation was like jumping into the ocean. "I am the Kepress of Brithnem," she said with the strength of desperation and the voice of a queen. Her gaze flickered to Firian, who half-turned. "And I order you to leave. I'm surrounded by allies here, and we're staying."

"I am a Tanyu," the man said simply.

"No," she said, fighting to keep her voice steady. "'*To the Tanyu I have given the task of protecting the people of God and their Keepers.*'" The passage flew out before she realized she was quoting.

A hint of amused annoyance passed over the man's face. He tipped his head. "Not this time." The man nodded with parting deference. "Master Firian," he said, and closed the door behind him as he left.

37

FIRIAN

THERE WAS A HORRIBLE SILENCE. Firian realized he still had the knife in his hand. It felt heavier than usual. He put it in its sheath.

Conflicting thoughts overlapped each other as Kiria stared at him, aghast. The buzz he'd felt when he entered the fortress made more sense now. At first, he had blamed the feeling on Kiria. Like an idiot, he hadn't recognized the obvious. Sentries. He knew what they felt like—he knew the difference. That meant that Tanyu were here. But why hadn't he known? And why did the Academy shield them from his mind? The messenger wore the outfit of a Carradoc soldier, not a Tanyu.

He had a feeling—not a terrible feeling, but a blank, sure feeling—that the Academy had planned all of this. In such a storm of thoughts, this fact only bothered him vaguely.

Kiria, his hostage? It had the taste of unreality. For a split second, he willed fire into his hand. In the Unreal, it would work. He looked down at his dark palm. No spark.

Belik's words came back to him: *Remember to do anything we tell you.*

He was done following demands blindly. But this put him on the world stage. Finish this, and he would be an equal to Belik and Jovan and all those others who had controlled him for so long...

He had to obey the Academy. Suddenly he wondered what Bard would say, but he had no idea.

Kiria's glare turned slowly from a clear, defiant question to fearful uncertainty. Firian lifted his hand and she flinched.

"You heard the man," he said. His voice sounded hollow. "Get your things."

He said it more to buy a moment away from her penetrating stare than because he really wanted to say it.

But Kiria still fixed him with a fierce look, unmoving, as though the sound of his voice gave her renewed resolve. She opened her mouth. No sound came out, so she closed it again and shook her head.

Whatever else she was, she was either braver or more reckless than he would have thought to stand up to him in this moment. The Kingdom couldn't stand against the Academy. "It wasn't a question," he said, a surge of anger welling up within him. He couldn't have said why.

"If you won't protect me, I'll protect myself," she said, her voice cracking.

"Then pack your stuff."

"I won't go." The simple statement cut the bond between them. They both felt it lashing. By just a little, her eyes grew sad. And the room grew cold.

"You will," he said, his rage growing.

Her small face pleaded with him. "Firian." The way she said it sent goosebumps over his skin.

"No. We're leaving. Now." He glared, willing her to follow his order.

Finally, with measured breathing, she stooped down to put on her shoes, never taking her eyes off him.

He felt like cursing and strode forward to grab their packs. Every shape in the darkness mocked him.

A scuffle of feet.

Kiria bolted for the door, grasping madly for the handle. With a lunge, he grabbed her, pinning her arms at her sides. She shrank from his touch as he dragged her from the door.

"Help, somebody! Help—" He clasped his hand over her mouth. She screamed hot in his hand, but no sound would reach outside the room.

"Shh, shh!" he hissed in her ear. Her nearness oddly soothed him. "They said move, then wait. That's all," he said, each word slow and distinct. "I won't hurt you."

Her wild eyes looked back in his. When she stopped screaming, he released her to speak. "You don't have to do this," she said quietly. Her heart beat fast in her chest. "The Keepers will kill you if you don't bring me home."

They can try. "I don't want to hurt you," he said, avoiding her gaze. "If you run away, there are Torithians. I'll still take care of you."

Her lip curled.

"You can't try this again. If you do, I'll know." He turned her around to face him, still holding her at arm's length. Although she looked him defiantly in the face, her hair fell disheveled and she looked distraught. That stupid messenger had ruined all he'd built with her and left him with far more questions than answers. He didn't want to threaten her. Experimentally, he let her go.

She didn't bolt, but walked back to her shoes with her head so high, it was as though she'd commanded him to let her go and, by the force of her authority, he had obeyed. At the very least, she acted the noble prisoner.

He ran a hand through his hair. *Gore.* What was he going to do now?

WATER AND MUD made slogging forward difficult. He couldn't run in water up to his hips, and she certainly couldn't with the water rising to her waist. Maybe this route was a mistake. But once people realized the Kepress and her bodyguard were missing, the first place they'd check would be the walkways—the only easy way through the swamp. This was the only other option.

Radiating anger, Kiria didn't speak. Maybe she'd never been so covered in mud.

"Nothing's changed," Firian said.

"Don't be an idiot," she shot back. "Of course it has."

His face flushed with rage.

Something slimy swam by. She jumped and whirled on him as though it were his fault. The movement was almost graceful.

They continued and sloshed around opposite sides of a massive, gray-barked tree.

You know I don't have a choice. But the words wouldn't come out. Mud and anger made him sullen.

Unbidden, Master Belik appeared in his mind as clearly as if he stood in front of him, an unreadable face in an unreadable room. He looked hard at Firian.

"Don't go to Archer's Point," he said.

"Hello," Firian said pointedly.

"Don't be a child. Archer's Point has more Kingdom allies than Carradoc. Until we have this sorted out, you'll need to stay away from populated areas." Belik spoke as though reading from a list.

"Why didn't you let me know this way? Why did you send that fool? He was surrounded!" Firian pointed furiously behind him into the darkness.

"*I* didn't send him," Belik said. "But I understand it. The princess needed the fear of God put into her."

Firian's eyes narrowed. He spat a curse. "You're just breaking all ties with the Kingdom, then." *And putting a target on me.*

"Not if they do what we say."

Firian looked into the familiar face of his Master, the one he had trusted. How much of this plan had he engineered? And now he threw Firian to the wolves. Why? Because he thought he could handle himself, or that he was expendable? "You knew about this," he said, accusation dripping from every word.

The Master ignored the comment. "The Head made me your contact. It makes sense."

"No," Firian said, "you *knew* this would happen."

"It was always a possibility," Belik admitted. He took off his glasses and rubbed them clean on his shirt. A disarming gesture, unnecessary in the Unreal. Old habits. "Firian, trust me. Stay out of sight and nothing will happen to you."

"I can handle the city."

Belik settled his glasses on his face again. "Not when Brithnem starts sending troops. Even the best can't defeat fifty people at once."

Firian tried to picture it. It almost made him wish he had the chance. It would loosen the tight knot of anger in his stomach.

"No, you couldn't," Belik continued, as though reading his mind. "For now, don't kill the girl. I know you probably wouldn't want to anyway," he said, lifting his eyebrows a fraction, their message clear. Belik's insinuation only aggravated him. "But you might have to kill her eventually, a few weeks maybe. We'll let you know when."

Kill her. His body felt electric. "But it would be more useful to keep her alive—" he sputtered.

"We're not catering to your—"

"I mean she has the Talent," Firian snapped, thinking fast. "I could take her back to the Academy."

Almost imperceptibly, Belik's mouth fell open, the only sign this was completely new information. "At this point we don't need the risk," he said finally. "We know where her loyalties lie, with her family and her country. She'll probably make herself a martyr and help them. In the end we'd have to kill her anyway."

"I might... be able to change that," Firian said, his pulse quickening from the greatness of the challenge he issued himself. Belik could be right, but what if he really could sway her?

"Like I said," continued Belik, "you might have a few weeks. They'll crack. And if they don't, you'll have to eliminate her." He tilted his head down to see over his glasses, sending a warning. Surprisingly, lines of sympathy pinched the edges of his eyes. "You're overestimating yourself, Firian. If you follow what we say, the Head will promote you as soon as you get back. A Master by nineteen. Don't screw it up." He let the words simmer.

A Master by nineteen.

Despite everything, his heart leapt. Firian had fought so hard to hear those words. All his life, he'd practiced to become a Master. It was all he'd ever wanted. And, after one mission, it was within his grasp.

Surely the Kingdom would give the Tanyu more power if their Kepress was in danger. No question. They would yield, he would release her on good terms, and then he would return to the Academy a hero.

Belik rolled two fingers together thoughtfully before he continued, treading more carefully than usual, as though he felt the words needed to be said. "You have to be prepared to kill her." With that, the blank room dissolved. Murky trees and sky and Kiria seeped into focus.

Firian tasted blood. He'd bitten the inside of his lip. Disgusted, he spat into the swamp. As soon as they escaped Shifra, he would rebuild what he'd had with Kiria. She'd come with him before submitting to death. But hopefully it wouldn't come to that.

"Firian." Kiria looked at him in concern, as though she sensed his abstraction as he went into the Unreal. She probably did. She'd seen it often enough. "Firian." His name got softer in her mouth. The tips of her hair swished in the water.

He looked over the dark wetland, scanning for rescue teams or dangerous creatures. When he knew they were alone, he slowed his pace.

"I know what you want," she said quietly, her demeanor no longer angry. "I know you want to be the best. But there's more than one way." She laid a hesitant hand on his arm. "Think about what your sister would say. Her husband fights on our side. There's still time to turn around. No one will know we were gone."

"And then what?" he snarled. The mention of Brett sent him into a fury. If he did what Kiria said, the Kingdom *and* the Tanyu would have his head.

Kiria grew quiet and looked away, wading with him through the gloom. Swishing water filled the hollow silence. He felt his hands at her soft throat, a knife to her chest, a knock to the head—the relentless images played in his mind. He hated each one with visceral hatred.

His chest tightened. No one asked him what he wanted. Instead, everyone thought they knew best and could use him for their purposes. Grinding his teeth, he felt blackmailed by everything he cared about.

What do *you want?* Bard would ask.

I want to be a Master. I want Kiria.

I want all of it.

38

KIRIA

THE ROUGH BARK scratched the inside of her arms. Firian silently wound the sash around Kiria's wrists, tying her arms behind a tree. The black cloth tied around her wrist squeezed the circulation from her hand. Cold, howling wind blew hard through the grasses. "You could turn yourself in," she said, twisting to try to see him. "I'll make sure nothing happens to you."

He scoffed. "If you wouldn't run away, I wouldn't do this," he muttered, tightening the cloth. He laid his hand over hers when he was finished. Then, louder, "You could also give Tanyu a vote."

"Not after this." She settled back, grimly looking straight ahead. Defying him gave her an odd mixture of nervousness and strength.

Tanyu hadn't helped the Western Kingdom in any tangible way until Firian came as her bodyguard. At least not in her lifetime or her mother's. They sent ambassadors to keep informed, who were little more than vain warriors flexing their strength. They kept their talents to themselves, not offering to assist even in the Torithian War.

At least the Amir had served the Western Kingdom faithfully. If one group held more claim to a vote, they did.

The light faded, leaving deep, soaking shadows under the trees. Dark blue skies between blowing black branches.

He crawled to the front of the tree, facing her. "You know it's not my choice," he said, his face very close to hers. His dark hair whipped against her face.

"Of course it is." Heat rose along her neck, but she remained resolute. There was always a choice. Hopefully Firian didn't want to be involved in making her a hostage, but either way, he had betrayed her.

He sat up and crossed his legs, their knees touching. "Kiria, you should understand. Where would you be without me?"

The selfishness of his friendship became clearer and clearer. Irritated, she pursed her mouth. "At home with my mother."

He ran a hand back through his dark hair and took a deep breath. "I mean about the Torithians. You're not like the others. You have Abilities. Two of them."

"And you have one, but look what you're doing with it." She tried to tuck her legs closer.

His lip twitched in the waning light. "I don't want to be your enemy."

"You don't want me to be your enemy," she said slowly, in a voice of steel. Hopefully he would understand. Her mother didn't need any more heartbreak, but now the Academy had made her daughter a pawn in their political game. Kiria wouldn't stand for it. Not only was it a bad idea politically to give the ruthless Tanyu power over the Kingdom, but personally too. When she returned, she would make them pay for what they had done.

For a while Firian fell silent, looking over her as though she were a castle to be taken. She tensed, preparing for his next attempt to find an entrance.

"Kiria." He leaned close but she went rigid, flinching away from him. Out of sight, her hands twisted in their bonds. No use. As he brought his face to her ear, her heart hammered painfully. "I want to protect you from the Tanyu," he whispered, as though someone would overhear, "but I can only do that if you come with me. I want you to come with me."

Another wailing gust of air swept over her, sending loose strands of her hair flying across her face, sticking to her lips, her eyes. He let the words settle before checking her response. When she didn't answer, he sighed with frustration and sat down next to her. "You have to come with me," he said.

"Where? I have to go home."

"The Academy." The idea excited him, and he turned to her, his face alight. The intensity renewed her fear. His blue eyes flitted over her. "You have the Talent, Kiria. You could become one of the most feared leaders in the world." Goosebumps rose up on his arms. "I..." His voice trailed off.

"I can't do that." It would feel like betrayal. Strangely, their journey together had toughened her will enough to defy the danger gladly.

"You like me," he said suddenly.

The statement caught her off balance. It was true. But he'd chosen not to be the good man he could be. "And you care enough about me not to hurt me," she said, treading carefully.

He paused. They sat together, bound against their will to violent demands. Barely, he nodded—an admission.

She let out the breath she'd been holding. "Firian, it doesn't have to be like this," she said gently, his friend again. "I've seen what you can be. You can be a good man." She nodded encouragingly and scraped the sash across the bark, hinting.

Firian's eyes blazed. In the dim twilight, his eyebrows twitched downward in realization. "I don't want to be good," he said. "I want more than that. I want you."

He pursed his lips to a thin line, and suddenly moved. As she pulled away and shut her eyes, he pressed a kiss to her forehead. Her eyes shot open. Then she saw him lean back again and strip off his jacket. He balled it up for a pillow and lay down just out of reach.

WITH ONE SWIFT MOTION, Firian pulled out the pin that held up her hair. It came falling down around her shoulders, until he gathered up a fistful and held it against the nape of her neck. He guided her face to his, her mouth to his. Her heart pounded.

As they kissed slowly, she drew her hands along the ridges of his ribs all the way up to his muscular chest, and then dragged her fingers down his abs. A warm, insistent ache grew in her stomach. Her knees buckled under it and she fell onto her bed. He never broke contact with her, launching forward and propping himself up on his hands. His arms closed around her waist as their kisses became sweltering, urgent. His hand moved to her leg...

Kiria woke up gasping. The dark forest spiraled back to silence as the ache died.

How could he do this? How could he attack her in her sleep? First nightmares and then attacks? Red rage blinded her. Stretching as far from the tree as she could, she kicked Firian hard. "How dare you!" she hissed.

He jolted awake, bolt upright, hair flying crazily, a knife in his hand from somewhere. Seeing her, he exhaled. "Kiria," he said, half relieved, half accusing. She could barely hear him over the wind. He lowered the knife.

Her mouth went dry. He was asleep? Could he attack someone when he was asleep? Tanyu could do a lot of things—it might be possible.

Darkness hid her deep blush. "Firian," she said, now having no idea how to proceed, "were you in... the Unreal, just now? You *can't* just..."

He looked at her in confusion for a moment, but even the darkness couldn't hide the smirk that slowly spread over his face. "No, I wasn't."

She wished she could shrink into a hole. "Oh. Okay. You know you can't..." Her last attempt failed just like the first one.

"I wouldn't," he said, tucking the knife under his jacket pillow.

Mortified, she closed her eyes and prayed for no more dreams.

After a long time, the waves of embarrassment flowed less insistently. Firian's slow breathing told her he was asleep. She couldn't remember another time when he slept while she was awake. The simple realization made her stop short. How many opportunities would she have to get away? She had no idea how far the Academy was from here. It could be days; it could be weeks.

She curled her fingers inward toward the sash, feeling along its edges. Smooth fabric and then, a thread! She rolled it between her fingers, testing its length. With a slight tear she felt but couldn't hear above the high wind, the thread unraveled as she pulled it, passing it from hand to hand as it circled around her wrists. There was still the knot to deal with, but this should loosen the rest of the binding. She kept ripping at the thread, coiling it around her fingers, dropping the useless length, picking it up again, until her arms felt cool, freed from the top of the restraint.

Facing away from her, Firian didn't move. She held her breath as her nails caught the bulk of the knot, weakened by the shredded sash. She pulled, coaxing it to come undone. One end of the sash budged, widening the circle tying her arms together. Straining quietly, she pulled her hands one at a time out of the loop. The black cloth fell with the rest of the fabric.

Now to get away. The forest, so dark it looked burned, mocked her as she looked around for some indication of where to go. Shifra was the only place that came to mind, and she knew dimly where that was. The messenger, that double-agent, probably still lurked there, but most of the people in the fortress would support her. Hide her. Take her home.

That was it, then. She couldn't sit here deciding any longer. Carefully, carefully, she stood, distributing her weight so the twigs wouldn't crack under her feet. Her chest trembled with her jagged heartbeats. With shaking hands, she took one painstaking step and then another. And then another.

When she was out of earshot, she ran.

39

FIRIAN

Alone with his thoughts, Firian had no choice but to sprint, trying to exhaust himself out of his black mood. Despite the cold, he felt hot.

Kiria was gone.

How could this happen? She'd floated before his mind constantly as they traveled. He could sense her like the direction of the sun with his eyes closed, her fear, her resolve. But when he woke, he felt her presence getting farther and farther away.

His thighs burned as he sprinted as fast as he could through the forest where he'd grown up. He fought the urge to scream, barreling toward the field of yellow grass. It grew tall, but the sound would give her away.

Dimly, a voice shouted in his mind. He shoved away the summons. Later, after he'd caught up with her and left anyone who'd helped her escape in a bloody heap, he could face another Tanyu. Not now.

Now... there were eyes upon him that he knew. It wasn't Belik's call but Kiria's look. Like a man dying of thirst, he dove into the Unreal. The color and power of it gushed over him.

On the Unreal mountainside, Master Belik appeared, furiously working his glasses. He shouted something but Firian, his mind crammed with bloody rage, couldn't tell what he said to him. Belik stood huge before him, filling the space with his presence as though to block Kiria from view. "I said stop, you damn idiot!" he said.

"No," said Firian.

"Listen! If you stop, you can get information. There's little you can get out of the girl while she's running around with you."

This all seemed like gibberish to Firian. A mad urge to strike Master Belik surged up in him. He had to calm down. "What?" he demanded, slowing to a walk.

"They refused to surrender in exchange for the girl," said Belik, very distinctly.

Firian furrowed his forehead. That didn't seem right.

Why wouldn't they?

"You did what you could," said Belik. "Let her go back to Brithnem. The Amir will let their guard down. You come back to the Academy." He worked his jaw. "I know you think about her. So, *think* about her. Tell us what you find out."

Firian's chest heaved with the effort of running so long. His lip curled. "I'll find her," he said.

"No, you won't." Belik took a step forward, seeming to shrink to his normal size. "You and the girl have a *katah*, or am I wrong?"

Firian blinked. He hadn't intended to declare one on her. He and Kiria *had* practiced focusing on each other for days. Even now, he sensed where she hid, saw the trees, felt her fear as though he could see everything happening. Unintentional *katah* meant weakness; using it could mean strength.

"I thought so," Belik said, a tinge of irony in his tone.

"But we didn't—"

"Maybe you should have."

Firian popped his jaw with frustration, opening his eardrums. A *katah*-level connection could give him power since Kiria wasn't strong enough in her Talent to counteract him. If he wanted to spy on her, he could.

Belik cracked his thick neck. "For now, watch her and find out what she knows. If you follow her now, your mission will be a failure." He spoke each word distinctly. The last one lingered in the air like smoke. Firian hated the stench of it, comprised of all his mistakes and all of Belik's. A shadow seemed to fall over the Master's face.

Picking flakes of skin around his Defender ring, Firian sucked his teeth and looked down, over, anywhere for answers. His chin jutted forward, his breaths coming short.

He couldn't fail.

"As you would have it, Master Belik."

When the Academy loomed above him, all dark stone, his mouth tasted sour as though he would be sick. After hurrying to get back, he found himself wishing he were anywhere else.

I'll get her back, he reminded himself. Kiria would come to him. That would shut them up.

Standing before the enormous wooden doors, he felt stripped of everything. Bitter hatred gnawed him. After all that work and anticipation... He closed his eyes and set his mouth before going in.

The fountain splashed in the courtyard, staircases rose along the walls, leading to the rooms on the upper floors. Learners formed little groups, walking to class or talking by the fountain. He rushed past them, hating it all. His eyes flickered over the faces to find Tiev, Bard—someone he'd have to respond to. A few acquaintances, but that was all. None of them Defenders.

His rage led him to the one who had orchestrated it all. When he reached Belik's door, he didn't knock.

Belik knelt next to a man lying unconscious on the floor. At the sound of the door crashing open, the Master opened his eyes in the slow, conscious way of a swimmer after he breaks the surface. In a silence that spoke louder than a shout, he slowly turned around. "You'll have to learn respect," he said. Firian had never seen him so angry. His mouth was a hard, cold line. "I would hate to have to teach it to you."

Firian was in no mood to be criticized. "Yes, Master Belik," he grated.

Belik raised his eyebrows at his tone and stood up. "I could have left you out there," he said meaningfully. The words would have had more effect under different circumstances. Belik's hand clenched. Striking the back of his chair with a sharp crash, he cried, "I should have left you out there! But I scrambled to find a reason to keep you. Direct access to the princess's mind."

"Yes, Master Belik."

"Then finish your mission and the Academy may forgive your gory stupidity!"

At the noise, the man on the floor rolled his head to the other side and his eyelids fluttered. Firian saw milky whiteness underneath.

Belik pointed at the man. "Thank your stars he wasn't Lost," he said, as though he didn't want a reason to blame Firian for anything else. Master Belik turned away from him to the man on the floor.

Firian's chest felt tight as he stormed back through the courtyard to the stairs. Eyes followed him as he rushed past. By habit, he checked the Unreal. No eyes there. Kiria was not among those watching him.

Had they counted on a connection between him and Kiria? Belik acted as if he hadn't known about her Talent, but the Academy had lied before. At least this war wasn't Belik's idea. He didn't have that much power. The Head had to be behind it.

That coward.

Bard wasn't in the room when Firian got back. Probably all for the best. Bard would be glad to see him, and Firian couldn't say the same thing. At least not until he'd calmed down.

40

KIRIA

Gulping for air, Kiria opened her eyes. Darkness. Where was she?

Her fingers spread open into deep, soft blankets. A pillow scented with lilies and musk cradled her head, now covered in her sweaty hair. She's slept in Brithnem, in the palace, in her own bed. But she still had nightmares. The disembodied sense of panic came from Torithians, from weapons rushing through thin air, from strangers in a pub, from Firian.

What time is it? She rolled over and tried to gauge any light coming in from the window. Oddly, it looked far away. Her room was enormous. She had woken up before the sun, even before Candrae and Vayci.

They had been so happy to see her yesterday. Against protocol, they had both hugged her, laying a dark, bare head and a dainty blonde one against hers. Shocked by how thin and bedraggled she'd become, they gave her a bath and clean clothes. The bath revealed that the raised, misshapen arrow scars in her left shoulder and thigh were here to stay. Her skin had darkened and her hair lightened in the sun.

Kiria's return to the palace was a bright blur of voices hushed and shouted. Jori brought her food, Atty glowed, Daelon smiled and brewed tea.

Her mother cried and fell on her when she first saw her daughter in the hallway. Kiria cried too, deep, heaving sobs. One person couldn't welcome her back.

In the darkness, she squeezed her eyes shut. A tear leaked out, streaking down her face into her hair. She made it back safe, but so much had happened that she couldn't relax.

They had caught the Torithian on the grounds of the castle, they told her. A couple from the city who hated the Keepers' leadership had helped him gain access. For weeks he had hidden in the wine cellar and adjacent storage rooms beneath the palace. Both the Torithian murderer and the traitorous couple had been instantly put to death.

Restless, Kiria sat up and struck a candle. When she and Firian had left Carradoc, she'd forgotten to take her notebook. It was still there when she returned, hungry and caked in mud. She thought she would remember the traitor-messenger's face, but she never spotted him. Still, an armed escort of five randomly chosen soldiers marched her back to the palace. She picked them herself, hoping that she could avoid, or at least break up, a contingent loyal to the Academy.

She picked up the notebook from her side table. With her mother still recovering from grief and shock, someone needed to contribute for the Second Line. A few comments yesterday made it sound as if she hadn't been in most of the sessions since Father died.

Her pen scratched along the page until gray light dawned. A click of the door—her head shot up. Quietly, Vayci and Candrae entered the room, carrying candles. Candrae's pale eyes widened at the sight of another light and Kiria sitting up in bed.

"My Kepress," she cried, rushing over to her, "are you unwell?"

"No, I'm fine," Kiria replied, closing the notebook on her finger. "I need a drink of water."

"Of course," Vayci replied, leaving like a dark shadow.

Candrae remained by her side. "Why is my lady awake so early?" she asked softly.

Firian's hour. "I just couldn't sleep." She pushed thin hair out of her face. Her Ability didn't need to emerge again until she went to a session. For now, being plain gave her a different kind of comfort, of invisibility.

Candrae laid a comforting hand flat on the blankets beside her. "We have posted extra guards for your safety," she said, "and we will catch Defender Kess for what he did to you."

Kiria looked down and quirked her lips. Candrae put it nicely. Others, yesterday, had cursed his name, promising to rain down torture. She understood, but she couldn't join them. In fact, their threats rankled. She knew the better man he could choose to be.

Vayci returned with the water. Kiria drank it gratefully.

A warm, black shadow entered her consciousness. Surely it was nothing. She raised the cup to her lips again, seeing if the feeling would leave. It didn't.

The girls started gliding around her room, preparing it for the morning. Tentative, Kiria closed her eyes.

In the Unreal, Firian waited, a dark figure with nothing behind. He wore the same fitted black shirt as when they first met, sleeves rolled up to the elbows. His thumb drummed absently against his leg. Despite that slight tick, confidence radiated from him, as it always did. *Almost always.* She remembered the pain in his eyes when he had looked in his mother's face.

Her breathing quickened as she ran through a mass of emotions: fear, anger, relief.

He's not here. He's not here, she reminded herself.

Surrounded by guards, she had felt safe when she came back to the palace. But she was still alone in her mind.

"What are you doing here?" she snapped. When he didn't answer right away, she said, "You can't take me back."

"I know," he said calmly. His look said otherwise. He fixed his gaze and his mind on her. The space he occupied held only the two of them. No scenery, no sense of place. When he noticed her looking around, a peaceful wooded area blossomed around them, perhaps to make her feel more comfortable. "I just wanted to see you."

She responded with stony silence. That couldn't possibly be the only reason.

"I miss you."

She cut him off. "Why are you here?" she demanded, done with his flirtation.

His voice dropped to a confidential undertone. "The Academy's making things difficult for me."

"I did what I had to."

"I know," he said again. "I don't want anything from you." His voice drifted off as though he wanted to say more. His blue eyes stared into hers, willing her to understand.

She refused. "You made your choice," she said, softening just a little. "You could have helped me."

Looking down, he ran his tongue thoughtfully over the top row of teeth. She knew that something about the situation didn't feel like a choice to him.

How could his loyalty run so deep to the Academy? Could he not see that their methods undermined trust? How could they have a vote if they were willing to coerce the Kingdom into it? What else would they try to force the Keepers to do? Over the years, the Tanyu had had the chance to help the Kingdom, but they chose to remain aloof and separate. This bid for power ran false, self-serving rather than loyal.

"I am going to help you." His eyes lifted to hers, and his lips flattened in a half-smile. His damned overconfidence made her want to punch him in the arm. She drew in a breath to tell him off.

"You're glad I'm alive," he said, rushing to beat her to the words. His thumb stopped drumming as he waited for her confirmation.

She deflated. He knew it was true, so there was no sense in denying it. She let her head drop in a nod. "I am glad you're alive," she repeated, deadpan. She didn't want him dead, but she didn't want him anywhere near her either. He'd shown his character loudly at the end.

Firian smiled and crossed his arms, the muscles cording in his forearms. "And you're back safe," he continued. A step on a path to a conclusion. "Kiria, I didn't mean for all of this to happen. We can help each other now."

Iciness ran through in her veins at the suggestion. She shouldn't be talking to him. Politically, it was a terrible idea. The Kingdom had surely passed out his death warrant to every city between here and the Eradi Desert, and with good reason.

But if he was having second thoughts about the Tanyu, she could encourage him to change and not to fight against them... A precarious plan. If it succeeded, though, she would have won a major victory for the Kingdom.

Firian was stubborn, but hadn't she seen him change over the weeks they traveled together?

"I don't know," she said. "I'll take information you give me." There was no way she'd give him any more information about Brithnem than he already knew.

"Sleep on it." His eyes sparkled with the reminder that her habits had changed because of him.

To give herself more time to think, she nodded and opened her eyes. Trying to be extra quiet, Candrae and Vayci had opened the curtains. They must have thought she had fallen back asleep. Kiria squinted against the light.

If Firian came again, she wouldn't discourage him unless he tried to get information from her. If he did, she would never speak to him again. Simple as that.

She sensed the shadow, like an exhaled breath, leave her mind.

IN THE PALACE, the celebration over her return gave way to serious thoughts of war again. Kiria attended every session and she got the notes from Hada, one of the Main recorders, about what she had missed.

Her initial elation at being reunited with everyone—her mother especially who, despite her joy, looked more worn and haggard than she had ever seen her—melted slowly away into dark foreboding. She began to realize that if they did not win victory on both fronts, they would lose the Kingdom. Brithnem would cease to be the center of noble leadership, of learning, of beauty. Her beloved city would fall.

As hard as she could, Kiria tried not to feel guilty for the time lost worrying about her when she was a hostage. The Second Line had suffered. After the ultimatum came, her mother could think of nothing else. From what Kiria could piece together, someone had discouraged her from attending sessions, since her only thoughts were for her daughter. Something about a lack of clarity and impartiality. The very idea sent Kiria combing madly through more notes, determined to show the Second Line's worth every way she knew how.

"They treat me as though I cannot think," Mother burst out one day, as though to herself.

Kiria squeezed her hand softly as they walked to the Main. "I'm sure you'll be welcome now," she replied, disturbed she had to say anything like that at all. Her mother should always be welcome. Yet this marked her first session since Kiria's danger.

Although Kiria had only been gone a few weeks, she caught guards and servants openly staring at her, their heads tracking her movement past them. It felt good to be Beautiful again. *A woman is strong when she realizes she's beautiful.* She smoothed down her dress with her free hand, the line from the Scroll resonating inside her. General Brishen had spoken the words to Mari in Carradoc —*Carradoc!*—on the night Shane fell in love with her, though Kiria grew up thinking he loved her long before that.

Kiria wore Beauty differently now, with more purpose, like armor. Since her ordeal, she felt more solid, like a white picture filled in. Her Beauty no longer covered emptiness.

As the two of them approached, guards swung open the ponderous doors. Cúron already sat on his throne and she heard Atty's footsteps shuffle over the long rug behind them.

The Ariocs entered the Main coldly. The many-paned window had been soldered shut—Kiria automatically checked every time. Daelon had already arrived, sitting in the front row. His face split into a smile when he saw them. Also in the front row sat the royal Amiran advisors: Parohim, Chetana, and Reynard, each now with a vote. So far, nothing had really changed, the advisors siding with their respective Keepers.

Searching the faces, Kiria hooked her mother's arm through her own. Did someone want the Second Line to die? Everyone knew that two Keepers would quickly lead to one. Atty would never wish that. Cúron? It seemed odd to suspect him, because he had always been an upright man, good to her, although distant and sometimes condescending. But who else could it be?

Merian strode, stately, to her seat on the dais. Moments later, Atty hurried in wearing a fur-collared Keeper's robe. Kiria settled herself between Daelon and Hada, directly below her mother's chair.

The session began with formalities. Parohim introduced the day's topics (mostly war-related again.) Kiria watched everyone's reaction to her mother's part in the proceedings and piped in with her own thoughts. Her mother barely spoke, but she had always been reserved, content for others to make most of the decisions. Passivity galled Kiria now more than ever, but she had to show as much support as she could. All in all, everything seemed normal.

And then the shadow came.

Kiria shifted in her seat, listening to Cúron's ideas about food shortages now that so many key farmers had become soldiers. Hada's scratching pen ran over the page. Trying desperately to shake off the feeling of dread creeping over her, Kiria cleared her throat, too low to be heard. Daelon noticed. Of course he would. She nodded to assure him she felt fine.

"...until they return from the front. Sublets will..."

Focus on something else. Cúron, with his commanding voice, kept airing his opinions but she found it harder and harder to concentrate. The warm shadow tickled her mind like a hair fallen on the back of her arm—unfindable but unmistakable.

If Firian watched her mind *during* sessions... Her body seized into a tight knot of frustration. She should never have been kind to him when he came the first time.

"Excuse me," she said, almost tripping over Daelon's knees as she hurried over the mosaic floor. Guards obediently pulled open the doors to let her out.

In the hallway, she pushed her hands to her face. Someone gently touched her elbow. Daelon. His blue-gray coat floated to a stop around his ankles.

"You are unwell," he said, uncharacteristically skipping her formal title. The scholarly lines on his face had deepened since the Torithians attacked her in the garden.

"No, no."

"Come. Sit," he coaxed, leading her to a bench along the wall. She relented and sat with him. "My Kepress, something's wrong."

The closest guards stayed by the massive doors, just out of earshot if she spoke low. "I can't go to any more sessions in the Main," she said, avoiding his eyes. His immediate confusion irritated her. Even though she knew that he had done nothing wrong, she was tired of feeling like a liability.

"My Kepress," he replied slowly. "Now more than ever you need to go. This is the time—"

"I'm being watched." She didn't take her eyes off the patterned rug running almost to their feet.

"Who's watching you?" he cried, brow furrowing. "We'll take care of that. Tell me who. You know we'll protect you."

"I know *you* will," she corrected him. Someone—Torithians or Tanyu or Kingdom—was targeting her Line. First the attack, then her father's death, then the hostage situation. Through it all, her mother had been gracefully but definitely shattered. Now would be the perfect time for Kiria to ease into a Keeper's responsibilities, begin to lead the people... "But it's my thoughts. My thoughts are being watched."

"Ah," he said with dawning understanding.

Kiria finally looked up. Would Daelon understand? She wasn't shying away from her duties; she was trying to do what was best for the Kingdom, even if it made her feel useless. "I'm counting on you to be at every session. Do what you must to get them to listen to you. But don't tell me anything until I can figure this out." Anger twisted like a beast inside her.

His eyes softened and she almost regretted her anger. He was her teacher, after all, and one of her best friends. She couldn't afford to alienate anybody.

"You know what I would say. I trust you," she said pointedly.

"What do you have to do to get rid of him?" he asked. So he did understand, in a way.

"I don't know," she admitted. "I'll figure something out. You don't... know what to do, do you?"

"I'm an Amir," he said, with a strange mix of pride and regret. "I don't have the Talent. But apparently you do, so remember the words of the Scroll and let me know if I can help you in any other way. If you can figure out where he is, we'll send someone there. If it helps, we'll find someone who has enough Talent to help you. Maybe the Watchman, or my mother."

Warm relief washed through her. She sighed deeply, unable to stop herself from going on. "I don't know what to do. He comes and... talks to me. I thought I could control it, but just now I felt him there. He might overhear everything. I can't risk it. He's probably hearing this." Her chest tightened with claustrophobia. She fought the urge to check the Unreal.

Daelon put his hand reassuringly on her shoulder. "Don't be afraid. There has to be a solution. I'll pray; I'll be your voice in the Main. The Second Line is safe with me."

She inhaled another deep breath. "You're right." She was still frustrated, but the choice seemed right. It felt satisfyingly like defiance. She would dedicate herself to mastering those things necessary to being a great leader. Let them try to snuff the Second Line. They would have to kill her first. "You're right."

"He's in your mind to spy on you?" Daelon asked significantly, after a pause.

And other reasons. "Well... it seems that way," she said bitterly. "He listens. It's all the same, isn't it?"

"And you know when he's there watching you? Can you do the same?"

"I usually know," she said, catching on. "I know what he's thinking sometimes, but I'm not as good as he is. He had only just begun to teach me how to use the Talent."

"You say he's probably overhearing this conversation." He chose his words carefully. She appreciated his caution, but he didn't fully understand that Firian couldn't just hear words if he wanted to, but might also see her thoughts. Still, maybe it would help. Daelon continued, "I get the feeling that he may be watching you for more than information. Don't take offense, my Kepress."

She didn't answer him, and that was answer enough.

"If that's the case," he went on, "he might come to you sometimes even when you aren't attending sessions. If he does that, see if you can make anything of it—carefully, of course." Daelon came out of his thoughts as he seemed to realize his plan could be dangerous.

"I can do that," she reassured him. In fact, the idea excited her. She could turn Firian's visits to her advantage, rather than feeling like a pawn. "I may as well make the most of this."

"Until we can find another solution," said Daelon. He seemed to think she was too enthusiastic about the idea. "Be very careful. He's double-crossed you before. You know he's dangerous."

She chewed her lip. "I do, but I'm glad I can still be useful. Don't tell the Keeper about any of this," she added. Her mother didn't need to worry about anything else just now. Let her think that Kiria stayed away from sessions out of grief or illness. If Kiria's spy work yielded any results, it would just come as a good surprise.

41

FIRIAN

One thing was clear. Firian couldn't tell Master Belik that Kiria would provide no new information. It was out of the question. The only thing to do was find some way around it.

"Which is a lie?"

"Is this another exercise?" Bard looked down from the top bunk. Dark bags puffed around his eyes.

If this practice didn't matter so much, Firian might let him sleep.

Back at the palace, Kiria had started to use her Ability again. He drank in her Beauty any time he had a spare moment. Though he was careful, she got better at sensing his presence. Like someone half-turning her head to listen, she would lean into him just enough to confirm he was there.

She didn't speak to him. But he remembered the look in her eyes in Shifra. In the golden brown, piercing gaze of her full beauty, that look could stab him through with pleasure. He watched her incessantly, craving that gaze, her attention, a respite from darkness.

In his first rage, Firian hadn't noticed the changed mood in the Academy. Now he saw that fewer people roamed the halls and courtyard. The Tanyu he did see were either quiet with a new kind of weariness, or excited with loud, hollow desperation.

Entire hallways downstairs had been designated as war zones. Retrieving the Lost kept Master Belik occupied most of the time, since few had that specialty. Firian had little contact with him besides giving the information he learned from Kiria—not a task he enjoyed. Especially now that Kiria kept herself out of the Main.

"Yes," he said. "Pay attention. I kissed Alani today. Rian got moved to Erron's regiment."

"You didn't kiss Alani," Bard said without hesitation.

Firian squinted. "Did someone tell you about Rian? I could have kissed Alani."

"No. Nobody told me. I'm just playing along, like you said. Aren't you going with Maya?"

"How did you know the answer so fast?"

"It's pretty easy, if you're paying attention." Bard was telling the truth. Hopefully Firian wasn't as transparent.

Slight emphasis on the last word revealed Bard's defensiveness. His initial happiness at Firian's return had faded since he refused to say anything about the mission. Bard seemed to take it personally, but stopped asking questions after the first day.

Firian cracked his knuckles. He tried a few more and Bard knew the answers instantly. The options must be too easy. He would try something from the mission. Let Bard figure that one out.

"I broke a man's nose with a spoon. The Keepers gave me a dagger as a gift before I left."

Bard's black eyes widened as he considered his answer. He'd never been good at hiding his curiosity.

Finally, some hesitation.

"The Keepers didn't give you a dagger."

"How can you be this gory accurate?" Firian cried, yanking Bard off the bunk.

Bard crashed to the floor, and hopped to his feet. "I'm sorry, I thought you wanted me to do this!" he snapped. The war must really have gotten to him.

"One more," Firian said. A lie.

If Bard could see through his deception, Belik could. If Belik didn't swallow the false intelligence he had to give him... He didn't want to think about it. It wasn't an option.

He dipped into the Unreal for a glance of Kiria.

"Is that her?"

Firian hurdled back into reality. Hatred choked him before he realized it was Bard. Bard, who had never done anything wrong, possibly in his whole life. Still, what business did he have looking into his thoughts?

"One more," Firian repeated. The little stone room they shared had never felt so small.

Bard crossed his arms and prompted him with his eyebrows.

No idea came to him. Bard knew almost everything Firian did. "Which one is a lie?" he said, stalling for time. The lengthening shadows mocked him. Almost time. "Enderin sent more reinforcements to the Kingdom. I stole food from the palace." He hesitated. "My mother is dead."

Before he even answered, Bard's eyes told the answer. "Fir..."

The door opened. Firian had seen the blond man before but didn't know his name. "Bard," he said, "Tiev needs you in the War Zone."

Suddenly ashen, Bard nodded once and the stranger left. His skin's pallor made his spiky black hair more startling. "Later, Firian, yeah?" he murmured.

Firian watched him go, not trusting himself to speak.

Tiev led a regiment now, but he shouldn't be able to take Bard away when Firian needed him. What good could Bard do in battle anyway? He was never a fighter. And wasn't he studying *katah*? Focused special missions, those fitted him better than combat.

Those fitted the war better than combat. The Head's decision to launch this fear campaign, killing civilians in their sleep, made Firian's stomach turn. There had to be a better way to settle this conflict.

The dark orange sun angled through the window, casting deep shadows. Belik waited for news.

Firian swallowed and slipped out of the room. Uncomfortable silence met him. Many had questions about his mission but he'd shut down every one. Only Belik knew the truth.

As he strode slowly to the staircase, the heavy pain hovering over the Academy crept into his bones. Before, pain had sparkled in service of something better, more powerful. Firian had almost longed for it, loving the power it gave him. Now it felt futile.

Several Tanyu had died in the war already, mostly in circumstances more shameful than heroic. Losing to an Amir was already embarrassing, and whispered rumors blamed the Head's mismanagement as well. All of it gave Firian a sour taste in the pit of his stomach.

He expected more from the Academy. If he were in charge, he would end the war against the Kingdom. Or if the royals refused the terms, he would fight on both fronts, mental and physical. He would bring in people who had no Talent or very little and train them to be fighters. Surrounding towns would fear the name of Tanyu absolutely; he would punish incompetent leaders. The Academy would become a place of action, not intrigue.

Belik's door.

Firian calmed his mind, emptied it. Clarity, changeable and lucid as water, filled him. He took a deep breath and heard Belik tell him to come in.

This time Belik was alone. He wasn't Retrieving anyone; instead he sat just as he always did his plain wooden chair as though it were a throne. It felt like so long ago that Firian had taken lessons with him. Belik, however, hadn't changed like Firian had. The Master glanced inscrutably at him over his glasses. "So," he said, "what do you have for me?"

Firian stepped forward. The Master didn't stand. "The Second Keeper is distraught over the loss of her husband," Firian recited. "She hasn't been attending sessions. Kiria suspects that someone may be trying to undermine the Second Line."

"Emotional," Belik interjected.

The word briefly interrupted Firian's calm. He went on. "They are planning to have her take over the Line from her mother very soon." If only that were true. They could end the war together.

"Anything military?"

"Kiria is scheduled to go to the Main tomorrow morning to discuss war strategy, Master Belik." It could be true.

"It sounds like spying on your lover is paying off so far," the Master said, standing. "So why are you nervous?"

The room was really very small. Firian stood up straighter. "I'm not nervous. I'm anxious that this mission be successful." It sounded too much like an admission of defeat. But at least the idea was plausible.

Belik blinked slowly, almost luxuriously. "She already knows?"

Ice shot through Firian's spine. He hadn't even begun to feed Belik information. "Are you comparing her Talent with mine?" Firian demanded.

"You like her, yes?" Belik said. "Odds are that you of all people wouldn't be content to watch her from a corner but would rather get the information in a more... intimate way. Where she could see you. Tell me I'm wrong."

"We don't talk about politics or the war," Firian protested. *We hardly speak at all.* "She thinks I come to support her, that I'm on her side. That kind of trust is hard to create." The muscles in his throat felt stifling. "I'll watch her and gather information. After a while I'm sure she'll even confide in me herself."

"Oh, I'm sure," Belik sneered. "Feed you false information, and you'll eat it too."

Firian flexed his hands open and closed. "No one else can do this job."

"You will address me as Master Belik. And yes, we have others who can do this job better than you can. She knows that you're watching her and plans to spy on you now." Suddenly his eyes seemed to turn black with dangerous rage.

Firian tensed for a fight.

"Could you be any more of a disappointment, Firian?" Belik yelled, letting out each word separately, like he was restraining himself from saying or doing something worse. "You...!" He pointed at him furiously, then stood to jab him hard in the chest with a blunt finger. "You were...!" One deep breath composed him enough to speak. "Don't go back to the girl. Someone else will take care of her. You'll go to war under Tiev."

Firian opened his mouth. Belik's quick, murderous glance was enough to let him know that he was fully aware of how much pain his order caused.

"The War Zone. Now." Belik shooed him out with a wave of his hand.

Firian burned hot and his muscles ached with sickness. Any words of protest stuck, choking, in his throat. He couldn't think without feeling poisoned by every thought.

He could see himself, just arrived at the Academy, convinced that he would grow powerful, that all would respect him, look up to him, follow his orders. He grew up before his eyes. He could see himself training, becoming more dangerous. Even Jovan didn't scowl at him. Girls were intoxicated by him, his body and ability. The Scroll was a weapon in his mouth. Few Tanyu knew how powerful those words were. Belik gave him a mission. There they were in the pub, equals. Master Gerand flashed before him and faded, leaving the two travelers, Tanyu and Kepress. Kiria was Beautiful now with a Beauty that burned his eyes. He saw it like the negative image of the sun, always before him, coloring his vision. There was his family—Brett with the baby, his mother crying, and his father not saying he was proud. A wave of sickness. And she was gone. And he was here.

He stumbled backward and caught himself against the wall with his hand. He'd found the War Zone. People began to come into the hallway and disappear quietly in different rooms. They could have been pictures for how much he noted them.

Bard, he finally thought, *is under Tiev too*. If he could find Bard, he would be in the right place. Maybe he would never have to speak to Tiev at all. He knew that thread of comfort would break, but he held onto it until he had to let go.

Unbidden, Bard appeared in his mind, as though he had been waiting to hear his name. Firian knew exactly where he was.

He walked in the large unused classroom without knocking. Motionless Tanyu filled tight-packed rows of chairs. Tiev, looking years older, stood at the front with his eyes closed as well. Bard sat toward the back, with his eyes shut tight and sweat standing out on his clammy face.

A girl named Xan woke up, coming out of the Unreal. With no word from anyone, she came over and took Firian out of the room. He had seen her sometime before but didn't know her well. She was several years older than he was, tanned and fierce-looking with her hair back in a braid.

"Master Tiev sent me to tell you what to do," she said.

He stiffened but wasn't capable of suffering much more just then.

"We are part of the intimidation force," she explained.

Dreams. No real threat. Kiria was right. He should have taken her back to the Kingdom. He had no future here.

Xan ignored the seething fury rippling off him, and continued her explanation. "We fight at night because we aren't going against anyone with real Talent. You will be assigned your target. Most of them fight back, but aren't trained. You can't let them wake up and be able to describe you. Understand?"

He nodded once, glaring blackly at her.

"You're supposed to start immediately." She opened the door and gestured toward an empty seat in the back.

He sat deliberately, setting his arms slowly on the rests and pushing his spine against the wooden back of the chair. His body was the only thing left for him to control.

He closed his eyes. Nothingness washed over him like a thick wave. He sucked it into his lungs like a man eager to drown. The relief was immense.

Then he saw Brithnem. He recognized the houses from Parohim's tour. It was an old part of town near the outer wall—nowhere near the palace, he noticed.

There was Tiev. For a moment they both remembered the last time they had been in the Unreal together, and the houses flickered into a tall round room. In the next breath, the city returned.

"Your targets," said Tiev, pointing to two houses separated in the dark by several streets. The Unreal afforded clarity denied to ordinary existence; Firian knew exactly what he meant. As clearly as he understood which men he was to kill, he also knew that they were strategically meaningless. He was part of a mindless campaign of fear. If people began dying in their sleep, the others would panic and urge the leaders to give up this Tanyuin war.

Any drone could do this. They had no Talent to fight back with.

Tiev, who obviously had no desire to stay longer than he had to, disappeared and left Firian alone in the phantom streets.

He would rather fight than think, so he went to the first house. A young bearded man slept next to his wife. He had the sprawling look of an oncoming hangover. Numbly, Firian let nothingness come over him again to search for the man's dream.

It came slowly and hazily. Firian hated him for its indistinctness. He couldn't accuse the man of anything else and he needed something to fuel his anger. *No Talent at all*, he thought. The man was helpless. Victory over him wasn't anything to live for.

If the Western Kingdom had been stronger, this fear campaign might do some good, but he knew that divisions threatened to crack it from the inside. If the Academy wanted to take control of the Kingdom, Firian could do it faster than this. But he didn't want this gory war at all.

The dream materialized. The fogginess was maddening, but Firian knew suddenly that he couldn't be apathetic here. Later he would figure out exactly what to do. Now, he would be the best fighter they had. He knew how to do that even if his world was crumbling around him.

Mist floated over his vision, but he saw the bearded man, walking by the edge of a wooded cliff. Could he have made it any easier? Firian joined him, gauging his reaction. The man saw him coming from far off and a large knife appeared in his hand.

So the man had been warned about nightmares.

This man wasn't a threat. He was just a man. One who didn't deserve to die.

Something inside Firian sank. The red rage that had pulsed through him cooled. Pausing, he peered into the man's face through the murk of his dream, observing him almost clinically. What did this man have to do with this conflict? Nothing.

This wasn't what Firian signed up for. This wasn't honorable. No one would respect him for killing a defenseless civilian. Kiria would hate him for it, and he would hate himself.

Tiev and the Academy could go to hell with their instructions. If they wanted him to fight, then he'd fight someone who was actually an enemy.

He focused on the palace.

42

KIRIA

By the time it was clear what Firian was doing, Kiria had already watched him for too long. He was somewhere in the palace.

If he had been looking for her, he would already be in her mind. No, this was a military assassination.

He seemed to be by the Amiran rooms. In the darkness she saw the round lamps and the colonnade. He entered one of the rooms. Not one of the primary advisors' rooms. Not Daelon's. She didn't know whose it was.

Rather than stall to figure out the target, she bolted down the hallway toward the door. Her serving girls and ever-present guards followed behind. "A doctor! I need a doctor!" she cried. Candrae peeled off from the group to fetch one.

They ran out of the palace into the gardens and around the colonnade. "This is it!" she cried, turning the knob. The door wouldn't open. "It's bolted! Do something!"

The guards didn't require an explanation. One threw his weight against it, but the door wouldn't move. Again, and the door hardly budged.

She pounded her fists against the door. "Wake up! Wake up! Open the door! Wake up!"

A few Amir jogged around the corner at the din. Daelon's high-necked coat was unlaced in his hurry. "What's wrong, Kepress?" he demanded.

"Wake him up!" she said. "Tanyu..."

Daelon understood immediately and pulled out a key. Kiria almost fell into the darkened room. She half expected to see Firian standing there, but the little cell was empty except for the sleeping Amir. Daelon violently shook the unconscious figure on the bed. "Wake up! You're under attack!" he yelled in his ear. But the figure merely slumped out of bed onto the floor.

The Amir was dead.

It was my idea to give a speech, Kiria reminded herself as she faced the sun in the ceremonial box at the arena, looking down at an enormous crowd. So many people came that they could barely fit in the arena. Every night, men and women died in their sleep, and people from all over the Western Kingdom were panicking. Someone had to commiserate with them and put their fears to rest. Kiria could do that without knowing any specific war plans at all.

Behind her stood Daelon and Chetana. Her mother's advisor looked more than ever like a general these days. Her long neck and high cheekbones gave her the aura of an immovable statue. She hadn't been idle during the Keeper's stint out of the Main. In fact, from what Kiria could gather, Chetana played a pivotal role in planning the Tanyuin War, as significant a role as the man Firian had assassinated. Daelon, who looked more like a Kingdom man than a Khelê like his mother, always preferred peace. In their own ways, they gave her courage.

Looking down, she saw faces she recognized from open sessions and servants who had come and gone during her time at the palace.

She breathed a prayer and began:

"People of Brithnem, I know that many of you have come here for comfort. I have little comfort to offer, since I also am one of you. I have experienced your pain and your anxieties. What I can offer is what has comforted me. I can think of no greater comfort than these words from the Sacred Scroll: *'Do not fear, for redemption will come to you. While you are surrounded and the shadow of your destruction overcasts your skies, salvation will come.'*"

Beneath the banister, Kiria's fingers fidgeted with the sleeve of her ocean-blue dress.

"We may be at war with the Torithians and with the Tanyu, but the people of Brithnem have always been hardy. We stand with the strength our founders had, the strength that says that we will tolerate no injustice. We are people willing to sacrifice for what is right and in the end we will be victorious."

Jori's face appeared in the crowd, uplifted with the rest. For all his flippancy, he needed comfort too.

"We stand with the strength of hope," she said, her voice rising. "Those words were spoken over our city. The strength of our soldiers may falter but not the strength of our God. When our enemies have fled in shame, we will rebuild our lives with singing."

That line reverberated inside her. When she wrote it, she had hoped it would sound poetic enough to remember but direct enough to reassure the people. If nothing else, it calmed her a little.

"I say these things not to diminish your suffering, but to remind you that it is not in vain. When we rise up with this strength, it is not we, but our enemies, who should fear."

She blinked slowly to check for Firian's presence. Deep shame and sadness filled her when she thought of him. Clearly, potential for good was not the same as goodness. *May we rise to goodness.* In the Unreal, she sensed no sign of him. Only blank haziness in that direction.

She continued. "See the beauty of this city and the people you fight for. Let it fill you with courage to defend them. These are the things that comfort me now and will continue to comfort me through this fight. Join me in looking to God and to each other in our need. At the end of this struggle we will rise again, strong in the justice of our cause and joyful because we have seen the fulfillment of our hopes."

Silence followed. Her eyes were filmy with tears.

Applause roared up from the arena, coursing around the great statues in the center. She may have reassured them with the speech, but they also reassured her with their trust. All these people believed in her and she believed in them. Her life's goal, briefly eclipsed by Firian, came back into focus. Preserving this Kingdom was worth living and dying for.

43

FIRIAN

Just outside the battle room, Firian glared into Tiev's slanted eyes. "I killed an Amir! A strategist!"

"That's why I'm not throwing you out," Tiev cried, keeping his voice low to prevent it from cracking, "but I'd rather have ten Bards who do as they're told than one gory insurgent!" His teeth flashed white in a snarl.

Firian swore at him and stalked away. He wouldn't stay to hear more abuse. Not today. Not when everything crumbled around him—everything he'd built, every relationship he had. Let Tiev try to stop him. Firian had less and less to lose.

Bard was already snoring when Firian got back to the room, even though he had only left minutes before Firian's run-in with Tiev.

Firian felt too filthy to touch anything, even the bed. With something like despair, he threw himself down anyway and gave into exhaustion.

A long night passed in fits of sweat. When morning finally came, enough to give up the fight for sleep, Firian lay on his back. Vague memories of the night before gushed over him.

When he had gone to the palace, he saw the swish of a silk nightdress in the corner of his mind. Kiria had been very near when he killed the Amir. Why hadn't he stopped? The Amir plotted against the Tanyu, and hated them with unreasonable passion. Firian knew that as certainly as he knew the man's name: Salaar. But his gut clenched with the idea of what he'd done, and that she had seen it all. She might hate him now. Odd that, in the moment, stopping hadn't occurred to him. Rage, desperation, and frustration had thrilled through his body enough to shut off his brain.

He reached, tentatively, toward her. All he found was a soft but alarming buzz. He sat up in bed and held his aching head in his hands. His eyeballs stung and the scabs stretched along his back. How had everything come to this?

"Heard it was a tough night," said Bard quietly, jumping from his bunk to the floor. When Firian didn't answer, he continued. "Me too. They woke the guy up before I could do anything." Relief and bitterness edged his words. He shook his head and hissed a breath through his teeth. "Gore, I hate this!"

Sometimes Firian thought that almost any trade would suit Bard better than being a Tanyu.

"You know," Bard said, "what did that guy do to deserve this, hm?" He pointed at Firian with both hands as though he were one of the targets. "He's not even fighting. I've seen kiddies running around." He looked meditatively at the floor before sitting and pulling on his shoes. "I thought war would be different."

"I know. And you're right. It shouldn't be like this."

Bard shot him an amazed look. "You agree?"

"Yeah, definitely."

A moment of melancholy passed between them. There was very little they could do about it.

"So, I'm off for the day," Bard continued. "Honestly, I don't even mind. You want to get a pint?"

"Yes, I do." Firian tried Kiria again. Another buzz, different than sensing a mind in the Unreal. This humming felt persistent, unmoving, charged with pain if he got too close. The realization left him sick and breathless. He'd felt this once before. A Sentry.

He hurled himself against it. He grunted as blinding pain seared him from the inside.

"You okay?" Bard asked.

"Yeah," Firian murmured. "Let's go." Like birds of prey, his thoughts circled around the Sentry. Without Kiria, he had nothing. He felt like the desert cat in its cage. Even the sky seemed lower. How to break the Sentry...? It was just a strategic problem, like all those others in Master Asoka's class.

The answer broke over him like a wave. He would find them. Sentries were people, punished Tanyu. Funny that he had never thought of them that way. To everyone at the Academy, they were tools, threats, objects of pain. They protected warriors from getting Lost like Anewa and punished others by tearing away the right to the Unreal. But they had to be nearby. He would follow the buzz, lean into the pain even if it broke him. Then he would be free.

PAIN PULSED in his skull as Firian wandered behind the Masters' stone houses, keeping his mind on the threshold of the Unreal. Nothing looked like it would house Sentries, just more pine woods. But the sickening buzz definitely began somewhere out there.

"You okay, Fir?" Bard's light feet crunched the pine needles as they went. His forehead creased in concern.

"I need to... find something." He rubbed his temples hard for a few seconds, but it did nothing to alleviate the pounding in his brain. Just concentrating enough to approach but not hit the incapacitating barrier gave him a headache.

"You look awful."

Firian didn't bother to send him a dirty look. He was right. Of course he looked awful.

"What are we looking for?" Bard had known Firian a long time, so he stopped prying, and began scanning the ground as though the answer would present itself.

Firian stifled a groan as the droning ache intensified. "Over there," he said, pointing to a dense clump of skinny trees. They walked together to the source of pain. Firian gritted his teeth, the world swimming in red.

Bard cocked his head and crouched down. "Look, Fir, there's something here." He swept away a layer of pine needles and dirt. A trapdoor.

That had to be it.

"That's it," Firian said, clearing his head, leaning back into reality. Relief swept over him. He hadn't noticed the sheen of sweat over his body.

"What is it?"

Firian considered a moment. Bard would figure it out soon enough. "Sentries."

Bard paled, the black freckle on the top of one ear standing out in stark relief. A curse word escaped his mouth. "Why? Firian, this..." He shook his head.

"I have to." Bard didn't need to know why.

His friend lowered his voice just above a whisper. "We could get kicked out for this."

"I know. We just won't be caught." He knelt down and yanked open the door. Dim earthen steps with only darkness beyond. He walked down. "Coming?"

"There's a reason we're not supposed to know where it is," Bard called out in an undertone. But Firian was already treading down the stairs. After a pause, he came too.

Bard closed the trapdoor over them, shutting out the only light. Not only was it too dark to see, but a disturbing haziness grew in Firian's mind. Feeling their way down the uneven steps, they approached the source of the painful buzz, the Sentries who blocked him from Kiria.

Dull red light dawned as they went deeper. Heat rose too, as if they were descending into a furnace.

"Firian," said Bard, from close behind him, "this is crazy. Why do you need to go down here? We should turn around." After a pause, he said, "It's—hm—isn't it? The Kepress?" In a lower voice, "Why are they blocking you?"

Oddly, Firian didn't mind the words coming from Bard as much as he would from anyone else. "It doesn't matter," he muttered. "I'll fix it."

A whisper. "What are you going to do?"

Before Firian could answer, they came around a bend into a cramped room with a large fire on the far earthen wall. It was filled with grimy men and women, all pale with the clamminess of earthworms. The darkness of their burning eyes made them seem like another kind of being altogether. Most of them had long, muddy-looking hair, but a few had haphazardly shaved their heads, even some of the women. Many had scars and burns but the ones who did looked tired, rather than in pain. Some sat, others were standing. Two of them tended the furnace. The air was filled almost visibly with the painful and disorienting buzz of Sentries.

Firian stopped short, as though he were interrupting something. It took him a moment to remember why he had come.

"Who's assigned to me?" he said thickly.

Without a word, the people turned their sunken eyes to a large man. He must have been strong once, but now he looked overgrown and flabby. Now that Firian was paying attention to him, he seemed vaguely familiar. Most of these people had once been Tanyu. The thought horrified him.

The large man nodded, a shade of curiosity on his face.

Firian walked forward. The people shrank from him as oil shrinks from water. "Take the Sentry off me," he said. In the atmosphere of mental buzz, it would be difficult to tell whether or not he did. Experimentally, he tried to reach Kiria. No, the man still blocked his way. "Stop blocking me."

The man still didn't speak. It was almost as if he couldn't.

"I will hurt you," Firian said, looking into the man's dead eyes. For all the effect it had, he may have made a comment about the weather. Bard, however, made a slight noise. Firian had almost forgotten he was there, the only other person alive in this tunnel of the dead. He kept his attention on the large man. Now that the Sentry had a face, Firian knew he could be beaten. "Take it off or I'll kill you," he said. And he would. Horrible resignation settled on him like a weight.

"You'll just be reassigned," said a woman sitting to his left. She had shoulder-length matted hair. It was almost impossible to tell how old she was. Maybe it was just the fact that she had spoken, but she seemed to have more life left in her than most of the others. He definitely had seen her before, many years ago, but he couldn't remember her name. It didn't matter.

He looked to the large man, completely indifferent to Firian's threats, who confirmed what she said.

Firian couldn't kill them all. He wouldn't, even to free his mind. The Sentries were unarmed, hopeless, and clearly abused. The Academy used them shamelessly. If he ran the Academy, he wouldn't let this go on.

I won't let this go on. Excited, he tossed a look at Bard before saying, "If I could get you out of here, would you let me go?"

The Sentries looked at him impassively. He took that as a yes. "You!" he yelled to the furnace workers at the back. "Everybody! I can get you out. There should be no more of this."

This garnered a little more reaction. "They'll bring us back," someone said.

"I'll tell you where to go," Firian insisted. "If you all leave at once, they won't have enough Tanyu to bring you all back. We're at war. The last thing we need are people blocking access to the Unreal. We'd be better off without you." He warmed up to his new role. "I'm sorry I threatened you," he said in a burst of generosity.

"Where could they go?" Bard asked.

Firian turned around. "If they split up and go into the bigger towns around here, it will be really hard to catch them all. I think it's worth the risk, don't you?"

Bard still looked uncertain, though eager.

"Who do you know who really needs a Sentry?" Firian urged.

"The Head."

"People who would get Lost…"

"Let them get Lost. Losing one person because he has no self-control is better than losing all these people, don't you think?" He gestured around the room. He knew that Bard would give in when he took another look. These were some of the most beaten and dispirited people Firian had ever seen. If Kiria were there, she would set them free too, for the sake of basic justice. Bard couldn't hold out for long.

"You really think it's a good idea?" Bard said quietly. "We could just leave."

"No. Look at them."

Reluctantly, he did. Then his expression hardened with resolve. "Then let's do it now."

"We're going," Firian announced.

Until then the Sentries had listened to their argument blankly, as though it didn't concern them at all.

Bard pulled an old woman to her feet.

"Come with us," Firian said. "We'll get you out of here. Don't break off the shield until you've gotten a little distance away. Can you do that?"

He got no response except a look of genuine curiosity. Affirmative, then. He told them where the nearest towns were and made sure that they all knew not to stay in Tánuil. It was a quick and confused shuffle. The men left their fires and the creatures limped their way up the dark steps.

Above the trapdoor, they almost looked worse. Most of them squinted at the light, such as it was. Only one woman murmured a thank you. When over half of them emerged and headed deeper into the woods, Firian drew Bard back to town. The Sentries could take care of themselves. They needed not to get caught.

Firian waited a moment in the clean air. Then he tried the Unreal again. There she was, standing on a platform, radiant in the sun, wearing a blue dress that flowed like water over her hips and gathered gently at her bust. Her lips spoke of compassion and resolve. Servants had drawn her rich hair back in braids that circled her head. She was nervous. But not because of him.

Bard kept trying to catch Firian's eye as they took a long way back into Tánuil. Would the Sentries be all right? Would they be caught? Now that Firian had access to the Unreal again, the questions didn't seem to matter.

They stopped to have that pint before going back to the Academy. By now somebody would be checking on the Sentries and they couldn't be caught strolling back at the same moment. Besides, Bard looked like he could use a drink.

"This one's on me," said Firian, smiling as they walked into the pub.

"Yes, it is. Bard, leave." It was Master Belik, standing by the entrance.

Firian's blood froze. Bard slunk carefully away, leaving Firian alone.

"Come with me," Belik said quietly. He was shaking. Firian had never seen Belik's eyes so full of rage. An old rage kindled new and irreparable, like family betrayal, needing only a nudge into violence.

Firian obeyed.

The Master led him to the edge of town where the woods began. "Don't come back," he said.

Cotton-mouthed, Firian stood, not understanding.

On the verge of explaining, Belik returned to the safety of the words he had already said. "Don't come back."

Firian's legs took him away mechanically. He had no thought of direction. Just as Bard had predicted, he was kicked out of the Academy. He was no longer a Tanyu.

44

FIRIAN

For a long time, Firian had known what happened to people who were kicked out of the Academy. They were too much of a liability. They had to be killed.

He ran for hours without seeing anyone. His hands numbed. He opened and closed them mechanically as he went. Normally so full, his mind was blank. Only confusion and disbelief flooded in. Muttering like an insane man, he finally slowed down and started pacing back and forth. It wasn't possible. It wasn't possible.

He had failed. That was it. He had failed at his one shot to be important. He had no love and no control. He had nothing.

He sucked air in through his nose and felt the nip of the cold wind. So what if Tanyu murdered him? It didn't seem important. A hard lump rose in his throat and he swallowed frantically.

He was only passively interested in what was happening, as though his body wasn't involved at all. Almost wishing he felt more attached to what was going on, he thought that any physical sensation was better than the torture of the despair oozing up in his thoughts.

Every new thought brought new pain. Bard, the one who was there if he ever got in trouble, stayed beyond his reach now. It was only a matter of time until they brought back some of the Sentries. If the Academy didn't kill him, they would at least keep him out of the Unreal. He had just killed an Amiran strategist the other day and would no doubt be seen as a potential threat to the Academy.

Bard... He would probably never see him again.

Firian's reputation of power was shattered. He had been popular. Now no one knew him.

Belik had seen potential in him. Being disowned by Belik was one of the most painful things. Firian felt sick thinking about it. The Master, for all his bull-necked stubbornness, was one of the best Tanyu in the world, and he had taken Firian under his wing for years, and now...

What could he do now?

Ahead of him, a small stone hut. He entered it blindly and sat down on the floor, trying to concentrate. There was nothing to hold onto, as though he'd slipped down a dark hole in a dream.

But the Unreal was still there. It would always be there. No... No, it wouldn't... He just couldn't picture life beyond it. There probably wasn't life beyond it. Nothing was beyond it.

For now, he could dive in, drown. He closed his eyes.

At first only darkness filled the space. Dim gray shapes appeared, growing and shrinking confusedly, fighting each other. He shook his head, pushed the hair out of his face, took a deep breath, and tried again.

There it was. The fountain in the center courtyard, full of clear water. It was peaceful, like death, in that large courtyard that held no one but himself, the only sounds trickling and splashing. He cupped his hands and dipped them in the fountain. They came up dripping. Carefully, he poured the cold water into his mouth and wiped his face with his sleeve. His eyes strayed to the upstairs room. He had the strange feeling that Bard was in that room still, training or cleaning or sleeping. Just beyond the edges of his mind.

Kiria was still out there too. Why hadn't she come to mind first? Now that he was out of the Academy, there was no added risk in seeing her. The worst had already happened.

Unbidden, the face of the Amir rose before him. He scrunched his eyes tightly together at the memory, even in the Real, and chewed his lip. She would never agree to see him after what he did. With the persistence of despair, he searched anyway. She might ignore him but she didn't know enough of the Talent to block him.

Before he saw her, he heard music. Around her was the music of a stringed instrument, starting at a low somber hum and then delicately soaring into higher notes. She touched each one as though she were singing. The song was the deep maroon and blue and silver of his own sadness. Yes, that's what he felt—sadness. But in her hands, it was beautiful. The song ended on a silver note that hung in the air and swept past him like a spray of mist. Solemn peace flowed around him and he breathed in the silence. The Academy faded away and there was only blackness, emptiness. He took breaths in the void and he saw her, standing as she held the wooden neck of the lyra, feeling the last note and not thinking to look for him. He sat quietly for a moment looking at her.

Then she started peering around as though something was wrong. With wide eyes, she spun around to face him. "Firian!" she cried. Tears of rage welled up in her eyes, which unnerved him. Firian had only seen a dry, hard-edged rage among most of the people he had known. This was different. "How dare you show your face here? *How dare you?*"

"Wait! I... I'm not... I'm not at the Academy now." He couldn't bring himself to say it more plainly.

"Good!" she snapped. "I can't believe..."

He started to walk toward her through the darkness, but she hardened and turned away. He kept walking. She was all he had, now. She was his only hope.

"Never come here again," she said grimly, and she meant it.

"Let me tell you what happened..."

"No! Let me tell *you*." She turned toward him fiercely, red eyes alight. She wielded the instrument like a sword. Just for a moment, her authority made him feel like a child. "Salaar is dead because of you. The people of Brithnem are dying in their sleep and the ones who aren't are panicking. It doesn't matter *what* you say." Her voice rose with heartbreak. And then she breathed. "I won't listen."

He steadied himself. "I'm not... with the Academy any more—"

"I don't care."

"I will talk to you like this or while you sleep," he said, gaining momentum, "but I am not going to leave. The Academy was just using me! I *know* we shouldn't be at war. I know there's a better way than this."

"You seemed to like them well enough! You seemed just fine with their war when you were the assassin!" By just a fraction, her tone softened. "I can't trust anyone who has done what you've done."

"Let me prove it to you."

"No." There was a tiny hesitation. "I wish I could believe you, but I can't." Her raised eyebrows punctuated the statement. "I won't."

He interlaced his fingers behind his back to keep himself from reaching out to her. If he grabbed her arm, she might see it as a violent gesture. She was driftwood to a drowning man, but he had to look non-threatening.

He nodded and stepped back. That was enough for now. She had spoken to him—a small consolation—so he let her go. She shook her head at him as she slowly, slowly disappeared. He watched a wisp of her hair that waved as she cast her disapproving look, and saw her light freckles fade to nothing. Left alone in the darkness, he felt suddenly heavy and lay down to sleep.

WHEN FIRIAN WOKE UP, it was dark. Time to move. Moonlight covered the tree trunks with a luminescent film, enough to see by. He got to his feet, crunching the pine needles, and walked toward Raewhith. Refreshed after sleeping, he scanned the trees for anyone who had come after him. The evergreens provided good protection for the Academy, but also made it difficult to see if anyone was lying in wait. Everything was an opportunity and a liability. What mattered was controlling the environment.

Yesterday he wanted to die, but today was a new day.

First, he needed a weapon. His mind and strong body could go far, but only so far against someone with a knife. Since no one had come back to the Academy to warn against the dangers that awaited those who had been disowned, he knew he had to be ready for anything.

He bent down and picked up a large stick, rough and relatively straight. This would have to do for now until he could get something better.

At Raewhith he would come up with a new plan. He could always escape to a remote corner of the world for a while as he thought of some way to get back at the Academy. Or did he want back in?

Both. I want both.

His heart pounded as he pictured his lessons, his mission, the admiration of the other Tanyu... Aching, he swung the branch in his hand, feeling its weight bend powerfully outward. *All that I've done for them...* He grabbed a fistful of his hair as he pushed it back out of his face.

Deep breath. All he needed was a new plan. All was not lost yet.

Black turned to navy turned to blue, and the stars shone brightly before they winked out above the netted branches.

A head of black hair ducked behind a tree.

Shock coursed through Firian's body. Both hands on the stick, he carefully backed up to higher ground. Let them try to kill him. Shivers ran down his back and neck like spiders. Eyes watched him.

For so long that his heartbeat began to slow, nothing moved. Well then, he would go to them. With long, measured steps, he stalked carefully forward, dark against the gray of the early morning. He had killed before.

Here was the tree where he had seen the head. Were there more of them? He still felt the eyes. Like an animal, he raised his head and turned it cautiously, smelling, listening. No one, but he still felt a presence.

He flexed his hands against the branch, tensed, and swung to the other side of the pine. Nothing. The expanse near the tree was open enough that no one could have run without being seen. He glanced up. The branches were too high and thin to climb. Had he imagined it all? No, there had definitely been something. The emptiness of the forest did not calm his apprehension. If anything, he was more alert. The back of his head prickled. Out there, someone was watching him. He hadn't studied at the Academy over seven years for nothing. He knew when he wasn't alone.

After a few minutes, nothing happened, so he jogged off toward Raewhith. At his pace, he could reach it in less than a day.

Sooner than he expected, he reached the outskirts. Low, brown buildings grouped like gossiping children, ready to give him away. The open spaces between them blazed white with the sun. He would be visible from anywhere. And, since it wasn't an enormous town, surely many people would know the Kess family and be able to spot the resemblance. Besides, he was wearing Tanyuin clothes. That, at least, was something he could change.

Tracing the backwood path to the tailor, he crept up behind the building. With the sun already setting, he could simply wait until dark and then take an outfit from the shop. Maybe he could sleep there too if he got up before morning.

The tingling touch of a gaze had never fully left him, but he'd seen no sign of anyone on his way to the village. Crouched under the window, he faintly heard the murmuring of the tailor and a customer rise and fall, and the light pattering of pins in a bowl. The tailor's voice rose one last time as he bid the other man farewell. The dull thud of fabric staves being put away, the soft creak of boards as he did his final check, and then, finally, he closed the shutters and blew the candles out. Firian waited a few more minutes before he crept in, just to be sure the man didn't double back to get something.

The little store was simple, more for repairing than selling new clothes. Only a few finished pieces were strewn across the two heavy wooden tables or hanging on human-sized frames. He chose a pair of brown pants (which didn't allow for the same range of movement as the Academy-issued ones) and dark green shirt. It would have to do. Inspecting himself in the dim copper mirror, he thought he could pass for an ordinary citizen well enough. A traveler, maybe. From here, he would head to one of the surrounding villages, working his way east until he could find a safer place to stay for a while.

As a child, he had heard of some interesting places. The most he had ever traveled was on his mission with Kiria. Left on his own, he could go anywhere he wanted—the island of Torith, Phlaxtin with its silver trees, the small islands of Shee where nymphs lived, the Watchtower Mountains across the Kheltor, the night colony of Qib in the Eradi Desert...

He pulled out a large bolt of fabric from its place in the wall to use for a pillow, then grabbed both hands behind his back and stretched. Night had fallen. Maybe Kiria was asleep. He turned his mind in her direction. Nothing. That was strange. That also meant that no Tanyu was very close by, which, now that he thought of it, surprised him.

A red flush of shame washed over his face. He had gone back to his home village. The most predictable move. Ignorant moves like that had cost him his dream of the Academy.

The Unreal waited for him like a breathing beast, or like dark waves of water. The dark silence in the Unreal, despite its apparent message that the Academy hadn't discovered him yet, unsettled him. He closed his eyes to focus more intently. Maybe Kiria was asleep but not dreaming. That happened sometimes, but it was rarer than people thought. It was probably too soon to see her anyway. Her red-rimmed eyes meant that she needed time. At least, hopefully that's what that meant. She had optimistically thought he could live up to her expectations, that there was greatness in him. He had seen it in her mind, beautiful and full of light. She might have been projecting her own potential for good onto him, but he wanted to be near that affirmation.

He fell asleep thinking of her but had no dreams.

THE NEXT DAY, Firian, his belly full of a meat pie from the Raewhithian butcher, struggled not to shy away from everyone on the road. Now, when a man appeared coming toward him, he stiffened but stood up straighter as he walked, holding tightly to whatever dignity he had left. He was a Tanyu, whatever the Academy may think of him, and Tanyu shied away from no one.

The man, large and bearded, carried a heavy pack on his back but seemed cheerful. His thick legs fit into deerskin leggings and boots that were both splashed with mud. He wore a round cap on his head, and he gripped the straps of his pack with muscular arms. He had obviously been traveling for some time. As they passed each other, the man nodded to him. "Where are you headed?" he asked with a gruff but friendly voice.

"Imlin," Firian replied truthfully.

"Is that far from here?"

"No, it's just half a day's walk."

The man turned around so he could walk in step with Firian. Something clanked in his pack with every trudging step he took. He didn't seem very threatening, but Firian watched him sideways. "I bet they have an inn and alehouse?" the man said.

"I think so," said Firian, starting to realize that this man really meant to travel with him.

"Then I'm coming too. I've been without company for a long time. That is, if I may." The man looked at him with bright, questioning eyes, sparkling above his whiskers.

Firian should say no and travel alone, but it was a relief to find someone who didn't know about his stigma. "That's fine," he said.

"What's your name?" the man asked, readjusting his pack.

"Belik," Firian replied, choosing the first name that came to mind.

The stranger's eyes darkened for a moment. "I used to know someone by that name. In another life. Older than you, though. Belik, you said?"

Firian nodded.

"Strange. My name is Anewa."

45

FIRIAN

Anewa was a surprisingly chatty travel partner, and as minutes turned to hours Firian got grumpier from a lack of food and water. He cracked his neck and reached to scratch his shoulder under his shirt.

"So, it shouldn't be much further, from what you said," Anewa continued, clanking along.

"No."

"Where are you from, if you don't mind my asking? It's just that I'm interested in that name of yours, and it's good to know who you're with in times like these."

Firian realized that he didn't know where Belik was from. He grunted noncommittally, getting more uncomfortable by the minute. Why did this man ask so many questions? And why did he constantly feel like he was being watched? It was like having a fly near his face that he couldn't shoo away. A constant irritation. He inhaled slowly, took a dip in the Unreal. Hopefully Anewa would be silent long enough for him to have a little respite.

He made the Unreal space into the Eradi Desert and looked up at the stars. The moon-washed dunes surrounded him, smelling like cooling dust and a fresh-cut melon. The black night sky was speckled and splashed with light. Tipping his face upward, he let the breeze flow through his hair. This was better. Maybe he would go to the desert after all. Then he looked down.

With an impassive expression, Master Belik stood there.

Firian almost tripped as he backed away. *A sandstorm might take him by surprise.* He immediately felt one brewing, ready for his command.

"What are you doing here?" Belik asked.

"I left," Firian said.

"Where are you now?"

If Belik didn't know, he wasn't going to tell him. "Not near the Academy," he answered.

The Master ran his hand roughly over the lower half of his face. "No, I mean, where are you now?"

"On the road."

"So you can hear me?"

"Of course." These inane questions must be some trap. He watched Belik's empty hands. "Why are you here?"

"You're not on the road," he said. "You're Lost in the Unreal."

Firian snorted and shook his head. The suggestion was ridiculous. "Don't mess with me." Belik had nothing more he could take. Was he targeting Firian's sanity now too?

"I'm not," he said. "You're in the Second Level. Look around. There's no one else here. Look for your roommate or the Kepress. They can't reach you here."

It was true. Those two presences so constantly on the edges of his mind had vanished. Not even a buzz or an image. No wonder the desert was so quiet.

"You've gone beyond the First Level of the Unreal."

The Second Level. Last year, Firian had tried for months to reach it, but he kept passing out when he got close from lack of air. Even he couldn't muster the concentration. Belik had had to get him out every time, like a parent saving a child trapped under a frozen pond.

Firian had never consciously entered the Second Level. Arriving at this peaceful landscape would have been a great accomplishment a few months ago, but now, realizing suddenly where he was felt like going deep under water, running out of air, lungs straining, the panic completely at odds with the strange, serene environment around him.

He was alone with Belik, who had no incentive to save him. Firian's head felt stuffed with fear and his knees ran icy cold. Heart beating hard, he opened his eyes to drowning darkness. Desperately, he tried to ascend to the road between Raewhith and Imlin, but he only managed melding the two landscapes. With a shock, he remembered where he had heard of Anewa.

"Where am I, then?" he asked steadily. "Get me out."

"I will."

Firian balked at the slow significance of those words.

Belik stood confidently, with no doubt that he could save him. But he was waiting for some response. Firian couldn't read his face. It didn't seem angry. In fact, there was—maybe—a glint as he had seen in his first lesson. Yes, there was pride.

He squinted. "Why are you helping me?"

"We'll see," Belik replied brusquely, as though awakened from deep thought. "Right now, you're in a hut in the woods. You've been Lost for days."

Firian's head spun. His words sounded too far-fetched. Even now, Belik could be trying to kill him. "So, what do I do?"

"I'll go up one level and you turn your attention to me, you understand? The road from Raewhith?" He lifted a corner of his mouth to criticize the choice. "Were you with anyone?"

"Anewa."

Belik's eyes widened. "You have good senses. What did he look like?"

Firian described him.

"Toward me, not away," the Master repeated, looking sternly at him, and then his image faded into the desert sand.

Firian closed his eyes and obeyed Belik, as much from curiosity as anything else. *Toward me, not away.* At first there was nothing but stifling darkness, followed by stifling light. He jerked violently for air. Squeezed between two worlds. Panic seized him. He *was* Lost. Just as he started to drown, the light began to look like the sun. The sun on a road. He fell, gasping, onto a dirt road similar to the one he had just left.

"Good," he heard behind him. Belik. And he sounded genuinely pleased. "One more. Close your eyes."

Almost against his will, he obeyed the Master again. For all of his manipulation, there was no one better to learn from, and he had done Retrieval a long time. Besides, Firian had nothing to lose.

"You're lying down in front of a fire," he heard Belik say. "You're in a small stone hut. I'm here, making sure you don't die." There was only a touch of irony in the statement. "I'm going there. Follow me up."

Through the emptiness, the familiar presence of his Master moved away from him. Firian followed in his mind.

Firian opened his eyes. Squinting against the fire, he turned away to the darker side of the room. The light seemed oddly bright, brighter somehow than the road on which he had been traveling. He lay on an uneven stone floor, cushioned only with a thin, rough blanket. The round hut, already small, felt smaller because of Belik's gigantic figure sitting over him. Belik's face came into focus as the Master bent over to peer in his face. "You'll be all right," he said in a father's voice.

Pain gnawed Firian's stomach. When he tried to move, he felt how much strength had sapped from his muscles. Even rolling over took more effort than he expected. But pain meant reality, and often led to greater things, so he didn't complain. "Why did you do that?" he said, trying to sit up. Belik had no reason to save him.

A sigh escaped Belik's lips. "I've always liked you, boy. So I checked on you. You weren't there, and you weren't dead. So you were in the Second Level." He shrugged a large shoulder. "No one gets to the Second Level and gets back out. It's too dangerous."

"You did."

He just smiled and adjusted his glasses. "Could you do it again?"

Firian hesitated. "Yes."

"When I first saw you," said Belik, feeling expansive, "I thought you had something. You're insubordinate and Talented. If you can get to the Second Level again, I have a proposal."

This new mood made Firian suspicious. Where had all his rage gone? Anyone who could dam up and re-route his emotions that completely had frightening, enticing control. One day, Firian could be the same, but too often his feelings and opinions showed on his face.

Now, for instance, he was sure he looked dazed, flooded by the shock of being

Lost—him, Lost!—and the longing to be accepted back into the Academy. He felt the two familiar presences again, but he didn't pursue them. Belik needed all of his attention. Firian sat fully upright. "A proposal," he repeated.

"Yes. We'll give this one more try." By *this*, Firian suspected he meant him.

Before diving back into the Unreal, he observed all his surroundings closely. He had to have a better grip on the Real to give himself a way out.

After going into the familiar darkness of the Unreal, he sank to a lower level of consciousness beyond it. By the time an island materialized, the journey had left Firian lightheaded. The two of them stood on a large green wedge rising out of the ocean, a slope sliced off with a knife. Firian could see other islands off in the distance and briefly wondered if this were part of the Shee or Sharb Island chains, or if it was just part of Belik's imagination. They stood together at the apex, looking down the cliff into the ocean. Even with the smell of salty grass and the surge of waves, there was an almost unnatural silence and emptiness there, as though whispering voices had just ceased.

"You're here." Belik stood beside him, looking out at the mist hovering over the gray ocean.

"Yes. Just as you said."

"And it wasn't a problem for you?"

"Not at all." The new environment just took a little longer to materialize. Nothing to worry about. He would get even more adept with time.

"Good, that's very good," he said, with a teacher's smile in his tone. "When you were younger, I thought you might be able to, given time. When you weren't fooling around."

Firian stayed silent.

"I'll have to be hard on you when you get back, of course, but you still have many supporters," he said meditatively. "Soon, the Head will still promote you."

"You won't send me back to the same assignment?"

"Under Tiev?" he scoffed. "Tiev's a fool. He has no vision at all. The Academy needs vision. Even Sias is reactionary. But you have ambition."

"Yes, I do."

Belik looked at him approvingly. They both knew he spoke the truth. "The Head is growing older," he said, "and soon he won't be capable of leading. He hasn't set up a clear successor but will have to choose someone before the spring. Without establishing that, the Academy could suffer with all those Masters vying for the position." His tone turned regretful and bitter. "I, myself, am not in the running. Past indiscretions. But you've always seen the Tanyu for what they are and the Academy for what it could be. I've looked for someone like you for a long time. I tried to prepare you for this moment, so I want to help you."

Firian felt hot with coursing blood, trying to find the trap. His breathing came ragged.

Belik sensed his hesitation and went on. "We're both tired of being used. I believe in you, Firian. If you don't muck this up, you could be next in line."

"I'll do whatever it takes," he heard his voice say, but it seemed disconnected from him. How could this be happening? It was the fulfillment of a dream. He realized he knew exactly how he would lead, what he would change. He'd played idly with those ideas for years.

Enough with being blindsided. He could end the wars against the Kingdom, get Kiria back, and shape the Academy to have the power it deserved! He felt like flying, letting the island ground plummet beneath his feet as he shot up and up through layers of cloud and light, but he had to stay rooted to the shared environment. At least until he got better at controlling the Second Level. All these thoughts would stay here, he knew. Nothing on the surface could indicate that he dreamed of becoming the next Tanyuin Head.

He beamed at Belik, eyes shining. "Let's go back to the Academy."

46

KIRIA

Kiria huffed out a breath and set down her lyra. Firian stood like a negative image before her mind, his tall, black-clad figure white like a ghost. It didn't seem possible that he had murdered Amir Salaar. He was the same Firian she had known. His eyes seemed sincere—redder than she had ever seen them, and he sounded desperate—but she had been too quick to trust him before.

If she saw him again, she would just ignore him. Before she went to bed that night, she would have to remind herself not to entertain the thought of talking with him, even in a dream. Thoughts and actions were one.

At least now she didn't have a reason to keep watching him. If he really was kicked out of the Academy, then he could offer no new information helpful to the war. She could cut him off completely.

Quickly, she brushed the angry tears from her eyes. Daelon must have seen the gesture, because he stepped tentatively forward, his brows furrowed. His gray-blue robe swayed a little behind him. Feeling heat rising in her face, she pretended to take special care to put the bow away properly behind the neck of the instrument.

"Is My Kepress unwell?" he asked. He always became more formal when he was uncomfortable. He probably knew what was going on.

She shook her head. "No, Daelon. I'm fine. I was just thinking about the composition and... about more ways to help the Kingdom, since I can't attend the sessions." There was only a small note of bitterness in her voice. She needed to occupy her mind right away.

Morale—that's one thing I can offer. Contingency plans. Internal unity. Better war tactics. Strong Keepers...

"Bring me pen and paper," she said as the ideas came, now flowing like water. *Let Firian spy.* Brithnem needed her to be strong. "Right away."

"Of course, My Kepress," he replied, sweeping briskly out of the room.

She clapped her hands together as though wiping off dust. Fueled by the challenge Firian's presence presented, she felt suddenly energized. Even without the official title, now was her time to be a leader.

Atty had lost weight, and his hair lay flat, almost colorless. His splotchy eyes betrayed the fact that he wasn't sleeping. As supportive as Kiria tried to be, he struggled with being a Keeper. She tried to remember if he had ever offered an original idea in the Main. He hadn't even come up with the idea to give the Amir half a vote. That idea was Cúron's.

But he could still attend sessions. She couldn't, at least not quite yet.

"Is he there now?" Atty asked as they walked away from the great carved doors where Kiria found him exiting. Like Jori, Atty alluded to Firian with some bitterness. They had both wanted to be Tanyu and it rankled that they were now the enemy. Disillusionment always hurt.

"No," she said laconically.

"Then I can tell you something," he said, touching her arm to invite her into his suite of rooms. "I want to know what you think." Servants opened the double doors for them into a grand room with high ceilings and rugs. "Come in. I've been thinking." The door closed with a click behind them.

"What is it?" Kiria had come to give *him* information, but he seemed excited.

"He's not there?" he confirmed.

She shook her head. No, she hadn't felt Firian's presence in days.

"We need to strengthen our alliance with Charäkhnem to have any hope in these wars." The vocabulary of a Keeper, not the Atty she knew. "During the next session, I'm going to propose that I marry Shear Ganesha's daughter." He looked tired but proud, and nodded at her, anticipating her disbelief. Shear Ganesha was the king that held the pass between the mountain ranges. Kiria remembered the prince's visit well.

She knit her eyebrows together, scanning Atty's faded fur robe. Having a supporter would suit him. It might bring life back into his eyes. But only if she were kind and understanding. "Have you met her?" she asked.

"No. She's never come to the palace before."

"That's a big decision..." she began slowly, "but it could be good for us. Hm." She wasn't sure what else to say and looked down at the carpet. If he wanted to sacrifice for the Kingdom, who was she to stop him?

"Isn't that a good idea?" he prodded.

The last thing Atty needed was more responsibility. He was still finding himself. "You know I'll support you," she said, managing to give him a smile.

He nodded again, distractedly.

"I was thinking," she began, getting to one reason she tracked him down after the last session, "what if one of the Lines leaves no heir? I'm thinking about me now. You very well might have an heir with the princess."

He smiled at the thought, and his eyes crinkled.

"Right," she continued. "My Line has been targeted more recently and I realized that there is no provision for appointing heirs that aren't in the bloodline. That's crazy!"

"Oh, I'm sure..."

"Hear me out, Atty, please. I could have died last month. I *am* the Second Line. There's no one else."

They looked into each other's eyes furtively. They both knew her mother's time was over.

Kiria cleared her throat. "We need a contingency plan. I want the ability to appoint someone after me if I don't have a daughter of my own. Just in case."

"That doesn't sound so crazy," Atty mused.

She punched him lightly in the arm. "Why would my ideas be crazy? Of course it's a good idea! That's the first one you could present to the Main. And it could be good for you too, in case the Charäkhni don't take to your idea of marrying the princess. No one else has three leaders. It's a tradition worth preserving even in desperate times." She felt her face flush with subdued excitement.

"I'm a Keeper of Brithnem," Atty replied, latching onto her comment about the princess, a little offended but passing it off as a joke. "Of course they'll like my idea. I'm a catch."

"That's not what I meant. It's just—"

"—in case. I know. I don't like to think about 'in case.'" He unclasped the ceremonial robe he had worn to the Main and swung it off his shoulders, tossing it aside onto a chair.

"You're thinking ahead too," Kiria encouraged. "It's what we're all doing. Another thing we need is more widespread education about resisting attacks in dreams, especially for the men left in the city. They seem to be the ones targeted the most. I can help with guidelines."

"Because you have the Talent." Another twinge of jealousy.

"Because I have the Talent. I also..." she lowered her voice, "have an idea where the Academy is."

Atty's eyes widened, then narrowed. "You do? No one knows where the Academy is."

"I was heading in that direction when I escaped. I don't know exactly, but it would be worth sending a few scouts to the area to investigate. They're elite fighters, but I don't think there are very many of them." She stepped into her mind. Still no Firian. *He can't hide his presence, can he?* The thought made her feel naked, but she risked continuing anyway. The words spilled out of her. "Send people over the Charúnin Thôr and check the woods west of Shifra. I could be wrong, but I think it might be there. What do we have to lose?"

A slow, lopsided smile spread over Atty's face. Finding the Academy could mean a swift victory for the Kingdom.

47

FIRIAN

INVIGORATED, Firian marched back to the Academy at a great pace, as though walking faster would get him more quickly to his goals. He couldn't remember ever having been so happy. Belik walked much more slowly behind him and was soon out of sight.

The air smelled beautifully of pine, and the gray, cloudy sky hanging low over the trees cooled him, promising rain. The soft earth yielded under his rapid feet. If Belik was right, his work was about to pay off. He couldn't wait to be back.

Striding confidently up to the main doors, he let himself into the cavernous hall and leapt up the left-hand stairs to his room two at a time. Before he reached the door, Bard came out and jumped up, catching him in a squeezing hug. Today Firian didn't mind.

"Fir!" Bard cried with a grin as Firian pushed him off. His smile melted away into a frown of fearful concern. "What are you doing here?" he whispered.

"I'm back," said Firian, opening his arms and letting them drop. "No need to explain."

But Bard apparently wanted an explanation. His dark eyes questioned him.

"Just forget about what happened. It doesn't matter." Firian pushed past him to their room, but he had nothing to drop off and he didn't want to sleep. Electricity pulsed through his body. "Do they still have you in the war?" he asked over his shoulder.

"They do, yeah. Same as before." Bard lowered his voice. "I haven't... killed anybody though. Intimidation, mostly."

Firian turned around to face him. Bard, who was nodding, certainly didn't look intimidating. Maybe to the untrained eye he could pass as a fearsome Tanyu, but he was a stickler for the rules, who drooled for his mother's cooking. "I'm sure you're doing well."

A smile flashed over Bard's face which still radiated confusion. "What's going on with you?"

Firian realized he was grinning. He wanted to go for a walk—get out some energy, see more people... "Nothing."

Bard followed him and shut the door behind them. "Why did you disappear for a few days?" He said it like someone who knew the answer but wanted to hear a different one. "Where were you, hm? I couldn't see you anywhere."

"What, are you watching me?" Firian asked, sniffing a new shirt. It smelled like cinnamon again. Bard must have been up to his old habit of putting cinnamon sticks everywhere since he left.

"I know you don't like answering questions, but something's up."

"I'm going for a walk." He pulled the black cinnamon shirt over his head, feeling the soft fabric against his body. He needed to find Maya.

Bard stood steadfastly in the doorway. Firian reached over his friend's shoulder and pushed open the door while Bard puffed air out of his nose, frustrated. After his first burst of energy, Bard had become more subdued and Firian noticed more lines on his forehead, now gray-tinged pale. His normally shining eyes were dimmed with cares beyond the worry that Firian would break the rules.

"I'll tell you later," he conceded, moving past him.

Soon, he would be able to end the war and expand the power of the Tanyu. He just couldn't let anyone know yet.

As he ran back down the stairs, he passed Belik, who had just entered the main hall and was heading slowly back to his little room down the side hallway. He flicked Firian a practiced, impassive glance over his glasses. Firian met his eyes.

The events of the past few days seemed almost dream-like. The unreality of his shifting circumstances was beginning to form a tiny crack in his happiness. If this was another move on their part...

No, he wouldn't be tossed around anymore. The Academy had lied to him and used him too often. He was better prepared now. If they tried to kick him out again, he wouldn't leave. From now on, succeeding Sais Jairon was the goal.

He had to. It was the only way to change everything.

It was the only way to make things right—to make it all worthwhile.

He paused to splash his hand in the fountain.

The huge room was uncharacteristically empty, which surprised him until he remembered that Defenders fought most of the war at night. He could deal with the war later. He ached for company. Maya's upstairs room lay at the end of the hall opposite his, where it began to curve away from the balcony overlooking the courtyard. He ran quietly up the staircase opposite his own and strode down the hall. Tesni, a Charäkhni girl with whom he had shared classes, nodded a greeting to him, but he saw no one else.

"Maya," he hissed at her closed door, darkened by the shadow of the recessed hallway. He had not spent time with her since before going on his mission, he realized. That seemed so, so long ago. Maybe she hadn't waited for him. He knocked quietly.

Almost immediately the door opened. Her tousled hair suggested that she had been sleeping, but her heavy eyes widened when she saw Firian. "Firian, where have you—"

He wrapped his arms around her back and pulled her roughly against him for a kiss. It only took her a moment to respond. He reached his hand into her warm hair and pressed her head against his. Too long since he had tasted a woman like this. He felt a knot in his stomach begin to uncoil and relax. This was what he needed. Thought gave way to sensation, violent well-being. She leaned into him, grabbing a fistful of his shirt. She still loved him, would wait for him when he needed her, would do what he told her. Others would too.

"Master Firian Kess," Belik announced as they stepped through the doorway two weeks later to meet the Tanyuin Head.

"Our latest Master. Well done!" said Sias Jairon, standing as Firian entered the room. It was just a stone room like any of the others, not even much bigger, with a large desk toward the back wall. When Firian imagined what the Head's office must look like, he had pictured more. Still, the austerity was just what he would have chosen. The focus wasn't on luxury, but on the man himself.

Sias Jairon was smaller than Firian remembered. He looked frail, just by virtue of being human. His skin was light, almost translucent in places, and thin, blue veins branched along his temples. He kept his dirty-gray hair short. He had quick eyes with a joke in them, almost like a bookish man. A slender iron circle with a square opening at the forehead provided the only evidence of his power. Although his bones were steel, his aging flesh reeked of introversion. Stooping, but only very slightly, he sat back down.

Firian dipped his head.

"I remember meeting you," the Head continued, "when you were a boy. I saw you coming."

"You looked up at me," Firian confirmed.

"Such a fiery young boy. I'm not surprised that Master Belik" – he nodded toward him – "decided to promote you to Master."

Firian, despite himself, could hardly stifle a smile.

"The title is well deserved," Belik stepped in, "after he investigated the escape of the Sentries, and provided key information about the Kingdom's movements in the war."

Firian's gut curled. Bard still didn't know about the Sentries. He'd have to explain that he and the others tracking them down had given them a choice: swear allegiance to the Academy and be allowed to serve in Tánuil, or defy it and suffer a double burden of Sentry work, almost sure to make them brain-dead over time. Maybe Bard would think it was cruel, but it was merciful too.

The Head made a sound that wasn't a groan or a sigh—it indicated discomfort. "Yes," he mused.

Firian realized that the Head hadn't been noticeably active in organizing the movements of the war. He usually stayed in his quarters and busied himself with new recruits, a part of the job he obviously relished. Master Belik, Jovan, and others had taken over most of the war planning.

Firian sucked his teeth. How could this man be an effective leader if he wasn't directly involved in the war? He certainly had not been a visible presence during most of Firian's time at the Academy.

Belik broke the silence. "He has, I understand, more information on that front. It could be crucial to us. Firian?"

"Yes," Firian said, snapping back to attention. "I've learned that the Kingdom plans to make a physical attack on the Academy. They are sending scouts now. They don't know the exact location, but they are aware of the general area. Unless we act quickly, one of the scouts might find us."

The Head knitted his brows together and worked his jaw back and forth for a moment. His temples bulged around the modest crown. "Well done, Master Kess. I'll consider what you've said." Almost wearily, he looked down at his hands.

The Master seemed far too disturbed by the news. A Tanyu was imperturbable, strong, undefeatable. Anything but weak. All they needed was action to negate any threat.

A creak behind him meant Belik had opened the door again to go out.

Firian's breathing quickened. Then the words burst from him. "I suggest—"

"Firian!" Belik hissed.

"—we raise a larger army in case one of their scouts gets through. Even if they don't, we might not be able to maintain perfect secrecy forever. It makes sense to have more trained men ready in a standing army. Plenty of people in nearby villages would jump at the chance to serve us."

Close to his ear. "That's enough."

A warning even glittered in Jairon's eyes. "All good thoughts for another time," he said, an ironic smile twisting his mouth. "Master Belik?" With that, he waved them both out.

Silence weighed on Firian as he walked with Belik down the hallways leading back to the main courtyard. Belik's bad leg thumped an irregular beat.

A subterranean grumble, almost like an earthquake, grew in Firian's mind. He checked the Unreal. Not there. His mouth dried up. One more level. It took far more concentration to go down further. Lost, he had actually believed the Unreal was reality, so going down one more level had been intuitive. As easy as entering the Unreal on a normal day. Now that he intentionally plunged more than one level at once, and tried to walk at the same time, the effort almost gave him a headache.

When he arrived, Belik stood in a black landscape, just black. "You want him to like you, remember?" he growled.

Strangely, Firian didn't share his concern. "I don't think it matters. I think I could be the Head whether he likes me or not," he retorted with no emotion.

He knew he was right. In fact, ever since he had returned from banishment a couple weeks before, he had felt stronger, almost untouchable. A deepening well of resolve opened in Firian's chest. He lifted his chin. Even here, in the Second Level, he felt the strength alive in his body as he rarely had before. It coursed in his veins, in his arms and legs and hands—it kept him still, it made him quick. He felt it burning.

Belik examined Firian's face for a few moments. Firian could see his own distorted reflection in the Master's glasses as Belik's searching eyes stared back into his own. Barely lifting both eyebrows in surprised resignation, Belik stepped back again. He always walked with no difficulty in the Unreal.

"Maybe so," he said. His tone was uncharacteristically soft. He opened his mouth again to speak, and then closed it.

Firian swam up toward the surface. Where was the First Level? He only saw blackness. Then he remembered. He hadn't visualized anything for the First Level. This would be tricky. He held the blackness around him like a cloak and stood firmly up. Hopefully that would be enough.

He opened his eyes—he hadn't realized they were closed—and gasped as the wind of his walking blew on his face. Blurry reality came into focus around him. Belik was nowhere to be seen.

48

KIRIA

"No, no, I've got it." Kiria untangled her hair with her spread fingers. Smoothing it as she divided it into sections, she waved Candrae away. She didn't want any help. Maybe her thin hair could be braided into the same impressive design she had seen on someone else earlier that day. It was just the kind of mindless work she needed to go back over the clues to the Academy's whereabouts.

Even without dipping back into Firian's mind, she had many pieces of information she could use. The last part of their journey had been a circuitous path to the Academy. She pictured the maps she'd studied that morning. Two mountain ranges surrounded Brithnem, which was situated on the southwestern coast. Charäkhnem filled the pass between them. Charúnin Thôr, the range where she and Firian had traveled, slanted down from the north and the Somul Mountains up from the south. The Academy had to be past the mountains, near the woods where she escaped. Firian seemed at home in forests. The scent of trees clung to him even in cities.

She looked at her braid bending at odd angles with pieces sticking out like a frayed knot. "Come here, Candrae," she said. Kiria could practice on her. Candrae had long blonde hair while Vayci had none.

Candrae came forward obediently, expecting to fix the braid, but Kiria instructed her to kneel in front of her chair instead.

Only Firian could give her more accurate information, but he hadn't spoken to her since the night with her lyra. The memory made her grit her teeth. She closed her eyes for a moment, her hands piecing out Candrae's hair, and went into the Unreal. Nothing and no one appeared. She wished she had enough Talent to see through Firian's eyes at will—to steal information from him as he had from her—but she was still new at this. He wasn't thinking of her.

A knock at the door. She opened her eyes as a guard announced Jori.

"Let him in," Kiria replied, handing the unfinished braid to Candrae.

Jori ambled in, embroidered vest undone, no urgency in his movements. "Isn't this supposed to be the other way around?" he asked, seeing her fix her handmaid's hair. Candrae stumbled to her feet, embarrassed by his comment.

Kiria ignored the question. "Here," she said, leaning over to the desk and hastily scribbling a note. "Take this to Atty. He'll know what it is." She thrust it in his hand.

"Hello, Jori," he said in a high imitation of her voice. He crunched the note in his hand. "So good to see you!"

"This is serious. Make sure he gets that." She looked into his eyes and pointed to the note.

"All right." He uncrumpled the note and held it up to his face. "'Northwest from Charäkhnem. Past Shifra. Pine forest. More than one scout.' Do you two have secret meetings now? Is this a code?" He sat down on the end of her bed, pretending to scrutinize the paper.

She stood up, took the paper from him, folded it pointedly, and handed it back. He set his mouth, apparently irritated that she hadn't liked his joke, and stuffed it in his pocket. "All right. I'll get it to him. But what's there, I wonder?" He sat up straighter. "Wait, is this where you went with...?"

"Not exactly, but I think it may be where he is now." She kept her sentences short. Who knew if Firian would appear again, spying on her thoughts?

Jori raised both eyebrows. "I'll make sure he gets it," he said, meaning Atty. "Then we can finally kill that gory traitor!"

"Well, that's not... It's not just about him. If we know where the Academy is, we can end the war." It sounded simplistic, she realized, as she sat back down and took the braid from Candrae's hand.

"We'll get him, though. Don't worry," said Jori.

Kiria focused her attention on the braid. It was much easier to braid another person's hair than her own, she thought as she folded the strands over each other. "I need pins," she muttered. Vayci hurried forward and got them out of a drawer.

"I'm sure you want to see him caught more than I do," he continued, uncharacteristically serious. "I heard four more people died in their sleep last night."

"It wasn't him," she said absently.

There was a pause. "Why do you do that? It could have been."

She shook her head. She was getting to the end of the braid. Vayci handed her a pin and showed her where to put it in. "Is everyone ready for the presentation?" Kiria asked. Tomorrow, every neighborhood block would gather in the arena for basic information on staving off mental attacks. More awareness would hopefully result in fewer casualties. She would teach part of the lesson.

"I don't have anything to do with that. I've already been briefed," he replied shortly. "Do you still care about that Tanyu?"

"No, of course not."

"Sometimes it seems like you do. He's a monster, Kiria."

"Okay," she said, exasperated. She didn't need another person telling her that. She knew better than anyone else what he was.

A buzz just beyond the edges of her consciousness made her heart drop. Should she check if he had overheard her plan?

Jori shifted his shoulders uncomfortably. "Maybe it's a good thing you aren't going to the sessions."

"Excuse me?" Kiria snapped.

"It's like you don't mind that he's there, just watching you."

"Of course I mind!" She was doing everything she could. Her mother, overwhelmed, only went to about half the meetings. Daelon spoke as often as he could in Kiria's stead. But it still felt like the Second Line was dying. It broke her heart. "Jori, I will give everything to this kingdom. *Everything*."

Jori set his mouth in a line. She felt him surging away from her. He closed his fist on her note.

A SHEEN of sweat covered Kiria's forehead after giving her part of the presentation. She fanned herself in the cool of the arena passage. Again, she mouthed the words she had used in her lesson. They tasted dusty. Words seemed poor, but she had offered what she could.

An odd feeling crept over her. It settled in the pit of her stomach. She fanned more furiously as it became harder to breathe.

He knew.

She knew it as certainly as she had known about Amir Salaar.

Returning quickly down the passage through the arena, Kiria called Daelon over to her. She squinted at him, her eyes still adjusting to the inside darkness. He walked in silence with other high-collared Amir, one of whom had also presented. Mental battles almost always took place either at sunrise or sunset, so he could be spared to speak during the middle of the day.

Daelon hurried over to her. "Yes, my Kepress?"

The fabric of her dress strained against the length of her strides. "Tell the Keepers and the Amir in charge of mental warfare that the Academy knows we're coming."

"You're sure?" he replied, matching her hushed tone. His eyes admitted doubt.

"Absolutely."

KIRIA STARED AT HER MOTHER, who was sitting in a chair by the window. Mother's long, brown hair glowed in the light, but her skin was ashen. She had missed another session, claiming a headache. Kiria hated the voice in her head that told her that was a lie. Her forehead scrunched with frustration. Her mother had to see that on her face, but she couldn't help herself.

Seeing this weakness in her mother pained her. She felt the Second Line dying by the day.

"Don't look at me like that," her mother began, lowering her voice.

Kiria took a deep breath. "Why are you giving up like this? We're in the middle of two wars and *you* can actually go to the Main."

Merian gestured for Kiria to sit down next to her, but Kiria didn't respond to the invitation. Instead, she stood, looking down at her mother from a little across the room. Merian seemed to realize that Kiria would not obey and continued, "You know it's been difficult for me these past few months…"

Kiria felt a twinge of regret. She shouldn't speak to her mother this way, especially when her disappearance caused so much of her pain. "I know," she said softly. "But the Kingdom needs a Keeper."

Her mother wilted, bobbing her head in a nod.

"Mother." Kiria walked up and put her hand on her shoulder. She swallowed a few times before speaking again. The words had grown inside her. Now ripe, they were ready to come out. "I can do it."

Dusty lines covered her mother's face as she looked up. The weighty whisper had left little room to doubt her meaning. "But Kiria…"

"I want to serve the Kingdom. We're facing wars on two fronts. I know what's at stake, and I think I can do it." Her eyes burned with passion. They *could not* lose. Not now. So many people needed justice—innocent men and women slain in their sleep, soldiers in Torith, Firian, her father…

Kiria took her hand off her shoulder, waiting for a response. Was that sadness or relief on her mother's face? "I know you've wanted this a long time," she began slowly, not meeting her daughter's gaze. Some thought seemed to crush her under its weight. Her mouth lined with grief. With deep love, she finally looked up. "You have more to give than I do."

A lump filled Kiria's throat. "I don't want to take this from you if you're not ready."

Her mother gestured for her silence. "No," she said. "I believe you can do this. Ever since you came back, I've seen the change in you. The fire."

Kiria nodded.

Her mother's eyebrows met, suddenly concerned. "Is that Tanyu still watching you?" At this point, everyone knew about Firian's invasion of her thoughts. Happily, her mother didn't know many details.

"Yes, but not for long." One way or another, she would make sure those words were true.

Tenderly pulling her arm, Mother drew her into a chair next to hers. This time, Kiria yielded. Her mother's eyes glistened as she gazed in her daughter's face. "I missed you," she said, pushing hair away from Kiria's forehead.

Kiria's eyes prickled. "I missed you too," she whispered, "especially when I heard…"

Her mother nodded so she wouldn't have to finish the sentence.

"I just want to do the right thing," Kiria said. It was the closest thing to an apology she could muster. Hopefully her mother would understand.

A kind hand in hers told her that she did. "I'll talk to Chetana so she can prepare for your coronation."

Kiria folded her mother's hand in both of hers. "Thank you," she said, and sighed.

49

FIRIAN

No more light streamed through the little window in his room. Firian pulled off his shirt and rubbed it absently over his hair. Tomorrow morning, he would start fighting one-on-one with the best mental warriors Brithnem had. To fight made his mind and blood tense in a satisfying way. His breathing shallowed thinking about it. But he already knew that a victory would be two-edged. Kiria would know. Fighting Amir almost seemed unfair, like Masters fighting Learners. They could only struggle for so long.

And ever on the edges of his mind was the old Tanyuin Head, looking down at his unmoving hands.

"*Master* Firian!" He looked up. Bard, with his face still wet from the washroom. "I heard! So, you're not going to get one of those houses in town?"

"No need," Firian said. After they freed the Sentries, Bard seemed alight with a fresh sense of purpose. If he knew the truth, he'd be horrified.

Bard grinned and closed the door behind him. "Good for you, mate," he said. "So, you got to meet the Head and everything?"

"Yeah." He threw his shirt in the corner and sat down on the bed.

"It's about time! Everybody knew you were going to be promoted." He checked himself, remembering Firian's stint outside the Academy. "You know, except…"

"Let's not ever talk about that."

"I need to know sometime," Bard said, uncharacteristically combative. Maybe the war had changed him a little bit, made him less submissive.

"Sometime."

Bard cocked his jaw and climbed up to the top bunk.

Firian heard shuffling at the top. "I'm going into the war tomorrow," he said.

"As a warrior or a leader?" Leaders, like Tiev, organized Defenders in their subversive campaign, while warriors fought against other people with the Talent.

"Warrior," Firian answered, lying down and rubbing his hand over his face.

"Ooh."

"Yeah."

"What was the Head like? I hardly ever see him."

Firian grunted. Unreasonable anger smoldered in him. The meeting had almost felt like betrayal. Firian had given his life to the Academy, to the Tanyu, and the man in charge seemed too weak to defend it.

Kiria was smarter than he liked to admit. She could figure out the general area of the Academy without too much difficulty. If the Head did nothing more to fortify it, one of the scouts would surely find it. What then?

"Firian?" Bard's voice prompted from above.

"Oh, he was all right. He's getting old." He suddenly wished he could tell Bard about his intention to succeed Sais Jairon as Head. Better to keep it to himself for now. Bard would support him, no matter what. He needed other Masters on his side, though, so he wouldn't have to vie against too many others for power. Jovan came to mind. Balling his hand into a fist, Firian flexed his forearm in the dark. Especially after his days spent Lost, he knew he might not be able to take Jovan in a fight. They would be closely matched at least.

"Hmm." More shuffling. A deep breath. "Well, good luck tomorrow. Don't wake me up, okay, huh?"

"Okay." Firian rolled onto his side, but he couldn't sleep.

THE OLD MAN was obviously of Khelê descent. He had nut brown skin, reddish hair, and a short, white beard. Firian wouldn't have feared him face to face, but often the older someone was, the better they could use the Talent.

They stood on a flat, sun-baked rooftop made of stone as red as the man's hair. It felt rough under Firian's feet—the man was good at details. Above them, the sky looked as clear and hard as a gemstone. Ponderous dark mountains rose hazily in the near distance. It could have been somewhere in Charäkhnem.

"Do you see it?" the man asked.

"Yes," Firian replied.

At first the man didn't move. He just shifted his weight a bit from side to side as he stared back at him. Did he expect Firian to attack him first? Well, if that's what he wanted...

Firian gathered energy into him, felt himself expanding, growing taller. Now he was looking down on the man, who seemed unflustered by this turn of events. Firian, now huge, easily straddled the entire width of the building, with one foot on each of the far edges of the roof. *Crush him like an ant.*

As Firian lifted his foot, the man flew suddenly, impossibly, around and up into his face, wielding fire and smoke that obscured his vision. Firian swallowed a cough—none of it was real anyway—and transported himself, now normal-sized, to a nearby rooftop. He almost liked this spunky old man. *What now? Ah yes. Water.*

Firian placed his hands calmly behind his back as the man bulleted toward him, running at twice the speed of a normal man. *Water.* He commanded it to gush from behind him as though a tidal wave had risen above the rooftop. A pulsing wall of liquid flowed, roared, in, sweeping away dust and flags and baskets. As though he were in a glass bubble, Firian stood untouched. The man's eyes dilated in surprise. Caught off guard, he flung heavily upward with the waves. His body suddenly looked like a child's. Firian watched him for a few moments as he struggled to disbelieve his circumstances, maintain the environment, and think of a counter-move. Belik had put him through similar tests when he was younger. He had almost choked. At the memory, he twisted his mouth to one side.

This wasn't a fair fight. The hot pulse of strength didn't live in his arms anymore as it had that morning, when he had woken up hungry to battle. He could let the man live.

The waters subsided. The rooftop instantly cleared and dried again as the old man stood up in dripping clothes. He looked small now. If Firian wanted to, he could kill him. The man believed too much in the Unreal. More even than Salaar had. Strange for an Amir, or at least that's what he assumed the man was. As they looked at each other, he noticed a familiar brightness in the man's eyes. Brown skin crinkled around them, but they looked dark and shining, almost like Bard's.

They both knew in that moment that the fight was over. No needless bloodshed. Firian had won this round.

Everything dissolved and re-formed into the small plain room where Firian stood alone. He took a deep breath through his nose. Bard was onto something when he said he didn't like this war. He agreed with the premise that the Tanyu needed more power in Brithnem, but this war seemed like such an indirect way to get there.

Belik's words burned almost tangibly in his mind. Now, to gain power in the Academy, *that* was a worthwhile cause. He stretched his back, looking up at the ceiling. Who were his competitors? These fights with outsiders felt hollow—empty flexing. Even the deaths so far were no reason for glory. His real competitors were inside the Academy, the others angling for succession.

SITTING on the edge of the fountain, Firian stared at the floor, his hands clasped between his knees. Scouts came nearer every minute, and still no word of reinforcing the Academy's defenses.

Sais Jairon was too passive. Too passive where it mattered and too violent against innocents. He had war strategy turned completely on its head. If Master Jairon would not protect the Academy's interests, Firian would.

The thought had come to him last night, inevitable but surprising. He couldn't really be considering it, of course...

It took about three weeks to travel between Brithnem and the Academy. There was still time for the Head to move. But would he?

There were easier ways to get things done.

Like a man going underwater, Firian plunged into the Unreal. Down one more level. A moment of struggling to breathe and then... space opened out like a subterranean cave, cold and dark and vast. He waited. The glint of wetness glimmered on the sides of his cavern. Here and there, a drip.

Why was he even waiting here? Maybe Belik was busy. Besides, he wouldn't tell anyone about his idea. It wasn't even a real idea, more of a hypothetical situation. His breathing sped up. No, he couldn't seriously entertain the thought.

Dismissing it with a wave of his hand, as though his idea had flown toward him with new-grown wings, he kept waiting.

Was that...? It was. The dark shape of Belik slowly materialized near him.

"Progress?" he asked gruffly.

"Some, maybe. I talked to Master Jovan yesterday. He's going to give me more training." His words sounded empty, probably because his thoughts didn't fill them.

"That's not what you need."

"I think that's the only way he'll give me his support," Firian said.

Belik shrugged his head to one side. "The man does need his precious pride to be stroked. And you're right. He will probably suggest himself when the time comes."

Firian nodded, cracking his knuckles. *What am I doing?*

"Anything else?" Belik prompted, lowering his head with a look alternating between annoyance and curiosity, as though he guessed something.

"The Head still hasn't... taken my advice, has he?"

"No. I think the border patrol will take care of the scouts."

"But you saw my point?"

"I do."

They were silent for a moment. The cave dripped.

Part of him wanted Belik to read his mind so he wouldn't have to say the words that grew louder inside him. Just by proximity he should be able to hear them. Firian's blood pulsed as the certainty grew. He had to say something.

"When do you think the..." He cleared his throat. "When do you think the Academy will be ready for new leadership?"

The line of Belik's mouth softened. It could have been a smile. "It's not about when they're ready." He shook his head. "People are never ready for change. But good leaders make it anyway."

"You think I'm ready now," Firian said in a low voice. It was a question.

"I think you're ready now."

They paused again, the realization growing like weight upon them. Could he really do it? The fulfillment of his dream, the strengthening of his Academy, the power he had always wanted, the ability to protect, to command...

"I think you're ready now," Belik repeated.

Firian looked him seriously in the eyes. "Will you help me?" he whispered. The meaning was clear.

Belik began to nod, first slowly, then with more conviction. "Yes, I will."

So it was real—his idea was real.

The face of Amir Salaar came back to him like sickness. He had died for no true purpose. He killed him only to prove that he could serve the Academy better than everyone else—that he could assassinate their enemies. Rage had fueled him so ineluctably that he hadn't considered Kiria's face, her disappointment, her anger. Where was the strategy? What had they won? Fear in the Kingdom? That was nothing. They could achieve that in other ways if necessary—if Firian thought it was necessary. There were other, truer, reasons to kill. Necessary reasons.

Change wouldn't come on its own.

Together, they would kill the Tanyuin Head.

50

FIRIAN

When Firian walked back into his room, Bard was digging through the drawers of the dresser. The distinct smell of cinnamon wafted up from them.

"Hey, Fir," he said. "Have you seen my Tanyu figure?" He held up two fingers to show how big it was. "I can't find it."

Firian smirked. "Is it with your Indisfate game?"

"No."

"I haven't seen it. Do you want me to look?"

"Yeah, check your stuff," he said, arm-deep in clothes.

Firian dropped to the floor and lowered himself to see under the bottom bunk. Dust and hair and crumbs of food layered the ground, but no wooden figure. Bard was funny about his stuff from home. So attached. Firian pushed himself up, got to his feet, and waved his blanket around once. "Not here," he announced.

"Oh, how was this morning?"

"What?" He snapped around to look at Bard.

"The fight? How'd it go?"

"Oh." That seemed like weeks ago. "I won. He didn't... die, though."

"You know, that's good," Bard said thoughtfully, scratching his head and giving up his search in the drawer. He picked up the lumps of dark clothes from the floor and shoved them back in the dresser. Pushing the drawer closed with his elbow, he turned back to Firian. "Are you all right?"

Where did that question come from? "Yeah, of course."

"You just seem a little off. You've been weird ever since you came back. Did you check the bed?"

"Uh huh."

"I wonder where it went..." He scrunched his face to the side thoughtfully before returning to his last idea. "Yeah, I know you're always thinking about something, but it's like you have all these secrets. More than usual."

Firian shrugged, figuring it was best not to speak at all. Bard, sometimes, made him feel exposed. No one else but Belik had spent so much time with him. Other people found him mysterious, but Bard knew him too well. Not that he knew everything, of course.

"Fine," Bard said. "You can keep your secrets. Maybe I'll find out sooner or later."

He would, Firian realized. This was one secret he couldn't keep in his mind. Eventually, in a day or two, the wheels of power would turn to him. Lightheadedness passed through him like a ghost and he smiled.

"What?" Bard asked suspiciously.

"Nothing." He shook his head. Waves of excitement flooded over him, alternating waves of terror, happiness, surprise... Hopefully Bard didn't see into his mind.

His ascension would be a surprise to many people. Let it be. Longing to give voice to his thoughts in the Second Level, he lay down and pretended to rest. He could barely get to the Second Level if his eyes were open. The last time he tried, he almost ran into the wall. No, better to be completely still.

He heard his name as though the sound came from underneath the earth, or inside him. Belik already waited for him. He dove in.

"I think we should do this quickly," Firian said, not waiting for the other Master.

"I agree," Belik said. They stood close together. The landscape wasn't important.

"When?"

"I have two Retrievals in the morning. Damn fools," he muttered. "Tiev's one of them."

For a moment, the surprise didn't register. There were bigger issues at stake now. "Tomorrow, then?"

"Night."

"Right, tomorrow night," Firian said breathlessly.

"Without the Sentries, he's vulnerable. Of course, they've brought many of them back, but I don't think they've found the one that normally covered Sias during the night." He gave Firian a meaningful look. Was that amusement? Reprimand? Congratulations? "He kept himself protected when he slept," he explained.

That was common knowledge. Firian had bypassed Sentries before, so he figured that nighttime would provide their way in. He had a few ideas.

"This is your parade," Belik prompted.

"Right, there are a couple ways I've thought of. One of us could get him to go to the Second Level—use some excuse—and the other could go into his room and do it." The guard outside Sias Jairon's door came to mind. Losing a fighting man would be a shame. "But a better way," he continued, "I think a better way would be to make him think he died in his sleep. It would be tricky, but the two of us could do it, disguised, of course. The suggestion from the lower level that his heart is slowing and stopping, and his breathing..." He stopped and shook his head like a dog shaking water from its fur, shocked by his own words. They burned like liquor and went to his head. He wanted more.

"It would take two of us..." Belik said. "But it could be done."

The concentration to achieve what they were talking about would be almost impossible with one. Alone, getting Lost would be inevitable. Belik's face, almost luminous with hope, seemed to search the ground for his thoughts, to gather them. Light glinted off his spectacles as he turned his head from side to side. It felt strange to count on him so heavily.

"The war will be enough of a distraction for the rest of the Tanyu. I don't think they'll interfere," Firian said. His chest rose and fell with his breath and he stretched his numbing hands. "We'll meet at midnight."

Belik hummed, his gazing turning inward for a moment. "Once it's done, the first person to claim responsibility will become the new Head. Everyone will know what happened." That someone killed him. Firian's heart felt like a heavy cord of firewood. Belik scoffed, almost to himself. "In his sleep!"

"In his sleep," Firian said, the words suddenly empty. He tried to fill them up with meaning.

"The Masters will support your nomination. Don't worry." He eyed Firian as a bird would, beetle-black pupils inhumanly focused, yet detached.

Firian nodded, more to expel his manic energy than to agree. "They always talk about needing young blood. And who else is there?" Tiev was Lost. Jovan and a couple others would put in their names, but Firian was the future of the Academy.

"Who else is there?" Belik echoed. "Just you, Kess."

MIDNIGHT CAME QUICKLY. Bard was used to Firian leaving in the middle of the night, so he probably wouldn't notice if he snuck out now. Firian knew he should lie in bed and do everything only in his mind, but, as he lay there, heat and chill chased each other over his body. Even pushups would be better than being immobile. Besides, it felt right to be closer to the Head when he met Belik. What if something went wrong?

He slipped into a classroom near the entrance to Master Jairon's hallway. His room was attached to the office Firian had seen, so he knew exactly where it was. As he stood in the dark, the expanse of open air washed around him, feeling more unreal than the space where they were about to fight. The quiet, too. It was as though the darkness washing against him in its cavernous silence pressed him up against the wall where he stood, listening. Blood churned in his ears. His neck bones creaked.

The sense arose that he could walk away from all of this, and yet... he couldn't. Something like fate gripped him. No, not fate. A choice. He'd made a necessary choice. One life for true, lasting change. One life in exchange for many. He was about to become the strongest Tanyu—the strongest Tanyuin Head—that anyone had ever seen. He was the one who could bring the Academy to its full glory, and give the Tanyu the esteem they truly deserved, and win Kiria's respect. He could end the war and still bring the Academy's glowing potential to light.

Didn't he want that change? Didn't he want both Kiria and the Tanyu?

Yes, I do.

He took a deep breath. Right—the Unreal. He had to meet Belik.

He sank down into himself. Belik was there, in the darkness. The Master's grim eyes glinted but he didn't speak. They both knew what to do, but the operation would be tricky. The first step was disguise. They couldn't seem to be themselves. They had to work almost exclusively in the Second Level, where they would be hidden. But to find someone else in the Second Level... someone who didn't know they were coming... Only very, very few could attempt it.

Firian almost tangibly felt Belik's mind reaching out with his toward the Tanyuin Head, cautiously but resolutely. Like a snake. Recognizing the Head's subconscious was like encountering a familiar smell. They circled it, drawing closer. There it was.

Firian's shallow breathing sounded hoarse in his ears, though he stifled the sound as much as possible. They were swimming through the Head's subconscious now. The sensation was similar to entering someone's dream, as Firian had recently done to those in Brithnem, only the shapes were less distinct. Thick fog covered everything. Dark colors swirled, and emotions swept across them like wind. Dark blue peace, red lust, black fear...

Time to emerge from the Second Level, disguised as stifling vapor, thumping like a heart—an incredibly difficult manifestation to maintain.

Firian looked at Belik, nodded, and went first. Though he had practiced water drills many times, maintaining a vapor state to suffocate the Head took all his concentration. Subtlety was the key. Slowly building, building, enveloping his dream until it turned to darkness. Just an old man asleep in bed.

Struggling to keep his form, Firian felt a sudden rush of power—Belik to help him. With the other Master, he kept his concentration. Pressure built in his head.

There, just then, he slipped, perilously close to revealing himself. Just in time Belik sent the energy he needed, as he had during Tiev's practice fight.

Sais Jairon lay sleeping, his mouth slightly open. Fighting through the headache, Firian stretched himself further, harder. Nothing in his life had been more crucial than this moment. The fog thickened, the thumping became a heartbeat—loud blood.

How long would he have to keep this up? He was losing his grip, too much strain on the last knuckle of his mind as he climbed.

...Help! Help! His frantic thoughts toward Belik, his momentary loss of concentration, made the fog shimmer like a mirage.

He froze. No breath. The thumping got quieter.

The sleeping Master rolled onto his back and looked up. Straight into his eyes. "Firian?"

51

FIRIAN

Firian opened his eyes, gasping in the darkness of the classroom. His hands were shaking. What had he done? What could he do now?

He couldn't let the Head tell anyone. He couldn't let his secret out.

His entire life... all he'd endured, all he'd done, would be for nothing. He'd never do any good; he'd never change the world. He'd end up dead or back in Raewhith.

Firian moved mechanically out of the classroom. There was no choice but to finish it. This time, Belik was too far away to help. He patted his clothes, almost distractedly. He had no weapon with him but a small knife he always carried.

There are many ways to kill a man...

Jovan's words on his first day.

His legs felt heavy as they took him closer to the Master's door. It was like walking through pudding.

The knife shook in his hand. *Wait, wait... What about the guard?* He hadn't planned to kill him. But now he had no choice. The pit of his stomach grew leaden. Another life on the altar.

The guard would sense him coming. That prickle of the Talent would reach him before he saw Firian. So Firian could use that. He had to.

Surprise was his best chance to overpower a man who was no doubt better armed than Firian. Maybe he even wore armor. Firian suddenly felt naked. His thin black shirt rubbed against bare skin, both so easy to tear. Surprise. He had to have surprise.

Rooms and hallway, all darkened except for tiny flames, floated by like something in a dream. Mutant shadows reached across the walls and ceiling, calling him into their dark ritual.

The only ideas breaking through him seemed juvenile. Would they work?

Where was his center, his stamina? He drew a slow, shaky breath into his core, where blood thrummed like a heart in his stomach.

He could do this. *I can do this.*

Around the corner from the Head's office, he stopped. Time to decide. Best just to do it. There wasn't anything supremely unusual about a Master staying up late and roaming the halls. So he would be an ordinary Master. Simplicity often succeeded when complicated plans failed.

He walked casually by. Maybe the guard wouldn't notice the turmoil in his mind, or the knife ready on the far side of his body. He didn't remember the guard's name, but he knew his face—long nose, splotchy tan birthmark on his neck. His neck.

The guard didn't issue a challenge. Firian calmed himself as much as he could, which wasn't enough, and strolled to face him. Without a word, quick as a snake, he sliced the knife upward and plunged it behind the guard's neck, where the spine meets the skull. Hot blood gushed over his hands and the guard, his sword half-unsheathed, dropped like a puppet to the ground.

Wiping his hands distractedly, mechanically, on his clothes, he stepped over the guard and passed into the office, and then opened the inner door. Sais Jairon was his main target.

Now speed was his ally. He strode in and grabbed the pillow from beneath the old man's head. Without looking at him, Firian smashed the pillow against his face, gripping the edges. When he flailed against him, Firian got on the bed and held him down with his body. Sais kicked and twisted under the blanket, scratching at Firian's arms, trying to pull the suffocating pillow off.

Although he had some strength born of panic, the Head did not continue for long. Slowly his actions subsided. The frantic breathing under Firian's legs deflated, leaving nothing but emptiness.

Firian remained rigid. Moving felt like an admission of guilt. The dead weight under him made him nauseated and confused. Firian rolled off the bed as the room tilted and spun unevenly. When he released the pillow, his hands stayed clenched in the same position. It was almost painful to open them.

His hip bumped into something metallic, sliding it forward on the side table. The iron circle, Tanyuin crown, rocked gently back and forth.

It was a sickening thought to rearrange the pillow. But he had to, he had to. He grabbed the soft edge of the pillow with one hand, smearing it red, and with the other lifted the heavy head of the Master, replacing the pillow where it had been. Did he look asleep? He looked ashen, eyes squeezed shut. Was that a normal way to sleep?

Would they know?

The idea of touching the man's face or getting his body on its side made hot bile rise up in his throat. A massive wave of chills splashed over him. He couldn't bear to stay in that room. He stumbled out. If he could make it back to his room, he would be safe. His hair was drenched with sweat so he passed his sleeve over his forehead to soak it up. The wetness on his sleeve just made him colder and clammier.

A call from deep within. He jumped. He'd forgotten all about Belik. *No. Not now.* He had to get to his room.

He was in front of his door. *How did I get here so fast? Which way did I go?* There must not have been other Masters in the halls, or else someone would have challenged him, shaking him out of his daze with a question about the dark blood on his hands and sleeves that stuck to the hair on his arms.

His heavy breathing still came in ragged gasps. The door rattled once under his shaking hand as he opened it.

Inside was only silence. Bard didn't seem to have heard the noise.

If I can just make it to bed...

He flung himself forward into the darkness.

SOMETIME IN THE middle of the night, Firian had woken up, covered in someone else's blood. He snuck to the washroom, scrubbed his hands and arms raw, almost vomited, changed his shirt, and went back to bed.

He woke up the next morning with a fever and a headache. but he went to fight anyway. The day felt like a dream—mental warfare, training with Jovan (who told him the Head had been killed in the night), meeting with Belik.

By the time he went to Belik's room, his legs trembled from work and cold. Pain pounded his head. He creaked the door open.

"What's wrong with you?" Belik asked, looking up at him.

"Nothing. Sick," Firian grunted.

They hadn't met since before the incident, even in the Unreal.

"I thought you'd lost it."

"Yeah." Firian was in no mood to talk. He sat in the chair opposite Belik's and closed his eyes. If he wanted to talk to him, he could do it in the Unreal. He dove down into depths of clear water. One landing, two...

When Belik arrived in the same shapeless cavern where they had made the plan, his eyes were shining. "People are eager to put a new Head in place," he said. Though his tone was business-like, he shifted his weight eagerly.

"Okay."

"Have you heard anything?"

"No."

Belik blew out an exasperated breath. "Gore, Firian! Do you even hear what I'm saying to you?"

Firian looked back in his eyes deliberately. This man knew what he had done. Suddenly, he hated the power Belik held over him. "Yes."

"I've been talking to the other Masters," Belik continued. "And there is no heir apparent. I thought more discussion would gear toward you." Something in Belik's tone tried to prepare him.

Firian licked his dry lips, feeling the light leave his eyes. *Was this all for nothing?*

"You have to tell everyone what you've done, how you've saved them from tyranny, all that stuff. They'll have no choice once you take the position."

Firian felt his pulse in his Adam's apple. *Tell everyone or it will be for nothing.* He picked the skin around his new ring.

"Should I do it today?" The voice came as a whisper. Firian couldn't muster more.

Belik regarded him, looking over him as a strategist would look over a map. Suddenly, he smiled. "No regrets, Firian." He leaned closer in fatherly confidence. "Remember why it needed to be done. You've done well." The lines around Belik's eyes softened compassionately. "And you'll continue to do well. The Academy needs you, and so do I."

Then he reached out and put a heavy hand on Firian's shoulder. The simple act had more affection in it than he would have expected. How could Belik even reach him across the chasm he'd created by his murder last night? He felt adrift and hollow. Other people seemed to live across an unbreachable space. Yet Belik found him there, and still believed in him. Hadn't left him. Hadn't rejected him.

Firian nodded in acknowledgement, feeling his face grow hot. His eyes stung. He sniffed hard, trying to rid himself of his welling emotion. Belik patted him once and turned away, almost ashamed of his outburst.

The rush of the idea came back to him. Control of the Academy. Make it better. Make everything better.

He could ignore the racking chills for one day and pretend that his head didn't hurt so bad he could barely see. Mental warfare was his specialty. That was all it took. Shove it into the Unreal and carry on as though nothing had happened, as though he couldn't see his face, and his knees didn't still feel as though they were straddling a dying man struggling to be free from under the covers, and his hands weren't sweating and slipping little by little down the edges of the pillow, and he didn't hear the subterranean muffled gasps.

One day. He could pull himself together and take control of the Academy. He couldn't let it be for nothing. It had to mean something.

No regrets.

52

KIRIA

Atty, for one, was thrilled. "I won't be alone!" he cried.

What an odd thing to say.

"You were never alone," Kiria replied. Atty did always act as though he were alone, or somehow on the outside. Yet he technically had more say than anybody, Cúron excepted. She loved Atty, but sometimes his victim attitude got under her skin. "Cúron and my mother were always there, and Jori sometimes, and all the Amir. And you're friends with Daelon, right?"

They were sitting in the dining room where they only sat for more formal occasions. Candles hung in the chandelier above the long wooden table that was clearly meant for hosting large parties. Stretching on like a garden row, a refulgent bouquet of blue and purple lilies bloomed along the center. Official announcements and arrangements often happened here before being announced in the Main, at least when it pertained directly to matters like the coronation. All of the Keepers' families were here—a small group—their advisors, and representatives from the army and palace staff. In all, about twenty sat solemnly eating their shrimp and pickled lemon.

At a nod from Kiria's mother, Amir Chetana stood up. She had pulled half of her curly reddish hair up for this occasion, which was beautiful but made her cheekbones and dark eyes more severe. "My Keepers," she began, "I have the privilege to announce that Kiria Arioc, heir to the Second Line, will become the next Keeper of Brithnem in three days' time." This was not new information to anyone there, but applause erupted across the whole table. "Her coronation will take place in the Main at midday. All the arrangements are being made; you all have your assignments." Chetana scanned the people sitting at the table. "The rehearsal is tomorrow…"

Under his breath, Atty whispered, "It'll just be nice to have someone on my side."

"I've always been on your side," Kiria said. Even though she'd chosen a very loose dress for the occasion, the new tattoo still burned along her shoulder blades. "Maybe you should stand up for yourself if you feel nobody listens to you. You're a Keeper."

"Yes," he mused, then lowered his voice so it was barely audible. "But Cúron never listens to what I say. If I disagree, he ignores me and follows his idea."

"All Keepers get the same vote." Maybe their whispering was starting to look conspicuous. Kiria smiled across the table to look more at ease.

"I've won the vote and he still goes ahead with his plan."

"That's not how it works." She took a bite of shrimp.

"I'm telling the truth!"

Maybe he was overreacting, but she had seen Cúron charge ahead with his plans and avoid bringing them to the Main at all if he suspected there would be opposition. With everyone, there was a bit of political maneuvering if they thought it was for the good of the Kingdom. Too much, and the other two would check him. That was the strength of having three leaders. "If that's happening, why haven't the Amir said anything?"

"I don't know. Maybe they're on his side. You haven't been in the Main for a while."

She set her jaw and squinted as she looked at him.

"...Head, Sias Jairon, is dead." Chetana's voice suddenly invaded her consciousness again.

Kiria spun around in her chair. The Tanyuin Head was dead? How had she not known about that? Apparently, others around the table had the same question, because they immediately looked at her. A twinge of relief registered in some of their faces as they saw that she'd had no idea.

"He has been succeeded by Firian Kess. It is of the utmost importance that we find out his position on the war as soon as possible."

She flushed cold, then hot. Breath was hard to draw. How had she not known? How had this happened? He had said he would end the war. Was this his way of doing it? She had too many questions. They buzzed like insects, relentlessly, and made her dizzy.

Atty put a hand on her shoulder. Eyes looked back into her own as she focused on the faces around the table again. "I'll find out immediately," she told them.

THE NIGHT before her coronation came sooner than she had expected. All alone in the Main, Kiria stood beside the enormous statue of Mari. As a child she had liked this statue the most, because it showed a woman as big and strong as any of the men.

Servants had already cleared the chairs away for the ceremony. Because of the gulfs of darkness, the room looked as enormous as it had when she was young.

She saw a young man in rags wash the feet of the lowest serving man. *"Thus will I serve my country, thus will I serve my God."* It had happened right over there.

"A robe... shoes... crown..." So they would all call for her. She would rise and her mother would fall.

She craned her neck to look up at the statue. Mari had a sword on her hip and regal bearing. Standing up straighter, Kiria knew she would have to embody that strength for the people of Brithnem. The time had finally come—the moment she had awaited with such excitement, dread, and anticipation. Finally she could utter the words that had dogged her, pleased her, all her life: "I swear to serve my country, the Western Kingdom, and its capital, Brithnem, to the best of my ability, to guide her through war and peace, freedom and judgment, with wisdom and integrity, for as long as I live."

But first, a matter of business, of war and peace. She closed her eyes. He would be there. He hadn't been for a while, but she knew better. With her coronation the next day, he would want to make an appearance, whether to congratulate her, taunt her with his own new position... something.

She recreated the Main in her mind with its floors glossy and lanterns lit. An almost exact representation. Careful to hide her Beauty in the Unreal, she sat on the middle throne, her throne, waiting for him. Firian might be Head of the Tanyuin Academy but she was still a Keeper of Brithnem. Her power exceeded his.

Where was he? She waited a few beats, and then said, "Firian?" Her voice echoed in the empty room.

He appeared, standing on the mosaic of the First Line. Nothing about his appearance had changed. He still wore simple black clothes and boots. Wait—was that a crown? A thin metal circlet with an open square in the center sat on his head, overlapped by his dark hair. As he strode up to her, his eyes gave an almost chemical glow, unhealthy but beautiful and bright. He jumped up the stairs to the dais and stood looking down at her.

"Firian," she said coldly, diplomatically.

"Kiria."

"I hear you are the Tanyuin Head now." She had questions about his ascendency but now was not the time to ask. More important was the kind of leader he would be now that he had the position.

"I am. And you are about to be a Keeper of Brithnem." A smile curled his mouth. Was he proud of her or of himself? Maybe both.

She nodded and continued the speech she had rehearsed in her mind. "That puts us both in a position to make good on our promise to end the war." His looming over her was becoming bothersome, so she stood to face him. "I have called you to find out your official position on the war as Head of the Academy. We could start peace terms right here."

"I agree," he said. "We have your scouts" – her breath caught – "and I intend to send them to you with my terms in writing. I won't hurt them."

She set her mouth in a hard line. Of course he had terms. "What are your terms?"

"To end the war immediately."

Her tense body relaxed, but she still suspected a trap.

He wasn't finished. "And to help you in your war against the Torithians, as long as you give us some of your troops to work with, and allow us to have the Torithian prisoners of war. That's all."

"And the vote?"

"We haven't earned a vote with you yet. You know that." His mouth twisted ironically. Maybe that was a flash of regret in his blue eyes too. "And we don't need it. We're going in a different direction for now. More independent."

"The Tanyu have always been independent," she agreed. "You're not... rejecting the Kingdom, then?"

"No." His fingers flexed forward, but he drew them back again. "We're simply acknowledging that we haven't really been part of it for a long time. We're different. But we can be allies again."

She digested that idea. "And you're sending all of this in writing? With the scouts? All of them?" If he allowed them all to return, that could mean revealing the location of the Academy, and they both knew it.

"All of them," he repeated. "It's a new age for the Tanyu. We aren't going to keep our location a secret for much longer." He lowered his voice almost to a whisper, looking straight into her eyes. "I said I wanted to show you."

Her heart beat quickly and her stomach knotted. "What you would do as a leader. I remember. I'll show you, too."

They stood silently a moment. The awkwardness reminded her of how young they were—very young and very powerful. Together they had the power to make peace... or war.

She cleared her throat. "So now we're allies," she said slowly, puzzling out the risks and opportunities.

He nodded.

"I'll wait for the writing," she said.

"I know."

She almost didn't believe it. First the Tanyuin War ended—she would check the terms and make sure there were no unreasonable demands—and now a chance to end the years-long Torithian War? Her beautiful city could find peace. Her dreams could come true.

She looked back at Firian, at the throne, at the statue in the corner. For the first time, she truly felt worthy to lead.

53

FIRIAN

FIRIAN STEPPED into the Head's office, his heart thumping hard and slowly, Belik following behind. The room smelled like dusty paper and wet stone. The blank rock walls, identical to all other rooms except for the second door, provided nothing but a backdrop for power. There was a flash of that power in them, wavering like heat. Firian felt more solid and real than they were.

He stepped around to the back of the desk. Taking a deep breath, he sat in the chair. Belik stood silently before him, his expression almost obedient. Firian smiled. "Get me some official paper, and a pen."

Belik nodded, a slight smile running over his mouth, and turned to leave. As he went out the door, Bard almost ran into him but jumped to the side in time. Firian hadn't seen Bard in days. Ever since the announcement, Bard wouldn't look him in the face.

Firian waved him into the room, but he didn't come.

"The Tanyuin Head..." He ran both hands down his face in place of words, his black eyes wide.

"It's true!" As Firian stood, he flicked a glance at the other door leading to the bedroom.

His roommate leaned into the office, open-mouthed, looking from floor to ceiling, and at Firian, awestruck. His eyes searched like conscience. "Fir, I can't believe it!" he said. "How could you do it?"

For a second, Firian squirmed. *So many reasons.* "I wanted to end the war with Brithnem."

Bard eyed him skeptically. Then he shook his head.

"No, I'm doing it today."

"I'm not an idiot, Firian." Bard hardly ever used his full name. His eyes continued to roam around the room, as though searching for something that would justify his friend's decision. His gaze lighted on nothing.

He should send him away. No Tanyuin Head courted the favors of a Defender. But this was Bard, who should stick by him. "I can do good here," he said, remembering Kiria. "You can help me."

His friend still stayed like a shadow at the door, dressed head to toe in Academy black. Something like pain crossed his face. "Fir..."

"I'm serious about the war."

Bard walked forward, one hand over his mouth, his eyes welling with tears. Light shone on the bottom lids. He swallowed visibly and turned his red face away. "That would be..." He couldn't say what, because his voice broke. "Ah, Firian!" He lay flat on his back beside the desk and folded his arms over his eyes. It didn't mean forgiveness, but friendship was a possibility again.

Firian laughed through his nose. The air felt fresher.

After a moment, Firian kicked Bard in the side. Bard's supine figure suddenly seemed out of place. "Get up! You're in the Head's office."

"Right, yeah..." he said automatically, scrambling to his feet. "I can't believe it."

"Master Kess?" The earnest voice was new. A grizzled man with tan, leathery skin stood in the doorway. Firian had seen him before in Tánuil, hadn't he? Anyway, he looked familiar.

"Yes, what is it?" Firian quickly returned behind his desk.

The man looked pointedly at Bard, as though asking whether he should wait until they were finished meeting. Apparently his information could not be given in company.

"I'll talk to you later," Firian told Bard, who took the hint and left.

The man closed the door behind him with a strong, rough hand. He spoke in an urgent undertone. "We've found and captured the last of the three scouts from Brithnem. Should we execute them now?"

"No, bring them to me."

"Yes, Master Kess." The man exited the way he had come.

For now, he would send the scouts back to the Kingdom with his demands. After he helped Kiria win the war and brought Torithian fighters back to the Academy, where all the best fighters belonged, he would announce their location. No more hiding.

These next simple moves would mean the end of two wars: Tanyu and Torithian. At the end of them, Firian would have the makings of a powerful military that didn't rely solely on mental warfare, and Kiria would love him for it. His breathing quickened and a smile spread across his face.

The door opened. Belik walked heavily in and set the paper and pen flat-palmed on Firian's desk. "Don't get used to me getting you everything you want," he said, smiling.

"Can you watch the door for me? The Kingdom scouts are about to get here."

Belik grunted, but his face wasn't as hard set as it usually was. He was proud of the new Tanyuin Head, but he wouldn't say it again. "You're making quick work of this."

Firian nodded. Watching the Master follow his commands tasted sweet and sent a thrill through his bones. When he was alone, he leaned back in his chair and took a luxurious breath. He had made something of himself. That little boy in

Raewhith would hardly recognize the man he was today. He, Firian Kess, could change the world. To what extent remained to be seen. Soon, everyone would know it. But for now, he'd content himself with just a few.

Leaning forward, he grabbed the pen, smiled, and started writing.

To Yanon and Lithia Kess...

INTO THE UNREAL

BOOK 2 OF THE TANYUIN ACADEMY SERIES

1

FIRIAN

To Yanon and Lithia Kess,
I am the new Head of the Tanyuin Academy. Come with the bearer of this letter.
Firian Kess

THAT WAS ALL the message needed to say. Firian set down the pen, took a deep breath, and looked down at the curve of the letters. When Sias Jairon's invitation arrived in his parents' hands years ago, each lilt of the strong letters had spoken of promise, magic.

Did the last Head's message look so short?

Firian sat back in his chair, running his thumb against the armrests. The Tanyuin Head's office in the Academy was small and stark, but powerful. The blank stone walls, gray like every other room in the Academy, suited him. Scarcity, simplicity, cold—these all made Firian feel more alive. They called attention back to the hot blood coursing through his veins, his own strength, his own stamina. The superiority of the Unreal.

The Unreal. Its colors put reality to shame. And the possibilities... He was a god in that imaginary space. And now he was in charge of its best warriors, those who could take out generals and tacticians through mind warfare, spread fear through dreams, communicate with the farthest reaches of the world in an instant.

His eyes strayed over the page one more time. Stamped red at the top of the paper, the Tanyuin seal confirmed who he was. It left no room to doubt the position he now held, one of the greatest and most feared in the world.

This note would prove his father wrong. Firian had amounted to something.

Brett should come too. The realization flooded his mind like the forgotten answer to a question. His sister, at least, would be proud of him.

Recent memories crowded in and his stomach clenched uncomfortably. *Will she be proud of me?*

The last Head had steered the Academy into darkness, into war and confusion, clinging to fearful traditions, using its warriors like they were property. He had deserved to die.

Firian's heart thumped as the image of the man's face returned. The wide eyes, the ashy skin, the struggling legs kicking for breath, the one word uttered in disbelief— "Firian?" The memory moved as he blinked like the negative image of bright light, bright darkness.

Firian flexed his clammy hands and stood. He leaned over just to add *Bring Brett*.

Taking the letter to the door of the office, he fought the urge to look at it one more time. He couldn't help feeling that the little piece of paper didn't properly convey its own importance. A little note couldn't express how hard he had worked every day to earn his skills, or the sacrifices he'd made on behalf of the Academy to get to this point.

Well, maybe his family had already heard about when he took Kiria hostage. It was news across the continent. Only his promise to work with her instead of against her, now that they were both in power, had created a tenuous truce.

Master Belik sat just outside in the stone hallway. He must have dragged a chair from a nearby room so his leg wouldn't bother him.

I need to appoint a new guard. Firian didn't want to think about what had happened to the last one.

Belik turned when he opened the door, his bull neck craning. Light from the hall torches reflected off his glasses, hiding his eyes. "Wrote a letter, did you?"

Firian handed it to him. "See that it gets to my family in Raewhith."

The Master moved his head just enough that Firian could see Belik's eyes rove around his face, evaluating where they both stood in this new relationship. Belik wouldn't suffer himself to become an errand boy. But this was important to Firian.

The Master hummed deep in his throat, almost a growl. Then one side of his mouth lifted. "Telling them the good news?"

"Yes."

After all they'd done, they couldn't afford to mistrust each other now. If prodded, Firian still felt rage like a deep bruise from the lies Belik had told. But the Master was also one of the only people who had believed Firian could end up here, in this office.

After Firian moved out of their shared room to stay in the very place where he'd suffocated Sais Jairon in his bed, Bard had hardly spoken to him—as though Firian had done something wrong, when he had only taken drastic action for the good of the Academy. Bard's cautions still echoed regularly in his mind, but the two of them spent no time together anymore. Strangely, he wished Bard would understand. Firian wouldn't admit it, but he missed him.

Still seated, Belik stretched his jaw. "So, do you want me to send this"—he held up the letter, the bottom of it scrunched in his hand—"or wait for the scouts?"

"Send that. Right away. I'll wait for the scouts."

Belik had told Firian what to do thousands of times. Now it was Firian's turn.

Clearly grumpy, Belik rose from the chair, cursing the stiffness in his leg as he walked away toward the inner courtyard.

His uneven footsteps overlapped with the patter of new ones getting louder down the hall. A border patroller marched three people bound in front of him. Bold of him to conduct all three scouts himself. Firian found himself liking the patroller.

The scouts from Brithnem wore brown and green and tan clothing. Firian scrutinized them from their heads to their dirty boots. No weapons.

Unlike scouts from other countries, people from Brithnem almost never matched. Too much Khelê blood. In fact, one of the scouts, the only woman, was definitely Khelê. She was stout but attractive, a few years older than Firian, with a milky white eye and tattoos on the side of her head that didn't have a wave of blonde hair. The two men varied as well. One, the tallest of the group, had a beard and was muscled like a seasoned fighter, while the other reminded Firian of a deer, thin and graceful.

Firian waved them all into his office. The door clicked closed behind them.

"So these are the Kingdom scouts." He strolled once again behind his desk, the one where all the leaders had sat since the Tanyu split from the Amir so long ago.

None of the scouts showed fear. Didn't they know what he could do to them? What any other Tanyuin Head *would* do to them? But he had promised Kiria to send them back unharmed. She'd be waiting for them, for the end of the Tanyuin War, for proof that she could trust him. Firian took a deep breath.

The border patroller forced the three of them to their knees.

Firian's face flushed. "You've come on secret land," he said. "No one has come from outside and lived."

The thin man leaned, almost imperceptibly, toward the woman in the center as though for protection or comfort. The woman's white eye grew wider, but she bared her teeth, almost animal-like in defiance. Their sweaty stink began to fill the office.

Firian had to watch his words. The border patroller carried a large sword, unsheathed. Firian couldn't let him misunderstand and stain the floor black-red.

"But today," he continued, "we have the same goal. I am the new Tanyuin Head, and my plans are different from my predecessor." His lip curled with the word *different*. "I want to end the war between us." Already tired of the desk between them, Firian came back around it to stand directly over the scouts. His body cast a torchlight shadow across them. "As proof, I will let you live."

The woman's chest rose and fell, the only sign of her relief. The patroller's hand didn't relax its grip on the sword.

"Tomorrow, you'll return to Brithnem with my terms, and the Academy's location will no longer be secret."

He felt the force of the patroller's surprise. His mouth slackened and his knuckles burned white on the hilt. The hum of unsaid questions whirred through the air.

Firian stood taller, sure in his decision. The Academy would be exposed, but this decision would provide undeniable proof that Kiria could trust him. He could recruit soldiers from neighboring towns, fend off bands of curious mercenaries, or even whole armies with the Kingdom on his side. Open trade would bring more wealth and power to the Tanyu. Though he hated giving up a long-held secret, he would just hold tightly to the ones that remained about his famed warriors. "Bring my terms to the Second Keeper. When she accepts them, the war will end." Kiria. He wouldn't let the other Keepers make such a crucial decision. What did they matter? He ended this war for her. Together, they could use their power to do whatever they wanted. She probably still had that notebook of ideas of how to lead the Kingdom with justice, peace, order... Warmth, almost a caress, snuck up the back of his neck into his hairline.

He jerked his head. "Get them up."

The patroller kicked the woman's heels and the three of them trundled to their feet.

"You'll stay with the border patrollers tonight. In the morning, I'll give you the terms." He caught the man's eye as he turned the three of them away. *Don't hurt them.* The patroller nodded, disappointment in his eyes.

2

KIRIA

KIRIA ADJUSTED her crown and swung around to check it in the glass. It seemed to be centered. She couldn't help wanting every minute detail to be perfect. Today was her first official session as Keeper. Though she had been coronated, today she would take her throne.

"It looks perfect," her mother crooned, touching one of its silver points with a finger. Kiria could see her and her Amiran advisor Chetana standing in the middle of the bedroom floor behind her.

The only one missing was her father, killed by Torithians a few months before. He would have been so proud of her. She fought back the memory of getting that news, when Firian had tried to comfort her, holding her as she wept, but nothing was enough. Her mother had been even more devastated by his death than she was.

After clearing her throat, Kiria turned to look at her mother. Not long ago, she had worn this crown. Kiria didn't have any regrets about taking over the throne, but seeing only pride in her mother's face made her smile.

"This is a big day for you," her mother said, squeezing Kiria's hand. "Why haven't you changed?"

"I will in a second." Kiria bit the inside of her cheek. While she got ready, putting on the trappings of a Keeper for the first time since the coronation, she didn't want her Beauty yet. She wanted a moment for the title to seep into every part of her, to let its glow be beautiful enough. In the Main, she would appear with her official face, the one blessed by God with painfully complete Beauty, but for a second she was just Kiria. This part of her wore the crown too.

As though she'd been summoned, Candrae, one of her serving girls, rushed to check the fastening of Kiria's dress. Kiria flinched as Candrae touched the buttons.

"Oh, My Keeper!" Candrae cried, laying a palm gently on Kiria's bare back.

"The tattoo's still a little tender. It's not your fault." Kiria's design covered the upper part of her back and shoulder blades. She'd chosen a design similar to the one Mari Calthwaite had received in Carradoc. Artists kept a record of all the designs, and she'd always admired the beauty and ferocity of the founder's. Delicate swirls ending in claw-like points adorned her upper back like jeweled armor. Kiria had added a subtle laird flower in the center to symbolize the peace of Brithnem. The final flourish, a graceful point, rose up the nape of her neck.

Since she'd had the procedure, she'd worn open-backed dresses. This one, all light blue, made her appear every inch a Keeper.

"I'm sure she won't do it again," said her mother, eyeing Candrae, who dropped her gaze.

Kiria squeezed Candrae's hand gently to reassure her that she'd done nothing wrong, then turned her attention to Chetana. "Do you have a tattoo?" She'd never noticed one on her advisor's dark skin, but her advisor was fiercely proud of being Khelê. Most Khelê had tattoos in recognition of their heritage. It was in solidarity with the mismatched race of Khelê that the tradition of royal tattoos had started all those years ago.

Chetana tapped the side of her head with an elegant finger. "Right there. Not all allegiances are obvious to the eye." She pulled down the high-necked collar of her Amiran robe. Beneath her hairline of dark, rusty curls, the edge of a tattoo unfurled. Although impossible to see the whole design, it had the signature curls, dots, and points of most Khelê tattoos.

"You used to shave your head?"

Chetana smoothed the collar back up and patted the sides of her close-cut hair. "For a very short while."

"I didn't know that, Chetana," her mother said, drawing her brows together.

"It's not always best to give every detail of one's past. The present is more important."

Kiria was about to ask why when a voice cut in.

"You know, compared to Atty's, yours is very nice."

Kiria whirled around at the sound of Jori's voice. True to form, Jori wore the finest clothes in the sloppiest ways. His embroidered vest was undone as though he were just arriving at home. How he could manage to seem at home no matter where he was remained a mystery to Kiria. "Atty's is exactly like your father's, though. That has to mean something."

"And? I think it must be something about the skin," he said thoughtfully. He sauntered up beside her. Blushing, Candrae backed up against the vanity.

Despite herself, Kiria smiled. "You're ridiculous."

"The Keeper is right," Chetana agreed with no hint of levity.

"Of course," he replied. Giving into his penchant for theatrics, he bowed his head.

"I'm surprised they let you in," her mother said, with a little more amusement.

"*I'm* not." Jori flashed a mischievous grin. "Well!" He turned again to Kiria. "I just wanted to wish you good luck. With those two, you're going to need it." *Those two* were Cúron and Jori's brother Atty, the other Keepers.

"Hardly," she said. "I can hold my own."

He winked. "That's my girl."

"We need to finish getting ready for the session," Chetana said pointedly.

Jori flourished a hand. "Point taken. You might start talking politics at any moment." He headed toward the door. "All my best, darling," he cried as it shut behind him.

Candrae returned to fiddle with the ties of Kiria's dress. It felt secure back there. Maybe Candrae just wanted to feel like she had something to do.

"Speaking of politics," her mother said, "have you done your research?"

Kiria fought not to roll her eyes. "Yes, I've done my research." She'd dived into the issues until she could barely see by the candlelight. The past week had been packed with nothing but study punctuated by checking for the scouts Firian had promised to send.

She wouldn't know if she could trust him until all three scouts came back unharmed, with peace terms and news of the Tanyuin Academy's location. She prayed he was as good as his word. If her gut was right, and he was telling the truth, then the war against the Tanyu would be over, and they could potentially end their war with the pirates as well. What a victory that would be—peace on both fronts!

If her calculations were correct, it took about two weeks to travel between Brithnem and the Academy. One more week to wait.

She came back to the present and closed her eyes. A tingling covered her body as she put on her Beauty. When the change completed, her mother gasped softly behind her. No one quite got used to the Ability. Beauty revealed everything Kiria was, but more. She'd seen it over and over again in the glass. Her light brown eyes turned golden, her mousy brown hair rich and full, her skin flawless, her figure immaculate. It was everything she was *meant* to be.

Candrae stopped fussing over the back of her dress.

A satisfied smile curled the edges of Kiria's lips. Despite the dangers of war, of wrong decisions, of future anxiety, she felt ready, eager to begin.

"Is it time?" her mother asked, smiling.

"Let's go."

Guards flanked them as they left for the Main, the enormous meeting room for the three Keepers of Brithnem. Kiria couldn't count how many times she had snuck in there as a child, then sat in on sessions when she was older, but now... now she was a Keeper.

When they arrived, two guards opened the grandly carved double doors. Blood hummed through her veins as she saw a familiar sight, now glowing with possibility. The dais in the center of the room held three thrones: one for Cúron, one for Atty, and the center one for her.

From the ceiling hung the blue and purple flags of Brithnem. Movable walls portioned off part of the room so it didn't look as cavernous as it had during her coronation. A collection of chairs ringed the bottom of the steps, spreading back onto the intricate floor mosaic. Daelon, her tutor, smiled encouragingly at her from the front row.

Her mother and Chetana took their place near him in the front row with the other Amir, nobles, and generals. Kiria climbed the steps to her throne between the other two. Surely this was a dream. Atty, dressed in a fur robe much too warm for the season, pursed his lips in a reassuring smile as she took her seat. Not too long ago, he'd had his first session too.

As soon as Kiria sat, Chetana rose to begin the session with a prayer. She quoted part of the passage from the Sacred Scroll carved along the edge of the ceiling.

With the session open, Kiria spoke. "Keepers, Amir, and dignitaries, I am so pleased to be here today to carry on the long tradition of the Second Keeper." She looked at her mother. "I pray that I can bring honor to the position. I know that I'll do everything in my power to better the Western Kingdom, and to protect it, as I swore at my coronation. I look forward to serving you all the best of my ability."

The small crowd gave polite applause.

"We're sure you will," Cúron replied, smiling at her. "Now onto the matters at hand. Because of the Tanyuin threat to our citizens, I have discussed with our military strategist Petra Madola about allowing people to sleep during the day and work at night, since that is when all the nightmare attacks happen. Our normal economy will be temporarily disrupted, but it is important to keep the people of Brithnem feeling safe."

"There haven't been any attacks since the new Tanyuin Head took over," Kiria pointed out.

"No one has reported an attack," Cúron admitted, "but we assume that he's just getting settled. Firian Kess is young and no doubt took the position by force. Once his crown is secure, he'll turn our way again."

When Kiria turned to Atty, he nodded almost apologetically.

"I don't think he will," she insisted.

"Don't forget what he did, to you, to all of us." Even as Cúron turned dramatically to the little crowd, there was a clear warning in his voice.

How could she forget? *She* was the one taken hostage, not him. She bit back a retort. Diplomacy, even when Cúron was condescending to her, was the best way. He wasn't a bad man, she reminded herself, just ambitious.

"I think it works as a solution for now," Atty said, referring back to the sleeping schedules. He raised an eyebrow at her, a friendly nudge to get her back on track.

"There!" said Cúron. The word was a warm reward to Atty for having said the right thing. Was this how Cúron spoke to Kiria's mother when she was the Keeper? To leave everything to Cúron, the oldest and most experienced leader, must have been tempting, but Kiria had known since she was a child that she wanted to be a different kind of ruler than her mother.

Kiria's brows twitched downward. Dimly, she noticed the attention shift to her. Every gesture she made was magnified with her Beauty.

"So, if no one has anything else to say...?" Cúron let the question hang in the air as he regarded the advisors, the generals, the other Keepers. He ran his hand once over his white beard.

"I have something to say." Kiria's own voice surprised her. She shouldn't be rankled by something so small. But this was her first session. Everyone needed to take her seriously as their leader, not push aside her voice.

"I would like to announce that I have received hopeful news from the new Tanyuin Head that our war may be at an end."

Surprised shuffling. Her mother stared at her with a warning in her eyes. Bold moves, according to her, often led to danger. Maybe that was the reason she never proposed any.

That look made Kiria falter, though she was no less sure of what she wanted to say. Surely her mother had to feel proud of her once she heard the plan.

Cúron turned to her with another admonishing expression. "When did you receive this news?" he demanded.

"The day before my coronation."

"From what source?"

She hesitated, just for a moment. "The Tanyuin Head himself." *I stood here and he stood there.* She glanced at the spot on the dais as though she could still see his shadow.

"And you trust this news?" Cúron began.

"What did he say?" The fact that Atty talked over Cúron proved his surprise.

Kiria turned to Atty. "He said he had our scouts, but that he would send them all back safely with terms to end the Tanyuin War. He also promised to help us in our efforts against the Torithians as well."

Cúron's eyes narrowed.

He was probably thinking that, mere months ago, Firian had double-crossed them. The Academy had ordered him to do it. Now that he was in charge, though, things would be different. Probably. Hopefully.

"What does he want in return?" Cúron asked.

"He doesn't want a vote like the Amir. He just wants Torithian prisoners of war." Anticipating their next question, she added, "The scouts should be here in a week to confirm if he's telling the truth."

"Until then," said Cúron, his voice booming now, to include everyone in the small crowd, "we will refrain from negotiations with Tanyu."

He said it as a parent would to a child. There was something final, non-negotiable, about it. Kiria bit her lip. It would be extraneous to add anything else, wouldn't it?

Gathering her courage, she said, "I hope this will mean the end of both wars for us. If we don't broadcast the alliance, then we'll be able to surprise the Torithians. Though it's unlikely, an alliance with the Tanyu could be the most advantageous move for us right now. A risky one, but if it pays off, well worth it."

Obviously a little irritated that Kiria got the last word, Cúron smiled broadly. She met his gaze. Especially since the death of Atty's father, Cúron was used to being right, to being the one to run these meetings. It was true that he did have more experience, but Kiria planned to contribute just as much as he did.

Parohim, Cúron's advisor, stood, holding a piece of paper. "Next on our—"

With a huge crash, a window exploded into shards. Kiria's arms shook once against the carved armrests as pieces of glass shattered across the floor.

Parohim ducked. She thought she caught the flash of an arrow and her heart turned to ice. But no. Just glass.

Everyone at the foot of the dais twisted to see the many-paned window. Two guards patrolling the door sprinted outside. Others ran protectively toward the Keepers on the dais.

Kiria's spine stiffened with fear. She let out a shaky breath, fighting the urge to touch the wound on her shoulder. No other crash followed, but threat billowed like smoke through the room.

Shouting came through the empty window. Cúron and one of the generals stood. The distortion and height of the glass didn't offer a good view of what was happening, especially now that the dais was surrounded by guards poised to fight. From her seat, Kiria could only look between them.

"What was that?" Atty asked.

Kiria looked at him but couldn't answer.

After a few more seconds, one of the guards returned.

"What happened?" Cúron demanded.

"There's no danger, My Keepers," said the guard, bowing. "We apprehended two protesters throwing rocks at the window. They are being held outside, bound."

Kiria's brow furrowed. She stood to see around the guards, who parted respectfully and stepped halfway down the steps so she could get a clear view. "Protesters? What were they protesting?"

"Please forgive me, My Keepers. They were protesting your ascension to the throne."

Something like guilt threaded through her. She'd heard a passing comment to that effect before she was coronated. Her mother Merian was well-loved by the people. But this disruption took Kiria completely by surprise.

Her mother stood angrily. "Tell them my daughter has my full support." Her tone was strained, as though the anger wasn't directed only at the protesters, but at her daughter too.

"Of course, My... lady." The guard turned his full attention to Kiria. "What shall we do with them, My Keeper?"

All attention shifted to her. She felt herself pale. *This is it.* So soon, she had to make a hard decision on her own.

Why had these protesters snuck onto the palace grounds? Why couldn't they have stayed home? She couldn't let them go. To solidify her reign, she had to show that this threatening behavior wouldn't be tolerated.

It would be easy to execute them. The thought made her still. What a horrible thought! It would be simpler than a just solution, but she wanted justice more than simplicity. The temptation snagged at her consciousness, but, finally, she stood. "Keep them in a cell for two nights. After that, bring them here to me. If they swear allegiance to me as their Keeper and beg forgiveness, I will show them mercy." *Swear allegiance, beg forgiveness...* The solution sounded self-centered. But this wasn't just about her, it was about the Second Line.

She glanced around quickly for affirmation—her mother, Chetana, Daelon, Cúron... To her relief, they all regarded her with a little pride. She looked at Atty last, who seemed like he wanted to clap her on the shoulder in congratulations. She let out a furtive sigh of relief.

"Of course, My Keeper," said the guard. "Right away."

3

FIRIAN

Blood coated Firian's knuckles as he pounded the mattress leaning against a tree. He needed something to beat, some way to release the aggression welling up like oil under his skin. The mattress would do. At least he wouldn't break his hands.

Today, the Unreal wasn't enough.

His family was coming today.

The scouts wouldn't arrive in Brithnem for a few days. Though there was plenty to occupy his time, this visit was the most urgent. Some of the older Masters grated against his authority, but he could deal with them after he confronted the monster lurking in his past. After that, he would rid himself of fear and put them all in their place.

Now, though, memories filled him like a disease. His father storming in, coiled as a wire. The sight of him made Firian taste salt in his mouth and scan the objects in the room so he'd know what he might have to prepare himself to face. The fury in those eyes looking for an outlet for his rage.

His sister Brett always sensed the danger immediately too. She touched Firian's upper arm for him to back up, his little body shadowed behind hers. He stumbled back a step, wincing at the fumbling sound it made.

His mother leaned back, placing one palm on the table as Father approached. She looked empty, fragile, like a doll. Firian's throat constricted until he was fighting to breathe. Mother had no power to fight, either for herself or for them.

Father sneered and violently grabbed her wrist. "Don't act like you're afraid of me, Lithia," he spat, flinging her away. "God, it's no wonder your son is such a coward."

Though Father didn't look at him, Firian tensed at every movement. He burned with shame at how thankful he was to have Brett standing in front of him. Father never hit Brett.

His mother, shaking, didn't respond.

"Did you hear what I said?" Father snarled, bending to stare Mother in the eye. The motion made Mother seem like a little girl. "Or are you stupid?"

Mother dropped her eyes, shuffling her feet, maybe to start doing something else. The whole room began to smell sharp and sour. When Firian was very small, he had thought the smell came from the forge, maybe the coke burning, or the panes of glass before they were cool. He learned better eventually.

"Gore!" Father swore. "Look at me, Lithia! Look at me, you idiotic woman!" He squeezed her chin in his hand so hard it distorted her face.

Something touched Firian's arm. He jumped. Brett again. He pressed her hand lightly enough that Father wouldn't see the movement.

"I have to put up with this after working all day? I don't know why I bother to feed you."

"I'm sorry, Yanon," she whimpered.

He struck her across the face. "You know why? It's because nobody would buy you even if you offered."

"I'm sorry..."

"Oh, are you?" He came at her like a man possessed.

Firian knew this part. He shut his eyes tight, trying not to listen, but every attempt just amplified the sounds. The half-strangled screams ripped through his little body. Every muffled thump bruised him in dark, dark places...

Firian swiped sweat off his forehead with the back of his hand, willing the memory away, but it was like sound. Trying not to notice just pushed it into sharper relief. Growling, he swung and hit, over and over, leaning into the pain, into the anger that fueled him. Anger, not fear. His knuckles ached and stung as they made contact.

The mattress ripped. Straw stuck out of the holes at crazy angles, slicing Firian's hands. He pulled back and grunted with another hard swing. The punch made the mattress wobble and almost fall.

He swung lower, jabbing upward, bobbing up and down on the balls of his feet. A red smear appeared where his fists had touched, as though there had been a murder.

"So that's where it went."

Firian twisted violently around. Bard. He'd stolen the bottom bunk mattress from Bard's room. Only Bard's room, now that he had moved into the bedroom attached to the Head's office. He didn't answer.

"When are they coming?" Bard asked softly.

Firian bit back a curse. Bard always knew. He glanced at the sun, rubbing his hands on his pants. "Now."

Bard turned around, preparing to walk back to the Academy with him. He preserved a wise silence for a moment before asking, "What are you going to do?"

Firian pursed his mouth and ran his sleeve across his face. What a time for Bard to talk to him! They hadn't interacted much at all since Firian had killed Sias Jairon. Maybe even before, when Firian had tracked down some of the Sentries they'd freed together.

He still didn't know what he was going to do with his family. He wanted to make his father pay. It would be the first time Firian saw his father since he'd taken the entrance test when he was eleven. The pit of his stomach tightened again.

Still breathing hard from boxing the mattress, he answered, "I don't know."

"You're not going to...?"

"I don't know."

The breeze blew the shirt-sweat cold.

"You got what you wanted," Bard said. "There's no need to hurt them."

Firian lifted his chin. He'd played versions of this meeting in his head for years, but now that the moment had come, he wasn't sure what he would do.

"Fir?"

He gave Bard a pointed look. He would decide when his family stood in front of him. Should he invite them into his office? It wasn't very grand. That was just Firian's style, but at this moment, he wished it were covered in tapestries and heraldry and trophies from the defeated. At least he would wear his crown. He had brought it with him, tied to one of the straps of his black coat. Reaching back, he unknotted it. The hard metal felt cold against his forehead. Who was worthless now?

"You don't want regrets, yeah? Firian, I'm serious."

"I know you are. You're always serious." Releasing his thoughts even that much started to relax his tense muscles as well. He resettled the crown into a more comfortable position. Maybe he shouldn't hurt him, but only threaten...

Maybe they were already here.

His throat started to close. *Damn it, you're the Tanyuin Head! They'll do anything you say.*

Bard looked up at him solemnly, black hair wild. "I'll be just outside."

Firian started to protest, but stopped. If Bard were outside, he might find the self-control not to order his father's death. Brett and his mother would probably be horrified if he killed his father, even though the scut deserved it. They didn't need to see that side of him.

A warm droplet leaked down his finger, pooled on his fingertip, and dropped into the pine needles.

"Okay."

A black figure strode from the Academy toward them, darker than the fortress's dark walls. As he got closer, his features materialized into Ryker, a Learner, about fourteen. More white than usual ringed his brown eyes as he approached Firian. He softened toward the boy. "Master Kess," he said, "your visitors have arrived. They're just outside your office."

Even though he'd been expecting the message, his insides leapt. He nodded, his face uncomfortably hot. "Tell them I'm coming."

"As you would have it, Master Kess."

Ryker ran back to the Academy to deliver the message, and the two of them hiked back at a greater speed. Firian fought the urge to run the rest of the way.

Within minutes they had breached the enormous wooden doors and swept through the fountain courtyard with its chandelier. Learners made way for them.

Firian's pulse beat in his throat as they turned down the hallway to the Head's office. His office.

And there they were. Belik and the door guard flanked the three of them, who all looked soft by comparison. His father's brown hair had grown peppery gray, his thin frame more like human gristle than muscle. His arms were so narrow. Those eyes, those accusing eyes, were exactly the same. They widened only a fraction to see Firian, grown and strong and crowned, coming toward them.

He remembered his mother from the trip to Raewhith with Kiria. Now, though still washed out, she was dressed in her best. The faded yellow dress hung limply on her body.

And then there was Brett. Her baby hadn't come with her. He had almost forgotten his sister was coming. Despite all the anticipation for his father's arrival, she was the one who caught and held his eye. She stood sturdy and vibrant compared to the others. The long, glossy hair he remembered was tied back in a braid. Her lined eyes regarded him with an unreadable expression. She could have been proud or wary or glad or condemning. He tried to find the words there that he'd tacked to his bedpost and then fastened to the Sacred Scroll. *Now you'll be a warrior—a Tanyu—one of the bravest and smartest people in the world! I love you. I won't forget you.* The memory of them made him swell with pride. Brett had believed in him when no one else did. And now he was the Tanyuin Head. He lifted his mouth in a half smile for her.

Though her ambiguous expression didn't change, her eyes twinkled back.

Feeling bolstered, he turned to his father. "Come in," he said, his tone turning cold as he passed them to enter his office.

His father shifted. "Firian—"

"Shut up!"

His mother jumped at the ferocity of his comeback. Firian almost did too. He was a dam about to break.

He would deal with the others later. His blood coursed hot as his father's eyes strayed to his knuckles. Remembering the time Father had struck him for coming home from school with bloody knuckles, Firian could barely see through his rage. That had been one day—one day!—before he went to the Academy. The last insult he would suffer from that man. He couldn't begin civilly. Now, he needed retribution, payment for all the years of torture he and his mother had endured at the hands of this monster.

"Come in," he repeated more softly, burning with the pain of holding in the fury he felt.

Without a word, his father followed him inside. Both Belik and Bard stayed outside with the rest of his family. With a wave of his hand, Firian ushered in the new armor-clad guard, who closed the door behind them.

Now practically alone, he stepped heavily toward his father. They were the same height now. Snarling, he stopped less than a hand's-span from his face. All of his practiced speeches disappeared. What were words anyway? They couldn't make up for what was done, all the sleepless nights, the noises he heard from his mother in the quiet, his life-long fear that his father might have been right about him...

He paused just long enough for his father's stare to flash up to the open iron square on his forehead. "Get on your knees," he whispered.

"Firi—"

"On your knees!" Firian roared, stepping back. His chest rose and fell as though he had run for hours. He ground his teeth, staring down the man who had made his entire family feel like nothing.

Steadying himself, he took a deep breath. "I am the Head of the Tanyuin Academy. If I tell my people to kill you, they will. Without hesitation. So get on your knees."

Hatred radiated from his father as he lowered himself down slowly, tentatively.

Kneeling before him, he looked so small, and Firian hated him more for it. "Now beg my forgiveness."

"I didn't do anything to you."

Heat burst into Firian's skull and he pulled his hand back only after he realized what he had done. Father's temple was dark red, and a welt beaded up where Firian's Master ring had struck him.

He blinked in horror. What had he done? For an irrational moment, he thought his father would retaliate, grow large as he was in his dreams, and beat him.

As Firian had just done to him.

Fresh disgust, this time at himself, flowed through his thoughts. He was a warrior getting justice, someone who'd learned violence as a force for power and respect and doing good. But for a sickening moment, he felt like he was looking in a glass at a distorted image of himself.

I didn't do anything to you.

He refused to explain all the times his father had called him worthless, had beaten him and his mother, had talked down to him, had not believed in him. He would not itemize his pain. But he would have his revenge.

Collecting himself again, he remembered his purpose. "Beg."

Silence from the head bent downward.

"Beg or I'll kill you." It was still probably true.

His father cleared his throat. "For whatever you think I did..."

"Start over," he growled.

"I'm sorry." The words wrung out of him, grating, quiet, forced.

Firian waited.

"I'm sorry for... hurting you in some way." Even from this angle, his jaw clearly worked with agitation.

Firian cut a grim look at the guard and nodded once. The guard struck his father on the back of the head. The blow made him lean forward and catch himself on his hands.

Firian's blood beat at the sight. *Yes, beg.*

"I'm sorry." Now his voice had more of the right tone. Maybe he thought he was begging for his life. He was. "I'm sorry."

The picture became disgusting. Repulsed, Firian kicked him lightly on the wrist. "Get up."

His father did, coming back into himself like a second skin. Here he was again, the demon from his past, his hate-filled eyes rimmed unhealthily with red. His sallow cheeks paled like a fever victim's.

Firian nodded again to the guard, who opened the door. Firian's mother stood with her hands to her mouth. Brett glared through the opening, her forehead a mass of tight wrinkles. They must have heard the whole thing. Good. Now they knew this monster could be beaten.

His father didn't spare them a glance, but his skin flushed pink with the knowledge that they were being watched.

"You can't hurt me now," Firian said, "but if I hear that you've hurt *them*, I'll harm you in ways you've never heard of. I'll torture your dreams, I'll send Tanyu to fetch your fingers one by one..." He stopped because he was shaking.

Though his father didn't quail, Firian noticed that he barely breathed as he stared back at his son. Firian would make good on every threat. He felt the complicated looks of all four watchers as he glared at his father: Brett, his mother, Master Belik, Bard.

He willed himself back to calm. His hands stilled. "Get out."

When his father turned around, Firian knew that was the last time he'd ever see him. And he was glad.

The guard widened the door for him.

As his father stalked out, his mother's eyes rounded, huge as a doe's. Fear, not relief or thanks, radiated from her.

A wave of grief, surprising in its strength, assaulted him at the sight of her. As a child, he'd reserved some of his anger for her because she hadn't stood up for him all those nights when his father came home and struck him and called him a scut and screamed that he never should have been born. But she was a victim too, even more than he was. How had he never seen it? Trapped in that cruel marriage, it was all she could do to be kind to them. She had never been strong enough to protect them. Firian's eyes felt hot.

He turned to Brett. She stared back, disbelieving, her eyes full of angry shock. The total effect made her look almost like a Tanyu. Despite the accusation in her expression, the sight made him a little proud of her.

"Bring them in." He wanted to be able to talk to them, reassure them, without Belik and Bard overhearing. The women came in and stood where his father had. When the door closed again, he met Brett's glare. "He deserved worse."

"Firian," Brett began, her blue eyes mirroring his own. A dozen questions died on her lips. "Firian, how could you?" They must have overheard through the door.

"You can stay here if you think he'll hurt you."

"We can't stay here." She took a tentative step forward. "We can't live at the Academy. I have a family."

"Bring them."

She took a small, exasperated breath. "We can't." Her eyes softened, a version of the look he'd been waiting for from her. "I was excited to see you. When we got the letter, it felt like the first one, but this time *you* wrote it." She looked down in a sort of disbelief before continuing. "I knew you could do it. Even when kids made fun of you and you weren't sure, I knew you could do this." Her voice was soft and earnest, dropping now to a whisper. "But you don't want to become like him."

His insides curled as she reflected his own thoughts back to him. "I'm not like him."

"You have power now, Firian. If you hurt people with it, you shouldn't have it." She shook her head.

He forced his twitching fingers not to reach for the crown to readjust it again. "I didn't hurt him. And even if I'd killed him, he would have deserved worse. You grew up with him. You know the kind of man he is! He's scum, trash."

Brett lowered her voice even further. "Firian, he'll hurt Mother."

"He already does!" Anger flushed him. Why was she questioning him? Somebody finally put Father in his place, on his knees, begging forgiveness, where he belonged until his miserable life ended.

"No. We're going back."

"No, you aren't."

"Sabir is there." The baby.

"Bring him too. Live in Tánuil. And if he comes back—"

"Listen to yourself. You can't make everything better by controlling it. I can protect myself. Gaius can protect me." The words made a soothing chant, as though she were putting a child to sleep.

Suddenly Firian was eleven again. "I'll protect you," he said, a low whisper through barely parted teeth. The purity of the words filled his body with light. There was something whole about it. Maybe this is why he had become the Head in the first place.

A tight smile passed over Brett's features. "I know you want to."

The idea struck him suddenly. "I'll protect Raewhith." He turned his attention to Belik and Bard in turn. All of them would approve. "It needs us. There's no city wall."

She didn't protest.

"Brett." Here was something she couldn't argue against. He took her hand gently in his, and something inside him twisted with emotion. "I promise I'll look after you and mother. My Tanyu will guard the city and check up on you. I meant all those things I said, so I'll figure it out."

She pursed her lips as she listened. "Okay," she said, his sister again.

He dropped her hand, smiling grimly. "Okay."

4

KIRIA

"I can't believe you were communicating with that Tanyu!" Kiria's mother muttered, setting down her coffee. The cup rattled in the dish. "It was entirely unsafe." Light from the ceiling-high windows of her bedroom crowned her.

"But look what we got from it," Kiria replied. Technically she'd gotten very little yet from talking with Firian, but she had a decent idea of the Academy's location as well as his promise to end the wars.

Her mother shook her head, flinging the unpleasant thoughts away like water droplets.

The palace had buzzed with the news of Kiria's first session, both the ill-planned attack and her announcement about an alliance. Sessions in the Main were usually guarded secrets, but people weren't guarding their words as closely as they should. At least if quick silences and pointed glances were any indication.

Taking another drink of lukewarm coffee, Kiria eyed her mother. She had something on her mind, though Kiria couldn't figure out what it was. An eager, abstracted look kept flitting across her mother's face. It made a stark contrast to her usual demeanor of resigned grace.

"Now that you are the Keeper," her mother began, as though she'd practiced.

Kiria took a protective sip.

"You need to think about marrying."

Fighting not to cough, Kiria swallowed. "Now?" she asked. She was still eighteen. In all the excitement of the past year, she'd barely given marriage a passing thought. For a second, she envied Kader, Cúron's son, who was too young to be pestered about such things.

"As soon as possible. It's the best way to secure the Second Line." Her mother folded her hands in her lap. "Is there anyone you have an eye on?"

The way she asked the question suggested she wanted to be in on the secret to make up for Kiria's excluding her before.

A brief image of sitting with Firian on the night-dark wooden walkways of Shifra came back to her. He had leaned in, brushed back her hair, breathed against her mouth... She shook off the unwanted memory as a servant approached to refresh her coffee with some newly boiled. Firian had betrayed her almost immediately afterward. It didn't matter that they'd shared a moment, had almost kissed. "No," she replied.

Her mother's face fell a little. "Well, there are plenty of men interested in getting to know you. You should invite some of them here, or even host a party to meet them."

"I'm sure there are." Kiria wasn't using her Beauty now, but she knew how alluring it was.

"You don't have to decide today or this week," her mother said, "but it would help the Kingdom accept you as their leader if you showed a dedication to continue the family line."

Would it, though? Would marriage prevent unrest like they saw at the session? It seemed unlikely. A small part of her was insulted that her mother would play on her weaknesses like that. But maybe she was right. Marriage was a good idea. Before, Kiria was too young to consider it seriously, and then she was swept up in the danger of assassination when Firian had to be called in as a bodyguard.

Kiria tipped her mouth. Her mother never meant to hurt her. They were each other's only family left. Kiria couldn't let small things come between them.

"I'll think about it," she promised.

Her mother's smile turned mischievous. "I have a couple young men in mind that you might like."

Curious, Kiria struggled to think of who they might be. "Who?"

"Don't look at me like that, Kiria," her mother said lightly. "I know you've never been very interested in the guards or ambassadors' sons." Her face fell just long enough that Kiria could tell she was remembering her own husband, a general. The pause lasted long enough for memories to clog their throats before passing away again. "In fact," she continued, "part of me is glad. A Beauty like yours can be dangerous if used the wrong way."

Kiria nodded, waiting for the names of her mother's suggested young men.

"Have you met General Madola's son Warrick?"

She struggled to remember. The vague image of a tall, thin boy flitted across her memory. "Once, I think."

"What about him?"

She considered. "I'd have to meet him again." She accidentally allowed a slight grimace on her face as she spoke.

"Or what about Tierney Oscal?"

"I'd rather marry Jori!" Every time Kiria saw Tierney, he ogled her openly and she'd caught him more than once making bawdy comments to his friends.

"Don't joke," her mother said, frowning. "He comes from a noble family that has donated generously to help Brithnem through the years."

"I know who he is," Kiria said pointedly. "Have you met him? Aren't Keepers supposed to stay pure until marriage? Stay true just to one person?"

Her mother blushed. "Yes! Is he...? If he's like that, then of course I wouldn't recommend him. But his family..."

"Not everyone is like their family." A meaningful hush fell between them, and Kiria took a final swig of coffee.

A knock at the door interrupted her thoughts. A guard stepped inside. "Pardon me, my lady," he said, addressing her mother before turning to Kiria. "My Keeper, the scouts have arrived."

The cup clattered in the saucer as Kiria stood. "Where are they?" She could feel her mother's gaze on her, scrutinizing her enthusiasm, but she didn't care.

"They're meeting with Keeper Cúron and one of the military strategists now."

"Take me there." *How is Cúron always the first to know?* She turned to her mother, who still sat. "I need to go."

"Yes," her mother replied, arching her eyebrows. But then she softened. "You're right. You should go. I hope we all hear good news."

With a nod, Kiria swept out the door, donning her Beauty as she went. The scouts were convening in the dining room, which sometimes doubled as a small meeting chamber. She arrived in a rush.

Three scouts, still dirty from travel, sat at the table. Two men and one woman. Cúron and Petra Madola sat opposite them. The scouts stopped talking when they saw Kiria, hastening to their feet.

"Ah, I'm glad you could join us!" Cúron exclaimed. He didn't stand.

A guard emerged from his post by the door to pull out a seat for her. She sat and regarded the scouts who appeared weary but unhurt. The woman pushed a shock of white-blonde hair out of her face, revealing one empty-looking eye. Kiria inspected them for bruises, cuts, anything that would indicate that Firian was less than his word. A tinge of fear colored the smaller man's face, but she was used to that look. It faded with time and exposure to her Beauty. A bearded man sat on the other side of the woman, his positively cheerful demeanor a marked contrast to the others.

Kiria addressed him. "Did you reach the Academy?"

"We did, My Keeper." He reached into his travel-stained coat and pulled out a map, which he laid on the table. He jabbed a calloused finger at the forest just north of Raewhith, where Kiria had gone with Firian when they had been attacked.

Her stomach warmed and the corners of her mouth lifted. Just as she thought.

"We'll have it added to all the official maps," Cúron said, as the man kept jabbing with his finger.

Petra waved to see the paper more closely, and the bearded scout passed it to her.

"Did you see the new Tanyuin Head?" Kiria asked. She didn't glance at Cúron, but knew that he'd have a reaction to her question. Firian's conduct toward the scouts would either support or weaken her announcement of an alliance. Despite everything, she had acted like she trusted him.

For a second, she wondered where Atty was. Had he gotten the same message she had?

"We did," the Khelê woman replied. Her words came out measured and slow, almost like a question.

"What did he say?" Kiria was getting impatient. She didn't want to ask any leading questions, but rather to hear their version of events first, the true version.

"He wants to end the Tanyuin War," said the bearded one with a smile.

Kiria realized how heavily her heart had been beating. Heat flushed her cheeks.

"He said," the woman added, as though to clarify.

"He wrote out terms." The thin man nodded, and another paper appeared from the bearded man's jacket.

Kiria took it before the others, feeling almost greedy. The terms. What had Firian said? He wanted to end their war and help with their conflict against the Torithians, as long as he could keep the prisoners of war. That was it, right?

Her mind whirled. She tried to focus on the paper. It lacked the niceties that usually came with diplomatic documents, but cut straight to the point. As she read, she could practically hear Firian's voice. There were no extra demands. All was exactly as he had promised. It looked as though, for now, it really was a new age for the Tanyu.

She fought to control her excitement. Her mother and the rest of Brithnem would have to respect her decision now. The gambit had paid off. One war was over, and she could engineer the end of the second with Firian's help.

She wanted to laugh. She wanted to see Firian, but she couldn't get ahead of herself. Instead, she beamed a huge smile and handed the paper deliberately to Cúron.

5

FIRIAN

FIRIAN LOOKED himself in the eye, and another, and another. His mind strained to keep all the copies of himself intact in the blank mindfield. It felt like a good stretch or a fall when adrenaline cushions most of the pain.

That copy didn't act naturally. Its chest caved in and its knees bent slightly to the side. *Stand up.* Slowly, the version of him straightened, the broad shoulders brought to attention. Firian looked from face to face. Light skin grazed by the sun, dark eyebrows, dark brown hair just longer than his ears...

He tried to create a sixth. The whole construction wobbled. *Five for now. Not too bad.* Later, he would make them move separately. He had heard of Tanyu employing a decoy in a fight, but never more than one. Dizziness swirled around him as he animated the five Firians.

Gasping, he swam back to the Real. Cool air from his office drifted across his sweat-sheened face. He drummed his fingers once over the armrest of the chair.

The door opened with a tentative stutter that could only mean Bard was coming. He'd walked in on Firian before in compromising positions. "Fir, hey," he said, his hesitancy falling away as he saw Firian was alone. "You okay?"

"Just practicing."

"You're always practicing." His friend scratched his spiky black hair. Something else was on his mind.

Firian leaned back. "Is something wrong?"

"No." The word trailed off into a forest of unsaid things. "I was just thinking. About the war on Torith. You know, the one we're joining now, for Brithnem." He looked up from the floor into Firian's eyes. "I want to help, any way I can."

One side of Firian's mouth lifted. Bard sounded so earnest. "How?"

"So I've practiced *katah* for years now and I've never used those skills. People usually tell generals to watch out for a female presence"—his ears turned red—

"and I'm not. I don't... I wouldn't do everything, of course. But that's not what Master Gerand taught me. She knows I'd be terrible."

Firian burst out laughing. "You want to seduce a general?" Calling *katah* on someone usually included seduction to speed up the victim's belief in the Unreal, making them easier to kill.

"No! No, obviously. Fir, I'm serious. Do you think I could? I've practiced on you more than anybody." He writhed a little as his explanation didn't take the smile from Firian's face. "No!" he repeated. "That's not... Okay." He pulled up a chair and sat across from him. His eyes caught the green and brown flag Firian had taken from Raewhith when he went to visit Brett and see the new recruits there. He felt it between his fingers. "You're in charge now," he said thoughtfully. The statement set distance between them, but distance Bard was willing to breach. At least there was a glimmer of hope they could remain friends after all that had happened.

When Firian had murdered the Head, he felt as though he'd fallen into a place so dark that Bard wouldn't be able to see him. He didn't regret killing him, but he didn't want everything else in his life to die too.

Bard fanned out his fingers on the desk. "So I want to help you end the war."

Firian nodded. "Your family."

"Yeah, they're in Enderin and Jac's on the front line. I think. Haven't gone home in a while." He scratched his head again. "I'm pretty sure they hate me."

Firian scrunched his forehead skeptically. Bard's family couldn't hate him.

"They do," Bard protested. "Or I think... sometimes... they would just because of what I am." He didn't say the word. Tanyu.

Bard's presence at the Academy had always baffled Firian a bit. Not everyone there had extraordinary ability, but Bard's skill set didn't seem to match the Tanyu at all.

"The Academy isn't at war with the Kingdom anymore." *Or its allies.*

"I know. It's just..." Bard looked down at his feet. The faint smell of cinnamon wafted off his clothes. With a deep breath, he drew his splayed hands into fists on the tabletop. "I want to do some good. I want to help you make the Academy great."

You want to make up for what I did to the last Tanyuin Head.

Using a *katah* to gain information was actually a good idea, though. Bard wouldn't attract as much suspicion as a woman or Firian himself. There wasn't enough time to set up a full *katah*, a full death sentence, but Bard could still get somewhere with the general.

"I'll get you the name," Firian said.

Something hard eased in his chest when Bard smiled. "That's great!" Bard jumped up from his seat. "Oh, okay, I can do this. I'll get the information about the Torithian general or strategist or whoever you give me, and then you can finish it." He flashed another grin, black eyes sparkling. "Wanna get an ale?"

Everything was like before. *Well, not everything.* But Firian had to admit he missed this easiness. These days, Jovan stiffened at his authority, Belik spoke only of strategy, Tiev was broken from his time Lost in the Unreal and rarely spoke to anyone.

Firian nodded. "I'll meet you there. First, I'll get the name."

"All right," Bard agreed, darting out of the room.

He closed his eyes again. *Kiria, Kiria...* She beat against the inside of his eyelids and he sent his mind toward that energy.

Closer now, he heard music. The melody wasn't as sad as the one he had heard her play before—still like silver, but now living instead of mourning. He waited until the last note sounded. "Kiria," he said gently. As Head, he could finally afford to be patient.

Her image grew sharper, but not more beautiful. Still, he liked her like this— her little heart-shaped face turned to him. It felt natural. She was standing in a room of the palace Firian had never seen before. About the same size as her bedroom, this one was full of musical instruments.

When she saw him, gladness, like light, shone on her features, though she didn't smile. She adjusted her long russet skirt, an unnecessary gesture in the Unreal. "Firian. I was going to contact you. The scouts arrived today. They seem safe and they had your terms." She tripped almost playfully over the last few words.

"As I said."

"You said a lot of things." A note of caution shone now in her light brown eyes, like a lens carefully placed there.

His eyes wandered to the silver tiara she wore. "I did." He realized he was tapping his thumb against his leg, and stopped. "I also said I wanted to end the war. Both wars. So you agree to the terms?"

"Yes. We read them and all three of us agreed they were reasonable." She drew herself up. "We are willing to make a conditional alliance."

He frowned. "Conditional?"

"Assuming you follow through on your end of the terms."

"Ah. That's actually what I came to talk about. About Torith." He tripped over the last words, but rallied when Kiria didn't seem to care.

Instead, she stood, coquettishly waiting at attention, eyebrows raised.

"I need the names of the top men on the Torithian side. I have somebody ready to gather better information for you."

She tensed. The royal tattoo peeked black over her shoulder. The idea excited her too. His stomach tightened a little. "Who?" she asked.

Information for information. "Bard."

"Your friend?" The name was like a spell to cast them back to how they used to be—the best time, between the attack and the Academy's ultimatum that involved taking her hostage. Bard was a safe subject, an intimate subject.

Firian smiled. "Yeah. He practices *katah*." He hoped she recognized the trust he had in her to share that much.

"*Katah*?"

Firian considered how much to tell her. "Bard will be able to... read his mind, sort of." That wasn't right, but it was the explanation that would probably make the most sense for now.

She dropped a bit of her royal bearing. "You're serious? He'll relay information to you and—"

"I'll tell you everything."

She gave him a searching look that reminded him of that moment outside Carradoc when they had almost kissed.

"You can't betray us," she said. "We have the exact location of the Academy." She lifted her chin as she said it.

He took a step toward her. He could almost smell the citrusy musk of her hair. "Are you threatening me?" he teased.

"Yes," she replied.

A strand of her hair fell loose across her collarbone. He could sweep it back behind her ear, a move he knew would quicken her pulse.

He smiled again, gazing down at her. "You'll see I'm telling the truth. So"—he lowered his voice to a whisper—"those names."

Little goosebumps rose on the skin of her bare arms. He skimmed his gaze over them, just to show he noticed.

She backed up, raised her chin again. Her eyes grazed him up and down before answering. "Tibor Wat," she said, pronouncing the name clearly. "He's more of a captain than a general. You know, pirates."

"Perfect." He drew out the two syllables. Her lovely face held so much potential. In her eyes he saw all that he could be—not only the Head of the Academy but the lover of a queen. "I'll come back with information."

As though she were coming out of a trance, her shoulders relaxed and her attention refocused. Her lips lifted in a small smile.

Suddenly his demeanor felt like a mask, the one he wore when he was flirting with somebody else. That honest smile seemed to pierce its armor and give her the high ground. It made her more of a friend than a target—a co-conspirator.

He caught his breath and the vulnerability washing over him passed. When she didn't speak, he said, "Look for me soon. Get your soldiers ready." He nodded once and opened his eyes.

Silently, he prayed Bard could make good on his offer. They'd see to it, he assured himself. Bard never lied.

He shivered pleasurably and grabbed his long black coat. The guard at the door nodded at him as he passed. Everything was fine.

His encounter with Kiria hadn't lasted any longer than five minutes but he didn't see Bard. Must already be outside. With long strides, he hurried into the fountain courtyard. Learners made way; Masters had mixed reactions. Though no one openly defied him, he caught the edge of several dark glances. He would deal with those later. Feeling lighter than he had in a while, he swept out the massive double doors into the cool spring air.

Helping Kiria would set the world right again. Everything from the sky to the sizzling energy under his skin all felt different since he assassinated the previous Head. But all these shops and faces and roads hadn't felt the world shift as he had. They all looked the same, but as though he were peering through a window that distorted certain details and minimized others.

The Old Pub hadn't changed either. Wind moved its hanging sign with the wrong proprietor's name on it. Would Hyrum ever change that?

Firian creaked open the door, his hand brushing against the groove in the wood worn by thousands of visitors. Raucous talk and the smell of ale swept over him as he entered. Dozens of patrons squeezed into the space, almost everyone sporting gaudy colors. Normally, citizens of Tánuil wore gray or brown, easy colors to make and maintain, but here everyone had bright red scarves or green hats or yellow streaks of paint on their faces. The planting festival. He'd forgotten that was today.

More than one person turned when Firian entered. Tanyu rarely participated in parties like this even though many Masters technically lived in town. The Academy stayed insulated. Still, one or two others in black stood out like blotches on a colorful canvas. Rian was the only one Firian recognized. Not surprising. He was going with Maya now, so she was probably nearby. The idea should have aroused more jealousy than the tiny twist of his stomach, but it was curbed by the possibility that he could soon be with Kiria. Kiria outshone Maya in every way except availability.

Bard waved to catch his attention. Firian held up a hand at him before ordering at the counter. A man in garish red face paint made way for him, colliding into a pale woman with fuzzy-edged tattoos wiping down tables. The smudgy quality of her hair and the listless awareness of her gaze announced she was a former Sentry.

Firian flicked one token onto the counter and Hyrum shoved an ale over to him.

Before going to sit, Firian spun back. Bard wouldn't say that Firian owed him anything for helping with the war. Still, why not? "Another," he said, holding up payment. Raewhith's tribute coins were fresh in his pocket. "And a sticky bun."

Hyrum's glare darkened. "Old Danior's got those. None here."

"Just the extra ale, then." Hyrum obliged and Firian brought both mugs to Bard, who beamed at the sight.

"Thanks, Fir!" he said, taking the brimming flagon. His nose stopped just above the foam as he smelled it. "I forgot all about the planting festival."

Firian slid into the seat opposite, facing the rest of the room. "Me too."

"Why don't you bring the guard with you when you go out now?" Bard's black eyes flitted to the iron crown.

Honestly, it hadn't occurred to him. He'd always taken care of himself. He shrugged off the question just as he used to.

"Maybe you should," Bard continued. "You're... more important now." A shadow fell across his face, almost his whole body, as he said the words.

Firian tipped his chin. It wasn't a terrible idea, but losing his autonomy sounded stifling. Autonomy was one of the reasons he became the Head in the first place. But power had its cost. He couldn't forget what he had done to get here, and that others could do the same. "Maybe," he conceded.

"Did you get the name?"

"Yes, I did." He leaned back luxuriously and took a deep draught while Bard waited.

Bard gestured with his ale, barely moving away from his face as though anxious to keep it close. "There was no need to do this."

"It's fine."

"So, did you ask the Keeper?"

"Right. Who else?"

"So? Who is it?"

"His name is Tibor Wat." He pronounced the odd name carefully.

Bard smacked his lips meditatively, casting his eyes to the ceiling.

Firian felt eyes on him and looked up to see Devanie, the herbalist, her hair done up in braids around her head. She touched her yellow scarf suggestively as she eyed him. He raised an eyebrow. Tánuil's planting festival went until sunrise the next morning, with dancing and coupling and feasting and general abandon. Later, maybe.

He turned his attention back to Bard, who said, after a pause, "I'll start right away. Tonight I'll find him." He gave a quick succession of nods as though agreeing with himself.

Firian grinned, something he'd done a lot lately. "That's great. Let me know." An odd sensation gripped him that here was something easy and good. Two people walking in the same direction.

"I will." Bard brought his voice down. "Do you know *katah*?"

Kiria and their accidental connection didn't count. Most Tanyu saw an unintentional *katah* as weakness. "I never took Gerand's class."

"I know, but can you do it?"

Could he connect to another person so completely that their lives intertwined, that he gained the ability to kill the other or be killed because of all the reality between them? Could he practically read the other's mind and emotions? "Maybe," he answered.

"I bet you could." When Bard sipped again, a little foam got on his lip, sticking to the shadow of facial hair covering his jaw.

"Probably. I'm sure if I tried." The gravity of his order struck him. "Find out if the general has more Talent than they normally do. Be careful."

"I'll just get information. No worries, yeah?" Bard hated war. If his ability to beat Firian at Indisfate was any indication, he could handle strategy or tactics, but he wouldn't kill.

"Okay, good."

"When are the soldiers from Raewhith coming?"

"Three days."

"And then Torith?"

"I'll organize with Kiria. A few weeks, probably." Firian downed the rest of his ale.

"A few weeks," Bard repeated. "Okay. I'll get it done." He reached out, grasping his hand in a promise.

Firian's mouth quirked. This was just what he needed. His best friend was on his side again.

6

FIRIAN

THE NEXT DAY wore away as swiftly as fire burnt paper. Two more days until the volunteer troops from Raewhith arrived and he had to plan the Torithian attack in earnest.

Belik stood before Firian in the Head's office, rubbing one hand over his rough chin. "Bard is going to declare *katah* on the Torithian captain?" He asked the question in a slow, thoughtful way. Digesting, perhaps criticizing. His eyes, narrowed behind his glasses, offered little clue.

"He has the skill to do it," Firian said.

"I know he does."

Firian sat back in his chair. He could still smell Devanie's musky perfume on himself. In the new daylight, the smell bothered him, as though he had done something wrong. But that couldn't be. At least Devanie wouldn't say so.

Belik, despite his bad leg, continued to stand. The old feeling that the Master held power over him because of his secrets, his decades of knowledge, crawled over him. It was time to take some of that power back. "You used to be the lead strategist," he said. It wasn't a question. Belik had dropped enough hints about his past that it was almost certainly true.

Belik didn't deny it, but shifted, waiting for the point.

"I'm going to reinstate you to that position. I need to know what you know." As much as he hated to admit it, Belik had far more experience than he did, and he needed support if this new mission was going to succeed. It had to succeed.

Apparently unsurprised, Belik eased himself into the chair across from Firian. The movement meant agreement. "What do you want to know?"

"How many fighters can we spare for the Torithian War? How many Tanyu do we have, including those on mission?"

Belik raised his eyebrows. "You think I know about everyone on mission?"

"Don't you?" It was a challenge. A man like Belik wouldn't abandon his job of knowing everything, only the title.

Belik pursed his lips with amusement. "Yes. We have about three hundred battle-ready Tanyu here, if you send them all."

"And abroad?"

"Almost two thousand."

Firian leaned forward, his brows lowering. "*Two thousand?*" That wasn't possible. Memories of Belik's lies came back to him like poison and Firian's hand became a fist on the table. The small white scars stood out in relief. "Don't lie to me."

"I wouldn't," Belik replied easily. "The others are on mission or embedded strategically across the Western Kingdom and beyond it. Remember the man in Carradoc?"

The one who had told him to keep Kiria hostage. Yes, he remembered. "Where are these people?"

"Everywhere. Tanyu have infiltrated even closed societies in case we need someone on the inside. The movement started just before my time."

"So they're all older."

"Most of them."

He thought of how young the Tanyu in the Academy tended to be, apart from the teaching Masters. Had all the rest gone on missions? "Do we have someone with the Torithians?" Since the group was more of a pirate organization than a race or country, it was unlikely.

"Yes, there's one man."

Firian's face flushed hot. "Who? Why didn't you tell me before?"

"You were so smitten with that Kepress and so angry at me that I thought it better to keep it to myself. What good could that information have done you?"

"You don't get to decide—"

"*Now* I don't. Now you're the Tanyuin Head. And never forget who helped you get there. I'm on your side, Firian." Belik held his gaze long enough that Firian felt seen, man to man. The recognition made his stomach crawl—did he want others to see him this intimately?—but he saw Belik's humanity too. Another person sat before him, not an obstacle or a book of answers.

Firian's fist relaxed.

Belik resettled his glasses on his nose, a soothingly familiar gesture.

"So, how many can we spare?" Firian asked.

"I wouldn't send more than half. You announced our location to Brithnem, so they have every opportunity now to attack the Academy if they want to."

With Kiria on his side, he hadn't given the idea a spare thought. Other cities or nations might come to test their strength or steal their stores of tribute, but not Brithnem. "I told you I ended the war."

Belik's voice was carefully steady. "Still, you need a standing army here, as you said before."

To the Tanyuin Head. Those were some of Firian's last words to Sias Jairon before smothering him in his bed.

"Half," Firian repeated. "I'm not going to pull everyone from their stations around the world for this. They need to stay in case I need them. So I only have a hundred and fifty? That's not many."

"Not for an ordinary army." One side of Belik's mouth rose in a smile. "But these are Tanyu. You know what we can do. A soldier is a rainstorm. We are hurricanes."

7

KIRIA

Kiria stared at the map, at the pieces on it, and tried to remember every detail, to make everything as realistic as possible. The edge had been folded accidentally when Daelon carried it from the room in the Amiran Academy into the palace. She added a triangular crease. The trees of Á Quihilmar were a tiny bit smudged from the oil in people's fingertips. A couple of the colored pieces representing troops had spider fractures through the wood. She smiled. Even the arena hadn't been this precise. She didn't need to go to the Tanyuin Academy to practice her Talent in the Unreal. She could smell, just faintly, the wooden table on which the map lay.

That's it. That's as close as I can make it. So far.

She traced the route her coronation tour would take through the Kingdom when this conflict was over. As it was, she couldn't afford the luxury. Now was the time for planning and for war.

Firian's dark form, wearing black as ever, materialized beside her. Right on time. Had he meant to appear so close to her? She stepped sideways to make room for him to admire her work.

It still felt odd offering him information, but he had kept his word. The scouts had all returned safely, and there was a new marking on the map for the Tanyuin Academy. If he was willing to risk the location to a former enemy to prove his loyalty, and then offer help in the Torithian War, who was she to doubt him? After a little more convincing, even her mother reluctantly agreed that this was the best way to end the war and bring peace to the Western Kingdom. Kiria longed to be able to say that they had achieved peace, and that she had helped orchestrate it.

Politically, she would work with the Tanyu. Personally, she would stay wary around Firian.

He cast a quick look at her and then gazed at the map. His dark brows shadowed his sharp eyes as he ran them over the cities, rivers, ocean, troops. He briefly scrutinized her work before turning to her, his closed lips pursed in a smile. "This is good work."

"Since we need to talk about precise strategy, I knew it had to be correct," she said, not sure how else to take the compliment.

"No, I mean, you've been practicing, haven't you?" His head fell a little to one side as he looked at her, a cross between an amused puppy and a man conducting an experiment.

"Well, of course," she said, squaring herself toward the map. "I mean, you know it's better to hone your abilities if you have them..." He had said something very much to that effect when they were alone in the wilderness.

He hummed, obviously pleased. Turning to the map as well, he somehow had closed the distance between them again. Their arms nearly touched.

She reached hers out of range as she pointed to the Tanyuin Academy on the map, beyond the northern mountain range of Charúnin Thôr. It would take the Tanyu several days at least to reach a sea port. "How many troops do you have to offer?" she asked, all business.

"One hundred seventy."

She whirled on him. "That's it? That's nothing!" She blinked as she realized he might be insulted by her tone. Regardless, one hundred seventy was a measly number. Her gut sank at the thought of it. Endrians disappeared almost daily, soldiers, trade ships... All were in continued jeopardy if they didn't succeed. The two of them knew firsthand how ruthless the Torithians could be. They bore the scars.

Maybe she never should have trusted Firian. That seemed to be a common theme.

"Nothing?" he asked gently, meeting her gaze. "These aren't ordinary soldiers."

She looked over his face, searching for the truth behind the arrogance. Searching for the lie that she could call him out on. She felt her pulse beating as she stared at him—his dark hair falling over his forehead, his blue eyes, his lips, his jaw... She clenched her teeth. "Our soldiers are excellently trained," she snapped. "How are the Tanyu so much better?"

The lines in his face softened. He was sure of his answer. This was his life, his anthem. His eyes glowed as they did when he first appeared in that iron crown. "We see everything. We see the body"—his eyes flickered over her plain form—"but we also see the mind. We see the whole person... and we see the whole world. There are possibilities all around us. Every window is a door. Every object can be a weapon or a shield. We can do more, endure more. We are the ones that can bring justice and peace. That's why so many people still revere the name, our name. And that's why I'm proud to be a Tanyu."

Her shallow breath matched his. That level of intelligent warfare on behalf of justice and peace—the idea swam like liquor, intoxicating her mind.

An uncomfortable clinging sensation left her feeling that she was being dragged toward him. The heat from his body welcomed her.

She planted her feet in the carpet, felt the fibers rise up around her embroidered pointed shoes. "We'll see." She cleared her throat. She had no time for these destructive thoughts. Without fully trusting him, she couldn't entertain foolish ideas. "So you only have one hundred seventy troops." She rolled her fingers together and a new piece appeared between them. She placed it on the tiny Academy with a click. "Your friend Bard will gather information from the captain. I suggest that you set off either from here or here." She pointed to two ports along the western coast, Redshore and Enderin. "Ships can transport you from either location. We'll take care of that. Your job will be to locate the top men on the island and eliminate their leadership. You know, they're basically pirates. All men. Just a group that stays together because they can terrorize resources out of others. Without leadership, they'll continue to pillage, but, if they don't have a strategy, we can stop them one by one if we have to. And you can take those who resist as prisoners of war, per our agreement."

"Where are they on the island?" Firian leaned forward as he studied the map. Torith was a large, misshapen island almost directly west of Brithnem over the Kheltor Ocean.

She drew her nail gently over the southeastern area of the island. "Right there. It's a fortress."

He turned to her. "Bard can get us the interior layout if you need it."

"How long will that take?"

Firian paused. "I'll let you know when he has it. Where are your troops now?"

"We have quite a few stationed in Enderin." She touched the top of one of the wooden pieces. "To—"

"—protect the citizens," he finished.

She nodded, glad he saw the necessity of that. "Right."

"What about the others?"

"We have some ready to move on the western side of the island. The residents have been gracious enough to let us move into their villages. They don't want the Torithians either." Kiria realized it was a shame that everyone called these murderers Torithians as though they belonged on the island, when the real islanders had been terrorized for a decade.

"So why haven't you attacked the east side already?" Firian tapped one finger on the pirates' base.

"We have. Obviously we have. We've been at war for years."

"And?"

"And their base is too heavily fortified. We just end up sacrificing lives. We need a more surgical approach."

Firian lifted his chin in acknowledgement. The Tanyu were the surgeons. He inhaled deeply. "It seems like a simple plan."

"Sometimes simple is best."

"Sometimes it's predictable. How do you know they won't see us coming?"

She was almost glad he didn't agree with everything she said. She had started to get the sense that he would pretend to agree just to draw her in. Now he was acting as any other ally would. "No one outside the palace and the Academy knows that we're working together now. The Tanyu will be a complete surprise."

He smiled and so did she. "Perfect," he said. "Make sure it stays that way. I haven't informed anyone from Raewhith."

"Raewhith?" That was the little town Firian came from. Why would he mention it?

"They're sending soldiers to assist."

"Then how could they not know about this alliance?"

"I offered them a chance to exchange soldiers for safety. It was a general offer. Everyone there wants to be a Tanyu but very few get the chance, so now they can fight on our behalf—whatever battle we see fit."

She peered up at him. The Tanyu had taken over Raewhith, a small conquest, but something about it felt off. "Will any of them go with you to Torith?"

"A few. The majority will be Tanyuin warriors. Don't worry."

She wanted to defend her soldiers who had risked their lives for years to accomplish peace. They were well trained, maybe not to the obsessive level of the Tanyu, but they deserved respect. Firian's confidence suggested he underestimated them. "Our men are spread too thin. Their priority is protecting the civilians."

"There's no need to explain. They have their job. We have ours."

One hand on the map, she faced him. The colors were more saturated here. The black of his clothing was deeper than in real life, his eyes bluer. Maybe her hair looked less mousy here than it did when she was plain in real life. She had still never intentionally shown him her Ability when they were alone. But maybe, to him, she was beautiful, even when she was herself. Without Original Beauty.

Their business mostly done, they stood in silence for a moment, neither making a move to leave in case the other had something to say. She tried out a couple of lines in her mind: *We'll meet again once you have more news. I'll watch to see what kind of leader you become. How did you become the next Head? Why are you helping us?* None of them made it into the air. Part of her knew that she wouldn't want to hear the answers.

"Do you want to float?" Firian's voice took her back to the present.

"What?"

"You said when we were traveling that you wanted me to show you." His boots left the carpet and he levitated easily, almost insolently, a hand's-breadth above the ground. His long black coat flowed around his legs in a phantom breeze.

She chewed the inside of her lip. Yes, she did want to learn. But she didn't want to get too familiar with Firian again.

He held out a hand. He was already taller than she was by a head. Now, floating, he towered over her. He beckoned with his fingers, flicking them open and closed over his palm. Those little white scars, small details, crisscrossed his rough hand.

Stifling a smile, she lifted her chin, avoiding his hand. "How do you do that?"

He touched down on the carpet again, light as air. The look he gave her, that knowing, teacher look, reminded her strongly of their time in the mountains. She could almost smell the piney air. Almost as though things were normal again. As though her history with the Tanyu weren't as rocky or as heartbreaking.

"Is this real?" he asked.

"No," she said automatically.

"Are you sure?"

"Yes."

"Then you can manipulate what you see. Change the background." He brushed his fingertips over the map. A small compliment.

"Okay." At her thought, the little room melted away—the map, the table, all gone—and a wooded clearing appeared in its place. She had seen something like it in Á Quihilmar outside Brithnem. Sunlight bathed the tips of the yellow-green grass. Seeds or insects floated like dust in the streaming light. Around the meadow stood tall trees, not pines but tulip poplars.

"You've gotten better." Genuine pride edged his voice. "So you can change where we are. You can also change yourself."

She seized up, a rock forming in her stomach.

"You know that," he continued, one side of his mouth lifting. "You can change where you are, what you look like. Even size is no barrier at all. You always envision settings in the correct dimensions." He gestured to the air and glanced up. "Let me."

The meadow fell away so quickly that Kiria got dizzy and almost collapsed. It became the size of a soft rug below her. The trees came only to her knees. She felt the urge to crouch. In the clouds she was too visible, too vulnerable. She softened her knees, but fought the feeling enough to stay upright.

"See?" he said, standing as he would in any other space.

With a crush of gravity, the ground rushed up to meet her again and she found herself in the same clearing as before. Slightly nauseated, she nodded.

"Levitating is a bit easier."

Once again he approached her, hands outstretched. This time she took them. The sudden changes had made her knees watery, and she couldn't risk falling over.

Soft but firm, he closed his fingers over hers. "Just let it happen," he said, rising from the ground.

She stayed resolutely earthbound. She had to raise her arms to keep hold of Firian.

"Let go," he said. "Come with me."

Still nothing.

"Close your eyes and open them again."

She ran her tongue over her teeth, bristling at his commands. But she wanted to learn this aspect of the Unreal, even if it was from him. She shut her eyes barely longer than a blink. When she looked around, she was floating with him.

"That's it, that's it!" he said with a real smile.

She squeezed his hands reflexively, afraid to fall. "How are you doing it?"

"Anything you can picture, you can do. Remember that the same rules don't hold you back in the Unreal."

A place with no rules. What a frightening, intoxicating thought! A thrill ran through her. He seemed to sense her thoughts, that they ran to more than physical laws.

She waved her feet. "So I could become invisible or glow or anything I want?"

"Anything you want."

"Let me try it myself." She untangled her fingers from his and floated backward, the air like a water current waiting for her command. She picked up speed, rushing around the clearing near the tree line. Her dress and hair whipped in front of her. When she stopped in front of Firian, her arms tingled with the rush of wind. He waited for her, standing on the grass. She checked her hands to make sure she hadn't changed. Windblown and happy, she grinned at him. "Thank you."

His eyes softened. She'd seen that look before when they were traveling and he said he could protect her dreams. She'd believed him then. He paused a beat too long before answering. "Any time."

She swallowed, dismissing the invitation in his eyes. She hated to admit it, but being with him validated all she had worked for. Plus, they met in the Unreal with its heady freedom. It (and he) reminded her about what set her apart, what made her uniquely suited to rule. And no one could reach them here. That edge of danger, as long as she went with a purpose, thrilled her.

"I need to talk to you about one more thing," she said.

He raised his eyebrows, cuing her to go on.

"If we're going to be allies, you need to send someone to Brithnem to swear loyalty on your behalf."

He clasped his hands behind his back in a thoughtful posture, digesting her words for a few seconds before replying. "I see."

"Since our troops are scheduled to leave soon, you should send someone immediately."

He looked back up at her. "Anyone you would prefer?"

"No," she said, meeting his gaze defiantly. She paused a moment too long as well. Gathering herself, she explained, "Obviously someone loyal to you and to our cause, as I assume they all are." She assumed no such thing, but Firian seemed to be able to keep the Tanyu in check, so she wanted to promote the best in them.

"If I came, would you pledge your loyalty to the Tanyu as well?"

The question struck her in the gut.

The Tanyu had to prove themselves to her first. She owed them nothing until the war was won.

For a moment she squirmed, hating that he would probably read her hesitation as indecision. He drummed his fingers against his leg as he waited for her response. He wore a dark ring with a red stone that he hadn't had when they left Brithnem together a few months ago. Maybe it was only for Masters, or just for the Tanyuin Head. A position he had gotten suddenly, too suddenly. Under those circumstances, she couldn't pledge loyalty to the Tanyu, even if Firian came himself. Hopefully that decision wouldn't jeopardize their tenuous alliance.

She shook her head. "No. Not until the war is won."

He stopped tapping his fingers and nodded slowly. "I would do the same thing."

She had never thought of their leadership styles as similar. "Then you understand. Let me know who you plan to send."

Firian would probably not come himself. The journey might put him in danger with people who held a grudge against the Tanyu for the all-too-recent war. Surely, he would rather stay at the Academy where he could rule in safety. The way he talked indicated that he was planning to go to Torith with the troops, though. Who would he put in charge in his absence?

"I'll come, and sail to Torith from your port."

What? She knit her brows. Part of her was relieved that she would know who they were dealing with, but another part seized up with anxious energy. She hadn't seen him in person since she was a hostage. Things between them were just starting to go back to the way they had been at their best. "Are you sure?"

A smile pulled on one side of his mouth. "Yeah."

He wasn't coming to swear loyalty. He was coming to see her.

Well, if that were the case, she would just surround herself with guards and advisors, and not allow them to be alone. He was too unpredictable, and, if she were honest with herself, she was too unpredictable around him. But she still needed his help. The Torithian conflict had worn Kingdom soldiers thin, so it was time they ended this war.

She raised her chin. "Good. I hope you can leave immediately."

8

FIRIAN

FIRIAN LOST NO TIME. Taking a horse and some provisions, he set out the next day. Only when he got closer did he consider that maybe Bard was right when he said it was stupid for him to go by himself.

But what better person to travel alone from the Academy to the capital? If Firian had brought someone else, they only would have slowed him down. Alone, he could make the journey in almost half the time it took him and Kiria to do it.

On his way, he'd received news from the Tanyu stationed in Raewhith to check on his father. No visible signs of abuse. The report couldn't be true, or maybe it just didn't matter if it were. His father had collected enough sins already in the past without new ones added on. On nights when Firian couldn't sleep, he'd haunt his father's dreams, dropping him from a height or chasing him as a mountain ghost. Once, he transformed into the sea creature that had terrified Shiro during their hall test.

Firian's sweating horse bobbed from a canter to a trot just as the familiar sight of Brithnem shone through the trees. The sun gleamed on the ocean he would cross tomorrow, almost too bright to look at, silver and burning. He gathered the reins in one hand and slowed the mare to a walk. He had pushed her hard that day. Now that he could see the city walls, he felt less anxious to hurry.

Kiria's warm presence lingered there in the palace, like drink or strong perfume. He didn't submerge himself fully in the Unreal, but he touched her mind lightly, reaching out almost as though he were brushing her with his fingertips. Just a few more minutes.

He crossed the fields and farmhouses of the outer edge, getting closer to the wall. At the familiar scenario of the guards about to challenge him, he bristled. Maybe he should have taken Jovan, in case the soldiers gave him any trouble. The Master often bragged about being the Charäkhni king's personal bodyguard before he became a trainer. He resented Firian's leadership, though. He could see it in his eyes every time he looked at him. As though he deserved to be the Head. But Firian, not Jovan, had smothered the life from Sias Jairon, giving up a portion of his humanity to lead the Tanyu toward a better future. No, it was better that he go alone.

He sat tall, kingly, upon his horse as he rode toward the Abrecan Gate. Ten soldiers flanked its towering doors adorned with elaborate metal designs, only a few more than was needed to get the doors open or closed.

A guard with a square face, almost like Belik's, stepped forward, hand on his sword hilt. "State your business with Brithnem." Exactly the same greeting as before.

"My name is Firian Kess. I'm the Tanyuin Head. Your Keepers are expecting me."

A second guard came forward to whisper in the ear of the first, then stepped back to his original position. "You come alone?" said the first guard.

Firian's throat tightened just a little. He was a fool not to bring another Tanyu, after the Academy's dangerous recent history with the Kingdom. "As you see."

Unbidden, the memory of blood running down his hands thrust him back to a month ago. Master Jairon's guard had had no clue that Firian would murder him. And Firian had had no clue that he would murder the guard until seconds before. The idea that he could not know in the morning who he would kill in the evening made him feel dizzy and sick. The power gave him an unhealthy vigor, like metal in his veins, but the thought nauseated him.

More whispering and finally they began to open the ponderous double gate for him. "Very well. You may enter."

Firian swept his black coat back over the horse's flank as he rode through so he would have easier access to his boot. He'd only brought the same two weapons he'd carried on the trip with Kiria—one small knife and one large. He needed to be able to reach both of them. Just in case.

The dusty smell of the city wafted through the air, a clear change from the fresh Gray Forest from which he had come.

As he entered, a stable boy took his mare, leaving him to go the rest of the way on foot. Two grim sentinels flanked Firian on either side and he had the odd sensation of being a prisoner. How could he incapacitate the two of them if he needed to? The guards wore armor, but their heads were exposed. Moisture glinted in their eyes. Yes, if he had to, he could take care of a couple guards.

They followed stone streets leading up to the palace. Banners flowed on its battlements, tiny and dark in the distance against the bright sky.

One woman they passed seemed familiar. She could be no more than thirty, with dark hair tied up in a kerchief. Her lively eyes glared as though she could murder him with the force of her hatred. Then he remembered. The wife of the bearded man he had been ordered to kill in his sleep. He hadn't actually hurt the man, though he could have, choosing instead to defy orders. She didn't know to be grateful for his restraint. Maybe someone else had finished the job.

She wasn't the only one radiating anger. From an upper window, a large man watched him as a hawk would watch a snake.

Something struck his shoulder blade hard. Hot fury rushed through his bones as another object hit the back of his calf. "Tanyu! Tanyu!" cried children's voices. "Get out of here!"

The guards on either side of him didn't react except to wave a languid hand in the children's direction, shooing them away. It hurt to keep walking in measured strides rather than respond. The children must have thought he was a prisoner, or else they wouldn't dare throw stones at him. The guards could treat him like a prisoner now, if they wished. After he helped them win the war, he could parade through the streets and they'd treat him like the king he was.

With the deliberation of a predator, Firian turned his head to look at the children out of the corner of his eye, and left them alone.

Like last time, the sun was setting by the time they reached the enormous castle. His gaze traced the stone walls up to the battlements. How many times he had seen this place in the Unreal? Reality made it simultaneously bigger and smaller—bigger because it was undeniably, unshakably in front of him, and smaller because the colors were muted and it would never be more than what it was right now.

Unlike last time, they led him not to a side door, but up a private stone-paved road up the lawn to the front entrance. Children played and families picnicked on the grass, keeping a respectful distance from the castle. The space seemed meant as a public park. It was strange to see such a grand place open to the entire community. Gardeners tended flowers and hedges that became more elaborate the closer they grew to the palace. The smell of grass and sea filled the air.

Magnificent double doors, three times the height of a man, fluted with statues and script, were flanked by enormous blue flags. Guards opened the doors in unison. Firian stepped ahead of his conductors just for the joy of going in first. His blood hummed in anticipation.

A high-roofed gallery lined with potted trees and finery led down one of the wings. Through his roiling thoughts, he still paid meticulous attention to the layout of the palace as the guards took him around corners to return to his quarters. He knew where Kiria slept and his room was far from it. *No surprise.*

It didn't take long to reach their destination. "You may clean up in time to meet the Keepers at full sundown," said a guard who reached to open the door for him, his metal armor oddly silent. "These are your quarters, Master Kess. I hope they are to your satisfaction."

They weren't. But it didn't matter. There were some good elements. Its size, for instance, fit his importance as the Tanyuin Head. This had to be the largest state room in the palace. A gigantic four-poster bed laid with pillows and dark purple silks dominated one side of the room. Opposite was a fireplace, already lit. Tapestries fell from two walls, depicting scenes from Brithnem's history, including the coronation of Cúron. The image showed a much younger man, brown haired, but with the same distinctive beard and commanding eye. *This must be his wing of the castle.*

Lush rugs covered the floor and a marble step led down to the washroom. A claw-footed tub, almost large enough for two people, was just visible through the arched opening. With the washroom attached, Firian had no reason to leave the room and go roaming through the palace. Probably part of the reason they gave him something so nice. No doubt guards came with this arrangement.

He never would have chosen these furnishings for himself, but he found himself seduced by what they represented. Wealth and power. To one who could offer a guest something so magnificent, the world bowed.

"This will do."

FRESHLY WASHED, Firian resettled his crown on his head. The motion reminded him of Belik and his tic of fixing the glasses on his nose. He had nothing to worry about with Belik in charge in his absence. They had the same vision for the Academy, the same drive to make it better with Firian's leadership.

A suit of fine clothes had been laid out in the mint-scented washroom for him, but he chose to wear his all-black outfit, though it was stained. The clothes made him feel like a Tanyu.

One glance out the window told him the guards would reappear any moment to take him to the Keepers. To Kiria. His head swam with the thought of it.

Before they could summon him, he stepped out of his sumptuous room to join the small group of guards outside. "Are the Keepers ready to see me?"

One of the guards, this one a woman whose skin was matted with freckles, nodded curtly. "Yes, Master Kess. We were just about to fetch you."

Something about the word *fetch* annoyed him, but he didn't respond. Instead, he walked quickly, not waiting for the guards to lead him. He knew where he was going. If the Keepers weren't going to meet him in the Main, then they didn't know the importance of the man they were dealing with.

Sure enough, more guards stood on either side of the soaring wooden doors leading to the throne room where the Keepers held their audience. Scenes of the Kingdom's history were carved in relief on the huge slabs.

He recognized most of the figures from the Scroll. He had partially memorized the rare copy he had back at the Academy.

"Wait here, Master Kess," said the freckled guard as she went in to announce him. The name "Master Firian Kess, Head of the Tanyuin Academy" reverberated through the room beyond.

He fought the urge to clasp his hands victoriously as he passed through the massive doors and into the Main, with its soaring ceiling that rose even higher than the one in the fountain courtyard. His bootsteps echoed through the room, empty save for the Keepers, their advisors, and a coterie of guards lining the walls.

One guard stood directly in front of a glass pane Firian recognized. He had removed it on his last visit when he had snuck the younger royals into the Main. Lantern light glistened on it now like a secret.

Though the enormous Main dwarfed him, every sound was magnified, every decision enhanced. There was an expansiveness to the power he felt here, and he wanted more of it. Now, he was the Head of the most powerful group of warriors in the world, but he had no kingdom.

All three Keepers of the Western Kingdom sat on their thrones on the raised dais in the middle of the room. At the foot of the steps leading up to the platform stood their Amiran advisors. Firian immediately recognized Parohim, Cúron's advisor, who had led him aimlessly through the streets on his first visit. The dark-skinned woman with short, rusty curls looked familiar as well. He had definitely seen her last time, but couldn't remember her name. She had the eye of a Tanyu, not an Amir—dark, piercing, and unafraid. And the third was a new face, standing below Atael's seat.

Crowns—bronze, silver, and gold—perched on each Keeper's head. Cúron wore flowing light blue robes edged in fur, which gave him an impressively regal aspect, especially since he was so much older than the other two Keepers. Atael wore a dark purple cape clasped around his neck, a bad idea for practical reasons.

He saw it all in a blink.

Once he saw Kiria, his attention for anything else melted away.

A sound as though he were clearing his throat ripped out of him. Very little could make him stop dead in his tracks, but the sight of her Beauty almost did. He willed his legs to move forward, toward the center throne where she sat. His heart hammered in his chest and dry throat. It hurt to look at her.

He wanted to stop time, to linger and memorize her. Every line was perfect, suggesting the Kiria he knew, but elevating her to a goddess. She looked back at him, her piercing gaze showing no apprehension or hint of changing back.

Those lips seemed made for truth and justice. He'd believe anything that came out of them. Any word—any kiss—would be fierce and right.

Golden brown hair twisted up around her crown as though that symbol of authority were rooted to her head. The crown only confirmed she was a queen; it didn't make her one. Light blue gems edged in gold dangled from her ears, matching the blue of her dress. Its wide neckline revealed her collarbone and the tip of her royal tattoo, just visible on her shoulders. The gown gathered around her bust and flowed down over her knees, sexy but not self-consciously so. Anything she wore would have highlighted her body, whether she intended it or not.

There was something primal but pure in her bearing, like a queen from a story, or how he had imagined the great heroes to be before he met them and found out they were flawed.

Power and Beauty. He fought to keep his breathing even. She was everything he wanted.

When he reached the foot of the dais, he stopped and dipped his head to her. His stomach knotted and re-knotted.

"Thank you for joining us, Master Kess," someone said.

He flicked his gaze to see it was Cúron, whose expression wavered from magnanimity to suspicion.

"I understand that you are here to swear your loyalty to the Western Kingdom."

Coming from him, looking down from his high seat, the words chafed unexpectedly.

"My Keepers," Firian said, "now that the war between us is over, we can benefit each other." The heat from Kiria's gaze made it difficult to focus on anything else.

Speaking was difficult, but her attention elevated his words. For a moment he'd been afraid that his words would sound small next to her, but they didn't. "The Tanyu have a long history with the Western Kingdom, and this is just the next step."

"Before you proceed," Cúron again, "Parohim will speak of that history. For without God, our efforts fail."

Kiria and Atael both bowed their heads slightly in agreement. Firian already guessed which part of the Scroll the advisor would recite. The Amir were so predictable. But Kiria's reverence cast a seriousness over the words that made him listen, as though he would find answers there.

From memory, Amir Parohim began. It was a lengthy section, passed among the advisors like a long-practiced chant. They spoke of the Exmorei, of the defense of the Khelê, of the sacred responsibility to God. The words, half-remembered, kept Firian's mind occupied as a game would, with just enough mental stimulation to keep him from becoming agitated.

"Therefore," spoke a musical voice, Kiria's voice, after the passage was complete, "what do you swear?"

He'd waited for that voice, familiar yet transformed by Beauty as her body had been. She gazed down at him from her throne, the delicate points of her crown adorning that head he wanted to take in his hands.

The tall, dark woman stepped in. "You will kneel before the thrones as you pledge your allegiance."

He set his jaw hard. Kiria should have been the one to say those words. He had known this moment was coming, but kneeling before anyone went against his nature. Soon, he would win the war in Torith, win more troops, win Kiria. To do that, he had to kneel. *This is just a step toward more power, not less.* Still, it took him a moment to convince himself to bend. The Tanyuin Head should bow to no one.

He stared at Kiria, at that Beauty that went beyond the bounds of the world. That woman, that ruler, would soon be his. He wouldn't bow to Cúron, and still less to Atael. But he could make himself do it for her. If their positions were reversed, how much this would make him want her...

His long black coat spread out over the floor as he went down on one knee, never taking his eyes off her. She remained impassive, but he suspected she enjoyed the sight.

"Master Kess." It was Atael this time. Atael, who was always out of his depth. "You will repeat the words of the oath."

Parohim spoke again, pronouncing the words of the pledge. Firian repeated, and kept his eyes fixed on the center throne.

"I swear to serve my country, the Western Kingdom... to the best of my ability, regardless of danger... and should I betray her, may the punishment be death."

The brief ceremony over, he rose to his feet. A greater ease filled the room now that he had pledged his oath. Now there was nothing left but business.

Firian spoke first. "I will sail to Torith in the morning with your troops. Tonight I'll inform the Academy that they should leave too. When we return"—Kiria met his gaze—"we will earn your allegiance as well."

Her eyes brightened. Did he imagine it? "Do so," she said, a smile playing on her mouth.

His chest rose and fell with a deep and satisfied breath.

Cúron dipped his head courteously, not agreeing with Firian's words, but rather closing the meeting. "The guards will show you back to your room, Master Kess," he said. "The ships will be made ready for a dawn departure."

Firian cracked his knuckles. This dismissal felt too familiar. His whole life had been about proving himself, and now he had to do it again. At least he knew how.

He allowed himself to be led away. Boots tapping the mosaic floor, he wondered if they all knew where he was about to stay the night. Even now, Kiria's consciousness hovered on the edge of his mind like the buzz of a Sentry, but kinder and more familiar.

Evening light glinted on the polished floors of the Main, the refined atmosphere of the place almost condescending. Well, there was external luxury, and there was internal strength. He knew which he preferred.

The ponderous door swung after him as he left, Kiria's presence still coloring all he thought or saw. He almost shook his head. He wanted her. There was no doubt about that—her beauty, her warmth, the way she saw him and didn't look away—but his feelings couldn't outstrip hers. She had to come to him. They already had an unintentional *katah,* something that Tanyu viewed as weakness. Though she tempted him to trust her, to fall hard, he had to keep the upper hand to maintain control. He had already resolved: if she didn't show that she cared for him, then he hadn't won.

Sometimes he felt as though he were looking down from a height, staring at the view, longing for it, but then he would waver, just the slightest muscle spasm, and he'd realize how close he'd gotten to the edge. The same feeling had overtaken him in Shifra. That same vulnerability, of falling. No. He couldn't let her have so much power over him.

Once inside, he stripped off his jacket and threw it on the bed. Huffing a breath, he dragged his fingers through his hair. Something hard, metal, hit his hand. His crown. He threw it beside the coat.

Needing to flex his own power a bit after dwelling under the authority of somebody else's, he sank into the Unreal—just the First Level, no need to strain himself. He had told Belik to be ready to report at sundown.

In a few moments, his old mentor appeared. Belik's jaw twitched. Maybe he had to remember to change his greeting. "Master Kess."

"How is construction at the Academy?"

With the influx of new soldiers to be trained in the Tanyuin fashion, and the imminent return of more after their battle against the Torithians, Firian had planned to build a barracks and training facility in Tánuil.

"It's coming along." Something odd, distracted, flitted across his face.

"What?"

"Tiev got Lost in the Unreal again."

Firian gritted his teeth. "But there's no war!" Tiev was always a liability. He'd gotten Lost a few months ago too.

"He might have wanted it this time. I went in once to get him. Wouldn't come out."

"How long?"

"Four days. The Head is the one with the final word."

Keep him alive or let him die. Firian felt oddly stoic about the decision. Tiev was always a gory pain, and hurt him even in his lowest moments, but he hadn't made life easy for Tiev either. He worried the inside of his lip. "Do whatever Bard says."

Belik scoffed. The sound made Firian flush hot with anger. "You're leaving the decision to him? He's not even a Master."

"He will be once he gives us information on that captain," Firian bit back. "Just do whatever he thinks."

"You know what he thinks." The reply came almost too quickly.

Keep him alive. Firian drew his fingers into a fist. "Then try again. Don't let him die. We need all the Tanyu we have."

Belik grunted. "We need *more*, with your plan."

That was true, but first Firian needed to see how many Torithians he would be able to take back as prisoners of war. "By the time it would take anyone to mobilize against us, we'll have enough."

"We need more."

The repetition grated on him, as though he were a child again, listening to his teacher.

Belik must have sensed Firian's mood, because he changed the subject. "Have you seen the Keepers yet?" He only meant one, though he said the plural.

"I just came from the Main."

"And?"

"Everything went well."

"You vowed your loyalty? Something about death after betrayal?" He said it almost mockingly.

Firian sneered back, refusing to be mocked. "Yes. You know this alliance helps us. Or would you rather be at war?"

"I'd rather know you weren't following the whims of a certain princess." Something darkened in Belik's face. "Be careful, Firian. Don't let—"

"She doesn't control me."

Belik just tipped his chin. Apparently, Firian's protest had been enough to prove the point. The silence stretched thin. Coming from the quiet, Belik's next question sounded clear and loud, the low, almost raspy tenor of his voice filling the Unreal. "Are you seeing her tonight?"

Firian had thought about it. In fact, he'd started running through plans in his head. He simply hadn't considered those plans until now, like remembering a dream.

He didn't answer.

Belik continued. "Don't trust her. Working together doesn't mean she won't betray you. Just get what you can and get out."

He said it with such finality that looking back at his Master was like looking at a wall. "She won't betray us."

After a beat, he said, "You're young."

That old condescension filled Firian's body with lightning, anger coursing through his veins and muscles. He glared. "She won't betray us." He said each word more slowly this time.

Belik let out a humorless laugh. "Ha, but what about the others?" As though he had won a hand at cards, he removed his glasses and rubbed them with his shirt between his fingers.

Cúron. Atael. Only Cúron might have the balls to betray the Tanyuin Academy, and he seemed like someone who wanted to keep the populace happy. Taking that kind of risk might not be worth it to him. What could he gain?

A knock sounded at the door.

Without another word, Firian left Belik alone in the Unreal to discover a guard standing in his room. "Your pardon, Master Kess. The Second Keeper is here to see you."

9

KIRIA

KIRIA WATCHED the guards lead Firian toward the doors.

Hopefully he wasn't able to tell that her chest tightened when she saw him again after all this time. It felt as though they had just spoken—they had!—but seeing him in person was different. More shocking and emotional than she had anticipated. The last time they'd seen each other in person, he'd tied to her to a tree. And now...

She was on the throne and wielded power she didn't have last time. For appearances' sake, she stayed Beautiful. That was, after all, her royal face. To become less beautiful, to shrink to a lesser target for his gaze, would have been cowardly.

Seeing him again reminded her not only of the recent hostage trauma, but also of his greater moments. That pledge was one of them. Now that he ordered the Academy, things might be different. *He* might even be different. Honestly, she missed the better parts of their rocky relationship. He challenged her, in good and bad ways, it was true, but there was almost a game to his kind of challenge compared to the difficulty of ruling a kingdom. A piece of her fancied a taste. Or just an interaction, a question. That would be enough.

How did you get this power, Firian?

His answer would tell her if she could trust him. Or would at least give a better idea. Whether he inherited the position or took it by force, she had to know. If his answer wasn't what she hoped, then she would pray he could help them gain peace in Torith. Afterward, they would have almost no dealings with each other. The Kingdom would not pledge its loyalty to the Tanyu, as he wished. It was a foolish, radical request from an organization so small, no matter how influential or strong.

But it didn't surprise her that he'd asked.

That desire for control, for order, flooded even her own thoughts at times. The protesters at her first session came to mind. If everyone could just do as they should!

The door shut with a reverberating click.

Cúron shook his capacious sleeves up over his wrists. He turned to Kiria with a stormy face. "I'm glad that's over with," he said, rising from his throne. Atty did the same.

Frankly, Kiria was glad too. Her shoulders had felt tense all day and she longed to stretch them now that the meeting with Firian had passed. "He'll be a great asset in the war." She hoped that dispassionate summary would be enough to end this meeting, which had begun hours before Firian even arrived.

Cúron didn't reply to that, but his eyes narrowed enough to show his skepticism.

"Will he?" It was Atty who asked the question. The Amiran advisors stalled and shifted their weight, redirecting themselves from the exit back toward the Keepers, all now standing on the dais. None of them betrayed irritation, but she thought they must be tired of this topic. Amir were no fans of the Tanyu, but they had put up with her idea to have them help in the war. She suspected they all just wanted to go to bed.

Atty gave her a searching look. He, at least, must have noticed that Firian didn't take his eyes off her the whole time, as though he were swearing allegiance to her alone. In fact, anyone who didn't notice didn't belong in the Main. He hadn't tried to hide his infatuation.

"He's been very cooperative so far," she replied.

"He has to be cooperative." Cúron's voice boomed. "The Tanyu were never going to win their skirmish against us. We outnumber them a hundred to one. It's in his best interest to form this alliance."

A few of them nodded out of habit. It was almost impossible to disagree with him. His stature, his voice, his logic—all of it was more regal than Atael and, she suspected, herself.

"We can't take him for granted," she protested.

Chetana set her face in a hard frown. She would put up with Firian, but she wouldn't praise him for making what she would see as the obvious choice.

"Maybe *we* can't." Atty stepped off the platform like an angry child.

Abandoning decorum, she called after him. "Atty!" He had to know the target he painted on her with that remark.

Parohim drew his hands together in a request to speak. "Master Kess did seem more interested in one of you than the rest," he said carefully.

Kiria ground her teeth. *Obviously.* But was it that much of a surprise? They had gone through that ordeal together a few months ago, had gotten to know each other, and now she was his point of strategic contact in Brithnem. Of course he would pay her more attention. Didn't other dignitaries when she was Beautiful? Perhaps it was a silly reason to command the attention of a room, but her royal Beauty did draw the eye and sometimes the hearts of palace visitors. It put Brithnem in a wholesome, shimmering light.

Atty whirled around. His fur-lined cloak, much like Cúron's, flew around him. "I don't trust him. I don't like that he's staying in the palace. I say we put extra guards on him while he's here. Public opinion is against the Tanyu, so we can say it's for his safety." The *s*'s began to slur at the end of his declaration.

Cúron held up a hand. "I second that."

It wasn't a bad idea. She knew Firian's unpredictability well. He was a dangerous young man. Guards would help, but unless there were very many, they couldn't guarantee they could contain him. She raised her hand as well. Chetana and the other advisors followed suit.

"Unanimous!" Cúron said, striding down the steps. "We'll set up an extra guard right away. Then they will conduct him to the ship in the morning. Let him fend off these Torithian barbarians. Or die trying. Either way's our gain."

Strangely, she hadn't considered the possibility that Firian could die. Only that he would succeed. His confidence had made her confident. Her hands grew chilly at the idea. How could Cúron talk about him like that, as though he were just a pawn, or a tool to be used?

Coming abreast of Atty, Cúron turned to face her again, the only one left by the thrones. A different, new idea lived in the lines of his face. "If this works and we win the war, we'll have you to thank for coming up with this"—he laughed, a jovial sound—"this fool alliance!"

She put on what she hoped was a smooth smile. "Yes, you will," she said defiantly. *This will work, this will work...*

Cúron's large frame bustled across the floor, robe flowing. Atty walked beside him. The advisors' attention was still on Kiria, who hadn't moved. Realizing they were waiting on her, she hurried out.

Guards acknowledged her as she paced out of the Main, down the long hallways, toward her bedroom in the Second Keeper's wing. She had chosen to keep the second-best room, while her mother remained in the Keeper's suite. There was no need to move a couple spaces down.

Once alone with her girls, she paused. One look around the room confirmed that she wouldn't be able to rest until she had answers. Firian was here, actually here. This was the time to ask about anything that could get in the way of an alliance. Until now, she had tiptoed around some of the harder questions, reaching only for a peaceful interaction. And even that had made her feel daring.

She stretched and yawned, an excuse to close her eyes. Nothing. That was strange. She assumed he would be waiting in the Unreal. Had she misread him?

It didn't matter. She had to find out about his rise to power. Better to find out late than never.

"Candrae, Vayci." She drew herself up as they came forward. "Come with me."

The girls obeyed silently as she exited the room again and strode back to the First Keeper's wing. No one had told her where Firian was staying, but she had a good idea. Flanked by her girls, she headed quickly in the direction of the Main, trying to ignore the voice inside her that said that this was a bad idea—a dangerous, self-indulgent, irresponsible idea.

Guards. She slowed. There were extra guards posted outside Cúron's main guest suite. Lanterns glinted on their armor. That had to be it. With more confidence than she felt, she approached a man with a dark goatee. She had seen him many times before but couldn't remember his name. He lowered his head respectfully at her approach.

"I need to speak with Master Kess."

"I hope all is well, My Keeper?" the man responded. Stalling, maybe. Though she hadn't given an order that he was to see no visitors, Cúron might have.

"All is well. But I need to discuss something important with him before he leaves with the ships in the morning."

"Very well, My Keeper. Would you like one of us inside?"

It would be wise, but that would mean another ear for Firian's story. *Would that help or hurt?* "I'll be all right," she heard herself say.

"Very well, My Keeper," the guard repeated, and he conducted her past seven other guards to the door.

He knocked. A courtesy. Then he went in to announce her.

In a flash, tingling crept all over her body as her Beauty fell away. Though her plain face wouldn't give her the same leverage, it was the face he knew, and still the only one she felt comfortable showing him one on one. Candrae laid a soothing hand on her arm. Seconds later, she and her girls walked in after the guard.

Firian betrayed no emotion when she walked in, though she captivated his attention. "Thank you," she muttered to the man with the goatee, who didn't respond.

After he exited the room, silence fell.

Firian took in the presence of Candrae and Vayci, who stood a little behind her, and he raised one dark eyebrow to demonstrate his curiosity. He had thrown his black coat on the bed but still had his boots on. The Tanyuin crown lay beside it. Firian's dark hair, shiny and clean, looked a little mussed from wearing it so long, as though he had just woken up. Pieces of hair arched around the invisible iron circle.

She felt oddly embarrassed as he waited for her to speak. "Firian," she began. It didn't feel right for her of all people to refer to him as Master Kess. To her, he was just Firian. "You're only here for a short time, so I wanted to talk to you about something before you leave." A couple chairs lined the walls by the fireplace. She gestured to them. "Please, take a seat."

He pushed up his sleeves to the elbow and grabbed two chairs, setting them in front of the hearth. His tentative silence kept her on edge. She settled in one chair and he sat angled beside her. Candrae and Vayci stood at attention nearby. The fire popped and crackled.

She drew a breath to speak, but the air didn't seem right.

He stretched out a hand and touched hers, cracking a smile. "It's all right." He suddenly was as easy as he'd been at the best point of their journey together. She saw no bitterness for her escape or dangerous lust or any of those things she was afraid she would find. Instead, here was her friend. Almost as though he invited her to forgive the past too.

The presumptuous gesture was oddly comforting. Something unwound inside her, and she could speak. "Before you leave, I need to know." She glanced at the crown on the bed. "I need to know how you became the Tanyuin Head."

Distraction passed over his face a moment, his blue eyes going hazy. Normally he was so present that the shift was striking. "Is that why you came here?"

She nodded.

His eyes passed again over her serving girls.

"We can trust them," Kiria said. *We?* Brithnem and its citizens and Keepers should be *we*. Firian shouldn't be swept into that pile. Not yet, at least. Not until he proved a worthy ally. Warmth filled her cheeks, but it could have been the fire.

Flickering orange light played over one half of his face as he spoke. "There are only two ways to become the Head. I chose the harder route."

"I don't know what that means." His words felt like a riddle, drawing her in to ask more questions, which annoyed her.

One side of his mouth stretched crookedly. "You can be appointed by the current leader, or you can take power by force."

Force, then. She dropped her voice almost to a whisper. "Did you kill him?"

His chest rose and fell a couple of times before he answered. "Yes."

Her breath caught before she could stop herself. She looked at those hands that had committed such a deed, now spread over his knees. Nothing had changed about them. Thin, white scars still laced his rough knuckles.

"I had to do it. You know what he was doing to your people." He leaned forward as though willing her to understand. A spark of vulnerability showed through his eyes.

"I do, yes." So many people still reeling in pain, still afraid to sleep at night for fear their nightmares would kill them. As they killed Salaar. Firian wasn't innocent. "But is that why you did it?"

He rubbed his fingers over his knees. On the pointer finger of his right hand, he wore his new black ring with the tiny red stone that she'd noticed in the Unreal. "Why else would I do that?"

"Power. Control."

He blinked, not in shock but like a cat at ease. "Is that why you took over for your mother?"

"How could—"

"I can do a lot of good now. You understand that. Power isn't evil."

"No," she agreed. The heat of the fire was starting to make her face sweat a little, but she didn't move her chair back. "The decisions, the people in power..." She left the thought unfinished. "How did you do it?"

He lifted his chin and straightened his back, leaning away from her. "I don't think you want to know."

"That's why I came here."

Sardonically, he raised an eyebrow. She kept her expression at a practiced neutral. The fire cracked and hissed. When the flame flared up this time, she saw it shine on something. A knife in Firian's boot. She'd forgotten about that. He arched his back in a stretch and then relaxed. His face, however, looked more drawn. "I'd rather not talk about it."

"I need to know. I'm the one who brought you here, back in good standing with the Kingdom. So tell me."

"Are you reminding me that you are my Keeper?" he asked, almost purring.

Her insides twisted. Was he being disrespectful, or seductive, even with these others watching? "Just tell me."

He let out a sigh and crossed his arms, sitting back against the chair. "I killed him in his sleep." He said the words quietly, clearly, without remorse or pride.

"How?"

"I suffocated him."

Her lips twitched. *How horrible.* But what had she expected?

"Is that enough?" He set his mouth in a line.

"Yes, that's enough."

"Not everyone can request power and have it given to them."

"I know."

"So I did what I had to." He shifted in his seat. "Do you hate me for it?"

"No," she answered. Too quickly.

He smirked conspiratorially. He'd known exactly how she would answer the question. His ability to read her was simultaneously unnerving and comforting. A game with high stakes. The small jolt of adrenaline that coursed through her at those moments was addicting.

"We'll see," she revised.

"It's good to see you," he said, leaning forward again.

Reality was full of little details that didn't always manifest in the Unreal, at least not with her level of Ability. The fabric of his pants wrinkled under his forearms. He'd sat on the back of his long-sleeved shirt, so, when he leaned, the shirt pulled tight across his chest and the sinews of his neck. A slight sheen of oil shone on his forehead in the firelight, and an eyelash had fallen on his cheek. Hopefully he would rub it off.

She wouldn't be bated. It was *interesting* to see him. *Good* went a little far. "Why did you come alone?"

"You know I don't need anyone else."

She blew a breath out her nose. She recalled a few times when another set of eyes could have helped him, but she let him have his arrogance.

Another silence fell between them. Memories populated the space. As the seconds drew on, it became more and more apparent that she should leave. Her business was done here. But she didn't move.

She drew her hand over the side of her skirt, the side that faced the fire. It had grown hot during their conversation. Perhaps that would damage the silk. Normally, she didn't sit so close to fireplaces.

He scrubbed his cheek—the eyelash came off—and drew his fingers through his hair. "Is there anything else?"

It had long since gotten dark outside, and he was rising before the sun to sail across the Kheltor to Torith, where he would fight on her behalf. She chewed her lip. Part of her was angry at herself for not leaving, but something made her want to stay, to see what he would do next, to see if their horrible past could be put right by greater things.

She rose. "Be careful," she said.

"Will you be there to see me off in the morning?" He gave her a knowing look. The flames flickered in his bright eyes. He laughed a little as he rose to stand beside her. That precarious easiness was back between them. That part of them that knew each other's strengths and weaknesses in a way that others were afraid to point out, like partners. "I'm going to win this war for you. It's the least you can do." Perhaps he was joking, but probably not.

She weighed whether to call out his cockiness or let his confidence soothe her. Despite herself, she smiled. "You know I'll be there."

10

FIRIAN

The morning sky had turned from black to dark blue. Firian scanned the beach for Kiria. She'd promised to be here. Chilly air rose from the sloshing waves beneath the *Talori*. Above the beach on the crest of a hill, Mon Párinath looked down, lights beginning to wink to life through its windows.

The deck pitched unevenly as he secured the final provisions for the trip. The voyage would not be long, they'd assured him—just a matter of a few days—but they couldn't be sure how long they would need to be on the island. He was already glad that their time on the sea would be short. He'd never spent time on the ocean, and he disliked the thought of being at its mercy.

Pulling a knot hard, he looked again toward the beach.

Kiria walked down the steps from the palace gardens, the train of her dress falling behind her. Even in this pre-morning light, the line of her jaw, backlit by the palace lights, told him she wore her Beauty. It was in her silhouette, the way her hair fell, the power he saw in her movements.

He stood up straight so she could see him over the deck rail. With her attention falling fresh on him, he felt like a hero. All the rush of power with none of its consequences.

Together, they had engineered this alliance. Together, they would win this war.

He stood still a moment, torn between wanting all the soldiers to notice them gazing at each other, or turning away so they could keep this secret. This connection between them, this desire she held at bay. There was no mistaking the signs last night. He was almost there.

All that stood between them was a war. A battle, really. What had she said? Tanyu would be the surgeons. The others from the Academy would arrive about a day after the *Talori* with its Kingdom soldiers. Then they would find and kill the Torithian leaders in their fortified base. It sounded simple, a small hurdle on his way back to her. When he thought that way, he knew he was showing his inexperience. But hadn't he proven himself before? One or two battles, with over a hundred Tanyu at his back... It sounded thrilling, not frightening.

He walked to the rail and touched it. A farewell. A promise. Exhaling, he strode to his cabin on the main deck.

A laugh almost escaped him when he opened the door. Across the bed lay a full suit of silver and blue Kingdom armor. For a second he considered trying it on, but only to feel how clumsy it was. The large breastplate and shoulder guards had to restrict movement. The smiths in Brithnem were talented enough to make the armor all but silent, but that was the best thing Firian could say for it. Light blue cloth draped across the top in a flourish that would make him feel as if he were wearing the Western Kingdom's flag.

Firian stacked and folded it as best he could and shoved it under the bed. His long black jacket might not turn a blade, but it sure as hell looked better.

Shouts from the deck and the flap of sails announced they were pulling away from the dock. How long would Kiria watch from the beach? Until they disappeared over the horizon of black water?

As though on cue, he felt the small thrill of her presence. Immediately he dove into the Unreal. Seeing her standing on the beach in the Unreal made him grin. She'd stripped away her Beauty, he saw with a pang of disappointment, but he liked this face too. This was the face he could look at straight on, the one that knew him best. They were alone with the sand and sea. She made the sun peer up behind them, casting light on the empty waves. Apparently she didn't like the dark.

The waves were actually passable. He didn't tell her that creating believable water was one of the first truly difficult tasks of being a Tanyu. Light struck the waves in a too-predictable pattern, and the line between sea and sky was too marked. But, all in all, he was impressed.

"I thought you'd wait until I was gone," he said.

Her face was alight with a smile that didn't show and nerves that didn't break through the surface. The result was fascinating and fixed on him. He fought not to stare.

"You told me to come and say goodbye," she said. "And I wanted to make sure you remembered everything. The Torithians aren't ordinary fighters."

"Neither are we."

She nearly mouthed the words along with him, as though his response was imminently predictable. "I know, but we've tried to take their fortress before. I'm a little worried."

"About what?" He stood his ground, longing to soothe her concerns away with a touch.

"It's almost impossible to get in. And Torithians use human shields..."

"We'll be careful. Bard has the whole layout. You've told me this before." The waves rolled further up the beach at his command. The next surge soaked his bare feet in cool water. Kiria stepped back. "What did you change?" he asked.

She pointed. "Do you see that shell?"

It was small and pink, half buried. "That's a good one. It didn't stand out."

"Isn't that the point?" she said, trying to sound matter-of-fact but only managing to sound pleased.

"Yeah." It really was impressive. She didn't practice obsessively like he did, but she learned quickly, even when he wasn't actively teaching her.

They both turned and watched the artificial sea. She shivered beside him. Since she wasn't wearing her crown, the gesture made her look helpless, a marked difference from a moment before.

"You're not cold, you know," he said.

She pressed her lips, casting him a sardonic glare. "I know. You said I was doing so well a second ago. No, I was just thinking... about what we'll do if you can't stop them."

"We will."

"But what if you can't?" She reached out and touched his arm.

His skin burned with the knowledge that her fingers had been there. She had chosen to touch him. Even though this was the Unreal, it felt as though it had really happened. Why did he react so violently? She wasn't touching him in a romantic way, but somehow this friendly closeness felt even more intimate. He'd had plenty of romantic encounters, but he had few friends. He let his heartbeat return to normal. "What would happen?"

She played with her bracelets before answering, one hand straying up to her shoulder. "A lot would happen," she said quietly. "People would still be taken from their homes in Enderin... all those people... all those livelihoods would still be trapped on that island... and I'm not sure where else we could go for help."

And Brett's husband could be killed. Firian didn't care about the man, but he'd like to spare his sister heartache.

Kiria looked up at him. "Some people aren't happy I asked you."

He nodded. "They will be soon."

She dropped her gaze.

"What about Charäkhnem?" he asked. The waves touched Kiria's shoes now too. "I thought I heard you had an alliance with them."

"We're friendly, but they've never agreed to supply troops for us. For a long time we didn't even have that, so I guess it's better than nothing. At least we can trade now, and our people can get through the pass..."

She looked abstracted again. She really was worried about this war. "It's different being the Keeper, isn't it?" he asked gently. Her title felt intimate to say.

She rallied, looking out at the piercing bright sea against the darker sky. "It is. I'll be glad when this part is over."

"When I end two wars for you?" he teased.

"When *I* end two wars." She whirled on him with an impish expression.

"I'm the one who's going."

"I created the alliance and gave you information."

"I sent the peace terms."

"Would you have sent them to anyone else?" She blushed bright red and stepped back. Somehow they'd come to stand very close to each other. Even though Kiria was the one blushing, Firian found he had to catch his breath. Close to the edge again.

He didn't answer the question. Instead, he looked at the pink shell to ground himself. *This is not real.*

"I really hope this works," she said, digging her now shoeless toes in the sand. "Thank you for going. I probably sounded ungrateful just then. But I'm not. I'm really, really thankful that you're willing to help me."

"Of course."

"Not of course. You make your own decisions." Her careful tone revealed which decisions she was talking about. Siding with the Academy when it told him to take her hostage, killing a strategic Amir during the war... Maybe she even counted the Tanyuin Head.

He tipped his chin in an admission.

"So I'm glad you're with us now," she finished. Something like fear flashed over her expression. It was quick, almost too quick to see.

"And I will be," he said.

He should have been triumphant, but the same fear made his stomach feel light. He hated how much he loved it. He'd been with girls before, but never had they made him feel on the brink of losing control, of falling completely under their spell. The challenge made his blood race.

If he hadn't promised himself he'd let her come to him first, he would have kissed her right there.

She gave a nervous laugh. "If you don't get yourself killed because you're so cocky."

He shoved down the small rise of irritation. "I know what I'm doing."

"It doesn't always seem that way." She gave him a teasing look.

His insides melted. Few people could get away with saying that about him and being right.

He had to back away from the cliff now. He'd let this go on for too long. As long as he just wanted her body and her admiration, he wasn't in danger. But looks like that made him want to let down his walls, to give her everything. It was time to reestablish his position. "Don't let that be the last thing you say to me."

She opened her mouth in angry protest.

He smiled and leveled his gaze. "Don't worry, Kiria. There's a reason you sent me. I'm the best, and I know exactly what I'm doing."

Catching his stare, she colored. He couldn't tell if it was from desire or anger. He almost didn't care. Her eyes and thoughts were locked on him.

She didn't speak for a long time. Maybe it was only minutes. He didn't speak either.

Finally he shifted, preparing to go.

"Come back, Firian," she said.

Heat flushed his face. *Is this it?* The ocean faded away. Just the two of them left suspended.

"That's what I would say," she added quickly, clarifying. "Come back."

A promise echoed in the words. He would definitely come back. He would come back for her.

11

FIRIAN

Firian gripped the guardrail of the *Talori*, pretending to look for Torith on the horizon. When would that cursed island appear?

His stomach roiled. Why had no one told him about seasickness? By the end of the first day aboard, he'd felt horrifically sick. Staying in his cabin hadn't helped. The only thing besides the Unreal that mitigated the bile rising in his throat was being out in the fresh air. It was an improvement, but not much of an improvement. He'd waited until the crew and soldiers were out of sight before he vomited over the side.

Rubbing the back of his hand over his mouth, he wearily straightened. With his skin feeling so clammy, he had to be paler than usual, but since these soldiers didn't know him well, they hopefully wouldn't notice.

Kiria had told him the voyage would take about three days. It was the third day now. Give him a horde of angry Torithians before another day on this ship. It creaked all night and rocked all day. The wind, the food, and the small space didn't bother him. But the everlasting rocking that turned his stomach did.

A crewmember, a boy no more than fifteen, scrambled down the rigging from the crow's nest, landing with a thud. "Land spotted, sir," he said to the captain. The captain shouted directions and the deck came to life.

Finally. Firian pushed back from the rail. He didn't know how to sail, but at least he could get lost in the bustle. He could lose no more time contacting Bard to see what he found. Before they landed, he needed to have a better idea of what he was getting into.

Nausea churned inside him. He pressed it down. His practice with the Unreal had gotten him through the night, but when his attention slipped, seasickness irresistibly surged up again.

He took measured steps to his cabin and shut himself in.

"Bard!" Firian waited in darkness, considering a setting. He could switch it to—

"Fir, hey."

Bard materialized before him. His hair was frazzled and his eyes ringed with gray, as though he had just woken up. *Katah* was serious business, never-ending vigilance.

"What do you have for me?" Firian asked.

"Tibor Wat," he began wearily, almost grimacing. "He's in the compound."

"Where?"

A map appeared in Bard's hands. He rolled it out in the air and pointed to the same area of the island Kiria had shown him. Confirmed, then. "The base is right there. Fir, it's..." He turned his dark eyes to Firian's, almost pleading.

"What?"

"It's terrible."

"Where's Wat?" First things first. The fortified base, including the interior layout, took up the majority of the map when Firian looked back to it. "Is this correct?"

"It's all I know."

Some of the edges of the plan were pale and hazy, but a few particular rooms stood out in sharp relief.

"So where is he?"

"Right now?"

"Right now. We're coming up on Torith."

"Aren't you going to wait for the other Tanyu?"

"Yes." He would need at least a few minutes on dry ground before he'd be at his best.

Bard pointed again. "He's right there. He moves around, but he's usually there." Something haunted passed over Bard's face.

"What?" Firian asked again.

"So I've followed him around. He doesn't have the Talent," he clarified, rubbing his knuckles over the back of his head. "Not a ton, but some, I guess. It's all hazy. I can't get a full *katah*."

"Headache," Firian sympathized.

"You'll have to be careful, Fir. There are a lot of people there."

"Obviously."

"A lot." Apparently Firian didn't react the way Bard wanted, because he went on. "Innocent people."

Firian paused. "Kiria told me there are human shields."

Bard nodded rapidly. "Yeah, and... women."

Firian raised an eyebrow. "Prostitutes?"

"I don't know. It's not..." But whatever it was not, he didn't say.

Firian turned his attention again to the map. "So, what's this?" He pointed to the room Bard said held Tibor Wat.

Bard sighed. "I think it's his bedroom, or office, or something. He talks to his lieutenants and has a lot of the treasure is there. Yeah. And he meets with ladies."

"*Ladies?*" Firian smiled sarcastically at his choice of words.

Bard colored.

"Well, that's good to know," Firian said, feeling seasickness return. "And he's usually there?"

Bard nodded again.

"Have you gotten a layout of the entrances and exits?"

He touched the map at a few points. "These are some of them. They might be all. It's actually pretty secure."

"So I've heard."

"What are you planning to do?"

Honestly, he wasn't sure. He'd been waiting for Bard's intelligence. So instead of answering, he asked, "What about the lieutenants?"

Bard named them and gave descriptions.

Maybe sensing Firian's confidence, Bard gave him a warning look.

"I'll be fine," Firian protested.

"Just be careful. These people aren't like a normal army. They're like…" Bard searched for a word, didn't find it. "They're out for themselves."

"Isn't every army?"

"It's different. They're just…"—he searched for a word—"marauders." That one seemed to satisfy him. "They're not really an army at all. They just want what they want, you know? They want treasure and so they kill or steal or whatever they can to get it. Some of them steal people and just keep them. It's…" He winced.

"That should make them easier to beat."

"They don't have rules. At all. They'll kill their own people, yeah? But they've gotten good at fighting together too."

"If they can get money and women."

Bard nodded, obviously remembering a number of specific incidents.

The troubled look on his face made something squirm in Firian's gut. Was that nerves? He couldn't afford nerves. "So you've had to watch this captain with girls, have you?"

Firian thought he could feel the heat from Bard's deep blush.

"We'll get him," Firian said, stifling a laugh. With Bard's prudishness, this *katah* was truly a sacrifice for him.

Firian's thoughts grew serious again. If Bard continued to give information of this caliber, he would definitely have to promote him to Master when he got back. Even a partial *katah* developed this quickly would be difficult for the best Tanyu to pull off. "When we land, I'll come again to check things over."

"Okay," said Bard, still not looking at him, as though he were ashamed.

"Just keep the information coming." *And then we can win the war.* "It's not so bad, is it?" he needled again, unable to help himself.

Bard hit him on the arm.

Firian laughed. "It's good for you."

Bard puckered his lips in an expression that said it definitely wasn't.

At least Bard's misery would be over soon. Firian had the captain's location. All he needed to do was land, wait for the Academy ships to land, and then the Tanyu could be the expert war surgeons they claimed to be.

12

FIRIAN

Firian crawled on his elbows to see over the ridge. Rocks dug into his arms and the mud coated the front of his black shirt. Huge leaves dripped leftover rain on his face. He wiped off the drops with a grimy hand so he could see.

Most of the compound seemed no taller than a single story, but it stretched back and back into the trees for an undetermined distance. The building was well established, no doubt there before the Torithians arrived to use it as their base. Jungle foliage crawled over the roof until the two blended into one seamless blend of shadowy green.

Firian pictured the plan Bard had shown him. This was the south entrance. Captain Tibor Wat's room lay in the center.

Lowering himself further, he peered at the visible door. Only one man stood guard, partially hidden in the shadows. His head was shaved like every other Torithian. Since they came from different places and had no distinguishing uniform, their shaved heads seemed to mark their allegiance to the gang.

His heart squeezed. The last time he had seen a Torithian was when he and Kiria had been ambushed in Raewhith. Red streaked across his memory. Raewhith, his hometown. He never would have guessed they'd go so far inland, just to get Kiria. They'd been minutes away from Brett. Huge dead bodies must have been big news in the little town. She'd certainly heard about it. Did she realize he left the corpses there?

He forced himself back to the present. The fortress had very little evident security. Firian had expected much more, based on Bard's description. Seeing almost no one was more unnerving than facing a clear army.

"There are hundreds inside," Bard had told him, "and civilians."

It wouldn't be as difficult to rush in like a wildfire, burning the murderous pirates where they stood, but working around innocents was completely different.

He stared for a while longer, envisioning all the ways he and Bard planned their attack. First, they would backtrack to the Torithians' ships and burn their escape route. Then, he would sneak in and kill the captain while more Tanyu blended in among the prisoners. Using the Unreal for communication, Tanyu would direct Endrians and Kingdom soldiers to surround the remaining pirates as the spies revealed themselves and new troops barged in the front.

Now that he was looking at the fortress, though, he could improvise a few more opportunities. They could go in from above, if there were any crack in the stone.

Firian edged backward down the embankment, his elbows sliding in the muck. Tanyu, Brithnem, and Endrian soldiers all stood ready for his command. Many of them were fully twice his age. He stifled a smile.

"The base is below us," he said.

A few Brithnem soldiers all but rolled their eyes. They'd been here before. They'd lost friends. Firian had heard them swapping stories on the *Talori*. Though no one complained, the Brithnem soldiers didn't stand very close to the Tanyu, who had just arrived that morning and had barely disembarked before coming here to the fortress.

He scanned the troops in black and picked five out of the crowd, all girls. "Get to the roof. See if you can find a way in." Bard hadn't mentioned any, but then he wouldn't know if the captain never thought about it. The way the huge stones stood piled on top of one another suggested that there probably would be a crack somewhere. Someone like Tesni, tall but skinny as a candle stand, would be able to wedge herself through even the smallest of openings. The five girls disappeared silently, as though they had never been there.

"You," he said, pointing now to the Endrians, "burn their ships. Give them no place to run." Firian had already left soldiers from Brithnem, as well as a couple Tanyu, guarding their own ships, well hidden in a jungle cove.

"Where do we begin? They always hide their fleets in several places," said one Kingdom soldier. When Firian continued looking at him, he added, "Master Kess."

"We'll find them all. Like we planned, the faster they burn, the better. I'll come with you." He swept his gaze over the remaining forces. "The rest of you, stay here. Create a perimeter around the fortress. Stay out of sight. We'll be back before nightfall."

As the army broke into its tasks, Firian relished the snuff of thick leaves, the mud underfoot, the wetness trailing down his hair. The ships would not be difficult to find. His troops left footprints, but so had the careless Torithians.

The first fleet was in plain sight on a sandy beach not far from the fortress. Tall-masted ships with huge hulls for transporting weapons and people and treasure floated serenely on the lapping waves.

Firian crouched down at the edge of the tree line and frowned.

A general from Enderin came up beside him, his leather shoulder guards dark with moisture. "They never guard the ships," he said in Bard's lilting accent.

Firian whirled to face him. "Then why haven't you burned or taken them before?"

"We burned them once, three years ago." He licked his bearded lips and his gaze grew far away. "We didn't realize then, but the brig was full of children tethered to the bars. By the time we heard the screams, we couldn't save them. We tried again last year, but the captives alerted the Torithians and our troops got trapped against the water when they arrived. All killed but two who jumped overboard and swam."

"Prisoners are in the brig?" Firian confirmed.

The man didn't nod, but his stern look conveyed that he thought so.

Simple enough. Couldn't these people think through any problem? If the captives alerted the Torithians, then they had been threatened. Since Firian's soldiers had no way to knock out all the prisoners—no gases or space to do it all at once—they would just have to threaten them with something worse than the Torithians had. Then they'd untie them, burn the ships, and let the people go free, unharmed. Were Kiria's soldiers unwilling to threaten people even to save them?

Firian crooked a finger toward Master Nedi, the tallest Tanyu in their company. He could inspire fear if he wanted to. "You go first," Firian instructed. "Find the brig. Make sure no one down there makes a sound. If they do, stop it." He paused. "But don't kill them."

The Endrian general shot Firian a glance that he ignored. "We go in just behind," he announced in an undertone to everyone else with them.

When Nedi left, Firian counted under his breath. When he reached fifty, he sprinted, staying low, across the beach. His running footsteps were just the crunch and rainy spray of sand.

The ship was anchored just off shore. As Firian charged into the bay, the water got deeper more quickly than he anticipated. In three steps it came up to his waist. He kicked off the sandy bottom and did his best to swim toward the ship. Why did Bard like swimming so much? He always talked about how he missed it at the Academy. It was so much slower than running, or even climbing.

Happily, Nedi or someone else had left a rope dangling from the deck into the water. Firian grabbed hold of the rough, slimy hemp and hauled himself up, walking up the uneven boards of the ship's hull.

It didn't take long to find the brig. Firian jumped down into the hold, skipping the ladder entirely. In the blackness, he heard shifting people, a couple gasps, a child softly crying. The brightness of the sun and water and sand had blinded him. Though he squinted, he could see nothing for a few seconds. A horrible stench of human feces and rotting fish made him gag before he could stop himself. His blindness put him on edge. What if this were a trap? What if he had sent some of his best people right into it?

He started to breathe again when shapes began forming in the gloom. Tiny children, some no more than three years old, sat on the ground, one wrist tethered tightly to metal bars, both inside and outside the square cages that lined most of the space. They were dirty and skinny, without shoes. Their eyes seemed to grow larger in the darkness. Firian fought the urge to shiver with the sense of being haunted. The eyes reminded him of the Sentries, buried underground, listless and hopeless.

There were adults too, all men and boys. Most of them had ratty beards. Nedi stood face to face with the largest man, who looked as though he had lost a significant amount of weight in a short time. Heavy skin hung below the bicep of his raised arm tied to the bars. The hand itself was discolored, too light compared to the rest of his dark skin, like the hand of a corpse.

"Make a sound and you're dead," Nedi whispered.

The boy next to the dark-skinned man trembled, but the man acted as though Nedi hadn't spoken. He began banging his dead hand against the bar, almost as though it were a spasm, an automatic response, and not a conscious choice.

Firian stepped in and grabbed his hand to silence him. His flesh was hard and dry—a thing, not a person. But others started clanging against the bars too. It was odd that they didn't raise their voices.

They don't care if they die, Firian realized. "We're going to get you out," he hissed, hoping that would be enough motivation for them.

The banging continued.

Desperation surged inside him as the prisoners started to wail. Unearthly sounds. Horrifying sounds. The Tanyu and Endrian soldiers who had come in behind him snapped into action, covering mouths, barking quiet directions. One soldier yelped and shook out his hand. The prisoner must have bitten him.

"The kids," Master Nedi said. "We'll kill the kids if you don't shut up."

All sounds ceased.

Firian had said to threaten them. He was glad he hadn't been the one to say it, but even before Nedi spoke the words, he dreaded the inevitability of them. The men might not care about their own lives, but they would care about the children.

Firian sensed the shock of the Endrian soldiers as they turned toward him. He couldn't reassure them yet or else the prisoners would start their din again. "Yes," he said, but he felt like he was going to be sick. *This lie will save them. It'll save them.* "Now shut up and we'll let you go. You don't want to be on these ships when we burn them." This was war. Sometimes justice and victory required people to do hard things. People killed in war. Surely this was no different.

He nodded to the Tanyuin warriors closest to him, and they began slicing off the leather bonds. Salt and age glued the knots together. Some had been tied so tightly that they couldn't cut them off without harming the arm as well. But freedom was freedom. No one cried out from the pain. Maybe they couldn't feel it. One man—probably the oldest, judging from the white in his beard—nearly collapsed once his arm was free. The prisoner beside him, a man with milk-white eyes, held him up.

"Check the upper deck and take them out," Firian ordered the Endrians. The words tasted like stale fish. He swallowed, his eyes sliding to a boy a few years younger than he was, whose forearm was sliced near his wrist bone. Blood, black in the darkness, flowed over his hand onto the ground.

Again, sickness rose up in Firian's gut, but that could have been the swaying of the ship. He'd had enough of that aboard the *Talori*.

"Get them up," he said again.

Up above, a yell. A clank.

Firian's stomach lurched and he dove toward the ladder, pushing past brown-clad soldiers to see out. Two Torithians, looking as though they had just crested the railing, stood at the edge of the deck, swords drawn against three Endrian fighters.

Potatoes spilled out of a sack and rolled across the planking. The pirates were here to feed the prisoners.

Firian jumped out of the hold and drew his sword with a grating ring. It didn't feel quite balanced, although he'd practiced with it before he came. He preferred knives. If he needed them, he had one at his belt and his small blade tucked in his boot.

When the two men saw Firian and the others crawling out of the hold, they stopped fighting and jumped overboard toward the beach. Without thinking, Firian launched himself over the railing after them. The water went over his head, sucking him down into silence. He kicked and broke the surface again. The pirates were almost to the beach. He thrashed after them, pinwheeling his arms. His pace was maddeningly slow. Bard should have taught him how to swim. Too late now.

One of the men looked back and stopped, while the other continued. Firian realized he still had the sword in his hand. He tightened his grip on the cold handle as he muddled forward. This was ridiculous. His thoughts stilled. This was just like the Unreal. When he was fifteen, he swam in the test against Shiro. He could swim now. He just had to use the elements to his advantage, like anything else. Everything was his ally, if he knew how to use it. He kept himself afloat and took a deep breath through his nose, grateful that it no longer smelled like human waste.

Eyeing the young, bearded Torithian who had stopped, Firian reviewed his options. They weren't good, but he was a Tanyu, and he had come with other Tanyu. Even now, he heard a splash behind him. He blinked and the Torithian was gone. Frowning, he scanned the beach. The second pirate disappeared into the tree line, no doubt to warn the people at the fortress, but there was no sign of the first man.

Another splash. A soldier swam up behind him. Firian pointed to the beach. "Stop them! Go!"

An Endrian soldier, and then another, swam powerfully past him. He almost resented them for their skill, but he was glad someone could go faster than he could. "Get to the—"

Something grabbed his ankle and yanked him under. Water rose over his head, cutting off the air before he could fill his lungs. He kicked, hit something, some*one*, but he didn't move toward the surface. Now someone tugged at his wrist, his neck. Firian arced his sword, but it moved through sap, like a nightmare. He heard the muffled swish of something breaking the surface. Pressure pushed on top of his head, holding him down.

Panic welled up in him. His lungs already burned. The more he kicked, the less energy he reserved for holding his breath just a little longer. He opened his eyes and saw legs treading water in front of him. He grabbed at them, missed, switched his sword to his left hand, grabbed again, was kicked off again. Finally, in desperation, his eyes getting blurry, his nose and mouth aching to take in air, he dropped the sword. It sank gracefully into the murky depths below. Firian lunged with both hands, got a firm hold, and bit as hard as he could. The instinctive thrash that followed was enough for Firian to break the surface.

Sweet air filled his lungs with a loud gasp. Sun beat down. The first sound he heard apart from his own breath was a foreign curse.

Panting, Firian drew his curved knife, lightning quick, and plunged it into the pirate's chest. Again. Again, just to be sure. Red billowed like smoke underwater.

He spat blood and kicked his way to shore. When he reached the soft sand, he turned around to see the first ship on fire and a lifeboat taking the prisoners away.

13

FIRIAN

"You all right, mate?" Bard's voice sprang to Firian's mind as he sprinted back along the beach, trying to erase the memory of his incompetence in the water.

Hopefully no one saw him flailing in the water and then gasping for breath on the beach. He had spent a full minute lying on his back before he had enough air in his lungs to run after the man who'd escaped. He would fix the problem. That was all. He would learn to swim, learn to hold his breath, to fight in water. He would fix the problem, as he had fixed all his other weaknesses. It just rankled that he kept finding more.

"Yeah. Get back to the captain," he replied, still running but also dipping into the Unreal.

Bard's spiky black hair looked almost hazy. Could that happen with too much concentration? The *katah* was clearly wearing on him. "You're almost there?" His shoulder twitched restlessly.

"On my way." Firian's clothes were soaked. He'd stripped off his dripping shirt as he ran, but he'd have to stop before he had the chance to wring out the rest of his clothes. Water made his boots feel heavy and sluggish.

Bard hesitated, but didn't leave. "Be careful."

"You've said that before."

Bard hummed, admitting but not apologizing.

"Be ready," Firian said. Bard was instrumental in this plan. He was in the captain's head. He had the layout. If he had created a successful *katah* connection, he could incapacitate Tibor Wat, their leader, from where he was at the Academy.

Bard's Adam's apple bobbed. He nodded grimly and vanished.

Firian focused on the present. It wasn't far back to the compound. He didn't catch up to the two Endrians and the fleeing Torithian. If the man reached the fortress before his troops could enact their plan... He pumped his legs harder.

He'd left the rest of the soldiers behind to free the other prisoners and burn the remaining ships. The wind against his bare skin began to dry the seawater.

Through the Unreal, he contacted the nearest Tanyu and ran to her hiding place. It was Xan, a serious girl with a long braid who had fought under Tiev mere months ago. That time felt like a different life. She fixed Firian with a look so fierce it seemed as though she strove to be like Master Gerand when she was older. Now, she stood in a hollow with perhaps a hundred Brithnem soldiers, whose armor sparkled in the sunlight.

Firian wiped his wet hair out of his eyes. "Any word from the roof?"

Xan shook her head.

Firian bit the inside of his lip. No news from the roof, a loose Torithian who knew of their presence... His plan was unraveling at the edges. But Tanyu were adaptable.

His lungs and throat still burned raw from his near drowning. If any others had seen him, their confidence might be shaken. He had to show them what he could do. His whole life, he felt, had been that endless fight.

"I'm going in," he said.

Xan's brows twitched downward.

"We can't wait. One was going to alert the others." The Tanyu were Kiria's last hope of defeating this threat. If he could do this—he, Firian—then he would save them all.

Firian considered the layout of the fortress again. The south-facing door opened into a series of passages full of blind corners and partial walls.

He was the only one who could sneak in through the front door, navigate the maze, and kill the captain. He'd been communicating with Bard, the one whose *katah* would help them succeed. And he wanted to prove he could do it. This was a delicate task, a surgeon's task, and he was born for it.

From Xan's hiding place, he could peek above the long ridge he had climbed earlier and see the pirate's base. Somewhere inside there was supposed to be a Tanyu, secretly implanted years ago. Belik said his name was Moryam Cashel. Though they'd tried to contact him before landing on the island, no one had been successful. Maybe he was already dead.

"You need to distract the guard," Firian whispered. "Don't kill him or alert him that we're here. I just need to get inside."

"As you would have it, Master Kess," Xan replied.

Firian faced the leaf-covered stone building. The door opened left-handed, so he would sneak around the side on his right. He pointed to the spot. Xan nodded.

Firian's black clothing blended with the shadows as he picked his way through the jungle. A bird called. Something dripped on him from above and he ran a hand through his hair. It felt gritty with salt.

When he reached the side of the building, his body tensed, energy bunching in his arms and legs and core. But he saw no more guards. He found a dapple of bright sunlight and pivoted his Master ring until the red stone reflected a dot of light. Xan was sure to see it on a tree near where her company waited.

What felt like a long time later, the lone guard went to investigate something just off to his right, away from Firian. Firian's chest burned, his vision almost

Into the Unreal

blurry with excitement. He edged around the building and slipped through a crack in the door.

Bard had warned him about the two additional guards that stood just inside, but his heart still lurched to see them. Drawing on the inner stillness he had cultivated at the Academy, he bashed the head of one, disorienting him. Then he turned his attention to the second, who was stirring to attack. Firian grabbed the front of the man's clothes and gagged him with it, swinging him by the back of his collar into the first man. One more blow and the two guards lay nonconscious. Firian stood without a scratch. The whole exercise felt nearly graceful, like a stretch or strategy exercise.

Laughter and music greeted him inside. Energized by action, he slid to a dark corner behind a half-wall. This sounded like a party, not an army. *These are the people who almost murdered Kiria.* He remembered the raised scar on her left shoulder and flushed red with anger.

He recalled the map Bard had shown him. Above him was a square wooden door covering a long, continuous storage space that ran most of the length of the first room. From there, he could avoid a few blind corners on his way to the center of the compound.

Shimmying into the tight space, he started to elbow his way along. Bright slivers of light streaked across his face from the other cabinet doors. Edging the tobacco, candle stands, tankards, and pouches of unnamed things out of the way proved to be the most difficult part of navigating the tight tunnel.

Closing one eye, he peered through a small knot in the wood. The room was full of men of all ages, bristling with weapons, some on their person, some hanging on the wall or leaning in corners. The assortment was staggering: swords and axes and pikes and maces, all cruel and many dirty. They bore the markings of many different cultures, some of which Firian didn't recognize, although he'd met people from all around the continent at the Academy.

And with them were women, all in various states of intoxication or undress. They sat on knees or lay on the floor. Although they moved with little prompting, most of them did so without smiling, obeying automatically. One girl, beautiful, no more than sixteen, wore nothing above the waist but a necklace of enormous rubies. Dark purple burn marks peppered her midriff. The man whose lap she sat on smoked gaily, gesturing to his friends and laughing obscenely. Firian's blood boiled. A couple boys, distinguishable as separate from the Torithians by their long hair, served the gaudier pirates, apparently following some code of rank.

Even if his troops told the slaves to run, many of them probably wouldn't understand or be able to move before their captors grabbed them. Firian looked back toward the entrance he had used. Eight guards, apparently sober, stood with two or three wickedly curved blades at each of their belts. Firian thought of the sword he had lost in the water.

The light was dim. If there had been windows, they were now overgrown or covered up. The only light came from torches bolted into the wall or candles dripping wax onto thick wooden tables. Though it was still midday, fully half the men appeared to be drunk. The better to kill them.

Was Moryam among these disgusting people? The thought made Firian's lip curl. How long would someone have to live a debauched life like this before they didn't acknowledge other loyalties? The Academy might be the only place strong enough to demand instant allegiance from men like these.

Belik had described the Tanyu, but Firian saw no one who matched his description. He was almost glad.

Treasures lay piled in corners too, along with the weapons. An Endrian carving of a tree, partially gilded, hung on the wall as decoration. Bard, if he were here, would have pointed it out. Firian had never given much thought to the fact that the Torithians had been attacking Bard's country for years. No wonder he was so concerned. Now that he thought about it, that group of girls lounging on the carpet had Bard's coloring. Firian had only offered to help with the war because of Kiria, but he could actually help many people before the week was out.

A splash of liquid hit the stone floor and a chair scraped back. A couple girls shrank away, but two nearby Torithians stood, their hands full of weapons. One pirate held a tankard in one hand and a short ax in the other.

The man who'd lost his drink gave a lengthy curse. The man he accused barely spoke the common tongue, but he managed to curse right back. Waving a dagger, he pressed the point of a blade against the first man's chest.

Violently, he shoved the offender's hand away, and the swift movement broke into a full-blown fight. More men stood either to watch or get into the action. One girl was hurled off her captor's lap to the ground. Her mouth moved with feeble protests, but she was clearly not lucid enough to fully comprehend what was happening. She drew her legs in a little, hiding them under her skirt, which had obviously been a grain sack before it was clothing.

Though Firian wanted to see how far the fight would go, he used the distraction to mask the noise as he crept to the end of the storage area.

There was a gap between him and the hall that led to the rooms beyond. Here, he would have to get out of his hiding place.

The captain's room was in the center of the compound. Bard's map had shown a series of large spaces, all similar to the one he had just left, circling around a cluster of smaller inner rooms. He'd have to cross at least one more repulsive cache of people and weapons to reach his objective.

A scream pitched through the air. Heart in his throat, Firian eased open the cabinet door and grabbed hold of a wooden beam in the ceiling. The shouts became instantly louder in that open space. Scented smoke floated in a haze. Though it strained his muscles to hold on, he would be out of reach of most weapons here. He reached from one beam to the next, hiding as best he could in the gloom.

The ceiling showed no sign of excessive age or wear. He didn't even feel a draft. The possibility of a rooftop entrance seemed slim.

Easing himself down, he slipped through a doorway—and bumped straight into another guard. The man reached for something but Firian had already crooked his elbow and smashed it hard against the man's nose. Disoriented, the pirate stumbled back and yelled, the sound blending with the others in the next room. Firian punched his head against the wall a few more times before the man slumped, unconscious, to the ground.

Firian shook out his hand, as much to wind down his adrenaline as to mitigate the pain from hitting bone on bone. His heart skipped unevenly and he melted into the shadows of an alcove to get his bearings.

"There was an extra guard," he told Bard sourly, keeping his eyes open as he went into the Unreal. He let out a slow breath until he felt all his wits again.

"I told you they're all over."

Despite the danger and Bard's snarky comment, a smirk spread over Firian's face. He felt like himself again. "I'm headed to the center room now."

"Remember the outfit."

He flashed Bard a crude gesture before coming fully back into the Real. Heat pumping through his blood again, he moved forward carefully. There were so many entrances, openings leading to half-walls somewhere else.

More raucous laugher and clinking of tableware sounded from the next large room. This time, Firian knew exactly what to expect. Bard was so sensitive that one half-dressed dancer would have made his skin prickle. But he wasn't joking. This place really did have many people enslaved for the pleasure of these pigs. Everything here was a mockery of luxury. It would be sumptuous if it weren't so tainted.

Smells of roasting meat wafted on the air. Part of him hated his automatic hunger.

Firian returned to the man he had knocked out. Faint breath barely fluttered from his nose. Alive, then. As quietly as he could, he yanked off the man's long tan vest and he put it over his own clothes. The pirate's body odor clung to the fabric, but the stench still wasn't as bad as the ship's brig. Then he unwound the silk scarf around the man's neck. Pausing, he chose to tie it at his waist like a belt. The man's red pants were baggy enough to fit over Firian's slim black ones, so he pulled off the man's heavy shoes and then the pants.

Casting around for an excuse to go in, he found a wooden box full of flints. Good enough.

He pulled the small knife from his boot and hid it under the flints before closing the lid. The borrowed pants had too much fabric that could get in the way of his hands.

He ran his fingers through his dark hair a few times, so it would look more like the servants' did, smoothed back and curled at the ends. His hair was shorter than that of the boys he'd seen, but it would have to do. With what he hoped was a servile attitude, he approached the doorway. He'd have to keep his head down, even seem meek.

Guards would be posted outside this room too. These he would probably have to bring down. He could already feel their hot, sticky blood on his hands.

Would any of them recognize him? Had his description gone out after the encounter at Raewhith?

The air seemed to grow thinner the closer he got to the roasting meat and the cackling men and the bare-legged women. Firian was tall. Would that matter?

Willing himself to perfect calm, he crossed the threshold.

14

FIRIAN

"Wait up!" Someone plucked Firian backward by the neck of his shirt. He bristled, and his lungs felt like rocks in his chest. He turned and found himself face to face with three leering men.

Was he too late? Had the pirate from the beach already come?

"What's this?" asked one with onion on his breath. His head had been unevenly shaved. A few rogue hairs sprouted up at crazy angles, only visible in certain light.

Firian held up the box with both hands. "Someone asked for flint," he said softly.

A different man, skinny, with a scar along the length of his head, threw back a laugh.

Firian's face heated. He could kill this man in the span of a heartbeat.

A guard who'd stood out of sight leaned forward. "Probably Yotar," he said to the rest.

Nods of suggestive acknowledgement.

"He said to bring one to Moryam too," Firian added quietly, shoving down his disgust.

A chorus of laughter met the name. No answers, and no luck finding the Tanyu so long hidden among their ranks. So Moryam was dead, or at least gone, then. He'd be no help.

"Always had a sense of humor! Yotar's over there," said the one with the scar, pointing, altogether too close to Firian. His finger grazed Firian's chin as he pulled it back.

Choking with rage, Firian nodded, unable to hold back a sneer of contempt, and turned away. He wanted to spit, to curse, to destroy it all.

He wove his way through pirates pawing at their captives, smacking at their meat, asleep in magnificent velvet chairs. The men had pointed to a man with a birthmark covering half his face. Even his lips were two-toned, dark and light. *He's Khelê.* Firian wasn't sure why, but the presence of any Khelê surprised him. The man's outfit hung down in strings. Firian hadn't heard of a culture that dressed that way, but the matching pants and shirt—if it could be called that, since it revealed his whole chest—were clearly made of a single fabric.

Firian realized he had forgotten to keep his eyes down. His boldness had drawn the looks of several Torithians. He lowered his voice to make up for the mistake. Flipping open the box, he said, "You asked for a flint. To... smoke."

The pause that followed made Firian's insides squirm. Had Yotar even heard him over the din?

When Firian glanced up, he was relieved that the man wasn't reaching for a weapon. A smile curled across Yotar's face. His gaze took in Firian and he languidly shuffled through the flints in the box, seeming to touch each one. The knife was buried deep enough that the pirate's wandering fingers wouldn't find it.

Don't kill him. Don't kill him.

Finally, the man chose a stone and flipped the lid of the box down himself. Unsure of what do to, Firian gave a fractional bow and backed away. His arms shuddered with anger. He could hardly see. But he had free reign of the room now. No one noticed he was out of place. They must have brought in new captives all the time.

And there—there!—was the captain's room. Without breaking his step, he called to Bard in the Unreal.

"I'm here."

"In the center room?" Bard's voice echoed through his head.

If he was focused enough, he could hear other Tanyu's voices without picturing them in his mind. Besides, it felt like Bard's voice was always echoing through his head.

"Yes. Is there any way in through the roof?" Firian knew it was a useless question.

"I dunno. Maybe?"

"I have people on the roof. I'm outside the captain's room now. Is he with any guards I should worry about?"

"They rotate in and out. Right now there are six with him. Yeah, six." A pause, and then, "That's a lot. You should have told me when you were going in."

Firian ignored him. "What's the captain doing?"

"He's planning a trip. He's charting... to Enderin."

"Okay." Firian's mind spun with the possibilities. Seven people. With extra weapons and an enclosed space, he didn't like the odds. Difficult, but not impossible. "Explain the guards to me."

Bard didn't answer right away. It was challenging to maintain a *katah*, get information, and communicate with someone else at the same time. Pride washed over Firian at the thought. He and Bard would be the ones to take down these gory pirates. He wouldn't have pegged Bard as such a helpful ally, but he was glad this time that he'd been wrong.

"There are two right next to him, helping him plan... and two by the door. Mm hm. Another one is on the other side of the room, against the wall. Another guy is sitting on the bed. I think he's drunk."

Firian numbered them off in his head. Two with the captain, two by the door, two extra. Six in all. His mind spun with strategies. Seven at a time... Even with Firian's elite training, it would be close.

In the Real, Firian offered his wares to another group, four people reclining together in a tangle on a luxurious rug made of the fur of some exotic animal. A young man who looked little more than seventeen took a flint from the box and invited Firian to join them. He pretended not to hear him.

The encounter made him feel more on edge. While in this compound, he constantly went from confident to nervous to excited to enraged. Now, as he bought a little more time to consider what he would do in the captain's room, he felt an odd fluttering of nerves. If there had been three guards plus Tibor Wat, he would have felt assured of victory. Surprise was on his side. One of the men was drunk. But six?

"Fir?"

"If you take Tibor Wat, I can take the guards. It's a *katah*, right?"

"I don't... I don't know."

"You don't know?" Firian demanded, tension making his words sharp.

"I don't know if it's strong enough."

"Bard, it has to be! You want to be a Master?"

"Yeah."

"This is where you do it. I'll count to thirty."

Weaving aimlessly through the revelers, Firian offered flints to anyone who asked. Mostly they just wanted a closer look at their new slave. A few called him over, glanced at him, waved him away. The girls noticed him with dead or vaguely pitying eyes. Not the responses he was used to. The whole place made his skin crawl.

He had to use the knife under the flints to stop these men. The Torithian War wasn't something talked about in taverns and debated in the Main anymore. It was something that roiled black rage through his blood. Bard had been right. This *was* different. They weren't an army. They were pleasure-seeking murderers that banded together for power.

Killing one man wouldn't destroy their influence. It would just hamper their unified decisions. But it was a start.

He lay a palm against the captain's door handle. Scenarios played through his mind. One against six. Hopefully not seven.

After a deep, steadying breath, he knocked.

A grim-faced man, bald like the rest, scowled as he opened the door. Firian heard a voice. Maybe the second guard. "Did you ask for someone?"

Keeping his head down, Firian crossed the threshold as though he had been called inside. The guards didn't stop him, but rather shut the door behind him. From the corner of his eye, he tried to take stock of weapons. The space crawled with shadows and smelled like sweat.

The chamber was as eclectic as the rooms outside. Two beds sat pressed together side by side, covered with an assortment of skins and blankets. In the

Into the Unreal

opposite corner, locked wooden chests had been piled in two stacks as high as the ceiling. A painting of four men against a landscape of yellow grasses and lakes dominated one wall. Carvings in the background made Firian think they had been stolen from Enderin. An oddly tooled piece of metal—it might have been tarnished gold—leaned unceremoniously against a tall round table where three men stood. One had a pen in his hand, evidently writing down what the captain said, while another stood closer, pointing at the map in a studied manner. A recorder and a map expert. He recognized the men at the table from Bard's descriptions: Tibor Wat's lieutenants. An elaborate colored lantern hanging from a tall stand provided enough light to see, but the room was still dim, even for Firian.

A drunk ruffian sat on the edge of a bed, clutching the neck of a bottle. Another man propped himself sullenly against the wall, as though he weren't part of the group, or they weren't doing what he suggested.

The talking man at the table looked up sharply when Firian entered. Tibor Wat. It had to be. He was thin and rigid, perhaps in his forties, with discerning eyes. A diamond shone in his ear.

"Did one of you call him here?" Wat asked. His raspy voice was captivating.

They all shook their heads.

"I heard you wanted a flint," Firian said, ushering as much humility as he could into his tone.

"No," said Wat, shooing him away. "We'll call you if we want you."

Firian's stomach tightened. He had counted beyond thirty. It had to be close to seventy by now. Still, the captain stood unharmed. "Now!" he told Bard in the Unreal, not losing his focus on the men in the room.

The captain wavered. It was a small motion, but enough that Firian could see him grow momentarily weak. That was all he needed.

He flipped open the box and grabbed the knife, letting the box and the sharp stones clatter to the floor. Ammunition for later.

He stabbed the scowling door guard in the neck before anyone had a chance to draw a weapon. Warm blood spattered out over his hands.

Ducking down, he let the second guard charge at him, lose balance. He slashed at the tendon in the man's knee. With a scream, he faltered, giving Firian enough time to stand and kick him out of the way.

Others were coming. No time to finish him off.

A fist slammed against his ear and the world spun. The room pitched like a ship's deck on a stormy sea. Firian staggered to the side until he hit the wall. The captain had backed away and was digging through a pile of blankets beside the motionless drunk. What was he looking for?

Pushing off from the wall, Firian slashed at the man in front of him. The recorder. Had he been the one to punch him? No matter. He barreled into the man, using their momentum to crush him against the table.

Behind the table, the map expert backed up a step, slipping on one of the fallen flints.

The crack of splintering wood sounded through the room. The table had split, but the recorder only winced before straightening again with his pen held firmly in his fist. Firian faced him. The captain was still burrowing through the blankets and the drunk only stared, uncomprehending. The map expert struggled to get back to his feet.

Behind Firian, the man who had languished against the wall approached, sword in hand, quick but clumsy.

They had him surrounded, but Firian had practiced this. He stomped hard on the insole of the man behind him, ducking to avoid being stabbed by the recorder. The sullen man grunted in pain. Firian brought his knife up with him when he straightened, drawing an uneven line from crotch to neck. The man screamed and stumbled back, thrashing until he fell to the floor.

When the map expert, now standing again, didn't make a move, Firian spun to face the man with the now broken foot.

A sword. A sword was all he saw.

He dodged to the side. He was fast, but not fast enough. Surprise more than pain sent a shockwave through his body as the sword sliced into his right ear. Was it still on his head? Did he still have his ear?

Firian savagely hacked at the man's sword hand. His little knife didn't go all the way through, but it was enough to disarm him. The sword clattered to the floor. Rather than pick it up, exposing his back, he drove the knife into the man's heart, all the way up to the hilt.

"Hey!"

The slur in this one word told Firian it was the drunk. Almost annoyed at the interruption, he spun and stabbed the man before he'd gone two steps.

The bottle rolled across the floor, chugging out reddish liquid over the floor.

Now with time to grab the sword, he snatched it from among the skittering flints and quickly finished off the injured guard and the frightened map expert.

He was shaking by the time he turned around to find the captain unconscious on the bed. Behind him, a girl shook, holding a blanket up to her face. She stared, terrified, at Firian.

He scanned the bodies, blood still burbling out of the wounds. The captain's chest didn't rise. When Firian stepped forward, the girl squeaked. A flint skittered forward. He hadn't needed them after all.

"Don't worry," he said, reaching out to touch the captain's back with his knife. After poking him a few times, he was content that the man wouldn't get up again. With his other hand, he gripped his shoulder and rolled him onto his back. Wide-eyed surprise was branded on Wat's face.

Firian sighed, almost giddy, though there was more to do. Bard had come through. And so had he. Barely. He raised his hand to his ear, but couldn't bring himself to touch it. He could feel the warm blood oozing down his neck. It was starting to hurt.

He cocked his head to the side, feeling oddly playful. "Is it still there?" he asked the girl.

She didn't answer.

"The ear," he clarified, before realizing that she might not speak the common tongue.

"Yes," she breathed.

Into the Unreal

He let out a sigh of relief.

A thump in the other room caught his attention. He held out his hand for her to stay where she was—on a bed with two dead bodies—and listened at the door. Another thump followed the first. He smoothed back his hair, wiped some of the blood from his neck onto his red pants, and opened the door.

The sight sent a smile over his face.

Two Torithians lay dead. Several others were already facing the wall with hands on their heads. The knives aimed at their backs kept them in line. Tanyu, disguised as he was, dealt with the remaining pirates as others threw bewildered prisoners to the far side of the room. None of the slaves appeared injured at all.

"Master Kess."

He turned to see Erron, his former hall master, at his side. Unlike many of the others, Erron was still dressed in Academy black. The knife he held in one hand gleamed with blood.

"We're subduing the other areas now."

Grunts and ringing steel echoed through the cavernous rooms. His Tanyu were brutal and quick, using all means to force the pirates to surrender. Firian adjusted his grip on the sword. The hilt felt sticky with blood. From his vantage point, all he had to do was watch as victory became his. It was mesmerizing.

"Can you see any of this?" he asked Bard, whose presence he could still feel as close as he could feel his own tripping heartbeat.

"See what?" The voice was faint.

"You did it. You killed the captain."

When Bard didn't respond, Firian went fully into the Unreal to picture him. Bard stood in a blank space, shoulders hunched, arms trembling. "You did it," Firian repeated.

Bard nodded, then he looked up at Firian. "Did they surrender?"

"It's happening now."

Bard's chest rose with ragged breaths. "And the slaves...?"

"All fine."

Firian could see Bard swallow hard. No wonder. He had just killed someone for the first time. Though he was reeling, he had helped win the war.

Standing up taller, Firian addressed the room. He still felt blood trickling at his neck, but he almost relished it now. He would wear any scar that came from today as proudly as he wore the iron circle. "Captain Tibor Wat is dead," he announced from the doorway.

The news spread rapidly as the Tanyu passed it to the other Talented minds in and around the fortress. He felt it buzzing. After the Torithians' surrender was official, he would tell the Western Kingdom of the victory.

No, not the Western Kingdom.

Kiria.

15

KIRIA

KIRIA WRUNG the moisture from her hair with a towel. Hanging her head sideways, she squeezed until her fingers felt damp. A few candles had been lit around her room, but it was still dark since the setting sun no longer shone through the multi-paned windows. She could barely see her own reflection in the glass. But she didn't care.

She hadn't heard from Firian all day. She had checked the Unreal compulsively, but he was never there. She knew he was on the island, that this was the day he was planning to storm the Torithians' compound. What if he rushed in on his own? It wouldn't surprise her. Firian always wanted to seem the hero. But, if he could manage this—if he could end the war—he really would be.

When would she hear from him?

She realized that she was gripping the towel in frozen fists. Easing it off her head, she waved Candrae over to brush out her tangles. The seat felt hard as she sat on it, wrong somehow. How could she sit, how could she do anything, when the Torithian War hung in the balance?

She squinted at her reflection, trying to see if the raised scar from the arrow wound were visible through her thin night dress. She didn't think so. Not only had the Torithians attacked her, but they had killed her father, and killed or imprisoned hundreds of Endrian and Torithian citizens. It was time for this conflict to end.

She pictured Firian standing in the Unreal throne room just before her coronation, both of them new world leaders. *I said I wanted to show you*, he had said. *So show me, then!* Although she was getting ready for bed, no sleep would come to her that night without news. *Come on, Firian!*

Maybe he didn't come because...

Her gaze shifted back to the darkening window. It wasn't late. He could still come to her. She wouldn't fear that something had happened to him until many more hours had passed.

She gave a small smirk. Firian wouldn't let anything happen to him. He was too cocksure and, frankly, too talented. At least from what she'd seen. She shoved away her fear. *He can do it.*

A small mental tug sent her tumbling into the Unreal, checking for him again. As soon as she closed her eyes, Firian appeared. Intense relief coursed through her. The halls of the palace materialized around him as he walked toward her.

Firian wore dark clothes, stained with brushed-off mud, his hair disheveled from fighting. He hadn't bothered to clean up his appearance for her, and he looked better for it.

She caught her breath enough to ask the question. "So?"

"It's done," he said in a low voice.

Her hand flew to her mouth and tears started in her eyes. "They surrendered?" she whispered, hardly daring to believe it.

The background wavered as he half-smiled at her. "I said I could end the war."

"You did say that," she replied. "And I told you *I* could end it. Remember?" She paused. Face to face, they said nothing more for a while. A thin streak of red leaked down his temple. She craned to look closer and saw that one of his ears was covered in blood. "What happened?" she asked, raising one hand to hover over that ear.

He brought her hand down again. The touch burned. "War. I'm fine."

"You always say you're fine." She barked a laugh to calm her mounting nerves. Why was she nervous? "We did it." When she blinked, tears stung her eyes.

He lifted his mouth in a smile. "Your wars are over."

Both of them. Faces passed before her mind—people who had lost loved ones, those who could now come home, those who never would...

When she came out of her reverie, his face was very close to hers. Maybe too close. He looked unwaveringly into her eyes. Her heart pumped hard in her chest. He had light freckles, this close. She didn't move away. She should go, tell the other Keepers... but she stayed. The moment stretched, warm and tingling, between them.

She closed her eyes and hugged him tight. The hug was a decision, a leap. A sob escaped her as all the tension started to ease away. "The war is over," she murmured, her voice almost breaking. She pressed her face to his chest as she held his strong body in her arms. *Is it okay to do this?* They had been through so much together, for and against each other.

He smelled like sweat and trees, not pine this time but something more tropical, like the smell in the solarium. She backed up to look at him. "Thank you."

He leaned forward until their foreheads touched, his strong arms reaching around her. It was hard to breathe.

Then, slowly, she tilted her face forward. Her nose rocked against his, and then her lips. As she pressed closer, his lips felt soft against hers. Heat flushed through her body.

After a beat, he responded so intensely it made her stumble backward. She grabbed onto him for support, feeling his back tense under his thin shirt as he pulled her into him.

With a sort of desperation, he raked his fingers through her hair as he kissed her. She felt the heat of his breath against her mouth as he thumbed the shell of her ear from top to bottom.

Her fingers closed around the neck of his black shirt. Tentatively, she felt his chest, his neck, his hair. When she reached his ear, he tensed and squeezed her wrist, bringing her hand down to his chest again.

Firian had bound her wrists another time too.

"Wait, wait," she murmured, stepping back, looking at the ground. *What am I doing?* Her wide eyes found his, mirroring the confusion she felt. "Wait, I..." Her cheeks flamed and she glanced away, feeling small and winded.

A few moments ticked by. "Have you never done this before?" he asked, betraying surprise.

She shook her head solemnly. "No."

"It's just thoughts," he said, mouth twisted in a smirk. The background materialized again. Palace hallway. She glanced at the *sachion* tree, the patterned rugs.

Her face burned.

Just thoughts. He's right. It's just thoughts.

She changed the pattern of a rug from purple to blue and back again. Her gaze traced a few leaves on the tree. Hard to believe this was all Unreal. She had forgotten.

She looked back in his eyes. They were shining with the fight and the victory and the kiss. The kiss. She released a deep-held breath as he held her and closed his mouth over hers again. Her insides ached as she craned into him.

He walked her backward until she hit a hard wall. His body followed and pressed her against it. She gripped him closer, closer. His brow furrowed as he bent his head to hers, sucking the kisses from her lips, dragging his hands through her hair. She arched against him, wanting more.

One of his fingers traced a gentle line over the side of her neck. His hand slid down her neck, her collarbone, her ribs, her hip, and into the open space at the small of her back. His dangerous hands. They knew where to go to make her crave just a little more. More heat, more pressure, more weight of his muscular body against hers.

Breath came hard as she reached for his hair, soft and dirty, and scraped her nails gently across his scalp.

With a moan, he pulled back and drew his shirt over his head in one swift motion from the back of the neck. He was on her again, muscles straining as he touched her in a thousand small ways.

She wrapped her arms around him and felt the muscles slide under the skin, his shoulder blades shifting as he held her and pressed his lips to the hollow of her neck. Raised, calloused scars punctuated his skin like notes, and one long scar she remembered. She traced them with her fingers, playing him like music.

Her core grew hotter with every hungry kiss. He kissed her like he needed her, like he had practiced before. She let herself sink into his expert hands. Yes, no inner voice telling her...

Inner voice.

"Wait," she said breathlessly again. "Wait, Firian." The dry-mouthed huskiness of her voice surprised her and sent a fresh ache to her stomach.

He licked his lip absently as he stood up, barely a finger's width between them. The panes of his strong chest, his disheveled hair, his sultry blue-eyed gaze, the muscles over his arms, his abs, his hips, ripped away her words.

She fixed a flyaway hair as she caught her breath. "We can't."

He sidled closer, his legs against hers. "Why not?" His voice was low, teasing.

Her burning face betrayed her. "We can't go so far." Keepers had to stay pure.

He hummed and she felt the vibration in his chest. An agreement and an invitation. "I've waited a long time for this. You"—he licked her bottom lip—"are so beautiful." A firm kiss on the mouth. "And we"—he drew close, lingered, the point of his upper lip barely grazing hers, drew back again—"ended two wars together."

His breath played on her mouth, waiting. Her heart pounded painfully. He thought she was beautiful, just like this. Her chin tilted up to meet his lips again. He pressed her back with new passion. She gave into the kiss, letting her hands roam over his body, running over the white scars on his torso and adding to the ones near his neck. Relief and pleasure blended together as she stopped thinking of anything but his hands, his mouth, his warrior's body on hers.

Finally they released each other and stepped back, breathing heavily. Neither spoke.

But they'd admitted something to each other that they couldn't hide anymore. More than the war had changed.

KIRIA'S STOMACH still felt twisted as she ran out of the room to tell the other Keepers that the war was over. Not about Firian. She'd keep that a secret for now, but hopefully not for very long. The excitement of the kiss was still burning off, but so slowly that she thought she could live on the high for several days.

The look in his eyes, the relief of accepting what she had felt for a long time, longer than she wanted to admit…

She sighed. Firian Kess could be a good man after all—still a dangerous one, but a good one. At least, he'd followed through on his promise to help with the war, and that counted for something.

Okay, she thought, remembering the Tanyuin War and the last Head, maybe Firian wasn't a good man, but he was on his way to becoming one. And their tryst had only been in the Unreal. These were tempting, luxurious thoughts. That was all.

But that wasn't all. Something about that kiss had gone beyond the Unreal. To her, he was darkness and thrill. And very real.

The way he had kissed her… like he'd longed to do it for months.

She could be rational about it later. Today, the Torithian War was over, and she could still feel Firian's lips on hers.

Stopping outside Atty's door, she grinned, sure she was practically glowing with happiness.

16

FIRIAN

FIRIAN SMILED to himself as he walked up the moonlit gangplank onto the ship. It creaked and thudded, echoing through the chilled air. The breath of the water lapping below floated over his face and through his hair.

His heart was still thumping fast. *Finally!* He laced his fingers behind his back and leaned back a moment to peer at the star-splashed sky. *Finally.*

"Master Kess?"

He looked down. The source of the accented voice stood at attention. He was a lithe young man, one of the Endrian recruits, dressed not in the silver and blue armor of Brithnem, but a more subdued bronze and brown. The buttons on his uniform shone in the dim light.

"Yes?"

"Shall I bring the prisoners aboard?"

"Yes, bring them up. Put thirty in the hold of each ship."

"Yes, sir. I'll bring them up now."

Firian nodded once to the young man as he sped away. There was something familiar about his black hair.

Moments later, an escort of armed men led a line of shackled pirates down the darkly pebbled beach to the ship. The men, stripped of their weapons, now looked like marooned sailors, smudged with grime. Some smelled strongly of alcohol and not all of them were dressed. Others were huge and muscular, with thick necks and jutting jaws. Their eyes darted dangerously, but the guards' swords kept them in check.

Firian stayed by the gangplank to meet them. He had been the Tanyuin Head for only a few weeks and his forces had defeated these men, now subject to him. If he told them to kneel, or to wait, or to fight, they would have to do as he said without question. He scrutinized their hard-set, sunburnt faces as they plodded on board. Fresh images of debauchery assaulted him like a disgusting smell.

The slaves would be safe now. Enderin had been placed in charge of sorting them out and getting them off the island safely over the next several weeks. It would take a monumental effort to bring each person back to their home, if they had one, but, from what Firian understood, they were going to try.

If the Academy hadn't needed more soldiers to defend it, he would gladly have left the pirates to fend for themselves, trapped on a tiny island somewhere. But they were proof of his victory—the victory he and Kiria and Bard had engineered together.

Kiria had looked so beautiful as she adored him. A pleasurable chill covered his body. Kissing her had been so much better than he'd imagined that he'd almost forgotten himself. Even as he reminded her that they were in the Unreal, that she could lose herself in him without consequences, he'd flinched when she touched his injured ear. He would be more careful to keep his bearings next time.

Impatience flooded through him. He was already tired of being around these pirates who had prodded and debased him, who had killed Kiria's father and attacked her without a thought. A shudder of hatred replaced his reverie.

As the Torithians came back into focus, a wad of thick spittle flew to the end of his boot.

Heat rushed to Firian's face. "Who was that?" he shouted.

The column of plodding men marched on.

Firian breathed heavily through his nose, knocking his defiled boot against the planks. He turned to one of the nonresponsive guards. "Who was that?"

"Who was that?" they echoed, prodding the closest men.

One man writhed from being jammed in the rib, but no one looked up.

Firian surveyed them as though staring hard enough would reveal the culprit. How dare they spit at him! He was the Tanyuin Head. He had taken his position by force, and—if he had to—he would maintain it the same way. Tanyu would not suffer indignities.

Overcome by the strength of his anger, he stepped back. He had to think. If he didn't calm down, he would hurt someone.

He turned and stormed across the deck to his cabin, a large one right beside the captain's.

Pulling the door hard shut, he glared at the painting on the wall, tempted to rip it down. Who needed luxuries at sea, anyway? It reminded him too much of the pirates and their spoils.

Shaking with rage, he leaned down and rubbed the grime off the toes of his boots. Hot blood still coursed through his face. It shot down, tingling, to his fingers.

With deliberate mindfulness, he took a deep breath and stood up straight. The effort constricted his throat, but he slowly felt himself getting calmer, though not forgiving.

The pirates thought they had a rough life, thick-skinned, not showing respect to anyone but their bull-headed leaders. Idiots. They were like animals. He would show them how respect worked. They would give it to him one way or the other. An army wasn't built on anarchy. He had won their services fairly.

Something else bothered him about these men. Their expression. He'd seen the same contempt edging glances back at the Academy. The same venom. Firian had the Academy under control, didn't he? He'd considered threats from outside so much that he hadn't looked inward. He crossed his arms. Anyone could harbor the same disrespect, the same desire for him to die...

Many people had seen the man spit. Firian bit the inside of his lip until he tasted coppery blood. If he was going to remain the Tanyuin Head and see Kiria again, he'd have to give into his first impulse to strike back hard at the offender. It was almost calming not to have to hold back.

First, he would have someone alert him when they were over the deepest water between Torith and Brithnem.

Convinced his face wasn't as flushed as it had been before, he stepped out of his cabin. The young man with black hair—why did he think he was a young man? He might be older than he was—marched past him on the deck.

"You!"

The man stopped. "Yes, Master Kess?"

"What's your name?"

"Jac Tanery."

Firian blinked. "Tanery?"

"Yes, Bard's brother."

Firian furrowed his eyebrows. They had heard about each other for years, but had never met. He felt almost territorial, and Jac had some kind of challenge flash across his face as well. It took a moment before he replied, "Tell me when we sail over the deepest water."

Jac tilted his head down in agreement. "Of course, sir."

"Master."

"What?"

"It's Master Kess, not sir."

HANDS BEHIND HIS BACK, swishing his long black coat, Firian paced in front of the line of men. None of them seemed repentant for the outrage he had suffered earlier. At this point, he didn't care who the culprit was. They would all pay for it.

He slowed to a stop and faced them. All these Torithians looked similar in the blackness—bulk-headed sailors with veins across their temples. A lantern swayed behind him, casting a pale glow over the waiting figures. Where Firian blocked the light, there was deep darkness.

He separated his words carefully. "Prisoners! The Academy and the Kingdom should have ordered your death, but you have the privilege to become soldiers in the world's greatest army."

One man in the line shifted uncomfortably. Another's mouth twitched. *A laugh?*

Firian felt himself flush again. Did these men have no respect at all? No, they didn't respect his authority or even human life.

Ignoring the fear pushing at the edges of his mind, Firian pointed to the second man. The Kingdom soldiers brought him forward.

The man brought his small eyes up to meet Firian's. They glinted defiance beneath the submissive exterior. Firian stared back, feeling heat rising to his cheeks. He brought his hands to his side.

"I am the Tanyuin Head," he said, "and I decide who lives and who dies." Saying those words calmed him a little, despite the pesky feeling that they may have sounded childish.

He swept a meaningful glance across the other men standing on the creaking deck. The Kingdom soldiers looked back at Firian with open suspicion. His comment must have rattled them. A few of them had even laid their hands on their weapons, waiting to see what he would do.

Though their threatening attitudes should have unsettled him further, he didn't fear what the soldiers would do. An open threat sent the blood of battle zinging through his veins with grim pleasure. Hidden threats, unknowns... those were the stuff of nightmares. Sias Jairon hadn't seen Firian coming.

As the highest-ranking person in this fleet, Firian had every right to put these Torithians in their place now. The soldiers would do nothing but watch and obey. They'd been trained for it. Scanning the ranks of shaved heads, Firian calculated how much it would take to send a message strong enough to subdue them all. In a commanding voice, he said, "Three of you will die tonight."

A few of them cried out in mixed languages, blaming the man next to them. Had their arms not been bound, a fight certainly would have broken out on the spot. Several of the men seemed to indicate one person in particular, whose loud protests almost drowned out the others.

Firian held up a hand for silence.

The undisciplined pirates didn't even notice at first. Firian's muscles tightened in frustration. Finally, they simmered into near silence. Firian suddenly couldn't wait to be back at the Academy, among the Tanyu, who knew how to be still.

The prisoners' chests rose and fell heavily. They darted glances across to each another. Even the Endrian soldiers knit their foreheads.

Firian turned his attention back to the man in front of him. The laughing man. Drops of sweat beading on his head betrayed his anxiety.

"That number will increase if anyone else disrespects the Tanyu, your protectors."

The sloshing sea was like a heartbeat.

The memory of the welt-covered girl and the emaciated children hardened his resolve. "Throw him in."

After only a fractional hesitation, the soldiers forced the struggling man to the railing and looked back at Firian.

"Throw him in," he repeated.

He was a large man, writhing against his ties, bending his knees to stay low. Ultimately, it took three soldiers to lift him over. He dropped heavily, as the first sound ripped from his mouth. A scream only started, then cut off in a merciless gurgle.

Firian's stomach flipped at the sound, but hopefully no one could see his discomfort. That Torithian deserved it.

When he turned back to the men, not one of them moved, soldier or prisoner alike. Waves splashed against the hull; sails flapped and strained against the masts.

Covertly, Firian took a deep breath, steadying his voice. "That leaves two."

That night, Firian reached his mind toward the Torithians as they lay asleep in the hold of the ship. Not one of them had the Talent. Too bad. He had almost hoped for a fight.

Whirring anger buzzed red in the Unreal, like a film over his eyes, sinking deep into him. He tried to picture the man who had spit. The First Level, the Second Level... He hadn't gone to the Second Level often since he and Belik had managed to take power from the last Tanyuin Head. A little out of practice, he dove down into the Unreal from where he was.

A brief sensation of choking.

Breathe, breathe! He sucked in a shaky breath. It had been too long. He should have every meeting with Belik in the Second Level so he never fell behind. Belik was his right-hand man—now managing everything back at the Academy—but he could never give him an excuse to lord over him.

He cast his mind once more toward the sleeping Torithians. Now he saw something, like objects in a murky pond. These men didn't have the Talent, but they did have subconscious minds that could be manipulated even below the level of a dream. Here was the small slice of them that intersected with the Unreal.

Firian's heart started racing, blood pumping frantically through his veins. What could he do to them?

Throwing the man overboard had scared some of them, but if he killed two more in a way that none of them understood, that would be even more frightening. He remembered the prisoners they kept shackled to protect their filthy ships, and the young girls they abused for their amusement. These men deserved to die. None of them deserved the distinction of fighting on the Tanyu's behalf. If he didn't kill more of them, they would turn on him. One day, in the dark, a pillow would smother him in his sleep...

He let those ideas circulate a couple more times before advancing. He was not killing innocent people.

Experimentally, he turned toward the farthest room in the hold, focusing all his energy on the two figures sleeping there. He slowly willed the image to change. Now they were corpses. Not asleep, dead.

His heart jumped in his chest. The pulsing of the figures—their breathing, their heartbeat—skipped. One of them woke and bucked upright.

Firian pushed against the figures again, even harder this time. *Focus. Focus.* It felt like bending a thick branch. Bit by bit, splinter by splinter, their minds gave. A startled cry sounded far away. Firian kept his focus.

Something burst.

Firian jumped. *What was that?*

He swam up through the narrow channel to the Unreal he knew, with its vibrant colors and endless space, and then opened his eyes in the real world.

For some reason, he lay sprawled on the ground. His legs felt too heavy as he tucked them under himself in a crouch. His crown had rolled to the edge of his reach. Shaking, he hooked it on the nearest bedpost.

No one had ever done what he just did. At least, he'd never heard of anyone doing it. He squeezed his eyes shut. What had he even done? Had Belik ever mentioned this before? He flipped through years of memories, of practice, of goals. No, he'd never heard of something like this.

That break had devastated the Torithians, both of them. A familiar sinking in his gut told him they were dead.

He settled back on his heels, chest heaving, bothered that his hands were still trembling. He splayed his fingers against the floor to still them. Uncharacteristic exhaustion settled over him, and a mix of emotions so strong that they resolved into confusion. He had figured out a new deadly ability even Belik didn't know. How far could this power go? Did this mean he could hurt *anyone*, just with a thought? Pride and revulsion warred inside him.

The next morning, two Torithians lay dead in a pool of their own blood.

17

KIRIA

Kiria shoved a large bite of soft-boiled egg in her mouth, too preoccupied to realize it was unladylike until afterward.

Amir Parohim gave her an imperious look veiled as concern. She met his glance, daring him to comment, and turned away. Candles lined the center of the grand table, the soft light flickering. Despite the hour, this room was still dark. A freshness in the air and the bags under Jori's eyes spoke of the morning, but here, in this windowless banquet hall, time seemed to stop.

Cúron's familiar, booming laugh sounded a few seats down. Since news of their victory broke, it was as though a bottle had been unstopped. Guards smiled and clapped each other on the shoulder as they went to their posts. Jori kept Kiria updated on all the extra parties in the city. Rejoicing followed her everywhere.

Because of the war, her coronation tour had been put on hold. Now that it was over, she could leave immediately, to meet and rejoice with people all over the Kingdom. Her mother had debated whether to come along. She would have been welcome, but, in the end, they decided Merian might take some of the attention that was meant to establish Kiria as the new Keeper. So she graciously stepped aside.

True to his word, Cúron had also publicly credited her with the victory. Because of her successful treaty with the Tanyuin Academy, she was the face of the alliance.

But this victory was Firian's as much as hers. Her skin tingled with the memory of their kiss. If her mother asked now, she would admit that she was interested in someone. But she wouldn't say who. Not yet, anyway. Despite all Firian had done for them, the people around this table had extremely mixed feelings about him. She could hardly blame them for their doubts. In the past, he had done terrible things.

He hadn't appeared the past couple nights. Probably busy with Torithians.

There was no way he regarded their kiss as a mistake. They'd both wanted it. She would try to be patient, but even now, she wanted to check the Unreal for him.

Atty burst out laughing, bringing her attention back to the table. He pressed his hands over his mouth as Jori leaned to whisper something else to him. Jori's face distorted into the mockery of a fancy noble. The brothers both looked furtively at the faces around the table.

She couldn't even tell them about Firian. The knowledge brought a slight sinking to her stomach. It wasn't as though she were doing anything wrong, was she?

Jori saw her watching them and winked. He couldn't let them in on their joke with the table between them, but she already suspected she knew what he was saying.

More than once, he'd whispered in her ear, mimicking the voices of two people at a party. Since they were out of earshot, he could invent any wild story he liked. "Oh, my dear, I must go off to see the nymphs on the Sharb Isles." In a higher voice, "Darling, don't think of falling in love with them!" A lower voice. "I already have. Her name is Mephi...bosheba." A laugh at his own absurdity, soon collected again. "I couldn't help myself. After we both rode the fish around the island, it was all over." "You rode fish?" "Yes, saddles and everything." "Oh! No one could ever be as charming as you. I'll never love anyone again." But the woman's mouth hadn't stopped moving and he had to think of more. "The way you smell like an ocean god," he continued in his high voice. "And... make love like a... dolphin." The man began speaking. "Oh, Penelope, you'll always be in my heart. We'll name our half-nymph child after you." "Even if it's a boy?" "Of course, my dear."

The memory made her chuckle. She kicked him under the table.

He finished what he was saying to Atty and then cast her a furtive glance. Atty caught on immediately and looked at her with a question in his eyes.

"You want to come on the coronation tour next week?" she asked Jori in an undertone. She hadn't spent much time with him in recent months, since she had been so busy learning all the duties of a Keeper while being the main point of contact in planning the war.

Atty turned to his brother. "That's a lot of traveling," he explained, as though it weren't obvious. The realization must have hit Atty hard on his own tour. "Never enough hot water."

Jori straightened and faced him. "Why didn't you invite me on yours?"

"My coronation tour?" Atty's eyebrows scrunched downward in thought. "I wasn't sure I was allowed to invite anybody."

"You can invite anyone you like when you're Keeper," said Jori.

Atty half-shrugged, not exactly apologetic, but a little ashamed of his past naiveté. "Well, I didn't want to bother anyone."

In mock astonishment, Jori put a hand to his chest. "Are you calling me a nuisance?"

"Well, you're not exactly cut out for Kingdom business."

Kiria waited until no one seemed to be looking before shoveling her side of capers onto the plate Atty held out for her. He was the only one who liked them. Jori had already added his to the little green pile.

"We both know that." Jori turned to Kiria again. "So where are you going on this tour?"

She described the route that started south and made its way northeast and finally back again, roughly in a large circle.

Chetana, her serving girls, and a host of guards and servants were the only ones she knew would accompany her. She couldn't relax with any of them. If a friend didn't come, she would be tempted to spend all her time with Firian. Eventually, someone might find out she was seeing him, and that couldn't happen yet. That is, if he ever came back.

"I didn't go south," Atty said, waving for another egg. "I wonder why they're adding King's Heights to your trip. It's nowhere near Charäkhnem." Atty had formally requested the Charäkhni princess's hand in marriage, but he hadn't talked about his plan for a while. The match would strengthen their most important alliance, he claimed, and Kiria thought he was right. That is, if the King of Charäkhnem agreed. As far as she knew, Atty hadn't heard back.

"I wish it were Shifra," she said. "That was beautiful." She stopped short, realizing they could draw the connection to Firian and ask about him. Thankfully, neither did.

"That's too far away," Atty replied. He nodded thanks as a servant placed another egg cup in front of him. He tapped the shell with his spoon. "But King's Heights. I'm sure they haven't been included for generations, maybe at all."

That was partially the reason it had been added to the itinerary. "They're still part of the Kingdom," she said. Honestly, it didn't sound like it would be her favorite stop either. The people of King's Heights were so private, and their reputation (real or not) wasn't flattering. One could spot someone from that city anywhere. They were stronger, meatier versions of Kingdom Dwellers with their dark hair, light skin. Stories had it that they were proud of their ability to survive, their tough blood, and they were mistrustful of visitors, particularly Khelê. But those were old stories. It was time to repair some of those fractured reputations on both sides.

"You still haven't answered the question," she said.

Jori placed both elbows on the table and peaked his fingers together. Atty rolled his eyes at his brother's theatrics, but there was a smile in the corner of his mouth as he took a bite of egg.

"Hm," Jori hummed, resting his chin high on his fingers. "I'm terribly busy."

She kicked him again. "Liar."

He brought his hands down. "Fine. You're right. I'm not sure I would like it, but you know I like adventure."

"And parties and parades. There will be parties between all the meetings and ceremonies."

Jori turned to his brother. "Can you do without me for a while?" His question was joking, but the slightest bit of seriousness crept into his tone. Sometimes Atty got lonely, especially since their father died.

"I think so," he said stoutly. "Don't make me look like a fool when you go to Charäkhnem!"

"Oh, you can do that all by yourself, I'm sure."

Kiria leaned forward and lowered her voice. "Did you hear back from Shear Ganesha?"

"A few days ago." The announcement gave Atty a glowing smile.

Kiria grinned. "Why didn't you tell me? That's wonderful!"

"The letter talked about 'final negotiations,'" Jori said, "so it's not finalized."

"But I'm expecting another letter before the end of the week," Atty said. "If he agrees, then Princess Haved will travel back with you."

"Oh, Atty, that's... I'm so happy for you!" She reached across the table to pat him on the arm, the one laced with tattoos from his fingers all the way up until they disappeared beneath his sleeve. She knew Atty had been longing to do something positive for the Kingdom, to prove to everyone that he could make his father proud.

"Have you met her yet?" she asked. "Is that something else you're not telling me?"

"No, he has not," Jori said impishly, separating each word. Atty responded with a look that said the two of them had had this conversation before.

"So you don't know what she looks like?" Kiria asked.

"Hag," Jori muttered.

Atty smacked him. "No, but I've seen a painting and met Prince Amrit, her brother."

"Does she speak the common tongue?" The thought hit her with some force. How would Atty communicate if the girl didn't speak the same language? Atty had always been a hopeless romantic—hopeless, in the sense that he almost never knew what to say or do except follow girls with his moony eyes. She had witnessed it dozens of times. His poor heart. Maybe he could communicate through kind gestures. He'd never been very good with words anyway.

"She's been practicing," Atty said. "I heard she's as good as Amrit."

The last time the prince had come with the Charäkhni ambassadors, his speaking skills had much improved. Apart from his thick accent, his knowledge was fluent.

"I'm glad," she said. "Good."

Atty swallowed another caper-peppered bite of egg and waved his spoon in the air in an almost Jori-like gesture. "See?" he said. "I can't have you messing anything up for me."

"What am I going to do?" Jori protested.

"Flirt with anything that moves, probably," Kiria said, laughing.

Atty gave his brother a pointed look.

A smile slowly widened across Jori's face. "I don't see what the problem is."

"Are you sure you want to invite him?" Atty asked her, half-teasing, half-pleading.

She paused, taking stock of the people already scheduled to leave with her. Jori would be more of a help than a liability. Probably. She nodded. "Absolutely."

18

FIRIAN

Curiosity to see the famed Academy piqued as they got closer. Firian read it in their body language. He was eager to get back too. He had ordered new training barracks to be built, but he'd only seen the plans. The best place for them was the relatively tree-less area behind the bakery, where the festival had been last month, where Old Danior kept his bees.

Firian marched in front now, guiding The Endrians and the prisoners along the path to Tánuil that he knew so well. Although he'd overheard several Kingdom soldiers talking about wanting to see the Academy too, they had all been ordered to sail back home immediately after they docked to let off Firian and the rest.

The Academy rose before them, a sheer face of dark rock in the fading light. A smile played on his lips as he gazed up at it. Finally his. How different this entry was to his last mission. Now it felt more like coming back to a kingdom. Well, almost. The decision to make its location public changed the face of world politics, tilting it a little sideways on its axis. All because he had decided it would be so. Because the trade was worth Kiria's trust and loyalty.

For a moment, all those years of ingrained secrecy recoiled at having so many strangers with him. He forced himself to stand straight and walk like a returning king.

As they all came closer to Tánuil, Firian adjusted the iron circlet on his head so that the open square faced forward. Behind him came some of the best Masters, then Endrians in brown leather and mail jackets, then Torithians in the center (still shackled), then more Endrians, and finally more Tanyuin forces at the rear. If they walked three abreast, the line of troops would stretch practically the entire length of Tánuil.

Pride ran through Firian's entire body as he stepped into town, the Academy rising above him like a huge shadow of himself. The dark stones were soothing, impenetrable. Something that had been tight in his gut since the pirate's defiance on the ship started to loosen.

Whole families came out of their houses to see them. A man stood in his doorway with one arm around his wife's shoulder and the other across the chest of a small boy standing in front of them. As they passed, Hyrum the pub owner considered them thoughtfully, picking the grime from his nails with his apron. All eyes flitted over the Torithians, the Endrian soldiers, and the Tanyuin troops, but they rested on Firian. Something like fear emanated from the crowd. Firian caught a glimpse of Devanie, watching them through the window of the herbalist. Her eyes blazed. He smiled at her.

Tánuil barely had streets, much less military processions. It was no wonder the townspeople were awed. The strange thing was the silence. Word seemed to spread without anyone speaking. With the caution of animals unused to the sight of people, everyone came out of their homes and businesses until the majority of Tánuil stood gaping at them. The people seemed utterly unsure of what to do. Proud but afraid.

Though he didn't like speeches, Firian knew he should tell the people of Tánuil what had happened in the war, and how to treat these strangers. Some of them had grown up never having seen any, apart from the new recruits at the Academy. Their wide eyes said they would hang on every word. Suddenly, speaking sounded much more palatable.

He turned back to the men following him. "Lead these men to the barracks!" he commanded as they came abreast of Danior's bakery.

At his voice, more people emerged from doorways, swelling the crowd. Men and women in black appeared on the darkening road from the Academy. Even Tanyu wanted to see him.

His breathing quickened with excitement and he hopped on a slope so more people could see clearly. The Endrian troops started to lead the bound Torithians away. Firian turned to a nearby Tanyu. "Get everyone outside."

In a shockingly short time, more Tanyu and the few townspeople who hadn't noticed the parade came out to hear him. Slowly, everyone gathered around the slope where Firian stood.

Firian scanned the crowd, blood beating in his fingertips. "These are the Torithian pirates," he cried. "Now part of our army. Because of us, the Torithian War is over!" He scanned the darkest portion of the listeners and found Belik, whose eyes shone hungrily, full of amazement. He felt lightheaded. "Too long we've stayed in secrecy and fear. The Tanyu are the greatest fighting force in the world, and we shouldn't be afraid to show everyone what we are. Starting now, our location will no longer be hidden. You can trade freely with other nations."

Astonishment rippled across the townspeople, who all looked at each other. Some frowned, outraged; others acted overjoyed.

"Any strong man or woman can join our army, share in our greatness. All we ask is absolute loyalty." He laid special emphasis on the last two words as he watched the brawny backs of the prisoners disappear into the darkness. If the need arose, he would show everyone what he meant by those words.

A current of energy sparked and hummed under his skin, and he almost wished someone would challenge him right there. No one rose up, but his heart kept beating fast, ready for a fight. He took a deep breath. "Tomorrow, we announce ourselves to the world." An idea struck him. "But tonight, a war is over. Tonight, we celebrate!"

Scattered applause built to a roar. Even the Tanyu joined in. If Firian hadn't let the surrounding cities know about the Academy, this deafening noise would announce them just as well. The screaming became frenzied, the sound of shouting long subdued. Someone whistled.

Firian stepped down the slope and waved over the nearest Tanyu, Master Makai. He lowered his voice and told Makai to gather a few Masters to help watch the Torithians. He didn't want the pirates taking advantage of what was bound to turn into a wild night.

"Making a name for yourself, I see."

He turned around and found himself face to face with Belik, his eyes alight with pride.

"We haven't had a reason to celebrate for too long," Belik said.

Firian suddenly remembered the small funeral the Tanyu had held for the Sias Jairon, the last Head. They'd held it almost guiltily, but with an understanding that the Tanyu were great enough that any leader who had served for so long needed to be remembered and not left for the birds. He was buried too deep for wolves to dig him up, near the other Tanyuin Heads in an unmarked grave. A few Masters had attended. Firian had made an appearance, presiding as the current leader. The whole ordeal had been dreamlike.

Master Belik patted him heavily on the shoulder, his gaze flicking up to the circlet on his head. Firian touched it, almost unconsciously. Something over Firian's shoulder caught Belik's eye. "I'll leave you to it," he said. Not one for celebration, Belik began walking slowly back to the Academy.

Firian looked over his shoulder and saw Devanie. She had come out of the spice shop, skin flushed. She came up to him, breathless. Before she spoke, she paused, maybe considering how to address him. Should she call him Firian or Master Kess, the Tanyuin Head? The idea left him flushed as well. He took in her eager body—thin dress that clung in all the right places, soft brown hair, scent of musk and sage...

Not long ago, he would gladly have taken his cue and spent a torrid night with her. But now his mind wandered back to Kiria. Since that night in the Unreal, it never strayed far. The mere thought of her left Devanie's beauty hollow. Well, not entirely hollow. *Kiria doesn't have control over me.* The thought ran like a chant through his mind. He could spend the night with Devanie if he wanted to. The thing was, he didn't want to.

"I'm glad you're back," Devanie said, her voice husky and unsure. Her gaze searched his face, his eyes, his lips.

He stood before her for a heartbeat as she waited, anticipating his response.

A shorter Tanyu pressed his way through the crowd, his eyes full of happy tears. "Fir!" he cried.

Glad for the excuse to turn away from Devanie, Firian broke into a smile and clapped him on the arm. "Bard!"

Bard pulled him in for a hug. When he let go, Firian said, "Your layout worked. The job you did here..."

Bard's grin waned. In the poor light, his skin looked grayer than usual. "Thanks, mate. You okay?" His dark eyes gleamed, despite the circles under them.

Firian remembered his sliced ear, invisible under his hair. "Yeah. Just a few scratches." He felt invincible.

Apparently realizing Firian wasn't going to pay attention to her, Devanie turned away and acted as though she'd seen someone she knew in the crowd.

If this hadn't been a night for celebrating, he would have returned immediately to the Academy and dived into the Unreal to see Kiria again. He hadn't seen her since the kiss. His mind had been occupied with the Torithians dead because of his new ability, and, honestly, his vulnerability needed to subside before he encountered her again. Everyone knew a *katah* was dangerous if it went too far. Denying himself the right to see her, even for a few days, had been one of the greatest tests of his self-discipline. Maybe he was being overly cautious, but it would pay off when he saw her and the balance of power had returned safely to him.

"You hear about Tiev?"

Firian snapped back to reality. "No. What happened?" But the answer the clear from the moment he asked the question.

Bard swallowed. "He never came out of it. We couldn't do anything."

"Did Master Belik try to help him?"

"He said Tiev didn't want to come back." His bottom lids filled with weary tears. He cleared his throat and scrubbed at his eyes before they could fall.

"It's okay," Firian said, clapping him on the back and guiding him away from the other Tanyu so they wouldn't see Bard cry. Curious stares followed Firian, conspicuous in his crown. "You won a war!"

Bard sucked in a breath and nodded. He had just killed his first man, and Tiev had always been more Bard's friend than Firian's. He shouldn't have been surprised that Bard was in low spirits. But tonight was a night to celebrate.

"Come on. What can I get you? I'll get you an ale or a sticky bun or whatever you want. Five sticky buns!"

Bard's wide smile returned.

"Oh, and I brought your brother," he added.

"Where?" Brightening, he craned his neck to see.

"He's here. I think he's with the Torithians." Catching Bard's eagerness, he said, "Why don't you watch the prisoners tonight? I need a few Tanyu to make sure they stay under control."

"I'll just say hi." Bard didn't need more incentive. He sprinted off into the darkness. Firian followed behind, more slowly, a smile tugging at his mouth.

They'd really done it. Some of the tension of the past weeks started to melt away. Yes, Bard didn't agree with everything he did—especially the way he had come into power—but they'd won the Torithian War together. Enderin and others would be free from the pirates' oppression. Kiria had kissed him. All that work had mattered. Firian Kess, the boy from nowhere, had made all that happen.

By the time he caught up with Bard at the barracks, he felt lighter than he could ever remember feeling in his life, except maybe when he got into the Academy for the first time.

The barracks weren't finished, but they were coming along. They'd constructed them just where Firian had commanded, and they looked just large enough for the influx of Torithians. Dozens of Endrian soldiers stood outside. Others came and went with supplies and information. Commanders gave instructions. Some looked around with the same hungry curiosity Firian had seen earlier when they'd marched into town. Most of the soldiers noticed Firian with rapt attention when he approached.

A brief pang echoed in Firian's chest. Had anyone told Bard about what happened on the ship? He wasn't ready for him to know about his newfound ability.

Firian found Bard talking animatedly with Jac in the deep shadow along the back wall. Jac stood at attention when Firian came around the corner.

"...So Edom got married?" Bard was saying.

"Yes."

Something about Jac's response made Bard give a puzzled look before turning around and seeing Firian. He waved him forward. "Fir! You've met Jac? Well, yeah, you have." He turned back to his brother. "It's so weird to have you here!"

Jac cast Firian a glance with a hint of apprehension or defiance in it. "Master Kess," he greeted. It was a moment before he continued. "Yes, Edom got married a while ago. You know how he is."

Bard cut him off. "How old's Aline?"

"She's twelve."

Bard rolled his eyes in happy surprise. "Can't believe it! Oh, what's Edom's wife's name?"

"Istia. They're having a baby soon. Or they had it already. I've been away for a few months, so can't be sure."

"Ah, that's wicked! So happy for him." The lilting Endrian accent came out stronger in both of them as they talked together.

"Hey, why weren't you on the island with us?" A small but unmistakably cold note entered Jac's tone. He looked over Bard's black Tanyuin outfit with a falsely lighthearted smile.

Someone in a group of young Endrian soldiers behind him called out, "Jac! You on duty? Come with us! We're going to find a drink, if they have those here." A second boy laughed as though he'd told a joke.

Jac shot them a dazzling smile, a different version of Bard's. "Be there later!"

With dismissive cries, the group disappeared into the darkness, apparently eager to get on with the celebration.

"I thought you would be," Jac continued, "after everything that happened." His eyes flickered to Firian and then back to his brother.

Firian imagined he could see Bard's blush in the dark and his mood darkened. *Everything that happened?* Jac must be talking about the brief war between the Kingdom and the Tanyu. To Firian's knowledge, the Academy had never attacked Enderin, only the capital. And now that he was Tanyuin Head, all of that had stopped.

"I never wanted to be at war, yeah?" Bard replied. "It's over now, anyway." His shoulder twitched as though he were casting off gloomy thoughts of the past. A smile split his face again as he glanced back at Firian. "It's all over. And you're here! It's so good to see you again."

"Well, you never were a fighter." Jac punched Bard lightly on the arm, but his tone had become even more acidic.

Firian stepped forward and asked sharply, "Do you know what the Academy does?" A beat of frozen silence met his question. "Bard was working for me here. Tanyuin business you wouldn't begin to understand. He wasn't on Torith, but he didn't need to be. It was on my orders that he stayed. Without him, we wouldn't have taken the compound and won the war."

"I apologize, Master Kess. I didn't mean—"

"It's okay," Bard said quickly, but he gave Firian a grateful look.

"I'm going for some ale," Firian said. Bard cared enough about Jac to spend more time with him, but Firian didn't. "Come over when you're finished here. Let me know what I can get you." He gave one more pointed glare at Bard's older brother. "You earned it."

A KNOCK POUNDED on the door. Firian's head pounded with it. He opened his sticky eyes. Still dark.

As he sat up in bed, the room swam. This is why he avoided getting drunk—it made his mind fuzzy. Faint nausea churned in his stomach. Celebrating had been good while it lasted, but now all he wanted to do was sleep.

The knock sounded again. He set his jaw in frustration. *This had better be important.*

When he opened the door, Bard was there. He should have known. There were only two people the guard would let through without question: Bard and Belik.

"Firian, we're missing one of the Torithians!" he hissed. Urgency was written in every line of his face.

Firian cursed, unreasonably angry.

"He got out the window. They told me they thought everyone was asleep."

"Tell them all to find him," he said with a hard edge in his voice. His thoughts came piecemeal. "I don't care when it is. Tell me immediately and I'll come. Bring him to the place we were earlier. And wake everybody up if you have to!" He slammed the door.

Instantly, he regretted slamming the door in Bard's face. This wasn't his fault.

Firian pulled on a shirt and shoes. The crown and coat went on last before he left the room.

What gory timing! The first time outsiders see the Academy and one of them defies me. He couldn't let it stand. Ice raced through his veins. He'd have to make an example of the pirate once he was caught.

An hour later, Maz the border patroller found the Torithian in the woods. It took two men to bring him to the spot Firian had specified. The gray light of dawn shone just enough to see by. Trees and houses looked black in the chilly air.

Bard had apparently told the others what Firian said because everyone was up —people of Tánuil, warriors of the Academy, troops both victorious and defeated —and gathered where they had the night before to hear his speech. Colors were sluggish to return. Everyone moved slowly, some clearly fighting off hangovers. Firian wished their celebration hadn't been quite as short lived. Hopefully this display would instill confidence in him, though, and give them a reason to celebrate loyalty in the future. Or at least fear insurrection. They would be on his side after this, unquestioning, because no one could withstand the new Tanyuin Head.

Maz and another border patroller dragged the huge Torithian in front of the slope where Firian stood. The pirate's bald head reflected the dim light. He bared his teeth in defiance as he was forced to his knees.

Firian regarded him in silence for a moment, letting the gravity of the situation sink in. A light breeze waved his coat and made people in the crowd gather their sweaters and shawls closer.

This silence was different than last night's. Now, no one dared to breathe. They all waited to see what he would do. Tanyu had cut off heads of those who opposed them, but not since Firian had come. Now they preferred to work in the shadows. Nothing was more frightening than what people didn't understand or expect.

Firian closed his eyes.

If only he could do this with his eyes open, as he could with almost anything else in the Unreal. He might get there, but for now, he had to do it with his eyes closed. Maybe that added to the drama of the moment. After all, he wanted them all to remember this.

As Firian reached for his subconscious, the man shifted uncomfortably, apparently aware of pressure building inside him. Firian heard his knees in the dust. Feet began scrabbling against the ground, all in vain because he was held down. Panicked curses escaped his lips. They were in a different language, maybe Eradi, but curses always sounded the same. Firian felt the man's blood run faster, his breathing turn to terrified, angry gasps. *Focus.* He was almost there. The man's panting became screams, and Firian's heart beat harder to hear them. A warrior's scream held infectious fear. *Focus.*

Something released, and the man's screams stopped. A few new, shocked ones from the crowd sprang up in their place. Firian came up and up and opened his eyes into reality.

Mothers had turned away, hands to their faces. Children started crying, and a few Tanyu had their mouths hanging open in surprise. The Torithian lay face upward with his hands balled into fists. Through his eyes and his clenched teeth, blood seeped out. Black blood slowly soaked the ground beneath him.

Firian swallowed, feeling almost manic. He looked at the remaining prisoners and hoped they'd had a good view. This would happen to them too if they disrespected the Tanyu's gift of letting them live. Firian's hands shook and his tooshallow breathing wouldn't allow him to give another good speech. Light-headedness came on quickly.

Without a word, he marched off the slope and headed back to the Academy.

From the corner of his eye, he saw Maz bend down to scoop the lifeless body off the ground.

Everyone knew better than to talk to him. He saw the questions in their eyes, but everybody gave him a wide berth. He stalked down the path to the huge double doors and, by the time he reached them, his arms were shaking visibly. At least he hadn't fallen down this time.

Agitated, unable to stay still, he paced the length of the fountain courtyard and back. Almost no one was in the building. They had all come out to see his demonstration.

As the Tanyu began to come back, he retreated to his office. He almost dismissed the guard, but thought better of it, closing the door instead. He needed to feel alone. Leaning on the chair behind his desk, he sucked breath deep into his lungs and exhaled.

The door opened. Firian's head shot up as he prepared to pour curses on anyone who dared interrupt him. It was Belik with a glass of water. Firian's energy wilted and he fell into his chair. Belik wordlessly set the water glass in front of him on the desk. Firian took it and drank. The water tasted sweet on his dry mouth.

"Gory Torithians," Belik growled, settling into the chair across from him.

Firian nodded.

"I have Jovan over there now, heading up the training. He won't be easy on them either." He paused, looking at Firian with subdued eagerness. "I've... never seen anyone do what you did," he said. "If someone was thinking about going against you, they won't do it now."

Firian frowned. "Is anyone?"

"No, no." Belik waved a conciliatory hand. "Not now."

The next pause was pregnant with a question. Firian was too exhausted to ask what it was.

"Did that man have the Talent?" Belik finally asked.

Firian shook his head.

The answer excited his old Master. Pride shone on his face. "Then how did you do that?"

"I figured it out on the ship."

"Do you use the Second Level?"

Firian was too tired to feel the right amount of satisfaction. His knowledge had outstripped Belik, who had taught him everything he knew about being a Tanyu. Right now he just wanted to sleep.

When he didn't answer, Belik's enthusiasm faded back into his regular stoicism. "You'll have to tell me later," he said, rising to leave.

"I will," said Firian, and he fell asleep on his desk.

19

FIRIAN

THE ENDRIAN TROOPS left the next day, ready to spread the news about the Academy's location. The thought spread like fire in Firian's chest. Tanyu had kept the secret for over a century, and people all over the world went to great lengths to get it. Men had even lost their lives. The soldiers should count themselves lucky to be among the first to see it.

There could be no turning back now. The scouts, and now the Kingdom's Endrian allies, knew where to find the mysterious Tanyuin Academy, with its heroes and treasure stores of tributes.

In his castle, Firian felt safer than he had on the nausea-inducing ship, but the widespread news of the Academy's location would bring new dangers. Nothing he couldn't handle.

Part of him was glad that everyone had gotten to see his new ability. Now that he felt better and had had a while to think about it, he wasn't sure he wanted to explain it to Belik. This could be his and his alone.

His new power exhilarated him, running like hot metal through his veins, but it made him feel dangerous or even sinful. Unpredictable even to himself.

If Kiria hadn't already heard about it, he decided he wouldn't tell her. Had it been only a week since he'd seen her in the Unreal? It felt longer. Whether or not he felt completely ready, he had to see her again. Any more waiting and he'd go mad, or Kiria's feelings would turn, killing any chance he had to be with her.

Sitting back in the chair at his desk, he closed his eyes, an indulgent gesture when he hadn't needed to do that to reach the First Level in years.

Inhaling a deep breath, he wrapped a setting around himself. This time it was the island. He could show it to her first-hand. Well, second-hand. The space he built was purely fictional, drawing on the elements he had seen on Torith: the fragrant earth, enormous leaves dripping with moisture, refulgent flowers, crash of distant surf. Maybe that part would feel like home to her. Trees and foliage crowded the hollow he created. Smells from the Academy, like a hint of cinnamon and pine, joined the rich leafy odors. He tinkered with a detail here and there, with the blue of the sky and the call of birds.

Something hitched in his gut. How many of his own favorite things had he included? Glancing around, he saw a portrait of one naked corner of his soul. Each sight or scent felt like a key she could use against him, opening doors he wanted closed. With a thought, he smudged the edges of those personal touches.

She didn't respond. Maybe she was busy. It was mid-morning and she couldn't sense the Talent as clearly as he could. Still he waited, absently stroking a leaf that hung beside him.

The soft silence became pointed. Did she not want to come? Impossible.

He saw himself as another would have seen him, waiting for a girl all alone when there were so many other things to do. If someone needed him to check on the Torithians or talk strategy, they would make themselves known. Even so, restlessness began to irritate him, the aftereffect of his successes leaving him oddly hollow. Kiria was the only goal he had yet to solidify.

"Kiria?"

She appeared, beaming. "I'm about to go to a meeting," she chastised.

Relieved, he grabbed her arm and pulled her toward him for a kiss. She melted into it.

When he pulled away, a smile still played on the corners of her lips. She had a confident air that hadn't been there last time. "I'm practicing my tour speech in a couple minutes. Is this..." Understanding dawned in her eyes as she looked around, seeing the forest for the first time. "Is this Torith?"

"Do you like it?"

She pulled her shoulders upward in a pleased gesture. "It's beautiful. It's too bad so many horrible things happened here."

"Not here," he reminded her, glancing at the bright red flower he had placed in the clearing to ground himself. No subtleties this time.

"Well..." She cocked her head from side to side, disagreeing. Then her expression changed into something more vulnerable. "I'm glad you're here. I didn't see you for a long time..."

"I was busy." The excuse came too easily. "The Torithians arrived last night."

"Oh!" she said with the speed of someone ready to accept whatever reason he gave.

They were both quiet for a moment. For a reason he couldn't pinpoint, he felt awkward. Kiria was here. She had answered his call and gazed at him expectantly. He had won her, or very nearly so. Then why did he feel a twinge of nerves?

He needed to go back to something he knew. "I'm glad you're here now," he said, tipping her chin up. He felt her breath catch as he lowered his head. "All the soldiers toasted to you last night, for what we did."

"There's more justice in the world because of us," she said dreamily, ready for kisses.

The comment took him by surprise, but it shouldn't have. "You're right. There is." Pleasure glowed anew in his chest.

She raised a hand, shyly moving his hair. "How's your ear?"

For a second, he couldn't think clearly enough to answer her question. It hadn't been like this with Maya or Devanie or the others. Their presence had burned, not turned his brain to mashed potatoes. "Fine," he managed, taking her hand and brushing his lips against her palm.

"Firian." The voice came from outside the hollow. Kiria didn't seem to hear it, so he ignored it.

Time pressed in on them both. Her meeting, this gory intruder on his peace...

She wove their fingers together. Another gesture he wasn't used to, as intimate as an embrace. He squeezed her hand and kissed her hungrily, as though he could devour time.

"Firian." Tap, tap.

He swallowed a curse and broke away. "Kiria, I..."

"I have to go too," she said quickly, face flushed. "I just wanted to see you first."

So many unsaid things lingered in the air that Firian felt he could catch them if he reached out. She was hiding something. It was in her start-and-stop way of speaking. And he wasn't saying everything he was thinking either. He never did.

He nodded. Hopefully there would be many more opportunities. He gave her one last kiss on the cheek and disappeared back into the Real.

Belik stood over him, one eyebrow raised and a finger pressed against the desk. Sitting up straight, Firian rolled his shoulders, shaking off the weakness that had settled on him over the night.

Now that Firian was lucid, Belik took his chance to sit down. He dragged his chair closer to the desk.

"Jovan has the Torithians on their feet this morning," he began in a jovial way that didn't match his body language.

"He should." Almost as soon as Firian had risen, his guard had informed him of potential threats to the Academy—just whispers. But a lot of whispers.

"The people of Raewhith are just trying to keep up."

Picturing Caedmon, his childhood friend, doing laps alongside a Torithian pirate was a funny thought.

Belik grunted, getting to his real point. "But we both know these troops won't be enough. Really, we need some that are already trained. We need an existing militia."

Firian waved his hand. "I know." His brief experience of war was enough to solidify his understanding of that.

"Now that you're back, I can tell you," Belik said, he placed one meaty hand on the tabletop, an invitation to strategize with him. To share with him. "I've scouted other locations to find willing soldiers. Imlin seems like a good starting place, and Archer's Point."

For Brett's sake, Firian wouldn't mix Raewhith's soldiers with those from Archer's Point, which had often vandalized and terrorized his little town when he was growing up. He had only struck a deal with Raewhith in order to keep it safe for her. The Tanyu he'd posted there kept him updated on his father as well. Even though Firian hadn't heard any reports of abuse, he still haunted his father's dreams sometimes when he couldn't sleep, sending him nightmares.

No, for his mother and sister, he wouldn't recruit soldiers from Archer's Point.

Imlin would have been more promising, except for one thing. "Imlin belongs to the Kingdom."

"So do we," Belik replied quietly.

An odd silence fell. Firian's limbs went cold at the accusation. One of the main reasons he had taken power was to help the Western Kingdom win the war against the Torithians. He had to pledge his allegiance as a sign of good faith, or the Keepers wouldn't have let him near their troops.

"Do you object?" Firian asked slowly, fixing Belik with a steel gaze. Almost unconsciously, he reached for his power beneath the surface. But he would never use it against Belik, no matter how much he aggravated him. They both knew it.

"No, Master Kess." The title grated from him, revealing the only reason he agreed.

"It's worked well so far. There's no harm in having a strong alliance."

"It hasn't started working at all. They used us to win their war. If a militant group comes for the Academy, do you think they'll step in?" Belik shook his head sardonically. "The Amir will make sure they don't. I just hope they don't ask us for any more favors."

Firian opened his mouth.

Belik spoke again, "Do they owe *us* any loyalty?"

At that, Firian drew a measured breath and smiled. One of the Keepers did.

Belik's face, however, fell. He squinted. "Firian," he started carefully, "you know I'm on your side. I want to see the Tanyu with the power and respect they deserve. Glories like in Corso's day, or Naedra's. We've fallen so far from our purpose. And together we can do it." He regarded him and turned his head to one side, deliberating, while keeping his eyes on Firian.

For an uncomfortable moment, he wondered if Belik was reading his thoughts.

The Master's next words were even more deliberate. "What do we really gain from this?" His eyes darted to the scrap of Raewhith's flag on the desk.

Sensing a challenge, Kiria's word rose to his lips. "Justice."

Belik's brow rose in amusement.

Firian clarified what he was really asking. "I've gotten Brithnem on our side, not just the other way around."

"It's the girl, isn't it?" Belik's question cut like a knife.

"Of course it is."

"What did I tell you?"

Firian worked his jaw. "To take what I can and get out."

"And did you?" Hope and disgust alternated in Belik's face. He curled his lip.

Firian hesitated, letting Belik color in the silence as he wished. "I want her as an ally."

Belik scoffed. "An ally! You want her in more ways than that!"

"And if I do?"

"Damn it, Firian!" he cried, but his voice was soft.

Firian didn't reply.

"If you don't think she controls you, you're a fool. What if this is her plan?"

Firian knew what he meant. A *katah*. Did she mean to seduce him in order to get information or kill him? That was the real question.

He sat back, remembering the kiss in the hallway, every sensation rushing back. That was no plan. He shook his head. "Trust me. She didn't plan this."

"Do you forget when she spied on you for the Kingdom?"

The back of his throat tightened. "No."

"And you still think she isn't capable of guile."

"What is it to you?" Firian snapped. When would Belik get to the point?

"If the Academy falls, so do I. I've been screwed by a woman before." Belik held up a hand when he heard his word choice. But in a moment, the tension broke. His shoulders rounded forward, his perfect posture snapped. "You think she won't turn on you. You'd better be right. Tread carefully or she'll rain hell."

Firian would almost like to see the full might of the Keeper Kiria, above and against the other Keepers, without inhibitions or restraint. He forced himself out of his seductive reverie. "Did you just come to criticize me?"

"Firian." He said his name like a curse. "I keep hearing about small groups of mercenaries coming to investigate us. So far, it's not enough to raise alarm, but the idea of the hidden Academy with its tribute stores and fame is enough to whet everyone's curiosity from here to Bosha."

Firian raised his eyebrows. "We'll invite Imlin to join us."

Archer's Point was known to be more belligerent. Their Lord Ruler would never give into a mere threat, and probably wouldn't respond to an invitation either. Maybe later he could try it. Now that he considered it, if he could control Archer's Point, then he could protect Brett on both sides of their little conflict. Their father would have less reason to rage at their mother. But then, his father would just find a new reason to be angry.

Firian shook his head, freeing his thoughts from the sticky hold his father still had on him. "Let's start with Imlin. It'll be easier to keep an eye on them since they're so close to Raewhith. Everything is adjoining. I'll send some people to demand fealty tomorrow, along with a couple Sentries to act as new Watchmen."

Belik tipped his mouth. "Sentries?"

"They have nothing to do, and their time as Sentries has made them unfit for most jobs." He lowered his voice. "Technically, I helped to free them, so they owe me loyalty, not like the Watchmen there now. I'm sending a Sentry to Raewhith too."

"Well," said Belik, finally pleased. He had been leaning far over the desk but now sat back as though he had finally gotten the answer he wanted. "Let's make it happen."

20

FIRIAN

"That's not..." Firian's voice faded as he realized the move had been a fair one.

Bard cocked his head, a grin tugging at his lips as he tried not to gloat. He'd rubbed the back of his head with his knuckles so often when he thought about his next moves that his hair looked particularly impish.

Observing the wooden Indisfate board on the desk, Firian sucked his teeth. He drummed his fingers once against the desk and sighed. "Fine!"

"Another game?" Bard started settling the pieces back in their original places on the board.

Firian narrowed his eyes. Bard had won two in a row. He would hate for Bard to win every single game. This time, he'd been watching closely. If they played another, Firian could best him. "Set it up."

Even without windows, Firian could tell the sun was setting. When would Master Makai get back from Imlin? Hopefully he would arrive soon. Imlin was larger than Raewhith, and could supply good soldiers for his army. More rumors of looters and foreign armies curious about the power of the Academy came almost daily—small rumors, but enough to put Firian on edge.

After one more game of Indisfate, it would be totally dark outside. A good time to see Kiria. Her nearness could charge through him and relax him all at once.

Impatience shuddered through him. Focusing on the game pieces, he breathed deeply through his nose. A Tanyu was patient, could be patient forever, like a creature of the forest, still until propelled to sudden movement.

Kiria had left for her coronation tour today, parading through the Western Kingdom to demand new loyalty. She would couch it in kinder words, no doubt. Words like Bard would use.

To have a kingdom waiting to adore and serve... Firian felt the heat of it by association. Hadn't he seen a glimpse of that fearful awe in Raewhith, in Tánuil? Together, they could—

"You start." Bard knocked him out of his thoughts.

Firian moved the piece that Bard had touched first in the previous game.

A toothy grin split Bard's face.

"Gore," Firian swore, reading his loss in that look. The word came out as an irritated chuckle. It was no wonder Bard liked this game.

Bard's hand flashed across the board with his move.

What pattern was Bard establishing? Firian still couldn't see it, and it annoyed him.

"Hm, we should add a coin for stalling," Bard said, cautiously nettling him. He reached deep in his pocket for a token.

"No, no." Firian moved his piece, starting to sense a strategy that might work.

Bard's next move tore it down, blocking his Viper.

When Firian groaned, so did the door.

Belik limped in, moving quickly considering his bad leg. Firian could see the guard standing on the opposite side of the doorframe as he let the Master in.

Firian sat up. "Is it news from Imlin?"

"They won't come."

Firian's face went bloodless. "What?" Even Bard's mouth opened in surprise.

Belik's expression was set so hard that his mouth looked like a crack in a boulder.

"Why not?"

"They didn't give a reason." He came closer, a confidant. "Firian, you can't let this stand."

"But if they don't want to come..." Bard's word faded under the piercing glare of the two other Masters. Firian realized he still wore the blue-stoned ring of a Defender.

"If they don't want to come, then we'll make them," Belik said. "You know they can't deny you."

Firian drew his brows together. Belik was right. Any command from the Tanyuin Head had to be followed. The Academy needed their standing army. The Tanyu couldn't trust that the Western Kingdom would send troops at every whispered threat. And besides, they were too far away for soldiers to reach the Academy in time if there were a crisis.

"You can't look like a weak ruler." Belik pronounced the biting words almost too clearly.

Firian's gut twisted, feeling the condescension. He should rage, kick him out... But he was right.

He hadn't come this far to be taken lightly. If the Tanyu required loyalty, then it should be given gladly and without hesitation. Like the people going to see Kiria on her coronation tour.

Belik, not one to waste words, seemed to understand Firian needed a moment to think. "We'll come up with a plan in the morning," he said, turning to go.

"First thing," Firian responded as the Master disappeared.

Bard chewed his lip. "I don't think you're a weak ruler," he said quickly, as though he were trying to stop Firian from taking drastic action.

"I'm not." Firian edged another piece on the board forward, sensing that it wasn't the best strategic decision but wanting to keep the game moving.

"I don't think you need anybody from Imlin. All the people from Raewhith were volunteers, yeah? And we got a lot of those. We don't need more."

Firian shifted in his seat. If it were just about troops, Bard might be right. Without an imminent threat, they had enough of a standing army for the moment. But this was a matter of principle. "They can't say no to the Tanyuin Head," he said.

Bard still hadn't made his move. Instead, he crossed his arms on the desk. "Is it just the two, then? Just Raewhith and Imlin?" The question felt like a move in a new game—strategy in the Real.

When he asked the question, something jumped in Firian's core. It was never just Raewhith and Imlin. "For now, that's all we need."

Bard raised an eyebrow. He could always tell what Firian was thinking. How could he always tell? At least he couldn't go to the Second Level of the Unreal. There was still one place where Firian could be alone with his thoughts.

"But look how much you have," Bard said. "The whole Academy!"

"It's your move."

Bard meant well, but Belik was right. The Academy would not be pushed aside. Imlin would bow to Firian's wishes.

Only the weak were satisfied with what they had. And what kind of message would it send if Imlin could just refuse?

Despite Firian's effort, Bard won another round of Indisfate. Tired, with a roiling mind, Firian declined to play again. Night was falling, and he needed the comfort of a queen.

He didn't call for her in the Unreal. He waited, picking up little details of the setting, adding to them, changing them. This time he wanted to meet in his office. He knew every corner of the place. The two deep scores in the top of the desk, the lighter patch of stone where something had hung on the wall, the design of the rug on the floor, the scrap of Raewhith's flag still draped across his desk. He marked one of the stones on the wall with an extra scratch.

She flickered in easily, like a piece that belonged there. Today she wore a fawn-colored set of breeches and a tight purple vest over light, billowy sleeves. Her hair was tied back in a braid. Those bright eyes found him first, and then roamed around the office. Her mouth quirked as she approached him. "What's all this?"

A small pang of discomfort struck him when he remembered the Main in all its grandeur. This space exhibited a different kind of power—elemental, not heraldic. Hopefully she would see what he saw in it. "This is the Tanyuin Head's office. Mine." A stab of pride lanced him when he said it.

"You have all your meetings in here?" She pivoted on her toes to take in the space. Divine.

"People come to me, yes."

"People." There was a question in the repeated word.

"Yes." He didn't elaborate.

She spun around the desk and sat in his chair. Those breeches were unexpectedly lovely on her, hugging all the right places. "You look very serious," she said.

"I have serious things to think about."

"Even with the war over." The thought that began as a question became agreement. Every trouble didn't evaporate because the Western Kingdom was ostensibly at peace. "I'm on my coronation tour now," she said, changing the subject.

"I know. Happy to be traveling again?" He came close so he could stand over her.

"It's very different this time."

"I'm sure."

She groaned, running a hand over her face. "Our trip... It was such a mess."

"Not all of it."

"Were you there?" she teased, her eyes sparkling. "No one in Brithnem has gotten over it." Though her mouth still crinkled in a smile, her expression darkened.

It shouldn't have surprised him that the Kingdom still didn't trust him, but the confirmation rubbed him a little raw. What more could he have done to prove his loyalty? And he didn't like the idea of voices in Kiria's ear reminding her of his past sins.

He paused, weighing whether to ask the question at his lips. Had she gotten over it? Could she ever forget what had happened, what he had done to her?

He licked his lips and tried a different tactic. "How would the war have ended up if we hadn't met? And you liked Shifra."

"That's true. I did. The first time." She had returned there after escaping from him. When they'd first arrived, though, she was so incandescently happy that he ached to watch her.

He offered his hand to pull her up. As she took it, her short fingernails slid across the skin of his palm and sent goosebumps up his arms. Even without her Beauty, she had the confidence of a Keeper.

She gazed into his eyes with a knowing look. Air stuck in his throat, that short-of-breath vulnerability buzzing inside him. She commanded too much power in that moment, looking at him, seeing him.

Slowly, though his mouth had gone dry, he drew his thumb over her jawline. Her eyes glazed a little with the action. "You know," he whispered, "I like you like this."

"Like what?"

He just smiled and bent to kiss her.

21

KIRIA

Thank goodness Jori had come along. He didn't ask questions about how she would handle potential dissenters, or whether she was nervous the Kingdom would accept her over her mother, or if she was in a secret relationship with a former enemy.

Instead, he made their stops more interesting, although the guards weren't always happy with his antics. With so much time to think, she was glad for the distraction. Late at night, and sometimes early in the morning, the Unreal provided excellent distraction too.

In all, fourteen people accompanied Kiria on the coronation tour. The luggage alone required three people to look after it. They brought banners, diplomatic gifts, and elaborate outfits. Guards, servants, a guide, a doctor, and a cook all made up the traveling party.

The experience was far different than when she had traveled with Firian. Now she was waited on and fussed over by everybody. The result was a much slower pace. Or perhaps the pace was the same, but it felt slower because they took main roads, rather than cutting through wilderness. The traveling itself felt like a parade with no spectators.

It took a full week to move past the forest of Á Quihilmar to the rockier plains in the south. Strange mountains reared up in the distance, higher than the Charúnin Thôr to the north. Even though it was springtime, white snow still covered the peaks, like the flat stroke of a painter's brush.

No wonder it had been so long since anyone had added King's Heights to the coronation tours. It was so far out of the way. A few years ago, Daelon had taught her the history—that the people of King's Heights had objected to the reestablishment of the Kingdom as a Khelê sanctuary, still thinking that Kingdom Dwellers were superior. They had broken away and formed their own colony, preserving Kingdom blood and traditions, unmixed with the Khelê. They didn't share in any of the Abilities God poured out on the Khelê afterward, Daelon said, because they refused to associate with them. Largely isolated, King's Heights kept its reputation for suspicion toward outsiders, but it was impossible that they could retain the same level of racism that they had started with hundreds of years ago. After all, they officially became part of the Western Kingdom about ninety years before.

People from King's Heights still rarely traveled to the capital, but Kiria was beginning to see why. The road was long and, after the forest ended, rather barren.

During the day, Jori vacillated between jovial fun and irritable boredom. Chetana said very little, unless Kiria asked her a question. She rode her horse like a queen, but as they got closer to King's Heights, something about her perfect posture and long neck became not only regal but stiff, as though she were bracing herself. Something was wrong with her, but she deflected any question about it. Candrae and Vayci never complained, and actually seemed excited to be traveling outside of Brithnem. Candrae's aunt was also a servant in the palace, and she got to come too. When the girls weren't tending to Kiria, they twittered quietly and happily with her.

Finally, they saw it. King's Heights, nestled at the foothills of the Somul Mountains, so far inland that the sea wasn't even in sight. An immense stone wall encircled the city. The buildings themselves were stone, blending in perfectly with the landscape, with light gray walls, smooth as if they'd been carved out of boulders, and dark gray roofs. The city obviously wasn't as large as Brithnem, but it was larger than Kiria had pictured it.

This also was part of her Kingdom. She had been so focused on a few aspects of her Keepership that she had all but forgotten the rest. Her priorities had been Brithnem, the Tanyu, and the Torithians. That was it. But there was so much more. Rather than making her shrink with the additional responsibility, seeing new parts of the Kingdom filled her with warm pride.

Jori rode up slowly beside her, open vest flapping. It was drier and warmer here than either of them was used to. "Finally!" he said. "I can have a proper shave. Where do you think they'll put us up? Do they have a palace, or a government building?" He pulled a wry face. "A government building—doesn't that sound dreary? Let's hope it's something more festive. Yes, a shave and a glass of wine."

Jori had been shaving along the way, but he did look more bedraggled than usual. She laughed. "First we have a speech."

"A speech?" He brought his horse closer to hers and leaned confidentially toward her. "Darling, you look like you could freshen up yourself." He scanned her Beauty and said, "I know, I know. But they're putting you on stage the instant we arrive? No rest for a Keeper?"

The bottom of her ivory dress was caked with dirt, and her gold threaded shoes covered in dust. Until today she had been allowed to wear more practical riding clothes, but since they approached King's Heights, she had been strongly urged to wear one of her finest dresses and her crown.

She tossed her shiny hair and smiled, though she agreed. Hopefully there would be at least a little time so she could smell fresh and feel good before presenting herself at this first stop. "You know," she said, "not many people would tell me that."

"I'm not many people." His lips twisted in a smile.

The sound of another horse approaching made both of them look back. Chetana eased her bay mare forward, making the space between Kiria's four guards feel a little cramped. Jori made way for the Amir.

"That is King's Heights," she said, gazing forward. The sun glinted off her laced metal septum ring, bright against her dark skin. She set her brow, almost antagonistic. Memory stirred in her eyes as the breeze stirred her short curls. After a moment, she remembered herself. Not often did she get lost in her memories like that. "Our first stop on the tour." Her face resettled into a pleasant neutral, not a smile, but enough to dispel the terrible energy that had begun to emanate from her. "They will be glad to see you, My Keeper."

"They all will," added Jori, unnecessarily.

"Yes." Chetana spared a look for him. "Now, My Keeper, your flagbearer must go in front, and all must demonstrate unwavering support, smiling, gladness..." It was only when she used words like "gladness" that Kiria saw the family resemblance between her and her son Daelon.

Kiria nodded politely. She'd heard this all before.

As they rode closer to the city, it seemed to come alive. Now they could hear bustling in the streets and see smoke coming from chimneys. Figures, small in the distance, moved between buildings and guards walked along the walls.

"We will support you in all things, My Keeper. First we'll process to meet the mayor, and then you'll give the speech, and then to our quarters for the night."

Jori leaned far forward to see around Chetana. He caught Kiria's eye and bared his teeth with apologetic disgust.

Kiria looked away from him. "No party afterward?" That was going to be the protocol in Charäkhnem.

"Not at this stop, My Keeper. We will not stay long, and I'm sure you are tired."

Kiria popped her eyebrows up at Jori, who leaned back in his saddle with resignation. Jori would have his share of parties later, but for now, Chetana was right. Kiria would hardly be excited for a late-night revel after a long day of traveling. This was almost a practice stop, just to show goodwill. Hopefully it would resolve the apprehension that sometimes settled in her stomach.

When others didn't question her, it was easy to pretend that she was the Kingdom's darling, but the constant reinforcement of "unwavering support" made her wonder. She had to be more careful to hide her visits with Firian. Especially now, she couldn't give anyone a reason to doubt her.

When the guards on the wall saw the flagbearer unfurl the royal banner of Brithnem, they opened the gate at once. Kiria felt grand looking at the blue and purple flag with its symbol of a laird flower flapping in the wind. The sweat and horse smell didn't bother her as much as she thought it might when all the guards of King's Heights stared at her, open-mouthed. Despite the drawbacks of travel, she was still their beautiful Keeper. Now was the time to impress, to embrace her visibility. Holding her head in what she hoped was a dignified manner, she rode slowly into the city. A crowd had gathered just inside the main gates, so thick that people had to move just for the horses to ride forward. It was like swimming through heads.

Her guards were clearly on alert with so many people. "Make way!" they cried. "Make way for the Second Keeper of the Western Kingdom, Kiria Arioc. Make way!" They rode forward in a practiced formation to shoo the crowds to the side.

The sea of faces was monochromatic. In Brithnem, everyone looked different —at least there was a wide range of body types and skin colors and hair styles— but it had never truly occurred to her that other places might not be. She had heard the rumors about King's Heights, of course, but the sameness struck her differently in the face of such a large crowd with uniformly light skin, grayish brown hair (shoulder-length, for the most part), and wide gray eyes. Seeing so many together was like an odd version of Jori repeated indefinitely. The facial expressions varied, but the most prevalent was an intense, almost hostile curiosity, as though she were an exhibit in a zoo.

Kiria felt off balance, but she smiled. A few people responded in kind and smiled back. Others tried to touch her, but the guards batted them back.

This was hardly a civilized way to welcome a Keeper.

Up ahead, she saw a huge, flat-topped boulder with stairs carved into the side. A canopy had been erected on the top, light blue and dark purple. The stage for her presentation. She kept smiling and giving demure nods to the crowd as they slowly approached the platform. At the stairs, she and her entourage dismounted and she went up with Chetana, Jori, and her guards. The others faded into the crush of bodies.

A man waited for them at the top. He had the same light face and ashy dark hair, but he wore a ponderous necklace of thick golden threads over a dark robe, almost reminiscent of the Keeper robes, but plainer.

The man touched his heart with respect as he approached Kiria. Although the guards wouldn't let him approach too closely, the brief gesture calmed her growing nerves. "What an honor it is for us to meet our esteemed Second Keeper! My name is Brontes Meaburn. I'm the mayor of this city," he said. His voice was a little higher than she had expected. He looked around. "Did our last Second Keeper, your eminent mother, not accompany you?"

"No, she did not," Kiria replied, surprised by the question.

"Would you have me announce you, My Keeper?" There was something almost tentative in the question.

"My Amiran advisor Chetana will announce me." Kiria indicated whom she was talking about, but the mayor of King's Heights didn't follow her gesture.

"As you wish." He scrunched his nose, maybe a nervous or impatient gesture, but it passed quickly, and he stepped aside as though he were opening a door to his city. The flourish reminded her a little of Cúron.

Kiria, Chetana, and her guards stepped forward, just within the shade of the canopy. Jori hung back at the same distance as the mayor.

After the whispered comments died away, a hush fell over the crowd. Faces craned upward. From this height, about two stories above the street, Kiria realized that the crowd wasn't as enormous as she had thought. Hundreds of people packed the streets, overflowing into side streets, but she could see where the crowd ended.

Her heart beat quickly in anticipation. Giving speeches didn't make her afraid anymore, as they did when she was younger, but she still felt a current of adrenaline. *All this, for me.*

Chetana stepped to the rim of the rock and lifted her chin. "*From the gloom of oppression will rise my people, my chosen ones,*" she began. "*From the dust of scorn, my people will look up and their lips will be cleansed with truth. In that day, I will help them, says the mighty one, the God of all. My Khelê will found a great kingdom. They will build upon the ruins of the old, stone upon stone. Wisdom will rise with its walls, and shepherds as its keepers.*"

Kiria sensed unease among the people as Chetana recited the passage from the Sacred Scroll. Some in the crowd squinted suspiciously. It could have been from the sun, but Kiria thought she sensed animosity toward Chetana—a Khelê who reminded them of their historical preference for the losing side of the War of the Kingdom Rebels. Chetana quoted the Scroll with particular gusto, as though she had been waiting to say just these words to just this crowd.

"People of King's Heights!" she cried. Kiria had never heard her shout before. Her voice was like a battle cry. "It is my distinct honor and pleasure to introduce to you your new ruler, one deserving of all your allegiance and praise, the Second Keeper of the Western Kingdom, Kiria Arioc!"

Deafening applause followed, an almost violent sound.

Now it was Kiria's turn. When she walked back into the light, many people gave another gasp and the whispering started again. Apparently her dust-stained dress didn't bother them. Her Beauty overwhelmed other thoughts the first time one saw it. She waited until they quieted.

"People of King's Heights, it is my pleasure to come to your city. I see before me a city of industry, of hardworking men and women, of people loyal to the thrones of Brithnem."

She gave her rehearsed speech just as she had practiced it in front of her fourteen travelers days before. She praised the particular strengths of the area, reinforced their loyalty, informed them of her promises as leader and their duty to serve.

She left her favorite part until the end. "Most of all, I am pleased to inform you that, since I ascended to the throne, the Torithian War is won!" She beamed, and light shone in the eyes of a few at the foot of the stone platform. Applause scattered through the crowd. "Through a strategic alliance with the Tanyuin Academy, I was able to help bring our forces to victory. All troops have already begun to come home from Torith, Enderin, and all the other fronts where we have fought and died to protect innocent people from harm." Her body warmed with pride. "I love this Kingdom and am proud to serve it. I hope, in that way, that we may be united. Thank you." She stepped back, almost stumbling on her dress.

She made it through her first speech. Blood raced through her veins. The thrill of ruling the Kingdom washed over her anew. She had done so much good for these people already. The thought filled her with satisfaction and brought a grin to her face. Jori smiled back when she looked at him, but Chetana's face was grim and wary as they all marched down the stairs to find their quarters for the night.

22

KIRIA

KIRIA SLID into Firian's lap. He gave a relaxed smile and wrapped his arm around her back. Happily, they had chosen to meet in the evening. If they met during the day, she was bound to get caught eventually. With all the anti-Tanyuin sentiment in the Kingdom even after the success on Torith, she couldn't risk her reputation by revealing her relationship with Firian.

The watery swamp sloshed against the pylons of the wooden walkway. Twilight filtered dark blue light through the mossy trees of Shifra. Bugs skimmed across the water. The humid air clung to the two of them, soft on her damp skin.

Hanks of moss hung unevenly on the closest tree, and a cluster of lily pads floating on the water included two with browning leaves. Even the smell took her right back to Shifra. Firian said she was advancing quickly in the Unreal, but she couldn't have conjured this many little details.

The difference—she always tried to find the intentional change he placed there—seemed to be the extra lanterns, but she liked that, and he knew it.

"How was your speech?" he asked.

"I think it was all right. You don't have to give speeches, do you?"

He shook his head, his face so close to hers that they almost touched. "No."

"Not if you don't want to," she teased, a little jealous.

He pursed his lips together in a smile. His hair smelled like soap and pine sap. "Exactly."

"That would be nice," she mused lightly, turning away. "But a Keeper has to do more than a Tanyu, I suppose."

He let the comment slide, but she felt him pick at the skin around his ring.

"How do you like being a Keeper now?" he finally asked.

She considered. "You know, before I left"—she didn't need to explain that she meant with him—"I looked at being a Keeper and thought about everything at once. I knew there would be violence and pain and unpopular decisions, and I tried to hold it all in my mind at one time. I tried to comprehend it, to steel myself." She drew a finger lazily down his arm. "As though, if I thought hard enough, I could understand it all, and swallow it in one bite." She puffed out her cheeks to mimic a full mouth. "But it isn't like that. Everything comes one by one, a day at a time. And you can't predict it all." She met his gaze and felt warmth crawl up to her temples.

Firian had certainly been a surprise. The idea brought uncomfortable thoughts to the surface. She liked Firian, perhaps even more than she had thought at the beginning, but she still didn't fully trust him. Wouldn't she be willing to show him her Beauty if she did?

His nearness made it easier to silence the voices in her head that warned her against getting too close to him. He was warm and comfortable and made her forget her worries of the day. They both liked being together in the Unreal, so there was no harm.

Something small ran over the boards, maybe a lizard. It was hard to see in the dim light. "What's that?" She reached past him to point at it.

He caught her as she leaned and kissed her on the cheek. "Doesn't matter," he murmured.

"No?"

"No." He traced one finger up her back until he reached the exposed skin of her shoulder blades.

She shivered at his touch, but shook her head, smiling. She gently pushed away a lock of hair from his forehead. His eyes closed with the motion. How did she have this great of an effect on him?

A niggling doubt, like a lingering sore throat, ached in the back of her mind. Something wasn't right. She scanned the area around them. Nothing could hurt them here. Nothing could hurt her.

She looked around the wooden platform that appeared so much like the actual one where they'd sat together before. A lantern had disappeared.

An odd feeling, like she was back in time, came over her. The terrible things that happened a few months ago were just a dream. She and Firian were really together, now.

She snuggled up closer to him and he responded with kisses. Like people drunk, or in a dream, they held each other. Her stomach tightened. Her shoe moved over the soft, splintery boards of the walkway, catching on the rough edges as she tucked her feet in. She felt his heart beat in his chest and his neck. Nothing else seemed to matter but this.

She jolted.

Firian pulled away for a moment, running his eyes over her to make sure she was all right. It must have been a muscle spasm, because she didn't feel that she was about to fall. Rubbing a comforting hand over her back, he leaned in again and she leaned to meet him.

A buzzing sound, like shouting in the far distance, made her break off again. "What was that?"

"Nothing." He twirled a piece of her hair in his fingers.

"I heard something."

"I didn't hear anything." But his interest was clearly piqued. He stiffened and looked past her, scanning for what, she didn't know.

She sat up, listening more intently. A strange feeling, as though she had forgotten something, came over her again and made her restless. The noise might be the key.

Her face suddenly went cold. Her hands flew to her cheeks, but they felt normal. Was she afraid? Did she realize something before her conscious mind could catch up? Vague fear covered her body, but only because her body was acting of its own accord. Something was wrong. But then, nothing was real.

Real.

Her insides squeezed tight as she realized what she had forgotten. *This isn't real.* She'd let her guard down, blurred the lines. She stood up, sucking in shallow breaths of air. She couldn't let that happen again.

"What's the matter?" asked Firian, jumping lightly to his feet.

"I have to go."

Without waiting for a response, she opened her eyes. For a second, the Real didn't come. Her heart skipped. *No, no.*

Then the light seeped in, blinding though she knew it was dark. She squinted up from a bed. Her hand touched rabbit fur and the ceiling was slate gray with faint designs etched into it. *King's Heights. That's where I am.* Three people peered down at her, horrified concern etched on every one of them. Candrae and Vayci looked the most distressed. Tears edged Vayci's brown eyes but she quickly sponged them away with a damp towel she was holding.

Chetana was the third. When Kiria looked at her, something unmistakable flashed across her expression. Realization.

She knew.

"Oh, My Kepress!" Candrae cried, handing Vayci the candle and actually hugging Kiria across the bed. In her relief, she'd forgotten to call Kiria by her proper title.

"We must move. Now." Chetana offered her heavily-ringed hand. "People are rioting in the streets and they are headed here, if they haven't already arrived."

Kiria sat up groggily, confused.

"Quickly!" Chetana snapped.

Vayci and Candrae clutched their own bags as well as hers, packed and ready. They waited by the bed, bobbing up and down with nervous energy. Candrae's face was white with fear. Kiria took Chetana's hand and allowed her to pull her out of the room.

Most of the lights were out, but patterns like water grew brighter against the stone walls. From the corridor, she could see down into the street. The mayor's manor had been carved into the mountain itself, so the hallway where she ran rose more than four stories above the street. Despite her vantage point, she saw nothing distinctly but the bobbing of tiny torches in the gloom. The simple, elegant carvings in the rock wall looked sinister in the moving shadows.

Glass broke. Wails like wind rose and fell, angry shouts, a few voices at a time speaking in unison, but she couldn't hear their words. They sounded like a storm, like a tidal wave. The noise got louder and louder, even as she and the others broke into a run. The sound brought terror to her throat. She fought to keep her breath steady as she shed her Beauty. The tingling feeling didn't leave her fingertips even after the transformation was complete.

Why were they rioting? Something in the snarled voices echoed back her name. Why were they coming for her? What had she done?

She gripped a stone bannister as she tripped lightly down a long, spiraling staircase. Around and around it went, doubling back on itself so many times that she began to feel claustrophobic. Once at the bottom, she sped after the growing group of guards and servants showing them the way.

She tried to run quietly, but it was almost impossible with so many people. Others joined them as they ran—the guards, the cook, the porter. There was Jori, tugging on his shoes. Even the mayor appeared. This scenario seemed less real than Shifra had felt just a moment ago.

They emptied into a fenced stone courtyard ringed with stables. "I'm so sorry," Mayor Meaburn whispered in a rush, slowing to a halt beside their stamping horses. "If you would just move to my other location, already prepared..."

Vayci shoved a coat into her arms, and Kiria realized she was only in her nightdress. Pulling her arms through the sleeves, she glared at the mayor. "Who are these people? Why are they coming for me?"

He scrunched his nose as though shaking off a fly. His plea came out as oily assurance. "Oh, My Keeper—"

"Tell me!"

He looked down at his leather slippers. "There are many here who disapprove of your reign. I am not among them! I invited you here, and if you would—"

"I am not staying here."

"But my other house..." He caught her glare and twitched again, huffing with frustration. "Small factions don't agree with your decision to forgive the Tanyu after the war... and others... think you killed your mother."

"What?" The word came out louder than she intended. "I never—"

The mayor put his hand over his heart again, a habitual gesture, apparently. "I am so sorry. I think no such thing. Please grant us forgiveness."

Kiria pressed her nails into her palms. His words were devolving into political pleading and there was no time.

"My Keeper." A guard prompted her to mount her horse. Over half of her entourage was already in the saddle.

With no idea what to say and no time to say it, she turned away from the mayor. Moments later, Kiria, Jori, and Chetana, holding her secret, escaped the walls of King's Heights.

23

KIRIA

THE CORONATION TOUR finally made camp about five hours later. On the ride, Kiria's throat had closed and the air had leaked out of her mouth and lungs and she couldn't breathe and her vision narrowed. It was the same panic she'd felt in Raewhith after the attack.

She'd sent a guard back to King's Heights to gather information and their remaining belongings from the mayor's manor—she needed to get to the bottom of those rumors, find out what had triggered the riot. Their Watchman could report back to Brithnem that Kiria was safe.

As Kiria got ready for bed in one of the large, comfortable tents, her heart rate finally began to slow

Now on her bunk, she looked forward to sleep. Deep breaths. Her racing mind didn't slow as her body sank into the soft blankets. Every fiber rubbed against her skin; every wrinkle suggested it would take longer than she wanted to actually become comfortable.

A cool breeze wafted through the tent flap as it opened. Chetana entered, still fully dressed. After she closed the fabric behind her, she fixed Kiria with an implacable gaze. Kiria sat up.

"You're seeing the Tanyu." Chetana said the words with such conviction that Kiria knew she had figured it out, though how she had done it, Kiria didn't know.

"What?" Kiria said stupidly.

"You have a *katah*."

"What's a *katah*?" The word sounded vaguely familiar, but she couldn't remember what it meant. Firian's friend Bard had done something with a *katah* to help them defeat the Torithian captain.

Fear flashed over Chetana's face. Or maybe it was regret. "It's a connection in the Unreal, My Keeper. A dangerous connection."

"It's not a dangerous connection," she protested, knowing that her comment was as good as an admission. But then, was it so bad that she visited Firian in the Unreal? If no one knew about it, it couldn't harm the people's opinion of her as a ruler. And it looked like that was already shot anyway. Why would Chetana accuse her like this, as though she were putting herself and the Kingdom in danger?

Chetana rubbed her full lips together, clearly unconvinced. "A *katah* is a Tanyuin death sentence, a connection that grows between two people in the Unreal. The Tanyu target their enemies that way, manipulating them until they cannot tell the difference between imagination and reality. The Unreal becomes their reality. They believe it. And then you can get hurt."

"That's not what this is."

She gave her a pointed look. "How do you know?"

"I—"

"You can't!" Chetana's vehemence was almost frightening.

Kiria sat straighter. "I can tell the difference between imagination and reality!" The stress of the day made her more irritable than usual. Maybe she should send Chetana away, demand she quit these accusations. Kiria knew what she was doing with Firian... didn't she?

"My Keeper,"—Chetana sat down on the edge of the bunk, less threatening but more unavoidable—"we couldn't wake you." It looked like she wanted to say more, but decided against it, instead setting her mouth in a line and sitting back a little.

Kiria frowned. "How do you know so much about this?" She picked up her pillow and held it in her lap.

"It doesn't matter."

"Do Amir learn this much about the Talent?" Daelon rarely talked about it, except as a feature of history.

"Some do." For just a second, she dropped her eyes. "That mob would be furious if they knew."

Kiria flushed. Now Chetana was being condescending. "Why should we care what they think?" Kiria snapped more harshly than she intended.

The mob was wrong about her anyway. She had to do right by them, but they didn't have to agree with all her choices. That angry group had terrified her, and they were already furious, so why would Chetana bring them up again just as she was beginning to relax?

"That connection could hurt you, hurt the Kingdom..."

"How?" Chetana had no right to dictate her private life. Kiria valued her wisdom, when she asked for it, but being an Amir didn't automatically give her a say in every aspect of her life. Besides, the lies and unrest centering around her were the more important issues. Unless... "Is there something in the Scroll...?" If God had forbidden such a connection, then it would be her duty to stop seeing Firian, but if Chetana's prejudices forbade it, she didn't care.

Firian's affection sometimes felt like temptation, but right now, she wouldn't give it up. Despite whatever darkness he had, she cared for him. He excited her, motivated her, soothed her. And he'd proven he was on their side when he helped them end both wars.

Chetana hesitated, glassy-eyed as she reviewed the holy words in her mind.

Into the Unreal

Kiria's heart sank. As the Amir gazed into nothingness, Kiria was reminded of a soothsayer. No one could look into the future, but Chetana's wisdom seemed to supersede this moment and understand what was to come.

Chetana seemed to settle back into her own skin again. "No," she finally admitted.

"Then I will do as I please."

Chetana lowered her head, breaking some of the veneer of an untouchable military and spiritual leader. She looked at Kiria woman to woman. Something about her gaze arrested her. "My Keeper," she said in a low voice, "he *will* hurt you."

Kiria's stomach dropped, but she didn't lower her eyes. Chetana made it sound inevitable, indisputable. But was it?

Most of the palace nobles and staff hated Firian—wouldn't trust him to wash their clothes. Everyone had been so angry after the hostage situation that Kiria couldn't talk about him even after he took over the Academy, turning it in a new direction. Knowing that Chetana knew what she was doing simultaneously relieved and concerned her.

Chetana waited patiently for her to speak, but Kiria didn't know what to say. Then the Amir gently took her hand. After a moment, Kiria squeezed her hand back, and something in her broke. "I like him, and I just want to be wanted, for me," she said. "If it's only in the Unreal, why do you care so much?" Shame flooded her cheeks with heat.

"I know." For such a severe person, Chetana showed a touching amount of empathy. "But we both know the Unreal isn't only in your mind. *It's* real also."

Understanding dawned. Kiria's eyes widened. "You have the Talent too."

"Since I was a girl."

Kiria stared. How had she not known? "Then why... why are you an Amir? Your sister is a Tanyu, and you have the Talent..."

A confusing mix of emotions flashed across Chetana's face—pride, anger... "The Amir follow God. They are not selfish. They have not neglected higher things," she said simply. She bent her rusty head in a prayerful posture and stroked Kiria's hand once. "I became your mother's advisor around the time you were born. I already knew the honor of serving your family, but when I saw you, I knew the joy of it. I hadn't felt joy in a long time, but your presence reminded me of the hope to come. *That* is what you offer your kingdom. And that is why I cannot stand by and let you fall prey to a Tanyu who cares for nothing but his own gain."

The words fell like weights on the coverlet. Their hands felt heavy together.

Kiria breathed in the thick silence, unsure of what to say. A breeze blew around the circular fabric tent in low, dense sounds. A tree branch moved outside. The corners of her eyes blew cold with unfallen tears.

She squeezed Chetana's hand once more and let go. "I love this kingdom, and that will never change," she said solemnly, like a vow. "I wouldn't jeopardize it."

Chetana sighed. Straightening, she looked a queen herself. "You know my mind, Lady Kiria. A *katah* is never something to be taken lightly. Even the most careful person can be deceived by it." She stood, her delicate septum ring shining dully in the light. Her lips twitched once as she gazed down at Kiria, as though she were considering a new way to convince her.

Steeling herself, Kiria found that her heart was beating fast.

Maybe her advisor sensed that she wasn't open to any more input on the topic. Tonight, at any rate, Kiria wasn't going to change her mind.

Chetana inclined her head. "May you have peaceful sleep," she said, and left the tent.

When she was gone, Kiria exhaled slowly and spread her fingers over the covers. Chetana's parting words didn't sound threatening, but the implication was clear.

He will hurt you. She spoke the warning as though it were as sure as fate.

Her heart pounding heavily, Kiria felt small against the pillow. She would get no sleep.

24

FIRIAN

Bard held up the black ring, inspecting it in the sunlight coming in through the windows. "What do you think, Fir?"

"It's exactly like all the other ones. It's great." Firian tapped a fingertip against his own ring.

Firian had thought Bard would be ecstatic to pick up his Master ring, but he had spent the last few minutes asking the elderly jeweler questions and inspecting it for flaws instead. The tiny shop had a sharp metallic smell that grated on his senses.

He'd been on edge since last night, when he felt a surge of panic coming from Kiria. When he couldn't find her in the Unreal, unease had followed him and made him irritable. Though he would know if something drastic had happened, her fear still unnerved him. She wasn't a Tanyu, but she wasn't often afraid. He would check for her again after meeting with Jovan.

"I don't want it to be too tight."

"There's nothing wrong with it," Firian insisted. Jovan expected him any minute at the barracks to inspect the new troops.

Firian had sent Master Makai and a few others to Imlin to demand their allegiance. They would relent one way or another. Soon enough, Jovan would have brand new soldiers under his command, even less tested in Tanyuin methods than the Torithians or men from Raewhith. Firian had to make sure preparations were going smoothly. Firian and Bard didn't have time to waste in a jewelry store.

Torvas, the jeweler, took the ring back in his hand, cradling it as though it would break. It bounced off his knobby knuckles as he eased it from one palm to the other. He bent his liver-spotted head over it with an oddly paternal care.

Firian watched him impatiently. The rings never broke. There was no reason to be so careful.

"It won't be too tight," said Torvas, "Master—?"

"Tanery." Bard beamed, as though the new title were just dawning on him.

"Very well. Master Tanery. We'll need more Masters here with the borders open," he said, voicing a common opinion in a soft, shaky tone. People of Tánuil were nervous that foreigners would come to loot and kill, now that everyone knew where to find them. It was like leaving a castle door wide open at night. If a Tanyu with an army stood on the other side, though, no one would get through. "My family has made the Tanyuin rings for generations. They're never too tight."

"You sure?"

"Very sure." Torvas nodded solemnly. That should be enough for Bard, who was now bouncing up and down on the balls of his feet. He took the ring back and put it on his finger. Wiggling his fingers in front of his face, he looked at... what? The ring again? Surely he'd seen enough of that. And he'd see it on his hand his entire life.

"Okay," said Firian, turning to go.

"Wait, Fir."

Something made him glare at Bard. In this shop so focused on rank, it felt wrong not to be addressed by his title. Bard didn't revise the name. He just thanked the jeweler, waved goodbye, and trotted after Firian as he walked quickly toward the barracks.

"This is great!" said Bard, coming up beside him. "I never thought I'd be a Master already." He smiled up at Firian, his dimples widening.

"Well," said Firian, softening a little, "you deserved it."

Bard kept sneaking peeks at the black ring on his finger, with a private look of pride and achievement. Firian laughed to himself. He knew the feeling, and Bard hardly ever had the chance to revel in his own success.

They went behind Old Danior's sweet shop. The barracks had been hastily put together and looked it. The large, low wooden building stood fairly solid, but it wouldn't be difficult to kick through a board and escape. Most of the Torithians Firian had seen were certainly big enough to demolish part of the outer wall. Firian would talk to the carpenter about converting the walls to stone before autumn.

A tent had been erected against the tree line for meals. Once the cold weather returned in a few months, a tent would be insufficient, but it functioned for now. Loud talking and pots clanking filtered through the air. One company of soldiers ate under the tent. Jovan wasn't among them. His huge form would have been easy to find among the bodies.

"Bard," he said, "run inside and tell Jovan I've arrived."

Without hesitation, Bard did as he was told.

Moments later, Bard emerged from the barracks with Jovan and a line of Torithian thugs. Jovan wore his typical black Academy shirt with the thin sleeves pushed up past his elbows. His swelling biceps were as thick as his own neck. The sun had baked Jovan's face tanner and more rugged than the last time Firian had seen him. He glowered at Firian as he approached. Had a few weeks really taken this toll on him?

Bard walked assertively beside him, probably energized by his new title, but his ashy face betrayed his nervousness. Jovan and Bard had never liked each other.

The line of Torithian soldiers behind them all wore some variety of Academy-issued clothing, but they still looked mismatched. Some of the black had faded to gray, and a few of the outfits were torn. Firian scanned the line carefully. These men were as much his project as Jovan's. Several bore purple or yellow bruises. All looked tired. But none looked ready to spit on his boots, so that meant some progress.

Jovan stopped in front of Firian. "Master Kess," he said curtly. Turning back to the men behind him, he barked, "Form lines!"

Jovan's shout made Bard shudder in surprise.

The Torithians shuffled dully into lines, about twenty by three. Could Jovan break these men down and build them up to a fighting force? Right now, they seemed too listless to be much good in a battle.

"Attention!"

Some raised their heads. All put their hands behind their back. Firian caught the eye of one, younger than the rest, whose shaved blond hair had begun to grown back. He had a long, bony face and large, watery, wandering eyes. When he looked back at Firian, his face blanched and he dropped his gaze.

Firian pursed his mouth and walked to the end of the line of men. Bard stayed there as Firian strode deliberately along the line, considering each man. He lingered on some hardened faces, his eyes zigzagging over them until they straightened or looked away.

"Jovan," he said, omitting the title and waving him over with a hand. "How have you been treating these men?"

"They run for two hours every morning, strength training in the afternoon. No weapons training yet. They need to earn the right, and they're still a bunch of gory insurgents." Anger radiated from him as he stood beside him, just a little taller than Firian.

That anger didn't seem directed only at the Torithians, but took in Firian as well. *Why?* Firian took a deep, steadying breath.

Jovan, who had been such a terrifying figure when Firian first arrived, now had to answer to him. The thought sent energy coursing through him. He felt strong, strong enough to beat Jovan in a fight. Well, almost.

"Of course they are," Firian said. "They have to be broken before they're built up." After a pause, he added, "Don't hurt any too badly."

He ushered Master Jovan out of earshot of the troops. "When do you think they'll be ready?"

Jovan scoffed. "It'll be months at least. These idiots are unorganized, undisciplined, wasteful thieves."

The implied criticism hung thickly in the air. It was no wonder they were thieves. They had been pirates mere weeks ago. "Make them my army," Firian said, meeting Jovan's eyes.

Jovan ground his teeth, barely getting out the next words. "As you would have it, Master Kess."

Firian stared for a beat longer before turning away. Jovan felt like a loose animal, like Imlin's defiant leaders. *Small problems,* he insisted to himself. He felt the Master's eyes follow him as he strode back to Bard.

Every attempt to control his world peacefully became harder and harder. At least he could still soothe Kiria's fears, and she could bring balance back to him as well.

25

KIRIA

KIRIA HAD NOT SETTLED DOWN. One day had passed since the attack at King's Heights, and questions still swarmed within her. It was three days to the next stop on the tour and she could already tell that she would have to wrestle with her questions and concerns and insecurities the whole way.

Chetana rode close to her, as she usually did, with Kiria's four guards. The enormous entourage grated on her today. Could she get no moment to herself? She had to think about Chetana's words last night, about the mob's accusations, about her position in the court of Brithnem. She had to think about Firian and her mother.

She had to think.

Alone.

But there was no alone in the center of this tired procession. Eyes regularly shifted to her. Servants tended to her needs. She found herself wanting to be invisible.

The day passed slowly. Irritable, she snapped at Jori more than once for trying to make light of the riot. By the late afternoon, he backed off, though his absence didn't leave her feeling the right kind of alone.

Did people really think she had usurped her mother? Was she really a worse leader than her mother had been?

The rocking of the horse beneath her stirred her thoughts into a rhythm.

They thought she had killed her mother... deserved to die... led the Kingdom into ruin...

No, she remembered. She won the war... allied for peace... helped the Kingdom...

No matter how much she considered what had happened, the angry mob still left her on edge. Unexpected noises made her jump.

By the time night fell, a mix of fear and annoyance and guilt had settled in her gut like undigested dinner. She didn't stay to sit around the fire with everyone else.

From her tent, she heard Jori telling a story. She couldn't hear the words, but occasional laughter punctuated the quiet. If only she felt so lighthearted. But for now, she needed to be alone. Words burned into her skin as though they were part of the tattoo on her back. *They think you killed your mother... This fool alliance... He'll hurt you.*

She ground her palms, still gritty from the horse's reins, against her eyes. Her Beauty fell away from her like a cloak. A warm presence, never far out of reach, pressed against the back of her eyelids.

For just a moment, she froze with indecision. Firian was only a moment away. She could call and he would answer.

Wiping the dust from her face, she opened her eyes again. Her serving girls hadn't come in from the campfire yet, and Chetana probably wouldn't come again. But was she right about what she had said last night?

Kiria exhaled a frustrated breath. She knew Firian much better than Chetana did. He had his faults, but didn't everyone?

She would be careful. And she would see Firian.

She sat on the bed and closed her eyes, letting the Unreal close over her. In the darkness, she whispered his name. That should be enough.

In moments, a pine forest materialized around her. Soft evening light sifted through the trees, making Firian's black clothes look light gray as he walked toward her. The self-assured glint he usually had in his eyes betrayed some concern. When they were face to face, he took her hands. Releasing a breath that tousled the hair on her forehead, he asked, "Kiria, are you all right?"

She tucked herself against him. He wrapped his arms around her and his solid warmth comforted her like nothing else had that day. "I ran into some trouble on the tour."

"I felt something like that," he said. "Were you hurt?" He ran his fingers along her back and arms as though checking for himself.

The Unreal wasn't like reality in all ways. Even if she had been hurt, she could have hidden those wounds here. Yet he felt along her sides, picked up her hand and pressed the palm open. She didn't protest.

Despite what others thought, their alliance had helped both parties. And despite what Chetana thought, Kiria saw little harm in meeting him in the Unreal. *It's just thoughts*, he had said that night when they first kissed. It was only thoughts. Delicious, dangerous thoughts that took her mind away from the relentless troubles of the day.

"No," she murmured against him, watching a dust mote glow across her vision. "I wasn't hurt. There was a riot in King's Heights." She grimaced at the fresh memory. "We got away. We're fine now." Then something he said struck her. She pulled away enough to look up at him. "You said you felt something? You could tell something was wrong?"

His chest heaved up with a deep breath, almost a sigh. This whole place smelled like him. "Yeah, I could tell you were panicking, but then you didn't come to meet me. I didn't know what was happening." He planted a lingering kiss on her forehead. "If something bad happened... maybe I could fix it."

A smile curled the edges of her lips. "You can't fix everything."

"No?" He tipped her chin up and kissed her until she was breathless.

Afterward, he led her over to a tree, where he sat and pulled her down with him to sit against his chest. Her roiling thoughts had muted, leaving hazy comfort in their wake. But everything with Firian felt fragile. Fears would creep back in soon. She felt them at the door of her mind. Some fears were reserved for him—what he might do back at the Academy, the kind of person he might still choose to be...

She finally said, "I don't think I should call on you every time I'm having a bad day." This hadn't been the first time. Stress had overwhelmed her suddenly about a week before. Angry that her usual resolve had been replaced with a pounding heart and unfocused mind, she'd excused herself to her tent and gone into the Unreal. He'd come right away. It was just like this. In an hour, her anxiety had disappeared.

"Why not?"

"It's just..." How honest could she be with him? Even the strongest person couldn't deal with every trouble on their own—that wasn't it—but she already had friends, family, people who were close and willing to support her. People who sat outside her tent around a fire. She bit her lip. "I'm afraid I'm using you. I still can't forget those things that happened." All the reasons she couldn't trust him.

She felt him tense. He leaned to the side so he could look in her eyes. "Do you like being with me?" he asked, not vulnerably, but as though he knew what she would say.

That insufferable pride. How had she come to like it? She sarcastically stared back the answer.

"Then use me," he said.

She suddenly understood Firian's obsession with power. She clamped her teeth shut as her heart started pounding. A declaration like that wasn't like him. He hated to be used.

This could lead to nothing good. She felt his lust for power leeching into her. But the darkness called, and she cautiously answered, bringing her mouth to his.

THE NEXT COUPLE stops on the tour went much more smoothly. They had proper parades, speeches, parties... Men she didn't trust wanted to talk to her, to dance with her. She tried new foods and heard new music. The air was full of new perfumes from new plants and flowers.

Most of the people she met were polished nobles, the wealthiest and most powerful from the towns and cities they passed. From them she caught the aura of the place, but she wondered about the people who didn't have such privileges. Kiria grew up in Mon Párinath and was used to luxury, but, to rule, shouldn't she know the difficulties faced by common people as well?

A few times, she thought she saw distrust in someone's eyes as they looked at her, so she adjusted her speech to emphasize that her mother had willingly handed her the crown for the good of the Western Kingdom. Part of her wished her mother had come along to corroborate her story. A snide comment here or there implied that her alliance with the Tanyu was ill-advised as well. So she added a bit more about the merits of that decision to her speech too. Chetana kept silent at her side, supportive but not overly so where the Tanyu were concerned.

Chetana's warning about the *katah* still echoed in Kiria's ears, striking her at odd times—breakfast with the Lord of Rantoul, when her serving girls were lacing up a dress for a formal event, the middle of the night... The intrusion annoyed and unsettled her. She would be careful. Her vow to keep the Western Kingdom safe had been sincere. She knew that, but the part that bothered her most was Chetana's certainty. *He* will *hurt you.*

Three weeks on the road had taken its toll on everyone. The initial excitement had worn off, and their travels felt like a job. Kiria missed simple things like having the rest of her clothes and talking to Atty. Even the ability to relax without fuss or scrutiny or adjustment sounded heavenly. Servants and guards surrounded her at the palace too, but here they were forced into tight quarters that made it feel as though she couldn't fully be alone. She hadn't played her lyra in a month.

Under her breath, she hummed a traditional song she often played back home, tapping the horse's leather reins with her thumb in time with the music. They'd ridden on the plains for several days already, and the bright, far horizon strained her eyes. Mountains rose along their right side in an almost unbroken line that swept ahead out of sight. The Somul Mountains to the south were strange. Seeing the Charúnin Thôr, even the unfamiliar end of the mountain range, felt like they were getting closer to home.

Up ahead, the grasses faded away to what looked like a long swath of white water. The air shimmered above it. The group began to twitter amongst themselves.

Still humming, Kiria looked behind her. Jori was riding confidentially between Candrae and Vayci. Her serving girls were both smiling, but Candrae's smile was shy as she pulled a curl of blonde hair over her shoulder.

Kiria rolled her eyes at Jori. *Incorrigible.*

She turned to Chetana, who always rode as close to her as the guards. "Are we getting close?"

"Charäkhnem is two days away," her advisor replied. "We are approaching the Salt Flats."

Kiria sighed, hopefully low enough that no one heard. She remembered the Salt Flats from the one other time she had gone to Charäkhnem as a child. They were unforgiving and boring. They would have to stop soon to gather extra feed for the horses because nothing grew in the Flats at all. Daelon had taught her the origin of the Flats, but she didn't remember much. Something about the rebels salting the earth of those who sided with the oppressors after they won the great war. A reminder of how the two kingdoms hadn't always gotten along.

"Have you ever been to Charäkhnem?" Kiria asked.

"I haven't, My Keeper. There isn't a large Khelê population there."

That seemed an odd reason not to go. Hadn't Chetana lived in a city like that before? "I went once. King Ganesha has a zoo inside the palace."

"That sounds very interesting."

"It is! I hope it's as great as I remember. Sometimes things aren't as grand and magical as they seem before you grow up."

A smile played on Chetana's full mouth as though she were thinking that Kiria was still young. "I'm sure it will be."

The guard at the front of the column held up a hand to halt the travelers. They all slowed. She heard Vayci laugh, a rare sound.

Chetana continued. "Some things are even better when you grow up."

"Like what?" Kiria struggled to think of a good example. The confidence she had gained from the journey with Firian was more of a reclaiming than anything truly new.

Chetana sat still, considering an answer. Her bay mare tossed her head.

The things Kiria could do now that she was grown—become the Keeper, drink wine, see Firian in the Unreal (which she kept dead secret from everyone except Chetana)—had merit, but also an edge that could quickly turn them from sweet to sour. As a child, she had pictured becoming a Keeper or falling in love as unequivocally good and fun. That wasn't so. With pleasure came pain or uncertainty.

Chetana, in a good mood despite the dark secret she held about Kiria, waved Jori forward. She hardly ever approved of Jori's flippancy, being so serious herself. "Tell our Keeper the benefits of growing up," she said.

He trotted forward, leaving the serving girls behind. "Ah," he said with a grin. "I wouldn't know. I haven't tried it."

A twinge of irritation crossed Chetana's face.

"One thing that's better now than when you were a kid," Kiria clarified.

"Hm." He looked up at the too-bright sky, tipping his chin. "All my powers are greatly improved." He gestured to her. "And yours, of course, as well."

"Your powers?" Kiria said, knowing she was setting him up for a ridiculous comment.

He ticked the items off with his fingers. "I'm faster, taller, hungrier, more eloquent, and better looking." He scrunched his gray eyes as though daring her to disagree.

Kiria laughed. "I don't know about hungrier. You ate everything when you were little."

"That still leaves four solid ways that I'm better now. You can't argue that I'm shorter."

"No, that's true."

Chetana silently peeled away from the conversation, staying close enough not to be rude, but excusing herself from this nonsense.

"And me?" she asked.

"Oh ho!" he exclaimed. "Don't make me give a full list, my dear. We'll be here till supper."

She waited.

He rolled his eyes. Holding up his fingers again, he said, "You're incomprehensively more beautiful—but you knew that—you're more powerful, you're also taller, also more eloquent, and also hungrier—"

"Do you even remember that one time with the tarts?"

"—and you're tougher too." His eyes strayed to her left shoulder, where the misshapen, raised scar from the arrow attack just showed from beneath her clothing. "Is that enough?"

"That will do," she said imperiously.

His eyes glinted in fun.

She pointed ahead. "We're getting close to Charäkhnem."

"Finally."

"Yes, those are the Salt Flats."

"They sound charming."

"Oh, they are."

"Now, if you don't mind"—he heaved himself off the saddle to the ground—"I'm going to stretch my legs a bit." A groom hustled over and took the reins from him. Jori gave a fractional bow from the waist before walking away, back to her serving girls.

She watched him take each one by the hand, helping them dismount. Jori wouldn't disapprove of her meetings in the Unreal. He might even be proud of her. At least he couldn't say she would be ruined by her decision to let Firian ease her sorrows and stresses away.

She wouldn't tell him just yet. There was still a chance—a small chance—that he wouldn't understand, and she preferred to think he would be happy for her. Not everyone thought she was making a mistake.

26

KIRIA

Huge tan domes and turrets of Charäkhnem's royal palace rose ahead of them. It was at least as magnificent as Kiria remembered. Long red banners rimmed with gold embroidery stood on gonfalons on either side of the enormous metal doors. They must have been three stories tall, decorated with round studs arranged in the shape of wings. Four guards, all wearing traditional pointed helmets, flanked the doors.

A pathway with guardrails, like a waterless bridge, led to the entrance. On the railing burned dozens of small candles. Wax coated the metal edges in a look both messy and religious. The guardrails must have been erected to keep those foolish enough to invade from having too many escape routes.

Kiria glanced at the armed escort that had come to lead them to the palace. These guards had conspicuous swords strapped to their belts and red sashes around their waists, looking fearsome in their shining armor. Her own guards' armor still gleamed, despite the trip. She'd spied them polishing the pieces at night and washing spots out of the blue cloth slung around their shoulders.

She was used to being the one who could call or dismiss guards with a word. Four Kingdom soldiers still surrounded her, but Char Visil, Charäkhnem's capital city, was so much grander than any of the other towns or cities they had passed, that she felt small. These days, she didn't often feel small.

Even amid the places where normal citizens seemed to live and work, huge pillars and sky bridges rose like oversized aqueducts to awe and intimidate. Much of the architecture was sandstone. Understandable, since Charäkhnem faced the Desert of Erad on its eastern side. The reddish tan buildings made the sky seem bluer and fresher, despite the dust and heady spices in the air.

It was a good thing they had planned to spend more than one day here. Kiria wanted to explore.

The tall, narrow metal doors creaked open on ropes to let them enter. Inside was a surprisingly small antechamber, again for defense. Kiria wondered if Char Visil had always been so intent on security, or if they made modifications because her ancestors fought them hundreds of years ago.

The Charäkhni guards stood at attention in two perfect rows on either side of them as the group shrugged off their riding cloaks and generally made themselves more presentable.

The metal doors swung shut. Though it was broad daylight, the tiled antechamber was almost completely dark except for golden bowls full of fire standing on stick-thin pedestals. The darkness became quickly claustrophobic.

Happily, one of the Charäkhni guards pushed open a door that let in some natural light. Apparently, there were actual windows in the next room. Kiria moved with her group into the opening, a short hallway, and into a lobby. Staircases led up in a few different directions and hallways disappeared around corners, but at least this area was more spacious. In front of them was another set of golden-plated double doors. This had to be the throne room.

She swallowed, but found that the roof of her mouth had gone dry. In seconds, she would be presented to Shear Ganesha, the king whose approval she needed most. The grandeur of his palace made her nervous that he might not accept her. Prince Amrit's flippant attitude toward her when they were children rushed back. She was a girl and therefore not a natural choice for a leader, but rather someone to forge marriage alliances. But that was years ago. Maybe Amrit and his father didn't think that way now.

Everyone but Kiria, the four Kingdom guards, and Chetana followed servants to their quarters in the palace. Jori pulled a face as he was led away. Obviously, he wanted to see his brother's bride-to-be. Kiria was eager too. There would certainly be another opportunity for Jori later.

Kiria dusted off her dress and lifted her chin. She wore her Beauty like power, like armor. It would help legitimize her in the presence of this established king. Although she shouldn't *have* to have it, it did make a striking first impression.

Someone announced her arrival in Charäkhni. A flourish of instruments and the doors opened once again to admit them into the presence of Shear Ganesha.

The long throne room shone like gold. Guards and musicians stood in columns on either side to usher them in. Some of the instruments had been dyed red, including one that looked almost like her lyra at home. Lampstands lined the enormous hall. Despite all the fire, the cooler air of the open space washed over her as she stepped in.

The vaulted ceiling met at a peak that stretched as high as the Main. At the far end was a platform, raised off the floor by several stairs, where Shear Ganesha sat on his high-backed throne. His expression betrayed none of his initial opinions about her. Most people had a visible reaction to her Beauty, but the king remained impassive. In the shadows behind the throne stood a man all in black. Did the king have a Tanyuin bodyguard? She would have to ask Firian later.

At the foot of the stairs were two seated figures. Amrit was the one on the left. Kiria hadn't seen him in several years, but he had the same reddish hair. He had filled out and was no longer that scrawny boy she remembered. When he saw her, his mouth went slack and he leaned forward, almost unconsciously, before sitting back again. She suppressed a tiny smirk.

The figure on the right was a young woman. Atty's fiancée, Haved. She had the same sandy-colored skin as her brother. She wore her dark reddish hair long, but tied it back to reveal large golden earrings. She had a square jaw and an expression difficult to read.

An alliance with both Charäkhnem and the Tanyu would render the Western Kingdom all but undefeatable.

The six visitors approached the throne. The king had a stony face, a hardened version of the expression she had seen on Haved. Over his shoulders he wore a stole that fell like a golden set of wings, the pinions stretching in front. Each feather glowed in the light with remarkable detail. Clearly, it was something only the kings of Charäkhnem wore.

Chetana and the guards bowed at the waist. Chetana spoke first, her words flawlessly diplomatic. "Your Majesty, King Ganesha, please allow me to introduce the Second Keeper of Brithnem and the Western Kingdom, Kiria Arioc." She stepped aside and Kiria went forward.

The king bowed his head a fraction to acknowledge her, but he did not stand. "Welcome to Char Visil," he said in a deep, gravelly voice, accented like Amrit's but more refined. "My Keeper, I am pleased that you have chosen to visit us."

"The pleasure is mine, Your Majesty," she replied, dimly aware of Amrit staring at her.

"Our countries are fortunate in such an alliance, which soon will be even stronger." He looked down at his daughter. "And news has reached us that you have subdued the marauders?"

It would have been easier if his people had assisted in the war, but she still felt glad when he mentioned the victory. "We have, Your Majesty."

"That is surely something to celebrate." He didn't smile or break the polite but mechanical cadence of his voice. "In two days' time, we will host a celebration in your honor, both for your ascension to the throne and the pending alliance between our two kingdoms. My son and daughter will attend, and you may bring those who traveled with you."

Two guards, as though summoned, left the room in unison, perhaps to tell the others about the celebration.

"I thank you," Kiria said, though the word *pending* still rang in her ears. "God has truly blessed the Western Kingdom with your partnership."

"Have you brought Atael with you?"

Kiria looked over in surprise. It was Haved. She appeared unashamed about the interruption, but not brash. "No, my lady," Kiria said.

The only evidence of the princess's disappointment was a slight dimming of her eyes.

Perhaps Atty should have come. It was a shame that so many would get to meet her before he did. "But his brother is here." Kiria added the words before picturing the two of them meeting. Hopefully Jori would behave himself.

"The Kepron, Jorrim?"

"Yes."

"Then you will bring him to the celebration, My Keeper."

"Of course."

"Will the late Second Keeper join us?" asked the king.

The late? He made it sound like she was dead. "No, my mother elected to stay in Brithnem." *She's in perfect health. She supports my ascension to the throne...* "She gladly supports me there, but wanted me to experience my coronation tour without other Keepers." *Did that sound odd? That sounded odd.* She bit her tongue to keep from saying anything more. Her mind buzzed a little with shame.

The king shifted in response, the golden wings moving with him.

If he was going to move forward in letting his daughter marry Atty, he had to like Kiria, or at least consider her a legitimate ruler.

Chetana stood forth again. "Your Majesty, we have traveled many days and My Keeper would like to rest."

"Then rest shall be granted," said the king. He turned to the guards. "Take them to their quarters." He said the words grandly, not dismissively. But he still gazed down at her from his throne as if unsure what to think of this beautiful new Keeper. She would have to make a better impression at the upcoming celebration, winning over both him and his daughter, for Atty's sake.

"Thank you, Your Majesty," she said, turning with the rest of them and letting the guards shepherd them to their rooms.

KIRIA HAD EXPECTED the party to be held in the throne room, since the Keepers always held their large gatherings in the Main. Little could have prepared her for the larger, grander room, covered in intricate gold leaf. The floors shone. The ceiling soared above them, lost in dimness. Servants in gold and red took capes, offered food, refilled glasses, brought messages. The wealthier guests, both male and female, had lined their eyes in coal black. She didn't know where to look. Several times, she realized that her face was stuck in a dumb, awestruck grin.

Amrit had the same grin on his face when he approached her, dressed more magnificently than any other guest, the king excepted. His golden vest was cinched at the waist. Beneath it, the shirt had maroon silk sleeves. Heavy metal plates formed in the shape of wings hung around his neck. The same design wrapped around his forearms. His lapels and skirts had matching intricate embroidery in black thread.

The Kingdom guard she kept with her moved to the side so she could speak to him. "Lady Kiria," Amrit said, "are you enjoying your party?" His speech still wasn't as smooth as his father's, but his fluency was far more advanced than when they had first met. It helped that he was home and had the ease of a host instead of a guest.

"It's amazing," she said sincerely. "Everything is beautiful. Please thank the king for me."

He spoke above the rising noise of the party. "I suggested the extra fabric. The red." He gestured to long, thin tables gathered on one side of the enormous room. They all had deep red tablecloths that matched the Charäkhni flag.

"That looks good."

When she looked back, he was staring at her. She couldn't think of a way to fill the silence. There had to be something that would promote goodwill between their countries without making it seem that she was interested in him...

"Yes," he finally said. "A beautiful color."

"Couldn't agree more."

Someone grabbed her hand and spun her around. Jori, of course.

"Look at that dress," he said. He all but winked at her.

Amrit waited for a second more but saw that Jori wasn't going to float onwards quickly enough for him not to be conspicuous. Appearing to see another important dignitary, the prince excused himself and strode away.

"Button your vest," Kiria whispered. "This is a diplomatic event."

Jori raised both eyebrows at her but stiffly and pointedly obeyed. He spread his arms when he was finished. "Is this acceptable?"

"Yes, just... be good."

"I thought this was a party."

"It is." But their alliance with Charäkhnem shouldn't be tested. They had to leave King Ganesha with no doubts about the Western Kingdom or her leadership.

"Why don't we meet Atty's girl?"

She hissed in his ear. "Don't say that! She's not 'Atty's girl.' Especially not here. And not yet, so *be good*."

He gave a crooked smile. Maybe he had meant to rile her up. He whispered back. "You have to relax. Have some fun." On his breath, she could smell a hint of the fermented honey drink the servers kept offering.

She adjusted her off-white dress with gold and purple trim. "I will."

He waited.

She sighed. "I'll try." She brought her voice up to the normal volume. "It is gorgeous here."

"And all for you, darling."

"Well—" Why was she about to protest? It was true. All of this was in her honor: the new Keeper of Brithnem. It felt too grand, as though there had to be an ulterior motive. If stronger alliances were an ulterior motive, though, that wasn't bad at all. She smiled.

He leaned forward again. "You've already impressed them. If you go too far, they might start feeling bad about themselves."

She stopped herself from smacking him for the joke. "Go on," she said, laughing. "Have a good time. And thank you." She inhaled deeply. Honey and lamb and roasted vegetables mingled in the air. So far, no one had accused her of usurping the throne or fraternizing with Tanyu. Maybe she could actually relax and enjoy the party, follow Jori's advice.

Jori suddenly strode away, walking with purpose. She followed his eyeline and found Haved, dressed all in gold with a deep red sash. Her hair, darker than her brother's, fell almost to her waist with a simple golden ornament twined on one side. Jori all but ran toward her. Kiria followed.

When Jori reached her, he bowed without a hint of irony. A good sign. Haved regarded him stoically. "It's an honor to meet the princess of Charäkhnem," he began. "I am Jorrim Calthwaite, brother of Atael Calthwaite, the Third Keeper of the Western Kingdom."

His title sounded pretty impressive when he put it like that. Why was he always complaining about lacking prestige?

"You can call me Jori."

"Atael's brother?" she asked, suddenly interested. She drew her dark eyes over him, inspecting, as though she expected to find a family resemblance there. He waited without shame for her to finish looking.

"Yes," Kiria said, drawing even with them, "but the brothers are very different."

Haved's eyes widened at the sight of Kiria's Beauty and she dipped her head respectfully. "Lady Kiria."

"Princess Haved."

"How are they different?" Haved seemed fairly stoic but Kiria decided that she liked her. Haved was so self-possessed, so unashamed of who she was. Her boldness could border on rudeness, but her words had no cruel edge.

"Atael has more power." Kiria cast a glance at Jori, who raised his eyebrows at her in a question. "He's more serious-minded, and he's a little taller."

"Not much taller," Jori said.

"He's bigger," she revised, casting him a glance.

Jori shrugged one shoulder.

"Is he kind?" Haved didn't ask the question in a timid or fearful way, but with genuine curiosity.

Kiria smiled. Yes, that was more important. "Yes, he is."

Haved's stoic face thawed into a smile too.

"Unless you mention that one Dedication Day," Jori said.

Haved, a little concerned, glanced at Kiria for confirmation. Kiria shook her head. That incident was years ago, when they were all little. Atty would never cry about fasting now.

"He's a wonderful person," she said.

Haved turned to Jori, though her eyes frequently went back to Kiria. Beauty was hard to ignore. "You are his brother. Tell me about him."

"I was actually hoping to learn more about you," he replied. "We can trade. I'll tell you something and you tell me something." He winked confidentially.

The arrangement seemed to please her. "All right. You begin."

Jori crossed his arms and shifted his weight as he thought. "We don't call him Atael. We call him Atty."

That information didn't seem like enough to warrant something interesting from her, but apparently this was the first time she had heard of it. "Atty?" she asked, emphasizing the *t*.

"Yes," Jori said. "Now your turn."

He didn't hesitate. "I love learning about the heavens, the stars. Do you have any Qib Navigators in Brithnem?"

"What?"

"Qib Navigators," Kiria stepped in. "They're the best ocean navigators, from the Desert Colony of Qib...?" She hoped this would jog his memory. Apparently, he hadn't paid enough attention to his Amiran tutor as a child. "I haven't heard of many," Kiria said to Haved, "but I did see one once, a long time ago. The army uses them, and I think a couple trade companies do too."

The princess beamed more broadly than Kiria had seen so far. "That's wonderful! I thought there would be more Navigators near the ocean."

"The Amiran Academy is there too," said Kiria. "They could probably teach you more about the stars if you're interested."

"Oh yes. Our own teachers are very good, but if there is any new information I could learn..." The passion shone in her face. "I like to chart the stars. Brithnem is so far away. They might look different." She wrung her hands, not from distress but anticipation.

"That's true," she said. Kiria wished she knew enough about the topic to satisfy her. Her love for the subject transfigured her from a wooden royal figure to someone she could see as a friend. When was the last time she had stopped to look, really look, at the stars?

"Does Atty go on the ocean? Does he know the stars?"

Honestly, Kiria wasn't sure if he knew constellations. He didn't often go out on the ocean, and when he did, it wasn't very far.

A server passed by and all three of them took a honey drink from the platter.

"I'm sure he doesn't know them as well as you do," Jori said.

"What does he do?" she insisted.

"He serves his country," Kiria said, filling the space she knew would be silent too long. Atty wasn't particularly good at many things. He was passable at many things. But that didn't make him sound like an exciting match. "He enjoys being outdoors."

Jori sucked his teeth, clearly holding back the comments welling to the surface.

"He must be thoughtful to like solitude," said Haved.

"Yes," said Kiria, a little too quickly. She loved Atty like her own brother, but this woman, despite her childlike frankness, seemed so grand, and Atty's destiny had always seemed too big for him.

"Well," said Jori, "that's—"

Kiria gasped as pain rushed through her chest. As though she'd heard a shriek, her heart beat so rapidly that it felt unstable. Panic surged through her. Her mind blurred with dread. The danger wasn't just inside her ribcage; there was something out there too, on the dance floor. She knew it as surely as she felt the breath clawing in her throat. Someone watched her, preparing to strike. She was too visible. Her Beauty made her a target. Instinctively, she ducked, searching wildly for the threat.

Someone was here. Someone would kill her.

The space between her and the other guests now seemed like huge gulfs exposing her to all eyes. Everywhere she looked, people were looking back. Heavy dread flowed thick in her veins and covered her mind, immobilizing it. She had to get to cover. Without a word, she ran through the huge room toward the nearest door. Maybe there was a place to hide, to think. Why was no one screaming? Why were there no sounds of death?

She sucked down air but none of it seemed to stay in her lungs. All its healthy qualities were gone. She was drowning.

She reached the door but her strength had left. She couldn't pull the handle. She was trapped. The door wouldn't open. Her heart pounded so hard and fast it hurt. She had to sit down.

As she began to sink to the floor, someone grabbed her arm. Was it her guard? Someone else took her other arm and half-walked, half-dragged her across the floor. The open floor.

Her head began to clear. Looking around, she saw no one else in a panic. The two men at either side were her guards. Chetana had joined them, following behind.

What had happened? The truth hit her in a wave of nausea. This was someone else's panic.

Firian.

Firian was dead.

27

FIRIAN

Water closed over Firian's head. It was late enough that no one else was likely to use the washroom, especially this one in the Head's secluded hallway. It was the perfect opportunity to practice a skill he hadn't mastered yet.

Thirty-four, thirty-five, thirty-six... Without water, he was able to hold his breath for two hundred counts. He calmed himself, feeling the warm bathwater lap over the crown of his head. Some of his dark hair must be floating on the surface. This was the closest thing a body of water for him to practice.

His heart slowed. Calm encased his mind. If Bard could do it, so could he. *Seventy, seventy-one, seventy-two...*

All it took was control, above or under the water. The warm, soundless space lent itself to serenity. *Ninety-five, ninety-six...*

Later, he could think about which towns to take and save. Later, he would check on the state of his growing army.

New recruits from Imlin were coming soon, thanks to Makai, so Jovan had to be ready for them. Firian suspected that Makai had to threaten more than one person in order to gain control of Imlin, but he didn't ask any questions. When the Tanyuin Head demanded allegiance, refusal wasn't an option.

This was the way forward. The Academy needed a new direction, a direction toward justice and power. There were bound to be people who resisted. Bard's and Kiria's thoughts were never far from his own, though, and they didn't understand the cost of success.

Firian could think about it later. Now, he could just practice his skills in and out of the Unreal. This was where he thrived.

One hundred twenty, one hundred twenty-one, one hundred twenty-two...

His chest started to feel tight. He redirected his energy to the calm tick of the numbers. He didn't mind a little pain. He swished one hand through the water, feeling the weight of it press back against his hand. *One hundred thirty-two, one hundred thirty-three...*

A faint pulse meant that someone had jumped or moved nearby. Probably out in the hallway. The feeling barely registered.

One hundred fifty, one hundred fifty-one...

A feeling of eyes on him. He dipped into the Unreal. With all the Talent in the building, any distinct individual was unclear. Everything hummed with life. He still had to master that skill as well. Belik always knew he was coming, even when he wasn't using the Talent. "Come in, Firian," he would say, before Firian had touched the door handle. One day, he would be able to do that too.

One hundred sixty-eight, one hundred sixty-nine...

He was just being paranoid. Almost everyone supported his Headship, and those who didn't feared his ability. No one was watching him. He was alone.

One hundred seventy-two, one hundred seventy-three...

He willed himself not to speed through the numbers. Control in all things. Even a bath could sharpen his wits, if he had enough patience.

One hundred seventy-nine...

Patience. Control.

One hundred eighty...

With a sucking, surging sound, something plunging into the water close to his head. He thrashed to the side, sliding just out of reach of the fingers that brushed against his temple. Panic gushed through him. The tub was suddenly the bay where children were left to die and the Torithian pushed his head down so he couldn't breathe. He couldn't breathe.

He kicked against the tub to push himself out into the air again. When he emerged, his gasped breath came too quickly to fill his aching lungs.

Jovan stood huge over him. Weaponless, the Master lunged again, his massive hands reaching for Firian's neck. Jovan didn't need weapons. He could kill him. In a physical fight, Firian stood no chance. *There are many ways to kill a man.* Jovan knew them all.

Firian was naked and weaponless too, but not helpless. Even before drawing another breath, he closed his eyes and dove into the Unreal—one level, two levels —and savagely attacked Jovan's mind, his body, his subconscious.

Vague pressure pressed on Firian's throat, pressure on his eyes and his tongue...

Firian doubled his attack, feeling his own heart beat under the water so loudly that the whole Academy must have heard it. His fear and rage turned red and black. He hurled all the violence he could muster. He could feel Jovan, feel himself, bending like a tree branch. He *would not* give first. He might not have strength or air, but he had power. He pressed with all his mental strength in one last heave.

The branch broke. Firian gasped. Air. Air filled his lungs. He hurtled upward through the levels and opened his eyes.

Jovan lay half in and half out of the bath. Pink water floated out of his ears.

Furious and horrified, Firian shoved Jovan's shoulder and threw him out of the bathwater. His skull cracked against the floor. Blood leaked from his closed eyes and open mouth.

Firian stood, grabbed a towel with a trembling hand, and got out of the tub. He could barely wrap the towel around himself. He kept blinking, impotent adrenaline spiraling through him.

Unable to stand, unable to shake the panic, he sat on the edge of the bath, watching the red blood pool around Master Jovan's head.

When he had finally gathered himself enough to stand, anger took the place of panic. No one would blame him for what he had done. He'd acted in self-defense. Jovan—he cursed loudly—made him do it. He didn't want to kill him. How *dare* he try to murder him? And why?

He could barely see through the black haze of rage as he marched back to his office, not even dressed. "Get me Belik!" he snapped at the guard outside his room. He hated the guard. Why hadn't he protected him? *I told him to stay where he was.* At the memory, he cursed himself, and then Jovan, and then the guard again.

The guard hurried away.

Firian slammed the door behind him. Almost feral, he checked every corner of the suite of rooms, looking behind doors, crawling to see under the desk and the bed. He ripped off the blankets and threw them against the wall. He needed to scream, throw something, kill Jovan again.

His hands shook. He bit his tongue until it bled. The pain helped. Taking a few slow, shaky breaths, he calmed himself enough to put on his Academy-issued black clothes. Something about the sharp edges of the iron crown made him rethink putting it on, so he left it in his bedroom.

The door opened in the office. He practically flew to meet the newcomer. It was Belik.

"Sit!" Firian roared. That posture would make it harder for someone to attack.

With shame, he felt angry warmth pool around his eyes. Hopefully Belik wouldn't see it. But he would. He always noticed.

Belik sat without saying a word.

The strength of Firian's voice had given out. The next words were quiet. "Did you know about this?"

"What happened?" Belik asked evenly.

Firian couldn't bring the words to his mouth.

Understanding dawned in Belik's blunt face. "Who was it?"

"Jovan."

Belik bit out a curse word. "No, I didn't know." He looked down. "I should have suspected. Firian, I should have warned you."

"Yes, you should have! Who else is there?"

"I don't know of anyone else."

"Liar."

"Firian, I swear. I knew that some people didn't approve of you, but I thought they were all too afraid to act against you."

"Get me a list." His power flowed through him like an evil spirit.

"I can do that." Belik said the words slowly enough that Firian doubted his sincerity. He was trying to calm him down and the effort just infuriated him more.

Firian was about to snap at Belik again when he cut him off. "Where is he?"

Suddenly exhausted, Firian deflated. One of his mentors lifeless as a monstrous sack on the floor. Gray hair mussed by a pillow. Stiff legs under blankets. Blood dribbling from a useless mouth. "The washroom," he said.

"I can get people to take care of that for you."

A wave of gratefulness overcame Firian. A hard lump formed in his throat.

Rage was better than this. Rage could eliminate the problem and show no weakness. All he could do was nod.

"It's done," Belik said with the self-assuredness of a god. He was security itself, someone to trust so Firian could rest.

He rallied his roiling feelings. "Thank you. But I still need that list."

28

KIRIA

Chetana and the guards led Kiria back to her room. Tears flowed down her face against her will. Grief and humiliation filled her so she could barely breathe.

Everyone had seen her panic in the great hall, but no one else could sense the danger. Even without strange actions like that, everybody noticed her because of her Beauty. They must all think she was unhinged.

She definitely felt unhinged. Something was deeply wrong. Maybe Firian wasn't dead. Maybe he was alive. Maybe it was just... She couldn't come up with a good scenario that would have caused her breakdown. Whatever had happened, it was serious. She had to check, had to see him right now.

Chetana, her arm across her shoulders, guided her gently into the diplomat suite. Guards stood at attention outside. Everything happened far too slowly, as though their legs moved through thigh-deep water. Once inside, Kiria gulped down air and pulled Chetana into a fierce hug. "Okay," she said, pushing her away. "Everyone needs to leave. I have to be alone." Her advisor would already know that her episode had to do with Firian. Kiria didn't look at her again, turning instead to the bed.

"My Keeper, may I get you a glass of water?" It was Vayci, eyes full of concern.

"No," she answered automatically, wanting them gone as well. "Yes." Her mouth felt sticky and her throat burned.

Dutiful as always, Vayci slipped silently through the door after Chetana.

"Please leave me alone," she told Candrae, who waited at the ready. Candrae didn't protest. Kiria knew she would stand just outside.

Finally, she was by herself. She rubbed hot tears off her face with the back of her hand as she changed from Beautiful to plain and shut her eyes.

All was darkness. Slowly, she reached her mind in Firian's direction. Her fingers trembled with apprehension. It felt like opening a door with a murder victim behind it. She didn't want to find his dead body, but she had to know.

"Firian?" she whispered. Even that volume sounded loud in the nothingness. Tears started at the corners of her eyes again. "Firian?"

Her heartbeat pulsed around the lump in her throat. He was dead. He had to be. And she wouldn't find out how it happened until they got the news from a Watchman in a few days. She couldn't wait that long.

"Firian!" She risked saying his name more loudly, though the silence was so charged that it felt as though a hundred people were listening.

A figure in black appeared.

She recoiled, heart pounding. Breathing hard, she leaned forward and squinted. The lines of the person's body became more distinct. She knew those shoulders, that hair, that walk...

She ran toward him, feeling as though her feet were floating. They might have been. "Oh my god!" she cried, and hugged Firian hard around the neck. He was solid. He was there.

Wrapping his strong arms around her back, he held her against him.

"Oh my god!" she said again, her breath hot against his shoulder. "I thought..."

His heart beat hard under hers. Something awful had happened. But they didn't want to talk.

He clung to her as though she could save him from whatever horrible thing stalked him. His hands were hot on her waist. She began to melt in his arms.

The kisses came fast. Her face and body flushed at his touch. She wanted him closer as he bent down over her. He drew one finger all the way up her side, over her neck, her cheek, sending shivers over her body. When he reached her hairline, he raked his fingers through her hair.

She hugged him tightly. Maybe she was cutting off his ability to breathe, but she needed him to know she was there. She could barely breathe either.

He moved his lips from her mouth to her hot cheek, greedily kissing up to her ear. "Show me," he said hoarsely.

She could barely respond. "What?"

"Change for me." The humid warmth against her ear distracted her from the words he was saying.

If she showed him her Beauty now, she knew what it would mean. Even in the Unreal—*the Unreal, they were in the Unreal*—she couldn't let him take her body. Neither of them could withstand the temptation if she changed.

She caught her breath, slowed it down. Her arms trembled with the force of what she felt, but she had to be resolved. Fractionally, she released him.

He swept her hair back around the nape of her neck as he attended to her ear. The back of her neck. It was almost too much.

"No."

"I need you. I need you today," he said in an undertone, not looking at her but running his hands back down over her sides. His fingers fiddled at her waist. He brought his face close for a kiss.

She sank into it a moment. Those lips... but no, she couldn't.

"What happened?" she asked.

At the question, the heat in him died down. He took a deep breath that made his shoulders hang lower and his hands stop moving. He was silent for a moment, head bowed, gently holding her.

Then he bit his lip, probably to keep from swearing, and his eyes darkened. After a few more moments of silence, he looked at her. "Someone tried to kill me."

Even though she had expected that answer, the words still made her stomach drop. "I thought so," she whispered.

Curiosity sparked in his unhappy face. "Did you feel something?"

She nodded. "I did. I thought... you had died." It was hard even to say the words. But it was the truth, and she could forgive herself for the embarrassing display at the party more readily since she had thought him dead.

He pursed his mouth. "No," he said simply. He was alive.

She wanted to repeat her question since he hadn't given an explanation.

He sighed and rubbed her sides, preoccupied with thought. His hands against the fabric, almost as though he were wiping them off, brought to mind another time they were together. In the woods outside Raewhith. When he had killed those men.

She fought off a shudder. "Did you kill him?" she asked, her voice tiny.

He just nodded a small, honest nod. It wasn't boastful this time. It might have been afraid. Dark hair fell down over his forehead as his eyes found the floor.

Almost motherly, she pushed his hair out of his eyes and hugged him again. He warmed up in her arms, like an animal waking up. She felt him take her into him.

She let go and pushed back against his chest. "I can't do this," she muttered.

"Why not?" The question came out rough and husky.

She wasn't sure how to answer him.

As the silence lengthened, anger flickered over his features. Then he softened and grabbed her hand to pull her back in.

She stood her ground, feeling cold. "I can't. But I'm so glad you're still alive."

His fingers recoiled from her into a loose fist and back again. His eyebrows lowered, uncomprehending. "Why are you never Beautiful with me?"

The question stung.

Neither of them made any sort of background. Behind him was only darkness, and he blended in as though he were part of it. The pit of her stomach felt sour.

Today, he had survived an assassination attempt. He wasn't himself. He shouldn't demand that she become Beautiful, or that she give herself to him. She still wanted to be with him, but they had different ideas of what that meant.

Based on everything that had happened, she was fragile too. It was a bad time for either of them to make rash decisions, even in the Unreal.

She swallowed. "It's different with you," she started, not sure how she would explain. "If I... changed, with just the two of us, it would feel..." She cast around for a word. *Frightening, vulnerable, wild, like a promise...* A promise. That was it. It would feel like a promise she wasn't ready to make.

He waited for her to finish. His jaw was clenched tight. The longer she stalled, the more he frowned, not understanding.

You still like me this way. She willed him to say something, but he stayed silent.

"I can't," she said again. "Not... right now."

She felt his surprise follow her as she disappeared back to reality.

She sat on the edge of the bed, heavy as though she had just come back from a swim. A glass of water sat nearby. The torches guttered. Mindlessly smoothing the blankets, she hung her head. All her thoughts were disconnected, more like images than words. Impressions. Desires and regrets bubbling up like the ocean. Wave after wave.

Her eyes felt crusty with dried tears. At least Firian wasn't dead. That was something to be thankful for. But the Charäkhni royal family must think she was insane, maybe unfit to lead. And Chetana knew there was a connection between her and Firian. Though her advisor didn't mention it, she knew Kiria's outburst had to do with him. Would she bring it up again?

Firian acted as though he wanted her to put back his broken pieces, but it was too much to expect of her. He would see her actions as a rejection. She read it like a bold sentence in his eyes, the cut of his hard-set jaw. How would he respond?

Glad she was alone, she put her face in her hands. The golden bracelets she had worn to the party tinkled as they slid down her wrists.

"...said she wanted to be alone."

"We all know that doesn't apply to me."

"It applies to everyone."

"Just open the door. I need to see her. Make sure she's all right."

"Sir—"

"Is she all right in there? You can tell me that at least."

Jori was arguing with one of the guards. Wearily, she stood to her feet and went to assuage his worry.

When she opened the door, he bolted inside, followed by a guard. Jori quickly made a pointed face at the guard before turning to her. He reached out and held her shoulders, observing her face. "How are you, darling?" He searched her eyes as though he could unravel the mystery of her behavior that way.

"I don't know," she replied, suddenly helpless. What was she supposed to say to him? Exhausted, she sat on the edge of the bed again.

"Are you all right? You don't seem all right. Gave everybody a scare in there." He sat down beside her, still maintaining comforting contact.

"I gave myself a scare." She could barely look at him.

This was the part when he would normally make a joke about Haved not wanting to marry Atty now. It was a testament to his concern that he didn't say it. "Ah." He gave her shoulders a squeeze. "You're safe now."

She looked at him and grimaced. "What's happening in there now? Do they think I'm crazy?"

Apparently encouraged about her mental state, he winked. "You've always been a little crazy."

She groaned and linked her ankles.

"Shh!" he soothed. "They'll be fine. And besides, who cares? I just need to know you're all right."

"Jori," she said, suddenly resolved, "I need to tell you something."

His gray eyes widened slightly, surprised by her seriousness.

"Actually, I need to ask you something."

They both waited in silence for a moment. Jori scooted away from her in a listening posture. He picked a feather off his sleeve and flicked it away. "What do you want to ask me about?"

Kiria squirmed. It was an uncomfortable confession. Hopefully he'd support her decisions. She couldn't continue without at least one person telling her that she wasn't doing anything wrong. "It's a little tricky…"

A smirk passed over his face. Leaning toward her, he gave her a confidential look. "That's my specialty."

She shoved him. "No, it isn't. You're never serious." Maybe he expected juicy gossip. In a way, now that she thought of it, that was what she was offering.

He set his face in a serious neutral expression. "Oh, I can be serious, darling. Keep secrets. Kill as necessary."

She rolled her eyes. But he did make her feel better. "Okay." She steeled her nerves with a deep breath. It was time for the truth. "You can't tell anyone, even Atty."

Curiosity blazed in his eyes.

"I… have met Firian in the Unreal."

"More than once?"

"Yes."

"Romantic?"

"Yes."

Jori, impressively, kept the neutral expression intact. A wave of relief swept over her when he didn't judge her right away. Not that he'd have any room to do that. Mon Párinath was filled with rumors of his romantic escapades. More than half of them were lies built on all his obvious flirtations.

"Do you love him?" he asked.

She blinked. She hadn't asked herself the question so bluntly. Firian impressed her. She thought about him often. Together, they were electric. But did she love him? She thought of his face before she disappeared. Vulnerable but angry. "I don't know."

"That means no," Jori said. "Always."

She opened her mouth to protest, but he held up a hand to stop her. "No, it always means no. If you loved him, you'd know it."

"I care about him."

"Of course you do," he said quickly, as though it were obvious. "You're a decent person. Much better than I am. I don't care whether he lives or dies. But he *isn't* a decent person. He was willing to turn on you."

"It's not the same now. He's in charge of the Academy. It's different."

Jori threw his head back in an exaggerated laugh. "Do you"—he readjusted his sitting position—"do you remember when he came to the palace the first time?"

"How could I forget?" Jori had practically skipped with excitement to meet him.

"So you know I want to believe you. The Tanyu. Kiria, the Tanyu! I wanted to be one. I wanted them to be perfect. But after I heard…" He dropped his gaze and fiddled with the buttons on his vest. His voice turned into a mutter. "I'm glad you didn't see me. The pubs got to know me very well."

Jori never talked like this. Almost as though he realized the same thing at the same moment, he tossed his head as if to free himself of the dark thoughts. "You, my dear, are light. Sweetness and light."

She scoffed, feeling anything but those things.

"But he has darkness. If you don't love him, don't let him in your soul."

Though he said the words flippantly, they fell between them like a curtain. Firian had made her a better leader. His drive encouraged her to start earlier, try harder. She pictured the way he had looked at her before the Academy made him take her hostage. Even her plain face fascinated him and opened something inside him. She could see it. And the Firian she saw in those moments took her breath away. He was a warrior, strong and capable, with the focus to topple systems and right injustice. She thought of Firian's hands at her sides, his kiss on her mouth. She wanted more of both. If only it were easier to do the right thing. Or even to know what that meant. "I have some darkness in me too," she confessed.

Jori snorted. "Impossible! My girl?"

"Jori, it's true." She looked into his eyes.

A smile crinkled the edges of his mouth, but he met her gaze.

"I know there are problems with seeing Firian," she said. "I know. Like tonight."

"That was him?" Jori sat a little straighter on the bed, as though he would charge after Firian that minute.

"It was, it was," she said, soothing him back down. "But not what you think. He was almost killed today. I felt it." She laid a fist on her heart, trying to make him understand.

He frowned.

She continued slowly. "I felt his panic. And I thought... Once I understood what was happening, I thought he died." She dropped her gaze.

"Hey, that's not good." The way he said it made it sound like he meant their connection, not Firian's attack. "This isn't good," he repeated. "He's taking you down with him."

"It could just as easily have happened to me," she said in a small voice.

He took her by the shoulders again, forcing her to look at him. His face was serious. "Hey, no. You survive. You live, free and easy. Always. He should keep his problems with him."

"It's not that simple," she said. "I care about him. This connection isn't what we planned, but I think you have to be ready to suffer with another person if you care about them. And I want that closeness. He looks at me like I'm beautiful."

"But—"

She cut him off with a look. She hadn't transformed for Firian in the Unreal.

"None of that means that you have darkness," he said. "Everybody wants to be close to someone."

"You certainly do," she teased, trying to laugh around the lump in her throat.

He pursed his lips ironically as she lapsed into silence. With a theatrical bow of his head, he let go of her. "There you are. What more proof could you need?"

She wrinkled her forehead.

Jori squeezed her hand. "Everyone wants to be wanted."

"So what do I do?" Her voice had dwindled almost to a whisper.

Jori sat up again, away from her. "Trust me, darling, you don't want to take my advice. Just do what you think is right."

"Is it wrong if I keep going? Secretly? Oh!" She threw her hands in the air. "It's not even real. It's just in the Unreal anyway. The whole thing. I'm not even doing anything!"

Jori's eyes narrowed. "What aren't you doing?"

She blushed. "We're just... nothing!"

He held up fingers as he ticked items off. "You meet secretly in the Unreal. It's *romantic*, you said. You're eaten up with guilt. You said you have darkness in you. Are you sleeping with him?" Jori's expression didn't change, except for a slight crinkling around his eyes.

"No! No, not quite." She dropped her eyes.

"I'm glad you haven't given him the satisfaction." Jori stood and took her hands, guiding her to stand. "You should value yourself more highly, even in the Unreal. I hate him, but you have to judge for yourself. He doesn't deserve you. No!" He held up a hand as though she might protest. "No, he doesn't. The world may not care about a Keeper's brother, the black sheep, but you do. A lovely girl like that deserves someone better than a man who would trade you for more power without blinking." He cocked his head. "You know he would."

"I don't know," she said again. Jori couldn't know the way Firian looked at her. But Firian had looked at her like that *before* too...

"Yes, you do."

She put her hands on her hips, teasing. "Who made you so wise?"

He trailed his pointer finger in the air like a flying bird until it landed, briefly, pointed at her. "I know you'll do the right thing. I, on the other hand, will do the wrong thing and you can just live vicariously through me."

She smacked his arm. He leaned forward and laughed in answer.

"You're terrible," she said.

"Incorrigible." It had become his byword. He rolled his eyes in mock surrender.

Something in her chest loosened when he went back to his normal self. She could have some space to think, and he wouldn't shun her in the meantime.

"No telling," she said, feeling eight years old.

One hand on his heart, he repeated her words. "No telling."

29

FIRIAN

The door burst open, slamming on its hinges.

Firian jumped to his feet, a knife in his hand. Adrenaline pulsed through his body like a lightning bolt. Who else was after him?

He pulled his hand back just before it was too late.

"Bard!" he said, throwing the knife to the other side of the room. It clattered on the floor near his bedroom door. He couldn't get another word out. All he could do was bring his hands up to his face. Though his hands felt hot, his face was clammy.

Bard, who had cowered before, now stood up tall. "What happened, Fir? Something happened. Are you okay?"

The alarm in Bard's voice annoyed him. His chest rose and fell heavily as the shock of adrenaline wore off, the edges of his vision hazy from the moment of horror. Finally, he cursed. And again, more loudly.

"Firian?" His whole name. The Bard he knew normally would have left him alone. But here he stood, searching his face with his eyes brimming with concern. "What happened, mate?"

What *had* happened? Everything seemed like a dream. Even Kiria, just now. Why had she left? His skin had gone cold when she pushed him away. *Why did she push me away?* She knew he needed her. He felt the heat in her kiss. And then she left. Always, before, girls had given into desire or had stayed away from him altogether. What was this?

The chair scraped back as he slumped into it, his energy completely sapped. He looked up at Bard, who had approached the desk.

"You have to tell me."

"I don't have to do anything," Firian snapped, before realizing how juvenile that sounded. He ran a hand back through his hair. It was still damp. He rubbed two fingers together to get the moisture off. Sighing, he said, "It was Jovan."

Bard's face became a mask of concern, his forehead bunching down from his spiky black hair. He leaned forward and put a hand on the desk near the flag of Raewhith and the new yellow flag of Imlin, which he had requested from Makai when he went to demand allegiance in person.

"He attacked me in the washroom." Hopefully Belik was getting the body out of there now. Even so, Firian wouldn't go in there for a few days at least.

Bard gasped. "How did you...?"

"I took care of it."

"You killed him."

"I took care of it."

The momentary silence was so pronounced that Firian could hear other Tanyu far away down the hall.

"Was he the only one?"

Firian's heart beat faster. That was the question. "Just now, yes."

Bard pursed his lips, his gaze bright and piercing. Those black eyes... they could see right through him most of the time. It was as though Firian could never keep a secret. "Yeah, but you think there might be others."

Firian looked down. They were both silent for a while, thinking of Jovan, thinking of Master Jairon...

"What are you going to do?" Bard finally asked.

Fire burned in his brain again as he thought about it. *I'm going to stop it. I'm going to find anyone else before they get to me. I'm going to...* But he couldn't tell Bard any of that.

"I'm their leader," he said. "They all have to see me that way." Something about Bard made him confess the truth. At least, something close to the truth.

Bard eyed him warily. Did he know he was leaving something out? The scrutiny suddenly rankled. Bard had no right to judge him.

"What do you want me to do?" Firian shouted, standing.

Bard's hand popped up from the table, shrinking at Firian's sudden movement. "I don't know." His voice was more hard-edged than Firian was used to.

Firian felt sick. "Then let me get on with it!" Maybe he honestly wanted Bard's suggestion. With certainty, he knew he would hunt down every person that wanted him dead, but Bard's world was softer. These kinds of decisions didn't exist in that world. If Bard could make all threats just disappear, he would.

"I only wanted to make sure you were all right," Bard said.

Firian looked down at him. If Jovan really had managed to kill him, Bard would have cared. And Kiria, and Belik. Maybe some others. Many would have cared out of respect for the office. There weren't many when they buried Sais Jairon, but he had been a bad leader, and had died in bad circumstances.

He glanced at the knife on the floor. "I'm all right," he said softly. But he wasn't.

THE BODY WASN'T THERE ANYMORE. Firian didn't know what Belik had done with it, but an unusual number of crows circled overhead, so he had a guess.

Staying close to the stone walls of the Academy, he went through his exercises.

Balance, strength, precision, patience. He normally did this sequence inside, but he needed fresh air.

Slowly, he lifted himself into a handstand, facing the forest upside down. He closed his eyes, blocking out the light. *Just breathe. In and out.* Spreading his fingers against the hard-packed ground, he carefully lowered himself until he balanced on his forearms. Jagged pieces of dirt and rock dug into his arms. Through slitted eyes, he saw the birds wheeling above the trees, just in his line of sight. He bit the inside of his lip and closed his eyes again. Darkness could help him focus on the strength in his body. Keeping his core tight, he bent his knees. His back arched, following the movement. He brought his feet forward until they dangled over his head.

Still the crows cawed, calling to each other.

He inhaled through his nose. His shoulders began to ache from the position he was holding. *Good.*

"Firian."

His eyes shot open. Dropping his legs, he jumped to his feet. Belik stood in front of him. The Master had a limp. How had he not heard him coming?

Blood rushed from Firian's head. "Do you have the list?" he muttered.

"You don't need one."

He was in no mood for riddles or games. Usually, Belik wasn't either, and yet here he was without the list he promised.

"You need to solidify your power outside the Academy."

"Gore!" Firian glared, rubbing the back of his neck. He had enough to do to hold onto power over the Tanyu. As it was, trying to hold the Academy, Raewhith, and Imlin in his mind at once made him feel physically stretched and vulnerable.

"Hear me out." Belik's eyes shone with excitement. Maybe this idea was the reason he followed him outside. "You don't need to chase down every threat one by one. Don't be a fool. You need to threaten them all until there's no one to challenge you."

Now Firian was interested.

"You want more soldiers," Belik said.

After he waited for confirmation, Firian nodded.

"Good. We need more. The world knows where we are, so they'll test their strength against us. People don't need a better reason for bloodshed. So you'll make a show of it."

"Of what?"

"Show our strength. We have Tanyu stationed all over the world. We can't expose them all, but it could strike fear into any would-be enemies if you set a few of them loose." Belik leveled a gaze. The intensity of it was almost unnerving. But wasn't this exactly what Firian wanted when he'd taken control—awe of the Academy's power?

"What are you saying?"

"You know what I'm saying. If you show you're the strongest, then no one will rise against you. That's why you need to be involved. You can't just send people. You have to pick a place and subjugate it in full view."

"We don't need to subjugate people." He could just hear Bard's objections.

"Subjugate—maybe you don't like the word." A muscle twitched in Belik's cheek, an almost mocking gesture.

Firian's face flushed.

Belik held up a conciliatory hand, and then brought it up to resettle his glasses. "But Jovan—and you—showed that people will kill to be the next Tanyuin Head. I'm trying to protect you. You're the one who deserves to be in power, and if you don't let people know it, they'll see you as weak."

Firian hated that word, and Belik knew it. He cracked his knuckles and took a shaky breath. Would it be so bad to take over another town if that would protect him from being vulnerable? "What would I need to do?"

"We can wait until another person attacks you if you want." The Master tilted his head down as though he were reading Firian's hesitant thoughts. In the following silence, the bird calls and the gravel crunching beneath their shifting weight echoed loudly.

Frustrated, Firian cocked his jaw. "No. Just tell me."

"Archer's Point is close but far enough to feel immune from us, I'd guess. They're known for their fighting men. We take that."

Something about Belik's voice was almost too confident. Archer's Point wouldn't be as easy to take as some of the other smaller towns. It was its own city-state just outside the Western Kingdom's borders and their leader was known to be strong, even brutal to his enemies. Understanding hit Firian all at once. "You have someone inside."

"We do."

Firian frowned, wiping the grit from his hands and forearms. "So I order that person to kill the Lord Ruler and then I walk in?"

"Something like that. That's the simplest way. String him up as a message. Let everyone see that you commanded his death. Word will spread quickly."

Firian wasn't convinced it would be that easy. Belik must have seen the doubt on his face.

"The harder way would cost more lives," he persisted. "No one wants more death. War is an ugly thing." Above Belik's head, the crows continued to glide in wide circles.

"If I order the leader to be killed, they'll want to kill me immediately. It won't be that simple."

"Bring the Scroll."

Firian frowned. "You know about that?"

"Of course. When Tiev didn't have it, I knew you had to. The people there are very religious. Practically Amir, all of them. Bring the Scroll and have all the leaders swear on it. Threaten their people for good measure. Be specific about the kind of pain you could wreak on them. You won't actually have to do any of those things, if you're worried." A sardonic glint shone in his eyes. "They'll listen to you the first time if you do it right. They'd rather have you rule them from afar—barely a change from their lives now—than put up a fight. Just flex your strength, that's all, and you won't have trouble."

Firian stood silent. He could threaten if it meant safety, but the plan sounded so drastic. The cities he had conquered so far, even Imlin, hadn't put up a real fight at all. What was one more?

Walking into the city, a conqueror, with almost no shedding of blood, his black coat flowing behind him, as everyone bowed. The image soothed him, like a mountain at sunrise. He gazed at it in his mind for a moment.

"I can't answer now," he said, coming out of his reverie like a trance.

"I'll post more guards, if you'll stay with them," Belik added, grumbling, "but they all need to see you as a leader. You're young. Untested."

"*Untested?* I helped win the Torithian War. I have... my power."

"*You* are tested. Your people's loyalty is not."

Firian regarded him sullenly.

"Everyone needs to see that you command all the Tanyu," Belik continued, "no matter where they are. That your word will be obeyed."

That all sounded good. But to take over another city, to kill its leaders... If it was the only way, he would do it. But only if there were no other option. He'd investigate first, ask someone less accepting of violence. "I said I'll think about it."

30

KIRIA

A DESERT CAT paced back and forth in its cage, working its long, toothy jaw with the last of its meal. The tip of its snout was square and its back legs bent lower to the ground than the front legs. She'd forgotten those details when she showed Firian this place.

With the day full of rebuilding trust with the royal family, she hadn't had time to see Firian since their encounter the day before. Besides, she needed a moment to think about the attempt on his life, about their connection, about his desire for her. Any time she started to think he was safe to love, his intensity made her step back again, check her own feelings.

Kiria glanced at Haved walking beside her. The princess had smudged her eyes with dark charcoal and pinned back her hair in a complicated knot. She looked as dressed up as she had been yesterday at the party. Memories of her behavior filled Kiria with heavy apprehension. Haved had to trust her after tonight, or she and her father might rethink the marriage with Atty. Kiria couldn't bear it if she were the cause of breaking so many hopes.

Together they strode through the palace zoo, now populated with exotic plants as well as animals. This was the first time since Brithnem that the air didn't feel so dry. The whole place ran humid, which felt good on her cracking skin, but also meant a rank smell rising from the animal cages.

Besides the desert cat, which was Kiria's favorite, a massive gray-green lizard lounged on a rock, each claw as long as her pointer finger. Two blue and orange birds with sweeping tails three times the length of their bodies sat side by side on a branch. A furry creature with small, rounded ears and paws shaped almost like hands paced in another cage. She wasn't sure what to call it. The closest association she had were pictures she'd seen of bears.

"Do they ever get to go outside?" Kiria asked.

"Sometimes," Haved replied. "Normally they stay in here."

Kiria tried not to read too much into Haved's clipped reply. A respectful distance away walked four guards—two from Brithnem and two from Charäkhnem. It seemed that there were always more people to overhear her conversations. "It would be nice if they could have more freedom," she continued.

Haved nodded solemnly, twitching the train of her dress with one hand so that it didn't drag. It seemed as if she were thinking of something else. Her eyes were far away, not angry or cold, but wistful.

"Are you all right?" Kiria asked.

Haved turned her serious gaze to her. "Are you?"

Kiria wasn't exactly all right, but she was in her right mind, if that's what Haved wanted to know. "Yes, I'm perfectly all right."

The desert cat's claws scraped along the floor, a dry, rasping sound. The tiny bear creature gave an answering yowl.

Haved tipped her chin with uncertainty but didn't contradict her. "Let's go outside."

The guards followed them, blue and red, out of the zoo area, through a ribbed, vaulted doorway and into the night. A large garden with flowers smelled strong and green, welcoming summer. It was obvious that they were young flowers by the wetness of them. The walled garden held trees as well. Colorful paths cut through the foliage.

The air was cleaner out here. Dust flowed on the warm breeze, perfumed with exotic flowers.

Haved's head tipped back. She didn't say anything, but a private smile grew on her face as she gazed up at the stars. With a confidential look, she invited Kiria to see them as well.

It was darker here than in Brithnem, so the stars shone more brightly. On her tour that consisted largely of the wilderness, Kiria had noticed the stars, but only in a passing way.

"That one is Sito." Haved pointed upward. "The Cat."

Kiria tried to follow the line of Haved's finger, but there were so many tiny stars that she soon despaired of figuring out which constellation she meant. Still, this shift from doubting her to cautiously drawing Kiria into her confidence seemed like a positive step.

"She's rising." Haved said the words reverently.

So she really had meant what she said at the party. Hopefully she would have the chance to talk to many Navigators one day. Brithnem was a good place for that. Usually, there was one at the docks, dark skinned and moon eyed. Their light eyes had frightened Kiria as a child, so she stayed away from them. They didn't scare her anymore, but she had kept the unconscious habit of avoiding them. Perhaps that was unfair to them, she realized.

"Is that your favorite constellation?" Kiria asked.

"Favorite?" Haved seemed confused by the question. A line formed between her eyebrows as she turned her attention back to Kiria. "No, I do not think so."

A thought struck Kiria. "Do you know if the constellations will be the same so far west in Brithnem?"

Haved nodded knowingly. "Most of them will be the same. And I will get to see

Kandormet, the great hero, I think." She looked pensive, as if thinking about the constellations she'd have to leave when she left her kingdom.

Watching Haved with the stars was like going to the upper room in the Amiran Academy. Golden and dark blue. Reverent.

Kiria hummed. She couldn't think of another response for a while, and Haved didn't seem to need any. Finally, she said, "Atty will love to learn about the stars with you."

Haved turned to her, her expression pleased but skeptical in the darkness. "Will he, though?" She said it more like a statement than a question.

"Absolutely." After a pause, Kiria added, "He'll love you."

And he would. Kiria could picture it without even trying. Though not a great sportsman, Atty liked to be outside, and to be with a pretty woman, and to feel strong. He would love watching the sky with her. He would love her.

A complicated emotion filled Kiria's stomach. It wasn't jealousy for Atty's affection—she'd never wanted that, and besides, he was her cousin, very far removed. No, it was something else. Atty would take care of Haved as well as he knew how. He was probably planning ways to please her back at the palace. And he'd be loyal, adoring, all their life long.

Haved took in her statement stoically at first, her head held regally, but then one corner of her mouth flinched with happiness. "You do not seem crazy," she said.

Kiria laughed with relief, and she realized how much she had wanted to earn Haved's trust. Atty's future should never be compromised because of her actions.

Haved laughed too, but quietly. She was an odd person—privileged and naïve, yet wise and queenly all the same.

"I'm glad you think so," Kiria said.

Taking a large purple bloom between her fingers, Haved bent to smell it. "I am too."

31

FIRIAN

It was tempting just to open the door without knocking. The whole town of Tánuil was his. But he scuffed the dirt with the toe of his boot a few times and knocked. At first, no one answered. Rian had told him Bard was here. Firian should have known better than to trust him. He was going with Maya now, and had always had a strained relationship with the truth.

The door opened. Finally. A stranger looked out. Everything about the man was thin—his body, his brown clothes, the hair on his face. Even his lips and fingers were thin. The wavy and distorted skin around one of his ears suggested that he had once been badly burned.

His throat bobbed when he saw Firian, happiness and fear alternating on his face. The end result was confusion.

"Is Bard here?" Firian asked. Something about the man's eyes and forehead seemed familiar, as though he'd seen him before.

"Hey!" Bard's voice called from inside. The thin man opened the door a little wider and Bard's face appeared in the opening. He gave a wide grin. "What are you doing here? Is everything okay?"

"What are *you* doing here?" His eyes flickered over the stranger.

"Oh, have you not met? This is Wells. No, you've seen him. Yeah, he's a... uh..."

A *Sentry.* "Ah." Heat flushed Firian's face. Firian wasn't searching for them anymore, but he had very recently hunted them down to get back in Sias Jairon's good graces. Bard's hesitation suggested that he'd known where this one was, but didn't tell Firian when it could have helped him to know.

He batted down the small stab of betrayal he felt. Bard had broken a rule. It almost made Firian proud that his friend was so steadfast, even to strangers who deserved none of his loyalty. Though somewhat annoyed, Firian was right to come.

Bard beckoned Firian inside as he turned away. "I just made tea for us."

The thin man scurried ahead. Firian leaned toward Bard. "Isn't this his house?"

"I was showing him how," Bard whispered back.

Who didn't know how to make tea? Firian had never done it and yet he knew. The years in captivity must have made Wells little more than a shell.

Together they walked to the small stone fireplace with a kettle hanging over it.

Bard grabbed a thin stick of firewood from the stack nearby and handed it to Wells. "Just use that and take the kettle off."

The man betrayed no embarrassment at being so ignorant. Despite the fact that he was older than either Firian or Bard, his movements showed subservience, but he went ahead boldly with the kettle.

"Yeah, like that." Bard watched Wells closely before continuing. "This is... uh, this is my friend." A fractional pause as he looked at Firian, eyes drifting to his forehead, now crownless. "This is Firian. He's... he's the Head."

Wells's neck bowed lower at the mention, like a dog fearful of being struck. His shirt hung down, waving as though it were empty.

"It's all right," Bard repeated reassuringly, gesturing to the tea. But he didn't mean the tea. He turned his attention back to Firian. "So, Fir, you didn't say. Why are you here?"

"I just wondered where you were."

Bard gave him one of those scrutinizing looks. It would be fine today if Bard could see into his inner thoughts. How could he ask for advice without asking for advice?

"Have you known each other very long?" Firian asked.

Another grin. "Yeah, ever since we, uh... freed them, you know." Bard gently patted Wells's shoulder as he gingerly moved the stick and placed the kettle on a small table. The *sachion* tree design on the kettle showed it to be Endrian work. The kettle wobbled as though Wells didn't have enough strength to hold it steady.

"You've been busy," Bard said, getting cups out of a knapsack. "And Wells is really funny, once you get to know him."

Firian glanced at the man, who had rarely raised his eyes above the floor. He doubted he was funny.

Bard dug deeper in his bag as though he had forgotten something. "I only brought two cups," he admitted.

Firian waved his hand. "That's fine. It doesn't matter."

Bard set the cups on the table, one for him and one for his new Sentry friend. "In Enderin we drink the leaves, but some people like their tea smooth," he explained, picking up the kettle. "You can just put cheesecloth in front of the spout if you don't like leaves." He poured Wells's first and then his own. "There you go!" he said cheerfully. "I'm going to talk to Firian for a minute."

They silently went to the doorway of the little house, leaving Wells to drink his tea.

"Okay, something's going on," Bard said in a stern undertone.

"Something's always going on." When Bard wouldn't be deflected, Firian continued. "I need to figure out what to do about this problem. I think I can take out all threats at once."

Bard opened his mouth.

"Without killing them all," Firian added.

Bard shut his mouth again and took a sip from his cup. "What is it?" he asked, eyes bright now with interest.

"I need to prove our strength, my strength, all at once."

The lines deepened on Bard's forehead. "What are you going to do? You know we could just put a Sentry on you when you sleep. Protect you, you know?"

Firian's skin crawled at the thought. And no. That wouldn't help. "No. That's stupid," he said. "I need something bigger. I wasn't asleep last time."

Bard dropped his eyes. "That's true, but it's not a bad idea."

Firian ignored him. Wasn't Bard supposed to be good at strategy? His attempt at a solution was halfhearted at best. After a silence Bard didn't fill, Firian went on. "Yeah, so I thought maybe taking over Archer's Point."

Bard barked a humorless laugh.

"We have someone inside," Firian insisted. "We could control it completely within a few days."

Disbelief clouded Bard's eyes. "How?"

"It would be mostly in name, and good for them."

"How would you take over?"

"Just Thraddock." The Lord Ruler.

"Firian!"

"It's just one person," Firian insisted, beginning to wonder why he had come. If Bard didn't like it, why didn't he suggest something else, something that didn't pretend everything would be all right? "The Academy can't be threatened or unstable. We have to show that we're united, that I know what I'm doing."

In the next pause, Bard's look sent shivers down his spine. "Do you?" he asked quietly.

"What would you do, then?" he snapped. "You weren't there when Jovan tried to strangle me. When I had to kill him or drown. And I almost..." *I almost drowned. I almost died.*

Bard nodded. "I just don't want..." He sighed, as though unsure how to continue. "Fir, are you sure you don't just want Archer's Point, you know? What would happen if you left them alone?"

"I need to choose someone strong."

"You could get hurt. They could get hurt."

Firian scoffed. "They need to see me as a strong leader. If the Tanyu follow me in this, the Academy can keep doing all the good it's doing." His words felt too much like a plea for Bard to understand.

But he didn't understand. He would never endorse Firian's decision to kill the leader of Archer's Point to unite the Tanyu and scare off potential threats.

Why had he come here at all? He'd known what Bard would say.

After another minute that Bard didn't fill with a workable suggestion, he stiffened, and his hot temper hardened into bitterness. "Isn't your friend waiting for you?"

Except for Belik, all those close to him were slipping farther away. Didn't they care that he had almost been assassinated? If not for his new-found ability, he would have been. And Kiria and Bard didn't seem to care at all.

"Yeah." Another concerned question formed on Bard's lips, but he let it die away. Then he rallied. "You can't do this, Fir."

Firian's heart thumped hard in his chest. One corner of his mouth rose in a snarl. "I have to, so I will," he said distinctly.

"There has to be another way to get rid of any threat to you—"

"We're great warriors. People like Jovan are not going to back down because I ask them nicely."

"That's not what I—"

"Everyone has to know what'll happen if they *dare* to threaten me." The power of the words robed him like a cloak of darkness. He felt like a king, so he knew he'd made the right decision.

Bard didn't shrink away, but he did fall quiet. Something hardened in his dark eyes. Disappointment. "I'm going to make sure Wells is okay." And he closed the door, shutting Firian out of the stone house.

Distant birds cawed and a pinecone thudded softly to the ground.

Firian gripped his hands into fists. Despite what Bard thought, he had to do something to protect himself. Great power didn't stay there by inertia, but by continual effort. A small breeze of exhaustion blew through him and passed. He had always been relentless. Becoming the Head wasn't a stopping point, but a stepping stone. The momentum had to continue.

The leader of Archer's Point had to be sacrificed.

Bard wouldn't like it, Kiria probably wouldn't like it, but hopefully they both would understand later, when the Academy was united and he still lived to tell them about it.

THROUGH THE HAZE, Firian watched his nephew Sabir play in the grass. He picked up pine cones and leaves in his chubby fists and brought them to Brett, who sat cross-legged on the ground. When he brought her a tiny purple flower, she smiled, cooing over the gift as though it were worth piles of tribute.

Sometimes Sabir toddled close to danger as he gathered treasures for his mother. A flash of wolves' eyes in the woods, or a steep embankment. A mother's worry.

His sister didn't notice Firian there. She didn't have the Talent, after all.

Normally, Tanyu didn't invade dreams without a reason, usually instilling fear into an enemy, or killing him. They weren't supposed to watch. It was like seeing a person naked and not turning away. But tonight, he had to remind himself of what had gone right during his reign. His conversation with Bard a few days before left a taste like ashes in his mouth. His friend didn't support his decision to take over Archer's Point, but he also didn't offer a different road to victory and safety.

Brett swept Sabir up in a hug, the image surprisingly touching. Did his mother ever dream like this about him? Maybe not. With Brett, he sensed no new fears.

Her dreams were good. Gaius, her husband, back from the Torithian War, slept peacefully by her side.

"Firian."

The voice came from elsewhere in the Unreal.

"Why are you up so late?" he asked Kiria, who stood in the palace hallway where they had had their first kiss. Was she here to apologize for pushing him away when he needed her most?

"I couldn't sleep," she said, meeting his eyes. "I know I should be able to, since we're riding all day, but I can't stop thinking."

"Tell me."

Something softened in her look, but they didn't move closer. This dance was a precarious one. One false step and he knew she'd back away.

"People keep telling me you're dangerous. I even heard a rumor the other day..." Her voice trailed into a laugh edged with nerves.

"I am dangerous," he said, "but not to you." He gave a lopsided smile, his stomach suddenly in knots. He should tell her his plan, see if she approved. But he knew – he knew – what she would say. Taking over Archer's Point was worth solidifying his power, even if Kiria didn't see it.

"You can't go around saying things like 'I'm dangerous,'" she laughed.

"Aren't I?"

"That's what they say." She sighed, tugging at the ends of her long sleeves. Even now, in the middle of the night, she dressed in finery, a backless blue gown, a flag of the Kingdom. A reminder that her choices were not always her own. "Did you mean it before?"

"Mean what?"

"You said... you wanted me to change for you. I won't do that until I'm ready."

He searched her heart-shaped face, her light brown eyes, so earnest as they looked back in his. The knots inside him loosened a fraction. She wasn't here to apologize, but she did say *until I'm ready*. Despite his dangerous reputation, she wanted to stay. That would do for now.

"Okay."

"That's all right with you?" Another question lurked behind that one, the true question. Almost a dare.

"Yes." He waved her forward and she came, head held high as though protecting her dignity. It was true that he wanted her Beauty, but this was the face that had captured him, the one he saw most when he thought about her. They were both Kiria.

He settled his hands on her shoulders. "It's definitely all right." Slowly, he peeled down her left sleeve to reveal the raised scar. Kiria held very still but didn't pull away as he rubbed his thumb over the wound and kissed it.

They stood in silence for a moment after that, something clicking into place between them. She pulled her sleeve back up and trailed her fingers lightly down his arm. He caught her hand when it reached his.

"You are dangerous," she said, little more than a teasing whisper. But she seemed to have found the answer she was looking for and wasn't afraid.

"Mm hm."
That was truer than she knew.

32

FIRIAN

FIRIAN HELD the bound Scroll tightly in one hand as he strode to Archer's Point. The front page stuck out a little beyond the others, propped up by the wax holding the note from his sister. He would live up to its words. He would protect her in Raewhith from those raiders in Archer's Point, he would solidify his legacy, and he would protect himself.

And this is how to do it.

He forced himself to remember the bathtub. Brett would understand why he had to do this.

Belik's suggestion that Firian conquer this town was a good one. Though he was harsh, he had always kept Firian's best interest in mind. Even after he kicked him out of the Academy, Belik had followed to make sure he didn't die in the Unreal. Few Tanyu would do that.

He flexed his fingers slowly, one by one, against the book of the Scroll. One, two, three, four, five. One for each black-clad Tanyuin warrior that flanked him on either side. Ten in all.

Now that he was resolved, he stepped with greater purpose. His black coat floated behind him. Why had he hesitated? This power was heady and pleasurable. Threats were far away. Rebels would be afraid to face his greatness after this.

He felt his heartbeat across his chest and in his throat. Even Kiria was one of three leaders. He was the only Tanyuin Head.

By the time the walls of the town appeared, a thin smirk had crept over his face. He liked this feeling too much. He'd said something to Bard about doing good after this, but right now, all he wanted was this power. Apprehension at his own excitement thrummed beneath his skin. Later, he could give into his better tendencies. At this moment, he had to make Archer's Point bow.

He stuffed away his smile as they marched closer to the main gate. High above, guards shuffled hurriedly along the wall. A flag flapped above the gate—bright green with the black figure of an archer in the center. Only two stood by the entrance to the city, one on either side of the gate. They both wore brown leather armor and a metal chest plate. No helmet. A sword and small round shield for each. This was a poor people's armor, but it would do if circumstances demanded it. Firian wore none at all, so maybe, he thought, he shouldn't judge their choices.

He and his ten followers strode to the main wooden gate. Coming from a slightly different direction, a man pulling a cart of hay stopped awkwardly before the gate as well, paralyzed at the sight of Firian's entourage.

"Halt!" cried the guard on the left, bracing one foot back. His shoulders and face were wider than the other soldier. "You must declare yourself and your business before we allow you inside."

All the Tanyu flanking Firian remained perfectly still.

"I am Firian Kess," he said. "The Tanyuin Head."

The guard's mouth formed a small, unconscious O.

"Why have you come?" It was the guard on the right. His receding hairline and scarred mouth suggested a battle-ridden life. Still, he watched Firian's entourage warily.

Firian squeezed the book a little harder. He flicked a quick glance at the top of the hand that held it, covered with white scars. Scars he had earned fighting in both the Unreal and the Real. He raised his head. "I must speak to the Lord Ruler immediately."

"On what matter?"

"Someone has a knife to his throat." he said calmly.

Both guards gripped their sword hilts now. Broad Shoulders collected himself. "How do you know this?"

"I ordered it. So bring me to him."

With a metallic hiss, the guards drew their swords. They bent their knees, grim and ready to fight.

"You dare to threaten the Lord Ruler?"

Firian didn't move. He was too aware that one of his hands was occupied with a large book. The tendons inside his wrist pressed against the cover. He could use it to fight, but he didn't want to, which made that hand all but useless if they decided to move against him.

More soldiers joined the two at the gate, running down from their positions along the top of the wall.

Firian saw the guards almost passively. He could kill them just by thinking it. Did they know? The fact made swords less frightening. But his skin still felt like thin protection.

He didn't deny their accusation. Instead, he held up his free hand. "We don't want to kill you," he said slowly, truthfully. His hand was starting to sweat around the book. "I have many people loyal to me. In many different places. Hill House, for example."

Slight movements—some forward on the balls of their feet, some slackening of jaws, some rotating of weapons—told him that Belik had been right about the man embedded in Hill House. It looked like they were starting to believe him.

Hill House was the place where the Lord Ruler of Archer's Point sat in state. A

Tanyu named Jaddeo had been installed there years ago. Belik said he started as a minor retainer, but had later taken a kitchen job as a way to be closer to Lord Ruler Thraddock.

Broad Shoulders advanced. Firian held his ground. "I've decided to take this city. So I will take it." Every word he said felt as solid and true as the words in the Scroll. He sensed the power of the ten Tanyu behind him. "Let us in and we'll spare you all. Harm me and the Lord Ruler dies." He locked eyes with a stony-looking guard in the middle of the others. If he had to kill anyone, Firian chose him. His hardened expression and central placement would ensure the greatest impact. "I extend the honor of being part of the Academy's territory. I don't want slaughter."

He reached down into the Unreal, like a man fishing in his back pocket for a weapon. One step further and he could level anyone here. He caressed the Second Level in his mind, holding it loosely, making it accessible. Being surrounded by this many clear threats was almost a relief after fearing so many phantom ones. These people he could manage. These people he could kill before they killed him.

"Show me to your leader," he said, extending his arms as though they were harmless. *Bind me. See if that works for you.*

The guards couldn't risk killing Firian and putting their Lord Ruler at risk, but they couldn't let him go after such threats either. Binding him would probably seem like the safest choice.

He shook his hands a little, one still clutching the bound copy of the Sacred Scroll. A few of the guards noticed with curiosity.

Three men approached cautiously, swords unsheathed. Firian didn't flinch as they gripped both of his arms hard enough to bruise, wrenched the book from his grip, and tied his wrists behind him.

He held his head high as they paraded him through the gates into the city. The rest of his Tanyu followed behind, also bound. Despite appearances, Firian was still the one in charge.

The smell of glue or tar wafted through the streets, alternating with soap. Most of the buildings they passed were made of slatted boards fitted together without seams. Some were painted with plants or creatures or designs. Clothing hung thick from lines strung between buildings, even the larger ones that cropped up every few hundred steps that Firian guessed were communal dining halls. The men and women coming and going seemed defined by their level of hunger, hurrying in, sauntering out.

People came out of their houses and shops to watch the little procession go by. Eleven Tanyu had probably never come here all at once. And never the Tanyuin Head.

A child appeared from behind curtains of hanging clothes. She had a mop of white hair and gripped the nearby fabric oddly. Only three fingers on that hand.

Again, Belik's intelligence was correct. The people of Archer's Point didn't look the same—different body types, skin colors, tattoos. Khelê.

Hill House lived up to its name, springing up on a little hill at the end of a maze of streets. It wasn't as grand as Firian expected, except for the red and green painted patterns on the walls, and the large trees growing around the bottom of the hill in a ring. Layers of history overlapped each other in a chaotic mix. From the trees hung mementos and flags. Even the trunks had been branded with the now distorted faces of past Lord Rulers.

A back-of-the-throat smell like boiling cabbage with tangy notes of sharp peppers floated by. Maybe Jaddeo had been cooking. The cabbage odor took him back home to Raewhith for a moment. How was Brett doing now? It had been over a month since he'd seen her.

"Up the stairs!" said a short guard behind Firian.

Wordlessly, Firian climbed the long, well-cut stone steps through the ring of trees, up the slope to Hill House. Smaller mounds dotted the hillside, adorned with elaborate displays of twigs, rocks, paints, and flowers. Burial sites.

An armored woman at the door stood waiting for them. She threw her shoulders back and stood with the rigidity of someone who had been bent over a moment before. Stiffly, she opened the door for Firian and his conductors. She scowled at Firian's entourage of Tanyuin warriors and whispered something to the guards as they passed. Whatever she said made Firian's guard twist the ropes holding his wrists until his bones popped.

Incense covered and magnified the dusty smell inside. The interior looked like a mansion, brighter and cleaner than Firian thought it would be—entrance with room for cloaks, kitchen to the left, enormous main room with open fire pit in the center. The guards led him toward the fire.

As they muscled him toward the open flame, he felt placid, utterly composed. They wouldn't burn him. Dull metallic surfaces reflected the fire and other small light sources strategically placed around the room. The result was a blazing space, screaming yellow and heavy with heat.

Firian blinked away moisture forming in his eyes from the warmth. When he could see more clearly, he stiffened. Six—no, seven—guards lay dead around Jaddeo, who held the Lord Ruler in place with one enormous arm over his neck.

They resisted. They deserved it.

Firian had known that this would probably have to happen, but any justification still sounded hollow. The guards would have ganged up on Jaddeo, killed him, and the whole plan would have been ruined. He ran his eyes over the slumped bodies and fought back a shudder.

Jaddeo and the Lord Ruler stood on the platform beside a modest throne, barely large enough to look significant. It was a child's version of the thrones at Brithnem. Hanging behind it was another green flag like the one at the gate.

A thin line of red trickled down Jaddeo's forearm from a wound in the Lord Ruler's neck. Blood leaked onto Thraddock's leather clothes—not the robes of a king, but the clothes of a working man or a warrior. Lord Ruler Thraddock was a large man, rough and tan, with a trimmed beard and blazing eyes, the kind that would make anyone quail. Firian fought not to swallow, to show any apprehension in his manner. But the Lord Ruler's heavy-browed stare bored into him. The moment passed, and Firian's calm returned. This fearsome man was entirely under his power.

Despite the bodies, power made Firian feel peaceful again. Was something wrong with him?

With Firian and the Lord Ruler face to face, the heat in the room seemed to double. A long line of sweat trickled down the scars on Firian's back. The people of Archer's Point were wound like a spring, but the Tanyu stood emotionless. Broad Shoulders kicked the back of Firian's knees and forced his head down. His palm, gripping Firian's hair, had a slight tremor. Though the guard was nervous, this was the first time he'd had anything like the upper hand. The situation suddenly reminded Firian of his helplessness when he'd been grabbed, choked, drowned… Blood rushed to his face until it felt puffy in the heat.

He had to do it now.

"Release Lord Thraddock or we will kill Master Kess," demanded a voice above him.

Firian lifted his head. The back of his neck touched something. A blade. The smallest misstep meant death. His mouth felt sticky as he locked eyes with Jaddeo, who stared at him, awaiting a signal. Firian nodded.

Jaddeo's eyes darted to others around the room. As the guard forced Firian's head back down, he heard a swift, struggling gasp and then a heavy thump like a body slumping to the ground.

Feet scuffled. Surprised noises. A clang. A yell.

A nudge.

Firian stood to see all ten other Tanyu on their feet, the guards on the ground. The guard with the scar and receding hairline stood above Broad Shoulders. Jaddeo stepped gracefully over bodies on his way back to the unconscious form of the Lord Ruler.

A knife slid between Firian's wrists, slicing off the bonds. As Firian rubbed life back into his hands, he ran his eyes over each new slumped figure, looking for signs of life. He had ordered the Tanyu not to kill unless it was absolutely necessary. Besides the initial dead guards, all the forms, including Lord Thraddock, seemed to be breathing. A small, terrible, burning part of him wanted to kill them all because he could. But then he'd see their faces, one after the other, in his nightmares.

They didn't deserve to die. But the sacrifice was small in the face of all he could accomplish with the Academy united in their fear of rebellion. Violence was short so peace could be lasting.

The scarred guard offered him back the Sacred Scroll. Firian wiped his hands on his coat and took it. The incense put the scene and his mind in a dreamy haze.

"Get the people," he said. "Anyone left with authority. Bring them here." He tapped his fingers against the cover of the book. "I'll meet them outside." The Tanyu already knew what to do, but it made him feel better to say it. "They'll swear on the Scroll not to oppose me, or the Lord Ruler dies."

33

KIRIA

"I have it the way I want it," Jori said, stepping backward.

Kiria's mother stopped trying to fix the collar of his leather jacket. She smiled placidly and shot a glance at Kiria, who stood just behind her.

Kiria smiled back. "There are scuffs," she said, picking up where her mother had left off. She vaguely indicated her own neckline. "You don't want to look scruffy today."

Jori raised a chin. "How else will they know who I am?" A laugh almost broke through his twitching lips, but Kiria could tell he was nervous. No, not nervous. Antsy. Tightly wound.

Atty was getting married today.

"By your handsome face," her mother replied.

Jori smiled as if he'd just won an argument.

It was good to see her mother looking so... alive. Since General Rhet's death, she had faded and faded until Kiria almost felt that she couldn't talk to her anymore. That she was an orphan. But she wasn't. Her mother was still here, even though Kiria was now the Keeper. They both were happy with the unorthodox arrangement, even if some people in the Kingdom had the wrong idea about it.

Today, her mother wore a long, deep purple dress with a gold belt and gold embroidery. It made a delicate V at her neckline, revealing her collarbone. That outdoor beauty her mother had shone out clearly in her twisted braids. The flyaways didn't look like mistakes but evidence of adventure and life.

When she'd offered to accompany Kiria to see Jori, she hadn't known why her mother wanted to come. Though her mother never said it, it was clear now that she wanted Jori not to feel alone, to feel that he had family. Because he had. Despite all his flippancy, he was surrounded by people who loved him and didn't judge him harshly for his flirtation and bad habits and light manners.

Atty was the only person left in his immediate family, though, and his affections would be pulled toward Haved. Inevitably, Jori would feel a little bereft. He hadn't sunk into one of his moods yet, but the Ariocs knew it was coming.

"Are we all ready?" her mother asked, just as she had when Kiria was a child.

Kiria checked herself. Beauty intact, silver and blue dress flowing like water, unsnagged on shoes or jewelry, silver belt, silver earrings, silver crown.

Ready.

Jori offered her his arm as they walked out of his room. The walk to the Main seemed longer than usual this time. Extra guards had been posted at the doors, some of them Charäkhni.

Kiria and Jori led the way, her mother walking imperially behind them, and behind her, more guards.

It was odd that at a time of peace there should be more guards in the palace than she could ever remember seeing.

She separated from Jori as they approached the carved doors of the Main. Heralds announced their names as they entered one by one.

It was warmer inside the cavernous Main, a byproduct of so many bodies and candles and torches. It smelled like lamp oil and lilies. The late afternoon sun had burned away, so the large space was left in that hot time between the light fading and the cool of night coming in.

As always, voices rose and fell at her entrance. Some of the guests had never seen her in person. Her Beauty was shocking, moving—even to her, even after all this time. It had taken danger and escape and a trip over the mountains to grow into her body. For fleeting moments, she sometimes still felt like a fraud. But it had not gone back to the pervasive feeling it had been a year ago.

Her long dress whisked across the mosaic on the floor as she processed toward the chairs at the foot of the platform. Where the three thrones normally resided, the three Amiran advisors stood: Parohim, Chetana, and Reynard. To either side of them, two young Amir in training, probably nine or ten years old, held poles. Across the poles was draped a gauzy white and blue fabric embroidered with blue laird flowers.

The symbol of peace.

The symbol of Brithnem.

She'd want to get married with the sun still up, so it could come through the colored panes of glass in the windows.

Get married. She'd always considered getting married inevitable, but now the idea hit her like a weight.

Could she marry Firian? For the Kingdom, he was a risky choice, still volatile. *Then what am I doing?*

Music began, sudden and loud. The first few notes were unfamiliar, even a little clunky. A wry smile tugged at her mouth. Atty must have written the first few bars. *You hopeless romantic.* The song soon turned into a melody that everyone had heard at other celebratory events. Jori knocked into her lightly as he swayed to the tune.

From behind the same closed doors that had opened to admit her on her eighteenth birthday when she demonstrated her Beauty, and that she and Atty had gone through during their coronations, came Atael and Haved. The double doors flung wide open, glad to reveal their secret.

Atty wore an all-white robe with some kind of fur mantle on the arm not wrapped around Haved's waist. Someone had pressed his curly hair down so that it shone like his bronze crown. His smile shone most brightly of all.

She knew he would like Haved.

The Charäkhni princess came out all in red, her country's color, with yellow-gold shoes. A large red gemstone gleamed on her bosom. As though Atty needed another reason to look there. Haved's dark eyes, though wise and sober, gleamed with happiness too. The edges crinkled up when she looked at him.

They approached the dais where the three Amir waited. When they had topped the steps, Atty and his bride, who looked like she had Beauty herself, knelt under the fabric. Parohim sang the words etched along the walls near the ceiling. Only during joyous occasions would Amir sing the words of the Scroll rather than saying or chanting them.

"...Be wise, therefore, and follow no other words but those of God. If you do not chase after other gods and invent them for yourself, He shall remain present among His people. Then you shall all be as the Khelê, seeing God's goodness in the ways that He chooses you for Himself.

Forever shall you worship God. In whatever you do, worship Him."

Charäkhnem had never believed in the same God that the Western Kingdom did, but those last sentences before the repeated line had some inclusiveness to them. Neither Haved nor the guards seemed bothered by the verses, anyway. Kiria was glad. Those lines had molded her childhood, subconsciously guided her decisions, her whole life. The Amir were here to make sure no one forgot them.

Atty shifted his shoe just a little. He looked confident with Haved beside him, but that shoe shift reminded her it was just Atty all along. Her friend Atty was marrying a princess.

After the recitation was complete, the couple stood. All five people under the draped fabric took hands in a circle, and then the Amir on the ends brought Atty's and Haved's hands together. Complete support, complete family, a complete couple.

The vows to each other were similar to the vows Kiria had made to the Western Kingdom. They were formal, with much talk of loyalty and children and death.

As the Amir took turns speaking, Kiria watched Atty's face. Wonder radiated from him as he stared at Haved, barely reacting to what they said. He looked so happy he could cry. He'd just met this girl, and yet he wanted desperately to bind himself to her, to create a family with her. He held her hands firmly but gently in his tattooed ones. Atty was many things, but disloyal was not one of them. He was simpler than Kiria or Jori, with their complicated temptations. All that simple love and admiration glowed on his face and reflected on Haved's. Naturally more reserved, she appeared perfectly contented. She was fairly tall, so the couple was almost the same height. She had to tip her chin up just a little to look into his eyes.

Kiria breathed shallowly as she watched them, gut twisting a little. Atty deserved to have something good in his life, *someone* good. Though the oldest son, born heir to the throne, Jori had always gotten more attention. Atty tried harder to be good, though, a struggle Kiria knew intimately.

After waving of hands, more reading from the Sacred Scroll, and ceremonial washing, the formal portion of the wedding was finished. Applause erupted from the crowded room. Beside her, Jori clapped without irony. Joy prompted a fresh wave of noise.

The party began immediately. Servants brought out wine. Tables laden with meat and fruit were uncovered. Plates of fish and delicate bits of candied lemon peel seemed to materialize in every corner of the room.

"...yes, I think so!" Cúron's voice boomed from the far side of the platform. With a glass in one hand and lemon peel in the other, Kiria went to join him. He was talking to a woman whose name Kiria didn't know. She had seen her in the Main before. Maybe an Amir.

The woman ran one long-fingered hand against the other in a movement that looked like a ritual or part of a dance. "But the number of Khelê in Charäkhnem is quite small," she replied.

"This marriage will open up roads." He said it with such confidence that Kiria pictured roads currently being built. "Keeper Atael is ecstatic. Charäkhnem is ecstatic. The Amir have never had such easy access to new documents and research."

Kiria had not known Cúron to sound so excited about "documents and research," but when he used his expansive, kingly voice, he could sound interested in anything.

"Ah, Lady Kiria!" He looped an arm around the air as though he were drawing her forward. "Don't you think this alliance will be wonderful for the Amir?"

"Of course it will." It was hard to think of a group that would not benefit from it. And it was all Atty's idea. A swell of pride grew inside her.

Daelon was on the other side of the room. Even he smiled broadly as he spoke with some of the younger Amir. He would certainly appreciate any additional documents that could aid him in interpreting the Scroll. It seemed like he was always reading, always learning.

When she focused again on the conversation, Cúron was saying something about extra defense. "...in case of another conflict. The Charäkhni are excellent soldiers." He scanned the room approvingly.

"With the Tanyu and Charäkhni, we're almost untouchable," Kiria agreed.

At the mention of the Tanyu, a breath of cold air passed over the little group, or maybe it was just a chilling of tempers. *What did I say?* She drew her brows together, surprised that a casual mention of their alliance could cause such an immediate reaction.

"Yes," Cúron continued, the moment passed. "We're in a very strong strategic position."

"No one is ever impervious to attack, My Keepers," the woman said diplomatically.

"No no no," Cúron said quickly. "But let us feel a little optimism." He smiled broadly.

Kiria took a sip of her drink. It was better than the stuff Jori usually had in his cabinets. The wine had been prepared decades in advance for this occasion.

Excusing herself, she turned away. Politics were important from far away, but close up, she had a friend to see.

He was easy to find. Glowing like a candle flame in bright white, standing beside his bride, Atty talked and laughed at the center of the room. He held Haved's hand as though they'd known each other for years.

Kiria rushed up to him. She paused a moment, and then gave him a hug. The wine in her glass sloshed a little as she cast her arms around him. A drip might have gotten on his white fur mantle, but it didn't matter. It also didn't matter that it wasn't proper for Keepers to hug. The blissful tilt of Atty's mouth and the creases around his eyes made the hug unavoidable. She had only seen that look a couple of times in all their years together. Tonight, it was the purest joy she'd ever seen in him. She felt she might burst, she was so proud.

"Haved," she said, and gave her a quick hug too.

"Kiria, I..." But Atty was never good with words. His whole being was speaking for him. He reached out and squeezed her arm.

She just nodded. The joy was so intense that it felt almost like pain. "Congratulations." The word felt too small to house all the meaning she wanted to put inside it. "I'm so happy for you!"

Jori swooped in from behind his brother. Delighted, Atty turned. Nothing could dampen his spirits, even being startled.

For a second, Atty and Jori just laughed. This inclusiveness and joy felt fragile, bound to crack at any minute. Nothing could be this good for long.

"Atty, Atty," Jori said, catching his breath. He bounced on his toes. Drawing himself up, he became theatrical again. He slicked down his leather collar as though it had water on it. That was for Kiria's benefit. The scuffs. "This is a day I never thought I'd see. Atty marrying someone who's actually very passable."

Kiria and Atty huffed. Haved took the words stoically.

"Very passable," he repeated, more loudly. "And even more than that." He looked at his brother's bride, standing there like a goddess in red. "You, my dear, are perfection. I don't know how he pulled it off. Atty"—he clapped his brother on the shoulder—"you can't screw this up. Make this lady's life magical so she can bear to look at you day after day." He said it jovially, and even Atty laughed.

"I will like to look at him," Haved said, peering at Atty sideways. Her voice was quiet but firm, and cut through the chatter around them like the note of an instrument. Atty grinned.

"Ooh!" Jori bobbed again on the balls of his feet. "Kiss him, then," he demanded.

She did. As they kissed, she brought one hand to his lightly bearded cheek. Atty, eyes closed, looked like he was in ecstasy.

Kiria smiled, but her heart clenched. It wasn't the same with Firian. Theirs was a fiercer, darker connection, but she suddenly wondered where he was. She wanted somebody to hold her hand at this party and not shut down at the mention of Tanyu, or shy away from her because of her power, or grow jealous because of her Beauty, or accuse her of usurping her mother. She wanted to be kissed like that.

"Congratulations," she said again, smiling at them both after the kiss was over.

She hurried over to the side of the room, where the space wasn't so bright. After draining her glass, she passed it to a servant. In the back was a table covered with creatures made of sugar. These had been Atty's favorite when they all were small. Kiria's favorite was fruit tarts, but Atty loved the intricate sugar animals. They tasted strangely bitter, but she had to admit that the shapes were charming. Squid, dogs, fish, birds. The squid had always been Atty's favorite. He liked to pull off the legs one by one. The brothers had tormented her with them when she was little. Squids were creepy.

After Kader, Cúron's nine-year-old son, scampered up to grab a sugar dog, only guards occupied this area of the Main. Not many people wanted to eat bitter sugar squids. She leaned against the wall, debating whether to close her eyes. Even if she did, and Firian was there, this wasn't the time or place to meet just because she suddenly felt lonely. With her Beauty and position, she wouldn't be left alone for long. And there was that time in King's Heights when she hadn't woken up. Haved had already seen her frightened because of her connection with Firian. She didn't want to go limp and require multiple people to wake her up. Unbearably embarrassing.

So she felt the solidity and coolness of the wall and watched the party. The music seemed farther away than it had a moment ago.

"Kiria?" It was her mother. A slight frown spread over her face. "Are you all right?"

"Yes, I'm fine."

"Did you hear?"

The way her mother said it made Kiria push herself off from the wall. "Hear what?"

She dropped her voice not to be heard over the crowd. "Firian Kess took over the town of Archer's Point and killed the Lord Ruler. You didn't know?"

Kiria felt numb. She swallowed and narrowed her eyes, trying to understand. "He did what?" she whispered.

"You didn't know?" Her mother lowered her eyes. "I'm sorry. I thought Cúron would have told you." She stepped closer, almost speaking in Kiria's ear. "I think he just got the news." It came out as an apology. She hummed, an understanding, motherly sound. "I'm sure the Amir are talking about cutting ties with the Tanyu. It was a good idea while it lasted."

Kiria stared blankly at a pot of laird flowers by her mother. Rousing herself, she looked up again. "Are you sure?"

"Sure of what?"

"Sure that he killed the Lord Ruler, that he took over the town? Was it his idea?"

Her mother pursed her lips. "From what I know. Ask Cúron or the Watchman. They can tell you." Her tone suggested she was a little insulted by the question.

Kiria was the Keeper now, so she should have been the first one to know about this.

It was a good idea while it lasted. The words echoed in her skull. No wonder being the face of the Tanyuin alliance felt off sometimes.

A weight in her gut told her that her mother was probably right, that Firian had taken over Archer's Point and killed the Lord Ruler. He had given into his darkness.

34

FIRIAN

FIRIAN STOOD with his back against the wall. His paranoia hadn't gotten better after being declared the new ruler of Archer's Point—it had gotten worse.

For a while he had carried around the bound copy of the Scroll, as though it could fight for him. All the ministers and generals and heads of different sectors of the town had knelt, touched the book, and sworn loyalty to him. The scene almost made him angry because he couldn't enjoy it. They'd made him order the death of the Lord Ruler first.

No one would listen until he did it. He screamed at the gathered leaders but they wouldn't budge, glaring at him as the Torithians had with their blunt, defiant faces. They believed in Thraddock. Even after Firian ordered his death, some of the ministers wouldn't pledge their allegiance until they'd seen his body for themselves.

All those people acknowledging him, trembling before him... That was a moment he should have savored. Some of his most self-indulgent dreams come true.

But he hated it. They swore to him, yet he couldn't trust a single person. They had only lined up by force. Nobody had come until Firian had ordered Thraddock's head strung up in the main square. The image made him queasy. Why hadn't they all just surrendered?

His ribcage felt as though it were tightening around his organs. Breath came in fits, though he didn't show it. Why did he think this was a good idea?

Other places had followed his orders too. Belik had communicated with the Tanyu embedded in three other towns to enact a similar show of power. Threaten the ruler, swear loyalty to the Tanyuin Head... It was enough to make people suspicious of those they had known for years. Firian saw the uneasiness among the remaining guards and servants in Hill House. They barely spoke to each other, and it wasn't just because Firian was there, pressed up against the wall, silent as a black ghost.

He wanted to go home. He needed the Academy. Compared to this place, the Academy sounded safe.

But it wasn't safe. He had opened the borders and upended expectation. Anyone could find him. Kill him. Drown him in a bathtub.

The fire in the center of the room had dwindled to embers. Tanyu had put out some of the blazing candles, so it was finally a comfortable level of semi-darkness that Firian was used to.

He locked eyes with Erron, the former hall master, now promoted, who immediately strode over to him. His questioning look awaited orders.

"Are the new Watchman and regent set in place?" Firian asked.

The Master nodded curtly.

"Then we'll leave at first light."

A warmth unconnected to the hot, incense-filled room eased up the back of Firian's neck. Kiria waited for him.

"Go. Pack," he barked, keeping his eyes partly open as he swam into the Unreal.

As soon as he arrived, it seemed like a mistake to come. Their interaction after Jovan's attack flooded back to him. He had wanted her, *needed* her, and she pushed him away.

He approached her cautiously. She wore a long, flowing dress that looked realer than some of her other clothing. That meant she was actually wearing this one. He took it in. Flowing skirt that moved when she moved, silver stitching around her waist, a neckline that hinted at an open back. Elaborate earrings and a crown implied an important event.

Her heart-shaped face shot him an accusing stare. "Firian," she began, clipped, "where are you?"

"Right here."

"No, where are you now?"

Oh. That was it. "Archer's Point."

He watched her breaths become shallow and labored. "What are you doing there?"

"You look wonderful." She did. After the long day of feeling as inflexible and twisted as a wire, he longed to hold her. He wanted a long moment of timelessness, to lose himself.

"Please answer me."

"Remember what I told you? When you could feel what was happening with me?" He scrubbed his bottom lip with a finger, waiting so she could conjure up the image of Jovan looming over him. "There's more than one."

"More than one person who...?"

He nodded. "I had to send a message to anyone else who might want to kill me."

She was silent for a long time. Her eyes darted for a while as she thought, and her chest rose and fell fitfully. That dream-falling sensation came upon him again. He actually backed up one small step to steady himself. He couldn't rely on her this much, need her this much. Somehow, her silence felt more dangerous than any of the guards had yesterday.

"Did I interrupt something?" he asked, changing the subject. She'd contacted him but, since she was dressed up, it seemed natural to ask.

Her eyelids fluttered a few times before she looked up. "It's Atty's wedding."

That's right. He'd heard that somewhere.

"What do you mean, 'Send a message'?" She raised an eyebrow.

"It's just the one time," he said, hating to have to explain himself. He already felt unsettled enough. "You understand. When the Torithians attacked you, you had to strike back."

"But this town didn't attack the Academy." Standing aloof, she made no move toward him. She might as well have been walking away.

He leveled his gaze. "I have a lot of enemies. This shows them that I have people loyal to me. That they can't take my crown." Watching her face, he tried to make out if she was one of the loyal ones. *Be one of them.* The others could all go to hell as far as he was concerned, as long as she was on his side.

Again, she paused. Then, finally, "But you killed him." She meant the Lord Ruler.

Ordered him killed. But to her that would seem the same thing. Briefly, he wished he had talked to her before making the final decision to come here. Maybe she could have offered something better than Bard's flimsy suggestions—something strong that left the blood off his hands. But he'd feared the scenario playing out in front of him now.

He stood bone-still. "You understand," he repeated. "You're the Keeper of Brithnem." He loved that title. It slid off his tongue like a kiss. He took a cautious step forward. "I didn't do it because I wanted to. If the town had just surrendered—"

"They were not required to surrender," she said clearly, separating the words. "You aren't their king. They weren't even rebelling. You killed to make a statement."

"It was necessary." Molten heat roiled in his chest. He already felt sick in this godforsaken city. For Kiria to accuse him of doing something evil was almost too much.

"Killing innocents is never necessary."

Killing innocents? Is that what she thought of him? A corner of his mouth rose in a defensive snarl.

Her voice intensified as she continued. "I want to believe in you, but you keep choosing the most selfish things!" One of her hands balled into a fist at her side.

Don't do this. "Teach me, then," he said, trying to keep his voice smooth and even. Bitterness and sincerity warred within him as he tried the gambit. Once the words were out of his mouth, he realized he meant them. He took her hand. It lay dry and limp in his.

She shook her head. "I can't. I've already taken this too far."

His stomach dropped. This was like the last time, but worse. There was something final about her words.

She slid her hand out of his grasp. Her voice became small. "I'm sorry."

Into the Unreal

Confused rage grew in him like a disease. He furrowed his eyebrows. "What do you mean?" he asked dangerously.

"The Tanyu and the Kingdom can still be allies for the time being, but we will not meet like this again." She lifted her chin.

"Like what?" It was a challenge. He would make her say it.

She flushed red, hesitating.

He stepped closer, feeling the heat of her blush radiate against his skin. He drew her into him, one hand on her back. He had been right. Bare skin met his fingers where the dress plunged. She was shaking a little. Every part of him wanted to hold her like that for a long, long time. "Like what?" he asked again, lower this time.

"Like this." She stayed only a moment longer and then twisted out of his arms. "I can't."

"Then who's being selfish?" he snapped, unable to restrain himself.

"Firian, I can't," she repeated, anger and regret in her eyes. Regret that she had been with him, cared about him, kissed him. His heart thudded and ached as she faded away. Her eyes were the last to go. They stayed locked on him.

Months of memories washed over him, drowning him. His whole body hurt, all the blood in his veins. Faces flashed before him—Salaar, Torithians in Raewhith, the Tanyuin Head, the prisoners in the boat, the escaped pirate, the Lord Ruler... Then other faces, all of them judging him—Bard, Brett, his mother, Belik, Kiria... Kiria. She looked at him as no one else could. She saw his power, his past, his weakness, all of him.

And said no.

When he came out of the Unreal, he couldn't breathe. Air came back to him as though it were black rage. His arms tingled with fury, aching to destroy.

He could barely see through the haze of his pain. Lifting the pathetic little throne, he hurled it across the floor. People skittered out of the way like bugs. He hated them. The chair leg hit the fire smoldering in the center of the room and threw up embers. A couple guards bent to take the fiery pieces and move them where they wouldn't burn.

"Leave them," Firian growled. "Leave it! Let the whole place burn." He was burning. Why shouldn't Hill House do the same? It was just a symbol anyway, not power itself.

Hesitantly, the guards stepped back. Small tongues of flame licked at the chair legs. In the dark fire he saw his father's forge, the coke glowing dangerously under containers of sand. Sand that melted and crystalized, mesmerizing as it transformed. His chest felt as molten as new glass.

Firian looked up, caught the eye of another Tanyu. He ripped off part of the flag that had hung behind the chair and stuffed it in his pocket. "Burn it all."

35

FIRIAN

Pensively, Firian ran the green flag of Archer's Point under his fingernail. Although he stopped picking at his bleeding finger the night before, the raw skin around his black ring still looked ragged.

"I noticed you've been experimenting with duplicating yourself," Belik said across the desk.

"Yes. I'm up to six now." Firian felt ragged everywhere. Declaring himself the ruler of Archer's Point hadn't made him feel better and more secure, but worse. He had new faces to fear. A few of the soldiers had backed down like obedient puppies after they witnessed his strength, but he couldn't check them all.

And all of that didn't matter. The new city didn't matter.

"That's impressive. I've only ever gotten up to seven. Even that wasn't very successful, though." Belik cleaned his teeth with this tongue, lightly smacking.

The noise grated against Firian's memories of Kiria moving resolutely away from him, her expression leaving no room for doubt. He'd had his chance, and he had lost.

"Are you here?"

Firian glared murder at Belik. He wasn't in the mood for condescension today. He could hardly stand his own presence, much less somebody else's.

Belik's face took on a more diplomatic air. Light reflected off the panes of his glasses when he tipped his head up. "Why didn't you use your new ability on Thraddock? I heard you made Jaddeo do it."

His new ability. Firian flushed hot with pride and shame. The room felt small, as though it squeezed the two of them together. He didn't want to kill someone else that way. He was proud of being able to kill, yet sick of killing. He wanted this murder done without his having to see. "It drains my energy," he said, instead of truer things.

Belik ran a hand over the stubble on his chin, flicking one finger up to resettle his glasses. "It drains your energy?" He asked the question carefully, as Firian had tried to be careful with Kiria.

Firian's anger at himself, at Belik, burned so hot that he took a drink of water to calm himself down. The Real felt dusty and colorless, but he tried to imagine that it was the Unreal, where he could be as calm as a tree or a mountain. "It does," he replied blandly.

Belik clearly wanted more information. Ever since Firian had returned from Torith, he had eyed Firian like a squirrel with a nut, puzzling how to get it open.

"Is it like what we did with Master Jairon?"

All Belik's prying was suddenly too much. Firian's awful, amazing ability was his, no one else's. It was the only thing that protected him when Jovan had nearly crushed his windpipe in the bathroom. "If you can't stop asking about it, get out!" Firian shouted, rising to his feet.

Belik looked infuriatingly unperturbed. "No need for that. I understand."

He didn't. He couldn't. Firian had nothing. No safety, no Kiria—just more responsibility, danger, confusion, and worthlessness. The crown bit into his forehead as though it didn't belong there. What good had he done?

He settled the circlet a little higher on his head. He still had this, he had control of the Academy, he had the ability to kill anyone at will...

He hated all of it.

That list would have made his heart race mere months ago. Now it felt like sand and blood. A guilty, heavy, lonely life.

He shook off the weight. It was stupid to be sad. He controlled—protected—several towns on top of Tánuil and the Academy. Many were on his side. Belik, for all his secretiveness, was on his side.

Belik, he realized like a lightning strike, could have killed him a long time ago. But he hadn't. For all Belik's own ambition, he'd supported Firian's Headship the entire time. The realization gave Firian a modicum of comfort.

The two sat in silence for a minute. Firian began to pick at the flag again. It was silky, like Kiria's clothes.

"I think this will have a positive effect," Belik said.

Firian nodded without looking up.

"Did the girl disapprove?"

Belik asked the question gently, but it still made Firian furious. It was a low, ember fury, though. He didn't answer. He would never admit that Belik had been right, that he'd let down his guard and now that she was gone, he felt a piece of him was gone too.

"The Kingdom should have helped you. After Jovan, they should have helped you. Made a proclamation or some gory thing."

Firian glanced up.

"I knew they wouldn't." Belik stretched his back a little, getting his leg in a more comfortable position. "I don't know your girl, but I know enough people up there—" He ground his teeth and slowly forced out a curse. When he laughed once, there was no joy in the sound. It was harsh and murderous. Echoes of Firian's father when his supplies were stolen. "I knew they'd do nothing."

"Who do you know there?" The obvious question hadn't occurred to Firian until now. He'd been too blinded by Kiria to care. The furrowed brow that cared but not enough, the warm hair across her bare shoulders, the moment they sat in the hollow after Torithians had attacked them, tired, dirty, but together...

Belik seemed to roll the question around his mind as someone else might roll a drink around their mouth.

"Walk," he said, rising.

Intrigued, Firian followed him out of the office.

Belik led him slowly down the hall, past empty classrooms, through the fountain courtyard—Bard caught his eye coming out of their once-shared room—and out the main doors.

Promotions and banishment rose up like old dinner. Memories.

They swept more quickly now, toward the house Belik owned but rarely visited. The grade of the sloped path assisted Belik's limp. They stopped at the door, but Belik made no motion to open it. How could this be more private than his office? Maybe Belik just needed to clear his head.

Unlikely. Everything he did was deliberate.

"Do you remember your first day?" Belik looked up at Firian, his expression unreadable.

"Yes." He bit back a joking "sir."

"The woman?"

She was one of the first things Firian had ever seen in the Unreal. Some details of her face and clothing remained in his mind, though he'd forgotten her name. When he pictured her, his memory jogged, as though he'd seen her face somewhere else too.

Belik waited for Firian to put the pieces together.

"From Brithnem?" Firian asked, trying to picture everyone he had seen on his two trips to the capital.

Finally, his thoughts gained purchase. The dark-skinned, tall woman wearing yellow shoes and a septum ring had been so out of context in Brithnem that he had let the sense of familiarity pass. The Amir.

But why was Belik being so secretive? Belik was secretive about a few things: his injury, his past, and his agenda. What did this militant-looking Amiran advisor have to do with those?

Belik nodded at Firian's dawning understanding. "I was worried when you went to Brithnem that she would kill you in your sleep."

None of this made sense. Firian shifted, and the gravel crunched under his boot.

Belik leaned a little closer. "Chetana hates Tanyu."

36

KIRIA

Kiria sat at the session the next day feeling hollow and alone. She looked out at Cúron and Daelon and Chetana, but felt they couldn't see in, as though she sat in a transparent cage.

How had she allowed her thoughts to go so far with Firian? At random times, her memory assaulted her with images and tastes that she didn't want to relive. She had been selfish, and she wanted to be selfish again.

Cúron sat next to her, tall and regal. Atty wasn't there. He had been allowed a few days respite with his new bride.

The Main was back to normal—thrones on the platform, dividers put up so the space didn't feel so overwhelming with only a few dozen people in it.

She never should have gotten involved with Firian. He'd always been violent and self-seeking. She felt the danger hum under his skin. She'd known it from the first moment they met, when he came to be her bodyguard. He'd walked in like a predator—careful, graceful, deadly—and met her eyes. She remembered wishing he were different. He wasn't easy to dismiss as a mere helpful precaution. As he was, Firian demanded a response. She'd given him one.

Cúron's loud, low voice crept into her awareness. "The Amir and the people of Brithnem demand a response."

They were talking about the attack at Archer's Point. She suddenly realized that Chetana was staring at her. Her dark, intense eyes spoke of Firian. Kiria hoped no one else noticed.

"No one expected he would use those soldiers to build his own empire." Cúron's words were grand. "We looked the other way after Raewhith, one of our cities but small."

City was too great a word for it. Kiria had been there. *Hamlet* would have been more accurate. There were many reasons including his family for Firian to trade protection for troops at Raewhith, so Kiria hadn't held that against him. Now, like a fickle god, Firian thought he could do everything, good and bad.

"And when he demanded allegiance from Imlin, we merely began to watch him more closely. But this blatant act of conquest leaves no room to doubt his intention." Cúron shifted importantly on his throne, readjusting one edge of his long robe. His eyes flicked to Kiria. "What say you?"

"He shouldn't have done it," she agreed, "certainly not while connected to us." Saying the words made her feel hollower than before, as though they had filled her and now were gone on the air.

The following pause filled her with apprehension. Was Cúron planning to propose what she thought he was?

She lifted her head. "We need to contact the Academy to understand why they've done this. Answers are what we need. Diplomacy before rash action. It's what we would expect of them."

Cúron waited a moment for her to say more. If he wanted her to apologize for forging the alliance in the first place, he would be waiting a long time. "The Second Keeper is right," he said. "He may not be allowed to continue his conquests while under our protection. Tanyu are violent and volatile, and have hurt many of our own." Now he didn't look at her. "This act of killing Lord Ruler Thraddock of Archer's Point seems to me an imminent threat against the Amir and the people of the Western Kingdom. If negotiations fail, we must cut off this alliance and stop him before he reaches closer lands."

She felt a little sick. "What do you propose?"

He observed the Amir at the foot of the dais. "That we terminate our connection immediately, and replace Firian at the Tanyuin Academy."

Replace Firian. That meant they'd kill him. Over an alliance that she had helped create. *Idiot!* she thought bitterly. The word could have been for Firian or herself.

Had Cúron planned for their alliance to end this way all along? The placidly aggrieved look he cast over the Amir suggested that he would gain favor by this decision. The Amir didn't visibly react to his words, but they all showed alert attention. She gritted her teeth.

"The matter, to me, seems clear," he continued. "These Tanyu have harmed our citizens, targeted the Amir, and now aim to start an empire. It isn't too late to act, if we act quickly. I say we put the matter to a vote."

Everything was moving too fast. Cúron had a good point, but she had to think, to digest, to do... something. "Wait," she said. "We'll vote if we have to. I'll communicate with the Academy myself if no one else will. This is an important vote, to send troops out again, breaking our new peace," she continued, sounding extra formal as she tried to gather her thoughts. "I move that we wait for Keeper Atael to return before making a final decision. I will gather more information and we can all consider until then." If worse came to worst, she could definitely convince Atty to side with her, not to kill Firian right away.

She became aware again of Chetana's dark eyes on her. Had her advisor told anyone else about her secret relationship? They'd all seen Firian's undivided attention when he came to Brithnem, but only Chetana and Jori knew that she had accepted that burning attention for a while. Despite herself, she blushed.

Daelon glanced at his mother and seemed to notice the message she was sending Kiria, though he couldn't read its contents. He gave Kiria an inquiring look.

Beside him, Hada, one of the session recorders, hunched over a piece of parchment, recording the proceedings. Every word set down where one could read it later. Something about the finality of that bothered her.

"He returns in two days," Cúron said. "We can all consider the merits"—he put extra emphasis on *consider*—"but I think we know what he will say. Keeper Atael highly values the security of this kingdom."

"As do I." Kiria pursed her mouth. She could barely stomach the veiled accusation. "It was for the security of this kingdom that I formed the alliance in the first place. I don't appreciate the suggestion that I am anything less than loyal."

"Of course you are," Cúron conceded, holding up his hands as though he had meant no such thing.

Amir Parohim stood up. The light coming in through the windows made the vertical lines on his face appear deeper. "Then I move that we reconvene later. In two days, we'll cast a vote about what to do with Master Kess."

THE NEXT MORNING, Kiria lit a candle and yawned. Her limp hair, all askew, cast huge frazzled shadows on the wall from where she sat up in bed. She stretched her arms toward the ceiling and let them fall to her sides. Pressure built up vaguely in her head, despite the lack of light.

This time before the sun rose inevitably brought Firian's face back to her mind. She couldn't save him from himself. She might be able to save him from the Kingdom, though.

For all his violence and arrogance, he had helped them win the war against the Torithian pirates. To kill him would betray their gratitude.

She didn't just think this because of their times in the Unreal, did she? She sat, staring blankly into space, taking inventory of her soul. She wasn't just Kiria Arioc. She was the Western Kingdom, and she had to act like it.

Archer's Point was outside their borders. Firian had never threatened her or the Kingdom directly. Even now, she doubted he ever would. She'd heard no complaints about his treatment of the conquered towns, except for his brutal takeover of Archer's Point. But would those cries reach her, if they did exist?

What had he done with the Torithians? Was he doing the same thing to the people he conquered? Did she know him at all?

She leaned forward, face in her hands. She needed more information.

If she failed, Cúron would stick to his vote, apparently hellbent on ridding the world of Firian, since he hadn't suggested diplomacy himself. If he proposed an idea, he voted for it, even if he knew better. Parohim was guaranteed to vote with Cúron, as every Amir voted with their Keeper. Atty was the swing vote. He almost always went with Cúron, but Atty was her friend—she could get him on her side. He might be feeling more generous now since the wedding.

Steeling herself, she hopped out of bed, swinging her arms to wake them up. Closing her eyes, she let the darkness take her, then the light, then the nothingness...

Firian was there in an instant, before she could even conjure a background. In a black room, he sat on a huge chair that might have been a throne, his expression grim. Coming closer, she saw hints of longing cross the blue of his eyes, though his face was hard set.

Did he know what they had talked about in the session? Firian was almost always guarded, but now he acted like a tower, looking out from impenetrable defenses.

"I'm here in an official capacity," she began, and then realized she hadn't worn her official Beauty. Maybe it was all for the best.

A muscle twitched in his cheek. "Official?"

"Yes." She cleared her throat. "We have some questions about what you've done since the end of the war. You said you took over Archer's Point." He leaned forward like an animal cornered but she went on. "Why?"

"I told you."

"It had to be for more than sending a message."

He was silent.

Her lungs constricted. This wasn't Firian. The Firian she knew was proud and selfish and determined, but not monstrous. At least, she knew he could be better than this, but he kept regressing, giving into his worst tendencies, his greatest vices. She waited defiantly for him to speak.

"Are you dissolving the alliance, then?" he said flatly. "Did your advisor suggest it?"

His manner continued to shock her. "Firian!" she said, breaking her professional guise. "Talk to me. This isn't you—"

"This is me."

She was standing over him now, and she saw that the crown he was wearing had grown into his head as though he were made of metal himself. They stared at each other, the air between them crackling.

"You're wearing a mask," she said. She'd thought it many times when they were together, even during the good times when they had talked and kissed away evenings. Now she couldn't see him through it. Wishing she could rip it off to see the real Firian beneath, she tried a different tactic. "You took over Raewith to help your sister. That's what you told me. What about Imlin?"

They'd start with something less violent. *Please let him have a good reason.*

He licked his lips thoughtfully, cutting his gaze away from her. "I needed more soldiers. The Academy is open now." He looked back into her eyes almost accusingly.

Her brows lowered. "The Tanyu weren't enough?" She couldn't resist accusing him back.

He went still. She had thought he was still before. Only now did she realize that there had been soft movements. Those were gone. Anger and pain reflected in his unblinking gaze.

His voice was chilly when he finally spoke. "One Tanyu can take on twenty, but not a hundred."

Kiria's throat had gone dry. "All right." It wasn't a great reason, but it made sense. "Is that why you attacked Archer's Point?"

"We didn't attack Archer's Point. We threatened the Lord Ruler in exchange for security for the Academy and everyone else." Something in Firian appeared to deflate. All his rigidity from a moment before dissolved and he stood, face to face with her. "It was a small sacrifice to keep us all safe."

She wanted to believe him, to agree with him so Cúron wouldn't get the vote he so desperately wanted. But Firian wasn't giving her the answers she needed. With each word, she became more and more convinced that he was lashing out in his paranoia. He was dangerous, just not quite in the same way the other Keepers suspected.

For a while, she didn't respond. They both knew she wouldn't take his side on this. Her mouth felt gummy as she remembered her words to him. She'd been so hopeful, so smitten. *There's more justice in the world because of us.* Was that true now?

"How would that keep us safe?" Her voice was smaller now as she searched for cracks of integrity and goodness in Firian's armor.

"No one doubts my strength."

"Only your kindness."

A few painful heartbeats later, he said, "I could have your kindness."

She ached to see the longing in his eyes. Firian Kess didn't beg. He didn't ask for things. Here was that crack of honesty she was looking for, but it wasn't directed the right way. Their time together was over. She wanted to find goodness, respect, justice in the way he made his decisions and dealt with his people. Instead, all she'd found were fear, ambition, and excuses.

"Is there no more you can tell me?" she asked.

He pressed his mouth into a line and sat back in the enormous throne. For an instant, she wanted to comfort him. She was near enough to take his hand or touch his shoulder or lean down and plant a kiss on his forehead. Or his lips.

She scolded herself for the thought and stood straighter. "If not, I'm going back. I was hoping to understand you better."

"Officially." He said the word softly, like a curse.

"Yes, officially."

It struck her that this might be the last time she saw him. All in black, on a black throne in a black room, with fear driving him to give into his worst impulses. A lump lodged in her throat. She couldn't help him. It wasn't for lack of trying.

She tried to study his face without his noticing, to memorize this moment in honor of who he had been to her and who he might have become, had things been different.

She fumbled for parting words. "I wish you... all the best, Firian," she said, sounding too hesitant and formal.

He seemed to understand, though all he did was grip the armrests of his seat as he held her gaze.

With tumbling emotions, she forced herself toward the surface. Negotiations had failed. All that was left was to convince Atty to side with her not to kill Firian.

The girls came into her room moments later. Vayci's glance at the candle prickled with guilt, but Kiria didn't need to explain why she had woken up so early and lit the candle herself.

She felt in a daze as they washed and dressed her in a cream-colored two-piece dress. Tingling covered her body. When she opened her eyes, she checked her hands. They glowed with Beauty. Everything that had been out of place now radiated in its perfection.

Fully ready, she went to Atty's room. At the door, she stopped. Was he in there with his new bride? She cleared her throat and cast a questioning look to the nearest guard, who shifted his shoulders back, the blue fabric shifting with them.

"I want to see Atael," she said.

The guard acknowledged her and nodded, opening the door.

She passed into the room. Small, feminine touches edged the corners where they hadn't before. Atty had always been stolid, more about substance than style, and he had not owned many beautiful things. It wasn't that the look of his room had changed drastically, but she noticed hints everywhere that someone else had moved in. Small things, like the way a pillow had been arranged, or a piece of lacy fabric sticking out from a drawer, or embroidered slippers by the bed.

Haved wasn't there. As much as Kiria liked her, she was glad. Part of her felt that she would never be able to have the same friendship with Atty that she once did after seeing the wedding. His dewy eyes full of joy had said that nothing would be the same again. It wouldn't, but at least they could still talk without Haved present sometimes.

Atty sat on the edge of the bed, putting on his boots. "Kiria, good morning!" he said in a clear voice.

"Good morning. Haved is still wonderful, I assume."

He nodded almost shyly. "Yes, that was the best decision I ever made."

Kiria never would have chosen to marry for an alliance, sight unseen. She inevitably would have ended up with someone far less desirable than Haved Ganesha. "I'm so glad."

Atty finished tugging on one boot and sat up. "She's everything I ever wanted."

"Well, I'm sure she's not perfect..."

"She made me this this morning." He twisted backward and picked up something tiny from the bedspread. It was cream-colored like her dress. She came closer. It looked like a tree made of paper. Atty's palm dwarfed it. The little tree was twice the height of his thumbnail. He gave a private smile as he stared at it.

"Was there a note on it?" Kiria asked.

"No." The dopey smile didn't leave his face, but he put the folded tree to the side. It flopped sideways, immediately lost in the covers.

"You should take her to the docks," she said, prompted suddenly by a memory. "She said she wanted to meet the Navigators."

"She did?" He bent down to grab his other boot.

"Yeah, I told her that we had some here, and she got excited to meet them. She loves the stars."

"I know." The way he said it made her ache a little with the love he had for her. How could those two have known each other for such a short time? Atty wanted to know Haved, and to love her the best he could. Maybe pure intention was enough to make up for time.

"You're coming back to the Main tomorrow, I hear," she said, sitting beside him.

"Yeah." The angle of his shoulders bent slightly heavier with the answer.

"Have you heard what we've been talking about?"

"I haven't asked, and no one's told me." His words didn't have the injured, accusatory undertone they sometimes did. He just didn't care about politics at the moment.

"The Tanyu are... causing problems," she began.

His eyes darted to hers, and he bit the inside of his cheek. He didn't say Firian's name, though. A moment passed.

She continued. "They took over Archer's Point. It's just outside our borders. Very close. Officially, that's the third town that's sworn allegiance to the Academy. A couple others are set to follow. So Cúron's getting nervous."

"The Academy's conquering all these places?"

"Right."

Atty sat up again. The mattress bounced a little with the motion. "What do you think about that?" He didn't add any more to the question, but much was implied. Kiria was the face of the alliance, after all. The touchpoint for the war effort. The one who knew Firian best.

"He has taken over those towns, but I'm not sure why," she said. Firian *could* be building an empire. Everyone had the potential for corruption. "But Cúron's going to suggest that we remove the current leader—"

"Firian Kess." Apparently Atty was done using vague pronouns in place of the name.

She nodded. "He wants to remove him. And I don't think we have enough information to break our alliance like that. I want us to be true to our word. They did help us win the war. Both wars. He called off the other one too." She liked the pronouns herself. They felt safer.

Atty hunched a little as he leaned toward her. "Does Cúron want to kill him?"

Her heart jumped at the words, although the idea had been swirling in her mind for hours already. An almost physical longing to know if Firian was eavesdropping tugged at her. "Yes."

Atty's thick eyebrows twitched together as he understood. "You need my vote."

"Yes."

"If he's taking over towns, doesn't that make him a threat to the Kingdom?" He asked the question without malice, not like Jori would have asked it. Atty hated to think about killing anything.

"Not necessarily. That's the thing. Not *necessarily*. We don't have enough information." It struck her that this conversation, which felt fairly normal, could hold Firian's life in the balance. Firian's wide blue eyes when he had seen his mother for the first time in years flashed over her memory. The tinge of betrayal and longing that made him seem like a child in that moment. His comforting arms around Kiria after the news that her father had been killed. He had stroked her hair.

"We can't order him killed," she said, voice thick.

Atty looked straight in her eyes. She looked back, hoping her face didn't betray too many of her thoughts.

The side door opened. Haved emerged from the sunken washroom, wearing only a robe. Her long dark hair, wound into twists, hung wet over her shoulders. She regarded Kiria politely. Haved didn't often smile, but she observed and there was intensity and kindness in the observation.

Kiria stood. "Please don't make any drastic decision before we know everything," she said, turning back at Atty. Hopefully, hopefully he understood what she said. His familiar puppy eyes had returned.

Kiria turned to leave, tempted to run from this potentially intimate moment between her friends, but she couldn't go without his acknowledgement. This vote was too important. "Atty. Atty," she prompted.

He finally looked back at her, calm but a little annoyed.

"I need you. I need you to vote with me."

But his thoughts clearly weren't on the next day's session.

She ran her thumbnail over her fingers, irritated. "Say you'll vote with me."

Atty held out a hand to Haved. "I need to think about it," he said, not looking at her anymore.

"It's important," she pressed. When he didn't answer, she swallowed the dread beginning to settle heavy in her throat. "I'll see you tomorrow."

37

KIRIA

Kiria's heart beat a shallow rhythm in her throat.

Firian's life. Should they replace him or let him live?

The three Keepers sat on their thrones. Advisors, military officials, and several others had been invited to this special session to decide Firian's fate.

Cúron, as usual, was the first to give his side. Firian had become a threat because of his apparent ambition. He had taken over Archer's Point. He had killed its Lord Ruler and left his head in the town square. He couldn't continue to be associated with Brithnem if he was building his own empire in the north.

She'd heard all this before. The news about the severed head had come a little later, and it made her sick to think about. She had mulled these things over and over in a nauseating loop. But she held firm to her decision that they should end the alliance, and probably stop him, but not take his life. It wasn't selfish. It wasn't just that she knew him. She felt he didn't deserve to die.

Cúron finished his argument.

Kiria stood up. "Keepers, advisors, distinguished guests," she began, feeling winded, "what the First Keeper says is true. Master Kess might be a threat. But that's the part we need to consider. As a fundamentally wise and peaceful society, we cannot strike without an imminent threat and due cause." She tried to catch Atty's eye, hold his gaze, but he seemed almost distracted, looking all around the room. Her entire back felt tense. Would he vote with her or with Cúron? "Master Kess might be a threat to us, but there is no evidence that he intends to continue. When I questioned him after our last meeting, he indicated that his violent actions at Archer's Point were intended to quell the need for any more conquest. I'm not excusing his behavior, only pointing out that it would go against our principles to murder him now."

Cúron hummed in consideration of her words. Her heart skipped. Had Cúron *ever* changed his mind after it had been made up?

"At most," she concluded, "we could dissolve our alliance." Saying that felt like a defeat. The alliance had been her idea and everyone throughout the Western Kingdom knew it. She tried to swallow the rock in her throat.

Cúron spoke without rising from his seat. "Wouldn't that anger the Tanyu as much as replacing their leader?"

"No," she replied, still standing. "I don't think so. But we do have to count the cost as well. Kingdom lives will be lost if we follow your plan. The Tanyu would know we were there before we reached the Academy. Sending one or two assassins wouldn't be enough, unless you're willing to sacrifice them and not guarantee success." The military leaders didn't stir, but hopefully they considered her words.

With a sweeping look, Cúron brought the knot of people seated at the foot of the dais into their discussion. "The question is about the safety of the Kingdom above all. We all make sacrifices."

He said it as though she didn't know. They had all made massive sacrifices for the Western Kingdom, and would continue to make them throughout their lives. He didn't need to inform her of the difficulty of ruling.

"It's a castle full of trained warriors who won't hesitate to defend their leader. Archer's Point proved their loyalty," she persisted. "We'd have to send an army and make the Tanyu our enemy again."

She accidentally caught Chetana's eye. Her advisor looked back steadily. Without changing her expression at all, she reminded Kiria of the *katah* she had with Firian. They didn't have to send an army. Kiria could kill him in the Unreal.

Kiria's eyebrows twitched downward as she dismissed the thought and turned away from Chetana. Where in the Scroll could it demand something so heartless?

Cúron passed a hand over his gray beard. "General Lincome, given what we know about the Academy, how many soldiers would it take to accomplish this mission?"

The general, a square man with pale birthmarks dotting his skin, stood respectfully. He wore armor similar to what the guards wore, all metal, leather, and blue cloth. "My Keeper." He gave a small bow. "I can foresee no less than three hundred if we attack the castle itself."

They were already planning the logistics of an attack? Again, Kiria fought to lock eyes with Atty on her left, but he wouldn't look at her. She felt sick.

"He has been traveling often lately," Cúron said, as though alone in a meeting with the general.

Kiria spoke up. "We haven't decided whether or not to replace him. Until then, all this planning is unnecessary and morbid." She paused and felt her mind. She didn't go into the Unreal—closing her eyes would have been a giveaway—but she wanted to see if she could feel Firian waiting. The signature warmth was gone.

Cúron nodded for the general to sit, and then turned almost cheerfully to her. "Then shall we vote?"

A hollow feeling carved into her chest. Firian wouldn't have a future with her, but he could still have a future.

Atty had said nothing. There were essentially two sides to this issue, and Cúron and Kiria had expressed those sides already.

To keep or remove Firian. That was all.

Into the Unreal

Kiria gazed around the Main. The soaring ceilings, many-paneled windows, grand statues, gilt lanterns... Something about its grandeur didn't match the occasion.

Firian was probably in the office she had seen in the Unreal, all gray stone. That room felt closer to the reality of what they were discussing. They were all so detached from the violence they calmly discussed in this room.

The mosaic in the floor drew her gaze. Through the chairs of advisors and generals scattered over it, she could see Maril clearly, holding lavender and a dagger. The image brought prayers to her lips.

Cúron voted first. Yes, they should remove Firian.

Kiria, dry-mouthed, voted next. No.

Atty came third.

Her heart pounded. He had never told her what he intended to do. Maybe *he* didn't know what he intended to do. He stood. She couldn't breathe. A yes from him would mean Firian's death. She wordlessly pleaded with him as much as she could without drawing the attention of the others in the room. He flicked a glance her way, but she couldn't read his expression.

"No."

Breath escaped her and she deflated against her throne. Others must have noticed her relief, but she didn't care. Brithnem wouldn't send people to kill Firian. He could live. Firian would live. Now that the danger was past, she realized how afraid she'd been for him. A surprising amount of emotion gathered in her throat.

Parohim, Cúron's advisor, voted yes, of course.

Chetana stood and voted yes.

Chetana stood and voted yes.

Kiria nearly rose to her feet. Advisors always voted with their Keepers. Always. Even Daelon's forehead creased in bewildered surprise at his mother's pronouncement. This had never happened before. How could Chetana defy her? The lump in her throat turned to anger. Chetana, tall and regal, had an air of independence, but she had never wielded that power against the Ariocs. She loved them. She'd said so.

Before Kiria could think of the right reaction, Reynard stood next. At least he would do the right thing.

"Yes," he said, not looking at Atty.

Her blood was fire. She counted votes in her head: she and Atty counted as two. Cúron, Parohim, Chetana, and Reynard counted as two and a half.

They had won.

Against the will of two Keepers, Brithnem would murder Firian.

The rest of the session passed in an angry blur. Kiria could barely focus enough to nod or respond when her time came. As soon as it was over, she jumped to her feet and practically ran out of the Main.

How could this happen? How could Chetana vote against her? How could her mother, when she was Keeper, have allowed the Amir a vote at all?

The questions raged inside her like the sea. Somehow, she made it into the hallway. When she realized that she was heading back to her quarters, she spun on her heel and stormed instead toward Cúron's room. His guards didn't have time to bow before she opened the door and went in.

Varinna, Cúron's wife, spun around at her entrance, startled. A tall serving girl with pale skin, even pale eyebrows, stopped lacing up the back of her complicated dress. A small bottle tipped back and forth on the vanity table in front of them. The surprise didn't fade as Varinna's eyes flicked over Kiria's face. "Lady Kiria," she said, a question in the tentative way she said her name.

Kiria knew she looked irate. She took a calming breath. None of this was Varinna's fault. "I need to talk to Cúron."

Waving the girl away from the dress, Varinna adjusted herself in the seat, squaring herself at Kiria. Apparently, she had gathered her wits enough to look disapproving. Her disapproval was smooth-edged with diplomacy, even at its most severe. Kiria had grown up around stares like that, and she was too angry to care now.

"He should be back from the Main any moment," Varinna said with the slightest edge to her tone.

"I'll wait for him here." Kiria made no move to sit. The hot blood coursing through her veins wouldn't let her relax.

"Is everything all right?"

"I have an urgent matter to discuss with him," she hedged. No, everything was not all right.

Varinna gestured toward the servant, who began tugging at the lacing again.

After taking three breaths, Kiria wondered how long the man could talk and cajole with others in the Main before coming back here. After all, he had just sentenced a man to death. How could he be in good spirits?

Finally, the door opened.

"Cúron!" Kiria snapped, surprising herself with the volume of her voice. She shrank back into herself. "Lord Cúron. How could you let this happen?"

His brow furrowed into deep ridges as he stepped over the carpets of his room. Kiria realized she couldn't remember the last time she had been here. She must have been a child.

"How could I let what happen?" he asked wearily, reaching for a clasp at his throat.

"How could you let the Amir shout down the Keepers? How could you order Firian's death when two of us voted against it?"

He handed his royal robe to a waiting manservant. "They didn't 'shout us down,' Kiria. It was a fair vote."

"Without the majority of Keepers?"

"It was unusual, but not unfair. We agreed that they could have half a vote. Your mother agreed to the notion."

The news prompted a humorless laugh. "She wasn't even going to sessions then."

"She trusted my judgment." He gave Kiria a pointed look.

"I don't," she replied. Her words came recklessly. "In this, I don't." She stood a little taller and stared back at him.

Something black flashed across his expression. "What is this all about, Kiria? You don't like that the Amir can vote? That was already decided on. Sometimes being a Keeper means living with decisions that you don't agree with."

"I know." She hated the heat she felt rising in the corners of her eyes. This was not a time to cry. "But you used the Amir to override us. You're used to being right, but you aren't right this time. You can't kill Firian because he took over a town that isn't even part of the Western Kingdom!" All the frustration that had built over months of small political moves, small condescensions, boiled out.

"I'm sorry you feel that way," Cúron responded in a familial way, like an uncle, which, far enough back in the family line, he was. "I'm surprised you seem to care about him after all the Tanyu did to Brithnem, and what he did to you."

"Of course I care. I don't want to kill an innocent man."

"Innocent," he scoffed, looking away from her.

He was right. *Innocent* went too far. She slowed down her words, trying not to sound quite as desperate as she felt. "You can't let this stand."

When Cúron turned back to her, both he and Varinna gave her stern looks that left no more room for discussion. "The decision is made," he declared in his deep, regal voice. "All you can do is abide by it. Remember that to warn the Tanyu would put our soldiers in additional danger. It would be tantamount to treason."

Her face went cold. To warn Firian of the assassination would be treason against her people? She knew it, but to hear it put so bluntly... She searched the room, as though it held answers about how it had come to this. Cúron's words felt like a puzzle box she couldn't assemble. Firian didn't deserve to die, but if she told him the Kingdom's plans, he would move the entire Academy against the soldiers they sent. Either Firian would be killed, or a company of the best troops in Brithnem. She couldn't breathe.

Cúron's face softened. "I know you love the Kingdom. With the Tanyu acting as erratically as they are, our citizens are restless again. Some are going with almost no sleep. The least we can do as their Keepers is ensure that someone responsible has the Headship of the Academy."

Her mouth felt dry as she tried to force breath in her lungs. She could hardly speak. "Don't send them," she managed. "We'll tell the people... tell them not to be afraid."

"It's done, Kiria."

His statement brought images unbidden to her imagination: Firian lying dead in a pool of his own blood, his head tipped sideways by itself... Her hand flew to her stomach as she felt suddenly sick. It wasn't only the violence that bothered her.

She knew Firian.

She... loved him. To whatever degree, there was part of her that loved him, despite his mess and the shadows lurking in him. The truth struck her like a knife. The timing of this realization could not have been worse. Now there was nothing she could do to save him, either from the Kingdom or from himself.

She shook her head at Cúron. How could this be happening? *Tantamount to treason...*

Only one thing would have kept her from warning Firian, and it was betraying the Western Kingdom. As long as she lived, she would never do that.

38

KIRIA

AT BREAKFAST THE NEXT DAY, Kiria didn't touch her food. She couldn't eat if she wanted to. Even the sweet scent of the laird flowers along the center of the table stuck in the back of her throat.

It was the same group that had eaten merrily together before her coronation tour—Keepers, family, advisors, a few others—but this time was different. Cúron didn't look at her, busy instead with his wife, Atty, and the Amir.

Chetana didn't avoid her gaze, but any time their eyes met, an electric current of challenge ran between them. Kiria felt it in her bones. The challenge wasn't loud or harsh, but constant and undeniable. Chetana could vote as she saw fit, it said. *But you cost him his life!* Kiria wanted to scream. They hadn't spoken since the vote. Kiria felt too hideously bitter. Today, though, she needed to call an audience with her advisor.

In two short weeks, the troops would reach the Academy. The thought of warning Firian popped up, unbidden, all the time. When she was at meals or sessions, talking to friends, falling asleep. But she hadn't. More lives would be lost that way, and besides, he could take care of himself.

He should be stopped, but not murdered.

Her hands trembled under the table. They felt dirty, coated in blood. Others chattered around her. She didn't hear what they said.

When she lifted her eyes, Jori looked back at her from across the table. His trademark cavalier attitude had been replaced by honest concern. She nodded a little so he would know she was okay.

Jori and Chetana. Those were the only two who knew about her continued connection with Firian in the Unreal. She'd called it off, but she knew she could summon him and he'd appear in an instant, never far away.

I'll feel his death.

The thought struck like a kick to the chest. She was going to be sick. When she was in Charäkhnem, she'd known his panic during the assassination attempt. Surely, she'd feel this too. She'd know before anyone told her because she would panic, lose her breath... Would she black out?

She looked back at Jori and revised her response. She slowly shook her head. *No, I'm not all right.* She pointed to her food. *Want it?*

He reached for the plate she handed him.

"You're not eating your breakfast?" her mother asked beside her.

"I'm not hungry this morning. I might be getting sick," Kiria replied.

The meal finished quickly. As everyone rose to leave, she found Chetana. "I need to talk to you," she said in a stern undertone.

Chetana's expression didn't change. She'd expected this conversation. "When would you like to talk, My Keeper?"

"Now." Kiria was tempted to stay behind, but the smell of flowers and breakfast turned her stomach. She needed fresh air. "In your quarters." That way they could walk across the gardens before reaching the Amiran Academy. There was also a hint of symbolism or justice that the conversation happen outside the palace.

"Very well," Chetana replied, and they left the room.

Kiria's girls followed her into the gardens, but she told them to wait outside the room while she talked to Chetana alone. Because she was an advisor, she lived in the Amiran Academy itself, in one of the private rooms, near Daelon's. The curved side closer to the palace held the personal rooms, the side facing away was for education, and the large domed room upstairs was for religious study and prayer.

Amiran bedchambers were tiny and ascetic. Chetana's barely fit the two of them comfortably. Handwritten notes and passages from the Scroll lay in a neat pile on the desk next to two candles that Chetana lit so they wouldn't be in darkness.

Tanyu and Amir were more alike in some ways than they liked to admit. Neither group cared about worldly comfort. It was easy to see how they came from the same root, although they focused on such different things now.

Chetana waited for Kiria to speak first. She loomed over her, especially with her curly hair, and some of Kiria's fury cooled a little. She sucked her lip for a moment before asking the question that had been plaguing her thoughts day and night since that session. "Why did you vote against me?" She revised. "Was there anything in the Scroll that meant I was doing the wrong thing?" *And if so, why didn't you tell me?*

"*God uproots the tyrant,*" Chetana said evenly.

"*And blesses the one with mercy,*" Kiria finished, glad she had played that Scroll game so often with Daelon during their lessons. He would give half a sentence and she had to provide the rest. She became very good at it.

Chetana's expression didn't change. "My Keeper, the Tanyu have to be stopped. This greed... I know what this greed can do. They pledged loyalty to the Kingdom but they will not keep their promise."

"Your duty is to God and then to me, and what I think is right to do for the Kingdom. I chose mercy. You should have too." She swallowed, but her throat didn't move the right way. "A man will be dead because of you."

"More than one, I think, and not because of me." Chetana leveled her gaze at Kiria. In the candlelight, she looked otherworldly. "You know what I say is true, but you care too much for him to order his death."

Kiria opened her mouth to protest, but nothing came out. Darkness pressed in, thick and physical around them. "You're supposed to be peaceful," she said. "Wise. God-fearing."

"I hope I am those things now."

Now? What did that mean?

Chetana went on. "I admire your mercy, and I knew you could be as stubborn as the First Keeper."

Kiria almost reprimanded her for being so blunt, but it felt good to be blunt, real. "You're saying that, but you sided with him."

"He sided with us."

Kiria paused. Some of Cúron's decisions clicked into place. It was his idea to give the Amir a vote; he had funded more copies of the Sacred Scroll, sent for research from Charäkhnem, vocally supported expanding their education to include the poorer areas of Brithnem. Most of them were great ideas, so Kiria had missed the pattern. He had wanted the Amir on his side all along. They gave him all the power. She and Atty were tagalongs in his plan. Dull anger simmered inside her.

Chetana was no fool. She had to have seen it happening and allowed it. Did Daelon see it too? Kiria didn't think so. He would have told her.

"There were other ways to get rid of him," Chetana said softly.

Kiria stood silently. A cool draught from the door breezed through the tiny room. She refused to understand Chetana's meaning.

"The *katah*." Light flickered on her septum ring. "But I knew you wouldn't take action. And that's all right. It is much to ask."

She would have Kiria kill Firian herself. The suggestion was repulsive. How could she betray his trust so cruelly?

Kiria's chest ached. She already had betrayed him by not warning him about the coming troops. The conflict inside her made her want to scream.

"My only regret," Chetana went on, "is putting you in danger, My Keeper. But you still have time to extricate yourself from his hold. I know the strength of a *katah*. You are just as strong."

"Chetana," Kiria said, breath coming harder, "your violence and disregard for me demonstrate you are unfit to be my advisor."

Chetana's dark arms flexed, but she showed no other sign of emotion. "I understood that you might feel this way, My Keeper."

Kiria fought to keep her voice from shaking. She reached backward and laid her hand on the cool door handle. "I want someone who will respect me and who will do the will of God. You've followed your own prejudices and it will hurt innocent people."

Chetana lifted her chin a fraction.

"Daelon will be my new advisor. He has greater respect for the Scroll than anyone I've ever met."

Despite everything, a gleam of pride for her son flashed in Chetana's dark eyes.

"And he cares for me. He wouldn't do anything to hurt me unless he knew that God would will it so."

"The same is true of me," Chetana said. "I will always love and serve your family, My Keeper."

Kiria set her mouth in a line, unconvinced. Until a few days ago, she would have believed anything her advisor said. Chetana was mysterious and strong, but had always been loyal.

Light streamed in as Kiria opened the door and walked out.

39

FIRIAN

FIRIAN PURSED his mouth as he looked at the dead rabbit.

Its gray-furred back arched in a U, its black eyes still wide. Around it, the pine needles had been shuffled in its death throes.

A fox or raven would come to take it away. What bothered him was that he kept finding these animals, killed but not yet eaten.

The breeze ruffled the rabbit's fur backward, showing more fluff. A healthy rabbit, broken in its prime. Maybe its neck was squeezed like his was underwater. The creature's stiff limbs made him a little sick. No one had threatened Firian since Archer's Point, but the echo of betrayal still wouldn't leave him. It played relentlessly in his head, waking and sleeping. Sometimes even in the Unreal.

It had to be a person killing these animals. He wouldn't have minded if the rabbits and squirrels were eaten too, but they all lay at the edge of the forest, left to rot.

Some Tanyu had anger, but they all had restraint as well. He couldn't think of anyone who would kill like this for no reason. Even Jovan, prone to violence, needed an excuse.

It must be Torithians. Who else could it be?

Firian turned away from the rabbit and headed to the barracks. He needed to talk to the new instructor anyway, make sure he was pushing the troops until they were ready to jump, to dive, to obey the slightest command. No more killing without cause.

His boots crunched the dead pine needles as he strode toward Old Danior's sweet shop.

Speed kept him from thinking about Kiria. Not completely, but it helped.

Belik hadn't said anything more about Chetana, but the bitterness in his voice told him they must have had a *katah* too.

An old *katah* still rankled, seared a person's insides like the aftershock of a burn, even after the initial sting went away. At least that's how someone had described it to him years ago. He couldn't remember who it was.

Belik had always seemed above such things. Even his regard for Firian felt like an exception to a life without attachment.

Firian still felt the sting. It stabbed him now, touched him constantly. Keeping busy just helped him to push it to the background, an irritating ache, demanding attention. It would rush back in any quiet moment. The Unreal pulled him toward her and he had to wrench his mind in other directions.

If he was going to get her back, she needed some time. It had only been eleven days—eleven and a half days—since she had pulled away from him, said goodbye, severed their connection. He would get it back. He just had to be more patient than he felt.

Firian stepped between the shops to the barracks. Already the carpenters had started building rock walls in front of the wooden ones as he had requested. It could have been Firian's imagination, but they seemed to work faster after he burned Hill House. Either way, grim satisfaction made him nod as he looked at their work.

The new instructor, Master Nedi, came quickly out of the main entrance to the compound. He walked, but gave the sensation of running. Exceptionally tall with long limbs and big hands, he had the look of a man cobbled together from several other people. He kept his brown hair short above his small eyes and big nose. Despite the awkwardness of his appearance, he still moved like a Tanyu, silent and sure. His size and formidable voice, helpful on Torith, now made him the right candidate for instructing drills.

"Master Kess," he said, approaching him.

"Master Nedi, how's my army?"

"Torithians are days away from weapons," he replied. His deep voice sounded as though it resonated through a gravelly cave. Even his voice at an ordinary volume gave the impression of being much louder than it was.

"Good," Firian said, getting louder himself. The people from Raewhith and Imlin must be practicing with weapons already. "Before you give them any, talk to them for me."

Master Nedi's pause asked why.

"Someone's been killing animals. Until that stops, none of them get weapons. My army does not kill without a reason." The Lord Ruler's face appeared in his mind. *He was a sacrifice for order. There was a reason.*

"As you would have it, Master Kess."

"Push them hard."

"As you would have it."

Warmth trickled onto Firian's neck. Or maybe it was just the Unreal. Kiria.

He nodded curtly to Master Nedi and turned to go. If Kiria was thinking about him... if she wanted to *meet* him...

He ducked between some shops, looked to see that no one was close by, and closed his eyes. This demanded his full attention. Immediately he saw her. He sucked in a breath. Beautiful, like a cool drink after a run. Her shining hair was in braids. His eyes slipped down to the jeweled slippers adorning her feet. His chest ached with the desire for her to look at him, but she was talking to someone else. The Third Keeper's brother, Jori. They sat on the edge of her bed in the middle of a heated conversation.

She hadn't come to the Unreal to meet him. A sour wave of disappointment mingled with his curiosity. Why did he think she had called him?

"I can't," she was saying, her gorgeous face contorted in pain. She held her hands open in her lap. "I won't." Her chest heaved with a heavy breath.

Should he make himself known? Should he comfort her?

Jori looked her over sympathetically. He was sitting too close to her. Firian stayed out of sight in case Kiria checked the Unreal.

"I know I can't... do anything now," she said bitterly. "The troops are already gone." A tear washed down her face. Another chased it, and another. She leaned into Jori's shoulder, and he wrapped his arm around hers. Quiet sobs shook her.

Firian's mouth went dry and his hands numb.

"You did what you could," Jori said, rubbing her fine skin. "It could be the best thing. Never know."

"I can't risk them," she said, her voice muffled against him. It was as though he hadn't said anything. "And I didn't... want to risk him either. But they're almost there."

Firian frowned, feeling sweat coat the back of his neck. *Him?*

"Nothing you can do now, love."

"I replaced Chetana," she said, straightening. Her face looked like justice. "She had no right to vote against me, not for something this important. Life or death, Jori!"

Firian wasn't breathing. Whose life was she talking about?

Jori tapped her a few times on the shoulder and let go. "I hate it for you, but you can't—"

"You know I won't!" she snapped. Her hands shook. As though holding in a curse, she bit her bottom lip. "He didn't have to die," she said quietly.

"He didn't have to take over all those cities either," Jori replied.

Cold washed over him. All that planning, all those precautions, all the fear he had battled in the past months, and now this. It was dread come to life.

Firian fought his way to the surface of the Unreal, floundering for the first time in years.

His mind was full, too packed to fit another thought. He might be sick.

They're coming for me.

40

FIRIAN

FIRIAN ROLLED IN SWEAT-COVERED BLANKETS. He hadn't slept for two days. Gray light leaked in through the small, high window in his bedroom. Morning again.

Every time he lay down, his mind churned. On the edge of sleep, his heart raced. A dream might start and he'd jerk awake, afraid he was Lost in the Unreal. His muscles ached from tension.

Thirteen and a half days.

Kiria had shown only disappointment in him back in Archer's Point, not fear for his life. She hadn't known what was coming. She wasn't cunning or evil enough to hide something like this so well.

Assuming they didn't send their whole army, it would take about fourteen days to travel between Brithnem and the Academy. At worst, he had one day left. At best, twelve.

His chest constricted and he kicked violently against the blanket wrapped around his leg. Blood raced through his arms, his hands, his fingers, but it didn't feel like strength. It felt artificial, as though he could stand like a dangerous warrior, large against the backdrop of the Academy, glaring lightning, but then the slightest thing would make him fall.

Nausea welled up in him and he sat up, cradling his head in his hands.

He'd told Belik and Bard and all the others to get ready for an attack. Bard also knew that Kiria had voted against killing him, but he'd acted aloof ever since the victory at Archer's Point. It was like Sias Jairon all over again. Bard would be civil if he had to, but he didn't seek out games of Indisfate with Firian anymore. A silent protest.

Belik didn't care about Kiria's innocence in the plot when Firian told him. "It doesn't matter for our plans, does it?" he had snarled. They tripled the border patrol, taught the new soldiers maneuvers, and set one of Gerand's best *katah* students to reach out for the leaders' minds. They were ready.

But how much of that would matter if Brithnem sent the full force of their army, now detached from any other conflict?

They wouldn't. They wouldn't do that. It didn't make sense. Belik had to tell him this a few times. They were only after one man, the one who posed a threat.

In the half-light, he bared his teeth. He could be a threat if they wanted one.

So why was he worried? He'd trained his whole life for this moment. Naturally, conflict would come. He had known that the moment he opened the borders of Tánuil. He just hadn't thought it would come from *her*.

Why didn't she fight for him?

He played the conversation over and over. Kiria had voted against sending the army. But she also hadn't warned him. She voted the way she did because it would save soldiers, and because it was right. She didn't love him, or want him, or save him now.

Her image burned behind his eyes. He wanted to look at every detail of her: the woven gold belt around her waist, the line where her shoulder joined her neck, her gaze both sympathetic and commanding... He scrubbed his eyes with his fists until he saw bursts of light.

Firian couldn't live like this. He jumped out of bed, pulled on some clothes, and rushed out of the Head's suite of rooms. His heart knocked against his ribs as though he'd been running or holding his breath. He needed something to make his thoughts shut up. A plan. Anything.

When the soldiers come, we'll defeat them. I'll frighten any army from coming close, any nation from breaking an alliance with the Tanyu. And then I'll get Kiria back. I've done it before. I'll do it again.

Firian almost knocked someone over as he sped around a corner. It wasn't his guard.

"Oh, hey!" Bard cried as he moved out of the way.

"What are you doing here?" The jolt of adrenaline made the words cruel.

Bard's eyebrows got closer together for a moment. His black eyes, rimmed with lack of sleep himself, looked hurt and even reproachful. "I came to tell you that the *katah* isn't working. Gerand sent me to tell you. I don't think they brought anybody with the Talent."

So Kiria couldn't call them off. It would be harder for the Tanyu to sense them coming too.

Bard mused, "I've never heard of an army with nobody who touches the Unreal *at all*." He looked up at Firian. "Anything yet?"

"No." He wanted to tell him to go back to sleep. Bard loved sleep. But he couldn't. When they were attacked, Bard had to be awake or risk getting killed.

Firian shook his head rid himself of these thoughts. The soldiers weren't after Bard, and they wouldn't get inside the Academy. But still, for some reason, he *needed* Bard to be awake when the attack happened.

Bard tipped his chin and lowered his voice. No one was there to hear. Firian had the odd feeling that everyone else had left, that it was just the two of them in the massive Academy, left to fend for themselves. "The patrollers will let us know, yeah?" he said. "How much time will we have then?"

"Not much." Firian caught himself picking the skin around his Master ring and stopped.

Bard's uneasiness seemed to have more to do with the idea of taking lives than it did with the possibility of losing. An Academy full of Tanyu wouldn't lose.

They wouldn't lose. They weren't weak. Still, this felt far more frightening than going to Torith or getting Lost in the Unreal when Belik had gone to get him out. This gnawed at him in ways he could hardly explain to himself. These soldiers, when he pictured them, didn't look like the metal-plated palace guards or the soldiers he had fought alongside on the island. They looked like mountain ghosts he used to battle in his childhood imagination—impossibly strong, supernaturally driven, unbeatable. They could walk through walls and kill at a touch.

"You never told me what you wanted me to do," Bard said.

Hadn't he? Firian flipped through his memory. He'd spoken to almost every group, from the people of Raewhith, to the *katah* Masters, to the veterans of the War Zone and even the Watchman. Bard wasn't good in a fight; he was too compassionate. *Katah* wasn't working. Intelligence might suit him, but Firian had border patrollers and Belik for that. "Just stay with me," he said finally. "I'll be heading operations and... you'll stay with me. In case I need you for something."

Bard regarded him oddly, his face dark in the shadowed hallway. "You sure?" His piercing gaze asked questions that his mouth didn't. *Aren't you going out to fight? What do you really want me to do? Are you afraid?*

"Yeah, I'm sure."

FIRIAN SPLASHED his face with cold water from the basin in the washroom. He only closed his eyes the moment he threw the water, then opened them again.

Coming to this room required an act of will. He'd avoided it since that day in the tub. Before others were awake, he would go to the washroom on the second floor, down the hall from Bard's room, where he had once beaten Tiev. No one had hurt him there.

Jovan's ghost wasn't watching him, but the bones at the top of Firian's spine prickled as though it was. He often felt watched, but there were different kinds of watching.

Kiria had watched him, her eyes like a caress in his mind. There was the time patrollers had interrogated him to test his loyalty to the Academy—they had watched him too. Someone besides Belik had watched him when he was Lost in the Unreal. He still wasn't sure who that was.

Lately, though, the sensation had been like a haunting. As though the watcher were a predator and Firian prey. It was something unholy that made his guts writhe like a scaly creature. At least he'd managed a few hours of sleep last night. It wasn't much, but it was something.

The door behind him opened quietly. He whipped around, slicking off his face as he did.

A border patroller. He had a thick mustache and unevenly chopped short hair. Malto, was that his name?

"Master Kess," he said.

But before he could continue, Firian knew.

They're here.

"Get everyone in position!" Firian cried.

Malto didn't need another command. He hurried to carry out the plan Firian and Belik had ordered.

Firian practically ran out of the poisonous washroom. He felt each wet drop run from his hair down his chin, gather, and drip off.

Crown and swords. He ripped open the door to his office. Heartbeats pounded against his ribs and throat. The Head's crown was in his room next to the bed. He gripped it in his fist. For a moment it felt like a weapon. It could become one if he needed it to be.

Swords next. In a box at the end of the bed was a long sword and a mid-sized curved knife. He'd worn the looped sheaths every day since he'd overheard Kiria's conversation. He already had his boots on, with their compartment for a small, everyday knife. Three weapons. That was more than enough. He could use the crown, the walls, the sun, his legs, anything to fight if he had to.

His mind, if it came to that.

No one would touch him.

When he came out of his bedroom to the office, Bard was already there, all rumpled, breathing as though he had just run. A crease in his face showed how recently he had been asleep. "I'm here!"

Firian was breathing hard too. He couldn't settle down. He had to move, though Bard's presence did calm him a little. It meant that all the Tanyu were being alerted to the threat. Plenty of people to defend the Academy.

But he had never been the kind of person to stand by while others had a chance at glory. He itched to run out, to fight. *Damn these weapons.* He wanted to *feel* the struggle. His blood was high, his power was back, and he knew he would win.

Belik stumped in quickly behind Bard. "They're here," he growled without further greeting. "Tree line. Master Nedi has the Torithians in front, as we discussed. Other soldiers behind. Tanyuin volunteers surrounding."

The words sounded like music, every syllable in its place. Firian had come up with this plan, and it was time. Seeing Belik with his heightened energy caused a profound, almost unearthly calm to come over Firian. "Perfect."

He set his crown on his head. Now he was ready.

41

KIRIA

It was starting. Kiria could tell. It had been exactly fourteen days. The jarring sensation came that she had anticipated and dreaded. It wasn't the panic she had felt in Charäkhnem, though. It barely registered. If she hadn't been waiting for it, she might not have noticed. But now it took her out of her reverie.

She stood in the upper room of the Amiran Academy, looking up at the ribbed blue ceiling edged with gold, praying. She didn't exactly know how to pray. There were the prayers the Amir led during special occasions. She knew portions of the Scroll. The passage that Chetana referenced echoed over and over again in her mind. *God uproots the tyrant and blesses the one with mercy.* She wanted... what? She wanted the horrible ordeal to be over. She wanted it all to be a mistake, for the Kingdom soldiers never to find the Academy, for Firian to show them all mercy, for the small force of elite guards not to kill him, for there to be no bloodshed. But there would be.

She held her breath inside her ribs. Daelon sat beside her, studying the Scroll and making notes. He was so focused that it took her a while to catch his eye. When he noticed her holding his gaze, his mouth set in a resolute line. Almost imperceptibly, he nodded at her, in a gesture of solidarity. They were in this together. Daelon was more peaceful than his mother. Blood on either side would wound him, cause him to lift up prayers.

Kiria knelt beside him. He quickly stood and offered his chair. But right now she didn't feel like a Keeper. She felt like a woman who needed help. Sitting back on her heels, she whispered, "Daelon, how do you pray?"

A grim smile tugged on one side of his lips, crinkling his cheek. He helped her to her feet. There were a couple other Amir sitting quietly in corners of the holy place. He glanced at them quickly and then whispered back. "You know the prayers I taught you, My Keeper?"

She nodded. She remembered them, but she needed new prayers now.

He had to lean closer for her to hear. "Always begin with reverence." Daelon lived his whole life with reverence, so it didn't surprise her that this was his first piece of advice. "Acknowledge God's will above your own. He knows better than we do."

She prompted him to go on.

"That's all. Then speak as you would to a ruler." He gestured vaguely to himself and then to her.

Speak as though I'm Daelon speaking to me. "That's simple."

"Truth is often simple. It's just difficult."

His words hung in the air like heavy clouds, resonating inside her. She never should have kissed Firian. Cúron never should have ordered his death. Simple, but difficult.

She cast her mind north again. It was as though thinking of him and the Kingdom soldiers could protect them all. Her duty lay with all of them, with the simple but difficult truth that none of them deserved to die today.

Reverence came first, then submission. But when it came to the part when she could offer her request, she had no words at all.

KIRIA ALMOST ASKED if there was any news, but there couldn't be. The army hadn't taken a Watchman with them, or anyone else who could convey information that quickly.

She knew someone with the Talent who could give her the answer to that question. But as soon as she asked him, he would know they were coming. Moments flashed by when she wanted to give him the chance to defend himself. But it was too late now.

Prayers had helped—they were all she could do—but she still felt sick. At odd times her stomach would drop with the reminder that she would feel Firian's death. The knowledge made her not want to speak to anyone or appear in public spaces. If her response to his panic had been so violent, how would she react if he died? Would she scream? Collapse?

She couldn't risk it, so she stayed in her room. Cúron probably thought she was sulking. Maybe others did too. There were many, after all, who hated her because of her sympathy for the Tanyu. Those people would rejoice to see Firian's head on a stick. She swallowed something bitter.

She'd find a way to make this better. Her throat caught. *How can any of it be better?* Hot tears filled her eyes and spilled down her cheeks. She let the Beauty seep away, tingling back into her old skin, plain and real. Her hands balled in her lap reminded her of him. She always checked her hands to make sure they were plain in the Unreal. For all his selfishness, he thought her plain face was beautiful.

Sobs came hard and thick. She gulped air convulsively. Snot ran onto her chin. Pounding the blanket on her bed as hard as she could, she cursed him and mourned him at the same time. She understood him. In some ways, she *was* him. His darkness crept through her chest as well.

She sniffed horribly, rubbing away the tears from her eyes. More took their place so she left them.

"My god, are you all right?"

She looked up in time to see Jori set a bottle down on a table as he rushed over to her. She didn't answer.

He sat beside her and took her by both shoulders, peering into her eyes. "Are you sick?" He ran a hand over her forehead and through her hair. His touch soothed her enough to calm down.

"No." She hiccupped the word.

Understanding dawned. He bit his tongue lightly in a grimace. "Is it time, then?"

She nodded.

He hugged her sideways. "You'll make it through," he said. "There's life on the other side." Because he didn't usually talk about difficult things, even the trite words made it sound like he was trying. "Come on." He switched his manner abruptly. "Haved invited us to the garden. It's a good day for it."

"It's early," she said, eyeing the bottle.

"Ah, you have to spice up a picnic," he said, a mischievous grin spreading across his face.

She wanted a distraction, but his flippancy grated against her worry. "I can't."

He ignored her, looking off to a different point in the room. "You know, Haved is too good for Atty. She's really wonderful."

Kiria didn't agree with the first part, but she did agree with the second. "She is," she said.

"So how about a picnic?"

"Jori..."

His eyes darkened a little, the gray turning stormy. He pulled his legs onto the bed, suddenly looking more at home than she did. "You know I want you there, love, but if you have to wait and see then I'll struggle on alone."

"That's very good of you," she said, and sniffed again.

He spiraled out his legs and jumped off the bed. In an elegant twirl, he grabbed the bottle once more. "I hope you get what you're waiting for." The tinge of a challenge in his voice made her go cold.

Maybe she would go to the picnic. Maybe...

Even as she thought it, she knew she couldn't. Tomorrow. Once it was all over, whatever *it* was, she could go out.

Jori made for her again, as though he thought of something new, or else couldn't leave on such terms. "You know I hate to see you suffer." He patted her leg. "I'll send up a fruit tart. Never too early."

She gulped away more tears. "Thank you." She suspected that it would taste like nothing at the moment, but fruit tarts were her favorite, and Jori knew it.

He winked and went out, leaving her alone to await Firian's death.

42

FIRIAN

Tanyu rushed by like a flock of ravens, tucking weapons into boots and sleeves. The deadly flashes reminded Firian of sneaking out to the inn to see a Charäkhni traveler do slight-of-hand. Their silent feet beat out the rhythm of Firian's blood, charged and ready.

Bard followed him out into the fountain courtyard with its huge chandelier and terraced upper floor. The sprinting warriors disappeared down side passages so they could emerge unseen on their way to the battle.

Belik couldn't match Firian's pace, so he had stayed behind in the Head's office, ordering the counterattack from there. The fact that someone else commandeered the space would have bothered Firian on a normal day, but he was so eager to get out and see the Kingdom troops that he barely spared it a second thought. He couldn't have sat there through it all. Besides, if Firian appeared on the battlefield, and they still couldn't get to him, it would make the victory more delicious.

Firian and Bard passed alone through the massive double doors. Tánuil looked empty, except for the Sentries bustling from house to house, sounding the alarm for citizens to stay in their houses.

It was early, but no one slept. There was a wakefulness in the air as everyone waited for the fighting to move closer. Each muted scream and clash of ringing metal caused a thrill along Firian's bones. He felt Bard tense beside him.

The sense of blood and danger filled Firian's nose and made the hair rise on his arms. That same haunted feeling crept over him again, but it was different this time. Weakness didn't threaten his mind. His senses sharpened and muscles tensed. He felt big and visible in his black coat, as though he were a famed mountain ghost himself. Something to fear. And he was.

In the gray of the morning, standing on the earthen bridge to the Academy,

Firian could just make out figures moving along the tree line. Brown patroller outfits against blue. Black figures knew enough to stay hidden until it was time.

Between the Kingdom soldiers and the border patrollers, it seemed like a fair fight. Firian watched almost disinterestedly. *Is this it?*

"Let's get inside," Bard said in a low voice. He must have felt how visible they were too.

It was the smart thing to do, but it sounded boring, if not cowardly. Firian hesitated. Bard hit his arm. "They'll see you."

"I know." Curiosity kept him outside a moment longer, as though he were watching a simulation in Strategy. What would the Kingdom forces do next? This couldn't be their entire plan.

Belik's words from the day before came back to him. "It's likely that they'll bring a secondary force, divert your attention, and then attack."

A secondary force. He swept the panorama before him with his eyes, but saw no one else.

"Firian!" Bard whispered.

Restless, he followed Bard back into the Academy. Walking fast, he strode back to his office for more news. They passed a couple of Tanyu—Rian, Tesni, Ardal—who had been instructed to remain in the Academy. There weren't many guarding the interior.

The guard opened the Head's door for them without a word. Belik sat behind the desk, bent over papers as though he belonged there. Something inside Firian squirmed at the image.

"News?" Firian asked. Really, what he wanted was a fight. Man to man. To get this over with. The lack of action frayed his nerves.

"The army approached from the south, the most direct route." Belik's mouth twisted disapprovingly. "Border patrollers are handling it now. Tanyu will pick off any stragglers."

"And the secondary force?"

Belik cleaned his glasses and put them back on. "We haven't observed one, but it's probably there."

Firian ticked off entrances in his mind, as he had the past few nights when he couldn't sleep: main doors, kitchen deliveries, Jovan's back hallway…

"We have guards at every entrance," Belik said, meeting Firian's gaze.

"What about the windows?" Bard asked.

"Most of them aren't on the first level."

"Get people on it," Firian said. *Every window can be a door.* "I want every window watched."

The guard outside overheard and sprinted to carry out his command.

"Should I check?" Bard asked.

"The guard's doing it," Firian answered.

Belik's eyes flicked between the two of them in a question he didn't ask. "The soldiers won't get in," he said instead.

"Fir, have you… talked to them?" Bard asked seriously. "Found out what they really want?"

Into the Unreal

"Me!" Firian retorted. Bard knew that already. What was he playing at?

"I mean, can you call off the fighting and try to negotiate something?"

"They're past negotiation," Belik muttered, looking back at his papers.

Firian opened and closed his hands. He didn't want strategy or maps or planning or talk right now. He wanted action. The Kingdom might not expect him to go out into the open and join the fray. *So what if I'm the person they're fighting to protect? Everyone fights to protect themselves.* Maybe they thought he'd stay here in this cramped room instead.

The thought made him claustrophobic. "I'm going out."

"Don't be a fool," Belik said quickly.

Bard nodded in rare agreement.

"I can't just stay here," Firian said, turning toward the door.

"You *will*."

Firian glared at Belik. The Master was wise, had practiced strategy for longer than Firian had been alive, but he was not Firian's father nor superior. Belik had no authority over him.

Without a word, Firian swept out of the room with Bard trailing after him. If there was a second force out for his life, he'd find them.

Only a few steps out of the office, Bard spoke up. "Fir, I think this is too obvious. We're underestimating them."

Firian slowed to walk beside him. "What do you mean?"

"They're coming from the south. That's too obvious. It's not the best place to attack from anyway, you know?"

It wasn't, but Belik hadn't seemed surprised. Bard looked uncharacteristically serious as they continued through the hall, inspecting each of the exterior doors and windows. Remembering Kiria's arrow wound, Firian scanned every corner high and low as they moved.

Bard's eyes darted to and fro. It was the same look he had while playing Indisfate. His mouth fell open. "The Sentries!"

Firian checked for the horrible current Sentries created to block the Unreal, but there wasn't a hint of it. "What about them?"

"You made the Sentries Watchmen."

Firian tried to put the pieces together, getting impatient now. "Yes. So?"

"They must have communicated with the army."

"The Sentries are loyal to me." Even as he said it, he felt a prickle of shame. What if he was wrong?

"Yeah, yeah," Bard said quickly. "They are."

"And these soldiers don't have the Talent. You told me."

"Yeah. But the Sentries didn't know about the plan to attack beforehand, when the Kingdom could have asked about the Academy." Bard reached out and touched Firian's shoulder, spinning him around to face him. "The Sentries... their underground tunnel. It leads into the Academy. It has to, or else what was that fire for? Isn't there a—"

But Firian was already running. There was another entrance, if it could be called that. A narrow passage led from the Sentries' prison to the furnace and tribute stores beneath the main level. Bard followed close behind. Firian could count on one hand the number of times he'd been to the vault, even as Head.

The staircase led down from the hallway that held Firian's office and the cursed washroom. How had he not thought of this before?

As they passed his rooms again, he cracked open the door. "Get out," he told Belik. "Go to Jovan's room." There was a guard already stationed down that hallway, as well as an exit if he needed to run. Though he'd never seen it, Firian doubted Belik could fight half as well as the others with his bad leg.

He heard the soft, stumping footsteps leaving in the other direction as he and Bard approached the tiny staircase. Kingdom soldiers put themselves at a disadvantage here too. Without the element of surprise, they trapped themselves. And there was always a guard for the tribute. Maybe Bard was wrong.

The unmistakable sound of metal against metal filtered up the stairs, followed by a keening groan. He cut a glance at Bard, then at the hall leading back to the courtyard, where most of the reserve Tanyuin forces waited. *Get the others*, he instructed wordlessly. Bard understood instantly and sprinted off.

Firian unsheathed the curved knife at his waist and spread his legs, waiting for the first soldier to show himself coming up the stairs. His heart pounded, keeping time in a violent trance. Though his body acted afraid, he didn't feel afraid. Certainty calmed him. They were coming in through the Sentries' entrance.

No one appeared. If the soldiers really had killed the guard, then they'd have had plenty of time to reach the staircase by now. Why weren't they coming up?

He stilled, breathing slowly, feeling every vibration in the floor, listening for every sound.

Movement caught his attention. A strange mix of pride and concern churned in him at the sight of Bard leading a column of Tanyu, most of those that remained in the fortress. Rian took fewer strides with his long limbs, Tesni's braid waved behind her, and Ardal the World Events Master had a short and stocky frame that made him almost invisible as he moved through the rest.

Firian pointed down the stairs.

Ardal nodded curtly, going first. Tesni went next, grim as death. Others followed carefully but without hesitation. Bard shifted on his feet, staying beside Firian as he had promised. Furtive sounds of fighting came through the space.

Fire burned in Firian's veins. Unable to hold himself back any longer, he plunged down the steps.

Only a few torches lit the space. It felt hot and suffocating, not as bad as the Sentries' dungeon, but the sensation was too close to be comfortable. Most of the treasure stores lay behind locked doors, so the large chamber's floor was usually unobstructed. Figures moved in the gloom. Flames reflected against metal armor and blades. It was as though half the Tanyu had disappeared, melted into black shadows.

Perched on the last step, Firian scanned the fight. Three Kingdom soldiers lay on the ground and no Tanyu. About twenty opponents. The Tanyu were making quick work of the small force, lashing out like vipers, cracking necks, stabbing eyes and armpits and anywhere else the armor was weak.

Into the Unreal

The appearance of Firian on the stairs galvanized the Kingdom soldiers when they saw him. They doubled their efforts, fighting more savagely than before.

"Hey!" Rian yelled. A Kingdom soldier holding him in a chokehold. Flinging himself backward, Rian crushed his attacker into the stone wall behind him. A torch rattled in its holder. When the soldier kept fighting, Rian smashed him again.

Sounds on the stairs made Firian turn. The darkened stairwell filled with faces and weapons. "Block them!" Firian ordered, jumping down.

Tanyu whirled at the coming forces.

More soldiers came, not just from one side, he realized, but from both. More troops crawled through the Sentry opening at the same moment soldiers flowed in down the stairs.

They must have already snuck into the Academy before they figured out the plan. Firian's blood ran cold, then hot.

They were surrounded. Firian stood in the center of fighting and blood, trapped in this underground room. Rage coursed through him. He had let this happen. The ploy was so obvious. He never should have ordered so many of the reserve Tanyu to the same place. Only Belik, new recruits too young to fight, and a few guards weren't in the fray. Unless Bard had set aside some Tanyu for other purposes, everyone else was here.

There were too many Kingdom soldiers coming through both entrances to block them completely. They crawled like bugs out of holes. The small space became stiflingly full of bodies.

As he called in the Unreal to the nearest guards to come help, a soldier muscled past Rian, who still battled, and rushed at Firian sword first.

Firian whipped out his curved knife and met the blade on its way to him, forcing it around and down. Bringing it sharply up again, he sheared the sword hand off. The man screamed, a terrible sound. Firian silenced it. Dark blood slicked the floor.

The Tanyu could outlast them. He knew it in his bones. Guards were coming to deal with any soldiers in plain sight in the hallway. It was a short staircase, so they just needed to empty it. He jumped toward two men coming at him, almost glad. The walls, the floor, the blind tunnel, the tightly packed bodies, the knives... All weapons. All pieces in a game.

The Tanyu drove the Kingdom soldiers back in both directions, black against silver and blue, vicious, relentless, forward, barreling the men backward into their companions. A flash of eye whites. Airless pressure filled the room as they pushed them back, getting heavier as more bodies were added. Boots crushed over the slippery obstacles of dead soldiers.

Were Tanyu dead too? Firian couldn't look around but he thought he saw a pile of black clothes from the corner of his eye. He didn't take out his sword. It was too long for such close-quarters fighting. The curved knife felt right.

Jumping up using the neck of a man's armor for leverage, he kicked off the wall to get above the fray. As he landed, he flung his knife in a wide arc that sliced through two man leaping down the steps. They fell with the others, choking and reaching futilely for his wounds.

Firian took a breath and realized that he didn't see any more people coming down the steps toward them. Craning his neck to see up, he spotted the dark figure of a Tanyu further up the stairs. A drop of sweat fell from his neck as he turned it. They'd cleared the stairs.

Now the Tanyu had one side of the room, and the Kingdom the other. An eerie quiet settled over them all, save for the sputtering torches and the panting of fighters. The rank, coppery smell of blood assaulted him through the heat. Firian shot a glance to the side. He saw five Tanyu with him: Bard, Rian, Tesni, Ardal, and Makai. Bard was shaking. He had a small knife in his hand.

Were the others alive?

It would matter later. Not now.

He scanned the room. No one else was coming in through the tight opening to the Sentries' furnace. Six against at least forty.

His mind whirred, cycling through strategies. Could they leave them here and set the room on fire? Was it too late to send Tanyu to the Sentry entrance in the woods? He pictured himself coursing forward at impossible speeds, impaling them all cleanly in one motion. But this wasn't the Unreal.

A Kingdom soldier stepped forward. One hand held a sword and the other was raised in a gesture of truce. "We only want Master Kess!" the man announced.

A bland, false quiet fell. Hearts beat in chests. Hands tensed around sword hilts.

Firian snarled, scanning the room full of people again. So many, all poised to kill. No one had sheathed their weapon. Their stances said clearly that they wanted to kill all the Tanyu. Firian peeled back his lips in a grimacing, defiant smile.

The Tanyu wouldn't give him up. Fear and loyalty prevented them. Nobody answered the man. Firian ran his thumb along the side of the knife blade.

The speaker stepped closer, one hand still raised, a moving figure among statues. His face was smeared with dirt and sweat, his expression diplomatic.

Firian tensed as the man took another small movement forward, approaching him as he would a cornered cat. The hairs on the back of Firian's neck stood up. Two of the men behind the spokesman edged forward too, their boots sloshing against shallow pools of blood.

Why was everyone pausing? Why weren't they protecting him? They said the purpose of this assault was to kill him, only him. The man tightened his grip on his sword. Close enough now to strike...

"We just want—"

Firian swung hard, slashing the man across the chest and shearing off his hand. Blood spurted across Firian's chest and face. He spat as the room erupted into chaos.

Kingdom soldiers charged. Rian screamed and rushed headlong toward them.

Two Kingdom soldiers ran forward, already too close when they emerged from the storm of battling bodies. They filled Firian's vision.

Bard jumped forward, blocking him.

Something in Firian snapped. "Get behind me!" he roared, shoving Bard sideways. "Get behind me!"

Into the Unreal

He risked closing his eyes. The soldiers could slice his flesh at any moment. Quickly, down, down...

He reached out, saw them all. So many... Could he do it?

He let go of the urgency, his imminent death, his fear for others, everything but the beating hearts and brains in front of him. With measured breaths, he leveraged all his strength, all the burning power of the Unreal sucked inward like it had done with Tiev years ago, a pillar of light and intensity, enough to destroy, to shred, to blast to skeletons...

Then, with all the life he had, he burst like a firestorm over them all, breaking as he went.

He was death itself.

In the Second Level, he watched them fall, all of them, ruined from the inside. They broke one by one like huge black branches overcome by a crushing tidal wave. The roar of it—was it a real sound?—thundered in his ears.

Firian had barely opened his eyes when the ground rose sideways to crash into the side of his head. As he fell in a mangled heap, the wave of darkness took him too.

43

FIRIAN

The first thing Firian knew after losing consciousness was walking slowly down a hallway. Everything ached. His body was a bruise. At first it felt like dreaming, a nightmare, but the details were too real, crawling over him like insects.

The stiffness and sheen of his pant leg crusted with dried blood. The scuffling of feet as more Tanyu behind him took away bodies. The sweat that beaded in his eyebrow and dripped into his eye. The pulsing headache that made him acutely, terrifyingly aware of each blood vessel in his skull.

How did I get here?

Stone walls passed by in a blur. Hands stronger than his own gripped his elbows on both sides, guiding him forward.

His head weighed almost too much to turn. The effort made him squint. On one side, Master Ardal, with blood plastering his hair down near his ear. He cast a grim eye toward Firian. Looking to the side made him dizzy, but he needed to know who held his right arm too.

Bard.

Blinking sweat out of his eyes, Firian blew out a shaky breath. Bard was alive. He was too tired to smile, almost too tired to stand. Were they all safe now?

Images of the soldiers falling around him set emotions bubbling like a cauldron. How many had he killed? How could he not know them all? An urgent, childish urge to count, to look into their faces and ask their names, almost sent him running down into the storerooms.

Were the Tanyu all right? He had an odd feeling that he had murdered everyone, including himself, and he almost started crying. His eyes felt like hot stones. Tears probably couldn't come from them. Still, he wouldn't have had the strength to stop if another memory hadn't taken its place.

Perfect, fiery power shooting like liquor through his veins. He had stared at an army and taken it down. He had known he could kill them all. He'd wanted to drink that liquor until he burst, but it left him sick.

Heavy exhaustion threatened to crush him. He just had to lie down. The Academy was safe. Bard, Belik...

Still covered in blood, Firian wearily pushed open the door to his office. His fingers trembled against the handle as though someone were shaking him. His muscles strained against the weight of the door. Ardal pushed it open with him and then let him go in alone.

No, not alone. Bard guided him inside. He knew he was leaning on Bard enough to strain him, but at least it was no one else.

In the empty office, Bard let go of his arm. Firian righted and steadied himself, his head pulsing, legs shaky.

Despite the exhaustion and pain, he sensed something dark lingering between them. Bard's black eyes narrowed and his chest heaved as he stood in the middle of the room, more than it should from the strain of helping him. A crackling in the air told Firian that he was there to advise, to criticize something he did.

"Not now," he slurred, moving toward the room where comfort, or at least unconsciousness, awaited him. He could wash the blood off in the morning.

"Fir. It has to be now." Steel wove through Bard's tone. His words were soft, but there was a strength, an urgency, that Firian had never heard from him before.

Firian turned, unreasonably angry. He summoned his energy. "What can't wait?" he asked, separating each murderous word. The pit of his stomach constricted with the knowledge of those he had just killed. He breathed in deeply through his nose and let the air out through gritted teeth.

Even from the opposite side of the room, Firian saw that Bard swallowed, his Adam's apple bobbing. His hands were fists at his sides. "You.... How could you?"

"Did what I had to." He had seen it all. Why did he ask?

"No. No..." Bard shook his head. He looked taller, somehow. "You... didn't have to do any of that."

"They were attacking us!" Firian's face grew hotter. He caught the door jamb to his bedroom to steady himself.

"They stopped! Maybe they would have talked, I don't know. You didn't have to kill them all. And Rian...!"

Rian. So he had killed a Tanyu. Furious shame almost made him vomit. He couldn't stand here another minute.

"And it's not just this. It's the Sentries, and Master Jairon, and Archer's Point." He was breathing hard, but he caught himself. He shuddered back into stillness. "You were like family to me!" Tears welled in Bard's eyes.

Firian caught the past tense. He gripped the doorpost harder.

"Like a brother, Fir." Bard's voice caught and he lowered it. "I want to stand by you. But I can't."

Firian brought his voice low too. "What are you saying?"

"You can't keep doing this. You can't."

"What—?"

"You're a monster, Firian."

His breath stopped. *A monster.* The word stuck, covering him, oozing into his lungs. Bard would turn on him too? His best friend? But he saved him. He'd done this *for him.*

Flashes of the attack came back to him. Faces smashed against the floor. An arm flung at a weird angle over a torch bracket. His own arm twisted underneath him where he fell. Blood pooling on the ground and dripping from stairs. Wild, bleeding eyes left open. He weighed as much as a boulder, couldn't sit upright. His body hurt wherever people touched it to raise him. Foggy layers of horror.

Firian's face felt like wax and his heart beat faintly under thick layers of his body muting the sound.

Bard, stronger now, looked into his eyes with resolve. Tears trailed down both sides of his face.

"Get out," Firian whispered.

Bard breathed shakily, even his fists trembling. "You have to—"

"Get. Out." Firian felt a black abyss under him as he said it.

After a beat, Bard nodded. "Yeah, I know." As though dragging a weight, he turned toward the door. Firian watched him step off the carpet, reach for the door handle, open the door. Time moved sluggishly, pounding in time to the pain in his skull.

Bard looked back once. His forehead creased with anger or disappointment. "I wanted to stay."

Firian didn't reply as Bard disappeared and shut the door behind him.

44

KIRIA

Kiria stared at her lyra, but no music came to her. The pain had subsided, but it still racked her whole body with a dull ache.

For hours she'd sat, waiting, knowing that any second...

The stabbing knowledge of Firian's pain had struck more quickly than she expected. She'd tensed, bracing herself for the pain to pitch higher and higher. Maybe she should have called for a doctor.

If only she'd understood the depth of Firian's ambition sooner. She knew what he was, of course, but what if there were something she could have done to prevent this? The thought echoed loudly as it would in a hollow room, again and again. No one could blame her for her grief. She'd chosen the Kingdom above Firian. Even above herself.

"Petra Madola," a guard announced.

Kiria, tired from the ache, looked up to see him opening the door for the military strategist. The tall woman walked forward swiftly and bowed to her. She was clad all in armor as though she were a guard herself.

"My Keeper," she greeted. "I bring news from the Watchman."

Kiria knew what it would be. The only question now was who they put in place of Firian.

"The removal of the Tanyuin Head has been unsuccessful."

Kiria sat up, confused, shocked. "What?"

Petra inclined her head. "All our troops were killed."

"No... they couldn't have been."

"I'm afraid so, My Keeper. We're holding another session today to debate our response."

Kiria put her fist over her mouth. How could this be happening? If Firian was alive, then what pain had she felt? *All* of their soldiers? "How did the Watchman get the news?"

"The young man with the supplies apparently ran to the nearest unoccupied city."

She couldn't think. It didn't make sense. She hadn't known what to hope for, but it wasn't this.

"I will see you in the Main at midday, if My Keeper can attend," said Petra.

"I'll be there," Kiria replied, her mind still spinning.

"My Keeper, Atael Calthwaite," said the guard at her door.

Petra bowed and exited as Atty entered. He wore a simple buttoned tunic, not like his royal robes. His hair was mussed. When he reached the bed where Kiria sat, he turned and indicated that the guards should shut the door. They did.

"Did you hear?" she asked.

"I did." His brows furrowed deep. He didn't look at her. "Just now."

Something was wrong besides the defeat at the Academy. Something that had to do with her.

He paced a couple times. She waited, unsure of what else to do. The blackness of Firian's pain still flowed unevenly through her mind. It wasn't as acute now. He was alive. Just like last time. The loss of soldiers left her little space to be glad.

"Did you tell him? Did he know?" Atty said quickly, his words slurring a little.

"What do you mean?"

He looked into her eyes. The fear and aggression there took her aback. "Did you warn that Tanyu we were coming?"

She went cold. "Who told you that?"

"Just answer the question, please. I hope you didn't."

Jori told her secret. The knowledge left her a little more broken than before. "No, I didn't," she said clearly.

"Are you still... Were you ever seeing him? Secretly?" Coming from him, the idea sounded ludicrous.

"Not now," she said. "How did you know?"

He pursed his lips. "Haved told me."

"Haved?" The surprise brought her to her feet. She had never told Haved her secret. The only people who knew—she *thought*—were Jori and Chetana, and Firian himself. "What did she say?"

"She heard you and Jori talking about it." He looked away for a moment at his brother's name, as though he felt betrayed or left out.

"I didn't warn him," Kiria repeated.

"You've been in your room all day. Nobody's seen you."

Kiria's fingers started to go numb. Atty didn't believe her. Her breath felt shallow, barely filling her chest. Ever since he became a Keeper, she'd sensed him drifting away from her, but it was just his responsibilities, his busyness, his insecurities that drove him to Cúron. She understood all that, and adjusted. Now, though, he didn't believe her.

She couldn't explain why she wanted to be alone. It wouldn't make sense to someone without the Talent that she still had a connection to Firian even though she didn't go to the Unreal to see him anymore.

"I'm telling the truth," she said. "I'm not lying to you."

"But you didn't tell me about you and the Tanyu before."

"It was..." She sighed in frustration. "You didn't need to know at the time. I didn't tell anybody. Please don't tell anyone else, Atty."

He leaned against the wall by the headboard and crossed his arms, regarding her as he would a stranger.

"I'm still me," she said, guilt settling behind her ribs. She touched his arm, willing him to understand. "And I *didn't* tell him we were coming. I don't know how we lost."

Atty still stood impassive. "Why didn't you come out this morning?"

She could lie. She could say she was sick. "I was waiting for him to die," she said quietly.

Atty pulled away from the wall and drew his eyebrows together. His forehead wrinkled with confusion. "What? What do you mean?"

"I could tell." Her voice was a whisper now. Embarrassment and sadness wouldn't allow her to speak any other way. "I don't see him in the Unreal, the space in our minds, anymore, but I'm able to feel when he gets seriously hurt. Did... did Haved tell you about Charäkhnem? When I panicked?" She knew the answer before she finished the question.

He nodded.

"He was almost killed right then. I didn't know what was happening until later. It was *his* panic."

Atty drew a knuckle over his stubble, digesting her words. "So you can read his mind?"

"Not exactly."

"Can he read your mind?"

She paused. "Sometimes. I think so. Only sometimes."

His gaze pinned her where she stood. "He knew we were coming." His voice grew stronger now, accusatory. If he hadn't been pointing this intensity at her, she would have been proud of how Keeper-like he was.

Was he right? Could Firian have read her mind? She hadn't sensed him there since Atty's wedding, and she could usually tell when he waited in the Unreal. She hadn't told him, but what Atty suggested wasn't impossible. She felt sick.

"I didn't tell him." She could barely get the words out. The protest sounded feeble now.

"I know you wanted to wait until we had more information before attacking. I did too. But these were our people. They're dead now."

"I know!" Her chin trembled with anger and sadness. If Atty felt betrayed, now so did she.

"You said you can tell if he gets hurt," Atty said after a pause. "Did he get hurt?"

It felt like a test. "Yes."

"Will you tell them about your connection to him at the session?"

She took a few breaths. Atty was prodding an open wound. Maybe he didn't know how much he was hurting her.

She didn't answer. She didn't know.

"Kiria," Atty sighed, suddenly younger again. "It's the right thing to do."

He knew that mattered to her. Despite her indiscretions, she wanted to do what was right. She wanted to be good, but she failed over and over again. No wonder Cúron tried to get more done on his own. He had experience, and Kiria kept making the wrong choices for herself, for Brithnem...

"If you don't tell them, I'll have to do it," he said. He lifted his chin as though convincing himself to follow through.

"Please don't." Her heart was in her throat. If everyone knew about her connection with Firian, they might not trust her again. Not after so many had died.

"I have to." He started backing toward the door.

"Please."

He stopped, almost drooping with exasperation and disappointment. That tired look he'd had before Haved crept back in gray shadows over his face. "Kiria, why did you do this at all?"

The question felt painful coming from him, happy in his love for Haved. She couldn't explain. Not to him. She stood silent.

He tipped his mouth, not saying anything either. Instead, he left.

KIRIA'S MOUTH felt dry as Atty took his place on the throne to her left. Today's agenda was to figure out what to do about the Academy now that their attempt to unseat Firian had been unsuccessful. There was no reason for him to tell her secret, that she'd had a secret relationship with Firian. That was all over now. Though it hurt terribly, she hadn't warned Firian about the soldiers. She had chosen the Kingdom over him. To drag her secret out now would damage her reputation for years, if not for her entire reign. If Cúron found out about it, it wouldn't be from her.

The atmosphere was solemn. So many good soldiers. All dead. Their memory filled the room as though their corpses were present.

Parohim opened the session with a prayer for the dead. Daelon followed with a passage from the Scroll. Reynard completed the Amiran contribution by another prayer for guidance.

After that, Cúron, as usual, began. "As you all know," he said, addressing the small crowd, "our campaign against the Tanyuin Head has failed."

In her peripheral vision, Kiria saw Atty chewing his cheek.

"News has reached us that even the one who survived to give us the message passed away a short while later." He bowed his head in silent remembrance.

A fresh wound of sadness sliced into her, as she pictured the young face that she might have seen in the garden, training with the guards.

"What remains is to react," he continued. "With all our soldiers killed, it is clear that the Tanyu are no longer our allies." He didn't acknowledge Kiria, but most of the people at the foot of the dais did. "They are clearly against us. We know where the Academy lies, and we know, although they have more soldiers at their disposal than they did, that their forces are still small compared to ours."

Kiria felt empty, the wood of the throne hard under her arms, biting into bone.

"But a smaller force can still succeed if they have better information," Atty said, bold yet hesitant.

She looked at him. *Please don't. Don't do this.* He returned her look like an apology.

"Very true," said Cúron. Kiria breathed again when his gaze didn't cut to hers.

She scanned the little crowd. Chetana briefly met her eyes. The touch was enough to let Kiria know her thoughts. Chetana probably suspected the same thing Atty did, that she had told Firian everything. Did no one trust her?

"Considering the destruction of our last force, we will have to create an entirely new plan, and send greater forces, if we want a guarantee of success."

Kiria nodded, trying to look engaged. Trying to look as though she weren't petrified that Atty would shatter any confidence the Kingdom still had in her.

Parohim spoke up from below. "Is there any evidence that the Tanyuin Academy plans to attack us here in Brithnem?"

A murmur from the crowd. They had wondered the same thing. Would more people die in their sleep, as they had last winter?

Petra Madola answered, "No direct evidence at the moment, but given their reputation as mercenaries, I doubt that they'll let this statement go unanswered for long. We only just smoothed over the last war with them."

"Lady Kiria could find out for us." Atty again.

She couldn't swallow, though she tried. Everyone watched her expectantly. Some of them knew she had the Talent, at least. "I can see what I can find out," she said.

"You could ask the Tanyuin Head," Atty pressed.

A marked interest angled in her direction. She froze. Some of them knew about her spying during the first war, knew she had the Talent and had communicated with Firian, or at least watched him. "Yes." She cleared her throat. "I watched him for information during the war. I could do the same thing again."

"But he watched you as well," Cúron said. "Would the same thing happen again?"

When I couldn't come to any of the sessions? She hoped not. "I don't... think so."

Cúron turned back to his audience. "But the question remains, what will we do? The Tanyu might strike now or later, but it seems very likely that they will strike. We cannot give them that opportunity."

"Kiria." It was barely a whisper. Atty.

She didn't respond.

Petra said something about numbers and maneuvers or something like that, but Kiria wasn't paying attention. Her own thoughts and blood beat in her ears too loudly.

"Excuse me," Atty said, standing. "I'm not sure that Lady Kiria should be at this session."

Her arm shook against the hard armrest. She dug her short fingernails into the wood to ground herself.

Atty looked at Cúron before he continued, as a son would a father. "She could alert the Tanyuin Head about our plans."

"I'm sure she wouldn't—" Cúron began indulgently.

"I think that's how the Academy knew about our plans today." He lisped the s's, the only clear evidence of how uncomfortable he was sharing this information about her. He, like her, chose the Kingdom over companionship. He thought he was doing the right thing. She was a traitor and he was their savior. He might as well have stabbed her. She could barely breathe around the lump in her throat, much less speak. If Firian learned about their approach from her, it wasn't intentional.

A hush fell like a smothering blanket on everyone in the Main.

Finally, she said, "I would never tell them." She hated the weakness and hesitation in her voice. The sound made the whole picture real, as if remaining silent could have frozen the moment and prevented it from moving into reality. Tears sprang into her eyes.

Atty continued, sounding choked up as well. "It's the only explanation for how things went."

She mouthed his name, pleading.

Atty tore his eyes away from hers. "She was in her room all morning, and the Tanyu were clearly ready for us. This was no surprise attack."

Warm tears fell freely down her face now. She stood beside him. "I didn't tell them!"

He turned back to her, his eyes tired and mournful. "But you care about the Tanyuin Head. You didn't want him killed."

"No, but I would never betray the Kingdom."

"He knew we were coming." The softness in his voice almost broke her.

Their soldiers were all dead, and it was her fault.

She couldn't answer for a moment. Steely anger rose up in her slowly, starting from her fingers and feet. "How could you accuse me of treason? Because that's what you're suggesting. I said that I would never betray the Kingdom. I vowed it. Do you not believe me?"

"He knows your thoughts. You meet him in the Unreal. You love him."

Again, he stunned her to silence. She wasn't sure which accusation to deny, if she could deny any with certainty. Every second that passed sealed the destruction of her reputation. As surely as if it were a piece of fabric burning, she felt each strand frayed end eaten away like smoke.

"Is this true?" Cúron asked.

She had almost forgotten he was there. She and Atty might as well have been alone. Her stomach turned over itself.

"I don't meet him now, and I didn't warn him about our attack," she said with all the strength she could muster. "I swear." She held up a hand and cast her eyes up to the Scroll passage etched on the ceiling.

After an awkward pause, Cúron said, "We'll adjourn the rest of this meeting until tomorrow."

Now that her secret was out, they didn't want to continue with her in the room. Somehow it was worse that they knew after the relationship was over, when she could feel the full brunt of her mistake.

She cared about Firian, still did, but she had known his ambition was bigger than any feelings he had for her. She knew he was dangerous. That was one of the reasons she liked him. She wasn't proud of it, or herself, but at least she could own up to the truth.

She looked at Atty one more time before stepping off the platform. He looked back with love in his eyes. She loved him too, but he had broken their friendship. It could never be as it was before. He had ruined her.

45

FIRIAN

"Sit up," said a voice above him, brusque but not unkind.

Firian angled his arms so he could push himself up without opening his eyes. The blanket and pillow were damp with sweat. At the movement, his head swam. The room tilted when he pried open his eyes.

"That's it. Have this."

Firian took the cup of water Belik offered him. He brought it to his clammy lips. The cold liquid made him shiver. Had water always been so tasteless? It was as though his senses were heightened and dulled at the same time. He was always *feeling*—the weave of the blanket, the ache of his bones, the piercing light in his eyes—but some of his senses had left him completely. Time, for example. He had no idea how long he'd lain there. It had to have been more than a couple days.

At least Belik was taking care of things in his absence. Firian hated being useless, but he had no choice now.

After a few sips of water, the room stopped spinning so much. He rested his back against the headboard as he looked at Belik. The Master's presence scared away the monsters in his mind, so a weak wave of thankfulness came over him.

Belik's mouth flattened in a smile as he regarded Firian through his glasses. "The doctor says you'll live," he said.

Firian didn't reply.

"That was quite a performance. I'm surprised you'll pull through. But you were always strong." His tone was fatherly.

Firian let the words wash over him like a balm.

You're a monster, Firian.

Those words had repeated, echoing through his skull through all the long nights of his illness. *A monster, a monster, a monster...* Bard could be fearful, but he was rarely wrong, especially about him. But Belik knew him too. He was one on a very short list of people who understood him, at least better than others. And Belik thought he was strong, not a gory monster.

He wished he could hate Bard, curse him for those words, but he couldn't. When Firian thought of that day, he felt shame, not hatred. Shame and sadness were worse than hatred, but he couldn't make himself feel any differently.

"Of course the Kingdom isn't happy about it." Belik breathed a mocking laugh through his nose. "There was a riot yesterday. Nothing serious, just a few broken windows and enough to scare the princess and her friends."

"Riot?" In his feverish state, Firian couldn't piece together why there would be rioting in Brithnem.

Belik brightened at his response. Firian wondered again how long he'd been lying in bed, feverish, clinging to life. "The alliance," Belik said. "The princess. Something about how she's pro-Tanyu."

Keeper, not princess. He kept back the retort to save his energy. Instead, he shook his head. She wasn't on the side of the Tanyu, not since their last meeting.

Belik raised an eyebrow, reading Firian's face.

"Some people want Merian back in power," Belik continued. "Fine by me. She never did a gory thing."

Firian held the cup tighter. He couldn't help thinking that Kiria would agree with what Bard had said before he left for Enderin.

"Either way," Belik continued, "it doesn't take a genius to figure out war's coming again."

Dropping his eyes, Firian felt the uncomfortably slimy sensation of wet sheets on his legs. Nausea welled up in his throat, went back down.

Belik jabbed his arm lightly with a blunt finger. "You did what you had to do. Few casualties." He meant Tanyu. "But Brithnem isn't happy. They'll come again, now." He paused and pulled on his earlobe thoughtfully. "And I can't ask you to do this again. It isn't practical."

And I'd probably die.

"When you're up, we need to talk about a counter-strike. It's the only way to get the upper hand here. Offense, not defense."

What would Bard say to this? Normally, Firian had two voices, even though so much input often annoyed him. Attack Brithnem? Is that what Belik was suggesting? It was much larger than anything they had overtaken before. They had more soldiers. They had Kiria...

At the thought of her, his whole body ached again. He was losing everyone. Her presence was like medicine. If she held him like she had done before, he would heal. His need almost overwhelmed him.

For a second he forgot what Belik was talking about.

War. That was it.

He looked dully back at his mentor. Time had little relevance right now. Surely he could sleep and think and no time would pass. Or he could reach out to Kiria and avoid war altogether. Slowly he brought the cup to his lips again and nodded.

"You know your little friend left," Belik said.

"Don't go after him," Firian rasped. Hopefully no one had been sent to track him down already. In his delirium, the possibility hadn't crossed his mind.

"I know. You two had a connection or something. Where did he go?" Belik's casual tone revealed more interest than it hid.

Home. Firian didn't say the word. Belik hadn't promised to leave Bard alone. Even if he had, his promises twisted too often into lies. Bard didn't deserve to have Belik go after him for disloyalty. Disloyalty wasn't the right term anyhow. How could Bard ever be disloyal?

"You don't know?"

But Firian was done talking.

Belik hummed and stood, favoring his good leg. "I'll be back tomorrow," he said. "You look like shit." Then he smiled and walked out.

46

KIRIA

Kiria laid her palm on the new glass pane. She stood by a potted *sachion* tree, half hidden from anyone who might walk through the wide palace hallway. The glass was cool against her hand. It looked clearer than the other smudgy panes, criss-crossed with black metal.

How could she lead a nation if the people didn't trust her?

Atty had done what he thought was right. It's what his father Aylmor would have done. Atty thought she was a threat to security, and he had always cared about safety, even more than she did. Kiria, at least when she was younger, took risks that made him shudder.

Firian was one risk she never should have taken. How else could the Tanyu have known that they were coming and had time to prepare? She was the weak link. Her face felt hot and she laid her forehead against the glass.

Days before, the window had been shattered by protesters. Rioters were a better name. People of Brithnem had reminded her of the crazed mob at King's Heights, shouting her name, throwing any hard object they could find. Finally, guards had to put them down, disperse the crowd. The memory still seared.

They hadn't screamed for anyone else. Only her. She was the enemy.

Looking through the window, she saw the green lawn sloping down through manicured hedges to the main streets into the city. Almost out of sight, her favorite statue peeked above the stone buildings. *People need to remember their heroes...* Her own voice came back to her like something out of a dream. Then she remembered when she had said those words, or something like them.

"You keep talking about doing good. What will you do when you're the Keeper?"

She had told him. A good beginning, he had called it.

"You only live one time. You get one shot. Is that what you're going to do with it? Or do you have the courage to do what isn't safe?"

It certainly seemed like she'd wasted her time as a Keeper ever since ending the two wars. Here she was on the brink of a new one, and this time it was her fault. She breathed in the clean scent of the tree beside her. She couldn't do this.

Where was Daelon? He was her new advisor and now was a very good time for advice.

She pushed off from the window and turned. To her surprise, he already stood behind her. His long robe settled in a way that suggested he had just approached. Daelon wasn't one to spy on her.

"My Keeper," he said, and bowed. "You weren't in your room." His face was neutral, his posture characteristically stiff. Her request that he take over for his mother didn't seem to fluster him. Chetana had accepted it as a necessary consequence for her actions. Maddeningly, she seemed to think her vote was worth being dismissed.

"They want my mother reinstated." She didn't realize those would be her first words to him.

"They don't know what they want," Daelon said kindly. He walked closer beside her. "It's easier to see out now." He peered through the window.

She sighed. The pane didn't match. It would snag her gaze every time she walked this way.

"Lovely view." He side-eyed her. *"Those who keep their eyes above—"*

"*—will never want for wisdom,*" she finished. Despite herself, she smiled. She'd always loved the Scroll game. She'd been good at it, and they hadn't played for so long. "Is that what I'm missing, Daelon? Do I need perspective? Or prayer?"

He considered, weaving his fingers together behind his back as he continued to look through the glass. "It's always difficult for those who have compassion big enough for both sides of a conflict." He turned to her, smiling sadly.

"What should I do?"

"Continue to love the Kingdom. It may take years, or even a lifetime, but they'll see it. You don't serve the Kingdom for praise."

"No, of course not," she said quickly, realizing the words weren't as true as she wished they were. "It's not wrong to want to be loved, though, is it?"

"Even Keepers are still human," he replied.

"That doesn't do me a lot of good."

He cast his eyes to the ceiling with an expression that reminded her how young he was. "I remember a little girl," he said, "who caught fireflies one night. I think she got more than the boys."

Kiria shook her head. Atty had gotten the most.

"All right," he amended. "As I recall, she came to me afterward, angry because she was afraid the boys would squish their fireflies to see if the insides glowed. I told her to go to bed, but then I heard the next day that all the boys' fireflies had disappeared in the middle of the night. It was a great mystery, until you were late to my lesson. Didn't your mother find you playing the anthem of Brithnem to those poor fireflies? Your skills on the lyra were... not as polished back then. Perhaps they felt more patriotic after you freed them into the garden."

She laughed, a little embarrassed at the memory.

They started to walk slowly back down the corridor together, abandoned but for the guards. "I know you, My Keeper. You wouldn't betray Brithnem. My mother doesn't think so either."

Kiria's chest tightened. Chetana thought she was wrong, but not a traitor. Her own mother, Merian, had looked horrified as soon as she found out the truth about Kiria's connection with Firian. Since then, even their relationship had been strained. "Thank you, Daelon."

"The best leaders continue to serve even when they are maligned. *'Does a man want power?'*"

"*Greatness is found in service and majesty in love.*" She'd always pictured that service done for an adoring public. Or, if not adoring, then at least not hostile. "I know, but it's harder in real life."

"My mother has told me that joys are better in real life too." He cast a glance at her as if to ask if he were bringing up Chetana too often.

Chetana, at least, knew the lure of the Unreal, so she could compare them. Kiria missed the Unreal. She couldn't share it with anyone besides Firian, and now she couldn't even do that. Its freedom was intoxicating, exhilarating. The air flowing past her dress as they walked reminded her of flying around the field. Her feet moved heavier at the memory. She hadn't experienced many joys lately.

Daelon stopped walking. "Not everyone hates you. There are many who still believe your word. I'm one of them."

At that, she hugged him tight, squeezing her eyes shut and pressing her face against his shoulder. He smelled like soap and candle wax. For a moment he held his arms out, unresponsive, but then he patted her back gently. "It'll be all right." He nodded against her hair. "You'll be all right."

An unmistakable dark shape materialized behind her eyelids, growing in her mind. She felt as though she were being dragged into the Unreal after it. It was hard to tell if Firian forced her down, or if she made the decision herself. She swam toward the surface, but found she couldn't quite reach it. Like a drowning woman, she could see the way out but darkness pressed in all around her and she gave into it. Just for a moment.

"Kiria." Firian stood in front of her, close. He said her name in a fragile way that made her think he wasn't feeling as strong as he looked. She didn't either. Damn it—despite everything, part of her still loved him. "I don't want war with you," he said. So, he wasn't going to pretend everything was normal. He must have known he only had seconds to speak.

"Then you've fooled us all," she sneered, surprised by the bitterness that nearly blinded her.

He opened his mouth.

She didn't want to hear him. "There's nothing I can do, or would do, for you. War's coming." The thought turned her bitterness into black sap, heavy and exhausted. War, again. She pulled on the edges of the darkness with her mind. The arena turned into Shifra turned into the hallway where she stood now. The power of the Unreal rippled under her skin. The control distracted her from the misery trying to cling to her.

Firian looked at her as if he knew what she was doing. The hallway turned into bridges over treetops and islands with waterfalls and far off deserts. He'd always loved the Unreal too. "It doesn't need to. I don't want to hurt your people. I just want you."

She scoffed, backing away. Her feet sank in the sand of the dune. She almost stumbled backward. "You killed everyone, and I'm being blamed for it."

"You? Why?" He didn't deny it.

She leveled a look at him.

Understanding lit his face.

It occurred to her that if he overheard her thoughts in order to prepare for the assassination, then he would know that she chose not to warn him. He already knew her choice, so why did he persist? Why did he want her this much? "Leave me alone," she said. "Don't drag me back here again."

"Or you'll kill me?" His face was hard to read. Sadness, amusement, and anger all barely surfaced one after the other in the blinding light of the desert sun.

She didn't answer. Which meant yes. She'd have no choice.

He raised white-scarred knuckles toward her face. She flinched away from his touch. He extended a finger in time to touch her jaw, but she shoved his hand away.

"I did what I had to do," he said in the same tone he'd used to describe killing the last Tanyuin Head, Sias Jairon. The only difference was a stronger note of sadness. "I don't want to hurt more people."

The repetition grated against her skull. It was meaningless, like a child's nursery rhyme. He'd proved himself more than willing to hurt her people. She was right not to keep him by her side.

"What you say doesn't matter anymore," she said, her strength spent.

A long silence stretched thin.

"I'll come for you," he finally murmured.

A threat? A promise? A declaration of love? His tone almost suggested that he said it to himself, not to her.

Open your eyes! She practically shouted the words out loud as she struggled to get out of the Unreal.

Then—victory!—she emerged and lay in the darkened corridor with Daelon again. He was fanning her face.

"I called for the doctor," he said steadily, though his eyes were tinged with the wild fear she had seen in them that day Torithians attacked her. "You fainted, My Keeper."

"I didn't faint. I'm fine."

"He'll check you out."

"I'm fine."

Daelon stopped fanning. "Were you...?" He hesitated, apparently not wanting to finish his question. Still he waited for a response.

"I haven't seen him in weeks. He forced me to stay and talk to him. I told him nothing. We're nothing." The confession came out quickly and angrily. Somehow the truth would get out anyway. It was best to rip it off like wax. He helped her carefully to her feet.

Running footsteps sounded through the hall. Two men jogged toward where Kiria and Daelon stood—probably the doctor and an assistant.

"She'll be all right," Daelon assured them, raising a hand. Then he looked at Kiria, speaking so only she could hear. "You'll be all right."

47

FIRIAN

Firian took a tentative step. He could walk today, but he hated the weakness in his limbs. His sinews trembled a little when he put weight on them. Still, he preferred to focus on that than anything else.

Forty-two people.

And Bard gone.

Kiria wouldn't see him.

Rian was dead.

And he had killed forty-two people.

He jumped up and down, testing his legs. The effort burned his calves in too short a time, but he kept going anyway. The headache started to return, and still he kept jumping. It wouldn't take long to get back in shape. He'd devote all his time to it.

No, not all his time. He had to get Kiria back. He would come for her, just like he promised. Despite the pain and accusation he'd seen in her eyes the day before, there was care and desire too. She wanted everything to be all right between them. And she was good, maybe even forgiving. He jumped faster.

A cramp in his calf made him double over, cursing. Stars spotted his vision, along with all the images he tried to block out. Gripping the sheets on the side of his bed with one hand to steady himself, he replaced the horrible images with her. Her hair, her eyes, her heart-shaped chin...

"Feeling better?" Belik stood over him, favoring his good leg.

Firian stood, letting out a breath. "Yes."

"So maybe we can finish that conversation, hm?" Belik didn't wait for an answer, but went out into the office.

Firian followed. The room smelled dusty and abandoned. A large scrap of green fabric caught his eye. It was the new addition from Archer's Point, part of their flag. It lay next to the green of Raewhith and the yellow of Imlin.

Into the Unreal

Belik settled into his usual chair across from Firian's. Firian eased into his seat, rubbing his hands along the armrests.

"I've been directing things in your absence," Belik started. "A few of the troops were hurt in the fight, but not many. All the burials are complete. I've been preparing for our counter-strike."

"I never authorized a counter-strike." The past days, maybe weeks, were a blur. Had he said something in a moment of delirium?

"It's the only way to move forward," Belik said, not minding him. "If we allow this to stand, it means the end of your reign."

Firian regarded him darkly.

Kindly, confidentially, Belik leaned toward him. "I know you can take on an army by yourself, but clearly you can't do it over and over again. You're a human, not a god." He paused. "You know I could help you. Having someone else with your abilities means we could be twice as powerful. Think of that!"

Firian ran the three flags through his fingers, feeling the rough fabric, checking his fingertips for dyes. He didn't answer.

Belik continued with some derision in his voice. "A strike against Brithnem would be tricky, but they're not as secure as they claim to be. The outer edge farmland and the docks are the most vulnerable."

"What do you want to do, scare them?" Firian wanted revenge as much as anyone, but even he hadn't considered taking over Brithnem in the name of the Academy. It was an impossible target.

Belik shrugged one massive shoulder. "You've seen how easy it is to control a city." His eyes fell on the copy of the Scroll lying on the desk. Its pages were warped and yellowed, its stiff cover propped up with Brett's note. "Brithnem is particularly religious. In three, four steps, it could be ours."

Belik's meaning was slow to connect in Firian's mind. "If that's true, then why didn't we do that during the last war?"

"You know why," he retorted. "Sias was a coward. He never knew what was good for the Academy. Tanyu deserve better." He gestured with a meaty hand. "They got better."

Firian pressed his lips together. Belik rarely stooped to flattery.

Take over the capital? That still sounded too outrageous to be true. His gaze darted around the room as he tried to process the idea. If he controlled Brithnem, he could rule with Kiria. The Academy *and* the Western Kingdom. The concept was so enormous that it confused him, but that might have been the lingering weakness from killing all those people. The idea felt unreal. A tantalizing thought experiment. A lesson in strategy. "What are the steps?" he asked carefully. He realized he was gripping the green and brown flag of Raewhith in a tight fist.

Belik blinked knowingly behind his glasses. Though Firian hadn't told him about the state of his relationship with Kiria, he felt sure Belik already knew. "You look tired. We could talk about this another time."

"No. It's all right." Firian released the flag, trying to seem nonchalant.

"I'm not sure you're well enough yet." There was a hint of challenge in his tone.

Firian lowered his eyebrows. "I'm fine. Tell me the steps."

"Does it bother you that your girl is there?"

"Tell me the gory steps," he growled.

Belik ran a thumb through a blackened score in the tabletop. "Threats alone might do it. Offer to burn the outer edge."

"Dreams," Firian offered. Just like they had done before. The thought was distasteful, but he knew that had to be part of Belik's strategy.

The Master nodded. "The palace next, from the sea. There would be no need to fight more than a few guards at the palace. Once the Keepers knew we were serious, we'd have them swear loyalty on the book." He looked again at the Scroll.

That was far too simple. He was leaving steps out. Even taking over Archer's Point had required killing the current leader, burning Hill House. Well, he hadn't strictly needed to burn it.

A vein at Firian's temple started to pound again. He shook his head. "No, that's... that's not enough." Simmering anger bubbled up inside him. Belik was always hiding something, always keeping something back from him.

"I admit it would be easier if you'd let me carry some of your weight for you."

Firian eyed him, considering. Killing was the only ability he'd ever had that was all his own. Belik hadn't taught him that. A sick kind of pride made him protective.

But Belik was right too. If they did get into another battle, or if the Academy was attacked again, it would be helpful to have someone else who could take the brunt of the fighting too. Obliterating Brithnem's forces had almost killed him. Had they brought a back-up force, he would have been useless to defend everyone. Bard would have been on his own. The thought made him bite the inside of his lip hard. Coppery blood leaked onto his tongue.

"It's directional," Firian admitted. "You have to be facing them in the Second Level."

Belik sat motionless, but his eyes were alive with anticipation.

Firian hesitated. Any measure of control he had over Belik came down to two things: the crown and this one skill. "That's it," he lied.

Belik's cheek twitched. "I taught you the Second Level," he said tightly, but didn't press him further. He stood. "Just say the word and we can be mobile within the week."

Within the week. Firian felt lightheaded. He wanted Brithnem like he wanted to fly: it was a stupid dream, no more than that. Yet here was someone claiming to have the magic words. He couldn't let himself believe it, or he would make a fool of himself.

Despite all his rational thoughts, his heart thumped hard against his ribs like a chased animal. "I'll tell you when," he said. He'd meant to say something else, not *when*, but the sentence poured out of him naturally. Desire for the Kingdom began to pulse through him, growing stronger despite all the reasons he knew it couldn't work, it wasn't smart, it didn't make sense...

You're a monster, Firian. The words came again. He wished he could claw them out.

Maybe Bard was right. Kiria had seen it too.

Maybe he was a monster.

Into the Unreal

The door clicked closed as Belik left. Again, the memories came, thick and fast —the faces of all the people he'd killed, Kiria's terror when he'd held her hostage, Hill House going up in flames, Master Jairon kicking against him as he smothered him in his bed. Sickness pressed against his throat.

They were right.

A blank moment of self-awareness stilled him. The sickness subsided. No anger rose up. Instead, he felt oddly calm. Darkness throbbed in his veins, his thoughts, terrible and powerful. Maybe this is where he'd been heading all along. He'd never meant to be a villain. He had just wanted to matter, to be the best, to get what he wanted and help other people with his power. Certain people, at least. He'd sacrificed his life for those things. The thing was, he still wanted to matter, to be the best, to get what he wanted. Now he just had to do it alone. His breaths were shallow as he considered it.

All right, then. I'll be a villain.

48

KIRIA

Jori, from across the table, took Kiria's glass and filled it with sparkling wine. He winked at the servant standing behind her who no doubt felt snubbed or ashamed at shirking that duty. Kiria didn't protest when he handed it back.

The atmosphere at dinner was tense. Kiria's mother had invited Chetana, although she wasn't normally invited to such intimate gatherings anymore. Daelon sat beside his mother, his eyes often on Kiria.

Atty was the opposite. He could barely look at her. It had been well over a week but the tension hadn't softened.

She took a sip of wine and spoonful of the hearty soup in front of her. It smelled like creamy onions and beef with the slight tang of fish sauce.

No one talked about the inevitable conflict with the Tanyu. It was heavy on everyone's minds, so she suspected they kept silent because of her. Well, not silent. Atty talked to Haved, Cúron to Parohim, her mother to Chetana. Jori slyly exchanged money with the servant standing behind him. Jori's latest passion was going to footraces on the beach and betting on the outcome. When he learned the competitors' names, he asked everyone he could for information. Servants knew the most, he told her. He had competed in a couple of the races himself, but had placed very poorly. At least he would say so. She had gone down to see one of the races. Jori, shedding his embroidered vest for the occasion and running with his arms pumping more wildly than the rest, had finished in the middle of the pack. She was even a little impressed, but he had gone back to betting rather than running.

A guard entered the dining room, wearing full armor, including his helmet. He wasn't one of the two who normally guarded the door. The chatter hushed then died. "Please pardon the intrusion, My Keepers," said the guard. "We apprehended a Tanyuin man outside."

"What's his intention?" Cúron demanded.

"He wants to meet with you."

Cúron's eyes flashed to Kiria. "I don't think it's necessary for all of us to meet with him."

"With respect," interrupted the guard, "he says he wants to talk to you, My Keeper."

He, and then everyone else, looked at Kiria.

Her heart stopped for a beat. She set down her spoon. Was Firian here?

The reactions around the table ranged from accusation to protective kindness. Some of them must have sensed her fearful uncertainty, because several of the harder looks transformed into something more curious than angry.

It might not be Firian. It could be someone coming with a formal declaration of war, as though the events of the attack hadn't been clear enough on both sides. She straightened.

"We'll meet him now. In the Main," she said. No need to wait.

Chairs scraped back and everybody rose. Cúron whispered something to Parohim, and Atty nodded to Reynard, his advisor. There was a tacit agreement that anyone in the room could come as they received the Tanyu. Kiria almost hoped they would all join her. When they observed her interaction with whoever it was, they would see she loved the Kingdom and wasn't itching to sell it to any handsome Tanyu.

In the end, there were a few who elected to stay behind, but most of them came, even Jori, who could rarely contain his curiosity. Normally the sessions in the Main bored him, but this wasn't a session. This was a Tanyu. Kiria wasn't surprised that he joined the small group as they trekked from the dim dining room through the sumptuous hall to the Main.

The three Keepers settled on their thrones. Kiria glanced down at her hands on the armrests. Beautiful. If it was Firian… It crossed her mind to change back to being plain. No, she would stay as she was.

"Let him come in," she called to the guard at the entrance.

Small against the massive wooden doors of the Main, three figures entered—a Tanyu flanked by two armored guards on either side. She knew in an instant it wasn't Firian.

Why had she thought it was? She would sense his presence getting closer if he came to Brithnem. And there were enough people who would recognize him that they would have used his name.

This young man held his head lower, keeping his eyes on the ground before him. His black hair was wilder, his skin darker than Firian's. A light beard covered his jaw. The guards had bound his hands behind his back. Unlike Firian, he didn't wear a long black coat. Presumably he had one, but the past few days had been hot. The knees of his dark pants were light with dirt, and his boots left crumbs of dried mud on the pristine marble floor. When they got closer, she saw the young man wasn't as tall as Firian, still strong but not as broad in the shoulders.

He looked more and more familiar.

The guard on the right grabbed the boy's arm roughly and flung him forward, at the mercy of the Keeper.

Immediately he knelt on one knee, his head still bowed. "My Keeper, Kiria…"

His faltering voice echoed around the Main's empty expanse. The accent was lilting, foreign. Maybe Endrian.

"What is your name?" Cúron demanded.

The young man cleared his throat. "My name is Bard—Bardhon Tanery—and I..." He looked up and his eyes widened when they settled on Kiria. Awe glowed in his face. "I want to help you. With the war." He spoke as though he had almost forgotten what he wanted to say.

Kiria remembered where she had seen him. "Bard?"

He nodded vigorously. He didn't smile—he seemed too nervous—but his eyebrows rose hopefully.

She had heard of him. But what was he doing here? Was this a trap? She knit her brows. "How would you help?"

"I...um..." His dark gaze, almost completely black, moved briefly around the enormous room and then to each of the figures standing around her—Cúron, Atty, the guards, Chetana, Jori—before returning to her. He moved with some of the grace of a Tanyu, but he didn't have their trademark arrogance. In fact, his face turned ashen, and he dropped his eyes. His hesitation became pointed.

"This is ridiculous," Cúron muttered. The light in Chetana's eyes showed that she agreed with him. Cúron flicked his sleeves as he always did before he called the end of a meeting.

"Wait!" Kiria held out a hand to stay them. "He came to see *me*. I want to hear him out." She probably shouldn't have called more attention to the fact that this Tanyu was appealing to her rather than the other Keepers, but at that moment, she didn't care.

Bard looked up gratefully and a grin seeped sideways across his mouth—a little glimpse of joy. It was a wide smile that split his face even though he didn't show teeth. He rolled his shoulders. One of the guards looked sharply down at him when he moved.

She nodded at him to continue.

"I just want things to be right again... between us and... I think you know."

He was talking about Firian. Neither of them wanted to use his name in case the mention of him snapped his tenuous thread of credibility. She nodded again.

"I've, uh, I've got a lot of information about the Academy and I think they need to be stopped. No bloodshed," he added quickly.

A muscle in Cúron's cheek moved with skepticism. Kiria wanted to be skeptical too, but found it difficult. It was odd, but she wanted to trust this strange Tanyu. His eyes were sincere rather than cunning. *He's a Tanyu. You can't trust them, especially under the circumstances.* Brithnem and the Tanyuin Academy were moments away from declaring war on each other. This could be a trick to gain information. If so, it was a clumsy one.

"Stand up," she ordered.

Bard hopped easily to his feet, his hands still bound behind him. The two guards moved in.

She regarded him. He had a nervous energy that showed in many small ways: how he blinked and looked around, moved his mouth, resettled his shoulders, shifted his weight... His very hair seemed mobile, full of static. Dirt smudged his cheek, and the faint smell of body odor wafted from him. He'd traveled far. How was he still so antsy? She'd made that trip before. It was a long and tiring one.

"You'll give us information about the Academy?" she asked.

"Yeah. Yes. Just don't kill him."

He sounded like her own thoughts the past few days. That someone else felt the same way—or said he did—made warmth blossom in her chest. Could they really end this conflict with minimal damage to both sides? The idea tantalized her. Even if it meant publicly associating with another Tanyu, she would follow this lead. Serving the Kingdom wasn't about her own image, after all; it was about serving the Kingdom.

Kiria looked for a sympathetic face in the small crowd at the foot of the steps —Jori, who watched Bard with unabashed interest. "I think we should hear what he has to say," she said. "He knows a lot about the Tanyu—how the Academy's run. We could use him." She ran her thumb over her other fingers to steady herself. "He can stay in my wing until we find out all he has to tell us." She turned to the guards, avoiding everyone else's gaze. "You two stay with him. You can release his hands."

Silently, the guards obeyed.

Bard's arms fell to his sides and he flexed his fingers with grateful vigor. "Thanks... thanks! Thank you so much. I'll help you. I promise."

As soon as the guards led Bard out of the Main, Atty turned to Kiria. "You think we can trust him?" His expression was openly skeptical.

"I'm not sure, but if he is telling the truth, then we should listen to him."

"Do you know that young man?" Cúron asked, his tone accusatory.

"We've never met," she said. She had seen him before, though. Firian had shown her his image when they first started practicing in the Unreal, and his name had come up a few times in their travels. But she left all that out.

"None of us should meet with him alone," Cúron said, his meaning clear. Atty nodded. "His appearance is too suspicious. He must have left the Academy immediately after the massacre of our soldiers."

"What information do you think he would have to give?" Daelon asked softly.

"I'm not sure," she replied, feeling the growing weight of all eyes on her. She hadn't engineered this meeting. She wasn't in charge of it. But she always stood at the epicenter of all the Tanyuin movement around Brithnem, and there was no way to move out of the eye of the storm. "Like I said, he'll know more about the inner workings of the Academy than we do. Something there could help us." Kiria longed to find out what Bard knew, but didn't want everyone staring at her while she talked to him. Nothing could look more suspicious than meeting with him alone, though.

"Is it safe to let him stay in the palace?" Atty asked.

"I'll set extra guards outside his room," she said, a little exasperated. Bard didn't strike her as dangerous, but she'd been wrong before.

Cúron stood, shaking his sleeves in that peculiar way. Kiria and Atty stood as well. "He can't be allowed to wander the halls," he said, with an air of finality. "Meals will be brought to him, until we can figure out what to do with him."

As the group began to disperse, Kiria called to Daelon. "Would you come with me to make sure that the Tanyu is settled into his room?"

His eyebrows rose just a fraction at the request. "Of course, My Keeper. Is there anyone else you would like to bring?" The question was a suggestion. Daelon understood her reputation well.

She thought for a moment. "The Calthwaites." Jori would take the edge off the conversation, and Atty could see that she wasn't betraying them by wanting to hear Bard out.

A fragment of bitterness lodged in her throat for a second as she turned to Atty. "Would you like to come with me to check on the Tanyu?" Her tone might have come off as haughty to compensate for sounding too indulgent toward Tanyu before.

His eyes darted over her face. If he read anything there, he didn't say it.

"Daelon's coming too," she said, in case his hesitation had to do with caution. "And Jori, if he'll come."

"Ha, he'll come," Atty said humorlessly.

Most of the crowd had disappeared through the doors on their way back to supper.

"Will you, too?" she asked.

"After dinner."

"Right. After dinner."

"Okay. I just won't stay long." There was always Haved to get back to.

Kiria, perhaps strangely, didn't feel bitterness toward Haved for eavesdropping on her conversation with Jori back in Charäkhnem. She'd had a good reason to worry about Kiria then. How could she have known the damage that her gossip would cause? No, it was Atty, her childhood friend, who had hurt her the most. Their relationship could never go back to its innocent beginnings, but it seemed right to reach out and try to repair the breach, at least. They would have to rule together for the rest of their lives.

The meal passed swiftly. Opinions passed freely. Most didn't like or trust the new guest at the palace. His appearance was too coincidental, his offer too outrageous, his focus on Kiria too reminiscent of recent events.

Across the table from her, Atty leaned over to his brother and said something in his ear. Jori's face lit up in surprise and he looked at Kiria, who nodded. A mischievous look crossed his face. With Daelon, Atty, and Jori in the room, she could count on balance, or at least something like it.

After dinner, she rose and went out with her serving girls. Daelon followed with the Calthwaites. There were several guest rooms in every wing of the palace, most situated near each other, so she knew approximately where Bard was staying. The small group didn't speak on the way there, although the air buzzed with questions and, from Jori, snarky comments left unsaid.

Five guards outside one room reminded her suddenly of Firian's last visit.

"We are here to see the Tanyu," she announced to the guards, who immediately let them all in.

The room was very like the one where Firian had stayed. A fireplace crackled, and the sumptuous carpet ended in stairs leading down to a private washroom.

At the announcement of the visitors' names, Bard bounced off the large, four-poster bed where he had been lying on top of the blankets. His eyes grew as round as plates when he saw them enter and his wild black hair stuck out in every direction, smooth with the dampness of a recent bath. Judging from the messiness of the sheets, he had been pretending to swim the backstroke.

His mouth moved with greetings and responses he didn't say aloud. Instead, he tightened his robe, Brithnem blue and purple. His Academy clothes lay balled in a corner on the far side of the bed.

Kiria avoided looking over at Jori, who no doubt was trying to catch her attention with a private joke. She held up her hand toward Bard in a peaceful gesture. "Hello, Bard. We're just here to see how you like your quarters."

His chest rose and fell, his nervousness palpable but fading. "Very much. Thank you." He craned his neck to peer around the room as though to demonstrate how much he liked it all.

"Can I have the servants get you anything?" she asked. Bard was essentially under house arrest, so it seemed like a kind gesture.

The word "servants" seemed to catch him off guard. His eyes darted around the room with the alertness of a Tanyu, though with none of their predator instinct. "Could you—" He stopped, his cheeks turning darker. "Do you have cinnamon bread?"

Beside her, Jori beamed. "We can have that sent right up," he answered looking back and winking at Candrae, who left silently to fulfil the order. "Are you from Enderin?"

Now it was Bard's turn to grin. His wide smile split his face. "Yeah, yeah! I saw... I saw some Endrian stuff here. The trees in the hall."

"*Sachion* trees," Atty offered. His small contribution made Kiria glad. Atty wasn't withdrawing. He might even be open to peaceful talks with Bard after all. She wanted to squeeze his arm encouragingly, but refrained.

"Yeah," Bard said again. "They're wonderful. I've never seen them inside." In a moment, he seemed to remember whose presence he was in, and fell silent, shoulders stiffening.

Daelon stepped forward, formal as always, but he spoke warmly. "Enderin has been our strong ally for a long time."

Bard nodded rapidly. "I know. My brother... he fought in the Torithian War. Jac is his name. Jac Tanery." He said it as though he expected one of them to remember him.

"Jac Tanery," Kiria repeated, hoping Jac had made it out of that conflict alive. She'd never heard of him.

"Yeah, he joined the army a couple years ago."

"Why didn't you go back to Enderin instead of coming here?" Jori asked. His tone was curious rather than insulting, but, without knowing him well, it was hard to tell the difference.

"I wanted to," he began. "But I knew what would happen if I didn't do anything, so I thought..." He swallowed and left the thought unsaid.

Kiria didn't know that any Tanyu had emotions this transparent. Their training seemed to harden them all, or at least every other one she'd seen.

After a moment, he continued. "Someone needed to... make this right. Or stop it before..." It looked like he wanted to say more. His black eyes flitted to hers, dropped again.

"Well, we certainly want an end to this conflict as well," Daelon said kindly, breaking the silence. "If you can help us, then you are very welcome to the palace."

Bard gave a watery smile as the door behind them opened. Candrae was back with the toast. Her blonde head weaved by Kiria as she brought it to Bard, who could only nod happily at her, too overwhelmed to speak. The scent of cinnamon filtered through the room.

"We'll leave you for now," Kiria said, sensing he was out of words. He needed to rest after his long trip. "We look forward to hearing your ideas."

He took a crunchy bite of toast. His shoulders instantly relaxed at the taste. "Okay." His voice dropped to a whisper. "What... what should I call you?"

Atty looked at Kiria strangely, trying to interpret the question.

"My Keeper," Daelon replied, bringing his hand respectfully to his stomach in a bow that didn't materialize.

Bard bowed low from the waist. "My Keeper," he repeated, balancing the toast in one hand.

Jori glanced at his brother with a raised eyebrow when Bard bowed deeply to him next.

"We'll let you sleep. Welcome to Mon Párinath," Daelon said.

Everyone filed out the door, leaving Bard alone with his meager meal.

Jori bounded over to Kiria. "I think I like him," he said. "He's nothing like that other one."

On both counts, Kiria had to agree.

49

KIRIA

Bard had been at the palace for a few days, and still neither Cúron, Atty, nor the generals made a serious attempt to find out what he knew. It became clearer and clearer that they had no intention of taking his help. He was allowed to stay in the palace to appease Kiria, to make her feel like she was doing something toward the war effort, and nothing else.

She had brought up the suggestion to talk to him several more times, but no one responded. Suddenly meals and meetings and nameless appointments dominated everyone's schedule. So Bard was left alone.

Frustration built up in her as she sat at her vanity. Cúron, Atty, and Chetana wanted Firian dead. They weren't even open to other options. Justice demanded that she at least find out if there *was* another alternative.

Candrae leaned toward her in the mirror as she arranged Kiria's hair. "Is My Keeper well today?" she asked quietly.

Kiria forced her face into a neutral expression. She was too easy to read. A Keeper couldn't afford for everyone to know her thoughts. "Very well, yes." The rebellious streak that characterized her childhood rose up, furtive and exciting. "We have a meeting this morning."

"With whom?"

"Master Tanery. You and Vayci are coming with me." She'd noticed Bard's red-stoned ring when they'd met, so she assumed the title matched Firian's.

"The Tanyu?" Vayci's voice was small on the other side of the room where she trimmed the candles. Kiria saw her turn away, as though her question had been impertinent.

"Yes, the Tanyu. He might have information that will help us, and no one is asking him about it."

She glanced at the white-yellow light streaming in through the window. It was still early. Cúron would certainly be awake but might not see her in the hallway yet. The sooner they could meet with Bard, the better. Fewer prying eyes.

"It can be simple, Candrae," she said, touching the hair just above her ear.

Candrae finished rapidly, twisting her hair back from her temples and pinning it in a simple bun at the nape of her neck. The simplicity matched the purple-gray dress she wore, plain and therefore underscoring her Ability.

Vayci finished preparing the candles and fireplace and joined the two of them as they left the chamber. Bard's guest room wasn't far from her own.

She'd sworn to serve and protect the Western Kingdom. That's what she was doing, she reminded herself. Words and warnings swirled through her mind.

Do you have the courage to do what isn't safe?

"Tell Bardhon Tanery that I am here to see him," she told the nearest guard, heart thumping.

"Of course, My Keeper."

After her announcement, she and the serving girls went into the room. Dishes cluttered the open surfaces and corners of the floor. On the bed a boardgame and its pieces had been meticulously set up, though unplayed. The room smelled like cinnamon and old vegetables.

Bard had shaved his beard, which made him look younger. He was probably her own age, though, no more than twenty. "My Keeper," he said, bowing low and keeping his eyes on the floor.

She held back a smile. He held his hand exactly as Daelon had the other night.

"It looks like you're getting comfortable here."

His tan skin colored a little. "If you need me to clean up..."

"No," she laughed. "It doesn't matter." Between the ages of eleven and fourteen, Jori's room had looked ten times worse. The servants played betting games to determine who would clean it. She caught them at it once. "I've come to hear what you have to say about the Academy."

He looked up, then away again, unable to hold her gaze. He clasped and unclasped his hands as he stood before her.

"Please sit down." She waved toward the bench at the foot of the bed. It opened as a trunk for extra blankets and had a pillowed top embroidered with the same *laird* flower as the flag.

Obediently, he sat. She settled beside him.

Bard's nervous energy didn't wane. He twitched as though he wanted to hug his knees to his chest, but forced himself to stay still. Candrae and Vayci hovered by the door.

"Has anyone come to speak to you?"

He shook his head.

She pursed her lips in frustration at the confirmation. "I want to know what you came here to say. Can you tell us about the attack?"

He sucked in a long breath through his nose, lifting his chin as he did so. When he let it out again, he looked more composed. "Thank you." His eyes widened in fear. "My Keeper," he amended.

"Kiria when we're not out with the others."

He nodded, relieved—he seemed to do that a lot—but didn't revise her title.

"So you want to help us," she prompted.

"Yeah, yes," he said, catching hold of the opening she gave him. He balled his hands into fists in his lap. "I'm glad you came. I thought you, more than anybody, would know what I meant. I just didn't know..." He crooked his jaw, his gaze darting to the floor.

"If this makes you that uncomfortable, I can change." The Tanyu already knew her other appearance, so changing back wouldn't compromise security. "It's an Ability," she went on, "Original Beauty, but I can always go back if I want to."

"Beauty," he said, "is not a grand enough word." He blushed at his own boldness.

She smiled. Closing her eyes until the tingling sensation covered her, she became plain again. "There," she said, feeling deflated. "Now we can talk."

Recognition flashed across his face as he looked at her now. Had he seen her image as she had seen his, in Firian's mind?

"How well do you know Firian?" she asked, all pretense gone.

"Better than anybody, or most people. We were roommates." He seemed genuinely more at ease now that she wasn't using her Ability. "What about you?"

The returned question surprised her. She wasn't sure how to answer. "I'm sure you know we traveled together," she said carefully. "I'm not sure what Firian told you."

"Not a lot, but he was different when he got back. He thinks about you all the time."

A flush of regretful pleasure filled her cheeks. It was strange hearing about this from a stranger. His confirmation made her loss more real. "We got to know each other fairly well during the trip," she said.

"And you must have the Talent, or else he wouldn't think about you so much."

This nervous Tanyu understood more than he let on. "Yes," she admitted.

He watched his hands as he spread them over his knees. Bard was wearing brown and blue, she realized. Firian wore black even in the Unreal, but Bard was someone else underneath the Tanyuin training. "I don't know you, really, but I figured you might be the one to talk to about... stopping him. Because you probably care about him. Do you, at all?"

"I don't want to kill him. So you are talking to the right person."

His mouth quirked. "He's... he's done some terrible things. I know that. I know he has. I was there. But I thought we could make it right, you know?"

"When did you leave?" she asked softly, guessing the answer.

He gulped and for a while he was silent. When he finally answered, his voice was quiet, almost a whisper. "He's gotten more afraid, lately. Which makes sense. There are people out to get him. But it's made him different." He paused again, unwilling to go on. He flexed his bare feet up and down.

She felt the weight of the silence. If Bard left when she thought he did—after the Kingdom's attack—then explaining all that could feel like he was betraying his friend to the enemy.

"You said he needs to be stopped," she prompted.

"He does." The words came out flat and sad.

"Why do you say that?" The Kingdom had their reasons, but Bard's might be different.

"He's... I think he's panicking. But it's made him..." He trailed off again, tipping his head toward the ceiling as though he could find answers there.

"Power hungry?" she offered. "He was always like that."

"Yeah," Bard agreed. They smiled at each other, the instant bond of people who had the same intimate knowledge that they'd never shared before.

She needed to ask what Bard knew about the attack, but he didn't seem ready. "I think we're on the same side, Bard."

By the door, Vayci shifted her weight. Bard's sharp eyes noted the motion.

"But," she continued, "he killed our soldiers."

"You attacked us," he said very quietly.

"After Firian took over Archer's Point."

Neither of them seemed to like this exchange at all. She felt her dinner roiling in her stomach, and Bard looked queasy too.

He scratched the back of his head, almost as though he were clearing his thoughts. His black hair spiked even more. "I told him not to," he said.

Kiria resisted the urge to squeeze his hand, to thank him if what he said was true. Firian needed more voices like his. "I found out too late," she said. She squared her shoulders at him. "What made you leave?"

His brows lowered and jaw clenched. After a while, he said, "I tried to stay, but... It was a lot of things. The day your people came, I couldn't..."

"Couldn't what?"

When he finally looked up at her, his eyes shone glossy with tears. Her eyebrows shot up in surprise. "Did I do the right thing?" he asked.

The question reverberated inside her too. *Yes. You got away. We need to stop him. We're in the right and he's in the wrong.* But all the words rang false. Right and wrong, good and bad, didn't describe Kiria versus Firian. Both terms described her, and both described him. The difference was the choices they made, the side they took day after day. "I don't know," she said finally.

"It's just, you know, he's... he's like my brother. And I thought, if I need to stop him, I had to come here. That maybe you would understand."

"I think I do." She gave a sad smile.

Bard turned to face her, and their gaze connected in understanding, as deep as coming home to family. The strength of that understanding startled her.

He warmed up to the conversation as though he had held it inside him, just waiting for somebody to listen. "I want him to change," he said. "To go back to how he was, or more. He could be better."

She wanted the same thing, but that was looking more and more impossible. How could they stop him without killing him? Did they imprison him? Exile him? Replace him with someone else? Or would he listen to two people who cared about him, and give up this ridiculous quest for control?

"What do the other Keepers think?" Bard asked.

The change in direction was noteworthy enough that she felt they had strayed too close to something Bard didn't want to talk about. A secret about Firian? She burned to know what it was, but she'd have to earn Bard's trust first.

"Well," she said, "you can see that no one else will talk to you. Understandably, they don't like Tanyu at the moment."

He nodded again.

"Hopefully they'll try to get to know you."

"Like you're doing," he said.

"Mm hm."

"Do you trust me yet?"

About to say no, she stopped herself. She did trust him for some reason. He seemed completely ingenuous, with none of Firian's calculated responses. It probably wasn't a good idea to let him know, in case she was wrong.

"That's okay," Bard said after she paused.

"I want to," she said, and smiled. "But first you have to tell me what you know about Firian and the Academy."

He chewed his bottom lip, considering. His shoulders twitched as he thought for a long time. The secret wanted to come out. Kiria waited, perfectly still. "You don't want to kill him either?" he confirmed.

"Not if I can help it."

"He... Firian, he..." Bard cracked his neck, stalling. "He can kill, um... I don't know how, but he can kill people just by looking at them."

Heat flooded her body, disbelief, fear. "Just by *looking* at them?"

"It's something with the Unreal, obviously, but I've never heard of it. I don't know how it works."

Her gut sank. Firian was even more of a threat than the other Keepers realized. How could she justify a plan that would keep him alive now? Their only hope was negotiating until he was on their side, with terms phrased like an ultimatum. Break this agreement and it would mean instant death. But if he could kill someone with his mind, then who could they send to carry out an execution? Her head swam.

"We'll figure out something," she said, just above a whisper. But she didn't know whether even a Keeper and a Tanyu could figure out a way to save Firian from himself.

50

FIRIAN

EVER SINCE FIRIAN agreed that they should capture Brithnem, Belik seemed charged with tireless energy. "Tanyu originally *were* the army for the Western Kingdom," the Master explained as he led Firian out of the barracks. The stone walls, far sturdier than the wooden ones, had been completed while Firian battled the fever. Bright morning light washed them white. "Bad leadership led us away from that position. It's always been something we deserve, that we could do."

"I know." A clump of gray fur caught Firian's eye. Another dead rabbit. He frowned.

Men and women scurried out of their way as they strode out into the light of the field beyond. It was harder now to tell who used to be a Torithian pirate. Most had grown out their hair. A couple still insisted on shaving their heads, but many of them didn't bother to continue.

"Didn't we want to expand to other nations besides the Western Kingdom, though?" Firian asked. He'd heard their history before. "We could do more that way."

"Make more money too," Belik growled contemptuously. "The Amir hated us for it. That and a lot of other things. Can you think of an Amiran hero, anyone who turned a battle or saved somebody? No? That's because they're all Tanyu. Corso, Naedra, Anewa... Of course we wanted to expand beyond the Western Kingdom, but we deserve to rule there more than anywhere else. Amir are jealous, and pissed that we don't waste our time memorizing the Scroll. Have you heard of Original Plan, Firian?"

"Yes." This wasn't the first time Belik brought it up. They were a radical group that hated Tanyu. They used the word "Original"—like Kiria's Original Beauty or Firian's Original Talent—to suggest that they had some extra ability, like understanding the will of God. There had been a fierce conflict in the Unreal between the Tanyu and Original Plan before Firian was recruited.

Belik cursed the Amir in an undertone. "They were a gory scourge when I was your age. And now they practically rule the place."

They took the dirt path through the shops that led back to the Academy, dark in the near distance. Firian's legs had tired from a hike that would have been nothing to him mere days ago. He forced his breathing even.

His decision to assert control in the Western Kingdom was about respect for the Tanyu, not revenge against the Amir. Belik was harping too much on the past. Firian didn't need these explanations. "I don't think they ordered the attack on the Academy."

"The vote, Firian. Use your head!"

Firian ground his teeth, biting back a reaction. Maybe Belik was right. He had assumed that the male rulers had banded together, as they often did, in spite of Kiria's protests. She must have protested on his behalf. The thought made him wish he'd seen it. Now his breathing had little to do with their swift walking pace.

Belik limped quickly between the standing carts that choked the road. A two-week trip required provisions for three. With a small army on the move, the trip wouldn't go as quickly as it would when Firian was alone. Firian edged through, glad it was warm enough not to wear a jacket that might catch on the wheels.

Belik started explaining the waves of transportation and logistics the army would implement, but Firian was barely listening now. They had already talked about the big ideas—the outer edge, the demands, the almost peaceful transition, the banishment of the Amir. It was all quite simple. They hardly needed an army at all. The existing leaders would pay homage and tribute to the Academy, obeying their demands but continuing to function in their current roles, subservient to Firian's will.

He planned to solidify the plan through Kiria, but he kept that part to himself. Belik might see that as weakness, after all his warnings about her having power over him.

As the dirt road sloped upward to the main entrance to the Academy, Shiro came out through the main doors. His stare flashed first with fear, then hatred. Firian returned his gaze long enough to show he wasn't intimidated. Shiro was Rian's good friend. Was. Firian found himself picking at the skin around his ring again. He stilled his hands and paced into the castle with Belik.

He allowed his mind to drift down into the Unreal. Where was Kiria? She wasn't hard to find. Her imaginative mind glowed like a new color. She came into focus, beautiful and windblown, walking. Firian stayed hidden. Her surroundings were slower to appear—they mattered less. In fact, they didn't matter at all, except to flesh out the picture. Sand, water, sky. She was on the beach, her expression serene.

She had extra guards around her. That made sense, since she had been attacked near the beach when she'd been struck by a Torithian arrow. Had Firian really learned about that in World Events less than a year ago?

There was someone else too. It took Firian a moment to tear his attention away from Kiria to realize that he knew this person. It was just so radically out of context that his mind couldn't make the connection at first. He was so constantly on his mind that Firian could barely distinguish his presence from his own thoughts sometimes.

Bard.

Bard was there with Kiria. What was he doing in Brithnem? A confusing storm of emotions raged through him. Bard talked about his family back in Enderin all the time. Why didn't he go there? Firian thought he remembered Bard telling him where he was going. But Firian had barely been conscious at the time. His memory could be playing tricks.

The two of them walked side by side, not close. Bard didn't wear Academy black, but something else. Something breezy but fine, as though he'd gotten it at the palace. Was he staying there?

Firian struggled to understand. He felt wrong, almost dizzy.

Bard was in Brithnem. With Kiria. Jealousy flashed through him. Kiria was Beautiful for him. Clearly they weren't in an official meeting. He studied their hands, their body language. All innocent.

What was he thinking? Bard would never go after Kiria in a romantic capacity. He had to have gone for a different reason.

You're a monster, Firian.

Had he... defected? Turned his back on everything the Academy stood for? Turned his back on *him*? It didn't seem like Bard to help the Kingdom kill him, but what other explanation could there be? Rage and betrayal ripped through him like a wound.

Just before the surface of reality, he screamed with fury. The corners of his eyes were wet with the sheer force of his anger. They'd left him—*left him*—and now they were conspiring against him. He was shaking.

"...ready tomorrow." Belik's voice seeped back to his thoughts.

"What?" he snapped. His vision blurred.

"We'll be ready to move tomorrow."

It felt like someone was grabbing his throat, choking him. Bard was in Brithnem, and the Academy's forces would move tomorrow. The possibility that the Keepers wouldn't agree to their demands broke through for the first time—a thought he hadn't allowed before. What if this conquest wasn't bloodless? He could save Kiria. She was valuable enough to bargain with. But Bard?

He couldn't swallow, couldn't breathe.

Belik came into focus near him. He stood close, as though shielding him from prying eyes in the hallway. Which hallway? Which way had they come? "Firian." He frowned at him, looking genuinely concerned. "Get yourself together. Do you need to lie down?"

Firian bared his teeth.

Belik raised his chin knowingly, brought it down in a nod. "We'll push back the departure one day. You need to rest." He was again alive with control as he turned away from him, shouting at various people to delay their preparations.

One day. That wouldn't nearly be enough time to come to terms with what he saw.

51

KIRIA

Four guards seemed excessive.

Kiria and Bard walked along the beach behind Mon Párinath. Despite the grim soldiers around them, Bard's grin hadn't left him since they reached the sand. Shoes dangling from his right hand, he looked out at the ocean as though he couldn't get enough of the sight. His toes dug into the wet sand with every step.

His happiness was contagious. Kiria found herself letting go of her spiking worries too as she gazed out to the hazy white line where the sky met the calm sea on the horizon. At that moment, Bard's horrifying information about Firian didn't matter. At that moment, she could forget.

This was a false peace—no, just a temporary one—but she relished it.

Bard turned to her, a breeze shuffling his wild hair. "This is great," he said. "Why are you being so nice to me?"

"You've been helpful," she said easily. She didn't feel that she'd been that nice to him. After all, he'd been relegated to his room alone for days except for when she asked for information. This was the first time he had been allowed to go outside since he arrived. If he was from Enderin, it made sense that he missed the sea. The Academy was landlocked. She'd missed the soothing splash of waves when she traveled over the mountains—the sun glaring almost too bright on the water, the smell of salty air, fresh seafood...

Bard pried his eyes away from her. Since they were outside, she had worn her Beauty. After a few conversations, though, Bard seemed much more comfortable with her than he had been. His uncertain words and nervous tics had settled into greater confidence. He gave information piecemeal, as though trying to figure out what could help and what could hurt his former friends. The idea of doing the wrong thing haunted both of them, simmering just below the surface. That nagging doubt that they were betraying people they cared about. So they treaded carefully.

"I used to swim all the time," Bard said, looking over the water. Despite living near the ocean, Kiria rarely swam. "I'd have competitions with my brothers and sisters. Jac." He turned around to see if she remembered the name from the other day. "I was pretty good. But I haven't done it in ages." He moved his jaw as though he were chewing on something.

"I think it'd be all right if you wanted to swim," Kiria said, glancing at the nearest guard for confirmation. He remained stone faced, which she took as a yes.

Bard smiled wide. "You sure?"

"Go ahead."

Kiria settled herself on a boulder nearby as Bard carefully folded his shirt and shoes in a pile and leapt headfirst into the water, not bothering to wade out first. Twenty breaths later, he reappeared, breaking the surface gleefully and shaking his hair like Jori did after it rained. Then he went back down. He made it look easy, as though he were a sea creature himself, full of joy.

"What are you doing down here?" When she spun, she saw Atty, hand in hand with Haved, walking down the steps in the grassy embankment toward the sand. He carried a satchel in his free hand, perhaps food for a picnic. Two of the guards parted to let them through to the beach.

Though Kiria didn't come down to the shore as often as she'd like to, Atty frequently did. He enjoyed being alone in nature. Or alone with Haved. She suspected his new favorite was both.

Haved saw Bard first. "Oh, look," she said. "Is that the Tanyu in the water?"

Bard was far out now, but his hair gave him away.

"Yes," she replied, an edge of defiance in her voice. "We were talking."

Atty made a noncommittal noise.

"He keeps giving helpful intelligence."

"And you believe what he says?" Atty asked.

The question stung. "He said that the Head has a new ability that could change our odds in the war."

"Positively?" Haved asked. The word was delicate in her Charäkhni accent.

"No."

The two of them didn't come close to the rock where she sat, their distance mirroring the distance she saw in Atty's eyes. But he had to hear this.

"Atty, come here." She waved him forward. "This is serious. He said that he can kill people... with his mind." It sounded almost silly when she said it.

"Isn't that what the Academy is for?" Atty asked, a little irritated.

"No, this is different. He can just look at someone—they don't have to have the Talent—and they'll die."

"He just looks at them?" Haved knit her brows.

"I don't exactly understand how it works, but Bard told me about a Torithian—"

"I think he's messing with your mind, making you afraid," Atty said, shifting the bag in his hand, clearly ready to leave. "You shouldn't listen to them."

She stood and faced the couple. "He's given us good information. The layout of the Academy."

A splash sounded in the distance, and a laugh.

Atty was unmoved. "Why do you trust them? Why do you side with them?" His voice was strong, no slurring at all. "You're becoming friends with this Tanyu. Do you meet him in the Unreal too? That didn't work out last time. It's like you're trying to join the Academy."

She blushed angrily. "I'm trying to do the right thing, Atty," she said, glaring. "And you were the one who wanted to join the Academy when we were little. Don't pretend you don't remember. I'm just trying to make sure that we have all the facts before we rush in and kill people. There's nothing wrong with that."

"There is when our people get killed instead," he said softly.

Her mouth worked. "You know I didn't mean for that to happen."

Atty gazed back at her, as though he were embarrassed on her behalf.

Kiria's mouth went dry, but she couldn't think of anything else to say. Miserable, she sat on the rock again.

Haved put her hand on Atty's broad shoulder and leaned close to him. "I think I see a place over there," she said, apparently unruffled by her husband's tense conversation. Haved had the kind of calm that Kiria aspired to.

As they headed across the beach, Kiria looked back to the ocean, where Bard still splashed in the waves like a ten-year-old. How could he find joy in this moment when, to her, everything seemed so dark?

She hadn't even thought about meeting Bard in the Unreal. As a Tanyu, he had the Talent, but she hadn't considered it. Firian and the others who came to the palace held it like a precious secret. Bard's ability must be an aspect of his personality that he didn't cultivate to the exclusion of everything else. She glanced at his neatly folded shirt, golden tan this time, lighter than his skin.

Even surrounded by guards, she felt alone. Without the comfort of friendship, she kept all the accusations and pressures inside her, packed close, insulating her from the world until she felt that she was looking in from outside. Bard was a new friend because she needed one.

The warm breeze blew across her face. She breathed it in. She'd never been good at choosing romantic relationships. There was Tanis the guard-in-training, Anton the soldier, and Firian the Tanyu. Why couldn't she find someone kind, who loved her as she was? Instead she was apparently drawn to arrogance.

Loud splashing announced that Bard was trudging happily back to the shore. The sun glistened on his dark tan shoulders. His smile was blissfully happy. When he arrived on the beach, he looked a little out of breath, judging from his back's rising and falling. Other than that, he was surprisingly still. He didn't seem so ghostly or antsy anymore. This was a glimpse into who he was away from the Academy, from Brithnem, from all those things that had tried to define him. It was clear the Tanyu had only done that poorly. It was strange that the two of them shared so much without actually knowing each other. They both cared for a dangerous, broken young man enough to put their reputations on the line for him.

Part of her wanted to ask Bard more about Firian's new killing ability, but a sense of peacefulness fell over her. The sea stymied any more serious talk. The rhythm of the waves was like the rhythm of her blood. She sat silently for a good while. Nearby, Bard did too. The sun warmed her feet around her leather sandals as they looked out at the Kheltor Ocean.

The sky changed slowly as they watched it. Bard was the first to move. He threw on his shirt and walked back toward Kiria. She felt the guards tense around her.

He nodded before he spoke, that odd, quick nod he always did. "This has been the best. The best."

"I'm glad you liked it."

"Would it be okay to do this again? Or... it doesn't have to be tomorrow or anything, but I really loved this."

"Sure." She had loved it too. A moment of peace, away from Firian, away from judgment, away from all of it.

His eyebrows darted downward. "Don't you have other things to do?" He asked the question as though it had just occurred to him that a Keeper shouldn't be able to give him any time at all.

"I always do. But I'm the only person who will talk to you, so it's probably a good idea to get all the information I can out of you." She gave him a teasing, sad look.

He caught a glimpse of Atty and Haved, who were enjoying their meal almost out of sight along the shoreline. "They don't believe me, do they?"

She stood. "No, but they will eventually."

"You believe me, though?"

"I do."

He nodded, more slowly this time, and they started to walk back up the steps to the palace. It rose above them majestic, wreathed in gardens. The domed Amiran Academy sprouted up on the left. Kiria wondered if Daelon was inside reading.

"I think I saw you brought Indisfate all the way from the Academy?" she asked Bard. "That didn't look like a palace set."

He beamed. "Yeah! I play all the time. Used to." His face darkened. "Before the war, especially."

"Were you there?"

It was clear what she meant. *Were you there when all the Kingdom soldiers were massacred?*

He sucked his teeth. The sun shone on a black freckle directly on top of one of his ears. "Yeah. It was awful." He scratched the back of his head. A few droplets sprayed in her direction. "Oh, I'm sorry!" he cried, holding out his hands. He accidentally touched her arm and he yanked the hand away as if she burned him.

She waved away his apology. "I'm fine." The lawn grass gave way to paved walkways. "Did you see him?"

"I'm with him all the time." He bit his lip, amending. Not anymore. He looked down at the bright path in front of his feet.

She waited in anticipatory silence.

He twisted his fingers together before continuing. "They came into the Academy," he said in an undertone. "I guess you have to know what happened. They came in, and Firian—" He paused, glanced at the guards, then at Kiria, who nodded encouragingly. "I was with Firian. He asked me to be there, so I was."

Kiria tried to picture Firian asking Bard to be by his side in a fight. Was Bard a better fighter than he let on? He did have surprising skills, like his adeptness as a swimmer.

"They came in from both sides. We all knew they were there to kill him, so... we had to defend him, you know? We all had our jobs. But then we got trapped downstairs. I was afraid..." He closed his eyes to steady himself. "I was afraid that there were too many. None of them had the Talent." It was almost as though he was talking to himself now, getting out the images he'd held with him. "There were so many in that tight space. I thought it might be over, that there was nothing I could do. Firian was fighting, and the rest of us." He seemed to remember Kiria was there, maybe thinking of the map he had provided her the day before. "There were even more coming in on both sides."

She felt a confusing swell of pride at the idea of her army doing their job so well, overwhelming even the Tanyuin Academy. Of course, if this were true, then how were they defeated? She pictured rows of blue and silver soldiers in a large room made of the same stone as the Tanyuin Head's office, where she'd stood in the Unreal. A little ashamed of the memory, she knit her brows.

"I thought that was it, that we were going to die. Or maybe barely win. We had some good warriors with us." Bard skimmed one hand over the top of a hedge, still not meeting her eyes. "I tried to help, but Firian wanted to take them all at once. I didn't think he could."

She found she was hardly breathing. Firian took on her troops *single-handedly*?

"And then"—Bard squeezed his eyes shut, his voice hitching—"he just closed his eyes and the whole room felt tight, like my heart wouldn't work right. And... everyone just died. They just died. There was screaming."

A lump rose in her throat.

Bard's hands traced parts of his own face in a haunted way, as though he remembered something about the way they died that he couldn't say aloud. His words thrilled into heavy quiet. Birds chirped in the trees. Their footsteps sounded loud over gravel.

Was that the moment she had thought Firian died, when he killed all those men? Had the process hurt him somehow? But Bard had subsided into a profound melancholy, and she doubted he would say anything more.

They made it all the way to the palace before either of them spoke again. She hated to leave on this dark note. Bard was something positive in her life right now, even though her friendliness with him made others suspicious. Let them think what they wanted. "You'll have to show me how you play Indisfate sometime," she said as the guards began to conduct him back to his room.

"Whenever you want." He resettled his shoulders, back and forth, considerably lightened. But the worry didn't leave his eyes.

52

FIRIAN

FIRIAN CRACKED HIS KNUCKLES. When he squeezed his fingers together, small raised scars snaked across them. Only the slightest noises sounded behind him in the dusky pines. Anything louder and he would go back and remind his warriors what was at stake. If Brithnem knew they were coming, the Kingdom could plan for their arrival. If they planned for their arrival, more of the Tanyuin army would die. He let out a slow breath as he gazed out over the shredded clouds.

Under normal circumstances, Tanyu only made camp after dark, but the Torithians were having trouble continuing after the sun had gone down. After eight agonizing days of walking, he had finally conceded that tonight only, they could make camp early. A child could have gone faster than this new army. Firian's pulse raced when he thought of it. He went three times as quickly on his own. But he couldn't execute a full counter-attack by himself. He could fantasize, but it wasn't realistic.

A shadow rose next to him. Firian knew him by his presence as much as his shape. "Belik."

The Master settled on a rock near him. "We could have gone until the moon was up," he grumbled.

"I know. Gory Torithians." Honestly, he knew Belik struggled with the march too, despite getting one of the only horses, but he never liked to admit it pained him.

Belik shifted, looking over the rocky landscape. "Secrecy is the most important thing," he said, as though it were an admission. "Speed is secondary."

Firian pursed his mouth. Belik was right, but this delay bothered him. He couldn't have said why speed seemed so important. Maybe it was his pent-up energy, all that he had lost over those feverish days. Or he could be rushing toward what felt inevitable—his confrontation with Kiria and Bard—though he didn't know what he would say when he got there.

Into the Unreal

They didn't talk for a while. Soft sounds of camp filtered up behind them. A clank, a curse, a footstep. None of the voices were Tanyu. They knew better.

"I always worked in strategy," Belik mused. "It's been a long time since I've done something like this."

Firian drew his brows together. Belik was almost never forthcoming. So, he stayed silent, waiting for more.

"You could go mad around so many people," Belik growled.

Firian smiled at the small rush of warmth in his chest. He felt exactly the same way.

"You take after me, I think."

The mountains rose in front of them, stony with patches of green, growing black in the deep shadows. A chilly breeze blew past.

Belik angled toward him. "You're done with that girl, aren't you?"

"Yeah." It was mostly true. There was no need to tell him how often he still thought of her, how she dominated his thoughts of Brithnem, even now. How the only future he envisioned was one where he earned her adoration, and she told him it would be all right, and her arms weaved around him, and he pressed her to his body...

"Good. No distractions."

He realized he hadn't told Belik about Bard. He doubted he would tell anyone. No clear ideas filled his head at the thought. It was wordless pain.

"This will fix our problems," Belik said, stooping down to pick up a knobby pine twig. He ran a thick thumb over its rough bark. "We've deserved this a long time, and I could wait a long time." He caught Firian with a piercing look. Above his eyes, the clouds reflected in his glasses. "You were a godsend. You idiot," he said almost affectionately.

Firian scraped his heel against pine needles and mulch, digging a hollow that he covered back up. He didn't want Belik to be his only ally, but he was glad he had one. Belik was a powerful ally to have.

"Almost there," Belik continued. "Soon years of injustice will be... improved." He stood and clapped Firian on the shoulder. "Almost there." With that, he stumped back to the camp.

Almost there. He breathed. Almost to Kiria. The takeover moved his blood, but Kiria was the real goal. Firian could force people to give him what he wanted. He'd taken the Academy; he could take Brithnem too. But Kiria was different. He couldn't take her. He had to coax her, seduce her, make her see all he could offer.

Hadn't he tried all that? His words didn't seem to impress her. It was when he was out of his element, stumbling, vulnerable, that her eyes softened.

How could he get her to look at him like she did before? Was that before she realized how monstrous he was? How hungry? Need burned inside him, not only for power, but for the shadow of goodness that followed her and filled the shadowy places within him.

Maybe if he acted gentle and inviting ... What if he caught her when she was happy and generous, like that time in Shifra? The memory, once sweet and heady, tasted like ash.

She couldn't be fully his until she looked into his eyes and loved him. Then he would burn and she would burn and nothing else would matter.

He cursed, almost laughing. He couldn't lie to himself anymore and say she didn't have power over him. She did, it was true, but she wouldn't use it against him.

The clouds had disappeared into the dark blue of evening. She would be going to bed. Maybe she'd even be sleeping. Tonight, when he was sure she was asleep, he'd steal into her thoughts, kindly, and start to win her back.

53

KIRIA

KIRIA RECOGNIZED THE FAMILIAR WARMTH. Where was he? She turned around but everything had the haze of a dream. Knowing that her dreams met the Unreal, she solidified her surroundings so she could see shapes and lines clearly.

She stood on the Salt Flats. The empty stretch of land mirrored the sky above so it seemed like she was floating or walking on a still lake. Firian was a distant black line shimmering on the horizon, growing larger as he walked toward her. His coat swayed behind him. He wore more confidence than she had seen in their past few encounters. It was as if he expected her to welcome him.

Bard's words from the day before rushed back to her. *And... everyone just died.* Something Firian did made all her troops fall dead.

She was nervous, but something—probably something naïve within her—was sure he wouldn't kill her. As Chetana had predicted, his actions had hurt her, but now he probably wanted her to forgive him and take him back.

He was close enough to talk now. *Why am I not moving? Why don't I just wake up?* But she had the detached curiosity of a dream, yearning to know what would happen next, and that was all. It was as though she watched herself. She hoped that she wouldn't say or do the wrong thing, as she would wish observing another person in an important meeting.

When she looked down, the Salt Flats had morphed, just slightly, into actual blue sky. The change didn't surprise her as it should have. Firian stopped walking. His feet angled downward a little to show that he was hanging in the air too. One side of his mouth lifted, teasing, and he floated backward as she had done in the field. She followed him, swinging her legs in the expanse.

Firian increased his speed, flying through misty clouds. Tendrils of white clung to him and dispersed. She reached out to touch them but they dissolved, a spray of cool mist, before her fingertips reached them. Firian didn't seem to be going anywhere, just flying, enjoying the sky. The bright light made his eyes burn blue.

He halted. She couldn't stop before she collided against his firm chest. Unfazed, he scooped her in his arms and held her there. As though sinking into mud, he sank backward. The mirror of the Flats had returned. Or something that looked like it. Now it was a shallow pool of water that reached in all directions like glass. He leaned back into it. Warm water lapped at her feet, her ankles, her calves. She wanted to sleep in the comfort of the water and Firian's arms. She lay on his chest, feeling his heart beat beneath her. His warm breath played on her cheek and ear.

Maybe if they didn't speak but just held each other, it would all be all right. The moment felt like a memory, one that had to be told carefully, leaving out details that would ruin it.

Firian kissed her hairline. His touch had two effects. It made her want to stay, and it made her more conscious, which made her want to leave.

For a second, she lay very still. Then something in her hardened against him, slowly growing more upset.

As she started to wake up, finding her way to the back of her eyelids, she shuddered at the dream. Firian had actually been there. She was sure of that. He had engineered the dream as a nonthreatening way to get her to warm to him. Hopefully that was all he meant to do. With the semi-consciousness of a dream, she hadn't been thinking clearly, couldn't tell him off as she would have if she had been awake.

She opened her eyes in darkness. Dim shapes of the bedposts and draped fabric ghosted her vision. Slim moonlight came in through the window of her bedroom. All was sleeping beneath its bluish glow.

Bard's story came back to her again. Firian had killed all those people. She smacked her lips as if she had eaten something bitter. This back and forth was tiring. She didn't want to love him.

How could she guard herself against his advances? Was there more she could do before she slept to resist him? Or could she fight? As soon as the thought came to her, she shoved it aside. If Firian was an expert in anything, it was fighting in the Unreal. She would stand no chance. But surely she could improve in closing her mind against him. Tanyu had to have their methods.

She rolled over beneath the covers. The stalk of the candle on the bed table stood cold and dark. Her mind roiled.

After a few minutes, she sat up, folding the soft blankets over her crossed legs. There was one more person she could ask. Did Bard keep the same hours as Firian? Bard confessed to being Firian's roommate for a time, so it was possible.

She closed her eyes again and tried to remember what Firian had taught her about creating a space to meet, reaching out with her mind… It became easy to do with him, but she had never attempted it with anyone else. The palace hallway materialized around her, a setting she had created multiple times. Would she recognize Bard's mind when she came to it?

Yes, there it was! It was like meeting a familiar smell—not easy to describe, but unmistakable nonetheless. "Bard?" she whispered.

He flickered into view, his eyes puckered with sleepiness. Drawing the back of one hand across them, he frowned in confusion as he looked at her.

She realized she was plain again. She'd never intentionally used her Original Beauty in the Unreal. She wasn't going to start now.

"My Keeper?" he said uncertainly, more questions forming in his expression.

"Could you show me how to get someone out of my dreams?" She ignored how vulnerable the request sounded.

Bard blinked a few times and scratched his head. Studying his fingernails, he said, "Fir? Is it Firian?"

Fear? At first she was going to protest that she wasn't afraid, and then she realized that "Fir" was a nickname. The idea would have amused her if she weren't so troubled. "Yes."

"*Katah?*" he asked through a grimace.

"Yes."

"That's hard, yeah." His fatigue made him act more familiar toward her than he ever had.

"Did I wake you up?"

He shook his head widely, like a shaggy dog shaking water out of its fur. "No, I was, um... I've been trying to stay awake through the night."

"Why?"

He licked his lips, finding the words. "I left the Academy, so, I figure they might try to kill me. Dreams, you know? But I take naps during the day. Hopefully they can't find me then." She could tell he was trying to keep his lilting words casual, but true fear edged his tone. He gave a huge yawn, an honest one.

Watching him made her yawn too. His plan didn't sound foolproof.

He squinted as though the hallway were bright with light, but every time she had imagined it, she'd seen it at night, dark with shadows.

"So there's no way to prevent him from getting in my mind?"

"Sentries would do it," he said.

Dimly, she remembered what Sentries were. "We don't really have any."

"Then I don't know."

"Would he really try to kill you?" she asked after a pause. The idea made her shudder. Bard seemed so innocent, and he had been Firian's friend.

Bard's jaw worked. "I didn't think so, but then he killed Rian..."

"Who's Rian?"

"A Tanyu. He was there. At the attack. Just in the way, I guess. He didn't get behind him." Bard began floating absently above the floor. "He wouldn't kill me, though."

"Then who would? Why are you afraid?"

He looked at her as though he'd never asked himself the question, but, now that he did, he knew the answer. "It's Master Belik, I guess." He clamped his lips together and bit down on them. "Yeah, he'd do something like that. Say I was a traitor to the Academy or something. He'd do it."

The name lingered between them. Master Belik. She'd heard that name before. Wasn't he the one Firian left in charge of the Academy while he was fighting in Torith? This was the first time Bard had mentioned him. If he could kill

Bard without Firian's approval, then he must have massive influence at the Academy. She tucked the information away.

Though the hallway was dark, the only light coming from the sconces along the walls, the colors seemed more vibrant in the Unreal. She'd missed this. To find someone non-threatening to meet felt suddenly liberating. She floated too.

His face split in a grin when he saw her do it. "Hey, look at that!"

She smiled.

"What else can you do?" he asked. Without waiting for a response, he shrank away to nothing and a streak of blue light shot across the hallway.

She gaped. "How did you…?"

Bard reappeared, holding a small ball of blue light in his hand. It licked up like fire but held its shape, reflecting the light oddly and casting wavy shadows. She realized it was made not of fire, but water. "This is one of the first things they teach. You know, once you have the basics."

"No, he didn't show me that." Had Firian been withholding things from her, or was she just not advanced enough?

"Here, hold out your hand." His blue light vanished and he held his empty palm face up. It looked almost black in the nighttime corridor.

She did as he said.

"Then you picture it. Believe it's there."

She stared at her hand, the lines on her palm. She waved her fingers as though that would help the light appear.

He screwed up his face in confusion when nothing happened for her. He tested it in his own hand, the ball of light appearing and disappearing quickly once, twice. His face looked unearthly, underlit with blue. "Okay," he said, having an idea. "Okay. It can't just be the way it looks. You have to think about how it feels, or if it weighs anything. Focus on it like it's a real thing. Act like it's a real thing. That's when you stop thinking so hard. It'll work then."

She followed his instructions the best she could. A feeble blue glow grew between her globed fingers. She stared at it, mesmerized, then up to Bard, who was smiling. When her attention shifted, the light went out like a dying ember.

"That's all right," he said. "That was good! You're not a Tanyu or anything." He cut himself off, embarrassed. "I mean—"

"I know. That's fine," she said, stretching her fingers. "I'll practice that."

"There's a game with it, once you get it down."

"A game?" She was intrigued.

"Yeah, I used to play with some friends. Not Firian, usually. He was too serious most of the time. Other people."

That didn't surprise her. Firian was always serious. His focus, as he liked to say, made him the best. But it probably cost him some fun at the Academy. She'd not considered that people might have fun there, but Tanyu were people, just like everybody else. Bard certainly broke the stereotype.

"I do know how to play Indisfate, though," she said.

"I thought you wanted me to show you." He alighted on the rug.

"Show me how you play. Not teach me."

He scrunched his face in an impish expression, bothered and almost impressed. The board appeared between them, all its pieces in place. Bard changed the background subtly to a place she didn't recognize. It was a cliff of tufted grass that sloped down to the sea. The grass waved in the breeze, but she didn't feel cold. The air smelled like horses.

"I did that with Firian too," she continued.

Bard laughed. "I bet he hated that!"

"Yeah, I beat him."

He doubled over with high-pitched, barking laughter. When he straightened, he pressed the heels of his hands to his eyes. "Oh, that's wicked. I beat him too." Peeling his palms away, still gleeful, he looked at her. Mischief glinted in his eyes. "Okay, let's have a game."

BARD WON the first game of Indisfate. Kiria won the second.

She and Bard had both beaten Firian at this game before. Maybe strategy wasn't his strong suit. Maybe it was sheer force, in the Real and Unreal. If she could outthink him somehow...

The later it grew, the clearer their situation became. Firian—and Belik, from the sound of it—wouldn't suffer an insult like the Kingdom's attack on the Academy without retaliating.

She blew a breath through her nose as Bard magically put the pieces back again. The Vipers and Men and Falcons all moved, very slightly. At first it seemed a trick of the light, as though a new shadow had fallen across the intricate figures, but then she saw that they actually ruffled their feathers or stretched their bows or snaked out forked tongues. An unconscious smile crossed Bard's face as he looked at them. She hated to ruin his calm.

"Bard," she said quietly.

He raised his eyes to her.

"Has Firian used his... ability... any other time?"

A tiny horse walked across the game board. "A prisoner escaped, one of the pirates. That was the first time." He corrected himself. "The first time I saw it. But he knew what to do, so I'm pretty sure he'd done it before. Maybe on the island."

Her stomach clenched. "Is that it?" *Isn't that enough?* She picked up the Man gingerly and set him down. She couldn't will the pieces to their positions yet.

"That's all I know. I think he probably did it one other time, but I'm not sure."

"When?" She wasn't sure she wanted to know.

"Um..." He hesitated as if he wasn't sure how much she already knew. Bard understood that the connection between her and Firian was strong. "There was a... another Master who wanted to control everything. Yeah, so he almost killed him. A big guy. He was huge, so I don't know how Fir could have gotten out of it unless he just..." His voice faded away again. The Viper coiled around and around in a circle.

"It works on a lot of people, then," she said. The words were empty, but maybe they would jog some idea that could solve the problem.

"Yeah." His piece moved on its own to the correct spot.

Kiria recognized the same pattern he had used before to win the game. "What do you think he'll do now?" It was a question she'd avoided asking, but she couldn't put it off anymore. She needed to be a strong Keeper for her people. The Western Kingdom was far more important than one man, no matter who it was. She couldn't let anything get in the way of Brithnem's safety. Mercy had to have a limit.

Bard twitched one shoulder upward, shrugging. "What do you mean?" he muttered. Apparently, he didn't want to think about it either.

"Will he stay there or come here?"

"I left right after, so I didn't hear."

He paused, but she refused to play her turn.

"But you have a guess. You know him better than I do."

He gave his signature rapid nod. "He'll do something soon. He was sick for a while."

"When?" This surprised her. He hadn't seemed sick in the dream. But everything could be different in the Unreal. She could make herself plain when she was using her Beauty in the real world. Firian was so advanced, he could probably make himself look like anything he wanted.

"Right after the attack," said Bard.

She raised an incredulous eyebrow. "Didn't you leave?"

"Sometimes I know what he's doing anyway. Or I check, just check up on him." He waved at the board.

"Do you know what he's doing now?" she demanded, annoyed that he hadn't mentioned this before.

"Not right now." He seemed oddly hesitant as he drew figure eights on the floor in front of his crossed legs. Lines tightened around his mouth and eyes. He cleared his throat.

"Could you look?" Firian had the ability to spy on her, but she could never get the hang of doing it the other way around. He always knew she was there. But if Bard could watch him, that could be exactly what they needed.

Bard looked up at her meaningfully, chin tilted down. What if they both found what they dreaded? Even if Bard found Firian making a speech at the Academy about how he wouldn't attack Brithnem, they still couldn't trust him not to turn on them. He had that killing ability, so no matter what he said or did, he was a threat.

Was there anything Firian would trade, or someone he would listen to, in exchange for peace? Besides Master Belik, who seemed to hold some sway, the only options she knew were paying Indisfate on this cliffside. She searched her memory. Was there really no one else? Then she remembered Firian's sister, and their emotional reunion. She might be another one to add to the very short list.

"One of us should talk to him."

"Yeah, I know," he said, as though he had been waiting for her to say that, but hoping she wouldn't.

She moved her game piece. The Falcon flapped in her gentle grip. "We don't have a choice. This is bigger than us."

Bard's nostrils flared with the force of his intaken breath. Then he nodded again, more slowly this time. "Sorry I didn't do it sooner," he said quietly.

"I don't blame you."

He gave her a wan smile.

"But we have to do it now. We'll both talk to him." She couldn't watch Firian the same way, but she could get his attention. She was sure of that much.

A Horse ran off the board. Bard cupped his hand to lead it back where it belonged.

"Not at the same time, obviously," she continued. "Do you think he knows you're here?"

"I don't think so. I think I would know." The Horse settled in place.

"Separately, then."

Nothing definitive changed about Bard's breathing, but she suddenly noticed it. It seemed more careful. He was nervous.

"We have to," she said.

"We have to," he echoed.

When they looked at each other, they had a grim understanding. They would do it for the Kingdom. They would do everything they could, but Firian would choose his own fate. She prayed he chose the right one.

54

FIRIAN

FIRIAN TRIED to ignore the blisters on his feet. Surely they were bleeding into his boots by now. When they stopped, he would try to find running water and bind them. If anything, the pain reminded him of where he was going and anchored him to his surroundings. He'd grown too soft.

He jumped lightly up a cluster of boulders on the side of the path where his army trudged. Below him, heads bobbed as they moved by.

Higher than some of the smaller trees, he knew he was conspicuous, should anyone else be traveling in these mountains, and he didn't care. Belik would tell him he could just use his extra ability. The thought made his blood curdle, so he pushed it away.

Even at their worm's pace, they would arrive in less than two weeks. Brithnem. What had Kiria said? It meant Beautiful City, or something like that. It had been beautiful, he supposed, but he hadn't focused on that when he was there. Beneath its appearance was power, the kind of power he'd felt in his test with Tiev, when all the light and wind and intensity spiraled like a tornado.

He turned at the sound of a familiar voice. But it wasn't a voice. It was the Unreal. Someone was waiting for him. Quickly, he dove in.

Bard stood in their room back at the Academy. For a mad second, Firian wondered if Bard really had gone back, only to find most of the town and fortress emptied. He looked around the little room for the tell, the change. The bunk bed with its dirty sheets, the dresser, the candle, and even the faint scent of cinnamon and sweat were all the same. Bard scrubbed the back of his head, sending his spiky hair flying. Then he spotted Bard's wooden figure of Corso, the Tanyuin hero, on the window ledge.

"I told you to get out," Firian said, relief and anger battling for dominance.

"I did." The same edge of defiance that he'd had during their last interaction punctuated his response. "I wanted to see how you were, mate. You weren't... feeling good when I left."

An unexpected swell of emotion caught Firian by the throat. He swallowed it roughly down, waiting to see if Bard would admit where he had gone. Maybe he was going to tell him what he was doing at the palace.

"Is there a reason you came?" Firian prompted.

Bard's black eyes grew visibly nervous. "To see how you were," he repeated. "And to see what you're up to. I was thinking, Jac's in the army, you know, and I just... wondered about the Kingdom. I was hoping you wouldn't... after everything that happened..."

Firian fixed him with a glare. So that was it. Bard was trying to learn how he would retaliate because of the recent attack. He had officially gone to the other side. The side that had sent soldiers to ravage the Academy. That had tried to kill him. Firian felt his fingers tremble with rage.

Bard was the one friend he never thought would betray him. He'd doubted Kiria and Belik and all the rest, but never Bard. That he would ask for information to give the enemy... Firian could barely see, his vision spotted black and red.

Bard seemed to realize Firian's intention the moment before he struck. He crouched to avoid a sheet of flame shot from Firian's hands. "Wait! I only—"

But the landscape shifted away from their small room at the Academy. The fire flared to nothing as the Pillars of Awel materialized, at least the way Firian had always pictured them. Impossibly tall stone pillars overlooking the ocean, with a four-posted room cut out of the top for spying ships.

Firian stood at the top of one of the pillars, Bard at the top of one nearby. Firian threw a dagger at him. It evaporated in the air, as he expected. He didn't mean to kill Bard, but to send a clear message: *Leave me alone. Take your gory questions and never come back.*

"Firian!" Bard wrapped one arm around the nearest post, as though he anticipated what Firian would do next.

The world tilted hard, tipping the two of them to the right. Firian almost tripped at the force of his own illusion, but he stepped carefully from the stone floor to the wall to the ceiling as everything turned around.

Bard hung onto a thin stone pillar holding up the roof, as though he thought the world would keep turning. From upside down, he stared at Firian, but didn't move to fight.

Firian hopped to the lip of the roof, the drop from that ledge now impossibly far, into the dim sky and out of sight. Above him, the dark ocean churned, its spray falling like light rain. He liked this. He just needed to give Bard a lesson.

The ocean released. As water fell with a roar, Firian jumped. The adrenaline of falling subsided into something like calm as the sky lightened around him.

He slowed and landed on the roof of Mon Párinath. Long blue and purple flags snapped around him. Toward the sea, the Amiran Academy looked a perfect circle from up here. On the other side of the palace, a green lawn reached down to the city streets. Just like he remembered. It was close enough to the real thing. The only addition he made was adding grass in wide swaths along the flat rooftop, with walkways of stone along the sides.

Bard appeared in one corner of the roof, popping into existence like a bubble. He eyed Firian but didn't cower. Firian was proud of Bard's courage. What guarantee did he have that Firian wouldn't hurt him?

When Bard merely set his jaw, Firian summoned more fire. It burst from his hands in two thick orange streaks.

Bard stumbled back, struck. Firian's heart turned over. Recovering his balance, Bard conjured a shield of water. It was an elementary move, almost comforting. The water spread out as though as though it splashed onto a circular pane of glass, though nothing was there. Beads of it sprayed up and clung to Bard's face. That, or he was starting to sweat. As Firian's fire disappeared into the water shield, he realized that Bard hadn't gotten wet from the falling ocean. He must have disappeared in time to avoid it.

Firian's veins, raised and glowing red, felt like the firestream. Why didn't Bard fight back? Firian snapped away the fire. He'd try something new. One by one, he replicated himself until six Firians stood on the palace roof.

Bard's water shield evaporated. Without that barrier, Firian could see blood dribbling from one corner of his mouth. Not much. He would be fine. Bard's eyes widened as he looked from form to form, all identical, all staring back at him. "Firian!" he shouted. "Stop! I don't want to hurt you!"

Firian's mouths curved in a bitter smile. At last he got a reaction.

Bard's chest heaved as he looked around at the copies of Firian. His face betrayed his belief that any one of them could strike if he wasn't paying attention. "Firian, where are you now?" His voice had grown hard-edged. He didn't mean which copy was the true Firian. That wasn't the right question. He meant in real life. Was he on the way to the capital?

"Where are you?" The words sounded eerie coming out of so many mouths.

They both knew the answer, but he waited for a few heartbeats, freshly aware of where they stood. If Bard were honest about going to Brithnem, at least Firian would know Bard hadn't changed as much as he feared. Firian clasped his hands behind his back as his Masters used to do, waiting patiently for the correct response.

For a second, he thought of warning Bard to get out of the city, but that would just alert him to their plans. So he stayed silent.

Quiet surged around them, as though there had been white noise during the rest of their confrontation. Now it was truly still, even breaths muted.

The implication was clear: *You betrayed me.*

And you're a monster, Firian.

They stared at each other, neither one backing down, though the longer they looked (Bard had chosen the center Firian to stare at), the more the silence gained the color of memory, and Bard's eyes rimmed red, and Firian started to fear that his own eyes looked the same from rage. Firian found himself wishing he could erase the past couple weeks completely, maybe the past couple months of his reign, and start over. At the beginning, he said he would do this right. That was why he had killed the previous Head. Yet here he was, having lost everything that mattered.

Into the Unreal

When no one spoke for a few beats longer, Firian opened his eyes. Squinting against the bright sunlight on the rock, he cursed.

55

KIRIA

The conversation at the session had exhausted her. Charäkhni trade agreement logistics seemed trivial compared to the secret project she and Bard were working on. Two days ago, Bard had tried talking to Firian first. When Kiria went to get information from Bard later that day, he didn't want to talk about it. He almost looked as if he'd been crying. That was so rare among Tanyu that her heart had jolted with fear—they were lost, Bard had told him everything, Firian was going to retaliate and kill them all...

Bard did admit that Firian knew he was in Brithnem, and then he said he couldn't go again. It wasn't new information that had broken his heart, after all.

Enough time had passed that Kiria hoped her visit wouldn't seem suspiciously connected to Bard's. The possibility existed that he would figure it out, but she had to try anyway. The Kingdom needed to know any plans he'd made against them. And the list of people Firian cared about enough to tell grew smaller and smaller.

Reaching her room, she startled to find that someone already stood there. "Oh!" she cried. "Jori, where did you come from?"

"Here. That's what they tell me."

"I told the guards not to let anyone in tonight."

Obviously chewing on something, Jori gave a lopsided grin. "You underestimate my powers of sweet talking."

"They still wouldn't have—"

"They *might* have, but I got in a different way. Lots of ins and outs in this castle."

Kiria didn't know of another entrance besides... the chimney? She felt instantly foolish for thinking it. There was an emergency escape tunnel as well in all the Keepers' rooms, strictly off limits unless the worst were to happen. "Tunnel?" she asked.

He pointed at her, still chewing, as if she'd won a point.

Now that she looked, the knees of his blue pants looked particularly threadworn. He'd also buttoned his vest, which he only did for some special occasions and, apparently, when he didn't want the front dragging in the dust as he crawled through a tunnel.

"You should know better than this," she said. He was nineteen and acted like he was nine.

"I doubt that'll happen any time soon," he said lightly. "There's a party just outside the palace wall tonight. Unsavory characters, flowing ale, non-royals. I thought you might be interested."

"You know I can't."

"I don't know that."

"I have things to do."

"Tanyuin things?"

She tried to stop the creeping blush. Her hesitation was enough of an answer. Had she promised never to see Firian again? She felt like she had. Well, this time it wasn't selfish. In fact, she'd have gotten out of it if she could. But the Kingdom needed information, needed her.

Jori's face fell. "I'm sorry Atty's treating you like an idiot, but you do run off to the Tanyu more than you should."

Her mouth fell open. "Excuse me?"

He raised his eyebrows almost into his hairline. "You want to invite the Tanyu too? I'm sure that would go over well."

"You don't know what you're talking about."

"I do, I do," he said, spinning on the balls of his feet to look at something at the side of the room. "You've told me."

But you don't know everything. You don't know that I'm dreading this meeting but I'm doing it anyway for you and the rest of the Kingdom. She couldn't say any of that, so instead she said, "Jori. Jori!"

He redirected his languid attention to her.

"Do you trust me?"

He paused to consider the question, looking first at her, then around the bedroom, as though searching for an answer. Maybe he just wanted to make her squirm. If so, it was working. He met her gaze again. "I think," he said deliberately, "that the Tanyu irritate me, but I also think that you are one of the best people I know." In his eyes was a challenge, as though it was up to her to keep it that way. "So yes, I do trust you."

"Thank you," she said, the relief too obvious. "Okay then. I need you to trust me now and leave me alone. I have to do something."

"Will this something take all night?"

"I hope not."

"Then ask for Tanis Restino at the north gate when you're done and they'll point you in the right direction. I'll be there. Possibly drunk. You might want to tone it down a bit before you come." He scanned her with his eyes.

At the mention of Tanis, the first boy she'd ever liked and the first one who had suggested that her Beauty was all that mattered, she knew she wouldn't go to his party. Years had passed, but he still reminded her of bad decisions. Hopefully she was better at reading people now. Thinking of the task ahead, she wasn't so sure.

She nodded at Jori. "All right."

He headed toward the door.

"The guards will hate you," she said.

He turned around and winked. "They love me." When he yanked open the handle and let the heavy door settle into place after him, she heard him say, "Boys, you miss me?"

She shook her head, stifling a grin, and turned her thoughts to the task at hand. She'd played it over in her mind a thousand times. Firian was rarely forthcoming with information. Even on his best days, he preferred to keep an air of mystery about him. Now, with more at stake and less reason to trust her, he would probably stay as tight as a barnacle.

She bristled at the idea of coaxing the plan out of him in more devious ways. The best she could come up with was to appeal to his better side. It was naïve, and quite possibly wouldn't work. She knew that already. The army of Brithnem was at the ready if he refused to side with her, though she didn't want to use them, or even bring them up, if possible.

Somewhere deep inside him was a man who could see the value of peace. It had to be true. For a moment, she had the odd sensation of looking back at herself with pity, as though her failure had already happened.

She took a few deep breaths.

Reverence, submission, prayer. *Let there be peace in the Western Kingdom.*

The words sounded childish. Was peace even possible? With so many moving and vying groups, the possibility felt remote. But she still wanted the same things she had wanted as a child: peace, goodness, wisdom. Maybe it was good that she didn't have strong political instincts, that her vision for Brithnem and the rest of the Kingdom was so simple. Someone had to hold onto that vision.

Now, though, it fell to her to secure it by finagling information out of a dangerous man.

She shook out her hands and rolled her neck. She could do this. She *would* do it. If Firian really was planning a counter-attack against the Kingdom, she might be their last hope of finding out.

Weight pooled heavily in her gut as the implication hit her. She had to do all in her power—*all in her power*—to get him to talk.

She blew out a quavering breath as she closed her eyes and wove a setting around her. She'd already chosen it. The hollow where the two of them had stayed the night after the attack in Raewhith. He had comforted her during a panic attack. She had bandaged a long sword wound down his back. She remembered him gazing bleakly at his sword sticking into the dirt, running his thumb along the crossguard. Red blood had soaked his bare back, and then the sash she'd used to clean it off. It was one of the only places where they had both been vulnerable.

The memory, oddly, was a good one. That day marked the first time she'd seen who he could be without his swagger and arrogance. She liked that version of him, the one who saved her from Torithians and spoke kindly to her when she didn't have the strength to keep walking.

As she set the little stream in place, and the rock where Firian had sat, a pang of regret or mourning struck her like a stomachache. She missed this Firian. Maybe she should have chosen a different place to meet.

A dark shape snagged her attention. Firian stood on the lip of the hollow. At the sight of him, she stumbled one foot back. She hadn't called for him. He looked at her with a confusing expression on his face, at once glad, desiring, and careful.

Dealing with her imaginary scenarios already seemed easier than dealing with the real thing. Regaining her composure, she stood tall, reminding herself to breathe.

What was she thinking? She actually could grow taller here. She rose up until she was about as tall as Firian. Everything looked a little different from his height.

Her skin prickled with nerves as he strode down into the hollow toward her. When he reached her, he scanned the length of her, clearly noting the height change.

Her heart thudded. "I was hoping you'd come," she began, unsure of what else to say.

His eyes lit up with hope and irony. "Were you?"

"Yes..." *Now what?* She couldn't just ask him outright. He'd refuse. All the practice conversations she had invented completely abandoned her, left her alone with him. Her cheeks heated. Then an idea came to her. "Firian, I need to know if I'm in danger."

He frowned and touched her arm just above the elbow. Realizing she had been wringing her hands, she dropped her arms to her sides.

"Why would you think that?" he asked.

"I... know what happened at the Academy," she said, looking up at him. How had she become smaller? It was probably too much to focus on both keeping up the illusion and directing this conversation.

He kept his expression neutral.

"And I was afraid you might do something rash," she continued.

"Did you make the order?" he asked, almost deadpan.

"No!"

A flutter of eyelashes signaled relief on his face.

"No." She amended the word with less emotion. "I didn't."

"Then you wouldn't be in danger." He sidled up to her, even closer, barely a whisper of distance between them.

She held her ground, despite her dry mouth and roiling insides. She turned to the side to speak. Body heat from his chest warmed her left cheek. "Is anybody else? In danger, I mean?"

"There's always someone." A fingertip near her temple sent chills down her body. Firian gently drew stray hairs behind her ear, taking his time. Right now it felt like that she was that someone.

Angry now—at Firian or herself, she didn't know—she tried to clear her cloudy mind. "There doesn't have to be," she said.

"Are you begging for your kingdom?" he asked smoothly, bringing her face up to look into his. "Or do you just want information?" His lip curled on the last word. His steel gaze meant he had guessed the reason for her visit. Dark hair fell into his blue eyes.

Her pulse galloped. "I want you to be the man you could be, without letting this go too far."

He deflated a little, releasing her chin. Kiria stepped back, giving herself room to breathe.

He thought for a moment. "I won't tell you anything. Today," he said. "Maybe tomorrow."

His meaning was clear. She had to return if she wanted him to reveal anything useful. She set her jaw. "*Will* you tell me tomorrow?"

"Let's say I don't." He clasped his hands behind his back. "What would you do?"

He was playing games now. Lives were at stake. He had to end this flirtation and come to some peaceful understanding. "I have an army."

He smiled as though she had just put on her Beauty. "I don't think you'd use it."

"I think I'd have to." Suddenly, it surprised her that he rarely won games of Indisfate. Now, at least, he didn't seem averse to risky strategy.

"Then we'll see tomorrow," he said. He looked at her for a long moment, until his cocky demeanor turned to pain, before he disappeared.

56

FIRIAN

She smelled like lavender and sweet oranges and musk. Firian tried to breathe it in again as he walked through the darkness, past skinny black tree trunks. It took a few seconds for his heart to stop pounding after he left the encounter with Kiria in the hollow.

She was coming back tomorrow. It didn't matter that he made her do it. She was angry; so was he. She hadn't warned him about the attack against the Academy and now she wanted to know his plans, as Bard had. But now he had leverage to make demands.

Forcing her to meet him tomorrow was the kind of thing Bard would probably think was monstrous. Well, if it was, then it was worth it.

His disparate troops had crested the mountain and now had the arduous task of going down the other side. The pirates kept gasping in the thin air and drinking the extra water reserves. Firian found himself hating them more and more. But the Tanyu didn't give him any trouble. In fact, now that he thought about it, he hadn't worried about a mutiny since before the Kingdom attacked. Even Tanyu weren't fool enough to fight him now, it seemed.

Belik stumped up beside him. "We need to find a place."

Firian didn't see a spot to make camp, but there was probably a cave not too far away. He and Kiria had stayed in several of them on their trip, and he had taken shelter in one on his way to Brithnem later.

Tomorrow. The word beat like a drum. He would see her again tomorrow. After going for so long without her presence, even their time in the hollow felt delicious. He wanted more.

"You're still seeing her, aren't you?" The question came like something from his own mind, but he caught Belik's eye and knew he'd asked it.

Firian didn't answer. They were far enough away from the others that they wouldn't be overheard, even if he did speak.

He heard tiny sounds of the army behind him. Belik looked at him, but Firian didn't acknowledge him, instead focusing on the long, thin clouds.

"You have to break that *katah* if it kills you," said Belik in an undertone. "Cut her off, set a Sentry—"

"Shut up. I'm handling it."

"You aren't handling it." Belik set his glasses fiercely. "You told me you were done. But I can tell you aren't. You have to free yourself before we reach the city or you'll put everyone here at risk."

Firian glowered at Belik. His connection to Kiria hurt no one but himself.

"That's ten days. Cut it off. Kill her if you have to, but get out of there."

Firian's blood burned with rage. He imagined grabbing Belik by the throat for that comment, but he did nothing.

"Your allegiance is with us," Belik continued, as though he didn't sense his danger for speaking to him this way. "The Tanyu need you. The world looks up to us. Kingdom be damned. But if you're still entertaining that *katah*, she will take us all down. Do you understand me?"

"She's not—"

Belik said it slower this time. "She will control you, and take us all down."

"Damn it! If I want her, why does it matter to you?"

He felt waves of anger radiating from Belik. He grated out, "I thought, at one time, that it didn't matter. It didn't matter what I did. I was above it all. And that was true, mostly." His voice fell until it was uncharacteristically small, rising just above the sound of their own footsteps. "I was the Strategy Master, so sometimes Amiran groups, radical groups, would send women after me. Declare *katah*. I killed them, Firian, to protect the Academy and its reputation."

A chill washed down Firian's spine.

"But..." Belik hesitated, watching the dark ground before them for a while before going on. "There was one who was different. I entertained her for a while. I thought I would kill her later, but she wasn't afraid and she didn't pose like the others. She looked me in the eye. She could have been a Tanyu if she weren't so gory stupid." Firian thought the comment seemed unwarranted, but the statement seemed aimed also at himself. It took Belik a moment to collect himself from a choking bitterness. "So the *katah* took," he said in an angry sigh. "I should have been more careful, but I thought she wanted me too, after a while. We talked about being together. That's always how it goes. They make you believe it. She even came to a place nearby—I never told her where the Academy was, but I was traveling—and we met in the Real. Several times. I thought she'd stay there." He spat. "When she got pregnant, I thought she'd stay there. It was my son. She should have stayed. But she wanted him to be an Amir." He cursed creatively. "My son, an Amir! I told her she had to stay, that my son would never be less than a Tanyu." He took a couple breaths as he finished his story, slow and deliberate. "We could have fought in the Unreal—I would have won—but she broke my leg, left with my son, and destroyed my hope of becoming the Tanyuin Head."

Firian hardly dared to speak. Chetana. It had to be Chetana, Kiria's advisor. The one he had seen on his first day in Belik's room.

"She's still in my gory head!" Belik pounded his skull with a finger as he hissed out the words, more sound than talk. They walked on in silence as the words spiraled out. "So," he said, his voice clear now, dark with meaning, "it doesn't matter if she's nice or tells you everything you and your dick want to hear. You will break off the *katah* before we reach the capital."

Firian swallowed, but it didn't wet his dry throat, not even enough to tell him off. With anyone else, that would work, but not Belik. Belik had been there for too long. He'd seen too many things. And suddenly parts of Firian's memory clicked into place.

Firian saw a large cave opening ahead on the left. Belik saw it too and left to order the army to stop and make camp.

Belik's horrible history with Chetana didn't have any bearing on Firian's situation. Kiria was different. He felt complete when he was with her; every moment excited him. And she was good. Despite everything, she still cared about him.

A whiff of pine floated past on the cool breeze. Nothing would go wrong if he saw Kiria again. He *would* see her again, and he only had to wait until tomorrow.

57

KIRIA

Kiria found Cúron emerging from a meeting with his advisor. They had been drinking strong coffee in the solarium that looked out onto the gardens and the ocean beyond. At the sight of Kiria, Parohim took Cúron's small porcelain cup and set it clattering on a tray with his own.

Kiria started to walk into the solarium before she paused. "Lord Cúron," she said, "I'd like to have a word with you about something important." Hopefully if she didn't look at Parohim, he would realize that he wasn't invited. Bitter-scented steam from the coffee rose from the cups.

Cúron pursed his mouth. The short white hairs around his lips stuck out. "Is it particularly important? I was just going to—"

"Monumentally," Kiria said.

Cúron paused a moment, and then turned to Parohim with a look that said he would fill him in later.

"Thank you," she said, descending the two steps into the solarium. Plants and flowers and trees from the farthest reaches of the known world grew there. Large, pale pink, tubular flowers that drooped over their bases, plants with leaves as long as Kiria's arm and three times as wide, stalks that brimmed with thorns from the base to the top, its arms sticking out at fantastic angles. From the roof hung fruit and long, trailing vines. Half of the room was sided with thick glass that gave onto first a barrier and then the landscape beyond.

She and Cúron settled into chairs. His sharp eyes took her in when he thought she wasn't looking. When she faced him, he fixed his expression as an indulgent father would. She set her jaw. He had to believe her, but lately that hadn't been in vogue.

"I think he's coming here," Kiria said, without preamble.

"Who's coming here?" he asked, loudly enough to suggest there were more people in the room.

She quickly looked behind her, but they were alone. "Firian."

His bushy eyebrows rose, then lowered. "How do you know?" He asked the question as he used to do when she was a child, soothingly, disbelievingly.

"He plans to take revenge. On you. I don't want that to happen."

"How do you know?" he repeated, obviously knowing the answer but wanting her confession anyway.

She breathed in the thick green scent of the room. The humidity was already starting to coat her skin. She wondered how Cúron could stand to be here wearing his favorite heavy blue robe. "I'm one of the only people who can get information out of him. I knew this was a possibility so I went to talk to him. For the Kingdom."

His blue eyes became cloudy as he looked at her. "For the Kingdom? Kiria, you know he's dangerous."

"I know." *But Keepers should be willing to face danger.*

"You shouldn't have gone. He's done nothing but hurt us, and yet you run to him every chance you get. It's like he's cast a spell on you."

She felt her face getting red. "I didn't *run* to him. I went to see if he would retaliate for our attack on the Academy. I think he will."

"You think? Did he say so?" He sighed, settling his sleeves. "Kiria, I'm worried about you. You keep thinking the Tanyu are good, but they're our enemy. All the advisors see it."

"They're all Amir."

"Which is why they make such good advisors. You trust Daelon, don't you?"

"Absolutely."

"So do I."

Running her thumb along the intricate ridges of the chair's armrest, she looked out the window.

"We have our own ways of getting information," Cúron continued, "so stop putting yourself in danger by talking to those Tanyu." His ideas came out as though they were the only logical option. "How many guards do you have for the one staying in your wing?"

"Four."

"I thought there were more."

"There used to be, but four is enough." She turned back to him.

He cocked his head in blatant skepticism. "See, you're even sympathizing with that one. They're master manipulators. I'm going to add a couple more guards to his room."

"Bard wouldn't hurt us." The very suggestion sounded ludicrous.

He returned an almost pitying look that made her shoulders tense. She was trying to help the Kingdom and she got pity. Deep down, she cared for Cúron. He'd been there for her when she was growing up, but his condescension became more pointed as she got older.

"He wouldn't!" she cried. "Have you met him? He's nothing like the Tanyu that used to come here, or like Firian. I think Firian might hurt you. You have to get ready."

He regarded her for a long moment.

"You should mobilize the troops." She rolled her eyes. "Don't say it was me. Don't tell them where I got the information, but you have to be ready."

"Have you told Atael?"

"Not yet." The truth would just drive a deeper wedge in their friendship. "Would you do it?"

"Have you told the other Tanyu?"

"Not yet."

"He could tell the Tanyuin Head our plans. You can't tell him what we plan to do."

Remembering Bard's desolate expression after his last encounter with Firian, she doubted he would tell Firian anything. "I won't give him any details," she promised.

"And I'll inform Atael," he said, rising with bustling finality. His head brushed against one of the trailing leaves. "Stay away from the Tanyu, Kiria. Brithnem doesn't need any more unrest. You are with *us*, not them."

She hated that the words echoed some of her own thoughts. She'd never wanted to go against the Kingdom, or betray it. But she still found it oddly difficult to think about the Tanyu in such black and white terms. Life didn't work like that. Everyone in Brithnem wasn't good and everyone at the Academy wasn't bad. Their choices made them what they were.

Her choice was to see Firian again, to risk her reputation to get more facts Brithnem could use to protect itself. The idea rattled her with nerves, but it was the only way forward. It might not be good enough—her efforts rarely were—but it was something.

"I am with you," she agreed.

58

FIRIAN

FIRIAN'S HEART lurched when Kiria appeared. During the entire day's march, he'd been dipping in and out of the Unreal, testing different settings. It took away the monotony and kept his skills sharp.

The current setting was an indoor pool casting patterns of light on the ceiling. Water could be difficult to reproduce correctly in the Unreal. A shadow would be wrong, or a swell too perfect, and the illusion would be shattered. Kiria did well at the beach for a beginner, but Firian had practiced for years.

Kiria appeared on the opposite side of the pool, her head instantly tipping up to see the dancing webs on the ceiling. She had her hair tied back and wore a simple linen dress that covered her from her collarbone to her ankles. He couldn't even see the tip of her royal tattoo rising over her shoulders. Most of her dresses dipped down in the back to highlight it, but this one didn't. Still, the blue and white and black reflections encircled her, caressed her. He watched them for a while, savoring the quiet moment. Soon enough, they would speak and things would get more complicated.

She seemed entranced by the vision he'd created, gazing around before her eyes lighted on him. "Is this a place you know?" she asked, remaining still on the opposite side of the space. Her voice echoed around the room.

"No." A smile grew across his features. She was here with him. He didn't move to go around the pool either.

A line formed between her eyebrows. "I'm back. So...?"

She didn't waste any time. They were often alike in that way. Today, though, he preferred to waste time. "Relax," he said, sitting at the edge of the pool. "You seem like you could use it, Kiria."

She didn't sit. "I'm just here to find out what you know so the people I care about don't get hurt."

"I won't hurt you," he said, feeling like he'd repeated himself a dozen times.

"What did you do to Bard? Whatever it was, that hurt me."

"Did it?" he said through clenched teeth. She wasn't going to pretend, then. "Sit."

"I prefer to stand."

"Kiria." Her name came out in exasperation. She was fighting herself, fighting him. Couldn't things go back to the way they were? "I didn't hurt him," he said.

She grabbed her elbow with her other hand. "There's more than one way to hurt somebody."

His jaw flexed as he remembered Chetana. They stayed in awkward silence for a while. She stood, he sat, separated by the dark pool. This conversation was already going badly. "Yes, there is," he agreed, fixing her with a look to remind her that she wasn't innocent either.

"I didn't have a choice."

"There's always a choice." Her words from when he took her hostage for the Academy. *Always a choice.* His life had felt like a series of inevitabilities. What choice could he have made to make Bard stay, to make Kiria love him?

She must have recognized the words because she bit her lip as though biting back a response. The gesture brought memories that made Firian's stomach swoop.

"How did you know?" she asked, meaning the attack.

"I listen."

"I'd listen," she said, now with both arms around herself, "if you'd tell me anything."

I'll tell you everything. He almost said the words, but they were a blatant lie, and she'd know immediately. Other girls he'd been with expected lies, almost demanded them. It was the language of flirtation, but Kiria knew better. She wanted something real, and he didn't know what to give her.

To buy time, he stripped down to his underwear and jumped into the pool. Its cool water enveloped his head and swirled against his skin. Tiny bubbles zigzagged up the hairs on his legs and over his chest. *One, two, three, four...* He held his breath, but it was suddenly gone. Water meant death. To suck in air through his nose or mouth would drown him even as he tried to save himself, water burning thickly in his lungs as he choked.

He thrashed to the surface, gulping. The splash of his head and arms sounded as loud as a scream.

Kiria, sitting on the edge now, looked down at him with concern. Her arms weren't crossed anymore. She even leaned forward toward the water. Her thin veil of pretext was torn.

His shame dissipated quickly. He lapped up the look, holding her gaze.

"Are you okay?"

Still trying to catch his breath, he made the pool shallower. His bare toes gripped the rough floor. "Fine."

"You sure?"

He half-swam, half-walked to her side of the pool. Reaching it, he slicked back his hair. "Yeah, I'm okay."

The moment suddenly reminded him of a few months ago.

I'm glad you're alive. She hadn't liked admitting it then either.

"Why do we do this?" he asked.

The skirt covering her crossed legs moved as she flexed her feet underneath it. "Because you're probably coming for revenge and won't tell me."

"I might tell you tomorrow."

She huffed. "This isn't a game, Firian!" A flush of anger or sadness darkened her cheeks. "If you don't tell me... if you don't leave us alone... we'll have to kill you, and everyone who helps you. I won't be able to stop it, and..." Her voice trailed off. She looked away.

"And what?"

"I don't think I would."

He stepped back. The water swished with the movement. "Does Bard think that too?" Of course he did. Firian was a monster, after all.

"I don't know," she said. Did they talk about him all the time? How well did the two of them know each other?

"I can look out for myself," he found himself saying. He was done with talking. It was getting them nowhere. He didn't intend to tell her where he was or what he was planning. She didn't want to talk about anything else. Blue patterns webbed across her sullen face. Seized by a desire to touch her, it took considerable strength to hold himself back.

Maybe just one more question. It burned inside him. She, like Bard, tried never to lie. She put up a front sometimes, but she couldn't hide how she truly felt. And he didn't know how she would answer.

Those seconds in the water looking up at her felt like adoration, like judgment. "Come in with me," he said, surprised to find his voice a whisper. The sound barely reached the walls, quieter than the drips echoing from somewhere.

She shook her head, but there was a tiny hesitation. He latched onto it. "It's the Unreal," he said, reaching out a hand toward her, reminding her and himself. Her dress wouldn't even get wet. Not really.

"Firian..."

"Come on." He tried not to sound too desperate, but he wanted her close for this question. He wanted her close even without anything to say. Holding her would calm his heart a little, or at least make it beat from something other than nervousness. His stomach twisted. He had to know the answer, but asking felt like jumping from a height and hoping for water instead of stones at the bottom.

His hand wavered in the air for too long, but he didn't take it away. She regarded it, focused on his dripping palm and fingers. She couldn't understand the power in that look. "Will you tell me what I want to know?" she asked.

"You first. I have a question."

Wary creases formed at the corners of her eyes. She took his hand and with the other held her dress down as she slipped into the pool. The wet fabric clung to her legs. It was thick enough not to outline the shape of her body, but his heart thumped anyway.

He could drown her, he realized, immediately disgusted by the thought. That meant, though, that she trusted him, at least a little. Little was better than nothing.

Her face was still impassive, not inviting him any closer, but he drew her toward him anyway. Despite the water all around them, his mouth felt thick and dry. Surely, he was strong enough to ask a simple question.

He wrapped one arm around her back to speak in her ear. He was right that the dress revealed no bare skin. A shiver passed through his body as a finger gently touched the long scar on his own back. A moment, and it was gone. The touch pushed him over the edge of that high place.

"Kiria," he breathed, "do you think I'm a monster?"

A long silence. Too long. He tightened his grip on the fabric of her dress to steady himself, staying by her ear. If she had the worst to say, he'd rather hear it than see it on her face.

Then she whispered, "You always have a choice."

59

KIRIA

Kiria and Jori sat on the floor of Bard's guest room, playing a game called Slug. It required acting quickly to collect matching objects from the floor. Players took turns, but the turns were often so fast that they almost overlapped. According to the Calthwaite boys, there were times when it was acceptable to skip someone's turn. Every year, the rules multiplied. Kiria had grown up playing the game, but she suspected Jori had invented it himself. The origins of Slug had long since fallen out of memory.

Bard caught on quickly, his dark eyes darting over the small objects strewn in the middle of their little circle. He seemed particularly focused. Maybe he was glad to had something mindless to focus on as well.

Kiria's meetings with Firian frustrated her. He refused to tell her anything substantive, though she'd seen him multiple days in a row. For so many reasons, she no longer wanted to be with him, but her body betrayed her. Her pulse raced and she fantasized about being in his arms, but only in the Unreal. She'd gotten used to it as a secret space, where it didn't matter what she did. But obviously it did matter. The Unreal, despite its name, could be just as real as this moment, now, with Bard and Jori.

Jori lashed out a hand to grab a ring and drop a token. Kiria was collecting stones, so his move didn't help her. Bard seemed to be trying for a collection of small figurines of the royals. Kiria rarely went for that set. It was dumb, she knew, but it felt a little weird. Jori knew that, and used her preferences against her. Try as she might, she had never become a master of Slug. Jori basically controlled the game every time, reminding them all of "rules" they had forgotten, so she might not have stood a chance anyway.

With one hand, Bard grabbed a ring and a figurine of Kiria. With the other, he blindly took a bite of cinnamon toast. He'd ordered tons of the stuff ever since his meeting with Firian almost two weeks ago. Since he didn't eat with the Keepers or the servants, Bard seemed to live on orders of cinnamon toast and oranges.

She refocused her attention on the game in time to see Jori snatching a coin aloft, stretching it toward the ceiling in triumph. "Ha! I won!" He laid out five coins neatly in front of his crossed and booted legs.

Kiria and Bard showed their hauls. She had three stones and two tokens. Bard had four figurines and a ring. The face on Cúron's figure had almost rubbed off completely from years of playing.

"Ah, you were close," Jori told Bard, "but I'm the king of Slug."

Bard gave a broad, close-lipped smile.

"You know what I just realized?" Jori said, pointing to them both. "You have the Talent, you have the Talent, and you also have that Beauty. I'm the only one without an Ability. What are those others? I could have had one of those." He looked down and snapped, trying to spark a memory.

"Knowledge, Harmony, and Language," Kiria said.

"Right, right!" He hesitated. "There are five? What's Harmony? Maybe I have that one."

"Nature can't hurt them."

He smiled. "Well, maybe. I do like rain."

"It's different. You could still get struck by lightning."

"Thank you, darling. Always the optimist." He winked at Bard. "And why is yours called the Talent? Aren't you born with it? I find that supremely unfair."

"It takes practice to do it right," said Bard.

"Is that so?" Jori turned to Kiria, who nodded.

Some of the smaller pieces bounced over the rug as Jori swept them all toward himself with his hand. He produced the badly sewn leather bag where he kept the pieces. When they were younger, he had scraped his name near the bottom in uneven letters. Above it, in larger and slightly more mature handwriting, it read "SLUG."

"Is it getting late for you, my darling?" he asked Kiria.

She peered at the window. It had been black for some time. Out there somewhere, the troops were ready to stand against an Academy attack, according to her orders. Well, according to Cúron's orders. The rumor around the army was that she had warned Firian about the impending assassination and so she had indirectly doomed the soldiers who marched to Tánuil. They weren't quick to trust her now. She had to gain back that trust, drop by drop, over years.

But she didn't have years. Each time she met with Firian, the more certain she became that the Tanyu were marching to the capital. At least all the Keepers could agree that they should prepare for the possible threat.

"Kiria?" Jori prompted, readjusting one of the larger figures so it would fit in the bag.

"Yes, it is getting late." Her eyes felt grainy and rough. Sleep had been hard to find the past few nights. It took Firian about two weeks to travel from the Academy to Brithnem. That time had come and gone, but that meant she didn't need to add extra time for travel. Tanyuin forces could theoretically arrive at any moment, if that really were their plan.

Into the Unreal

"Thanks for coming by," Bard said, scratching his head with both hands.

"Eh, you're not miserable company," said Jori, standing, with a roguish smile.

Bard hopped to his feet. It almost always looked like he jumped, rather than stood, as though he were weightless.

Jori tightened the strap on the leather bag. "I think it's time we said good night."

A swell of appreciation for the two of them rose in her. They hadn't abandoned her. They weren't the best political allies, but they cared and she loved them for it.

When she gave them each a quick hug, Jori hugged her back but Bard stiffened in surprise. "Good night," she said. "Thanks for the game."

Bard waved awkwardly as she and Jori left the room.

"What was that?" Jori asked, meaning the hug. He looked past her to smile at a guard, who didn't smile back. "Feeling lonely?"

"Something like that," she said.

He lowered his voice. "I think Atty will come around, the idiot."

He said it lightly, but she took it seriously. "I hope so." To lose a friendship that had meant so much to her growing up pained her more than she liked to say. Even Haved would be welcome into their little circle. She had hurt her, but Kiria still didn't think that Haved was fundamentally mean-spirited. Kiria admired the courage it took to marry a stranger for the sake of her own kingdom and then to love rather than resent him for it. Kiria thought of the little paper tree. Just the other day, she'd seen a corner of delicately folded paper sticking out of Atty's breast pocket.

They reached her room in seconds and Jori said goodbye. Candrae and Vayci helped her wash and get ready for bed. She couldn't have said why her stomach was in knots.

As she put her head down on the soft pillow and closed her eyes, she found out. The Unreal engulfed her as though she had fallen through the mattress into darkness beyond. The force of Firian's call overpowered her.

Something was different this time. There was no setting. There was only Firian, dressed in black. His agitation was palpable. She looked, expecting to see dark circles under his eyes, since his presence gave the impression he hadn't slept, but the Unreal washed away those imperfections.

His blue eyes blazed. "I'm going to tell you everything."

60

FIRIAN

Blood oozed from a torn piece of skin under Firian's Master ring. He hadn't realized he'd been picking at it again.

The few lookouts in the Gray Forest were easy to find and subdue. Now, if he got closer to where the woods thinned, he could see Brithnem. Yellow lights peeked through the dark like an inverted sky. At the crest of the hill sat the palace. Flags on the battlements waved like ghosts in the thin light. Bard's black eyes when they'd both stood on that roof came back to him. He ignored the memory.

Belik hadn't caught him meeting with Kiria during the rest of their journey. His fury wouldn't change Firian's mind, but he kept the secret anyway.

Before them lay the farms of the outer edge, sprawling to the thick city wall. This was the first step to taking over Brithnem. His lungs contracted as he glared through the trees covered with a mix of unfamiliar pine needles and leaves. Desire and anxiety battled within him. Governing the Academy had gained him enough enemies. But to have a kingdom...

A kingdom.

His breathing grew shallow with longing. It was time to issue the ultimatum: surrender or suffer the outer edge to burn.

The demand would send the army out to meet them. His army was ready, mismatched though they were. They'd trained for anything, including a conflict with the largest military on the continent. Belik suggested that he send the message early in the morning, when everyone had rested. That meant Firian would get no sleep.

A tent had been set up for him near the center of the camp, but he was far from it now. He couldn't keep his eyes off the palace glinting in the distance. To demand loyalty was one thing. To win it was another.

Now that they were here, something felt wrong, as though he'd thrown a bone out of joint. Everything would be fine if Brithnem surrendered, but the odds of that were so small. Belik acted as though it were the most likely scenario, but they both knew better. It would take more than a threat and a book to make the capital bow to him.

If he could find some other way... He shivered, but it wasn't cold. The answer came slowly, inevitably, irresistibly. His pulse pounded. The buzz of his mind came into focus around one idea, an idea that could satisfy him, and satisfy her.

Kiria was the key. As Keeper, she *was* Brithnem. With her power and beauty, influence and honesty, she was everything he wanted. As long as he had her, the rest of the Kingdom could go to hell.

He wiped his bloody finger on his pants. What a victory it would be to steal a Keeper! She'd come willingly. He'd seen it in her eyes. She just needed a strong reason that it was better to come with him than to stay. He could give her that reason. Now.

His heart raced with the strength of the new idea that didn't feel new at all. Kiria always talked about his using power for good. This way he could do that. Lives would be spared. He could call off the rest of this conflict. She'd love him for it.

He licked his dry lips. Why hadn't he seen it before? Kiria for the Kingdom. It was a fair trade.

Plunging into the Unreal with so much force that it felt like some of the night went with him, he searched for her. She appeared quickly, as though he had torn her to this level with him. She looked around disoriented for a moment, glanced at her hands, then at him.

"I'm going to tell you everything," he said.

The force of the words hit him like an aftershock. He knew it was true, but for a heartbeat he didn't know which "everything" he meant.

He pulled out of the Unreal far enough to see both her and the city beyond with double vision. The beautiful lights of the palace and surrounding buildings twinkled behind her. Brithnem and Kiria. The power he yearned for, the person who consumed him. His soul ached.

He paused so long that she considered him as though he were an apparition, as though he might not have said those tantalizing words. Her light brown eyes looked up at him in that heart-shaped face and he melted.

If he demanded the Kingdom first, she might run or fight back or... he wasn't sure. Sometimes she was easy to read, and other times he couldn't anticipate her at all. The choice was clear. He had a choice, and it was Kiria.

"We're outside the city walls," he said.

Her hand flew to her mouth before she forced it back down. Words formed on her lips, something like "I knew it." Angry tears formed on the base of her eyelid.

He hurried on. "The Tanyu are set to take over Brithnem. In the morning we'll burn the outer edge if you don't surrender." His words sounded horrible, all wrong. "But you, you can stop it."

His heart jumped painfully in his chest. He felt naked.

She glared at him, chest heaving, as though every nerve strained toward hearing what he would say next. Was she hoping for the same thing he was?

"None of that needs to happen," he said, his voice irregular and frantic. He forced himself to calm. "There's an abandoned farmhouse on the edge of the Gray Forest. It's east of the Abrecan Gate. I'll be there until dawn." Tanyu had found it sweeping for scouts. It was a safe place to wait. Belik wouldn't suspect that he was gone during the night. But he couldn't let a whiff of his plan reach the Master. He would tell him once it was successful, then Belik would see Firian's *katah* wasn't like the one he had with Chetana.

"If you come to me, I'll call everything off. But you can't tell anyone. No one. I'll know." His skin burned with adrenaline.

Her lips parted with amazement and her eyes widened until white showed all the way around. "Firian, I..."

It wasn't clear which part she protested. This was the best solution. This would save lives. She just had to have the courage to give into her desires.

"You can't tell anyone," he repeated. Firian refused to be a diplomatic debate. The most disgusting option was for her to yield because government officials and Amiran advisors told her to. He wanted her passion or nothing. He had to choose him. Their combined choices would save Brithnem. "Come to me, secretly, and I'll leave the city alone."

She was shaking, gripping the long sleeves of her gown. "How could you do this?" she gasped.

He recoiled. He hadn't expected her to look at him with such horror. Even now, when he would call off an attack on her city that he had every right to make. "You have until dawn to decide," he said, then he softened. "Kiria, come to me."

She didn't bend. Instead, she disappeared.

He came back into reality, heart hammering. It wasn't a long walk to the farmhouse he'd mentioned, but it felt like he was walking through sludge. The heft of his thoughts weighed him down. She might refuse.

She might refuse.

The ground seemed to tilt beneath him. If she did, then he would give into the monster clawing inside him. This felt like his last chance to do something merciful. Wouldn't she approve of that? And this allowed them to be together, to finally free their bottled passion. They could rule together, make plans, comfort each other. He could teach her to fight in the Unreal and she would be the voice of kindness. They could start a dynasty. Belik would eventually see she wasn't a threat to them.

He looked back toward the trees. Dawn was a long, long way off.

She might refuse. The thought intruded again. She'd denied him before, but despite it all, she still cared about him. He could see it in her eyes, in her answers, in her studied posture. Those tiny assurances had been his lifeline.

What if they weren't? What if they were just the desperate hope of a person too far gone to see the difference?

Why did he make this deal in the first place? If dawn came without her, it would be difficult for him to contain the rage he'd want to unleash against the Kingdom. All his monstrous instincts would have precedence. He knew what he was capable of. He could tear through the city like a hurricane. Part of him wanted to do that now, instead of waiting there, subject to her whim. That exposed feeling came over him again, as though she could overhear all his anxious thoughts, tear him open and mock every weakness.

He weighed the options as he pushed open the heavy barn door. Either she loved him and fought against her feelings because of the politics of the Kingdom, or she didn't love him and now he was demanding to own her in exchange for the safety of her people. In both scenarios, she would come to him that night. Savior or monster—the question wasn't as urgent as whether he would hold Kiria in his arms.

Sadness crept over him. He remembered his eleven-year-old self, so anxious to create a legacy, and regarded himself through those eyes. Would he be proud of the man he'd become, or would he recoil too?

61

KIRIA

KIRIA REELED, sitting bolt upright in bed. She couldn't catch her breath. She would have let out an angry scream if her serving girls wouldn't come running.

How could he? How could he?

His last betrayal—betrayals—had been bad enough, but this was beyond enduring. He dared to threaten her city to blackmail her into being with him? It seemed impossible, even for him. Before, he had been paranoid about threats to his crown—something she didn't agree with, but to some extent understood. She felt similar stresses in her own reign: the desire for control, the inability or unwillingness to give up her own interests... But this!

Time seemed to slow, every movement suddenly comprised of creaking bones and flexing muscles and the wisp of air past her skin. She felt every place her nightdress touched her and every hair falling on her shoulder.

She had not acted carefully around him—not enough, anyway. She'd known that he wanted her and she gave into that part of herself that wanted him.

That part was gone. For a fleeting second, she regretted that their soldiers hadn't completed their mission at the Academy and killed him when they could.

Now she couldn't tell anyone about this. She had to make the choice on her own. To go to him and possibly save the Kingdom from domination, or to refuse and risk hundreds if not thousands of lives in the conflict?

Something wet hit the blanket beneath her with a tiny thud. Furious, she scrubbed away the tears. What if Firian was bluffing? What if the Tanyu weren't poised outside the city at all?

But that wasn't possible. He said he'd be at an abandoned farmhouse. He was certainly there, and there was no reason for him to come alone. So other Tanyu were there too, and their reason had to be retaliation, as he said.

If she didn't go, the Tanyu would demand that Brithnem surrender. None of the Keepers or advisors would agree to that, so they would have to fight back.

Firian said that he would set the outer edge on fire. Her blood seethed. They'd have to put out the fires and fight, potentially, hundreds of Tanyuin soldiers.

Would Torithians be there too? The thought struck her like a fresh wound. When Firian had asked the question several nights ago, she should have answered differently. *Yes. Yes, you are.*

She sat numbly on the edge of the bed, only her thoughts and her own body real to her. What if she told someone who could sneak to the farmhouse instead of her and end the conflict that way? Firian would know. He said he'd be watching.

She feverishly flipped through options—a note, a signal, a weapon of her own? Nothing would work.

She turned to the option she'd dreaded. What if she gave herself up to him? What if she snuck through the city and met him at the farmhouse? Even with all his twisted desire and horrible decisions, she couldn't fathom that he would attack Brithnem after he had her. He was telling the truth when he said he'd trade her for the Kingdom. The idea didn't make her feel at all comforted.

And if she was still being naïve, like Cúron thought she was, then she could escape from him again, and the conflict would start as though she'd never gone. That was an idea too terrible to contemplate for long. Firian was a tyrant, but she saw sincerity in his eyes, an almost fearful vulnerability that made his evil more tragic.

Brithnem could be safe if she did this. Probably. Nausea grew in her gut as she considered logistics. Since her mother was still alive, she could step in as the Second Keeper, so the Line wouldn't end with Kiria, at least not right away. She could disguise herself fairly easily to go through the streets and out the main gate. Even if the best were to happen—she went with Firian, who treated her well, and Brithnem was safe—everyone would think she had betrayed them all. Those who knew her background with Firian might think she had chosen a passionate love affair over the good of the Kingdom.

She made it to the sink before she wretched. There was no good outcome here. The best she could hope for was to be viewed as a traitor and pariah who'd left all her friends, her family, her subjects...

Her friends. They'd all be in danger if she didn't go. But none of them would understand why she did it because she couldn't tell a single soul. She wiped her mouth with the back of her hand, still tasting vomit on the back of her teeth. She spit. Jori, Atty, Bard, her mother—the catalogue of people seemed to grow every time it cycled through her thoughts. Servants and guards were added, people who rarely spoke to her. They all seemed to matter so much now.

If she could only talk to Daelon, or someone else who was wiser than she was, to help her make this decision. She wasn't good enough on her own. The certainty of that made her sink to her knees on the hard floor of the washroom and give into sobs. They shook her violently, tears washing in a steady stream down her face.

A sound made her look up. It was Vayci, her face underlit by candlelight. Her dark brows announced deep concern. "My Keeper, you are unwell?" She knelt before her, feeling Kiria's brow and pulse.

Kiria stopped crying long enough to respond. "I got sick," she said, gesturing feebly at the sink.

"Let me help you to bed," Vayci said, crooking her arm for Kiria to take.

Together they stood. Vayci's thin, strong arm steadied Kiria mentally as well as physically. By the time she reached the bed, she had made her decision.

"Thank you," she said. "I think I just need to sleep."

"I'll bring you a cup of water."

Kiria didn't protest as Vayci rushed to fetch her water and returned with Candrae by her side, her blonde hair glowing in the flickering light.

"What happened?" Candrae asked, gently taking Kiria's hand. Kiria couldn't help thinking how dirty that hand was, but Candrae didn't seem to mind at all.

The truth almost spilled out of her, but she bit it back. The overwhelming desire to say *something* filled her until she could barely breathe. "Are you ever afraid that you'll never be good enough?" she said, hiccupping with the sobs that still threatened to overtake her.

Candrae smoothed a strand of hair away from Kiria's wet face as Vayci handed her a cool towel. "I don't think anyone thinks they're good enough, not for the job you do. If they did, then maybe they wouldn't be fit for it."

Kiria sniffed, an unflattering sound.

Candrae let go of Kiria's hand to allow Vayci to press the water cup into it. Trembling, Kiria brought it up to her lips. With all the shaking, some of the water splashed onto her cheeks and nose and dress, but she managed to drink some of it down.

Vayci chimed in. "We know you love the Kingdom. Those protestors don't know you like we do."

Kiria took another sip. Though they misunderstood, their words felt like medicine. She swallowed thickly before thanking them.

The girls smiled serenely, promising to check on her later that night, and left her to her own thoughts again. Her mind was not so kind, but it was made up.

For Candrae, for Vayci, for all of them, she would sacrifice herself. They'd all see her as a traitor, and she wouldn't have time to explain, but that was the choice she had to make. What had Daelon said? *"You don't serve the Kingdom for praise."*

It was better if they thought she'd betrayed them. The Keepers would be less likely to start a war with the Tanyu—she would be the only casualty.

She tried not to think about what Firian would do with her. She gazed around her comfortable, lonely room by the light of the candle Vayci had left, dwelling on details she hadn't noticed in months, if not years. A corner of her vanity table was discolored from the time she dropped oil on it when she was fifteen. One of the session recorders, a girl named Hada, who was about her own age, told her it would make her eyelids an attractive color. In the heaviest blanket was a tiny snag whose threads formed a shape like a dog's face. She used to trace it with her finger when she was younger to help her fall asleep. She must have been only six or seven.

If time had gone slowly before, he seemed suddenly to speed up. Even on a fast horse, it would take her an hour to get to the outer edge. Longer to find the right farmhouse. Her chest ached with the desire to linger but she had to go.

Hastily, she threw a couple simple outfits and necessities in a bag. She hesitated. Would carrying a bag draw too much attention to herself? She had to pass several rounds of guards. Her plain face would disguise her in the city, but not in the palace, where she sometimes switched back and forth. She sighed as she realized with certainty that she would be Beautiful when she met him. This was official business, Keeper business. She would wear her official face. She was tempted to curse and leave the bag lying on the bed.

Poised precisely between taking and leaving it, she stood frozen in the middle of the room. These things were the least of her worries and they angered her for being so trivial. Spite finally decided for her. She unpacked so as not to rouse suspicion too early, violently jamming her clothes in their trunks.

Breathing deeply, she composed herself before going out for the last time.

62

FIRIAN

Firian couldn't remember a slower night. It was like four nights strung together, shot through with anxiety. Fear and anger and hope chased each other like rabbits through his mind. His shoulders ached from all the tension.

The farmhouse reminded him a little of the abandoned structure where he and Kiria had stayed one of their first nights away from the palace. Only a few rooms composed its simple layout. A structure attached to the outside of the house clearly had saved harvested crops when it was in use.

Firian stayed in the main room because the only external door led into it. Kiria could find him without searching.

His gaze found a messy mouse nest in the corner, strung with hemp and thread and grasses. Maybe the house was abandoned during the Tanyuin War. That timeline would be logical, since the house wasn't completely overgrown. Nature had only started to move in. The layer of dust on the floor was thin. Waving cobwebs glinted on the ceiling when he moved, like a trick of the eye. He'd struck a few lights around the room. It was still dark, but he was used to darkness. It was like the barrier between the Real and the Unreal, so it didn't bother him at all. He did want to see her, though, when she came in. If she came in.

He could sense that she was on her way, but it didn't feel real. She hadn't talked to anybody else. Even if she came, would that mean what he thought it did? His fears were illogical, but they consumed him, nerves inhabiting his body as though it were haunted.

He huffed out a breath. Taking over Brithnem would burn power through his veins, but it wouldn't be voluntary. It would be won with blood, and he'd already had enough blood.

He pushed his hair back from his forehead. Rian, Salaar, Master Jairon, the unnamed Torithians in Raewhith—the everlasting images assaulted him again.

Into the Unreal

He hadn't meant to kill Rian. One second they all lived and thought, and the next they were just a thing. Firian's throat tightened. *There are many ways to kill a man.* Jovan had been right. And then Firian killed him too.

Kiria wouldn't come. He had done too much. His hands curled into fists and his core hardened into a painful knot. He couldn't go back to change anything. Even if he could, would he? He would make most of the same decisions again. He would take over the Academy, he would kill the Amir Salaar, he would defend himself against Jovan. The knowledge calmed him. It wasn't the calm of peace, but the calm of closure.

She might love a monster anyway.

Bard didn't.

He worked his jaw, spinning the Master ring on his finger and reopening the wound there. He watched as a dark drop of blood beaded against it and overflowed down his knuckle.

It would all be all right if she chose him. It would all have been worth it if Kiria Arioc, Keeper of Brithnem, chose him, Firian Kess of the little backwater town of Raewhith.

He cursed. Why dwell on the past? It held pain he had no desire to relive.

To shut up his thoughts, he fell to the floor and did push-ups until his arms burned. Physical pain was always better than other kinds. More helpful too.

The crunch of a soft footstep.

He froze, listening. Had he imagined it? The silence seemed to deepen in response to his intense desire to hear.

The sharp intake of breath. No, he hadn't imagined it. He leapt to his feet, heart thundering. He reached out in the Unreal.

It was her. It was Kiria.

He could barely hear over the blood pulsing in his ears. The door opened slowly, arcing over the dust-free semicircle on the floor. Her presence grew stronger as though the farmhouse were the Unreal and she were materializing into it. He felt her in his mind, but couldn't feel his own hands.

When she slipped into the room, he felt weak, stomach flipping. There were no words. She was light in darkness, soul in a lifeless body, meaning in life. Better than he imagined. The Unreal didn't carry the glorious force of her Beauty. It was like a shadow in comparison. This reminded him why he was alive.

Pain like a sword thrust winded him. He wanted that pain to last forever. She was Beautiful. For him. The air between them tasted like victory. Life when he had eyed certain death. He could breathe again and he was moving, rushing to close the gap between them.

They collided and he held her tight with trembling arms. He pressed his lips to hers with fierce passion. Tasting her warmth, he realized this was the first time they'd kissed in real life. He dug his fingers into her sides as he held her more firmly. Her lips felt different. He tried to memorize the feel of them, the peaks and edges.

She was here, she was here! He pressed himself against her, desperate to get closer. Feeling drunk, he smiled in his kiss, teeth against lips. Everything floated hazily around them, darkening like an Unreal setting until only the two of them remained, enclosed in each other's arms. He licked at the salt in the corner of her mouth.

Then it struck him. She wasn't bending into him. She wasn't even kissing him back. That salt, was it tears? Still holding her, he gave her one more soft kiss before pulling away. It took a moment for her expression to register. Those golden eyes, so full of wisdom and truth, looked back at him through tears. Fear, anger, sadness. The wide eyes and wary expression had been set in determined lines, afraid but immovable.

He dragged his hands around her back and sides as he let her go. She didn't speak aloud, but her rod-straight body and defiant look spoke for her.

She hadn't consulted anyone before coming. He'd checked. This decision was hers and hers alone. She had chosen to come to him. But she didn't love him.

A rock ached in his throat. He felt his world fall, almost as though he were dying. He didn't want to speak, but the question forced itself out. "If you don't love me, why did you come?"

A tear fell from her eye, down her flushed cheek. He should have noticed she was distraught the moment she came in, but he had been too overcome with relief and joy and her Beauty to think of anything else.

She could barely answer, her voice catching. "Because I love them."

Heat drained from Firian's face. She loved *them*, not him. The emptiness inside his ribcage stretched and echoed the words back to him. Time stopped. All the triumph he had felt turned to dust. He wasn't sure if he would tear the room apart or kiss her again.

The charged silence dragged on. Neither he nor Kiria moved.

Slowly, thoughts started to form coherently again out of chaos. She had given herself up, but not because she loved him. She considered it a sacrifice to save the people she actually cared about. He had promised not to conquer Brithnem. But she didn't love him. She didn't love him. Relentless pain beat in every muscle at the knowledge, the news he never wanted to hear.

He could keep her anyway. Her Beauty burned and allured him as nothing ever had. It would fit the deal they'd made. His foot moved toward her. His fingers twitched forward, then fell. Another drop of blood fell from his finger onto the boarded floor. What a monster he'd be then. The temptation made his insides curdle, pulling at him like a clawed creature.

He looked in her eyes. They'd never turned away from him. She still knew him, even the darkest parts. Maybe she feared he would take her for his pleasure. It would be a lie to say the idea didn't eat at him. She knew his other sides too, though. In the pool, she'd said he had a choice.

He wanted Kiria, but if she didn't want him, then at least he could resist the monster in his chest. He could be the man she thought he could be. Maybe she still thought there was hope for him. There had to be.

But that meant he'd have to send her back, to get nothing, to return alone. The notion made him feel weightless, hovering over darkness.

Still she waited.

He couldn't help himself. Furrowing his brows, he kissed her again. "Go back," he rasped, pulling away. He teetered on the edge of taking back the words even as he said them.

A light, followed by confusion, came into her eyes. "What?"

"Get out," he said again, straightening.

"You won't attack Brithnem?"

"No." He threw out words like weapons. They felt more dangerous, more reckless. "I won't. Go." It was the best he could manage, and he regretted it already. He longed for her even though she hadn't gone.

She twisted, eyeing him experimentally as if he would attack.

"Go!" he cried, furious now. If she stayed any longer, he would change his mind. She had to run or his will would dry up.

She turned and ran.

When sounds of Kiria and her horse had faded into the distance, Firian stirred. Hollowness made him move like a corpse.

What did I just do? He could have kept Kiria for his own. He could have experienced that burning Beauty and those understanding eyes, that skin and those lips, for as long as he wanted. Doing good was supposed to feel good too, wasn't it? He didn't know what had made him think so. Bard often seemed so worried, and Kiria looked heartbroken and afraid just now.

His promise felt oddly unbreakable, stronger than the strands of his life. He wouldn't burn the outer edge or threaten to take over the city. Now all that was left was to tell Belik.

His gut sank further. What a travesty this trip had become. But he was still the Tanyuin Head. If he told his armies to return to the Academy, giving the Kingdom nothing but a warning, then they would. Firian felt weak, but he wasn't in a bargaining mood.

Somehow he got himself back to the camp, ignoring the pull, like a snagged thread, of checking on Kiria. She would warn her military, telling them where the Tanyuin forces camped. That was fine. They would be gone before a battle could start.

He ducked into Belik's tent without ceremony. The Master lay under a thin blanket with his meager provisions haloed around his head. His glasses balanced on a waterskin just in front of his nose.

"Belik, wake up," Firian said, softly but clearly, toeing him in the side.

The blankets bucked under the speed of his waking. Belik grabbed his glasses and glared at him, a look that would have crippled Firian's younger self. A red crease lined one side of Belik's face where his pillow had folded under it. "Gore, Firian!" he swore.

"We're calling off the attack." He felt beyond the reach of consequences.

Belik grunted as he trundled to his feet before answering. He stood a little shorter than Firian but he could still look him in the eye. "We are not calling anything off." He frowned, eyebrows ticking downward. "Have you learned something?"

"They just need to know we could have conquered them. We'll release one of those scouts from before. They'll run home. That's enough. We're leaving."

Belik grabbed Firian's shoulder in a meaty fist. "We are not leaving," he said through gritted teeth.

Firian plucked the Master's hand off his shoulder. "We are. Get them ready."

"Damn it, Firian! We've all marched through the gory mountains to do more than send a message! These people tried to kill you. Did you forget?"

"No," Firian said, fury rising.

"Tanyu have deserved this for years and you're just going to throw…" His voice faded as realization made Belik's face go slack. It hardened again and he lowered his head, dangerous intention through every pore. "What have you done?"

"I've made a decision you're going to follow."

"It's the girl. It's Kiria." Belik snarled with rage. "She convinced you to do this. Because you wouldn't be such a *gory idiot* otherwise. What did I say? I said this would happen."

Somehow Belik was closer to Firian than he had been. Firian saw Belik's fisted hands. There was a wildness to him that Firian wasn't used to, an unpredictable violence. Firian tightened his muscles.

"Master Belik," he said calmly. The hollowness was coming in handy now. "You will do as I say. Let our troops know to pack and leave before first light." He stared steadily back at Belik's furious face.

Firian had just made fists too when Belik's demeanor suddenly relaxed, though the change didn't make him seem any less dangerous. "You don't think the Tanyu deserve this?" he asked, almost teacherly.

"I think it's unnecessary to make our point."

"And it would hurt your little girl."

Firian's elbow went back almost before he realized what was happening. He smashed Belik in the jaw, the impact rattling up his arm.

Belik stumbled and fell to the side, catching himself on his hand without making a sound. The Master stood, slowly, and looked Firian in the eye again, as though the violent outburst had never happened. Finally, Belik sighed. A yellow bruise was already blooming under his skin. "Okay," he said. "We'll march back in the morning." His red, watery gaze took in Firian from his hair to his sternum. "Have you been up all night?" He acted as though he knew the answer, and the reason.

Firian didn't respond.

"We have a few hours," Belik said dismissively. "Have a drink. Get some sleep. It's a long march back." Belik didn't disguise his bitter disgust.

Firian doubted he could sleep, even though his eyes ached at the suggestion. When he found his own tent, a bottle had already been left for him. The strong liquor burned his throat as he shot it down. Chucking the bottle against the wall of the tent, he flung himself down and fell into a dark sleep.

63

KIRIA

Kiria shed her Beauty as soon as she left Firian, but she still felt wildly exposed in the streets of Brithnem as her horse clopped up the quiet roads to the palace.

He let me go. Her thoughts wouldn't settle. Of all the scenarios she had considered, this wasn't one. She was too confused and upset to be relieved. Now she only had one course of action—to tell the other Keepers that Tanyuin forces were camped right outside their door.

She got back as soon as she could, making flimsy, unnecessary excuses for the guards who let her into the palace. The hall rugs felt softer than usual under her feet as she ran back to her room.

Stopping short, she saw Bard arguing with her guards, who circled around him. He waved animated gestures in the air. Though the shortest among them, he clearly held his ground. Something about his composure reminded her he was Tanyu.

When she approached, he turned and his face brightened. The guards saw her too and their postures relaxed enough to show they were relieved to see her.

"What's going on?" she asked. Nobody should have been awake at that hour. Had something happened?

"Are you all right?" asked one of the guards, stepping on Bard's question coming at the same time.

"I'm fine," she said, realizing that her face still had to be puffy from sobbing. The way down to Firian's abandoned farmhouse had been blind and punctuated with smothered screams of frustration.

Bard's quick eyes didn't buy her answer. "I need to talk to you," he said quietly. "They won't let me in your room."

"Let him in," she said wearily, passing through the guards, who opened the way for her. Bard followed behind.

Both her mother and Chetana whirled around when she entered. With a cry, her mother jogged forward, catching Kiria in her arms. "Oh, Kiria! I thought you were gone!"

Kiria glanced at Chetana over her mother's shoulder. The Amir was glaring at Bard, who had entered after her. "I'm fine," Kiria repeated.

"Chetana told me you were missing," her mother said, her red eyes probably mirroring her own.

"Chetana? How did she know?" Kiria realized that her response basically admitted that she had been away. "I just... went for a walk."

"Was it Jori again?" her mother asked, drawing a sleeve across her eyes. "I swear I'll kill that boy..."

"No, no," Kiria said. "I just went for a walk." She gave the excuse more strongly now. Glancing at Chetana, who looked imperious in the dim light, she remembered the crucial news. Speaking more loudly, she said, "I got a message. The Tanyu are here. They're camped right outside the wall. We have to get our soldiers out there."

Her mother's eyes widened in fear and surprise. Chetana, however, betrayed no surprise at all. "I'll tell the general immediately," her mother said.

"Yes, go," Kiria agreed, not sure she had the strength herself. "As soon as they're ready, they can go. They'll start with the outer edge!" She yelled the last instructions at her mother's back as she disappeared through the door.

Alone with Bard and Chetana, Kiria wasn't sure where to start. Chetana probably wouldn't want to speak freely in the presence of a Tanyu, and the feeling might be mutual. At this point, it didn't matter. Now was not the time for pettiness.

"What did you come here to say?" she asked her former advisor. She probably had arrived first, so she got the first question.

"My Keeper," she hedged.

"Ignore him," Kiria replied, her tone clipped.

Chetana rubbed her lips together thoughtfully, but she obeyed. The rusty accents of her curly hair glowed dark orange in the candlelight. She straightened her back as she spoke. "My Keeper, I came to warn you about the Tanyu, but it sounds like you found out more than I could tell you."

"How did you know about them?" Kiria asked.

"There's one I could tell was nearby, nearer than he'd been in years, and he's dangerous, My Keeper. Very dangerous. If there are more of them, then you were right to summon our military."

"A *katah*?" Kiria asked, putting the pieces together. So this is how she knew so much about it when Kiria hadn't woken up in King's Heights. She had one herself.

"Very old," she said. "Daelon's father."

Kiria's eyelashes fluttered. This was too much to process at once. She turned to Bard beside her instead. His wild hair revealed how distracted he'd been with his news. "What about you?"

"Same thing. Well, not really." He cast a glance at Chetana, but didn't shy away from her withering look. "I knew Firian was close by. I didn't know if you could tell, so I thought you should know. Somebody should know."

She almost asked the same question—*katah?*—but stopped herself. After Bard finished, Chetana's eyes softened just a little from hatred to mere skepticism.

"They're all here," Kiria affirmed.

A glow flared in the corner of her vision, drawing her attention to the window, where unnaturally bright orange light rose and fell in the dark. She gasped and clasped a hand across her mouth. Chetana turned to look too.

"They're burning the farms!" Kiria cried. Firian promised not to. Was it too late to help them? Hopefully her mother's message would mean instant action. But that wouldn't be good enough.

Despite how haggard Kiria felt, she had to warn more people—Cúron and Atty, at least. Her mother was only one person. News had to travel faster than that.

She tore out of the room, telling guards as she passed them. A couple of them sprinted off to spread the news too. Fast, quiet footsteps told her that Chetana and Bard followed her. Maybe her serving girls. She didn't look back to see who it was.

Cúron's bedroom was in the front wing, so it wasn't as far to run. Everything inside her was chaos, but the wide hallways were eerily silent. Darkness dampened the sound. Her own ragged breathing was the loudest noise.

She passed Kader's room. Cúron was just around that corner. She sped past the portraits and trees, skidding to a stop in sight of his door. She felt a bolt of ice stab through her. Sprawled in unearthly shapes, like demons about to rise and crawl on many hands, lay his guards. They slumped where they'd fallen, black against the floor. Her heart beat mercilessly against her ribs.

Chetana rushed past her and knelt by one of the guards, putting two fingers to his throat. She looked up almost instantly. Dead. They were all dead. Chetana rose and pushed open the door to Cúron's room. As though she were in a nightmare, Kiria's feet wouldn't move to join her.

One peek and Chetana rushed back to Kiria. "Go. We need to go!" she hissed, grabbing Kiria by the hand and dragging her back where they'd come.

Tingling covered Kiria's body. It felt like putting on her Beauty, but she knew she was going numb with shock. What had happened to Cúron? Was his wife Varinna all right? Kader?

The castle seemed even quieter this time. A tomb. An abandoned structure with no one left alive. Kiria couldn't hold onto a thought for longer than a second at a time. But they circled back, and back, and back. She caught them with feeble hands each time they flew by. *Outer edge is burning. Cúron is dead. We're under attack. Firian lied. I have to warn everyone. Where's Mother? Where's Atty? Where is everyone?*

Time slicked by like oil, sticking to her and moving erratically. She forced her feet to move, one in front of the other. Chetana was leading her back to her room. Were they going to escape? Would this hellish vision fade into unreality once they reached the safety of her bedroom?

What she saw made her shake. The guards who had remained at their posts were dead outside her door. Shock rose from her core to the back of her eyeballs. It didn't make sense. They hadn't been gone more than a few minutes. Who was doing this?

Chetana pulled her forward, making her step over the guards on the way to her room. She forced down bile as it rose up in her throat. There was less blood on the ground than she had thought would come from so many bodies. But they were dead. They were dead.

Bard and her serving girls picked their way around the bodies after her. Kiria gasped in relief when she realized that Candrae and Vayci had followed her when she'd run out. Otherwise, they might have been dead too.

Chetana went in first. She seemed to know exactly what to do, fiercely alert but otherwise calm. Kiria watched her every movement, ready to do what she said.

In the middle of the room, Chetana stopped and raised her head like an animal, listening. She gestured toward the serving girls. "You, open the hatch."

Vayci and Candrae hurried to the emergency tunnel on the far side of the bed, their legs only a little unsteady. Together they pried open the small square opening, disguised in the wainscoting, easing it back and forth until it gave.

Where's Jori? Kiria's chest hurt. There were too many unknowns. She caught Bard's gaze. It was wild, but beneath the panic was a center of calm or understanding.

"...wasn't here." Faint voices sounded from just outside, too calm to be on their side.

"She's here," answered a gruffer voice.

The second voice made Chetana jump. "Go!" she said, pushing Kiria roughly toward the hole. Candrae and Vayci crawled inside. "Go now!"

"You go," Bard told Chetana in a breathless voice. "Make sure they're okay. I'll... hold them off."

Chetana didn't argue. She nodded once in grim acknowledgment before turning to the escape tunnel.

Kiria looked back at Bard once before wedging her body into the opening. His dark figure rolled his shoulders and his neck as he faced the door and made to open it. Her abdomen hurt from worry. The man on the other side of the door had made Chetana afraid. What could Bard do against someone like that?

He's dying for me, she realized.

"Go! Get in!" Chetana whispered, shoving Kiria all the way into the tunnel. She didn't remember stopping.

Crawling forward into blackness, her knees kept catching on her skirt. She hauled up the front, gripping it in her fist so she could move faster. Chetana wedged the square panel back into place behind her, shutting them in complete darkness.

64

FIRIAN

FIRIAN WOKE GASPING. Reality refused to spiral into focus, but his heart still beat with panic. He hauled himself up on one elbow, panting out breaths as he tried to remember what was a dream and what was really happening.

A soft crackling sound guttered outside. Too slowly, his eyes adjusted and he saw orange shadows crawling like phantoms over his tent. He staggered upright and ran outside. The camp was abandoned. The farms were on fire. He ran to the edge of the fields, scanning the tree line for the person who had acted against his orders. *What was going on?*

The drink. Belik had sent him a drink. There was no way Firian would have slept through a moving army, even one as silent as Tanyu could be, and setting the outer edge ablaze. This sleep was induced, forced on him by whatever was in that bottle. Which meant that Belik had drugged him in order to take control.

His blood surged again with panic, unconnected to his black and red rage. He wasn't panicking. He was thinking it through. He was going to take his army back. He was going to find Belik and kill him.

Then the panic couldn't be his own. With a jolt, he realized he felt Kiria's fear. He dove into the Unreal toward her, simultaneously running toward the city walls. Avoiding swaths of flame and men riding horses and blackened fields of smoldering heat, he leapt across the outer edge as fast as his legs could carry him. He barely stayed upright in his speed.

Where is she?

There! He saw her in the Unreal. She wasn't alone. She was surrounded by others with the Talent. One presence Firian knew almost as well as his own: Bard. Some of the fear was from him.

He forced his divided attention toward Kiria. She was in her room... no... disappearing through a hole. Would she be safe there? Firian felt his way forward in the passage where she was and hit the faint buzz of another mind. He didn't recognize it. It wasn't one of his Tanyu. Chetana, maybe? Odds were that she wasn't going to harm Kiria, but he shouldn't take a chance.

Firian skirted a burning field, charging onto the main road, not caring if he was seen. Oppressive heat pressed in on both sides. Smoke swelled on the air, making it difficult to see if anyone was coming. Shouted orders in the distance meant soldiers were on their way, probably to put out the flames.

The great city wall loomed closer. Guards would never let him in through the gate. He would have to climb the wall.

His attention wrenched back to the room where Bard was. Bard rolled his neck and shoulders, facing the inside of Kiria's door. He walked out and Firian knew instantly why he was so afraid. In the hallway, Belik and Shiro stood there beyond a pile of dead guards.

Belik splayed a hand toward Shiro, who looked ready to pounce like a cat.

Firian increased his speed, ignoring the heat that threatened to blister his shoulders down to his forearms.

"You can't come in," Bard said. His voice was surprisingly even but his brow furrowed as though he were staring at something bright.

Belik's face showed curiosity but also, most of all, frustration. He shifted his weight to the other leg, then limped forward a step. "It's by order of Master Kess."

Firian hissed a curse. So they didn't know he hadn't ordered the attack.

Though the news sent shock flickering over Bard's expression, he stepped forward too and set his palm on Belik's chest, jutting his jaw defiantly. Bard's Adam's apple bobbed a couple times before he spoke again. "You're not going in."

Shiro made to walk past him, but again Belik signaled for him to wait. What was he waiting for? Did he want Shiro to watch him make an example of Bard? Firian didn't know what damage Belik could do. He'd never seen him in a physical fight. Next to himself, Belik was the best fighter in the Unreal, but they weren't in the Unreal now. They were in that palace, on that hill, past that wall.

Firian slammed into the wall, stifling a grunt as he reached high for a handhold. He climbed recklessly, aware that one misstep could send him crashing to the ground, dead if he fell from too great a height. But he still practically jumped from stone to stone, calling on all the strength his fingertips had as they wedged into the mortar. His arms were faster than his legs, which did little more than steady him.

He hauled himself over the top, scraping his abdomen across the metal guardrail. His lungs and muscles burned, and he came out of the Unreal long enough to contemplate the way down. It was too far to jump without breaking bones. He sprinted along the top until he came to an attached stable. It was hard to judge distance in the dark, but it looked close enough that he could jump and roll onto the roof with enough power left to get to the palace.

He hit the stable a heartbeat past his expectation, his teeth clacking together. Painfully, he let himself fall off the peaked roof. He landed on his side on the flagstone street below, but was up before the impact fully registered. The stable would have a horse. There would be no time to saddle it. But it would be faster than his own legs.

The space smelled like hay and mature. Most of the stable doors were already open, and a girl no older than fifteen stood in the shadowy recesses near a wall where large poles were sticking out. She wore a cap over her short hair. As she turned and saw Firian, her hand rested on the only remaining saddle as though she forgot it was there. Were all the horses already gone?

Casting around for a remaining mount, he heard a muffled snort. A horse was left in a stall close to the doorway where he stood. Snatching the lead rope and throwing the gate pin to the ground, he dragged the mare outside. The stable girl came alive as soon as Firian vaulted onto the horse. Her shouted protests followed him as he kicked the skittish horse into motion.

Once he was flying through the streets, another pang of fear sheared through him. He looked back at Bard and Belik. Belik's face had hardened into a murderous stare. Bard met his look with determination, his light brown hands balled into fists.

Then Belik closed his eyes. Why would he do that? It was tactically stupid. Unless he wanted to go into the Unreal. But Belik could do that with his eyes open, as Firian was doing to watch them.

Neither of them could go to the Second Level with their eyes open, though. The thought hit Firian like a punch to the gut. Why would Belik go into the Second Level now?

Dread pooled inside him until he felt full of black poison. No. Belik didn't know how to...

Bard's eyes widened. A cry of surprise escaped him as his spine bent unnaturally backward.

The rabbits. Firian couldn't breathe, kicking his mare with enough force to leave marks.

Soundlessly, Bard's mouth opened wider. Shiro glanced nervously at Belik, who concentrated with his eyes still closed.

Then the screams started. The noise shredded through Firian's whole body. He wanted to scream himself at the horror.

The horse became slick with sweat beneath him.

Bard's screams didn't last long. Falling silent, he arced backward. His head hit the carpet with a sound that was too quiet, too final.

Belik opened his eyes. Shiro looked at him, awestruck, but Belik didn't look back. "Now you can go in," Belik said.

As Shiro stepped past the unmoving forms littering the entrance, Firian snapped back to the present. He had to focus on getting to the palace.

It took too long. There were too many streets. The hooves clattered up and up. Behind him, the glow of the firelight was growing. People were starting to come out and gasp or scream. Guards ran quickly in unison down toward the gate. A few cried out when they saw him but he evaded them, his reflexes sending the horse down side streets before a hand could grab him or a something could knock him to the ground. The automatic movement made him feel precise and dangerous, but detached. His body was accurate, but his roiling mind couldn't focus even on his own peril.

When he reached toward Bard again, he sensed nothing. No word, no thought. Mouth bone dry, he reached toward Kiria instead. He couldn't let his mind wander too far into possibility. The weight of it could crush him. Belik, Bard, Kiria...

She was there. She was alive. Her shock and sadness and anger burned like the flames behind him, but there was no fear or pain. For now, at least, it seemed she was all right.

Soldiers sped down the main streets, forcing Firian to keep taking side roads. This ride was taking too long, too long... Shouldn't the sun be rising?

Finally close enough, the shadow of Mon Párinath, awash with red light, blocked out the sea and stars. Firian skidded the horse to a stop and vaulted to the ground in the same movement. His feet scrabbled for purchase on the gravel, the first few steps too slow. Then he was racing.

An armored guard blocked the nearest way in. Firian didn't slow. The guard yelled for backup just as he hurdled forward, aiming the point of his elbow at the guard's face. As a wet crunch sounded in the helmet, the hand reaching for its sword released its grip on the hilt. With no time to finish him off, Firian shoved him up against the wall and left him crumpled behind him, wrenching open the door and flinging himself inside.

The cool dark of the corridor felt ghostly as he ran and ran. Extra soldiers must have emptied to put out the flames. Kiria probably told someone the Tanyu had camped just beyond the outer edge. They'd go to meet them head-on, unaware of the enemy already within their gates.

One more guard peeled away from a door where he was stationed to block his way, rising before Firian's narrowing vision. This one already had his sword unsheathed. "Where are you going?"

Firian didn't answer. The man's eyes grew larger when he saw who it was: Firian Kess, all in black, the Tanyuin Head.

The man swung his sword. Firian rushed into his arms and wrapped the man's sword arm in front of them, prying at the fingers. When the man wouldn't let go, Firian jammed a heel into his instep.

Armored boots. He jammed harder. Again.

Finally, the guard cried out and loosened his hold just enough for Firian to send the sword sailing to the ground. It skidded across the carpet and hit a pedestal, which tilted crazily from the impact. Its fall sent a vase of flowers crashing. Water spilled out on the floor.

Firian made for the sword but a hand yanked him back. Furious, he launched himself backward, aiming to headbutt the guard, but the man moved in time to avoid him. Firian stumbled and fell. The man kicked him in the side on his way to the sword.

Flexing his foot, Firian locked his ankle around the man's foot and sent him sprawling to the ground. The wet carpet squished as the man fell, wheezing as the wind was knocked out of him. Good. A few more seconds before he called for help. Leaping up, Firian left the sword and the man and continued running.

He only fully realized where he was going when he arrived. Bodies were arranged in front of Kiria's room just as he had seen them in the Unreal. Belik and Shiro were gone. A moment of confusion threaded through him. He expected himself to pursue Belik in revenge. The thought passed as he fell to his knees before Bard's prostrate form. Too much time had passed since he'd crumpled to the ground. *Be alive, be alive, be alive.*

It was a slim hope. Bard's spine was still bent backward, not as violently as the rabbits' had been, but enough to make Firian's skin crawl with the comparison. Bard's fingers curled in on themselves, his teeth showing in a grimace. A dribble of blood leaked from one tightly shut eye.

"Bard." Firian grabbed Bard's arm tightly, feeling for a pulse. The arm was limp but it felt warm. Something hardened painfully in Firian's chest as he pressed his thumb into Bard's wrist. Nothing. He pressed harder, as though Bard were a lever that would give if he pushed hard enough.

Firian willed his own frantic heartbeat to slow, so he could distinguish Bard's pulse from his own. He still couldn't feel anything. He cursed under his breath and brought his fingers to Bard's neck instead. A beat. Firian's heart skipped. Had he imagined it? He put the back of his other hand against Bard's mouth and nose. Another beat.

Firian's breaths came fast. He must not have been breathing before. He shook Bard lightly, gripping his forearm again. Now he could feel a faint heartbeat in Bard's wrist and the crook of his elbow. Raised veins pulsed in Firian's arm—he could see them—and Bard had just a whisper of life. Firian held on as though he were the one giving Bard the strength to keep living.

Muted running down the hall meant that more guards were coming.

A small movement focused all Firian's attention on Bard's right hand. Weakly, the fingers closed around Firian's arm.

"I'm sorry." Firian's own words surprised him as they came out. "I'm sorry." Firian couldn't manage anything else. His face felt red and bloated as he looked down at his friend.

Bard opened his blood-stained eyes enough to see. Taking a real breath, he squeezed Firian's arm, the pads of his fingers barely but unmistakably tightening. The meaning was clear.

Everything grew hazy. Firian couldn't see.

Footsteps and clinking metal grew closer.

Firian swallowed, blinked, and hauled Bard upright. It was obvious that Bard wouldn't be able to hold onto consciousness, much less walk. He felt heavy as a corpse. Bracing himself, Firian manipulated Bard's body until he lay across his shoulders. A faint, wheezing breath gasped at his ear. If Bard was alive, he should stay that way.

Galvanized into action, Firian took off away from the sound of the approaching guards.

Belik. Belik did this.

Rage gave him strength. Belik had tried to kill Bard and Kiria. He was a traitor. There was no excuse he could give that could persuade Firian to show him mercy.

Blood roared in his ears. Bard hardly slowed him down, though the hands that held Bard's wrists and ankles trembled.

Firian knew his next steps with diamond-cut clarity: save Bard's life, and then kill Belik where he stood.

65

KIRIA

THE CRAWL through the tunnel seemed interminable. Without light or enough space to stand, the journey felt as dreamlike as a nightmare. Everything Kiria had witnessed didn't seem real, but it had to be, or else she wouldn't be making her way to the safe house.

Her knees rubbed raw, and she was sure that her hands and shins and dress were covered in filth. With darkness covering her, she had let hot tears fall, careful not to be loud.

Who's left?

Chetana's reaction at Cúron's room left little doubt about his fate. He, and probably Varinna too, was dead.

She had escaped. Maybe Atty and Haved had too. Maybe they were crawling through a similar tunnel, running for their lives. Maybe they would all meet at the safe house together.

Nobody spoke. Kiria wanted to ask if the safe house really was safe against the Tanyu, but she couldn't make herself breach the silence. So they all just went forward on hands and knees, on and on. Serving girls, Kiria, Chetana.

Her hand splashed in a puddle. The air in the tunnel was stifling with disuse. Maybe the sun was starting to rise now. This night was as long as several long days.

Jori had used this tunnel recently. It couldn't be much farther. *Jori.* Was he alive?

Exhausted, she couldn't consider the questions as deeply as she should. She didn't have the strength. Her head felt sore and hopelessness threatened her with the inevitability of sleep.

She took another shallow breath, crawled forward another step, and refused to give into despair.

Whoever was in front, Candrae or Vayci, stopped suddenly. Kiria's face rammed into the fabric of someone's dress. She sat back on her haunches like a dog, waiting.

Ahead of her, lines of white light cracked open, forming a perfect square. Blinding light pierced the space and she squinted. Her serving girls crawled through the opening.

Kiria followed them, and Chetana came out last. All four of them stood gazing at their new surroundings. It was a nicer space than Kiria had envisioned from the tortuous crawl through the tunnel. There were tapestries on the wall alongside lanterns and provisions. A hall led away from this small storage room to the rooms beyond. It felt as though they were underground. Maybe they were. The only window was a small slit near the ceiling. The wall around it radiated murky firelight.

Kiria tore herself away from the group and pushed a chair against the wall. Ignoring the dirt and protests, she leapt up and tried to peer through. Only on her tiptoes could she see.

The palace was burning.

Horror seized her throat. "The palace..." she breathed in a gasp. Her mother was in there. Everyone was in there.

Firian lied, Firian lied. Relentless and violent, the thought joined the tumult in Kiria's brain. *Did anyone else make it out alive?*

Legs suddenly watery, she sank down into the chair she'd been standing on. Vayci offered her water. She thought she said yes. Her shaking fingers closed around a cup. The liquid did little to wet her gummy mouth and dry throat.

She looked at Candrae and Vayci, both standing at attention. There was something hollow and fearful in their faces. Their friends, their family, were in the palace too. Kiria gripped the cup harder.

Plans started swirling through her mind. Guards had to be here, right? They were probably just outside. "Chetana, tell the guards we're here." The Amir hurried to obey.

Kiria took stock of the situation as best she could. They were at war. The First Keeper was dead. She was alive. She didn't know about Atty. Her train of thought hitched into vague but intense pain at the thought. The three Keeper Lines needed to be saved. They had to find a safe place to go. They should control communication and supplies...

She became lightheaded and realized how quickly she was breathing. Vayci seemed to notice it too, because she knelt beside her and gently took her hand. Kiria squeezed back, taking another small sip of water.

She took a deep breath and stood, resolve hardening inside her. Letting go of Vayci's hand, she turned again to the window that flickered orange with fire shadows. The air started to smell thick like distant smoke.

The Tanyu—maybe Firian himself—had killed Cúron and taken over the palace, her home. She would not let this attack go unanswered. There was still at least one Keeper left alive.

And she would get back her throne.

KINGDOMS ON FIRE

BOOK 3 OF THE TANYUIN ACADEMY SERIES

1

BELIK

Master Belik had three reasons to burn the palace.

It would demoralize the people of Brithnem, bring its soldiers to him, and split their attention as they tried to salvage treasures and lives from the castle. If he hit the right pressure points, surrender would come quickly.

Belik limped down the wide, shadowed hallway of Mon Párinath, flanked by high-ranking Tanyu, and weakened from his encounter with that traitor Bard. Though his breath came labored, power ran like iron through his veins after watching the boy bend backward through the sheer force of Belik's mind. It should have been gruesome, but all he'd felt was grim fascination. Rightness.

Finding the royal bedchambers when he'd arrived had been easy. The buzz that constantly vibrated at the corners of his mind spoke of traversing these halls a thousand times. He didn't remember consciously following Chetana in years, but as soon as he set foot in the palace, he knew the layout like a memory.

The First and Third Keepers had been in their rooms, in bed with their wives. Each had a coterie of four soldiers guarding the door. One problem with royals was that they lacked imagination. All the guards were exactly where he expected them to be. When the black-clad Tanyuin warriors had arrived, striking out of the dark like vipers with their knifing teeth, the soldiers had no time to scream, much less draw their weapons. They dropped like sacks.

Belik ordered the Keepers to be killed painlessly. Mercy had gripped him at random. It didn't matter if they bled or not, if they suffered or not. The only thing that mattered was that Cúron's and Atael's deaths be undeniable and deliberate.

After the chaos, he would escort the soldiers off the palace grounds. The Tanyu would station themselves inside the beating heart of power, with the sea behind them, giving themselves access to limitless resources.

Most of the work of conquering a kingdom wasn't physical, but mental. Once the people believed the Tanyu had won, then they had. Resistance would wane, and everyone would become more and more convinced that this was how it ought to be.

All it takes is belief.

Tanyuin Masters had repeated those words over and over again. Belik set his mouth hard as he took another uneven step, cursing his bad leg in frustration.

Belik had believed in Firian. The moment he first saw the boy, he knew this was the one who could make the Tanyu great, could make *him* great.

Belik's earlier protégé, Anewa, had gone far but ultimately failed, getting irreparably Lost in the Unreal, despite Belik's efforts to save him. Belik needed someone even stronger. And for a long time he didn't think anyone could live up to his expectation.

Firian was the exception. His intensity had been obvious from the moment he arrived at the Tanyuin Academy. He would do whatever it took to become a Master. Too many Learners started by doing what was asked of them and assuming they would rise through the ranks. Idiots. A Master was not only a master of the Tanyuin arts, but of his own fate.

Firian had practiced often enough and hard enough to earn even Belik's grudging respect. Firian might have more scars than Belik did on his own body. Scars proved his effort—that he pushed himself to the edge of what was possible. More than once, Belik had been forced to grab Firian out of the Unreal before he believed in his own death.

He took a sharp breath through his nose at the memory. The air was filled with an underlying must. It had seen blood. He huffed it back out again, eyeing the shadowed corners. This hall wouldn't be quiet for long. Even now, footsteps and shouts filtered through the hazy air. Took them long enough. He halted in the center of the elaborate corridor. Master Nedi, the leader of physical training after Jovan died a few months ago, towered on his left. Shiro, a young Tanyu about nineteen, Firian's age, stood at his right.

There had obviously been questions about Firian's whereabouts. Most thought that they were acting on Firian's orders.

In the few seconds of peace they'd had since they entered the palace, Belik told several of them that Firian's true plan had surfaced—using them to eliminate the other Keepers so he could rule with Kiria alone.

Close enough to the truth.

In a different way, Firian had betrayed the Tanyu by suddenly acting the coward. Belik included some vague nonsense about Firian's exhaustion after using his killing ability, so the others wouldn't be as afraid to attack him if he showed his face. When he showed his face.

Belik's chest felt hard as stone with disappointment. How could Firian fall prey to the same vice Belik had years before? The injustice of it scratched at his heart. He'd been so careful to make Firian loyal only to the Academy. He'd raised him as he would have raised his own son, if he'd gotten the chance. And *still!* He gritted his teeth.

That girl had gotten her claws into him so deeply there was nothing Belik could do. Waiting outside the capital city of Brithnem, ready with an army, Firian had simply called off the attack. Called it off. Because some girl told him to. It didn't matter that she was the Second Keeper. That should have made her opinion matter *less*.

It was almost impossible to think that Firian could be so spineless. Especially when justice was this close.

A group of armored Kingdom soldiers appeared around the corner. Only fifteen. Over half of them had light blue cloth across their shoulders marking them as palace guards. One of them caught Belik's attention. He wore many insignias the others didn't and was the first to direct the others toward the Tanyu.

Belik needed to speak to Kingdom generals. He could start here.

The approaching soldiers rushed forward, swords drawn. The Tanyu didn't move. A corner of Belik's lip curled upward. These soldiers had such fierce expressions as they came on. Despite their fervor, they would attack in a spearhead formation, probably all using their right hands to wield identical swords.

At a twitch of his head, two more Masters materialized from behind him to stand by his sides. He communicated with their minds in the Unreal, out of earshot of the charging soldiers. "Everyone but the leader."

The fight was brief. The Tanyu, both in black, whirled through the crowd of soldiers like ghosts. A couple missed opportunities—Belik's eyes narrowed—but the warriors exploited vulnerabilities in the armor and the soldiers soon dropped. The leader, who appeared to be a general, at least, stood with his arms wrenched behind his back, face to face with Belik.

Shiro ripped off the man's helmet and threw it away with a clank. The leader was middle-aged and sandy-haired, with high cheekbones and almond-shaped eyes. To the soldier's credit, he didn't openly quail before the Tanyu, but a white rim shone around his irises.

Belik resettled his glasses on his nose. The air was getting smokier. "I would like to speak to the other generals."

The man's mouth closed in mute defiance.

Belik sniffed. There was no time for this. "Tell them I'll meet them just outside the barracks in an hour. I have an offer for them."

Confusion replaced the insolence in the man's face, which was an improvement, at least as Belik's plan was concerned.

"Something good," Belik clarified, as though speaking to a child. "Of course, they can refuse it." He regarded the man meaningfully. Refusal meant death—surely he could understand that. He'd just watched all these men die.

The man eyed the weapons around him warily, as though he could fight them off with mere awareness. But more than everywhere else, his eyes landed on Belik's face, meeting his gaze.

"The Keepers are dead," Belik explained, "and I don't want this to be bloodier than it has to be."

"Lies!" the general spat, the word ricocheting out of his mouth.

Belik backhanded him casually. "You'll see their heads in the arena square before sunset tomorrow."

The man's pale lip twitched convulsively, though whether from sorrow or horror, it was difficult to tell. Faint crackling sounded in the distance as Belik let the moment stretch, grow heavy with significance.

"It's done," Belik resumed. "The Tanyu have control of the city. You can take my offer and be part of restoring peace, or you can doom your soldiers to painful deaths. You know our reputation, what we can do. There's no Keeper to stand behind. One hour." He growled the final words one by one.

The Tanyuin Master released the general and gave him back his sword. The gesture seemed to baffle the man, but he slowly sheathed his weapon and left.

When the general was out of sight, the Master trailed him down the hall and out the door, silent as smoke, which was filling the space.

"Outside," Belik told the others. He had an hour before he could deal with the other generals. The Masters around him could stop anything but a fight with truly overwhelming numbers. And it took more than a few ordinary soldiers to take down a Tanyu. If he moved quickly, they wouldn't have time to plan an attack coordinated enough to take him down, and now the military leaders had the draw of his offer. Imminently generous, and most of them would see that. What were riches for except to direct power?

Shiro opened the exterior door as Belik passed through. Even the glass in the door was decorated. Were these Keepers trying to compensate for their lack of military imagination by keeping everything pretty?

Apart from a couple indiscreet Torithians and border patrollers from Tánuil hauling loot from the burning palace across the gardens, it was a quiet night. Even now, with two of the three thrones standing empty.

He needed to empty all three. They'd find the girl soon enough. He'd make sure of it. His mind shuffled backward a few paces, a few minutes.

Bard, that deserter, had bought her enough time to get away. In the rush of the initial attack, no one could sense where she'd gone. Firian knew, but he'd already made his preference clear. He'd choose her safety over the Academy.

Honestly, Belik didn't regret the time it took to kill the boy. Another Tanyu could have done it quickly, but Bard seemed like he would make a good first victim, since there had to be victims. A little smaller than male Tanyu tended to be, and too weak for violence, he was unlikely to fight back. And he had betrayed the Academy. Run off to spill their secrets to Kiria, the girl who had her barbs in Firian. No one betrayed the Academy to that extent and lived.

Belik had felt young and powerful again as he showed off his new ability for the first time. It was simultaneously horrible and thrilling to open his eyes and find Bard's spine bent backward and blood leaking from his ears. Shiro was the only one near him at the time, but he had been suitably impressed. Impressed wasn't the word. As Bard's body collapsed, Shiro was terrified, awestruck.

Hopefully Belik would never have to use that power against another Tanyu again, past or present. That part rankled. That, and the fact that little Bard had been a friend of Firian.

The perfume of flowers softened the air around him as he moved quickly across the flagstone patio of the garden. This false peace wouldn't last. Time was against him. Right now, he needed to get inside the one place he swore he'd never go: the Amiran Academy.

2

FIRIAN

Firian heaved out a shaky breath and readjusted the body he carried across his shoulders. Bard's limp form was surprisingly heavy and unstable, even though Firian grabbed his wrists tightly. His arm wrapped around the crook of Bard's knees, even though that meant limited mobility for that hand. If a guard came to kill them both, he would have to drop his friend and fight.

No, the guard wouldn't come to kill Bard. Only Belik wanted him dead, and he thought he had finished the job. Only the faint warm breath against Firian's left cheek suggested Belik was wrong. Bard was alive, but barely.

Something warm and wet slid down Firian's temple and dripped off his jaw. Blood. Bard's blood.

Firian bit back a groan as he picked up his pace. He needed a doctor. Now. The only one he could remember was the doctor who had come for Salaar, the Amir Firian had killed in his sleep several months ago. He barely recalled what the man looked like, much less his name.

With palace guards after him, and Belik no longer an ally, Firian was on his own. He fought back panic. Getting out of this enormous tomb seemed like it had to be the first step.

Which doors would Belik and the other Tanyu have used? Judging from the silence, they would still be unguarded for a few moments. Firian conjured a map in his mind, ticking off the options. Belik wanted to kill, to conquer. One choice stood out. It was what Firian would have done.

If Firian had had a bad leg, that is.

There were high windows no one bothered to guard that could be easy entrance points, but Belik couldn't reach them. Firian had shown Kiria last year. Her two friends had been there, too—the Third Keeper and his brother.

His brother, Jori.

Firian blinked hard, willing himself to come out of the Unreal. He hated to admit it, but shock sometimes thrust him into the Unreal without his knowledge. If he didn't realize his mistake about reality, he could be Lost forever in that imaginary space.

He'd realized quickly this time, at least. Jori Calthwaite sprinted toward him in a radically unlikely way. His billowy white shirt and open embroidered vest flowed around him in his speed. His gray boots rose to uneven heights on his legs. When he saw Firian, he skidded to a halt and drew himself up like a fighter in a children's story. Like he'd never really fought anyone before. His face was chalk white.

"Where's Kiria?" he demanded, too loudly. "Is she alive?"

Firian couldn't break out of the illusion, so he spat back, "Yes! Where's a doctor?"

Jori's chin trembled with his next words. "You didn't kill her?"

Firian adjusted his hold on Bard's wrists, jogging him further up on his shoulders. "No. A doctor!" At this point it didn't matter if what he saw was real. Bard was dying.

Jori squinted at Bard, as though seeing him for the first time. "Is that Bard?"

Firian cursed. "Yes. I need a doctor *now!*"

Jori waved him forward, breaking into a run. "Here, here," he said.

Firian followed Jori's kicking heels, eyes darting to all the details he and Kiria had changed. The purple of the carpets, leaves of the *sachion* trees, frames of the portraits, panes in the windows—everything was right. He wasn't in the Unreal. This was really happening.

Jori ducked into a small storage room. He jumped high-kneed over bags of dried food and piles of silk blankets like someone who had done this hundreds of times. Bundling sheets in his arms, he threw them out of the way, revealing a small square door underneath, set low into the wall. It came up to Jori's thigh.

Firian calculated whether he could crawl through with Bard in his arms. It was challenging, but he could make it work if this was the only way. "This leads to the doctor?" he demanded.

"We have to get out," Jori said, his voice desperate as he started to force open the door.

Bending forward so Bard would stay in place from his own weight, Firian grabbed Jori's throat and forced him to his feet. "Is this the quickest way?"

Terrified tears streamed down Jori's face. "Please…"

"Is it?" Firian gave him a shake. Bard's legs began to slump off his shoulders. He let go of Jori to catch Bard behind the knees again.

Jori fell to the floor, gesturing helplessly to the tiny opening. "There's a doctor through here."

"Then go." Firian kicked him, galvanizing him into action again. He had no time for panic, no time to think. Bard's body was still warm against the back of his head, but he couldn't be sure he felt breathing anymore when his own was so erratic.

As Jori lunged headfirst into the opening, Firian eased Bard to the ground, considering all the ways to haul him through this space that must be only for emergencies. He took Bard by the armpits and dragged him to the opening, getting himself inside first, and then Bard after him. It was an awkward arrangement. Bard was lying partly on top of him with his back against Firian's chest, but Firian found he could push his way along with his legs while still holding onto Bard.

There were no lights in the tunnel and very little air. The claustrophobic smell of mold and dampness permeated his nostrils. "How far does this go?" he hissed.

Jori's voice sounded far ahead of him. "Just this way."

That didn't answer his question, so Firian just focused on going as fast as he could, pushing off with his feet as he dragged Bard's limp body. Again and again and again. A faint heartbeat pulsed beneath Bard's arms. He was still holding on. The earthen floor of the tunnel scraped Firian's back as he forced himself backward, heedless of anything in his path. Part of his shirt ripped loudly, shredded by the pebbles.

Finally, light fell over them. Firian's head cast a black shadow over Bard, so he couldn't see his friend's face, couldn't see if more blood leaked from his eyes like tears. With renewed energy, Firian kicked against the walls and tumbled out onto wet grass. The light had come from the moon. They were outside the palace walls, though where exactly, Firian couldn't tell. Surf crashed in the distance and the shadowy shapes of buildings rose over the grassy basin where they'd emerged.

Jori was already sprinting away. Firian cursed repeatedly under his breath as he bent down to pick up Bard. Jori had to be running for the doctor. If he was running to get away from the Tanyuin invasion, he was a gory coward who deserved worse than what Bard was enduring.

Firian's breath seized. Bard's light brown face had gone gray. He still had a pulse, but he was fading fast. Even a doctor might not be able to save him. "Come on," he muttered as he pulled him up again. The flowing breeze cooled his back and confirmed his suspicion that much of the shirt had been torn away. He was probably bleeding, but it didn't matter.

He eased Bard's unconscious body to the ground. No warm air feathered against the back of his hand when he held it against Bard's mouth. Too much time passed between thick heartbeats before a sign of life appeared.

From the top of the knoll, Jori and a man ran toward them. "Here's a doctor. It's a doctor," Jori said when he reached them.

The doctor was tall and thin, middle-aged, with a hanging lip and a wary eye, like some homeless travelers Firian had seen. Despite looking as though Jori had woken him from a deep sleep, the man looked at Bard with precision and concern, and Firian had no other choice. This doctor had to help, or there was no hope to save his friend. Maybe hope had already left.

The doctor knelt next to him, checking his vitals.

Firian stood above them, unable to walk away. But a second task assaulted his mind, now that this one was done. He couldn't do anything more to help Bard. His life or death was out of his hands now. He'd done what he could. Even with those reasonable words, he lingered. Was there nothing—*nothing*—more he could do?

Bard's eyes were glued shut with blood. The backs of his hands were filthy from rubbing against the walls of the tunnel. Firian watched his chest to see it rise and fall, just once. Then he could leave. It felt like a long time before he saw it.

He swallowed. "Give him the best treatment," he told the doctor. "He lives." He said it like an ultimatum. When he glanced up from Bard, Jori had already gone.

Spinning around, he saw the palace rising behind him. They'd gone just past the wall enclosing the palace grounds. In there was Belik.

Without looking back, he dove into the dark passageway, running like an animal on all fours. Belik had defied him, tried to kill Bard, taken control of his men, gone after Kiria... The crimes went on in an endless list. All the lies and manipulation he had endured came back like bitterness on his tongue. How had he not seen this coming? "Gore," he muttered and pushed himself to speed up.

He burst through the other side of the tunnel, colliding with a basket of candles in his speed. They rolled across the floor as he leapt over them to get to the hallway.

As he emerged from the storeroom, he grabbed a long strip of cloth, tying it around his palm as he ran. Where was Belik? He tightened the end of the knot with his teeth.

Belik wanted the Tanyu to have control of Brithnem. He hadn't given the Keepers a peaceable option, so he would take what he wanted. That meant that he would follow the method he taught Firian: disable the leaders and have the public swear you in on whatever they deemed holy. In this case, the Sacred Scroll. Firian hadn't brought his copy from the Academy since Brithnem was known to have duplicates. If those tactics didn't work, he'd threaten their lives and the lives of those they cared about.

Belik had already gone after the Keepers. Firian cast his thoughts toward Kiria again. He still felt the distinct buzz of her presence on the edge of his thoughts. She was in distress, but not dead. For now, anyway, she was safe. Hopefully she'd found someplace to hide until he could put this right.

He looked down at the carpet rushing beneath him and took a slow breath. *This is the best way to help her. She might not take my help now anyway.* The thought did little to dissuade him from going to find her, but it did enough. He would find out more about Kiria later.

What about Cúron and Atael? There was no time. Checking on them would mean wasting time looking for Belik. Belik was the one who needed to be stopped. He had betrayed Firian in the worst way possible. Even the thought brought the taste of blood to Firian's mouth.

He had to be at the Amiran Academy. It was the only place guaranteed to have copies of the Sacred Scroll. Few of the Amir would consent to crown Belik the leader, or Keeper, or whatever he demanded. But he had to be there.

The closest exit brought him past Kiria's bedroom again. Hopefully no guards would slow him down.

Even as he thought it, he heard footsteps behind him. It didn't matter whose they were, Kingdom or Tanyu. Firian stopped dead and whipped out his knife. Eight Kingdom guards in silver and blue ran toward him, swords in hand. Behind them was a strange orange glow. The fire on the outer edge couldn't be raging so fiercely that its light reached that far.

The truth dawned. The palace itself was on fire.

But that wasn't why the guards were running. The fight in their eyes showed they were coming for him.

He spread his legs in a fighting stance. Eight against one. Normally, those weren't great odds, but the fire in his veins made him feel superhuman. He had to find Belik. These people were just roadblocks. There wasn't time to explain that he wasn't the enemy. They wouldn't believe him anyway.

He sliced a warning in the air with his knife as he scanned the space. If he used his killing ability to wipe them out at once, he'd weaken himself too much to go after Belik. He wouldn't risk it.

Statue, window, plant, chandelier.

Creativity and simplicity. The words of Master Asoka, the woman who'd taught strategy at the Academy, came back to him. *Those make the best plans.*

The first two guards reached him.

With his wrapped hand, he grabbed the first soldier's sword by the blade and swirled it around into the man's knee, where the armor was vulnerable. *One down.* His other hand dug the dagger under the second soldier's arm.

Crouching by the injured bodies, Firian made the next soldier hesitate, unwilling to swing a weapon so near his writhing comrades. Mistake.

Firian slid the sword and dagger forward, parallel on the carpet. The hesitant soldier looked down. It was the entry Firian needed to vault over the men on the ground and plant a hard kick in the man's chest, sending him tumbling into the man next to him.

Both blades were in Firian's hands again. With another precise kick, he left the two men nursing broken bones. *Four down.*

A thrown knife incapacitated a fifth.

He parried a thrust from the next soldier. Most Kingdom guards heavily favored their right sides. Firian's observation over the last year had detected five primary moves that all seemed to master. Such a limited repertoire.

Keeping his eye on the two others, Firian fought the largest guard, probably the most experienced as well. Each parried thrust flung his opponent's sword in the direction of one of his comrades. Such action hamstrung both enemies at once.

Use everything at hand. You are part of the environment.

But he couldn't let the fluidity and rush of battle distract him from his mission. He didn't have time to waste here.

He switched the sword to his left hand and disarmed the man with his right, protected by the cloth. A slice across the front of the helmet left his opponent crumpled on the ground.

Releasing his energy in a yell, he yanked down one of the large potted trees between them, leaving Firian with the exit. They stumbled out of its way, momentarily distracted. Firian raced in the other direction, watching the view from the windows.

He'd seen the Amiran Academy on the palace grounds before. It wasn't hard to find. He didn't wait for a door that might be guarded. The tied cloth guarded his hand against glass shards as he leapt through the nearest window frame.

Belik would have other people with him. If the Master had gone alone, palace guards would kill him for treason. If he went with a group of armed Tanyu, they could fight off the guards or hold Amir hostage, or however he thought best to get their attention and their pledge of loyalty.

The dome of the Amiran building rose beside the manicured gardens behind the castle. Columns surrounded its covered portico and round lanterns hung around the entire circumference. He knew those lights. His father, a glassmaker, had sent Firian to learn the family trade. All those white lanterns came from Raewhith, his hometown, but they were patterned on the colored lanterns of Shifra that Kiria loved so much.

His heart thundered as he charged toward the building. It was foolhardy to run in a straight line and in plain sight, but he didn't care. He could take down any Tanyu one on one if he had to, and it was a matter of extreme urgency. He couldn't slow his blood enough to hide in the shadows. Kiria, Bard, now Belik—it was too much. His body was alight with urgency. He barely felt his feet fall on the flagstones.

As he vaulted a green bush, he spotted the first Tanyu. It was just the sliver of an arm behind a column—there, and then out of sight. Almost a trick of the eye in the darkness. Without those globed lights, he might not have noticed it. Nothing else stirred.

He flew toward the column, catching the ankle of the traitor and then gripping them by the neck. He spun around to see Xan, a Tanyuin girl a couple years older than he was, stone-faced, hair braided back. She had fought with him under Tiev when the Tanyu had launched a fear campaign against the Kingdom. Before Firian became the Tanyuin Head and called off that war, which Belik had started up again. He tasted coppery blood in his mouth.

"Where is he?" he snarled in Xan's face. She looked confused rather than afraid, though her pulse raced in the web of his hand.

She could have brought her arms up to snatch his hand away, but didn't. Unable to speak, her eyes flicked from his face to a spot to his left. Adrenaline shot through his body. His hand flexed under her jaw as he turned around enough to see over his left shoulder. No Belik.

Until today, he had never had bad blood with Xan. For a heartbeat, he wondered what to do. Then he boxed her on the side of the head, knocking her out. He caught her as she fell so she wouldn't hit her skull on the stone floor. Belik was the only one who should die for his crimes.

He swiveled to the door directly behind him and yanked it open. A narrow, winding staircase led out of sight. There was no way to see if anyone lay in wait above.

Belik had taken control of the Tanyuin forces against Firian's will, so he had to know Firian would retaliate. Belik had pitted them against one another. Only one of them would make it out of the capital today. The thought made him catch his breath in a rush of emotions he couldn't name.

"Firian."

He whirled at the sound of his name. He knew that voice. It sounded as measured as ever.

"I'm glad you joined us." Down the walkway stood Belik, flanked by Tanyu.

Shiro and Nedi were at the forefront. Blood speckled both their faces and their hands were stained dull red. Light from the burning palace lit Belik's face, highlighting the bruise purpling his jaw. Firian's heart pounded against his chest, the sound rushing in his ears. Before he knew what he was doing, he hurled himself at the Master.

Something hit his shins and he vaulted face-first to the ground. His arms were immediately pinned behind him and bound. White spots burst in his vision, but he tucked his knees under himself, getting ready to spring. He tried to explode upward, but the weight of many bodies held him down.

He reached toward the Second Level. These people were blocking his way to Belik... that traitor... that murderer...

"Firian." That hateful voice again. "They're just doing what I ask. If you kill us all, you'll kill good Tanyu and maybe yourself if you're not goddamn careful."

A shard of deliberation sliced through Firian's rage, and it said that Belik was right. Choking on fury, Firian opened his eyes. He was on his knees, his wrists attached to his ankles. Air felt trapped inside his ribcage. Stars still followed his vision as he narrowed a glare at Belik.

"There," said Belik. "I figured you'd be angry, but I finished our mission. I removed the Keepers and the city belongs to us. So don't be an idiot, and join us."

Rage clouded Firian's sight. He spat in response. Behind his back, he writhed his hands. Shredded bits of his shirt blew against them, but he wouldn't be able to slip the bonds unless he broke his thumbs. It wasn't time for that yet. He might still need his thumbs.

"This is what we've been working for all this time." Belik inhaled through clenched teeth. "We know what you did, but there's still time to... atone." He fixed Firian with a look, impressing on him his crime of letting Kiria persuade him not to attack Brithnem. What Belik didn't understand—among many other things—was that the decision had been Firian's alone. It pained him, even now, but any other choice would have broken her heart, made him the monster he didn't want to be.

Firian would never apologize.

A muscle in Belik's jaw twitched and his nostrils flared. "Firian, I'm giving you a chance. Take it."

If the choice was between death and joining this man, the choice was easy. But Firian was fairly sure there was a third option. He didn't like it, but it lay in wait down in the Second Level, where everyone's brains and hearts and lungs pulsed with life. Firian suspended himself above that abyss, ready to plunge in if Belik made a move.

When Firian didn't answer, Belik's eyes narrowed. He nodded once to the Tanyu next to him, Master Nedi.

Nedi, huge and imposing, walked forward with purpose. Firian realized what he was going to do a second before it happened. Pain exploded in his temple and everything went black.

3

BELIK

Belik drew his mouth into a tight line as he watched the limp body of Firian being carried away, bound. All that strength, all that potential, tied up in another girl. He saw his own mind in those bonds. Chetana held a string he could never shear away, no matter how much he wanted to, no matter how much he hated it. Hate was easier than fear, more powerful, so he had chosen that a long time ago. He would kill her if he ever got the chance. The one who had seduced him, betrayed him...

Belik's lip curled. They were so close—literally moments away—from making their dream a reality and Firian had to screw it up out of a misplaced sense of... what? Honor? Lust? Whatever it was, Belik wouldn't beg. His road had been much longer than Firian's, though he had grown fond of the boy. Maybe Firian would realize his stupidity.

"What the gory hell was that?" Master Ardal demanded from behind him. "He's the Tanyuin Head. He'll kill you. He'll kill *us*."

Belik tore his eyes from Firian, whose hair flopped over his face, mouth lolling open as he disappeared past the light of the everlasting round lanterns.

"I didn't see you stepping in," he responded coolly. Master Ardal had never impressed him. He taught World Events at the Academy, but he was rusty in action.

"I know not to put a target on my back."

"As you're doing now?" Belik raised one eyebrow meaningfully.

Despite a flash of apprehension, so quick it might never have been there at all, Ardal didn't back down. He'd argued with Belik before, although most Masters knew better than to try. "What did he do? If this is a coup, it's messy. Master Kess has many people on his side."

Messy? Maybe. Belik shrugged his massive shoulders, setting his expression into a glare.

Shiro stepped in to answer. Belik had told enough Tanyu to accomplish the initial mission. Word just needed to spread. "He only ordered the Keepers killed so he could rule with Kiria. That's why he disappeared. He helped her escape." The younger Tanyu's eyes flashed with hatred. He felt Firian's betrayal more than most, since Firian had accidentally killed his friend Rian when Kingdom soldiers raided the Academy.

"He wants to distance himself from the strike now," Belik added. "It's all right, Ardal. He lied to all of us. Turns out he had a *katah* with her." He felt his own anger rise with the word. This part was truth, and it made him seethe. "Firian was going to leave us all to rot. No justice for what the Kingdom did. You knew the victims of the attack on the Academy. I did too! So I'll get revenge with or without him." There was no one who could refute his story, but he'd have to remember the details so he could repeat them. His lie might as well be truth. "How else could she have known we were coming? Coward," he spat. "She left them all to die."

"She wants to be with Master Kess?" someone else asked. They were like children, all lapping up gossip. Firian had had plenty of girls. Why were they surprised about one more? Kiria was a child, no more than eighteen. Of course she'd want to be part of the grand play Firian promised with his power and his name.

Belik tried to prepare for the unpredictable, but was often disappointed when people acted exactly as he expected. No one was original anymore. Firian could have been. He could have gone somewhere...

"She won't show us mercy after this, if Firian gets his way." Belik grunted. "Hopefully he'll come around."

"He could have killed us all just now," Ardal insisted again.

"He could do that before." *Before the killing ability made it easier.* "I'll put it right." *And hopefully Firian will start thinking with his head and not his dick.*

Belik was tired of talking. There was work to be done. Right now, the generals in the barracks were no doubt arguing among themselves about the best course of action. That, or following attack protocol. Belik had stationed many Tanyu there to settle things before he arrived.

Belik turned to Shiro. White light from the round lanterns warred with the waning firelight, dominating opposite sides of the Defender's face. The sky had turned gray with the morning, but none of that light bled in. Belik was already sick of this soft place with all its religion and reminders of her.

"Advisors," he grunted. Shiro and another Tanyu ran to gather them.

He loped after them slowly, rounding the corner away from where they'd taken Firian. The weakness in his leg had gotten worse since he used his new ability on Bard. Someone appeared around the corner. His stomach jolted with nerves.

Just a Tanyu. He cursed himself. Death didn't frighten him—his plan would work, he was reasonably sure—but his body reacted with anxiety now that he was so close to his son. Seething anger layered under his skin, at himself, at her... He hadn't seen his son since he was a baby, and since he was three-quarters Khelê, he didn't have to bear any resemblance to either of his parents.

Shiro and his companion returned with three Amir in tow. They stood with regal dignity, as though standing before Belik were beneath them. Belik fought the urge to spit on one of the gory prisses' boots. They all wore the same grayish blue robes, but the one on the left was the oldest, with dark, thinning hair slicked back. In the center was a younger one who looked like a stereotypical Kingdom man, deep-set eyes, fair skin and dark hair. On the right was another man who might be the same age as the one in the center. It was difficult to tell. He was clearly Khelê, having very large eyes and a small mouth. His irises might have been tinged with purple.

Belik scrutinized the ones on the center and the right. The man on the left was too old. Surrounded by the buzz of the other Tanyu, it was difficult to tell if any of these men had the Talent. Any son of his had to have it. "The Keepers are dead," he said. It would be true of all three soon enough, and the more people he told, the more plausible it sounded.

All three let out cries of horror.

Belik studied them impassively before continuing. "I need one of you to announce this to the people, and to inform them that the Tanyu will take ownership of the city at the next new moon."

"What proof do we have?" the oldest demanded hesitantly.

Belik stifled a smirk. "We'll show you later. Which of you will give the announcement?" Fractionally, he paused. "What are your names?" In the silence that followed, his heart started jogging in his chest. This was it. If he was right—and he was rarely wrong—this would be the moment he would meet his son.

"I am Parohim," said the eldest, "and this is Daelon and Reynard."

Daelon. Belik locked eyes with the one in the center, taking in the high-necked collar, the scholar's hands, the lined eyes, the youthful mouth, the straight nose. Daelon's skin wasn't dark like his mother's or pockmarked like his. A hint of defiance was the only sign Belik could detect of his parents' deadly personalities. His breath caught in his throat as Daelon looked him in the eye. His eyes had the tired look of someone who read too much but hadn't yet gotten glasses. He would need them in time. He was Belik's son, after all. A royal advisor. An Amir.

No scars at all.

He swallowed down the trapped air. Chetana had ruined their son. Daelon was a man of words, not action. He couldn't defend his home against the Tanyu. He couldn't even help his princess, or Keeper, as she was now. His only son, and she had twisted him with her own priorities, told him that the Tanyu were bloodthirsty and cruel, while the Amir were soft and merciful. His face grew warm with blood. His son. His only son.

He shifted his weight, his badly broken leg throbbing as though the fight with her had been yesterday. Daelon was the prize he had lost. By then, he'd already lost Chetana.

"Which of you will give the announcement?" he asked again, willing for Daelon to speak.

All three remained stonily silent.

About to call on Daelon, he stopped himself. He had to make an example of anyone who refused. "You," he said to Reynard.

"I will not," the Amir replied calmly. "I will not sanction a cruel leader while my Keepers might still live. God would not have it so."

Belik ground his molars. He should have expected this pigheadedness. "You will, or we'll kill you."

Constriction in his neck tendons revealed the Amir was nervous. "I can't betray my Keeper, my kingdom, or my God."

Before Belik could respond, Daelon spoke. "*God supports the just man's cause and dawns upon him light in darkness.*" In his eyes burned a fire, admittedly small, that made Belik almost proud. It had to be about the Sacred Scroll, though. Everything did with these people.

Belik turned back to Reynard. "You won't do it?"

The Amir's huge eyes widened almost comically. "No."

Chewing his cheek, Belik gave one nod to the Tanyu behind Reynard, who went down in seconds, his neck cracking loudly through the night air.

Daelon and Parohim recoiled in horror, shuffling away from the body and uttering guttural sounds of dismay. But they didn't fight back. Did they have any nerve, any mettle at all? Who could watch one of their own go down and not attack the one who did it?

His gaze brushed past his son again, standing tall but too docile beside Reynard's body. Had Chetana ever told him who his father was? About to call on Parohim, he stopped. His curiosity burned him from the inside out.

"You," he said.

Daelon stiffened.

Belik's heart hammered. To be announced by his own son would taste more like victory than any other part of this so far. Someone had to recognize the greatness of the Tanyu. If not Firian, then his biological son.

"My name is Master Belik, a Tanyu of the Academy," he said, staring into his son's eyes.

Something in Daelon's expression went slack with recognition and dread, but he didn't say anything.

"I need you to announce that the Keepers are dead, and that the Tanyu have taken the city. It will be made official at the next new moon."

The recognition in Daelon's eyes gave way to pain. His mouth strained as though pulled by misery. Belik could see his shallow breathing. All the little adjustments resulted in a horrified grief.

Was he this sad about the Keepers? Belik considered for a moment if he could allow that as a legitimate reason to be so upset.

"No," Daelon managed. His brow lowered and he glared up at his father with a clear message: *How could you? My own father!* So he didn't want to admit the relationship. Fine.

Belik felt pressure building in his blood. His gaze ticked to the Tanyu standing behind his son. He didn't nod.

"The Tanyu have taken the city," Belik repeated. "You can support what's inevitable—" *Or you can die.* But the words stuck in his throat.

"I will not sanction you," Daelon said again, more clearly this time.

"Do you have another quote for me?" Belik barely hid the derision in his voice.

He might have imagined it, but it looked like Daelon leaned forward. "*God uproots the tyrant.*"

The Tanyu behind him started forward. Holding up a hand, Belik was barely quick enough to stop from breaking his neck as he had broken Reynard's. Belik's mouth had gone dry. Anger swam in his thoughts, but he couldn't have his own son killed. It shouldn't have mattered so much, not when there was so much at stake, but he'd found an unexpected weakness in himself. Later, he would redress the issue, but for now, he couldn't do it.

Flicking a look at Shiro, he said, "Daelon will send food down to Firian. Show him where he is."

It was a dangerous job, but it accomplished Belik's purposes: throwing Firian an obvious lifeline, and keeping his son alive. If Firian threatened Daelon or injured him in his reckless anger, at least Belik wouldn't have to watch.

Two weaknesses.

Fatigue lapped against him. After a few more hours, Belik could rest and start the hard work of prying them off his mind.

4

KIRIA

Kiria tore herself away from the thin, dirty window where she had been watching the palace burn, a billowing black plume just on the other side of the walled grounds. If she ran out of here, she could be there in minutes. But what could she do? How could she save the dead, or take her kingdom back?

Tears burned like smoke in her eyes. She sniffed them back and steadied herself on shelves laden with emergency provisions.

The tunnel through which they'd all escaped fed into this storage cellar. A larger room with more finery was visible through an open doorway. That was it, the entire safe house—just some basic supplies in this room and the second room large enough for several people to lie down. A temporary reprieve.

Her serving girls, Candrae and Vayci, took her arms gently and steered her toward the bigger part of the compound.

The main room had no windows at all. Stifling. This room had been decorated to be more comfortable, but it still felt sparse and unnatural, despite the purple and blue flags of Brithnem draped from the ceiling. A few formal but utilitarian pieces of furniture had been arranged, grouped into a sitting area, working space, dining area, and a bunk, all in a space no bigger than her royal bedroom.

With the four reserve guards in there already, the space felt cramped, a mockery of her title as the Western Kingdom's Keeper. Hopefully not the only one still alive.

Candrae, quietly crying, settled Kiria into a chair. Her long blonde curls fell disheveled in her smudged face. The upholstery of the seat suggested luxury that Kiria wanted no part of right now. The city was under attack. Horrible things were happening. She couldn't let herself think about all the possibilities. The likely possibilities. The memory of Chetana's horrified expression after coming out of Cúron's bedchamber made Kiria's throat close until she couldn't breathe.

She couldn't breathe.

Gasping, she stood and waved to Vayci, who already stood by her other arm. Her eyes stung as panic crawled up through her chest.

"Just breathe," Vayci said. "In through your nose... that's it... and out through your mouth."

Kiria repeated her shuddering attempts until she could drag air into her lungs again, feeling deflated as an empty set of clothes. Who else had escaped? Was her mother okay? Was Atty? Jori?

"Is Chetana back yet?" she whispered. Her former Amiran advisor had disappeared through the cramped emergency tunnel as soon as she'd deposited Kiria in the safe house. She didn't say why she was going back.

"Not yet, My Keeper," one of the guards replied before Candrae had the chance. He was young, with a large tattoo on his face. She didn't recognize him. Maybe a newly inducted recruit.

Kiria shook as she took another breath. Chetana would risk her life for more than one person in the palace: her son Daelon or Kiria's mother Merian held the top of the list. It was possible that she would go back for Atty too. As the Third Keeper, he was technically the most important person there, since Kiria was in this compound and Cúron was...

She sank back in the chair as her strength left her. Leaning forward to look back to the other room where they'd emerged from the tunnel, she hoped to see Chetana's short reddish-brown curls coming through the opening. But there was nothing.

A loud noise jolted her out of her seat. Legs trembling, she shot glances at the serving girls. Their wide eyes confirmed she hadn't imagined the sound.

The guards leapt to attention.

Again, someone pounded against the safe house. Her heart leapt into her mouth. Chetana would return through the tunnel, wouldn't she? Who else knew she was here?

A sudden alarming idea hit her. Firian would know. Their connection often allowed him to know what she was doing. Was he coming for her? Why? Hadn't he done enough? Watery rage engulfed her. Or was it violent sadness? Firian had no right to come after her, not after she'd willingly given herself up to him to save her people. Maybe he'd changed his mind, not only about ruling the Kingdom, but also about owning her.

Earlier that night, he had given her an ultimatum. *Was that tonight?* It felt like weeks ago. He said he wouldn't attack the city if she gave herself up to him. He promised. Eventually the solution was painfully clear. Brithnem was worth more than her life and reputation. Without telling anyone, she had gone to the abandoned farmhouse where he told her to meet. He had kissed her, and then... he had let her go.

If she'd thought this outcome was even a possibility, she never would have left. She wouldn't have jeopardized her city and the people she loved. The thought flushed her dark with anger and regret.

The events of the night had been so breakneck that she hadn't had time to think about the meaning of that encounter, except to see that Firian had broken his promise.

He had attacked her beloved Brithnem, breaking her last shred of trust. The memory of loving him tasted bitter in her mouth. Rancid. Piece by piece, he'd ruined something that could have been so good. She should have known it could end this way. She knew him better than most, and she'd seen the creature that tugged him toward greater violence. He'd given into that monster within. Maybe he was coming for her now.

Her stomach clenched painfully, emotions roiling like an ocean in tempest. Even she could never have predicted how far he would go in his quest for dominance. In a far corner of her mind, she doubted he *could* go so far, that he'd ordered this attack at all. But that was just more evidence of her weakness. She should be far beyond those delusions now.

The pounding had stopped, but a small scraping like a rodent's nails took its place. No one moved toward the door except the guards, standing with weapons raised.

As they all watched in horror, it burst open and someone fell inside. Kiria gasped. Vayci stumbled backward a couple steps and Candrae covered her mouth with both hands.

Dust billowed in after the figure, obscuring him for a moment. A pick, like a hairpin, dropped to the ground.

"Jori! Oh my god!" Kiria flung herself toward him, wrapping his neck hard in her embrace.

"Kiria!" He held her tight, shaking, planting rough kisses on her cheek. One of the guards hurried to shut the door behind them.

Sobs rushed out of her. She let them go on Jori's shoulder as she clung to him. Tears poured faster than she could wipe them away. One of the metal buttons on Jori's vest pressed against her collarbone.

Jori's back hitched. He was crying too. How had it come to this? Were they the only ones left? Time froze as they cried into each other's clothes and hair.

Sucking in uneven breaths, Kiria let him go. "You got out," she said. "Did you see anything? Do you know what's happening?"

Jori looked like a man haunted. Even at his worst moments, she'd never seen such desolation on his face.

Her gut twisted. Her instincts were wrong. They had to be wrong.

He swallowed convulsively, as if trying to force the words out of his throat. They stuck for a while, and he couldn't speak.

"What happened?" she made herself ask.

He fluttered his fingers, the only gesture that looked recognizable, as he summoned up his words. Kiria's chest felt tighter and tighter the longer he paused. The pressure built through her entire body.

A noise behind her made everyone jump. In the next room, Chetana stood tall and dark. Almost grateful for the interruption, Kiria dashed toward her. Her feet skittered to a stop when she saw Chetana's face. The Amir looked like a harbinger of death.

Penned in by bad news, Kiria steeled herself as best she could. She had to know more. It was her duty, and those were her friends. "Did you learn... anything?"

Chetana's expression filled with pain and horror, but in her eyes was a fierceness that made even Kiria quail before it.

"They got Atty!" The words ripped from Jori like an arrow.

Kiria's knees went weak as she turned back to face him.

"I saw. And Haved..." Jori was shaking violently.

Candrae scrubbed the tears from her face and helped him sit. His arms and legs convulsed at random as though he were freezing.

Kiria came closer. Jori pressed his palms to his eyes, shuddering again, and then reached for her hand. Her presence seemed to calm him, though she felt anything but calm. She squeezed his fingers.

Breathing heavily, he continued. "I was... going out. And I saw Tanyu. Just..." His eyes became perfect circles. He snapped with his free hand. "They were fighting Atty's guards. So I ran back—all those tunnels—you know I know all the ways."

She nodded.

"I was going to warn him." He gritted his teeth as more tears came. Kiria felt them in herself too. Jori's voice broke as he said it again. "I was going to warn him." Inhaling sharply, he crushed her hand in his grip, not realizing he was hurting her. The rings she wore dug into her skin. "When I got there, I... They were... They were dead on the bed." He closed his eyes, his breaths coming faster now.

In a daze, she motioned for Vayci to bring him water. Kiria could barely understand his story. She felt like she'd been stabbed, that life was draining out of her, but she couldn't cry. Something worse than sobs sat heavy in her chest. *It can't be true. They can't be dead. Atty's not dead. He's my friend.*

Candrae beat Vayci to the task and pressed a cup into Jori's trembling hand. At the touch, he opened his eyes again, meeting Candrae's gaze. He didn't smile, but there was gratefulness in his look. The water splashed as he brought it to his lips. He lowered his cup to his lap, his attention on Kiria again. "I tried to find you, to make sure... I ran, but you escaped. I'm glad he was right. I knew it, or I would have come after you."

"What? Who was right?"

"Bard..." He stopped, winded again. He tried to take another drink.

Was Bard still alive? Kiria waited impatiently. In the whirlwind of her thoughts, she hadn't thought enough about him. She sensed Chetana stiffen near her.

"He needed a doctor," Jori continued, shaking his head. "It was that Tanyu. He said you were all right."

She scrunched her brow, confused. "Bard said I was all right?"

"No, Firian."

Shocked, Kiria let go of Jori's hand, her attention instinctively drawn toward the door. "You saw Firian? With Bard? Is he here?"

"Here?" Confusion and grief distorted his features.

A tiny breath of relief escaped her. "They were together?"

He nodded, gulping the last of the water like a shot of liquor.

"What was he doing?" Her head spun. She had too many questions. Shooting a look at the door, she added, "Bolt it. If it can be bolted any more."

"Taking Bard to the doctor. He didn't look all right."

Did that mean that Firian wasn't behind the attack after all, or just that he didn't expect Bard to get caught in the crossfire? "Was he... ordering the attack?"

Jori waved his head back and forth, almost in a stupor. "I don't know."

"Did he talk to any other Tanyu, or...?"

"Just saw him with Bard."

Helping Bard wasn't definitive proof that Firian wasn't behind the attack, but even the hope of it gave a little water to her parched soul. Maybe she didn't have to add another betrayal to the list of evils done tonight. *And he didn't harm Jori, a member of a Keeper family.* Her tiny hope grew brighter.

There were more urgent questions than wondering about Firian's moral limits. "Do you know about anybody else?"

"No." Another tear squeezed from his eye as he handed the cup back to Candrae.

Sickness overcame her. She turned away, afraid she might throw up. Atty was dead. Haved was dead. Jori was alive. Firian was alive. Bard may or may not be alive...

She swiveled to Chetana with the same question.

Chetana's glowering sadness proclaimed her news before she told him. "Cúron," she said grimly, as though beginning a list, "and Varinna."

Jori cried out.

Kiria fought to remain composed. "Kader?" Kader was their ten-year-old son, heir to the first throne.

"I didn't see him. Without a body, it's likely that the Kepron was able to escape, but I don't know with certainty. I'm sorry, My Keeper."

Her title sounded odd in this safe house. She wished Chetana would call her Kiria. The familiarity would be comforting, especially considering the way Chetana was still looking at her. They all needed as much comfort as they could get. But more than that, they needed justice.

Kiria flexed her hands, nails digging into her palms. "We have to make a plan."

One of the guards, a large blond man, stepped forward. "We must take you farther away from the palace," he said in a low, clipped voice. "Your safety is the most important to the Kingdom."

That was true. With Cúron and Atty gone, she was the only monarch left. But the passivity of the suggestion made her skin crawl. Despite grief filling her like a lethal disease, she had to do something. She couldn't let her city burn. "Okay," she said. "Where?"

"We have a place prepared," answered the only female guard among the four.

The memory of Carradoc swarmed over her. A Tanyu in the fortress hidden in plain sight. Would all Tanyu side with the invaders, even if they were in different cities or countries? It was a stupid question. Of course they would.

So where could they go that was safe? Safe from Tanyu, safe from Firian? If he was hellbent on finding her, he would do it. They could only buy time.

Weakness overcame her. She sank into the seat next to Jori. His nearness was comforting even though he was holding his head in his hands. When had she last slept? She didn't feel tired, only weak, but she knew she hadn't slept for days. Or maybe one day?

Dimly, she noticed a change in the light streaming into the storage area by the tunnel's mouth. She stood up hazily, and went to see.

Chetana followed her. She hadn't told Kiria her news yet. Kiria didn't want to hear it, because part of her already knew that the tragic news hadn't stopped coming.

The Amir set a dark hand comfortingly on Kiria's shoulder as they both peered up at the smudgy window.

"It's Mother, isn't it?"

Chetana's fingers tensed. Answer enough.

Emptiness had replaced Kiria's earlier desperation, like the undertow of a wave that would surge again into mad whitecaps with time. Her poor, lovely mother.

"Daelon?"

"I don't know."

The grayish-yellow morning fought with the violence of the firelight through the high, narrow window. Despite everything, the sun was rising.

"We'll take it back from them, My Keeper." Chetana's profile was red-eyed and resolute.

Kiria's thoughts fluttered unevenly. *Them.* The Tanyu. Firian, who, despite helping Bard and not murdering Jori, still led the army. The boy she'd once loved who had become utterly unrecognizable. How could he do this? How could she have not seen what he was?

Her insides weren't large enough to fit all the grief. But they could fit the same tenacity she saw in Chetana's eyes. That burning resolve to make things right. To take back the Kingdom and save the friends that remained.

5

FIRIAN

Firian woke with a jerk. His head throbbed. The air felt acrid against his nose and throat but he wasn't bound anymore—a small mercy, but it was mercy. Why hadn't Belik just killed him?

He jumped to his feet. His vision narrowed with the quick movement, tilting the ground beneath him. He caught himself and focused.

The events of the night rushed back, almost collapsing him under their weight. The offer to trade the Kingdom for Kiria, letting her go, the attempted murder of Bard, Belik's betrayal, realizing she didn't love him... How had it come to this?

He was in a cell, the air smoky and dark. Judging from the haze, he must be in or near the palace. Floor to ceiling bars blocked him from the rest of the small space. On the other side of the bars was nothing but a blank antechamber, a space for standing. His was the only cell. The quality of shadows at the end of the rectangular room suggested a bend leading to steps or a longer hallway. Yes, there was the jut of the lowest stair. He was alone.

Firian thrust his arm through the bars, feeling for the lock. On one side of the crisscrossed bars was a box with a large keyhole. The burns he'd received on his arms as he ran through the fields of the outer edge a few hours before protested against the rough treatment. They weren't deep, but still stung with any pressure. Firian hadn't noticed the pain until now.

He shoved his finger into the keyhole and felt around. No latch gave; no hint of its internal mechanism brushed against him. He scanned the walls for hooks, shelves, ropes—anything that could help him, but there was nothing.

If his environment couldn't help, his next recourse was to communicate through the Unreal. He could feel for someone he might be able to trust. Bard was incapacitated, but Firian had still been popular among many of the other Tanyu, even those he didn't often talk to. He lunged below.

The force of the shock flung him stumbling against the wall. In his desperation, he hadn't immediately felt the Sentry placed over his mind. This was worse than anything they'd done to him so far. He yelled and punched the stone wall. The blow broke the skin on his knuckles but kept his bones intact. A dark smudge smeared the wall and the bite of pain felt good.

He sucked in a breath. Did he believe Bard and Kiria were alive because he hadn't felt their panic, hadn't felt the pain of their leaving? Was a Sentry strong enough to hide a truth that devastating?

He forced himself to stay calm, but the effort left him trembling. He hadn't felt so helpless since he was a child hearing his father's drunken footsteps coming toward his room.

No one had placed a Sentry on Firian since... Belik. It was his fault last time too. Firian's bloody hands curled into fists. Belik had ordered a Sentry after discovering that Firian kept spying on Kiria even after she gave no new information.

That had been months ago. He was stronger now. He could go to the Second Level. He could kill from there. He had practiced skills no other Tanyu could achieve. Even Belik hadn't managed to kill Bard. Not yet.

He had to get through. Standing tall with legs spread, he brought air deep, deep into his lungs. Setting his jaw, he closed his eyes, calling on his considerable focus. With all the violence he could summon, he dove down again.

For a few seconds he knew nothing but pain, bursting from his head to his extremities. Sheer willpower kept him there a second longer. He burned from the inside out, pain ripping from a thousand exit wounds. Another second. Maybe he would die. *All it takes is belief.*

With a gasp, he released his hold. Opening his eyes, he landed heavily on his hipbone as he collapsed. Another gasp brought up vomit. He wiped his mouth with the back of his hand, reeling from the smell. His headache had spread to the base of his neck, throbbing along his skull. He refused to die. Not when he had to kill Belik.

Pale light, then quiet footsteps cut through his pain. He froze and then forced himself to stand. Through the metal grating he saw a figure wearing the high-necked robe of an Amir, holding a torch and something else in its hands. As his vision cleared, he recognized the man.

It was Kiria's—what? Friend? Advisor? Daelon was his name. Firian felt a handhold, a crack in Belik's plan. He knew something about this Amir. "Daelon?"

The man's expression remained bereft and wary but he approached Firian without slowing or angling away. He laid a cup of water and hunk of bread on the ground just outside the bars. Belik didn't intend to kill Firian now if he had someone bring him food. Perhaps this was a peace offering.

"What's going on out there?" Firian tried to keep his voice kind, but the question came out as a demand.

Daelon ground his teeth. "Your people are taking over everything," he said. "They've profaned the holy place."

"What did they do?"

"You don't deserve to know."

Firian glared but kept his composure. "I won't be in here long," he managed.

"If you tell me, I can stop them." Seeing the indecision in Daelon's eyes, he added, "I'm obviously not on their side."

"They've killed the Keepers," Daelon said thickly, going greenish pale.

Firian's gut dipped. The blackness of the shadows reached out for him, constricted his throat. *No.* "Is there proof?"

"I haven't seen it." The desolation didn't leave his eyes.

"Kiria's still alive." The words came out before Firian could bite them back. Maybe he needed to hear them himself, like a fresh breeze through this forsaken, fetid place. The Amir needed to hear them too. If Belik had shown no proof, then Kiria wasn't dead. She couldn't be. Firian refused to believe it.

Daelon's mouth fell open. He blinked with raised eyebrows. A tear slid down his cheek. When he closed his mouth again, he muttered something under his breath. A prayer, maybe. Then suspicion entered his gaze again. "Are you sure?" he asked, each word clear.

"Yes." Kiria was alive. Bard was alive too. A Sentry couldn't hide something so monumental from him. That belief kept the last bit of ground from crumbling beneath his feet.

Daelon wrung his hands before dragging one over his face.

A moment of panic took Firian. If Belik actually thought that Kiria had been killed, then he had just told someone a fact that could send new assassins after her. One more look at Daelon dispelled his fear. This man, at least, wouldn't tell Belik. He was loyal to Kiria. Besides, Firian doubted Belik would allow an Amir into his presence when it wasn't necessary to his plan. "Don't tell anyone," he said, just in case. His tone bore a threat he didn't verbalize.

In his place, Kiria wouldn't threaten Daelon, but anything that could give her additional minutes to escape had to be tried. What would Kiria do, if she were locked here? She wouldn't accept the fate of Brithnem. Just hours before, she showed what she was willing to do to save it. The memory tasted like shame.

Daelon's pupils contracted, flame flickering across them from the torchlight, but then he gave a sad smile, as though death wouldn't be so bad after all he'd witnessed. Then he nodded. "I don't have a key," he admitted.

It wasn't an offer of help, exactly, but it was close.

Quietly, the man turned to go, leaving the torch burning in a bracket and providing helpful light. Soft footfalls faded to nothing in the distance.

Iron rust from the bars had left bloody-looking red marks on Firian's arms, which he hadn't been able to see before. He grabbed the two items and pulled them inside his cell. They could be poisoned. The drink Belik had sent him after Firian had called off the raid had some kind of agent in it that knocked him out. This could be the same. He'd get water after he was out of this prison. He crushed the bread. Just hard crust and doughy insides. Nothing else.

All he'd needed to do was alert some of the Tanyu that this *wasn't* his plan the moment he realized Belik acted in his name. They would have pulled back, even disposed of Belik for him. Now he couldn't contact anyone. Panic had made him stupid.

Black despair threatened to close around him with the finality of death. He was trapped. Belik was taking control of Kiria's city. The only people he cared about were as good as dead, and they hated him. He had failed. He had failed. Just as his father had predicted. The words he'd heard as a child played in a hectic, overlapping loop.

Why'd we even keep this scut? Worthless, gory, stupid kid...

He felt hollowed out. The echoes bounced inside him until he couldn't take the noise. He screamed. He even startled himself with the shredding sound. The worst things he could think of, all the curses and all the pain he kept inside his head, burst out in barely coherent shouts. Wrapping his fists around the bars of his cage, he rattled hard until the veins stood up on his arms and blood from his knuckles dripped down to the floor.

Deflating, he grimaced. His heel hit the bread crust on the floor as he backed up.

He would not give into despair. He would not. Belik would not win.

6

KIRIA

THERE WAS no time to mourn. The five people in the safe house had pulled the upholstered seats into a rough circle. One guard stood by them. Three others had stood by the door after Kiria voiced her fear that Firian might try to find her. Candrae and Vayci sat back as though abashed to sit in such company, but Kiria and Chetana sat forward. Jori lounged, listless. Half the time he seemed not to be listening or following their train of thought.

"So no one knows whether Kader made it out of the palace?" Kiria looked at the guard nearest to her, the blond one who held seniority over the others, but got no answers. That had to be their first priority, to make sure the three Lines were safe. "How can we find out?"

"I'm sure the Tanyu will announce which leaders they eliminated," Chetana said bitterly.

"We can't wait that long, if there's a way to find out sooner," Kiria replied. Besides, the idea of waiting for such a horrible report turned her stomach. "We should try to find him now. The Tanyu will be looking for him if we aren't."

"And us," said the soldier with the face tattoo.

The big blond guard, old enough to be the younger one's father, shut him up with a look.

What they needed was more information. God knew Kiria didn't want any more bad news, but if the heir to the First Line was alive, then they needed to make sure he stayed that way. If they knew what the Tanyu did, they could make better decisions. With her sanity hanging by the thinnest thread, she needed all the help she could get.

Firian would know all about the attack. Kiria wrung her hands, running her thumbnail along the length of her fingers. She didn't want to see him, not when he was probably the engineer of all this horror, despite being seen with Bard. What if he made more demands? What if he found her even as they were talking?

"I don't think I should contact Firian directly. It could just draw him here. We need a plan first." Her muscles tensed at the thought. She didn't need to explain further. The rumor of her relationship with Firian had run through all the palace personnel.

"I don't think he's in charge," Jori struck in.

"He's the Tanyuin Head," Kiria said drily, surprised that Chetana hadn't replied first, considering the Amir's hatred of him. Instead, Chetana's expression implied that she agreed with Jori. Kiria raised a brow at her.

"Yeah, but I saw him carrying Bard out of the palace," Jori said. "Why would he do that?"

"He was *carrying* Bard?" It would be hard to direct an attack and save someone at the same time—someone the Tanyu harmed in the first place.

"And he didn't harm you. Did he?" Chetana asked.

Jori shook his head, shifting uncomfortably in his chair.

Kiria's mind whirled. It felt like betraying the memories of those she lost to consider that Firian might have kept his word after all. What did it matter now anyway? "But he must have ordered the attack. Who else could have started something like that?"

"I know who it was," Chetana said. She had that faraway look she often got, as though she were about to prophesy. Even the serving girls stared at her, hanging on her next slow word. "Belik." The sounds of the name rolled in her mouth as though she'd already tried every variation, tasted and spat each syllable.

Master Belik was Chetana's *katah*, Daelon's father? The one who had incapacitated Bard outside her room?

Kiria knew that name.

Firian trusted him. Belik had been his teacher when he first arrived at the Academy. He had taught Firian about the Unreal. Did that mean he knew more about it than Firian did?

"Master Belik?" she echoed. "He and Firian are close. Are you sure they aren't working together?" The idea made her shudder. Anyone who could frighten Chetana was truly dangerous.

"I don't know. They could be, but Belik killed our family." She meant multiple things by those words. "He is... treacherous. He is capable of turning on the Tanyuin Head, of taking power for himself. I am surprised he didn't do it sooner."

"Maybe he couldn't."

"Oh, he could have."

The others watched their faces in rapt attention, bouncing from the Keeper to the Amir and back. The room felt airless, as though everyone held their breath for fear of missing a crucial word.

Jori swiped a hand over his face. "How do you know him?" he asked Chetana, who ignored the question.

"Something's gone wrong with his plan," she said stiffly, with almost a twinge of fear in her voice.

Jori looked at Kiria next, who didn't supply an answer either. If Chetana didn't want everyone to know about her *katah* with the enemy, she would respect that desire. She knew it all too well.

"Do you know what his plan is? His next move?" Kiria asked instead.

"I think he has a few objectives," Chetana replied curtly. "The most obvious is taking control of the city. That's what we need to focus on."

"So, there's a new Tanyuin Head?" asked the tattooed guard. This time, the blond one didn't shush him.

"For our purposes," Chetana said, "we'll act as though there are two."

Reluctantly, Kiria cast her a look. Chetana seemed to divine its meaning at once before Kiria even asked the question. "Could you find out more about his plan?"

Chetana's dark eyes hardened. "I can't gather information from Belik. He'll know where we are immediately. It would just draw him here."

So there it was. The truth. Anyone in the room who knew about *katahs* would understand now. Jori straightened a little out of his slouch.

Belik had been the one outside Kiria's room during the brunt of the attack, the one Bard had confronted to give Kiria a chance to escape, the one who had made Chetana so afraid. Firian, on the other hand, had saved Bard, left Jori alone... Certainty solidified within her.

She dropped her voice and her eyes. "So Firian didn't order the attack." Something stirred in her, writhing and alive. The emotion was strong but unnamable.

Firian was still at large, his allegiances unknown, she reminded herself. Based on their last intense but confusing meeting, he could go either way. And still had the means to find her if he wanted to. *When.*

Jori shrugged a shoulder.

The female guard wasn't so nonchalant. "If he didn't order the attack, does that mean he's on our side? If this Belik has turned on him, wouldn't he want some kind of revenge, if not justice?"

Kiria heard the real question: *Could he be our ally?* She'd hung onto that possibility so many times and the rope hadn't held her in the end. If she could avoid another disastrous alliance, she would. Yes, Firian was powerful, but with so much at stake, she couldn't take the chance. "It's too soon to tell," she evaded.

Chetana mirrored Kiria's meaningful look from before.

"Once we get farther away from here, then we can discuss the possibility," she added, to end any more prying. Calling on Firian, now, would break the fragile hold she had on rational thought, the ability to plan and mobilize those under her command. As it was, horror and sorrow and rage and exhaustion pressed in around her like stifling blankets, kept at bay only by the jabs of her forward motion, her planning.

Chetana's dark eyes fell to the floor as though she were searching for something. Her full lips wrinkled with a sneer that touched the bottom of her septum ring.

"We could leave the city." The voice sounded small and far away. Kiria smiled. Vayci never gave her opinion, but if there were ever a time, this was it.

Chetana looked kindly at her. Vayci looked down to avoid her gaze. "If the people find out the Keeper has left, they could lose hope. That cannot be our first resort."

"But it's not a bad idea," Kiria added, though she agreed with Chetana.

"Belik will try to set Tanyu at all the exit points of the city," Chetana continued. Her expression was bitter and knowing. "Until we know the danger, we should not run toward it. Our duty is to Brithnem, in Brithnem." She looked at Kiria for confirmation.

She nodded back.

"We have to stay here?" Jori stretched backward on the seat, craning his neck to see the room upside-down. Clearly, the idea didn't appeal to him.

"Yes," Chetana snapped, "at least we've chosen a more secure location."

"Yeah, this one's not the most secure," he admitted, scratching his ear.

Kiria cast a nervous glance at the outer door. It had been relocked, but it still felt like flimsy protection.

"Are there any other ways out of here?" she asked Jori. She didn't see any, but that didn't mean they weren't there.

Jori gestured toward the tunnel. "No. Just those two."

"Will you be able to hide me when we move?" Kiria asked the guards. The only other time she'd been in hiding was with Firian, and she'd been far away from potential enemies most of the time.

"Both of you," Chetana corrected.

Kiria knit her brows. The insistent words were slow to register.

"Both of you need to be protected. The Kepron is the heir."

Kiria felt faint, each realization disorienting. Even after Atty had been crowned, she hadn't given the idea much thought. That Jori could become a Keeper of Brithnem was beyond imagining. Yet here they were. Atty was dead. His dream of having a family to succeed him had died also. The only clear option for the Third Line was Jori. Kiria was the Second Line. *Where's Kader?* she wondered again. *Has he been killed too?*

Jori rocked forward, running a hand through his hair. He shook his head a few times as though shaking his words loose. "No," he said simply.

Chetana was businesslike. "It is not your—"

"No!" Jori leapt aggressively to his feet.

Kiria sat back, away from him. The longer she watched his strained face and flashing gray eyes, the more she softened with understanding. In his place, if Atty were her brother, she would probably act the same way. Her heart contracted with shared pain. "We don't need to worry about that yet," she said. "You need to stay safe one way or the other." She laid a hand on his arm. "I need you."

He jerked away. Slumping back in the chair, he inhaled a few shaky breaths.

Candrae was on her feet, ready to serve. The girls weren't used to sitting by while others needed anything. Jori needed more than a cup of water this time, and Kiria wasn't sure that anyone could get it for him. "A pillow," she said, just to give Candrae something to do.

One of the guards—a round-faced man with pink skin and dark hair—stepped forward respectfully. "My Keeper, I could go and investigate Kader Calthwaite's location."

Kiria drew her hand into a fist, considering. They had few guards as it was, but Kader's safety had to be a priority. That way, at least, there would still be one person alive from each of the three Lines. She cleared her throat. "Go. Once he's safe, we'll have a clearer path to regain power." *If he's safe.*

She looked sidelong at Jori. His hair tumbled over one eye, and he didn't meet her gaze.

7

BELIK

BELIK GRIMACED. All these stairs were killing his legs. Why did all Watchmen need to be in the highest place in the city? They had a sputtering level of Talent, but that Talent could be used anywhere. Still, people liked their mystical beliefs about the job. They liked to believe that all the news coming from these high cells was perfectly accurate, removed from the biases of the world.

As though they've never met a person before.

"Do you want to pause?" Shiro asked just behind him.

Belik started to snarl at him but thought better of it. "Maybe to answer that stupid question. No."

Behind Shiro's head of dark hair were two more Tanyu. Only one was visible in this blindly winding staircase. In front of him walked one more. Four should do it. Maybe he'd add a couple more.

The problem was that no one could be spared from their duties. There weren't enough capable people as it was for all the tasks that needed to happen simultaneously for a smooth takeover. Manning the city wall alone took too many people. Several others stationed themselves around the barracks to keep the army true to their word to back the new reigning champions. Some had resisted, of course. Skirmishes. What rankled was that the Tanyu hadn't closed the net, plugged all the holes to prevent renegades from escaping. Dozens of soldiers had. Belik's forces could deal with them when they showed their faces again. The rest of the military's doubt was in Belik's favor, and they were held in tentative check by the few generals to whom he had promised generous riches.

During the raid, a few Tanyu had stood out as his most loyal supporters. They were the ones who cut the Keepers' throats, who didn't cry and moan about where Firian was. Weapons in his hands.

He struggled up a few more steps. He was being a fool—pain subsided in the Unreal. In an instant, he was there. Thoughts of Chetana floated like damned ghosts in the corner of his eye. It was all he could do not to whirl around and fight her, but he knew she wasn't really there. If she had been, there would be no mistaking it. Instead, he swirled colors against the black like flavors in a pot of soup. He floated in the midst of them, touching the silky texture of the colors floating by. This is where he went if he wanted to completely forget where he was. It was as good as sleeping.

Almost. Belik hadn't slept since this raid began. After this crucial task, he could rest for a short while before continuing. Delegate to Master Nedi and Shiro until he could join them again.

His foot reached the top landing. He came to himself again. The room at the top of the palace was large and circular, ornate and white. Around the windows there was yellow discoloration. A man sat cross-legged on a lush deep purple rug. The Watchman looked placidly at them as they entered, his old face scored with deep wrinkles.

"Are you the Watchman?" Belik asked, though he already knew the answer.

"Yes." The voice was husky from disuse. The single word came out clearly, but a little like a sigh.

One of Belik's eyes squinted behind his glasses. "What is your name?"

"My name is not important. You are the Tanyu who have ravaged my city," he said, making no move to attack or defend himself. The Watchman's breath sounded loud in the quiet. How much had he already told neighboring cities?

"I would like to know it," Belik said.

"My name is Velmay Rancin." The man's tone was the same as before, even and breathy.

That was enough. Belik jerked his chin in the direction of the old man. He averted his eyes at the moment Shiro snapped his neck. The man's death was necessary, one of a short list along with the Keepers, and the soldiers who resisted. The Watchman controlled information.

Belik scratched his ear, trying to replace the sound of the crack with something else, then looked carefully at the man's face. Slowly, he came closer. The impending trip back down the staircase occupied as much of his thoughts as the man slumped in front of him.

The man's skin was smooth like tooled leather. His eyes had been gray. That much he'd noticed as soon as they'd walked in. He sat with the quiet poise of a man who had never had anywhere else to go. Typical Kingdom bone structure. He'd just gotten a haircut. As Belik circled, he saw the perfect edge to his hairline. The man wore chipping paint on his nails. That surprised him, though he couldn't have said why. He stretched his jaw, ready to begin.

With the ease of a bird in the air, he entered the Unreal. Instantly, he had sharply-cut hair, badly painted nails, and soft leather skin, scored with age. He knew the Tanyu with him were doing the same.

After taking a moment to modulate his voice, he reached toward the Watchman in Redshore. "Lady Kiria, the Second Keeper, has run away with Firian Kess, the former Tanyuin Head, compromising the safety of Brithnem in this time of crisis..."

8

KIRIA

EVEN WITH THE GUARDS' help, the journey from the safe house to the tannery was a frightful one. The sun was up, shining traitorous light on their passage. All the neighborhood buildings served to shelter them, but also became a terrifying maze of blind corners.

The young guard with the tattoo on his face gave Kiria the swath of blue fabric that draped across his shoulders. She wound it across her own and over her head. She'd dispensed with her Beauty before the attack began, which deepened her disguise.

Jori had no God-given power to change his looks and, until now, never would have wanted to. Even in his listlessness, though, he moved with a secrecy even the guards couldn't rival. He'd always known about every nook and exit, every hiding place around the palace. Sneaking into places he shouldn't was his forte.

Chetana also seemed to melt into the air any time Kiria wasn't looking. For all her height and imperiousness, she could be stealthy too.

As the sounds of waking people, opening shops, alarmed voices, and marching feet surrounded them, Kiria's heartbeat tripped and her feet felt as though they'd been attached the wrong way. Phantom pains from her long-ago arrow wounds surfaced and ached.

They only saw one figure in black.

Not Firian. Still, Kiria stopped moving at the sight. It was a man with a light beard, standing in front of one of the main warehouses in Grand Market Square. A small crowd surrounded him, as though to ask for news. The agitated postures of those in front of the Tanyu told her they knew some of what had happened in the night. Something like a wail rose from among the voices. Hands gripped other hands.

Jori shoved her from behind, forcing her beyond the gap between buildings that allowed her to see. The strip of light passed over her face and left her in shadow again. Had the man seen her? What was he telling her people?

An irrational part of her wanted to march up to the man, dramatically reveal her identity, and confront him for all the evils he'd taken part in. She wanted to be a hero, not this skulking fugitive.

But there was nothing more foolish she could do than that, she reminded herself, the intrusive image of dead guards rising to her mind. They had to take this carefully.

Words, light as dust on the breeze, floated across her as they snuck forward, keeping to alleys and backways. Many reflected shock and mourning in their sound; others, serious discussions about what to do. But only one conversation, close enough to their destination that she could hear more, stuck to her after they entered the tannery.

"My cousin says the heads are in Arena Square."

A gasp. "All of them?"

"Not the Second Keeper."

A noise of pain. An obscured reply, and then, "Do you think she's with them?"

"I thought she might pull something like this." Machinery drowned out the next words but caught up at the end of the sentence: "...sympathizer."

"Are we safe? Will she keep us safe?"

"Looks like Tanyu are the ones in charge, not her. Just keep your head down."

The tannery was situated close to one of the smaller gates to the north, far from both the palace and the Abrecan Gate. Its position, unattached to the palace, made it more secure than the safe house, but Kiria didn't feel safer. The interior was unsettlingly alien and also small to house her, Jori, Chetana, Vayci, Candrae, and the guards who assisted them. One of the guards—the only woman, with freckles and narrow eyes—said the tannery belonged to her uncle and that it was easy to defend, at least temporarily.

The floors and walls around them were stone. Raised rock platforms rose to Kiria's hips, covering about a third of the floor space. As soon as they arrived, Jori jumped on one to get some breathing room, but he stumbled backward into a pit cut in the rock. Three identical square pits had been carved into the platforms, like huge basins. Judging from the foul-smelling swill left behind in the bottom, they'd been used for one of the more unsavory steps in the tanning process. She didn't want to know exactly what.

Large wooden paddles leaned against one wall along with an assortment of metal instruments Kiria was glad weren't in the hands of the enemy. The guards concentrated themselves at the entrance, blocking enemies' way in but also blocking their way out. The round-faced guard left to check for news of Kader as soon as they'd arrived. How long would they have to stay here?

The morning-bright room smelled tangy with animal musk. Outside, she could hear people in Grand Market Square working, haggling, hauling—all far away but echoing through the stillness of the room. The tension she'd heard in their voices on the journey here persisted, as did their words, which echoed, echoed, echoed in her mind, pinging uselessly but forcefully against her thoughts. She had no room for more pain, but it lurked at the door, ready to pounce whenever she found reprieve. *I thought she might pull something like this. Will she keep us safe?* How could anyone think she'd have a hand in this? Did her people know her so little? How many others felt the same way?

She suddenly wanted her mother there to tell her it would be all right. The longing for her grew into physical hurt.

Jori sat on the lip of a cold brick oven built into the wall, one knee propped up. He looked almost insolent, halfway between depressed and carefree.

The smell, the small space... It all felt oppressive. The ceiling made the room too low, too cramped. Anxious energy kept Kiria from relaxing.

When a knock came at the door, she started but was almost glad for the interruption. No guard moved to welcome the intruder. A loud voice came from the other side. "Amir Parohim has informed the people that the Keepers are dead! Tanyu have taken over the city! Come to the palace Mon Párinath at the next new moon to witness the crowning of the new ruler!" The end of the rehearsed announcement faded as the stranger moved onto another building with the news.

Tense silence fell. Kiria's chest constricted. The voice repeated the news farther down the street. With every repetition, the betrayal became more and more real.

"You look all right to me," Jori said.

Kiria caught his eye, but she was too stressed to smile. Instead, she turned to Chetana. "Why would Parohim make that announcement?" Cúron's advisor had always hated Tanyu, which made him happy to support the First Keeper's anti-Tanyuin agenda.

"They threatened him," she declared.

"But you wouldn't give into their demands if you were threatened," Kiria said, refusing to accept such a simple explanation.

"Not if they threatened *me*," she replied.

Whom could they threaten that would make Parohim overturn so much he had striven to build? The Amir didn't have any family. He had chosen to dedicate his life entirely to the spiritual wellbeing of the Kingdom. And, although his personality grated at times, he had done a good job of it.

Her breath caught. "Kader." Cúron's son. It had to be. Nothing else would make him spread these lies, this propaganda. "Do you think they have him?"

Chetana lowered her eyes in confirmation. Thick black lashes shadowed her cheeks.

A hissing sound at the door meant that the round-faced guard had returned. His companions let him slip inside. The man stood at attention, his helmet gleaming in the morning light. "My Keeper, the Tanyu have taken control of the Abrecan, as well as the Elidyr and Drein. They seem to be moving in both directions away from the main gate in an effort to control the outer wall."

Kiria pictured the city, arranged roughly in rings leading out from the seaside palace all the way to the city wall. Five primary gates and a few other minor doors provided exits. Chetana was right. Master Belik was cutting off their ways of escape one by one.

"They haven't reached Ana'h Gate yet?"

The man shook his head, but his expression was doubtful.

Her mouth went dry. "We'll be trapped."

Chetana looked grave. Jori shifted uncomfortably in the oven opening.

"We were not planning to leave the city, My Keeper. This changes nothing," Chetana replied.

Still, a new kind of claustrophobia sent her thoughts spinning. If they were going to take back the palace and regain control of Brithnem, they had to formulate a plan now. The new moon, had he said? That was in two days. That left no time for coming and going from the city. Her guards could drum up the surviving military still loyal to her...

Her head hurt. When she had studied military strategy with Daelon, she hadn't imagined it would feel like this—less like a game of Indisfate and more like jumping off a cliff and hoping for water instead of rocks.

"What about Kader?" she asked the guard. He hadn't led with information about the Kepron, so she didn't expect anything hopeful.

"Nothing definitive," the soldier replied, "but it looks like he may have escaped through his emergency tunnel as you did. No telling whether he could get out of the city." His face darkened.

Unlikely. Kader was so young. Was he afraid, waiting for someone to help him? "We have to find him."

"A few of us are attempting to find him."

The Tanyu would be on the same scent. The soldier's stormy expression halted her bleak train of thought. "A few of you?" she asked. "Where's the rest of the military? What else did you find out?"

He wet his lips. "Master Belik has promised land and wealth to the commanders in the barracks. He killed two who didn't take his offer and tried to revolt. The rumor is that you're all dead, all the Keepers. There was nothing left for them to fight for." Maybe he was close to those rebel generals. His words definitely sounded like excuses for people he cared about.

Or they think I'm a traitor, she thought bitterly. "Then we have to let them know I'm alive," she exclaimed. "And Kader too, probably. That we're both on the Kingdom's side."

Jori raised one hand, a small, reluctant gesture to add his name to the list. Kiria nodded in acknowledgment. She hadn't gotten used to thinking of him as the Third Line representative. Neither had Jori.

"That will let Belik know," the tattooed guard piped up.

"He already knows," Chetana replied drily.

"Some managed to get out during the fighting, looking for you," the guard told Kiria. "Not everyone has gone over to the Tanyu."

That anyone would defect, and so quickly, made her gut feel heavy. They probably felt that they had no choice after hearing the Keepers were slaughtered. Doubt plagued her, though. Before the attack, her leadership was heavily questioned. And after it too, apparently.

Now that she was the only living Keeper, would she have enough clout to reestablish the thrones? She had risked more than anyone realized for Brithnem already. She'd been prepared to sacrifice everything, and would do it again if it would guarantee safety for her country, and especially for her friends. Even if it meant working with Firian. She cast a glance at Jori, whose lip curled in disbelief.

They were desperate, and time was against them. They had to try to contact the Tanyu who might be on their side.

If the people in this tannery didn't get the upper hand somehow, Tanyu would hunt them all down and kill them, and, based on the depraved style of the attack, they wouldn't deal justly with her people either. She thought of Lord Ruler Thraddock. Firian had set up his head in the square, just as Belik had made a spectacle of the Keepers. The thought made her ill.

No, it was too soon to contact Firian. He was power and skill, but not strategy. For all his brute force and Talent, he hadn't studied large-scale warfare as she had.

Casting her eyes around the unfamiliar space, she wished Bard were here. Bardhon Tanery. She wondered if his name had any connection to a real tannery like this one. Bard could beat Firian at the game too. He wasn't a fighter, but he had the same goals as they did: beat the Tanyu and take back the Kingdom with minimal loss of life.

She cringed at the memory of his back as he faced death on her account. "Jori." He lolled his head in her direction. "Do you know where Bard is?"

"There's a doctor." He flicked his fingers in a vague direction.

"Could you find him again?"

"Kiria," he said, screwing up one side of his face in a grimace, "I don't know..."

She set her mouth in a firm line. "Can we try?"

"What's the point?"

Chetana nodded once toward Jori. "You remember what the Kepron said. He's probably not alive."

Kiria rounded on her former advisor. "Could you check?" Chetana had the Talent. Maybe she could feel Bard's thoughts. Kiria wasn't sure she was advanced enough to do that yet, without knowing right where he was.

Chetana let out a breath and closed her eyes. The last expression was admonishing before her lids shut.

Kiria waited a few breathless seconds as Chetana's lids fluttered. When she looked back at Kiria again, the answer written there made Kiria wilt. "I don't sense him anywhere. I think he is dead."

Tears pricked at Kiria's eyes.

Seeing her distress, Chetana added, "He died nobly. He redeemed himself from those Tanyu at the end and helped to keep you safe." She set a hand on Kiria's shoulder. The words barely comforted her.

"Yeah, we don't need him to come up with a plan anyway," Jori said, but his tone was far from cheerful. When Kiria turned her attention to him, he was staring at the wall above the pits, glassy-eyed.

Everyone here deferred to her to make the decision. Of course, it was only right. She was the Keeper, the only one left. She squared her shoulders. "Belik is supposed to be crowned on the new moon," she began, looking at Chetana. The thought mortified her, but running through ideas like this hardened her resolve and strengthened her hope.

"And the whole city will come out to see him." Kiria mused for a moment. "Do you think we could overcome the Tanyu at the gates during the coronation?" As soon as she said it, she realized that, although the people of Brithnem would come to watch a coronation, there was no guarantee that other Tanyu would come too. In fact, securing the perimeter would be one of their first concerns. She waved a hand. "Never mind. You say that Firian isn't in charge. It's only Belik?"

"It seems so."

Kiria looked at the guard who had gleaned information, who offered no more surety.

"Firian wasn't exactly subtle," Jori struck in.

Seems wasn't good enough, if they could afford better information. The uncertainty was maddening. She had to check. Chetana had said that contacting Belik would alert him to their location. Firian could find them without Kiria's cooperation. As it stood, he was the one with the power—to find them, to battle Belik, to turn the tide of the coup—and she needed to take that power back.

"I'll see," she said thickly, and closed her eyes. She hated the thought of feeling Firian's presence again, calling for it, but she would just check quickly if he was alive, at least. And if he really wasn't behind the attack, if Belik had acted of his own accord, and Firian had only come to the palace to save Bard, then there was a cobweb's chance that he might want to help them depose Belik. That would mean he meant what he said when he let her go in that farmhouse, his skin flushed with desire and mind obviously roiling against itself. It would mean that he finally denied his baser impulses. A fierce longing seized her for that to be the truth. She'd wanted there to be hope for him for so long, had defended him when no one else would, defended him until there was no excuse for him anymore...

She angled her mind toward the palace, though she could sense Firian from anywhere. At least, that's how it had been before.

Now there was nothing. Nothing at all. The darkness of the Unreal wasn't just empty of his immediate presence, but it was as though it had no knowledge of him. The familiar sense of his mind, always so close, was absent. It was like going home only to find a stranger who claimed to have lived there for years, with the furnishings to prove it. It was confusing and *wrong.*

"Firian! Firian!" she called. "I know you're there."

He didn't answer or materialize as he always did, dark-clad shoulders and knowing look. Blue eyes under heavy brows.

"Firian!"

No whisper rose to acknowledge her cries. Just a blank, endless emptiness tinged with pain, as though small but painful shocks webbed over her skin.

Firian was dead? It was the only explanation. He wouldn't leave her alone like this. Killed, then, either by Kingdom soldiers or Tanyu. Kingdom soldiers had never been able to match him. Even if they had, the news would have spread quickly. Her guard would have learned about it, along with the news of the commanders. The likelier scenario was that Belik, another Tanyu, had killed him.

Firian had kept his word.

This wasn't how she thought Firian's death would feel. His last agony must have been covered up by her own. The hope that she and Bard had held for him was gone, all that potential squandered.

Fury, hard and rough as charcoal, filled her gut. Belik killed Firian the moment he chose to do the right thing.

She opened her burning eyes and shook her head. "Yes, just Belik," she confirmed. Her voice was a croak. "We have to stop him before the coronation."

"Sounds easy," said Jori. "We'll just sneak in and stab him in the back. It's not like the Tanyu control every entrance." He brought his legs off the ledge to the ground. Leaning his forearms on his knees, he eyed Kiria.

She barely registered his words, tilting to the side as weakness overcame her. Jori couldn't expect her to have every answer. He wasn't the only one who experienced a traumatic night.

Releasing a breath like someone fighting not to drown, she turned to Chetana and the guards. "How do you think we—?"

"You need to rest, My Keeper," Chetana said, hovering her palm above Kiria's hair as though she would touch it, but then dropping her hand.

When Kiria blinked, her vision went blurry. She needed to tell them, but the words wouldn't come. Weariness settled in her limbs but the spastic movements of her mind kept her from lying down. Her thoughts sputtered like a dying fly—at rest one second and flailing the next.

"Yes," said the blond guard, "for now we'll see how many soldiers we can muster to your cause. We'll let everyone know you're alive. We can plan after you rest, My Keeper."

Kiria's insides formed a knot. "I think Firian's dead," she said, swallowing.

Chetana cut a serious look in her direction, more concerned about Kiria's well-being than the news that Firian had died. There was a hint of fearful determination too, since Belik was now unequivocally in charge and there was no hope of Firian as a temporary ally.

Jori raised tired eyebrows as he dragged three pelts into the enormous cold oven. "You all right, my girl?" he murmured, laying them out without his signature flair. Something told her he couldn't handle the weight of anyone else's grief right now, so she didn't answer.

No one else responded to her announcement, instead regarding her with grim looks. To them, Firian's death was a key bit of news, something to consider when moving forward. It was something different to her, a private world of confusion and anger and sadness for what might have been.

Kiria felt heaviness and grief transform her motions into the movements of a mannikin, hard and stiff and automatic. Exhaustion pressed on her aching head. As she helped Chetana work one of the wooden paddles off the wall, unconsciousness sounded like welcome relief. Perhaps sensing her fatigue, her serving girls came up on either side and took it from her. It was surprisingly heavy, so she was glad of the help.

In a short while, they had used the paddles to cover the raised stone pits, creating more spaces to sleep. Kiria still chose to sleep in a corner of the floor so she could feel the press of walls against her back and know that there was no mysterious animal substance underneath her. Besides, it was darker here, more sheltered from the sunlight filtering in.

The rolled pelt crackled as she laid her head on it. From her corner, she could see Jori, already asleep on his perch. If none of this had happened, they would have been preparing for Dedication Day today, instead of figuring out how to stay alive while Tanyu hunted them. Amir would choose selections from the Sacred Scroll and musicians would compose new pieces. Jori and Atty would eat extra helpings in anticipation of the fast.

A hot tear ran down her temple into the stiff fur. *"Do not fear, for redemption will come to you. While you are surrounded and the shadow of your destruction overcasts your skies, salvation will come."* How was that possible now?

9

KIRIA

The *sachion* trees in the wide palace hallways had been stripped to skeletal sticks. Pictures hung askew. Broken glass littered the ground near the walls. Beams of light crisscrossed madly through the windows, casting green and blue light. The end of the corridor looked as blackened as the depths of a well.

Kiria picked her way barefoot through the debris, observing each piece of wreckage as if it held the clue to a mystery. Confusion, more than fear, filled her at the sight. The blackness of the hall, though, unsettled her more than anything else. Monsters could be lurking there and she wouldn't know until they sprang out, like creatures of deep water.

The shadows beyond converged into a figure made of smoke. She squinted at it, but it just regarded her as a wild animal would. Although the shape had no eyes, she could tell it was there for her.

She stopped walking. The niggling feeling that she should do something about this quiet intruder worried at her mind, but she couldn't remember exactly what she was supposed to do.

The curls of smoke floating off the figure made her aware of an acrid smell in the air. It felt sharp in her lungs. As the air became thicker, she focused her attention on breathing. Dragging in a breath became more like exercise than reflex. It was interesting, like an experiment. How far would this go?

When she looked up again, the shadow was almost close enough to touch. The darkness drifting from its shoulders ribboned into her lungs. She pulled it in as she saw some men do to their pipes in neighborhoods near the wall.

Smoke surrounded her, obscuring her vision. Was she the shadow? Had she been looking in a mirror? Tendrils of smoke wreathed around her arms. Her hair floated up like a ghost. She'd stopped breathing, but it felt natural. She was suspended in darkness that trailed its fingers over her skin.

White light, sudden and violent, blinded her and she fell back, skidding over pebbly glass. The back of her head hit the rug before it bounced up so she could see what had happened. She eased herself up on her elbows, breathing heavily. Clarity returned to her vision.

Chetana floated near the roof like a goddess of war. Her orange dress waved around her ankles. Glaring down at the shadow creature, she held her hands in front of her as though they were weapons.

Another ball of white light exploded from Chetana's hands. Kiria squeezed her eyes shut, unable to stand the brightness. When she opened her eyes, a red dot followed every time she blinked.

The distortion made it harder to see when the hallway stretched, becoming enormous. Or maybe she shrank. Either way, the ceiling rose out of sight, though only the shadow had grown to match the building. It loomed huge above her. Kiria cowered, no bigger than its foot. Smoke from its body snaked toward her.

With a loud, grating ring, a three-pointed blade appeared in the hand of the shadow creature. One point of the crossguard-style edges could pierce straight through Kiria's tiny body. Her hands and forehead went clammy.

Chetana's determined expression didn't change. Nothing so far had surprised her. With a start, Kiria realized she had grown too, or maybe they both had. The creature still looked huge, but Chetana matched it. Its blade swung forward.

Kiria clasped her hands over her mouth to stifle a scream. Horrified, she couldn't look away.

Chetana's image flickered like fire and the blade fell harmlessly through her, lodging deep in the hardwood floor below.

Kiria jumped to her feet, finally understanding. This was a dream.

When she moved, Chetana flicked a glance toward her. For a second, the Amir looked glad. She flashed three fingers down at her sides.

Two fingers.

One.

Kiria woke up gasping. The pelt she'd used for a pillow lay unrolled against the wall. Panting, she sat up, placing a sweat-slicked hand on her chest as she struggled to calm down. The smell of dust and fur and dung filled her nostrils.

Chetana appeared, crouching at her side. Their eyes met in understanding.

"Thank you," Kiria whispered, holding onto the vain hope that she hadn't woken anyone up.

Two guards, the young one and the blond leader, instantly stood above her. "Is everything all right?"

Chetana looked up at them. "The Tanyu attacked the Keeper in her sleep. I'll watch over her."

The guards didn't move from their position close to Kiria. They loomed over her, hemming her in. The tattooed one shifted as though he wanted to help but didn't know how.

"Thank you," Kiria told Chetana again. "I didn't know you could do that." The image of the Amir floating so menacingly, so self-controlled, still filled her mind.

Chetana pressed her lips, offering no explanation. "I'll watch so you can sleep a little longer. It'll protect your mind from any intruders."

Now that she had caught her breath, Kiria sat up more fully. It was bright in the tannery, perhaps midday. Her heart still beat hard with the aftershock of the nightmare. "I need to know how to do that."

"It takes a long time to learn, My Keeper."

"You'll teach me later," Kiria said, not minding her protests. Chetana had the Talent; so did Kiria. Maybe she couldn't shoot light from her hands, but she could fight in the Unreal somehow. She could learn helpful tactics. Besides ordering the army, she had nothing to do here but wait and pray. And learn to fight.

Chetana must have sensed Kiria's resolve, because she didn't protest again. "As you wish, My Keeper. Get some sleep."

10

BELIK

AFTER MAKING his announcement as the Watchman, Belik somehow made it back downstairs, pain shooting up his bad leg with each step. After getting no sleep the night before, he needed to rest, to make his mind sharp again.

A few hours later, he emerged from one of the smaller, fresher bedrooms, which he'd kept heavily guarded, and exhaled. He'd sent Shiro and Nedi with jobs so the takeover didn't flounder in his temporary absence. The weighty exhaustion brought on by lack of sleep and killing Bard had lifted, and Belik felt ready to begin again.

Daylight came through the windows, along with talking and footsteps and screams. Everyone busy.

Belik nodded at Master Nedi, who'd returned from his duties at the barrack and now stood closest of the four he'd tasked with guarding his room. "The cell," he grunted.

He couldn't get Firian out of his mind. Something like guilt jabbed the back of Belik's sternum. Somewhere, he had failed Firian, who had believed him with reckless confidence. Firian was many things, but temperate wasn't one of them.

Belik knew he should feel bad for egging Firian on, but he couldn't force any feelings of remorse. Years and years ago, he and Sias had been friends, but that was before. Before his leg was ruined, before the *katah*, before he was demoted to a teacher. Firian *was* a better Head, while it lasted. Taking over the city and ultimately the Kingdom was going to be their crowning achievement, the glory of the Tanyu on full display.

While he caught a few hours of sleep, the blaze in the palace had been put out. Belik had ordered that fire only be set in the Main and a few other strategic locations. Most of the smaller areas of the palace, like the Watchtower, weren't badly affected. The issue was spectacle.

The five of them trod through the bright gardens where there was less smoke in the air to a partially hidden hatch in the ground near the barracks. Master Nedi heaved the trapdoor up with one huge hand, revealing a darkened staircase leading below. Belik indicated that they should all stay above while he went down alone.

The air grew smokier in the humid space. Firian's energy coiled like a snake waiting below. He waited for his eyes to adjust before he stumped down the final two steps.

At the bottom of the steps, he turned to see the cell. Iron grating covered the space at the end of the cave-like narrow room, a body's length of space behind it. The door looked secure, reaching seamlessly from floor to ceiling. A rancid smell turned Belik's stomach.

Firian crouched behind the door, glaring hatred. The fire in his eyes would have extinguished Daelon's quiet resistance.

His gaze moved to the crumbs at Firian's booted feet. "You didn't eat the food I gave you."

Firian didn't answer, except to stand, muscles tensed, ready for a fight. Belik didn't intend to give him one. It was odd. Firian's energy and drive should have been broken, at least temporarily, by Bard's death.

Belik's failsafe hadn't worked. Gerand's insistence that a *katah* would serve as useful insurance was nothing but wasted work. Well, maybe not as much work as he had anticipated. Firian had always been attached to his little friend, though Belik couldn't understand why. Bard's classes had only solidified their connection into something potentially deadly.

Young Firian, who claimed he didn't have those kinds of attachments, had two *katahs*. Belik hadn't planned his connection with Kiria. With Firian's reputation, he'd assumed that Firian would seduce the beautiful princess and leave without the mark of a *katah*. Bard he'd planned. Firian was like a son to him but Belik was also a Strategy Master—he always had to know people's weaknesses. And Bard was Firian's weakness. Unless...

Belik walked closer to the bars. The Sentry protected him from a Second Level attack. Behind the bars, Firian could do nothing but yield or rot in this cell. "It's working," he said, much as he would have back at the Academy. "The Amir have announced that the Tanyu have taken over the city." He was going to add that the Keepers were dead too, but if Firian's *katah* was anything like his had been with Chetana, the constant rumble of her presence, even with the Sentry, wouldn't let him believe the lie.

Firian's heavy eyebrows lowered over his flashing eyes. His hands became fists at his side. If Firian weren't acting like a child, he would understand.

Belik continued, lowering his voice. "These people are used to having multiple rulers. I could figure something out for you if you stop being so gory stubborn."

Every minute that passed made Firian's redemption less likely. If he didn't get on the right side, Belik would have to have him killed. He'd be too great a threat to their plan, even if he later pretended to agree. Belik chewed on something caught between his teeth. All this time, all this work... He liked Firian. Why couldn't he see reason?

Finally, Firian spoke, his voice low and menacing. "You went against my orders." His jaw flexed as though he wanted to add more, but choked back the words instead.

"We had a small window, Firian," he explained, trying to be patient, but he bit off the words with increasing bitterness. "Attacks can only be this painless if you act quickly. You weren't in a state to make demands, so I acted, knowing you'd come around."

"I told you to turn around and leave the city alone!"

"We were at the gates!" Belik came so close to the bars that he had to angle his head up slightly to glare into Firian's eyes. "We couldn't—"

"You murdered innocent people." Firian's chest was heaving.

"So have you."

A crackling silence, thick as oil, fell between them. As Belik felt the force of it, numbness shot through his hands. Certainty began to settle in his mind. He tried shrugging it off. He'd examine it another time.

"Revolutions take sacrifice, Firian," he said, more gently. The ice in Firian's glare hadn't melted. Gore, he had a strong will. Belik found himself wishing he'd given Firian more time to cool off before attempting to turn him around.

"I saw what you did to Bard."

Firian could only mean one thing. Belik twitched one shoulder in a shrug. "I figured it out."

Firian was trembling. Belik would get nowhere with this boy. That sense of certainty hadn't left him. It kept settling slowly, like a feather he kept blowing upward to keep it from touching him. There had to be a way to redeem Firian, to make him see that the Tanyu deserved to rule Brithnem, to put the Amir in their place, to right all the injustices they'd endured over the years. Firian *had* believed those things until Kiria convinced him otherwise.

Belik exhaled in frustration. In all ways, Firian was more his son than Daelon had ever been. A disappointment now, and a danger, but he'd handled him up to this point. He wouldn't give up on Firian now. Not yet.

He turned to go.

"I'll kill you."

Firian's words made him turn back. The tone and expression left no room for doubt. Rage radiated off him like heat.

In anyone else, the threat would have been laughable. Belik held the power here. Maybe Firian knew that Belik wouldn't kill him now—couldn't, because of their bond, all the hours and days and weeks and years spent together. Did Firian know him so well, or was he really so reckless with his own life?

Why did he have to make this so difficult?

"I don't think so." Belik climbed the steps to the fresh air without looking back.

11

KIRIA

Kiria woke well before the dawn as she usually did, though this time she had wasted almost an entire day. Rubbing her eyes, she sat up and wrapped her arms around her knees. As she looked blearily around, pre-dawn quiet lay heavy over everything. The freshness of the morning turned the faint body odor into something not quite as offensive as it had been in the heat of the day. Two guards stood at attention by the door. Candrae and Vayci lay snuggled together against the raised pits. She hadn't woken them. Jori slept too, sprawled messily in the oven opening, one arm hanging out and a look of concentration on his face.

Beside her, Chetana sat cross-legged. A slight hunch of her shoulders as she opened her eyes revealed how tired she was. Amir always maintained stick-straight posture.

"Thank you," Kiria mouthed, realizing that she should give Chetana the opportunity to nap before diving straight into her fighting lesson.

The quiet in the room suddenly became even more profound, as though her ears had stopped working. Chetana had taken away the Sentry.

Kiria gave her a pointed look, indicating the other sleeping forms around the tannery. She had permission to sleep.

Chetana's expression showed little relief, just steadfastness. But after a moment, she laid two fingers on her temples and began to rub them wearily. Kiria leaned forward and breathed, "We'll do it after you get some rest."

Chetana nodded and lay down, her breaths deep and measured almost from the moment she touched the floor.

Getting up this early was awkward now. She didn't have space to herself, she couldn't leave, and Firian would never meet her again... It was unwise to practice in the Unreal alone after Chetana had done so much to protect her mind as she slept. Her advisor should at least be able to sleep one time without worrying about her.

Her advisor.

Her insides twisted. Chetana wasn't her advisor anymore, not since the vote to get rid of Firian as the Tanyuin Head. Her son Daelon was. He didn't have the Talent, so none of them could be sure he was still alive. Were the Amir all hostages? Had they burned in the fire? The options were almost too terrible to contemplate. Yet Chetana still maintained her composure. Kiria doubted she could do that if not only the Keepers, but also her only son, were dead.

This morning there was little to do but mourn. The round-faced guard, whose name was Merrick, had started to alert the commanders and soldiers still loyal to her to get ready for a meeting, but some needed time to escape the palace grounds, if they were able to manage it. In the meantime, they all had a deep breath before sprinting again.

Everyone else woke up slowly: her girls first, who tried to be helpful as best they could, then the extra guards, who replaced the ones who had stayed up all night, then Chetana again, and finally Jori. Kiria had been awake for a long time before they all received water and a bite for breakfast.

"Okay," she said as she stuffed the last piece of biscuit into her mouth.

Chetana didn't need more prompting. "My Keeper," she said, as though these words had been simmering in her for some time, "it's been a long time since I learned how to fight."

"You did a good job last night."

"But I might not be the best teacher. I gave up that life long ago to pursue the ways of God." It looked like she wanted to say something else, but stopped. When Kiria didn't respond, Chetana sighed. "It's best if we sit," she said, crossing her legs and spreading her skirt over them.

Kiria did the same.

"What are we doing?" Jori asked, jumping down from his perch with a kind of cheerless enthusiasm.

Chetana cast him a sharp look. "*We* are practicing something dangerous and difficult that you cannot partake in."

"But those are my specialties."

"It's the Unreal," Kiria explained, freshly glad for these lessons. Jori's dreams were in more danger than her own since he had fewer tools to use to defend himself. *Thank goodness they didn't attack him last night!*

Jori rubbed his hands together and sank cross-legged next to them. "Oh ho! Then I'm going to watch."

"You'll just see two people closing their eyes."

"Fascinating," he replied, staring at them as though they'd already begun.

Chetana set her jaw and resolutely turned to Kiria. "You will have to tell me how much you already know."

After a glance at Jori, Kiria felt almost self-conscious. She hadn't worked on this Ability with anyone but Tanyu. It felt weird to do it in front of anyone else. "Let me show you," Kiria said, closing her eyes.

She created the palace hallway, as she'd done a hundred times. No, she realized with a painful twist, this was the palace hallway as it had been. This version of it didn't exist anymore. She set everything in place, checking the details. Would Chetana notice something she had left out?

The Amir appeared, exactly as she'd looked in the smelly tannery a moment ago. Even so, she couldn't help looking regal. After gazing around the room, she shifted her attention to Kiria. "This is quite well done," she said.

Pride bloomed in Kiria's chest.

"Now, what do you know of fighting?"

She shuffled through the things she'd heard and seen.

Bard's ball of blue light. *Focus on it like it's a real thing. Act like it's a real thing.* Firian's cryptic hints. *Every window is a door. Everyone has weak points, so exploit those. The eyes, the throat, the groin.*

"Not very much," she admitted. Fighting here wasn't like studying war tactics with Daelon.

Chetana rubbed her lips. Apparently, she wasn't surprised Firian hadn't taught her to fight. She was silent for a while, considering. "The key is to make the other person *believe* they're hurt," she said finally.

"How?"

"You have to believe it. You have to create it. There can be no doubt."

It sounded easier than it was. Her disastrous first attempt to recreate Bard's ball of water proved that. Her heart sank. "These are Tanyu…"

"They believe," she said, raising her eyebrows. "If you surprise them, you can win even against a Tanyu."

Kiria longed to ask how Chetana knew all this, but she didn't want to derail the lesson. "How?" she asked again.

"They always believe they have the upper hand. They believe their training is their luck, that they are gods in this space." She paused. "You show them they are not."

"Give me an example."

"Of course, My Keeper." The royal title created distance between them again. Kiria eased back. "You are sleeping. You see a Tanyu come. Do not be passive. Change the background to something you know better than they do. It will take some of the strain from your mind."

Kiria nodded. The hallway they stood in was already one of the places Kiria knew best, so she didn't switch it to something else.

"Can you change your appearance in the Unreal? Have you used your Beauty?"

"Not there, but I think I could."

Perhaps the shimmering moonlight glinted against Chetana's dark eyes, but it looked as if she were astonished by that answer. It was natural, Kiria supposed, for people to assume she'd used her Beauty around Firian when they'd been together. There was a lot that others didn't know about them.

"Maybe that's how you could surprise them," Chetana said.

"What do you mean?"

"You had a *katah* for several months. Could you look like Master Kess?"

Kiria cringed. She hadn't had time to process her feelings about Firian's ultimatum and his too-recent death. To look like him felt too vulnerable, an admission of how much she had studied him. Maybe even a violation of whatever was left of his memory. "I've never tried," she hedged.

But Chetana had latched onto the idea. "You won't be able to outfight them in a couple of days. You must resort to those tactics that will give you the best chance of winning. You said you wanted me to teach you. This would be a good first step."

Kiria had pictured doing what Chetana had done—levitating, shooting weapons from her hands, but not this. But she didn't have the luxury to protest.

She concentrated on her memory of Firian. He was a head taller than she was, blue eyes, dark hair, lean but muscular... She put each thing in place, including the black Tanyuin outfit and the little white scars. Even this slight height difference gave her something like vertigo. She compulsively pushed the hair out of her eyes and almost startled at the sight of the large, calloused hands. She flexed them open and closed once, assaulted by an odd mix of emotions.

When she looked back at Chetana, who stood at eye level now, she seemed impressed.

"Won't they be able to tell, though?" Kiria asked in Firian's voice. It wasn't always Firian's appearance that alerted her to his presence; it was something distinctive about his mind, something else that she could feel before she could see. Surely Tanyu were better at distinguishing people than she was.

"Eventually," Chetana conceded. "But all you need is time."

"What if I need to hurt them?"

"You just need to stop them."

Kiria had a strange feeling of déjà vu, like she'd had this conversation before. "Okay," she said. Stopping an attacker long enough to wake up unharmed was the first step. It sounded weak compared to what she knew others could do, but at least it was something. She thought of Bard's game with the glowing ball. "So, if I turn into Firian, then what?"

An idea came into Chetana's eyes. "Surprise them. Do something simple, like this." She stepped back, giving Kiria a look that warned her to get ready, which was difficult since she didn't know what to get ready for.

Hot, white light exploded from Chetana's core, drowning the space in blindness. The glare faded as soon as it had come, but Kiria couldn't see anything but vague dark shapes.

"You changed," Chetana said from somewhere in the murk.

Kiria sensed rather than saw that she was right. In the shock, she had returned to the plain appearance she usually had in the Unreal.

"Try it again." A new, commanding tone took over.

Kiria obeyed, piecing together the Firian illusion again. It was easier the second time. She also had to replace items in the hallway that had puffed away like smoke in her surprise.

"Ready?" Chetana asked.

Kiria nodded, feeling stronger this time. Maybe she was just channeling Firian. She did feel that she could do more this way, but that was foolish. In the Unreal, anyone could do anything.

Light consumed her again.

In the ensuing darkness, Kiria rubbed her hands together, feeling for the raised scars. She'd kept the disguise intact.

"Very good," came Chetana's voice.

"How do you do that?"

"It's fairly simple, but effective, as you see. And it harms no one."

At this point, with everything that had happened, Kiria didn't think that was an advantage.

Her arm twitched. It twitched again. Immediately, she looked for the difference she had planted in the background to remind herself that this wasn't reality. Her muscles seized with nerves. The last time she'd felt odd sensations like that, she had blurred the line, even forgotten the line, between what was real and Unreal. This time, though, she was in no danger of forgetting where she was.

Without telling Chetana what she was doing, Kiria opened her eyes. The brightness of the tannery actually matched how far her eyes had adjusted from the last assault of light.

"There you are. I thought you had fallen asleep." Jori was poking her in the arm.

She swatted him away, annoyed. "Jori! I told you it doesn't look like anything."

Sitting cross-legged across from her, Chetana opened her eyes as gracefully as a swimmer. She didn't even acknowledge Jori. "Is that enough for today, My Keeper?"

"No." Kiria shot Jori a look. "Let's keep going."

Jori's fragile jollity broke. With a sullen look, he slumped back to the oven.

12

FIRIAN

The encounter with Belik left Firian breathless with anger. *As though anything could be the same!* But Belik had insisted on talking to him as he always had, the careful, ruthless advisor. Firian didn't think that Belik's keeping him alive was much of a mercy, but his old Master clearly thought it was.

Firian hadn't lied or exaggerated when he said he would kill him. He would find a way to do it, if Belik didn't give up trying to convince him and killed him first.

Time stretched on. The stink in the dungeon from emptying his stomach earlier only intensified. Without a window, there was no foolproof way to tell how much time had passed. Since that first meal of bread and water, no one had brought him food. He'd gone without before, but the lack of freedom and information grated on him.

Most of all, he missed the Unreal.

He couldn't even check to see that Kiria was still safe, that Bard had managed to save her after all. All of Belik's Tanyu were probably searching for her. How long could she survive? He closed his eyes, fighting against despair. He couldn't check on Bard either, though he grew more hopeless by the minute. Even with the aid of a doctor, Bard was probably beyond recovery.

There were other reasons Belik cut off his access to the Unreal. Without it, he couldn't deny his lies or recruit others to his side against Belik. Skipping over the First Level to the next was impossible, so he couldn't use his killing ability either.

Stripped of his mental weapons, he resorted to the physical. He ran through muscle strengthening positions until he made himself sick with exertion. Push-ups, sit-ups, everything he could think of to keep himself in perfect shape as he waited like an animal to be unleashed.

His black shirt had been ripped up to his mid-back in the tunnel. Edges of the torn pieces felt stiff with blood from his reopened cuts. Disgusted, he threw the shirt to the side.

Again and again and again, his gaze darted to the base of the steps, illuminated by Daelon's guttering torch as well as thinly filtered sunlight. He couldn't stop staring, hoping someone would appear. Anyone but Belik. He needed news, allies, supplies, *something*. Wouldn't anyone come to him? Many Tanyu would stand by him if they knew he was alive. And Daelon had said something about a key.

Hours later, he stood fitting one of his boot clasps into the keyhole, fishing for a latch. The Tanyu had taken his boot knife, of course. Pinching with his fingertips, he swiped the piece of metal from side to side, trying to scrape all the walls of the lock, but the clasp was too shallow to find purchase. Cursing, he snaked his seared arm back through the bars. The crook of his elbow was red and raw from hooking it around the iron grating.

Crouching, he reattached the fastener to his boot. He refused to give up, but he was running out of options.

A door squeaked. He jerked his head up and stood. Someone was coming down the stairs in a pool of light. It was day, then.

The footsteps were lighter and more even than Belik's. Amir Daelon appeared, holding a platter of food. He paused at the foot of the stairs, squinting like a blind man before moving forward. The flame had gone out hours ago. If Daelon struggled to see, others would too. Firian tucked away the small advantage in case he needed it later.

Daelon's face looked gaunt as he approached the bars and set down the food. A misshapen piece of meat, though it wasn't clear what kind. Firian's mouth watered, but he didn't grab for it. The last time Daelon was here, Firian had ordered him not to reveal that Kiria still lived. Something about the Amir's expression said that he kept the secret. No sign of a key, though.

"Have they found her?" he asked, hating that he had to rely on this Amir for information.

"They haven't told me," Daelon replied. He sounded as though he hadn't slept in days. "I think they would inform us all if they did."

Firian agreed. Belik would want to make it clear that the people of Brithnem had no other ruler to pin their hopes on. Belik's war was psychological as much as it was physical. Kiria was a neat end to tie up.

The news should have made him feel heartened, but the gnawing unease didn't go away. They hadn't found her yet, but it was only a matter of time until someone did.

Daelon's hands hung limp at his side. Those hands could do something to turn the war, but the Amir hadn't practiced beating his body into submission, learning to be a weapon. What use was the Scroll now? Brithnem needed a hero, someone to fight against these injustices and win. Yet Firian stood behind bars in this tiny cell and Daelon walked free.

Energy burned beneath the surface of Firian's skin as the longing to be released came over him in a rush. With Daelon, he had a little leverage, at least. A temporary ally. Another chance.

"I could check on her," Firian offered, angling for friendship.

Daelon frowned.

"In the Unreal. Like your mother has."

Skepticism twisted Daelon's expression, but he waited for Firian to continue.

"I can find out where she is. I just need you to help me."

Daelon's gaze softened, still distrustful. "You took the Keeper hostage, you killed our soldiers, you led your troops here... There is little reason for me to believe you."

Firian didn't try to deny the Amir's accusations. Laid out like that, his crimes sounded horrible. Was that how Kiria saw him too? As a dangerous war criminal?

"I'm in here," he said, spreading his arms. "We're not on the same side, or they would free me." He licked his dry lips. "I want revenge."

"Revenge is not the same as justice."

Amir had a comeback for everything. In this case, revenge was justice. "You obviously need help, and I can help you. I understand how they work, what they'll do next. I can communicate with Kiria. I can kill Belik. You need my help." His pulse was racing. Daelon had to see he was right. What other chance did they have?

Still, Daelon fiddled with his sleeve for a while before he answered. When he looked back into Firian's eyes, his face was hard. "You could kill my Keeper, so I can't take the risk. You act as though Brithnem doesn't have anyone willing to defend it. We will prevail in this conflict, and we'll do it with those who are loyal to us. Maybe you can one day prove that your words aren't lies, but it's not today."

Firian vibrated with anger as he watched Daelon turn and shuffle back up the steps. Darkness settled over him again.

If Daelon weren't so blind and stubborn, he could help him find the Sentry, at least.

Mental claustrophobia closed in. Firian had nowhere to go. Drawing in a deep breath, he ran a hand through his greasy hair. Getting Daelon's help was the obvious solution. Maybe it was too obvious. Remembering the years of strategy and mental warfare he had taken, he ran through scenarios in his mind.

Possibilities are currency. Always think of more. The words were Belik's, but they were right.

He sat cross-legged and pulled the plate of food through the bars. The hunk of meat wouldn't fit through the square, so he had to yank it hard by the bone to make it squeeze through. Reddish rust coated the meat from being scraped over the grating. He sniffed the offering. It didn't smell rotten or poisoned. In fact, the roasted meat smell made his mouth water. He forced himself to eat slowly, savoring the juices. Long ago, he'd found that he could survive on less food as long as he focused on what he had.

The meal had to be a weak gambit from Master Belik. Good meat wasn't cheap, yet Firian, a prisoner, got a large share. It gave him energy and bought him a little more time before Belik snipped his life like a loose thread. Two good things in a world where everything had gone horribly, unthinkably, wrong.

Despite chewing slowly, even sucking on the fat and gristle, the food was gone too quickly. Just a bone left in his hand. A memory prickled the back of his skull. Something about a prison cell and a meat bone...

His eyes went wide when he remembered. Three good things. Bard played Indisfate with one wooden figure that didn't match the set: Corso, the great Tanyuin warrior. Long ago, before the Keepers, he had been imprisoned—*in this city!*—but he made a miraculous escape. In all its variations, it was Firian's favorite story when he was young.

He stared at the meat bone in his hand. It was knobby on both ends. Gripping one side, he cracked it against the ground once, twice. On the third strike, the bone broke, leaving a jagged edge, needle sharp. A smile spread over his face.

Kicking the smaller piece skittering to the side, Firian stood and wrapped his arm around the bars again. He fit the pointed end of the bone into the lock, careful not to press so hard that it snapped off. Feeling around, the point scraped nothing but the flat walls of an empty box. Readjusting his body, he tried a different angle, one that eased the raw space inside his elbow.

Then, there! There! The point caught on a small protrusion in the keyhole. He held his breath, pressing himself harder against the bars. With tiny movements, he traced the bone fragment around the latch. One side had a groove deeper than the others. That had to be it. Hooking the point into the groove, he pried the bone sideways. The thin point would break off any second. The groove was so deep in the lock that it might be a long time before he found anything else to do the job. *Stay on. Stay on. Work!*

A heavy groan of metal and the door eased forward.

13

FIRIAN

Firian's heart skipped. The door was open. He was free.

Fire licked through his veins as he ran to the bottom of the steps. He had to regain control of the Tanyuin forces, take them from Belik, but first he needed to find the Sentry holding his mind hostage. Then he would know if Kiria and Bard were alive.

Even freed from his cell, he felt the claustrophobic, low-hanging buzz of the Sentry in the corners of his consciousness, its white noise replacing the music of possibilities.

Still clutching the bone fragment, he crouched at the foot of the stairs and listened. A tiny sliver of bright light rimmed one side of the trapdoor at the top.

Where would Belik keep a Sentry? He swallowed down a lump of humiliation at his ignorance. He'd trusted Belik with the details and had been too distracted by Kiria to learn them all himself.

The white-hot image of her Beauty appearing in the farmhouse struck him like a physical blow. He hadn't allowed himself to dwell on her, but now the memory of her filled him with longing. She had only come to protect her people from invasion. She didn't want him. Would all this have been different if she'd loved him?

He wished he could hate her. That was an emotion he knew well, but instead he was filled with a chaos of thoughts. Could he blame her for not loving him?

From this distance of time, her stricken expression and trembling fear spoke more of courage than anything. He could have taken her for himself, and she knew it. Yet she'd come anyway. Bard's voice, insistent and clear, had told him to let her go.

But it was all for nothing. Belik attacked the city anyway. Firian balled his fists.

Beyond the trapdoor, people were talking. He should have asked Daelon where his dungeon was. Kiria, to his knowledge, had never been down here, so he had no sense of where it might be on the palace grounds. It felt hot and humid, but so did all areas of the castle just before autumn came. If he was close to the Kheltor, then the door muffled the sound of waves too much to prove it.

He could burst out and hide, unless they'd set a guard above the entrance. Voices suggested that he was close to a populated area. Well, an area populated by Tanyuin forces, at least. Now, Shiro, Xan, and Makai spoke to each other in clipped voices. They would notice if the trapdoor swung open.

"...loitering when there is so much to do!" This, from Master Makai's deep voice.

"I've been stationed by Master Belik," Shiro replied.

"He's not the one with the orders. That's Master Kess."

"He's turned," said Xan. "Not with the Tanyu anymore."

"Not with the Tanyu," Makai scoffed, his disdain for her comment clear even though the conversation was muffled.

"No, he helped the Keeper Kiria escape," Shiro supplied.

Below, Firian blinked. Did people believe all this?

"He hasn't been here," Shiro continued, as though that proved his point. That snake.

Something about the silence made Firian guess that Master Makai was the only one who didn't realize that he was practically standing on Firian's prison. If only he could reach out with his mind.

Other sounds, running, a brief fight, more conversation, now overlapping, made it maddeningly difficult to hear any more.

His isolation was an asset. As he craned to look up through the darkness, he knew no one was coming. If he waited until nightfall, he'd have a better chance of slipping out unseen.

Despite practicing patience all his life, the wait sounded interminable. His muscles grew taut and his breaths shallowed at the thought. *I can do it. I'm the Tanyuin Head.* He looked up in defiance at the glowing exit. This time he whispered it aloud. "I am the Tanyuin Head."

Even if they set a guard above him, *he* was their rightful leader. They should see that. Someone should challenge Shiro's gory lie and find him.

Belik could only have taken over because the other Tanyu were used to taking Firian's orders from Belik's mouth. Apparently, during the attack he'd undermined Firian's reputation enough that they were willing to accept Belik as their new Head, but that would be short-lived.

What had he said? Firian's blood heated to think of it. Had he told them all about Firian's *katah* with Kiria, how he had let her go with a promise not to conquer the city?

Did that decision make him weak? Maybe it did. At the time, though, he knew —he *knew!*—that his decision was the only one that wouldn't make him a monster. He had done it for Kiria, for Bard, for that part of himself that rebelled against being the villain.

His thoughts swirled as he waited for the light to change and fade. He shucked his black shirt back on, despite the rips in the back. Easier to hide that way once it got dark. The stifling presence of the Sentry made it hard to take a full breath.

Finally, the voices sank to silence and only the palest glow, perhaps night lanterns from a nearby building, seeped around the side of the trapdoor. He quieted his breathing, straining to listen. Nothing. Adjusting his grip on the sharpened bone, he clutched it in his fist, the scars on his hands barely visible in the darkness. Taking a steadying breath, he felt adrenaline course through his veins. He might not get another chance.

3... 2... 1...

He burst through the door, catching it before it flipped against the ground, and set it back in place. All silent. Though it was night, the darkness of his cell made everything look bright in comparison. Amiran Academy in the distance to the left, farther away the ocean, palace behind, a low building closer on the right, grove of trees ahead. Kingdom soldiers moved around the low building. A barracks. Then why weren't they fighting against Belik? Had they accepted his rule? What threat or promise had Belik made them? Firian scowled at the passive soldiers and sprinted lightly over the grass to the trees.

The buzz of the Sentry was coming from the palace.

Across the lawn toward the palace gardens, small movements probably meant Tanyu were patrolling it. If he had organized this attack, he would have made sure that the palace grounds were locked down despite the partially unusable palace. Wisps of ghostly smoke still floated on the air, eking from paneless windows blown out by the fire.

This was his test. He turned the pointed bone in his palm. He only needed to disable the Sentry. It would be easier to kill his way through, but the thought made him sick. Who would he be killing? Shiro was with Belik. Though not a friend, Firian didn't want to kill them.

He followed the trees toward the castle until their shelter disappeared. The ornately carved walls showed many entrances—doors, windows, cellars—but which would be unguarded?

By virtue of being a Tanyu, any soldiers that remained loyal to Kiria would want him dead. By virtue of being Firian, Belik wanted him neutralized.

With each step he considered who would side with him and who would side with Belik once it became clear that everyone had to choose a side. The groups played like drumbeats in his mind.

Tanyu would be split. Friends of Rian—the Tanyu Firian had accidentally killed when the Kingdom invaded the Academy—would probably side with Belik, as well as those who were more ambitious, unwilling to give up the current plan of conquest. Some would come back to Firian out of loyalty or fear.

Torithians and border patrollers would side with Belik because he'd give them free reign for their bloodlust and greed.

If Firian could go back to the Academy, the Sentries would help him. He freed them, after all. In that moment, he realized just how helpful—and how gory frustrating—they could be.

Belik had suggested that Master Gerand look after the Academy in their absence. Did that mean she was on his side? Firian wouldn't be surprised. Gerand had never thought much of him, but she was a capable commander, which is why he'd agreed to leave her in charge. She was also the sister of Kiria's advisor—what was her name?

The answer hit him with force. Chetana. Belik's *katah*. Firian had never put that together. Belik hated Chetana but worked closely with Gerand, a *katah* Master. Was Gerand trying to free him from the mental bond with Chetana? Firian didn't think that was possible.

In any case, regaining rulership of the Tanyu might not be as easy as going back to the Academy.

Firian crouched and sat back on his heels. What would he do in Belik's place? As much as he hated to admit it, he and Belik thought very much alike. The main doors would all be watched, since the Kingdom always guarded those, taking care of the most obvious routes first. He cast his eyes up. The roof was too risky to climb. Which meant no one guarded it.

With the bone, Firian drew three lines in the dirt at his feet, one straight with two adjacent wings, like an unfinished octagon. Inside the shape, he drew a small circle—the Amiran Academy. He enclosed the drawing in two parallel lines representing the city and the sea. If he did climb the palace walls, he needed an angle where he would less likely be seen.

All the flourishes in the stone work made for good camouflage, if he could just find a divot or alcove that stretched all the way up. He looked up from his drawing to the palace itself peeking through the trees. Shouldn't there be a drainage system or something?

But of course it wasn't so easy. Glancing back at his drawing, he obliterated it with his hand. He had to go and hope he could find a spot like the one he envisioned. It was that simple and that difficult.

Nothing facing the road to the city. The Keepers would want the most visible part of the palace pristine. Same with the ocean-facing side. The edges, then. Those were his best chance.

He stilled his breathing to observe the space in front of him. No immediate threats.

Quick as a shadow, he ran.

The palace wall offered one-directional protection, so he sprinted to it, arms pumping. At the wall he turned like a mouse, sticking close to the stones. His muscles tensed at every door, but their modesty meant that they were servants' entrances. No visible guards.

Just a few more seconds...

A door opened toward him. Without thinking, Firian slammed into it, crushing whoever was emerging outside. A scream and a foreign curse. Torithian.

Firian gripped the door with his free hand, yanking it back. He was right. A Torithian he barely recognized slumped against the wall, clutching a broken arm. Blood poured down his forearm, dripping into the pile of fabric at his feet. No, not just fabric. Tapestries of the royal families. How had those survived the fire?

The dark room was meant for some kind of food preparation. Wheels of curing cheese sat on the floor and on shelves. Beside the pirate's left shoulder was a pile of cheesecloth. The man's eyes bulged to white as Firian stuffed the bone in his own teeth to free his hand, grabbed one of the cloths, and rapidly gagged him as he kicked and cried out in pain. The gag pulled the man's face tight. Considering more restraints, Firian determined that the looter was in no condition to run. One of the legs looked broken too.

Knocking him out, Firian left him and moved on, shutting the door quietly.

No one else appeared as he raced to the narrowest part of the palace. Heart hammering, he turned and tipped his face upward. Mon Párinath was taller than the Tanyuin Academy, maybe even twice as tall. A flap of movement revealed the edge of one long flag. There was no recess for drainage here, as he'd hoped. But there was a section that had reliefs on either side that would at least shelter half his body. It would have to do.

Throwing away the bone shard, which would fall out of his clothes, injure him, or get crushed if he held it in his teeth, he started the climb. His adrenaline was starting to wear off and even the practice in the cell hadn't made his muscles optimal, as they'd been before the Kingdom attack. Before Belik had killed all those people...

He pushed the thought away and kept reaching for the next handhold. He needed speed even more than secrecy. His biceps burned and his fingers strained to hold onto the stone. Falling wasn't an option. It didn't matter how much it hurt, or if his shoulders dislocated. Pain was temporary. He couldn't fail.

If he didn't get inside the palace, he might never taste the Unreal again. If he didn't disable the barrier, he couldn't have all his powers to stop Belik for his treachery both against him and the Kingdom. Against Kiria. Against Bard. People he wouldn't see unless he survived this climb.

Another burst of energy brought him near the top. The resonant flapping of the flag sounded loud now.

He wrapped his arm around the topmost stone and dragged himself over. Rolling onto the roof, he leapt to his feet.

No unsheathed weapon. No cry of alarm.

His vision of the palace roof when he had fought Bard hadn't been far off from the truth. He must subconsciously have seen Kiria here. The roof was covered in patterns of walkways and miniature green lawns, like its own garden. On enormous poles the long blue flags of Brithnem swung in the breeze. It was almost peaceful.

Scanning the parapet, he found a door. Resisting the urge to rush toward it, he focused again on the pain just out of reach. Where was that Sentry?

His vision went blurry as he pressed into the web of pain blocking him from the Unreal. As his physical senses dulled to fire, the Sentry's location became clearer.

He broke off his focus, gasping from the effort. His mind felt shredded. But he knew where to go.

14

FIRIAN

Apart from the burned stairs and the acrid smell of smoke and two more Torithians carting off treasures, Firian reached the Sentry without much incident. He was being kept in a tiny room on the ground floor by himself to focus. Firian entered swiftly and closed himself inside. The space was so small that the two pressed against each other. In his trance, the Sentry didn't try to move away. The smell of parsley wafted up between them.

Firian's head felt squeezed tight. This place was black as blindness, not only to the eyes, but to the mind, and he hated it.

"Let me go," Firian demanded.

No answer.

"Can you hear me?"

A change in the cadence of the man's breath told Firian he did, but the barrier remained immovably intact.

Firian reached for the man's throat and held it. "Let me go." This scenario felt uncomfortably like when he and Bard had raided the Sentries' prison and freed them all. Firian had later tracked some of them down to appease the previous Tanyuin Head. Little good that did.

Giving the Sentry's neck a shake, Firian squeezed harder. The message should have been clear. Did the Sentry think he had no hope of freedom, of doing anything but this mind-numbing, dehumanizing job?

"I'm going to kill Master Belik," Firian whispered. "And then you'll be free."

The man swallowed under Firian's palm.

"Let me go." Firian said it more slowly this time, as though he were easing open the cell door latch.

"You won't give me freedom. You're Tanyu," the man rasped, barely audible.

"So were you."

The Sentry broke off the barrier. The dam broke, letting in the flood of the

Unreal. Firian fought back a gasp of relief, releasing the man's throat. So there was really hope he could do this. He hadn't realized any doubt before, but it must have been there, because now it was gone.

"If you don't free me, then kill me," said the man in the darkness. He was deadly serious.

"What's your name?" Firian asked, feeling the dark weight of his words.

"Lev Aramin."

"It's done."

The Sentry fished for Firian's hand, solidifying their pact.

Eager to go, Firian said, "I'll get you out of the palace, but you never saw me."

"If they find me..."

"I can't do any more than that. I need to end this, and I can't have you around." Normally, he would have told the Sentry to stay to buy more time, but Firian's absence was sure to be missed soon. There was no guarantee Firian would come back to this part of the castle to free Lev unless he did it now.

Before opening the door, Firian felt in the Unreal for Kiria. Was she alive?

A knot balled in his chest in the grasping second before he sensed her presence.

Then, there it was! Relief flooded him. It was faint and wreathed in too-familiar sadness. She had a Sentry too, but not a very good one. Had Belik set up both of them? Firian could break through this Sentry if necessary, so there was no need to track down whoever was blocking Kiria's mind. At least she was alive. She was alive—not panicking, not hurting, not dying. Despite the odds against her, alive.

And Bard? His chances were slimmer.

Almost fearfully, he cast his mind toward Bard next. Right away, he found him. Alive too!

But the brush against the Unreal made Firian pause and go further. The setting solidified around him. Yellow grasses, worn dirt paths, high-pitched roofs with intricate wooden carvings... This was Enderin. Dust motes floated above the surface of the ground, glowing in the sunlight. White clouds spaced themselves evenly across the bright blue sky. Firian knitted his brows. Something about the light or colors was wrong.

Bard was here somewhere. "Bard!" Firian called, ignoring the fake people who turned to look at the disruption. One woman with a kerchief shook her head at his brashness.

From behind a grassy hill that bent the road, Bard appeared. He wore a rough-spun gray shirt with worn brown leather accents. His black eyes grew wide with surprise and delight as he broke into a run. "Fir! What are you doing here?" he cried, colliding with Firian in a hug.

Firian stiffened. Had Bard forgotten their last encounter in the Unreal, the one that felt like a door slammed shut?

Bard let go and spun around. "Have you been here before? Why did you come to Enderin?" His lilting accent sounded even more pronounced here. Then his expression darkened. "You're not planning to take it over, yeah? We don't need the Academy. Look!" he said. "It's too big. You're here for something else."

A chill crawled down Firian's spine. Some details here were too perfect. A loose thread jutted from the neck of Bard's shirt, gnats swarmed around Firian's face, a broken piece of pottery—maybe a plate—lay halfway buried in the dirt beside the road.

Bard was Lost in the Unreal.

"Bard," he said, keeping his voice steady, "where are you?" Belik had asked Firian the same question not too long ago. Since the Master was the only person he knew who had practice in Retrieval, he took the same tactic.

Briefly confused, Bard pointed behind him. "I'm staying at home right now, if that's what you mean." His face lit up. "You're welcome to come! You should come. Meet everybody!"

"No, where are you really?"

Fear tinged Bard's expression like a film. "What are you talking about? I'm here."

That was all the confirmation Firian needed. Staying in the Unreal, he returned to reality enough to function in both. He left the Sentry's closet, Lev behind him, keeping his eyes open for soldiers. Freeing the Sentry meant shattering the illusion that Firian was still under control. But it was what Kiria would have done, and it took mere seconds to coax the man to follow him.

If Bard was Lost in the Unreal, that meant he would lie comatose in real life. By Firian's calculation, which was flimsy at best, the doctor had taken Bard a full day ago. Maybe two. Even when Firian dropped him off, Bard had been unconscious. How long would the doctor try to keep him alive if he wasn't regaining consciousness?

Firian's head spun as he tried to remember where to find the storage area with the tunnel that had led him to the doctor the first time.

In the Unreal, Bard still regarded him suspiciously.

"You're not here," Firian said carefully. Based on what he knew of Belik's work, it was delicate—more than a matter of turning the sky green to prove a point. If he made some grand gesture, Bard would assume he was dreaming, retreat deeper into his delusion, and be even harder to convince the next time. Bard had to come to his own conclusion, realize for himself that he was Lost.

"Fir, I have no idea—"

"Think! Where are you?"

Now annoyed, Bard nodded rapidly as he answered. "Why do you keep asking? I'm right here. I'm in Enderin." He looked like he was casting around for another sort of answer that would satisfy him. "My family's back there. The ocean is that way." He pointed.

"How did you get here?"

"What are you talking about? I took a horse from the Academy."

He was running out of questions. "Where's the horse?"

"Do you want it back, or...?"

"No, I just want to see which one it is."

Bard scratched the back of his head, sending his hair spiking in new directions. "Okay. Stable's this way." He walked past Firian on the path.

Firian gazed a moment longer at the perfect recreation of Enderin, so similar to what he'd seen when he docked there after the victory on Torith.

A scrabble of rocks made Firian whip around to see Bard on his hands and knees in a glowing cloud of dust. Firian's heart clenched. People didn't trip in the Unreal.

"You're okay," he said tersely, reaching down to help him up.

Breathing hard, Bard stared at the ground, as though he were too weak to reach up until he caught his breath. When he clasped Firian's forearm so he could haul him to his feet, Firian's gut flipped with the memory of Bard lying all but dead in front of Kiria's bedroom. *I'm sorry. I'm sorry.*

Firian swallowed hard. "What happened?" Hopefully he sounded unconcerned.

Bard dusted himself off before walking ahead at a slower pace. "I just rolled my ankle or something. I'm fine, mate."

But Firian couldn't shake off the terror that his friend was dying.

BARD SEEMED to forget about Firian's concern after they'd been walking for a while. Firian was glad, but not sure how long Bard could keep limping along this dirt path to the stables.

As quickly as he could with the Sentry following, Firian snuck down the hallways of the palace back to the storage area where Jori had shown him the tunnel leading to the doctor. Tanyu, Torithians, and Kingdom soldiers appeared now and then, but Firian expertly evaded their notice. A few he had to incapacitate, leaving more evidence of his escape, but with Bard's life running out like grains through a sieve, Firian couldn't afford slower stealth. He suspected that most didn't want to be in this section of the palace, still smoky and more badly burned than others.

The space was just as he had left it. White tapered candles littered the floor, now partially melted from the heat of the earlier fire. He hadn't bothered to return the cover last time, so the tunnel entrance sat exposed. Firian gestured to Lev Aramin, and then to the hole. The Sentry wasn't fast, but he was silent, a shadow of a person. This was where he could make his own way. Now Firian had to run, and he did, dashing through first, but not before he caught a hint of gratefulness on Aramin's face.

"Rissa thinks she's as tall as me now," Bard went on. "But I don't think so. We'll have to measure. She is tall for a girl..."

"Mm hm."

Firian kept the Unreal in view as he hurtled through the tunnel, running on all fours. The damp earthen wall pressed down on his spine whenever he bounced too high.

"I'm definitely taller than Elsi. And Aline's just a kid." Bard winced, a pain unconnected to his inane conversation.

"Mm hm." He had to keep him talking. "What about Jac?"

That sent Bard on another life update for a while. He half-listened as Bard explained how a local carpenter had asked Jac to help him restore homes that had been damaged in the Torithian raids, but Jac had refused, choosing instead to extend his stay with the Endrian army.

Surely the end of the tunnel was getting close.

"...staying in his room until he gets back from the war. Mum says we'll have to share when he gets back. Yeah, he won't like that very much, I don't think." Bard laughed and coughed.

The tunnel exit! Firian could see it in front of him, glowing softly in the moonlight. He vaulted toward it and burst through into the grassy hollow. Springing to his feet, he circled once, sucking in a breath of fresh air. No Tanyu, no Torithians, no Kingdom soldiers.

The doctor had come from over the lip of that hill, away from the direction of the palace.

"You okay?"

Firian's attention snapped back to Bard on the dusty road. "Yeah. Yeah, I'm fine."

Bard squinted at him, obviously doubting his flippant answer. "The horse is over here. You know, if something's wrong..."

"I'm fine." He was sprinting over the night-darkened grass. A line of buildings edged the field at the top of the hollow. Which one was the doctor? He wished he could ask Bard, but his friend wouldn't even understand the question.

Cautiously, Firian slowed. He would have to check them one by one. The delay set his teeth on edge.

Firian crouched against the building on the end of the row, hoping to sense Bard's presence. No. The next building. They almost looked like houses. No. Impatience clawed at his throat. No. No. No.

"Thass not... my horse..."

Firian's heart froze. The voice had come from the real world. He knew that murmur. Bard was talking in his sleep. A well of memories sprang up to choke him but he pressed it back down. The sound had come from the next building. He scanned for entrances. Of course, he could just use the door. Doctors always kept their doors open.

Would there be guards inside? He considered how he looked. Even those who hadn't seen him as the Tanyuin Head would know he belonged to the Academy, the enemy. The back of his shirt was shredded from crawling through the hole the first time. He quickly rubbed the red rust off his forearms. It gave him a murderous look. Some of the color remained stubbornly embedded in his skin. *Oh well.* He usually had a murderous look.

The doctor had seemed willing to help Bard without knowing who he was. Maybe he didn't take sides.

Firian smiled grimly at his own thought. Everyone took sides.

He pushed the door open. It gave easily.

The room smelled like powders and chemicals. Heat from the torches made sweat break out on Firian's skin. He felt painfully visible. Dark hallways led to more small rooms beyond. Physician's assistants moved between them, reacting smoothly to the moans of soldiers.

The hang-lipped doctor appeared. He quickly took in Firian's bedraggled appearance, betraying some surprise. "Hello, how can I—?"

"I'm here to see the patient."

"He's not well."

So the doctor did remember him. He followed Firian into the smaller rooms, protesting faintly. "You're... one of them. I'm afraid you can't—"

Firian silenced him with a look. The man closed his mouth, but his watery eyes brightened with defiance on behalf of his patients. Firian liked the doctor more for it.

He turned back to the short row of doors, nose crinkling at the smell, significantly worse than in the brightly lit entry. Four rooms, each neatly appointed with a bed and various medical tools. Every room, Firian realized, bore some hint of Brithnem colors: light blue and deep purple. Maybe the man was an official doctor of some kind.

In the darkness of one room, a figure lay on its back, covered with a sheet up to its neck. It had black hair.

Firian rushed in. Bard didn't respond or wake. Strands of hair stuck haphazardly to the sweat on his forehead. At least blood no longer crusted his eyes. The doctor must have washed it off.

Looking down at his friend, a moment of helplessness washed over him. He couldn't just snap at him to get up. He couldn't shake him until he woke, grumpy and sleepy. He had to convince him of the painful truth first, that he wasn't at home with his family, but on the verge of death because of a brutal attack. Despite the heat, a chill coated Firian's body like rain. It could take a long time, and he had a demand for vengeance that couldn't wait much longer.

"Gore," he breathed, rubbing one eye with his palm.

"He hasn't regained consciousness since he was brought in," a voice behind him said gently. "It's unlikely that he will."

Firian turned his head only enough to look at the doctor from the corner of his eye. "I said he lives. So he lives."

"So you did."

He turned his attention again to the brightness of Enderin. Bard was staring at him. "What is it?" Bard demanded.

Firian considered, breathing in the faint smell of horse manure. This illusion really was a masterful piece of work.

But there was no time. "You're Lost in the Unreal."

Bard's lips twisted in annoyance. "That's just mean."

"No, you are."

In the doctor's room, Bard slurred a few incomprehensible words.

"Seriously, Fir, stop it." He looked irritated rather than afraid.

Firian drew his bottom lip between his teeth, looking for a way to get the truth into his friend's skull. He had to be subtler or he would make him retreat further into his own mind. Inspiration struck.

"Look over there." He pointed to a barn-like structure ahead of them. It had a hitching post in front. The lintel and post were both carved in the Endrian style.

"Okay, I'm going to count down. When I say 'one,' a white horse will walk out the door by itself."

"Is this some sort of game? You want a wager?"

"Sure," he conceded. Anything to make Bard pay attention. "I bet you ten coins."

Bard's eyes rounded. "I don't have ten coins. I just have..." He fished around in his pockets, looking a little embarrassed. "Four tokens."

Firian waved his protest away, staring at the barn door. "Shh! Look!" He waited until Bard was staring too. "Three... two... one."

A magnificent white stallion trotted out of the building, dancing with Firian's own agitation.

Bard rounded on him, his heel scraping the dirt as he pivoted. "How did you know? I can't pay you, you know. I never agreed to the—"

"Bard! You're Lost in the Unreal. That's how I knew that horse was there. I made that horse!"

"You're not God." Bard didn't meet his eyes now, almost as though he were talking to himself.

Seriously? This isn't enough? Firian huffed a breath through his nose. When he spoke, he softened his tone. "I'm not trying to trick you. You got attacked. So..."

"Attacked?" Bard asked distantly. He was getting further away, sheltering more firmly in the depths of his own mind.

"Do you remember anything?"

"About what?"

Firian had no idea where to begin. Did he remember the Kingdom attack on the Academy when Firian had killed all those people? Did he remember abandoning Firian, calling him a monster before going to Brithnem? Did he remember seeing Kiria's Beauty, which she didn't hide from him? Did he remember stepping out in front of Belik to give her time to escape?

Instead, he said, "Do you trust me?"

The question seemed to jog a memory in Bard, who looked like he suddenly doubted his answer. Uncertainty crept into his eyes.

"Trust me now. I'm trying to save you. Just follow me." He closed his eyes dramatically, encouraging Bard to imitate him. "Go up, not down."

"There's a down?"

"In real life, you're lying in bed in a dark room. I'm standing there. That's what you should see."

Firian heard Bard's breathing quicken with fear. "Really?"

"I'll explain it all later. Just follow me."

Firian opened his eyes and exhaled. Strong herbs permeated the space. Bard lay lifeless before him. *Up, come on!*

Nothing.

Movement, not of trees or clouds or lanterns, stirred outside the window. Black forms headed toward the medical building, unmistakably Tanyu. Firian's chest seized. What reason could they have to come here unless they had found him or were coming to kill Bard?

He licked his fingers and put out the lantern by the door. Darkness would give them momentary cover.

The Tanyu outside disappeared, heading apparently toward the road that opened to the building's main entrance.

Firian rooted himself beside the bed, though every fiber told him to jump through the window and escape. Another moment more. Firian himself had been Lost in the Unreal. It could take a moment to orient himself. *Come on, Bard. Damn it!*

Seconds ticked by like the footsteps of approaching Tanyu.

Behind his lids, in the faint light of a dying moon, Bard's eyes moved.

15

KIRIA

"Let me out."

Kiria rolled over to see Jori facing the guards by the door in a brutally petulant mood. It looked dark outside.

Her eyes felt as scratchy as the pelt beneath her head. She must have just fallen asleep. The long, tense day trapped in the tannery, waiting for word from the military to begin concocting a plan in earnest, had sapped her strength. A strange buzz assaulted her senses, unconnected to her exhaustion. Chetana looked down at her and she remembered the Sentry.

"My Kepron, we can't let you leave."

Jori touched the blond guard, who blocked his path, more to make his point than to move him out of the way. He lowered his head. "I'm about to lose my mind. The least you can do is give me a couple hours of freedom." There was something fragile in his voice. He was begging.

"I'm sorry, My Kepron." The guard made to lay a hand on Jori's shoulder.

Jori twisted violently away. "You are going to let me out." He sounded close to tears now.

The closest guard opened his mouth.

"Then bring me something to drink." Jori held up a hand, ticking off items as he had done with Kiria since she was young. He jutted up his thumb for number one. "I've been through hell the past couple days... we all have." It seemed as though he wanted to add more to his list but couldn't bring himself to voice it. His fingers crumpled in on themselves. He got close to the guard's face instead. "So let me out or bring me that drink. I'm going mad in here."

"Jori," Kiria called from her makeshift bed.

Glowering, he turned to her. His waistcoat was soiled by hours spent in the oven opening. His red-rimmed eyes almost scared her.

"It's late," she said.

He cursed and kicked over a roll of leather like a child before turning back to the guards on full alert by the only door. After regarding them a moment, he held up a finger. "You know I can figure out a way." He raised his eyebrows, some of the old Jori coming back.

Two of the guards exchanged glances. Apparently, they did know.

"My Kepron, I—"

Loud knocking reverberated through the tiny room. Kiria started, sitting full upright.

"See, fate has spoken!" Jori cried, as though he were already drunk.

Urgent voices from outside the door demanded to come in, identifying themselves as Kingdom soldiers. The guards opened the door cautiously, then gratefully, as they saw two of their own outside. They bustled quickly into the already crowded space. Jori was forced to back up to make way for them.

Kiria trundled to her feet, anxious for information.

The two newcomers searched the room for her. When they found her, they bowed respectfully. "We have news of the Kepron."

Kader. "What is it? Is he alive?"

"He is alive. He escaped the initial attack and is on his way north."

Kiria let out a breath. A motley semblance of the Keepers still lived. Ten-year-old Kader represented the First Line, she the Second, and Jori the Third.

"Who's with him?"

"His guards."

Kiria's thoughts faltered. If these soldiers had been able to find out all this, surely the Tanyu also had means of figuring it out. Kader was very likely being followed, and what could a child do against a Tanyuin warrior?

She set her jaw. "We have to make the Tanyu think he's dead, and we have to make sure everyone knows that *I'm* alive. That may give them hope, and prevent more soldiers from giving in to Belik's leadership. The new moon is tomorrow. Tell the commanders still loyal to us to meet in the paper warehouse today at sunset." Earlier that day, they'd worked out the next location, this time large enough to house a sizable meeting and close enough that they wouldn't have to travel more than a few buildings over. Sunset would give enough time to relocate and rally. "We'll need a better place to meet. And get me something to write with."

Her notebook with all its ideas about bettering the Kingdom still lay in her bedroom, probably nothing more than smoldering ashes. A list, or a visualization of a raid on the palace, would help center her swirling thoughts.

"As you wish, My Keeper."

"And?" Jori prompted.

The guard hesitated for a moment, glancing at Kiria before responding. "And a drink for you."

16

FIRIAN

Bard's eyes were still closed as he lay back on a sweat-soaked pillow. The skin had a grayish pallor under his black hair. Firian frowned. What if Bard couldn't walk?

Well, they didn't have a choice. Tanyu were coming for them. He couldn't tell how many, and he didn't want to fight all of them by himself. Bard could too easily get caught in the crossfire, killed during a negligent breath. They had seconds to escape from the medical building, if they managed to escape at all.

He shook Bard's arm. There was something unnatural about the stiffness of the limb. Firian forced himself to keep his grip, bending down close. "Bard!" he hissed, pushing him. "Get up!"

"Aahgnn!" Bard exclaimed so loudly that Firian flinched.

At least that was a good sign.

His eyes darting to the door to check for movement, Firian pushed Bard so hard that he had to catch him from falling off the bed. Finally, the black eyes squinted open, focused on Firian, blinked. Bard had always been slow to wake up, but his evident concentration as he fought to keep his eyes open wasn't typical.

Firian swallowed on a dry mouth. Every second wasted meant they were both in more danger. By himself, he could take on a few Tanyu, but protecting Bard and preventing him from sinking irrevocably back into the Unreal complicated things.

"Get up," Firian demanded, a little more loudly than before.

Bard looked at him with the absence of sickness or distraction. "Where...?" he murmured, unable to form more of a question.

What if he couldn't carry Bard fast enough or far enough to save both of them? Could he still stop Belik, make sure Kiria was safe? The list of painfully urgent duties sent impatience like static webbing over his arms, his chest, his neck, his head. He could hardly bear it.

Bard winced and forced himself into a sitting position. He leaned back heavily on his right arm.

Firian's heart jumped. There was a chance. A chance that Bard could walk out of here.

"We have to go," he whispered.

Bard's expression didn't change.

Anxiety wormed back into Firian's body. Then Bard swung his legs over the side of the bed and stood. Unbalanced and still squinting, he wavered and fell.

Firian threw an arm behind his back to catch him. He didn't remember Bard's being so heavy. Gripping him around the ribs, he wrestled him fully upright. Instead of holding on, Bard's left arm hung heavily at his side. There was something dead about its movements.

Dazed, Bard stared straight ahead. He wasn't all right. But he wasn't dead either. He nodded, a small movement but enough to jolt Firian back into the urgency of the moment.

Their best chance was going through the window. Firian hauled in a deep breath. He'd have to get Bard through, make him stand again, and only then could they run as fast as Bard was able to go.

But he had no choice. *They* had no choice. Firian wouldn't leave him here. Neither Bard nor Kiria would die today, not while they had the true Tanyuin Head making sure of it.

A FEW HOURS LATER, Firian held Bard up, half carrying him through a wooden gate set in a low stone wall. Across a green lawn that stretched toward the beach lay a large manor house, though it looked too big for a residence.

Firian had crept painstakingly northward through the city, perhaps unconsciously following Kiria's mind, though he didn't actively search for her, focusing instead on getting Bard out of the city. Many of the shop doors were shut, making it fractionally easier for him and Bard to sneak through unseen. Knots of people ran through the streets, though, despite the hour, feeding the impression that violence lurked right below the skin of the city. Endless footsteps of soldiers and civilians reacting to the upheaval at the palace sent Firian hiding when all his training told him to go out and fight. But Bard couldn't fight, and his safety couldn't be risked. They spent too many long minutes crouched in alleyways or lying out of sight on cart beds or behind trash heaps, with Firian's hand over Bard's mouth to stop his sleep-talking noises. He wasn't asleep, of course, but he wasn't quite conscious either. It was like trying to run with a sleepy child.

Skirting Grand Market Square, which seethed with unrest, they finally made it here, outside the walls of Brithnem.

A tiny gate in the massive city wall had been patrolled by only one Tanyu, Bohai Lira, an Eradi Defender who used to live on Firian's hall. Hall Masters had tested them together when Firian was a Learner. Bohai couldn't hear well out of his right ear, and had grown to favor everything on the left. It was a simple matter of timing to undo the lock and creep through to the other side.

Here, the Gray Forest abutted these mansions, each like a tiny palace of its own. The leaves, some beginning to turn unseasonably yellow at the edges, hid the buildings from view. A fine place for Bard to lie low for a while.

Not a sound came through the many windows, but that didn't mean someone wasn't sleeping inside. The sun was rising on a cloudy, wet day. Everything looked gray, from the trees, to the grass, to Firian's own hand.

Moving like a blind man, Bard shifted a foot in front of him, and then another. He smelled like chemicals and herbs that made Firian's head woozy.

Firian stopped walking. Their escape had already seemed endless. Scanning the enclosed lawn, he spotted a copse of trees far enough away from the house to avoid notice. He sucked in another steadying breath and moved. *Just keep moving.* It was all he could do.

All the pieces—so many pieces!—out of his control.

He couldn't think about it. The possibilities blinded him. At least he hadn't gotten Lost in the Unreal again.

Had he?

He looked down at Bard's messy black hair that swept over Firian's cheek as he held him upright. *Turn red,* he ordered, and stared, waiting. The hair didn't change. Still black. A manipulation that simple would have been possible even if he were Lost. He puffed out a shallow breath of relief.

They reached the group of trees at last. He lowered Bard to the ground. Deep shadows slashed across his face, the dawn sun doing little to alleviate the darkness.

"You can sleep here," Firian said quietly.

Bard's eyelids fluttered, and then he cringed as though he hurt all over. Even that slight movement made the undergrowth crackle underneath him.

Firian's forehead furrowed with concern. "I can't get you anything else right now, but you're out of the city." The doctor had been just outside the palace grounds, not nearly far enough from the heart of the conflict.

Bard looked like he wanted to say something, maybe many things. Firian hesitated. Did Bard remember the moment he saved him from the palace?

Bard's eyes widened until he looked haunted. "Fir," he whispered. "I can't move."

Relief at hearing his voice gave way to deep-seated worry. Firian's stomach tightened. "You can move," he said. "You just—"

"My arm." Bard's gaze shifted down to his left hand lying in the dirt.

"Sure you can move." Firian squatted beside him.

After a moment, the fingers still hadn't budged. Firian didn't want to look up at Bard, who he knew was probably looking at him with panic. He couldn't take it. Not today.

"You can move," he repeated, this time rubbing Bard's forearm back and forth in his hands as though he were trying to start a fire. Bard's skin felt cool and damp. Probably the weather. When he let go, Bard's hand dropped uselessly back to the ground.

Helplessness threatened to choke him. This *had* to work. Something had to go right. He gestured for Bard to try again. Bard's chest rose and fell in quick gasps.

A finger twitched.

Firian jumped to his feet, pointing. "There!" he said more loudly than he meant to. "Keep doing that. You'll be fine." He glanced at the brightening sky and shook out the arm that had held most of Bard's weight during their walk. The Unreal beckoned, calling with poignant urgency. He had to take care of Belik. Now.

"What?" Weakness made Bard much less talkative than usual. But at least he was talking.

"If I'm not back in half an hour, get inside that house. There'll be food." He pointed to a hatch at the side of the manor. "I'm going to make this right. I'm going to kill Belik."

17

BELIK

Everything still smelled like mold and smoke. Belik only stayed in the gutted palace because the Amiran Academy made him feel trapped with its tiny monkish cells and domed upper room devoid of escape routes. From here, he could command his forces, prepare for the coronation, and quash the feeble resistance presented by the minority of Kingdom soldiers and civilians.

Leaning back against the headboard, Belik shifted against the sumptuous blankets of one of the royal bedrooms untouched by the brunt of the fire. The Main was conspicuous with too many opportunities for entry. Though he had slept in a smaller room before, this place served as his headquarters for now. Surrounded by other Tanyu, without closing his eyes, he dipped into the Unreal.

Master Gerand waited for him in the darkness. She looked no less severe than in real life. Her ashy brown hair met in a tight bun at the back of her head, pulling the light skin away from her eyes. Though only his own age, her thin lips faded in unattractive lines into the rest of her face. She wore Academy black without the long coat. The only hints that she was Chetana's sister were her height and her indomitable attitude.

Part of him loathed this woman, but she was a strong ally, and he'd be a fool not to admit it. She'd been on his side since the beginning, or at least since Belik's break with Chetana so many years ago.

"We got news that you had taken the city," she said. "Is that true?"

"It is." He had ordered all tunnels, closets, and rabbit holes searched until there was no cellar or safe house left. The Tanyu would finish their thorough search within a day. Security at the wall and harbor was strengthened until even Belik could hardly see a feasible way through. All the silly martyred civilians proved the strength of their position. "It will be finalized tomorrow."

"Did you get them all—the Keepers?" Gerand asked. "You don't want anyone for the people to rally behind."

Kingdoms on Fire

The straightforwardness that had initially drawn him to Gerand's sister Chetana grated on him now. The same thought had been eating away at his mind. *Kiria and Kader gone in the wind... Gore!* But he knew he could get them. Tanyu combed the city for them, starting with the medics and associates and moving systematically toward the wall.

A young boy and a teenage girl? How hard could it be? He'd eliminated all other threats. Well, Atael's dissipated brother hadn't shown up.

He fought to keep his face impassive. There were too many loose ends. The last thing he needed was Gerand nagging him about it. "Yes," he lied, and then amended, remembering the rampant rumors in the city about Kiria's survival. He couldn't keep those voices silent much longer. "By tomorrow all three bodies will be displayed."

"Well, that's something. Chetana?"

He clenched his jaw at the name. "Not yet. She ran."

Gerand narrowed her eyes. She suspected something. "She ran?"

They both knew Chetana didn't run. "We couldn't find her," he amended. "She's not our first priority."

"No." The syllable lifted at the end, unfinished. Belik knew Gerand felt almost as betrayed by Chetana as he did, and their bad blood went further back. Their goal was respect and power for the Tanyu, but the tantalizing idea of revenge tugged on both of them.

"We've secured the palace grounds," he said. "All we need until the coronation ceremony."

She continued to give him a skeptical look, but neither of them liked to mince words. The *katah* Master waited for more information. Then it struck him. According to Firian, the princess had the Talent. Gerand could declare *katah*, or send someone else to do it.

Firian already had one with Kiria, but he wouldn't kill her. His gut hollowed at the thought of his protégé. Firian was supposed to be part of this victory. Knowing Firian's implacable drive, it wasn't likely that he could make him come around. But it was worth one more try. Firian wouldn't completely turn his back on the Tanyu, but if he continued to fester in that cell with murderous thoughts, that's exactly what it would amount to. No, Belik wouldn't give up yet.

He eyed Gerand, considering. If he asked for a *katah*, he'd have to admit that he'd lied about taking care of all the Keepers. All they needed was a little more time to find her. If she became a problem, he'd turn to Gerand.

"You'll let me know," she said.

"Yes."

A sudden, rushing pressure squeezed at his chest, at his head. It threatened to crush him, to eviscerate him from the inside. His vision blackened. Without another word to Gerand, he sank painfully down to the Second Level.

Firian.

How the hell had he broken the Sentry?

In the Second Level, Belik could press back against the attack. It felt as though fingers let go of his windpipe. Now that he could breathe again, with nothing but a dull headache left behind, he created a background. The Main. Firian stood before him, legs spread, head tilted down with a murderous glare.

Belik curled his lip. "Are you here to kill me?"

But the answer was in the attack.

"Yes."

This time Belik felt as though his skin were stretching from the inside. It felt *wrong*. Like he would burst, entrails through skin. He calmed and pushed back.

Concern glinted in Firian's face and was gone. His posture now looked more forced than powerful. Belik had been practicing too.

"I don't want to kill you," Belik said. How close was Firian that his ability was working? During practice, Belik always needed to be within sight of the rabbits. If Firian weren't primed to assault him, he could warn his Tanyuin guards. No time now.

Firian flexed his jaw. He'd always been hasty, always grabbed for everything when he wasn't ready. "I don't care."

Belik searched his face. Not having a Sentry probably meant Firian was out of the cell. Sick pride welled up in Belik's gut. Where was the boy, then? "You have a right to be angry," he said in a measured voice, "and so do I. But you can't kill me."

"Watch," Firian snarled, lunging forward, growing larger, filling the space. His towering form gripped a sword. He swung.

"Wait, Fir!" Belik said in a lilting voice, in a body that matched Bard's. He threw up his hands in front of his face.

Firian halted, blinked just once.

It was enough of an opening. Still in Bard's body, Belik plunged a knife into Firian's shoulder. The blade cracked through sinews. Blood spattered his face as he tilted the room to make Firian fall from the shock.

Firian clutched his wound, biting out curses. The blades melted into nothing, but the pain was real.

"You're good, Firian, but I've been at this a long time, and I've shed my weaknesses." Now Belik was the one towering over Firian. "In real life I'm surrounded by Tanyu. Even you couldn't take them all by yourself. And here, I can match you."

Firian looked positively feral. Though Belik knew he was right, his heart stuttered, and he cursed it.

"You know I can get to you," Firian said through gritted teeth.

"But I know you won't. You're my only family, Firian. I've always taken care of you."

Firian spat blood and saliva on Belik's boot.

"I could have let you die a dozen times," Belik continued, his blood turning hot, "but there's something—something!—I saw in you. If it weren't true, you'd be dead now."

Glaring, Firian stood up again. Wetness seeped into a larger circle on his shirt.

Why wouldn't Firian see reason? Why wouldn't he join him? Belik was not a forgiving man, but Firian had an olive branch in his face and was throwing it away. "Think it through!" he snapped. "You kill me, and then what? You aren't an idiot, but your gory stubbornness is going to get you killed. Don't be blind! If you kill me, you'll have two options—take my place or countermand the order. If you replace me, you'll have the responsibility for all those deaths on your head." *And that damn girl will never forgive you.*

Firian had killed a lot of people, but he wasn't used to it yet. He would feel the weight of the Keepers. Belik had dulled his conscience for the cause a long time ago.

"I'd be a better ruler than you," Firian snapped.

"You *are* me, Firian! Don't pretend you'd do anything differently. If you didn't rule like me—if you let the princess back on the throne with you—you'd destroy what Tanyu have fought for." He scoffed. "She won't forgive you. Stop living in a fantasy." Belik drew himself up. "Say you kill me. If you pretend like none of this ever happened, go back to the Academy, you'd give up all we've gained here. The Kingdom will put such a target on our backs that none of us will get out alive. You'll be a traitor either way."

Hesitation finally shone in Firian's eyes. His chest rose and fell more quickly. He'd hit a nerve.

"Or," Belik said, speaking more gently now, "you can come back. I'm your only ally. We've always had the same vision for the Academy."

A new expression, something vaguely defiant, crossed Firian's face. Belik cocked his head. *Not his only ally?* Was he thinking of Kiria, or...? "Bard's alive, is he?"

It made sense now. Firian's strength, his ability to escape the cell. He didn't look weakened at all. Rage pulsed through Belik at his own incompetence, but he swallowed it down. Firian didn't need to answer. The answer was written over every line of his body. *Gore!*

"I'm the only ally who can help you," Belik revised. "I'll let you take the lead. I'll take the fall for the Keepers. This is happening one way or another." He rubbed his glasses between fingers of his shirt. The action always calmed him. Replacing them on his nose, he looked straight at Firian, all in black, coiled as a spring. Belik's mind raced through all the tricks he knew. Even injured, if Firian chose to attack, another fight would be even. "You're either with the Tanyu or against them. You have to make a decision."

Belik had too many issues to deal with already. He couldn't have Firian Kess of all people running around, mucking up his plans. He felt the foolish urge to pray that he would see reason. Not Firian's strong suit.

Across the patterned floor of the Main, Firian never broke eye contact. But he was wavering.

It's not a difficult choice! Even in the throes of his *katah* with Chetana, Belik had never turned his back on the Academy. Not once.

He had to make the choice even easier, apparently. "If you don't join me, then run. Go home." This would only stall for time, but if Firian headed back toward the Academy, it would be easy to waylay him, to use forces still at the Academy to stop him instead of his forces here, which were already stretched thin until reinforcements arrived. As his mind whirled, he liked the plan more and more. "When I could tell you were still dallying with that girl on our way here, I switched out the Tanyu in charge of Raewhith."

That got a reaction. Just a blink and a skipped breath, but enough to see he'd gotten Firian's attention. Belik's over-caution had paid off.

"She likes me more than you and will do what I say. At my word, she'll look for your arrival and report to me. I've been in contact with her every other day. If she doesn't hear from me... well, I would hate for anything to happen to your sister. It takes two weeks to get over the mountains, doesn't it? But you could do it in ten days."

He met Firian's gaze. *Come with me.* For once, the strength of his will might not be enough to bring Firian back to his side. Belik wouldn't stoop to ask again.

Firian's eyes flashed. "I'm going after Kiria." The words came out clearly, decisively. In an instant, he disappeared.

Belik stood alone in the Unreal Main, filled with nothing but the vapor of rage and disappointment. To run was to choose.

Firian could have wiped his sins clean, but instead he turned his back on the Tanyu. He chose to be a traitor.

18

FIRIAN

FIRIAN SUCKED IN A BREATH, clutching the shoulder Belik had pierced in the Unreal. He yanked down the neck of his shirt to see how bad the injury was. The movement made him grimace in pain. The cut was bleeding freely down one side of his chest. *Gore...* This wasn't good. He glanced down at Bard, who sprawled on the grassy ground, mouth open. His skin looked ashy, even in the rain starting to fall from streaky clouds.

Firian crouched beside him and put a hand on Bard's chest. Very slightly, it rose and fell. Firian's lungs ached with relief.

He stilled his trembling hands. Belik had looked at him curiously when he asked about Bard. He had expected Firian to be weakened from Bard's death. That was when Firian knew that Kiria wasn't safe either. Despite the news that she had died, Belik had to know she was alive. Otherwise, the question wouldn't have been about Bard—an inconsequential player in Belik's eyes—but about Kiria. So he'd made the only decision he could. He'd bought her time.

But how much time? Tanyu would be out looking for him in force, thinking he was headed toward Kiria's location, but Firian had to go north to save Brett too. He pressed the heel of his hand to his forehead. There was too much. He had to get to his sister, had to save her, had to save them all.

Again and again, Belik's words played in a dizzying, relentless loop.
Bard's alive, is he?
I'm your only ally.
You have to make a decision.
And then what?

He could have killed Belik, ended it all there. His nose flared with the force of his breathing. Was it cowardice? Firian had never run from a fight before. Others could accuse him of starting fights but never running from them. Now this was the second time he had failed to kill Belik when he had the chance. What was wrong with him? Why couldn't he finish the gory traitor?

Thunder rumbled in the distance. The trees didn't offer good protection from the rain, and the dark clouds presaged storm. He had to get them under shelter.

He scanned the length of lawn leading back to the manor. It looked abandoned, but all large houses did. He smacked Bard on the arm without looking at him.

"Get up," he said, gripping Bard's bad arm.

Bard's body twisted, forehead furrowed. Whether it was from sleep or confusion, Firian couldn't tell.

"We're going in there. This will be it, the last time." *The last time you need to walk.* He forced the thoughts away again. They led nowhere he wanted to go.

Wavering and disoriented, Bard struggled to his hands and knees, and Firian pulled him the rest of the way to his feet.

With a nod, they limped unevenly together from the semi-shelter of the trees toward the manor. It didn't take long to find a trapdoor at the side of the house with stairs leading down to a cellar. Firian's chest constricted as they descended the steps. This felt too familiar. Living in darkness, picking the lock, helpless against the Sentry...

"Fir."

Bard's soft voice made Firian realize he had stopped on the stairs. He forced himself to go down the rest of the way into the deep brown darkness. Wood rot and cool, moist earth made the space smell inviting compared to the hole where Firian had been kept. There was also the bready tang of ale. He swallowed. He hadn't eaten anything since the hunk of meat in his cell. It felt like ages ago.

Though rain splattered through the open door onto the stairs, Firian didn't close the door until he could light a lantern bolted into the wall. He'd had enough of darkness for now. Later, he'd overcome his inhibitions, but now he wanted something to go right. No more darkness.

The soft lantern light glowed over warm wooden barrels. Some had spigots. Piles of other miscellany sat in corners. Leaning towers of crockery, half-hearted stacks of rough-cut firewood, trunks with lids propped open by the amount of fabric inside.

He opened one of the trunks and threw a few blankets on the floor behind him. He ripped one into strips and bound his aching shoulder, remembering the times Kiria had passed her sash across his body to bind the cut on his back. He should run, send the Tanyu off Kiria's scent, but fatigue had caught up to him, and he was well hidden. As he reinforced the exit door so he would be alerted if anyone tried to get inside, his muscles moved sluggishly. In this rainless space, closed off from the rest of the world, exhaustion hit him hard. His breaths became labored and his mind dizzy from lack of blood and sleep. He couldn't run tonight. After a short, reviving sleep, he would decide what do to.

Almost before Firian rolled up two pillows, Bard had fallen asleep again. Firian lowered himself onto the blanket near him, scooted forward so his face was under a barrel spigot, and took huge mouthfuls of ale. He savored its heady coolness on his tongue.

Casting his eyes to the corner, he spied a cup among the dishes. Tomorrow he would make Bard drink too.

Wiggling back onto the makeshift bed, he curled on his side. A deep ache filled him like water in a drowning man's lungs. He took deep, steadying breaths as he looked at Bard asleep in the lantern light, and thought of Kiria in danger in her own city but willing to give her life to protect it. He should have been angry, but he was too tired. His eyes grew hot as he fell headlong into sleep.

19

KIRIA

KIRIA WATCHED the sun set through a slim slit in the cloud cover. Only a moment, but she caught it. Rays of light shot through the falling rain, shining bright against each drop chasing down the windowpane. The beauty of it made her heart clench. And then it was gone, black as midnight. She swallowed. The light spoke of what they had all lost, and all they still had left to lose.

She stood in near darkness, in a storage warehouse in Grand Market Square, larger than the tannery, with her top remaining military leaders. Chetana had come too, but no other Amir had been able to leave the palace grounds. Her group had moved as soon as word came that Tanyu had already searched the nearby building.

It had been a hectic and terrifying afternoon of trusting her guards to keep her safe. In a fight, Tanyu had the upper hand, so, to avoid one, the guards hid her and the others, sometimes separating them for long minutes. The tannery had fallen under ordinary notice, because the sweeps of the city took in even the lowliest outbuilding. Some of her people fought back against the sudden invasion, but the scuffles didn't last long, from what she could see. Near misses and huddling in alleyways and garbage heaps, her guards' instruction and her insistence that the Tanyu would be thorough, perhaps could track her down by her mind alone...

A breathless hush stultified the room. No chairs had been set out. A wooden stool sat squat in the midst of them in case someone needed to lay out a document. In this murk, it would be hard to decipher text. The walls, made of wooden planking and dotted with lantern brackets, were suggestions in the shadows, along with systems of pulleys in the ceiling. All the inky corners made her uneasy. A Tanyu in black would have all the shelter he needed to surprise them.

All eyes were on her. She wore the fresh clothes they'd found in the safe house, and she'd put on her Beauty for this official meeting. Still, her nerves felt frazzled and her fingertips numb. Without other Keepers and their Amiran advisors, the meeting seemed incomplete, as though they couldn't begin until experts arrived. But as she scanned the mismatched group, the earnest faces hungry for hope, determination welled inside her.

"Thank you all for coming," she said, clearly but quietly. "Master Belik says he plans to be crowned tomorrow at the new moon. As soon as he is, it'll be more difficult to get to him. The Amir, the military, and the people will swear to serve him. Many will believe that he's sanctioned by God." She thought briefly about how most people thought that about her too, and yet there were dissidents, even against her reign. There was a sour kind of hope in that now. "We have to strike before he's crowned, before everyone is forced to swear loyalty to him."

"We will not, while you live," said Lanthe, a Khelê military commander who, despite Belik's offer of wealth, had ordered her troops to fight back once they discovered the palace was under attack. Tanyu had killed almost all of the soldiers under her command before she changed tack and went to find any Keeper who remained alive.

Others, like Royce, the large blond guard with a square jaw who had helped Kiria since the safe house, joined in with agreement.

A wry smile rose on Kiria's lips. "Thank you. I don't doubt your loyalty. During the coronation, his security will no doubt be increased, but it will all be centered around him. We need to strike where he doesn't expect us if we're to have any hope of success." There was little hope to begin with, but a surprise attack could accomplish what they needed. The loyalty of a few talented soldiers might end this crisis. Doubt gnawed at her, as sickly as a disease, but they had to do something even if hope was slim.

She ran through the ideas she'd formulated in the hours leading up to the meeting. Everything Daelon and Firian had taught her, every game of Indisfate, everything she had learned about the Tanyu fed into her plan.

"On the night of the coronation, we'll send in an assassin, someone who can kill Master Belik from afar. Our best archer. As a precaution, soldiers in plain clothes will go posing as the audience. There's a cache of emergency weapons in the Main. The soldiers can use those if it comes to it."

The weak light from nearby buildings drew a slash across the blond guard's face as he shifted his weight. He held his helmet under his arm. "Excuse me, My Keeper, but what guarantee do we have that the Tanyu have not already confiscated those weapons?"

"We have no guarantees." The unbidden image of Firian floated before her mind, followed by the litany of those she had lost. The too-recent horror threatened to choke her.

She threw back her shoulders and looked at Jori to ground herself. He held one elbow in his other hand, abnormally uncomfortable. Before, he had never relished political or military meetings. Now, he had nowhere else to go and had to face the invasion head on. He returned her gaze with almost a pleading look.

She shifted her attention to Chetana. She needed allies, but, with each inspection of the room, she felt a little bolstered and still very alone. These people would do her bidding, even unto death, but who was there to tell her it would be all right? Who would hold her hand and give her strength? Take some of the terrible weight of responsibility that never should have fallen on her back alone?

"Then some of us should bring weapons to the coronation," the tattooed guard resumed. Kiria still hadn't caught his name. She'd have to ask later.

"You'll be searched," growled Royce. Always like an older dog with a young pup, those two.

"Yes," Kiria admitted. "Probably, but we'll arrive early, act natural. Our soldiers can take up the entire audience, leaving other citizens who come to watch unable to get in and having to watch from afar, if that's possible. If we take up all the space closest to Master Belik, any other audience members can be clear of the fighting."

"That sounds risky." As time had gone on, the tattooed guard spoke up more often, despite frequent looks of consternation from Royce.

"It is..." she agreed, waiting for his name.

"Viktor." He stepped a little closer so she could see him better. Viktor was the youngest among the guards. One half of his face was covered in a Khelê tattoo, this one an oversized *laird* flower, the symbol of peace.

"Viktor. But so is any plan that has our troops intentionally going into a Tanyu-occupied area."

"But what about the Tanyu on the grounds?" Lanthe asked. "We don't know how many there are."

"That's true," Kiria admitted. "Is there... Do you think that more of our own soldiers will join the Tanyu in resisting us?" The suggestion sent shivers spidering down her body. Could the dissent against her reign run that deep? If the conversation she had overheard meant anything, it did in some circles. This attack, at least, would demonstrate that she had done nothing to encourage this overthrow, the death of her friends... Again, bone-deep loneliness rose up to drown her as surely as the blank eternity of the Unreal.

Lanthe swallowed, the muscles in her bone-white neck tightening. "I think it's more likely that they won't engage."

"And wait to see who wins so they know who to support?" Chetana asked, disgusted. "Has anyone consulted the Amir about where their loyalty should lie?"

An awkward pause followed. Were the Amir even alive to consult? The air felt chilly around them. Rumors suggested they were alive. That had to be enough for now.

Kiria cleared her voice. "So the priority will be to kill only Master Belik."

"What about the Tanyuin Head?"

A lump of unexpected emotion rose to her throat. "Firian Kess is dead. Killed in the fighting. Master Belik has taken his place."

"But..." One of the commanders, a man with a lined face, looked skeptical, and even touched the stool in the center of the circle with his fingertips. "What about the Academy raid?" He spoke as though Firian were unkillable.

But no one was unkillable.

Kiria shook the hair out of her face. "He was dangerous, but someone managed to kill him." She wouldn't go into detail about his last day. "He's not a... a factor anymore." Thinking about his death made her deeply angry—at him, at the situation, and especially at Master Belik.

She wanted to scream, to be safe, to be alone, but she returned to the plan. Her words came out more labored, like a cart that had gotten something stuck in the wheel and had to work it free. "At the beginning of the ceremony, on Petra's signal, you'll form a unit and move in formation toward Master Belik."

"Do we know where he'll be located?" asked Lanthe.

"No, he could be in the Main. He could be on the lawn or on a balcony. We'll no doubt learn right before the ceremony begins, so we won't have time to adjust our plans. We'll have to be prepared for a variety of scenarios. My guess is that he'll do it in the Main. Regardless of the location, form up tightly enough that no one can get inside. The Tanyu's only options will be to attack from the side or from above."

Lanthe cast a quick glance to the general beside her. *Above?* her eyes seemed to say.

"Some of you will bring shields and weapons concealed in your cloaks, things that wouldn't immediately spark suspicion."

Viktor frowned, stretching the *laird* flower almost comically. Others shared his confusion.

"Like cooking tools, or farmer's supplies," Kiria supplied.

Jori's face twitched, though it was difficult to tell if it was from amusement, pride, or skepticism. The result was a dark, sardonic smirk.

"I know what it sounds like. But at least that way our soldiers won't be entirely weaponless in case of the worst." She banished the image of the guards lying dead outside her door. "We'll hope the weapons cache is untouched," she continued. "Use shield for above and weapons for the side. Even Tanyu can't break through that." *I think...* She did her best to be confident.

Bard's story about Firian's ability to kill people without touching them sliced through her thoughts. Could others do that too? She'd never heard of such a thing with anyone else. "Once you've killed Master Belik and gained a position of strategic advantage, announce your allegiance to me and the Keeper Lines."

The plan sounded simple enough. Too simple, in fact, but maybe that was the strength of it. The coronation was their best chance, with Master Belik on full display and the Tanyu coming out of the shadows to support him.

"Won't they be suspicious?" asked the skeptical commander. "We won't come across as a civilian crowd. There will be no children, no elderly."

Kiria chewed her lip. "We can't risk civilian lives in this."

"Of course not."

"Looks like it'll be cold tomorrow," Viktor piped up. "That'll give our troops an excuse to wear cloaks big enough to hide their features."

Kiria smiled at his support. "Thank you. I think this could work. We need to strike quickly, before they feel balanced, and before the people of Brithnem give up on us." *On me.*

20

FIRIAN

FIRIAN SUPPRESSED a groan as he woke. His whole body felt sore. The lantern had gone out during the night, leaving the cellar in darkness. A freshness in the air and light seeping down the steps said that it was already morning. How long had he slept?

He rolled to his knees and lit a lantern hanging from the wall for better light to inspect Bard lying beside him. Bard lay on his back with his mouth wide open. The angle of the rolled-up pillow tilted his head to the side. Some color had returned to his face. When he woke, would he be lucid? Would he be able to move his arm? Would he remember anything from the past few days?

Something pressed on the hollow of Firian's throat when he considered that Bard might not remember their reconciliation. Maybe he would wake up and call Firian a monster again, blame him for all this carnage, afraid and angry when he realized the two of them were alone.

The comfort of the musty cellar closed in around him. The feeling of safety had been a lie. Only exhaustion had convinced him otherwise. Whoever owned the house could come in at any moment and catch them sleeping. Thunderstorms usually didn't put Firian to sleep; they kept him awake. But he'd obviously slept for hours without waking once. That meant he had only nine days to get to Brett before Belik would make good on his threat. He had to leave as soon as he knew Bard and Kiria were safe.

Settling back on his heels, Firian eased into the Unreal. It felt true, almost cleansing. He'd spent almost no time there the past few days, and his mind was in need of space.

He hadn't seen Kiria, either in the Unreal or the Real, since the night he'd let her go back to the palace. His jaw tightened uncomfortably at the memory.

He deserved her opinion of him, since he just let her go on the run without helping her. But what more could he have done?

It was different now, as though more than just a few days had passed. Had his ruse worked to keep her safe? Now that the initial adrenaline had tempered down to uneasy embers, he cursed the feebleness of his plan. It was stupid. But hopefully it bought Kiria a few hours.

He had to check on her. It didn't matter if she woke and cursed him. At least he'd know she still breathed, still fought. All that life couldn't be snuffed as easily as someone lesser. Only his intimate knowledge of death allowed him even to consider the possibility, and it chilled him like sickness.

He reached toward her, mindlessly creating a wooded road around himself, morning sun casting shadows like black pillars across the path.

Through the trees, she appeared, fully dressed, fully aware of him.

Astonishment and relief made his breath halt. She was all right! She was here! His eyelids fluttered as though he'd forgotten to blink, and his hand ran through his hair to smooth it down. He knew the gestures were inane even as he did them, but his body felt foreign with surprise. When he'd let her go, he'd felt the pang of loss, assuming he wouldn't see her again. Yet here they were again, and she had never been awake before he was. The thought teased a trace of joy from him. Then he noticed her expression.

She stared at him as if he were a ghost, a fierce line drawn between her brows. One arm moved across her torso with an unconscious air of protection. Her eyes were fire, shock lighting their amber depths. "Firian?" she breathed, hardly audible. "I thought you…"

His words wouldn't come. She looked at him with intensity that stole his breath. The furious question in her gaze made him pause. Was she that surprised to see him here? Did she think he had died in the fighting?

As he looked at her, memories assaulted him—memories of her, distraught and angry as he kissed her. Memories of her glee when she beat him at Indisfate, or the way they held each other so desperately after he beat the Torithians, or her presence when she saw Brett and his mother for the first time in so many years, or when she pushed him away after his success at Archer's Point.

And now.

Now the recent past was hot between them, true and painful like a room ablaze. Like the palace.

"You're all right," he said, relief evident in his voice.

Lines fanned from her eyes, denying his statement. After all that had happened, none of them were really all right.

Because Tanyu had taken over Brithnem. His Tanyu. They'd killed the other Keepers.

"Did you do this?" Her voice was a hush; her body trembled down to her closed fists. The next time was a ragged shout, wet with emotion. "Did you do this?"

"No!"

Fearless, she charged him, snarling, eyes red. He didn't step back as she struck him hard in the chest. She glared inches from his face. "Where were you?"

Firian's face flushed hot with frustration and guilt. He should have been there to help her, but how could she think he had caused such horror, killed people she cared about? "Master Belik—I told him to leave and he refused. He took control of the Tanyu and... you saw what he did." There was no time for a full explanation.

"Are you with him now?"

"No," he cried, losing patience. "I'm not with him. I told you." The hurt and disbelief in her eyes were hard to look at, but he held her gaze. Low in his gut, urgency lurked. Words that needed to be spoken. But the most urgent was her safety. "Are you someplace safe?"

Her silence was frosty. She stepped away. "If you're trying to get our plans—"

"No," he repeated.

She wasn't safe inside the city walls. Belik would find her, and he would kill her. Judging from her demeanor now, she was still relatively secure, probably surrounded by guards. Otherwise she wouldn't be here talking to him. There was still time.

His breaths came sharp and quick. "You have to get out of the city."

Air puffed from her lips in a sneer, her eyes full of pain. "My people need me. I won't run at your suggestion."

"But you—"

"Remember that question you asked me?"

There had been many questions, but yes, he knew the one she meant. *Am I a monster?*

She let the silence draw out in the air between them. Answer enough. Every second dug into his gut.

"Okay," he finally said, his lip curling. He could deal with that later. Right now, Belik was stalking Kiria. This wasn't a game. Even Firian's pride had to halt for a moment. "Kiria, I'm serious. You have to get out. Belik knows you're alive."

She retained her new composure. "I'm not surprised," she said. "We've been telling the people."

"Kiria."

"They have to have hope!" A wild tinge of red came back into her eyes. Her chest rose and fell, heavy with emotion. Her voice quieted. "I need hope."

A confession.

An accusation.

So do I. "I didn't want this to happen," he said gently.

"That's why you brought your troops here," she said, deadpan. Her eyebrows rose.

He opened his mouth, closed it again.

"Unless that was only to blackmail me into being with you."

A muscle ticked in his jaw. Everyone he cared about was slipping away from him across a chasm he couldn't breach. He couldn't take much more. "Just... get out. He will kill you." He was surprised by his own breathlessness.

Her nostrils flared, sad but defiant. "He's the one who should be afraid. And you, if you come here."

She doesn't understand. He wanted to drag her out of the city himself, take her somewhere safe, turn back time... His fingers twitched but he held himself back. Taking her anywhere in the Unreal wouldn't accomplish his purpose.

"I..."

But she didn't want his help. He'd have to find some other way to coax her out of harm's way.

Out of options, the truest statement came out, bald and obvious. "I don't want you to die."

She gave him a curious look at that, her red eyes searching. Accusation and vulnerability at once. There was a breath of hesitation as her face cycled through myriad emotions. Maybe she would start crying. The look was hauntingly similar to the one she'd given him before running out of the farmhouse.

"I don't either," she finally said, the words quiet and almost confused. But then her expression cleared like the sky. "And we won't."

Before he could speak again, she disappeared.

We? She didn't mean the two of them. They would never be *we* again to her. She meant others. Who else had escaped? Maybe Jori had caught up with her. He was still alive when Firian had left him. The thought gave him a modicum of comfort. Kiria wasn't alone. At least, not completely.

After taking a moment to recover from the conversation, he came back to reality. He dug the palms of his hands into his eyes. His jaw was getting sore from grinding his teeth. She *had* to get out. How did she not see the danger she was in? Cúron and Atael had been killed by Tanyu. She had to see the risk. And yet, she didn't go. Even as he felt sick with worry, he was proud of her. Stubborn bastard that he was, he wouldn't have left either.

"F'r?"

He turned. Bard was sitting up.

Lightheadedness swept through Firian. Bard was sitting up on his own. Did he hate him too?

In hindsight, he realized that he should have told Kiria that Bard was with him. Maybe that would have proven his sincerity.

"What happened to your shirt?" Bard made a sound that might have been a laugh, but it sent him into a coughing fit. He leaned forward, bending almost in half with the force of his wheezing.

Firian rose to his feet and shoved a mug under a spigot. Dark brown ale sloshed and foamed into it. When the mug was half-full, he set the cup in Bard's hands. Only the right one curled around the handle. His stubborn left arm hung limp at his side. Still, seeing his friend conscious was a relief, and a welcome respite from the pain of seeing Kiria.

His mouth quirked up when Bard began to drink. He was okay. He was okay.

After a long moment, Bard lowered the mug again. He winced with his last swallow. "Where are we?"

"Some big house."

Bard's eyebrows drew downward. "I don't..." His half-finished sentence sounded husky, his voice creaky with disuse.

"Master Belik attacked you. But you're all right."

His face twitched a few times, as though he were trying out different movements. "I thought that was... a dream or something." As he said it, memories seemed to return. He stretched out his stiff thumb with his other hand. "Where's Kiria?"

"Inside the city somewhere."

"Are we not?"

Firian shook his head. "Just outside." After a pause, he added, "She needs to get out. Belik is looking for her too. It won't take him very long to find her."

Bard set down the mug, looking around as though seeing the room for the first time. He squinted, smacked his lips. Firian tensed, waiting for Bard's recognition that this was all wrong. The information seemed to take a long time to sink in. Bard's eyes grew large again. "My hand."

"I know," Firian said quickly. "You can move it. It's just hard." Crawling forward, Firian rubbed Bard's left arm. It had gone clammy again. "Here. Try."

The thumb twitched, more a tiny muscle spasm than a controlled movement. "See? You're fine."

Bard set his mouth in a line that silently disagreed. He stared at his hand for a while, his fingers making miniscule movements. A trickle of sweat beaded down his temple. When Bard's dark eyes met Firian's again, they were sharper than before. "What happened?"

The question held new weight. Behind it, Firian heard all the warnings from their time as roommates. *Don't do that or they'll kick you out.*

What was Firian's role in all of this? That was what Bard really wanted to know.

Honestly, Firian wasn't sure how to answer. He'd been so intent on stopping Belik that he hadn't asked himself how much of this was his own fault. Bard's gaze made him ask himself the question. He hated the uncertainty of the answer. He was the Tanyuin Head. Some of this destruction had to be his fault. He'd been spineless, foolish, weak. His nose flared at the thought of the last word. He worked so hard—*so hard*—not to be weak. His whole life was dedicated to it. Yet here he was. In a basement with one other renegade Tanyu while Belik stole his authority and threatened Kiria.

"I don't know," Firian said quietly.

Bard seemed to read the sincerity in his voice, and nodded. The two sat in silence a long time.

Firian's stomach felt hollow and his blistered feet ached. He hadn't noticed before. He also didn't remember taking his boots off, but he must have done so in the night. He flexed his toes.

Bard took another slow swig of ale. When he lowered the mug, his gaze flickered between Firian and his own useless hand.

Firian wasn't good with words. Nothing he had said to Bard, Kiria, or Belik had made anything better. With those three, he couldn't hide behind prepared lines and a sense of mysterious power. Of everyone in this world, those were the people who knew him best. He had no clue what to say to Bard, but something had to be said. The interior pressure made his empty stomach roil.

"Why were you here in Brithnem?" he finally asked in an undertone.

Bard blinked. "I had to stop you. But I... I didn't want you killed."

So you went to Kiria. Firian nodded, feeling oddly numb. The anger that he normally held so close didn't come to him now. It felt right to speak the truth. No more lies or posturing.

"I didn't want you to leave," Firian confessed. This cellar full of ale and junk had transformed into a space where there were no consequences for truth.

The only other time he'd felt this way was when he had talked to Brett in the room they'd shared when he was very young, maybe six. He hadn't thought about those times in years. After a particularly bad day, he or Brett could call a night meeting if they couldn't sleep. They'd wake up together and sit cross-legged on the floor and talk until they felt better. After the initial misery had worn off, they usually tried to make each other laugh. Silent fits of giggling meant that the night meeting was over and they could go back to sleep.

"Yeah, I figured," Bard said, echoing the words he'd said that day just before he abandoned the Academy.

Another bout of silence fell over them. A breeze tickled through the shredded back of Firian's shirt. Were these really the same clothes he was wearing when he met Kiria, and then carried Bard to safety? Maybe Bard was right to laugh.

"I saw you try to save her. That was stupid, you know." Firian smirked at him, proud.

Bard smiled back and coughed. "I know. Didn't get very far." His face fell again. His finger ran along the side of the tankard, and then he looked up as though realizing something. "You saw that?"

Firian shrugged. The word tugging at him now had so long smacked of weakness. Tanyu didn't get involved in an unintentional *katah*. He already had one with Kiria, but the evidence was overwhelming—he had two.

"Huh," Bard said, coming to his own conclusion, inevitably the same one. It was that uncanny ability he had to read Firian's mind, to know him almost better than he knew himself. "So you're going after Belik now." The statement held a question beneath it. *Where does that put me?*

"Yeah," Firian answered, standing and opening the chest full of fabrics. The new knife wound twinged under the bandage. He would just have to attack Belik from a different angle as he headed back to Raewhith and figured out allies that Kiria could trust to help her. "I have to. I mean, I ordered the Tanyu to stand down."

Bard's mouth quirked.

"Belik ordered the attack anyway. He killed... You were there." He looked away and exchanged his ravaged Tanyuin shirt for a new one from the chest.

"Would you have done it?" Bard angled his head with an evaluating gaze.

"Not all that," Firian said lamely.

"You would have burned the fields, yeah?" Bard murmured into his mug as he took another sip. There was a new fearlessness in Bard that took Firian by surprise. His boldness had grown back at the Academy, but it seemed to have solidified into a permanent aspect of his personality. He was still Bard—still cautious, still attentive—but now his strength of conviction was rising to the surface. He wasn't afraid of consequences anymore, not as he had been.

"Yeah," Firian admitted. "Maybe."

"But there was something with Kiria, I think."

Bold indeed. "Yes," he said carefully. He didn't want to think about it. What he thought was a mercy had made her distraught. So he'd changed course, gone against his impulses, and released her. The right thing, the good thing, Bard would say, and yet Firian felt like shit whenever the memory surfaced.

The night meeting had hit a wall.

"If I was in the palace..." Bard began. A sudden gasp sent him into a violent fit of coughing. He had to set down his mostly empty mug of ale to keep it from sloshing in his hand. The dead arm looked pointedly immobile when the rest of him was moving.

Firian waited until the fit passed. "I got you out," he explained, answering the unspoken question. A sharp smile twisted his lips. "That's how my shirt got all..." He gave a dismissive gesture.

Bard's black eyes sparkled, even though he still looked confused. "There was a doctor, though. I think."

"It's... There's more, but I did get you out of the palace."

Bard flexed his bad hand slowly. It had loosened somewhat, but it still looked like he was squeezing some tough, invisible object. "We need to figure out who's still on your side."

"I can't stay long, though. Belik said he'd... hurt my sister Brett. Remember her? I've got to leave." Belik's control bound him as surely as ropes. He cast a glance at the cellar trapdoor. Even this conversation was costing him valuable time.

"Once you gather support, then what are you going to do?" Bard asked. "You're not just going to kill Belik and that's it, yeah?" The implication hung in the air. *You could have done that already.*

"I don't know," Firian muttered.

"You do know," he said, not lifting his eyes from his own struggling fingers. "Kiria should be in charge." His gaze flicked up and then down again, not sheepishly, but pointedly. Her name sounded strange coming out of his mouth. He didn't even add "Lady" or "Keeper."

Firian froze. Admitting it would make it real. The same idea had crept into his thoughts, more and more frequently, coloring the choices he made, but he never looked at it straight on. It stayed in the periphery. He wasn't sure he was ready to turn his head and agree.

Did it really come down to this—him *or* Kiria? The question almost made him huff in impatience. Of course it was either him or Kiria. It would never be the two of them together.

But Kiria didn't trust him, didn't want his help, not after all he had done. He'd opened the door for Belik to kill the other leaders—not deliberately, but Kiria didn't see it that way.

He stayed silent. When he focused again on Bard, they gave each other a painful, knowing look. Firian's chest constricted. *I'd improve our defenses and alliances... and do my best to make peace... People will protect something they love...* He pictured the rioting and slander she had endured because of her alliance with him. The way she had defended him when no one else in Brithnem took his side.

The way she played like a sorceress to his better nature, taking what was hardened with fear and anger, and enticing him toward choosing good.

If you don't love me, why did you come?

Because I love them.

Bard was right. Something inside him struggled against it like a wild animal, but Bard was right.

He had to get Kiria, just Kiria, back on the throne.

21

FIRIAN

Firian nodded, dropping hard on his tailbone beside the chest of fabrics to steady himself. Words wouldn't come. That nod, that agreement, meant losing some of his identity—giving up a dream of power instead of feeding it.

Creases formed at the corners of Bard's mouth. Was that pride in his eyes?

Firian cleared his throat. "You can't travel very far, can you? Not very fast?" The words sounded empty and obvious, but it was something safe to say.

"Probably not." He shrugged apologetically.

"Then... maybe we'll figure out where Kiria is—I can find her—and you can communicate with the Tanyu for her." Kiria had mastered certain elements of the Unreal, but, as far as he knew, she had only met with him and couldn't communicate well with anyone else there. She would need a more experienced Tanyu at her side. She already trusted Bard—far more than she trusted him, at least—so maybe she would accept his help.

"Yeah," Bard replied. "Yeah, that's good." He stretched his fingers back with his other hand.

Firian would head to Raewhith and then the Academy, pick up anyone left there and in the surrounding cities, and head back down to the capital. On the way, he would communicate with the Tanyu and figure out whose side they were on. Without Bard, he could move much more quickly. With the urgency he felt, he could bring an entire force down to the Brithnem in just over three weeks. Hopefully before it was too late. Between new troops and Tanyu still loyal to Firian, they might have victory.

He would, he realized, have to tell his allies that they were fighting for Kiria. How many would abandon him?

"Fir, you're serious?" Bard wasn't just talking about having him work with Kiria. He meant conceding the throne.

In the corner of Firian's consciousness, a buzz sounded, another mind that wasn't Bard's. He sat up straighter, motioning for Bard to stay quiet. Bard's look of surprise soon gave way to understanding. He sensed it too.

There was definitely a Tanyu outside—maybe one who believed Firian's ruse that he was going after Kiria.

Firian hauled his boots back on, gritting his teeth against the searing pain. With another warning look at his friend, he opened and closed his hand, indicating that Bard should do the same. Bard needed to flex that hand if he ever hoped to use it normally again.

The pocket at the side of his boot was empty. No knife. He scanned the room, chose another tankard, and broke it. Bard cringed at the noise, but now Firian had a weapon. It was just a jagged handle, but it could do damage if necessary.

Something stilled in Firian before he jumped to his feet. This person was a Tanyu. One of his. He closed his palm more tightly over the curved handle, hoping he didn't have to use it. Better this than his killing ability, though.

Carefully, Firian snuck out of the cellar to meet their pursuer. The air was fresher outside, with the cool bite of afterstorm. The lawn grass looked greener, as though a layer of dust had washed away.

Firian's boots tread silently over the thick grass as he angled toward the other mind. Back toward the ocean, toward the front of the house. That was where he felt it most strongly. His stare skipped over the mansion's windows, the trees—anywhere a hidden person could be watching him.

The Tanyu wouldn't have gone inside the house if they could help it. Still, Firian avoided the view of the window in case the owners were home.

Down the embankment toward the sea? Firian ran swiftly toward the door in the low wall that opened onto steps leading down to the beach.

The little door slammed back against him.

As he'd expected.

He backed up and shouldered into it again, sending the unknown assailant tumbling backward before leaping again to their feet with a hissed "*yabesh!*"—a Charäkhni curse. Firian slipped through the opening to see who it was.

Tesni, the girl who had lived on the opposite hall. She had tan skin and dark reddish hair pulled back in a sleek braid. Her cheeks were flushed with exertion, as though she had run far before encountering Firian. Dirt smudged her black Tanyuin outfit. She didn't wear the long coat—better for tracking.

He held out an appeasing hand, the one without the jagged piece of pottery. "Tesni," he whispered.

She regarded him warily, a knife in her hand. Her gaze expertly scanned him from head to foot, snagging on the broken handle in his grip. But she didn't advance, didn't attack. Maybe she was thinking about the way he could kill her without a word or a movement.

"Master Kess," she replied.

"You were sent to follow me."

She didn't deny it. "Just to follow."

Did Tesni think that Kiria was here? Was it worth trying to keep up the charade a little longer for Kiria's sake? He decided not to mention it, to let Tesni draw her own conclusions. "Tesni..." He was hardly sure what to say. "I didn't give the order to kill the Keepers."

She betrayed little surprise. "No?"

"No. Master Belik acted on his own. I never betrayed the Tanyu. You know I wouldn't." Saying the words felt like drawing poison out of a wound. Grueling, painful, but cleansing. A relief.

She scrutinized him. "Then come back," she said finally. There was a question in her eyes, a genuine request.

Her look made a small flame of hope leap in his chest. "Not yet. The Tanyu are split. Belik has enough support that he'd go after me. And I have things to do."

"What do you need from me?"

Firian let out a breath, almost a sigh, and relaxed his stance. Tesni lowered her knife. "I need you to see who's still loyal to me. I am still the Tanyuin Head, but Belik's lies..."

Tesni nodded once, a soldier in his army. "You'll kill him for insurrection."

Firian paused. Yes, he did want to do that. But if so, why not simply order it now? Belik's words echoed in his mind—*what then?* He needed time to think. Killing Belik to offer Kiria the Kingdom would mean exposing the Academy to punishment or extermination.

"Eventually," he replied. When Tesni's eyes narrowed, he added, "Leave him to me."

She lowered her head at that, apparently understanding, though Firian wasn't sure he understood himself.

FIRIAN'S NEW REVELATIONS—AND probably the fact that he'd only had ale to drink in the last many hours—made him dizzy. If it had to be either him or Kiria on the throne, then she deserved to rule Brithnem more than he did. The truth itched, like a fine shirt against skin that wasn't used to finery.

He'd spoken no more than a few words to the Defender, but they were in accord that they had to stop Belik. She would be a valuable ally inside the walls while he rushed back to Raewhith to protect Brett and gather reinforcements, in case a few loyal Tanyu near Belik weren't enough. They had to be. A well-timed strike could end Master Belik. Kiria just had to be poised to take advantage of the opening.

That was where Bard came in.

Tesni had gone back to the palace, drawing Tanyuin eyes elsewhere while Firian reached out to other potential allies.

Soon, he'd take Bard to find Kiria, but the idea of treading carefully around Tanyuin minds while sneaking Bard back inside the walls sounded too precarious.

One thing at a time: allies, Kiria, Brett.

A plan was already forming when he ducked back into the cellar to find Bard leaning against one of the ale casks, half-asleep. His friend had gotten better, more aware, since Firian had brought him here, but the heavy way he slumped against the wooden barrel showed he wasn't fully recovered. Bard's hand, still claw-shaped, lay in his lap. The mug sat by his other side.

Only when Firian got closer did he stir. A few rapid blinks later as though his eyes needed to refocus, Bard asked, "Who was it?"

"Tesni."

Bard's eyes grew bright with the obvious question. *For or against?*

"She wants to help me."

Settling cross-legged across from Bard, Firian drew in a few breaths. It had been too long since he'd had the luxury of entering the Unreal like this, seated, fully focused. Mostly focused, at least.

Less than two weeks to get to Brett, but if all went to plan, Belik would be taken care of by then. No war. Just one quick battle.

Firian closed his eyes.

Master Makai first. The deep-voiced Tanyuin Master who'd led him to the Academy the first time seemed like a good place to start. Firian knew he'd been asking about him, at least, and they'd never had issues with each other.

Firian recreated the gray stone room of the Head's office in the Academy, and called to Makai. The man appeared almost instantly, the consummate professional, dressed in the customary long black jacket, which swayed around his booted feet.

"Master Kess," he greeted. The last syllable rose slightly, betraying his surprise.

Firian stood behind the desk he knew so well. Fragments of flags from Raewhith, Imlin, and Archer's Point festooned the front. Though urgency sang in his blood, he felt at home too. On his brow sat the metal circlet of the Tanyuin Head. Where was the real thing now?

"Master Belik defied my orders not to attack the capital," he began. "He committed treason against the Tanyu and against the Western Kingdom. I need to know whose side you're on."

Lines of concern scored Makai's dark brow. "Treason?"

"I chose you because you can see how horrible his actions are. I will stop Belik with or without you. Are you with me?"

Fractional hesitation.

Blood began to rise to Firian's face.

"If you'll take back the crown, I'm with you."

Neither Makai nor Tesni knew that it wouldn't be himself on the throne, but Kiria. Firian kept his secret for now. All he needed was enough allies to win a battle against Master Belik. He could deal with the fallout later.

Firian released a breath. "I thought so," he said approvingly. "Tell no one. Meet me in the Unreal in seven days, at sunrise. I'll gather others, and we'll end this."

Not everyone was as anxious to join Firian's cause without asking more questions. Firian didn't tell doubters about the meeting. He couldn't afford a greater risk of weak links.

In the next two hours, he found twenty Tanyu who overtly sided with him. Under normal circumstances, that would be more than enough. But Belik had beaten Firian head-to-head plenty of times, both in the Real and Unreal. The memories tasted bitter.

All that would change in seven days, when Tanyu loyal to Firian would attack Belik together in the Unreal. Seven days sounded like a long time to wait, but he couldn't guarantee Brett's safety any sooner. In seven days, he would be about two days from Raewhith, closer if he were lucky. The Tanyu waiting for Belik's response wouldn't get it, and Firian needed to be able to reach his sister before that person decided to take action against her. Seven days was risky, but it could work. In one week, Belik would be dead.

22

BELIK

AMIR PAROHIM CUT a nervous glance to Belik. The two of them stood together on the raised dais, dressed in finery, looking out over the remnants of the Main. The watered-down smell of smoke scratched against Belik's lungs, but at least a cool breeze whispered through the broken panes of glass. Metal lines arched through the empty spaces like winter trees. Charred remnants of Brithnem flags still hung high above by the ceiling.

The fire hadn't brought down the enormous statues of the founders either, but smoke had discolored them.

Sickly orange and dark gray settled into the grooves of the Scroll passage etched along the ceiling, enhancing the words. Belik pursed his mouth to look at them.

Ash—the burned remains of three thrones—had coated the floor until Belik ordered some of the remaining palace servants to clean it up. Most of the servants had survived the coup, and with Amir performing some of the least savory duties, there had been plenty of help for menial tasks. The room had to look splendid. Those Brithnem people liked pomp. This was just the sort of thing they'd lap up like dogs.

Belik was never going to be crowned at the new moon. Of course, it was important that all the citizens and the Amir thought so.

Tomorrow, Dedication Day, was a much better choice, more symbolically significant in the minds of the people, and a day when most of the city fasted, and would be less likely to fight back.

Today, the new moon would teach the people to fear. It was a temporary but necessary measure, to make sure the rebel faction of the military was killed or cowed.

A chair, salvaged from the wreckage, sat on the dais. Only one, not two. Belik looked at it almost mournfully.

Fury built in his chest. A *katah*, again. Firian really was like him. Except he was younger and stupider. Headstrong, with even more on the line. Tanyu were on the cusp of ruling the entire Western Kingdom, and Firian would rather be on the run.

Belik's mouth felt sandy. He fought the urge to spit.

Shiro jogged toward him, stopped, and stood smartly. "Shall I let them in, Master Belik?"

"Yes."

"As you would have it."

The huge double doors opened immediately and hundreds of citizens filed in. Belik scanned the ranks hungrily. No children. No elderly. Many wearing oversized cloaks. He almost laughed—would have, if it hadn't been so insulting. With Kiria and possibly Kader still alive, he expected some clique of the army to retaliate against his rule, but this was childish.

Warriors manned the entrances, searching all the visitors before they could enter, but they'd clearly allowed the people to bring personal items with them, even incongruous ones. Tanyu should know better than anyone that harvest flails or coin purses or even baskets could be used as weapons. Perhaps they thought these people too weak to use them well. It was unwise to discount an enemy, no matter how predictable.

A flicker of movement caught his attention. Turning, he saw more spectators outside the broken windows. *A little better,* he admitted. It would be more challenging to contain them all out there as it would be in here.

The flaming lanterns and booted feet shuffling across marble floors made the only sounds. Too late, he considered music. Eh, he'd already bowed enough to their delicate sensibilities. Silence was where a Tanyu lived.

Parohim seemed disturbed by it, though. His slicked-back hair was practically quivering with tension.

Belik leveled him a glance. The Amir would go through with this. He'd watched as Reynard, advisor to Atael Calthwaite, died instantly at Belik's command. Visible fear had stuck to Parohim like sap ever since, binding him to Belik's will until it dulled, which could take years if Belik kept giving him reasons for terror.

Parohim blinked long and steadyingly in reply. He could have been praying. Always God, always the Scroll, with these people. As long as the Amir planned to crown him, Belik didn't care how Parohim felt.

One more scan of the room assured him that the princess hadn't come herself, just sent her cronies to deal with him. A twinge of disappointment tugged at him but it dissipated quickly. Of course she didn't come herself. She'd have been a fool if she had. Kiria was naïve, but based on the way she was able to manipulate Firian so thoroughly, she wasn't a fool.

Once everyone had filed in, the people quieted, looking up at the dais with anticipation. Belik watched a line of sweat form at Amir Parohim's temple. Searing silence cut through the room like a dare.

Belik had Tanyu stationed along the walls, in front of the dais, around the building, in the hallways—all with strict orders to kill any Brithnem soldier they saw who didn't wear a sign of Tanyuin loyalty: a simple scrap of black cloth pinned at the neck of the uniform. Hesitation had flared in some of the warriors' eyes. Tanyu could be brutal, but this was a higher level of brutality than usual. These younger Defenders were largely untested in anything except rigorous drills, so Belik had made it known that disloyalty would come with harsh consequences.

Firian flashed through his mind again, staring at him with murder in his eyes from behind those rusted iron bars. It would have been cleaner to kill him, make him an example and start fresh. But he couldn't. Even now, he knew he wouldn't do it himself. Taking over the Academy and then the Kingdom hadn't initially been Belik's plan, but Firian was so perfectly placed to do just that that the temptation had been too much to resist. And why should they resist it? A more perfect opportunity would take another twenty years to materialize, and he'd done his share of waiting.

Belik nodded at the Amir beside him, prompting him to speak.

"Welcome," Parohim said, with a volume that sounded hollow in the large space. He wrung his hands.

Shifting from the audience. Hands reaching under cloaks.

"This is a... momentous day for Brithnem. Thank you all for coming." His eyes flickered up to the smoke-damaged words along the ceiling. He blinked hard as though he had to get rid of dust, and his throat bobbed. *"Forever shall you worship God. In whatever you do—"*

Outside, something hissed and thwacked against the building. Parohim halted his recitation to look. An arrow clattered down the chaos of metal lines in the window frame before falling out of sight. Heat climbed up Belik's neck, not due to the fur stole he wore for the occasion. That was too close. Accidents like that couldn't happen.

Two Tanyu vaulted through the openings in the window to drop on the other side before Belik halted any more from going. They couldn't all leave when there were enemies in here too. "Enough!" he snarled. The quiet inside the room allowed the word to carry.

Parohim looked at Master Belik as though to ask if he should continue.

A moment later, the crowd outside surged apart with gasps and screams of surprise. A huge black-jacketed figure led a man, half lifting, half guiding him toward the window that the arrow had hit. The Tanyu held the would-be assassin's arms behind his back. The archer's right bicep bled freely through his dark green shirt, and the paleness of his face made the stubble on his chin look like something that was drawn on. His expression, however, was resolute. The man, midforties maybe, had the look of someone who had seen war. It was a Tanyuin expression.

"The Second Keeper lives!" he shouted.

Tanyu could have simply killed the archer when they found him.

Pandemonium erupted. Shouting, men and women flung themselves at the bases of the four huge statues. The grating of swords being unsheathed rang through the Main.

The bases are hollow.

Why hadn't they checked more thoroughly for weapons caches? The carved-out bases of the statues were right under their noses. Belik clenched a fist as several Tanyu sprang forward to quash the predicted rebellion. The area behind the sculptures quickly became choked but the weapons still passed from the hands of killed soldiers to the living.

Parohim ducked and then straightened, clearly unsure of what to do. Belik hadn't warned him about what was coming. "You can go," he told him. The man ran to the opposite side of the room. There was no exterior door there, just an entrance into an office—a dead end—or statues and blown-out windows. The cowardly Amir would still be necessary for the real crowning ceremony tomorrow. It was best that he not get caught in the carnage.

In the commotion, no one else even saw the death of the archer.

The Kingdom soldiers fell back from the statues—*how did we miss a weapons cache like that?*—and threw back their cloaks, slicing out shields and holding them out in an overlapping pattern around and above them. The shielded mass of Kingdom soldiers pushed forward.

Then Belik lowered himself into the Unreal to speak into the Tanyu's minds. "Now."

At the word, shadows materialized into black-clothed Tanyu. They moved without the huffing and screaming of the Brithnem soldiers. Inner poise. Reigned-in rage.

Small knives darted from corners as the front of the mass of bodies reached the front of the dais. Two Brithnem soldiers slumped to the ground, leaving a momentary break in their shield wall. One of the shadowy Tanyu jumped into the opening, moving artfully and felling six more soldiers inside before falling back, injured. The opening was wider now. How long would they pretend that their shields were an impenetrable defense?

Looking down, he saw a Tanyu Defender standing in front of the dais run through by a sword, overwhelmed by the force coming forward. So far, the only one down. Blood leaked out on the stairs, dripping and smearing with the fighting.

His heart thudded in his chest, his new power just out of reach. Was it worth it to try again? Unless Kiria herself were here, it would be useless. Killing someone as Firian had been able to do was draining. And Belik wasn't good at it.

Bard was alive, after all.

A sword clanged against the top stair as someone fell forward with the force of his swing. Belik took a step back.

The shields over the heads of the Kingdom soldiers rippled like bronze and silver waves. It would be difficult to fight one-handed and keep that awkward position for long. The soldiers had considered unusual possibilities—an attack from above—but didn't consider what addressing them would cost. Maybe they were learning after all. Belik nodded at one of the smaller Tanyu, a young girl whose name he didn't know. Her eyes glinted back at him. She had the same idea.

With a leap, she landed on top of the undulating platform of shields. She stabbed downward just as she skipped to another shield a safe distance away. Stab, jump, stab, jump. By the time she'd killed a dozen of them, the shields angled down again, removing the flat surface she'd used to her advantage. The young Tanyu nimbly leapt back to the ground.

Without protection from above, the cloaked soldiers were twice as vulnerable to attack. Belik saw one more Tanyu go down, but the soldiers died in droves. They fought forward, always looking to their front. They parried and thrust as all good soldiers were taught to do, every move predictable, like a child in a sporting match.

He toed the blood leaking down the sword-made crack in the marble and waited for the din to die down. It didn't take much longer, and he was safe, surrounded as he was by a ring of warriors around the dais.

Shifting his attention, he spied a similar scenario playing out on the grounds outside. Without the enclosed space, it would be harder to herd the rebels all in. But he trusted his Tanyu to do what he said. Most of the time.

The metallic smell of blood washed through the room. The back of his throat rose in response.

If he was going to keep this power, and if the Tanyu were going to follow him despite not enjoying his every order, he had to make sure that they knew what would happen if they rebelled.

Firian had rebelled. Everyone knew it. He'd rebelled against his own, against all the Tanyu, leaving them leaderless.

Tesni had returned without information about Kiria's location. A ruse. Belik should have expected it. Firian's connection to the princess was the only excuse he had left to keep him alive. Based on this attempt on Belik's life, it seemed likely that Kiria was still inside the city, gathering support, raising hopes for the Keepers to rise again. Belik could find her without Firian. Every person she met was a leak, a weak spot in her hiding place. He already had Tanyu hounding her at night, filling her with nightmares. But the girl had some kind of Sentry now, so she'd parried their recent attempts.

Chetana must be the one standing guard over Kiria's mind. He hadn't sensed Chetana's death, and who else could it be? No one else in the Keeper's camp, besides the girl herself, had the Talent. His blood chilled at the thought.

With a jerk, he ducked, all instinct. Only afterward did he register the arrow he'd seen flying toward him. Another assassin? He glared from the weapon embedded at an angle in the window frame to the place where the attack had originated. This time, it came from the opposite direction, outside, removed from the fighting. The fight against the soldiers had died down enough that a couple Tanyu, including the girl who had leapt on the platform of shields, could be spared to race off in the direction where the arrow had come. His blood boiled.

Better, he thought bitterly.

Another arrow whizzed at him, aimed lower. This time he hurled himself sideways. The blood on the toe of his shoe painted the story of his movements. That he had backed away. That he had cowered.

No, not cowered—lived.

When no more arrows came, Belik tore his gaze from the view of the empty grounds where the second archer was hiding. The arrow had caught one of the

Kingdom soldiers in the leg. Tanyu had all but won the skirmish in the Main, with only a few holdouts.

A slim black figure, one who had run at the first sign of another attacker, leapt into the room. Running up to the dais, she stood smartly before Belik, a soldier to a general. "We got him, Master Belik," she said with a surprisingly girlish voice. "Would you like us to show you the body?"

"No," he said, waving her away. "Finish this."

His skin still sang from the near miss, but after a few moments, he steadied his breath and watched as the Tanyu utterly routed the rest of the Kingdom fighters.

Kiria's fighters.

The initial sweep of the city hadn't turned up the princess. At first, Belik was furious, but the more he considered it, the more he thought it would be better to wait than to send more people after her now. Secure the palace and later the city. Find out who was working with her, if there were any leaks in the newly submissive barracks. Use her defiance against her. Then they could crush any uprising more decisively, without anyone to view her and her cohorts as martyrs.

The hushed thudding of fleeing boots whispered outside. Belik nodded at a Master standing outside the broken window. Let them go. A couple survivors could tell the tale, run to other traitors and reveal their positions.

A ghostly quiet settled over the Main. Belik found three Tanyuin bodies. The rest were Kingdom. Spreading blood obscured the inlaid mosaic symbols of the Three Lines.

The girl approached him again. Other Tanyu fought to keep the horror out of their eyes, but not her. *Interesting.* "Where would you like us to move the bodies?" she asked.

"Set up a few outside the palace, by the street. Burn the rest."

"As you would have it, Master Belik." Her tone was clipped and efficient. Dark, silky hair fell in sheets to her chin. He recognized her dimly but they had never interacted in any meaningful way, despite her wearing a black Master ring. She couldn't be over twenty-five. A new Master, then, one of the last created under Sais Jairon's rule.

So far, Belik had Shiro and Nedi to carry out his orders. Another would be welcome.

"What's your name?"

"Enktuya Baloraat."

Eradi, if he had to guess. She had the eyes for it.

"Find me when you're finished. I have more work for you."

Power didn't materialize on its own. It was held by decisive action and a loyal coterie of followers. *Always have a backup plan. Even when you've just executed a company of soldiers.*

23

KIRIA

It was late but Kiria couldn't sit. She paced, her serving girls following her with their eyes. She could tell the two of them were tired, but no one would be able to sleep until they heard how the assault against Belik had gone.

Had the plan been too simple? Had it worked?

She rubbed feeling back into her hands. She wanted to do everything and nothing. What she really wanted was news, but none had come.

Except that Firian was alive.

Seeing him alive shot sparks through her veins. She hated him and loved him. It was enough to drive her mad. She needed to focus on the attempt to unseat Belik, but her thoughts repeatedly wrenched her toward Firian and the desperation in his face when he told her to get out of the city. It was in his best interest to get her out of the way whether or not he still pretended to care for her. He did seem sincere in one thing, though—he wasn't in league with Belik. In that, they were allies.

She had told the others right away, but that news had quieted in the wake of this infernal hush. This wait for news that didn't come. Firian had become nothing but a complication they could deal with if the attempt on Belik's life failed. Well, more than a complication, but something no one was ready to face fully just yet. Yes, he could find her here, but, judging from his former behavior, he wouldn't threaten them, and she could even play along, pretend to work together, until it became impossible to continue.

Guards watched her, Jori watched her, Chetana watched her. It grated on her thin nerves.

Kiria had gone over the plans again and again, self-soothingly, until the others were no doubt sick of hearing about them, about the contingencies, about what they would do if the soldiers succeeded, about what they would do if the soldiers failed...

Finally, she'd fallen silent, resorting instead to remembering the moves Chetana had shown her for defending her dreams against Tanyuin attack. She hadn't been able to master many of them, but she could levitate, disappear briefly, look like Firian.

Did the lack of news mean that there was no one alive to deliver it? Her head ached with nerves. Waves of thoughts flowed and subsided.

A knock.

She nearly flew to the door. With a hand against one of her shoulders, the blond guard named Royce stopped her from opening it herself. She couldn't show her face until it was clear who stood on the other side.

Her heart galloped as Royce cracked open the door. The words from the other side were maddeningly obscured, though she strained every nerve to listen. The door closed again. The guard turned a grim face to her. He shook his head.

She let out a breath, anguish pooling inside her.

"They failed?" Jori asked, incredulous. He turned to Kiria. "Belik is still alive? Didn't we send *two* archers to assassinate him? And all those soldiers?"

"Yes," she answered. She had known it would be a gamble, but she prayed it would be one that paid off. The company of soldiers would all have the same goal —to kill Belik. The risk was huge, but with that many, couldn't they accomplish that task?

No. They'd failed, the force of the Tanyu too strong. Chetana's expression mirrored the way Kiria felt—disappointed but unsurprised.

Immediately after the counsel when they'd met to decide how to kill Belik, Chetana had started to reach out to some of their nearest allies, but, without a clear directive, the effort petered out, depending on this news.

This failure.

"Because of the attack, Master Belik is still uncrowned," Royce added.

"Who was at the door?" Kiria asked.

"One of ours from the meeting."

The hair on the back of Kiria's neck prickled. Lowering her brows, she asked, "How many survived?"

"The final count is unknown, but it sounds like only a few. Civilians also got caught in the fighting. Tanyu slaughtered them."

Gut swooping, she traded looks with Chetana. "We should get out of here," she said, sparking Candrae and Vayci into motion. "If only a few soldiers survived, then they're definitely being followed. They're looking for me." She shot a glance at Jori. "And you."

Jori scowled but didn't argue.

"What's a place they wouldn't know about?" she asked him.

"What do you mean?"

"One of your places."

"Ah." He pivoted back and forth on the balls of his feet, the only evidence that he was pleased by the question. "For all of us?"

She raised her eyebrows in response. *Obviously.*

He cast his eyes to the ceiling. "There's a place not too far."

"Great, where is it?" she cut in, hoping he would speak more quickly.

"It would take us out of the city, though."

Kiria froze. Out of the city. She couldn't leave now, when her people needed her. "Where?" she asked again, cautiously this time.

He looked at her seriously now. His voice lowered. "Do you want to leave the city, darling?"

The guard with the tattoo on his face spoke up. "My Keeper, there is another safehouse, the one meant for the First Keeper and his wife. We could go there."

Kiria's heart sank, not just at the all-too-recent memory of Cúron, but at the impracticality of the plan. "No," she said, "that's too far away. And the Tanyu have surely found it by now. The other safehouse too," she added, cutting off any mention of Atty. Jori felt raw as it was. "Do you have any other ideas?" The question was directed at the guards, at Jori, at anybody who could help them.

Jori inspected his fingernails. "There's a tunnel beneath a house one street over. It goes under the wall."

Two of her guards exchanged furious glances. But this was no time to bemoan old security risks—it was time to avoid new ones.

She heaved a breath. *Another gory tunnel.* "You think it would be safe?"

Jori nodded, slowly at first, and then with more conviction. They would still be close enough to the city to influence it, to encourage the people. The important thing now was not to get caught by any Tanyu who had followed the messenger. There could be someone lying in wait at that moment. They had no time to lose.

"We'll take Jori's way," she said, turning to the guards.

Candrae and Vayci had already packed most of their belongings. There weren't many to begin with. Most of them had burned in the palace.

All eyes shifted to Chetana, the most experienced user of the Talent. Calmly, she closed her eyes. Maybe it was that Firian didn't always close his eyes when he did it, but there was something more mystical about Chetana's power.

After a few moments, she opened her eyes and nodded once. She sensed no Tanyu in the immediate area. They were clear to go.

A hand touched her shoulder. Jori was putting a cloak on her. "Don't forget our disguises."

"My face is a disguise." She hadn't worn her Beauty since the meeting with the generals. How many of them had gone to Belik's coronation themselves? How many of them would she never see again?

He hooked her chin with one finger. "You look like a Keeper to me," he said, his voice oddly quiet.

She closed her mouth. Unexpected emotion prickled at the edges of her eyes. Jori could be sour when he felt caged or down, but that look meant that he trusted her. That he would follow her. She nodded at him and cleared her throat.

He released her chin and took a packet of provisions from Candrae, who hadn't handed it to him.

Kiria gathered the folds of the cloak around her. "Show the guards where to go."

"Will do, love."

"Who owns this place?" the tattooed guard, whose name was Viktor, asked Jori, frowning.

He only waved his hand in answer.

It was a legitimate question, Kiria thought. The tunnel that ran under the wall had emptied them out into a space that looked like an enormous, low-ceilinged, underground house or bunker, with plenty of open spaces where many people could gather at once. They stood in one of the largest now. Everywhere she looked was an opening somewhere else. Cursory investigation had unearthed a makeshift kitchen and bedrooms laid with abandoned, moth-eaten blankets and enormous pillows. Haphazard decorations—expensive-looking colored lanterns and snagged tapestries—suggested that this was a place frequented by some of the wealthier families. Nothing had been cared for, only used for wild festivities. A great assortment of bottles and clothes and masks and dishes had been crammed unceremoniously into corners.

"Ah!" she cried, going toward one pile and holding up a lyra. Her instrument had no doubt burned. She squeezed the neck of the instrument and avoided looking at the others as she felt sorrow threaten to overwhelm her.

"I've come here a time or two," Jori said. "Always the best parties when no one knows."

"The partygoers know," Chetana replied acidly.

"But not the Tanyu."

"For now."

Kiria turned to see Jori spread his arms wide. "I found a place. Here. It's big enough for all of us." He pointed to the serving girls. "You could have your own room, darlings. Doesn't that sound good? There's probably even food around here somewhere." He bustled to a doorway.

"It does sound good," Kiria admitted. "Thank you for finding this place." Words hung thick in the air. They could stay nowhere for long. All their moves so far had been too short-sighted. Because of that, the Kingdom had lost good soldiers, some of whom she knew personally.

She cast a glance at Chetana, who seemed to understand exactly what she was thinking.

"We'll be safe here tonight, and tomorrow..." *Tomorrow.* Tomorrow was Dedication Day, a day of fasting and prayer and remembrance. How had she forgotten? Looking around again, she realized they all would be spending the holy day here, in this cavernous party den.

Sounds of items tossed carelessly across the floor crashed through the wide room. Royce set his jaw with obvious irritation. "Jori!" Kiria called.

He emerged, one brow raised.

"Tomorrow is Dedication Day."

His shoulders slumped. "Everyone's still fasting?"

"Well, we certainly need the prayer."

"Isn't there a story," he began, twirling one finger through the air, "about an army who lost because they were weak after fasting? Hm? Don't want to be caught off guard. I doubt Kader is celebrating."

The mention of Cúron's son sent a twist to her belly. They'd received no updates after learning that he had escaped north, a maddeningly vague report.

"We're observing Dedication Day," she said firmly. "We need a day to think, to regroup. And pray. We can use the time to contact our allies as well, see if anyone knows where he is." She held up the lyra in her hand and waggled it with levity she didn't feel. "I could play."

After choking back his first response, he said, "That wouldn't be so bad. Thank you, love." Apparently giving up his search in that area of the underground house, he approached her and took her free hand in both of his. "If that's what you want, it'll be lovely. Just..." He looked around. "Unorthodox." He shuddered, then brightened and spoke in an undertone. "I remember one party here last summer. Unbearably hot. But someone brought firecrackers—"

"Inside?"

A wry smile stretched his features. "Oh, you're no fun."

Here was a hint of the old Jori, the one she liked and leaned on. She gave Jori a sideways hug that lingered.

Chetana began speaking to the guards, and Candrae and Vayci tidied up to prepare the space for a Keeper. *Almost two Keepers*, Kiria thought again, holding Jori closer. He mirrored her movement.

Her plan had failed. Words came back to her as from a forgotten dream. *There are possibilities all around us. Every window is a door.* She would get up and try again.

"The Kepron is right." Chetana's voice—and, even more, her words—startled Kiria upright.

"What?"

Her advisor stood between two guards. All looked grim. "Belik will try to use the holy day to his advantage. I guess that he'll crown himself tomorrow when Brithnem has less strength and strategy to fight back."

Kiria swallowed. It made perfect sense. Even if Belik did crown himself—she shuddered to think with whose crown—it didn't change the ultimate plan to take back the Kingdom. There were the trappings of power, its symbols, and then there was the real thing. Belik crowned would present new problems, but nothing she couldn't face. She had to believe that.

"I'm afraid that..." Chetana closed her mouth.

"What?"

"My Keeper." Chetana's tone was deadly serious, one full of horrible confidences she needed to share.

Taking her cue, Kiria broke away from Jori and headed into a different room with Chetana, trying to brace for more bad news. How much more could she take? "What's wrong?"

"My Keeper," she began again, "I have made a decision."

Kiria froze stiff with dread.

"I must go back to the palace." She dropped her eyes. "I've given you what I was able, but I cannot continue. I will send a new messenger for you. I'll figure out a way for you to have all you need. But I have been away from my son for too long." Her face was etched with pain. "Daelon is still alive, and I fear Belik plans to use him to get to me. I thought my duty was with you, as it is, but blood cries louder." Anguish drew a fierce line between her brows as she gazed down at Kiria, not asking for permission but understanding.

Kiria's eyes had gone misty. She struggled not to feel selfish for forgetting the depth of Chetana's struggle. Kiria missed Daelon too, but she had the entire Western Kingdom to think of. They all had given what they had to give. "When will you leave?" she asked simply.

"I will sleep to gather my strength, and then I must go back."

Kiria bit her lip, mind whirling. Chetana had helped her defend herself in the Unreal, and she was the primary person who could communicate with Tanyu and Watchmen alike. Was Kiria strong enough in the Unreal to do the same? It would be better if someone other than the Keeper could convey messages. It would potentially keep their location more secure.

If Kiria commanded it, Chetana would stay. Probably. But she couldn't command it. If Daelon had more hope of surviving this storm if Chetana left to be near him, then Kiria had to let her go. They'd all lost loved ones. Kiria would sacrifice a slice of her own safety if it meant that she didn't have to lose one more. The trade wasn't even worth considering. The gain was infinitely greater than the risk.

"Very well," she agreed, an image of her own mother rising in her mind. Merian would have made the same choice Chetana was making now. "I just have one request."

"God willing, I will grant it."

"I would like one more lesson."

Chetana's eyelids fluttered with relief. "As you wish."

WHEN A KNOCK SOUNDED at the door, Unreal knives evaporated from Kiria's hands.

It wasn't a loud knock, but no one should have been knocking on the door leading outside. She opened her eyes, emerging into the Real. She sat cross-legged across from Chetana, to whom she gave a questioning look. Though she said nothing, Chetana's dark eyes went stern. Her advisor had much to worry about, but the look still sent Kiria's pulse racing. Kiria flexed her now empty hands and turned her attention toward the opposite end of the room.

A short staircase led up to the ground level. Royce and Viktor had turned cautiously toward the sound.

Kiria stood, feeling less vulnerable if she could run. It wasn't Belik, of course, or else Chetana would have sensed it. Was it a different Tanyu?

Royce cracked open the door at the top of the stairs. Then he stepped backward down the steps, alert but not afraid. Kiria let out a breath.

"It's Master Tanery, My Keeper."

Kiria laughed, here then gone, the noise bursting out of her before she recognized it. Joy and disbelief surged so strongly through her veins that she couldn't keep it in.

Bard appeared, ducking his head so he could see into their underground space.

Jori leapt up from the corner with surprising speed and took Bard's head in his hands. Bard tried to shake him off but Jori held on and turned Bard's face toward Kiria. "Ah! Kiria, my love, you told me he was dead! Look! Look! Why did you say that?"

Chetana had been the one to confirm it, but the Amir looked as bewildered as Kiria felt.

Jori didn't wait for an answer. He looked into Bard's eyes, finally releasing his face and instead resting his hands on Bard's shoulders. "Are you all right, darling? You look a bit wobbly."

It was true. To escape Jori, who was blocking his path, Bard stepped off the last two stairs sideways. Instead of having a Tanyu's sure poise, Bard had to steady himself. A smile crinkled the corners of his mouth, but he heaved a breath as though even that tiny exertion had cost him something.

"Get him a chair," Kiria ordered.

One materialized almost immediately. Bard looked grateful to sit down.

"What happened?" she asked, standing before him. The air was cooler by the door, even though it had been shut again. She didn't realize how much she longed for fresh air.

"My Keeper..." Royce spoke her title as a low warning. His meaning was obvious. Bard was a Tanyu. Was he not in on the coup?

Kiria shot the man a glare. Bard had risked his life to save hers. She wouldn't doubt his loyalty now.

"I thought you needed me," Bard said.

Jori flashed a grin, quick and sad.

"Bard..." Kiria felt tears well up in her eyes. She swallowed. "I saw you face Master Belik for me. How did you get here?"

"Firian found me."

Jori cursed joyfully. Kiria shushed him.

Although she was glad Bard was alive, she wasn't ready to hear a glowing report about Firian. She knew more about what had happened the night of the attack, and she doubted Firian had told Bard about it.

Bard was silent for a few seconds more, as though he wanted to say something else, but couldn't for some reason. His breath smelled like ale. Jori must have noticed too because his eyes sparkled as though laughing at the mad coincidence.

"He took me to a doctor and then got me out again before Belik's people could find us." He side-eyed the guards standing above him with a mix of apprehension and determination.

Beside Kiria, Chetana narrowed her eyes. "Were you with him just now?"

Bard closed his mouth.

Her heartbeat rushed. *Yes, then.*

The soldiers braced to run out, but Kiria gestured for them to stand down. Firian would already be long gone, and running out would only betray their location.

"You need a Tanyu, I think," he forged on. "For messages, and to know what's going on."

"They can find us through him," Chetana told Kiria quietly.

"They can find you through Kiria too," Bard responded.

Chetana raised an appraising eyebrow.

Kiria scrutinized him, looking for injuries, but found none to explain the weakness. He held his fingers oddly in his lap, as though he were gripping something that wasn't there, but his hand didn't look broken.

"I want to help you," he insisted. His black eyes bored into hers.

After a pause, Kiria said, "This is good." She turned to Chetana. "You can go back and Bard can stay with me."

Chetana's gaze darted across the floor, as if searching for an objection. Finally, she inclined her head. "As you wish, My Keeper." Relief laced her words. "But..." She sighed. "He's probably correct that you're being tracked at this moment. You need to get farther away from here."

"I think so too, yeah," Bard said. "They can find us here."

Jori looked aggrieved at the insult to his hiding place. "Then why haven't they done it already?"

Bard fiddled with his hands. Something wasn't right about the way his left arm moved. He lifted his forearm and hand all in one piece, as though it were made of wood. "I don't know. I can guess."

"Then guess," Kiria said.

He lifted his eyes to hers. "My guess is that Belik will want to use you, or call you, or want you on his side or something."

The suggestion made her stomach writhe. "On his side?"

He nodded, a little less rigorously than before, but it was such a familiar gesture that Kiria smiled. "Yeah. I'm not sure. But you're the Keeper, and he hasn't found you yet. I'm sure he's figured out you're alive."

Royce stirred. "Everyone knows My Keeper is alive. We told the populace, to keep their hope alive that this disruption will soon be over."

Disruption. He made the attack—the *murders*—sound like a bout of bad weather.

The guard's words merely seemed to deepen Bard's conviction. "Then he won't want that. Yeah, he'll want you for something... special."

Jori glanced at Kiria, almost fearful. She straightened her spine. "I want to be here to give my people hope," she said, her chest tight as she said it. The words seemed like the right ones, so she forced them out, but if duty hadn't tethered her to the city, she would have followed Bard's advice without question.

Jori set a hand on her arm. "You also want to live."

"Has Belik only taken over the palace grounds?" Bard asked.

"The whole city," Viktor answered.

"Is he crowned?"

A shadow passed through the room at the mention of the lost battle. Bard's brow twitched as he sensed the atmosphere shift too. "Yes?"

"No," Kiria answered heavily. "We think he'll do it tomorrow."

"That'll be it. Probably. He'll want to... get you before the coronation. Maybe for the ceremony."

Chetana's full lips had flattened to a line. It almost looked as though she had changed her mind about returning to the palace.

"You too," Bard said to Jori.

"Me?" Jori splayed his hands over his chest in a gesture of innocence. "What have I done?"

"You're the heir to the throne. Right? Kepron?"

As he always did when the topic came up, Jori turned touchy.

Without warning, Bard slumped over, his head heavy as a child's. Kiria and Jori caught him from falling off his chair.

"Water!" she cried, and Candrae went to fetch it.

Bard's dark eyelashes fluttered open and he gasped in a breath.

"You're not dying on me?" Jori asked, his tone artificially light. Lines Kiria had never seen on Jori's face until the past few days deepened.

"No, mate," Bard said, though his voice was barely more than a whisper. Maybe it was his word choice, but something seemed to remind him of where he was. A Tanyu among hidden royalty. He braced his hands against the seat of the chair and sat up as Candrae rushed forward with the cup.

"I think we've asked enough questions for now," Kiria said. "You need to rest."

"You've got to get farther away," Bard insisted, his voice a little stronger now. "Trust me."

Something dark passed through her mind. "Did Firian tell you that?"

"He's right, though."

"Would he follow me if I left?"

She and Bard were suddenly the only people in the room. Pretense was reserved for opponents, not allies.

"Not if you go east."

An odd reply. "Do you know what's going on between Firian and Belik?"

"Yes."

"You'll tell me as soon as you've rested." Kiria looked up at Chetana. Assuming Bard had the inside information he claimed, he could communicate as effectively as her advisor could. Now was as good a time as any for Chetana to return to Daelon. Bard could even check on Chetana to verify that Daelon was still alive. Kiria took a deep breath. "You can go," she told her.

This time, Chetana did not protest. She leveled a look that spoke more than words could. Warnings, instructions, and love passed between them. "I would have abandoned all else for you."

Kiria nodded, her eyes beginning to sting.

"Remember what I taught you, My Keeper."

"So many things," Kiria replied, squeezing her hand.

And without another word, Chetana was gone.

24

FIRIAN

Eight days.

Firian had eight days to get back to Raewhith; otherwise, Belik would order Brett hurt or killed. He could make the trip over the Charúnin Thôr that quickly at the peak of his strength, but he was weak from the knife thrust to the shoulder and little sleep.

One of the manor houses at the far end of the beach row had especially magnificent stables that were now one mare short. He rode furiously to the foothills, the pounding hooves beating his thoughts into an empty trance.

Bard was with Kiria. That would help her navigate the dangers of the Tanyu, at least. They both lived, for now. In a few days, the small group of loyal Tanyu would join together and attack Belik in the Unreal. And, as soon as he could, he'd return in force just in case to make Belik relinquish control. That was as far as his practical thoughts took him. Daydreams—of Kiria choosing him, of killing Belik before he hurt Bard—played through his mind like breezes through the air. Here one second, then gone, only to return minutes later.

Low in the saddle, Firian urged the sweating horse to go faster along the uninterrupted stretch of beach. The Gray Forest rose to his right, darkness turning the leaves a murky orange. It was faster riding this way than through the trees, at least until he reached Redshore, the seaport, which wouldn't be for another hour. He needed all the time he could recover.

It was already nearing autumn, which meant that, although it was balmy here, snow could fall over the mountains at any time, slowing his progress. The idea shortened his breath. Belik wasn't one to give grace. He'd probably only allowed him to get to his sister as a concession to the ways they'd served each other over the years. There would be no more mercy.

The horse's hooves splashed in the surf and the beast skittered to the side. Drops of sea water spattered Firian's legs. Firian was no expert rider, though he had ridden plenty of times before. His anxiety must have gotten to the mare. He lowered his voice, murmuring soothing words, and calmed his body, guiding the horse back on course. He'd switch mounts at Redshore. Once he reached the mountains, with their treacherous rocks and climbs, he'd go on foot, but for now, this was the fastest way.

Bard's familiar presence arrived like the scent of cinnamon.

"Everything all right?" Firian asked, momentarily taking his attention off his ride to find him in the Unreal.

"We're okay," Bard affirmed. He had created a low, windowless space made of sandstone. Looked like it could be the place where he and Kiria were hiding.

"Have you left yet?"

"No. We're leaving after Dedication Day."

Firian huffed. He'd forgotten about the holiday. A few people at the Academy celebrated it every year, but they were the minority.

"Fir, it's about the Kepron." No one else inhabited the large room, and it made Bard look small, though he stood up straight.

"Jori?"

"Kader."

The young one. "Did they get him?"

"We don't think so. Not yet. Do you think you... do you think you could convince Master Belik he's dead so they don't go out looking for him?"

This didn't sound like Kiria's idea. She was furious with him. But she would want the boy to be safe. With Kader, they'd have all three Lines accounted for. "Do you know where he is?" Maps flashed through his mind. He didn't have time for a stop. He barely had time to slow, as long as he could force his body to keep going.

Bard shook his head, sending black hair askew. "Heading north, is all they know."

Firian sighed. "Bard, I can't—"

"You don't have to stop. Can't you talk to Tesni or something? Figure out some proof that Master Belik would believe?"

In the sandstone room, Firian tapped his leg with his thumb, considering.

"It would matter a lot to her," Bard persisted.

If Belik discovered the deception, any plan could compromise Firian or the people he was starting to amass on his side. But Bard was right. Kader's safety was a priority for Kiria, a key step in pursuit of her goals. The boy didn't matter much to him—he'd never seen the Kepron before—but she could be worrying about him even now. Maybe he was one of those she'd given herself up for the other night. One of those she loved.

Something fierce tugged at his heart. "Okay, and if I catch a rumor of where he is, I'll let you know. I'll make sure Belik thinks he's dead. Don't tell Kiria it was me or she might not believe it. Just tell her the Tanyu aren't going after him anymore. That he's safe."

Bard gave a curt nod, his expression somehow impish and concerned at once when he looked up. "And tell me about your sister too, yeah?"

"Yeah."

Firian wished he'd come up with the idea to help Kader. Now that his mind spun with ideas about how to accomplish the task, it was definitely possible to do while he rode on his way to Brett. It was almost a blessing to be able to focus on something other than his own failures. Before long, though, a simple solution presented itself.

Firian talked to Tesni, to a couple others still in Brithnem who sided with him, and they divided tasks. Firian would contact Watchmen to the north, directing them not to make the Kepron's escape public if they saw him. Another Tanyu would find a personal token in the Kepron's room and another would cut off the small finger of one of the casualties of battle. Both would be sent to Belik.

Firian didn't fear that Belik was watching him. The Master was so busy mucking up everybody's lives that he wouldn't spare more than a thought or two on Firian now that he was headed to Raewhith. At best, Belik would think that Kiria was up this way too, that Firian was going to join her, as he said.

No, to make sure his plan was executed, Firian was watching Belik instead.

25

KIRIA

Kiria didn't sleep that night. She kept running her hand over the neck of the lyra until she was afraid she would destroy the strings with the constant friction. She had no appetite, so fasting wasn't a burden.

It would be a strange Dedication Day without Chetana. She had always been a key figure in the holiday since Kiria was a child. She and Jori and Atty would complain about having no food to eat, and then they'd all go to the upper room of the Amiran Academy and listen to the new composition. During the music and recitations, she, at least, would regret her earlier griping. The holiness of the moment would envelop her as it always did and she would thank God for all they'd been given. The day before usually gave her some trepidation because of the seriousness of it all, but she ended up loving it every time.

Last year, both her parents were still alive. They'd held hands in the upper room. Kiria hadn't yet revealed her Beauty, and she'd looked at their display of love with anticipation for her own future.

She scrunched her eyes tight and clutched the lyra close to her chest like a talisman. How much had changed in one year! It didn't seem possible. She had been a different person then.

Blinking back hot tears, she stood. If she was going to command her group to pause for a day of remembrance, they ought to make it a day not only to remember the trials of the founders but the trials they'd just endured themselves. They could honor the dead. She had to face it sometime or another. Shuddering a little, she turned the pages of her mind to the horrible list of those they'd lost.

Cúron.
His wife, Varinna.
Her guards.
The soldiers of yesterday.
Haved.

She stopped, choking on her memory. After a few sniffling seconds, she turned the last pages, the ones she didn't know if she could face.

Her mother.

Atty.

They deserved to be remembered. They all did. Jori wouldn't be ready, but there was never a good time to comprehend loss. Dedication Day was the best chance they would have for a while.

Candrae and Vayci slept fitfully on the other side of the space Kiria had chosen for herself. They didn't take up Jori's offer of a separate room. Kiria was surprised she hadn't woken them. It was no wonder they were exhausted after the past few days.

Vayci rolled over. When she saw Kiria already awake, she trundled to her feet, blinking sleep out of her eyes. As though the two were connected, Candrae woke up too.

"Girls," Kiria said gently, "today we'll make arrangements for a funeral service for the lost, just before the evening song. You can help me."

"Of course, My Keeper," they replied nearly in unison. Then Vayci leaned her dark head forward. "May we get you anything this morning?"

"No. It's Dedication Day." Kiria realized she still had the lyra in front of her as though it were some sort of shield. Now that Chetana was gone, Kiria would not only provide the music but maybe even the Scroll recitations. The thought brought a grim pleasure. Daelon would be proud of her.

The day passed in a blur of tears and prayers. Bard looked a little lost through it all. He'd never celebrated the holiday before, but he happily filled in wherever he was needed. In the afternoon, they prepared a service honoring the lost.

The ceremony was over too quickly. Everyone shed tears, several spoke about people they had known, prayers were lifted, but it all ended in a flash. Through most of it, Jori held her hand so tightly he bruised her fingers. To his credit, he seemed to realize how important it was for them all to face the tragedy they'd endured. Maybe it was good that the ceremony was so short. None of them could face the truth for long. Kiria squeezed his hand back. He sniffed loudly in response. Neither of them was a graceful crier. Even Bard, who hadn't known any of the causalities well, had tears running down his face as each part ended.

Afterward, Kiria needed to clear her head. The weight of her grief clogged her lungs, making everything sluggish. If she was also going to play the music for Dedication Day, she had to get some air.

Calling over two guards as she tightened the black mourning cloth around her wrist, she said, "I'm going outside. Just for a moment."

They seemed to understand because they didn't protest, but silently followed her up the stairs to the woods outside. Her skin instantly cooled in the twilit air. Trees rose around her and she could feel the ocean nearby, though she couldn't see it. She drank in the freshness, just breathing. Fireflies flitted under the green trees nearby, blinking in and out of sight like magic dust. The sight brought new tears to her eyes. Something about the beauty made her wish she could share it with those they had lost. Atty would have loved to show this to Haved.

As though on cue, someone emerged behind her. Probably another guard to call her back, remind her that being out in the open was unwise, especially tonight. She swallowed her tears and turned.

"I was hoping to be alone. Plan foiled, I see," said Jori, sauntering up beside her with his hands in his pockets. He didn't smile, but his words aimed at his signature levity.

"Don't act like you didn't hear me." She watched the fireflies silently for a few moments longer. "You'll never be alone, Jori."

He made a strangled sound, as though he were trying to swallow but couldn't quite manage it. He turned it into a barked laugh. "You always know the words to say."

"*I* do?" She faced him. "I've always thought that of you."

He gazed listlessly into the distance. "Today, you have the words, my dear. I don't... have much of anything."

She waited until he turned to her. "We've all lost too much," she said quietly, not wanting to spoil the forest's peacefulness. "But none of us are alone. We have to remember that."

He raised one skeptical eyebrow. "We're a small group now."

"Stop protesting. I've got you. We have each other. We can't forget what we still have."

A small smile crept its way across his features. "You could be a Keeper, with all these speeches." He gave her a quick kiss on the cheek. "Thank you, love."

They stood together in the quiet a few moments more before heading back downstairs. It was easy to forget that the outside world held so much danger for the two of them. She would think twice before going above again.

Most of the people, listless and thoughtful from sorrow and lack of food, hadn't left the common room, with its piles of random items in the corners. After being outside, the space felt hot and stuffy. A sheen of sweat clung to her skin.

Earlier that day, she had written a new piece of music for Dedication Day. With only one day to prepare, she thought it sounded rusty and a little cliché, but hoped that the others wouldn't think so. Viktor, with the Khelê tattoo, had volunteered to recite from the Sacred Scroll, and that took a bit of the pressure from her to provide yet another ceremony for everyone.

She took the lyra from the corner where she'd left it and started playing without any announcement. The few hushed sounds ceased. The interplay of minor and major keys matched her feelings. The lingering notes had a swampy, ringing quality as she drew the bow over the strings. Overlaying everything was sadness, but she couldn't forget there was still hope, and that she was the face of it. The movement of the bow soothed her, focusing her thoughts into melody.

At a key change, a spike of apprehension tore through her, unrelated to the music. She lengthened the note she was playing to buy herself time to focus on the feeling. Because it wasn't connected to anything directly at the moment, which probably meant that Firian was experiencing it instead. She didn't know what to make of him surviving the attack. Part of her had nearly collapsed with relief, but another part had burned with so much anger that it had been difficult to speak. Why should she be relieved, when he'd all but engineered the pain they were experiencing?

She closed her eyes, leaning into the melody, which she had practiced enough times that day to do automatically, and let herself sink into the Unreal. She didn't want to meet him, but if he had information she needed, then she couldn't let her feelings get in the way of helping her people.

No, not apprehension. She'd misread the feeling. It was anger, just as sharp and searing. He hadn't invited her to join him in his mind, so for a while she couldn't see anything. Where was he? Although she knew he could see her at odd times, she couldn't do the same with her level of ability.

"What's happening?" she whispered in the dark, risking detection.

Firian was instantly by her side. "Belik."

The darkness transformed into the partially burned-out hull of the palace façade. One of the balconies still remained stable. On it stood Belik and Amir Parohim, lit clearly by a row of lights constructed on the terrace. Belik wore a fur stole over his black Tanyuin uniform. The entire scene was hazy, as though she were watching a memory or a dream. Firian wasn't creating this himself, then. Belik appeared most clearly, so maybe he was watching Belik and she was able to see this only through their *katah*. Nothing seemed impossible with Firian.

Parohim was saying something, but she could barely hear it. Why was the advisor helping Belik? She and Chetana had never figured out why he would turn. Kiria had never liked him much, with his slicked-back hair and oily voice, but he had always been loyal to the Keepers.

Parohim raised his hands to the sky, clearly in a prayer. Where was Daelon? Was he all right? The dark oranges and blues of the sky moments ago had given way to velvety black. Belik stood silent and regal above a nervous, mixed crowd who had come out to see. It was no wonder that they looked anxious after what happened at the past coronation.

It was as they feared. Belik was being crowned today.

Her empty stomach churned. *God help us.* Was this really happening? She glanced at Firian. He wasn't looking at her, but was staring at Belik with far-seeing eyes, his hands clenched into fists.

She turned back. This was actually happening. Somehow, Firian was seeing it in reality. There was no time to ponder how.

The coronation wasn't as beautiful as the original ceremony, with its symbolism and vows. This was stripped down to the skeleton: a prayer and a crown.

Her skin prickled as she spied something metal in Parohim's hand. She squinted to see whose crown Belik had decided to use. They'd all been left in the palace during the chaos of the attack. Breath caught in her chest as she recognized the gold diadem Cúron had worn as Keeper, but it had grown, become more elaborate. Bronze and silver teeth made the crown menacing.

Bronze, gold, and silver.

She ground her teeth. The bronze belonged to Atty, the good ruler he had slaughtered. Gold, to Cúron. And the silver—that was a statement. He was coming after her power. He would crush whatever was left.

Parohim lifted the gorgeous crown high and placed it squarely on Belik's head. Something in Kiria cracked. This moment had seemed like a terrible part of a story, something looming but destined not to happen because the hero would ride in and stop it. But no one stepped forward.

Kiria turned her eyes again to the crowd. Black-clad Tanyu stood amongst them, glaring watchfully. Angry heat bit the corners of her eyes.

"As the God-blessed Keeper of the Western Kingdom," Parohim shouted, "Master Belik now requires every citizen to swear allegiance to him." The Amir glanced nervously at Belik as he spoke. There was an unspoken warning in the words.

Belik shifted his weight as though it pained him to stand. "You will take a knee," he said. His rough voice wasn't loud, but deep and carrying. "You will swear on the Scroll."

How many loyal soldiers were left? Kiria searched the crowd. Many had died the day before in the failed attempt on Belik's life. Were there others trapped inside the city walls? There must be.

Slowly, a few began to sink to their knees.

Did they really think that God meant for such a thing to happen, for such a ruthless man to lead them?

One man resisted, standing stubbornly, but three Tanyu approached him. They didn't have any weapons she could see, but the meaning was clear. The soldier's options were loyalty or death. One of the Tanyu put a hand on the man's shoulder. After looking at the Tanyu defiantly, he obeyed. More followed, until all the men and women, soldiers and civilians alike, knelt on the ground.

Kiria wanted to stand forward, to yell. *I'm still alive! Don't follow him. There's still hope!* She watched helplessly as Parohim led them all in a recitation of loyalty, the Amir first, the people repeating.

"Tanyu will make the Kingdom great," Belik continued after the vows were complete. "Rather than forcing our will upon you, we'll give you a choice. All the cities that belong the Western Kingdom will receive both riches and independence, provided they swear continued allegiance, if they choose to turn from their former queen."

A movement to her right made Kiria glance at Firian. He was mouthing the word *Keeper*.

"She ran away instead of helping you, but she can make it right. If she agrees with my order to give you wealth and independence in exchange for loyalty, she can come forward and we can make a bargain together."

"Don't go," Firian said sharply.

"Obviously not," Kiria spat back.

"If you help the fugitive queen, you don't deserve my offer."

Kiria felt cold inside. Belik was trying to turn her own kingdom against her. Would anybody listen?

"All this... unpleasantness can be avoided if Kiria comes to me and agrees to give you what you deserve. If not, you'll know what kind of leader she is. I suspect she will choose to rebel against you all, since she ran away with the last Head of the Tanyuin Academy. No matter what she does, I will restore order and justice here in the Western Kingdom, even if I have to do it myself." His gaze cut sharply to Parohim, who took it as his cue to pray an end to the ceremony.

Kiria was shaking. She had no intention of bowing to Belik's wishes, no desire to negotiate with someone who had killed her friends and family and stolen her kingdom. Her face felt hot with the force of her fury. She let out a few breaths as she watched the ceremony and the crowd slowly snuff out like a candle until only curls of fragrant smoke were left.

Belik's words played again and again in her mind. How many of her people would listen and feel that she was withholding something good from them? Would any of them hunt her? The thought made her dizzy, as though the ground shifted.

Firian spread out a hand toward her—maybe she actually had wavered on her feet; she hadn't eaten anything that day, after all—but he let it fall back at his side. His dark eyebrows were drawn down, his jaw cut in a hard line.

Watching him made her feel reckless. "You don't support him?" She'd asked the question before, but the answer was so essential that she had to ask again.

His expression didn't shift as he stared out at the empty place where the crowd had been. "No."

"Is this real?" Firian could create all of this if he wanted to, even the haziness of it, but why would he add details that would incriminate both of them?

"Yes."

"Then what are you going to do?"

He turned to her. His blue eyes burned with a fierce emotion she couldn't place. "What I have to."

"That's not an answer." Then, remembering Bard, she added, "Did you help Bard here last night?"

He hesitated before nodding, a small echo of Bard's repetitive nods. "You need him more than I do now."

This all felt odd. It was as if he was changing so quickly that she couldn't keep her eyes on him long enough to tell what he was doing. She knew Firian—she had thought she knew him. But that was all before he offered to trade her for Brithnem's safety. Now she didn't know who this boy was.

She narrowed her eyes but just said, "Yes, I do." *Are you on my side?* For some reason, she couldn't get the words out. The other questions had come out easily, all demands. This one question didn't feel like the others. It tasted like vulnerability and she didn't like it. "Is he going to tell you what we do?"

He tipped his mouth thoughtfully. "Not everything."

These non-answers drove her crazy. "I don't want him to tell you everything."

"That's fine. You could check up on me instead, you know, if you're worried." He spread his mouth in something that could have been a smile but wasn't.

"I trust him more than I trust you, so he'll stay with us."

His expression got smaller but turned into something closer to a real smile. "Okay."

Will you kill Belik? It was the other question she couldn't stomach. If Firian hadn't done it yet, something was stopping him. Whether it was inability, or the two were secretly working together, or something else, she didn't know.

A phantom pain pricked at her arm. She looked down but saw no stinging bug or anything else that could have bitten her. It must have been from the Real.

Up and up through the haze she went until she opened her eyes in the underground room lit by torches and faces, so many faces, looking down at her from above. She squinted against the firelight and took a big gulp of air. An arm wrapped around her back and helped her to sit up. She realized she was still clutching the neck of the lyra. It had fallen beneath her when she collapsed, its edges digging into the back of her upper arm. Pulling it free and setting it on her lap felt like moving through water. Voices were talking over each other.

Candrae and Vayci were there, of course, but they weren't among the talkers. Kiria looked at them and they ran off to fetch water and something else that would probably help far more than these people's questions. She stifled a grunt as she sat fully upright. "Belik..." she said. "He crowned himself the new Keeper."

26

KIRIA

"You're sure about that?"

Jori's question was sincere, but it still gave Kiria a headache. "Yes, I'm sure."

"How do you know? Was Firian there?"

She, Jori, and Bard sat cross-legged on the ground together after Kiria had been too shaky to stand. Her guards stood behind them protectively, as though danger were going to burst through the door at any moment. Maybe it was.

"That's how I could see. But he wasn't helping him."

The round-faced guard scoffed. "Well, he's not helping us."

"He's against Master Belik," Bard confirmed. "We talked about it."

The reminder did nothing to improve the guard's mood, apparently, since he eyed Bard with greater suspicion after that.

"It doesn't matter what Firian's doing right now," said Kiria. "What matters is what Belik has done. He's wearing the crown, and he made all the audience swear their allegiance. Even Amir Parohim was afraid to go against him." The mention of the advisor brought Daelon to mind. Hopefully they would hear from Chetana soon that he had survived the attack.

Jori pouted and shifted his weight, sighing. "Then what are we going to do?"

"The Tanyu are able to find me because of the Talent. I think we need to get away from here until we can regroup and attack from a place of strength." Kader's guards had the right idea after all. The idea of running from Brithnem brought her physical pain, but it could be for the best.

Bard stopped drawing in the dirt with his finger, evidently surprised by her shift in mindset.

"My Keeper," Viktor interjected, "isn't there still a way to communicate with our troops on the inside? I know many of them will still be loyal to you."

Many of them. She didn't like the implication. *Many others won't be.* But it made sense. Belik had made them swear on the Scroll that they would be loyal to him.

He threatened them and their families. "We need more firepower," she replied, shoving away the thought of Firian's ability to kill, the one that had obliterated the Kingdom forces they'd sent to the Academy several weeks before. He hadn't offered, and she wouldn't ask. "So we'll go to our other cities, rally the armies there. With troops on the outside, we'll have a better chance than relying only on those trapped inside Brithnem."

"Do you think they'll all come?" Bard had asked that morning when she suggested the urgent need for more allies.

"They'd better," she replied. "Can you communicate with the Watchman?"

He shrugged one shoulder. "Sure. What do you want me to say?"

She paused. The Tanyu had certainly gotten to the Watchman in Brithnem by now. She wouldn't risk their lives on the possibility of his disloyalty or death. "How about Watchmen in other cities?"

"Yeah."

"Then contact the ones in Rantoul, King's Heights, Redshore, and Arrow that we need their urgent assistance."

He nodded, slowly at first as he considered the names like a sum, then faster as he grew more confident. "Sure. I can do that right now, yeah. Is there a place I should tell them to meet?"

She looked down. "Nowhere yet. Just tell them to muster their armies. I need an idea of how many there are first."

"Shouldn't we bring them here, darling? It's the inevitable next step," Jori had interjected, overhearing their conversation. "We can hunker down, wait for reinforcements. Sounds like a plan to me. Better than gallivanting across the countryside."

"Not yet. It's not quite that simple. And we won't be gallivanting," she said. "We have to get out of reach of the Tanyu first, to preserve the Keeper Lines." She poked Jori's knee. "Yes, you too. And then we can come up with a plan of action. We know that the Tanyu are braced for an attack." Even as she spoke, she felt braced too, tension knotting the muscles in her shoulders.

Bard's jaw worked with the mention of Tanyu. Some of these invaders were his friends. The less bloodshed on either side, the better. But she would do what it took to bring justice back to the Kingdom, even if it meant danger or death.

"Where's Cúron when you need him?" Jori muttered. Kiria frowned at him, but he gave her a sad, impish smile.

Dedication Day was effectively over after Kiria's announcement about Belik. The services were over, the lyra put away. Royce, who had fallen into the position of head guard, talked urgently to the freckle-faced woman, Lilith. Hopefully they would have some good input later.

"So where are we going, then, if we aren't staying in this choice location?" Jori gestured to the underground room he'd been so proud of.

"Rantoul is the closest, if we go directly east. That's probably our best chance right now." It had seemed secure during her return stop on the coronation tour.

"The one with the racing track?" Jori asked. Their guide for that part of the city tour had been a cute, curvy girl Jori hadn't stopped flirting with until she handed them off to an older man with a short beard styled as his father Aylmor's had once been.

"How do we know that the Tanyu haven't anticipated that move?" asked Viktor.

"We can't know," she snapped, then felt bad for her tone. She rubbed her forehead. "But it's something, and we have Bard to look out for us."

Bard raised his chin slightly in acknowledgment, perhaps feeling the pressure of the position he held as the only Tanyu among them.

"We'll have a warning, at least," she clarified.

Jori popped up his eyebrows at Bard. "You can handle that, right?" he asked. "If my girl says you can."

He could. Bard had gone up against Belik himself when he'd come to murder Kiria. He'd stood his ground in the face of almost certain death.

Dimples appeared in Bard's shy smile. "Yeah, that's true," he agreed. "I can do that."

Bard's usefulness to her cause still didn't mean she needed to forgive him for keeping her awake now. They were all shipping out before first light, first to Rantoul to gather support from her own cities, and then onto Charäkhnem to join with their forces. The idea was to overwhelm any counterattack Belik could cook up. Between the Kingdom towns and the massive force King Ganesha could bring from Char Visil, it should be enough.

Kiria had elected to sleep in the great main room along with everyone else so the guards could take shifts looking out for everybody at once. After the evening they'd had, the unspoken consensus was that they wanted the company too. She nuzzled her head against the pillow. It had been found in one of the smaller rooms and smelled like pipe smoke.

"So you just... kept the shields under your cloaks?" Bard asked in an undertone. In a room as quiet as that one, any noise carried.

Royce sat across from him, temporarily off duty. With his helmet off, he looked almost more formidable. The tendons in his thick neck suggested he could crush Bard to smithereens. "That's what they did," he confirmed.

"And they didn't search you?"

"I don't know. Probably. They thought we were ordinary citizens." He heaved his large breastplate across his crossed knees and started polishing it.

Bard shook his head. "I... I could have told you how that plan would go."

Royce blinked at his audacity, the rag pausing in his hand. "Then tell me, what could we have done to reverse any of this?" It was a challenge more than it was a question.

"Well, the first attack was a surprise, so I don't know—"

"So was our move."

"Not in the same way."

In the pause that followed, Kiria started to drift off into warm sleep, sailing on that silence.

"Hey, any word from Adelisa? She's your daughter, isn't she?"

Kiria cracked opened her lids to see Jori settling himself beside Bard and Royce, breaking some of the tension between them.

"I haven't heard from her," Royce replied grimly. "We won't get a full count until we're inside."

Bard squinched up his face, trying to remember. "Is she the one—?"

"Runner," Jori supplied.

Kiria suddenly remembered where she'd heard the name. Adelisa, a young servant in the palace, was part of a squad who fixed broken things—broken pans, mortar, furniture—and she was one of the fastest in the beach races Jori loved. He'd bet on her more than once.

"What do you mean?" Royce asked, moving onto the next piece of armor.

"Have you never been to the races?" Viktor whispered from where he stood on duty above Kiria. She was getting to know all the guards well. Viktor was the youngest among them, only eighteen, like she was.

"Stay at your post, soldier," Royce growled before turning back to Jori. "What races?"

"At the beach," he said easily. "Nothing untoward."

Bard's mouth quirked in a smile.

"I beat Adelisa once," Viktor added.

Jori raised both eyebrows high. "Then it wasn't during one of the races."

"It was! Last spring—"

"Enough," said Royce, holding his shining helmet in one meaty fist.

After a moment, Bard asked, "She's your only daughter, yeah? I'm sorry you haven't heard from her."

"I have seven children."

"Busy man," Jori muttered.

"I'm one of six!" Bard quietly exclaimed, delighted.

The slope of Royce's shoulders softened. "Are you? Where are you from?"

"Enderin."

Jori leaned toward the soldier, imitating Bard's accent. "Listen to him. I thought that much was obvious."

"There's more than just Enderin up north," Royce replied. "I went there twice during the Torithian War."

"Did you?" Bard was leaning forward now too, his black eyes shining with news of his home country.

Jori frowned. "Am I the only one who hasn't been there? What is there to see?"

"Everything!" Bard's prompt response made Jori smile in surprise. "I'll go back when this is over, eventually, I think. I need to visit my family. My brother got married and I have... I have a niece or nephew, only we've never met. You understand, sir."

Royce looked pensive a moment before responding. "I do."

Jori squared himself at Bard. "So all there is to see is your family? That's not a long list of sightseeing options, unless they're spread out, hard to find, like mythical creatures." He looked far away at the wall past Bard's shoulder. "Oh, there's one! I think I spot a Tanery."

Bard smothered a laugh, but Royce rolled his eyes. "I wasn't there for sightseeing."

"Granted," said Jori. "But your eyes were open. There's nothing?"

"There's the ocean," Bard supplied.

"We've got that."

"But it's different."

"Bright pink?"

"Uh... wilder. We've got cliffs and *sachion* trees outside the main city. You should see the buildings. Your houses are just gray. Not... to be... not to offend anyone. But ours match the families. I think I saw some Endrian work in the palace. Woodworking?"

"Go on."

"Have you ever tried *orfinskal*?"

Jori plucked a handkerchief from his breast pocket and offered it to him. Bard shoved his hand away.

"*Orfinskal?*" Bard persisted. "It's like porridge, but with oranges and honey and nuts?"

"I had your cinnamon toast one time."

"That was you?"

"Of course it was. Pretty good. I ordered it from the kitchens next day." Jori turned his attention back to Royce. "Enderin can't be all bad. There's *alfinskat*."

"*Orfinskal*," Bard corrected.

"*Orfinskal*."

Royce set the helmet aside. "Yeah, I tried it. I could never get used to the way they keep the leaves in their tea, but we ate the Endrian food when we had to."

Bard's mouth flattened. Apparently, he didn't like his local cuisine insulted.

"We leave before dawn," Royce said, more gently now. Kiria heard fatherly care in it. "You two should get some rest."

"I never rest," Jori said grandly. "I only pause."

Bard quirked an eyebrow. "It's all right. You can sleep," he said, as though guessing that some fear lay behind Jori's declaration. "How are we traveling? Horses? I... I'll need to sleep sometime, but if I can ride with someone tomorrow... you know, sleep in the saddle for a while, I'll watch you tonight."

Jori's eyes widened in pleased surprise. "Oh ho! You want to watch me sleep? But we haven't so much as held hands."

Bard's cheeks darkened. "No. No, I mean, the Tanyu will come after you. You're their biggest target, after... My Keeper." His eyes shot to the guard. Maybe he felt he had to use her formal title in front of him. "They'll come in your dreams, maybe tonight, yeah?"

Jori grew serious, his gaze sliding to where Kiria pretended to sleep. "What about her? Kiria needs this more than I do."

"She has the Talent, at least."

"Check with her." Without waiting for someone else to do it, Jori crawled over to where she slept.

"My Kepron," Viktor began hurriedly, "don't—"

Jori gently shook her shoulder.

Kiria sighed and looked up at him. "Do you really think I could sleep through all that?" she whispered.

He smiled roguishly. "Then you heard, love. What do you think?"

She sat up slowly to look him in the eye. "Chetana taught me what to do. Or she started to before she left yesterday. I can take care of myself."

"Don't lie, darling."

"Never."

Jori cocked his head, unconvinced. "You're dreaming peacefully away and a Tanyu comes to kill you—you'd know what to do?"

"I have a plan, yes."

"So I should let this one watch me in my sleep?"

"Definitely." Her face warmed. Why hadn't she thought of suggesting it herself? At least someone had. "He can ward them off, or at least wake you up in time to avoid getting hurt."

"You're going to stay up all night?" Viktor asked Bard, dropping the pretense of whispering. More than one person groaned. For a guard that was supposed to be silent, he had a lot to say.

Bard gave one of his rapid-fire, repetitive nods.

Viktor reached in a pouch by his side, retrieved something small, and threw it at Bard. "Helps me stay awake."

In Bard's palm lay something that looked like a seed pod.

"You chew it," Viktor explained.

"Well, that's that," Kiria said, shoving Jori playfully away. "Now please, please, be quiet and go to sleep."

27

BELIK

SANDALWOOD. It was always sandalwood first. Belik snuffed, as though he could rid himself of the smell that meant Chetana was near. During this whole gory campaign, he'd felt her presence, but had successfully ignored it so far. A lifetime of practice had given him excellent skill at that. But he hadn't been crowned more than a couple hours before he started to feel it again in force.

She wasn't in the Amiran Academy—he'd had it searched—or else he would have killed her right there. If Amir weren't valuable assets, he would have burned the infernal place down with all of them inside, in honor of her memory. Except for Daelon, maybe. As it was, they made good servants.

As pacifists, the Amir didn't frighten him with rebellion, but as scholars, they could be capable of spying, so he ordered them locked in their Academy at night.

He pushed aside such gloomy thoughts, readjusting in the uncomfortable chair. The air still smelled smoky here, but this was the Keepers' quarters farthest from the worst of the damage. Third Keeper's quarters. He had all the bodies taken out days ago and placed in the arena plaza, but the room still had the uncomfortable feeling of recent failure. His most reliable allies—Shiro, Nedi, and the girl named Enktuya, who'd taken charge at the first coronation—stood around him. He'd just sent away the Tanyu taking care of the thin troops commanding the wall. If Chetana's presence got stronger, he'd send out a search for her, but at the moment he could hardly spare the warriors as he took total control of the city and crushed the mushrooming attempts against the Tanyu's rule. Now was the time to lock down the city tightly and to kill those who opposed him. Quick and simple, but requiring all hands. Finding Chetana was not the kind of job he'd trust the Kingdom troops to do. She'd once been part of Original Plan, the radical group that had sent her to assassinate him, once upon a time. No, if it became necessary, he'd find her himself.

"A Defender," said Shiro after checking the door.

Belik waved his hand impatiently. A ruler's work was never done. The crown, melded of all three royal diadems, sat on a cushioned pillow beside him, ready to be wielded like a weapon when necessary. One day the Tanyu would have the palace, have the wall, have the city, have the Western Kingdom, but he wasn't quite there. In the meantime, it was always meaningless interruptions.

"Master Belik," said a Tanyuin Defender, approaching him with head bowed. The stocky, light-skinned boy held out a carved wooden box. The markings didn't distinguish it as coming from any particular culture—no Endrian *sachion* trees or Charäkhni golden eagles.

"What's this?"

"It arrived... from Master Kess."

Belik's eyebrows darted downward. *Firian?* He was supposed to be on his way over the mountains by now. He snatched the box and opened it. Inside, next to a curl of paper, lay a small human finger severed at the second knuckle. He cast a shrewd glance at the messenger, but the boy looked back steady and guileless. The Defender hadn't manufactured this grisly present.

Belik pinched the slip of paper and read it. *Kepron Kader is killed and no longer a threat to you. Give Brett more time. Three days.* The handwriting looked masculine, but there was no way to test its authenticity.

"Where did you get this?" Belik demanded.

"Master Turgin, on the wall."

"Your name?"

"Lazlo Gram."

He'd have to question Master Turgin about where he received this package.

"It's a finger," Belik explained, gauging Lazlo's reaction.

The boy's features remained immovable. A good Tanyu, with no sign of guilt or innocence.

The bloody stump could belong to Kader. As he began to accept the possibility, his body felt alight. If the Kepron were dead, that was one less loose end to track down. Who else could it belong to, unless Firian had infiltrated the Tanyu here in Brithnem? There was no way to check if it came from one of the previously dead bodies, since all but the royals and would-be assassins, put on display, had been burned.

Kiria, then, was the only royal left. And the Calthwaite prince. Belik could deal with both of those in dream attacks. No Tanyu would even have to leave their post. It was elegant. Suspiciously easy.

He snapped the box lid closed. Oak. Still better than sandalwood.

28

BARD

BARD POPPED one of Viktor's seeds into his mouth. They tasted bitter, like fenugreek, a spice his cousin used to use in all her food. It was never his favorite. He'd always liked sweets better.

Slow breathing surrounded him, lulling heaviness into his limbs. But he could sleep in the morning. Now he had to defend Jori. Of course, being awake at night and asleep in the day like a barn cat reinforced that he was an outsider. He was already Tanyu—too soft for the Academy, too Tanyuin for his family. At least here his differences could help someone.

Jori slept recklessly. A small smile dimpled Bard's cheek as he looked at him. The Kepron's mouth was wide open, wavy hair falling back from his forehead. Never careful. If he was going to survive Belik, he'd have to learn some caution.

He'd suffered so much. Bard forced down the last seed, smile fading, trying not to think what he would do if one of his own brothers were killed, and slipped into Jori's dream.

Nothing was distinct, as though everything were happening underwater. The forest Jori wandered through looked born from the sea too. It wasn't made of trees like any forest Bard had seen, but sea kelp or upside-down jellyfish, the tentacles and transparent veils waving in an unfelt breeze. Red birds with slim bodies and long wings flew among the pale green appendages, squawking to each other.

The environment was incredible, as imaginative as anything a Tanyu would come up with. It set Bard's mind ablaze and brought an open-mouthed smile to his lips. So beautiful and strange.

Jori looked up for a while. Faces appeared between branches—fleeting glimpses gone in a blink. These seemed to confuse him, but the dream still felt tenuously peaceful.

Bard stayed out of sight. He could have set a Sentry instead of watching the weird, unruly beauty of this dream. Every murky corner was decorated with thoughts the way every Endrian house was decorated in carvings and strings of shells. Setting a Sentry would have been simpler. But the idea scared him.

The memory of those people, once Tanyu like himself, forced to become Sentries until their Talent and identity faded into nothing but pain. His heart squeezed. Back in Tánuil, Wells had told him a little, but Bard never pressed him. The image of pale, dirt-smeared people with hollow eyes was enough to haunt Bard for the rest of his life. He'd rather watch and defend every crazy dream Jori had than set a Sentry night after night.

One translucent branch bent down toward Jori as though curious. Its sinuous arm wrapped around him tight.

Was another Tanyu here? Was this an attack? Bard felt for another presence but found none. An ordinary nightmare.

As Jori struggled, Bard's breath grew shallow. Shouldn't he help him anyway, since he could?

Before he could decide, the ground tilted and spun, folding in on itself, the branch taking Jori with it. As though someone had turned a page, a new scene appeared. Jori was still bound by the plant creature, but now the space was smaller and emptier. It was a rectangular box, splashed with different colors. The walls closed in slowly, or maybe it was the colors themselves, but everything was contracting around them, getting smaller and smaller.

Another figure appeared nearby but Jori didn't seem to notice it hadn't been there all along. Bard looked closer.

Kiria. She looked already dead, purple-pale and wrapped in layers of clammy tentacles.

Jori called to the birds in the forest, the red ones that had swum in the air above him, but his voice was muffled. He tried to scream, his mouth open wider than it was in real life as he slept, but the sound grew quiet, instantly stifled.

Bard's stomach tightened. He knew that feeling. No voice. Shouting when no one could hear.

Then, the touch of another mind. Subtle. This Tanyu was probably older and more experienced. The buzz became more distinct, but Bard saw no one.

He raced to the surface of the dream and burst out into the Real again. Jori hadn't moved or changed his expression. Only Bard knew what was happening inside his head. He shook the Kepron's shoulder, but he didn't stir. When Bard shook harder, Jori only smacked his lips and rolled over.

Urgency pressed against Bard's chest. If Jori wasn't waking, then Bard would have to help him from inside the dream. Hopefully he hadn't lost too much time. Dream time was different than waking time.

In a flash, he was back. The dark walls were still lowering, getting closer to the prone forms of Jori and Kiria, trapped in their bonds. Bard's nose wrinkled. If the walls touched Jori, he'd wake in seconds.

This probably wasn't part of the Tanyuin warrior's attack, then.

Never wake them up. That was what his Masters had instructed Bard before they sent him to terrorize the people of Brithnem during the fear campaign. Ah, he'd hated that. Hated it. Done all he could to avoid hurting anybody.

Even though closing the room wasn't the Tanyu's primary tactic, Bard hated to see Jori trapped like that, about to be crushed. He eased into Jori's consciousness, made himself known as he gently directed the dream to change, for the ceiling and walls to expand.

Jori followed him with his gray eyes, curious, no longer panicking. A small spike of relief ran through Bard. But something was still wrong. The feeling of the other presence hadn't left. This was too easy.

The dungeon-like room shifted sideways as the forest had done, pitching like a wave into a variation of the scene. Kiria's body disappeared. The long ceiling became a wall hung with tapestries. A small blonde girl was kissing him. Jori's eyebrows rose in surprise and then delight.

Bard inhaled sharply. *Nothing like the captain, yeah?* He'd never forget what his *katah* with the Torithian captain Tibor Wat had made him witness. Images stuck to his mind like tar. Poor, used girls, naked bodies with bruises, sour kisses, and nights that brought pleasure only to the captain. He wished he could scrub his mind clean.

Jori wrapped his arms sweetly around the girl's waist, broke the kiss, and said something indistinct, a playful smirk on his face.

No, nothing like him. But it still felt invasive to spy. Bard squirmed.

The shift that followed was slight. Jori stopped talking. He stopped moving, and so did the girl. His eyes slid out of focus.

Bard snapped to attention. She was the Tanyu. Had she shifted the dream to this to distract him, lull him to airless sleep? Bard couldn't will away the girl—somebody must have chosen to look that way since she didn't seem familiar at all—but he could do something.

He sent an enormous red bird barreling at the couple, flying low enough to brush both their heads. Jori's eyes focused for a moment. Good.

But the Tanyu saw him too. "Leave us alone," she laughed in a girly voice.

Bard's skin crawled. "He's... needed at a meeting."

"Ha! Just two more minutes." The steely eyes belied her innocent words. Jori still held her loosely.

Make them passively accept what's happening, the Masters taught. He needed the opposite.

"What do you think?" Bard asked Jori.

"I think?" Jori replied, looking as though he'd forgotten something.

The girl planted another kiss.

Bard glowered. Jori wasn't catching on. Though it was risky, Bard rapidly took in the details of the little nook and added realism to it, solidifying it. It was a relief, actually. The dream had been so murky, Bard felt he had trouble breathing. Now the stone walls had depth, and the tapestries had clear design and texture. The air smelled a little like cinnamon. Why not?

Just like practice. But he hadn't practiced fighting in the Unreal for a while. Didn't think he'd have to again. He took a deep breath and released a piercing gust of wind from his palms. The tapestries whooshed upward and the Jori was slammed back into the wall with a grunt. The force made him release the blonde girl—the Tanyu, whoever it was—who whirled on Bard.

He brought the red bird back, its long gleaming beak clacking. The dusty smell of feathers joined the scent in the air. It picked up the blonde girl by the back of the collar.

Instantly, a spear flew at Bard. He shrank to avoid it. It didn't even look like the girl threw it, but the weapon definitely came from her mind. *Believable but unexpected.* That was a hard line to walk, but she apparently had practice.

Bard was no Firian, but he had practice too.

The huge bird dropped the girl. Instead of hitting the ground, she sank into it as though it were a pit of tar. The ground roiled and bubbled, pitch black and sticky. It covered the girl's arms and left angry red burn marks. Bard chewed his tongue but didn't let up. She was going to kill Jori, heir to the throne and one of his few remaining friends. Someone who didn't dismiss him or mock him or fear him. Someone who actually seemed to like him.

The image grew grotesque, but finally, mercifully, she disappeared. Hopefully her real burns weren't too bad. He needed to really frighten her so she didn't come back.

When he looked to the side, Jori had disappeared too. Bard came back to the Real, the mild scent of cinnamon replaced with faint body odor. Jori was stirring. Uninjured. Awake.

Bard smiled reassuringly when Jori opened his eyes. He had the same expression he'd worn in the dream, confusion, like he'd forgotten something important. He ran a hand through his hair and turned over to see where he was. His attention returned to Bard, who didn't feel as sleepy as before. Either the fight or the seeds had done the trick.

"That wasn't..." Jori trailed off, instead lifting one eyebrow in a question.

Bard nodded. "It's okay," he whispered. "You can go back to sleep."

Jori's mouth turned downward in perplexed amazement. "That was amazing. I'll try to get in more trouble."

"Please, don't do that."

The mischievous glint in Jori's eye offered no promises.

29

FIRIAN

When the box arrived for Master Belik, Firian immediately shifted his attention back to the Real.

As soon as he did, exhaustion cried out in his bones. He'd been riding as hard as the new horse could stand for a long time. Between his trips to the Unreal and the endless ride, he'd almost lost track of time. The sensation was like dizziness. Squinting at the horse's mane bobbing before him, he fought to find his footing, to remember how much time was left to save Brett. The ground swam. Even when he looked up, the mountainous landscape moved like water. He ground his teeth with frustration. Time to stop.

He pulled up on the reins and the sweating horse obeyed immediately. They were well clear of Redshore, traveling along fairly well-trodden roads. Despite wearing the brown shirt he'd taken from the chest in the ale cellar instead of his customary black, he knew he could be recognized. Still, it was faster this way, and speed mattered most now.

He heaved in a breath of sea-scented night air and dismounted. Beside him, the mare tossed her head in wide-eyed agitation. What would Kiria have named this horse? The question caught him as a more serious one would have. He faced the beast and looked into its deep brown, glossy eyes, rimmed with lashes. Keeping a hold of the reins steadied him. Gore, he was tired.

Move or sleep.

He gazed down the lantern-lit road running parallel to the sea. Was Kader safe somewhere north, or was he another corpse that Belik would soon find... or make? Belik was no fool. He'd suspect a trick, and if he caught Firian spying on his mind, that would only deepen his suspicion. Still, better to check to make sure that the ruse had actually worked, and that the young Kepron was safe from further pursuit.

He led the mare off the road into the trees, where he could sleep without prying eyes. The poor beast was covered with sweat. Pursing his lips, he stroked the mare's long nose. He should have changed horses more than once, he realized as he eased off her saddle and bridle. Well, at least they were resting now, and there was good vegetation for her to eat here.

As he lay down, his last thought was that her name should be Laird. Kiria would like that.

Firian had always regarded sleep as wasted time, but when he woke a few hours later, he had to admit that he felt much better. Now he could ride and trek afresh. Brett's life depended on it. Though he hadn't seen his sister since the shocking encounter in Raewhith, he knew she was on his side. When the world abandoned him, his sister never would.

Laird, the mare, wasn't happy to continue. She threatened to nip at him as he put her tack back on. He patted the side of her head once, reassuringly, before leaping in the saddle again. His muscles ached, which was good. He could regret the break less if he knew he had pushed himself far enough to hurt.

Now, maybe, he could sneak a look into Master Belik's mind. Was Kader safe? Could he tell Bard he'd succeeded?

Casting his mind back to the palace felt strangely off-kilter. That was the place his mind had gone to be with Kiria, but now it was Belik's domain. The knowledge burned. At least he could do this to help her, to show her that he didn't condone Belik's violent overthrow. Soon—but he reined in his mind. Thinking too far ahead was disastrous. The simple fact was this. Firian would kill Belik for what he had done. He would make things right. Beyond that, his ideas shied like a horse at an unexpected barrier. He couldn't ask himself why, not when there was so much at stake already.

A direct confrontation. It was a gamble, but it was best. If Firian had really killed the Kepron, he would own up to it directly.

Firian cleared his mind. *Meeting up with Kiria in the north, saving Brett, picking off heirs to the throne to buy time...* He inhabited the (mostly) false reality he wanted Belik to believe. Now, where to meet? Statues and tiles and stained-glass plates and soaring ceilings came together in a replica of the Main. He smirked in grim satisfaction at the sight.

Belik was not long to appear on the dais beside him.

The wound in Firian's shoulder shot pain across his chest.

The Master didn't wear a crown, but he might as well have. He scratched the side of his head casually and took in Firian, up and down. Though his posture was relaxed, his eyes shone bright with wariness. Apparently, he determined that nothing was different about Firian except his attitude.

Firian's muscles tensed, even in the Unreal, but he held his black rage in check. When they'd met before, his hatred nearly drowned him. Now, he was diplomatic—at least, as diplomatic as he ever got.

"I want time for my sister," he said. Could he kill Belik now? Maybe, but he needed Belik to call off his allies from harming Brett. And who knew if Kiria was in a position to retake the throne? Bard had said they'd leave after Dedication Day, and that was yesterday.

Belik grunted, waiting for more.

He'd have to sell it, then. *Okay.* "I..." He swallowed. "I found the Kepron. Kader. The young one." He allowed a flash of the hate he felt to surface in his gaze. "I made it fast. I had to kill his escort too, but he's gone."

"Where?" In the Real, Belik would have sat on the throne beside them, but here, his leg didn't hurt. They were on equal ground.

"I killed him in a tavern between Brithnem and Redshore. Where they were hiding before moving on."

"Which inn?"

"What?"

Belik repeated the words.

This was a game, a calculation. Firian fished for a name. Hadn't he passed an inn...?

"I don't know the names of all these gory places," he said.

Belik's law clenched. "And the body?"

"You got your gift," Firian snarled. The idea of killing a child... Disgusting.

Belik leveled his gaze, and the gravel in his voice deepened. "The body."

Firian's chest constricted with fury. "I gave you part of it. Do you want the rest?"

"Where is it?"

"Burned by now for all I know! I didn't stay. I doubt anyone would recognize him. He was wearing average clothes and the only royal token I found on him is the one I sent you. Now, do I have my three days?"

Belik scrutinized him longer. Firian didn't flinch. A deed as horrific as he'd claimed to have done would earn him, at a minimum, that extra time.

"Three days," Firian repeated, jaw clenching. He truly could use the time. With only seven days left, he could run out of time if snow had reached the mountains. It wasn't unheard of this time of year.

"The First Line is dead?"

At the words, a rabbit's breath of pause shook Firian. Had Kader been a shield for Kiria? She was all that was left of the Second Line, as far as he knew. Now that the threat of a living heir to the First Line had been dealt with, would Master Belik spare more Tanyu to hunt her down? The thought made him sick. Still, "yes" was the word he heard himself say.

Belik's barrel chest expanded in a heavy breath.

"Three days," Firian said again.

"Two," Belik replied, mouth quirking as though they engaged in some sort of game.

A hand might as well have gripped Firian's throat, for the rage he felt. He had to leave. Now. His curt nod might have come off as a twitch, but he didn't care.

He came to, sucking in the cold morning air. The leaves, ripening to orange as he went north, and clean chill brought him to calm as he rushed along the road.

He could do more than this. He'd saved the Kepron, but Belik had to be stopped. Soon, his own allies inside the palace would take care of that.

30

KIRIA

THAT MORNING, Bard lay slumped over the saddle horn of Royce's chestnut mount, bobbing with the movement of the horse. He'd stayed up all night defending Jori's dreams. Exhausting work, even at the best of times.

Kiria looked back at Brithnem, her city, right before it went out of view. Was it her imagination or was the air still hazy above the palace? The black sky was lightening to gray, cooling the tips of the far waves. City Beautiful.

Where was Chetana in that tangle of stone buildings? Was she safe? If her *katah* with Belik was anything like hers with Firian, Belik would know she was near. When Bard wasn't so drained, Kiria would ask him to check on the Amir, make sure she was safe. Maybe they would learn whether Daelon was alive.

Their group wasn't taking the main roads, so it would be slow going. The pace grated against her nerves. It was a straight shot east to Rantoul, then Charäkhnem, much more direct than her coronation tour had been.

"Kiria."

She turned to Jori, who looked more serious than usual. It was probably the earliness of the hour. Despite his claim the night before, he loved to sleep in.

"Bard told me he set a watch over Kader's dreams as well. Thought you'd want to know."

"He watched two people himself?"

Their words fell like leaves in the burgeoning autumn. Pre-dawn chill swept over their faces, and birds sang in the quiet.

"He said there was someone else to watch Kader."

She lowered her brow. "Another Tanyu? He should have told me."

"It was the middle of the night, darling. We had specific instructions not to wake you, if you remember."

"But another Tanyu!"

"I know, love, but maybe we don't have a choice."

"There's always a choice." The words echoed in her thoughts, dripping like an indoor pool. She shook off the feeling. "Who is it?" *It had better not be Firian.*

"He says he was a 'Sentry' back home. Abused by the Tanyu so he has no love of them. Blocks the dreams or something. Says his name is Wells."

"No love of the Tanyu?" Kiria replied. "He is one of them."

"So's our boy."

She chewed her lip. Bard was the exception. Theoretically, there could be more like him. She cast a glance in his direction. His mouth was open, eyes closed, crazy hair fluffed in the wind. Royce, holding the reins, towered above him.

"I'll speak to him later," she said finally. The two heirs were her responsibility. Hers alone. Atty and Cúron weren't here to support her. She stiffened her spine. "You shouldn't go making decisions like that without me."

He narrowed his eyes. "You can't have it both ways, love. You insist I'm important—"

"You are."

"—and yet I can't act like it. Which is fine."

But it didn't look fine. His expression turned sullen.

Kiria adjusted her grip on the reins. "You just... Jori, you know yourself. Have you ever been responsible?"

"I heard there was a time when I was eight."

"Lies." She smiled. "You are important. You are... the Third Line. But you didn't know where Qib was!" Her coronation tour had only been a few months ago, and the name had slipped his mind during the party when they both met Princess Haved for the first time.

He placed one hand on his chest in horror. "Oh, Qib! Well then, I can never rule."

Kiria rolled her eyes. "You know what I mean."

"Do I have to be more intelligent? I've heard I'm very dashing."

"Not the same thing."

"And fabulously brilliant."

She sighed. "You have to know where Qib is, and who our allies are, and how to enforce laws."

Halfway through her sentence, Jori's attention drifted elsewhere. He pointed ahead of them. "Is that a blue wren?"

"Am I boring you?"

"Oh no. Taxation and legislation have been my constant source of pleasure for years." He eyed her, deadpan.

"That's what I mean. You have to get more serious about this stuff."

"Many have tried. Many have failed."

"Jori!"

He released a breath and held her gaze now. "Don't squash my sense of fun. Not now." There was a hint of pleading in his tone.

For how long? Jori couldn't avoid responsibility forever, not with so much at stake. "Just think about it."

His attention lingered on her only for a beat before he gasped and fell back to maneuver around her. "Look who's awake!"

"Not awake," Bard slurred, closing his eyes again.

Jori clucked his tongue, casting Kiria a quick conspiratorial look. "We were just talking about that person you sent to help the Little One." That was their unofficial code name for Kader while they traveled. It wouldn't do to have strangers overhear that another heir was alive.

"Wells," Bard murmured, doubling over on himself in an apparent effort to get more comfortable.

"My Kepron," Royce said above them, snapping the reins, "let him sleep."

Jori held up a finger. "Very quickly, very quickly." His voice was soft, but he spurred on his own horse to keep pace.

Kiria followed, hedging Royce's horse in on the other side. "Does he know... if Kader is still free? If he's been caught?"

In an admission of waking, Bard raked a hand through his hair and scratched his head hard. Heavy shadows ringed his eyes. A pang of guilt sparked through her at forcing him awake. "He hasn't," he answered. "They won't get him."

Relief flooded her body. Then his effortless tone struck her. Was it just that he was still shaking off sleep, or did he know something more?

"Biscuit?" One appeared in Jori's hand. He broke it in half and offered some to Bard, who waved it away, but then thought the better of it and took it gratefully.

"So good," he said through the second mouthful.

"Only the best. It's old, but I always keep some in my—"

"How do you know the Little One won't get caught?" Kiria interjected.

"Firian," came Bard's swift reply. When he looked back at her, however, something like indecision wavered in his gaze a moment, as though he'd said too much.

"What about Firian?" She asked the question carefully, unsure what to expect.

Bard swallowed the last bite of biscuit. "He made Belik look the other way." A one-shouldered shrug. "Convinced him Kader was dead. He's not! He's not."

"How?"

"Do you really want to know how?" Jori asked, peering through the gap between Bard and the horse's neck. Then, to Bard, "You can tell me later—I'd love to know details."

"It's... It'll work," Bard said. "No one will look for him, at least not for a long time. He said not to tell you it was him." Something like defiance crossed his features.

Firian helped her? Helped *Kader*, who could do nothing to advance his cause? She held her breath. "Does he know where the Little One is?"

Bard shook his head and swayed in the saddle. Royce caught his stiff left arm before he fell.

"Sorry," Bard said, righting himself.

Jori patted Bard's knee. Royce glared at the hand so close to his own leg.

"It's fine," Kiria said. The landscape around her blurred, secondary to her thoughts. "Get some rest. Now we can all sleep easier, with that information."

Bard gave a wide smile that split his whole face. "Yeah."

Kiria trotted ahead of the guard, leaving Bard in peace. Hopefully Jori would follow her lead. Bard had more than earned the rest. It crossed her mind that she had forgotten to ask about Chetana. She'd ask him about her once he woke in a few hours.

Because of mysterious actions by Firian, Kader was safe somewhere. The Three Lines intact. She felt lightheaded. Glad. Confused. *How* had he done it?

And with the Sentry over Kader's mind, she didn't need to worry about a nightmare attack on any of them. She smiled, and it felt strange. All this time spent in terror and horror and grief. Finally, now, some good news.

Some very good news.

31

KIRIA

Rantoul lay on the far end of Á Quihilmar, the Gray Forest. The large town spanned the river. The mayor's residence rose like a miniature fortress on one bank. Beside it, threaded among trees, were shops and theatres and money changing stations. Well-dressed citizens bustled along the streets, stopping by the various businesses and entertainment options. Ordinary citizens lived across the river on the larger half of town, where the structures were noticeably more dilapidated. Warehouses, factories, smithies, and small farms took up that side. Two bridges spanned the Apothelin River, connecting the disparate sides.

As they approached from a distance, Kiria was struck by the beauty yet odd segregation of the town. On her coronation tour, nobles had ferried her from one sight to another, but they never crossed the river. From where they were, only the mayor's tall residence, and a sliver of the activity happening on either bank was visible until they came closer. Then the town walls shut out much of the activity within. A large portcullis closed the gap that allowed the river to run through the town's center.

Near it, outside the walls, children played along the riverbank on the poorer side. One small boy, shirtless despite the early snap of autumn, perked up to see Kiria's little group approaching the more affluent side. She waved at him. Without wearing her Beauty, there was little danger of being recognized. The boy waved back before screaming joyfully and rushing at the cold water with the other children.

After a few hours on the road, Bard had reluctantly woken up and let the Watchman of Rantoul know they were arriving. Their entrance that afternoon held little fanfare, unlike her last visit. This time, she was disguised with her plain face. With violence so close by, the guards at the walls had insisted on seeing their agreed-upon verification: the top of the royal tattoo, whose point ended at the nape of her neck.

Now they all sat around the mayor's large wooden dining table. Every guard but Viktor, who was carrying everyone's bags to their quarters, had joined them in the room, opting for additional caution. Bard was nursing a cup of tea, Jori a cup of wine.

The décor here had a seafaring flavor, though they were several days from the Kheltor. On a side table sat a large model of a naval ship. A row of cylindrical metal lanterns had been hung above the long table. This room had windows too, unlike the grand dining room in the palace. One was ajar, letting in cool air. Every other place she'd been to since the safe house had felt like a closed box, a prison. This felt open.

The mayor of Rantoul, a young man in his twenties with thick, closely cropped brown hair and a round emerald earring in one ear, sat with them. He stretched his long legs out, his chair angled sideways to the table. He was obviously trying to look relaxed, but he held his body tense and his shrewd gaze kept returning to her as though she were a puzzle to be solved.

"Mayor Emeric," she began, "thank you for taking us in during this time of need." The words felt false, rehearsed, although she meant them. Tonight, she could sleep in a real bed. For that alone, she was grateful.

"It was no trouble, My Keeper," he replied evenly, adjusting his posture and pulling up his chair. "In fact, it was a delight. It's good to be able to do something positive. I'm horrified by the events."

"Yes," she said, her limbs suddenly heavy, "but the Three Lines live on and the traitors must meet justice."

Jori dropped his eyes.

She picked up her tea and blew on it. "That's why we came to you. I need your army to assist us in taking back the capital. We must act quickly. We're calling on other cities as well, all around the Western Kingdom."

"I'm honored you stopped here first." He inclined his head, but kept his eyes on her.

Relief and suspicion battled for supremacy inside her. There was something scrutinizing about his piercing gaze, something that went beyond respect and loyalty. She needed these Kingdom cities on her side. The memory of Belik's promise to give wealth and freedom to anyone who refused to help her sat sour inside her.

"And who are my guests?" Emeric gestured to the others. An emerald ring flashed in the light.

"This is the Kepron Jorrim Calthwaite, and this is our friend, Bardhon Tanery."

His eyes lit up at Jori's name. "A pleasure. I thought I recognized your face."

"Yes, well, it's a memorable face," Jori replied.

"But *your* name," Emeric continued, turning to Bard, "I regret to say, I haven't had the pleasure of hearing before." Friendly dimples appeared in his cheeks, but his eyes sharpened.

The tea in Kiria's stomach made itself known. Should she tell the whole truth, that Bard was a Tanyu? As Keeper, she could do as she liked, but having a Tanyu by her side might undermine her credibility. Belik was already trying his best to do that without her confirming negative rumors.

"He was a Tanyu but he's on our side now," Jori piped up. "Bard's communicating to the Watchmen for us. Best of the lot."

Emeric cut a glance at Kiria. She saw his mind working.

"He's from Enderin," she supplied. Maybe the fact Bard's family was an ally would repair some of the damage Jori might have done by outing him as a Tanyu.

Bard nodded, absently twisting the black Tanyuin ring around his finger with his thumb.

Emeric noticed the action. "I see," he said, leaning back again. "I must say I'm surprised to see you traveling with a Tanyu after all that's happened. What, if I may ask, happened to the Tanyuin Head?"

Kiria set down her tea. A blunt question required a blunt answer. "Master Belik supplanted him when he attacked the capital," she explained.

"Did he die in the fighting?"

"No."

Their eyes locked, a challenge in the look. Why would Emeric challenge her? Did he not believe her? Again, Belik's speech rose to her mind.

She put her shoulders back. "He's not our concern right now."

"I think"—here, he tapped a finger against his lip—"that I have some right to know if I'm going to help you. Don't you think?"

It didn't escape her that he said *if* not *when*.

"He's heading over the mountains right now," Bard supplied. The last red rays of the evening sun fell in a slash across his cheeks and nose.

"I didn't help Master Kess organize any sort of attack, if that's what you're insinuating," Kiria said, when Emeric's attention flashed back to her. She swallowed. "My family were casualties in the fighting."

"Your private affairs are hardly my business, My Keeper. My apologies." He pressed a hand to his chest and briefly bowed his head.

Private affairs. "Accepted," she said flatly.

He waved a female servant forward. "Drienne, check on the dessert and tell us how long until it's ready." She swept from the room to follow his orders. It was early for supper, but Kiria had requested a meal immediately after all their traveling. "I'm simply looking out for the welfare of Rantoul. You must understand."

"Of course," she said.

"So, I have to ask. How do you come to travel with a Tanyu at all? Did he renege on his kind? I've never heard of a cowardly Tanyu. Wicked ones, we've seen ample proof. Again, I mean no disrespect."

Jori perked up, his eyes darting between Emeric and Bard as though he just realized what was happening. "Excuse me, you might not mean it, but you're managing it just fine. It sounds like you're insulting my friend here."

"I meant no—"

Bard tipped his mouth and waved his good hand to dismiss the slight, but Jori squeezed Bard's shoulder and shook him lightly. Bard rapidly set down his tea to keep it from spilling.

"Bard was with us during all the… unpleasantness. And before that night," Jori said. "He left the Tanyuin Academy before any of this happened. He saved my girl —your Keeper. He's more heroic than any of us, and takes less credit. You excepted, my dear, as always," he added to Kiria. "And with a little help, his hair could be better than yours." He leaned forward, scrutinizing the handsome mayor. "Probably. But that's not the point. If you're going to slight my friend, then you could find yourself paying higher taxes for a year."

Itching powders in bed, a duel, a public dunking in the river, Kiria might have expected from Jori to persuade him, but taxes? She wouldn't follow through with his threat, since the common people didn't need to pay for their leader's lack of tact. But maybe Jori was listening to her after all.

Emeric looked at her for confirmation. Was Jori someone to be taken seriously?

She smiled mirthlessly. Though she tried for her mother's easy grace, it didn't come as easily to her. Still, diplomacy seemed to be breaking down. Somehow, she needed to repair it, put Emeric's fears at ease. "We're not working with the Tanyu," she explained, "but we are working with Bard. He isn't like the rest."

Bard readjusted his shoulders as though his shirt were on crooked. His cheeks had gone dark, but his eyes shone with delight at the compliments.

The mayor's jaw jutted as though he were a reprimanded child. "My apologies."

Jori raised his eyebrows and took another drink.

"In fact," Kiria said to Bard, "if you could contact Charäkhnem and let me know how many troops they plan to send. Take a guard with you."

"Sure. I'll go right now." He bounded up from his seat so eagerly that a servant flinched as she gathered the mayor's glass.

Once he was gone, Kiria said, "He could do it at the table, but I wouldn't want you to be uncomfortable."

Jori looked at her approvingly over the rim of his cup, as though she'd just won a point.

"I assure you I wouldn't be uncomfortable…"

"It's the convulsing," Jori added. "That gets some people."

The mayor frowned, looking sorely ganged up on.

"Now that you know he's no threat," she said, thinking they might have taken their comments a little too far, "you know that you have nothing to fear from us. I want the Tanyu out of the capital even more than you do."

"No doubt." Emeric laced his fingers together. Taking a breath, he looked up again. "I should have known better than to question your judgment. I hope you will forgive me. With all the uncertainty surrounding the attack, and the conflicting reports about you, My Keeper, we have been warier than usual."

"I understand that," she conceded, although it was unsettling to hear more about conflicting reports about her. Would the mayor think like those citizens she'd overheard in Brithnem? Did he think she was a weak leader, sacrificing those she loved to succumb to her passions? No leader was universally loved, but that memory stung like a new wound every time she thought of it. "What are the conflicting reports, exactly? In Brithnem, I wasn't in a position to hear much news beyond what my guards brought me."

Emeric blinked a couple times before answering. Not a good sign.

"Sometimes they paint an unflattering picture," he admitted, running one hand through his short hair. "Now I see they were mistaken about your character."

"But what do the reports say?"

When the mayor hesitated, Jori said, "It's an easy question. Do they say she's as tall as two people standing on each other's shoulders? That she's a muskrat, a murderer? What?" He flung his hands in the air.

"They conflict," Emeric said delicately. Looking at a servant behind him, he said, "Bring out the dessert now."

Could he stall any more obviously? She stopped herself from crossing her arms in annoyance as the servant left the room. She hadn't come through the trauma of watching her world burn to be strung along by this man. The time for prevarication was long gone.

Emeric angled his chair again before continuing. "I had heard something about how you were... involved with the Tanyuin Head, and that you let them into the palace. I was shocked, of course, and knew you would never have done such a thing."

Jori glowered at the mayor. He all but said, *Damn right*. Kiria didn't deign to respond, but still felt heat creep into her face. Hopefully he wouldn't see her blush.

"I also heard that you refused to give aid to Kingdom cities who helped you," he said.

She quirked an eyebrow. Belik's coronation speech had traveled quickly.

"I knew right then that I was listening to lies."

"What aid?" she asked carefully. "We've always treated our allies fairly." The Keepers had always helped the other cities of the Kingdom—fostering trade for their economy, sending troops when they were in trouble, assistance after disasters—all with the assumption that the Keepers could rely on them to fight on their behalf. But Emeric sounded like he meant something else, something more.

"There's substantial danger in helping you," he said. "The entire force of the Tanyu is against you. It will cost great loss of life. The leader of the Tanyu said he would pay for our armies to stay out of the conflict, but I knew you would give more for us to help you."

"Pay?" Jori repeated. "We don't normally do that, do we, love?"

"We do. We give fair compensation," she said icily, finally understanding the young mayor's game. "We promise nothing extra for helping us. We depend on loyalty to the Keepers."

In her periphery, she saw Royce tighten his hands on his sheathed sword. Emeric saw it too, but he persisted. "A promise would be a show of good faith. Your reputation—pardon me—is tarnished at the moment. Not rightly, I know!" He opened his hands in a gesture of peace. "Giving from the palace stores could help restore some of that trust in your leadership. My suggestion comes from a place of loyalty, believe me." He laid one hand on his heart.

"Unwavering dedication to the throne would start to end those rumors too," she replied, her heart clenching.

"It's... difficult."

"Which part?" Jori asked. "Loyalty, justice, honor? I'm curious."

Emeric shot him a look. "None of those things." Then he added, "Kepron Calthwaite. You must see things from my position. Many people are believing these vicious rumors. I could mobilize them with the right... monetary incentive... but without it I'm afraid my hands are tied."

"Cúron and Varinna Calthwaite, Atael and Haved Calthwaite, Merian Arioc," Kiria recited. The names felt like ash on her tongue. To bring them up in the presence of this mercenary member of the Western Kingdom felt almost sacrilegious. But words came rushing out, her blood ringing. "The Tanyu have gutted the capital and we require your assistance. We have been good leaders to your town in the past. I believe we even assisted in the floods last year? I can't promise you riches if you come because I don't have access to my own stores, and even if I did, I wouldn't empty our coffers so you could feel more comfortable about doing the right thing."

Jori leaned forward as he listened to her, wide eyed, as though this were a sporting match.

She had too few allies to be rash, but part of her wanted to rise up—as Firian undoubtedly would do—and order Emeric to be arrested.

She was so tired.

Bard came back at the same time as the servants who held dishes of lemon-flavored ice. He looked like she felt, gray around the edges. Pressing his lips together tightly, he eyed Kiria, a request to speak with her.

Something was wrong. She sat up straighter. She would have been glad for the excuse to leave, except the reason looked like it could be nothing good.

"I'll hear this news. Save the dessert for another time," she said, standing. "Mayor Emeric."

Jori swiped a dish as he followed her and Bard out of the dining room. "He's awfully handsome," he exclaimed around a large mouthful of lemon ice. "Too bad he's a conniving bastard." His eyes grew large and he looked down at his dish. "Mmm! There's mint or something in this. We should ask our..." At the sight of Bard's stricken face, his words vanished on the air.

"What's wrong?" Kiria asked. Seeing a cadre of Emeric's guards posted nearby, she added, "Here, let's get to our rooms." Their floor of the tower wasn't particularly large, and they found their guestrooms quickly.

Gathered in her simple, nicely appointed bedroom, Kiria and Jori turned wordlessly to Bard.

"They aren't coming," he said.

Kiria's body went cold. "What do you mean they're not coming?"

Bard scrubbed the back of his head with his knuckles. "The Watchman said that the alliance is dissolved."

"But... Haved!" she protested. "They must want to avenge her death."

Jori made an uncomfortable noise in his throat.

"They... they said Belik's returning her to them, so they want out of the conflict," Bard said. "Those were his words."

This is impossible. "They just want her body, and they'll be satisfied?" The thought filled her with nausea. She hadn't pegged King Ganesha as a coward. Her hands balled into fists.

"No." Bard shook his head. "She's alive."

Jori went bone-white, almost blue.

Alive? Kiria clasped her hands in front of herself to keep them from shaking. She couldn't believe it yet, just in case. But the news sent lightness to her bones. "Didn't you... see her?" Kiria asked Jori gently. If Haved was alive, that changed everything with Charäkhnem and gave them one less friend to mourn.

Jori moved uncomfortably, as though itching to get out of his own skin—his neck, his shoulder, his arm. "Yeah."

"Are you sure she was...?"

"It looked like it." His voice sounded dry and hollow.

Kiria wanted to ask details, but Jori was on the verge of breaking already. She couldn't push him further. Instead, she turned to Bard. "Did Charäkhnem have proof? Could Master Belik be lying?"

"Yeah, they seem pretty sure."

"Is there a way you can check?"

Bard's attention darted around the room, searching possibilities. "Maybe."

"Try. Tonight. And tell us in the morning."

Whether or not Belik was lying, she could no longer count on Charäkhnem's support. Could she count on anyone's? Her mind flashed to Chetana. The last time Bard checked on her, she had said something about sending help if she could. But what kind of help could be enough if her own allies—her own kingdom!—refused?

"I've also got to..." Bard pointed at Jori, who was still too flabbergasted to speak, a rare look on him.

"Right." She sighed. "We'll find out soon. You take care of Jori."

Jori's dish of lemon ice was forgotten in his clenched fingers. "I thought..."

"It's okay," Bard assured him, tentatively patting him on the arm. "You know, maybe she's all right. That'd be good, yeah?"

Jori took a gasping breath as though he'd realized he was holding it.

"It's all right," Bard repeated, holding his arm now and leading him toward the door. "Which one's your room?" Bard's reassuring lilt faded as the boys left.

Alone, but for her serving girls, she took a fortifying moment to consider the day. After she contacted the Watchman, she'd return to her conversation with Emeric. It wasn't late, and she didn't have time to waste with his games.

32

BARD

Jori wrenched his arm out of Bard's grasp. As soon as he did, he patted Bard's hand absently, murmuring, "I'm sorry, darling. I'm not... I won't be able to sleep."

The past few days, only getting snatches of sleep, made Bard want to crawl into bed immediately, but he nodded. His news had shaken everyone. "At least Haved's alive, yeah?" They stood in front of Jori's bedroom in the mayor's residence but they made no move to enter.

Jori gazed sidelong at Bard, a vulnerable expression in his stormy gray eyes. "You didn't hear anything about...?"

Bard's throat tightened. *Atty.* "No. I'm... I'm sorry."

Jori tossed his wavy hair as though shaking off the thought. "I knew that. I knew that," he said quickly, breathlessly.

"It's okay," Bard said, bringing his voice low. It really was. If Bard lost one of his siblings, even though they hadn't talked more than a couple times the past few years, he'd be devastated. The very idea made his chest tighten. "It's normal." With the words came a spark of defiance. It had to be normal to grieve a huge loss, even though the Academy might deny it. Well, he'd defied the Academy in many ways. The knowledge gave him grim pride.

Muscles flexed in Jori's jaw as he looked away, dashed away a tear with a brusque hand, and straightened. He looked up and down the hallway but no one stood there but the two of them and Lilith guarding Kiria's door. Who was he looking for?

"We'll just get a quick drink, then. You're coming, of course." Jori said it casually, but Bard hadn't been chosen as a companion for a long time. Hadn't realized how starved he was for company until that moment. He felt alight. This was wicked—asked by the Kepron of the Western Kingdom. Jori's title jumped to mind as though they hadn't become friends already. Jori was kind to everyone, so the invitation shouldn't have struck him so forcefully, but it did. Why did so many powerful people want to spend time with *him*?

"Yeah. Yeah, let's go!" Bard cried.

Jori's mouth stretched into a dimpled smile as he pretended to clean off his cuffs. One side bulged a little where the sleeve hid the black mourning cloth he and the others had worn since Dedication Day. "We'll find out where they keep the good drinks in this place," he said, heading off down the hall.

Shouldn't they take a guard? But they were already out of sight of Lilith. Maybe there would be more of them in the next section of the tower. Even Emeric's guards would be useful as backup if anyone were to attack Jori. Not that Bard expected that, exactly. Still, it was better to be prepared, since Jori was being targeted, and he had no combat experience. Did he?

"We'll be fine."

Bard's attention snapped back to Jori, whose eyes laughed at him.

"You look worried."

"Can you fight? I mean, have you learned to use a weapon?"

Jori's smirked. "That's how I spend all my free time. That's why I have six knives currently strapped to my person. Care to guess where?" He paused and spread his arms wide.

Bard grimaced and laughed at the same time.

"We'll be fine," he repeated. Then he leaned close to Bard's ear. "Best case scenario, I get a little drunk and you have some impressive fights in my dreams. Worst case, I die."

His bluntness made Bard startle. "Yes, that is the worst case."

"Only a little," said Jori, resuming his walk toward the staircase. "I mean, it's generous to call that the worst case, isn't it?"

"No," he replied firmly, trying to catch Jori's eye, but he wasn't taking the bait. Did Jori mean that?

"Aw, you'd miss me. Say nice things about me when I'm gone."

"Don't joke."

They trotted together down the long staircase. At the bottom, Jori veered left, past two guards at the base of the steps. "I have a nose for these things. Ah!" He pulled up short, staring at a servant Bard recognized from the dining room.

Short and prim, with Endrian-dark eyes, she was just coming out of a side room, carrying a tray with little silver bowls on it. Sensing Jori's attention on her, she stopped uncertainly.

Jori approached her with his signature ease. Just moments ago he'd been in shock. No one could tell to look at him. It was amazing to have that kind of control, that command over himself. It wasn't the Tanyuin kind of control, the kind Bard always struggled with. It was the kind of thing that made a person popular, magnetic.

"Oh, is that the dessert from earlier?" he asked, grabbing one of the bowls off her tray. Disappointed, he set it down again. "Empty," he explained to Bard before turning back to the girl. "Darling, I was wondering if you could fetch us some of your best wine." When she hesitated for a beat, he added, "Jorrim Calthwaite," pointing to himself, "Bardhon Tanery," pointing to Bard.

Her face lit up with recognition. "Yes, of course. Shall I send it to your room? Would you like any food as well? Eggs with capers?"

"No, no, dear. Wine sounds lovely. What was your name? I know I heard it and I'm shocked at myself for forgetting."

"Drienne." She tucked a strand of brown hair behind her ear, clearly flustered at Jori's attention. The Kepron seemed to have that effect on most people. Candrae, Kiria's serving girl, couldn't look at him without blushing, anyway.

"That was it. Rolls off the tongue." Jori winked at her and turned back toward the stairs. "Easy as that," he said, speaking to Bard again as they headed up.

"How do you do it?"

"Ask for drinks? Well, you need the right vocabulary. Send. Wine. Sometimes ale. Sparkling's best."

Bard chuckled despite himself. "No, I mean, put everyone at ease."

"I hardly do that."

"You did just now."

"I suppose I could have yelled at her," Jori answered with mock thoughtfulness. "But she seems like a nice girl."

Bard made a frustrated noise. "You know what I mean."

"You, at least"—Jori stopped to point dramatically at Bard's chest—"aren't relaxed by my presence. Or, what did you say? 'Put at ease.' I keep you up all night, fighting on my behalf. Sorry that lot fell to you. Can't imagine." He raised his brows apologetically.

"I don't mind." Bard waved his hands, revising. "I mean, it's fine. I can do it, and I'm glad. I want to keep you safe." Finally, his Tanyuin skills used for something more than spying and killing. After he left the Academy, he missed the Unreal when he didn't have it, but, for a while, who could he have talked to?

Firian's expression as Bard closed the door to his office for the last time still haunted him. He'd seen that face before, but never directed at him. It cropped up in nightmares even now. Crazy that he and Firian were still friends after everything. He should give him an update about this stop, ask how his side of things was going. He'd find a moment before Jori went to sleep.

Despite the exhaustion and the stress, it was great to stretch out his mind again in the Unreal and feel powerful enough to help.

Jori smiled lopsidedly at him. "Could you fight? With all the knives I have on me?"

For some reason, the question made him squirm a little. It felt sincere, despite the fact that Bard's hand had stopped twitching when he tried to move it. It was stuck for good. Without it, how much of his limited physical training would still hold up?

"In the Real?" he asked. "Sure, yeah. I'm not..." He almost named Firian and stopped himself. Jori had good reason to dislike him. No point in extending that dislike to Bard too.

"Ah, I'd like to see that."

They reached the bedroom again to find Viktor so pale his tattoo looked like it was pasted on top of his skin. The guard exhaled with relief at the sight of them.

"My Kepron, why weren't you here?" he asked tightly.

"I had protection," Jori assured him, laying a hand on Bard's shoulder. Warmth filled him at the compliment. It was a compliment, right? Must be, after the nice things he said about him to Emeric earlier. The memory brought his hand up to his hair. Was it really that good?

"Always tell us where you're going," Viktor said, grumpy now. "I was about to tell the Keeper you were missing."

Jori flashed him a grin. "We're back, see? Don't worry Kiria about us." He pushed past Viktor to get into the room. "Unless you hear screams or something," he added as an afterthought.

After assessing the room, Jori bounded onto the chair in the corner and crouched there like a bird. His gaze took in the bed, the pictures on the walls, the chest of drawers. It looked a lot like Kiria's room next door.

Just watching Jori made Bard realize how tired he was. A yawn forced his mouth wide. He covered up the gesture by scratching the back of his head as though it didn't matter.

"If you want to sleep tonight—" Jori began.

"No." Bard stretched and shook out his shoulders. He gave a sniff to end the argument before it began. A second afterward, he realized that was a tactic he'd picked up from his mother.

"You know, with a Tanyu watching my every move—don't mistake me; I'm flattered—it's a lot harder to go where I want, sneak out a window, get away from all this." Jori gestured wistfully toward the window, raising himself enough to sit on the back of the chair with his gray boots on the seat. Bard didn't point out that they were at least three stories up.

"Sounds kind of fun," Bard admitted. "Where would you go?"

"I don't know. That's the fun part. Who knows what's going on out there?" After a moment, he said, "Not that I blame you. Escaping from a Tanyu, now that would be something..." A dreamy look stole over his face, the expression children got before stealing a treat.

"Don't try it, please."

"You can sit." He indicated the bed.

"I'll be sitting all night, if it's all right." Bard stood beside Jori and leaned against the wall to show he was comfortable.

Jori angled toward him. His open vest flapped to the side. "Once, I followed two Tanyu after they visited, all the way out of town. They never noticed."

"They noticed."

"I was wearing a servant's outfit."

"They noticed."

Jori huffed. "Thank you for ruining my great achievement, Master Tanery."

"I would notice."

"Point made."

A knock on the door meant that drinks had arrived.

Jori leapt off the chair. "Drienne!" he cried, opening the door and snatching up the bottle and two glasses before the girl even came in sight. "What a marvelous lady you are! Thank you, love."

"It was my pleasure, Lord Calthwaite."

At this, Jori shot Bard an astonished face, eyebrows raised. *Lord Calthwaite.* "This will be all," he said to her. "You've been wonderful." And he closed the door.

With practiced ease, he opened the bottle and poured two glasses, offering one to Bard. The dark red liquid smelled sharp and warm at the same time. Unpleasant memories jumbled in with the scent. Wine wasn't offered in Tánuil but Tibor Wat, the Torithian captain, had drunk it all the time. He swallowed and watched Jori down a large gulp before sipping from the rim. The taste wasn't bad. Grapes and herbs.

Jori refilled his glass and then held it out to Bard in a toast. "To exciting dreams!"

"How about no dreams? Help for the Kingdom? Something like that."

"This is supposed to be a fun moment, not a political one. Don't be yesterday's wet clothes!"

Bard tried out a few expressions, but none seemed to fit. He always found himself dampening other people's fun with caution, but wasn't *now*, of all times, the moment to toast to Kiria's success? The list of duties stretched before him, as long as the night—contact Firian, set watch over Jori while he slept, check on Chetana. He'd forgotten about that last one, or maybe he'd just put it off, since Chetana didn't like him very much. Kiria cared about her, though, and she'd been gone ever since Bard arrived. He needed an update from her too.

"Still here?" Jori asked, snapping his fingers.

"Yes. To... you," Bard said, clinking the glasses together. That would do. He'd be Jori's advocate, even if he didn't advocate for himself.

Jori beamed. "What an enlightened choice!" he cried, and tipped back the glass.

An hour later, after the bottle was gone and jovial stories turned sad by memories, Jori crawled into bed. Fuzz clouded Bard's mind as he settled cross-legged next to him on the blankets. *Shouldn't have done that.*

"Your eyes are cloudy," Jori said, sitting up again to peer at him. "Can't hold your drink, I guess." He sighed and flopped back down. "It's more impressive my way but more fun your way."

Jori didn't seem any more sober than Bard was.

"Maybe I could sneak out after all," Jori slurred.

"Just go to sleep." A hint of bitterness laced his tone. There would be no sleep for Bard tonight.

As soon as Jori closed his eyes, so did Bard. He had only minutes before the Kepron was unconscious, vulnerable to attack.

The responsible thing would be to contact Chetana first. He shifted his hips, bracing himself, and looked for her mind. It was subtler than other Tanyu, quieter. Location was more important, but he didn't sense her to the west.

Where else would she have gone? North, to chase after Kader? He checked. Not there either. She couldn't be further east than they were, or, at least that was highly unlikely. South? What was south? He cast his mind in that direction.

The pit of his stomach hollowed out the longer it took to find her. Had Belik killed her? How could he tell Kiria? Then, a whisper, like sandalwood. That was

Chetana! He moved his energy in that direction—almost due south—and the nothingness around him melted into a small room crammed with people, mostly older women. Though they looked nothing like one another, they acted like family, or perhaps an army, standing together in tight knots, others seated so close they were practically in each other's laps. Most of their attention focused on Chetana, who stood in a place of prominence. One scan revealed that Daelon wasn't there.

Who were these people?

Many of the women were well-muscled and all of them had shrewd expressions, like wild animals. Though some regarded Chetana with interest, others held open hostility for her. The uncomfortable quiet made it seem as though Chetana had just finished speaking.

"How is she different than they are?" asked one woman in the small crowd. "She fraternizes with them."

"We have the Talent as well," Chetana explained. "And we aren't Tanyu."

Someone spit. Bard heard the noise but couldn't see who it was.

"Yes, but we don't have relations with them either." The woman's tone was pointed. Chetana didn't quail, but her jaw hardened.

A white-haired woman, apparently the oldest in the room, raised her head. "Why have you really come back?"

"To ask you to help us," Chetana said in a low, measured way. "Your skill is needed in this war."

"It's a coup!" someone shouted.

"You have always wanted to end the Tanyu. Here is your opportunity."

End the Tanyu? What was Chetana a part of?

"It would be the illusion of victory," said the oldest woman. "Rumors state that there was a Tanyu in the palace even before—"

"Shh!" A woman with blonde dreadlocks, who must have been beautiful in her youth, jumped to her feet, head cocked as though listening.

An almost ritualistic silence fell over the group.

The dreadlock woman nodded to the oldest one, Chetana momentarily forgotten. "One's here," she whispered.

"I would never bring..." Horrified understanding entered Chetana's expression the moment before she looked straight at Bard. The vision of her was doubled, eyes open and closed. "Why were you spying on us?" she hissed.

Bard's heart thumped erratically. "I wasn't! I wanted to see how you were, what you were doing."

She deflated and rubbed her lips together. "Your timing may have cost us allies," she murmured. Then, more loudly, "Daelon's alive, but I couldn't get to him. Is that what My Keeper wanted to know?"

"Yes," Bard said hurriedly, wanting to ask about the group of women but sensing that the longer he stayed, the more danger he put Chetana in. "Let me know... anything else."

"Go," said Chetana bitterly. "I might be able to save this."

Bard didn't need further prompting. Who was Chetana associated with that would want to end the Tanyu? He looked down at Jori and fished a red seed from his pocket to stay awake. These women didn't sound like the best allies, but the Keepers could use whatever help they could get.

33

KIRIA

It was a common dream—at least, versions of it were. Big tropical leaves and rocky trails opened up to a place where she could see an open field far below where people practiced their powers like magicians. The colors were rich, like the colors of a storybook. A dark-haired girl shot light from her hands. The ground seemed to move with sparring partners and the air was alive with people flying. Everyone wore black.

This was the Tanyuin Academy as she'd imagined it as a girl.

At the edge of the huge clearing stood a magnificent castle, its size distorted to be both near and far at once. Mysterious caves and rivers and monsters prowled the forests around it, but the warriors were not afraid. No, they were too powerful. A boy shapeshifted into a bear as he faced off against his opponent, but, as he charged, his quarry vaulted over him with a quarterstaff, never touching the ground, but instead perching on its tiny end like a vulture, perfectly balanced.

The dream shifted its details, but the core was the same. Darkness would come over the scene any moment. Kiria felt it as surely as an ache in her chest. But the ache wasn't only for the coming darkness. Longing overtook her as she saw these people who so clearly *belonged*. These people with their strange gifts belonged together. They weren't abominations; they were magic. She couldn't remember why that made her sad, but it did.

To take advantage of the last sliver of light, she rose from the ground, as she had done with Firian all those weeks ago. At the thought of him, he appeared as though summoned. Quiet, intent, floating in front of her. The grass and wet leaves shook beneath them in the breeze.

The pang inside her intensified and eased all at once. "Firian, I..."

He came closer, nearly touching now, blocking the scene below with his body. They looked at each other, not speaking, and as she looked, his face changed. The expression was slow to catch at first, but the warm tenderness she'd first seen melted away, leaving his eyes hard and lifeless, full of fury and disgust. His carved lip curled. Looking at him became like looking into the face of all her mistakes, her failures, every bad thing she'd ever thought about herself since she was young. It withered her as she choked on her own thoughts.

"Stop!" she said, but the word was small and died on the air.

"No."

The voice wasn't his. It was baritone, like Firian's, but the timbre wasn't the same.

Anger replaced her shame and she stood up straight. Her feet touched back to earth. The choking sensation from a moment ago hadn't gone away.

"You think you can kill me?" she asked the thing in front of her. "Wait till you see who I am!"

Her form stretched and fell away to reveal Firian's instead, an even more perfect replica. The change was immediate. She could breathe again as the Tanyu wavered. "Leave me alone!" she said in Firian's voice.

Consciousness was returning. The barrier to the real world felt thinner. Knowledge that Firian was still, in a strange way, her protector, her talisman, infuriated her. She shook off his form and peeled open her eyes.

A dark room in Rantoul. One side of her face was cool from the autumn chill. Even the shapes of furniture weren't visible in the gloom. She might as well not have opened her eyes at all.

Rolling over, she cast up a desperate prayer for dreamless sleep.

"Wake up, darling."

Kiria snorted and shot upright in bed, her mousy hair falling over her face. Pushing it out of her eyes, she squinted into the face of Jori, who crouched next to her bed. "What's the matter? Who let you in here?"

"The guards, of course. They're doing their job beautifully."

She let her shoulders slump as Jori's expression registered. He didn't seem upset. It was as though yesterday hadn't happened. She, on the other hand, was in an acrid mood. Her night was filled with dream attacks and the second meeting with Emeric had not gone as she'd hoped. He had even delicately suggested an "alliance," which could only mean marriage, but not before he asked to see her Beauty. He did it all with pristine manners, making it sound almost as though it were Kiria's idea. Nothing was suggested outright, but rather alluded to as a possibility. She suspected it was so he could have deniability in the morning. She'd left in a fury. "Is Haved alive then?" Bard must have checked last night.

"Alive and well."

"Ah!" she breathed. Warmth rushed into her heart and she clasped Jori's outstretched fingers. He rubbed the top of her hand, grinning. She should have stayed up later last night to hear the news from the Watchman. She'd just been so frustrated with Emeric and so afraid that her hope would be dashed again, that Haved would be confirmed dead. But Bard was right. She should have trusted him.

Realization crashed into her. This meant the Charäkhni would stay firm in their decision not to help the Western Kingdom. They had none of their own deaths to avenge. The bitter, horrible irony of it!

Some of Jori's merriment seemed forced as he stood. "You look dreadful."

"I just woke up," she muttered. "Why did you wake me up?"

He held up one finger. "I got up early and hate to be alone."

"Isn't Bard—?"

"Two, Mayor Emeric has invited us to the racetrack."

"This early?"

"After breakfast."

"I'm the Keeper. I decide when breakfast is." But she was awake. Actually, now that she noticed the warm sun streaming in, it was a marvel she had fallen asleep at all. All night, she kept forcing herself to wake up to defend against attacks, but it looked like she'd gotten a few hours of sleep after all. Now, they needed to make progress on gathering their allies.

She took Jori's hand as he helped her to her feet. "I'm glad you're doing better today," she said.

He waggled his head from side to side, a smile tugging at his mouth even though there was something strained about the motion.

She tugged on a robe. "Now get out of here." As another thought came, she touched his arm before he could go. "Tell Royce to have Emeric invite his second-in-command to breakfast with us."

Jori cocked an eyebrow curiously. "Anything for you, love," he said breezily as he exited.

Moments later, she followed. When she reached the dining area with her guards and serving girls, Emeric was already there, as was Jori. Bard was not. The two young men sat on opposite sides of the table, leaving the chair at the head for her. This morning, Emeric had on a deep purple waistcoat and fawn-colored trousers, all immaculate.

Emeric rose from the table when she entered. He inspected her quickly but thoroughly. She frowned a little as she took her seat.

"Good morning, My Keeper," he said. "I trust you slept well."

"Yes. Almost too well, it seems," she replied, adjusting her skirt. "I don't usually sleep so long."

"I'm glad my residence could provide comfort to you." He sat as well, tilting his chair just enough to stretch out his legs as he had the day before. If he had settled his boots on the table, she wouldn't have been particularly surprised.

Despite his politeness, she didn't trust him. His words were too practiced, too perfect. The only time he'd said anything that revealed the man beneath was his suggestion yesterday that she pay him a substantial bribe for helping her.

"Yes, well... I believe I requested that your second-in-command be here too?"

"He'll join us at the racetrack," he said. "I'm sure the Kepron told you what I have in store for you today? If you should wish to go, of course."

"I can stay no longer than a day, and we have important things to discuss," she said.

"We'll make time for it, though," Jori said.

A plate of cured bacon and orange slices was placed before her. Her mind was still spinning with the news that Haved was alive. Wouldn't Charäkhnem want to fight against the people who had *almost* killed her? To back out of the conflict now wasn't good.

She picked up an orange slice with her fingers. "Have you given any more thought to what I said last night?"

Their conversation had circled in diplomatic spirals until she became too tired and frustrated to try for more headway.

"I've considered it," he replied, ordering more coffee for himself.

Kiria noticed a picture in the dining room that she'd overlooked before: an illustration of Cúron, her mother, and Aylmor, each standing with a protective arm over their heirs. Kiria looked a little too cherubic in the painting, with wide brown eyes and brown curls. Her hair had never been curly, and the expression of astonished earnestness was rarely on her face at that age. She'd be more likely to set her jaw when she felt stubborn or grin when she beat the boys. Jori, she realized, wasn't in the picture at all. Atty was there, the picture of young justice, and Kader, who, despite being so much younger, looked almost as tall as she was.

Was this how Emeric saw her? Just a young girl out of her depth, despite being the only Keeper left?

She refocused on him. "*How* have you considered it?"

"Carefully."

A dimple of laughter appeared in Jori's cheek.

Kiria was not laughing. "I hope you came to the conclusion that you misspoke yesterday."

"On what matter?" Emeric's coffee arrived. "Thank you, Drienne. I only want to serve you and your image, My Keeper."

Jori snorted, his amusement turned derisive.

"I don't appreciate being mocked," said the mayor, shooting a dark look at Jori. "In fact, you would do well to humor me." His eyes flicked briefly to Merrick and Lilith who stood guard opposite him. "If I do not overstep my bounds, I would suggest that to both of you. Given the current circumstances, it appears that I have the ability to make an independent choice for the good of Rantoul."

Kiria felt his point building to a terrible conclusion. He didn't need her; she needed him. "We will take back the Kingdom—"

He cut her off. "If you treat your smaller cities well. I have a powerful voice at this table. Perhaps the most powerful."

A cold silence blanketed the table.

Finally, after Emeric attempted a few casual bites at his breakfast and failed, he said, "My Keeper, I'm not suggesting anything extreme, only that you demonstrate your commitment to the Western Kingdom as well. There are some who think you have abandoned us." Kiria recalled the carpenters sent to the poorer half of Rantoul just last year to rebuild houses after the river had flooded. "The Tanyu's announcement has many of us on edge. Since you've come to the forefront of politics, things have been especially… unsteady. I hope you will forgive me for being frank."

"I always value honesty."

"Good. So I—"

"But if you're suggesting I'm the cause of the unrest we've experienced and that I have to make it up to you somehow, you're mistaken. By virtue of my crown, you owe me your loyalty. I'll compensate your soldiers fairly, but I won't give you extra gifts, extra bribes, to fight for me. You are not my Keeper. I am yours. The only question that remains is whether you will keep your position as mayor of Rantoul."

His skin blanched, and his brows dipped angrily. "My Keeper—!"

"Will you fight for me, or take the Tanyu's bribe?" Her blood sang. She wasn't used to making ultimatums. Her way had always been peace, but war demanded a firm hand. If her kingdom didn't rally around her, all would be lost.

Even Jori stopped eating for a moment to watch the two of them. After a too-long pause, Jori broke the silence. "We aren't going to the racetrack today, are we?"

"Only stopping by," she replied, "to meet the new mayor."

JORI HAD to wake up poor Bard before he got many hours of sleep. They were leaving Rantoul, and he needed to contact several other cornerstone cities in the Western Kingdom to determine their loyalties. The pull of independence and payment was strong. Master Belik had known which strings to tug. How had it been so easy to sow discord among her own people? Belik's version of independence would only be in name. If anything, it freed Brithnem from their part in helping other cities. It didn't free the cities from helping Brithnem.

Kiria took another bath even though she was clean already, knowing she wouldn't see a tub for a while. Freshly clean, with her few belongings packed, courtesy of her serving girls, she waited on the ground floor of the tower, ready to leave.

Her guards, as well as a few from Rantoul, stood in the foyer with her. The new mayor was on his way to see them off. Calix Blackwater was his name. He was short and bearded with a quick smile. Kiria liked him, at least upon first meeting him, though he was initially reluctant to replace Emeric. The younger man was popular in certain circles, he said. Kiria wasn't surprised and didn't care. Calix promised to support them in the war, as they ought to have done at the beginning. That was enough.

Jori tripped down the stairs faster than safety allowed. She feared he might jump on the banister. Outside the palace, it was bad form, but she'd seen him do it dozens of times on the coronation tour. Landing in front of her with a hop, he earned a glare from Royce. "Bard's coming," he said.

"I figured he was."

"When I went to wake him up, he was muttering something about a cat fighting a war game. I admit I waited to see how it would play out." He sighed dramatically. "I'm sorry to report that the story didn't go anywhere interesting. So much wasted potential. You know how I love a good story. Said something about buttons, incoherent sounds... Not sure, really. I've never heard someone talk so much in their sleep." Kiria had heard Bard a couple times herself, and she had to agree.

As though on cue, Bard appeared on the steps, rubbing his eyes but moving sure on his feet.

"You look a vision this morning," Jori said, holding out his hand to Bard, who ignored it.

"Everything sorted?" Bard muttered. Lack of sleep weighed heavily on him. He kept blinking his bloodshot eyes and rubbing them with his frozen hand.

"Yes," Kiria replied, "we're ready to go as soon as we say goodbye to the new mayor."

"New mayor?" Bard perked up at that, then understanding dawned. "He was pretty pushy."

"And insulting," Jori supplied.

Bard cleared his throat. "So, who should I contact today? Where are we going next?"

Kiria wished they could contact Kader, who was braving this ordeal without them, but she had to trust that Bard's word was good—that Firian had taken care of his safety.

"Oh," Bard said, "I heard that Daelon is alive."

Kiria's face split into a smile. "Oh, thank goodness! Is he still in the city? Is Chetana with him?"

Before he could answer, Royce leaned forward and spoke in an undertone. "The mayor of Rantoul has arrived, My Keeper."

She turned to see the man approaching, wearing a more sedate version of Emeric's flashy clothes. His face was fresh and he was beaming. With effort, she wrenched her thoughts from Daelon and onto the task at hand. "Mayor Blackwater," she greeted.

"My Keeper! We're sorry to see you go so soon."

"It's a matter of utmost urgency. It can't wait. You'll bring your troops no later than three weeks." That timeframe sounded so long, so many days of the Tanyu establishing their dominance in the capital, but they couldn't return much sooner than that from Charäkhnem. Despite Haved's being alive, breaking the strongest personal link to the Western Kingdom, Charäkhnem *had* to help them. There were rumors that the Tanyu would come with a second wave of warriors. Her only hope was to overwhelm them with numbers, and the neighboring kingdom would help her do that.

"I'll scour the logistics and inform you of our earliest meeting time," Mayor Blackwater said jovially.

Jori raised a brow.

"Within three weeks," Kiria repeated.

"Of course, My Keeper, and you will be there also?"

"We have a few more crucial stops," she hedged.

"To be honest, My Keeper, you might encounter a similar attitude in other cities as well, if you're going to collect allies."

Her heart felt hard in her chest. "Why do you say that?"

"Emeric is an ambitious man, but not a unique one."

Kiria's mind flashed to her decision not to jail Emeric, but only to depose him. Though clearly ambitious, he didn't strike her as a violent person.

Calix continued. "From my understanding, many Watchmen have received the same story about you. I don't know how much is true." He nodded in a short of apologetic shrug. "And perhaps more will think it kind to offer help in exchange for surety."

"Surety?" she said drily.

"Money. Promises."

She regarded him, trying to parse out the truth in his face. Was he as mercenary as the others he talked about? "You've always been a good member of the Western Kingdom. We will compensate your soldiers fairly, and continue to support you as well. But when my kingdom is in trouble, I expect cooperation."

"And you will get it from us. I just hope you find others as willing as we are. But you're a shrewd leader. I trust you'll get it done. Just don't expect the road to be easy."

She pursed her lips, thinking of the royal portrait in the dining room. "My road has not been easy, Mayor Blackwater." She turned to the rest of her group before facing the mayor again, who was still smiling, whether to appease her or because he was glad of his new appointment, she wasn't sure. She let out a breath, exhaustion seeping into her bones again. There was no time to determine everyone's motives or change everyone's minds. They had a job to do. "Thank you for your hospitality," she said, "but now we must be going."

Minutes later they were on the road again. Jori rode up beside her on his borrowed horse. He got by far the largest horse—an enormous mare with feathered legs—because he offered to ride with Bard, who lay slumped against Jori's back, trying to sleep. She didn't ply him with any more questions about Daelon. Just to know the Amir was alive was a tremendous relief, especially after she'd come to expect only bad news.

"Don't look so glum," Jori said softly, looking down at her from his tall mount. "All politicians are terrible."

"I'm a politician."

"You're a *Keeper*." He scoffed. "If you were a politician, I wouldn't be able to stand the sight of you." A mischievous smile quirked his lips.

"Do you think other cities will help?" The idea that she was alone in this war left her feeling heavy, as though she were dragging a weight, even when she wasn't actively thinking about the coup. It wasn't possible, was it?

"No, probably not."

She frowned. "No?" she demanded.

He flourished a hand. "Men are pigs. Women too if they're politicians. Everyone wants what they can get, and Belik is offering more than we are."

"Besides justice? Loyalty? Avenging the deaths of the Keepers? Probably saving the lives of the Amir?"

Jori's expression darkened. "I don't know what to tell you, love. I've suspected for a long time that it doesn't matter what we do."

She stared at him in disbelief. "Jori Calthwaite, how could you say something like that?"

He shrugged. "The sooner you believe it, the sooner you can try to enjoy the rest of your life."

"Which will be short and violent if we don't get back the throne."

"I wish it were different. I really do." He reached down to pet his mare's neck. His gaze shifted away from her in a way she recognized. This had been the look he had after his father died. He was slipping down into one of his dark moods. "I'd love to see myself with gray hair and grandchildren. I'd be magnificent! But I never really thought I'd get there." With a final pat, he took up the reins with both hands again.

"You will." The voice was Bard's. He straightened uncomfortably in the saddle. "You will. You're the Keeper's heir. You can't throw your life away."

"It's already gone." Now Jori's tone matched his morose attitude. No smile lingered anymore.

"Jori, you need to help your brother, yeah?"

Jori snorted.

"He would have helped you."

That made Jori still, though he didn't respond.

"So, yeah, come on. Don't be a coward when your kingdom needs you."

Kiria could hardly have said it better herself.

"I'm not a coward, but I'm not a fighter either, you leech." Jori's soft retort held no vitriol.

Bard lowered his voice to a whisper. "I know you dream about him."

For a moment, Kiria thought she should leave and not overhear.

Jori's eyes settled on the reins in front of him. "I dream about a lot of things," he muttered automatically, barely audible over the steady clop of the horse's hooves.

"It's chaos," Bard conceded, almost to himself. Rallying again, he continued, "But you're not a coward. You set off fireworks inside—"

"That wasn't me."

"You were inside when someone else set off fireworks. You challenged the fastest foot racer and bet on yourself. You snuck past guards that one night just to get a haircut!"

Kiria raised her eyebrows. Jori had told him that story? Evidently, he'd left out some details. Apparently sensing her look at him, Jori twitched his shoulders in a halfhearted shrug.

"You can do something. Don't pretend you can't," Bard finished. "You're the king of Slug."

That made Jori laugh. Just for a moment, but it was something. He looked behind him to acknowledge Bard's point. "I *am* the king of Slug." The game he'd invented as a child had inevitably burned with the palace. It was the last thing all three of them had done together before everything went to hell.

"No one knows the palace like you do. You've got Atty, yeah? Haved's out there. Kiria's right here." He gestured to her riding beside them. "So don't give up or I'll stop being your Sentry and finally get some sleep." He sighed at the very idea, a sound almost like a groan.

"You can sleep, darling," Jori said softly. The acidic pessimism had left his tone. Thoughtfulness creased his brow as Bard leaned forward again and closed his eyes. Jori needed some space to think, and Kiria was happy to give it.

Bard would stick by her side. She had allies who would die for her—he'd already proven that. A swell of gratitude filled her throat. Now if Jori could let go of despair and take up the responsibility passed down to him, she would feel stronger, ready to take on the Tanyu, ready to face her allies and her enemies.

34

FIRIAN

FIRIAN TOOK a deep breath as he tried out different environments in the Unreal.

This exercise of switching backgrounds normally calmed him, but the tension of knowing what he was about to do boiled inside him, insistent. His Tanyuin allies were almost all inside Brithnem, trapped in the cage with the beast while he was running north. Yet, against Master Belik, they would fight for him anyway.

Around him, a realistic depiction of the palace Main turned into the Torithian beach. Dust and salt mingled in his nose. Squinting up at the sky, he frowned. It was too bright here, with light bouncing off water and sand.

The beach melted away into a blank room with black walls, similar to the one he had created with Kiria once. This time he left out the large black throne. Let the outcome of this fight determine who deserved that.

A bead of sweat trickled down his temple.

Almost sunrise.

The others were set to meet him any minute. Fighting was the part he understood, the part he could do. But his conversations with Belik and Bard played over and over in his thoughts. Once he had the upper hand... killed Belik, an idea that still felt surreal and somehow wrong, then what?

The Tanyu meeting him today expected Firian to take the throne, not to fight only to give it back to Kiria. Doing so would feel like another betrayal to them. And Kiria had left the immediate area to chase down her own allies and keep her group safe. She couldn't step in immediately and rule in Belik's place. Someone had to do it in the interim.

Why not himself? Power's familiar voice called to him.

Panels of the slick, black room turned over, like scales on a snake, revealing dark purple undersides. The pattern of turning panels took his mind off his uncertainty for a moment. Not long enough.

Breath stuck in his chest. As much as he would enjoy lording over the Western

Kingdom—*the Western Kingdom*—would he be able to hand over the crown when it came time? The seductive lure of power had made him do horrible things before.

Kiria was the one who deserved the throne. Bard was right about what he'd said so calmly in the cellar. She wouldn't share with Firian, not after everything he'd done. She was willing to give herself up, to lose her reputation, all for the sake of the Kingdom. She'd worked hard to make it better. But he'd worked hard and sacrificed to rule too.

A crease formed between his brows and the rotating panels stopped, leaving the walls half purple and half a solid, glinting black. They couldn't rule together, but he couldn't see a different solution.

Shaking his head, he dispersed the dark room with a thought. For Belik's crimes, he would pay. He could figure out the rest later.

For a while he would reign in his place, just long enough to restore order. He would cut a deal with Kiria in exchange for executing Belik.

He longed to spend time with her, and all his traveling had pulled his mind again and again in her direction. She needed time to heal from their last interactions, to mourn her dead without his interruption. It's what she would have given him.

He should have seen this coming. How was he so blind to the danger Belik posed? Kiria shouldn't have to mourn anyone. He shouldn't have to track down his Tanyuin Master to kill him. None of this should have happened.

He expelled a hard breath.

What place would suit their mission best? The palace hallway. The carpets, the potted trees, the multi-paned windows... They would remind him what was at stake.

The sun was rising.

Beside the potted *sachion* tree, Vardalt appeared. He was a Master Firian had spent little time with at the Academy, an older Khelê man with a shock of white hair running even through his dark beard. His features lumped together, low on his head, which made the span of his scored brow look uncharacteristically large. Light from the mounted lantern near the tree cast flickering shadows across his face. A glint in his eye was the only indication that he was relieved to see Firian alive.

Firian nodded at him, feeling the familiar cold press of the metal crown against his forehead.

Makai came next, dark and inscrutable, but waiting for Firian's command. Others materialized silently around them. As though bound by clandestine silence, a few wordlessly looked to see who else had chosen to join Firian over Belik. Firian and Tesni had agreed not to give away any names until this moment. Several participants in this overthrow looked pleased to see each other there, comrades on the same side. The hallway, which had always held only Kiria, felt crowded. Firian's chest felt tight, but he couldn't say why.

"Master Belik betrayed me, the Tanyu, and the Western Kingdom—all of us," he said, addressing the miniature army. They reacted with fury and disgust at the mention of his name, brows lowering, grunts of assent.

"Today, we'll set it right. I am still the Tanyuin Head." He regarded the room of people he had known, all standing at attention, Masters and Learners alike, primed for the fight. The group numbered about twenty. Not everyone he and Tesni had talked to—Tesni herself was missing—but enough to end Belik's life. "I know you risked yourselves to join me. Thank you."

Makai stepped forward and gripped Firian's forearm in solidarity. Others nodded, grim but purposeful.

"Stay out of sight until I find him. He shouldn't have time to prepare."

"As you would have it, Master Kess," came a few voices. Usually the response sounded rote, but there was a poignancy in the way a few of them spoke the oft-repeated line now. *As you would have it.* It was loyalty, a spoken declaration. Master Vardalt caught his eye before he, like the others, obediently vanished one by one like steam on the air.

Firian cleared his throat. To demand allegiance was one thing, but this was voluntary, and it felt different. No time to consider it.

Though he was tempted to wait until Tesni arrived, enough warriors were here to continue.

Firian flexed his hands open and closed once, and then looked for Belik's mind. It wasn't difficult to find. It felt natural, like an old wound. In the silence of it lurked all the things he'd once told Firian as he grew up, a muted chorus of advice and condemnation and guidance and praise. These words made up Firian's life. What would happen when they were gone?

Firian squared his shoulders. He'd be better off, that's what.

His old Master turned to him with a deliberate, hostile stare.

"We've been through this," Belik said. "I assume you haven't killed any more royals. Are you coming back?"

But Firian didn't answer. He stood, muscles tensed, glaring.

Belik's eyes flashed to Firian's right and left, just past his shoulders. His allies must be arriving one by one.

Firian waited, motionless, as he felt more of them arrive, letting the full weight of Belik's predicament settle on him. But Belik's hostility didn't increase. It didn't turn to fear. If anything, it thawed into disappointment.

"Do you see it?" Firian spat, a Master to a Learner.

One eyebrow rose. "This display? Yes."

Firian's blood ran hot at Belik's attitude. Did he want to die?

"Go." The single word sent Firian's Tanyu hurling themselves forward. Light and dark and weapons and wind rushed past him. His skin zinged with the current of them, all in the Unreal at once. He felt weightless, all-powerful, alive.

Belik disappeared behind the crowd of attacking Tanyu. The air shimmered above him. Holes ripped in the fabric of space almost made Firian look away. There was everything and nothing there. Just like the Unreal itself. The eyes couldn't reconcile it, kept trying to fill it with something reasonable.

From down the hallway came a wave, improbable, huge, crashing toward them. Portraits and plants swept with it, ripped from their positions by the force of the water. It filled the space, almost to the ceiling. The grating roar made Firian's heart skip with panic. The wave would drown them all. In the darkness, where there was no air...

Firian shook himself and dismissed the counterattack, though he saw a couple Tanyu flinch. The hall was back to its original form, all pristine detail, down to the dust motes that floated in the meager light. A company of Tanyu couldn't be shaken so easily.

His warriors kept coming. Firian hadn't seen Belik since the moment of the attack. His form was invisible behind all the Tanyu on Firian's side. Maybe it was invisible altogether.

"Back!" cried Makai in his deep voice. The others obeyed. In the space they created, Makai conjured a thundering flame. It was a good tactic to force Tanyu to show themselves, if they had become small or vaporous for example, or at least to move. But there was no physical sign of Belik.

Firian still sensed him, clear as sunlight. Kaori, a boy he'd known since he arrived at the Academy, looked back at him uncertainly. Should they continue?

Then Belik was back. He leapt from the shadows with a light that made the fire seem dim. It screamed. That was the right word for how bright it was.

Despite some of the other Tanyu being disoriented, the fight ramped up again. Belik against all the others. Glass flew, bodies stretched and bent, weapons sought to crush, slice, stomp, burn. The Tanyu were in a frenzy.

When the attack continued, Firian's muscles tightened. What was taking so long? He would have attacked with them if not for the fact that the Tanyu needed Firian alive to take the throne, for however short a time. His hands trembled with the desire to rush forward. No matter his tricks, Belik couldn't overcome twenty Tanyu at once... could he?

New Defender Kaori fell back, bleeding and then blinking out of existence. There was something oddly final about his movements. Kaori, who always talked too much at meals. Was he...? Minet, his girlfriend, barely old enough to join them for the campaign, glanced backward at the body and roared, doubling in ferocity. Then she fell too.

Defender Fox, Master Vardalt...

Belik was killing them in the Real. In the palace. Firian's body went numb. They'd exposed their identities too soon. Had Belik recognized them all?

"Go! I've got this!" he shouted. "Get out of here! Everyone!"

A few looked at him in confusion. "We're with you," someone insisted. It was the white-haired woman who had attended Firian's first meeting with the Tanyuin Head. She was in her late thirties now, hearty and dangerous-looking. Master Jerica. That was her name.

Firian caught a glimpse of Belik behind her. All their attacks kept going through him like water. He flickered in and out of view, materializing solid to land a blow to one of his attackers. This time the attacker was Jerica. She clutched her chest as blood seeped through her clothes, dripping red down her hand. A good Tanyu, she straightened and tried to shake off the illusion. But then a new stab wound—a phantom knife—sliced through her and she jackknifed back before lying still. Firian thought he heard the echo of a far-off scream.

"Get out!" he yelled again. "All of you!" If there was a chance that Belik didn't know everyone's identities, then they might be able to return to the Real and escape before they were caught.

They all began to disappear, all their tricks and stratagems fading into the air like smoke, leaving just the two of them. Belik and Firian. Alone again.

Belik pursed his lips, apparently concerned about nothing but Firian's lack of foresight.

Firian cursed himself. He should have known. He should have thought things through, but he had been so angry, and the cause had been just, and he'd lusted for victory in these days when he'd had none.

"Firian." Belik said the name gently.

Firian realized suddenly that he didn't want to be the one to do it. He wanted Belik to be gone, but he didn't want to look at his face and snuff out his life. Like Sias. Like Jovan. But now necessity demanded it.

He closed his eyes.

The first hint of fear glinted in Belik's expression as Firian slid into the Second Level. Belik met him there, the only person who could. He appeared in the empty expanse, holding one hand up to halt him.

"We talked about this," he continued. "You won't do it. You had the chance before. It's all right."

Belik spoke as though he sensed Firian's pain and were trying to comfort him. Firian almost yielded to the permission to stop. Steeling himself, he reached deep as he had before, feeling the blood beat in Belik's heart, his veins. He felt the breath held in Belik's lungs. And he pressed. He pressed with all the crushing force he could summon. A whirlwind of darkness swept him up as he directed all his power into Belik, breaking him from the inside. His throat felt dry as a bleached bone, but he kept going. More. More.

But there were no screams for mercy, no panicked curses, nothing but a faster-beating heart. The tree of his life wouldn't split under Firian's tidal wave. It only bent, pausing like a held breath, and then returned to normal.

Exhaling, Firian opened his eyes again. Belik stood before him, panting as though he had just run, as Firian was.

He was alive. How could that be?

Firian had killed over forty people at once with his terrifying ability. Why not Belik, the man who deserved it most?

Belik sighed just enough to be noticeable. At least he had frightened him.

"Proximity," Belik growled, triumphant.

At the word, Firian finally realized his own gory limitation. Belik's nearness to Firian's allies had ruined this attempt and cost several their lives, but that wasn't what he meant. *Proximity.* The killing ability would only work at close range. Firian would have to go back to Brithnem.

35

FIRIAN

Without his killing ability, Firian and Belik were evenly matched. Firian's heart charged in his chest as he met Belik's level gaze.

He drew himself up like a diver about to plunge off a cliff, sucking in breaths to fill himself with strength. His hands were fists, his muscles taut.

But the space in front of him was blank. Belik had vanished.

"Belik!" he roared. How could he abandon this fight? Belik was the worst kind of gory criminal, but he was no coward. "Belik!"

Firian ascended to the First Level again. Nothing. His arms shook. All of his allies had disappeared when he told them to, though a few ghostly bodies lay slumped in the palace hallway, slowly fading from view. He felt like he was choking. "Belik!" he tried, but he knew the Master was gone. Even his ears felt hot from the shock and horror and rage. With a yell, he exploded the scene in a commotion of glass and fire.

Reality came back to him. He was jogging, though he hardly knew where he was. He glanced at the position of the sun, the rocks and pine trees around him. Still going north. But still two days away from Brett. Now that wasn't enough time.

The ruse of the Kepron's finger wouldn't buy him any extra days now. He'd tried to kill Belik, and the Master might get his revenge on Brett, who had nothing to do with this conflict. Firian fought for breath, still choked, still moving. His mind whirled.

As soon as he collected himself, he told the Tanyu who had revealed themselves in the Unreal attack to get out if they could, to act penitent if they couldn't, and wait for reinforcements. Tesni appeared with them, frantic to hear news, since she'd been called out at the last moment to stop a skirmish with citizens outside the palace. In that position, she couldn't slip into the Unreal without being noticed. All for the better, since Belik didn't connect her with the attack. At least there was one ally who might be able to help him in the future.

The killing ability didn't work at this range, but he had other options too. There were still Tanyu at the Academy who were loyal to Firian. Sentries too. As soon as he confirmed Brett's safety, he would gather them.

A pull behind his sternum drew him forward as though he were a fish on a hook. He barely slept. More than once he had no idea how he had gotten where he was. Maybe he slept as he walked. He knew his feet were bleeding now, but as long as he hurried, it wouldn't matter.

Plans and fears swirled like a nightmare through his mind as he traveled as fast as he could back to Raewhith. Time wasn't on his side. He would ensure his sister's safety and then go to the Academy to muster whoever he could to march down to Brithnem.

Brett, Academy, Belik. That was all.

Most of the time. All these hours alone made him think more about Kiria too. Bard confirmed she was alive and heading to Charäkhnem despite that kingdom's reluctance to send troops to help her. She was tenacious, hopeful in the face of hopelessness, as a Keeper should be. Even on his behalf, for a while. He wanted to see her, to talk to her, to comfort her. He wanted her to comfort him.

Their last physical interaction had broken something inside him. He wasn't worthy of her, and that knowledge cut almost as deep as Belik's betrayal. He was just Firian. Not a legend, not capable of swallowing the world. He was a boy with certain skills and certain weaknesses. She had known him far better than he had known her.

The days of travel, despite their speed, slogged on as though time had slowed or he was dragging all his recent history with Brithnem behind him. His thoughts and legs were heavy.

But he wasn't helpless. Others might not see him with a crown, but he could still save his sister—he had to believe it—and then kill Belik. Before, he had hesitated. Before, he had acted rashly. Now, he would be ready. He would think through every strategy the Master might use to protect himself, and he would overcome it. Even as Firian Kess—no kingdom or mythology—he could accomplish that.

He reached Raewhith well after dark, slipping in like a shadow. His town smelled the same as it ever did, like herbs and dusty fruit and faint smoke. Few lanterns lit the pathways, and jogging down the road set his teeth on edge. This place felt too much like the Unreal when someone else had taken control of the environment. Nothing felt solid, yet stores and houses rose up around him, everything in its place.

No one stirred but the night guard. Firian spotted him sitting at the crossroads that led to the watchtower, his bearded head lolling forward. It could have been the slight breeze through the pines, but it sounded like he was snoring.

Firian's house was right over that hill. *No, not my house.* With barely a thought, he bypassed the front door and went instead to the window of his old bedroom. Since his father was a glassmaker, they had some of the best windows in town—the toughest to break into, his father had said. As a boy, Firian had studied those windows, partially because he wanted to know how they worked, and partially because he wanted to break out of them. He never quite managed to figure out how to open them after they'd been locked on the opposite side. His father didn't use the same technique as the palace with its soldered, many-paned windows. Those he could figure out. The memory brought something warm into his chest as he worked.

Peering through the panes, he saw what looked like an empty room, but Brett could have just walked out, or be staying in a different part of the house. In any case, he wasn't sure where she lived if not here.

After examining the glass for a minute longer, he ran back to the garden, hoping the small stash of tools was still there. It was. He pulled out a simple iron bar with a flattened end, fighting back a wince at the memories it stirred, and brought it back outside his old bedroom. He pried off the strips of wood holding the window in place. Once that was done, he could pull the window down from the top, opening like an inverted door. He hopped onto the pane, now horizontal like a high step, and dropped inside.

"Brett," he whispered. The musty room felt unused. "Brett!"

His old dresser still sat against the wall, and his bed with its yellowing blankets. The sight didn't bring memories of fear like he thought it might. Instead, he looked back at his younger self as he would a different person, someone he cared about for a while.

Brett wasn't here. Where was she, then? Had she moved out with her husband, returned from the war?

He exited his room. For a second, he stood before his parents' door, which lay opposite his. Sounds used to come from this room, painful things. He laid his fingers on the door handle, feeling oddly like a child dared to enter a haunted house. Even then, he wouldn't have turned down a dare, though his stomach roiled with nerves. Never once had he opened this door, but now he had no time.

Brett, Academy, Belik.

He turned the handle and stepped inside, not bothering to be quiet. It was a plain room, similar to Firian's childhood bedroom, though a little larger. In the center, his parents' bed was barely big enough for two people, and there was a partially etched windowpane leaning against one wall next to a dark jug sitting on the floor. The room smelled a little like vinegar.

"The devil!" came his father's startled voice as he sat up in bed.

His mother gave a whimpered cry as she woke too.

"Where's Brett?" Firian demanded.

His father squinted into the darkness. Apparently, his eyes hadn't adjusted as Firian's had, because he said, "What? Who are you?"

"Where is Brett? I need to know," Firian repeated. He must have looked menacing as a black shape in the doorframe.

"Who is that?" he demanded again. Did his father not recognize his own son's voice?

Firian's face went hot with angry frustration. "It's Firian."

A momentary pause. "What's wrong? Why are you here? Is something wrong with her?"

His confusion was a good sign, at least. If Brett was dead, it happened recently enough that their parents didn't know. Alive, then. "She's in danger. I need to find her."

"Oh!" said his mother, almost a sob.

His father let out a furious breath as though steeling himself and swung out of bed. "You'd better be gory sure about this."

"I am." Firian's voice was steel. He fought the instinctual urge to step back as his father grabbed his coat from its hook.

"Is it something to do with the capital? Is that what you have her mixed up in?"

That his father knew anything about that was surreal. These were different worlds. Then he scoffed at his own naiveté. Of course they knew—this was world news, and Brett was in danger because of it. He didn't answer his father's questions. "Where is she?" he asked instead.

"I'll take you there," his father growled, lighting a lantern on a hook and taking it with them.

Firian frowned. This was the closest thing to kindness his father had ever shown him. The one thing, maybe, that they had in common was Brett. Neither wanted to see her hurt.

He walked with his father out of the house. They were alone in the night, the breath of the autumn wind whistling around them. The two of them walked abreast, his father refusing to meet his eye openly. Furtive glances shot apprehension into Firian's body. He tensed his hand and realized he was still holding the piece of metal he'd used to pry the window open. Good, he could defend himself if he had to.

Will he hurt me with no one around?

Firian studied his father's profile, scowling and lamplit. In Firian's dreams, he was always enormous, with energy that went far beyond his form, as though he could poison the air around him. His footstep, his voice, were enough to make younger Firian hold his breath. His father was a tyrant, calling down judgment whenever he saw fit, without anyone powerful enough to stop him.

Now, in the darkness, his father looked frail, unworthy of terror. There was a humanness to him that he hadn't seemed to have before. His voice was just a voice. His body just that of a man aging prematurely because of his unhealthy obsessions.

Neither spoke. Their footsteps—his father's shuffling and Firian's sure and quiet—made the only noises.

All his life, Firian had tried to become the best, and even now as Tanyuin Head, conqueror of cities, his father still treated him as though he were insignificant. There was nothing he could do to earn this man's respect. Why had he been trying at all?

Unbidden rose the image of Kiria's distraught expression when she'd entered that farmhouse, the salty taste of her mouth. All along, she had held the answer that could free him from the self-doubt that had plagued him all his life.

He didn't have to demand admiration from others. He needed to *be worthy*.

The simple truth of it, as he regarded his father's sneering profile in the night blackness, hit him like a revelation.

"There," said his father, pointing to a house as small as his own. "Don't let her get hurt!" An implied threat laced the words, but he was no longer terrifying. He was just a man, a broken part of Firian's broken past.

Firian grunted acknowledgment and sprinted to the house, not looking behind him.

No lights shone in the windows. He would contact the Tanyu after Brett was safely by his side. Who knew if the warrior was waiting here in the shadows? It would be easy enough to blend in, disappear. Firian himself had done it many times.

He pounded on the door. No one rushed to open it. Firian breathed once, twice, ten times, before someone answered. It wasn't a Tanyu in black. It was a shirtless man in his late twenties with a light beard. "Who are you?" he grumbled, leaning on the door jamb and squinting through eyes closed from sleep.

"I'm here to see Brett. Is she here?" Maybe he should have snuck into this house too. He pushed past the man, who tried to stay him with a hand on his chest. The man—Brett's husband, hopefully—was strong. Firian squared himself at him. "I'm Firian Kess. Let me in."

Frowning, the man stiffened but let his hand drop.

"I'm her brother."

"I'm her husband. What are you doing here?" His eyes were fully open now, wary, as though Firian might strike at any moment. Something protective flashed in his intense gaze.

A child started to cry in the dark recesses of the little house.

Gaius. Firian remembered the man's name now. Brett had told him her husband's name once. He had fought in the Torithian War. Where, Firian couldn't remember. Now that the Tanyu were public enemies of the Western Kingdom, how could he not resent the Academy?

"I'm here to save her," Firian said.

From the shadows, Brett appeared in a nightgown, holding her son Sabir, who still sniffled but had stopped crying and was now playing with the frayed end of Brett's braid. "Firian!" Her eyes rounded in fear.

Confusion shot through him. Had she been warned about a Tanyu who might take her life? But then he understood. Brett didn't fear the Tanyu. She feared *him*.

For some reason, Firian had assumed that his reputation had spread all across the world, except in Raewhith. His little town would stay the same, think the same thoughts about him that they had when he was a child. But even they weren't immune to the terror that accompanied the name Firian Kess after both his overthrow of Archer's Point and then the battle at the Academy.

A chasm opened inside him as he looked at his sister's face. In it he saw horror of his actions. Maybe she even thought the murders in Brithnem were his fault too.

Gaius moved protectively to his wife, moving her slightly behind him.

Cutting off his own roiling thoughts, Firian asked, "Has any other Tanyu stopped by here recently?"

"There was one that would sometimes go to Father's house…"

"No others?"

"No."

Relief crashed into him. Brett was safe. A wave of exhaustion hit him in the darkness, pouncing like an animal. How long had he gone without sleep? He wavered but righted himself. Hopefully none of the others noticed.

Gaius leaned forward. "Why would other Tanyu come here?"

Brett adjusted Sabir on her hip. He was getting big. "Before the end of the war, Firian had one of the Tanyu check up on us sometimes to make sure we were all right," she explained. There was a slight tremor in her normally strong voice.

It wasn't the whole truth, but it was correct. Firian had checked to make sure his father didn't hurt Brett or his mother. The Tanyu he posted in Raewhith hadn't been able to detect any abuse, but Firian was no fool. He knew it still happened out of sight, but at least he wasn't leaving visible bruises and black eyes anymore. Small comfort.

"Are they supposed to check up on *us* now?" Brett asked. Her unspoken questions were loud. *Why are you here? Why... why... why...*

"No." Firian scanned the dark corners of the room behind Gaius. "Light some lanterns."

Brett's husband didn't move.

"Do what he says," she breathed.

He fixed Firian with contemptuous look and exhaled before obeying.

"We heard you were in Brithnem," Brett said carefully. The first light flared in Gaius' hands and washed over her high cheekbones.

At her comment, Gaius cut a dark glance at him. Which lies had they heard?

"Can I talk to you alone?" Firian asked.

No." Brett's husband straightened.

Although Firian appreciated Gaius' protectiveness, it was a nuisance now. He didn't acknowledge the man. He could posture as a soldier all he wanted. Firian and Brett went further back.

Brett searched Firian's face. With her, he could tell the truth—some of it—and learn what she knew. And if they could be by themselves, he would feel less alone. Everyone he trusted had been peeled from him like skin from an onion. He was smaller now, and he needed his sister.

"It's all right," Brett said, reading his look. She passed Sabir to Gaius, who looked completely befuddled at her confidence.

"I can't let you do that," he said.

"You'll be right out here, love," she said, giving him a kiss on the cheek before turning away.

Firian followed her to her bedroom, where she lit a lantern. Square, painted wooden pictures hung from the walls in a geometrical design. The subjects were bright, most with high contrast and tropical patterns. They reminded him of the views in Torith. He hadn't given much thought to how beautiful they were at the time.

The door creaked as Brett closed it partway, stopping it intentionally so it stayed ajar. Crossing her arms protectively across her stomach, she turned and gave him a complicated look. When had they last been alone?

I was eleven. The thought struck him hard. So many years...

"Someone's threatening you," he began.

"A Tanyu? Father doesn't visit—"

"Not him." The mention made him want to spit.

"Why? To get to you?"

A chill spilled down his spine. "Yes."

Brett sat on the edge of the bed. She was barefoot. "Firian," she began carefully, "what happened in Brithnem? The stories I've heard... I don't want to believe them. I defended you at first. But then we learned about Archer's Point. I hope you didn't do that for us, out of some sense of duty. The vandalism doesn't matter..." She trailed off, shivering, pain and the echo of fear etched in her features. Stray hairs stuck out at odd angles from her braid. No longer meeting his eyes, she fiddled with the ends of her hair. "Lord Thraddock. Was that you?" She grimaced at her own lap.

His heart stuck in his throat. Did she already know the answer? Could he keep her from the horrible truth? It didn't matter that someone else's hand had been the one to end the Lord Ruler. They did it on Firian's order. He felt sick.

When he didn't answer, she took a shuddering breath. "What happened in Brithnem?" she asked again.

What happened in Brithnem? He hardly knew how to answer. "What have you heard?" He settled next to her, gently, slowly, with no hint of threat.

"That you killed the Keepers. That the Tanyu have been ruthless, killing anybody who opposes them, not letting anyone leave the city. But then we heard that someone else had been crowned, and that you'd run away with the Second Keeper. It's been madness, all these rumors. Some of them have to be true, but I hate it. Someone the other day asked if you could kill people just by looking at them." She half laughed at the absurdity of it. "That was a friend I'd had for years." Past tense. Her expression grew serious and sad.

"I didn't kill the Keepers."

She met his eyes. Nighttime chats to stave away fears. She dropped her voice. "Weren't you planning to? You were in charge of everyone, and they marched on Brithnem. What happened?" She rolled her eyes upward in a plea. "Everyone thinks you can murder with a thought!" Her words escaped as though she'd held them inside for a long time. "Some people treat us like pariahs."

Sweet Brett, having friends turn on her, because of him? He had no idea how to respond. Finally, he said, "I'll use it to save them, save the capital. I'll kill Belik."

She didn't look impressed. Always, she'd been strong enough not to be ruffled even by the biggest news. Now, she held him like an anchor.

"He went against my orders."

"I don't know what's going on," she admitted helplessly.

"Master Belik is the one who killed the Keepers. He tried to kill Kiria." It felt natural to use her informal name with Brett. "She's still alive." Was he asking Brett for advice? It felt like it, all of a sudden.

"But you came here."

"Belik said he'd kill you if I didn't leave," he confessed. "I had to check. And I'm going to the Academy after this to get ready to face him."

"But aren't the Tanyu fighting with Belik? Is anyone on your side?"

"There are some."

"You're going to kill the new leader?" She said the words as though they were in a foreign language.

"Yes, I will."

Tears glistened in her blue eyes now. "And then what?"

The echo of Belik's words struck a natural frequency inside him that snapped his attention to the question.

Her voice fell until it was barely audible. "You're killing so many people. I don't know you anymore."

Each of the faces of those he killed returned to him. It was no wonder Brett looked at him the way she did when he showed up at her door.

"This is what I was afraid of," she whispered.

She didn't add it, but Firian heard it anyway. *You're worse than Father.* His ribcage felt like bars closing shut. He could hardly breathe. He longed to protest, to justify everything he'd done, all the life he'd taken. *It was to protect you and Mother and Kiria and Bard. It was to secure the safety of the Academy. It was to win a war for Brithnem. It was to free slaves. It was to gain respect.* They all felt like lies, and the faces of the dead felt like truth. He could spend his life making amends and still fall short. He could have the admiration of the whole world and still not be worthy.

Where could he go from here? Was there no way to redeem his future?

Despair threatened to crush him under its black weight. He felt nothing and then... everything. He took a couple hard breaths like forcing water through a hole far too small, and then he collapsed over his knees, shaking violently. Not only did he see the faces of the dead, but Kiria's and Bard's too. He was bound to them and could feel their pain. He *was* their pain. Bard never would have left the Academy and been attacked if not for him. And Kiria...

He choked on a sob, close to vomiting with the need to cry. Everything that had been wound so tightly within him was unraveling, and all the reality he had held at bay with the force of his running and running and running rushed back in. He couldn't stop himself. Tears streamed between his fingers as he held his face in his hands. He couldn't gather enough breath.

He was broken, totally and irreversibly.

Sobs came thick and heavy. He was the Tanyuin Head. And he was crying to the point of being sick, bent in half over his legs next to the sister he had loved and had utterly failed.

He remembered her words when he first entered the Academy. She had been so proud of him.

But he didn't even have breath to apologize.

When the storm inside him abated to an emptiness, he felt her cool hand on the hot skin of his back, motherly. He let himself breathe, feeling that hand on him. Finally, he couldn't excuse himself anymore. He wiped his nose with the back of his hand and sat up. His eyes were hot and stinging when he upturned them to his sister's, the mirror of his own.

No forgiveness shone in her gaze, but the fear was gone and some of the understanding between them had returned.

"What should I do?" he asked, swallowing.

"Besides eat and sleep?" She shook her head. "It's obvious."

"What?"

"If the Second Keeper is still alive, you have to get her back on the throne. You have to find relatives of Lord Cúron and Lord Atael and reestablish the Three Keepers. That's what you have to do." Her tone was like a general's and her eyes flashed. As she returned her hand to her lap, a brief but intense stab of regret passed over her features.

Firian didn't have to tell her that the Keepers could sentence him to death once they were back in power. That, or sentence him to a lifetime of imprisonment. He'd pushed away the implications of his decision to fight for Kiria for as long as he could, but he couldn't deny the truth any longer. He and Brett both knew what the outcome would be. One way or another, if he did what she said, both his life and the Academy as he knew it would end.

Brett twisted her marriage ring, a version of his own nervous tic. Firian stayed very still, his heart aching.

"I know," he finally said, "and I will. No matter what happens, I'll make things right again." Tentatively, he took his sister's hand in his and gave it a gentle squeeze.

This final act for Kiria would be his last chance to do something truly worthy. Maybe, in the end, someone could love him in honor of what he had done, even if it was too late for him to experience it.

36

FIRIAN

Brett convinced Firian to spend the night before confronting the Tanyu in charge of Raewhith. "You're tired. You need to be in better shape." She used her motherly wiles until he came around to her way of thinking. Gaius didn't seem surprised.

Firian told Gaius to push their bed into a corner without windows, and to stand guard directly beside her, armed with multiple weapons. Brett insisted on holding the baby in her arms in case the danger was as real as Firian thought.

So he slept a few short hours in the front room, planning to wake early to meet the Tanyu who expected him to check in once he arrived.

Even that brief sleep was plagued by dreams. He and Kiria walked together through Charäkhnem. He'd never been there, but it was clear that Kiria wanted to show it to him. It was the kind of thing they might have done when they were together, before there was so much violence and hatred. He created the scenery and she directed him to place a turret there, a road going that way.

She wasn't really there. Dream Kiria was different than real Kiria, like the difference between looking at a person and viewing a painting. She acted like herself in the dream, but all the while he knew he was imagining impossibilities.

Beside him, Kiria smiled at one of his creations, a fruit stall that was a modified version of one he had frequented growing up. Instead of plums and potatoes and carrots, it sold fanciful jeweled grapes and made-up versions of lemons and apples in all shades.

He kept adding detail the longer they stood together. It was never right. They were never right.

Battered coins exchanged hands. The seller had bitten his fingernails to the quick and tiny hairs stood out on his knuckles. Dream Kiria whispered to him, "Almost everyone has dark red hair, not black."

He made the change in an instant. Delight lit up her face at his work. They moved on from the fruit seller, strolling down an empty street that curved out of sight through walled buildings. The air smelled like grilling meat and heavy flowers.

Kiria took his hand. There was something so easy about the gesture for her, as though this version of her had done it a thousand times. That she held his hand didn't surprise him—it was his dream, after all—but his own reaction did. The sense of intimacy grew like a knot in his chest. This was something different, not the heated passion of a kiss, but the comfortable love of a loyal friend. He squeezed her hand gently, the knot hollowing inside him.

They turned a corner into a large courtyard crisscrossed with wooden beams. The pergola cast shadows across the ground and across their faces, obscuring Kiria's expression in darkness. She went stiff as a statue beside him. When he looked up, the light and the warmth became like a bath with his head held underwater. His hand suddenly gripped nothing but air.

Above them hung dozens of bodies, dangling by their necks from the beams. Their arms and legs were bound as though they were encased in monstrous cocoons. They swayed gently in the breeze. Ropes without bodies, like tenantless nooses, hung in the empty spaces.

Firian knew each blank face. These faces had stared at him in dreams before. Sais Jairon, Amir Salaar, Master Jovan, Lord Ruler Thraddock... They were all there, but now there were many, many more. Atty Calthwaite hung closest.

Someone uttered a sharp cry and Firian knifed upward in bed, dread uncoiling in his belly. In the early morning light, Brett's home came into focus. He let out a breath and ran a hand over his face. Just a dream. Not even an attack, just an ordinary nightmare.

Rising, he checked on Brett. She must have finally given into sleep after a long vigil. Gaius and the baby were there too, all sleeping peacefully in each other's arms. Relief turned into an odd kind of longing.

Going to confront the Tanyu in charge of Raewhith would likely mean having to kill again. He didn't want more hanging figures, didn't want to hear another last breath because of him. And what if this were an ambush? It wouldn't surprise him. Belik had sent him all this way to protect Brett. He had to know Firian would protect her, one way or another. Nothing less would have torn him away from Brithnem.

A vengeful part of him, small but sure, was glad he was up to the task of stopping whoever was threatening her. Just because he didn't want to hurt the Tanyu didn't mean he wasn't glad to know that he could. He had the power to use his prowess for good this time, but his gut still twisted with apprehension, not for his physical safety so much as for the magnitude of the task in front of him.

As he left the house, he found a plum and a cup of water on the counter. When had Brett had time to put them there? Despite his title and his training, despite everything, she still seemed better than he was in so many ways.

She knew the truth before he explained it. He had to fight on Kiria's side, no matter what came of it for himself. Bard had said it too, but Firian had pushed the consequences of that thought out of mind, focusing only on being Brithnem's hero.

He plucked the plum off the counter on his way into the gray morning. The watchtower wasn't far. That would be the Tanyu's primary location, where he would expect Firian to arrive.

Firian had reached forward to sense the Tanyu's presence only once as he raced back to Raewhith. Without his killing ability, he did it mostly for his own sanity. He would confront the man when he arrived and not before, then he'd find out any information the Tanyu had to give on Belik, on Brett, on the Academy.

Tracing the steps he took as a child when he was tested for the Academy, Firian strode to the watchtower. He had no crown, and even his black top had been shredded in the tunnel, so he didn't wear full Tanyuin garb. But he was a Tanyu through and through. This person's leader, whoever it was. The Tanyu's mind hadn't felt familiar.

He met only a few people on their way to fields or workshops. Most eyed him as they passed, but no one challenged him, though someone must have recognized him. Raewhith was small. Everyone knew everyone.

His attention went immediately to the top of the tower when it came in view. That was where he'd taken his first flag. He hadn't planned to, exactly. The Watchman—woman, in that case—had stared and stared at him. He wanted decisive proof of his victory, so that's what he did. He ripped the little flag off the wall in front of her eyes. The hint of green in his office was supposed to remind him of Brett, but it usually reminded him of the rush of taking control. That same adrenaline coursed through his veins now.

In minutes, he passed through the doors. Once inside the watchtower, he sprinted up the stairs on silent feet to find the landing where he had met Master Makai all those years ago.

Firian arrived at the office he remembered so well. Behind the desk sat a formidable Tanyu Firian didn't know well, Master Gallevions, dressed head to toe in black, including the signature long jacket. Gallevions did something high level at the Academy, but he hadn't taught any classes Firian knew about. Belik oversaw him. A mistake in hindsight to give Belik so much unchecked authority. But Firian couldn't have known earlier how big a mistake.

The man had dark hair, gray at the temples, that fell to his broad shoulders. One hand rested on the desk near a shallow dish holding a couple items of jewelry: a ring that looked like a marriage band and a locket wrapped in several links of chain, amid sundry loose beads. The skin on that hand looked much darker than the rest of him, though the fingernails were light. At second glance, Firian saw it was completely covered by Khelê tattoos, even more completely than Atty Calthwaite's hand had been.

Gallevions looked up when Firian entered, as though he'd been expecting him. His face blanched, though, and his heartbeat pulsed visibly in the side of his neck. No other signs of strain. "Master Kess, I was told you might come."

"Gallevions."

The presence of a Sentry was intense, suffocating.

Bastard. He'd put one on himself, probably at Belik's urging, to protect against Firian's killing ability, which finally worked at this close range. Fine. At least he stayed somewhere predictable. Firian didn't want to kill him, but if it came down to Brett or Gallevions, the choice was obvious. One more rope.

"Were you told I would stop you for threatening an innocent woman?" Firian asked, equally composed. He picked up a round bead from the jewelry bowl and rolled it between two fingers. It was blue and ridged and reminded him of Kiria. Brithnem color, lantern shaped.

Surprise registered on the Master's face. "Innocent woman?" he repeated. "I'm keeping peace here."

Firian couldn't help but sense the man was being sincere. But he'd thought that before. "Are you always here, in Raewhith?"

"I'm the peacekeeper, the Tanyuin presence, and I'm the Watchman when the posted guardian can't be here."

"Who's the guardian?"

"Master Gerand. She comes every week or so. I report to her."

So Belik had only told a half-truth. Of course he had. Gallevions didn't plan to harm Brett, but Master Gerand would. She had always taken Belik's side in everything. But with a Sentry on Gallevions now, he couldn't report to her. "How often do you report?"

"Every other day or so."

Firian quirked a brow. "Even with a Sentry?" It was impossible to break through Tanyuin Sentries, as he well knew.

"The Sentry has only been in place for a couple days," Gallevions replied, not truly answering the question.

The barrier had to lift periodically, so he and Gerand could communicate back and forth. That would be when the order might come to harm Brett.

Firian furiously considered his options. Belik often lied, but didn't often make idle threats. Brett could be harmed physically or in dreams. Firian could defend her against both, but if he stayed to defend her from physical attack, that prevented him from going to the Academy and confronting the root of this problem: Master Gerand, who no doubt had plotted with Belik to have Firian killed far from the capital. The Academy would have more manpower than this to use against him, but he had to try. He'd come this far. For Brett, for Kiria. Dreams it was, then. He could monitor Brett's dreams from afar. Which left only the issue of immediate physical harm. Master Gallevions was the most likely to carry out that order, even if he seemed innocent now.

Firian eyed him. He'd seen too much death already, and more was to come. Gallevions was a big man, but Firian could subdue him if he were careful, leave him tied up, away from any means of escape. He'd eventually be found, even if it took a few days.

Protect Brett in dreams and then run to the Academy to retake power from Gerand. It could work.

Then the solution came to him. "Gallevions," he said, "leave everything. We're going to the Academy." Another person didn't need to die today.

37

FIRIAN

Returning to the Academy was like returning a ghost to its body, intimately familiar but lifeless. Its dark walls loomed among the pine trees. The needles whispered under Firian's boots like friends. With most of the Tanyu gone, it lay especially quiet.

Strength hummed through his arms. This was the place he had fought and clawed and honed himself into a weapon. Belik may have come up with backup plans or traps, but Firian refused to be caught by surprise.

Two brown-coated men, low to the ground, peered furtively through the trees at him and Master Gallevions following behind. Border patrollers—at least, what was left after most of them marched to Brithnem with the rest of the Tanyu. Firian shouted their names, and they stood, recognition dawning in their faces.

"Master Kess," the one named Soto acknowledged, hurriedly giving an awkward half-bow. His eyes darted to Gallevions. The Sentry, and therefore Gerand, would know that Gallevions had broken rank by coming back, but that was a small issue compared to Firian's return. On the way, Firian explained in a few words that the story Gallevions had been fed was slander. He never betrayed the Tanyu. Belik was the real offender.

The other patroller, Burrell, tried to look as if he weren't surprised to see Firian walking through the woods wearing something other than a Tanyuin uniform. "We didn't know you were here."

"I didn't tell anyone." Firian suddenly missed his crown, which he'd left in the tent outside Brithnem. It was gone for good now, unless he took it back from Belik, who'd inevitably stolen it. "Go back to your duties."

The patrollers were just turning away when he stopped them again. Burrell had new bruises and cuts on his dark face. In his haste, Firian hadn't immediately noticed.

stayed somewhere predictable. Firian didn't want to kill him, but if it came down to Brett or Gallevions, the choice was obvious. One more rope.

"Were you told I would stop you for threatening an innocent woman?" Firian asked, equally composed. He picked up a round bead from the jewelry bowl and rolled it between two fingers. It was blue and ridged and reminded him of Kiria. Brithnem color, lantern shaped.

Surprise registered on the Master's face. "Innocent woman?" he repeated. "I'm keeping peace here."

Firian couldn't help but sense the man was being sincere. But he'd thought that before. "Are you always here, in Raewhith?"

"I'm the peacekeeper, the Tanyuin presence, and I'm the Watchman when the posted guardian can't be here."

"Who's the guardian?"

"Master Gerand. She comes every week or so. I report to her."

So Belik had only told a half-truth. Of course he had. Gallevions didn't plan to harm Brett, but Master Gerand would. She had always taken Belik's side in everything. But with a Sentry on Gallevions now, he couldn't report to her. "How often do you report?"

"Every other day or so."

Firian quirked a brow. "Even with a Sentry?" It was impossible to break through Tanyuin Sentries, as he well knew.

"The Sentry has only been in place for a couple days," Gallevions replied, not truly answering the question.

The barrier had to lift periodically, so he and Gerand could communicate back and forth. That would be when the order might come to harm Brett.

Firian furiously considered his options. Belik often lied, but didn't often make idle threats. Brett could be harmed physically or in dreams. Firian could defend her against both, but if he stayed to defend her from physical attack, that prevented him from going to the Academy and confronting the root of this problem: Master Gerand, who no doubt had plotted with Belik to have Firian killed far from the capital. The Academy would have more manpower than this to use against him, but he had to try. He'd come this far. For Brett, for Kiria. Dreams it was, then. He could monitor Brett's dreams from afar. Which left only the issue of immediate physical harm. Master Gallevions was the most likely to carry out that order, even if he seemed innocent now.

Firian eyed him. He'd seen too much death already, and more was to come. Gallevions was a big man, but Firian could subdue him if he were careful, leave him tied up, away from any means of escape. He'd eventually be found, even if it took a few days.

Protect Brett in dreams and then run to the Academy to retake power from Gerand. It could work.

Then the solution came to him. "Gallevions," he said, "leave everything. We're going to the Academy." Another person didn't need to die today.

37

FIRIAN

Returning to the Academy was like returning a ghost to its body, intimately familiar but lifeless. Its dark walls loomed among the pine trees. The needles whispered under Firian's boots like friends. With most of the Tanyu gone, it lay especially quiet.

Strength hummed through his arms. This was the place he had fought and clawed and honed himself into a weapon. Belik may have come up with backup plans or traps, but Firian refused to be caught by surprise.

Two brown-coated men, low to the ground, peered furtively through the trees at him and Master Gallevions following behind. Border patrollers—at least, what was left after most of them marched to Brithnem with the rest of the Tanyu. Firian shouted their names, and they stood, recognition dawning in their faces.

"Master Kess," the one named Soto acknowledged, hurriedly giving an awkward half-bow. His eyes darted to Gallevions. The Sentry, and therefore Gerand, would know that Gallevions had broken rank by coming back, but that was a small issue compared to Firian's return. On the way, Firian explained in a few words that the story Gallevions had been fed was slander. He never betrayed the Tanyu. Belik was the real offender.

The other patroller, Burrell, tried to look as if he weren't surprised to see Firian walking through the woods wearing something other than a Tanyuin uniform. "We didn't know you were here."

"I didn't tell anyone." Firian suddenly missed his crown, which he'd left in the tent outside Brithnem. It was gone for good now, unless he took it back from Belik, who'd inevitably stolen it. "Go back to your duties."

The patrollers were just turning away when he stopped them again. Burrell had new bruises and cuts on his dark face. In his haste, Firian hadn't immediately noticed.

"What happened to your face? Did people come for the tribute?" His inner protectiveness over the Academy reared up again, as natural as a second skin.

"A couple days ago, after the news that most of the Tanyu were down in Brithnem," he explained. "A raiding party. We took care of them."

"Wasn't easy with how few of us are left," Soto added.

The treasure store hidden within the Tanyuin Academy had propelled thieves to search for it even before the Academy's location was public knowledge. Now their riches and secrets were exposed, vulnerable. Firian should have expected this, but the news still stung.

He gave the men a curt nod. Questions about whether any of the money had been transported to make good on Belik's promises died on his tongue. These patrollers wouldn't be the most reliable source of that information. "Good," he said instead.

They nodded back and disappeared into the woods, talking together in undertones.

Firian and Belik had brought most of border patrollers with them to Brithnem. They provided brute force, like the Torithians. What had he expected to happen at the capital, after all his forces marshalled there? Had he really thought the Keepers would relinquish power bloodlessly?

Now, at least, he could try to make it right.

Firian nodded permission for Gallevions to leave too. On the off chance the Master joined Gerand after hearing the truth of what happened, Firian had made it perfectly clear what would happen if he chose the wrong side.

Alone, Firian approached the main entrance. No need for secrecy. Master Gerand, who currently monitored the Academy, would know soon enough that he had returned.

He paused before the huge double doors, something aching behind his sternum as he looked at the worn wood he'd touched so many times. Setting his jaw, he pushed them open and strode into the fountain courtyard. It was eerily abandoned. Water splashed in the stone basin below the high chandelier.

Before he made a conscious decision, he found himself bounding up the stairs to the room he'd shared with Bard for so many years. He hadn't set foot in it since Bard abandoned him.

No, not abandoned. His mind leaned into the well-worn ruts that claimed Tanyuin superiority above everything, and he had to work to wrench out of them. The Tanyu weren't always right. He wasn't always right.

Silencing his thoughts, he slipped into the room. It smelled faintly of cinnamon and sweat. So, so familiar. Bard hadn't packed his things before going. Good. That meant there were still Tanyuin clothes in the dresser. Firian actually breathed a sigh of relief when he pulled a long-sleeved black shirt from the top drawer. A token fell out of it and clinked onto the floor.

When he bent to pick it up, a small object caught his eye, mostly hidden in the shadows of the dresser. Bard's wooden figure of Corso, the great Tanyuin warrior. Bard had lost it right before Firian killed Sias Jairon and became the new Tanyuin Head. He'd be so glad to have it back. He shoved both the figure and the token in his pocket before shucking off the shirt he'd found in the cellar and replacing it with the Tanyuin one. It fit all right, despite being Bard's. Maybe a little small.

He yanked open another drawer and another. A boot knife, and then... A smile spread over his face. A jacket. Putting it on, he felt like himself again, as refreshed as if he'd slept peacefully all night. He jogged his shoulders, adjusting the coat, feeling its comforting weight. He was home.

His reverie halted abruptly. He wasn't here to stay. He was here to gather whoever was left and take them down to Brithnem to fight for Kiria's throne. After that, there would be no Academy, at least, not as he knew it. Without Belik or Bard or dreams of power and respect, what was left here?

He allowed himself a moment to breathe. So much hadn't changed—the bunk, the courtyard, the patrollers—but everything else had. Everything under the skin had decayed, and Firian felt a tremendous sense of loss. A part of him was dying. Maybe all of him. His life couldn't be long now without identity or purpose. Once he got Kiria back her throne, that was it. If he survived his confrontation with Belik, she'd have to punish him to legitimize her own reign, and probably order the dissolution of the Tanyuin Academy. And could he blame her?

He cleared his throat and sucked in a deep breath. It wasn't time to think about this. He'd never been sentimental. Now would be the worst time to start.

Master Gerand. She would be the next obstacle. She and Belik worked closely together, so she wouldn't freely hand power back over to Firian. He'd have to take it.

THE GUARD AT THE DOOR, Master Shanson, let Firian into the Head's office without question. Either this was a trap, or some still recognized him as the rightful Tanyuin Head. Or they were afraid of him. Hopefully, he wouldn't have to use his killing ability now, but he reached back for it all the same, soothed by the fact it was there at his command.

Master Gerand sat in the chair behind the desk. An extension of Belik's power even here. Firian glared. Gerand's black jacket looked pristine on her shoulders and she had pulled her hair back, as she always did, into a severe knot at the back of her head. With her light skin and thin lips, it was a wonder she was Amir Chetana's sister. Khelê never looked alike. At least their severity seemed about the same.

"Firian," she said as he entered, pretending to look down at some paper or other that lay next to bright remnants of flags. She said it as though she were the schoolmaster and he were a student. Her eyes were unfocused on the desk in front of her. She knew better than to ignore his presence in the room.

He scanned what he could see for weapons. There could be several behind the desk, and she wore one in her boot like he did, if she kept the same habits as a few months ago. He let the stillness he had cultivated so meticulously consume him. He felt his hands, his legs, the air around him, and felt a part of it all, completely in control. His mind raced through scenarios, detached, as though they were strategy simulations.

Command her to gather whoever was able to fight so they could march on Brithnem and retake the capital.

No, she would warn Belik. Maybe she was doing that now.

Expose the evil of Belik's betrayal to win her to his side.

Impossible. Gerand had always been a weapon in Belik's hand, even before Firian had traveled with her on his first trip to Brithnem, when he'd been so eager to prove himself, and didn't realize he was merely a pawn in the Academy's game. Belik's game.

Imprison her and set a Sentry so she couldn't relay information.

Multiple people would have to stand guard and there was always the possibility that she could escape as he had. They shouldn't risk the manpower either.

The truth came into focus like a beam of light narrowed into a point. He had to kill her. He saw no other way.

"I knew you'd be here, sitting at my desk," he said, taking a pen off the desk, nonchalant.

"I've kept the Academy ready for you." The words were careful. Now she watched him openly, wary but unafraid, following the movement of his hands as he flipped the pen around his fingers.

"Not many left here, but thank you."

"What are you doing back?" She cocked her head, just slightly. "I heard you turned your back on the Tanyu, right after giving us the possibility of true greatness, all because of that princess." Now she couldn't keep the sneer from her voice.

That broke down quickly. "Keeper," he growled. She sounded just like him. "And Belik turned his back on me."

They let the silence stretch thin. "I would have killed you for that," she said. The words were quiet and distinct, unapologetic.

"You're speaking to the Tanyuin Head," he said in the same tone.

"Former."

"I'm not dead yet."

She pursed her mouth disapprovingly.

Belik had implied that Firian could live if he stayed out of Brithnem. But that couldn't be true. Firian was too much of a liability. He had to be contained. The point of light tapered into laser focus.

Gerand had always been meant to kill him if—*when*—he returned.

Firian flexed his jaw. Belik had woven nets around him, tighter and tighter—Brett, Kiria, Bard, Gerand... Even Tiev had been used as a pawn against Firian in the beginning.

He let calm sweep over him again. He had to think clearly. Yes, they had him in a trap, but he was a different kind of animal.

"We both know what's coming," Gerand announced, "so at least let's be civilized." She finally emerged from behind the desk and set two chairs opposite each other. She sat in one almost carelessly, except for her rod-straight posture, inviting him to take the other.

He could kill her now, but she was right—this was a better test of strength, a more decisive win. How could she be so confident going against him? Hadn't she seen him kill the Torithian who escaped? Was she planning to team up with Belik against him? For a split second, his heartbeat skittered, but then he set down the pen and sat opposite Master Gerand. This shouldn't take long.

Firian didn't close his eyes as he slipped into the First Level of the Unreal. He recreated the Head's office where they sat, finishing it to the last detail in a breath and overlaying it with what he saw. This was a tricky move. It would be easy to believe in the environment, since he was essentially seeing it with double vision—Real and Unreal. He changed one fastening on the desk.

"Do you see it?" they asked in unison. Firian gave Gerand a poisonous smile. Answer enough.

Right away, he felt sick and saw flesh begin to drip off his bones. After a flash of horror, he fought back the sensation. Firian shook his hand as if slicking off water. Skin flew from his fingers, leaving only bone at the tips. He met her gaze in a challenge. They were just warming up.

He healed his hand with a thought and stood, flashing around the room like a ghost, everywhere and nowhere. Gerand tracked him with her peripheral vision, not deigning to move her head. Belik didn't appear.

Why had he given Gerand this opportunity when he could have simply killed her while she sat in his chair? Always the desire to prove himself. The knowledge spread like heat across his body. Even as Tanyuin Head he hadn't outgrown the compulsion. Well, he was here now, and he'd do what he had come to do.

This was his time to show off. He duplicated himself five times, painstakingly creating unique movements for each. They all eyed Gerand.

He'd never used his copies to fight before, only intimidate and confuse. Might as well try it now.

One of the duplicates rushed toward her, knife in hand.

He fell through her onto the stone ground as though she were a ghost. A second Firian cocked back an arrow aimed at her head. If this also went through her, then she might not believe in the Unreal enough to hurt him, staying one foot in the Real. If that were the case, he'd have to shock her into belief, but then the fight would be over.

The arrow flew.

It embedded itself deep in flesh. But... it wasn't Gerand. Sitting in the chair across from him was Kiria, horribly gored by the arrowhead.

Stifling a cry of horror, he made the apparition disappear. Gerand's presence was only felt now, not seen. Where was she?

The bloody vision of Kiria stuck to his mind as it had stuck to the worst parts of his imagination over the past days, the fear that that might actually happen, and that he would be powerless to stop it.

He had to focus. Shaking his head, he assessed the space again. It had turned dark, not recognizable as the Head's office anymore. Two of his duplicates had disappeared with his concentration, leaving three. The one on the ground now lay sprawled in an explicit embrace with Maya, the girl he'd been seeing earlier that year, the *katah* student from the opposite hall. His stomach turned. Master Gerand would stoop to *this*?

More visions cropped up like memories, dizzying in their speed, none of them flattering. All featured Firian. There he collapsed from exhaustion, there he scowled at Bard, there he bled from a failed Unreal fight against Belik. It was mesmerizing and sickening all at once.

With effort, he banished the parade of images. Like a dust mote in the corner of his vision, he saw movement in the Real.

Just in time. Gerand leaned forward in her seat, fast as a striking snake, and pulled the knife from his boot. It seemed to happen very slowly and very quickly at once. The slight pressure, there then gone, against his ankle sheath. Her lips pulled back over her teeth in a focused snarl. There was an air of not only hatred, but desperation, in the expression, an admission of how much she feared that he would win the fight after all. The blade flashed dully in her hand as she pulled it back.

Automatically, Firian flung himself sideways to the ground, reaching for the Second Level. As it came to him, pulsing with life and breath and blood, other figures came into focus. More knives. Gerand was not alone.

Of course not. Why would she gamble her life on such long odds?

One, two, three more. In the room now. Firian's concentration wavered. Who were they? He had seconds, maybe two, either to kill the newcomers or to identify them and maybe give them the chance to live. Which would probably mean that he would die instead. Kill or be killed.

He propelled himself backward, out of Gerand's reach, giving himself another moment to decide, to think. His only weapons were his body and his mind. And that was enough.

Master Gerand flew forward at him, flanked by three others.

Firian sank down again into the Second Level, swathed in the calm darkness there, so at odds with the regret that already choked him.

Gerand hardly made a sound as she fell dead, burst from the inside.

Breathing hard, he angled up on his knees. As he watched blood dribble from Gerand's mouth, a strange mixture of relief and horror surged through him.

He remembered, as though he'd heard it beneath water, a man's scream. All four of his opponents sprawled across the floor of the Head's office, terrified expressions on their frozen faces.

Master Gerand.

Master Shanson, the only male.

Master Smyth.

Defender Ya'minat.

Firian didn't know any of them well, but the Academy was small, so he recognized them. The women were probably Gerand's students. Weapons littered the ground near their bodies. A growing pool of blood from Smyth's eyes and ears overwhelmed one dagger like a rising tide.

He'd won, but it barely felt like it. The afterimage of himself failing again and again, trying with rabid intensity to be worthy, admired, loved, left a taste of steel in his mouth, as though he were bleeding too. And Kiria. Would he really be too late to help her?

He pried the knife out of Gerand's dead grasp and replaced it in his boot with a shaking hand. The room tilted.

Brett is safe now. The thought should have comforted him more, but he just wanted to curl up on his side and shut out the world. The smell of blood filled the room. He couldn't sleep here. And someone would have heard the scream. Despite his depleted energy, he had to finish what he came to do.

He gripped the desk to haul himself up, eyeing both doors to make sure no one else came in. His vision sparked, blackened. Sucking in slow breaths of the contaminated air, he steadied himself. Behind his closed eyelids, he stumbled and rutted and cried. Kiria bled.

Firian opened his eyes and looked at the lifeless body of Master Gerand. *Katah Master indeed.*

Ten minutes later, per Firian's order to the man who answered the scream, all remaining Tanyu gathered in the fountain courtyard to hear him speak. It was mostly Learners between twelve and sixteen, though there were a few Defenders and Masters in the crowd.

Firian stood on the second-story balcony, looking down at the small crowd of a few dozen. Gallevions stood tall among them.

Not enough.

He'd bring Sentries too, who weren't present, but he knew Belik would summon Tanyu on mission whom he'd worked with as a Strategy Master. Who knew how many would come to bolster his position in the capital? Belik was always thinking of the next move. Had he thought of this, too?

Firian rested one scarred hand on the low railing. "Tanyu," he began, "Master Belik has betrayed me, betrayed us, and painted the Academy in a hideous light by killing the Keepers. His evil must be stopped. Master Gerand plotted with him, so I killed her." He didn't mean for the statement to come out quite so threatening. A few of the Learners held their breath, all movement stopping.

Here came the part of his short speech that made his mouth dry, almost unwilling to form the words. "I require every able-bodied Tanyu over the age of sixteen to be ready to march in two days." Sooner would be better, but securing enough supplies and food took time. More than two days he wouldn't consider.

There was a stir among the black-clad figures below. Others, like Erron, his former hall master, looked at him steadily.

"The younger ones will stay with families in Tánuil."

An outraged cry from one Learner.

Firian leveled his gaze at him. "Yes, without Masters and Defenders to protect it, the Academy will be open to attack, but this is about more than the fate of this fortress. It's about the fate of the nation, and of who we are as Tanyu." He felt Bard's figure of Corso in his pocket, a talisman. "We must defeat Belik."

The range of expressions revealed that most eagerly agreed with his conclusion, but there were some who glared questions, waiting for the end of his statement to dissent. Belik had fierce ambition on behalf of the Tanyu; others did too.

Firian himself would have balked at this announcement just months ago. He would have been a fool to think that all Tanyu would blindly go along with him, now that Tanyuin loyalties were split between himself and Belik.

"Excuse me, Master Kess," said one bold Learner. "Didn't we go to the capital to retaliate against them for attacking us? Isn't that what we're doing?"

The Tanyu next to the boy elbowed him hard.

The crowd went blurry, then focused, then blurry again. Firian gripped the railing. "They've paid for that already," he answered. "Everyone who attacked us has died. No one else has to suffer, but Belik is still ruling like a tyrant."

"Master Kess," said Erron, seriousness etched onto his large features, "may I ask a question?"

Firian inclined his head. Erron had always been fierce in the Unreal, but was ordinarily a silent presence otherwise. He hadn't come to Brithnem the first time because he could do more for the cause through dream warfare, and some Tanyu had to look after the younger ones.

"If we defeat Master Belik, will you also order us against the Second Keeper? Reports say she's still alive." His words were stiff but intentional. Wariness, like defiance, shone in his gaze. Something told Firian that if he were heartless enough to send Tanyu after Kiria, Erron would refuse.

It was a bold question. Inside it was the true one. Who would sit on the throne at the end of this? Were they fighting for the Tanyu or for Kiria? Everyone looked to Firian for his answer.

Pride in Erron's mild defense of Kiria, and apprehension about the other Tanyu's reactions to what he was about to say, roiled inside him. If he said this, then he made his position public, and probably doomed both himself and the Academy.

It's right, though. It's right.

Kiria's voice, Bard's voice, struggled to find purchase inside him. He'd wanted power and respect for so long—all those things that Gerand had showed him trying to get in those horrifying vignettes. Now, he gave more and more of it away.

He cast his eyes to the chandelier and over to the rows of rooms lining the second floor. Who would he be without this place?

Then he thought of her on the throne when he'd pledged his allegiance. She loved the Kingdom in a way he couldn't, saw the good in it despite the way it treated her. She sacrificed for it and labored to make it better and to make herself better for it.

Maybe that's what love was. Not torrid kisses in the dark, at least, not only. Maybe it was this—giving up a part of himself because he knew she was worth it.

"I will not order you against the Second Keeper," he finally answered. "She deserves to rule, so we're winning back the Kingdom for her."

38

KIRIA

OTHER KINGDOM CITIES had mixed reactions to Kiria's call for aid. More of them acted like Emeric than she'd expected. A few responded right away that they'd come, but most of those were small—too small to turn the tide on their own. Their tenuous alliance with Charäkhnem provided the best hope of overwhelming the Tanyu with numbers. Also, the prospect of seeing Haved again energized them all.

On Kiria's other trips to Charäkhnem, she had only heard of the Book of Names. She'd pictured an artifact, a bound book like a copy of the Sacred Scroll, housed in the enormous palace somewhere, but it wasn't an artifact. It was the palace itself.

Haved Ganesha ran her fingers reverently along the polished bronze wall scored with thousands of names in unreadable characters. It was beautiful. From floor to ceiling were listed names upon names, going back for generations. Here and there a name had been blotted out, a deep score covering the foreign letters.

In the center of the room were benches where several people now sat, chanting the names like prayers. They didn't wear a uniform, like the high-collared robes of the Amir. These people seemed to be palace staff, priests, soldiers, and even common citizens. One or two did as Haved did with her guards, touching the letters as they slowly strode the circumference of the space. Doorways on either side led to similar rooms.

Even with Kiria, Jori, Bard, and her coterie of guards, the room didn't feel small. She sensed awe coming from all of them, even Jori, who pointed to one of the scratched-out names. "What did this person do?"

"Unspeakable things," Haved replied, not looking at him.

Jori raised his eyebrows at Kiria.

Haved continued to look at the wall as though searching for something.

"Are you in here?" Kiria asked. "Is your name in the Book?"

"Of course," she answered sharply, as though the question offended her. "The Book of Names is not only for the dead, but for the living. They all live on in memory."

"Except that guy," Jori muttered, pointing to another unintelligible marking.

Bard shot him a warning look. Jori shot him a look back that said he didn't need to chastise him.

"Here." Haved stopped. Kiria's group stopped too and looked where she was pointing. It was a set of new markings, fresh, at least by the sharp edges that hadn't worn away by so many people touching it.

"What does it say?" Kiria asked.

"Atael Calthwaite." She said his name slowly, including every syllable with downcast eyes. The silence grew palpable.

"You added his name," Kiria whispered, running her fingers along the strange letters etched in the bronze. *Atael Calthwaite.*

Jori stared with a hard set to his jaw. Bard blinked a couple times and looked furtively up at Jori with concern written on his face. He moved a little closer to him and Kiria, pretending to get a better view.

"I insisted," Haved continued with a sad calm, "so he will always be remembered."

Kiria swallowed against the lump in her throat. "Thank you."

"Am I on here?" Jori asked, trying for levity.

"No."

He frowned. "Why not?"

Haved looked at him. "The Book of Names is for all the people of Charäkhnem, so they will not be forgotten. We value life, but cannot list every name beyond our kingdom."

"I feel that I'm moderately important," Jori huffed, crossing his arms.

Kiria laid one hand on his forearm. "You are. Atty's on here because of Haved."

Jori relaxed at her touch and nodded, giving up his feeble fight.

As they left the Book of Names, she caught him touching his brother's symbols. They passed through a vaulted doorway into a large corridor with molded trusses.

Haved drew close to Kiria as they walked under the arches of the palace. Her coal-lined eyes held concern. She had bad news.

"What is it?" Kiria asked.

"I wanted to show you the name, so you would know I loved him."

"I know you did."

Haved's eyes became glossy for the first time. What must it have been like for her to wake up next to her new husband's dead body? Kiria didn't want to think about it. The idea made her feel sick. She missed Atty too.

"The king will not help you."

"What?" Kiria stopped walking. "What do you mean?" She hadn't expected the refusal to be so abrupt, now that they had come all this way.

"He will not send soldiers to liberate Brithnem. Now that I am returned, he will dissolve this alliance completely." Her tone was matter-of-fact, but there was a hint of apology in her gaze.

Kiria felt like someone had punched her. She pictured Charäkhnem settled between the two mountain ranges. Without trade access, the Western Kingdom was essentially cut off from Erad. Without military support from their neighbors, they might not be able to stand against the Tanyu. No one was coming to help her. She was on her own.

How had everything fallen apart so quickly? She couldn't speak.

"Amrit and I have both spoken to our father," Haved continued, smoothing the front of her gold-laced russet gown. "He will not be moved."

"Let me speak to him!" Kiria insisted.

"He will not hear you if he does not hear his heir."

Anger grew like a bubble inside her chest, pressing from inside. "He will hear me," she said with a dangerous edge to her voice.

In her peripheral vision, Jori opened his mouth but wisely closed it again.

"I can get you an audience," Haved said, "but he is like stone. He thinks I was placed in danger, and so he does not feel kindly toward the Western Kingdom." She raised her eyes again. "I have tried."

"And I will try again," Kiria replied. Haved's jaw, square and dark, regal, was set in resolute apology. "We need you to make a decisive victory."

From somewhere nearby, the sound of trickling water echoed through the arches of the palace. "I have done what I can, and I keep trying. For Atty. But he will not be moved," she said again. "The king did not know his kindness." She swallowed and looked away again.

"When can I have an audience?" Kiria asked.

"I will ask him. I have told him about the way Atty treated me, so he allows us to talk"—she gestured to Kiria and those with her—"but I do not know when you may talk to him."

"Tell him I will meet him at sunrise," Kiria said. "He can move any other appointments." A Keeper of Brithnem was not an option, but a necessity, if one demanded a meeting.

Something hardened in Haved's look. Her strength was always beautiful and mysterious. How did she manage to be so collected? "I will tell him so." The princess of Charäkhnem was not one to be denied either. "I will have my servants lead you to your chambers. It is late, and your meeting will be early."

Kiria briefly clasped Haved's hand in thanks before she traced the familiar steps back to her guest room.

Jori waved the Charäkhni servants away once they reached Kiria's chambers. "I know where my room is," he said, barging into Kiria's. He turned to Bard, whose eyes looked shadowed with exhaustion and concern. "You don't need to stay."

"I don't know where to go," Bard replied. He looked at Kiria and bunched his mouth to the side apologetically.

"I'll show you in a minute." Jori and Bard would have to stay in adjoining rooms, if not the same room, because of their arrangement with Bard watching Jori's dreams.

Once the servants had left, Jori turned to Kiria. "Charäkhnem isn't going to help? This is ludicrous!"

"Yes, it is, but I'll have a meeting with the king."

"*Shear Ganesha*," he said, as though explaining something she hadn't thought of. The king was famously immovable on most issues.

Exasperated, she sighed. "Yes."

"No one's helping us."

"No." The weight of it lay heavy on her too. Her list of allies, once so grand, had dwindled to almost nothing. She wasn't desperate enough to call on Firian, but she was close.

"I wasn't surprised before, but this is getting ridiculous," Jori muttered. "We were nothing but good to Haved. She was one of my favorites. And we need them." Jori scrunched up his face, looking first at Bard and then aimlessly around the room as though searching for a solution. "Normally, you know, I wouldn't care," he continued. "But this is Brithnem, the palace!" He waved his arms, looking for words. Exhaling, he let them drop. "Atty."

She nodded.

He scratched his eyebrow. "I hate this, you know."

"I know."

"I hate politics and princes and alliances and laws."

That last one brought a grim smile to her face. "I know."

His jaw jutted thoughtfully. He looked like he was about to speak, but he just stood there, breathing and thinking. He turned to Bard. "Do you think there's a tattoo artist still available tonight?"

39

KIRIA

Kiria left all the guards she could spare for Jori and Bard, who still hadn't emerged from their room when the gray light of dawn began to melt into golden shafts of light. She wasn't sure who was sleeping and who was awake. Keeper tattoos generally took a long time, and Jori started late. Tattoo methods might be different in Char Visil too. That is, if he ever went through with it in the first place.

The thought of Jori getting a painful tattoo almost made her laugh, but she couldn't deny she was proud of him. If he actually did it, that would be a monumental step for him.

The throne room was practically empty when she arrived for her meeting with the king. A guard announced her and opened the golden double doors to admit them. At the end of the gallery stood the tall dais with its large throne. King Ganesha sat robed in dark red, with the golden eagle stole over his shoulders. Amrit and Haved sat at the smaller thrones at the foot of the steps. Had both been required to come, or were they here to support her? She nodded gratefully at Haved.

Just before the steps, she stopped.

"Lady Kiria," said Shear Ganesha from his throne, "you requested an audience." There was a clear note of annoyance in his tone. He used the least formal way to address her that didn't breach protocol. He adjusted the golden stole on his massive shoulders.

"I did. King Ganesha, my capital has been occupied by violent usurpers. The other two Keepers were killed, and I only just escaped with my life."

The king looked unmoved, just as Haved had predicted. He knew this story, but how could he not care?

"This evil action cannot stand. I need your help to restore the three Keepers."

"You have your own kingdom," he replied. "Why do you need mine?"

The muscles in her shoulders tightened. "They do not have the strength, but your kingdom is mighty."

He cut her off. "They refuse to fight for you, so why should I?"

He knew the truth, then, that many of her soldiers wouldn't help. Her face felt clammy. "They are being manipulated by the Tanyu. They need to see the strength that they still have in their Keepers. If you come to support me, they'll follow my leadership again."

The king pursed his mouth as he gazed down at her. Why did he have to sit so high?

"The Keepers," he began slowly, "are the descendants of those who salted our land and killed our people."

Kiria's mouth opened in disbelief. "That was many generations ago." Why was he bringing that up now?

"We do not forget those who have fallen. For us, the past is still here."

"Father." It was Amrit. He twisted in his seat to look up. "That is true, but Lady Kiria is not guilty of those deaths or the broken parts of our land. We have also been friendly with the Western Kingdom."

"Until now," the king finished sternly.

"If I hold no ill will toward the Kingdom, then you should not," Haved replied, eyes flashing. Her will could match her father's.

The king ran one hand down the golden pinion of the stole. "We gave you an opportunity. We even gave you our most precious gift, and you squandered it."

Heat rushed to Kiria's face. "Atty loved Haved," she said, dropping the formality. "He loved her more than life itself. And he was kind. He never would have let anything happen to her. A Tanyu snuck into their room and killed him as he slept. He didn't see it coming, or else he would have stopped it."

"Incompetent guards, it seems to me."

Kiria wanted to scream. "This enemy is well-trained and ruthless, willing to strike in the dark. That's why we need you. We can't take them on our own."

"Listen to her, Father." She had never been so happy Amrit was there. As heir to the throne, his opinion had to hold some sway.

"If your own people will not fight beside you, there is nothing to fight for," said the king. "If your enemies are as dangerous as you say, then you may stay one more night in the palace. No longer. Then you must leave Char Visil and handle your own war."

Kiria felt sick. The black fabric of the mourning cloth felt tight against her wrist. "Atael's name is in the Book of Life," she tried.

"I do not scorn his memory, but that name was a gift for my daughter, and I will not fight for his dissolute brother and an untrained girl."

For a moment, she was speechless. She couldn't feel her hands. Then words started to rise up inside her like a battle cry. "If you will not fight beside me, then I will fight alone. I would fight if I were the only one left. I am the Keeper of Brithnem, and whether or not they believe in me, I believe in them. I will die to get justice for them, if I have to. I think you know what's right, King Ganesha, and I think you fear losing someone close to you." She glanced at Haved. "I've already lost people close to me. So you can hide behind your insults. I'll show you who we really are." She didn't wait to be dismissed.

The red and gold throne room all but disappeared before her eyes as she stalked back out the doors. Haved was right. Her father would not be moved. He thought so little of Kiria and the Western Kingdom that he would rather cut off their alliance completely than honor the agreement they made such a short time ago.

The morning didn't become bright after all. Blackened clouds covered the whole city like smoke. By the time she reached her room again, the sound of pattering rain was echoing through the walls.

"My Keeper." Vayci rushed up to her when she entered. Kiria took in the room in an instant. Guards were moving purposefully, Candrae looked close to tears. Although nothing had been disarranged, there was a manic feeling in the air. "The Kepron has disappeared."

"What? Jori?" This was not the time for him to run off somewhere. "Have you checked with any tattoo artists?"

The door opened behind her. Bard looked relieved to see her. "Oh, you're back!"

"Yes," Vayci answered. "Master Tanery told them to look there first."

"And he's not there?"

"They didn't find him."

Kiria tugged at an earring. "Have you checked the kitchens?"

Royce appeared in front of her. "Yes, My Keeper, but we're trying to be discreet."

"I was sleeping," Bard said miserably. "I thought he'd be back later and then we could switch."

"So you don't know if he came back to the room."

"I don't think so, but…"

Kiria stopped. Something had seemed off, as though an essential fixture was missing in the throne room besides the king's compassion. Slowly, the pieces came together. The last time, King Ganesha had had a Tanyuin bodyguard standing behind him. Now, the black figure was gone.

Kiria whirled toward Bard. "The bodyguard!"

His black eyes went wide. Despite never having been to Charäkhnem before, he clearly understood.

"Go, check where he is," she told Royce. The guard was out the door immediately.

"He won't be here," Bard said. He was no longer sad, but serious, looking down with darting eyes as he shuffled through options.

"Okay, what do you think happened?" she asked. Bard had been trained as a Tanyu. He might know.

"If he took Jori, he'll take him to Brithnem."

"He won't—?"

"I don't think so. If Belik controls Jori, he has the biggest game piece. Except for you. He's trying to get you all. And you're the biggest threat to him. Jori's just easier to get alone. It must have been convenient to take him instead of you." His ideas made sense, although his words came out piecemeal. "He'll use him as leverage."

Kiria addressed her serving girls. "We're leaving today. Pack our things." The rain pounded against the window. Fitting. Jori always said he liked rain. Was he out there now? Did he get a tattoo marking him as a Keeper? She knew from experience that it hurt for a while afterward. Were they hurting him?

"Do you think the king had anything to do with this?" Viktor asked in an undertone, looking down at her.

Bard jumped in. "He would have no reason to side against you."

"He said he won't fight for us," Kiria said.

"But to actively go against you is something else." Bard was right. "It wouldn't make sense. I think his bodyguard worked alone."

"So, he just heard from Master Belik and ran?"

"Tanyu are loyal. They're always Tanyu first." *They*, not *we*. He paused, but didn't take back his statement.

Her mind spun. "When's the earliest Jori could have been taken?"

"An hour after he last saw you, maybe? He said he was going out, and I thought he would bring a guard. That was stupid, yeah?"

"Not stupid," she stopped him. "He should have. He knows what's at stake."

Bard rubbed the back of his head, sending his already disheveled black hair spiking in new directions. "I thought so. I've been trying to talk to him."

"It's a losing battle, sometimes." She tried to smile.

"He really was going to get that tattoo." Finally, when Jori was accepting his place as a Keeper, this happened. Could the timing have been worse?

The door opened without an announcement. Royce was back. "The Tanyuin bodyguard is gone. The king is furious."

Kiria put her fists on her hips. "How did he not know before? Doesn't his bodyguard follow him everywhere?"

"The man who filled in for him said he had terrible food poisoning, but then he wasn't in his room. No one can find him."

Viktor cursed under his breath, then shot an apologetic look at Kiria. She didn't mind. She wanted to curse too. "We're leaving," she said.

Bard stepped before her, serious. His expression made her pause. His face was set hard, lines around his eyes and between his brows. He thought she was going to argue. "I'm going to tell him what happened," he said, leaving no confusion about the *him* he was referring to. "We need him."

Movement swirled around the two of them—Kiria and Bard—as she considered his words. Firian didn't need to know how vulnerable they were, how much danger Jori faced. Helping Kader was wonderful, but couldn't this opportunity prove too tempting for him? "We don't know where he is," she stalled.

"I do," Bard countered. "He's farther west than we are. He could stop them before they get to the capital."

"No. You said it. He's always a Tanyu first." If only they could count on Firian to come down like a hurricane and deal with this threat... but she'd been down that road before. The very idea sent her heart beating harder.

"He's on your side."

"But he knows an advantage when he sees one," she said, getting angry with Bard now too. "Who can say if he'd give us Jori or not? I can't risk it."

Firian had helped them since the attack, by protecting Kader, by saving Bard... For those things, she was grateful, but Belik was still alive. Couldn't Firian have killed him already? Months of standing up for Firian when he ultimately betrayed her still stung like salt in an open wound. If there was the slightest chance he'd take advantage of Jori's predicament, she wouldn't ask for his help. Firian could continue to help them from afar if he wanted to, but she wouldn't rely on him. She had trusted in his goodness too many times.

Bard spoke his next words carefully. "You don't have a lot of options, you know? And I think he would help you. I know he would."

"I've thought that before." She turned away and started directing Candrae and Vayci as they packed. Tears streamed down Candrae's face. Kiria set a hand on her shoulder. "We'll find him. He'll be fine," she soothed, trying to believe it. That Jori was gone hadn't fully penetrated her thoughts. She couldn't dwell on it, couldn't process it. All she could do was act.

When she turned around again, Bard had disappeared.

40

BARD

WITH JORI, waking up was an adventure. Yesterday, when Bard squinted his eyes open, Jori's head had rested on the edge of the bed like the family dog had done in Enderin. Jori sighed with disappointment and told Bard he was just getting to the good part of the story. At least Jori didn't mind his rambling. Two days before that, a high, rattling roar sounded through Bard's dreams. When he'd finally sat up, Jori was sitting on the floor near the foot of the bed, rolling marbles ("I said the floor was uneven!") It was hilarious and odd. Before that, Bard's hand hit something cold and hard. He recoiled and found it was a porcelain plate with a scone on it. Jori was nowhere to be found. It was a delicious scone.

Despite the unpredictability, Bard was glad to room with someone again, or many people, as it was when they were on the road. When Firian had moved into the Head's office, he'd left Bard alone for the first time in his life. Growing up, he roomed with multiple siblings and eventually just his older brother Jac. At the Academy, he roomed with Firian. Then nothing. It was a bit lonely.

This morning, it had actually been morning when Bard awoke. Feeble rays of sun filtered sideways through the pouring clouds. That was when he knew something was wrong.

Now, as he reached their room, he pictured where Jori and the Tanyu might be. If he was taken as early as they feared, then they'd never catch up following in a straight line. Not with this many people. Not with the Tanyu's head start.

He shoved their belongings into their trunks. His clawed left hand slowed him down. Most of the time, it didn't bother him too much, but mobility had never returned. He hadn't realized how often he used his left hand until it was useless.

Where they had gotten trunks, he wasn't sure. Why were they so heavy and big? He wouldn't mind leaving everything but a jacket and snacks. He couldn't take on the Tanyu by himself, though. Master Jovan had worked as the bodyguard for King Ganesha for many years. Bard cringed at the memory of their first meeting. Master Jovan, a mountain of a man, had crushed the top of his foot just to make a point. Bard was eleven, and classes had been extra difficult for a week afterward. He limped everywhere. This bodyguard probably wasn't much different.

Firian could do this. Bard's chest felt like coiled wire. Firian would just have to think and he could free Jori, or he could rescue Jori without killing the man. You know, if he could avoid it.

Jori would be in far more danger once he reached Brithnem. Maybe Master Belik would do to him what he had done to Bard. He tried to swallow and couldn't. Instead, he scrubbed his eyes with bloodless fingers before closing them.

"Fir!"

Firian appeared immediately in the blackness, blending in with his Tanyuin uniform. "Hey. How's Kiria? Everything all right?" His gaze was piercing, his stance confident. It was good to know that some things stayed the same.

"Kiria's fine. But Jori... Jori's been taken."

Firian's dark brows lowered. "Taken?"

"We're in Charäkhnem. The bodyguard must have heard from Master Belik. He's gone, Fir, and Jori's gone too."

"To the capital?"

Bard gave a quick nod.

"Gore," Firian breathed. "Where are they now?"

"I don't know. I'm not great at locating people unless, you know, unless there's a *katah* or something." He had been careful not to create a *katah* with Jori, despite focusing on him so intently. It was difficult to do both—focus and not get too involved. After knowing what it felt like to break one off, even a weak one with an evil Torithian, he couldn't take it, not with all their lives hanging in the balance. He'd known for a long time that he had one with Firian, but hadn't said anything. The truth felt embarrassing. Surely Firian had figured it out himself by now. He was reckless and ridiculous and cruel sometimes, but his grasp of the Unreal was the best Bard had ever seen. It was probably the best anyone had ever seen.

"I have a group with me now," Firian said, changing the subject. "Sentries and some of the Defenders we left here. I have the Academy again. Master Gerand was running it for Belik. I took care of that. I'm headed back."

The words spilled out of him. Bard struggled to make sense of it all, to place the ideas into a pattern. "Sentries, that's good. Are you saying you're still at the Academy?"

"Yeah. Leaving today."

"Can you go ahead, help us take care of this?"

His lip curled, just a little. Not a good sign. "The Sentries were eager to go after I told them... I told them what we talked about, that the Keepers are sitting on the thrones at the end of this. Some of the others put up a fight, though. The Academy's divided, but I did what I could. I'm taking most of them with me."

"Nobody you can trust to watch everything, yeah?" Bard supplied.

"I'll look. I'll try to find someone who can lead them down while I go ahead." Exhaustion passed across his eyes for a moment, turning his light skin gray. But only for a moment. Firian could be wrong, but he was always tough. Bard wanted to be that tough, but he felt the opposite now. Hope of rescuing Jori before he reached Master Belik was dwindling. Even if Firian did find someone to lead the reinforcements, could he go fast enough to intercept them? Bard realized he was worrying his lip.

"Bard." Firian's tone was serious.

"Yeah."

"I'm taking everyone, everyone but some of the younger Learners." He looked in Bard's face with an odd expression. Understanding dawned. The Academy would be left completely undefended. Once this was over, there might not be an Academy to come back to. It would be gutted.

Bard's heart twisted, but not for the building. He'd already given that up. For Firian, though, doing this meant giving up who he'd been before. His identity was linked to the Tanyu, to the Academy. No one took more pride in it than he did. To Firian, the Academy was home.

"I think that's good, yeah?" He touched Firian's arm lightly.

"It better be," he said in a low voice. "Are you going after them too?"

"We're leaving now."

"And Kiria's with you."

"She's fine, yeah." He checked himself. She had the same gray expression as Firian these days, trying to stay positive in the face of overwhelming odds against her. "Well, except everyone's turned their backs on her. Charäkhnem won't help us. Even a lot of the Western Kingdom."

Firian's gaze went dark and threatening, as it did before a fight. "No one's backing her?"

"Just a few people. I'm not sure if it'll be enough." He wrung his hands. "Firian, this isn't good."

Firian lowered his shoulders and lifted his chin. At moments like this, it was hard to believe Firian could ever be beaten. This was the Firian who had defended Bard against cruel classmates, who had spent sleepless nights practicing, ignoring Bard's advice to rest.

"She'll win," Firian said. "She has us."

His words were threaded with that old confidence. Bard straightened. It was the kind of comment that would set up Jori for a smart remark. He'd toss his hair and grin and say something like *Can't lose then,* or *One-man army, that's me.* Probably something wittier.

They would save him somehow. At the Academy, Bard had practiced coming up with moves, countermoves, and backup plans, real and imaginary. He'd always had a knack for it, at least in games. Real life was a different matter, but his mind still spun, ideas sluicing through his mind. Two Tanyu and a Keeper could figure this out. They had to.

"Yeah," Bard agreed. "They have us."

41

KIRIA

Though they moved as fast as they could, the trip back to Brithnem seemed interminable. A dream-like slowness coated everything. Days felt like sleepless nights. Kiria's very bones were exhausted by the time they were halfway there. Bard, on the other hand, seemed to have manic energy now that he didn't have to stay awake at night and sleep during the day. His dark eyes filled with fire at any mention of Jori.

Today was another chilly one. It kept raining off and on as they rode, lifting no one's mood. The horses were slogging through mud since the roads had gone soft. They were worn out too.

Kiria sheltered under a canopy quickly constructed by her girls. Viktor helped them to get it attached high enough on the tree. Sighing, she tightened the black strip of fabric around her wrist, absently remembering that her aunt had Original Harmony, the Ability that allowed her not to be hurt by the elements. Well, the rain didn't hurt Kiria either, but this delay made her antsy. Still, they couldn't make the horses go any further without a pause. A stream ran nearby where they could drink and chomp dying grasses.

Bard scampered up close beside her, huddling under the square of fabric. He leaned out from its shelter to shake some of the wetness from his hair. Rainwater still streamed down his face and neck as he turned back to her. "I've heard from the capital," he said in a hurried undertone.

Her eyes went wide. "Is he okay? Did they do something to him? Did they get the Little One?" The questions poured out of her as she thought them. To hesitate was to lose her nerve. Was it possible that Jori had reached the city already? Her limbs went cold with dread.

Bard nodded quickly. "It's... not good." He held up his hands. "He's alive! I mean, but Master Belik is telling the Watchmen of other cities that he has Jori, that he caught him running away from the Kingdom. You know. It's all the things he said about you."

A coward. A traitor. Yes, she knew, and so did everyone else in the Western Kingdom. "Did he reach Brithnem already?" She calculated the time and distance in her head, as she had many times along the journey as she bobbed along on her horse. Only at a steady gallop could he have reached the city walls. Keeping that up in this chilly rain seemed impossible.

"I don't think so," Bard replied. "Right now it's just the announcement that they have him, but I'm pretty sure they'll do something to make you turn yourself in. You're the more important one, yeah?"

"Politically," she admitted.

"Yeah, exactly." Looking down, he rubbed the back of his head with his knuckles. "Kiria, I thought we could stop him from getting all the way there..."

"I hoped so too, but we couldn't have gone any faster." She couldn't keep the bitterness from her voice. She was shattering from the inside. If Belik demanded her life for Jori's, what could she say? As a friend, she would go. She had to. But as a leader, she couldn't leave her people under the control of this monster. Her heart thumped painfully in her chest at the thought. *Please, don't let it come to that...*

"No. Well..." Bard said, tilting his head. "I called someone who could."

A current jolted through her. Hope. "Bard, you called Firian?"

"It's life and death!" he cried. "And I thought he could intercept them. He could still be on his way."

"Here?" Then she realized it was a foolish question.

"To Jori," he said. "Maybe I shouldn't have mentioned it. I don't know if he was able to break away. But I asked him to go to the capital if he could. He was still north of the mountains when I talked to him..."

Her hope deflated. "He couldn't break away? What could be more important than this?" She sighed and slicked wetness from her hair. "I told you not to tell him."

Bard set his mouth in a determined line and stood straighter, puffing out his chest. "I had to do anything we could to save him."

If she didn't recognize the attitude as her own, she would have gotten angrier. "Is he coming in time or not?"

"Between the two of us, we'll save him," he said, evading the question. *Us* meant the groups—Kiria with Bard, and Firian on his own. "I just, um, wanted to tell you, in case he did it. Rescued Jori, I mean. And I've been thinking about what to do, now that... with everything that's happened."

"Tell Firian, apparently." She pursed her mouth. "Have you been telling him everything?" She knew the answer before Bard gave it, and her heart gave a twist. Part of her felt betrayed but another part had a new, irrational, foolish hope.

"Most things," Bard admitted.

She clenched her teeth against the wet cold and her annoyance. *But what if,* said a small voice inside her, *what if Firian can save Jori?* Firian would follow through with whatever plan he had in motion anyway. Why not help them too?

Glancing over at the horses still munching grass and the soldiers refilling their waterskins, she made up her mind. She'd give him five minutes in the Unreal, ask him to help them. Bard was right that it could mean life or death for Jori, and there was nothing she wouldn't do for him, even confront Firian again.

"I've been thinking about how to retake the city," Bard said quietly, bringing her attention back. "It doesn't have to be with Firian. Do you want to see my ideas?"

"Go and get them," she said. "We'll leave soon and I'll have a look."

With a nod, Bard jogged off into the rain. It pattered against the awning like an irregular heartbeat. She'd only have a moment alone, not enough time to contact Firian. *Tonight*, she promised herself. *I'll do it tonight.*

THE NEWS from Brithnem got worse as the clammy day went on. Bard communicated snatches of information as he gathered them—Jori had given up all of Kiria's plans, and therefore any diplomacy was off (as though it had ever existed.)

Kiria didn't believe it. She couldn't. Jori would never give them up, and he had to be getting close to the capital but couldn't have reached it already. Their efforts couldn't have failed yet.

Kiria's party stopped only when the horses and riders began bobbing with exhaustion. Despite their desperation, they had to regroup in the morning.

Alone, she couldn't help remembering how Firian seemed never to get tired, fueled by urgency in whatever he did. That, and many other things, made him a formidable enemy, but it also meant that he might be able to help Jori.

She wrapped a blanket over her nightgown and strode out of her tent into the shelter of nearby trees. On the way out, she waved at Viktor, who waved back. Her mind and body felt fatigue, but anxious energy kept her moving. Moisture dripped off the leaves above and landed, cold, in her hair. Maybe the worry would wear off if she just paced for a while. Maybe she wouldn't keep picturing and hearing all the things the Tanyu were doing with Jori at this minute. Sucking in a breath, she pressed her palms to her eyes until she saw red.

Poised before the Unreal, Kiria tensed. Firian was on the other side.

At first, all was dark—the nothing, rainbow dark of the Unreal. What was she doing here? Was she really going to Firian for help?

Kader, she reminded herself. *Bard. Jori.* All people he had helped or saved or spared after their own connection had been severed in the farmhouse. After creating an intricate deep purple dress to wear, she felt calmer.

He appeared easily, as he always did, details filled in. She scanned him to see how well she'd imitated him earlier during the dream attack. Same broad shoulders, black outfit (though tighter this time), scarred hands, dark hair and brows, bright and questioning expression in his blue eyes. He seemed both disarmed and still dangerous, if only because of his hyper awareness, the life that seemed to pulse at every nerve, making the moment crackle with possibility. Surely, she hadn't mastered the *force* of his presence. It hit her low in her gut.

Whose side are you really on? Always, always, he had his own agenda, but her mind kept inclining toward its old ruts—the insistence that maybe he could be good.

She swallowed the thought.

"I heard Bard contacted you," she began.

"He did." The question burned between them. Why was she here? A tinge of relief edged the words, and she knew that it was because she wasn't furious this time.

"He told you what we're doing? That... Jori's in trouble?"

The blank space around them transformed into tower ruins, the style reminiscent of ancient Haelben, the society that ruled the land long before the Western Kingdom. They stood on a stone platform surrounded by crumbling battlements and, below them, trees. One lantern hung on a ring bolted to a partially standing wall. Its light spilled over the area where they stood, staving off the night darkness. Above them were stars—more than she'd ever seen in a real sky. They crowded together in glowing, swirling clusters like cream in coffee. Haved would love this.

"Yeah, he told me about Jori."

She snapped her head down at the sound of Firian's voice. *That* was why she was here. To save Jori. It was desperately practical, not personal. Every word they spoke, though, prodded at her wound.

Was this setting meant to be romantic? The idea, now that time was so critical, repelled her. *Not now.*

"Have you gotten any closer?" he asked.

"Not close enough," she admitted. "We need... someone faster."

His jaw flexed. "I would, but I can't."

Her heart sank. "Can't?"

"There's snow on the mountains."

"Bard told me."

His eyes glimmered at that, searching. "If you want me to intercept the Tanyu before he reaches Brithnem with Jori, I don't think I can. And I—Did Bard tell you?"

"What?" Apprehension crawled up her spine.

"I'm bringing people down from the Academy."

"Who's left?" she exclaimed before he finished.

"Not many. Some Sentries. But I'm not bringing them for Belik. I'm bringing them for you."

She narrowed her eyes. "Killing Belik would have been helpful for me. Right now, all I want is to see Jori safe." She wanted a bit more after that. Taking back the Kingdom. But hopefully she could do that on her own, without having to rely on someone who'd hurt her so deeply.

She sighed, letting go of a bit of her armor. "I heard you helped Kader, though. That was... thank you." She shook her head. "Why did you leave so quickly? If you're telling the truth, you could have stayed to prove it." *Maybe*, she wanted to add, *Jori never would have been kidnapped.*

"I will prove it. But I had to go. Remember Brett?"

"Your sister."

He nodded, sinking down cross-legged. "Belik said he'd hurt her if I didn't go back to Raewhith. So…" He looked away.

"Is she okay?" Kiria liked Brett the one time they'd met.

Firian raised his eyes again.

She sat across from him on the shadow-dappled ground.

"She was all right when I checked on her. I did… what I could." He tossed hair out of his face, worried lines creasing his brow.

"I'll send a patrol that way to make sure she's not harmed. She doesn't deserve for that to happen." Someone was bound to be close to Raewhith, too far to help in her fight now. There were odd patrols in every Kingdom-controlled city.

Firian smiled, a surprised, genuine, hopeful thing.

Her pulse skittered and she adjusted her sitting position.

"Thank you," he said.

She waved off his gratitude. That gravity between them pulled at her, even as she fought against it.

"You can't reach Jori in time?" she asked. "I thought you could do anything."

His face fell, expression darkening. "No." The syllable was bitter. Firian always overestimated himself, but he couldn't do this thing she asked him to do, she needed him to do.

"You're not bringing your soldiers down for us, are you?" she asked flatly.

"I am. I'll show you."

Familiar words. For a moment, she was torn precisely between thanking him for helping Kader and telling him off for all the times she'd believed in him and he had failed her, preferring selfishness to love.

She had loved him, but he had never loved her. Not truly.

She had to get out of here. Firian couldn't help, and that was that. Her company would move out soon.

The warm night tempted her to stay, but she had to get out, rush to Jori's aid if she possibly could. She, at least, would do all in her power to save him, no matter who reached the city first.

"My soldiers might attack yours if they see them coming," she said, standing up. "I won't stop them. You're planning something, Firian. Surely, you can understand that I can't trust you."

A muscle ticked in his cheek. "I'll show you," he said again, this time more sincerely.

"Show me you can help Jori," she said, mimicking his inflection. "Show me you can stop Belik. Show me you can do the right thing for once!" Unexpected emotion flushed her face with heat and balled her hands into fists. The past few days had been so utterly frustrating.

He stood and a moment of uncertainty passed between them, something awkward during which no one spoke. The brightness of the stars made the black sky look blue.

She'd said what she needed to say. Of course she wanted him to demonstrate that he'd help her, to swoop in, rescue Jori, and then disappear from their lives, but it was all wishful thinking.

Finally, he said in a quiet, low voice, "Kiria, I—"

But something hit her in a gasp, scrambling her breath and thoughts like a high fall would do. Was she falling off the tower? Collapsing to the ground? Had she been stabbed?

One second, she saw Firian, concern in his eyes.

The next, red behind her lids.

And the next, nothing at all.

42

BARD

"Bard!"

He jumped as Firian's enormous form invaded his dream, sudden as light shining in his eyes.

"Kiria!" Firian said before fading to a picture version of himself.

The jolt had been too sudden. Bard was awake, heartbeat thudding quick and heavy. He pried his eyes open, though there was little to see in the darkness, just sketched outlines of bedroll, pile of clothes, sack with supplies, and the lightened sliver of the tent flap. The smell of stale bread still lingered on his fingers, and heavy drops still splattered on the fabric of his tent. He couldn't have been asleep long.

Kiria. The name returned to him after floating free for a second. He gripped it tightly in his mind, repeating it to himself as he rolled out of bed. *Kiria, Kiria.* Something was wrong.

He pulled on a shirt and stumbled outside in the direction of Kiria's tent. Merrick, standing guard outside his own, asked no questions when he passed.

What could it be? Was Jori...? No, Firian's message would have been different. He would have been more careful. Kiria must be in danger. Maybe a dream attack? But, if Firian knew about it, why wouldn't he defend her himself?

As consciousness pieced itself together inside him, reality came into focus. Fear clung to him as he picked up his pace, jogging now.

Viktor, standing by Kiria's tent opening, gave a confused smile when he saw Bard approach. "What is—?"

"Kiria. Is she all right?" Bard's words came out breathless, frantic. He pushed past the guard with his cold metal armor and peered inside. Invasive move, normally, but he had to know. He had to see for himself that she was all right.

The tent was frustratingly dark. "Kiria!" he called, louder than he'd spoken before. "Kiria, are you here?"

A lump of blankets came into focus and he cast himself toward it, feeling for her shoulder to wake her. His hands went deep into the soft folds and hit nothing solid. Bard's entire body went frigid. He patted down the length of the bed. Nothing.

When he turned, he met Viktor's eyes. "Where is she?" Bard asked. "Did you see her go?"

"The necessary."

"Where?"

"Over there." Now Viktor's tone held more professional seriousness. He followed Bard as he ran into the forest in the direction the guard had pointed.

"Kiria!" Bard hissed.

"Lady Kiria," from Viktor.

Nothing nothing nothing.

Kiria never snuck out for fun like Jori did. She was gone, taken. A noise like a frustrated animal escaped Bard. *Jori, now Kiria? No!*

Royce, his eyes steely with urgency, appeared beside Viktor. "Kiria's gone," Viktor explained, his voice almost lost in the haze of Bard's thoughts.

Desperate, he cast his mind in search of Tanyu. There!

Bard was moving before the conscious decision to run after her. The Tanyuin mind was retreating fast, much faster than Bard could sprint, or the guards could run beside him. He halted, bark spraying up at his sudden stop. Willing enough presence of mind to think, he stood still a moment, panting with terror. His own breathing obscured his ability to hear if there were fleeing hoofbeats, but it only made sense that Kiria would be taken by someone with a swift retreat.

"Horses, horses!" Bard cried as he turned around. Could he ride without tack? Getting the saddle and reins situated would take time, and they had no time. He wouldn't be fast that way, at least.

The mental signature of the Tanyu was just a blip on the edge of Bard's awareness now. He focused on Kiria instead. Maybe she would sense that he was trying to contact her. Maybe she could tell them where she was going.

But they all knew where she was going already. He might even compromise her safety more if she gave information. The Tanyu would be sure to figure out Bard was trying to access Kiria in the Unreal, probably before she did.

Bard found Firian instead, forgotten after the initial shout in his dream. "They have her," he said. No background, not even a body. Just voice. "I tried, but I think by the time we get the horses..."

A roar from Firian that mirrored Bard's own distress.

Jori and Kiria.

With both of them, it was no longer leverage Belik had, but power. The Master could kill them both and be done with it. Were they torturing them now? The memory of Firian's beaten body coming back from additional "training" filled his chest with dread. If that was training, what would Belik do to someone he really wanted to hurt?

Bard grabbed a cold saddle with numb hands. Time had gone hazy.

If Jori and Kiria died, there would be no defense against Belik, besides Firian. They could get revenge, but nothing could put this tragedy right.

His mind spun impotently. Voices rose around him, and fragments of rescue ideas circled like refuse in the waning tide. The kidnapper was too far away by now. They would chase, but they wouldn't find Kiria. Fear, icy-fingered and cruel, gripped Bard's throat. This night meant his friends' deaths and the end of everything Bard had been fighting for. Unless, unless...

The night passed in a delirious frenzy that left Bard shaking and cold and hopeless. By the time he and the soldiers returned to camp, it was well past midnight. Words had become empty of meaning. Something about meeting first thing in the morning. Plans. Trying... something.

Even though exhaustion had him gasping and seeing light bursts in his vision, Bard couldn't sleep for a long time after they returned. What if he had jumped out of bed faster? What if he had taken a horse to begin with? Could he have stopped this attempt to take Kiria? Belik wanted to kill her and Jori, probably even make a spectacle of it so anybody who still had the courage to resist would cower. What if they were both tortured and killed and he never saw either of them again? If he had tried harder, looked after them better, would they have lived?

He pressed his face against the pillow to stifle the sound of his racking sobs.

BARD LIFTED himself up on his elbow, yawning and scrubbing his hair with his free hand. His eyes were sore from crying the night before. Sunlight against the walls of his tent seemed to insist that there was hope. His mental protests against that stupid notion sounded grumpy rather than despairing. A tiny improvement. The air smelled like leaves.

Today, he would come up with a plan to rescue them. He wasn't much of a Tanyu, but he was a Tanyu, and he had people on his side. Corso did more with less.

On the ride toward Brithnem, he tried to keep his mind busy. Over and over, he ran through the cities and towns that had agreed to back the Keepers in battle. The list of *no*'s rang louder—Charäkhnem, and even Carradoc, held hostage by a few Tanyuin plants inside the fortress. Belik's promises won over some, and fear of the Tanyu silenced others. Another, smaller group also refused to help. Through his few checkups with Chetana, he learned she had tried to contact some sort of group who hated Tanyu so much that they refused to come on the grounds that they were working with Bard. After that, he didn't ask her for any more updates, afraid she'd blame him for the lack of backup they had.

At Bard's request, Viktor mapped out the city gates and palace layout. Royce described the original guard rotation before the Tanyu attacked. He learned more about the system the Western Kingdom employed for ships coming into the docks... Anything he thought would help in formulating a plan to free Kiria and Jori, assuming Belik held them prisoner for a while before killing them.

That was all before lunch.

By then, the wetness in the yellowing trees had evaporated, but the ground still sank slightly with each step. Bard stared at the little sandwich he'd made with their provisions, wrapping his fingers around it to keep the dried meat from falling out.

Shouting cut through his thoughts. Some of the guards had spotted movement. They leveled their swords at an area of thick trees. "Come out!"

Bard lowered his sandwich and rose to investigate.

From the foliage, a figure emerged with raised hands. A woman. Most of the guards relaxed their weapons.

Bard couldn't believe it. It was too much to take in at one time. Kiria was gone, but Chetana was here. Bard's last glimpse of her in the presence of those warlike women flashed through his mind, but they weren't with her now. He walked forward like someone in a dream. Others looked at her with the same confusion. After everything that had happened, she could have been a Shee nymph here to tell his fortune and he would have been equally surprised.

Then he saw who she brought with her. Bard barreled forward, crashing into Jori, holding him in a fierce hug. The Kepron's hair hung dirty and he smelled sour. His loose shirt and embroidered vest were smudged and torn, with loose threads tickling Bard's nose. He squeezed tighter, and Jori squeezed him back. Neither let go for a long moment.

"You're alive!" Bard managed. "You're back!"

"Of course I am, darling," Jori said into his hair with the same cavalier attitude he ever had. Only the hoarseness of his voice and the slight tremor suggested that anything traumatic had happened.

They let go of each other. Jori looked around at the gathered crowd. "Where's Kiria? If she's sleeping through this, she really should have anticipated—"

"She's missing," Bard said, blinking to clear his vision.

Alarmed, Jori turned back to him. "What?"

"They took her."

"The Keeper is gone?" Chetana asked. Bard had all but forgotten about the Amir. She must have rescued Jori on her own. When things settled down, he would ask them what happened. She began talking urgently with Royce and the other guards.

"When?" Jori demanded.

"Last night."

"Then let's go!"

Several of the servants went back to their duties. One asked if they could get Jori anything. "Nothing but a clean shirt and a bottle of wine, but that can wait," he replied.

"You're going to have to tell me everything that happened," Bard said carefully. Would Chetana be able to rescue Kiria too?

Jori's gaze hooded, but he set his jaw. "I'll need that glass of wine first."

Bard gave him a flat-lipped nod.

"And a snack."

"I can get that for you!"

Jori caught his arm. "Let someone else get it. We need to get Kiria and, until then..." His thought faded, but Bard warmed with the feeling that Jori wanted him beside him. "We've got to get going. Quickly."

Bard nodded swiftly, urgency lighting up his body again. "Yeah. As fast as we can."

"Then"—Jori clapped his hands, looking around imperiously—"let's not stand around." It was a performance, but one Bard was grateful for. There was too thin a layer that separated them from falling apart. Theatrics at least allowed them to put on a mask and carry on with what needed to be done.

Bard called over Candrae. "Food for Jori, please. On the road."

She nodded and disappeared to find some rations.

"Good of you," said Jori, clapping him on the back. He poked his arm. "You'd be proud of me. I got the tattoo." He rolled up one sleeve and lifted up the front of his shirt to show it off. The tattoo covered his chest and scrolled down one arm, the arm where Atty had chosen to have his. A raincloud poured into a goblet covered in a design like the one on Kiria's back.

"Looks good, mate," Bard said. "What does that mean?" Down Jori's arm, all the way to the back of his hand, beautiful script in an old language replaced the traditional swirls and points. *As elithäma kemai.*

"*May it rain hope always.*" He flexed his hand open and closed, watching the old letters move.

"From the Sacred Scroll?"

"My favorite part."

Jori still hadn't pulled his shirt down. "Wait," said Bard, "is that...?"

Jori gave a small, crooked smile. At the base of the goblet were four tiny letters, a throwback to their final night in the palace together: SLUG.

43

BELIK

Of course it was Chetana. Belik dismissed the messenger from the room.

Tanyu could have had both the prince and princess, but now he had only one, all because of Chetana and her terrorist friends in Original Plan. Was he twenty again? This felt too familiar.

At least she'd rescued the boy and not Kiria. The princess would arrive in Brithnem under heavier guard within a day.

Predictably, she'd chased after Jori, and then, like the teenager she was, had wandered off alone. And some people still thought she was fit to rule a kingdom. Well, finally, Belik would show them.

Consolation for the support he'd lost in Master Gerand. They'd been partners for years, allies at least, though they didn't get on personally beyond their shared mission. It smarted to lose the Academy, though. Another thing he'd have to put back together after all this was done.

Jori was useful, impactful, but Kiria was his perfect hand at cards. It would be simple to kill her, but better to use her first, briefly, to tie up his loose ends. If everything went smoothly, the prince and their allies would surrender themselves, and Firian, mustering feeble forces against him, would abandon his little army of Sentries and Learners.

Simple.

He stumped over to the door, where Nedi and Shiro waited on the other side. "Make sure the arena is ready by midday tomorrow, and invite citizens to come see something that concerns them."

Too few people had the acuity and tenacity to chew on a problem for years and, when they discovered the solution, stomach the actions necessary to make it happen. Belik had no such problem.

44

KIRIA

Kiria woke in darkness. Her head throbbed in time with her nausea. Faint breezes played around her wrists and ankles. She was moving.

Trying to shake the haze from her mind, she fought to remember where she was. Her own caravan wouldn't treat her this way, slung uncomfortably over something that bucked beneath her—a saddle. The horn of it dug into her ribs. A rough, warm body pressed against her other side.

She moved her head slightly and the rough weave of burlap touched her cheek.

They'd taken her.

Her heart thundered and her speedy breathing huffed against a fabric gag, warm and stifling. She could barely suck in enough air through it to feel grounded.

Twisting her wrists in their restraints, she felt around for anything within reach that she could use to get herself free.

Despair threatened to settle like mud in her stomach. She swallowed down the acid that rose up in her throat. Belik now had her and Jori. That left only Kader, who was still underage. No one could rally around him the way they could rally around her. Even Jori had followers. He'd started to embrace his destiny right before...

Fighting to keep her breathing even, she took stock of the situation. She was taken. Jori was taken. As far as she knew, Kader was still free.

She couldn't let them take her behind the palace walls. Tanyu controlled that entire area. It would get progressively harder to escape the closer they got to the capital.

She hadn't moved enough to alert the rider that she had regained consciousness. Her breathing had changed, and she had stretched her fingers, but those were small clues, difficult to notice on a cantering horse. She cast her eyes down.

Maybe there was an opening to see the ground, get a sense of where she was. Nothing. A string around her neck held the bag in place. No light meant no vision.

Not knowing how long she'd been unconscious proved a new problem. She couldn't calculate how close they were to Brithnem. Would they stop before they reached the city walls? If they did, then she could try to find a way to free her ankles and run.

With consciousness came greater pain. It built quickly as though making up for lost time. Her ribs, pressed against the saddle horn, spiked with agony every time the horse moved. Her legs flopped uselessly to one side, chafing the ties around her ankles. Over everything was a blurriness not due to hurt or exhaustion. Thoughts wouldn't stay in place. They blinked in and out like fireflies. Some kind of drug?

Hopelessness gripped her. There was no reason to keep her alive now. They must only be taking her to be murdered somewhere public. Firian knew she'd been taken, didn't he? She only remembered part of their conversation in the Unreal. Was he close?

But she heard no scuffle, and the horses didn't stop until their hooves beat on the stone streets of Brithnem.

No one took off her mask or restraints when they arrived. Instead, she was hoisted onto someone's broad shoulder and carried roughly into a place that smelled like cool mold. A hint of garbage tinged the clammy air.

She didn't struggle. Without a way to run or fight, all struggle would harm more than help. Iron squealed. Something rough scraped across stone.

When they threw her down, she landed on her bruised ribs and couldn't hold back a cry of pain.

"She's awake," someone said. An accented male voice she didn't recognize. "Let him know."

"Don't you want to see?" a new oily voice suggested. His salacious tone sent frost to her limbs. She lay very still.

"We're supposed to bring her intact," said a woman's voice, high, though commanding.

"I didn't say we'd break her apart," said the oily one querulously. Kiria felt a large hand run from her knee to her ankle, almost as though it were petting an animal.

"Shut up," snapped the first male voice.

"You're not curious?" the oily one insisted. "You don't want to see the famed Beauty?"

A moment of hesitation. "Show us, then."

The woman huffed. "I can't leave you alone with—"

"Go tell Master Nedi we've got her," sneered the oily one. "Don't worry. We just want a look. She'll be here for you."

After a snip by the back of her neck, a flash of indistinct light and cool air washed onto her face. She blinked a few times before her eyes focused. A hand rolled her roughly to face upward, her arms twisted awkwardly beneath her. Three people stood over her, dusty from their ride. Around them, she didn't see the main dungeon of the palace, but the little used rooms—more exhibitions now than actual prison cells—beneath the arena.

Her throat felt dry as chalk as she took in the three looming above her, two men and a woman. The woman wore black and she stood with the knife-sharp gracefulness of a Tanyu. Her bobbed hair was sleek and black and her coloring looked as if she might be from Bosha in the Eradi Desert. The men's heads were shaved. Both of them. Torithian. Somehow this made her anger and panic worse.

The taller man's lip curled. "That's it?" It was the first man, with the accent.

"Maybe it's hard to tell with all her clothes on," said the oily man, stooping down to run his fingers over her.

She screeched into the gag, rolling away from him. But he could move and she couldn't. She squeezed her eyes closed and felt something warm slide down her temple. Was she crying? All her thoughts followed those fingers, tracing their path, flinching away from them, expecting them to rip her nightdress open.

"That's enough," said the woman.

Kiria kept her eyes shut. When the searching hands disappeared, she lifted her chin. It was such a tiny gesture that she was probably the only one to notice. That was all right. The defiance felt almost mechanical, but she needed the reminder. They would not break her. She would escape and free Jori and take back the Kingdom. Or, if she could not, she would fight until the end. She would die with ferocity and dignity.

Squeal and scrape and silence. Something dripped far away.

Even during the attack on the palace, and after her father was killed, and she watched the Torithians go down as Firian defended her, death was a concept, a thing far away. Now it was a monster in this old cell with her, threatening to choke out her breathing and turn her existence into a fading memory.

She struggled to her knees. Was there anything sharp in here to break her bonds? All the old stone, more sandy than gray, looked smooth, and the iron bars had no sharp angles.

Soft bootsteps sounded down the hall. When the owner of the boots appeared, he was far larger than his quiet approach suggested. He was one of the tallest men Kiria had ever seen, although maybe being on her knees had something to do with that assessment. He had pale skin, a large nose, and large hands. He wore all black.

The sight of the Tanyuin clothes made her heart constrict. Something about it was insulting, wrong, as though the world were askew. During the attack on the palace, she had seen no attackers. Here was one standing in front of her, in league with Torithians. She glared.

After entering the cell, the Tanyu angled his head down to her, his small eyes squinting. Without ceremony, he stood her on her feet. She could have weighed as much as a cat. She barely kept her balance. Lightheadedness and her bound legs acted against her.

He pulled the gag over the back of her head and out of her mouth. Her hair mussed crazily, loose ends tickling her cheek. Part of her wanted to spit at the man, but she had to weigh her options before doing something drastic. Besides, between the gag and lack of water, she had no saliva.

"Kiria Arioc," he began in a voice like gravel. It was one of the lowest she'd ever heard. "That is your name." It was a question, though he didn't phrase it that way.

She didn't currently look like the image on new-minted coins or the wooden figures of her sold in Grand Market Square. Standing as straight as she could with her head swimming as it was, she lifted her head and glared levelly at him.

His hand shot under her jaw, rough and squeezing, catching her breathless in its speed. "Answer me." The scariest thing might have been his lack of anger. This man gave no clue about what he was going to do. Could he kill her so dispassionately?

"I am," she managed, wrenching her chin away.

"You are going to die, Kiria Arioc."

The words bounced off her awareness. She could not let them in. She would not.

"But you can still save your followers, few as they are, if you give us the location of the Kepron."

Which one? Did they know Kader was alive, and only needed him to eliminate all Three Lines? Or did they mean Jori? Impossible hope welled in her. Had Jori saved himself? Had Firian saved him? Every scenario that spun through her mind seemed too improbable to contemplate.

"We don't need you in order to find him, but you can reduce his suffering if you help."

She jolted away from her brief spark of hope back to the cold eyes of the Tanyu. She stayed silent, tasting rebellion on her tongue. She was the best hope the Kingdom had of restoring the Keepers. The thought should have bolstered her, but it made her feel so, so inadequate.

"Where is the Kepron?" The huge Tanyu kept still, but a simmering violence radiated from him.

Shaking, she kept silent.

The Tanyu's enormous hand sped forward again with the deadliness of a snake and caught her around the throat. Her head crashed against the cell wall. Her feet couldn't keep up and they buckled under her. For one panicky moment, the Tanyu held her entire weight by her neck. As she struggled to get her legs under her, he said in the same low, even tone, loud in the silence, "I told you to answer my questions."

Surely her nightdress was trembling with the speed of her frantic heartbeat. "I won't." Her voice came out choked and raw.

Red pain exploded in her left eye socket. The back of her head cracked against the wall again with such force that her hair must have become matted with blood. The Tanyu retracted his fist. "You will when we're done with you."

45

FIRIAN

Firian's boot sank into half-frozen mud. At least snow wasn't blocking his visibility as it had a few days before. He, along with his ragtag group of Tanyu, Sentries, and border patrollers, had finally reached the southern foothills. Almost due south was Brithnem, where Belik had Kiria.

Maybe he should have left everyone and run to help her. Even so, he wouldn't have been able to get there in time. It would take a few days with or without the emptied Academy trailing behind him.

Her eyes. God, her eyes as she looked at him. She thought he could do anything. He'd started to lose that belief in himself.

Would that Kingdom patrol still protect Brett just in case something happened to him? Doubtful that Kiria could have communicated that order so quickly. No, she'd been taken while they spoke together in the Unreal. But she'd cared enough about his family to offer it.

Firian stopped dead, his breath stuck in his throat. He could feel the tendons in his neck and the veins in his fingers. Panic. That could only mean...

He lunged into the Unreal.

When he spotted Kiria, she stood Beautiful, high in a balcony of the arena with her arms bound behind her, wearing nothing but a thin nightdress pasted to her body with sweat. A purple bruise blossomed over her left eye. She held her chin up, but her mouth trembled and her eyes were wide.

A small crowd had gathered below on the sand. The shadow of the great statues fell over the people, but the sun beat down on Belik and Kiria. They stood out like a glare on water. It was hard to look at them, but impossible to look at anything else.

Belik stood before her, saying something about giving her what she deserved as a coward and enemy of the capital. Then Firian saw Belik's knife. Was he really going to kill her?

"In exchange for her life," Belik said, not loudly but clearly enough to be heard as his voice bounced off the arena walls, "I will accept the surrender of Jorrim Calthwaite. In exchange for her pain, I demand that Master Kess abandon his small resistance."

This show was some twisted test of loyalty? What did Belik think would happen? That Firian would give up the fight?

His breath came choppy. He was too far away. He couldn't get there to help her. He was too far away. *No, no, no!*

Belik spoke louder, but Firian didn't hear his words. Instead, his gaze was locked on Kiria's panicked one. She knew the same thing he did. Whether or not Jori surrendered or Firian disbanded the dregs of the Academy, Belik would kill her.

He felt sick.

Belik held the knife idly against her face. Her chest rose and fell frantically and tears started spilling down her face as he pressed the blade into her lip.

"Kiria!" Firian called.

She looked at him. He changed the background to Shifra, something that might be comforting to her. In a flash, she stood in front of him on the wooden planking, holding his hands so tightly that the knuckles grated together. Her eyes pressed shut and her breath hissed through gritted teeth. "I can't do this," she managed.

He squeezed her hands back. "You can. Be brave."

Tears coursed down both sides of her face. He wanted to hold her, to comfort her, but he didn't come closer. With her Beauty and the clinging nightgown, any move toward her could be seen as an unwanted advance. "I can't," she repeated, her voice hitching as she braced herself.

In the distance, screams echoed over the water. Her screams. His stomach twisted into a ball. "You can push pain into the Unreal. It helps. You just have to believe it completely."

She grimaced again.

"Believe it," he ordered.

She was crying. "Help me. Distract me."

He watched her helplessly as she tried to do what he asked. He could run his hands up and touch her through the clinging nightdress, and then her body would be underneath his as they clung together, the only sound in the darkness their own ragged breathing.

But that wasn't what she meant. Not now, not with him. He dismissed the fantasy with a desperate curse, holding more firmly to her hands.

"Look!" he said, shifting the setting to Brithnem. Brithnem before any of this had happened. The city glittered below them in the sunlight, as they watched the city from an imagined height. Happy people walked the streets, new statues bloomed at the crossroads... He even put some of the people she'd lost far below. The palace was intact, flags flying in the ocean breeze. "Look!"

She opened her eyes. Blood dribbled from the corner of her mouth. It disappeared at his will.

"Be brave," he said again.

Her eyes devoured the sight. He held her hands tightly. Was this all he could do? He'd never felt so useless.

"See, there's a statue of you." He let go with one hand to point.

She laughed, but it was like a sob. She was trembling all over. Maybe she didn't want him comforting her, but no one else could do it. Maybe she still blamed him for everything. It didn't matter. Anything that helped her get through this torture was welcome for now.

He couldn't swallow the lump in his throat as she ground her teeth together again and squeezed her eyes shut. Blood appeared on her chin, painting a streak of red across her light skin.

If she died here, with him...

He couldn't think about it. Again, the blood disappeared, but her grimace remained fixed. She was trembling. *Gore.* She opened her amber eyes. With one hand, he cupped her face and smoothed away the new tears with his thumb. He couldn't help it. "Be brave. You can't give up now."

"I don't think I can." Her broken voice rose barely above a whisper. She had nothing left.

"Sometimes courage just means lasting. You can do it." He shook her hands, trying to bring her back to him. Her mind was clearly on whatever was happening in the arena. He refused to look. Rage and sadness already threatened to consume him. He was the only one standing on Kiria's side, helping her through the pain.

She looked into his face with gleaming eyes. "I can last. I can do it," she said, like a mantra. "Just stay with me."

46

KIRIA

When it was over, two Tanyu—the big one who had interrogated her and the woman with slim green eyes and black hair—threw Kiria back in her cell under the arena. She collapsed, shuddering violently. Blood pooled under her face. Revulsion paralyzed her. She ached to know the extent of her wounds, but couldn't bear the thought of touching her face. Belik had carved deep into her lips and chin, saying something about taking away her Beauty. It was all a trap for Jori and Firian.

She had to get up. Her mouth was filling with blood. She had to get her face above her heart. A strange breath of air touched her teeth in new ways, outside to inside. Crawling to the corner, she propped herself against the wall and spit. The trembling hadn't stopped. She felt cold and sick and afraid and alone. But she was alive. Barely.

Blinking a few times to clear her mind, she made fists as tight as she could, driving her nails into her palms to distract herself from the pain in her head. *Bind it. I have to bind it.* The black scrap of mourning fabric still wound around her wrist, but it would not be long enough to tie around her head. There wasn't much extra material in her nightdress, but it did go to her knees, so there was room to rip off the bottom without compromising what little modesty she had left.

Images of the arena assaulted her like a physical thing. She had been with Firian in the Unreal, but she had been in the arena too. Despite her best efforts to remain stoic, she writhed and screamed under the torture of having her face ripped open. For a split second, she had considered that it might not be so bad to die.

Sometimes courage just means lasting.

No one watching in the arena or hearing about her situation from afar could help her. Firian was her only choice, and she had clung to him like a drowning woman in rough waters clings to a floating board. And she had outlasted the storm. This storm, at least. But she wouldn't last much longer at the rate she was bleeding.

She spit again and tried to get her eyes to focus. It took her five tries before the delicate red-stained fabric finally gave when she tried to rip it. Her strength was all but gone. The dress tore unevenly but she was past caring. Sweat coated her skin, slicking the silk. Everything took so long, but a tiny part of her was grateful to focus on the repetitive movements of trying and failing to get the fabric to stay.

In the forest, she had known this method would help the wound on Firian's back. Would it work the same way on her face? At least it would stall the blood, and it was all she knew to do.

Besides observation, of course. She scrutinized each face that came in range. According to Bard, Firian had gathered some of the Tanyu against Belik, and when Kiria's forces took back the city, she wanted to be able to distinguish any good Tanyu from the bad.

With her face bound, she allowed herself to lean back—not too far, or else her mouth would fill with blood again. Her shuddering had begun to subside, leaving occasional violent jerks in its place. She was too tired to strategize, to do anything beyond surviving. But sometimes that was courage too.

47

BARD

KIRIA, tortured in the arena? It was unthinkable. Bard winced as Firian left, the news still sending shocks through him. Firian, who hadn't seemed to notice he had blood on his fingertips, said he had left her sleeping fitfully in her cell. She was alive, but oh! who should be put through that?

Determination flamed through Bard's veins. He squinted through the thick shafts of sunset light at the others. Royce could help, rallying the other guards. He knew the inner workings of the palace and the walls—Bard hadn't stopped asking him questions about it. Jori would join the cause of saving her, but his talents didn't lie in anything that seemed immediately helpful. His status as a Calthwaite was something, as well as his knowledge of the passages that the guards didn't watch over. He had a little working understanding of the seedier parts of town as well, if that came up. So there were a few things. Chetana was valuable asset, although her full set of skills was still a mystery even after hearing the story about Jori's rescue. The serving girls would do all they could, but they weren't fighters.

They might meet allies nearer to the walls. Would those armies be decimated already? A lump formed in the back of his throat. As soon as Kiria was taken, a sure voice had told him, *Bard, you knew it! You knew that following Jori the most obvious way would lead to trouble.* The voice sounded like his mother, with a tinge of Jac's ridicule. But they were right. He had known it, but had worried so much for Jori's safety and the pressure of time that he'd ignored the warnings in his mind and run forward with the others.

Now Kiria was in the hands of Belik. Tortured, Firian said. He hadn't gone into detail, but he hadn't needed to. Tanyu were marked by their imagination, and in that way, Bard was no different from the others.

Bard pulled his mount alongside Royce, who wore full armor, silver and sleek, with a sheaf of blue fabric across the shoulders. The ends of the fabric barely looked worn from all this riding. Bard, by comparison, felt grimy, his yellow shirt stained with sweat under his arms.

"Royce?"

The older man turned to him.

"Do you already have a plan to save Kiria when we get there? Did Chetana talk to you?" Ever since returning, the Amir avoided Bard when she could. She must have blamed him for ruining the chances of Original Plan helping them any more. But he hadn't known who those women were when he'd gone to check on her. How could he have?

"It's war," Royce replied simply, with a hard expression on his face. "We'll wait for our allies and then we'll strike."

"We can't do that," Bard said quickly.

Beside them, Jori rode abreast, interest and concern written deeply in his dark brows. "Is there news?" he asked.

Bard turned to him. "Kiria..." He stopped, although he should have kept going. The truth, though, was not much better than the horrible guess hanging in the air after his silence.

Jori paled. He looked immediately older, with dry lines forming across his smooth skin.

Bard soldiered onward. "She's alive. She was... tortured in the arena."

Jori's lips fell open in a silent, horrified sob, like a backward gasp. The skin around his eyes grew taut. "She's alive?"

"She's alive."

"Did the Watchman announce it?"

"Not yet. And you know we can't trust the Watchman. Belik will have gotten to him a long time ago."

His expression clouded. "Then how do you know?"

"Firian told me. You know the... connection. He witnessed the whole thing, but he isn't at the city yet either."

Jori clenched his jaw. "You *know* that he's telling you the truth?"

Bard put a hand over his heart. "Yes. Absolutely."

Sadness replaced Jori's hostility and he slumped a little in his saddle. Normally he rode tall and glorious, smiling despite his own pain to lift up other people. Bard was finally starting to see how he could one day be a Keeper too.

Bard turned back to Royce. "We can't start a full-out war until we have Kiria back. She'd be the first casualty. They'd kill her for sure. The people need to have someone they can put their hope in."

"They aren't putting enough hope in her," Jori remarked.

"The leaders aren't. We don't know about the citizens. I think more of them will be on her side, yeah?"

Jori cracked a smile. "Yeah. Hopefully! So how do we get her out?"

"I was hoping you would help me with that." He shifted his attention back to Royce, who rode with an impassive expression. The glittering of his eyes, however, told Bard that he was listening intently. "I'll consult with you too, and Chetana, if she'll meet with me. She has to. This is Kiria. Together we'll make a plan."

"Look at you, the general!" Jori wrapped the reins around one hand, leaving the other free for gesturing. He lifted one eyebrow until it disappeared into his hair. He was teasing, but a serious air permeated the words too. Was it pride?

"I don't have a glass of wine," Bard said.

"Make it a bottle owed."

"Deal."

CANDRAE AND VAYCI split a piece of paper and wrote in tiny, cramped handwriting while Bard and Jori sat at the edge of the bed and conspired. They'd add the ideas to the pages Bard had given Kiria, which they'd found afterward in her tent.

Jori's ideas were endless. Many of them would never work in real life, but he put them forward all the same. He had the imagination of someone who spent his life in the Unreal, except that his ideas weren't for war but for play. The fresh perspective sent Bard's mind spinning through new corridors, as though he just learned that Indisfate players could stack their pieces three high.

A single lantern hung from the center of the tent, casting a dimly glowing haze over everyone inside. They had all ridden until the horses were panting and covered with sweat. Jori had immediately climbed a tree against the soldiers' protests, to confirm that they were in sight of the city. The palace, he reported, wasn't on fire anymore. Bard did his best to usher him inside the shelter of a tent while the guards stood protectively at their posts.

It was late, and Bard was exhausted too, especially knowing that he was back to the duty of monitoring Jori's dreams, but this was too important to put off. He could always chew more of Viktor's dried seeds to keep himself awake. A few cities had vowed their support, but none of them would likely arrive outside the capital walls for several days. They had little help to rely on but themselves.

"Could we release an animal outside her cell to scare away the guards?"

Candrae's eyebrows rose and she scribbled something on her paper. Kiria's serving girls had been desolate but this task directed their efforts to something more helpful. Bard saw grim determination in their eyes.

Bard didn't say that getting a terrifying animal would be more trouble than help. Instead, he nodded. "What else?" Jori's words were like building tools. Some were bricks and hammers and beams, while others were wild decoration or wheels that would never fit on the edifice Bard was trying to build.

"Seduce the guards."

"Yeah, that would take longer than we have," Bard replied, as though considering the suggestion.

Jori gave a roguish smile.

Bard ignored it, looking down as he rearranged the strategy board again in his mind. "What else?"

"Flood the cell. Make them move her. Or we could go to the arena dressed as Tanyu and replace the guards. Do you still have your old clothes?" Jori picked at the front of his loose shirt, where his tattoo was etched underneath.

Bard shook his head quickly. They had been in the palace when it burned. "They'd recognize me. And you."

"I was thinking about Viktor."

"He has a huge tattoo on his face. He wouldn't fit in my clothes anyway. He's too tall."

"Well, he would *fit*..." Jori gave a short, hoarse laugh.

A tiny smile curled Candrae's lips, though she didn't look up.

"All right," said Jori, smoothing his shirt down in a fussy manner, like someone about to address a much bigger audience. "We go in as doctors to check on her."

Bard shot a glance at Vayci, making sure she wrote that one down. She nodded back at him in confirmation once it was done.

"Was that one good?" Jori asked, catching Bard's silent conversation.

"Maybe. Yeah." He scrubbed the back of his head with his knuckles.

Jori hadn't needed a doctor, since he was never tortured. Chetana and Original Plan had waylaid the Charäkhni king's bodyguard when he grew complacent near the city walls. The worst Jori had endured were days and nights of relentless travel, bound and gagged, with his fresh tattoo aching and itching. That, and the fear of inevitable death, which was enough torture for anybody.

Bard suspected that Jori hadn't told him everything, especially about Original Plan, but he had been specific about the conditions of his kidnapping, so Bard didn't pry. All he knew was that the group of women refused to help the Keepers beyond freeing Jori, and Bard had a sinking feeling that their decision to leave was all because of him.

"Or," Jori said grandly, "we could tunnel below."

Candrae started to write. Bard subtly shook his head no.

"What about that thing, that blocking thing you Tanyu can do? Blocking the mind? Would that stupefy the guards? I bet you could do that, dear. You're very good."

Bard blushed at the compliment. "No." He'd never trained as a Sentry, although he knew he could block someone's access to the Unreal if he tried. Being a Sentry was the opposite side of forming a *katah*—the painfully mind-numbing side. "That's not how Sentries work."

Jori snapped. "Sentries! That's the word."

None of Jori's ideas, Bard noticed, involved Firian. Bard could feel Firian getting closer, although he wasn't positive about his location. "Firian's coming, you know. He might be able to help."

Jori bit his tongue lightly, a clear message that he hated the idea. If that weren't enough, his gray eyes stormed at the mention. When Bard waited, Jori sighed and ran his fingers along the bedspread as though checking for dust. "He's on his own side, love. Surely you can see that. I will suggest nothing that has us count on *him*."

"But I could—"

Jori set a firm hand over Bard's useless one. "Not if I can help it."

Bard cleared his throat when Jori let go. It was foolish to ignore such a big player as Firian, but Jori had reason to dislike him. There was still a chaos of ideas that Bard could gather into strategy. "Then what else?"

48

KIRIA

THE SAME THING happened the next day. This time the cut was to her cheek, deep and horrible. Firian appeared again, transforming the Unreal into backgrounds to distract her. He offered her tarts and strawberries, took her to see glassblowers and to meet imagined versions of her past heroes. The statues in the Main became walking people she could talk to, lanterns around the Amiran Academy turned different colors, mirroring the ones along the wooden pathways of Shifra, the grassy plains of Enderin housed improbable animals, stars shone above, water below... And then she was left in her cell again, alone, and cold with the autumn and feverish terror.

Because of the pain, Kiria hadn't slept, though she felt weak from blood loss. Thirsty too. Cool water going down her throat—she fantasized about it but got little. She could hardly drink anyway. Her mouth didn't move correctly. As much as possible, she kept her whole face still so it could heal, binding it with the cloth when she could bear it. One day, she wanted to talk again without slurring. The awful scars were unavoidable. But they didn't concern her as much as everything else.

Was Jori really all right or had they killed him? Was anyone coming to rescue her?

She'd done her own inventory of the cell and the door, to see if she could escape by herself. Unless someone came to assist her, it was nearly impossible, as far as she could see. The best option for her to escape alone would be when they took her from the cell to the arena. There were so many more variables then, and she kept her eyes open for all of them. But before they took her out of her cell, two Tanyu would come—she learned their names were Enktuya and Nedi—and tie her arms behind her before they marched her into the arena. She had her voice and her feet, but barely. Even if she could run, where could she go that would be safe?

Her conclusion, and the best plan she had, was that she would escape from the two Tanyu however she could and run to a hiding place. It didn't matter what it took to get there. A fleeting indignity was worth the prize of freedom. Once she hid, hopefully behind a locked door, she would...

Here, her mind stuttered. She would wait until there were no sounds, perhaps in the deep of night, and get out of the palace to meet up with her caravan. Right?

Remembering Firian's and Bard's strange sleep schedules—each for different reasons—part of her knew that there would never be a time Tanyu weren't on guard, especially if she were missing. If she contacted Bard about her location, that could help, but that plan relied on his knowing which Tanyu were trustworthy enough to help her.

Kiria had tried to contact Bard, but it took so much mental effort that she hadn't been successful yet. She barely had enough presence of mind to pray. Hopefully Firian updated them all. He was the only one who truly knew what was happening to her. Despite Firian's kindness through the torture, she hadn't granted him a lasting place on the list of those she trusted. Being in the Unreal did soothe the pain—Shifra and an unblemished Brithnem, her own palace halls and her room in the morning—but the smart of his betrayals hadn't completely left her.

In the desperation of her pain, when she forgot she was a Keeper and had only one thought—to make it stop—she wouldn't have prevented him from embracing her. In fact, she'd welcome it. Anything to distract from the arena. In the past, his strong arms had felt safe. She could pretend they were back in that time, just until the blade was put away and the Tanyu's insults and demands subsided. But he hadn't done anything more than hold her hands, and she'd initiated that, squeezing with all her might as though he were the only thing anchoring her to this world. In the dizzy, shaking rush that followed the torture, she wondered why he hadn't held her, hadn't kissed her, pressing his body against hers so she could lose herself. Part of her was glad. It meant she could have no qualms about going back to him if she had to endure another day.

How many days? Her eyes welled. Carefully, she rubbed the tears from her left eye before salt could dribble into the wounds.

It isn't over.

The temptation to give up hovered around her like fog. She told herself again, told the darkness smothering her, the same words.

It isn't over.

In a hum that was more sound than buzz (since she couldn't fully close her lips) she began the anthem. It was the same soaring song they'd played at her coronation, the same song she'd played badly on the lyra for captured fireflies. This was her song. These were her people. She would make it through this and restore the rightful Keepers to their thrones. Violence and manipulation and cruelty would not have the last word in the Western Kingdom.

Her hoarse song got louder. Let them hear her defiance. The small part of her, like a ghost, that hovered above this moment, above this pain, welcomed anyone who would listen.

And someone did. Two people.

One was a young Tanyuin woman with a reddish-brown braid down her back. Her coloring was like Haved's, except that this person was lithe and coiled, rod straight and thin, as though she were made only of bone and strong sinew. Kiria had never seen her before. She wasn't in the usual rotation of guards.

The other looked unmistakably like Candrae, *her* Candrae, except that her long golden curls now looked dusty brown, like Kiria's, and she wore a nightdress reminiscent of the one Kiria wore as she sat looking through the bars of her cell.

Kiria blinked. She hadn't hallucinated, except perhaps to see flashes of light or moving shadows. Her Talent was too weak to let her get Lost in the Unreal. So what was this? She gazed at the pair—the Tanyu had one hand on Candrae's shoulder, and Candrae's tear-filled eyes were locked on Kiria.

Kiria was afraid to speak and break the spell. Or maybe this was a rescue effort that relied on her silence. Her ragged song of rebellion faded away.

The second guard standing watch leaned toward the new Tanyu. "If you're here to clean up, Tesni, don't bother."

Tesni, the Charäkhni Tanyu with the braid, replied, "Then let's move her. Just because we can take the smell doesn't mean we have to." She gestured to Candrae, whose changed hair was mostly obscured by a hood. "I found a servant who can do it for us."

Had they taken Candrae too? A scream of protest welled up inside Kiria but she forced it back down. They weren't treating her like a prisoner. And the only reason they'd have to hurt Candrae is if they knew it would hurt Kiria to see it. She clung to the dim hope that they didn't know their connection, pressing her thumbnails into the sides of her fingers. Meeting Candrae's gaze, she gave what she hoped was a heartening look.

"Are you here to clean too?" her guard cried to someone out of sight.

"Yes, sir," came an unfamiliar male voice. "These cells over—"

"You shouldn't be here."

"But I was told—"

Tesni cut in. "Tell them that we're moving her." She began unlocking the bars.

The other Tanyu didn't budge. "Master Belik said not to move her to safeguard against escape." Doubt bled through his words.

Tesni drew herself up to her full height, which wasn't much. "You think she'll escape on my watch? Look at her!" She flung one hand toward Kiria, still sitting, weak, against the wall. "I've already posted another Tanyu at the entrance. So you can keep your gory thoughts to yourself." At that, she turned away from him and finished unlocking the door. After a final appraising look, the other Tanyu disappeared. Kiria didn't even see him leave.

Through the whole exchange, Candrae stood silent, watchful as a spirit. If they truly were just moving her, then why was her serving girl here? The sight of her made Kiria's chest ache. Her own torture had smothered hope inside her, as though everyone else had died too. Here was a sliver of home, coming without comment into her cell.

Kiria still didn't dare speak, and wasn't sure she'd be able to anyway. The cloth made it difficult to breath, much less talk.

Candrae approached her, falling her one knee and kissing her filthy hand. "My Keeper," she said quietly, with tears in her voice. "We're going to—"

As Candrae spoke, Tesni pressed something soft and suffocating against Kiria's nose and bleeding mouth. Kiria thrashed once, and fell into nothing.

Something stung Kiria's cheek and she woke up grimacing, which didn't help the pain. As the room where she lay materialized around her, she found that she wasn't in her cell, or in the arena at all. The air smelled fresh, like trees and salve, and there was soft fabric over her arms. Her face felt cold. She was in new clothes in a new space and there were faces over her. With light behind them, she couldn't make out who they were.

One dove for her, kissing her uninjured cheek.

"Stop!" hissed a voice. "You'll hurt her."

Kiria didn't mind at all. Jori and Chetana. Jori was alive, and they'd both come back safe.

"You're awake," said Bard's glad voice. "Try not to move."

She gave a little nod, but it was hard not to smile or cry at the shock of being back. How had she gotten away? Scraps of memory felt more like dreams than sensible parts of a plan.

"Were you really singing the anthem?" Jori asked, his face growing clearer as her vision adjusted. The same as ever, he didn't seem to be injured or maimed. Royce and Viktor stood in the room too, along with Vayci and two other guards who had traveled with them. Chetana held a pot of fragrant salve.

She nodded again. Bard and Jori gave matching grins. "That's my girl," Jori said, swallowing hard. His face looked puffy.

For the first time, Kiria wondered what she looked like. Everyone stared as though she were an apparition. But she didn't want to ask and she didn't want a looking glass. Another sting surged through her lip and cheek.

"Where's Candrae?" she managed without moving her lips.

Jori looked grim. Kiria's breath halted. Had something happened to her?

Chetana cut off whatever response Jori was about to give. "She's not here yet." She dabbed more cooling ointment on the cuts.

From the corner of her eye, Kiria saw Vayci wringing her hands.

"She still there?" Kiria asked, still keeping her mouth still. Candrae had been dressed approximately like Kiria. They couldn't have meant to *switch* them... Master Belik and the other Tanyu who regularly watched her cage would have caught on immediately. Candrae would be dead already if that were their plan.

"Not in the arena," Bard explained. "She should be on her way to us." He and Jori shared a look laced with concern.

"It's a little complicated, and not what I would have liked," Chetana said archly, "but you're here now, and safe. You need to rest."

"Yes, safe," Jori echoed meaningfully, touching her arm through the blanket spread over her.

"You'll need to apply this to your cuts twice a day for the next two days, but you'll heal," Chetana said, closing the pot of salve. "We should leave her to rest."

"No," Kiria said. The word felt wrenched from her. She didn't want to be alone. Jori seemed to catch her meaning. "I'll stay."

Her neck and shoulders relaxed as Vayci said, "I'll stay too."

Chetana placed a soothing hand on Kiria's hair, cradling the top of her head as though she were a child. "Just don't let them keep you up," she said, running her thumb once over her forehead. For a moment, genuine love shone in her eyes. Kiria returned what she hoped was an echoing look.

As the guards took up their posts all around the exterior circumference of the tent—it was her old tent, she noticed—Bard looked uncertain whether he should go or stay.

"He came up with the plan to save you," Jori said quickly, following her eyeline.

"We did," Bard amended, though there was a flash of pride about him.

Kiria held out her hand to Bard, who took it and squeezed gently.

A smile softened the corner of his lips. "I'm really glad you're back. Seriously, I can't say. You know, we were worried. I can't even believe what they did to you." His eyes gleamed. "I'm so sorry. They're not all the same, you know. I just..."

Jori patted his back, not taking his eyes from where Kiria lay comfortably on the bed. "And you were singing the anthem," he said, a punctuation mark to Bard's apology.

"I couldn't do much else." It was freeing not to have a bandage around her face and the constant taste of blood. Chetana's mixture stung, but in a healthful, healing way. "Is anyone else here? The armies?"

"Not yet," said Bard, "but it'll only be a few days before most of them get here."

Disappointing news, but not the worst. She was in no shape to plan a battle today, anyway. Tomorrow would be a different story. She could already feel her body recovering just by lying down. And the best thing of all was seeing her friends and family still very alive.

"We already have some strategies laid out for when they get here," said Bard. "It's a combination of what we talked about and a bunch of other ideas. Mixed together, I think they can work, yeah?"

In this half-delirious state, she didn't know if she could remember all their allies or make sense of what best to do against this unprecedented enemy, so she tucked the question away for tomorrow.

Her next question felt frivolous, but had to be asked. "Do I look like myself?" Not once had she traced the lines of her face since the first demonstration in the arena. It had been too painful and she was afraid of what she might find.

She looked to Bard for an honest reaction. The Tanyu just bit his lip.

"You're beautiful as always," Jori said, dipping to kiss her forehead.

Not an answer. She sighed. Well, there were more important things. She was Keeper with or without the face she'd grown up with. And she had a kingdom to take back.

49

BARD

It was such a relief to sit with Jori and Kiria together that Bard almost forgot his worry. Almost. He never truly let it go.

Tesni and Candrae hadn't come back and the thought of the serving girl flushed his face with concern. The plan had been mostly his idea. Candrae was about the same height and build as Kiria, and they needed a decoy for the Tanyu to follow while a Kingdom soldier friendly to their side brought Kiria back to the camp. It was imperative that the Tanyu not follow her *here*.

It was a temporary solution anyway. As they talked, Viktor was checking to see if Jori's underground party hall had been compromised. If it was safe, then they would all move there, better hidden, once their allies found them.

Jori counted off with his fingers. "So, we have the soldiers still alive in the city, a handful of Endrian soldiers who are coming tomorrow, six Kingdom towns, and ourselves."

"That's it," Bard confirmed. Endrians weren't required to come, but some had volunteered to repay in good faith all that the Kingdom had done to help them during the past years' raids. Jac might be with them. Did his brother even know which side Bard fought on? "And the Tanyu on our side, like Tesni," he added.

"Yes, well, there aren't many of those, are there?"

Bard drummed his fingers against the side of his chair. Firian's troops were coming, Sentries and all, but the Brithnem guards had the order not to let him near the Keepers. *Well, he's not here now.* "Maybe more than we think," he went on. "Firian's coming back."

"He'll fight on his own side for his own reasons," Kiria said. Her speech sounded slurred since she tried not to move her mouth. The deep wounds on her lips and cheek had closed overnight, but she still sported wicked red lines. One began on her upper lip and pierced all the way down to her neck. No matter how she healed, one side of her mouth would be left twisted.

"I think he's for you," Bard insisted.

"Then he can show it." Her tone was steely, but there was a vulnerability in her eyes that said she really did want him to.

He couldn't blame her for her skepticism. Bard had known Firian most of their lives and he had trouble sorting out his motivations sometimes.

"And Belik has Tanyu, Torithians, and all the towns he coerced into helping them," Jori finished.

"And a couple that went willingly, remember?" Kiria said wearily. "Most are staying out of the conflict, though."

Bard's thoughts drifted to Haved and Atty and the Charäkhni king. "At least the fight's on a smaller scale, I guess," he said.

"It should be on a bigger scale," Jori grumbled. "This is our lives and our kingdom." His face brightened with a sudden recollection. "I never showed you my tattoo!" Standing, he lifted his shirt to reveal the image of a rain falling into a goblet. The color of Jori's design looked redder than Kiria's black one. Maybe they had different ink in Charäkhnem.

She winced good naturedly, waving for him to stand farther away. "I'm so glad you got it! We weren't sure if you made it to the artist or not."

"Oh yes. I made it." Jori beamed.

"What'll happen when you get old and fat?" she teased.

"Me? Never!"

"That's what drinking does."

"Bigger canvas."

"This design is complicated," she said.

"Like me." He touched the side of his face with two fingers in a gesture of pathos. Dropping his hand, he added, "It hurt worse than that hail storm. I had to keep thinking of happy, fluffy things to maintain my dignity."

Bard chuckled.

A head appeared through the tent flap. "My Keeper," said Chetana, "they're back."

Relief flooded Bard as he, along with Jori and Vayci, bolted for the door. He felt as if he'd been holding his breath until he heard the news. The worst aspect of the plan to rescue Kiria had been risking Candrae's life. He knew it was a risk, but she was willing and the best person to do it. Chetana had wanted to begin the inevitable war instead, to overwhelm the Tanyu after more of Kiria's allies arrived. But that would have meant bloodshed, so much of it, and no guarantee of success.

War was coming—Bard wasn't denying that—but it didn't have to come now, and it didn't have to come with so many casualties. He hoped. Remembering the black pit of horror he felt after snuffing out the Torithian captain Tibor Wat, he doubted he could ever do it again. Certainly not to other Tanyu. Happily, Jori had chosen his plan over Chetana's, and she had yielded, calling him "My Keeper" for the first time.

Tesni and Candrae waited in another tent—they only used three now, to be less noticeable. Tesni stood, all in black, her face set and alert. Candrae sat on the side of the bed, hunching over her knees, trembling slightly.

Vayci ran to her, lifted her chin, and hugged her. Candrae held on tight. A slight but unmistakable odor of human feces rose from Candrae's clothes.

"I'm so, so glad you're back!" Bard cried, resisting the urge to hug Tesni as well. She'd never acted affectionately toward anyone, that he knew of. Tesni regarded him warily. Bard knew what she might be thinking. *Traitor. Defector. Boy who turned his back on his own.* He'd accepted that the Tanyu might not love him. Hopefully they were beginning to see why he left and why he ran to Kiria for help.

Once the hug between Candrae and Vayci was over, Jori took a knee beside Vayci and looked Candrae in the eye. "You were very brave, my girl." He took her hand gently and squeezed it. "We're indebted to you." Candrae looked abashed, wide-eyed and filled with emotion.

Movement at the entrance signaled Kiria's arrival.

"My Keeper!" Candrae exclaimed, as though she were glad for something else to focus on besides Jori's piercing gray eyes. "You look so much better." At that, she fell into weeping.

Vayci embraced her protectively and the others left them alone to wash up and compose themselves. The whole group headed back to Kiria's tent, which was the biggest.

"Kiria, this is Tesni," Bard said, almost adding, *She's a Tanyu.* But that was obvious. Her poise and black outfit made Bard keenly aware that he wasn't wearing his.

Tesni inclined her head to Kiria while keeping her eyes on her.

"I'm glad you came," Kiria said. "Is Candrae all right?"

"She will be. She wasn't hurt." Her tone was flat, though whether from her business-like composure or distrust, it was hard to tell.

Firian's unspoken name sizzled in the air, crackling in their ears like static.

Two guards parted the curtains and allowed them all inside. One followed them in. The group stood in a tense circle—Kiria, Jori, Bard, Chetana, Tesni, Royce representing the guards.

Bard's Tanyuin training guided his attention to all the potential weapons. Tesni must carry a dagger in her boot—they all did—and Royce had a sword at his side. Jori and Kiria were weaponless, and so was he. As the clearest link between Brithnem and the Tanyu, he felt the weight to speak. But how could he, with all these important people here? He looked to Jori, who met his gaze.

"Well," Jori declared, clapping his hands, "isn't this a fun party? We were just in the middle of counting our allies. I hope we can count you." This last comment was directed at Tesni.

"I'm against Master Belik," she replied. "He supplanted Master Kess."

"Which means you're for us," said Kiria, casting a warning look at Chetana. Suspicion didn't leave the Amir's face, but the rigidity of her jaw softened. "You've made it clear by how much you risked to help me escape. I'm deeply grateful, and I'm grateful that you took care of Candrae."

"She's very fearful," Tesni said.

"She won't be going on any more missions, so it doesn't matter, does it?" Jori added. "I thought she was brave. Not sure if I'd do that." He stretched his back so he stood taller and turned to Kiria. "No, I take it back, darling. You know I'd do anything for you."

Kiria gave him a smile made lopsided by her cuts. The small gesture tugged at Bard's heart because he knew it was true. They'd each do anything for the other. If only their eyes would dart to him too.

"Tesni," she said, "once you swear loyalty, you're welcome to stay in our camp."

"Are there others like you, who could get out?" Jori asked the Tanyu.

"I said there were," Bard answered, his dark brows ticking downward, but only for a moment.

"Will they?" Jori revised.

Tesni's frame had relaxed a fraction since she'd entered the tent. Bard sensed less threat from her now, not that there was ever *threat*, exactly. Just excessive wariness on both sides. "We've been staying on the inside to gather information. I expected most of us would strike from there when there was a coup."

Three voices spoke at once to correct her. Bard faltered in astonishment when he realized the others deferred to let him speak. "This isn't a coup," he explained. "Kiria belongs on the throne. Belik usurped what belongs to her. To both of them. Kiria and Jori."

"How does the Tanyuin Head feel about that?" Chetana asked in a dangerously measured voice.

There it was. The unspoken name.

"Whose side is he on?" Chetana looked as fierce as any Tanyu Bard had seen. Her dark eyes flashed and the patterned septum ring in her nose shone like a war trophy.

"Yours," Bard answered. Their time in the cellar had convinced him of that, and every time they met in the Unreal afterward solidified his belief in his friend.

Chetana tipped her head at Tesni, prompting her to answer.

"Hers," Tesni said, looking at Kiria.

Bard was suddenly aware of Royce standing with them, shifting his weight as though to beg Kiria's attention. She granted it, but said nothing. No change in her orders.

"We want peace," Kiria said, addressing the group and looking them in the eyes one by one. Despite wearing a simple dress, plain face, and struggling to speak around her wounds, she looked like the Keeper she was. "We all want peace for Brithnem, as little killing on both sides."

"Master Belik is ready for you," Tesni said, sounding remorseful now.

Ready? How? Did Tesni know more than they did about his plans?

She continued. "There are four ships due in the port today to drop off new soldiers. I don't know all his plans—he only confides in three others—but I know he has allies coming, and he plans to crush you before you get into the city. Especially since the last plan failed to turn up the other heirs." She gestured to Kiria's face without embarrassment. "Or Master Kess."

The news affected them all instantly. Bard wasn't surprised, but still felt his chest tightening. Kiria stared at Tesni, not in challenge, but with a burning sort of courage. Chetana took in a slow, deliberate breath, and a muscle ticked in Jori's temple. The skin around Jori's eyes constricted and his pupils went small from fear. He still stood in his insolent way, but it was obvious that he'd never been around war. Bard's small taste in the storeroom of the Academy was more than he'd ever wanted to encounter in his lifetime.

"Now Belik will kill them on sight." Chetana's words were more of a statement than a question.

Tesni nodded, eyes narrow. "When are your forces coming?"

Kiria held up a hand to stop anyone else from answering. "We'll only give information as necessary. We're working for a solution that spares as many Tanyu as we can."

"Master Belik won't negotiate away his power." Everyone knew Tesni was right.

"I'm not talking about negotiation," Kiria replied. "But surely more Tanyu don't approve of Master Belik's methods."

"There are some, yes. He purged several already who made attempts on his life. He would have done the same to me if he'd known. Many of us still consider Master Kess the Head, not Belik."

"Well, now you aren't following him, are you?" Jori said. "You're following us."

"She still hasn't pledged her allegiance," Chetana observed icily.

Kiria lifted her chin. "There are two sides to this war," she said, her gaze fixed on Tesni. "For the Kingdom and against it. Keepers or Tanyu. Firian hasn't demonstrated his side clearly, but he will take one. I need to know that you are on ours."

Bard watched Tesni's hands, so capable. Royce seemed to tense beside him.

"We can't work with Tanyu," Chetana said abruptly, and then shifted to Tesni. "Thank you for your help, but we know we can't expect any more from you."

"Chetana," Kiria chided. "We already do." She gestured at Bard.

He fought not to fidget under everyone's renewed scrutiny of his Tanyuin background. "Yeah," he said. "We're not all the same. Some of us see the injustice of this. You need us. At least, we could be helpful."

"Already are," Jori added. "Honestly, I think it's a relief that we can count on some Tanyu. I always hoped they weren't all murderous." He said it lightly, but there was a pointedness to the words that made Bard feel bolstered.

Tesni didn't take the comment kindly, but fell neatly to one knee before Kiria anyway. "I swear loyalty to you and the crown."

"Let's rephrase," said Jori, stepping in. "Repeat after... her." He gave a theatrical flutter of his fingers to Kiria and stepped back.

Tesni repeated the traditional oath, with an addition. "I swear to serve my Keepers, Kiria Arioc and Jorrim Calthwaite, and my country, the Western Kingdom, to the best of my ability, regardless of danger and should I betray them, may the punishment be death." She rose, stern but resolute. "I'll be glad to see the thrones restored."

"So will I," Kiria said, motioning to Royce. "He'll show you where you can rest and wash."

Once Tesni was gone, Bard leaned over and spoke in an undertone. "Did you forget the words?"

Jori pretended to be affronted. "I never forget things. Also, yes." He winked. "At least I'm trying."

50

FIRIAN

Endrian forces, though not many, had arrived in Kiria's meager camp. At least that's what Bard had to report. He seemed antsy. Jac must be among the numbers.

Firian peered through a break in the trees. A couple other small Kingdom towns had swelled their numbers too. A little colony of tents barely hid among the full yellow and orange trees of the Gray Forest.

Though firelit guards were stationed around the perimeter, the camp looked woefully tiny considering what it was about to attempt. This was Kiria's army, barely a few thousand, and yet she planned to fight despite small chance of success. *Justice*, he could almost hear her say. He couldn't help but be impressed.

Tanyu are coming, he reminded himself. Sensing the final conflict drawing near, he'd told his Tanyuin allies inside the city—those who lived—to figure out a way to get out and meet them. Bard said he had plans for them. The way Bard talked suggested he was one of the main figures in charge of strategy. Maybe Indisfate was directly related to strategic ability. So far, though, Bard's plans had succeeded. Kiria was safe.

Per Bard's instructions, Firian had contacted Tesni and explained how to rescue Kiria. It was risky. A non-Tanyu took the real Kiria back to her camp, while Tesni drew all the attention with the serving girl posing as the Keeper. Firian never should have doubted it would work.

Bard had also said that Kiria hadn't fully warmed to the idea of accepting Firian's help.

"She said you'd have to show her," he'd told him, eyeing Firian with a curious look, a sort of sympathetic challenge. A look like he'd given him in the mansion's cellar. Bard believed in them both, but his belief had always been bigger than Firian's.

So he would show her. As he told Brett, he was on Kiria's side. No matter what happened, she was the one who deserved to be on the throne of Brithnem. She could establish justice over tyranny. His mind gave a little skip. He couldn't think about what would happen next to him or the Academy.

Firian mapped a trail of blind spots away from the guards. His black clothes would give him away as a Tanyu, even if they didn't recognize him as Firian Kess, the Tanyuin Head. Night shadows would be his salvation.

He had to appeal to her directly. If he went to Bard's tent or approached the nearest guard, there was no telling if the soldiers would let him near her.

Let. He hated that word.

He could get to her if he wanted to, but he also wanted to avoid conflict. The point of this exercise was to prove that he was on her side, after all. It would be hard to prove that if he had to fight his way to her.

Firian's own troops—if he could use the word—waited about fifteen minutes away. Sentries and Defenders and remaining Tanyu, all that were left at the Academy.

The memory of Kiria's pain tore through his gut. He hadn't known she would be tortured, but *that* was why he'd emptied the Academy. To keep her from pain and to help her get where she belonged.

Was she all right now? Her wounds had been terrible, but she had gritted her teeth and survived. Since she met him in the Unreal during her torture, she hadn't come again. Now he was actually here and could do more than comfort.

Belik's words in the arena had come back to him piecemeal. At the time, he had blocked them out, trying to avoid rage in favor of whatever care he could offer. Belik's demands for Jori and Firian in exchange for Kiria's life twisted like a familiar knife. The words sounded like Firian's own. *Just give yourself up.* He felt sick at the thought. Had he really said that and considered it mercy?

He was closer now, assessing the guards. Extra stood in front of a couple tents. Kiria and Jori. It had to be. Both tents were light blue, Kingdom blue, with dark purple edging and smudges that could be scrollwork along the top. One of the tents was a little larger than the other. He'd go there.

It was surrounded by many other shelters, almost at the center of the camp. Moving into position, he started edging between tents, avoiding the light of fires that punctuated open areas. A medley of smells ran thick through the air, campfire smoke and sour body odor and tanned skins used for new tents and melted cheese over the fire. His fast steps were silent.

Just in front of him, almost colliding, an Endrian soldier came out to take the air. Without thought, Firian reached up and silenced him—a painless cutting off of blood. He frowned and stepped over the limp body. The man would wake with nothing worse than a hangover.

Finally, he slipped into Kiria's tent, not through the proscribed opening, which was heavily guarded, but underneath.

A large bed sat in the middle of the dark space. A hint of firelight shadowed through the tent, playing over Kiria's sleeping form. Furtively, he approached. She didn't use her Ability as she slept. It wasn't the sumptuous silks and furs given to the only remaining Keeper that captivated him—it was the artless, defenseless, mussed countenance of the girl. Her mouth was open. Her hair was wild. And she'd never looked so beautiful.

He wished she could sleep without his interruption. For a few breaths, he took in her peaceful expression, careless of the danger around her.

She rolled over. Two wounds came into sharp relief, one on her cheek and the other dragging from her lips to her neck. Anger and pain shot through him at the sight. He had held her hands...

Maybe he gave an audible breath. Kiria jerked upright. Immediately, her eyes locked onto him.

He managed half a smile. He didn't expect a smile back.

"Firian! What are you doing here? Guards!" she shouted.

He stayed. His plan depended on it.

Moments later, after being thoroughly searched, he was tied tight to a chair, his wrists chafing against each other. He faced the big bed with blue and purple coverlets, and Kiria stood before him. She watched him intently, still in her night clothes. In the chaos and speed of his arrest, she hadn't bothered to change either her clothes or appearance.

"Why did you come here?" she demanded, eyes burning.

"I came to help—"

"Into my tent," she clarified. The words' edges blurred under her injury.

"I needed to speak to you directly, and I didn't know what your orders were... about me."

"They were going to arrest you."

That's ambitious. He almost said the words aloud, but now was not the time. His mission hung by a thread. She could reject his help completely, refuse to let him get involved, and then his decision to empty the Academy would be in vain, and her own mission might fail.

No, he would help her anyway, if not openly, then secretly.

Behind her, one of the serving girls lit a few candles by the bed to give the space more light. Judging from new shadows flickering over Kiria's face, the other girl was doing the same thing behind where Firian sat.

There was something like relief in the rigid lines of Kiria's body. He felt it too. At last, they could confront each other directly. No matter what happened, at least they would know where they stood.

She shivered.

"My jacket's over there," he said, indicating with his eyes.

She wrinkled her nose skeptically, but then moved toward the long black jacket the guards had taken from him.

When she pulled her arms through the sleeves of his coat, he had to remind himself that her wearing the jacket wasn't a concession to their earlier relationship, but defiance in the face of it. She didn't look like a Tanyu—she was too soft, too idealistic—but she did have a Tanyu's core of strength, tempered hard like cooling glass. She gazed down at him with those heartbreaking scars and his gut twisted. She was a queen.

"You could have spoken to me directly," she said softly. Her forehead was lined with concentration and anger.

"In person," he said.

"Okay. What are you here to offer? Can you kill Belik for us?" she asked, pulling the coat closer around her. The dirty hem dragged on the ground.

"I can try."

Kiria gave both the guards behind him a meaningful look. Her busy fingers did the buttons up the front of the jacket. Firian followed their movements with his eyes, realizing he could look at her like this for a long time, watching her do simple things. And world-shaking things. Eating strawberries or talking to Brett and then deposing a tyrant. He could picture her talking to his sister.

"Could you distract him?" she resumed.

"Yes. I can get to him."

"Can you?" There was a challenge in the words.

"I can," he replied. "We're the only two who can go to the Second Level."

She stuffed her hands in the jacket pockets. "The Second Level?"

"It's an advanced level of the Unreal." He twisted his bound wrists behind the chair to settle them more comfortably. "Trust me. I can manage it."

Trust. How much had she told the others about their encounter in the farmhouse that night? That had been their last time in person. Firian's demand that she give herself up for the safety of her people. The memory made him sick with shame. If he hadn't been so stupid, none of this would have happened. The Keepers would still be alive, and Kiria would still be in his arms. But he couldn't take it back now. All he had was a purpose, and a purpose had to be enough.

Kiria cleared her throat to freshen her tired voice. "We might be able to use you, then. But let me be perfectly clear," she said, touching her lip with a knuckle and checking it for blood. "My allegiance is with the Western Kingdom. It is not with you. Don't think that I'll make an exception for you because of our *katah*. You know exactly how far I'm willing to go to protect my people." She was leaning closer now, glaring at him with amber eyes.

He did know. He knew better than anyone else how much she would risk for her people's safety. At his insistence, she'd nearly sacrificed her body and reputation. And later, he had stood with her through the pain of withering torture. Despair had shone in her eyes both times, but she hadn't broken.

He didn't quail as he looked back at her. Then something between them softened. Everything in the room, besides the two of them—her standing, him sitting—blurred to hazy edges. His gaze dropped to the cut on her lip.

She blinked, cleared her throat again. "What's this?" she asked, drawing out Bard's wooden figure of Corso from his jacket pocket.

"It's Bard's. It goes with his Indisfate set. He was looking for it."

She closed her fist around it protectively. "He doesn't have his set anymore."

"But he'll still want that back."

After looking at the figure's bearded face, she guessed, "Corso?"

A corner of Firian's mouth lifted. "Yeah."

"Hm. I'll make sure he gets it." She put the piece back in the pocket. Did she plan to keep his jacket? Where was Bard now? "You still haven't said why you needed to meet in person," she continued, picking up the thread. "You could have just offered your help some other way." It was a challenge. Would he admit to doing all this in order to win her back? But it wasn't that simple anymore.

The moment stretched, her implied question singing like the aftereffect of a song's last note.

"I brought an army with me," he said. "They're yours."

She straightened again and froze, motionless, but in a way that made it seem like she would suddenly start at him. If only she would. If only she would see him like she used to. All of him. All the ugly parts, the selfish parts, the proof he laid at her feet now...

"To do with what you want," he continued. "It's Tanyu, civilians, Sentries..."

Her forehead knit together, her expression unreadable. She searched his face. Instantly he was transported to another time when she'd looked there for the truth and hadn't found it. They'd sat on the wooden walkway in Shifra, surrounded by the colored lanterns she loved. He had longed to kiss her, and she had searched his face, trying to discern his love or loyalty. He'd failed at both.

"I'll see where they fit in," she said, her manner business-like, but her fingers playing with the buttons. "But I can't let you go with them."

Emotion lodged in his throat. He'd expected this, but the reality didn't make it better. He nodded stiffly, wishing they were alone instead of being watched by so many others.

"They're still all yours," he repeated. "They're waiting for you about fifteen minutes northeast. You need to take back the throne. Just tell me what you want me to do."

Something lit up in her eyes. It was only there for an instant, and then her calculating expression was back. "We'll find a use for you."

A strange swell of pride bloomed inside him. She had become the confident leader he knew she could be. She had outlived Belik's torture. She was powerful. She had the Tanyuin Head tied to a chair. A bolt of desire, low and hot, shot through him as he gazed up at her. He dropped his eyes to her bare feet. Neither of them had time to revisit what had once existed between them, and she'd made it clear she didn't want to.

The jacket swished against the ground, it was so long on her, as she turned to yet another guard near the door. "Keep Master Kess under guard until we're ready to move tomorrow." She cheated a look at him that revealed she knew it was still Firian's choice to remain shackled.

He flexed his wrists, testing the restraints. It wouldn't take long to undo them, and it wouldn't be difficult to control the room even without being untied. But he'd respect her order. If he didn't prove how serious he was about helping her, she wouldn't use his prowess to take back the Kingdom. She might even order his incarceration early. Or execution. How many knew the extent of his crimes? But, with odds this slim, his participation could mean the difference between victory and defeat, especially with Belik at the helm.

"When was the last time you ate?" Her voice shook him from his thoughts. It was gentler than before.

He raised his eyes. "Yesterday."

One of her eyebrows twitched upward.

"I needed to get here quickly."

"And eating would slow you down?" she asked, her shoulders relaxing a little.

A tiny smirk threatened to spread over his face.

His eyes must have given away the smirk despite his effort because she looked away. Though composed, she had the smallest tinge of fear in her expression. Wavering balance on the edge of a cliff. "See that he gets food and water," she instructed.

Firian felt the rope tying him to the chair release as it was cut, though his wrists stayed bound. Two guards gripped both his arms roughly and heaved him to his feet. He held still under their control, though his instincts roared to break free. As they marched him out of the tent, he cast another look at Kiria. Her arms were crossed in that long black jacket, and she didn't look back at him, instead calling over one of her serving girls.

Helping Kiria regain her rightful place on the throne, doing something that could begin to make up for all the times he'd failed, was its own kind of freedom.

51

BARD

Concentration and haze made Bard's head pound. Jori's dreams always had a dark blur of unreality. He didn't have the least bit of the Talent, but none of that was his fault. Bard tried to focus on what was happening while remaining aware of possible threats. Chetana and Tesni and the nearby capital meant a constant faraway buzz of other minds, but nothing invading Jori's sleep.

Jori walked—or floated, it was hard to tell—along the edge of the palace roof. He held his arms outstretched, bobbling gently from side to side as he tripped along. In the way of dreams, it wasn't the gardens with the Amiran Academy far below but the roiling sea. Narrow warships had sailed right against the palace walls, tapping against the stone with every wave. The movement didn't seem to damage the ships at all. Every ferocious face tipped upward to watch Jori as though they had come so close only to watch him fall. The tenor of the dream wasn't terror, but a balance of levity and tension, like a hard knot of anticipation. Nerves for something long put off.

Would he jump into the churning sea? Crash onto the waiting decks and wake up?

Then Bard saw himself, waving for Jori to get down off the edge. The dream Bard held out his hand to help him down onto the safety of the roof, which looked similar to the one Firian had created when they'd fought—almost a plaza, with pavestone paths patterned through patches of improbable green grass. Maybe Firian had actually gone up there at some point. Bard never had, and he lived in the palace for weeks. But he didn't have Firian or Jori's penchant for troublemaking.

It wasn't unusual for Bard to see himself in Jori's dreams. He'd become almost a fixture, playing small parts in the strange things that happened. Kiria frequented the scenes too. And Atty.

As Jori approached dream Bard, steps appeared, leading him even higher until

Bard had no chance of reaching him. The steps materialized just before Jori placed his foot. This development seemed to distress him but he couldn't turn around. Something drew him onward. Dream Bard was small now, and the waiting ships looked like toys. The stairs, nearly invisible as they drew him up into the clouds, widened so that Jori could have lain down across the length of them three times. Creatures appeared on them, fantastical things, and people shuddered in and out of vision like flashes of shadow. The steps took on the quality of being indoors, and haunted.

Something was at the top, and the top was drawing nearer. Bard tried to see what it was, but the entire dream was so murky, and he couldn't see anything that Jori wasn't experiencing. The effort squeezed Bard's headache tighter. He took a couple slow breaths to clear his mental vision through the pain.

It wasn't something. Some*one* waited at the top.

Who? The question was invasive. But then, so was watching someone's dreams. Bard's curiosity made him breathless.

A long, fur-covered lizard slunk past Jori's legs and disappeared off the edge of the step, into the nothingness outside the dream. A large square of light lit an opening at the top.

Please reach it. Please reach it. Dreams had an annoying way of ending right before the exciting revelation.

A violent shudder ran through Bard.

Jori took two more steps.

Another shudder shook Bard, and he realized that the sensation didn't come from inside him but from the real world. So he wouldn't find out what Jori wanted so much.

He took quick stock of anyone nearby who might want to attack Jori in the dream space, found none. Exhaustion made returning to the Real like swimming through custard. His eyes felt sticky as his lids fluttered open. He cracked his neck. All night, he sat hunched over Jori's sleeping form. His back and head ached. It was easier to ignore when he had entertainment. Most nights he even laughed.

He squinted into the face of Kiria. Two guards flanked her. Her expression was serious but not alarmed.

"Firian's here," she said softly.

The revelation rushed in at the same time as her words. When he guarded Jori, his concentration was all-consuming. He hadn't realized that he had boxed out even his awareness of Firian, which usually waited just outside his own consciousness. Still recovering from dream logic, Bard hadn't noticed that Kiria was wearing a black Academy coat. What did that mean?

He couldn't hold back his smile at the news. "Where is he?" he whispered, slowly rising from where he sat on the big bed. "Is he here with the others? I told you he'd come."

She didn't answer either question. Instead, she tipped her chin toward Jori. Dusky brown waves of hair flopped over the arm where he rested his head. One bare shoulder blade peeked above the fine sheets. His face, turned toward them, had the seriousness of dreams.

Despite his new excitement, unable to stop himself, Bard yawned. Jori just looked so comfortable.

"I want you to choose a Sentry for him," Kiria said. "Someone we can trust."

Bard fought the urge to pump his fist in silent exultation. He could finally sleep again! Part of him would miss the odd sort of companionship that came with guarding Jori's dreams. "Wells, for sure," he said. "He's trustworthy. He was my friend back in Tánuil." And he hadn't needed to guard Kader for several weeks, ever since Firian convinced Belik that the boy was dead.

"We should take this conversation outside," Kiria whispered, indicating for the guards to precede her. "We'll wake him up."

"I mean, I doubt it." Bard shared a look with Kiria.

Her lips rose in a small smile. "He's hard to wake up," she agreed. Walking back to her own tent, she instructed one of the many guards to locate Wells and give him his instructions.

The soldiers seemed to multiply around Kiria and Jori as new troops arrived. The new mayor of Rantoul had sent some soldiers, though it looked a poor showing. Skirwith and Redshore too.

Enderin had sent volunteers to help as well. Only a few hundred, and Bard hadn't had time to welcome them. Casual questions revealed that his older brother Jac was among the volunteers. Bard's eyes darted among the firelit tents to find his brother's stylish black hair and confident attitude, but of course there was nothing. Jac was sleeping, most likely. What time was it, anyway?

He could find Jac in the morning, if he wanted to. He did want to. It was just that the last time they'd spoken, Jac had confirmed Bard's fears that his family held a grudge against him for being on the wrong side of the brief Tanyuin War against the Kingdom, the precursor to the war they were now about to fight. Home had evaporated like smoke with Jac's words, but Bard loved him anyway.

No time to worry about that now.

"Firian's under guard," Kiria said, resuming where they'd left off.

"You know that's—"

Kiria cut Bard off with a look. They both knew that Firian's killing ability made guards obsolete unless there was also a Sentry. Even then, keeping Firian in chains was difficult.

"I need to tell you something," she said.

Her seriousness filled Bard with nerves. Was someone hurt, dead? Was he in trouble? He ran through what he did over the past day. Nothing she could criticize, unless she wanted him to use her title, or never disagree with her or tease the royals.

When they reached the illusory safety of her tent, she turned toward him. Firian's jacket, too long for her, dragged in the dirt. Bard's mind roiled with questions like the ocean in Jori's dream.

"Oh," she said, "this is for you." She produced the figure of Corso Bard had lost back at the Academy.

He took it from her, beaming. It was in perfect condition, the miniscule knives crossed in front of the hero's chest and everything. "No way! He had this? Where did he find it?" It had been months since he last saw it, a piece of home. All his homes.

"I know you're excited that Firian's here," she began, "but I'm seriously concerned. We both know what he is, but there may be more that you don't know."

Kiria swallowed, circling her wrist with her fingers. "Right before all this happened, Firian... gave an ultimatum. Me for Brithnem."

"What?" Bard whispered. He knew something bad had happened between them, but he hadn't realized *this*.

Her eyes dropped and her voice grew smaller. "I couldn't tell anyone, or he'd take the city. I thought I could save it. Everyone would think I'd run away with him, but it wouldn't matter if everyone was... safe." Her lashes fluttered with memory.

The figurine felt heavy in Bard's hand. No wonder she didn't want him telling Firian what they were doing, even after he'd helped Kader get away.

"I went," she continued. "I thought it was the only way. There's a... farm-house... in the outer edge. We met there." Her eyes looked glassy and faraway. "I thought he'd take me away, like a prisoner of war. What else could happen? He'd demanded the trade of my life." The words snagged on emotion. Her brows lowered, lines forming between them. "But he let me go back." She looked up at Bard again. "That's where I was. I wasn't taking a walk. That's how I knew Tanyu were outside the city."

That night, Bard had known about Firian's presence too. No one had listened to him until Kiria appeared, looking like she'd witnessed a murder. Horribly ironic, Bard realized, since that happened just afterward.

"That's why I keep pushing back," she said. "Firian can say whatever he wants, but I can't believe him. Why do you?"

An unexpected question. It clung to him uncomfortably. He considered. Hopefully there was room both for comforting Kiria's terrible, legitimate pain, and the possibility of Firian's redemption. Bard had always assumed there was. Well, not always. But since Firian saved his life, yes.

"He's ashamed," he said, remembering the cellar. "Maybe he acts brave around you, but..." Bard shook his head. "He is brave. That's not my point. But not in every way. He's afraid there's no hope for him, that he started all this, and he can't end it, and he hurt you... and me." He didn't realize the truth of the words until he heard them coming out. "He knows you won't take him back, and I don't think he expects you to keep him around after this. I think..." The truth formed clearly in front of him and stole his breath. Sickness surged through his stomach. "I think he expects to die."

Kiria's lips parted in surprise. They shared a fraught silence.

"What would happen to us if he did?" she asked, her voice barely above a whisper. Her eyes were shot through with concerned determination.

Images of Tibor Wat sent bile crawling up Bard's throat. Everything had moved so slowly after Firian, in the pirate's compound on Torith, had shouted, "Now!" Bard extricated himself from the captain's mind, pulling pieces of himself out like sinew through teeth. Bard's life had replaced some of the captain's own, unbeknownst to Tibor Wat. A *katah*. A death sentence. It took Bard long enough to complete the job that he'd put Firian in extra danger. Happily, his friend was a good fighter. Otherwise...

Bard didn't leave his room for four days. Then he got news of Tiev's death, Lost in the Unreal. Four became five. He felt nauseated and cold, plagued by thoughts of the captain. He'd been a horrible man—stealing young men and women, forcing himself upon them—but he'd once been a child too. He had parents somewhere. And Bardhon Tanery had snuffed out his life. It was something he would never willingly do again. Even during the Kingdom's attack on the Academy, he had only injured, not killed.

He took a breath. When he spoke, his voice came out fractured. "Firian never *declared* a *katah* on us. It just... happened." It was the intention, the dismantling of another person's reality, that killed them. "So we would live. We would just be weakened. But..." *But I don't want him to die.*

Kiria nodded thoughtfully. "You can see him before you get some sleep," she said, cutting off any further discussion. "It'll be a short night. We're moving to the new location just before dawn."

That couldn't be far off. The darkness outside had the heavy, muted quality of deep night.

"I'm so sorry he did that to you," Bard said.

Her returning gaze was level, sad and regal. She didn't look like the Keeper he'd met at the beginning. Now, she bore the weight of the Western Kingdom. She was its tradition and royalty, everything standing in the space between her people and domination by the power-hungry sect of Tanyu. She straightened her shoulders.

Bard bit the inside of his lip, hesitating. Then he opened his arms to her.

She breathed a small laugh and took his offered hug.

Both feeling bolstered, Bard went to find Firian. It didn't take him long. The pull of Firian's mind made itself clear once Bard was focused on him. Again, no black hair appeared among the tents as Bard made his way. *Jac is asleep, and besides, he's not looking for you.*

In the quiet, Firian's voice filtered through the walls of a tent, listing names of Tanyu that Bard knew. He moved the flap aside to enter. Firian sat, bound, in a chair, and Tesni stood beside him. They both wore black. It was almost like being back at the Academy, except for the flip of power. Behind Firian stood three guards, and in front of them stood another, carefully writing down the names in a list. Could Firian really have done that to Kiria? Yes, in his desperation, he could have. But Bard saw a new aspect to his friend now. Something settled, determined, not frantic.

Firian lifted his head as Bard entered.

"Hey, Fir," Bard said, grinning as he held up Corso.

Firian's eyes brightened. "She gave it to you?"

"We had a talk, yeah."

Firian closed his mouth. Maybe he guessed what they talked about. "I tried to get here sooner," he said.

"I'm sure you went as fast as you could, mate."

"I did." He nodded toward the guard with the list. "Tanyu are going to meet us in the new shelter. I told them all to get out while they could."

"How many?" Bard was already adding calculations to his strategy and backup plans.

"Thirty-one."

The number fell heavy. So few. Bard nodded quickly, scratching the back of his head with his stiff hand. "Okay."

The movement caught Firian's eye. "How's the hand?"

Bard raised the useless hand in question, little better than a stump, and shrugged. The fingers had never uncurled since the cellar. It was a nuisance, but Belik's attack could have left him dead instead, so he was grateful.

"Who else?" prompted the guard with the list. "You said thirty-one."

Tesni gave another name. Firian gave the next.

"I'll see you later, yeah?" Bard said, turning to go. He didn't want Firian to feel alone among people who hated him. "Are they just gonna... keep you like that?"

Firian narrowed his eyes, a grim joke in them. "It looks like it."

"Okay, well..." He wanted to stay and talk, to thank him again for saving his life, for dropping him off to help Kiria. He wanted to see if his guesses were right about Firian's fears and expectations. He wanted to talk about his conversation with Kiria and see if Firian was still ashamed of his actions then. But those weren't topics for a greater audience. Later, he would see if they could get more privacy.

Tesni provided the name of another Tanyu inside the city.

"I'll be back, then," Bard said as he left, feeling the unsaid things like gnats in the air.

The sensation vanished almost as soon as he got outside. Bard didn't have his own tent. There weren't enough tents, for one, and for another, he and Jori slept at separate times so they shared. He headed back there. Now that sleep was imminent, he was so eager for it that he moved faster.

A mental buzz grew as he got closer and went in. Wells sat cross-legged on the ground, his eyes slitted open as though in a trance, his thin frame perfectly still.

A pang of regret lanced through Bard. He'd made Wells relive some of the horrible memories of being a Sentry, but he stood by his suggestion. Wells was trustworthy and would keep Jori safe.

The Kepron lay just as Bard had left him. Had he ever reached the top of those stairs?

Suddenly awkward, he realized they were both going to sleep at the same time. Should he make a bed on the floor? The idea of stripping off blankets and constructing something new filled his limbs with exhaustion. Jori only took up one side of the bed. And he wouldn't mind. He'd probably just make a joke about it in the morning.

Bard quietly took off his shoes and lay down on top of the blankets on the other side. Glorious comfort soaked into him as he laid his head down on the pillow. His upper back still groaned from the hunched position he'd held earlier, but now that he was lying down, his spine seemed to stretch. His limbs sank into the deep blankets and in seconds, he was asleep.

52

KIRIA

Kiria folded Firian's jacket. They'd just arrived in Jori's underground shelter again. After reconnaissance, it seemed not to have been discovered. Alone in her quarters, she felt the fabric with her fingers. A guard had informed her that Firian had thirty-one Tanyuin allies inside the walls. It was nearing nightfall now, and only seventeen had reached them. Eight were killed trying to leave, and six were unaccounted for. Seventeen. The number sounded so small, despite the fact they were some of the very best.

The remaining towns had sent their troops as well, but even those were small to summon a decisive victory against an enemy like this. All throughout the day, she kept getting reports of more cities coming to aid Belik. The Tanyu apparently had members in most large cities, and in every nation. Belik was leveraging that pressure now, using his influence with the older generation of warriors to come help him. Kiria's camp had no strong numbers, but the estimates of Belik's power were growing all the time.

It became clearer and clearer. The time to act was now.

She set down the jacket in a corner, the smell of sweat and pine coming off it. After a pause, she bent and fished in the pocket, where she'd felt something small as she'd interrogated Firian. She held it up to the light. It was a tiny blown glass bead about the size of a fingernail, Brithnem blue. Its shape, round with minute ridges, reminded her of the lanterns in Shifra. The trinket struck her in a way few objects did, as though she recognized a piece of herself in it. What was Firian doing with this?

Unwanted feelings bubbled up as she observed the tiny lantern bead, its workmanship so fine. Glass, that was going to be Firian's profession if he hadn't been recruited to the Academy.

She stuffed the bead away, only realizing afterward that she put it in her own pocket instead of his.

Firian himself was kept in another small room with nothing but a guard and a Sentry. He had a small but crucial role to play in the plan that she and Bard had laid out. Right now, Bard was communicating to the leaders of the different groups in the main room.

To highlight her belief in working with Tanyu who proved their loyalty, she had urged Bard to give the presentation instead of her. He wouldn't give all the details in this briefing. Those would go to individual groups. Only he and she would know the whole scope of what they planned to do.

Straightening her dress and putting on her Beauty, Kiria exited and followed the sound of Bard's voice. The tingling change was less comfortable than before, her scars stretching as a result. They felt much better today, though. The bruises on her ribs and face were dull, and the pain in her cheek wasn't as piercing. As much as she longed to be alone to process everything that was happening, Bard needed her presence for support.

She emerged into the main room. Bard stood on a crate at the far end, overlooking a sea of heads. Endrian soldiers in brown leather armor, Brithnem guards in gleaming metal, Tanyu in black. Heads turned toward her. The presentation momentarily stalled as exclamations resounded around the space. People touched their neighbors' shoulders to urge them to look. Was it her Beauty or her new scars calling up this response? Probably both. Now she had many reasons for people to stare. The storm of whispers slowly died down as she took her place near Bard's platform.

"Yeah, as I was saying," Bard resumed, "most of the Tanyu will remain here…" He outlined the plan with fewer stutters or stops than he tended to use, his lilting voice clear as he addressed the crowd. From where she stood looking up at him, Kiria could see an occasional tremble or extra blink, but Bard was doing exceptionally well for his first time speaking to a large group. Kiria even saw Chetana at the opposite end of the room, nodding in sincere agreement. Bard gestured and nodded and answered a few questions at the end mostly with, "That information is only for the people it directly concerns."

"Thank you. That's all." He stepped off the crate, and the crowd, dismissed, started moving around the packed space. Several people craned to get a better look at Kiria. Others immediately began directing their men and women what to do. Some vented the questions Bard wouldn't answer at each other instead.

"You did very well," Kiria said softly, leaning toward Bard so others wouldn't hear.

He gave a wide, closed-mouth smile. "Thank you."

Two male figures pushed their way through the mass of bodies to talk to Bard.

"Well, that was sexy," said Jori once he was free of the tangle of the crowd. He dusted off his embroidered purple vest with exaggerated care.

Bard barked an uncomfortable laugh, but his demeanor changed when he saw the person beside him. "Jac," he breathed. Then, stronger, "Jac!"

Bard's brother. He'd mentioned him multiple times but Kiria had never seen him. Jac had light brown skin like Bard's, and black hair, though his was tamed into an attractive coif instead of Bard's wild spikes. He wore the uniform of an Endrian soldier, brass-studded leather over a coat of mail. He stood a little taller than Bard and didn't seem to have Bard's charming humility. Jac's attention ricocheted from his brother to Kiria and back again. Finally, his black eyes settled on Bard, though it looked like it took some effort to keep them there.

"Hey!" Jac greeted, giving Bard a one-armed hug.

Jori raised an eyebrow at him, assessing. Then he pointed between the two of them. "Brother?" he asked.

"Yes," Bard confirmed. "This is my brother Jac. Jac, this is the Keeper Kiria Arioc and this is Jori Calthwaite."

"Also a Keeper," Jori said, shaking Jac's hand and tapping his chest where the royal tattoo lay beneath. "Almost."

Barely disguised amazement shone in Jac's eyes. He looked again at Kiria in disbelief, though whether it was because of her Beauty or because he couldn't believe his brother kept such high company, it was hard to tell.

"It's a pleasure, an honor," he said, unsure.

"I'm happy to meet you too. Bard has done great work for us," Kiria said, deciding the amazement was a good thing. Bard could stand to get more credit.

Jac turned once more to Bard, taking him by the shoulders and shaking him. "I'm proud to be here." Leaning closer, he said, "I wish Mum and Dad could have seen that. And Edom and Rissa and everybody."

Bard's dark eyes shone tearful and a line formed between his brows as he looked into his brother's face. He gripped Jac's arms. Words started to form but never fully materialized, his mouth twitching, opening, closing. He nodded instead.

Jac laughed and pushed him playfully away. "I've got to get back," he said, taking a furtive look around. Kiria could have sworn he was checking to see if people noticed who he was talking to.

"Will I see you again?" Bard asked in a rush. "I mean, I have to talk to the different leaders, but…"

"You know where I'll be!" Jac called, absorbed once more into the crowd.

Bard's question sent an ache to Kiria's chest. They all didn't have much time left. The plan they'd concocted began in earnest tomorrow afternoon. One day. That was all any of them had before the battle really began.

53

KIRIA

Of course it was Jori who suggested the party. Word spread as quickly as if everyone were Tanyu and could speak mind to mind. The large space all but emptied as everyone took an hour to get ready.

Kiria wasn't sure she wanted to be around so many people the night before they were going to put their plan into action. Her stomach was in knots as it was.

She couldn't keep strategy out of her thoughts. It swirled around like an unholy brew. Any time she paused, thoughts she didn't want came rushing in. The pain of the knife digging into her face, which still stung to the touch. Firian bound to a chair with a look so complicated that she couldn't unravel it to reach the end. The faces of all those they'd lost, and the faces of those she still had to lose.

Maybe the party would be a welcome distraction after all. In the days of Shane and Mari Calthwaite, armies traditionally held huge parties before campaigns. Only recently had the tradition started to fade. Even her father, General Rhet, had learned to dance for such occasions. They were a time of abandonment and gratefulness and joy when there was bound to be a scarcity of those soon.

The underground rooms weren't decorated—Jori complained pleasantly about the fact as he directed the placement of small platters of food—but the light of the torches looked friendlier than it had weeks ago when she and her coterie had hidden there from Belik's forces. Barren but inviting. Well, not barren for very long.

People began to arrive again in droves. Some soldiers abstained from the festivities so they could guard the entrances. She was thankful to them, but also glad to see the Kingdom soldiers, Endrians, a few Sentries, and even Tanyu. Several of the Tanyu greeted her respectfully when they entered, treating her as they would a general.

The room grew hot with all the bodies inside. She shed her soft jacket and wore only a sleeveless blue dress—the nicest one she had with her. This was her last moment to forget about being practical, if she could. The dress had frothy tiers of light blue skirts edged in silver embroidery. The back plunged, as most of her dresses used to do, highlighting her Keeper tattoo, the swirling, sharp-edged pattern of black that ran from the middle of her back to the nape of her neck. Candrae had twisted strands of her hair up into an elaborate knot so the entire pattern would be visible.

Kiria, with considerably less skill, had tried to return the favor, pinning up Candrae's wavy locks, now brown instead of golden. Already, Candrae's hair was falling out, strands trailing down her neck as she talked to Vayci near the hall that led to Kiria's room. Kiria had lent them two of her own dresses. They fit the girls imperfectly, but their eyes shone with excitement nonetheless.

Endrian soldiers in only their shirts and breeches began to play a lively tune on pipes and drums. Unlike so many others, who jumped up to dance, she couldn't rid herself of her worries so easily.

Bard looked like he felt the same way, chatting seriously in a corner with the commander of the Endrian forces. He could talk to some of the leaders tomorrow morning and that would still give them time to prepare, but he had used his hour conversing with the different groups, checking times, counting soldiers, tracking down friends from the Academy. His energy was up, despite the long night he'd had the day before.

From somewhere in the crowd, Jori emerged, his cheeks already pink with drink, and grabbed Bard's arm, dragging him toward the center of the room.

At first, Bard frowned, apparently peeved to have been pulled away from his conversation.

"You can't be solemn all night. There's dancing to be done," Jori said, then stopped. "Look, look!" He leaned down and pointed at something across the room.

Bard and Kiria followed his eyeline to two dark-skinned young women, laughing and talking beside the musicians.

"You know what they're talking about?" Jori asked.

Bard looked confused. "No, do you know them?"

Jori grinned wickedly. "Maybe I will later, but I'll wager they're talking about you. In fact, I know it. I know things. Look!" he repeated. He shifted his voice to a higher register. "Have you seen that Tanyu over there?" He laid a self-assured hand on Bard's shoulder. "Oh, the handsome one?" he made the other girl reply. "That's right. I hear he rescued the dashing Kepron. He's practically a general. So talented, and so good looking!"

Bard put his head down and pulled away half-heartedly, smiling. When Bard wasn't looking, Jori eyed him warmly.

He fished Bard back in with one arm and talked lower in his ear, almost too quiet for Kiria to hear. He was still mimicking the girls across the room. "Oh, if only he could hold me in his arms!"

Bard grimaced before his grin turned wider.

"Oh, darling," said Jori as the second girl, "he's too important and brilliant to dance with you. Can you imagine him coming over here?"

What he said next was lost in the noise of the crowd, but Bard blushed deeply as Jori stood straight again, his raised eyebrows showing he was satisfied.

A touch on her arm made Kiria startle. She spun to face a Tanyu she didn't know, a stern girl with bright red hair cropped short. "Master Kess has asked to speak with you, My Keeper."

Kiria's brows lowered. "Right now?"

"He said it's about tomorrow."

She sighed and followed the girl back through the labyrinth of passages to the room where Firian was kept.

The girl opened the door. Viktor trailed Kiria to the room and entered with her, standing dutifully by the door.

Firian sat in the chair in the middle of the room, no longer bound. In fact, he slumped forward, knees wide apart, hands clasped, head bowed. When she came in, he stood quickly.

Her heart hammered at the sight of him. His presence had always undone some of her composure, though she wasn't sure why that was still true.

"Is everything ready for tomorrow?" he asked. He didn't have the heat in his gaze that had characterized their interactions before the palace attack.

"Everyone knows the plan. All that's left is to do it. May God be with us." She raised her eyes to the ceiling. A familiar ache returned like a wave. She couldn't relax tonight, not with everything at stake and the final stand so close.

Firian drew his lips into a serious line. She looked away from them as he lowered his voice. "Belik put a Sentry on me. I just told Bard a minute ago."

A lump lodged in Kiria's throat. She'd learned a lot about Sentries lately. They blocked others from the Unreal, but Firian had said something about another level below the Unreal. Would Sentries prevent him from getting there too? "Does that mean you can't do it?"

His usually arrogant manner faltered and his eyes dipped to the floor, darting as though he had dropped puzzle pieces there. "We tried to locate him. Lev Aramin is his name. But his mind is out to sea."

"Out to sea?"

"On a ship," he explained.

They couldn't reach the Sentry in time, not without expending soldiers she couldn't spare. Her expression hardened. "You'll still try it," she commanded.

He nodded once, without argument. Fire without light. Almost hopeless.

She took a step forward. "Firian," she said, lowering her own voice to match his, "you are the most dangerous person I know. So be dangerous."

The slow intensity of her words made him raise his eyes to hers again, and a smirk tugged at the edges of his mouth. He pulled his shoulders back and stood tall. "You know I will."

"I know you will," she echoed.

The warm moment between them froze quickly. She was getting too close again. *Again!* Would she never be rid of him?

"Is that all you had to tell me?" she asked.

"No one's broken a Sentry before, that I know of." Though his confidence had returned, the words still felt like a confession. He could fail.

Regardless, he was their best hope of finding and eliminating Belik. "That was true of a lot of things, before you came along."

"Dangerous things," he said, apparently comforted by the idea.

Though he didn't step closer, she remembered the times he had. *Dangerous things.*

"Yes," she replied curtly, eager to get out of the room. "Let one of the guards know if you need anything else."

He breathed in as though he wanted to say something else, but then he just exhaled slowly.

She turned to go and remembered her Beauty and the tattoo on her bare back. Her skin flushed warm.

"My... Keeper," Firian said. Had he ever called her that before? It didn't feel like it. She turned. "I'll get it done. Good luck tomorrow." He clamped his mouth shut and nodded, as though biting back other things he wanted to say.

"You too." She paused. Though she kept reminding herself that she couldn't trust Firian, he was helping her. He'd effectively saved Kader by faking his death. He'd brought troops to her aid. It felt wrong to keep him always locked away—in the Academy, in her mind, in this room. "Do you have any other clothes?"

His brows darted downward. "Why?"

"You read the Scroll."

He nodded.

"Do you remember the party the founders had before the war started?"

"In Shifra."

"Right." Maybe she had told him about it too. She had been so giddy with excitement when they'd visited the fortress there together. "Since we're... taking the Kingdom back tomorrow, Jori started up a party in the common room."

"You did look dressed up."

She didn't respond to the comment, even though he said it more innocently than usual. Firian would have to prove himself with more than a couple weeks of good behavior. But he wasn't a prisoner, not really. She looked back at the guard by the door. There was another one just outside. "Get some of Jori's clothes and bring them here for Master Kess," she said. Though Firian was more muscular, they looked as though they'd wear approximately the same size.

"I have this," Firian protested as the guard left the room.

"Have you ever been to a party?" she asked, eyeing his dusty black shirt and pants.

"Yes."

"I don't know. You never let yourself relax." She could have been talking about herself lately. "Go ahead and change. Everybody's in there. I'll tell the guards it's all right."

Kiria relayed the message to the guard as she left with the Tanyuin girl. Tracing the dark path back to the party, she mulled over his new information. His ability in the Unreal was crucial to their success against Belik. She didn't understand everything about Sentries, but if Firian felt that he couldn't break through, maybe something terrible would happen if he tried too hard. He wasn't the kind of person to do things by halves. He wasn't afraid to die.

She emerged into the main space in a burst of sound and laughter and music and light. The room had gotten even more crowded than before. People had to walk sideways to thread their way through the mass of bodies. The smell of bubbling cider and meat and sweat hung heavily in the air. A raucous burst of laughter came from beside one of the bracketed lanterns. Every other light was intricately patterned, casting a multi-colored glow over the party. A small group of soldiers were placing bets on the comparative abilities of the Brithnem and Endrian troops. Their glittering eyes and loud voices as they held up their coins told Kiria they were already drunk.

Kiria made her way through the crush to the guards at the steps leading out, to make sure they knew that Firian was invited just like everyone else. Most of them didn't like Firian, but they didn't need to. They did all need to work together, though.

Everyone seemed to be having fun, but Firian's news troubled her, interrupting even the lively music trying to caper into her thoughts.

"So sour!" Jori acknowledged the female Tanyu with a wink as he drew Kiria with him into the throng of dancers. People pressed against her on all sides, moving to the beat. "This is your chance to relax, you know," he said once they were within arm's length of the musicians.

"I thought you were talking to Bard." She had to yell to be heard. Jori should just leave her to her thoughts for once.

"Here. Stay here." He disappeared and returned with something strong in a cup. "Drink this."

"You'll make a terrible Keeper," she said, thawing toward him.

He shrugged. "We all know that."

They shared a look. Then Jori's gray eyes turned impish as he started waving to the rhythm of the drums. She rolled her eyes as he took her free hand and shook her arm. Tension seemed to fall from her body as he made her dance like a rag doll. Once she was loose enough to start dancing on her own, Jori caught her in his arms and they whirled around the floor. She tripped a little as they spun. He'd always been the better dancer.

She pulled away to sip the drink he'd given her, half of which had already spilled. The bubbles rushed to her head immediately. When was the last time she'd eaten?

Jori was already dancing with someone else, and then she was too as the sparkling tune shifted into a different song, a familiar drinking ballad. Jori clapped and leaned heavily on Bard, who had reappeared. Although his voice was pitchy, Jori launched into a lusty rendition of the song. Volume made up for accuracy. His enthusiasm drew those around him to sing too. Even Kiria sang, glad that the others drowned out her voice. At first, Bard didn't join, as though he'd never learned the words, but then he came in on the repetitive chorus. Jori sang at the people around him, men and women, as though it were a competition he was winning.

When the song came to a warbling end, everyone cheered and clapped and threw back the last gulp of their drinks. Kiria laughed and did the same.

"You can sing. You can sing!" Jori told a few people around him who'd carried the tune better than he had.

Another song began. Some moved off to get food while others joined the dancers. Through the crowd, Kiria caught flashes of Firian walking along the side of the room. He'd actually taken her suggestion. He wore dark gray pants tucked into his Tanyuin boots, and an embroidered vest of dark blue over an off-white shirt. The white made his skin look tanner than usual. Rather than wearing it as Jori usually did—open and dissolute—he had buttoned the entire vest. The result made him look like a prince.

His too-straight posture was the only detail that gave away his discomfort. Otherwise, one might think that he owned the room and had suggested the party himself.

Stomping, not in time with the music, caught her attention. A small group from Erad hunkered together, slapping their thighs, stomping, clapping, in a dance they all knew by heart. They whooped when an Eradi Tanyu joined in.

When she looked back at Firian, Bard was by his side, beaming and chattering. Firian's expression softened, more at ease.

This was a night to forget what lay ahead, to delight in what they still had right now. Everyone had their own ways of doing that. Some arm wrestled, others danced, others drank or flirted or sang or laughed. But there was no talk of strategy, no dour expressions. Tonight they all had each other, if only for one more day.

Kiria went back into the midst of the dancing. She was instantly face to face with Jac Tanery, who looked abashed to be dancing with a Keeper. She danced with them all, even Viktor, who had eventually switched duty with Merrick so he could participate in the fun. When she looked over, Jori had joined Bard and Firian, all with mugs in their hands. He'd lifted up his shirt to the neck to show off his royal tattoo. *Incorrigible.*

Every time she spun around, Firian drew her eyes, but he didn't always meet her gaze. He was having fun of his own that didn't include her. She half expected him to stalk forward through the crowd and dance with her when the music slowed, but he made no move toward her. The more glasses she had, the more she wished he would try.

Jori began to lead another chorus, beckoning for Bard and Firian to follow. Jori had never liked Firian, so it pleased her to know he was trying to get along with him. To her amazement, Firian danced. He instantly caught the attention of some of the younger female soldiers, who eagerly danced beside him. Kiria kept one eye on him as she jumped and kicked her feet to the beat. Firian caught onto the steps quickly, and pulled many partners close, but not any one person for long. Not that it mattered.

When the song ended, Firian clanked his mug against a few others and drank. His smile afterward was everything. It made her heart skip with its openness and boyishness. It was the smile she'd wanted to see from him since the moment they'd met. It wasn't crafty or seductive or arrogant. It was a short glimpse beneath the mask. This Firian had a family, had friends that cared about him. This Firian could be different. The dimpled grin was gone in a flash, but it burned in her memory like an aftershock.

He turned his eyes to her, and she realized she was staring. She looked away. Her plan to help him have fun and to be more accepted into the group had worked—miracle of miracles! Still, a small part of her, a secret part, had hoped he would talk to her, not about the coming battle, but just to talk. It had seemed inevitable. He'd always had his fixation. They. Together. But seeing him like this, giving her space when she didn't act interested, reminded her of what she had loved in the first place. He was still dangerous, but now, it seemed, he might be able to show kindness too.

She took a break from the dancing to eat from a stack of buttered bread. She couldn't afford to relive feelings that had brought her nothing but pain.

Firian left early, while the moon was still high outside.

Kiria stayed, even when the music slowed down and leftover food was brought out when the new plates were gone. She laughed until her lip split open again. How long since she had laughed? Too long, she decided.

She ran her gaze over the remaining people, a fraction of those who had crammed the space earlier. Bard was still bobbing joyfully to the music with his brother and a few others. A couple kissed in a darkened corner. Two servants had begun to clean up dishes.

Jori sidled up to her, looking at the others. "Oh, love," he sighed. "I sincerely hope we don't all die tomorrow."

54

BARD

When Bard finally steered Jori back to his room after the party, the buzz of a Sentry already surrounded the Kepron's mind.

Wells wasn't sitting in a corner as before. Sentries didn't need to be close to the people they guarded, but they did need to get their assignments in person. Connecting to the Unreal in healthier ways wasn't something they could do after a while. It was all static.

Won't be long, though. Former Sentries could be free to live their lives without taking shifts at their old, mind-numbing job. If Bard's plan worked. If they all lived.

Familiar worry descended into his thoughts. Jac believed in him now. The knowledge had made him as buoyant as the wine. His home, which he'd felt slip further and further away with every passing day, was his again. But now his brother's life was at stake because of his plan. This had to work. They had too few allies to regroup if his scheme fell through. An ache twisted his stomach.

"Don't you look grim!" Jori exclaimed, poking Bard's face. "No grim... grimness. Is that a word?"

"I think so."

Jori tried to toe off his boots but they were on too tight. Giving up, he bent over, stumbled, and managed to undo the laces. "Your brother, he's not so bad."

"I didn't say he was bad, did I?"

"Brothers... are good," Jori concluded.

Bard chuckled, though his heart ached for Jori, who didn't have one anymore. "I like mine."

Jori fell into bed, gathering the covers up over himself. "Won't they all be jealous?" he said, curling up on his side.

"Hmm?"

"I took the strategist to bed after the party."

Bard's cheeks flamed.

Jori laughed at his expression. "I'm sorry, I'm sorry," he said, then disarmingly patted the blankets beside him. "Come here."

Maybe it was the bubbles still floating through Bard's head, but he did. Kicking off his shoes, he laid down on top of the blankets like before. Jori tucked up next to him and threw an arm over his chest. It was surprisingly comfortable. Feeling someone next to him reminded him of home, of sleeping three to a bed when he was a child in Enderin. It was nice to be held. It was nice to be held *by him*.

"There you go," Jori murmured, kissing the back of his head.

Bard hummed, feeling strange and relaxed all at once. He hadn't wanted to find a different room where he would be alone. Not tonight. Jori must have seen it written on his face.

Tentatively, he reached for Jori's hand with his good one and held it.

"Did you know you have a freckle on your ear?" Jori asked, barely audible, his breathing deep and slow. He was asleep before Bard could answer the question.

55

KIRIA

Kiria stared at the darkened ceiling, trying to summon prayers. The fizz of hope from Jori's party was wearing off—that buffer between her and the inevitable conflict beyond. She touched her lip and rubbed her fingers together. The split had apparently closed, because her hand felt dry.

Had she thought of everything? In this breathless wait before the battle began, her courage felt small.

Whispering into the dark, she repeated to herself the sacrifices and losses she had already endured. Compared to those, the task ahead became manageable. She could stare it down and see it through.

Candrae and Vayci, exhausted from the excitement of the night, slept nearby, ready to help her in a second. Her whispering might have already woken them up, but she knew they wouldn't grudge her for it. The Western Kingdom depended on her. Her body sagged with the weight, but sleep wouldn't come.

A soft knock rang at the door. Royce spoke through the crack as he opened it. "Amir Chetana," he announced.

"Let her in," Kiria said, sitting up and fumbling for a way to light the candle by her bed.

Vayci stumbled to her feet and helped a guttering flame appear as Chetana strode into the room with a bundle in her arms.

"My Keeper," she greeted in a gentle voice. "I thought you would still be awake."

"I was having trouble falling asleep," Kiria admitted, trying to puzzle out why Chetana had come. She hadn't been at the party, but that was no surprise.

The Amir set down the bundle on the bed. Layers of clothing and armor. It was difficult to make out all the details in the gloom except for the impression of gleaming blue and silver. "For tomorrow," she said. "I asked if I could bring it to you."

"It looks perfect." Kiria indicated for her to sit. Something was clearly weighing on Chetana too.

Candrae was awake now and standing beside Vayci.

"Do you want privacy?" she asked.

"No, that's not necessary," said Chetana, waving her hand.

"What's going on?" Kiria folded her hands in her lap and turned to her former advisor.

Chetana's posture was immaculate with her strong neck and imperious gaze. A slight crease appeared between her brows. "I owe you an apology, My Keeper."

"For what?"

"I underestimated your judgment. More than once. You were right to put your trust in Master Tanery. He has clearly demonstrated his loyalty. Kiria, I..." She pursed her lips and took Kiria's hand. "I never doubted your intention, but I doubted your strength, your ability to lead. I'm sorry for the ways that I have sown that doubt in others. You've fully shown your capability to be the Keeper of the Western Kingdom."

Kiria squeezed her hand. "There's nothing to forgive. You always considered the Kingdom before devotion to its leaders. I want more people like you around me. And I'm glad you've finally come around about Bard."

Chetana gave a wan smile. "I have... difficulties... with the Tanyu."

"Don't we all," said Kiria drily.

"But you," Chetana resumed, looking intently, "you deserve all the love and loyalty of your people. You are worthy of their devotion."

Kiria's forehead felt tight. Chetana said the last sentence with such conviction. *Worthy.* She'd fought to be worthy enough to lead the land and the people she loved. The layers of her sacrifices had started to confer that title on her, but to hear it from someone else's lips... She swallowed the rock in her throat. She couldn't respond.

"I was your advisor, but you are the one who has taught me. I have always striven to be worthy of love," Chetana began. The word *striven* made Kiria miss Daelon. Chetana wasn't able to contact him directly when she tried to go back to Brithnem, but rumors said he was working as a slave for the Tanyu. "My sister..." She cleared her throat, forcing out the words. "My sister and I grew up in King's Heights. Bastard children, both of us. We had no one but each other. And we... we loved each other." Her voice broke as she talked about Gerand, but she quickly recovered her queenly composure. "I thought she loved me. Our mother died when we were young, so we were left alone. You went there. You saw how different we would have been from everyone else."

Kiria pictured the sea of traditionally Kingdom-looking people with pale skin and dusty brown hair. Their suspicion of her had spilled into violence quickly. As far as Kiria knew, they were still angry because she had worked with the Tanyu to defeat the Torithians, and they didn't trust how quickly she had ascended to the throne.

Chetana continued. "Gerand fit in better than I, but we were both outcasts. We needed each other. We found a... small group of other Khelê to belong to, out of the public eye. They didn't mock or persecute us. They said we had Talent, and they fostered it. We both became strong in their ranks. Their goal was to dismantle the Tanyu, because of the ways they'd strayed from their purpose. I was devoted to that task. And then our invitations came to be tested at the Tanyuin Academy. I dismissed mine immediately. I think I burned the letter. But Gerand was lured by the glamour and power she perceived in it. So she went. We fought." Chetana's pained expression became abstracted. Lines pulled around her full lips. "We fought. She thought I should be glad for her, but I couldn't forgive her for abandoning me. Life with Original Plan was a hard one, and we had no other family. Now I don't know whether or not she still lives." A fraught silence fell.

Kiria's mind spun with the pieces of Chetana's life. Pieces clicked into place like machine parts. She had Talent that she'd used for Original Plan, a group Kiria had heard of in passing, always in negative terms. In reputation, they were just shy of a terrorist organization. And Chetana's *katah* with Master Belik. That must have happened as a result of something she was doing with that group. Daelon resulted. The depth of that history was more than she felt equipped to fathom. And then Chetana had turned to God and to serving the Keepers.

Chetana adjusted her face and pressed Kiria's hands once more. "I don't tell this story to unburden myself, but to demonstrate what you have shown me. Without you, my young Keeper, I would not know what unconditional love looks like. You love the unworthy."

Kiria wasn't sure which "unworthy" one she meant.

"Thank you," Chetana concluded with the seriousness of a prayer. The candle flame danced over her lace septum ring as she dipped her head.

Kiria's face felt hot. She hardly deserved such heartfelt confidence. Only Kiria knew the extent of her own weakness, how she nearly broke under torture, how she still sometimes thought about Firian despite all her good judgment, and how she was so, so afraid of tomorrow.

But she was a little less afraid now.

When she found her voice, she said, "You give me strength too, Chetana." Abandoning the protocol that the Amir so carefully maintained, Kiria leaned forward and grasped her in a hug. The bruises along her ribs protested against the contact, but when Chetana held her like her mother used to, the sting was worth it. Tears slid from Kiria's tightly shut eyes. She savored the warmth and breath of the Amiran woman who had endured so much.

Time seemed to spill into the space between them when they broke apart. Only hours left now. Maybe that was part of the reason Chetana had come. Time might be running out for all of them. They had to say what needed to be said. More tomorrows weren't guaranteed.

Kiria's grip on Chetana's brown hands grew tight.

The Amir extricated her fingers and laid one palm on Kiria's head, softly chanting words from the Scroll. "*Greatness is found in service and majesty in love. Remember a heritage of evil but a future of hope.*"

Kiria nodded stoutly. *A future of hope.*

Happiness pulled at Chetana's mouth as she stood to leave. "*God supports the just man's cause—*"

The Scroll game. Kiria smiled. "*—and dawns upon him light in darkness.*"

56

KIRIA

THE NEXT DAY was cloudy and a little cold, even into midday. Kiria tightened her grip around the small scroll she had just sealed. Her wishes, should she not make it out of this conflict alive. Really, there were only two wishes, that the struggle for justice in the Kingdom continue and its three thrones be restored.

After some thought, she had named a third cousin—the only relative she was sure was still living—to be her heir. Her cousin had married a wealthy merchant and moved to Hinter, north of Enderin, far enough from the fighting to be safe.

Merrick, armor-clad, took the roll of paper from her and tucked it neatly inside a pocket. Kiria's heart beat a dull thud in her chest. The leather tunic beneath her own armor left her plenty of room to breathe—she had checked when Candrae and Vayci helped her put it on—but it felt as though it were shrinking.

She nodded a thank you at the guard.

Most of the others had already left to their positions. No more soldiers from Rantoul or Redshore, Skirwith or Tarryall, remained in the bunker. Endrian troops were gone too. Bard had left early to check on the Sentries. Some of the other Tanyu remained, and a small company of Kingdom soldiers that would go with Jori. They'd arrived just yesterday. She didn't ask them how they got past Tanyu at the gates. Others had been waiting outside the city for Kiria to arrive, since it was safer outside than inside now. Firian was here too, still deep in one of the smaller rooms. As soon as Sentries blocked the mind of Belik and his inner circle, he would leave as well.

Chairs had been set up in the main room in a few short rows. Leftover from last night, the smell of tart and savory food tanged the air.

Boots hitting the hard floor of the hallway signaled the arrival of Jori. He was dressed in armor similar to hers, except that he had no swath of blue across his shoulders. The thin plates of metal moved soundlessly with him. Most armor

Kiria had seen looked bulky but Jori still managed to look lithe and dashing. His smirk as he approached told her that he thought the same thing.

"I know," he said, holding up a hand and then transitioning into pinwheeling his arm as though testing it out. "I look amazing."

"Did you take time to do your hair?" she asked, squinting at his perfect, dark waves.

He drew his hand through it. "Always best to be prepared." Despite his cavalier attitude, she saw the same edge of fear in his eyes that haunted her own thoughts.

"Speaking of that," she said, "we need your heir."

"So soon?"

It took discipline not to roll her eyes. She gestured to the guard. "Merrick will keep the names safe for us. I don't think we'll need them, but we have to be ready, just in case." She tried to keep her tone light. "I'm sure you'll have no trouble at all finding a girl you like after you're the Keeper, but we have to be prepared now, like you said."

"Hm, yes." His gaze darkened. "Who'd you choose?"

"Third cousin."

"I'm sure I have one of those. Does it have to be family?"

She considered. "Normally, but we're running low on them." They shared a look full of memories of Kiria's mother and Atty.

"Does it have to be a man?"

Her eyebrows shot up. "No." If they were abandoning the idea of bloodlines, then they could abandon the idea of two men and one woman.

He considered his fingernails. "Haved. I choose Haved."

A smile crept onto Kiria's face. "Jori, that's perfect," she breathed. "Write it down and seal it. Then..." *Then you can go.* But she didn't want him to leave yet. He looked strong and brave and she was so proud of him. "You'll do wonderfully," she said instead.

Someone handed Jori a slip of paper and a writing utensil. He scratched out the words, looking from her to the paper and back. When he was done, he rolled it up as she had and sealed it, giving it to Merrick for safekeeping. "I have no doubt," he replied, settling his hands on her shoulders, "that you'll make us all proud."

"I love you," she said, voice breaking.

"I love you too, darling." They couldn't wait any longer. Kingdom soldiers were waiting for Jori to arrive. "I'll see you in the Main!" he called as he let two guards usher him away.

When he was gone, she took a deep, calming breath. This was it. Now it had really begun. At the thought, her sadness and fear started to crystalize into something more, something different.

Since the attack on her home, she had run and hid and planned. No more. Now was the time for action, for justice, for her to shove the tyrant off her throne.

Tesni approached. "Master Tanery just said the Sentries are in place, My Keeper."

"Good. Thank you."

Moments afterward, Kiria found Chetana praying in a separate room, their time not yet come to leave. She joined her for a short while, then checked compulsively on the Tanyu in the front room and with her army preparing outside. Bard was next. It was difficult to contact him, but a good way to use the remaining minutes. He reassured her that everything was ready.

Finally, she strode down the hallway to Firian's room. The guard outside opened the door when he saw her coming. Firian sat on the floor, bent over one outstretched leg, limbering himself for the task ahead. He raised his eyes to her and came slowly out of the stretch. As ever, he wore the black uniform of the Tanyu. No jacket. Dust from the floor clung to his pants as he stood.

"Are you ready?" she asked.

"Yes." His blue eyes blazed with the intensity he'd always had, but there was a softness now that hadn't been there before. Strength and passion but no chemical lust. Either he had figured out a way to break off the Sentry, or he was confident he would find one.

"I assume you still have the Sentry." She wasn't strong enough to sense whether or not it was on him without trying to go into his mind.

He nodded, a faint note of frustration bleeding through.

"My sources say Master Belik spends most of his time in the front wing of the palace, near the Main."

"I'll take care of it."

"Sundown," she said. "You'll have ten minutes."

"I understand," he replied, tightening a cloth around his hand with his teeth. It was black like the rest of his clothes, but he wore it much like a gesture of mourning.

They would lift the Sentry on Belik's mind only for that long. One of their only advantages was their Sentries that could hinder communication on the enemy side. Ten minutes would provide Firian a window to use his killing ability. If he could break through or disable the Sentry on his own mind.

Kiria frowned.

Catching her look, he raised a questioning brow.

"Can you do this?" she asked intently, matching his stare.

"If anybody can," he replied.

He was right. So much of their plan hinged on someone who she didn't want to trust. The new foundation he had built in support of her instead of against her was still a tumbled ruin, but she could see its outline. She sighed, then gave a curt nod.

"Be brave," he said softly. His baritone voice cut through her thoughts, steadying her. He met her eyes. Strength and, if she didn't know better, admiration shone in the depths of them.

"Be dangerous."

A smile tugged at his mouth, crinkling the corners of his eyes. His effortless confidence bolstered hers. The leather jerkin under her armor didn't feel quite as tight. "As you would have it, Kiria." With that, he cracked his neck and swiftly left the room, silent as a shadow.

More pieces moving on the board.

She watched him go. He moved as someone who completely inhabited his body, knowing its every facet and point of balance.

She'd never heard him say her name like that. Soft, yet distant and respectful. Something definitive had changed in him since the attack. It was in the line of his jaw and the level of his gaze. He still had the awareness of a predator, but not the razor-sharp edges.

Tanyu were beginning to settle into their seats when Kiria returned to the main room. They spent no time shuffling or adjusting like people did in the Main, she realized. This pool of black figures simply took their places like frozen figures in a pantomime. She was transfixed. Without any external signal, they closed their eyes as one.

Hopefully, the presence of so many Tanyu would draw out some of Belik's from beyond the wall. Kiria's allies would be ready for them.

Seconds ticked away. Soon, her army would march on Brithnem.

Be brave.

Be dangerous.

KIRIA ADJUSTED THE FOREARM GUARD, tightening the strap that held it in place. Around her marched Kingdom soldiers and allies from across the continent. The force, to her, looked huge. Thousands strong. But she could see the end of the marching mass of armored bodies, and before them lay the walls of Brithnem, tall and thick and guarded by expert Tanyu and ruthless Torithians. Her blood went hot as she spied moving figures above the massive Abrecan Gate.

Her army wasn't quiet or subtle. Their boots whisked through the charred grasses of the outer edge, armor gleaming in the sunlight. In the absence of many traditional generals, Royce had taken charge of soldiers' behavior and cleanliness. He was with Jori now, along the northern edge of the wall. Jori needed him more than she did, having no combat experience and going into the heart of enemy territory—territory that rightly belonged to them.

Flexing her wrist, she forced her squeezing heart to slow. They would all do their best. No one could ask for more.

The army stopped. She, in the middle, couldn't see how much land was left between her forces and the gate. Enough to avoid arrow fire. Chetana stood somewhere out front. Too bad Kiria couldn't see her. The latent power in her former advisor would make her a terrifying foe.

"My Keeper," a soldier murmured reverently, offering her his hand.

She hadn't noticed them bringing the platform forward. A square stand made of planks lay at her feet, lined with men and women ready for combat.

She took the soldier's hand out of courtesy as she stepped up. Her veins hummed with life and something almost like gladness. Gladness—a word that belonged to Chetana and Daelon's vocabulary. Appropriate that it should come to mind now. Once she stood in the center, six soldiers lifted the platform and muscled it onto their shoulders. Brief vertigo rocked her, but she spread her feet and laid a hand on the sword at her hip.

For a long minute, she didn't speak, just stood there feeling like the statue of her ancestor Mari in the Main, gloriously beautiful, armed, and resolved to get her kingdom back. All her life had sharpened to this point. She would drive forward until victory or death.

The dark figures pacing the walls stilled and the line of them grew thicker as more climbed to see the Keeper held aloft. Could any citizens also see her? Hopefully they did and knew that hope was coming.

Finally, she spoke. "My name is Kiria Arioc," she cried. The scar stretched across her lip but she didn't slur. "Second Keeper of the Western Kingdom. I have a message for Master Belik, the pretender, the murderer, the usurper who took my throne."

A breeze blew across the seared fields, ruffling the stray hairs pulled free around her face. Its gentle hush revealed just how quiet everyone was. In the mass of people, no one made a sound. It was like being in the Unreal.

"Surrender now," she demanded, her voice rising above the silence. "Surrender, or we will take the city back by force."

She had considered many other things to say—addressing the torture, the manipulation, the way no citizens could speak against Tanyuin rule—but in the end, she had decided on those words. That was the heart of it.

"You have one hour," she called.

The soldiers lowered her down. The figures above the gate began bustling again, faster this time. She couldn't hear anything they said from this distance, but her threats had galvanized them into action, at least.

One hour.

It was enough time to hurry from the palace to the Abrecan Gate, enough time to send troops from other stations along the wall, enough time to focus Belik's every thought her way. Having Chetana in front would hopefully solidify that.

It was enough time for the others to get into position while everyone turned their attention toward her.

57

BELIK

The dull crackle of a Sentry slammed into Belik's mind. It was like cutting off air. His eyes shot to Nedi, Shiro, and Enktuya, who stood nearby in the Main, and they confirmed his suspicions. All of them had Sentries.

Shit. "How many others have Sentries?" he growled. "Find out."

Shiro disappeared to obey.

Like a new wound distracts from a duller one, the Sentry removed his *katah* with Chetana. He hadn't actively used it in years, but it festered in his mind, always a thought away from rekindling. Being so angry and yet having to be so careful had made him tense, always. That tension shifted now. The difference was slight, but it pushed some knowledge he hadn't realized a moment ago into relief. Chetana was here. She was in the army marching against him.

Of course she was. She was a warrior, and had chosen her side. His heart beat furiously in his chest. He should have dealt with them all sooner.

There was one primary reason not to attack the princess right away after he found her cell empty. Everything in his blood wanted to crush her decisively, to tear away the feeble hope that Firian and the people of Brithnem still clung to. But if he waited, he could flush out all her allies, destroy them at once. No lingering, petty attempts to unseat the Tanyu from their rightful place. This way, when he killed her, she wouldn't be a martyr, but a final note in a song that would never play again.

Her forces were approaching the main gate. A frontal assault. Always so gory predictable. Well, he could work with that. Early estimates from the walls suggested they were seven thousand strong. Not bad considering the offer he'd made to all towns in the Western Kingdom—money and autonomy. Very few people could resist such a potent combination. Especially when the alternative meant marching into death at the behest of a young girl who'd betrayed them all by running into the arms of the enemy and leaving her people vulnerable. His version of the story had spread, and no one had the facts to deny him. It was close enough that it had the smell of truth.

Seven thousand, and now Sentries. It was the Sentries that bothered him, more than an army's-worth of weapons.

Sentries meant that Firian was back from the Academy. Several Tanyu—traitors—had defected to Kiria's side, trying to leave the city. That should have tipped him off. He hated killing Tanyu, but what could he do? They were like Firian's spineless friend who left after the Academy was attacked. A liability.

Something gnawed the pit of his stomach. Not fear, but anger, frustration, disappointment. He'd said he would kill Firian on sight if he returned. The idea didn't thrill him, but he would stay true to his word. Sentries also meant that there were more than the seven thousand that met the eye.

Even if Kiria did have more people on her side, she couldn't win. They'd wear themselves out against the gate as more and more people sailed to help the Tanyu. It was more of a nuisance, though, like untangling a knot he thought he could cut clean through.

A Tanyuin woman approached the foot of the dais. "The Keeper's allies have reached the Abrecan Gate, Master Belik."

He grunted. "And?"

"She demands your surrender within the hour."

That actually brought a laugh to his lips. It came out humorless and grating. That girl dared to defy him so openly? The girl who had quivered and cried and screamed in pain in the arena? This was her last gambit. He was sure of it.

The buzz of the Sentry coursed along the line of his mind, whining incessantly. Already he couldn't stand it.

He flexed his jaw and faced the Tanyu. "Send all the Torithians and soldiers to the walls." Raewhith and Imlin and Archer's Point and myriad others whom he compelled to be there, to earn their place in his new world. The new world he was supposed to share with Firian. But it was better this way. Better alone. Attachment only made one weak.

"As you would have it, Master Belik," the Tanyu said, turning to go.

"And set up chairs in the Main."

"Of course, Master Belik."

Belik could throw all those forces at Kiria and not even use the Tanyu to defeat her army. Most of those he would keep inside the palace for now, the deadliest weapon and a precious resource. But Firian had Tanyu as well, and they wouldn't keep quiet in this fight. Better to address them head-on.

An hour? Maybe this battle could end before it began.

It would be a short fight. Kiria and Chetana would die, along with all their allies, and he would rule unopposed.

58

JORI

Jori felt like a hero in a book. Or, he would, if he weren't wedging himself between two muddy wooden planks like a child hiding from its nurse.

Armor was distinctly overrated. He'd suspected it already, though he couldn't deny its aesthetic appeal, but now the verdict was clear. Too clunky. Too hard to move in.

"Isn't this exactly what you were expecting?" he hissed at the trailing group of soldiers behind him, flashing them a grin.

Nobody answered. Spoilsports.

A small pang of regret lanced through him that so many people knew about these places now. He was giving up the best hideouts, after all. Parties, escapes, stolen kisses, places to be alone... He would just have to find new ones. He had the nose for it.

The armor protested as he finally squeezed himself inside. Turning around, he assessed the relative fitness of the other soldiers. They weren't pudgy, but some of them had manly barrel chests or women's breasts that he doubted could fit through the opening. Not that he was complaining. He bit his lip and drummed his fingertips together. "I'm sure if you just..."

The nearest man tried once to get through, failed, then crashed into one of the beams with his shoulder, pushing it aside.

"Marvelous," Jori said. "Just what I was going to do. Of course, we should also be quiet."

"*You* should be quiet," grumbled the soldier.

"That's hardly the attitude." They should be grateful that someone could lead them onto the palace grounds through undiscovered ways. *Undiscovered until now.* He sighed.

They'd been struggling on for two hours. The sun was setting. They'd come from the north, past the wall, the Maze—a neighborhood he frequented, inhabited by a colorful cast of poor and unsavory characters—then through Soldiers Way, and were nearing the palace itself. It wasn't easy taking a group of eight, even if they were the palace elite, through back ways secret enough to hide them. No Tanyu accompanied them, so Belik and his ilk wouldn't read their minds, or whatever Tanyu did exactly, though Jori could think of one he wouldn't mind having near him.

That morning, he'd woken up with Bard Tanery's hair in his mouth. It was wonderful.

Jori dropped his voice. "It's up here," he said, pointing down an earthen shaft. "Down and up."

His chest gave a twist of apprehension. They had nearly made it. He, Jori Calthwaite, had led troops to the enemy's doorstep. He smiled, even as his heart darkened. The end of his expertise lay straight ahead. As soon as they emerged into the cell of the Amiran Academy, his job was over. Then he became just the black sheep of the Calthwaite family, standing there in borrowed armor, suddenly a liability. If Kiria were here, she would say something lovely to him. Maybe that he wasn't alone. But he was. At this moment, he was.

I hope you appreciate what I'm doing for you, he thought to Atty. The memory of his brother galvanized him, and he wiggled his fingers to get feeling back into them.

Kingdom soldiers followed him deeper into the darkened tunnel, less regular than the official escape tunnels for the Keepers. There must have been some forbidden love story involved in its making. That, or smuggling. Jori hadn't used it for much except escaping his lessons.

The soldiers' skepticism about this route followed him but he slicked it off like water. He had one job, and he was going to do it. Feeling blindly above him, he detected a handhold, something more solid than the fragrant, loose dirt they crawled over. *Stupid armor*. Though he had to admit, he was devastatingly handsome in it. Gripping the handle, he pushed upward. The trapdoor stuck, leaving a sliver of fresher air trickling from the room beyond.

He considered his options. Something was blocking the way, so he'd have to call out. Was an Amir in there, or an enemy? He tried to squint through the opening but saw nothing. He felt dashing, but that was as far as his skills went. He couldn't fight a Tanyu or a pirate. The dim memory returned to him of a frustrated tutor explaining that it was strategically better to have the high ground in a fight. This, he concluded, was not the high ground.

"One of you lovely people want to take a stab at this?" he said, stepping back. Royce stepped forward.

Surely, Bard wouldn't have put them willingly in danger. It must be only an Amir in there, if anyone. Maybe someone friendly, like his frustrated childhood tutor. Jori clasped his hands behind his back and smiled encouragingly back at the other troops, though they probably couldn't see him in this gloom.

Royce laid a strong forearm against the trapdoor and pushed. He managed to get it wide enough that they all could see a piece of furniture balanced on it, its legs pushed to a tottering angle. Shuffling feet hurried over to right it. Long grayish-blue robe. The face came next.

"Daelon," greeted Jori, relief washing over him, "how are you?"

Jori was wrong in his first approximation that the air in Daelon's cell was fresher than the air in the tunnel. It was not.

A sour tang in the air made him scrunch his nose as he emerged from the trapdoor in the floor. Daelon had graciously moved the desk out of the way to let them up. The Amir grasped Jori's upper arm to haul him inside.

After his initial surprise and happiness at seeing Jori alive, his face was a mask of worry. "How many of you are there?"

Jori looked at Royce, who had come up first. "Eight? Nine if you count me." Looking around the space, it was abundantly clear that the foul-smelling cell could only hold perhaps two more people, unless they wanted to start stacking on top of each other.

Powerful memories of his own tutor returned to him. Jori, age eight, told to sit still and memorize figures. Age nine, presented with world maps. Age ten, quizzed on passages from the Scroll.

These books, this dust, those high-necked robes... He stiffened as though there would be a test. This, he supposed, was the test. He smoothed the place where his collar would be, though now it was just dirty leather and metal.

Daelon's brow creased. "You're taking back the city," he said in a quiet voice.

"You catch on quickly," Jori replied.

"With eight? I hope there are more of you." Then, an afterthought, a realization. "My Keeper."

Jori's heart flopped over at the title, though he couldn't have said if it was from pride or apprehension, or just the sense that someone else should have that name instead of him. He cleared his throat. "Yes, we plan to storm the capital and overwhelm them with eight soldiers. Me at the front. That should frighten them."

Daelon didn't even smile. "Where are the others?"

"Kiria and all them? They're safe." He hesitated and revised. "They're alive. We have more troops but no time to explain it all. Right now we need to get out of this room."

The lines across Daelon's forehead deepened. "I can't open the door. They jam the locks when we're not needed." His handsome scholar's face looked suddenly gaunt.

Jori squeezed his arm. "We'll get you out. Right, Royce?" He craned back to the soldier before leaning again toward Daelon. "He's a war hammer. You'll see." He winked.

Hope kindled in Daelon's eyes, small but firm.

Jori called quietly down the secret tunnel. "All right, lovelies. Stay there for a moment."

"How did you know that was there?" Daelon asked. "I didn't know about any passage."

Jori's eyes roamed over the tiny space—cot, desk, candle, Scroll. *Really, how could he not know?* But some people, he'd learned, weren't the same kind of curious as he was. They walked over mysteries without looking into them, looked at mysterious substances without tasting them. Well, he'd done that last one too many ill-fated times, but at least then he *knew*.

He turned his longsuffering attention back to Daelon. "Fate, love."

Royce had finished investigating the door, testing his massive shoulder against it without crashing through.

"Need a lock pick?" Jori asked. He wasn't particularly good, but he'd learned a few things.

"No," Daelon answered for the soldier. "The lock is jammed, not regularly locked. Otherwise, I could open it from the inside."

"Ah, yes."

After much fuss and altogether too many armored bodies wedging through the tiny space, someone managed to get the door open. Actual fresh air flowed in. Jori nearly moaned with relief. He took a long whiff of it and stepped toward the opening. Something closed like a vice on his arm. Royce.

"You stay here."

"Really? After all that?" he whispered back, but the soldier was already gone into the shadowy colonnade with its everlasting white lanterns. Jori and Atty had tried to put one out once. Amir Parohim, Cúron's severe advisor, had caught them, Jori on Atty's shoulders. The two of them had been consigned to nothing but lessons and kitchen cleanup for three days after.

Running a casual hand through the muddy hair that had been so perfect earlier, Jori blinked away the sharpness in his eyes.

More soldiers climbed up through the floor, improbable as a magic trick, and carefully filtered outside.

So that was it, then. All Jori was useful for. That, and being a charming figurehead. Staying alive, that was his job.

He blew out a breath and looked out the door. It seemed odd that there weren't Tanyu everywhere. After the attack, he'd alternated thinking about the palace as a silent tomb and a crawling anthill. Silent tomb it was, then. The Kingdom soldiers didn't reappear. Some of them were supposed to do reconnaissance to get Jori to safety, and who knows what else. Well, Bard knew. He came up with the idea. Damn, he was impressive. And shy. *Focus, Jori, focus.*

Jori scanned the horizon, just like when he waited for his father to come home from one of his trips. His longest journey had been to the Tanyuin Academy. He'd been gone almost two months when Jori was seven. Jori and Atty had been so jealous, and they'd missed him. That was a long time for a kid. The Academy's location was a close-kept secret then, so all that time must have been spent misdirecting him and blindfolding him and who knew what else. In retrospect, it was stupid for their father to go at all. But he was a good Keeper and was trying to do some helpful diplomatic thing, no doubt.

A speck of black on the horizon caught his eye. Clouds made dusk come on more quickly, so the sea already looked inky. Could be a wave. Jori blinked, in case the speck was in his eye. No. The little object didn't move. There were more than one, he realized. Four. Four ships.

He straightened, pushing himself away from the doorframe. Daelon and three soldiers had stayed with him—keeping him alive, that was their job too. They looked at him now with alert curiosity. Viktor peered through the doorway toward the ocean. From his reaction, he saw the vessels too. "We weren't expecting more help to come for Belik, did we?"

"No, they were all accounted for, we thought," answered another.

This wasn't good. If the strangers docked at the main port, that was uncomfortably close to where Jori and the others were now. He licked his lips, trying to wet his suddenly dry mouth. "Do we know those ships?" Their sails and flag were still shrouded in gloom.

"No. We have to tell the others to shelter in place until we can see what we're up against."

That sounded reassuringly competent. At the insistence of the others, Jori backed away from the door. There was nowhere to go, so the back of his knees hit the dingy little cot. His blood sang too loudly to allow him to sit.

A familiar face appeared outside. Royce. "We've opened the doors and confirmed that the upstairs is empty."

"There are ships inbound," said Viktor.

"We saw them. We should still have enough time to move the Keeper to a more secure location without being seen."

Jori needed to end up *inside* the palace. That was the deal. Preferably the Main, where the thrones were, if Belik wasn't already in there himself.

After all this talk of Belik, it was strange that Jori had never seen him with his own eyes. He pictured him like some half bestial warrior with impossibly broad shoulders, a wicked glare, and clawed feet. All with the Tanyuin uniform of black on black. Not a lot of creativity there. Jori didn't know what he would do if he saw Belik in person. Would he strike out, despite his woeful lack of military training? He'd want to, that was for sure. He'd want to flay off his skin and put out his eyes. The very thought made him shiver away from the gruesome possibilities his mind concocted. He could hear Kiria's voice ringing in his ears. *We aren't that kind of leader.* Or something like that. But Belik did deserve to die for what he did.

"If we go out through the tunnel," Jori said, "there's a way to get back to the palace." He pointed two fingers in the air and zigzagged them around each other. Apparently, his visual demonstration wasn't helping. "But that way is known by more people." He gave a little shrug, glancing back out at the sea. Four ships had become nine.

"We have a clear view from here to one of the servant entrances," said Royce. "If we take your way, the ships could already be here with reinforcements."

A cold thrill ran through Jori at the idea of running through the gardens, completely exposed. "These are Tanyu, you know." The warriors Jori had idolized as a kid. It would be much easier if there were separate names for the good and evil Tanyu. That they all had to be called the same thing played havoc with his childhood memories. Should they be good? Should they be—

"We know," Royce replied grimly. "But it's a short distance, and four of us will cover you."

He bit back a joke. "All right. Do I run flat out?" He might have finished middle of the pack on the beach with the racers, but surely that wasn't too bad…

"Flat out."

He knew the door they meant. It led to a small private kitchen attached to the formal dining room. Next door was the Main. That didn't feel very safe—more like running into the jaws of a bear—but he ran his thumbs over his eyebrows and prepared to sprint. *Stupid, stupid armor.*

Turning to Daelon, Royce added, "If you can, lock the door behind you when we leave." He counted down on his fingers. Three, two...

And they were off, Jori pumping his arms and keeping his head down as he vaulted over furniture and low hedges. The plants had grown wild around the edges with lack of tending. Chest heaving, he and the four soldiers surrounding him reached the side door. The soldiers laid hands on their sword hilts as Royce reached for the handle.

Across the garden, a dark shadow flew by, too big to be a raven. Jori's insides turned watery, the ghost stories of his youth welling to the surface like oil. The side door was partially obscured by a teardrop-shaped tree. One of the soldiers pressed Jori behind it with one rough hand.

Something clanged close by, metal on metal. Someone had seen them.

Jori was dragged inside the dark kitchen. It smelled like stale bread and pickling spice, but he couldn't see anything. Someone gripped the front of Jori's breastplate and pulled him down to the ground. Dizzying terror made him almost lose his balance.

Their barely controlled panting sounded loud in the room. Jori held his breath, trying to count the number of others in the room, but it was no use. The cacophony of breathing was too haphazard.

They waited and waited and waited. Jori's legs burned with the effort of squatting so long. No one spoke.

With renewed vigor, weapons crashing against each other sliced through the dark. It sounded like a battle out there. Jori knew little about battles, and had only seen the one black shape. Could one or two Tanyu do so much damage to the remaining soldiers? His mind whirled around and around, in a nightmare. He had no facts to ground him except that he was in this kitchen with Kingdom soldiers, he couldn't see, and the plan relied on his not dying.

Someone near him stirred. The movement made Jori jump.

"Tanyu are distracted," a low voice breathed. Royce, probably. "We need a room with better—"

The door flung open, deafening and bright. All four soldiers were on their feet in an instant, swords ringing out of their sheaths. Jori looked up at the intruder. It was a middle-aged man with dark skin, his eyebrows high with the excitement of discovery. He held a bloody knife. Jori felt the food from yesterday's party rising in his throat.

Royce pulled the intruder inside—*inside?*—and slammed him against the wall. He rested the tip of his blade against the man's exposed neck.

That was when Jori realized he wasn't wearing Tanyuin black. The outfit was gray and orange, lightweight for the weather, with a leather jerkin on top and a metal piece guarding shoulders and neck.

"Who are you?" Royce demanded in a hiss. If Jori hadn't been nearly afraid enough to wet himself, he would have appreciated the sexy impressiveness of the moment.

The man tried to jerk out of Royce's grasp. Viktor stepped in to make sure he stayed pinned to the wall. "We come from Galve, in Somul."

Jori struggled to picture a map. Must be a small town. It wasn't on the list of allies that he knew about. Outside, clanging continued. Someone screamed.

Viktor closed the door. Though Jori squinted against the darkness, he couldn't see what was happening anymore.

"Whose side are you on?" came Royce's stern baritone.

Small, huffed sounds of struggle echoed before a response. "We bring Tanyu," he said, "and you—"

His next words cut off in a strangled gasp of surprise.

Jori crouched back on his heels, away from the sound. Had Royce killed him? Did that actually happen?

"Lock the door," Royce commanded.

Jori said, "It's easy to—"

"Then bar it. Block it. We can't have any more getting in. Where is the Keeper?"

"Here." He felt faint. A coppery smell mingled with the cooking spices.

"Belik has more soldiers inbound. We'll stay here for now and make sure you're safe."

"Yeah, we'll make sure nothing happens," added Viktor.

Like killing someone in front of me? Jori's eyes had adjusted enough to see a lumpy dark shadow by the wall where Royce and Viktor stood. He laid a hand on his chest, trying to stop panting. No luck. This was already the scariest thing he'd ever done, and they weren't finished yet.

59

FIRIAN

The Apothelin River flowed under the city wall to the south. There was a checkpoint there, probably for trade, but it was still the weakest point in the city's land defenses.

Firian eyed the place where the river met the wall from his position among the trees. There were two guards, both on the same side of the opening, clearly talking to each other. Kiria's forces must have arrived at the main gate. His chest felt full at the thought of her in the middle of that army. It wouldn't be enough to take the city. They all knew that. If he took too long, if the other parts of the plan didn't work, then even the Tanyu who had sided with him wouldn't be able to save her. They'd be overwhelmed. Seventeen was such a small number when Belik had the force of everyone else on his side.

Firian couldn't fail.

He ran back through the trees, a black shadow among deepening shade, to test the water. The river ran though his hiding place before running to the Kheltor Ocean. The water frothed and glided, its noise a liability and a blessing. He dipped his hand into the swift-moving water. Frigid. And deeper than it looked. He regarded it sternly, his insides balling into a fist. Not the entrance he would have chosen. But he couldn't tell Bard now. He couldn't tell anyone anything. This damn Sentry was a bigger worry even than the cold river. No one had ever broken a Sentry.

Could he?

A faint light glowed in his tight belly, something pure. He would try. For her. And she was right—he could be dangerous when he needed to be.

He fell into familiar breathing patterns that magnified his calm, his presence, his ability to shove physical reality aside in favor of the making of his mind. He stood at the bank and pulled out a bag lined with wax from his pocket. Then he stripped down, the cool breeze playing across his skin, telling him about the cold rushing water splashing his feet. All his clothes fit in the bag. It wasn't heavy, but would it be enough to tip his equilibrium in the water?

He gripped the mouth of the bag in one fist and packed those thoughts down into darkness. Maybe the monster within would eat them up. *I am the Tanyuin Head*, he chanted to himself. *If anyone can do it, I can.* And Kiria's voice, *Be dangerous.*

She'd had the tiniest glint in her eye when she said it. She believed he could do it.

Sucking in a deep breath, he plunged in.

The cold hit him like a body blow. Everything was moving. Freezing water covered every inch of him. He bobbed his head to the surface and gasped. But he couldn't let the guards see once he got out of the tree line. The forest was already thinning. The lights of the palace glimmered through them against the blue and orange of the setting sun. He had to go under.

He mentally ticked his progress as he floated from one tree to another. Ten counts. Measuring the distance from initial visibility to a place within the city safe enough to emerge, his heart dropped. Two hundred counts at least.

If anyone can do it...

His bare feet had already gone numb. He could regulate his body, control his thoughts and his breathing. The flow of the water pressing against his bare skin became only sensation, his panic stuffed safely away. This was just another element he could conquer. He shut his eyes. No up, no down. Only one moment and then the next.

An undertow sucked him down a moment sooner than he planned. Out of tree cover now, he had no choice but to clutch the bag, hold his breath, and let the violent water bear him, lungs burning, into the city.

FIRIAN COULDN'T STOP the violent shaking and explosive coughing when he thrashed out of the river. His head barely stayed above the freezing line of water. In the dark, it almost felt as though he were still under, still sucked underneath with no light and no air. He pushed himself, arms scooping hills of water, to the side. With trembling muscles, he drew himself up on the bank and rolled onto his back.

He was in a warehouse built over a narrower part of the river. Crates filled most of the space, perfect to hide from prying eyes. Firian curled up into a sitting position, still clutching the bag with all his clothes. He heard nothing but the slosh and rush of his own ears. He popped his jaw to clear the water. It took a few tries, but he finally felt a slight sensation like a bubble bursting, and cool water leaked from his ears down his neck.

Still, he heard nothing. No one stirred among the crates. It was late enough in the day that whatever workers normally filled this building had gone home. The racket he made gasping and coughing and spluttering hadn't alerted anyone. He breathed deeply and coughed again.

That was it. He hated water.

He stood shakily to his feet and dripped over to a more hidden place among the crates to slick off his body and put his dry clothes back on. After a few pushups to get his frozen blood moving again, his head started to clear. He was in Brithnem and, so far, none of Belik's forces knew. A familiar feeling of empowerment began to warm him as he shucked on the black shirt. He knew it must be freezing but it felt warm against his icy skin. Pants and boots too.

Blowing into cupped hands, he approached the door. The space between the stone wall and wooden door was wide enough for him to spy through. The angle didn't allow him to see the palace, but a street lined with stalls and stores and food vendors. The few people he could see seemed to be closing their wares. Even during war, life went on. There was a quick and furtive quality to their movements, though, which told him that they'd probably gotten wind of Kiria's forces outside. They knew battle was imminent.

He glanced at the shadows. How much time had passed since Kiria made her pronouncement? He couldn't be sure because of the gory Sentry, but he guessed a quarter of an hour was already gone.

Time to get to the palace.

60

BARD

Just as he had that day in Jori's tent, Wells sat cross-legged with unseeing eyes as he blocked Shiro from the Unreal. His back nestled between the exposed roots of an enormous tulip poplar. All the Sentries were spread out around the forest. It was essential that Belik's forces not find them all together because they wouldn't be able to defend themselves. Their minds had gone to a steady buzz of pain and abstraction.

Bard hated to see Wells like that, but Sentries were one of their greatest weapons. Kiria's side could mess up communication between higher ups, but Belik didn't have that power. Except with Firian, apparently.

Bard bit his lower lip. Not good. But Firian had surprised him before. He'd figured out that horrible killing ability and had also saved his life, so anything was possible. And if not, the soldiers with Jori would finish the job, incapacitating Belik and the four people he kept in his inner circle. At least they'd try.

Bard had been very careful with his language when he spoke to Royce. *Incapacitate*, not *kill*. He knew killing was likely, and Bard wouldn't cry over Belik, but Shiro had been his friend. Or at least an acquaintance. They'd lived on the same hall for a long time. Shiro mostly teased him. He'd been the one to come up with Bard's long-standing nickname "Tawn." Bard didn't think he pronounced Tanyu that differently than anyone else, but apparently Shiro did. Everyone his age called him Tawn except Firian, who thought the name was stupid.

Shiro had been Rian's best friend. Rian, whom Firian accidentally killed in the whirlwind of his mental energy, protecting the Academy from Kingdom forces a couple months ago. When Bard left. He understood why Shiro was mad at Firian, even hateful toward him. Hatred didn't need to mean revenge, though. This took things to a totally unnecessary level of violence.

Some violence was inevitable, especially at the gate, and the thought made Bard struggle against guilt.

Restless, he mentally checked in with Makai who held the rear of the army waiting for Belik's answer to Kiria's challenge. The buzz of Wells' Sentry made pressing through more difficult, but he soon found the Master's mind.

"Anything yet?" he asked.

"Nothing," Makai replied. "Belik isn't going to respond."

Bard knew that. Master Belik was about as likely to surrender as the ocean. But an hour bought Jori and Firian time to get into position. Bard's mind constantly aimed toward them—a reflex—but he couldn't get in touch. Firian was blocked and Jori didn't have the Talent. Neither did anyone around Jori, by design. Bard hated not knowing what was happening, if they were okay. Jori didn't have fight experience. Would he have to fight, despite having soldiers to protect him? Jori was fun and inspiring and kind, but not vicious. It would take feral energy to beat any Tanyu they might encounter, and Bard doubted Jori had that in him.

"Yeah," he said to Makai now, "I know he won't. Just let me know if something changes, yeah? Have you seen any of Belik's Tanyu around?"

His mouth was dry. Worrying did nothing. He'd spent his whole life worrying. Would he get kicked out of the Academy? What would his family think of him? His family, he'd learned, was proud. And he'd walked out of the Academy himself. There was nothing left but to see this plan through, and get Kiria's crown back.

"No, but they'll come soon." The slightest edge of tension laced his deep voice.

"You'll be all right. Just give us time. Take as long as you can, unless you see an opening." *Unlikely.* "Then take it. We really could use the gate, but time is even more important."

"As you would have it."

Twisting his black Master ring, Bard came back to reality, to the little hollow where Wells stared unseeing. *As you would have it.* Younger Tanyu responded to Masters that way. Bard doubted he'd ever get used to that response to *him*.

After checking the status of all the other groups he could actually contact, which was harder than usual because of the fog of Sentry static in the air, he sat beside Wells. He felt short when he did because Wells sat higher on a cushion. It was the least he could give the Sentries. Their past had denied them the most basic comforts. Bard's good hand curled into a fist at the memory of their lifeless and beaten faces in that hot room underground. Burns and shaved heads and atrophied muscles. Inhuman. Once the shock had begun to wear off, that was the first time Bard thought he might leave the Academy if he could, but he'd thought at that time that he couldn't without becoming a Sentry himself.

A soft sound crackled in the hollow. They waited down an embankment, so no one should be able to find them unless they already knew where to search. Bard looked up.

A Kingdom soldier dressed head to foot in armor stepped down to meet him. Bard stood. The soldier looked vaguely familiar, but Bard didn't remember his name. He wasn't one of the few who had traveled with them to Charäkhnem and back.

Was this one of the soldiers he'd sent with Jori? Was Jori okay? If so, why was this soldier here? He belonged either with Jori or at the gate. A cool prickle danced down Bard's spine. "What's wrong?"

"Nothing," said the man, casting a wary glance at Wells, who didn't stir.

Something *was* wrong here. "What do you need?"

A weapon appeared in the man's hand. Something blunt. No blade. He swung it at Bard's head, but he dodged out of the way in time, gut swooping with confusion and terror.

In the split second that the soldier's arm followed through his motion, Bard scrambled for Kiria's mind, not the easiest to find since she was still honing her skills. Her lavender presence echoed from amid the army at the gate. "Take it," he choked out, hoping she would hear and understand. If he was hurt or killed or taken, she was the only one who knew enough to coordinate all the pieces of the plan. Most of the pieces could move on their own now, but they were crucial emergency measures.

He flung his eyes open again, but something was in them. Pain exploded across his cheekbone. He stumbled but stayed upright, looking for a weapon for himself. Nothing but the small dagger he'd brought. He bounded forward, landing on the man's foot, then hopped back and reached for his knife.

Wells hadn't stirred. Would the soldier kill him?

Desperately, Bard placed himself in front of his friend. His ears rang and the edges of his vision blurred as the soldier wound up again. A dagger was too small. He sucked in a breath to brace himself the moment before another blow hit him and he crumpled to the ground.

61

KIRIA

KIRIA SCANNED the darkening wall again. Now off the platform, she didn't have the best view. Forced to look around armored shoulders, a persistent tug of unease plucked at the nape of her neck.

More and more people had joined the others on the wall. A low sound indicated that crowds gathered just inside the closed gate. Hopefully the citizens living close to the gate would leave before the battle began.

A moment ago, she'd felt as though Bard were trying to contact her, but when she closed her eyes and found her way to the Unreal, he wasn't there.

Half of Belik's time had elapsed. Chetana shouted the update from her place at the front of the central column. Her clarion voice sent chills over Kiria's skin. Chetana was twice the warrior Kiria would ever be, but Kiria stood tall—as tall as she could—in her armor and encouraged the troops around her. She could be brave, but that didn't make the waiting any less terrible.

Every moment that slipped by grew chillier and made her brain churn with awful possibilities.

Movement ahead snapped her back to attention.

Abrecan Gate was opening.

She lifted up on tiptoes to get a better vantage. The huge double doors swung outward, helped by four men. One person appeared in the opening, then two, then three. Many, all in a row. They marched forward, pouring out like liquid and spreading to match the breadth of Kiria's army. None wore Tanyuin black.

She tensed. Was this it? Did this slow march mean the clash had begun? Maybe it just seemed slow with her heightened senses. Her right hand squeezed the hilt of her sword. Wearing it was a precaution, but she didn't know how to wield it in battle. She'd learned the basics on a week when Daelon caught cold. A guard close to her father had taught her the mechanics of swords and arrows and armor. She remembered that swords were much heavier than they looked. Her palm grew slick with sweat, and she adjusted her grip.

There were no cries of pain, no clang of metal on metal. Kiria's heart hammered as the enemy lined up to face her allies. There couldn't be more than the length of three people between the two armies. The dying sun gleamed on shaved heads. Torithians. Anger bubbled in her blood. Faces flashed once more through her mind. She closed her eyes in a promise. The Western Kingdom belonged to Atty, to Cúron, to her mother, to all those they'd lost.

Her fear fell away, replaced with determination, the cycle looping back to courage that grounded her. Master Belik killed her family. He drew Firian further into corruption. He used Torithians on the front lines, but not his own Tanyu.

They had hoped to draw Tanyu from their posts on other parts of the wall, thinning the enemy presence around the perimeter. Bard had insisted that Belik would send warriors to the underground den to flush out the Tanyu there. With the Talent, they'd be easy to find. Little did they know that there were extra Tanyu, soldiers, and Sentries waiting to ambush and neutralize whoever came inside. Were Belik's warriors still coming?

Maybe Bard had heard something. She closed her eyes, partly to contact him and partly to block out the enemy force in front of her that still streamed through the gate. They filled the streets beyond and all the space between her army and the wall. Seeing it in person was different than looking at plans with Bard. It was visceral and made her feel alive and fragile and strong all at once.

The Unreal was dark. She still didn't have the hang of talking to people without backgrounds, like the Tanyu could, and it was harder for her to find other people's minds. She'd only managed it with three people: Firian, Bard, and Chetana.

The darkness became the palace hallway, the easiest setting for her to conjure. "Bard," she called.

Maybe she was looking in the wrong place, not that space mattered in the same way here. Still, for her, it could be helpful to cast her mind in the direction of the person she wanted to talk to. She came back out of the Unreal and physically turned around.

She tried again. "Bard."

He could be busy with someone else, but he was a Tanyu, and knew to be attuned to her. Her heart was in her throat.

"Bard!"

Something was wrong. He wasn't there. Maybe he had tried to contact her earlier but she hadn't found him in time.

She opened her eyes, her mouth gummy. *Please, please let him be all right.* If Bard wasn't answering, she would organize the battle effort as best she could. Her level of Talent fell short of his, but she would do it.

She faced the army in front of her. The air smelled like leather and lightning with an edge of acrid smoke. They'd known the task could fall to her. Lifting her chin, she stared at the people who had taken her home and her kingdom, knowing with certainty that she would still be standing there even if she had been the only one to fight.

62

FIRIAN

Feeling had returned to Firian's feet and hands, though the black cloth around his palm kept one hand cold. He'd never seen the southern edge of the palace grounds. He'd always come and gone through the main entrance that faced east, toward the Abrecan Gate. Now he stared at the wall surrounding the palace grounds, scanning for Tanyu.

Mon Párinath was wrapped in walls—outermost were the city walls, tall and thick, then the walls around the palace grounds, and finally the walls of the castle itself. He'd breached the most difficult layer. Now came the second.

In the intensity of saving Bard and then his prison escape, he hadn't noticed just how much the fire had damaged the palace. Most of the glass in the windows had blown out. Smoke stains smudged the area above the openings. A pile of black char must have once been an outbuilding. The palace, made of stone, still looked stable, though. The fire damage only made it easier to breach, once he was past the wall.

Firian pushed experimentally against the Sentry again, a compulsion like tonguing a loose tooth. Jarring red pain shocked him. He cursed under his breath.

Proximity, Belik had growled.

The Master knew he was back. The only question was which of them would find the other first.

After scouting the palace wall as quickly as he could, Firian determined the angle that could be seen from the fewest vantage points. No window of the palace faced this section, and the hulking castle itself blocked the view of anyone patrolling the gardens or the seaports beyond. The only danger was someone directly on the other side. That, Firian could handle.

The palace wall wasn't as thick or high as the city wall, much more climbable. Running forward, he vaulted up, catching the wall with two steps before clinging to the top. In one swift motion, he pulled himself up and over.

His training took over as he dropped on the other side behind badly manicured trees.

Two figures in black ran past. One continued on toward the gardens but the other pulled up short. Firian stilled. The Tanyu looked around, up at the wall, almost as though she sensed exactly what had happened.

As careful and sure as a wolf, the Tanyu slowly strode toward Firian's hiding place. No one else was in sight. Firian rushed out from his hiding place, Jovan's drills moving him automatically. A fist glanced off the side of Firian's neck, but he was faster. Fighting felt good. One, two, three. Moves he'd practiced a thousand times. With surprise on his side, the fight was over almost too quickly, now that adrenaline raced through him. He dragged the unconscious body to the thick group of bushes where he had hidden moments ago.

His blood was high now. Youth and power filled him, directing his muscles as he ran surefooted toward the palace to find Belik.

Moments later, he was inside one of the guest rooms in the front wing. It wasn't as large as the one where he'd stayed only a few months ago, but it was similar, though starker. No tapestries hung on the walls, no chairs by the cold fireplace. Firian suddenly remembered the Torithian he'd caught running out of the palace with treasures in his arms. Had the whole palace been looted?

His lip curled. Belik wouldn't mind if it were. The Master depended on the riches at the Academy to pay the cities that wouldn't help Kiria.

The image of Kiria in armor stoked pride in him. Before everything had gone to hell, they'd talked about her future as a Keeper. She'd had such earnest love for her kingdom, despite her personal insecurities about ruling. How different she was now... The resolve in her eyes that afternoon fed his own determination.

He couldn't depend on this room remaining empty for long. Belik wasn't here. But he was probably nearby.

One look out the window told him he didn't have long to find him. Belik's Sentry would lift, releasing his mind and making it vulnerable, but only for ten minutes.

He quieted his blood and breathing, feeling the environment around him. Far away, he heard the dull sounds of conflict. That had to be closer than the main gate, which was nearly an hour away. Something was happening outside, maybe on the shore or in the gardens. He couldn't parse out its meaning. Any distraction was in his favor, but something told him this change meant nothing good. More allies for Belik, probably.

No footstep sounded just outside his room, so he gently opened the door. It swung on silent hinges. A side hallway, not the massive one he was so used to seeing in Kiria's mind. It provided more cover than the window-lined artery that led to the Main.

The nerves in his body were alive. Air flowed around him, bringing scents and sounds that made his skin tingle. Every tremor under his feet told a story.

"...roll of who's there?"

Firian's eyebrows twitched. It was too easy. That was Belik's voice. He froze.

"Well, look!" After a pause when someone else presumably spoke, he said, "It'll be quick." Another pause. "What?" he snapped. "How many?"

Firian inched closer. Maybe he could hear the other speaker.

"Five soldiers," Belik muttered. "From the barracks?"

The other speaker, it turned out, was Enktuya, a girl Firian didn't know well. She was a young Master but kept to herself in the Academy. "They're giving us trouble by the port."

"Then kill them. We don't need distractions. This should be over soon." A sigh.

Belik's voice grew further away. A door closed. Firian's lips curved. *Got you.*

The Master would leave a lookout, but probably only one. Firian dropped to the floor and peered around the corner, quick as the cold current that had borne him into the city.

One. He was right.

Hopping back to his feet, he didn't bother being silent. He made a small sound, like a breath when he needed to clear his throat. And he waited.

The Tanyu was swift, flying around the corner like a swallow. He gripped a knife in his fist, a flurry of winged black.

Firian used the Tanyu's own momentum to grab both his wrists and slam him against the wall, kneeing him hard in the diaphragm. The Tanyu gasped, only managing to give an impotent squeak. His eyes bulged as recognition dawned. Fear edged the anger in that stare.

Firian recognized him too. A Defender named Zhufal, Khelê, about twenty. He smashed the wrists against the wall again to loosen the knife. It fell from the Tanyu's hand, or maybe he just let go. They all knew about Firian's killing ability. Before the blade could clatter on the floor, Firian caught it out of the air and pressed it against the delicate skin at the man's throat.

Firian slanted his eyes across the hall in a command.

The Tanyu peeled away from the wall to walk toward the guest room Firian had just left. Still holding the dagger to the hollow of his neck, Firian wrapped his arm around the man's head and clasped his hand over his gasping mouth.

Even looted, the room provided enough cloth to tie and gag the lookout before knocking him out.

The sun still wasn't down, but it was sinking, marking time. Kiria's ultimatum had to be expiring.

He looked at the Tanyu tied at his feet. How could Zhufal side with Belik and his ruthless violence?

You did.

The unwelcome voice sounded like Kiria. She had been right about him all along.

Firian shoved those thoughts aside. He wasn't the same as he had been. His purpose burned, clear and difficult.

He slipped into the hallway again. No one had raised an alarm. No Tanyu came running. Belik was probably still in that room—maybe Cúron's? Its placement felt familiar, like a smell he couldn't place, but that was probably the *katah* with Kiria, who knew these halls so well.

If he was right, then there would be a washroom or servants' quarters attached. He ran his hand along the stone of the corridor, as if it would give up its secrets. Tanyu might meet in servants' quarters, but not in a washroom.

He cycled through options, picturing the sunken room with the claw-footed tub that the royals had offered him when he came to stay. He didn't remember any opening except for two small ventilation holes, one near the floor and one by the ceiling. He couldn't fit through those, even if he tried. They were barely bigger than a fist.

Was there any way to determine how many Tanyu were in the room with Belik, how many weapons, what configuration? Firian had nothing but two small knives. They were relying on his killing ability. It would only take a bloody moment, but he didn't want to sweep others into the carnage.

If he could reach his ability at all. With it, he could get close to that tipping point and sense how many people there were, their breathing, their heartbeats, the blood in their veins. But he had no access to it. Anxious energy spiked through him. *If anybody can do it...*

He laid one hand lightly on the door handle. He could storm the room, take his chances.

Belik would stand there, unsurprised, immovable as a mountain, staring him down. With his bad leg and the knowledge that Firian was after him, he'd keep as many Tanyu around him as he could until this was over. Tanyu that Firian had known at the Academy, people that had followed him, had admired him, had abandoned him to death when Belik lied to them.

Firian has turned his back on the Tanyu, betrayed you to the enemy so he could screw the princess.

Firian's heart beat too loudly in the hollow of his chest. Yes, he fought for Kiria, but he never meant to betray the Tanyu. The Academy was the only place he had ever belonged. Moments of belonging flashed like sunspots when he was with Bard or with Kiria, but that kind of life was for someone else. That was for people like them.

His fingers closed over the handle. The hall had become darker. Not quite sundown, but close.

In a flash, with his dagger in one hand, he opened the door.

The room was empty.

63

KIRIA

Kiria wandered in the dark emptiness, feeling like a blind woman. Panic threatened to claw up her throat. Bard could do this almost without thinking.

Finally, she felt something, a shift in the air, a new essence. "Tesni!" she cried, wrapping the palace hallway around her again. She'd abandoned that setting after she determined it was too distracting. The blankness that followed focused her mind on the search, but also carved a hollow in her heart. She didn't feel Bard anywhere. His absence weighed heavily on her. If something had happened to him...

Tesni appeared across from Kiria, who let out a breath, grateful to have finally found someone. "Tesni," she said, "can you see any Tanyu behind us?"

"See?" Tesni asked with a hint of haughtiness in her tone. "No, but they're there."

"Okay, can you check that everyone underground is ready for them?"

"As you would have it." She disappeared, leaving Kiria once again alone.

As you would have it. The same wording that Firian used. It must be distinct to the Academy.

She opened her eyes and the dying light seemed flashing bright. She squinted and her heart stuttered. Almost an hour had gone by. Belik's forces hadn't stopped coming, oozing around the edges of her army's formation, only a sliver of space separating the two.

What had she seen of battle? Firian killing the Torithians who assaulted her in Raewhith? An arrow, impossibly, flying at her face? She'd seen her share of pain, but never true battle up close.

All these people, she realized, looking around, were willing to die for her cause. That room in her mind had shut tight, self-protective, but it opened now. She turned to one of the Kingdom soldiers who had lifted the platform. He had dark brown skin, green eyes, and a tattoo covering both hands. She gently touched his metal-clad upper arm. "Thank you," she said quietly.

He looked down at her with a professional expression of care. She didn't know him, but he was with her.

Privately, she thanked a few others, asking their names so she could use them. Appreciation swelled larger and larger within her until she fairly glowed. Having her friends closer would have completed the joy that came out like hurt. But they were all far away, also fighting for her.

The hour elapsed.

A change moved over the crowd, a tensing of muscles and sharpening of senses. Chetana, now by her side, nodded solemnly.

Kiria stepped again onto the platform. Her joints felt like wood but her will was iron. The soldiers lifted her up again. From up there, Belik's army looked far larger than it had from her shorter vantage point. It flooded the streets of her city, a mass of bodies, ready for them if they were to breach the gate.

Her city. City Beautiful.

"The hour has passed!" she shouted. "Will you not surrender to the Kingdom's rightful ruler?"

She waited for a pregnant pause. No dignitary or Tanyu stepped forward to take her offer. If only they would. If only Belik weren't so hard headed...

"Then," she said, her voice carrying over the heads of thousands, "we are at war."

64

JORI

IN THE CRAMPED LITTLE KITCHEN, Jori began to wonder if he would ever race again. His legs screamed from being in the same position. Heroic Keepers—or nearly Keepers, to be unnecessarily scrupulous about it—didn't complain about leg pain when they were hiding. Still, his mind wandered to the sparkling wine he knew the cooks kept on the upper shelves, invisible now in the darkness.

As soon as Jori was sure the conflict directly outside was over, another sound echoed and the fighting renewed. Oh, to stretch! And they still didn't have a tally of who had made it through the gardens and was in here with him. Did soldiers just have a sense of these things?

"I thought you said we were going to move," he whispered, barely above a breath. The idea frightened him out of his wits, but those were leaving anyway the longer he stayed motionless in this darkness. Even his neck had a crick. If ears could be strained from listening too hard, he had that too.

A heavy hand descended on his shoulder. A warning to be quiet. The gesture was so authoritative that he wouldn't have been surprised if a finger had been laid against his lips. He shut up, though his muscles ached and his thoughts became increasingly edgy.

Maybe my legs will be stronger. And my shoulders from hunching. I'll look even better up there on that throne.

But the thought didn't soothe him. Picturing the throne inevitably conjured images of his brother on it, then the importance of this mission came flooding back.

On and on it went, a cycle that seemed to last ages.

Someone tapped his shoulder. Jori snapped out of his daze and the muscles in his thighs whined as he shifted. Questions bobbed to the surface of his mind, but he shoved them down. Keep quiet, they'd told him. They were the experts here, the ones making sure he didn't get killed.

Biting down on the words he wanted to say, he attempted to stand. A grunt escaped him. His legs spiked with pain. He stumbled lightly into the nearest guard, who caught him around the waist before he fell.

"Are you all right?" came the soldier's voice, too quiet to distinguish, almost too quiet to be heard.

"Fine." In the dark, he winced, flexing his feet to ease some of the tension in his muscles, like touching a bruise.

Dim light leaked over the shapes of bowls and counters and hanging utensils. There was the sparkling wine, glimmering on the top shelf as always. *I'll come back for you. We'll celebrate.*

He turned to see the soldier in the doorway leading deeper into the palace, who nodded curtly and opened the door wider. Still limping, Jori followed in the midst of the soldiers. Three of them, he now saw in the light of the dining room. Stoic Royce, Viktor with his flower tattoo, and one he'd just met before he led them through the back ways into Daelon's room. What was his name...?

Jori stopped short. Half of the long dining room table where he'd shared so many meals had burned completely away. White ash coated the floor by the main door. Near Jori, the room looked the same, everything in its place, down to the centerpieces, now holding crispy dead flowers. But the table ended in a jagged black rent. Jori's chest squeezed tight. He counted the chairs. No, he hadn't been mistaken. Jori and Atty usually sat where the table now looked ripped apart. *Don't think about metaphors.*

The warm, acrid sting of smoke still coated the room.

"Rather exposed, isn't it?" he whispered, eyeing the door to the magnificent hallway feeding into the Main. It looked warped. Did the lock still work?

He knew he had to be near the Main when they were victorious, so he could immediately resume the throne, settle the concerns of the people, wave and smile. All while his guards secured the symbolic location. The Main was such a big space, though. Tanyu probably swarmed it now. He pictured it all black with a portrait of that gigantic creature Belik instead of the wonderful statues.

Royce put his big blond face next to his. "Is there a secret way to the preparation hall attached to the Main?" To his credit, he didn't even grimace at his own suggestion that Jori knew the palace better than he did.

Jori mustered a smile for him. "Not through here, no, but there are a couple." He held up fingers as he listed, "Outside ledge, chimney (which I don't recommend), or the space between the generals' office." When Royce looked blank, Jori tutted. "Don't tell me you haven't noticed."

Royce's gaze narrowed to a glare.

"It's the shared opening with the light." Attached to the Main, on the north side, were two small rooms—the antechamber where royals waited for big events, and the head general's office. A window-like aperture between the two rooms opened near the ceiling, carving out a space that also looked out into the Main, like a missing puzzle piece connecting all three. When Jori, age twelve, had managed to get up there, he found a cold candle covered in dust. In the past, it could have been a signal or extra light source. He didn't particularly care, and had moved it to the side to continue exploring.

The soldier shared a look with the other two. They seemed to like Jori's idea, or at least they considered it better than the chimney. Through the generals' office, they wouldn't have to cross the ominous expanse of the Main until it was time.

A sound scraped outside the door. Tanyu were usually quiet as cats. Jori's blood froze. His legs, still burning, didn't feel ready to run.

Now a muffled sound, like someone talking behind thick walls. The soldiers drew closer to Jori and backed him up to the kitchen door. There were no windows in this room, either to see outside or into the hallway. Helplessness ate at the edges of his thoughts. He glanced at the ravaged table, briefly picturing the soldiers hurling it to the side to shield them all.

The noise grew louder, everything magnified in the stillness. A persistent murmuring. Now that it was closer, it sounded almost familiar, though no word was distinct. Words still didn't form as the voice passed within range of the dining room. Jori's guards laid hands on their weapons, shoulders rising, feet spreading. This would all be very exciting if it weren't so terrifying.

Then Jori's face went bloodless. He couldn't feel his fingers, and it had nothing to do with that horrible wait in the dark kitchen. Shock jolted through his core as he heard something he recognized. The quality of the muffled voice broke through in one indistinct syllable, and he knew.

The Tanyu had captured Bard.

Jori's mind suddenly filled with static and, floating like an island in chaos, one solid idea. *This cannot happen.*

He stumbled once against the table as he shot out of the room.

65

BARD

Ragged, brown-tinged Brithnem flags waved like ghosts as Bard got closer to the Main.

He was conscious now, gagged, wrists bound in front of him, but no Sentry. They knew there was no point in blindfolding him. He knew exactly where he was going. They were taking him to Belik. The Kingdom soldier who'd betrayed him walked on his left and a male Tanyu he'd seen before but did not know walked on his right.

What those two didn't know—hopefully!—was that Jori and Firian were in the palace somewhere too, waiting for their moment. Bard felt the pull to think of them as though it were a physical thing, but he leaned away from that worry, focusing instead on a less incriminating thought. The news that he'd been taken. If Kiria knew, then she would understand how to proceed. She could ignore any false message Belik might make him send.

Because Belik must want him to send a message. That, or reveal the parts of his plan that he didn't already know. Otherwise, Bard would have been killed already.

Twisting his wrists, pressed backward farther they should be because of his clawed left hand, he sensed Kiria's mind. It was in chaos. Was she all right? He couldn't sense anything clearly. She didn't have the calm mental center of a Tanyu, but he battled on, searching for purchase.

"Kiria! I've been taken."

A fierce sting lashed across his eye where the soldier had beat him. Pain dragged him back to the Real. The Tanyu glared at him, knowing exactly what Bard was doing. Masking his distress about Kiria and the others, Bard gave him a bloodshot glare right back.

"You know this isn't right," he said through the gag. It came out as a slurred murmur of indistinguishable sounds.

The Tanyu ignored him.

"It isn't right!" His heart was beating hard now. The Main was close. He didn't want to be afraid, but the last time he'd seen Belik, the Master had hurt him. He didn't remember most of the details, but flashes had come back to him in the past few weeks. Blood from the floor seeping into his hair, piercing pain in his back as though he were being pulled apart, Firian's white face filled with horror. And of course he had his useless hand to show for the encounter.

Bard turned to the Kingdom soldier, who looked pale and shadowy. "Kiria is fighting for you," he said. "Why would you do this? Did Master Belik promise you something?" Without magic, no one could understand what he said, but it felt good to say something. If he distracted them with his babble, then he could find another sliver of an opening to try Kiria again. Or, if he couldn't do that, at least he could take stock of the Tanyu they passed and gather information. It occupied his mind and pressed out the horrible voice that said he wouldn't make it out alive. If he could just—

A figure bolted from the room just behind them. Bard turned in time to see arms pumping with speed, close wavy hair streaming behind. Kingdom armor.

"Here!" Jori yelled, disappearing in the opposite direction.

No! No, no! He was supposed to be hiding. He wasn't a fighter. There was no way he could take on a Tanyu. Even Bard had learned moves that could incapacitate Jori quickly. Why hadn't he stayed hidden?

Three Kingdom soldiers followed behind. Viktor's Khelê tattoo shone black on his cheek as he sprinted after Jori.

Bard was going to race with him on the beach. They'd talked about it that morning, Jori flashing too many coins for a bet. Bard couldn't match it, but Jori grinned anyway, keeping the bubble of the fantasy intact. Neither mentioned the unpredictability of the next few hours. They would race. That was that.

Reality was slow to dawn. Jori was creating a distraction. For him. *You're more important!* he wanted to shout, but the gag and situation stopped him.

The Tanyu pointed. Another materialized from the shadows. "Get him! That's the Kepron." Without a word, the Tanyu obeyed, moving with animal speed and grace.

Bard's heart felt like a stone, but as everyone looked to the place where Jori disappeared, he crushed his heel into the bridge of the Tanyu's foot. Ducking and twisting from between his two captors, he turned to run back down the hallway.

With a tilt of vertigo, the purple patterned rug rushed up and smashed him in the nose. A solid hand pressed his face into the ground. Bard couldn't even turn his head. For a panicked second, he couldn't breathe at all through his gag. Judging from the boots in his peripheral vision, the Tanyu held him down. He ripped Bard upward by the hair and cracked his face down again. Bard's eyes streamed with pain.

The Tanyu whispered a few foul curses in his ear before hauling him up again. Blood streamed from Bard's nose into his mouth when he stood.

Where was Jori? They knew he was in the palace now. Did he have any chance of surviving? Bard didn't want his final memory of him to be his stupid, sweet bravado.

A shove to his shoulder got Bard moving again. The huge carved doors of the Main loomed before them. They opened and Bard felt his connection to Kiria, to Jori, to the others, all snapping away. His eyes darted around the huge space. He'd only been in this room once before, when he offered to help Kiria find an end to the war. All three Keepers had sat on the dais. Only Kiria had believed his sincerity. Hopefully that trust would pay off.

Now Belik sat on the platform, not on a throne, but on a plain chair like the many set up in rows across the mosaic floor. Shiro, Nedi, and a young woman he didn't recognize stood beside him. Wells had been guarding Shiro. Had they killed him? Could Shiro access the Unreal now?

Tanyu in black uttered soft noises of surprise or effort, some twitching like dogs in sleep. Someone cried out, slumping to the floor, her chest impossibly slashed open.

Bard felt sick, but also fascinated. If his plan worked, then the Sentries were bouncing from mind to mind at random—with the exception of Belik and his enforcers. Bard had never heard of such a thing killing someone, but the pain would be incapacitating for a while. Without access to the Unreal, Belik would just see the scream of pain as an ordinary battle loss.

As Bard drew closer to the steps and saw Belik's glare more clearly, he became eleven again. The Master looked as he always did, no added crown or finery—just the black outfit of a Tanyu and a hawk-like awareness behind his glasses. Wide-eyed terror clawed at Bard. He trembled with the effort to keep it at bay.

"Good work," said Belik, his attention slicing to the Kingdom soldier. Bard feared for him. He was in a room full of Tanyu—some guarding Belik, others fighting in the Unreal, still others patrolling the blown-out windows. Any one of them could kill him in a blink, and Belik was ruthless enough to order it.

The same realization must have filled the soldier himself, because he went paler, his skin like paper, though he kept his perfect posture. "Master Belik," he said, "I've only done this to ensure safety for my family. I apologize that they haven't always been sympathetic to... your cause. But we just want to live in peace. I need your word that this will be done." His throat bobbed as he said the words.

Belik pursed his mouth, his expression unreadable. "You would like them out of the city?"

"Yes... sir."

Belik's lips twisted at the word.

From below, a cry of pain split the air as a Tanyu grabbed his head and wavered in his seat. The soldier tensed at the noise.

"We'll see it done," Belik said. "The Tanyu aren't monstrous, as you've been led to believe." He nodded once to a female Tanyu standing by the opening that had once been a glorious, multi-paned window.

Even with the armor, the relief in the muscles of the soldier's back was obvious. Bard tried to catch his eye as he walked away, but the soldier refused to meet his gaze. Now, at least, Bard understood.

It was almost dark outside. The Sentry would lift soon, giving Firian ten minutes to use his killing ability on Master Belik. Bard scanned the space as subtly as he could, but saw no sign of Firian. He didn't think he would. Was he here? Was it even possible to break off a Sentry through mental will? His skin tingled with apprehension.

"Master Belik," the Tanyu holding Bard said urgently, "Jorrim Calthwaite is in the palace."

Belik's focus locked onto the words. "Here? Where?"

"We saw him just now."

"Saw him?" Belik stood, ready to issue commands.

"Tanyu are on it. It shouldn't be long."

Bard's breath hitched, only a little, involuntarily. It was enough to swivel Belik's attention on him. He glowered thoughtfully before leaning back in his seat. "What idiot put you in charge?" he muttered. "I hear that you are. In charge." His gaze dipped to Bard's clawed hand. "So this is what you'll do. Bring a chair for him." Shiro did. "Sit," Belik said.

Bard sat.

"You will tell them all that the prince is dead. He was found in the palace. His half-cocked plan got him killed."

Bard's blood beat so loudly in his ears that Belik's gravelly voice barely made it through. He huffed out a breath, clearing his nose of blood so he could breathe more easily. No one took his gag off. He wasn't supposed to argue.

He shook his head.

No one would believe the message if Belik sent it, even if he tried to disguise himself as Bard in the Unreal. Maybe a Watchman couldn't, but a Tanyu could tell the difference. It had to be Bard himself.

"This isn't a negotiation," Belik said, holding up one hand to stop the Tanyu from beating him again. "Jorrim Calthwaite is dead. He was found in the palace."

The words echoed like a nightmare song.

"No," Bard managed, speaking as distinctly as he could through the cloth. His lips tasted like salty blood. "He's alive."

"Tell them now, word for word, with no additions, or we'll kill you. As a traitor, you deserve worse."

Bard's brow furrowed as he looked at Belik. Suddenly, he realized that he wasn't afraid of death, if it meant he could help those he loved. He'd faced death before. After all his worry, almost every terrible thing he feared had happened. Yet here he was, still breathing, still defending his friends. Not terrified anymore. Just... a little afraid.

If he refused to tell the lie that Jori was killed, then the Tanyu would kill him instead. But if he gave the message, they might keep him alive. Kiria might already know that Bard was taken, and would know that the information was coerced.

She wouldn't give up hope even if she believed the message. She'd had plenty of chances to do that, and had chosen to continue.

Another moment meant another opportunity for freedom, for Jori's ridiculous heroics to mean something.

May it rain hope always.

The slice of sun sank below the horizon.

Bard set his jaw, a hard lump forming in his throat, and nodded.

66

FIRIAN

THE ROOM WAS EMPTY.

Firian's mind spun. He hadn't heard Belik leave, but he had been stowing the lookout Zhufal so maybe that masked the sound. His gaze flicked to the dying light. Kiria and her army were fighting now, and he had minutes before the Sentries lifted to give him access to Master Belik.

He didn't need to know exactly where Belik was. All he needed was proximity. He'd never tested the range of his ability, only that it worked when the targets were close. Belik had to be close by, probably in the direction of the Main, unless he had a good reason to go somewhere else. He would walk the paths Chetana took, probably without realizing it.

He turned on his heel and returned to the bedroom where Zhufal lay unconscious. There was no time to go searching for Belik, and the more Firian moved, the more risk there was he would be discovered. His body tensed with the familiar longing for a fight. That would be so much easier than what he actually had to do.

Silently, he shut the door behind him. His feet sank into the plush carpets, untouched by the fire. The feeling stirred a dim memory of being with Kiria. He couldn't remember what they were doing, but the memory was good. He burrowed into the feeling, leaning into the sensation of being seen, comfortable, enough. The memory turned inexplicably into a single moment at the party the night before, of her smiling. It was no more than a flash, her hair floating around her in a dance, a huge grin radiating her joy. Despite her scars, despite the danger, despite everything. Defiant joy.

His chest filled with tenderness. A new, brilliant pain. Her story would continue. He would make it so. His story, on the other hand, balanced on this knife's point, this single moment. Past it, he saw nothing.

Purpose flowed through him like air, like blood. Fortifying. He could break off the net of pain that hovered over his mind.

He stood in the center of the room, drawing strength for the task.

The light dimmed like an extinguished candle. It was time.

Skipping the tentative prodding, he dove straight in, hurling himself against the Sentry barrier. His hand flew to his mouth to stop a scream as he stumbled back a step. With effort, he righted himself. A violent shudder didn't soothe the searing pain in his head. The room pooled with black spots.

Firian sat on the edge of the bed. A human was creating this, so it had to be breakable. He gritted his teeth and tried again.

The shock of pain stole his breath. His whole being recoiled from it, like a hand jerking back from hot metal. His chest rose and fell with frustration. This was just like what happened in Belik's cell. It was probably the same poor Sentry, recaptured after Firian helped him escape. What more could he try?

His eyes rose to the window. Seconds slipped away. If he broke through the Sentry, he still might have to get closer to Belik for it to work. He had no time to lose.

He flung himself against the barrier. Again and again. He tried it in motion, lying down, slowly, quickly. He tried bringing the Unreal to him instead of going to it. He tried bleeding ordinary thoughts into the region of the Talent until they melded like dreams. He tried testing his endurance against the pain as long as he could, until he felt blood vessels bursting and skin melting away from the coke-hot heat. He was sand and the Sentry was a furnace turning him to liquid nothing.

He opened his streaming eyes on the bed, curled on his side, covered head to foot in sweat, nausea blurring his perception. His body, inside and outside, throbbed with overexertion, like torn muscles. He pressed one hand into the soft blankets and eased himself up. The room spun and he choked back the urge to vomit on the floor.

After one steadying breath, he tried again. Again, the impossibly strong force flung him down like a child's toy.

A shadow crept by the toe of his black boot as a stream of cold sweat ran from his neck down his back. He raised his face to the window. That split-second image of incandescent joy faded. Ten minutes had come and gone. He was too late.

67

KIRIA

Kiria's whole body was in pain, and she hadn't even fought yet. The helmet cut off her peripheral vision as Chetana and several other guards ushered Kiria away from the center of the army. There was a spot where she could watch and command, they said.

The center of the army felt safer, somehow, than this movement toward exposure.

Already, the buffer between her and the gate had thinned. She could barely think. All was motion. Battle sounded more glorious than this in stories. She hadn't believed the shiny veneer, but she hadn't understood the truth either. She wasn't a Keeper; she was a girl surrounded by jostling elbows and sharp blades. Moving feet had wakened choking dust that clogged her throat and dimmed her vision. Desperately, she dragged her cause back to mind, holding it in cupped hands like a bird in a storm. *Justice. My family. My friends.* The only part that made sense were the faces of the people she loved. She could fight for them, and nothing else.

The brunt of the attack would come from the front, and they expected Belik to send Tanyu to try to surround them. That was the reason Kiria and Bard had reserved some of the few Tanyu on their side to watch the rear of the army. But even in the center, screams reached her, the chaos of battle, the great surges forward, the madness of blood.

She needed to check for Bard one more time.

Guards surrounded her so closely she felt squashed between them. She gripped her sword and closed her eyes. It took her maddening seconds to get any sense of him. A cool wash of relief swept over her. Now, she realized the fear she'd bottled that he'd been killed. Other fears too, but she didn't open the bottle.

"Bard!"

They were nowhere together, suspended in a blank space, feet grounded only by will. Her elation faded when she saw Bard's expression. Devastation and fear pinched his black eyes.

Her flesh crawled. She didn't know what she feared most.

"Jorrim Calthwaite is dead. He was found in the palace."

Her breath was stolen from her chest. Her mouth and nostrils opened wide, but her gasps brought in no air. Her mind converged on one barely articulated word. No. *No no no. No!*

The last of her air expelled in a whispered scream. "No!"

Bard gave an odd quirk of his brow before he disappeared. Strange. On most people, it would be a casual apology. But not here. She grasped that tiny detail as if it held truth itself.

She couldn't lose Jori. She couldn't.

Did Bard mean he wasn't dead? The hope was like grasping a vein-thin root to stop from falling. But any hope was better than none. She would grasp at anything.

She opened her eyes. Chetana and the guards around her pressed even closer than before as they neared the edge of the army. She was almost thankful, since her legs barely kept her upright. Something was different, though, in the mass of bodies around her. *You have to care. Don't give up. There's life on the other side. You can think about Jori later.*

Jorrim Calthwaite.

That was what Bard had called him. She frowned, her whole face tight. Her mind moved sluggishly. It kept snagging on the news. *Jorrim Calthwaite is dead.*

Bard wouldn't call him Jorrim. Hardly anyone called him that. A new sliver of hope cautiously reared up.

Exclamations cut through her thoughts. She looked up. The bodies around her faced the wrong direction, all looking behind her. Thick horror coated her as she turned.

From the tree line came a new force. It wasn't a few Tanyu—frightening enough—but a new army. Not one of theirs, it sported a blue and black gonfalon. More were coming through the trees, but the mass of people looked huge, large enough to completely surround them. *But all of Belik's allies have come already*, she thought stupidly.

Obviously, he had more.

The new force quickly arranged themselves, shouting orders, as though surprised to see the conflict already underway.

She would have to fight.

Reckless rage surged through her and she screamed an inarticulate battle cry. It ripped through her chest and lashed her throat, drowning her fear. *Bring everything you have, you bastard, you murderer!* The Unreal seemed to merge with the Real, as though she could rise into the air like Chetana in dreams and rout entire armies, leaving nothing but scorched earth and a legend of vengeance.

Before her mind buzzed to blankness and battle fury, she reached for the Tanyu who were their allies to come and help. In her inexperience, she couldn't muster contact fast enough, but she shouted orders into the emptiness where they all waited to hear from her. Maybe they would hear.

Her feet started to move as the charge began. A slow dream with dark tree shadows.

Dark.

The bloody sky had no sun.

Her army just had to hold out a little longer. Firian had his window to kill Belik. He could do it with a thought. Without Belik driving the Tanyu, they could find victory. She sent up a prayer with no words. If Firian didn't succeed, it would be up to Royce and the others.

If Bard was right, then Royce, Viktor, and the other guards were gone too. Firian was their best chance.

Jorrim.

Pieces fell together. Bard's silence and then *Jorrim*. He'd been taken, told to say it that way. Did that mean Jori wasn't dead? Did that mean *Belik* wasn't dead?

Bard taken.

Jori alive.

Belik alive.

Then where was Firian?

The scraps of her thought fell away like shredded paper as the first wave of the new army collided against them.

68

FIRIAN

It wasn't in Firian to give up. Every nerve in his body burned, and the sun had sunk below the horizon, and the Sentry blocked his access to the Unreal as surely as a stone wall prevented someone from walking through it. But he stood up, shakily, to his feet. He flexed his fingers and bounced on either leg, trying to regain a sense of strength and balance. Killing Belik this way had only been the initial plan. It wasn't the only one that might work.

Zhufal stirred. His eyes opened, meeting Firian's. He didn't try to cry out.

In a second, Firian had crouched beside him and yanked down the gag. "Where did he go?"

Indecision warred in the man's features, though he remained composed. "The Main."

"How many are with him?"

"I don't know."

"Guess," Firian snarled.

"It's not a good place to strike. Most of us are there."

Of course Belik had made the Main a war zone. He could oversee more people from there. Then Zhufal's wording struck him. *Not a good place to strike.* This Tanyu wanted Firian to succeed.

"Why didn't you come before?" he demanded in a whisper, still clutching the gag around the man's neck.

"I couldn't." The simple response carried the weight of Belik's cruelty.

The Master's lesson came back to him. *Fear is the fastest way to power.* He'd been talking about nightmares, fear campaigns, debilitating an enemy, but its application extended far beyond that, it seemed.

"Will he stay in the Main?"

"Probably. Until this is over. I don't know his plans," he added hastily.

Firian replaced the gag. Would others side with him if they had the chance? It was a mildly encouraging thought. "I have to keep you here," he said.

The Tanyu's expression was impassive. He'd expected no less. Once the man was secured, far from anything that could help him escape, Firian knocked him out again to prevent him from contacting anyone and crept back out into the hall. His head pounded from his attempts to dislodge the Sentry, his vision narrowing and expanding. Sweat was starting to dry on his skin and clothes. He blinked a few times, then squatted and peered around the corner.

Belik would have noticed the absence of his guard. There was a good chance he knew Firian was in the palace. He had to assume they were looking for him. If that were the case, there would be several Tanyu close by, since they would search the adjacent rooms first. He exhaled an incredulous breath. How had they missed him in the guestroom? He had been vulnerable during those grueling minutes, and yet no one came. Gore, he was lucky.

69

JORI

Royce's grip on Jori's arm was a vise. The hold suggested Jori was a wild animal that would bolt at the first opportunity. But he had no desire to bolt at the moment. He fought to catch his breath as he crouched with the guard among garbage. His boots half-slid over nameless foodstuffs ground into the floor, peels and gristle and slimy pits.

Jori's frantic thoughts circled around the smell like a bird of prey. Thala was usually the servant who took care of the trash in the lower kitchen. He kissed her once. Had she been killed in the first attack too? Shame prickled across his skin like insect legs. He hadn't thought of her one time since the palace burned. His mind had been too full of Atty. But more than his brother had lost their lives.

Like Viktor.

After sprinting out of the dining room, Jori had barely caught Bard's eye before careening around a corner. He flung himself with the desperation of someone jumping from a height without looking. There would be no Tanyu because there *could* be no Tanyu.

He was fast, fast enough to beat Bard if they raced on the beach. Royce's daughter, Adelisa too.

Run, Bard! In the split second that he actually saw him, he took in the gag, the binds, and unfettered legs. Bard could run too.

Jori dove down a side stairwell.

Running footsteps followed. *Chuck chuck chuck* tripping down the stairs after him. He didn't look to see who it was. Many people. At least three.

Jori skidded to a halt. This wasn't a dead end, was it? There were rarely dead ends. Panic fritzed his mind and kept his eyes from focusing. They skipped like stones over water.

He turned. Royce and Viktor and the other guard and two Tanyu. No Bard, of course, but his mind had trouble grappling with what he saw.

The nameless Kingdom guard went down first, neck snapped as the Tanyu leapt up, more a predator than a person. The Tanyu landed on his feet. Reality blurred.

Royce and Viktor whirled on the two attackers. "Go!" shouted Royce.

Jori went, a destination finally locking into place. Trash heap. It fed into several areas below the main floor. He wouldn't be trapped. He kicked in the locked cupboard and lunged inside, tripping and bracing himself on his hand. He'd forgotten the short drop.

Through the opening, he saw the armored backs of his guards. Two Tanyu in black faced them.

"I'll cover you," said Royce.

"You go," Viktor insisted.

They didn't argue. Royce wedged his big body through the cabinet door after Jori, keeping his sword pointed at the entrance. His bulk blocked out all light. As it spilled back into the space, there was a lightning-fast movement of feet and steel outside. A strangled gasp and then a hand flopped into the opening, quickly kicked away.

Royce shoved Jori forward through the foul-smelling refuse. The force almost made him fall. Blindly, he ran.

That was a while ago, or a few minutes. It was impossible to tell. At first there were feet, but, after crouching and staying silent in an alcove for another long, stinking while, the sounds faded. It was so completely dark that no one could see them, even a Tanyu, and their special powers didn't work on him, he liked to think. At least they couldn't do that thing with their minds.

Viktor's death replayed in his thoughts. It was so short, so small. It didn't make sense. That's not how people died. They died after saying their last goodbye or a long, valiant fight. They didn't flop to the ground. They certainly didn't die because of *him*. He was Jori, the fun one, the unimportant one.

He smacked his lips quietly. His mouth was so dry he could hardly swallow. Royce's death grip on his arm tightened. He knew exactly where to squeeze, underneath his arm where there was no metal plate to shield him.

"My Kepron," he seethed into his ear, more warm breath than words, "don't run." The words were slow, severe.

Jori had to remember where he was, that this was a place to listen and not rebel against the wrong people. He almost apologized, but the words stuck in his throat. He wasn't sorry for running. He was more than sorry for the other two guards. Those words would ring empty. Instead he looked at Royce, or where Royce must be in this darkness.

They had to get to light. Jori was sick of darkness, and wasn't it more dangerous to stay put in the pitch black? Who knew if a Tanyu was lurking somewhere? They wore black, after all.

"Light," he croaked.

The image of Viktor's hand made Jori lightheaded. A person couldn't drop like that. It didn't make sense, not after a complex life. The hand turned into the blood-soaked blankets around Atty's ashen face. It could happen to anyone. It could happen to *him*.

He swallowed back bile. The sour garbage smell wasn't helping. He followed Royce without resisting as he guided him forward. "Left," Jori managed in a hoarse voice. They had to get to the Main. That was his goal, and the place they were taking Bard. Whatever happened, he needed to be in the right place when... when this was over, he supposed. Kiria would want him to.

His life had narrowed to a few things: Bard, Kiria, and the intrusive images of Belik's hulking form dominating the Main (imaginary) and Viktor's hand (real).

"What's to the left?"

"The general's office."

70

BELIK

Belik looked at Firian's roommate, black eye purpling, his only useful hand clenched in his lap. Red seeped through the cloth covering his nose and mouth. After Belik tried to kill him the first time—*had* killed him, but he'd clung to life somehow—he hadn't used the Second Level to kill anyone else. That exertion of his power dulled his wits, made him weak. But he would try it again on Bard once this was over.

He'd misread this boy. He had more iron in him than Belik expected. Hopefully he would fight back, then the others would see that Belik hadn't failed to kill a young boy who by rights should be a Learner, but a worthier adversary.

When Bard opened his eyes, the Unreal flooded back, pure as oxygen. Someone must have killed his Sentry. About time.

In a flash, Belik searched for Firian. Nothing but static. He was still safe.

He was too late to check that Bard had sent the correct message to Kiria, though, so he looked at Shiro for confirmation. He nodded.

"He told the princess and you told the Tanyu in the underground storeroom?" he clarified.

"Yes," Shiro confirmed.

Bard gaped, wide-eyed. Well, one eye was swelling, but the other turned perfectly round. Belik smothered a smirk. *Fight back. Show them you're made of something besides your mother's dinner rolls.* "Yes, we know," he goaded. "Let me be clear. I'm not worried about winning the war. We know almost everything about your plan. And I am the Tanyuin Head." He drew out each word. "My allies will never stop coming."

Tanyu embedded in cities and fortresses all across the continent were at his disposal, like Lord Ruler Thraddock was at Firian's. A simple command, and most of them would force their town to mobilize. One city from the Phlaxtin border was due about now, in fact.

Belik had waited for the princess' army to gather, to feel strong. There were at least two advantages to that: better intelligence and greater opportunity for surprise.

So far, the Sentries had been the only unexpected element, and that rankled. But it was temporary. For now, he could filter his commands through Shiro, who had championed him from the first moment he defied Firian's decision to leave the Kingdom alone. He was young and strong and held a grudge. It didn't matter that everyone knew Firian hadn't meant to kill Rian. Belik threw it in Shiro's face whenever he could. Hatred like that was so useful when harnessed.

It didn't matter that Belik had thought Rian was an idiot who deserved what happened. When survivors told Belik the story, most included that Firian had shouted for the Tanyu to get behind him. Rian didn't. Power like Firian's wasn't something to underestimate.

Enough pining over lost opportunities. He lowered his glasses and picked at the inside of his eye before issuing a few new orders, leaving Bard to stew in worry.

Finally, he returned his attention to his captive. "Take his mask off."

Shiro untied the cloth around Bard's face.

A shift in the quality of sound caught Belik's attention. Actually, the lack of sound. There were fewer grunts and groans and cries from the Tanyu seated around him like an enormous, blind audience. Fights had ceased or been won. A good sign.

Bard gasped and spit. Dark red streaks painted his face. Someone had broken his nose.

"We know the prince is here," Belik said, leaning forward. "He's probably dead. And we know Firian is here. Isn't he?" It wasn't a question. The moment the Sentries blocked his access to the Unreal, he knew, even before his lookout had disappeared from the hall. "Where?"

Bard's stained throat bobbed. His eyes darted to the window where the sunless sky darkened. "He's... He's with Kiria. Hidden in the army." His Endrian voice sounded thick and nasally.

That wouldn't be the worst place for Firian to be, since they were so intent on keeping their one royal alive. But his Talents wouldn't be best served there. He'd carve through armies, but his unique ability couldn't help unless he planned to explode and take everyone with him. No. He couldn't risk his princess getting hurt. Evidence and common sense would say Firian was in the palace, hunting down Belik. Judging from Firian's anger when they'd last met, he'd insist on it.

Before he could speak again, a Sentry electrified his senses. Again, the suffocating feeling. How many Sentries did they have? He barked an expletive. "If you didn't understand before, I don't need you. It will be easier to find him when he's weakened by your death."

Composing himself, he waved a hand for everyone to stand down, not to hurt Bard. Yet.

"We'll keep going until we get to our targets," he continued, keeping his voice more even, "but you can save a lot of people by telling me the truth." He readjusted his glasses. "This war doesn't have to go on. I know we're both tired of it and would prefer less bloodshed."

Bard just gazed back, steadfast.

"Firian abandoned you. He doesn't do what you want. Isn't that why you left the Academy? And now you're protecting him? Why?" Belik felt his blood rise as he laid out the arguments. Based on his observation, this was the way Bard thought, so why didn't he respond? "I'll ask you one more time," he said, "where is Firian?"

Blood ran down over Bard's chin, and his lip curled—barely perceptibly—in defiance.

71

BARD

BARD'S EYES streamed from the pain of his broken nose. A cold breeze flowed through the blank windows. The feeling on his skin was like the drafts that snuck through slatted boards back home.

During the party, Jac kept telling other people that Bard was his brother. He overheard him doing it twice. Bard had been trapped on the wrong side of the first conflict between the Tanyu and Enderin's ally, the Western Kingdom, but now he had put it right.

He was where he belonged. If everything he'd done had led him here, it was all right.

Trying to stay calm, he flashed through his options. Physically, he had no chance here. He scanned the space behind Belik. Where was Firian? The room was blurry through his tears.

At least Belik thought that the Tanyu in the underground room were under control. The problem was, they could be. Bard's plan had been to neutralize some of Belik's force in a secure location before the Tanyu on their side left the room and joined the fray. Not as many casualties and more chance of success. That was what he'd thought at the time. Hopefully the ruse was still working.

But now Bard's resources had worn thin. He could offer time—maybe minutes, unless they chose to interrogate him—and perhaps one real message to Kiria or one of the others. To get off the message, he'd need to distract Shiro or, better, get him out of the room. He acted like the only one of Belik's followers who had access to the Unreal. To buy time, Bard would keep Belik talking, focused on him.

You can save a lot of people by telling me the truth. If only that were true. The image of Jori running down the hall threatened to encroach on his new calm.

"This isn't what the Tanyu are supposed to be," he said.

"That isn't an answer."

A shadow shifted behind Bard, maybe Master Nedi. He didn't turn to look. He couldn't lose his nerve. They wouldn't snap his neck, right? Belik wanted to restore his reputation in front of his followers. And he couldn't do that until the Sentry was off him and he could do... whatever it was that had left Bard crumpled in a heap on the carpet. Belik was patient. He could wait for it.

This revelation bolstered Bard. He sat a little straighter. "I know it isn't."

Belik arched a brow.

"Corso fought *for* the Kingdom. He didn't try to take it over, yeah?" He tried to speak slowly, but the words spilled out as though a bottle had been uncorked. He ran through all the games he'd played as a child, the stories he'd heard at the Academy that made him proud to have the Talent. "Naedra defended it against enemies. They were heroes in the Lantern Rebellion. They prevented the rout of the Chrysï. Even Anewa stopped an ambush single-handed. Tanyu are defenders, not attackers."

Shockingly, Belik didn't interrupt, his expression perched between furious and bemused.

Bard hadn't thought he would get this far. "We were never meant to murder and conquer and... you know, control everything."

"You think that's what's happening?" Belik asked, his tone low and flat. "I saw the Tanyu disrespected and I'm not afraid to demand that respect. You ran. So when you say *we* shouldn't control our own gory property, you can leave yourself out of it." Belik's gaze dipped to Bard's Master ring as though he wanted to rip it off. "That's enough. Tell me or we're done with you. Where is Firian?"

Above Belik's left shoulder, a slice of a dark profile disappeared—almost a black spot in the vision or a shadow in the darkening space. It was too high to be expected, in an opening above a large side door. Bard might have missed it, except that he had stared at that profile for nights on end, chewing the seeds Viktor had given him in an effort to stay focused and awake.

Jori.

72

BELIK

BELIK DIDN'T NAME the cat he saw every week in the library, even after it started following him home. Being a two-person household, they had extra food, and his father often ate at the barracks, so Belik began feeding the creature. It stayed with him then, followed him everywhere, the perfect quiet companion. After long days of studying and pre-military training, he'd read with the cat on his chest, running calloused fingers through its soft fur.

It happened the day before Belik turned thirteen. A stray dog killed his cat.

He killed the dog.

That should have been it. Simple arithmetic. But rage and bitter sadness ate at him like acid. When his invitation to join the Academy came a few weeks later, he jumped at the chance to leave everything behind.

He had a feeling he was looking at Firian's cat.

Regret thrilled through Belik, a feeling all too familiar. This boy, Bard, could have been a Tanyu after all, his size and his hand notwithstanding. Belik considered his own bad leg.

"I'll tell you where he is if you call off the fighting," Bard said. "It's getting dark. Your people will..." He caught his breath, looked at the window looking out toward the sea. "Your people will just kill each other in the dark."

The balls on this kid. Unfortunately, he was right. Outright battle wasn't the best option now that the autumn sun had plunged the landscape in darkness. Subtler methods would achieve their aims better. "You're in no position to make demands." If he could reach the Unreal, he'd tell the others privately to contact the army, but that wasn't an option. "I know you have a *katah* with Firian. Find him."

"Lift the Sentry."

Either he liked Bard Tanery or he hated him. Lifting the Sentry meant giving

Firian power. But... if the royals insisted on blocking Belik's own mind with a Sentry, what did he have to fear?

"You'll have seconds," Belik said, jutting his chin at Shiro. "It's getting dark," he added. He would catch his meaning. *Stop the fighting. For now.*

Shiro closed his eyes to inform the lone Sentry to halt. They had sent him out to sea with another Tanyu to relay messages. Firian's Sentry would be much harder to track in the vast Kheltor and would be out of range for Firian's killing ability.

Belik tapped against the wall of his own mental barrier. Still intact. Firian couldn't reach him mentally or bodily.

Commanding the armies to stall would take a few extra messages than the one to pause Firian's Sentry. To do it, Shiro descended the steps and found an empty chair.

After a moment of silence, several of the other Tanyu stood from their seats, a hint of stiffness to their limbs. Bard's purple, swollen eyes caught the movement.

"How will I know when...?"

Belik didn't answer. If Bard had a *katah* with Firian, then he'd know without prompting. The presence of the other mind would present itself, not loudly, but clearly, like a breeze.

Bard blinked slowly a few times, growing more abstracted and looking less fearful. It was strange having no sense of what went on in Bard's mind. Unsettling. Belik closed one hand in a fist at his side. Finally, Bard's focus narrowed on Belik again.

"You called off the fighting, yeah?" His voice, less nasally with blood now, had grown small.

"It's black outside," Belik answered.

Bard worried his lower lip. This kind of hesitation usually meant a truthful answer. He didn't want to betray Firian. Belik hadn't wanted to lose the boy either, but Firian had betrayed them all first by choosing the princess over the Tanyu.

After a few more seconds of struggle, Bard released a breath. "He's... coming here. He's close to the east wall now, outside. Not the wall around the grounds, but here, the palace." He flicked his gaze at the wall he described. The broken window acted as an enormous entrance. Though guarded, it seemed a wider opening than before.

Here. Belik heaved himself to stand. "Look into it," he told Nedi. "Bring others with you. Go. Now!"

They obeyed.

Belik limped down the steps. "Bring him." Bard's Tanyuin guard hoisted him to his feet and pushed him after Belik. "Set up a room for dreams elsewhere. Guards where necessary. The rest can go back to their quarters." After a moment, he added, "Remember, Firian has a Sentry, so if you see him, engage."

The Tanyu all around the room began to end their fights and head out.

Shiro approached at the foot of the stairs. "It's done." The fighting had stopped for the night.

Behind him, Bard hung his head.

73

FIRIAN

"Go to the north side of the Main. Room on the north side." Bard's words were so fast they blurred together.

A question had half-formed on Firian's lips before the Sentry slammed back into place. He bit back a cry of pain.

The Sentry had faltered, or else Belik ordered that it be lifted for a moment. Why?

To find him. That had to be the only answer, or else Bard wouldn't have been there, giving him his desperate message. And Bard would only have known exactly when the Sentry would lift if he was with Master Belik.

That small taste of freedom, of success, shocked him as much as jumping in the Apothelin. He started running. He was outside and heading toward the Main from the west, staying close to the palace. From his vantage point, he could see gardens, Amiran Academy, and ocean. This was almost the same path he'd taken a lifetime ago with Kiria and Atty and Jori, when he'd broken them into the Main through a window.

Room on the north side. As he pictured it, its dimensions took shape. Kiria had been there. Firian dimly remembered seeing a door on the far side of the room when he'd gone to the Main himself.

Was that where Belik was holding Bard? He refused to consider the other reason Bard's message had been so brief. No, Belik could use Bard to find Firian. He wouldn't destroy an asset like that while he still needed him.

North side... north side...

The only light filtered up from the Amiran lanterns. Firian pushed aside branches as he moved with all the speed and secrecy he could muster.

As he got closer to the north side of the Main, he craned his neck to see entrances. Were there any unguarded openings? Considering the skeletal jaws of the blown-out windows, he knew they must be watched. The mourning cloth around his hand would let him enter without cutting himself, but it was too risky.

When he stilled, the sounds of people, quiet but distinct, flowed from inside. Tanyu. The sound reminded him of a home he could never go back to, one that never existed the way he thought it did.

If Belik and Bard were in the north room, then he would find a way to get there. He may have missed his window of time to kill Belik with the Second Level, but that didn't mean Firian wasn't physically dangerous. Bard wouldn't have led him there if it were a trap, or if there were too many Tanyu faithful to Belik. He could do this.

He prodded at the Sentry like an open wound, just checking, before curling his lip with frustration and surveying the wall that separated him from the place Bard said to go. It looked solid, no exterior entrances. But high up there were a couple openings, barely big enough to be called windows. More like embrasures. He could barely make them out in the dark.

Brushing spiderwebs off his sleeves, he measured the distance with his eyes. Too high to jump. Very difficult to climb. Even if he got up there, he could find the space was too narrow for him to fit through. The poor light and angle of the rough stone made judging their width almost impossible. He sucked his teeth. Belik was practically within arm's length, but a wall and a Sentry kept Firian from victory. Bard's life was on the line. If he didn't find a way in, then the Western Kingdom could cease to exist as he'd known it all his life. Kiria wouldn't find justice for her slain family, and would likely meet death herself.

Firian's cheeks flamed with heat. A wall and a Sentry.

Setting his jaw, he bent down under the cover of foliage and broke off a few thick stems from the bushes. They cracked as he split them off and rubbed the sticky sap on his hands. He avoided the mourning cloth, daubing his fingertips on that hand. Once done, he took one last look behind him. No one had spotted him. He wore Academy black, but his famous face would give him away even at a distance. Also, scaling the palace wall just might rouse suspicion, he thought bitterly. He had to be fast.

He inhaled and jumped. Most of the stones had worn smooth with age and angled gently outward, not up to create handholds. He kicked his boots into the grooves between stones and pulled himself up by his sticky fingertips. By the second handhold, the sap was already growing grainy and slippery with dirt. He reached as high as he could. Fewer handholds, less likely to fall.

He clung more than two stories off the ground when his hand slipped. His stomach plummeted. Pain shot through Firian's wrist and shoulder as he gripped with his other hand that had made it through the opening and grasped the other side. His legs nearly seized as they lifted him high enough to regain his hold. The toe of his boot slid free, wavered in sickening midair above the drop. His heart pounded fast, too fast, heavy and thick in his chest. He forced air into his lungs and reached with his other hand. Boots found footing. His muscles spasmed from the strain as he pulled himself up.

It was dark. Shadowy recesses pooled below in what looked like an antechamber, with several doors leading to other places in the palace. One set of double doors was particularly magnificent. Above them was another small opening into a lighted room. The Main, then.

No one was here. Did Bard try to hide him from a search party? Possible, but that didn't feel right.

Firian eased himself through the embrasure, a tight fit, and no way down but to jump.

Something moved in the darkness. A door adjacent to the fancy double doors slowly opened. A blond Kingdom soldier stepped inside. His armor gleamed dully in the gloom, and so did his sword, which he held in front of him as he scanned the small room. Then he looked up. Immediately battle ready, the man widened his stance and brandished his weapon.

"It's me," Firian mouthed, trying to maneuver so his face was more visible. Hopefully the soldier would know him. Even with so little light, Firian saw the moment the soldier recognized him. He lowered his weapon, though he didn't sheath it.

Firian lowered himself down from the little window, and then jumped to the floor.

"Master Kess?" the soldier whispered.

Firian nodded.

The soldier's face grew taut. "Master Belik is still alive. He has Bard. I was part of the team that was supposed to eliminate Belik if he wasn't dead by now, but that's become more difficult..."

For both of us. "My mind is blocked," Firian explained, ignoring the sting of criticism. Belik was supposed to be dead already. "Where is Belik now?"

"He just left the Main, but many of the Tanyu are still here." He cast his eyes toward the darkened door.

Just left? That didn't make any sense. Why would Bard lead him here then? "How many are with him? Did he say where he was going?"

"Only three Tanyu, and Bard."

Firian had handled four on his own before. But they hadn't been Tanyu. Especially not Tanyu he knew personally. Still, it would be easier to take care of Belik when he only had a handful of Tanyu around him instead of a room full of them.

Someone peeked around the open door to the next room. His wide gray eyes took in the situation—Firian talking to the soldier—and he straightened, eyebrows rising. It was Jori Calthwaite.

Firian's mouth opened in surprise and relief.

"The other guards with me didn't make it," the soldier explained. "I have to protect the Kepron first."

"Thought I heard whispering," said Jori.

"Then we'd better stop," said Firian. His mind whirled with a plan. The meaning of Bard's message wasn't perfectly clear, but it must have included helping Jori. Belik just left the Main. He had to be going to a small, less guarded location. The perfect chance for Firian to finally end this and restore Kiria's throne. But now he had Jori to look after as well.

The warmth of rightness settled in his chest as he looked at the others. This wasn't what he'd expected, but Jori was safer with him than with anyone else. The blond soldier looked capable, so he could help deal with any threats along the way.

It was time to be a bodyguard again.

74

KIRIA

Kiria unclasped her breastplate with shaking fingers. A single candle lit her tent, hiding the phantom shadows of the guards that stood in a tight ring outside.

She'd barely begun to fight, feeling the meagerness of her training, when the soldiers around her spotted an opening to spirit her away and fought to get her clear of the melee. The escape was grueling. Enemy soldiers by twos and threes kept appearing to track down their little group. Chetana felled several of them. Protect the Keeper—that was their duty. And they did it. She helped where she could, but her ability didn't stack up to the meanest trained soldier. So many attackers got close, though, spraying her with their blood, before full darkness settled and the battle paused.

Soldiers had put up these small tents while Kiria, Chetana, and the remaining leaders of her army met to talk about the day. She'd contributed, but each word was an effort. They all agreed that they couldn't sustain the same losses two days in a row.

She stacked the breastplate near the small cot, almost losing her grip on it as she set it down. Next, the arm and leg braces, each with buckles. This would be far easier to do with her serving girls, but they were away from here, out of reach of the fighting. Boots, sword belt, pants, leather jerkin, underclothes. Grime and sweat smeared her skin underneath.

She had to get clean, had to wash the blood and noise from her mind. A pitcher of water sat on the floor. It sloshed as she lifted it up and poured it over her head. With the breeze slicing through the tent, the water felt freezing cold. Moments ago, she had been hot in the armor, unbearably hot. She scrubbed ruthlessly at her limp hair, frozen cheeks, and stinging eyes, trying to clear her head.

Both forces had ceased, but not before it was nightmare dark. At first light, the war would begin again.

After all that fury, she'd remained a spectator, protected from the main violence of the battle. It might have been worse to watch without being able to get close. She couldn't help the wounded or hurt the guilty or raise the dead. *Am I a coward?* She gave her face an extra hard scrub, avoiding her new scars. No, she wasn't a coward. They fought to protect her, and she had done what she could.

But her mind was in the palace.

She'd barely caught it. As the fighting began to lessen and messages were being passed back and forth, Bard had come to her again in the Unreal. Even now, it felt like a dream. How much was real? When she'd tried to contact him again to confirm, there was no answer.

"Jori and Belik are still alive," came his frantic voice.

"Where are you?"

No answer.

So she'd been right. Bard was captured and Jori wasn't dead.

Water trickled from the ends of her hair down her back. She let her Beauty fade with it. For the first time since the news, she allowed herself to feel relieved. She held her face in her hands and breathed. Hot tears mixed with the dirty water. She couldn't lose Jori. Her poor, ravaged Brithnem needed his enjoyment of life. *She* needed it.

With a sniff, she grabbed a new set of clothes. No nightdress tonight. She would try to rest, but then her forces needed to regroup, finalize their adjusted plan.

Belik was still alive, and had more allies than they thought.

Firian couldn't break the Sentry, then. She'd truly believed he could. Bard's message hadn't contained any information about him. Presumably, he was still alive, and still near the palace. Bard would have told her about Firian's death, and they both would have felt it.

She laid down gingerly, as though she were covered with bruises, which was only partially true. Right now, her insides felt more fragile than the outside. A knock against the fabric of the tent made her bolt upright, clinging to the thin blanket.

"A visitor," said one of the guards. Not Royce or Viktor, whom she'd come to trust. They were with Jori.

A visitor? "Who?"

"Princess Haved Ganesha."

Kiria jumped to her feet, untangling her ratty hair. "Haved? Here?" Her mind was too full to understand it. "Let her come in."

The tent flaps parted and Haved, clad in a red tunic, strode inside the little space. Kiria's eyelids fluttered with disbelief. Haved might as well have been a ghost.

"Sister," Haved began, her typically stoic expression soft with concern.

"Haved." Kiria gulped back a sob and pulled her into an embrace. Haved stiffened with surprise before holding her tightly, smoothing her tangled hair and rubbing her back. Kiria soaked up the soothing contact. Haved's warm presence was a miracle, or maybe a mirage that would fade once they let go. "What are you doing here?"

"Amrit insisted on your behalf to our father," she said, backing up to see Kiria's face. "He told him that we fight for our own, and that Atael was one of our own. He is in the Book of Names." Her expression clouded with grief, but she didn't pause. "Every day my brother requested an audience with him, and it was granted. Finally, my father agreed, but did not allow Amrit to go himself, only to send an army to assist you."

Kiria was dumbfounded. "An army?"

"Yes, they wait in the forest, ten thousand strong." Haved said it so simply, as though it didn't change everything.

Ten thousand! "I need to tell the others!" About to run out of the tent, she paused. "And you came." It was a question. What wasn't Haved telling her? She wasn't a fighter. It couldn't be as simple as the narrative she proposed. Amrit asked enough times for his father to listen? Kiria doubted it. As Haved had said, the king was like stone.

"Yes." She shut her lips tight after the word. There was more she didn't want to say.

Kiria wouldn't push her. Not after this. "Thank you," she said, "and thank Amrit for his petitions. This... I can't express how much this means."

"The royal Lines of Brithnem deserve the thrones," she replied. A stern kind of smile curved her lips. Kiria ached to return it, but couldn't manage it. Haved reached for Kiria's hand. "Tell your people we are here to help. With us, you will have victory."

And Kiria wanted to believe her.

75

BELIK

Shiro's green eyes filled with shock. "Master Belik," he said as they walked away from the Main.

"Yes?" he answered gruffly, glancing at Bard. Did he need the gag put on again? The Endrian's nose and lip had swollen purple. They could offer the gag as a tactic to encourage him to carry out any last commands Belik might have. They'd leave it off.

"Charäkhnem is here."

Belik's attention swiveled to Shiro. "What? Fighting?" Enktuya put a hand on the knife at her waist. He hadn't summoned Charäkhnem. It was too large and complicated. That kingdom's strongest Tanyu had disappeared after failing to deliver the Kepron. He must have known how furious Belik would be, and what horrible consequences he'd face.

"Not fighting yet," Shiro said, "but camped, for the Keepers."

Bard's good eye lightened with hope and he panted once before catching himself.

Belik glared at him and then stretched his jaw. "How many?"

"No one's counted. More than we have, until our other allies arrive."

So Kiria had more bodies to throw at the problem. At first light, their ground forces would be overwhelmed.

Why hadn't Belik chosen a successor, someone to ensure that the Tanyu could fight on, that his dream of a globally respected Tanyuin Academy wouldn't die with him? He knew why. He'd been holding out, waiting for Firian to come around, and then the day-to-day business of securing the city had pushed the thought out of his mind. How did this conflict manage to find all the chinks in his armor?

"We won't wait 'til morning," Belik concluded. "We'll finish this now." In a perfect world, he'd crush Kiria's rebellion and every one of her allies as he planned. Now, speed was of the essence. Time to end this posturing.

"Tell all the Tanyu not to sleep. We're ending this tonight. Targets are the royals first, Sentries second. Send them out, physical and Unreal, and let me know when it's done."

He should have done this a long time ago, but he had to be so gory proud. Sometimes it was better just to finish something and be done with it.

76

JORI

Royce offered Firian a leg up to see into the Main from the candle opening. He didn't take it. Tanyu, or at least that Tanyu, didn't need it.

"I could have done it," Jori repeated.

Royce just scowled at him, one finger to his lips. He hadn't forgiven Jori for bolting and jeopardizing their lives. Jori hadn't forgiven himself either, but Royce didn't need to keep reminding him with rueful looks.

Without a sound, Firian perched on the ledge and looked out. When he stopped moving, Jori's eyes couldn't track him anymore. His black outfit blended into the nighttime shadows above, despite the faint light coming in from the gap overlooking the Main. Impressive. Jori hated that he was impressed. But... damn.

Firian dropped back to the ground as gracefully as a cat. "You said it was full."

"The room, yeah," Jori whispered back. When he had peeked through the opening himself, the Main had swarmed with Tanyu, like one enormous session. Everyone wore black, sitting and standing, except Bard, whose face was all bloody. Jori hadn't gotten a good view of him when he'd run from the dining room. Bard's wrists were bound. Why would they bind his wrists when he had a hand that wouldn't move? The memory of their unnecessary cruelty prickled over his skin. He adjusted his cuffs under the forearm guards.

"There's hardly anyone in there now," Firian said.

"I wonder why," Royce said.

"Three," Firian clarified, staring past them to the general's office with its desk and books and instruments, as though he would find answers somewhere.

Jori was just as perplexed. "You can take three, can't you?" Judging from the way Firian leapt up into the opening above them, and the obvious muscles in his shoulders, that should be no problem for him.

Firian turned toward him, a grim smirk on his lips. He nodded.

Jori shrugged and held his hands out to his sides. *Why wait?*

"There could be more," Royce said.

"He's right," Firian said. "We need to—"

"What?" Jori cupped his hand around his ear, genuinely surprised and delighted. When Firian didn't take the bait, he lowered his hand and merely grinned at Royce, who looked gruff as always.

"We need to find Belik," Firian continued, a slight edge of annoyance coloring his voice. He closed and opened his palm, his demand obvious. Jori handed him his sword. "We won't have another chance like this again."

"Where did all the rest go?" Jori could hardly hear Royce's objection, they were all keeping their voices so low.

Firian's lips pressed into a line.

"Sleep?" Jori suggested.

The Tanyu shook his head, his blue-eyed gaze cutting to the side. "I think they're looking for you."

The room felt suddenly colder. Viktor's arm had just flopped there like it was nothing.

Firian's hand was on his shoulder, giving him a light shake. He didn't offer any words of comfort, but he looked into his eyes. The force of his gaze made Jori understand Kiria a little better. Firian was indomitable.

After a nod to Royce, who laid his hand on the hilt of his sword, Firian went through to the waiting area—Atty had stood right there waiting for his coronation—and opened the double doors into the Main.

Jori squinted against the light. Firian was right. Only three. The Tanyu froze when they saw who it was. Firian Kess, Jori Calthwaite, Royce the palace guard, in that order.

Sweat coated Jori's neck and forehead. A bead dripped into his eye. He blinked it away, hoping it didn't look like he was crying. That would ruin the image of the moment.

Firian raised one weaponless hand, but every eye in the room looked at him as though he had crashed through with a battering ram. "I'm back," he said calmly, "as the true Tanyuin Head. I'll protect anyone who helps me, but I'm going to finish this." The unspoken threat if they decided *not* to help vibrated through the air.

Jori held his breath.

77

KIRIA

Kiria got no rest. If she fell asleep, Tanyu would attack her in dreams.

So she stayed up, talking to her commanders about the next day, and what they were going to do about the situation at the palace. If Bard was still alive, he was under Belik's control. There was no way to contact Jori, but Kiria was confident he must still be alive since Belik wasn't gloating about killing him. Firian was missing, either dead or trying his best despite the Sentry with no success. Kiria didn't want to admit how much she had counted on Firian to come through. The situation at the palace was tenuous, to say the least.

With the Charäkhni army, Kiria felt much better about their chances outside the walls. It looked like it would be up to her and her allies to breach the defenses and force Belik to surrender.

She ran her fingers through her hair. It had long since dried but still felt grimy. She rolled her fingertips together.

"You should get some rest," said Lanthe, one of the Kingdom commanders, rolling up the square of paper where she'd drawn a makeshift map. Several of her fingernails were dark purple, a shocking contrast with her white-pale skin.

The bearded Charäkhni general eyed Kiria with the same concern. Haved had started at the table with them but had since gone to bed. Kiria didn't blame her.

"I'm fine." Kiria looked at the general. "You have doctors rotating through your camp, right?" Besides twitching and other obvious signs, she didn't know what a dream attack looked like from the outside. Chetana, seated beside her, didn't know either. They'd given their best guesses.

"They are all looking into the tents," the general responded. His embroidered military crest—a golden eagle—gleamed in the dim lantern light. "It has become late and I have heard no reports of attacks."

"None?"

Chetana met her look.

"No, Lady Kiria." The general pursed his bearded lips as though to suggest that keeping the doctors awake all night was a waste of resources.

It was impossible that Belik didn't know about Charäkhnem's arrival. Now Kiria's army outnumbered Belik's own. He wouldn't go to sleep and hope for the best the next morning. He would try to weaken them, intimidate them.

"Please check now," Kiria said, gesturing to a soldier standing near the general. The soldier wore his pointed helmet, even though they were inside. After a nod from the general, he tilted his head and went to do her bidding.

Kiria put the back of one finger against her lip—habit now—but the wound had sealed for good. She turned to Chetana. "What does it mean if Master Belik hasn't sent any Tanyu after the Charäkhni army? Is there any chance he doesn't know they're here? It's been hours..."

"None," Chetana confirmed. "He knows."

The Charäkhni general's expression grew more pinched. Perhaps he was finally realizing something was wrong.

"Everyone has to sleep," said Lanthe.

"Yes, but the Tanyu will overlap so they don't miss any time." She and Bard had discussed this. "What are they all doing?" she muttered. Belik had to see the Charäkhni force as a threat. There was no reason for him to leave them alone. Unless... Unless there was nothing for them to fight for in the morning.

Chetana seemed to come to the same realization. "He's sent them after you and the Keprons."

Cold fear gripped her. "He wants to end this tonight."

"What can we do?" asked the Charäkhni general, shifting as if he would jump out of his seat that instant.

"Can you find out who they've sent? How many?" asked Lanthe, eyeing Kiria and Chetana, the only non-Tanyu with the Talent. Master Makai and Defender Erron sat with them too, recently come from the underground storehouse that now kept several of Belik's warriors secretly contained, but Lanthe avoided their gazes.

"It's not that simple," Kiria said, her eyes straying to an empty seat where Tesni should have sat. She had been targeted first when Belik's Tanyu invaded the space, one of only two casualties there, but sorely missed.

"What if Master Belik were dead?" her commander persisted.

"Then we could claim a victory," Chetana said, "and all that would be left are a few vigilantes. But I don't know that we could do anything in time." As a grim quiet took the room, her gaze turned inward, that all-seeing stare that used to scare Kiria when she was a child.

"We have Tanyu here as well," said the Charäkhni general, as though Kiria's fears were unfounded, "and our troops wait to serve."

"But he thinks he must only kill *two* to destroy the royal Lines." Chetana raised her head. Rage kindled in her expression. "He does not need a war. He needs an assassination."

"Then why fight in the first place?" asked Lanthe, frowning. Her eyes ticked to the cuts and bruises almost everyone sported.

"To show his power." The skin of Chetana's nose wrinkled. "To let everyone know that he cannot be beaten."

"Which means that you scare him," Kiria added, gesturing toward the Charäkhni general. The edges of his eyes softened with pride.

"He's using all his force to search you out." It seemed like Chetana was speaking to herself now. "The order might be countermanded if he were dead."

The look on her face was so singular that Kiria couldn't help but stare. Nerves bubbled up inside her at her tone. Kiria realized she was clenching her teeth.

The Amir turned her cool gaze to her. "My Keeper," she said, "take the Sentry off Master Belik."

78

FIRIAN

Firian didn't wear his crown, but he felt the rightness of the place where he stood, as though he'd found a jut of land in a violent ocean.

After announcing his return, a charged silence surged through the empty expanse of the Main. The three remaining Tanyu stared at Firian as though he were a ghost. Jori stood behind him, a clear symbol of Firian's intention to restore the Keepers.

He scanned the corners, the ceiling. If these three refused to help him, he could stop them. But he didn't think he'd have to. None of the three reached for weapons at their waists or in their boots.

"Master Kess?" one said incredulously.

A soft thud drew his attention to the eastern windows. Master Nedi, with more agility than his big body suggested he had, swung himself through the window and landed beside one of the huge statues of the founders. More followed. One, two, three... six more.

Firian's blood raced. He'd worked with Nedi on Torith, commissioned him as head of the Torithian troops after Jovan died, but the Master always had a bloodthirsty streak. He told the prisoners on the slave ship he'd kill the children if they weren't quiet. But Firian would have said the same thing if Nedi hadn't. Despite the bite of Nedi's betrayal, Firian saw his own decisions reflected back at him.

"Master Nedi," he said in a low voice, gripping Jori's sword. The name was slow, conciliatory.

Ignoring him, the older Master pointed and five ran forward swift as bird shadows. One hung back and unslung something from his back. A bow.

The next few moments happened in a blur of movement and heartbeats.

"Down!" Firian told Jori, bending also to exchange the sword for unsheathed daggers. He'd brought two this time.

The archer was far. Too far? No time to think. He flung the first dagger at the archer, missing the throat but hitting center mass, sending the man's arrow wide. It zinged between Royce and Jori before clacking to the ground behind them.

As the five sprinted closer, one of the Tanyu already in the room grabbed the arm of one attacker, simultaneously tripping him. With Firian, then. The enemy Tanyu fought back, kicking the other in the knees and earning a cry of pain. Firian didn't see the rest except as a fast-moving whirl of limbs.

The other four, and Nedi, were almost on him.

Clearly experienced, the Tanyu in front held two small knives in her fists. She had a shock of wavy brown hair that the tie could hardly wrestle back.

Behind her were three others—two Masters and a Defender—peeling off to the sides. They were going to hem him in and probably attack Jori. Nedi took up the rear.

Firian's heart pounded, though he held perfectly still. Fighting Torithians was one thing. Fighting Tanyu was something else.

Two knives. Three around the sides. Nedi at the back.

He had to even the odds. Who was the easiest target? And why did the others in the room just stand there?

Tanyu respected power. He'd give them a reason to pick a side.

He flung the other dagger, though he hated to lose it. One Master, headed toward Royce, went down in a gasp of blood.

The sole Defender, a mustachioed man in his twenties, had the least experience. The Kingdom soldier, Royce, could try to fend him off, or distract him, at least, until Firian could get there.

Firian gestured behind him without looking. "One on your left!" he cried.

Taking the one on the right means I'm open to knives, the one in front and I'm surrounded.

He stared straight ahead, his lethal training battling against his desire not to kill Tanyu. He'd known this was inevitable. Sweat formed in the hollow of his throat. Without giving himself another second to think, he threw himself at the front attacker, sword-first.

She parried with her knives hard enough to jump to the side, roll, and spring up again. The time lost while she rolled, he slammed his boot onto her hand, pinning one knife. She snatched her fingers away when he sprang back to cover Jori and Royce, but he had one of her weapons now, along with the sword. With so many Tanyu now so close, this would be his last throw. He flicked the blade. The Master would dodge, but she'd already given away the side she favored, so he factored that in. Slight right.

He didn't wait to see if the knife hit its mark, instead jumping back toward Jori crouched on the ground. Beside him, Royce fought with strength but no finesse. It would be seconds before he went down.

Firian couldn't spare time to help Royce with the Master closing in on the right. Could he get them closer to each other?

A dagger stabbed the air just over Royce's shoulder as Firian hauled him backward by the collar, toward Jori. With his cloth-wrapped hand, he wrenched the dagger from the Defender's grasp when he tried the same move again. Hopefully that save would be enough to see Royce through the battle.

Holding the knife by the blade, Firian whirled to the Master on the right, arcing both sword and bludgeoning hilt toward him. No contact. Momentum sent him kicking wide, bracing for impact.

With a jolt, Firian's body stopped. The Master had grabbed his foot.

A shock of hot pain knifed into his side. In response, Firian sliced behind him with his sword, an untenable position. No balance. But he got the result. The brown-haired Master gasped and went down, just as the other Master twisted Firian's foot while swiping at the other. Firian hopped in time to stay upright, but the combination of the two Masters somehow managed to make him lose his grip on his sword. It rang and clattered across the floor.

"Oh!" Jori exclaimed as one attacker fell.

Down to a dagger and one foot planted on the ground, Firian ran through his options.

Disadvantages: No control over footwork. Vulnerable. Injured. Advantage: One opponent has no hands.

Leaping toward the Master, Firian brought his knees up, one foot to meet the other, knocking him off balance and breaking the hold on his ankle. When the Master didn't fall, they grappled for a few seconds. *Balance, practice, strength.* The rest was muscle memory. Normally, that would have been enough, but this was a Tanyuin Master, not a brute Torithian. A waver gave Firian an opening and he smashed the Master's ear with the hilt of the brown-haired Master's short knife, recovered in the fighting, finally sending him crashing down.

Jori, still cowering, let go of the Master's pant leg. He'd tried to trip him. Firian acknowledged his help with a nod.

Firian had no time to relax. Royce still dealt with the Defender, now farther away, and Master Nedi had reached them. He lifted a chair – they were close to the place where the haphazard rows began – and set it down hard over Jori's head. That would protect him for a few more seconds from an attack from above, the most likely angle. Using the seat to get extra height, Firian jumped from it onto the Defender before turning to Nedi. The Defender wasn't dead, but he stumbled, disoriented, and the fight against Royce no longer looked like a certainty played out in slow motion. He had a chance.

Nedi, though.

Throw him off balance. Firian ran closer to disrupt Nedi's sense of rhythm but he went suddenly lightheaded. The room rose and fell. Nedi had ducked at the last moment and scooped Firian up over his back.

Nedi wasn't going for him. He was going for Jori, the easier mark.

Panic spiked in Firian's chest. *There are many ways to kill a man.* Flailing his arms, head spinning, he caught hold of Nedi's hair as he fell, sending him off balance, neck craned back. But Firian's balance wavered too. Both fell.

Not on the ground. Not on the ground.

They scrambled to get up. Firian met Jori's fear-stricken eyes. His face was pale, his expression pleading. He expected Firian to save him, to put things right.

With a roar, Firian leapt up. But he didn't land upright. Nedi shoved him down. The Master was so much bigger that Firian couldn't keep his feet. His dagger swung harmlessly in the air as he fell, missing its mark wide.

Master Nedi whirled on Jori. *No no no.*

Firian flung himself forward, hurling the knife. It lodged into Nedi's back. The Master grunted and slowed. Grabbing Nedi's leg to propel himself closer to Jori, Firian spun to face Nedi, shielding the Kepron with his body. No thought, just action. His mind crashed against the Sentry as it dove toward the Second Level. He bit back a scream.

Blood spattered Jori's face. Above them stood Royce, sword in hand, his chest heaving with heavy breaths. Jori, disgusted and shocked, shied away from the growing red pool beneath Nedi's bleeding body.

Royce helped Jori to his feet. The Kepron's mouth kept moving, lips rubbing together as he stared at the motionless bodies on the ground. Most of them weren't breathing. Firian nodded at Royce and clapped a hand on Jori's shoulder to assure him it was all right.

Firian's lower back throbbed and stung. He didn't investigate the feeling. This was for Kiria, and if he were injured or dead by the end, it would still be worth it if he succeeded.

"Where's Belik?" he demanded of the only two Tanyu left standing.

"I'll show you," said one, leading the way. Firian had never seen him before. He was old enough to have been sent on mission before Firian arrived at the Academy.

A direction. Finally! For the first time since he'd left Kiria, he felt optimistic and alive.

"Where are the other Tanyu?" Firian asked, moving fast in case the injured Tanyu in the Main woke and pursued them.

"They're all looking for the Keepers, Master Kess," came the reply with a glance at Jori.

So Belik sent most of his loyal Tanyu to find them while leaving the ones whose loyalty he didn't trust. All for the best.

Once out of the partially burned double doors leading to the main hall, a stab of pain lanced just above his hip. He stalked forward, not breaking stride, with Royce and Jori following. He'd had more than his share of scars.

Now, he felt more like the true Tanyuin Head than he had in a long time.

The end of the hall was doused in shadow. Brown smoke stained the walls and lined broken windows. The decorations Firian had seen so many times before in Kiria's mind were mostly gone. Looted, like that tapestry he'd seen the Torithian carrying when he first escaped the palace grounds.

"He's close," said one of the Tanyu, jogging ahead.

Firian's breath came more quickly. The Sentry still blocked his mind, and the stab wound created a new area of weakness.

"How can we tell which ones are with us?" Royce whispered loudly. His square jaw was set as hard as Belik's. Spots of blood dotted his pale skin and hair but his gaze was level.

"Just stay by him"—he nodded at Jori—"and follow my lead."

One blond eyebrow arched upward a fraction.

The Tanyu who had jogged ahead returned. "If your goal is to get to Master Belik, there are too many other Tanyu with him."

"How many?" Firian cut a glance at Royce, who had told him three.

"In and around the room, maybe twenty."

Firian backed up a step to shield Jori with his body, though they were almost the same size. "Any who could side with us?"

"We can't count on that."

Firian chewed his cheek. *Twenty.* "Belik's there? And Bard's with him?"

"Yes, Master Kess." The Tanyu's eyes shone absent for a second.

Firian knew that look. His brows drew together. "What?"

"You didn't hear it?"

"Sentry," he growled, then brightened with an idea. "Is there a Tanyu with Belik's Sentry? Can you call him off me?"

"He doesn't tell anyone but his enforcers where the Sentry is."

Firian reigned in his frustration. If they stayed in the open much longer, Jori would be killed and, if it were twenty against four, Firian might as well. Not to mention Bard in Belik's clutches. "What did you hear?"

"Belik wants an update on the Kepron."

"Tell him he's dead." Then Firian's breath caught with realization. "Who gave you that message?"

"Master Belik."

"Himself?"

"Yes." The Tanyu frowned at Firian's confusion.

Firian waved his hand. "Tell him. Tell him now. Jori is dead."

His thoughts raced. Belik's Sentry had lifted. Was the Sentry killed? Had the Tanyu gotten to Kiria's camp that quickly? His insides were ice and his wound burned. The other possibility was that Kiria decided to lift the Sentry again. Was this a new gap for him to take advantage of? Was Kiria expecting him to kill Belik *right now*? He had to believe the latter.

If Belik had access to the Unreal again, he could not only communicate with his followers, but also use the killing ability again. And Bard was in there with him. Bard had no further information they could torture out of him, if that was their goal. They wouldn't even need him as bait. Belik's presence was enough to bring Firian to them. Bard was disposable. Firian's muscles tensed.

Now. He had to kill Belik now. It didn't matter that he was outnumbered. If he didn't, then Bard and Kiria would die.

79

BELIK

MESSAGES CAME in at a dizzying rate at soon as the Sentry released. Most were variations of announcements about Charäkhnem coming to Kiria's aid. Belik was no fool. Although he had more allies to call on, they wouldn't have time to react before the princess' combined troops took back the city. His best chance to keep this power was to kill the heirs as efficiently as possible.

So when someone told him that Jorrim Calthwaite was dead, he replied, "Bring me the body." He couldn't gamble his fate.

With Firian loose on the grounds, he wouldn't risk having insufficient protection either. Every Tanyu was on duty, a slim number patrolling vulnerable areas or guarding him, and most searching for the heirs. Fifteen Tanyu stood in and around the room with him.

This excessiveness, he reminded himself with an uneasy adjustment of his shoulders, was temporary. Belik was the lynchpin of their success. He was the visible leader to the people of Brithnem and had more strategic experience than anyone else. That experience had taught him to trust no one. He alone could begin or call off attacks. The Tanyu could continue without him, but their victory —if they found it at all—would be bloody and chaotic. Chances were that either Charäkhnem would overwhelm them by sheer numbers or Firian would assert himself in Belik's place. And who knew what he would do as the leader? He certainly would accede some power to the princess, like he did before.

At least Belik had the Unreal again. Not knowing the reason made him wary, but it felt as though he'd had one arm pinned behind his back, and now he was free to move.

He turned to Bard, who looked back with wide black eyes. Still tied and bloody, he sat in a chair against the wall of the bedroom. This room was in a different wing of the palace from the Main, farther from Firian, and it didn't have as many windows as the larger room down the hall. Even though the expensive items had been stripped from it, and the dead guards of a month ago taken away, Belik knew very well whose room this had been. There was a certain rightness in winning this war from Kiria's bedroom.

"I haven't heard from the Tanyu searching the eastern wall," he told Bard. An absence of any report concerned him. Instead, Master Il'kamarse had informed him of the Kepron's death. Il'kamarse, who was supposed to stay in the Main. It felt suspicious.

"It's Firian," Bard answered simply, as though that were reason enough that they couldn't find him.

The door opened. Tanyu let four servants enter with trays of food. In all likelihood, this would be a long night. Tanyu could work through hunger, but Belik needed them at their best, and not everyone had the same capacity for self-denial as he or Firian.

Daelon was the last to enter. The other three kept their eyes down but his son met his gaze. Belik had given the Amir two choices: die or serve. Most chose to serve.

He snapped in Daelon's direction. "Feed him first," he said, jutting his chin at Bard. "Something from every plate. Quickly!"

Daelon hurried over and the other servants, who had actually been servants, not Amir, during the Keepers' time, gathered around him.

To Belik's annoyance, Bard ate the food Daelon put in his mouth with relish, as though he were starving. It didn't matter. This was the only task left for that traitor to complete. Belik hoped there was no poison to do his job for him.

He checked the Unreal again. Agitation rippled through but no words. He found the mind of a guard outside the bedroom. "What?"

"I think..." He trailed off.

"What?" Belik demanded again.

A sense of shuffled confusion.

Belik brought his notice to the bedroom again. "See what's happening," he said, eyeing Shiro.

The boy nodded and went to obey. Bard's eyes followed him as he chewed a bite of ham.

The door opened and Shiro grunted as he went down, folded from the middle.

All of Belik's senses went on alert. He pointed to several Tanyu behind him to take care of the problem. They moved stealthily and quickly as one, using multiple planes—high, medium, low—and protecting each other's blind spots. At least he'd chosen his guards well.

Belik's ears, both physical and mental, strained to hear what was going on. "Firian," someone managed to tell him, "and Calthwaite."

Belik sent more Tanyu to help.

Daelon straightened to his full height to listen too. He stood a little taller than Belik. He licked his lips. "Father."

The whispered word caught Belik's attention. *Not now.*

The door slammed open and everyone inside saw what was happening. Four Tanyu slumped on the ground, someone who looked like a Kingdom soldier blocking the Kepron against the opposite wall with his body, and Firian Kess fighting in front of them as Belik had never seen except in the Unreal. He was everywhere. It mesmerized him, made his breath stop. The fighting was almost perfect, each movement like a piece clicking into place.

Enktuya blocked part of Belik's view as she moved to protect him.

"Please stop this," came Daelon's voice.

Angry at the interruption, he turned on Daelon.

"Take me instead of the Kepron." The words were low and level.

Belik's heart thudded thickly in his chest. Soon the Kepron and the princess would both be dead. But this moment felt suspended, like the fall before a harsh landing. Why? He raised his lip in a snarl. He could kill both the Kepron and Daelon if he wanted to. But he didn't want to. His son was nothing but a disappointment and a reminder of his failures, but the possibility that this useless Amir could amount to something more snagged his thoughts more consistently than he wanted to admit.

Unless it meant the difference between victory and defeat.

"Bring them both!" he ordered, meaning Firian and the Calthwaite boy cowering behind the larger blond soldier.

The Tanyu must have misunderstood that *both* meant two and not three, because they finally subdued Firian's little band and wrenched their arms behind them. A meaty crack sounded and the Kepron screamed, his shoulder oddly configured in its socket, visible despite the armor. The boy was wearing armor and hadn't been fighting. He continued to grimace, eyes streaming, as Tanyu guided all three roughly by the hair and wrists into Kiria's bedroom.

Firian wrestled against his captors, almost pulling free. His leg hooked back, yanked forward, making the Tanyu holding him jackknife backward. Several Tanyu jumped on top of Firian, pinning him to the ground. With effort, they tied his limbs tightly together, their hands coming away bloody. That was interesting. Firian was injured, though Belik couldn't see where.

Belik crossed his arms. Maybe he should have ordered their quick deaths instead. Normally he would at least have had the Calthwaite boy executed without further fanfare. However, surrounded by reminders of his failures, he wanted something definitive and memorable, reestablishing his dominance.

All it took was a thought.

It didn't matter if he was weak afterwards, as Firian had been. He still had seven guards with him, and several Tanyu in the corridor were beginning to stir.

"So you lied," he said softly to Bard, whose gaze snapped from the captives back to him. "And you too." He signaled to Enktuya and nodded at the traitor who'd told him the Calthwaite boy was dead.

To his credit, the Tanyu didn't protest as his neck was broken. The display made the servants gasp and Jori sob.

Firian didn't register surprise or say a word, but his eyes flashed hatred.

"Father," Daelon pleaded.

"Over there," Belik instructed, ignoring his son.

Many pairs of eyes darted between Belik and Daelon at the word. Nobody commented, but only brought the prisoners against the wall near the fireplace where Bard sat.

His son wasn't the only one whispering hushed comments.

"I'm sorry," Bard said with tears in his swollen eyes.

"No, darling," murmured the Kepron.

"Take *me*," Daelon insisted.

"They all have successors," said the Kingdom soldier stoutly. "This won't end."

Belik's mouth twisted wryly. "And you think anyone will follow *them*?" He scanned the lineup. Firian stared murder at him, but there was something different in his eyes this time. A tinge of imploring. Belik looked levelly back. They both had wanted not to end up against each other. Why was that always the way? Why did everyone betray him?

Belik flicked his fingers. "Kepron first. Move the others out of the way."

"No!" came simultaneously from Bard and Daelon.

Firian fought against the Tanyu holding him, but there were too many and they had him completely bound. Desperation shone in his face. Even caged, he was dangerous. So why did he keep Firian alive? Belik was surrounded by his weaknesses—not only his failures, but also the two people he was most loathe to kill. That kind of attachment could be used against him, as he well knew.

Best to get on with it.

He closed his eyes and focused on the boy blocking his way to power. Dimly, he heard his son begin to pray. Pushing aside all awareness of the bedroom, he made himself in tune with the person before him. He found Jorrim Calthwaite's body in the Second Level, blood pumping violently and breath coming in gasps. Firian was right about their killing ability. It did work even on people who didn't have the Talent. All he needed was focus. He'd almost killed Bard, and Firian had done this many times. Belik could do it too if he concentrated.

But a strong sensation like sandalwood, always in the back of his mind, burst to the forefront, pulling him irresistibly upward. He fought like a swimmer against a current but the pull was absolute. To resist was like closing off sight, not by normal methods but merely by willing it. Couldn't be done. He had hoped never to feel the hateful smoothness of this insistent pull again. But it had to be dealt with. And it finally explained the absence of the Sentry.

Chetana was here.

80

KIRIA

"It's not up to you." Kiria put her hands on her hips. "I won't stand by while you die for me."

"You'd be in incredible danger," Chetana protested, tidying the few items in her tent. Her movements were brisk, efficient, almost too neat. There were no superfluous gestures, all was tight and rigid with nerves.

"I can just open my eyes," Kiria insisted. "I don't have to believe it." *You do.* The words remained unspoken. She gently touched Chetana's wrist. "I want to be there for you."

Chetana straightened and sighed. "I cannot guarantee that this will work."

"But you think it will?"

"I think it *could*."

Kiria bit her lip, shooing away images of Chetana lying lifeless on the ground. What Chetana needed was encouragement. "No one can get to the palace more quickly or effectively than you. Not even the Tanyu. Belik will pay attention to you. Didn't you say you broke his leg?"

The Amir's mouth tilted downward in a rueful smile. The septum ring settled in the bow of her lips.

Kiria took her hand. It felt like warm parchment. "I'll be right here."

They both sat down on the edge of the bed. "You can't distract me."

"I'll just stand there."

"That will surely get his attention." Chetana tried to laugh. Kiria had never seen her this uncomfortable. The strangled chuckle died away. She squeezed Kiria's hands with both of hers. "Forgive me for what you see."

"Of course." The brittle sound of the candle flame magnified in the silence. Kiria's heart pounded as though she were going to kill Belik herself. Somehow, Chetana had become her rock again. She didn't want to lose her.

Friendly Tanyu surrounded the tent and nearby area, but who knew how many Belik had sent to destroy her? This, at the very least, would give them all a greater chance.

Chetana still hadn't closed her eyes. "Tell Daelon," she said, breathing strangely, "that I... have always loved him."

A hard lump formed in Kiria's throat. She could barely manage a response. "I will."

Bending her forehead down to meet their joined hands, Chetana paused as though in prayer. When she sat up, her face was lined with determination.

"Ready?" Kiria whispered. She wasn't sure that she was ready herself, but she would go anyway. At least once, she had to see the man who had ruined the people closest to her and torn her city away.

Chetana took a deep breath through flared nostrils and slowly closed her eyes.

The setting was clear in an instant, with so many details that it felt practiced. A whitewashed barn. Hay littered the ground and filled the loft above. Bales made a barrier along one wall. Square wooden pillars with peeling paint held up the loft at intervals. In front of them was a warped double door with a complicated lock. The setting sun shot hard beams through thin gaps in the boards. It smelled like dried hay and oil.

Chetana now wore a green dress and yellow shoes. Her curly hair was even shorter. Kiria stayed carefully plain so she didn't attract extra attention. The setting was so convincing that Kiria swam up briefly to the back of her eyelids and spread her hand over the bedspread in the tent to show herself it wasn't real. All she had to do if Belik attacked was to open her eyes, to believe he couldn't hurt her. She might even be able to help, using the tricks Chetana had taught her.

A man appeared by the doors. Broad, medium height, glasses, a pockmarked though not unattractive face. He looked maybe fifty, and he wore all black.

This was Master Belik.

The same Master Belik who had killed her family and friends, taken her home, and threatened her life. The one who had shaped Firian into a killer. The one who had stolen her kingdom.

Her hands were shaking fists, but Chetana barely stiffened at the sight of him.

For a long moment, no one spoke. The fascinated hatred between Belik and Chetana made Kiria's heart beat quickly. She was an intruder here.

The two began walking at the same time, predators circling or dancers beginning a violent routine.

"I see," Belik said, his gruff voice low and commanding. "This was not a good idea."

"I hoped I would never see you again either," Chetana bit out.

"I can find you more easily now. Is it really worth it to try and kill me? That's what this is." The last sentence wasn't a question.

"Yes."

Then why weren't they attacking? They must have been sizing each other up, sensing weaknesses or something. All Belik's attention was focused squarely on Chetana, as though Kiria wasn't worth looking at. She was grateful not to receive such a glare of hatred.

"Your son is here."

Chetana stopped walking. Her face was suddenly ashen. "Where?" The question came out weaker than anything Kiria had heard before. Tears stung her eyes. Daelon.

"With me. In this room."

"You wouldn't—" Chetana cut herself off with a gasped breath. Her elegant hands flew to her collarbone. Then she collected herself, brought down her shoulders. "I see him."

Kiria didn't. All she saw was this barn. Since Belik had come in, even more detail permeated it until it was indistinguishable from a real place.

"He has nothing to do with this," Chetana continued. "You know it."

"Don't tell me what to do with my son!" The shout came out violent and Belik advanced on Chetana.

"He was never your son." Chetana raised her chin, imperious. "You only wanted him to atone for your own sins."

Kiria struggled against helplessness. Did Chetana want Belik to come closer so she could kill him? This didn't look good. Kiria could fight with a blade or turn into a Firian lookalike or levitate as Chetana had done in her dream. But her arsenal of tricks felt pitifully thin.

Belik stood even closer. "I don't have time—"

A scream ripped through the air.

It tore at Kiria's soul. Belik stopped to listen but Chetana didn't seem to hear at all. Only Kiria saw him. It was hard to pinpoint where, but the mirage of a falling boy in pain appeared. He wore Tanyuin black, with dark hair and light skin and eyes squeezed shut. His mouth was open in that dying shriek.

Time seemed to slow to the space between one halting heartbeat and the next.

Firian opened his eyes. They were blue, even in the haze, and fixed on her. She wanted to scream with him, to stop him from falling, to say new words. But all she had was a look. And all it said was goodbye.

81

FIRIAN

THE GROUND FELT HOT. The cheek pressed against it burned with the sharpness of shock. Firian's arms and lungs spasmed, muscles contracting at random. He shuddered as he drew the first mouthful of air into his lungs. Thoughts wouldn't form in his mind. His body could only feel, and it was hellish. It felt as though his head had been split open with an ax. Maybe it had been. If he wasn't dead, he was dying.

Events in Kiria's bedroom settled into his mind like butterflies, landing and flying away and landing again, bright as blood. He was here to kill Belik before he could take the Western Kingdom for himself. This was Firian's last stand.

But he couldn't stand.

He peeled his eyes open and turned his hammering head. Above him, darkness reached as far as the sky. The sight made him dizzy.

He wouldn't get out again.

Kiria had seen him fall. She would know what happened to him, what he'd tried to do. That he had tried his best for her, even if it hadn't been enough. There was no time to show her that he felt ashamed of how he'd used her, or that she impressed him with her courage, or that she showed him what it meant to be a leader. Or that he loved her.

Touching the floor with his palms to ground himself, he rocked upward, determined to stand up. He crouched with his feet under him and stood slowly, wavering.

Belik met his eyeline.

Firian's gut clenched. Belik's scornful look took in all of him, knew all of him, and dismissed it in disappointment. He didn't seem afraid that Firian still had the power to kill him. Or maybe Belik wasn't afraid of death. If that were so, Firian wasn't either. But this time, it wasn't the recklessness of desperation, it was the strength of knowing that his life was as small and large as other lives. The gigantic shadow of his own importance had shrunk into himself. Now he was Firian Kess, just Firian Kess, and he could save the ones he loved.

That assurance brought life into his limbs again and he stood more steadily.

"We both know you can't kill me," Belik said. He hadn't moved from his position opposite Firian. Neither of them created a background apart from the darkness. Each of their bodies glowed as if a light shone on it. "You're too weak." He held up a hand to stop a reply, but Firian still couldn't gather enough breath to say anything. "I know they stopped you only because you're outnumbered. You fought well out there."

Firian dragged air into his lungs, summoning all his strength, which was barely anything now. *Breathe.*

Still Belik didn't attack. Firian's mind spun. He had an opening then, something he could say to stave off the inevitable, to hold off the execution of Jori and Bard and Kiria.

"Then stop," Firian croaked, his voice a ragged, breaking whisper. He could barely see around the pain in his head. There was no way he could use his killing ability now.

Belik gave him a sardonic look and wiped the lenses of his glasses on his shirt as though deciding what to do.

"I could stop," the Master said slowly, not looking at him.

As he waited for an explanation, Firian felt like prey in the sights of a predator. He was the deer with a broken leg, or the rabbit chewing grass without sufficient camouflage. He tried to flex his hand around a knife, any weapon, but his joints only creaked. Breaking through the Sentry and falling, falling in pain had robbed him of all the ability he'd worked so hard to gain.

"I'll make you a deal," Belik said, repositioning his glasses as though he'd just made up his mind.

Firian struggled to keep his attention sharp. "What deal?"

"You're doing this for the princess, yes?" Belik didn't wait for a response. "What if I could give her to you?"

The pounding of Firian's heart just made his body hurt worse. "What do you mean?"

"If you come back"—the words seemed almost wrestled from him—" then I'll make sure you have her. That's my offer. I dispose of the other heirs, all of them, but keep her for you." His stare became earnest. "We could *make* something of the Tanyu, Firian. It's what we've always wanted. I saw you fighting out there. And..." He took a deep breath and leaned back, glaring as though Firian had said something defiant. "And I hate being against each other." He bared his teeth almost as if he were reprimanding himself for the words. "So that's my offer. Gory generous, is what it is."

Belik had said he wouldn't make an offer twice. In some part of his twisted brain, he couldn't let Firian go.

And then what? Firian had given that question a lot of thought. Belik's offer didn't describe something he could live with anymore. It was everything he wanted, and nothing. Now, despite his pain and despite the offer, was the warm certainty of what was right. But, if he played along, could he buy her time?

"Princess," he found himself muttering.

"Yes, Tanyu are almost there. I don't have time to waste, Firian."

"Keeper," Firian said more loudly. "You'd be better off calling Kiria a queen."

The two men looked at each other. Firian's answer echoed through the featureless darkness. He hadn't addressed Belik's offer, but by defending Kiria, he defied it.

Finally, Belik observed his nails, clenching his teeth. His brow creased in obvious anger.

Firian waited for the killing blow. His feet were stronger now. He felt them beneath him. His legs too. His head still pounded, but his body belonged to himself again.

He watched the man who had been his mentor, who had cared for and aggravated him, believed in him and betrayed him. Firian swallowed. And he summoned all the strength he had left, which felt so small, and directed it at Master Belik.

Firian had more experience killing this way. This was a slim chance, but at least it existed. As long as Firian lived, he would fight. All of Kiria's courage and sacrifice for her people would pay off.

Belik looked at Firian again, and Firian felt his own bones and muscles constrict, bending backward. Firian pressed harder through the headache and the pain shooting up his back.

The muscles in Belik's face twitched with exertion. *It's working!*

Firian kept on, throwing the whole weight of his mind toward Belik until he felt the fluttering heart, the straining muscles. His own body felt shredded open, but as long as his mind could focus, he fixated on Belik.

Firian's vision narrowed, blackening to a point. He couldn't breathe anymore. The pressure on his spine and skull and eyeballs was too much. He'd burst apart. He had to give one last try. Hopefully that would be enough.

Kiria laughing at the dance last night and Bard squeezing his forearm and Brett staying up with him until they could fall asleep.

He tried one last time and collapsed.

82

KIRIA

BELIK WAS GONE. Chetana and Kiria stood alone in the barn. The Amir looked at her with dark, skeptical eyes. Kiria didn't know what to say. Had Belik gone back to the real world, refusing to take Chetana's bait? Or had he somehow followed Firian's apparition?

"Belik!" Chetana called.

When there was no answer, Kiria said, "I saw Firian."

Chetana's forehead creased. "When? Where?"

"He fell." She traced his path with her hand. *He was screaming.*

A tiny measure of relief showed in Chetana's face. "His Sentry is gone?"

"I don't—"

Belik's big form appeared where it had before, stumbling once before righting himself. Kiria couldn't remember ever having seen a Tanyu stumble. He was wounded or exhausted. Firian told her about his bad leg, but Kiria hadn't noticed it in the Unreal.

Chetana wasted no time. She glided forward, seeming not to use her legs. Belik's expression was different. He looked at Chetana as a soldier might look at someone who could help him to his feet. Kiria could imagine Firian looking at her like that.

Chetana raised a hand and touched Belik's cheek. Then she shoved his shoulder so his back was pressed against the wall. Kiria was invisible behind them, intentionally so. The moment was strangely intimate. No words were said.

Chetana planted a fierce kiss on Belik's lips. Belik was a little shorter than she was, and the kiss was almost like a battle in itself.

When she pulled away, Belik was bleeding from the chest. The Tanyu sucked in a breath of disbelief and rage when he realized. As he fell awkwardly to the hay-strewn floor, light slicing across his body, he glared at Chetana, who held a blade in her fist. Then the glare lost its luster. His limbs settled horribly, small movements, into permanent positions. The barn itself seemed robbed of breath in the silence that followed.

Chetana turned around to face the place where Kiria stood unseen. The Amir seemed to know exactly where she was anyway. Her dark face was drawn and bloodless. She took a shaky step and stopped as though she couldn't go any further. Instead, she stood rooted to the spot, her gaze falling to the ground.

Kiria came back to the Real and squeezed Chetana's hand. Chetana still didn't open her eyes. Her mouth hung slack and a concentrating line formed above her nose.

"Chetana." Kiria shook her lightly with her free hand. "Chetana."

The Amir gave a shuddering gasp and opened her eyes, collapsing forward. She gripped Kiria's shoulder to hold her up.

"You did it," Kiria said, struggling with her weight. Finally, she had to lay Chetana down on the bed. It was odd to see someone weak who usually held herself as straight as a queen. "You killed him."

Chetana didn't reply.

Hot tears stung her eyes. She had to tell someone. She had to tell everyone. Without Master Belik's leadership, their way back onto the throne was clear.

After checking Chetana's pulse and breathing, Kiria left her on the bed, eyes closed as if sleeping. Drawing back the tent flap, she caught the attention of the nearest Tanyuin guard. "He's dead," she said. "Belik's dead. Tell the Tanyu. All of them."

Surprise and a curt nod followed her words.

It's almost over.

She went back inside the tent to check on Chetana, who was trying to sit up. Kiria gently took her hands and helped her.

"It was for Daelon," came her first words, an excuse for committing a crime.

Kiria nodded and rubbed Chetana's back like her own mother had done so many times. This should have been a moment of celebration, but Chetana drew her hands over her face and her back shuddered. Kiria hugged her tighter and spoke soothing words in her ear as she cried.

83

BARD

BARD WATCHED Jori writhe in the grip of his captor. His shoulder wasn't right, and the Tanyu twisted his arm cruelly. Panic showed in the whites of Jori's eyes. Belik's face was a calm mask of concentration as the other Tanyu in the room waited for his demonstration. Bard's bowels turned to ice. This wasn't supposed to happen. He remembered the Torithian who escaped the night Firian came back from the war. He had screamed, writhed, and fallen a broken man with blood seeping from his eyes and ears. It was awful to watch, and now Jori had the same edge of confusion and terror.

Down the line, Firian screamed, a bone-chilling sound. Never before had Bard heard such a raw noise. Bard trembled as he looked just in time to see Firian go limp. His head lolled back, mouth open. Multiple Tanyu held him, even with his arm and leg restraints, and they pitched as he fell as though unsure whether to hold him up or lay him down.

"Fir." The word was a breath. Bard couldn't manage any more.

Was Firian breathing? Bard stared at his chest. He couldn't tell. It didn't look like it.

Belik's ability had worked. On Firian. Time stretched and blurred.

A servant cried. Beside Bard, Daelon's steady voice chanted prayers under his breath.

Jori's eyes tore away from Firian's unmoving body—Bard couldn't think the other word—and lighted on Bard in a question, a plea for help. He didn't grow up trained as a warrior, bred to resist the fear of death.

It's okay, Bard wanted to say, but the words stuck in his throat. It wasn't. In seconds, the same thing would happen to Jori. Bard could hardly see him through his tears. There was nothing he could do at this moment but comfort him.

He cleared his raw throat. "Thank you... for running out. You would make... such a... such a good Keeper, yeah?" His voice kept breaking, so he paused.

Jori paused too. He heaved a deep breath that sounded almost like relief.

Bard shot a glance at Belik. His eyes were still closed, and the empty quiet went on a beat too long.

Jori still looked scared but no longer panicked. Had... had Firian broken through the Sentry? Impossible. It couldn't be done, and even if Firian had tried again, the attempt, or Belik's secret ability, had killed him.

Still, something had distracted Belik. If the other Tanyu hadn't noticed, then Bard didn't want to draw attention to it.

"Glad you think so," Jori croaked, attempting to smile. The result was horribly lopsided. "Took three people to give me the tattoo. I think they just wanted a look. It hurt so bad." He grimaced, apparently reminded of the greater pain he was in at the moment.

The Tanyu behind Jori looked uncertainly at Belik, who hadn't moved, or even changed his expression. An unspoken question hung in the air.

Bard ran through options in his head though he knew it was like looking over a lost Indisfate board, more to see how he could have won than to make a difference now. All his allies in the room were bound and hopelessly outnumbered. No one, that he knew of, was coming. It would take a miracle to restore the Western Kingdom to its rightful owners.

Daelon still prayed in the background. That might be something. Divine intervention. But it wasn't something one could count on.

The Tanyu grew more restless. What was happening? Even Royce looked at Bard as though he wanted direction. But Bard's throat was dry as chalk, and he was out of ideas. His plan hadn't gone at all the way he'd hoped. And now Firian was...

Belik fell hard to the ground. A deep stain spread through the front of his black shirt, just over his heart.

Bard stared in disbelief. Tanyu leapt forward to revive him.

"Is he...?" Jori asked.

Bard coughed once to speak. "Charäkhnem is coming!" he said as loudly as he could. His voice sounded odd. "You heard him. There are thousands coming this way. Belik is... dead." His face and fingers felt numb, but he kept going. "If you help us, maybe they won't kill you. We can tell them you helped us." He stopped, out of breath as though he'd been swimming for hours.

Two Tanyu still bent over Belik, trying to staunch the wound.

The same care wasn't given to Firian, but they did lay him down. Bard didn't see a stain growing over his skin, no blood, but he wasn't moving. His roommate. His friend. His enemy. His brother.

He swallowed against the lump in his throat, trying to keep his thoughts clear. He couldn't lose sight of the chance Belik's sudden death provided. Maybe the game wasn't lost yet.

"Yes, we'll tell them what you did," Jori agreed.

"You'll have no hope if you kill us," Bard added.

Their glances met, a secret between them. Jori's eager trust was enough to get Bard to the next moment, and the next. It probably would get him through many moments, if he lived so long.

Belik and Firian lay on the ground a body-length apart. The two acting Tanyuin Heads. Tanyu didn't stay leaderless for long, but their uncertainty told Bard that neither had clearly appointed an heir to take his place.

"We can't listen to this," wheezed Shiro by the door. "Who's a traitor to the Tanyu in this room?"

"You wouldn't be a traitor if you help us," said Bard, though he knew his word was as good as dirt to Shiro. "Tanyu are warriors, not murderers. I don't want you all to die."

"Do we have more coming?" one asked his neighbor in a gruff undertone.

"Not in time," Bard answered.

"Shut up. Do we?"

Shiro lifted his chin defiantly. "You think we can't hold this city? The new army isn't even inside the gates."

"But they have more than ten thousand. And Tanyu. Suicide isn't glorious."

"It isn't suicide. To win we just need to kill him"—Shiro stabbed a finger at Jori—"and the princess." Apparently, Shiro had taken his position as Belik's new protégé seriously.

"And we have backups," Jori said. "Mine's Haved Ganesha."

Bard clicked his teeth together. There were so many reasons why he shouldn't have said that.

"Princess of Charäkhnem," Jori pressed on. "I'm reasonably certain they'd send more soldiers if their princess were in danger."

Actually, it wasn't the worst plan. Putting a target on Haved just wasn't a particularly good one.

"Kiria listens to me," Bard said.

"And me, of course." Jori winked and immediately twitched as though the movement pained him.

"We'll ask her to show you mercy."

Shiro's face was red now. "Tanyu don't need mercy. They don't show mercy." His angry stare flicked once to Firian's unmoving body and then concentrated on Jori.

A knife was in his hand before Bard understood where it had come from or what Shiro was doing. Shiro flew at Jori. Royce yanked his body sideways to block the blow but only managed to knock Jori off balance. The armor clacked into the back of Bard's wooden chair.

Two large Tanyu held Shiro by the arms. A quick fight left three more Tanyu with their limbs bound. No one had let go of Jori or the others, but obviously the majority saw the sense in what Bard said.

Shiro spit in Bard's face.

Bard blinked the warm saliva away. "Call off the attack," he said. They all knew what he meant. If the Tanyu killed Kiria, they doomed themselves. All the Tanyu went vacant for a moment. The servants looked at each other in confused astonishment, still clutching their plates of food.

It was working. Bard's plan was actually working. The Tanyu were calling off the attack on Kiria. Lightheadedness took him for a moment and he swayed in his chair.

"Let them come back one at a time, or go back to the Academy," said Bard, righting himself again. He didn't need the confusion of angry Tanyu coming all at once. "And let Jori announce what happened."

"Before we have any terms?" someone asked, incredulous.

"We need something that benefits us both," said another.

"*Life* benefits you," Jori said.

Bard tried to raise his eyebrows in agreement but his face didn't work that way at the moment.

The argument went on for a long time. Bard negotiated with Kiria, who talked to the Charäkhni forces, promising no killing of Tanyu until a proper investigation had been done. Tanyu would wait until their judgment could be pronounced, and Kiria promised to show leniency to anyone who helped her cause and protected her people. The Tanyu had to promise afterward to be escorted from the city. Bard knew there were many who would rather run back to the Academy than stand trial under Kiria. Positions of power were there for the taking, and the guilty could prevent execution. They would deal with that later.

Finally, there was a tentative agreement, a truce strong enough to untie their bonds. Shiro and Enktuya were taken down to the dungeons. The bodies of Firian and Belik were carried from the room.

At sunrise, in a makeshift sling, Jori stepped onto the same balcony where Belik had been crowned, and he announced their victory.

84

JORI

Jori stepped back from the balcony as winded and flushed as if he'd just been thoroughly kissed.

From that height, he could actually see Kiria's troops marching toward the palace. An uncomfortable stab of apprehension lanced him before he could remind himself that this wasn't an attack. These people weren't coming to murder but to help. He strained to look for Kiria but she was so small, she could have been heading the column and still been invisible. A helpless little smile crept onto his lips. He felt nearly hysterical.

As he turned back to Bard, Royce, Daelon, and a few Tanyu, his shoulder throbbed. Bard's poor face, all smudged from beatings and crying. And still he'd managed to come up with a way to get the Tanyu to surrender.

"Could you change out of black, please?" he said, looking at the others. "You can see how that would make me uncomfortable." Personally, Jori doubted he would ever wear black again.

"We need to get ready to greet the troops outside," Royce suggested, completely ignoring the comment.

Together, still on guard, they all made their way to the palace's main entrance. Jori hardly ever used that entrance. The door always struck him as more of a decoration than something functional.

As they stepped outside into the morning sunlight, his stamp as the black sheep of the Calthwaite family took him with tremendous force. He hadn't even fought. He'd just struggled to stay alive, and that alone would inevitably leave him with suffocating nightmares of being pulled apart from the inside. Kiria should be here to do this. But she led the other side of this meeting.

The sun climbed as the army made its torturous way. Jori's life was an eternal wait, apparently. The rising sun gilded the stone houses and courtyards and side streets. He should have felt elated, but he only felt... lots of other things. He wanted to say something to the others but all his thoughts were half-formed sentences.

Bard gently touched his arm, his good arm, to bring him back to reality. Reliable, that one. Responsible and tender in a way Jori feared he would never be. Well, while there was life, he could still try. He gave Bard a crooked smile that felt weaker than what he deserved for his efforts today. Bard's cheek crinkled back, a mirror image of his own expression.

Up the long walk from the street below, Kiria was coming, with Haved, a couple friendly Tanyu, and members of the Kingdom guard. An un-Keeper-like sob escaped his mouth before he could stop it. He cleared his throat to cover it up, but no one would believe he was only coughing.

Kiria was a vision, Beautiful and tired. They both still wore armor, he realized. It felt like he had put his on a week ago. And Haved beside her looked nearly as lovely, with some of his brother's love reflected in her eyes. Others were there, but, compared to his girls, they didn't matter.

It wasn't diplomatic, but then, neither was he. Jori crushed Kiria and then Haved in the best one-armed hug he could manage, kissing their temples as something warm slid down his cheeks. Haved gently pushed him from her. "It was a close one," he said once he released them. "We've got the palace under control now though. Finally."

Just behind his eyelids were the bodies of Viktor and Belik and Firian and even that Tanyu who made to stab him and got cut through the neck. Did Jori still have blood on his face? He raised his good hand—even that motion earned him a stab of pain in his other shoulder—and surreptitiously rubbed his cheek.

"I heard," Kiria replied. "We'll get the final casualties soon."

Jori could have done without the numbness in her tone. "You, my dear, are Keeper again."

She mustered a smile that seemed to give her enough energy to grace the others with it too. "I was always the Keeper," she teased. "You're the one who's new at it." She lowered her voice so the people behind them couldn't hear. "And not forever. Haved just told me—"

Jori's mouth dropped.

"—she's pregnant."

"No!" His fist flew to his mouth. "Jorrim the Second! No, wait. Atael the Second!" He looked at Haved to see if he'd guessed right. A nephew! An heir! His brother's heir!

She smiled in that self-possessed way of hers.

"Atty the Second." Jori cast his eyes upward. *Are you seeing this?* So he only had to rule for sixteen or seventeen years. He could live with that. He could do more than live with it. It was perfect.

"I have the terms listed here," Kiria said, reaching behind her for a short stack of papers. "Shall we head to the Main?"

Right, they still had war things to discuss. Jori flashed a smile at Haved before looking at the paper.

"Obviously, they're basic now," Kiria explained, "but enough to call an official end to the war. I'll sign it." She nodded to someone over his shoulder. "One of the Tanyuin Masters has to sign it next."

"Please, I know all that," said Jori, handing the paper back to Kiria. He caught a glimpse of citizens coming out of their houses, tentatively looking at the palace steps. He gave them a regal wave before going inside.

"I'm glad you're all right," Bard said to Kiria, his comment oddly pointed. "You seem all right."

She was looking up at the ceiling. Jori tipped his head back too. Artwork, verses, and architectural features now spread unevenly across the vaulted interior. What had been uniform now was smudged or emphasized, based on the whim of the fire.

Kiria's expression was somber and thoughtful, alive with memory. "I will be," she replied.

Bard whispered something into another Tanyu's ear and the warrior ran off.

Jori asked for information with a look.

Bard just whispered, "Firian."

Formalities took place in the Main, with Kiria and Jori standing on the dais amid the improbable configuration of chairs. Haved, Bard, and others, including Amir freed from their cells, Parohim among them, stood as witness. A Tanyuin Master Bard told him was named Ardal filled the role of surrendering party. The Tanyu lost none of their gravitas during the exchange, almost as though many of them thought that the whole exercise of taking over the capital was below their dignity, and they just wanted to return home.

When all was done, terms read, marks written, and prayers said, Jori handed the paper back to Kiria. She acted distant, but positively regal. Battle did that to a person, he supposed.

"Charäkhnem has agreed to stay for a few weeks to begin escorting Tanyu out of the city," she said.

"Sporting of them."

"And I will stay here as well," said Haved in her low, measured voice.

"Even better!" He observed the sea of Tanyuin and Kingdom and Charäkhni people dispersing, several under guard, and turned tentatively to Kiria. "Is that all then? Can I have a drink now? I believe Bard owes me a bottle."

Bard nodded in that way of his.

"Let's have a toast," Kiria suggested, finally lightening around the edges. "*May it rain hope always.* And then off to bed."

85

KIRIA

FIRIAN HADN'T WOKEN UP. Three days had passed since Belik's death. Every day, Kiria and Bard called to him in the Unreal, but they were running out of time. What else could they do?

Even though the Sentry had finally been found and dismissed, Firian hadn't shown himself. None of the Tanyu understood the Second Level well enough to explain what was happening. Maybe the First Level was nothing but pain. Maybe he was trapped. Maybe he didn't want to wake up.

Bard had taken a break to rest, leaving Kiria and her guards alone with Firian. She had much to do to reestablish the Kingdom under her protection—new coronations to prepare for, judgments to pass on traitors, alliances to make and dissolve, building restoration projects to oversee... Yet here she was, with every spare minute, and even a few that weren't spares.

Firian's face looked gray, his lips cracked and parched. He couldn't survive much longer like this. His dark brows stayed slightly furrowed as though he were having a bad dream.

Come on, Firian.

Kiria would have to judge him, as she had judged other high-ranking Tanyu. Shiro had been executed, along with Enktuya, Belik's other enforcer. Some, as expected, had fled—another day's problem. She didn't know how she would judge Firian, but she knew she wanted him to wake up.

She brushed his hair away from his forehead. His skin felt feverish. Not long now. Closing her eyes, she went into the Unreal again. If their *katah* didn't save him, nothing would. Enveloped in darkness, she called his name. Again. Again.

Nothing.

The pit of her stomach roiled. Was there nothing more she could do?

When she came back to the cool medical room, her hand held his. She and

Bard would keep trying, but maybe this was it. He was dying in his effort to kill Belik and restore her throne. A beautiful crack of light.

She threaded her fingers through his. It was a fitting end, if it had to be the end.

His chest rose and fell more quickly, his eyes moving behind the lids. Kiria caught her breath and shot a look at the guard. "Get the doctor." She turned back to Firian's sleeping form. "Firian," she whispered. "Are you awake? Open your eyes." Remembering herself, she raised her voice so another guard could hear. "Get Bard too!"

Firian's throat moved as he swallowed. His lips parted sleepily.

"Firian, can you hear me?"

Squinting up at her, he gained his bearings, trying to angle up on his elbow. The blanket covering him fell, exposing his bare chest and revealing a thick bandage on his lower back. As he moved, his hand caught his attention, entwined with Kiria's. He looked confused more than pleased, as though he were seeing an illusion.

"I didn't get him. I didn't get Belik," he said quickly, in a voice husky with disuse. "I don't think he's dead."

"We got him," she replied. "Chetana stabbed him through the heart." Chetana had also been bedridden the past few days, but she was sitting up and eating now. She needed her strength to fill the place she'd earned as regent until Kader came of age. Her *katah*, even so many years removed, had made her pay a high price for executing Belik.

Firian squeezed her fingers gently, almost tentatively. She squeezed back. "So the Kingdom's yours again?" he asked, easing himself back down on the bed.

"It is. We won." She was still getting used to the idea, but she smiled.

His expression turned to a frown. "You came back for me."

She nodded.

"Why didn't you leave me there?"

The arrival of Bard and the doctor saved her from answering. She pulled her hand from his.

"Ah, he's awake," said the doctor, a good-natured Hinterlander, taking Kiria's place on the seat and easing his arm behind Firian's back to help him up.

"Fir!" It looked like Bard wanted nothing better than to hurl himself forward in a hug. Bard's broken nose looked purple and his hair, as usual, was wild. "You're up! You're out of the Unreal."

The effort of sitting took all of Firian's concentration. Even his eyes were shut tight in pain.

"Kiria and I called and called. I didn't know if you'd come out of it, mate. I thought..." He scrubbed his face with a knuckle, careful to avoid the splotchy bruises.

Kiria could only nod again.

The doctor pressed his thumb to Firian's wrist. "Dehydration."

"I'm okay," he replied, more to Bard than the doctor. "I heard..." He took a deep breath and hunched over, as though gathering his thoughts. With one hand on his forehead, he continued. "I heard you. Both of you." He didn't give more details. His pain seemed too powerful for him to focus.

The doctor ushered over some water. "And a stab wound."

"You heard us?" Bard came to stand next to Kiria.

"Yeah." He couldn't speak for a few more seconds. The doctor pressed a cup into his hand. "We won?"

Something in his tone gave Kiria pause. "You'll live, Firian."

"Yes," the doctor confirmed. "Liquids and rest will get you up in a couple days."

"Jori's alive too?"

"Yeah. Yeah, he's fine," answered Bard.

"Kader's on his way too," Kiria added. "We'll be all right."

"All right," Firian repeated, half-delirious. Small pangs distorted his face at intervals, as though he were bracing for a blow.

"Jori told me what you did, how you kept him safe. That's pretty amazing." Bard gave Kiria a glance as he said it. "And Kiria's army was ambushed right after sunset."

Kiria cut off his praises, which were inevitably coming. She deserved little praise. The people around her had made victory possible. "Without Bard, none of this would have happened. He negotiated the surrender."

Dimples appeared in Firian's slow grin. "Ah," he said, "I can't believe it. You're like..." He looked at Kiria. "You could take down a mountain ghost, couldn't you?"

She smiled, delighted by the compliment. Firian rarely gave them, so they were all the more precious. *Be dangerous. Be brave.*

"You too," said Bard.

"And you"—he looked at Bard—"your plan worked."

"Don't be surprised."

Kiria couldn't tell if Firian's response was a cough or a laugh. Then he hummed softly, disbelief and thoughtfulness echoing through the sound. The same question ran through Kiria's mind: What next?

As soon as Firian was up, she'd have to decide whether would she lock him up indefinitely, exile him, consign him to physical punishment, execute him... His ability to kill others with his mind made him a dangerous prospect for a prisoner. She relished none of the possibilities. Somehow, though, she sensed he'd bow to her wishes. It was an odd feeling. He'd found a cause and he'd stuck to it, to his own hurt. He'd always been extreme, but now he seemed to have found an outlet for his focus. And he chose to help her.

"You should probably leave him alone," said the doctor, startling her out of her reverie.

She looked up to find Firian already looking at her. They both looked away. She cleared her throat. "Of course. We can go."

"Just—" Firian caught her hand.

She pulled it away swiftly, but stopped to hear what he had to say. Her fingers felt warm.

He pinned her with his bloodshot gaze and his voice dropped, low and earnest. "I never should have…" His throat worked as he forced out the words. "You deserve more… than me."

She regarded him, his sovereign but also one of his only friends. The moment stretched between them, his words echoing like crashes in an empty room. She felt the presence of Bard and the doctor. Firian, on the other hand, seemed completely oblivious to them. Firian had had opportunities to apologize before, and she never thought she'd hear the words.

"I know," she said. "Get some rest."

Bard joined her near the door.

Jori met them outside, looking fresher than any of them, despite a few scrapes and his dislocated shoulder. "He's alive, I take it."

"He opened his eyes. He's talking!" Bard exclaimed.

Jori shot Kiria a look, almost wary, and adjusted his sling. It looked like it was made from a tapestry, it was so elaborate. "Does he remember his heroics or is he back to his insufferable self?" He said it teasingly, as though he couldn't decide whether to take himself seriously.

Kiria and Bard just gave wry smiles.

"You're not in love with him, are you?"

Kiria dropped her eyes, but the question was directed at Bard.

"No," Bard said firmly.

Relief crossed Jori's face. A barely perceptible smile flickered in and out. "Shows good judgment. Although you didn't see him fight those other Tanyu."

When Kiria raised her eyes again, Jori met them, sparkling laughter in his look. He was teasing, not criticizing. He hugged her sideways. "Keeper business is so serious."

She hugged him back. The first few days after the battle had worn her out. Justice was slowly being done, as much as she and Daelon, her new advisor, could reckon. But joy was yet to come.

"We all look dreadful," Jori said, wobbling his broken arm.

He wasn't wrong. Bard's hand flitted toward his face before he dropped it again. Kiria had almost forgotten about the scars on her own face. The reactions she got as she sat on her makeshift throne in the ruined Main hadn't substantially changed. Now she had not only Beauty, but Beauty that had overcome.

"I've come to a decision," Jori said suddenly.

"What is it?"

"My official coronation is… soon. Whenever we can finally get a good party going. So I've chosen my advisor."

Kiria had a feeling she already knew who he'd choose.

"Bard," he confirmed. "Has to be."

One person, at least, was surprised by this news. Bard raised both eyebrows so high they almost disappeared in his hairline.

"He's a Tanyu," Kiria pointed out, not because she disapproved—Bard was an excellent choice—but to goad him. "He'll have to learn the Scroll."

Jori held out his arm toward Bard and pushed up the sleeve. "What does this say, love?"

"*May it rain hope always.*"

Jori replaced his sleeve and gave her his most self-satisfied expression. *There, he seemed to say. No need for discussion.*

"I'm happy to take lessons," Bard said. "You know, if... if that's your decision. I've always been kind of curious. And I've read some of it. Firian's copy, remember?"

A Tanyuin advisor. An Amiran regent. Times were changing, but not for the worse.

"I think that's a great idea. I'd love to have you as our advisor—Jori's advisor." Truthfully, she'd like having Bard close by. Judging by the way Jori had started to look at him, that was likely one way or another.

"It could be good for relations between Amir and Tanyu," Bard added eagerly.

"Absolutely," Jori said, winking at Kiria.

And it would be. Kiria had big plans, ones that involved years of careful reconciliation between the two groups. Bard, with his Tanyuin training and Amiran spirit, would be the perfect ambassador.

86

KIRIA

Two days later, Kiria sat on the dais in a black dress edged in silvery blue. Beside her sat Jori, looking almost too pleased to be wearing that crown. On her right, the throne was empty. Kader, whose throne that would eventually become, would return shortly from Hinter, where he'd been in hiding. She couldn't wait to see him and get more involved in his life than she'd been before. In the absence of Cúron, Chetana was regent, voting with the other Keepers and advising in the Main, but she wouldn't occupy the throne. Instead, she sat in her usual seat at the foot of the short steps alongside Bard and Daelon. A Tanyu and an Amir. Who would have thought they could co-exist so peacefully?

Royce had requested to attend the final round of judgments as well. For all his help, Kiria agreed to his request. He sat a few rows behind, holding the hand of his wife and one of his daughters. After some of the dust had settled, Kiria found out that all but one of his children had survived the battle. The mix of joy and grief on his face when she told him nearly broke her heart.

Bard's brother Jac had survived too, though he was currently helping with the effort to escort pardoned Tanyu out of the city.

"Bring him in," Kiria commanded, and two Charäkhni soldiers opened the carved double doors. They were partially burned now, but she planned to have them reinforced with metal as soon as possible to preserve what was left.

Firian appeared, bound, flanked by six Kingdom guards and a new Sentry. Someone had given him clean clothes—tan and deep purple instead of his customary black. He walked with a straight back and a grim expression until the group reached the foot of the platform. He knelt down before her.

Jori shot her a furtive look. Kiria hadn't told him what she was planning to do. Even now, looking at Firian, she knew she could change her decision and no one would argue, not even Bard, the only one she'd told.

"Firian Kess," she said, "it's time to pronounce your judgment." Why was her stomach in knots? She had lost nights of sleep over this decision. Finally, she believed she came to the right one.

He looked up at her with resolve in his blue eyes. There were still shadows under them from his recent coma. Almost imperceptibly, he nodded. *It's all right.* She could almost hear his thoughts, despite the Sentry. *Go ahead. It's all right.*

She blinked before continuing. "You took me hostage, threatened the Kingdom, are responsible for conquering innocent towns, blackmailed your Keeper, and led an army of Tanyu to our walls."

He didn't look away as she recited his crimes.

"But, for your assistance in the last battle, I am commuting the death sentence which, in the past, you deserved."

His lips parted with relief and hope, and his gaze intensified with the obvious question. What, then, were they going to do with him?

"You are hereby banished, body and mind, from the Western Kingdom, all of its lands south of the Charúnin Thôr, for a span of three years. During that time, and for the rest of your natural life, you will work on behalf of the thrones, starting by gathering those who have committed crimes against the Western Kingdom. The first will be the former bodyguard to the King of Charäkhnem. Master Tanery will give you details. He is the only one you are allowed to have any contact with inside the area from which you are exiled. Should you enter our lands during that time or fail to continue your work for us then or afterward unless released by word of a Keeper, the punishment will be death."

His chest rose and fell in deep breaths. His lashes fluttered as he looked down for a moment. When he turned his attention to her again, his look was bright and intense.

"You will be escorted from Brithnem immediately," she continued, her tone automatic. "Then you will have seven days to get to the mountains."

She saw Firian's throat work as though he were trying to swallow.

"Plenty of time for someone like you," Jori added, rubbing two fingers together as though they had something sticky on them. He didn't look at Firian. "And Bard will be in touch."

There was something knowing in Firian's gaze when he looked back at her. He knew this was mercy. This was thanks.

She raised her chin and nodded back at him—the tiniest movement, like his had been. Then the guards turned him around and she watched him march out of the Main.

87

EPILOGUE

Firian knew he was born in the last cold stretch before spring, so that meant he had just turned twenty-three. When he had first come to the Academy, they told him he would have to work until he was twenty-four before he became a Tanyuin Master. Even with his exile, he beat their estimate.

It had been almost three and a half years—eighteen missions—since he received his judgment.

Everyone called it the Autumn War now. He'd heard his sister and her husband call it that more than once. Giving the battle a name made it sound like it should be written down in the Scroll. But his memory of the pain and cold and death couldn't congeal into a simple fact to be memorized. It was the life in his veins, more wholesome than the pure fiery liquor of the Tanyuin Academy. He belonged nowhere, but pieces of himself had slowly started to come back together, creating someone he liked more than the desperate boy he once was.

Before, breath had stuck tight in his chest. Always, he lived braced, tense, ready to fight. He still had that grace, that poise, but he could breathe again. Strange, for someone called the Ghost.

He'd hunted criminals, assassinated warmongers, protected innocents, stolen plans for weapons, and even encountered creatures that in the past he would have called monsters.

He was everything the Kingdom needed him to be—a one-man force taking care of the northern borders. Still a weapon, but now a weapon in a just hand. Most of the time, he didn't mind traveling by himself. He had always enjoyed being alone.

Last year, Bard and Jori had visited the Academy—Bard on official business as the liaison between the Kingdom and Tanyu, and Jori for the sheer joy of it. At least, that's what it seemed. The Third Keeper acted as though he could barely stay in his skin. Firian caught glimpses of them after their meetings and time at the pub looking at every detail of the fortress and the town beyond.

The Academy's power had diminished. Tanyu had returned to find the treasure stores looted and curious folk harassing those in Tánuil. The strangers were quickly dealt with, but the bigger change was the new integration with the Kingdom. Patrols of silver and blue soldiers were a common sight now.

On their trip, Bard was delighted to explain everything and Jori asked questions, hanging on every word. Bard brought the new Indisfate set his oldest brother Edom had hand carved for them. The woodwork was impressive, but Jori kept saying he looked like a hunchback compared to Kiria, who looked beautiful and fierce, holding a sword aloft.

"You're running," Bard had explained.

"No one runs like that. Why can't I hold a sword?" Jori tried out the pose.

Bard laughed.

Today was different. Technically, today's visit was for the Second Keeper to meet face to face with Master Erron, the new Tanyuin Head, to talk about integrating parts of the Tanyuin and Amiran Academies. Three years of work with the public had convinced the people of Brithnem to consider the idea. At least, that was what Firian had heard.

He'd kept his word, hadn't looked in on Kiria in the Unreal, though there had been nights in the first year when he couldn't sleep for the ache in his chest.

Of course, he listened eagerly any time someone brought news from Brithnem. The Main had been rebuilt, roads had been repaired, new statues crafted by the best artists. Much of the news, however, wasn't as positive. Events surrounding the Autumn War rent the Western Kingdom along many lines. Unrest filled the streets of Brithnem. Every report of Kiria and the other Keepers showed them handling the difficult situation the best they could.

The Charäkhni princess Haved lived in the palace with her little boy, who would inherit the throne from his father Atael, taking Jori's place when he came of age. Amrit Ganesha, heir to the throne of Charäkhnem, felt sympathetic toward Kiria and the others, so their official alliance with the neighboring kingdom would be reestablished sooner or later.

Kiria had made her good start. He felt her presence with every positive advance the Kingdom made. She ruled with compassion, but didn't hesitate to protect her own. She could be fiercely just, and it made Firian admire her more.

No one ever brought more than the thinnest rumors that she met a partner. The entire kingdom would know if she were engaged, would flame with the news faster than a wildfire.

He imagined her happier now. How could she not be? Bard certainly was. He was meant for Brithnem, not the Academy. Sometimes Firian suspected that it was Bard's happiness bolstering him on days when he would have felt sullen. In a strange way, Firian felt more satisfaction too. A veneer of regret slicked over him like sweat, but the spikes of anxiety and the black rush of rage were less common. He could sleep.

Except for last night.

Kiria was coming to the Academy for the first time. *The first time!* That didn't seem possible. After all they'd been through, all the times she had seen it through his eyes...

But first, a required meeting with Bard about another mission. When Firian slept at the Academy, he stayed in a small room at the end of the second-story hallway. Past the washroom, the corridor curled deeper into the fortress, like the curve of a shell. Firian spent only a small fraction of his time here, so it didn't make sense to reserve a better room for him. His was practically a closet, even smaller than the one he'd shared with Bard. Here, he sat cross-legged on the floor, Watchman-like, to ground himself. All day he'd barely heard a word. His ears had piqued only for Kiria.

"Master Kess."

"Master Tanery."

They began every session that way, partly because it reminded them of the seriousness of what they were doing and partly because it was funny, for some reason.

"Hey, Fir," Bard greeted again, grinning. He wore a light beard now, along with finer clothes, and his nose looked a little crooked from the break. His hair was still crazy. "Shifra, please."

Firian, who'd been there far more often than Bard, created the swampland around them with its great, mossy trees and wooden walkways, like endless docks, zigzagging through.

"The edge," Bard clarified.

Yellow grasses from outside the jungle became visible through the trees. Sunlight filtering down looked more yellow and less green. "Good?" Firian asked.

"Good. There's a little village near here—I don't know if you've heard of it. Probably, but it's small. Honesowel?"

The odd name sounded even weirder in Bard's accent. Firian's lips twitched. "Yeah, I've heard of it."

"We've gotten reports that a man is hiding there. He attacked several of Kiria's personal guards during a diplomatic visit to nearby towns, but he fled before anyone could get him. We need you to bring him in."

Pretty typical target, then. They discussed more details—names, faces, times, dangers.

"Has she arrived yet?" Bard asked after their official business was done.

"Hm? No."

"Should be today, yeah?"

"I know."

There was mischief in Bard's look. "It'll be all right, mate. You've done good work. I tell them everything."

Firian knew that. What he didn't know was why he felt so nervous. "I've got to go," Firian said, unable to wait any longer. The trees poofed into colored smoke.

"Tell me how it goes."

His heart beat thickly as he nodded and left, striding down the long hallway, then taking the stairs down to the main floors three at a time. Was she here? How many would be with her? Would they get a chance to talk?

As Firian jogged down the resident hall, he felt the shifted atmosphere.

Down in the fountain courtyard, Learners, Defenders, and Masters all moved more quickly, though Kingdom soldiers in their silver and blue armor stood at their customary posts. Part of the deal Kiria had cut with the Academy was that they would have to endure oversight, and that any attack on her soldiers would be tantamount to a declaration of war. Firian had watched from this vantage point so many times that the change, though small, was unmistakable. Daily disputes among warriors vanished in a concert of motion. This was one thing the divided Academy could agree on—preparing for the arrival of the Keeper.

Running a hand over his face, he wished he could look out a window. *Breathe. Maybe she doesn't care to see you.* He forced himself to calm down. The next steps he took one at a time. What was he running toward? Her? After all that had happened, her heart probably didn't beat faster at the mention of *his* name. Three years was a long time.

The soldier guarding the right side of the wooden double doors at the entrance peeled away from his post to approach him. The armor gleamed dully in the light of the single chandelier.

"Master Kess?"

Firian pulled his shoulders back, evaluating what to expect. "Yes?"

"The Second Keeper requests your presence after her meeting," he announced.

Firian tensed. He'd half expected her to leave without seeing him. "When?"

"She should finish soon."

"Then I'll come immediately."

The guard led Firian through his own Academy as though he knew its halls and secrets better. But the small indignity was swallowed up by the magnitude of what was happening. *Requests your presence?* For what? Was there a second judgment she would hand down? Did she want to say hello? None of that would match what they had been to each other.

The guard led Firian to the Head's office. He avoided this hallway when he didn't have official business. The memories rankled. His pulse pounded as he crossed the threshold into the familiar space. Two Kingdom guards, Master Erron, and a person taking notes filled the small room.

Behind the desk sat Kiria. Beautiful, perhaps even more so with the long scars that ran across her lips and cheek. The wound had healed into dark lines that proved she could outlast storms. Her face and posture showed she was a few years older, settled into her role as the most influential Keeper of the Western Kingdom. She wore a new crown of metal and glass, like something shattered that had been pieced together into something more beautiful. Little of that uncertainty he remembered from their first meeting remained. As he entered, Kiria's amber eyes fixed on him.

He'd forgotten—he always forgot—how much her Beauty affected him. It wasn't something he could imagine the right way, even in the Unreal. His throat worked as they locked eyes, deep recognition sparking there.

"My Keeper," he managed, and bowed. His voice sounded steady and professional. Years of practice kept his face even too.

"Master Kess," she replied. She seemed much more composed than he was. "How have the missions been going? Are they successful?"

Why did she even ask? She got updates from Bard regularly. "They've gone very well." One side of his mouth crinkled in a proud smirk.

"The assignment seems to suit you."

In the past, he would have taken the comment to mean that it suited him better than being the Tanyuin Head, and he would have bristled at it, but she was right. He was more effective than he had ever been, finally using his skills in a way that mattered. The job was dangerous, but he'd always liked the cold snap of danger. Now, he didn't have to ask himself if the danger was needless. His purpose was clear, and he sliced his way toward it like a bird through the air.

She had known him better than he knew himself. Was that still true? The buzz of her mind rested against his like white noise in the room.

"Would you be open to a change in position?"

He raised an eyebrow. She could simply command him, and yet she asked his opinion. "I might be."

"I need a new bodyguard. Mine's about to retire."

Firian's stomach flipped, a chaos of emotion running through him. He flexed his hands open and closed to retain feeling in them. He met Kiria's gaze, but words didn't come for several labored breaths.

Even with several years as Keeper, she was still a new leader. Firian was a legend, and more recently the ghost visiting justice on fled Tanyu and criminals. Everyone knew who he was, and what he had done. Well, no one knew the whole story. An eleven-year-old boy he'd met near Enderin said he thought Firian was the good guy, because he did the coolest stuff and killed the bad guys. But only his most infamous deeds were agreed upon by his few admirers and many critics. If he became her bodyguard, it could make other nations trust her less.

"My Keeper," he began, unsure of where his response was going, "what about your reputation?"

At that, Kiria beamed, stretching the scar across her lip.

For a moment, he couldn't think. She was so lovely. All that existed was Kiria and her smile.

"It's been worse," she laughed. "I know you wouldn't allow anyone to harm me." She gestured vaguely to her head. Their *katah*. Harm to Kiria would mean harm to himself too.

Was this real? This felt too much like dreams he'd had on the road. "Of course I wouldn't." The words came out more breathless than he'd wanted. He cleared his throat. "If that's what you want."

"You've proven yourself loyal these past three years. You have the chance to prove it again. Or do you know someone who would be better for the job?"

There was a slight challenge in her eyes, amusement on her lips. They both knew what he would say.

"No one, My Keeper." His insides burned. This was actually happening. Then he remembered. "I have a mission that will keep me away for a week."

"The transition doesn't need to happen immediately. I'll still send you on missions periodically, even after you are my official bodyguard. No one has been as effective as you have in catching fugitives and carrying out the will of the Kingdom in... difficult situations. When you're finished with your work here, come to Brithnem. I'll tell the palace guards to look for you."

"Thank you." He gave another small bow from the waist. Everything felt familiar and new. Even the tug he sensed in the Unreal. His skin prickled, but he didn't respond. She couldn't be waiting for him there. He already had enough of his dreams come true for one day.

"That's all for now," she said. "I'm leaving tomorrow. If I need you again, I'll let you know."

Her words were kind, but he felt the distance in them. After three years without communication, though, this proximity felt like floating interminably in the ocean and finally seeing land.

As he exited, the Unreal beckoned again. It was the matter of a thought to get there. Still, he hesitated. A true *katah* never went away, but that didn't mean that she wanted him inside her head. It was too dangerous to undo all that carefully cultivated self-denial. As her bodyguard... He smiled. Her bodyguard! He would have to continue keeping his feelings in check. It was worth it to be near her, to protect her, to do something worth doing.

"Firian."

This time there was no mistaking her voice from the Unreal. Heart thundering, he answered.

They stood far apart in a replica of the fountain courtyard. Kiria had recreated it almost perfectly. He blinked. Her skill had improved tremendously.

She no longer used her Ability, and stood as he knew her best—simple but breathtaking, the girl he had known and protected and betrayed.

There was something archetypal about Kiria, especially this way, as though other people were patterned after her. She made everything more real. Seeing her felt more like coming home than going back to the Academy did after a mission. It was a sense of rightness, of belonging, like the way he fit into his own body, even when it was in pain, just because it was his.

For a moment they stood in silence, the weight of all their history surging between them. Then, slowly, Kiria smiled, her look full of memories. His chest suddenly ached with them. God, he loved her. Without her, he wouldn't have become the man he was. A man he could finally be proud of.

She looked younger this way, with such raw thanks on her face, a mirror of some of his own feelings. In her gaze, there was a touch of the wonder he'd seen when they'd gone to Shifra. An evaluating kind of gladness, one that invited him to share in it. Since meeting her, he had seen her grow more determined, confident. Maybe he'd had a hand in that too.

Neither moved toward the other, but there was understanding and there was hope. Despite everything, despite how their story should have ended, they had made each other better.

And he smiled back.

ABOUT THE AUTHOR

Carly Stevens lives in beautiful Colorado, teaching English and writing immersive stories about the power of courage and hope.

To find out more about upcoming projects, check out her website: https://carly-stevens.com

Get free short stories—including one of Firian's Ghost missions and what happens after the epilogue—when you sign up for her author newsletter!

Also by Carly Stevens

Tanyuin Academy series (YA fantasy)
    Firian Rising
    Into the Unreal
    Kingdoms on Fire
    Tanyuin Academy Stories (short story collection)

Dark academia
    Laertes: A Hamlet Retelling

The Hamlet Reader (compilation of *Hamlet* research)

Printed in the USA
CPSIA information can be obtained
at www.ICGtesting.com
LVHW041603051124
795766LV00016B/154/J